T3-BNX-616

DISCARD

The American Music Handbook

The American Music Handbook

CHRISTOPHER
PAVLAKIS

THE FREE PRESS
A Division of Macmillan Publishing Co., Inc.
NEW YORK

Collier Macmillan Publishers
LONDON

The Free Press
A Division of Macmillan Publishing Co., Inc.
866 Third Avenue, New York, N.Y. 10022

Collier-Macmillan Canada Ltd.

Library of Congress Catalog Card Number: 73-2127

Printed in the United States of America

printing number

1 2 3 4 5 6 7 8 9 10

Library of Congress Cataloging in Publication Data

Pavlakis, Christopher.
The American music handbook.

1. Music--United States--Directories. I. Title.
ML13.P39 780'.973 73-2127

To My Wife, Betty,
for her forbearance
during the course
of this long and arduous
work

Contents

Part 5 Performers

Part 6 Composers

Part 7 Music Festivals

Part 8 U.S. Musical Contests, Awards, Grants, Fellowships and Honors

Part 9 Music and Education

Part 14 Foreign Supplement

Introduction

The plan of the *American Music Handbook* is to bring together information on all areas of organized musical activity in the United States within the limits of a single volume.

Its restriction as to time is the present; its emphasis is the field of so-called concert, serious, classical music—this field because it is heavily institutionalized and fairly well organized in units, because music institutions have assumed a national responsibility to continue a culture, and because there is a desperate need for information within this area of music. Or rather, this is at least the emphasis: one thing readily apparent in America's musical life (and, hence, in this book) is that its variety knows no boundaries and that neither "art" music nor "vernacular" music are completely separable. Thus, the reach of this book most certainly includes countless encounters with and references to American popular music. However, America's most telling music appears not to need a book of this kind as yet, and if the need can be established, our popular music will find greater representation in any future editions.

Included in this inventory of over 5,000 entries are service institutions and organizations of all kinds; performing organizations; individual musicians and composers; music festivals and competitions; institutions that teach music, store it, exhibit it, have information concerning it; communications media through which music is heard or read about; and suppliers and manufacturers of its materials.

The intent, therefore, is to encompass all these areas, present them separately in detail so they may be studied or referred to separately or in any combination with each other, and to strive for sufficient profusion so that a national picture is conceivable. The reason is simply to provide a single source of needed information. Hardly anyone in America possesses detailed knowledge about America's musical resources. Hardly any institution has taken it upon itself to develop, consciously, continuing files on such assets. The fact that at least two major music research libraries were of very limited help in the compilation of this book testifies to an enormous gap in this area of study.

The coverage outlined above suggests what can be meant by "resources." They include many aspects of the music world commonly ignored in music history books and in books attempting to study our musical condition. In this work, we see music commerce and industry occupying a great deal of space; we see also space given to the dance, an important sister art that cannot readily exist without music; we find myriad ways in which people contribute to and are involved in music and see how, apparently, this involvement occupies much of their lives. We see, therefore, that musical resources are more than performers and composers, who are most often placed in the forefront of historical musical documentation.

In a sense this is not a book about music, but rather about the activity music engenders: the people who are sustained by it, affected by it, and who produce it; what they have created to support it, continue it, present it, and to change it.

From the beginning, I had no preconceptions as to what ought to be included in the book, apart from those limitations already mentioned. It was my intention merely to gather from living people material as to what they are now doing in music and to organize it so that it may be studied now and in the future. Before the work was attempted its overall coverage was conceived in the most general terms only, and of my material I wished only, both for present and future use, that it be revelatory to the extent of its depth, historical by virtue of its breadth, and exemplifying by its variety.

The material presented was compiled from a framework of information sent to the author through the use of questionnaires. These, thousands of them, were dispatched in stages between the years 1967 and 1972 to organizations, institutions and performing groups (Parts 1, 2, 3, 4), composers, festivals, schools and libraries, firms in the music industries, periodicals, etc. Information on persons other than composers was gathered from a number of sources: references on organizational questionnaires, from concert managers, news releases, newspapers, concert programs, magazines, and, on occasion, standard works of reference.

The questionnaires, simple and carefully worded, were devised to yield first, basic facts of identification and second, distinguishing features. This is not to say that questionnaires alone provided the bulk of information. Such is not the case: they often merely yielded the skeleton. This was sometimes sufficient; in many cases, however, additional research was needed for flesh and blood. Much information had either to be confirmed, enlarged upon, or deciphered. In addition, it had to be correlated with other known facts and material elsewhere in the book.

Sometimes information submitted was either not clearly explained or was obfuscated by insubstantial claims; also, there were conflicts between questionnaire information and other printed matter received with it. In such cases, it was necessary to go to other sources such as press reviews, programs, etc. When none of these were readily available, it became necessary to write only a general description of the entry involved. Large, amorphous organizations were as troublesome in this regard as little ones, for sometimes the descriptive information they forwarded was so general or abstract in language as to appear to be machine-composed. This caused bedevilment to anyone trying to find the humanity behind it all.

For institutions or organizations of unusual stature, it was necessary to make special petitions for information beyond that obtainable from questionnaires. When this was not forthcoming or when the received information was discovered to be unsatisfactory, the writer undertook his own research. This procedure was necessary for a number of institutions, but it sometimes prevailed throughout whole sections. For example, the narrative text about festivals could not have been written exclusively from questionnaire information. There, much program information, news clippings, reports, even maps and atlases, were relied upon. Some of the extra information was supplied by the petitionee but often as well by this writer, who collected files for months before attempting the actual writing.

Although questionnaires (and letters) were dispatched between 1967 and

1972, the actual composing of the text did not commence until fall, 1968. All entries written earlier were updated during winter, spring, and summer, 1972 (and a certain amount in 1973) to the degree possible or necessary.

With respect to the text of this book, this point should be made: if information herein is not in direct quotes, not a paraphrase, not a rearrangement of conglomerate materials, it is, of course, original, and I am the author. I accept all responsibility for the selection and scope of the book's contents, its factual accuracy, and the nature of nuances that may accompany facts.

It is understood that inclusion in this book implies no special distinction on the part of persons and organizations. Throughout the volume are entries not so much the result of selection as of confirmation. Whatever is found in these pages actually exists; there is more of everything, but a book must begin and end somewhere. Some control and effort was exerted—not always successfully—to make certain that the largest, the best, the smallest, the oldest, and the youngest of every category of entry was included, but not for these reasons alone and not at the expense always of the organizations and persons that bear no such distinctions. The entries and information about them are, as mentioned, the result of search-and-find. One must allow for those who could not be located or, having been located, could not be convinced that they ought to provide information about themselves. It is hoped that future editions will see certain omissions corrected.

No one can predict the value of a given fact in a book of reference. What may appear to be trivial to one reader may be of some consequence to another. The writer has included as many facts about each entry as their availability permitted or the nature of the entry demanded. In putting facts into this book, certain requirements were followed. One requirement was that each item of entry actually be locatable, that, at the time of writing, the persons or institutions described actually exist and can be contacted, if need be, by mail, phone, cable, or whatever other means. In the case of individual persons, there are references to the organizations with which they are associated. Nothing is treated in the abstract.

This requirement will benefit the user of this book who wishes to know, for example: where a festival might be found in a remote rural area; where a publisher's imprint identified in a bibliography merely as "Boston," can be secured; where one can find a score of a specific musical composition; who distributes a model or brand name of a musical instrument or accessory. Individual persons such as composers and performers are shown in association with such institutions and organizations as schools, publishers, record companies, and concert managers.

Accordingly, this leads to another rule followed to a greater or lesser extent throughout this book, namely, the avoidance, as much as possible, of placing any organization or person in isolation in a field so obviously reliant upon interrelationships. Therefore, passing reference to a person or organization in one part can usually be followed in greater depth in another. Performers are shown in reference to concert managers, who, in turn, are identified more fully elsewhere; references to record labels in the section on composers, performing groups, and solo performers can be followed up in the section on record companies, etc. When an orchestra, chorus, or opera company is referred to under a solo performer's or conductor's entry, one can learn more about such ensembles in the appropriate section of the book. For more information concerning American or foreign contests won by performers in Part 5, the reader can consult Parts 8 and 14, and so forth.

This integrated format ought to add a new dimension of utility to this book and, at the same time, provide an overview of the music field.

Any Part containing entries whose information might be subject to varying interpretation or which is presented in a format requiring an explanation, will have an introduction which the reader ought to consult first.

All books purport to be useful. What existed in the music field prior to this work were various directories supplying names and addresses of some of the categories in this volume and frequently some of peripheral value. However, this book ought not to be compared with annual directories or regularly appearing publications containing lists of various kinds. Such publications have their value. Their prime usefulness is in supplying names and addresses, etc., which is to say, they point to where information can be obtained. If such basic information is not up to date, the entry is useless; hence the need to publish directories frequently.

In the present publication, it is obvious more is attempted. There is sufficient information to offset details which may change with the times. Thus, changes of personnel, telephone numbers, and other facts are of little consequence to the further usefulness of any entry that goes beyond such detail.

For this reason, the book ought to be useful for several years. This does not preclude its value as a permanent history of a specific period in America's musical life, for, even if this one edition were to be the first and last of its kind, its value would remain and very likely increase with the passage of sufficient time. It is expected, however, that revisions will follow. These will benefit from whatever criticism this edition earns. Errors will have been corrected and its form, if altered, will be shaped by the test of usage given this edition.

The final hope for this work is that it provide facts not generally known, that it can be used to resolve doubts and settle arguments, and that it provide substance for the image people have of an America that is a gargantuan purveyor and consumer of music on a level unprecedented in the history of that art.

An attempt was made to maintain a clear, concise language throughout, bearing in mind that this is not an interpretive work but a reportorial one, that qualifying, adjective-laden language would prevent the reader from getting to the facts quickly. Furthermore, stylistic indulgence would make difficult any subsequent revisions of the factual foundation of each section.

The style and format of this book vary with each Part and sometimes within Parts. There are narrative sections (Organizations, Music Festivals, Contests); there are simple listings (Concert Managers, Summer Camps, Music Tents) grouped in some logical arrangement, alphabetically or by states; there are sections written mainly in a kind of telescoped journalistic style so that facts are presented as briefly and leanly as possible, permitting the greatest amount of information to be corralled within the confines of a page. For such sections, syntactical satisfaction is a secondary consideration. Any reader hurriedly seeking some concrete fact will not miss nor be encumbered by very many "therefore's," "accordingly's," "the's," and the other articles and connectives, adjectives and adverbs that make our language whole and ringing but which also steal space from yet more nouns, proper names, and pronouns. For it is nouns, proper names, and pronouns that are the substance of this book.

My equivalent of:

> Cuero (kwâ-rō), city (pop. 7,498), S. Texas, on Guadalupe R. and N.W. of Victoria. Processes poultry, cotton, milk, and farm products. Annual Turkey Trot.*

is, to mention one example:

> **Webster Aitkin** (b. 1908), concert pianist, recitalist, and chamber musician; debut Vienna, 1929; U.S. debut, 1935; Recordings: *Lyrichord.*

The reader will understand this arrangement readily and may even discover more virtue than fault in this expediency: combining the sparcst use of verbs, adjectives, adverbs, etc., with the leanest form of nouns, proper names, and pronouns can force the reader to read and gather his facts faster.

Finally, there are sections containing a mixture of both a telegraphic style and a more expansive one. The writer hopes he used the latter wisely in order to better present the material in question. Thus, within the sections devoted to orchestras or opera companies, for example, there are some more fully developed entries, usually because the sufficiency of the information available permitted an exposition. It is the lapse into rhapsody that he hopes he avoided.

Abbreviations (except for everyday ones) are not used, since they would require the reader to consult their meaning elsewhere in the book. Only occasionally are the abbreviations of the words for street, avenue, states, resorted to. Others used in the book are "Tel." for the obvious and universally seen "telephone" and certain abbreviations for Latin words such as e.g., q.v., i.e., etc., and et al.—abbreviations which ought to be familiar to most.

Musical terminology is to be found in these pages but rarely. The term *a cappella* is used to describe unaccompanied choral music. There is no avoiding its use, particularly since it is found in the names of choral groups who sing in this style. *Collegium musicum* is found in the section devoted to schools. The reader is best referred to a good music dictionary for its meaning, since it is suspected that its use is not always consistent from school to school.

The use of "repertory" for "repertoire" and "theater" for "theatre" caused some awkwardness when used textually but was stuck to. It seemed not to matter which was used; either version would have been impossible to enforce, since, in the names of performing organizations such as opera groups and concert halls, both versions are found. They can only be quoted as they are.

Doctoral titles for musicians and educators are not used in this book. There is but one instance that comes readily to mind (there may be others), that of the title "Dr." applied to an M.D. who happens also to be a noted choral director. No one, least of all an American, would quibble with its use in such a case. Otherwise, it ought to be explained to foreign users of this book that academic titles outside the campus are not in daily use in American life, however ignoble that may seem. Furthermore, to all concerned, foreigners or not, it should

*The Columbia Viking Desk Encyclopedia. Vol. I, p. 327, Second Edition, 1960.

be pointed out that many holders of honorary degrees exist in the arts, music being no exception, and the indiscriminate or unidentified use of the title "Dr." only leads to confusion among the uninformed and dismay among the many in the music field who have earned the degree academically.

Some departures from normal editorial practices were found to be necessary for graphic clarity. Italics are used for journals, magazines, and other periodicals, for the names of record labels, and the brand names of manufactured goods. These are meaningful entities and they are legion. Italics should help the reader to spot them readily. Quotation marks are used for the titles of books and music.

Although it is usually explained in the introduction to the division within the book, it can be repeated here that dates appearing after the names of people signify the year of appointment to the post referred to.

Ellipses (. . .) are found as separators between entries in sections of the book where entries are especially brief or where there are too many to provide more generous space allotment. However, in such high-density sections, the use of capitalization for the entry titles ought to make them easy to find.

Bold type is applied only to living people and, at that, not in all cases. Its function is to delineate the present from the past and, in this way, present a new information dimension through graphic means. As stated, it is not consistently applied. Where it is to be found is entirely at the whim of this writer—the single whim he consciously permitted himself and the one he will most sincerely regret come revision time. The use of bold type does, however, follow some basic principles: it is used to point out the active participants in a given organization, performers at festivals and with performing groups, and so on. It is used for the entry heading of persons. It is not used for the section on solo performers except for the performer being described. To follow one name in bold type with another in bold type would be—well, tactless.

Finally, some random thoughts. Since I deny myself the luxury of opinion in the body of the book (with some exceptions), it is inevitable that this compilation, which (among its other designs) is meant to provoke thought, should provoke it in me. Let me limit my observations to a few and not necessarily the most important.

The active role women play in music ought to be acknowledged. We have come to expect their participation in the art as solo singers and instrumentalists, where they rank among the great musicians of our day. But chamber groups, symphony orchestras, opera orchestras, and bands have women lining their ranks in increasing numbers. Husband-and-wife duos—pianists, piano–violin, voice–instrument, and other combinations—are likewise proliferating.

Women compose the majority of private music teachers and are found on the music faculties of virtually every college and university. These facts do not really surprise us. But it is not generally known how often women are to be found in the top administrative echelon of important performing groups (Chicago and Boston opera companies, the New York Philharmonic), festivals, choruses, music industries, foundations, and music service organizations, apart from the likely sororities and other women-oriented groups.

The American Symphony Orchestra League was conceived by a woman, as was Wolf Trap Farm for the Performing Arts. The People-to-People Music Committee, the National Federation of Music Clubs, the Music Library Association, the Metropolitan Opera Guild, the Central Opera Service, to name some, are among the organizations of considerable influence in the field of music which have women in their top ranks.

A leading music publishing firm is directed and owned by a woman. The security of the seasonal survival of symphony orchestras and opera companies throughout the nation is heavily dependent on women as members of committees, fund-raising groups, and other supportive organizations, many of which are entirely composed of women. And, of course, there is a woman occupying the seat of the highest arts administration post in the country—that of the National Endowment for the Arts.

All this is amply documented in the pages of this book. Yet, for all this, we do not readily find the music of women composers on the programs of important symphonic and operatic groups, even those groups that have the active support of women which, for all practical purposes, means virtually all of them. It seems that women composers are ignored by both men and women.

That "no man [or woman] is an island" is particularly true in the field of music, where isolation is meaningless. Musicians in the United States are not immune to the seemingly native penchant for group activity and, as a consequence, any handful of people finding a common cause in a hectic profession are ready to found a society. The desire is strong both to organize and be organized.

Judging from the contents of this book and the effectiveness of many kinds of musical groups, one sees that the music professions and trades hold many able administrators, both men and women. One sees their ability to handle impressive physical plants (music schools, opera companies, symphony orchestras, concert halls, publishing houses, and factories); that they can handle payrolls, computers, and mailing lists; plan and successfully bring off conventions, tours of large numbers of people, fund-raising campaigns; understand the secrets of available information media and, in general, perform tasks normally not associated with their lives or professions. The expenditure of time and effort merely supporting music and engaging in its peripherals appears to be great. It would be interesting to know what other profession demands the same of its members.

It is affirmed everywhere that music is a universal need and that life without it would be unthinkable; the very hint of threat to its organized continuance brings us Music Institutionalized, and it is the Institution of Music—not music itself—that struggles daily for its survival. In that struggle, many mundane tasks are generated. This condition may well be worldwide. But it is in the United States, where the ultimate variety of problems and accomplishments exist, that the condition is classicized.

I am aware that I, as an individual, and not the federal government, or a foundation, or some study group or commission, have put together a long-overdue work that perhaps ought to have been compiled by such institutions and groups.

Having endured the experience, it is my opinion that the work could not have escaped from the hands of an imaginary committee without being bruised in the process. The special characteristic of this book is that its whole was created out of many parts, regarding each of which a single person had to have intimate knowledge; at the same time, so that no part would be thought of in isolation, an overall knowledge had to develop. This approach would be impossible in committee.

With the exception of a nearly negligible sum, all costs of this compilation were borne by me. Its plan and logistical operation were mine alone. The costs were high but would have been higher most certainly if this had been a communal effort.

Financial help was sought once. A noted foundation, permitting itself to review submitted plans for music research support, awarded, the year I submitted my plan, funds to a study of baroque (or was it Bach's?) ornamentation—undoubtedly a major lacuna keenly felt that year in the field of music.

That experience convinced me, however justifiably, that the contemporary cultural instrumentalities were not always geared to contemporary needs and that I ought to go it alone. It also occurred to me that foundations and their advisors in music, in this era of group activity, could have no faith in the outcome of any plan were its execution undertaken in a manner reminiscent of a monastic scholar. This depressing assessment was refreshingly counterbalanced subsequently when, in the course of petitioning thousands of people for information for this book, cooperation was willingly extended, and hardly a question was ever raised as to the validity of the enterprise or its need. Among these thousands were officials of that same foundation.

Acknowledgments

A great number of people listed in this book can be said to have taken part in its production. Without the information volunteered by them, the book would have been impossible to compile and write.

My gratitude goes out to the thousands of people who took the time and trouble to fill out what it was hoped were uncomplicated questionnaires. Most of them can be identified, as they are found in the pages of this book; some of them will remain anonymous to me, for they supplied information willingly in behalf of institutions or organizations with which they were associated without identifying themselves—nevertheless, they were careful to provide names of others who should be included in the book. Such selfless work requires a special measure of recognition.

My appreciation also is extended to those who not only sent me information about themselves, their organizations, and their work, but who also responded to special queries about other aspects of the music world with which they were familiar. They supplied statistics and other overviews which led me to yet other sources or which gave shape and perspective to information already at hand and to thoughts not quite formed. Among this group were Mr. Wangerin and his assistants of the American Symphony Orchestra League who, respectively, furnished information on the estimated number of orchestras extant in America and who double-checked against concert programs many of the concertmasters found in Part 2 whose names had been among my older files; in this regard, my thanks also to ICSOM (International Conference of Symphony and Opera Musicians), for providing yet further clues to verification of concertmasters; my thanks to the Music Teachers National Association, which supplied statistics on its membership; to Broadcast Music Inc., for its Orchestral Survey and other assessments; to the person at ASCAP who provided me with essential catalogues; to the American Music Conference, which provided me with miscellaneous statistics and summaries on the music industry and amateur music activities; to the American Music Center, for the use of their composer mailing list for the purpose of sending out questionnaires; to the wholehearted and friendly cooperation of concert managers and artists' representatives who inundated me with biographical data and other critical facts concerning the performers on their rosters (with regret that it was impossible for me to include them all); to the Record Industry Association of America for the submission of record sales figures; to the Electronic Industries Association of America for similar figures covering its field of interest; to Ray Norstrand, President and General Manager of Chicago's WFMT, who knows altogether too much about FM classical music broadcasting for me to have done no more than accept his list of radio stations and to contact some interesting ones among it; to Frank Little and Harriet Wagner at Public Broadcasting Service and to Susan Dudley-Allen at WNET/13 for materials sent; to foreign embassies and consulates for their assistance in locating needed information in Part 14; to all those who sensed I needed and desired more than sketchy data and saw to it that I was provided with ample information.

Finally, and above all, my unfathomable gratitude to Miss Diane Addison, young singer, assistant, and friend, who came upon my fourth year of lonely work to rescue my effort to meet deadlines; who performed enormously tedious chores with dispatch and good nature; who culled reams of information, pored over endless lists, questionnaires, and printed matter of all kinds; who typed the bulk of this manuscript and daily performed a veritable scenario of speed and efficiency that bordered on the supranatural—to her my thanks, forever.

The American Music Handbook

Part 1 | Organizations

The organizations that follow, arranged alphabetically, are those serving music or which are related to music, wholly or in part, directly or indirectly; dance organizations are among them. They include educational organizations, fraternities and sororities, foundations, trade unions, labor unions, professional societies, trusts, charitable organizations, honorary societies, amateur groups, and organizations which comprise yet other organizations.

Many of them are vital to musical endeavor in the United States. Without them, much of the diffusion, variety, and color in America's musical life would not be sustainable. Their multiple and sometimes conflicting influences are at once direct and indirect and can be seen or sensed in every corner of the music world.

Some of them are made up totally of musicians or others professionally involved in the field of music; many of them invite the participation of all interested parties.

The scope of interest and the avowed purposes of these organizations, most of which are nonprofit corporations, range from the extremely parochial to the universal, from those dedicated to a specific area in music alone to those serving the arts or mankind in general. Whereas some are devoted to practical, material, or financial problems within the music field, others are concerned with the aesthetic, spiritual, or intellectual realms. Some organizations, essentially democratic, functioning entirely from the strength and sanction of the entire membership and its collective devotion to a single cause, however more general their by-laws may read, are primarily self-serving. The reverse also exists: the organization which is really the instrumentality of one man or woman whose independent philanthropic actions can affect whole segments of the music field.

Foundations included here are the largest or best known in the field of music. There are innumerable others actively supporting some aspect of the music field. Some of these are mentioned in other sections of the book. The large, wealthy foundations often rely in musical matters on large-membership music groups to act as administrators or advisors in specific programs aiding music. This interrelationship is discoverable in the text.

Except for certain obvious ones, government agencies are not included here. There are surprisingly many state and federal government agencies that in one way or another support the arts in general and music in particular. The thread of government participation in music—only a hint of which is discernible from this book—can be traced throughout America's musical life. To describe the myriad programs and agencies of the federal government alone which, wittingly or not, involve music—in the State Department, Department of Health, Education, and Welfare, the Department of the Interior, and even the Defense Department, to name the Cabinet levels only—is simply beyond the scope of this book.

For some organizations the senior officer is not listed because correspondence and most other matters are dispensed with in care of the secretary or director, whose tenure is usually of greater duration and who generally is the chief executive for daily affairs. Where no headquarters address exists, the address listed is that of a responsible officer. Membership totals, when shown as round numbers, are presumed to be approximations.

For data about an organization's official magazine (if it is offered for sale or distribution nationally), consult the section on periodicals. Further information about certain organizations can be found in other sections of the book, principally in Parts 7 and 8.

ACCORDION TEACHERS' GUILD INTERNATIONAL (ATG), c/o President, **Mrs. Lari Holzhauer,** Rte. 4, Box 180, Traverse City, Michigan 49684. Tel.: (616) 947–6207. Founded in July, 1941. About 500 members. Membership is open to anyone interested in the progress of the accordion, but only accredited and active accordion teachers may vote or hold office in the organization, which is essentially teacher-controlled. Dues: $12 annually. Dues plus an additional annual contribution of $50 are required for sustaining members. Mimeographed bulletins issued about ten times a year. Annual meetings are held at the same time and location as the National Association of Music Merchants convention. ATG activities include support for national accordion competitions culminating in the National Championship Contest, participation in the world contest (Confédération des Accordéonistes Internationale, Coupe Mondiale), annual concerts, and annual teacher workshops.

ACOUSTICAL SOCIETY OF AMERICA, INC., 335 East 45th Street, New York, N.Y. 10017. Tel.: (212) 685–1212. Founded in May, 1929. Membership: approximately 4,200. Its purpose is "to increase and diffuse the knowledge of acoustics and promote its practical applications." Official organ is *The Journal of the Acoustical Society of America* (see Periodicals). Society Secretary is **Wallace Waterfall.**

AMATEUR CHAMBER MUSIC PLAYERS, INC. (ACMP), c/o **Helen Rice,** Secretary, 15 West 67th Street, New York, N.Y. 10023. (A new national office for the organization is being prepared at the headquarters of the American Symphony Orchestra League at the time of writing this information. The ASOL will keep the ACMP files and do all routine secretarial work under the direction of the officers of the ACMP.) Founded in 1948 by Leonard Strauss of Indianapolis, the ACMP functions as a voluntary, nonprofit educational organization, recently incorporated. Membership is open to anyone in any country who plays chamber music for pleasure and who would play with other musicians at his own home or elsewhere as a visitor. The organization publishes, every year or two, a directory of members' names, addresses, phone numbers, instruments, and degree of proficiency (members rate themselves according to ACMP's general classification system). Membership is approximately 7,000 with over 5,000 players in the United States and about 1,000 players in over fifty foreign countries. Many professionals are included in the membership. No dues are required; contributions are voluntary. There are no paid officers. **Samuel P. Hayes** is Chairman.

AMERICAN ACADEMY OF ARTS AND LETTERS, 633 West 155th Street, New York, N.Y. 10032. Tel.: (212) AU 6–1480. Founded in 1904, it is an affiliate of the National Institute of Arts and Letters, its parent body. The Academy's purpose is "the protection and furtherance of literature and the fine arts in the United States." Members must be citizens of the United States and be members of the National Institute of Arts and Letters. Academy membership is limited to 50. No dues are required. Among musician-members of the Academy are: **Walter Piston, Roger Sessions, Aaron Copland, Virgil Thomson.** The Academy awards grants of $2,500 for which no application is accepted. It publishes a *Yearbook,* for members only, and *Proceedings of the American Academy and the National Institute of Arts and Letters.* President (1972), **Aaron**

Copland; Secretary, John Hersey. Annual meetings are held in December.

AMERICAN ACADEMY OF ARTS AND SCIENCES, 280 Newton Street, Brookline Station, Boston, Massachusetts 02146. Tel.: (617) 522–2400. Founded in 1780; it is the second oldest learned society in America. Membership total: about 2,372. Among its purposes: "to promote and encourage the knowledge of the antiquities of America . . . to cultivate every art and science which may tend to advance the interest, honor, dignity, and happiness of a free, independent, and virtuous people." As an honor society, its membership is by election only and falls into four classes: physical and mathematical sciences, natural and physiological sciences, the social arts, and the humanities. Dues are $20 for resident Fellows and $10 for nonresident Fellows. No dues for Foreign Honorary Members. Publications: *Bulletin* (eight times a year); *Records* (annual subscription is $2.30); *Daedalus* (quarterly; subscription is $6.50). All publications are free to members. Other publications include those resulting from the work of special committees and study groups. Special recent projects include the Commission on the Year 2000, Seminar on Poverty, and International Studies of Arms Control. Musician-members include: **Leonard Bernstein, E. Power Biggs, Richard Burgin, Aaron Copland, Randall Thompson, Samuel Barber, Elliott Carter, Edward "Duke" Ellington, Ross Lee Finney, Elliot Forbes, Lukas Foss, Boris Goldovsky, Howard Hanson, Mantle Hood, Leon Kirchner, Erich Leinsdorf, Peter Mennin, Gian-Carlo Menotti, A. Tillman Merritt, Darius Milhaud, Daniel Pinkham, Walter Piston, Leontyne Price,** and **Gunther Schuller.** (It can be observed that many of the foregoing and others not listed here have had something to do with the musical life of Boston and environs.) Officers for 1971–72: **Harvey Brooks,** President; **Denis M. Robinson,** Secretary; **Thomas Boylston Adams,** Treasurer; **John Voss,** Executive Officer. President *ex officio* is **Talcott Parsons** (who served from 1967 to 1971).

AMERICAN ACADEMY OF TEACHERS OF SINGING (AATS), c/o The Secretary, 57 Winter Street, Forest Hills, N.Y. 11375. Tel.: (212) 261–6042. Founded in 1922. The Academy's goal is "To establish a code which will improve the ethical principles and practice of the profession, to further knowledge and culture, to promote cooperation and good fellowship." Membership is strictly limited and cannot exceed 40 (membership in 1971 was 36). Members are elected to the Academy by special invitation; election is based on the teacher's national reputation within the profession and his willingness to work for the goals of the Academy. Members are charged annual dues. Although the Academy has no regularly appearing organ or bulletin, it publishes what are called "pronouncements" about the profession of singing and the teaching of singing. These are distributed to some 4,000 interested people throughout the country. Since 1924, over 25 pronouncements have been published in addition to 12 song lists. Some titles are now out of print within both categories. All publications in print are available for sale to the general public. Pronouncements issued since 1950 include the following: "Ethics in the Field of Teaching of Singing," "The Sacred Oratorio" (published by Theodore Presser Co., and available there or through music dealers), "A Recommendation for the Creation of Music Sections in Public Libraries. . . ," "Classification of the Singing Voice," "Auditions for Singers," "Qualifications for an Operatic Career," "The High School Student and the Singing of Grand Opera," "Choral Singing and the Responsibility of the Choral Director," "Auditions for Singers—Problems of Adjudication," "The College Student and the Singing of Grand Opera and Recital," "Terminology in the Field of Singing" (published by G. Schirmer, Inc.), "Transition Period between the Student Years and Professional Maturity," and a recent revision of the 1932 pronouncement, "Singing in English." The Academy meets monthly from October to May on the second Monday of each month. It sometimes shares space with other organizations at certain national conventions. Officers are: **Harold C. Luckstone,** Secretary;

Dolf Swing, Chairman (15 West 67th Street, New York, N.Y. 10023); **Leon Carson,** Vice-Chairman; and **William Gephart,** Treasurer.

AMERICAN ACCORDIONISTS' ASSOCIATION (AAA), 37 West 8th Street, New York, N.Y. 10011. Tel.: (212) 228-7830. Founded in 1938, it is the largest organization of its kind. Its purpose is to raise the standards of accordion teaching and to acquire acceptance of the accordion among music educators. Among the AAA's activities has been the commissioning of new works for accordion by well-known composers. Current membership: about 400. Other activities include the sponsorship of the trip to Europe of the American entrant for the World Accordion Championship. Secretary: **Theresa Costello** (1973); President: **Elsie M. Bennett** (1973); Vice President: **Jacob Neupauer.**

AMERICAN BANDMASTERS ASSOCIATION (ABA), c/o Secretary, **Lt. Col. William F. Santelmann,** 7414 Admiral Drive, Alexandria, Virginia 22307. Founded in 1929 in New York City by Edwin Franko Goldman and others. Among its purposes: "promotion of better music through the instrumentality of the band . . . adoption of a universal band instrumentation . . . to induce prominent composers of all countries to write for the band." Membership is by invitation only. Total membership is about 250.

AMERICAN CHORAL DIRECTORS ASSOCIATION (ACDA), c/o Executive Secretary, P.O. Box 17736, Tampa, Florida 33612. Tel.: (813) 935-9381. Founded in 1959. The ACDA has a ten-point goal which includes promoting good choral music, better rehearsal procedures, important choral music research, and organizing and developing choral groups of all types throughout the country. The organization's membership is over 3,400 and consists of choral directors from schools, colleges, universities, community and industrial organizations, church and professional choral groups of radio, television, the concert stage, and the recording industry. Any interested person, institution, or business firm may join the ACDA as an Associate Member. The ACDA has members in all fifty states; there are state chapters with chairmen and six divisional chairmen for the United States. Dues are $10 for Active and Associate Members, $25 for Industry Associates, $15 for institutions, and $3 for students. Dues for Life Members are $150. All dues are annual. The membership year runs from July to the following June. The Association's official publication is *The Choral Journal* and is free to members. Subscriptions otherwise are $4 a year (to institutions only). The ACDA engages in a number of activities pertinent to its goals. These include the preparation of choral music lists in conjunction with the Music Educators National Conference, of which the ACDA is an associate organization and with which, in the past, it had held its national conventions; co-sponsorship of choral workshops and festivals throughout the country; co-sponsorship of the Vienna (choral) Symposium with the Institute of European Studies (for the symposia in 1969 and 1970) and the Council on Intercultural Relations (for the symposium held in Vienna the summer of 1971); the development of a Tape Bank of choral works infrequently recorded; the sponsorship of contemporary choral music. President is **Charles C. Hirt;** Executive Secretary and Editor of the Journal is **R. Wayne Hugoboom.**

THE AMERICAN CHORAL FOUNDATION, INC., 130 West 56th Street, New York, N.Y., 10019. Tel.: (212) 246-3361. Incorporated in 1954. The Foundation is a nonprofit service organization for choral conductors. Through its main membership organization, the Association of Choral Conductors (q.v.), which it established and administers, the Foundation seeks to promote performances of choral music, provide counsel to choristers and conductors, and publish reference works of use to choral musicians and conductors. It has sponsored concerts and has organized the American Concert Choir. Its official publication, serving the Association of Choral Conductors, is *The American Choral Review* (see Periodicals). The Foundation publishes a *Research Memorandum Series* which supplements the articles and reports of the *Review* and offers information to the professional choral conductor or chorister, particularly in the form of previously unresearched or unpublished choral music bibliographies. The *Memoranda,* which, since 1959 now total over 90, have covered such topics as: recommended editions of choral music published by various publishers (Memoranda Nos. 6, 7, 9 and 10 for the year 1959); a selective list of Baroque choral works in practical editions (No. 15, 1960); a select list of choral music for festivals (Nos. 27 and 35, 1961 and 1962); a bibliography of contemporary choral music for high voices, performable by children (No. 36, 1962); lists of contemporary American choral works respectively for men's and women's voices (Nos. 39 and 43, 1963); a list of choral music from operas, operettas, and musical shows (No. 41, 1963); a bibliography of polychoral music (No. 88, 1969); summer choral workshops and festivals (Nos. 86 and 87, 1970 and 1971). These, and all the memoranda, are published for the members of the Association of Choral Conductors and are available to the general public for sale one year after the date of publication. With a grant from the National Foundation on the Arts and the Humanities matched with grants from four sponsoring universities, the American Choral Foundation organized three so-called choral institutes during the summer months. The institutes were designed to offer the choral conductor an opportunity to gain experience in rehearsing and conducting a professional orchestra and to provide a course of detailed study and analyses of major choral works. The first institute was held on the campuses of the University of Wisconsin at Madison and the State University of New York at Binghampton in 1968. The University of Oklahoma at Norman and Temple University at Ambler, Pennsylvania were the locations for the 1969 and 1970 institutes. Project director was **Sheldon Soffer,** Administrative Director of the American Choral Foundation. The Foundation's Music Director, **Margaret Hillis,** took an active part in each institute.

AMERICAN COMPOSERS ALLIANCE, (ACA) 170 West 74th Street, New York, N.Y. 10023. Tel.: (212) 873–1250. Founded in 1938 with the efforts of such composers as **Aaron Copland,** Marion Bauer, **Roy Harris, Goddard Lieberson,** Douglas Moore, Quincy Porter, Wallingford Riegger, **Roger Sessions, Elie Siegmeister, Virgil Thomson,** and Bernard Wagenaar—to restrict the names to those who served on the first, and temporary, executive committee. The ACA is a licensing organization handling all of the performing rights of its members on a worldwide basis. The organization is member (composer)-controlled and -owned; the assets dealt with are the compositions of the members and the government of the ACA is completely in the hands of members. Membership is exclusively that of composers of "serious music" as that term is defined by the organization. Currently, 148 composers are members of ACA divided in the following classes of membership: Active (103), Associate (11), Limited (17), and Affiliate (17). The Active Member is a composer who is able to grant exclusive control of all performing rights to all of his work, i.e., who has not already assigned these rights to any other licensing organization; he must also have had at least one work published by a reputable publisher or performed "by an artist or organization of reputation." The Associate membership represents deceased member-composers whose rights have continued to their heirs, and those who control the rights in the compositions of composers who could meet the requirements of membership. This category is in the name of the composer, not the heir or rights holder. Limited Members are composers who cannot grant the assignment of performing rights of their works but who otherwise meet the requirements of membership (they may later become Active Members). Affiliate Members have assigned their rights exclusively with BMI, which holds the sublicense for ACA in general for collections and for supervision of broadcast and live performances of ACA music. Only Active Members have voting rights in ACA. Membership in the Alliance is through election by majority vote of the Board of Governors according to a fixed procedure and is subject to what is tantamount to a probationary period, during which there is a review of the elected composer's musical activity, that is, new works composed, the demand for his music, live performances, publications, etc. The activities of ACA are eminently on a practical level involving, for example, the maintenance of a library of members' music—some 3,500 volumes—which is at the disposal of any category of user. ACA handles all rental materials needed for specific performances of the music of members and the tasks of shipping, billing, and collecting of fees payable to the composer. In 1952, ACA established the Composer Facsimile Edition (CFE—see also Music Publishers), which functions as a publishing division of the Alliance with features distinctly different from those usually established in a music publishing operation. Composers may deposit copies of their unpublished works with ACA in the usual form of fair masters or inked transparencies which are kept on permanent deposit. These are used to print ozalid duplicates on demand. Royalties resulting from such sales go to the composer. The obvious purpose of this operation is to make the music of a composer available to the general music public prior to its commercial publication, which either may never occur or which may take many years to come about. Once restricted to the use of ACA members only, CFE, in 1967, permitted its services to be open to any composer. The ACA–CFE catalog, in terms of United States serious music representation, in its variety, scope, and concentration, is one of the most significant collections in the nation. Other matters of help to the members (e.g., copyright registration paperwork, publication advice, and the dissemination of information about the music and careers of the composers) are also handled by the organization. Regarding the latter service, the *ACA Bulletin,* now defunct (1938–1965) but some back copies of which are still available from the Alliance, was, in many of its issues, an informative periodical on composer-members, covering in detail the work of over 40 composers with musical analyses and lists of compositions, recordings, manuscripts, and instrumentation. Perhaps the most important accomplishments of the ACA as far as the general music public is concerned are the recordings it has sponsored under the aegis of Composers Recordings, Inc. (*CRI* label) (see also Record Companies) of which ACA is principal stockholder. Since CRI operates completely with subsidization, the support it receives from ACA and the American Academy of Arts and Letters, as well as from numerous foundations, is critical to its goals: that of issuing exclusively recordings of contemporary concert music and keeping the recordings permanently in the CRI catalog. Since its establishment in 1956, CRI has released more than 185 LP records of music by some 270 composers, a significant number of whom are ACA members. CRI has no peer on the American recording scene. Its catalog of American concert music is the most extensive in existence. The ACA holds its general annual meeting in May; the Board of Governors meets at least eight times annually. Members are charged dues. ACA officers are **Charles Dodge,** President; **Frank Wigglesworth,** First Vice President; **Harvey Sollberger,** Second Vice President; **Hale Smith,** Treasurer; **Joan Tower,** Secretary. Office staff consists of **David Cooper,** Executive Director; **Rosalie Calabrese,** Manager, Composers Editions; and **Albert Roger,** printer for CFE.

AMERICAN COUNCIL OF LEARNED SOCIETIES, 345 East 46th Street, New York, N.Y. 10017. Tel.: (212) 986–7393. Founded in 1919. The council has 35 constituent societies including some directly or indirectly related to music, such as the American Folklore Society, American Musicological Society, the Society for Ethnomusicology, and those for medieval and Renaissance studies. Publishes *Annual Report* and a monthly *Newsletter,* from October through May. The council gives awards and grants for research. President: **Frederick Burkhardt.**

AMERICAN FEDERATION OF MUSICIANS OF THE UNITED STATES AND CANADA, 641 Lexington Avenue, New York, N.Y. 10022. Tel.: (212) 758–0600. Founded in October, 1896. Affiliated with the labor organization, AFL–CIO, and is the largest United States musicians union. It has a membership of 315,000 (1972) which, in addition to the 50 states of the Union, represents Puerto Rico, the Virgin Islands, and, since 1900, Canada. The Canada membership is an important one to the Federation and has executive representation (see officers below). The stated purpose of the Federation is: "to unite all local unions of musicians, the individual musicians who form such local unions and conditional members, into one grand organization for the purpose of general protection and advancement of their interests and for the purpose of enforcing good faith and fair dealing, as well as consistency with union principles, in all cases involving, or of interest to, members and local unions of the federation." Membership is open to anyone who can pass the tests given by the AFM local union. These tests, as well as the dues charged for membership, vary widely with each local. The total membership is drawn from about 650 locals including those of Canada. The first president of the AFM was Owen Miller, who served from 1896 to 1900. Under Joseph Weber's presidency (1900–1940, the longest tenure to date), the membership grew from the original 6,000 to 134,372; thus, the last thirty years have seen the fastest growth for the AFM. Subsequent presiding officers have been **James Caesar Petrillo** (1940–1958), Herman D. Kenin (1958–1970) and **Hal C. Davis,** elected in 1970 following the death of Mr. Kenin. The work of the AFM goes beyond the internal areas of pensions, membership supervision, contracts, local union mergers, etc., and reaches out to play an important and influential role in the musical life of the nation. In 1948, the Federation helped to establish, after a period of much labor difficulty, the Music Performance Trust Funds of the Recording Industries (q.v. under this chapter), conceived to provide for employment of musicians in live performances to offset any loss of employment stemming from the burgeoning sales of phonograph records and other forms of recorded performances (since, it was argued, recorded performances were often used in lieu of live performances). The result of this agreement has been innumerable performances by musicians in concerts throughout the country offered free to the public. The effect of these concerts on the musical life of the nation has been felt in many concrete ways. The Trust Funds enabled many smaller instrumental ensembles, from concert bands to chamber groups—ranging from mixed amateur and professional, semiprofessional, to professional—to increase the number of their public appearances; they provided an opportunity for the formation of new (albeit often temporary) instrumental ensembles of all sizes. Money from the Funds has often been used to perform a program of works which, if admission were charged, would not be economically sound, particularly in the case of programs offering new, contemporary works or rare works from the past. In 1959, the AFM established the Congress of Strings, an educational effort aimed at alleviating the continuing shortage of string instrument performers, a shortage particularly critical in symphony orchestras. Each summer, 120 young string players are given the opportunity to study, practice, and play under the guidance and instruction of well-known professional performers, conductors, and teachers. The performers are often from the nation's leading orchestras, the teachers often from colleges and universities. The Congress lasts eight weeks and is held in two locations, each having 60 students. The 1971 Congress was held simultaneously on the campus of the University of Cincinnati College-Conservatory of Music and the University of Southern California at Los Angeles. The Cincinnati Congress was under the direction of **Henry Mazer,** Associate Conductor of the Chicago Symphony; the Congress in Los Angeles was supervised by **Daniel Lewis** of the faculty of the University of Southern California. Guest conductors were **Sixten Ehrling, Morton Gould, Izler Solomon, Miro J. Pansky, Henry Mazer,** and **Daniel Lewis.** (See also U.S. Musical Contests, Awards, ...) "Young Sounds of the AFM" is a program designed to accommodate the influx of young people into the pop music field, particularly rock and roll. Its purpose is to offset the likelihood of commercial exploitation of young musicians in the matters of contracts, bookings, agents, fees, etc. Briefings and advisory sessions are offered by federation locals according to specific procedures established by the federation.

Another program, called "Tempo," is a lobbying and promotional campaign, supported by voluntary contributions from the federation membership, whose main thrust is toward developing strong support for more live music performances and for opposing any job-destroying aspects of the music industry. Bipartisan support is given politicians who are sympathetic to the arts. In internal matters, the Federation has attempted to create various forms of financial security for its members. In 1965 it established, in conjunction with the recording industries, the Special Payments Fund. Recording companies party to the agreement contribute payments to the Fund based on their annual sale of recordings. Each AFM member who has performed in a commercial recording receives a dollar amount in proportion to his annual scale wage earned from recordings in relation to total wages paid all union musicians. (In 1971, $6.7 million was paid to some 20,000 union musicians.) Another employer contribution plan is the AFM Employers' Pension Welfare (EPW), established in 1959 and now covering some 90,000 AFM members who perform for recordings, radio, television, jingles, movies, etc. Beginning with $1 million in employer contributions the first year, and increasing to an annual level of payments of nearly $7 million (1971), the fund now has a value of $50 million. First pension benefits were paid out in 1964. From that year until 1971 some $2.5 million has been paid to qualifying AFM members who, in 1971, totaled some 328. AFM officers are: **Hal C. Davis,** President; **Victor W. Fuentealba,** Vice-President; **J. Alan Wood,** Vice-President from Canada; **Stanley Ballard,** Secretary-treasurer, Editor of the official publication (see below), and Congress of Strings Project Director. The AFM's official organ is *International Musician* (see Periodicals) published monthly.

AMERICAN FEDERATION OF TELEVISION AND RADIO ARTISTS (AFTRA), 724 Fifth Avenue, New York, N.Y. 10019. Tel.: (212) CO 5–3267. Founded in 1937, it is a branch of the Associated Actors and Artists of America, affiliated with the AFL–CIO. Executive Secretary is **Kenneth Groot.**

AMERICAN FOLKLORE SOCIETY, Box 5, Bennett Hall, University of Pennsylvania, Philadelphia, Pennsylvania 19104. Tel.: (215) 594–7352. Founded in 1888; it is a constituent member of the American Council of Learned Societies (q.v.). Total membership is over 1,500. Publications: *The Journal of American Folklore,* a quarterly with an annual supplement, Editor, **Américo Parades,** Parlin Hall 324, University of Texas, Austin, Texas 78712; *Abstracts of Folklore Studies,* published quarterly for the Society by the University of Texas Press, Editor, **Richard E. Buehler,** Memorial University of Newfoundland. Members receive both the *Journal* and *Abstracts* as part of their membership. Membership dues are: $10 individuals; $5 for students; $11 for husband–wife membership; $12 for institutions; $200 for life membership. Officers (1971): **D. K. Wilgus,** President, University of California at Los Angeles; **Linda Dégh** and **Dell Hymes,** First and Second Vice Presidents; **Kenneth S. Goldstein,** Secretary-Treasurer.

AMERICAN GUILD OF AUTHORS AND COMPOSERS (AGAC), 50 West 57th Street, New York, N.Y. 10019. Tel.: (212) PL 7–8833. Formerly the Songwriters' Protective Association, founded in 1931, it is an organization of composers and authors of musical works. "Membership is available to any person who engages in creative work as a composer or author of musical works as either a vocation or avocation. 'Associate' memberships are available for those who have not, at the time of application, acquired professional status." Membership is possible for any person "of earnest intention" who writes music or music lyrics. The membership of about 2,500 has a large and important representation from the fields of popular music. The purpose of the Guild is "to cultivate . . . unity of action and understanding among the members of the Association, and between them and corporations, firms or individuals with whom they have or may have business dealings, and to promote equitable adjustment of all matters relating to the professional work of the members." The Guild's special strength lies in its activities relating to the business rights and interests of its members, particularly in their dealings with music publishers. It was to end the inequities in such dealings that the original protective organization was established by a group of songwriters (Billy Rose and George Meyer among them). There are now some 1,000 music publishers who recognize the AGAC as the representative of songwriters and who have legitimized this recognition by signing the AGAC's main innovation, the so-called Basic Agreement. This agreement permits the publisher to use a "Uniform Popular Songwriters Contract," which outlines certain minimum provisions for the publisher and songwriter. The contract, in order for it to become effective, must be examined for any shortcomings by the AGAC after its signing by both publisher and songwriter and, if acceptable, is countersigned by the Guild. The result of this agreement has been better royalty and song exploitation arrangements for the composer or lyricist, that is, a larger royalty percentage minimum for recordings, motion picture sound tracks, etc. (50 percent versus previous percentages of from 10 to 33⅓ percent), and sheet music (a minimum of 3 cents per copy versus the former average of 1 cent); obligatory publication and exploitation of a song accepted by a publisher within one year or the return of the song to the author upon demand. Other secured privileges include more specific schedules of royalty payment to the author and the right of the author or his agent to examine the financial books of the publisher for sales verification, etc. The AGAC offers its members other services: copyright renewal service, hospitalization and surgical plans, group life insurance, and royalty collections plan. (No artistic, critical, or agency roles are undertaken by the Guild in regard to the writer and his proffered work.) The Guild offers four classes of membership: Regular (for the composer or lyricist who has had at least one song published or recorded by a recognized company; this category has eight classifications based on the author's output, with dues varying accordingly), Associate, Special Associate (for successors-in-interest of deceased writers), and Non-Resident Associate. Only the Regular Member has Guild voting rights. Some of the best-known writers of the AGAC include **Duke Ellington, Sheldon Harnick, Arthur Schwartz, Virgil Thomson, Johnny Cash,** to cite a very few. The Guild's official publication is the *AGAC Bulletin,* published quarterly and sent free to members, Editor, **Joan Whitney.** President of the AGAC is **Edward Eliscu; Burton Lane** is Chairman of the Executive Committee; **Robert Colby** is Secretary. (General membership meetings are held annually in November.) The Guild maintains an office at 6331 Hollywood Boulevard, Hollywood, California.

AMERICAN GUILD OF MUSIC (AGM), c/o Secretary-Treasurer, P.O. Box 3, Downers Grove, Illinois 60515. Founded in 1955; formerly the American Guild of Banjoists, Mandolinists, and Guitarists, which was founded in 1902. The purpose of the Guild is "to promote, advance, and maintain the artistic, music and mercantile interests of fretted instruments and the accordion." There are about 1,000 members, most of whom are teachers in independent, commercial music studios.

AMERICAN GUILD OF MUSICAL ARTISTS (AGMA), 1841 Broadway, New York, N.Y. 10023. Tel.: (212) CO 5–3687. Founded in 1936. AGMA is a branch of Associated Actors and Artistes of America, affiliated with the AFL–CIO. Originally a protective association for solo artists, it now extends its membership to include "all performers in the opera, ballet, oratorio, concert and recital fields." AGMA represents member-performers in their dealings with managers and employers; collective contracts are bargained for and various social plans are offered its members, including life insurance and a welfare fund. Areas of jurisdiction cover persons and organizations having agreements with AGMA in the United States and dependencies, and Canada. Signatories to agreements include opera companies, ballet companies, professional choruses and those amateur choruses which employ AGMA soloists, symphony associations, and concert managements. For those categories wherein are traditionally found many amateur or temporary performing groups (such as opera and ballet companies and choruses), a contractual agreement with AGMA is understood generally to identify that group as a professional one—or, in the case of the amateur chorus, a group with high performing standards. AGMA has 4,000 members. They include singers, dancers, opera and concert choristers, instrumentalists, and stage directors. Dues charged are based on a sliding scale of income earned by the member according to a fixed schedule and are due annually. There is also a varying initiation fee. Five times a year AGMA publishes *AGMAZINE*, which is sent free to members and has a total circulation of about 5,000. **Cornell MacNeil** is President; National Executive Secretary is **DeLloyd Tibbs.**

AMERICAN GUILD OF ORGANISTS (A.G.O.), 630 Fifth Avenue, New York, N.Y. 10020. Tel.: (212) CO 5–5630. Founded in New York in 1896, taking its precedence from England's Royal College of Organists (R.C.O.). The avowed purpose of the A.G.O. is "to advance the cause of worthy church music; to elevate the status of church musicians; to increase their appreciation of their responsibilities, duties, and opportunities; to raise the standard of efficiency of organists and choirmasters, by examinations . . . in organ playing, choir training, in the theory and general knowledge of music, and to grant certificates in Service Playing and in the respective classes of membership (Fellow, Associate or Choirmaster) to candidates who pass such examinations." The Guild is one of the few professional musical organizations which evaluate the practical competence of its members. Detailed examinations in practical organ playing and choir training are conducted in various parts of the country. Certificates earned (F.A.G.O., A.A.G.O., CH.M.) are held to be of significance to professional organists, since they attest to specific levels of musical achievement. Candidates are admitted to A.G.O. by examination, upon the recommendation of two members. The Guild, by nature of the work most performed by its members, is strongly oriented toward sacred music and the church, but is nonsectarian. Many of its members are concert artists, members of the music faculties of colleges, junior colleges, and universities, or hold positions, in addition or exclusively, as church organists, choir directors, and the like. Total membership is over 16,000 in some 300 chapters throughout the country. Annual meetings and elections are held in May each year. General national meetings are held biennially in even-numbered years. Membership dues are $15 for regular members, $10 for those over seventy or under twenty-one years of age, and $4.50 for new members and reinstated members. Fees ranging downward from $30 are also chargeable for examinations. The official organ of the Guild is *Music/The A.G.O./R.C.C.O. Magazine,* Editor, **Peter Basch.** The latter initials stand for the Royal Canadian College of Organists, which distributes the magazine to its members. The periodical, however, is owned by the A.G.O. Subscriptions are $7.50 a year (free to A.G.O. members). A single copy costs $1. The A.G.O. has published a number of items of use to members and interested persons. They include examination papers, a code of ethics, a membership list, and other items pertinent to members and potential members including the book "The Story of the American Guild of Organists" ($2.50). Some pamphlets are: "How Can I Improvise?" (50 cents), "Broader Horizons for Children's Choirs," (50 cents), and "Acoustics in Churches," (25 cents). A.G.O. officers are: **Charles Dodsley Walker,** President; **Ruth Millikin,** Secretary; **James E. Bryan,** Executive Director.

AMERICAN HARP SOCIETY, INC., c/o President, **Catherine Gotthoffer,** 43748 N. Waddington Avenue, Lancaster, California 93534. Founded in 1962 by **Marcel Grandjany,** famed harpist. The Society's goals are "to cultivate, promote, foster, sponsor and develop among its members and general public the appreciation of the harp as a musical instrument; to encourage the composition of music for the harp; and to improve the quality of performance by harpists." Membership is open to harpists and any persons interested in the activities of the organization. Current membership is about 1,600 in 45 U.S. chapters. Dues are $6 a year, which includes a subscription to the official magazine, *American Harp Journal,* published twice a year (Fall and Spring) and available to nonmembers for $3 annually. Editor of the *Journal* is **Gail Barber.** The Society, in order to raise the level of public awareness of the harp as a solo instrument and of singular characteristics, has commissioned new works from composers and encouraged publishers to publish better music for solo harp. Officers of the Society are: **Catherine Gotthoffer,** President; **Charles Kleinsteuber** and **Lucy Lewis,** First and Second Vice-Presidents; **Gertrude P. Hustana,** Treasurer; **Dorothy Remsen,** National Secretary; **Ann Mason Stockton,** Chairman of the Board. Annual conferences are held in June.

AMERICAN LISZT SOCIETY, INC., (ALS), c/o Chairman, Board of Directors, **David Z. Kushner,** Department of Music, University of Florida, Gainesville, Florida 32601. Founded in 1967 by David Kushner, **Robert C. Lee,** and **Fernando Laires** and others with the intention of developing "interest in the works of Franz Liszt through performance, recording, and publication of unpublished and out of print material and by providing a forum for the presentation of scholarly papers." The membership stands at over 100. The organization is open to anyone interested in the music of Franz Liszt and is not restricted to professional musicians. Dues are $500 for donor; $100 for life member; $10 yearly for active member; $20 for contributing member; and $10 for schools and libraries. A *Newsletter,* edited by David Kushner, is issued only to members once or twice a year. (The Society hopes to issue an annual journal eventually.) Annual meetings of officers and Board of Directors coincides with the Society's most important current activity, the annual Liszt Festival first held December 15 to 17, 1967 on the campus of Radford College, Radford, Virginia. Subsequent festival sites have been on the campuses of Brigham Young University, Boston University, the University of California at Santa Barbara, Southern Baptist Theological Seminary, the University of Florida in Gainesville (1971), and Westminster Choir College (1972). The events feature performances of the works of Liszt, stressing the less familiar works, and have offered performances by such soloists as **José Echaniz, Howard Lebow, Ozan Marsh, Alan Mandel,** pianists; **Georgio Ciompi,** violinist; **Louis L. Balogh,** organist; and many musicians from the academic world. Included on the festival programs are lectures, reading of papers, etc. Tapes of the festivals are available from the Society. Officers of the Society are: **Erno Daniel,** President; **David Z. Kushner,** Vice-President and Chairman of the Board of Directors; **Elyse Mach,** Executive Secretary.

AMERICAN MATTHAY ASSOCIATION, INC., c/o President, **Lytle Powell,** School of Music, University of Oklahoma, Norman, Oklahoma 73069. Tel.: (405) 325–3326. Founded in 1925 "to further and perpetuate an understanding of the work of Tobias Matthay [and his teaching principles]; to protect his genuine exponents and to encourage a high standard of performance and teaching. To foster a spirit of cooperation among his American pupils and adherents." (Tobias Matthay, famed English pianist and pedagogue, was born in 1858 and died in 1945. A number of pianists in the front rank of the concert world either were students of Matthay or studied under Matthay's students. Matthay wrote several pedagogical works outlining and utilizing what is called the Matthay System.) Membership is possible in the following categories: Active Members are those who studied personally with Matthay and who have been nominated to active membership by an Active Member and approved by the Board of Governors. Active Members must be citizens of the United States or Canada. Student Members are those of pre-college and college age who are studying with an Active Member. Friends of the Association are those contributing $5 or more each year to the work of the organization; categories of members in this group are Patron ($10 or more) or Life Member ($100 or more). A so-called Workshop Membership is open to persons who have attended two summer workshops on the Matthay System. Dues are: $7.50 for Active Members, $1 for students, $5 for Workshop Members—all annual. There are currently 160 members in the Association. Activities include the annual festival in conjunction with the organization's annual business meeting. The affair lasts one week and includes lectures, demonstrations, recitals and, since 1971, the Clara Wells Competition—all held on the campus of the University of Maryland in College Park (the 1972 event was the Association's fifteenth and took place from July 31 to August 6.) The organization's official publication is *The Matthay News,* issued three times a year to members only, Editor, **Chandler Gregg,** 19 Hundreds Circle, Wellesley Hills, Massachusetts 02181.

AMERICAN MUSIC CENTER, INC. (AMC), 2109 Broadway, Suite 1579, New York, N.Y. 10023. Tel.: (212) TR 3–7716 or SU 7–3300. Founded in 1940. AMC provides a center for the promotion of contemporary American music by maintaining an extensive library and acting as a clearing house for all information affecting American composers and their music. There are some 1,000 members of the AMC; about 650 are composers. The remaining members are music administrators, teachers (apart from those who may also be composers), publishers, conductors, singers and instrumentalists, students, and other persons concerned about the welfare and direction of American music, who may be in public life or who, privately and directly, offer financial or moral support for specific music endeavors. The AMC has the sanction to act as "the official United States information center for music," as designated by the National Music Council. President is **Ezra Laderman.** Other officers are: **Oliver Daniel** and **Martin Bookspan,** Vice-Presidents; **Claire Brook,** Secretary; **Arthur Cohn,** Treasurer; **Mrs. Toni Greenberg,** Executive Director. The AMC posts the following as honorary sponsors: **Leonard Bernstein, Senator Hubert H. Humphrey, Senator Jacob K. Javits,** and **Senator Claiborne Pell.** As a nonprofit organization it is not supportable through membership dues alone and, since it receives no financial assistance from governmental agencies, it is reliant on contributions from individuals and organizations. It operates on a budget of between $25,000 and $30,000, of which some $11,000 comes from members' dues. Modest contributions are made annually by some organizations totalling about $2,200, not counting funds contributed to AMC for carrying out specific programs such as the Composers Assistance Program (see below). Budget projections for the year 1971, the latest in available figures, indicated the need for AMC to raise some $6,500 in contributions. All of these sums indicate the extremely modest level of financing on which the AMC operates in view of the scope of the task it has assigned for itself, namely, "to foster and encourage the composition of [American] contemporary music and to promote its production, publication, distribution and performance in every possible way." The breadth of that goal, if a strict interpretation is applied—essentially the perpetuation of a musical culture largely unknown in its own country but a culture that, faced with constant preemption by its vernacular offshoot, struggles to establish itself as at least the "official" one on international grounds—is fundamentally a theoretical one in the light of AMC's operating budget and despite the impressive array of talent giving the Center its support. On a day-to-day basis, AMC's role is primarily a passive one of receiving information and making it available; cumulatively, its efforts have been effective. Composer-members of the Center are free to submit a reasonable number of their works for permanent placement in the Center's library, where they are catalogued and made available for loan and examination to interested persons without charge. Most of the works submitted are not generally available, i.e., they are unpublished and are usually available otherwise direct from the composers. The Center's library also has tape recordings of many of the works deposited. Currently, over 10,000 scores are in the library. AMC maintains an information library on United States composers consisting of biographical data; lists of works composed, published, and recorded; articles;

music publishers' catalogues; clippings, and so forth. For those seeking information about composers, the Center provides assistance through correspondence or, when possible, personal guidance to the use of the Center's information facilities. For the latter, the Center is open from 9 AM to 5 PM daily for visitors. Among the more active roles played by the AMC is the administering of the Composer Assistance Program under a grant from the Martha Baird Rockefeller Fund for Music, Inc. Under this program, financial assistance for copying and reproducing a music score is given to those composers who have secured definite performances of the work in question. An AMC advisory committee assumes the task of evaluating the financial need of the composer-applicant, the merit of the composition and the significance of the performance in general. Certain stipulations are applied to the program, although there are none regarding the composer's age or his professional status. To be eligible a musical work must be for seven or more performers and should be at least ten minutes long. It may be for any performing medium. The composer desiring assistance must secure a written invitation from a conductor or performing ensemble for at least one public performance of the piece either in the United States or abroad. He must also provide details of the performance, and an estimate of the cost of the work of copying and reproducing the music for performance, etc. In general, the majority of the grants are made to younger composers. Those having received grants who wish to apply for another can do so two years after the date of the first grant. The committee assigned to review grant requests and scores meets in October, February, and June and at other times when necessary. As of December, 1971 some 182 Composers Assistance Program grants were made totaling $73,825. The American Music Center publishes its *Newsletter* six times a year (subscription is $3 a year but it is sent free to members). An offset publication of from four to six pages, it mainly promulgates news of composers as submitted to the *Newsletter.* The news coverage is totally impartial, ranging from the trivial to the significant. Its regular features include lists of new performances, publications, recordings of the works of both members and other composers, contests, awards, festivals and contemporary music symposia; and announcements pertinent to the activities of the Center. Meetings for the Board of Directors are held six times a year; there is one annual general membership meeting, which is essentially an informal social gathering held during the Christmas season at which certain reports are read and members have the opportunity to meet one another. Dues for members of the AMC are as follows: $15 for composers, $15 for professionals, $75 for publishers, and $25 for orchestras and institutions. The AMC shares its quarters with both the National Music Council and the League of Composers–International Society of Contemporary Music (League–ISCM, U.S. Section).

AMERICAN MUSIC CONFERENCE (AMC), 3505 East Kilgore Road, Kalamazoo, Michigan 49002. Tel.: (616) 344–1697. Chartered in 1947 as a nonprofit, educational organization. Originally named, for a very brief time, the Music Institute of America, the AMC was formed as a result of specific music industry problems during the postwar period. It was created to act as the single promotional organization for the entire music industry; its formation was largely the effort of the National Association of Music Merchants (NAMM). Its prime goal is to help stimulate amateur music making in schools, communities, and in the home, thereby indirectly serving the interests of the music industry as a whole. In general, it receives its support from the music industry, its financial backing in particular stemming from dues paid by member firms. The AMC's formal declaration of purpose can be summarized to this extent: "To emphasize the public benefit of the greater use of music for educational, recreational, and cultural purposes, by stimulating music consciousness to the realization that participation in music activities is desirable in the lives of children and adults; foster interest in the extension of music instruction and administration, by informing parents and educators of the personal benefits of self-made music as a form of expression, a means of emotional outlet, a wholesome use of leisure time and a contributing factor in the development of well-rounded character and mental awareness; increase appreciation of the value of music by developing an active demand for music as a basic subject in all schools, readily available to children on the same basis as other subjects; stimulate groups to work for increased music activities on all levels, in the community, churches, schools, homes, and other character-building agencies." In practice, the AMC performs a wide variety of services for the public, educational institutions, the print and broadcast media, and the music industry. Probably the best-known activity of the organization is its annual surveys of the health of the music economy and the extent of amateur music-making activities in the nation. These surveys are always given wide distribution throughout the press—far beyond the confines of the press usually devoted to music news—and (undoubtedly because there are no similar surveys undertaken by any other organization) have been often interpreted strictly. In recent years, certain survey figures have been criticized by some as exaggerated or based on faulty projection of samplings. These criticisms and others coming from within AMC itself climaxed an extensive reorganization of AMC beginning in 1968 and culminating in a number of changes in an organization that had remained relatively stable for over twenty years. For a long time the surveys issued through the American Music Conference were the work of the public relations firm then retained, the Philip Lesly Company. When the association with this firm ceased in 1968, AMC temporarily availed itself of two other firms in succession before finally settling on the retention of its present public relations agency, The Public Relations Board, Inc., 75 East Wacker Drive, Chicago, Illinois 60601. A major responsibility of the new firm is the improvement of the method of gathering and interpreting survey statistics. To aid in this goal, AMC retains the services of the National Opinion Research Center of the University of Chicago, for the evaluation of amateur musical activities, and two part-time statistics specialists for studying the survey figures relating to growth within the music industry. Altogether, AMC allocates about $100,000 for public relations work. Some of the activities of the organization include: work with the National Recreation and Park Association (q.v.) for setting up techniques for planning community music events and parks activities; various "how to" manuals which were written by AMC and distributed to some 2,500 city recreational directors throughout the country. AMC participates in various conferences and conventions through exhibits and other means. Exhibits have been organized for display during the conventions of the Congress of Parents–Teachers Associations, National Association of Secondary School Principals, the National Association of Elementary School Principals, the National Association of School Administration Administrators, Association of Curriculum Supervisors and Guidance Counselors, National School Boards Association, and the National Catholic Education Association. AMC has produced two motion pictures, "Move to Music," and "Bringing Music into the Classroom," both available for loan to schools, teachers, and parent groups. A series of 11 hour-long radio programs entitled "Instrumental Odyssey," which outlines the history of music instruments, was written by AMC. First broadcast over WEFM, in Chicago (Zenith Radio Corporation) and later syndicated by National Educational Radio, the series won the Armstrong Award for the best FM music program series in 1970. The radio programs—tapes and script—have subsequently been made available to music stores, which may loan or give the programs to local schools. In addition to big productions such as this series, AMC has regularly provided the broadcast media with stories and interviews concerning music. Large amounts of material are also provided for the print media. In 1969, AMC participated as a member of the ad hoc Emergency Committee for Full Funding of Education Programs. This committee consisted of a large number of representatives of groups having an interest in education who lobbied to restore intended cuts in the House-approved appropriations for federal aid to education for 1970. The efforts of the committee were successful in blocking the cuts. Using Chicago as a test area, the AMC organized a so-called Youth Music Competition for the benefit of local amateur young musicians. In conjunction with the Chicago Park District, the first such event, with prizes awarded, was successfully brought off. The techniques used to produce the competition are being made available to other cities and parks throughout the country. An annual Advertising Awards Competition for creative use of musical instruments to promote nonmusical products in the print media has been awarded by AMC for over twenty years. Recently it began to offer the "Hugo" Award at the Chicago International Film Festival for the best use of musical instruments on-camera in television commercials. Other AMC activities include providing guitar clinics at the regional conventions of the Music Educators National Conference (MENC), supporting research into the medical claims that excessive music amplification was damaging to the human ear, and helping the University of Chicago conduct, in 1971, a seminar on the selection and maintenance of pianos and harpsichords. On a daily basis, the offices of AMC receive requests for information and assistance concerning a wide range of problems involving music. Recent publications prepared or published by AMC are: "Creative Approaches to School Music," "Music U.S.A.," a review of the music industry and amateur music-making activities, and, in conjunction with the National Recreation and Park Association and available through that organization, two booklets, "Community Instrumental Music Programming," and "Community Vocal Music Programming." The surveys undertaken by AMC are by far the most widely circulated of all its printed material. They are quoted extensively throughout the music trades and profession as well as general-interest magazines, popular magazines, consumer periodicals, and the like. Writers and speakers referring to the extent of music participation in this country are always at a loss to find any statistics other than those provided by AMC. Some of these figures are found in this book where they might provide a point of reference. The AMC is governed by elected officers, a Board of Trustees, and Directors. The Trustees represent various segments of the music industry. Thus, the following music industry organizations have representation in the AMC: the National Association of Music Merchants, National Piano Manufacturers Association, Guitar and Accessory Manufacturers Association of America, National Association of Band Instrument Manufacturers, National Music Publishers Association, National Association of Musical Merchandise Wholesalers, and the National Association of Electronic Organ Manufacturers. Officers of the AMC are: **Theodore M. McCarty,** President and chief administrative officer, whose offices are at the Kalamazoo address (AMC was a Chicago-based organization from its inception until 1970); **Elmer F. Brooks,** Chairman of the Board; **Jack J. Wainger,** Vice-Chairman; **Vito Pascucci,** Secretary; **Fred Targ,** Treasurer. **Mr. McCarty** is the first full-time paid president of AMC. Previous to the major organizational changes made by AMC from 1969 onward, the chief administrator was the Executive Vice-President, a post held by **James L. Bixby** for many years.

AMERICAN MUSICOLOGICAL SOCIETY (AMS), Office of the Business Manager, 201 South 34th Street, Philadelphia, Pennsylvania 19104. Registrar (for membership application, etc.) is **Cecil Adkins,** School of Music, North Texas State University, Denton, Texas 76203. Founded in 1934. The Society is the foremost organization of music researchers and scholars in the United States (and Canada). Members are mostly in the academic world (many with professorial rank) as teachers, music librarians, administrators, students majoring in musicology and its related studies; some are concert musicians. Among them are the leading music scholars in America, those with high professional attainment, as researchers, writers, and editors, beyond their institutional work. Membership, as of January 1, 1972, stood at 2,821 plus 1,019 subscribers (including in these figures 1,763 regular members, 869 students, 976 institutional subscribers, among other categories). The AMS has as its general purpose the advancement of musical research as an important aspect of learning and scholarship; by the same token, it can be said that it is also interested in learning and scholarship as an important aspect of music study. The growth of so specialized a society (fifteen years ago there were slightly over 1,000 members, twenty years ago, about 800) attests not only to the increase in interest in music scholarship and the realization of its need, but also to the ability of musicologists to cultivate that interest among young music academicians. The influence of music scholars in a very broad sense is manifest throughout the music field. The growth in kind and improvement in quality of undergraduate music history and literature courses and related music studies is seen in music departments and schools of music throughout the United States. These, along with graduate, particularly doctoral, music studies, reflect a generation of influence from the music scholar. The increase in scholarly music publications in America—both scores and books on music—the growing sophistication of library acquisitions in the music field, and the impact of music research and keener intellectualism in performance, composition, pedagogy, and even music journalism, is apparent. Since 1951, the AMS has been a constituent member of the American Council of Learned Societies and is an affiliate of the International Musicological Society. It works often in conjunction with such groups as the Music Library Association, the College Music Society, and the Society for Ethnomusicology. It is governed by an elected Executive Board of 11 members and a Council of 62. AMS produces publications, foremost of which is its *Journal of the American Musicological Society,* published three times a year and sent free to members as part of the membership dues (see Periodicals). This learned publication is a vehicle for the research findings of its members, which are published as full-length articles, or studies and abstracts. The depth of probing and particularity of the articles and their clinical documentation is usually expended on researches into music of the past which are intended for the specialist. The articles, extensively buttressed by footnotes, often have long quoted passages in foreign languages, including Latin, and feature diagrams, graphs, facsimiles and other accouterments of the thorough researcher; musical examples are sometimes in antique notation. These, and other factors, set the *Journal* apart from most of today's music publications and make it a permanent source of reference. The *Journal* also prints in-depth, scholarly reviews of new publications, communications from its subscribers, and other items. Until recently, it also published organizational news and reports. These are now published in the *AMS Newsletter,* issued twice a year. Co-Editors are **Claude V. Palisca** and **Frank Traficante** (editorial address is care of the latter, Department of Music, University of Kentucky, Lexington, Kentucky 40506). Other AMS publications (all for sale, with reduced prices for members) are: "Doctoral Dissertations in Musicology," 4th and 5th editions (1965 and 1971), edited respectively by **Helen Hewitt** and **Cecil Adkins;** "A Selective List of Masters' Theses," by **D. R. de Lerma,** 1970; "Abstracts" of papers read at 35th, 36th, and 37th annual AMS meetings (1969–1971), and the *Bulletin,* various numbers dating from 1937 to 1947. Studies and documents include "Quantz and his Versuch," by **Edward R. Reilly** (1971); "The Elizabethan Madrigal, a Comparative Study," by **Joseph Kerman** (1962); Volumes One and Two of the Collected Works of Ockeghem, edited by **Dragan Plamenac** (1966); and the Complete Works of Dunstable, edited by the late Manfred Bukofzer, 2nd revised edition, 1970 (published jointly with the Royal Musical Association, London). The studies and documents are made available for sale through Galaxy Music Corporation (see Music Publishers). AMS and the Music Library Association jointly sponsored the reprinting of the Schubert Complete Works (issued through Dover Publications); it has also sponsored a number of smaller publications through commercial publishers and reprint houses. AMS provides its members with a Placement Service: listings of candidates seeking employment or a change of position and institutions having vacancies for such. Other activities and projects of the AMS include the sponsorship of the Kinkeldy and Einstein awards in musicological writings (see Contests, . . .) and the highly successful International Josquin Festival–Conference held in New York City in June, 1971, which commemorated the 450th anniversary of the composer's death. The concerts, lectures, convocations, etc., were funded by contributions from foundations, private donors, and governmental agencies and received wide and highly laudatory press throughout the music world. The Society's three-day annual meetings and the regularly held meetings of some 20 regional chapters are events which provide the opportunity not only to conduct organizational business but also to hear professional papers, panel discussions, concerts of special interest and other activities relating to music research and learning. AMS often lends its voice to general causes affecting music, the arts and humanities; it makes curricula recommendations in consort with other music organizations. Officers of the AMS are: **Claude V. Palisca,** Yale University, President; **Charles Hamm,** President-elect, University of Illinois (term commencing in November, 1972); **Rita Benton,** Secretary, University of Iowa; **Alvin H. Johnson,** Treasurer, University of Pennsylvania. Business Manager of Publications is **Otto E. Albrecht** (at address above); Editor-in-Chief of the *Journal* (commencing with the Spring 1972 issue) is **Don Randel,** Cornell University. **Cecil Adkins** is Registrar and Director of the Placement Service. Dues are: $12.50 (regular), $6.50 (student); joint husband–wife is $3 additional.

AMERICAN OPERA AUDITIONS, INC., 4511 Carew Tower, Cincinnati, Ohio 45202. A nonprofit organization founded in 1957. Its purpose is "to discover, through national competition, outstanding new voices—and to prepare and launch them in operatic careers." (See also under Contests.) Auditions are open to American singers of professional vocal attainments who would benefit from further study and experience in the field of opera. Winners are trained in Italy with all expenses paid and receive an operatic debut opportunity there. The first auditions singled out 8 winners from about 1,000 applicants. Agencies cooperating with the auditions are the Cincinnati College-Conservatory of Music; l'Associazione Lirica e Concertistica, Milan; l'Associazione Italiana Diffusione Educazione Musicale, Florence; and Radio Cincinnati, Inc. President and Founder is **John L. Magro.**

AMERICAN SCHOOL BAND DIRECTORS ASSOCIATION, INC. (ASBDA), c/o **Dale Harper,** President, 24380 Oakhill Drive, Euclid, Ohio 44117. Tel.: (216) 481–1529. Founded November, 1953. The organization is made up of professionally trained and certified conductors and teachers of bands in schools. Its membership stands at about 956 with the majority being Active Members who are defined as being "men and women of established personal and professional integrity and reputation who are actively engaged in teaching and directing of school bands on the elementary school, junior high school, and senior high school levels." They must have had at least seven years experience. Other members are Affiliate Members (former Active Members who are no longer actively directing school bands), and Associate Members (interested persons and business firms, such as music publishers, manufacturers of musical instruments and so forth, who cannot qualify for Active membership). The goals of the ASBDA include the following: "To provide a common meeting ground and clearing house for an exchange of ideas and methods that will advance the standards of musical and educational achievement for the school bands of America and stimulate professional growth among school band directors. To work in close cooperation with school administrators as representatives of their individual schools and, through their respective administrative associations, to promote a standard of musical progress and achievement which will be of cultural benefit to the student in his school life and in his adult life. To serve as an authoritative means of liaison between the largest group of instrumental music teachers in the United States—the school band directors—and music publishers, musical instrument manufacturers, band uniform companies, school architects and suppliers of school building materials and equipment." Dues are $12.50 for Active Members, $5 for Affiliate Members, and $25 for Associate Members. National conventions of the ASBDA are held annually; state meetings are twice a year. The official publication is the periodical *The School Musician* (see Periodicals), a subscription to which is included in the dues of members.

AMERICAN SOCIETY FOR AESTHETICS, c/o Secretary-Treasurer, The Cleveland Museum of Art, Cleveland, Ohio 44106. Tel.: (216) 421–7340. Founded in 1942. Membership is over 750 and is open to all interested persons. The purpose of the Society is to "promote study, research, discussion, and publications in aesthetics [of all the arts]." Annual dues are $15 for the United States and Canada and $16 for foreign members; student membership is $5. All members receive the official periodical of the Society, *The Journal of Aesthetics and Art Criticism,* a quarterly (see Periodicals). The Society holds annual meetings in October and participates in the International Congress of Aesthetics held every four years in various countries (last held in 1969 in Uppsala, Sweden). President: **Bertram Jessup,** State University of New York at Buffalo (term expired December 31, 1972). Secretary-Treasurer: **James R. Johnson** (address above; term expired December 31, 1972). Honorary President is **Thomas Munro,** c/o Cleveland Museum of Art. Editor of the *Journal* is **Herbert M. Schueller,** Wayne State University.

THE AMERICAN SOCIETY OF COMPOSERS, AUTHORS AND PUBLISHERS (ASCAP), ASCAP Building, One Lincoln Plaza, New York, N.Y. 10023. Tel.: (212) 595–3050. ASCAP is a voluntary, nonprofit, unincorporated society of music writers and publishers which acts as a performance rights clearing house negotiating licenses with users of music who wish to perform in public for profit the copyrighted works of ASCAP's members. It was founded in 1914 by writers of music (this term in ASCAP's usage includes composers and lyricists) who sought to insure compliance with the 1909 copyright law, which recognized the compensatory use of published creative writings when the use was related to profit making in some form. Since compliance was commonly ignored in the earliest stages of the law's existence, the Society was formed to better protect the rights of writers and publishers. Members of ASCAP are 9,735 writers and 3,074 publishers whose collective repertories include all forms of music—symphonic, band music, jazz, blues, rock, film and TV scores, country and western, Broadway musical theater, folk music, religious music, educational music (see introduction to Music Publishers, Part 11), etc. The roster of members contains many of the prominent creators in each compositional idiom. Members are those who have at least one copyrighted musical work regularly published. To encourage new, young writers to join ASCAP, the Society now permits a writer who has a copyrighted work that has not yet been commercially recorded or published to join as an associate member who may then become a regular member whenever his work enters the commercial outlets. Publishers belonging to the Society are those actively engaged in publishing as firms or individuals who accept the normal financial risks of music publishing, that is, who do not require that writers pay for the cost of publishing their work. Both writers and publishers must submit as a condition for becoming a member of the Society a "regularly published work" in the form of a sales copy of the work published, or a commercial recording. Dues are $10 a year for writers and $50 for publishers. Associate members pay no dues. Dues payments are used for the relief of indigent ASCAP members or their dependents. The fundamental service provided by ASCAP is born of the size and complexity of the market consuming music. Essentially it has created the administrative machinery which enables the Society to issue single or blanket licenses, that is, to charge a single fee to users so that they may perform the works of any, or, theoretically, all of the writer-members of ASCAP. For large users of music, such as broadcasters and recording firms, the alternative would be an impossibility, namely, dealing individually with thousands of composers, lyricists, and publishers. A schedule of rates drawn up by the Society determines the amount of the fee charged for performance licenses with qualifying factors being the category of the establishment in which the music is to be performed (i.e., night club, bar, theater, amphitheater), its seating capacity, whether music is the featured entertainment or whether it is background to another entertainment form, etc. Although a blanket license holder, by paying a single annual fee to ASCAP, escapes the need to account for each performance of ASCAP members' music, it is possible for a more sporadic user of music to negotiate with the Society on a performance-by-performance basis. Fees charged in such cases are based on such factors as the user's performance income, the nature of the performance, etc. Income from all ASCAP's fees is distributed quarterly to the membership after operating costs are deducted (about 16 percent in 1966, a figure perhaps now larger). Net income is divided equally between writer- and publisher-members. Each group employs its own formula for apportioning its income. A Board of Review is established to hear complaints any member may have concerning his fee income. In general, the determining factor for allocating fee payments to any member is the number of performances a given work has received, a calculation that is made by an elaborately operated Survey of Performances, organized by an independent consultant firm and subject to occasional review by an appointee of the Federal Court, a court also used for redress by any user who is dissatisfied with the fee charged him by ASCAP. A rating system, which allocates "credits" for various categories of performance, is utilized. In its application, concert music, so-called serious music, is given a greater percentage of points and administrative costs are not deducted from royalty income. This is an agreement reached by ASCAP members voluntarily so that composers of symphonic music, whose compensation from their works is subject to altogether different economic factors from those of their fellow composers who write for popular music users, can enjoy the benefit of an improved income. The Survey system employs the greatest number of ASCAP staffers. In addition to income from licensing fees, ASCAP dispenses annual awards to its popular and standard (i.e., "serious") music writers. These are monetary awards, not exceeding $2,000 to any one member and not awarded to any member who earns more than $20,000 in royalties a year, which are granted to members on the basis of various meritorious factors such as number of performances of his work, productivity, recognition, honors, etc. For the year 1971–72, awards went to 580 writers in the standard field totaling $344,060, and $355,650 was distributed to 1,616 writers in popular music and lyrics. The large and important group of ASCAP license holders include symphony orchestras, which are charged a single fee for the entire season according to the orchestra's size, number of concerts, etc., or which may negotiate a fee for a single performance; the national network broadcasters, NBC, CBS, and ABC, whose total fee payment per year to ASCAP can be about $17 million; and the nation's colleges and universities which now occupy a crucial position as consumers of new (and copyrighted) music of all kinds. ASCAP only recently has drawn up an agreement designed to function for the particular case of educational institutions whose music consumption can include, in addition to concerts and staged productions involving music, such paid-admission events as football games and other spectacles involving the use of entertainment music. The license fee for colleges is based on a scale of student enrollment. Thus, the annual fee for a school having fewer than 1,000 students is $25; this sum is graduated to $200 if the school enrollment is over 20,000. The license entitles a school to access to the entire ASCAP catalogue and covers only public performances (accounting for which is done by the school's submission of the printed programs for such concerts). All single-fee licensees with ASCAP may utilize the music in the catalogues of ASCAP's foreign affiliates, who are the licensing rights counterpart agencies in foreign countries. The music of well-known and important foreign contemporary composers can be made available, therefore, to American performing groups and audiences. ASCAP has affiliate agreements with performing rights organizations in Argentina, Australia, Austria, Belgium, Brazil, Canada, Chile, Czechoslovakia, Denmark, England, Finland, France, Germany, Greece, Holland, Hungary, Iceland, Israel, Italy, Japan, Madagascar, Mexico, Norway, Peru, Philippines, Portugal, Puerto Rico, South Africa, Spain, Sweden, Switzerland, Uruguay, and Yugoslavia. ASCAP issues a number of publications: *ASCAP Today,* sent free on request, is a 40-page magazine covering information about ASCAP but containing a great deal of information about ASCAP members—composers, lyricists, performers, publishers, etc.—as well as general interest articles. Editor is **Walter Wager;** the magazine is issued four times annually. ASCAP also publishes a *List of Members,* a booklet listing all publisher- and individual members (including deceased members whose works are still viable in the ASCAP catalogue, e.g., Louis Armstrong and Sergei Rachmaninoff); two large and important catalogues, the three-volume "ASCAP Index" of popular songs and the "ASCAP Symphonic Catalog" (1959 with a 1966 Supplement and an Addendum to the Supplement), the latter a detailed 745-page catalogue listing the works of 3,000 composers for symphonic ensembles with title, complete instrumentation, duration, and publisher (ASCAP foreign affiliate composers are included in the catalogue); an 845-page hard-cover book, "ASCAP Biographical Dictionary" (3rd edition, 1966). The Dictionary is an invaluable compendium of biographical data on every composer and lyricist whose works are still in the ASCAP catalogues and provides a list of compositions of each member. Two competitions are administered by ASCAP: the ASCAP-Deems Taylor Award (see Contests . . .) awarded for the best writings on music, and the Nathan Burkan Memorial Competition held in law schools throughout the country, an award granted for outstanding essays on copyright law. ASCAP has branch offices and regional representatives in twenty-four cities in the U.S. including one in Puerto Rico. Major headquarters outside New York are the offices at 700 17th Avenue South, Nashville, Tennessee and 6430 Sunset Boulevard, Los Angeles, California. ASCAP's government is entirely composed of member writers and publishers. There is a 24-member Board of Directors, 12 elected by publisher-members and 12 elected by writer-members. ASCAP's president is traditionally a writer-member, currently one with an early legal background. Three of the publishers and three of the writer-members of the Board represent the field of serious music. The Board meets monthly. There are annual general elections for officers. Officers are: **Stanley Adams,** President (serving continuously since 1959); **Ned Washington** and **Salvatore T. Chiantia,** Vice Presidents; **Morton Gould,** Secretary; **Ernest R. Farmer,** Treasurer; **Arthur Schwartz,** Assistant Secretary. The Board of Directors (for 1971–1973) consists of the above-named plus **Harold Arlen, Samuel Barber, Cy Coleman, Vincent Persichetti, Richard Rodgers,** among others. The familiarity of these names indicates in some measure the nature of ASCAP's membership.

AMERICAN SOCIETY OF MUSIC ARRANGERS (ASMA), 224 West 49th Street, New York, N.Y. 10019. Tel.: (212) JU 6–2698. Founded in Los Angeles in 1938; the New York section was founded in 1944. The Society works to ease the problems that are peculiar to the professional arranger, particularly in his relationship to the American Federation of Musicians, of which he must be a member of good standing in order to retain his membership in ASMA. The organization publishes a monthly *Newsletter* for members only, holds annual general meetings and monthly luncheons and engages in various workshops and clinics related to music arranging. President is **M. Russell Goudey.**

THE AMERICAN SOCIETY FOR THE PRESERVATION OF SACRED, PATRIOTIC AND OPERATIC MUSIC, Suite 13–18, 2109 Broadway, New York, N.Y. 10023. Tel.: (212) EN 2–1796. Founded in 1941 by present Chairman and Musical Director **Charles Albert McLain.** The Society is nonprofit and noncommercial, organized "for the purpose of preserving the best to be found in sacred music and American patriotic music, of stimulating high creative endeavor in these classifications, of urging all American organizations to support American musicians, and of doing educational work towards advancing these purposes; and for the further purpose of establishing the American Music Library." Membership in the Society is only upon invitation by a board member and with the approval of the full board. There are no membership dues. The Society has sponsored concerts and international broadcasts and, from time to time, issues bulletins and circulars concerning its activities and interests. Board meetings are held quarterly; general meetings are periodically called by the Board.

AMERICAN SOCIETY OF UNIVERSITY COMPOSERS (ASUC), c/o American Music Center, 2109 Broadway, Suite 1579, New York, N.Y. 10023. Founded in 1966, the organization is made up of composers "who are or were affiliated with a university, college, school, or conservatory of music." Total membership is approximately 250. The primary aim of the society "is the mobilization of the resources of the academic community to the service of composers." Activities include local and national meetings during which concerts, lectures, discussions and a general exchange of information and ideas—professional and technical—take place. National conferences are scheduled in April of each year on different school campuses (the 1972 meeting took place at the Peabody Conservatory in Baltimore, the one in 1971, at the University of Houston). A Summer Institute is held in August each year (at Tanglewood, the University of Michigan, and other locations), when meetings of a more informal nature are offered permitting, however, essentially the same kind of activity planned for the national conferences. The Society publishes *Proceedings* each year, which is a digest of the discussions and presentations taking place at the national conferences and the summer institutes. *Proceedings* is offered for subscription to libraries and individuals at $3.50 a volume but is free to society members. *Newsletter* is the official publication of the society, appearing three times a year for members only. Other publications in process include the *ASUC Journal of Music Scores.* Three volumes will appear annually each containing an average of four to eight compositions in facsimile of member composers. Regular membership dues are $25 a year; student membership is $10; associate membership is $15. The latter two categories of membership allow participation in all society activities except voting and holding office. The society is governed in general matters by its National Council, representing members' various regions; daily operating activities are the responsibility of the Executive Committee. Both council and committee have their respective chairmen. Chairman (pro tem.) of the National Council is **David Burge;** Chairman of the Executive Committee is **Gerald Warfield.**

AMERICAN STRING TEACHERS ASSOCIATION (ASTA), c/o Executive Secretary, **Robert C. Marince,** 2596 Princeton Pike, Lawrence Township Public Schools, Trenton, New Jersey 08638. Tel.: (609) 882–7272. Founded in 1946. Has a membership of over 3,800, mostly string and orchestra teachers in public schools and colleges and some students. Members are located in chapters in about forty-three states and in some foreign countries. ASTA's purpose is to encourage amateur and professional performance of the bowed string instruments (violin, viola, cello, and string bass) as well as to promote the study, research and pedagogy, and teacher education related to the use of these instruments. Membership is open to anyone interested in the welfare of string instruments and their music. General dues for active membership are $6; other rates apply to students, institutions, contributing and life members. The activities of ASTA include, in addition to publications (see below), conducting research in the playing and learning of string instruments (in 1966, in cooperation with the University of Illinois and the government, a special study was initiated on violin teaching), development of a String Instrument Repair Institute, development of modern promotional materials, and cooperation with a number of musical organizations pursuing goals related to those of ASTA, such as the Music Educators National Conference, Music Teachers National Association, and National School Orchestra Association. In 1971, ASTA organized some 18 workshops at summer music camps and clinics for school orchestra teachers who do not play string instruments. Since 1963, ASTA has proffered an Artist-Teacher of the Year Award and a Distinguished Service Award. Recipients of the former have been **Isaac Stern, Pablo Casals, Ivan Galamian, Josef Gingold,** et al., and the latter award has gone to **Jack Benny, Heinrich Roth,** the Fine Arts Quartet, National Federation of Music Clubs, among others. The official organ of the American String Teachers Association is *American String Teacher,* which is free to members (see Periodicals). ASTA has issued the following publications, among others: "The Ten Piano-Violin Sonatas of Beethoven," by **J. Szigeti,** "Violin Left Hand Technique," by **Neumann,** "Dictionary of Bowing Terms," by **Berman and Seagrave,** "Modern Viola Technique," by **Dolejsi,** "Differences Between 18th Century and Modern Violin Bowing," by **Sol Babitz,** "Annotated Catalog of Contemporary Violin Music," by **Landsman,** plus various works of practical benefit to school string instrument teaching and playing. ASTA holds annual conventions in conjunction with Music Educators National Conference and organizes about six regional meetings annually. Officers are: **Ralph Matesky,** President, Utah State University, Logan, Utah; **Robert C. Marince,** Executive Secretary (see above); **Howard Van Sickle,** Vice President; **Phyllis Glass,** Secretary. **Paul Rolland** of the University of Illinois has had responsibility for the development of ASTA's list of publications.

AMERICAN SYMPHONY ORCHESTRA LEAGUE, INC. (ASOL), Symphony Hill, P.O. Box 66, Vienna, Virginia 22180. Tel.: (703) 938–2822. Founded in 1942. Founder (and now honorary president) was **Mrs. Leta G. Snow** who, with **Theresa Shier**—both from Michigan—set up the organization. From 1942 to 1950 the League was supported through the volunteer help of its members. In 1950, its first full-time executive was appointed in the person of **Mrs. Helen M. Thompson,** who served until 1970 (she now manages the New York Philharmonic). During that period the League established a national headquarters and greatly expanded its work, its membership, and its influence. It is today among the major nonprofit service organizations in the field of music. The League is the only unilateral music organization that has been granted a Federal Charter by the U.S. Congress (Public Law 87–817, passed October 15, 1962). Its purposes, as stated in the Law: "To serve as a coordinating, research, and educational agency and clearinghouse for symphony orchestras in order to help strengthen the work in their local communities; to assist in the formation of new symphony orchestras; through suitable means, encourage and recognize the work of America's musicians, conductors, and composers; and to aid the expansion of the musical and cultural life of the United States through suitable educational and service activities." Membership in the League is open to all who are interested in the current and future condition of the symphony orchestra. However, voting membership can be held only by member symphony orchestras (one vote each); persons, business firms, institutions, etc., are nonvoting (associate) members. Virtually all of the major symphonic ensembles and many that are active in secondary and tertiary ranks hold membership in the League partly because of the services the League provides and partly because of the need to join common cause with other orchestras in matters of benefit, if not survival, to orchestras. The ASOL has established a system of categorization of symphony orchestras in the U.S. (and Canada) which is widely accepted as a means of referral but which arose from administrative necessity in the matter of dues assessment and other considerations. Thus, the categories of orchestras are based on the budget under which each orchestra functions. The classes are as follows: Major Orchestras: those having an annual budget in excess of $500,000. (Beginning with fiscal year 1972–73, this category will undergo a change, to wit, that a major orchestra will be one which maintains a gross annual budget of at least $1 million for two consecutive years preceding the year of membership. It must have been in existence for a minimum of three years prior to the year of membership. It must employ professional musicians on a weekly basis whose principal employment must be with the orchestra; the orchestra must be able to perform the full range of the symphonic repertory. In addition, the major symphony orchestra must be defined as an institution operating as a nonprofit corporation, recognized as such by the Internal Revenue Service, for the prime purpose of serving its community by the presentation of orchestral concerts.) Metropolitan Orchestras: those having an annual budget from $100,000 to $500,000. Urban Orchestras: orchestras with an annual budget of from $50,000 to $100,000. Community Orchestras: those with budgets below $50,000. The schedule of dues payments assessed annually is as follows: $50 for orchestras with annual budgets from $100 to $9,999: $75 for the budget range of $10,000 to $24,999; $100 for $25,000 to $49,999; $150 for $50,000 to $99,999; $200 for $100,000 to $199,999; $200 to $999, or one tenth of 1 percent of any annual budget ranging from $200,000 to $999,999; $1,000 for orchestras whose budgets are $1 million or more. Dues for nonvoting members are: $10 for individual members; $25 for organizations; $100 for music business firms; $250 for nonmusic business firms; $25 for libraries; $5 for libraries receiving the ASOL official organ only (see below); $10 for Women's Council members of the League. Symphony Women's Associations pay $25 if their parent orchestra is a League member, otherwise the dues payment is $35. Current membership in ASOL is (as of January 14, 1972): 355 orchestras (which includes 28 major orchestras, 72 metropolitan, 28 urban, 163 community, 31 college orchestras, 26 so-called college–community orchestras—often consisting of college student and faculty players plus players from the community); 315 associate organizational members (150 symphony women's associations, 18 arts councils, 34 business firms, 77 libraries plus other groups); 1,371 associate individual members, more than a third of whom are orchestra conductors (536), the remainder made up of managers (226), musicians (200), orchestra board members (112), and others. Total League membership for all categories is 2,041. The activities of the League are often germinal. It was the first to establish a training course in orchestra management, which now continues annually (usually held in New York City), for those already having the responsibility of managing an orchestra or for those who are considering orchestra management as a career. Lasting a week, the course is taught by a large group of professionals involved in managing orchestras, as well as by concert managers, artist representatives, executives from the music industries (publishing, recording, etc.); 33 students attended the course in 1972. ASOL holds an annual Institute of Orchestral Studies at Orkney Springs, Virginia which offers highly concentrated training to about 12 young conductors (applicants can number as many as 100) under the guidance of a master conductor (for more details, see Shenandoah Valley Music Festival, Virginia). These workshops are designed to improve the professional skill of conductors of less than major orchestras or those who would most benefit from actual working sessions, under close tutelage, with a specially organized institute orchestra. The goal of the institutes is to improve orchestra playing and conducting in areas of the nation represented by the selected conductors, all of whom must already be highly talented. Funding for the institutes comes from foundations, arts organizations, and government agencies. All institute administrative services are provided by the League. The League has undertaken a number of basic studies, among them: the first study of the legal structure of orchestra organizations (resulting in a published manual of orchestra legal documents), the first detailed study of the governing boards of symphony orchestras (also resulting in a manual, on board structure and work), the first comprehensive analysis of symphony women's association activities, and a study of orchestra youth concerts. It conducts field analyses of orchestra organizations and various other surveys, sometimes in conjunction with other organizations, e.g., the annual Orchestral Program Survey of Broadcast Music Inc., which has always been done with the cooperation of ASOL. The League's central work for orchestras has spawned a growing information service covering not only matters pertaining to orchestras but to the larger performing arts field in the United States. As a result, the League is often called upon to provide supportive information for the use of arts councils, other music service organizations, cultural and educational agencies. One example of such activity is its closely maintained information service on legislative actions affecting the performing arts in general. The ASOL was among the front line organizations in the music field pleading for, first, the establishment and, then, the enlargement of the National Foundation of the Arts and the Humanities. Tax legislation adversely affecting performing arts groups, musicians, etc., is given notoriety in League publications which have helped to form joint action throughout the arts field for reversing such legislation. In all matters stemming from arts finances, law, etc., the communications from the League show a high level of sophistication reflecting solid legal counseling and an understanding of political and economic factors relating to the performing arts. An important affiliated organization established by ASOL in 1964 is the Women's Council of the American Symphony Orchestra League, an association of women-in-service to orchestras on the community level; members are past presidents of symphony orchestra women's councils. Membership of the Council is in excess of 200. The Council is active in strengthening the support basis of orchestras through fund drives, the enlistment of new members in orchestral associations and the many other characteristic activities that make the world of the American symphony orchestra unlike that of any other country. Among the publications of the League are: *Symphony News,* the official magazine, formerly called the *Newsletter,* which is sent to members six times a year as part of their membership privileges. Editor of *Symphony News* is **Benjamin S. Dunham.** The magazine serves as the prime source of communication between the League and its members. It is illustrated and carries some limited commercial advertising. Among the League pamphlets and books are: "Symphony News is Good News," a guide for publicity directors of orchestras; "Symphony Orchestras Abroad," by **Howard Taubman** (1970), a League-commissioned study of subsidy for European orchestras; "The Organization, Administration and Presentation of Symphony Orchestra Youth Activities for Music Education Purposes in Selected Cities—Part 1—Summary," published in 1968 and compiled by **Thomas Hill** and **Helen M. Thompson.** As of April 6, 1972, the League has issued some 624 *Memos,* which may be termed mini-monographs on subjects ranging from the use of the League's mailing lists and postal regulations covering them to extensive reports on Federal Government hearings on legislation related to the arts. The League financial reports and nominations for League offices and committees are also published in the *Memos.* For women's associations, there are several handbooks available. The complete list of League publications is available from its headquarters. (Some publications are offered at reduced prices to ASOL members.) The League presents an annual "Gold Baton Award" to persons making significant contributions to the cause of music and orchestras and grants the "ASOL/ASCAP Awards" for the best programming of contemporary music by orchestras (limited to ASCAP-licensed orchestras). The Women's Council makes its own awards for community services. Financial assistance has been received by the League from the Ford Foundation, Rockefeller Foundation, Martha Baird Rockefeller Fund for Music, Avalon Foundation, Shell Companies Foundation, Alice M. Ditson Fund, National Endowment for the Arts, ASCAP, BMI, and other organizations and foundations. The League's income for the fiscal year ending March 31, 1971 was $179,214.74; its general expenses were $194,426.39. Total annual disbursements for general and special funds amounted to $362,679.33. In February, 1972, officers were: **John S. Edwards,** Chairman of the Board; **Morton Gould,** First Vice Chairman; **Mrs. Hampton S. Lynch,** Secretary; **James Ravlin,**

Treasurer; **Richard H. Wangerin,** President and operational executive. In addition there are three vice chairmen, members-at-large of the Executive Committee, and 16 members of the Board of Directors comprised of orchestra conductors, managers, musicians, philanthropists, and persons active on boards of community orchestras. National conferences are held once a year for four days in June, in different cities in the nation. The sessions are attended by representatives of orchestras, patrons, friends, and associate ASOL members.

AMERICAN THEATRE ASSOCIATION, INC. (ATA), 1317 F Street, N.W., Washington, D.C. 20006. Tel.: (202) 343–8868. Founded in 1936. Formerly the American Educational Theatre Association. Membership: about 4,948. Membership is open to anyone interested in theater and related arts. Although its main purpose is to develop high standards in theater and related arts through education on all levels in schools, through tours, publications, conferences, projects, research, etc., it does support continuing projects in musical theater, opera, and dance when such projects may involve research or experimentation. Publishes *Theatre Journal* (four times a year, sent free to members); various bibliographies; teaching aids; rare books of the theater; directories; *Children's Theatre Review,* community theatre's *ON-STAGE,* and *Secondary School Theatre News* (all quarterly); and *Theatre News,* issued nine to twelve times a year. Regular individual member dues are $10; organizational membership is $30 a year. Executive Director is **Anthony Reid.** Other officers are: **Jed H. Davis,** President (through 1972); **Vera Mowry Roberts,** President-Elect (beginning 1973). Vice Presidents, respectively for Administration, Program, and Research are: **Ann Hill, William R. McGraw, Ralph G. Allen;** Secretary is **Karl C. Bruder;** Treasurer is **Harold R. Oaks.**

ASSOCIATED COUNCILS OF THE ARTS (ACA), 1564 Broadway, New York, N.Y. 10036. Tel.: (212) 586–3731. Founded in 1960. ACA is a nonprofit, incorporated foundation with a membership comprised of organizations—themselves nonprofit—which are engaged in the encouragement and support of the arts. Interested persons may also join ACA. Member-organizations are U.S. state and community arts agencies, arts councils, and arts centers. ACA does not disburse funds; its active role is in publishing and disseminating information pertinent to the support of arts and in providing guidance and assistance to anyone engaged in the arts. ACA's funds come from dues, earned income (e.g., in the sale of publications), grants from government agencies, and contributions from individuals, foundations, and business firms. There are over 500 members in the organization. Voting members are community councils, arts centers, etc. Nonvoting members (Associate members) are individuals who may or may not belong to such organizations but who represent only themselves as far as their membership in ACA is concerned; corporations, foundations, arts service organizations likewise qualify for Associate membership. Individual Associate members pay dues of $25 per year; organizational Associate members have dues of $50 a year. Dues for voting members (Participating) are $100 for organizations with budgets under $99,999; $250 for organizations with budgets from $100,000 to $199,999; and $500 for organizations with budgets over $200,000. The "arts councils" comprising the bulk of the voting membership of ACA are states arts councils and community arts councils (about 200 of which are members of ACA) of one kind or another—there is no fixed definition covering the possible variety. The state councils are now established in every state in the Union and all are members of ACA.* State

*New York State has often been credited erroneously with establishing the first state arts council. The "Survey of United States and Foreign Government Support for Cultural Activities" (U.S. Government Printing Office, Washington, 1971), prepared for the Special Subcommittee on the Arts and Humanities of the Senate Committee on Labor and Public Welfare—which specifically requested of official state arts groups that supplied information for the survey that they indicate founding date—reveals that the Utah State Institute of Fine Arts (its official arts council) was founded in 1899. The Minnesota State Arts Council is an outgrowth of the Minnesota Fine Arts Society, founded in 1903. Wisconsin's Art Foundation and Council was established in 1957. Puerto

Arts Councils are funded by appropriations from state legislatures, grants from the National Endowment for the Arts, (q.v.) etc. Their main role is to stimulate creative and interpretive arts activity and to develop audiences for them. Canadian arts councils, which have been in existence longer than American councils, are also members of ACA. The activities of ACA are centered around its attention to studies of conditions in America that benefit or hinder cultural growth. These studies are made available to those groups and individuals in a position to influence change and improvement in the way arts activities are administered, supported, and developed. References made by ACA and other arts administration organizations to "progress in the arts" and "cultural growth" have to be understood in the context of the work of these "activities-minded" agencies, for they ultimately seek to create a "consciousness for the arts" throughout society without meaning to form qualitative judgments as to the art forms themselves. Thus the arts within the range of interest of ACA and its council members are broadly categorized—music, dance, drama, visual arts, etc.,—and any viable institution or group of individuals engaged in the production or promotion of these art categories has the potential sympathy of ACA, regardless of the aesthetic roads such groups or individuals may take. The concern of ACA is that somehow arts production and consumption must flourish, and to create an environment favorable to that end is to understand such extra-cultural, extra-aesthetic factors that are economic, social and political in nature but which affect greatly such environment. To form a line of communication about such matters, ACA publishes a number of bulletins, reports, etc. They are available free to ACA members as a privilege of membership: *ACA Report* is a monthly newsletter, with news items of the work of arts councils, new publications related to the arts, ACA information, etc.; *ACA Word from Washington,* a monthly bulletin, issued at the same time as *Report,* covers pending federal legislation affecting the arts, and Washington issues and attitudes; *Arts in Common* is a quarterly newsletter for community arts agencies (sent out free to over 1,000 agencies the first year it was issued). Among the books published by ACA (and available for sale to anyone) are: "Persuade and Provide," by **M. Newton** and **S. Hatley,** 1970, a book about the creation of the St. Louis Arts and Education Council and its work; "Labor Relations and the Performing Arts, An Introductory Survey," by **Michael H. Moskow,** 1970; "Arts in the City," by **Ralph Bugard,** 1968; "In Search of an Audience," by **Bradley Morison** and **Kay Fliehr,** 1968, which uses the Tyrone Guthrie Theatre in Minneapolis as a case study of modern techniques for finding and developing arts audiences; "Politics of Art," by **W. Howard Adams,** 1966, a coverage of the organization of state arts councils; "The Arts: Planning for a Change," 1965, essays on arts and education, industry, etc.; "The Arts: Central Element of a Good Society," which includes articles on government subsidy, labor and the arts, legislation, financial support for the arts, etc.; "Directory of State Arts Councils," issued annually; "Directory of National Arts Organizations," a guide to national nonprofit service organizations in the arts, revised, 1971. ACA also sells publications of other publishers that cover the same kinds of topics as those mentioned. A film, called "Art is . . ." was produced by ACA with a Sears Roebuck Foundation grant. It is a visual primer intended to create interest in art and has been viewed by over 10 million people. It is available on free loan from the Audio Visual Department, The Sears Roebuck Foundation, 303 East Ohio Street, Chicago, Illinois 60611. Other ACA activities include the maintenance of a library, with services for research and consultation, open to any serious user and the organizing of annual national conferences, each built around some theme for discussion and exploration. The 1971 conference, under the topic, "Washington and the

---

Rico, which receives funding from the National Endowment for the Arts, founded its Instituto de Cultura Puertorriqueña in 1955. The New York State Council on the Arts, which has been provided with record levels of funding for the arts by the state legislature, was founded in 1960. All remaining state arts councils were apparently established since that date.

Arts," was held in the nation's capital and included an address by President Nixon which marked the first time an American President addressed a national arts organization. The 1972 conference was held in St. Paul with the theme, "Arts on Main Street." The income for ACA's fiscal year 1971–72 totaled $273,000. Earned income of this amount was $77,500, of which $17,000 (5 percent) was income from dues. Foundation grants amounted to $91,300, and corporation gifts totaled $45,000. Monies from state and federal governments came to $50,500. Government grants emanated from the National Endowment for the Arts, the Office of Education, the Federal Council on the Arts, and from the arts councils of Illinois, Missouri, Pennsylvania, South Carolina, and the Virgin Islands. The foundation gifts came from the Avalon, Biddle, Mellon, Quincy, Rockefeller, and other foundations. Corporate gifts included those of Alcoa, Atlantic Richfield, Bristol-Myers, Burlington Industries, Crown Zellerbach, IBM, RCA, Xerox and other corporate funds and foundations. Officers of ACA (1972): **George M. Irwin,** Chairman; **John Hightower,** President and Chairman of the Executive Committee; **Arthur Gelber, David Rockefeller, Jr.,** and **Bagley Wright,** Vice Presidents; **Suzanne F. Fogelson,** Secretary; **Louis Harris,** Treasurer. In addition, there is an 11-member Board of Directors of men and women representing various arts organizations or arts-interested groups.

ASSOCIATED MALE CHORUSES OF AMERICA, INC., c/o Executive Secretary, **Elmer C. Rehbein,** 1338 Oakcrest Drive, Appleton, Wisconsin 54911. Tel.: (414) 733–8650. Founded in 1924 as the Associated Glee Clubs of America, Inc., its intent was to act as a central organization for the glee clubs already existing at that time and as an agency for encouraging the growth of glee clubs. Clayton W. Old (died in 1964) was the founder and president until 1945, when, after his retirement, the organization was restructured, changing its name to the present one and altering its administrative formation. From the onset, support for the notion of a healthy amateur glee club movement came from a number of individuals including some figures then prominent in the music world. In addition to encouraging the "extension of male chorus singing among the men of North America," which is its basic goal, the organization seeks also among other things "to establish an American culture in male chorus singing . . . to help form Junior Glee Clubs . . . to help improve quality of male chorus repertoire and standard of performance . . . to bring about better industrial relations, by establishing or encouraging the organization of choruses and glee clubs through all industry." An important aspect of the work of the organization is the grouping of choruses in spectacular concerts using hundreds of singers. This is accomplished at District and Conference concerts and other special events. In the past, such concerts would feature as few as 540 singers (Carnegie Hall) or as many as 4,900 (Madison Square Garden). The norm currently is a District or Conference gathering of from 200 to 600 voices. The organization's membership stands at some 52 member choruses (down drastically from the total of earlier years) totaling about 2,000 men. Two or more clubs may form a so-called District (formed generally along state lines). Each District's presiding officer becomes a member of the Board of Directors of the national group. Two or more Districts form into Conferences, of which there are four representing the Atlantic, Great Lakes, Midwest, and Mid-continental sections of the United States and Canada. (Canada has 7 member choruses in the organization.) Conference presidents are vice-presidents of the national organization. District concerts are held once a year, and Conference concerts occur at least once every three years. Membership is open to any active male chorus or any person interested in the objectives of the society. The financing of the organization is achieved by a per person levy of a nominal sum for each chorus member of a member club. Two additional categories of membership are open to interested persons, Associate and Life memberships, dues for which are set at a higher rate. The organization publishes a monthly *Newsletter* from the office of the Executive Secretary during the months from September through May; it keeps files on music publishers, record companies, artists and agents, and in general provides information to member clubs to improve their organization and solve problems that may arise from their rehearsals and concerts. Officers are elected for two-year terms. Current (1972) officers are: **Charles Caldwell,** President; **Louis E. Eller,** Chairman of the Board; **Les Axdahl,** Treasurer. Historian is **J. Fred Rau.**

ASSOCIATION OF CHORAL CONDUCTORS, c/o American Choral Foundation, 130 West 56th Street, New York, N.Y. 10019. A nonprofit professional organization sponsored by the American Choral Foundation, it provides services for people active in conducting community, church, professional, school, and college choral ensembles. The association offers three categories of annual membership which enable others besides conductors to become members. They are: Full Members ($15 dues), Publications Members ($12), and Participating Members ($7.50). The categories involve varying privileges mostly having to do with the number and kinds of publications made available to members, the most important of which are the official journal, *American Choral Review* and the *Research Memorandum Series* (See American Choral Foundation under Organizations and the *Review* under Periodicals). A full member receives all issues of the *Review* and the *Series* as well as unlimited use of (a) the Foundation Library, a collection of over 250 choral works with a minimum of 40 copies of each on deposit in the library, which can be borrowed for a four-month period for only the price of postage needed to mail them; (b) the Drinker Library, additional scores which are available on a rental basis only; (c) the Advisory Services Division, a service designed to answer a wide variety of questions often raised by choral conductors, usually on a practical level concerning music, schools, choral groups, publishers, etc., and (d) the Reference Library Service or "Biblio-Center"—a service offering lists of reference books and the participating libraries located throughout the country that have them on their shelves. Members of the Association are found in all fifty states and throughout the world. Administrative Director is **Sheldon Soffer.**

ASSOCIATION OF COLLEGE AND UNIVERSITY CONCERT MANAGERS (ACUCM), P.O. Box 2137, Madison, Wisconsin 53701. Tel.: (608) 262–0023. Founded in 1957, the organization is concerned with presenting cultural programs of quality on college campuses. In 1970 there were about 360 member schools in the organization, represented by faculty members who have the responsibility of organizing campus cultural events booked from outside the college (only a small number of colleges have this activity controlled by a full time administrator). The formally declared purposes of ACUCM reads as follows: "to bring together representatives actively affiliated with colleges and universities throughout North America, who are responsible for the campus presentation of professional music, theatre, lecture, film and related cultural programs, in order to share information on the selection, promotion and presentation of such events on college campuses." Thus representatives from the United States and Canada are found in ACUCM, and their joint activities include sharing information concerning cultural events, fostering ethical standards and business procedures, encouraging young artists, fostering international exchanges, working to integrate all cultural activities of quality into the life of the campus and community, etc. One of the important goals of ACUCM is working to establish either full-time concert managers on campuses or, at least, chairmen relieved of most teaching duties. Membership application from representatives not on the full-time payroll of the college or university must be accompanied by a written statement from an administrative officer of the school confirming the designation of the representative. Memberships are approved by the executive board of ACUCM. The organization meets annually in New York City. A *Bulletin* is sporadically issued by the ACUCM containing information of practical value to campus managers. Annual dues are $25 for each member institution; $5 is charged for each additional representative from the same institution. From time to time various surveys are conducted by ACUCM with the intent to clarify and promulgate campus concert activity. These surveys cover such points as percentage of filled houses, the kinds of concerts drawing the greatest attendance, sold out events, and so forth. Executive Secretary of ACUCM is **Fannie Taylor** of the University of Wisconsin at Madison (address shown above). President is **James H. Wockenfuss,** Iowa University.

ERNEST BLOCH SOCIETY, 171 Marguerite Avenue, Mill Valley, California 94941. Founded originally in 1937 in London and New York. The American group's activities were interrupted for a number of years. In 1965, the society was re-established in Portland, Oregon. It incorporated in 1968. From its inception in England, the society enjoyed the support and participation of significant and influential musicians and scholars including Albert Einstein, Sir Thomas Beecham, Sir Arnold Bax, Sir John Barbirolli, Edward Dent, Serge Koussevitsky, Arthur Bliss, and Bruno Walter. The present Ernest Bloch society in America has on its Honorary Board **Leonard Bernstein, Nadia Boulanger, Pablo Casals, Yehudi Menuhin, Lewis Mumford, Georgia O'Keefe, William Schuman, Robert G. Sproul** and **Joseph Szigeti.** An Advisory Board is made up of **Helen Coates, Mrs. Walter A. Haas, Herbert Elwell, Abe Fortas, Nicholas Slonimsky, Paul A. Smith,** and **Harold Spivacke.** The aims of the society are the cultivation of interest and appreciation of Bloch's music by "encouraging and arranging performances of his work and by making available recordings of all his published compositions." The society intends to establish a library of Bloch's life work—his music, letters and other writings, and photography (Bloch was a skilled photographer). A *Bulletin* is issued sporadically containing information about new publications, recordings and live performances of Bloch's music, notes on Bloch's life, extracts from his letters, lectures, and writings, and activities of Bloch enthusiasts. Various other publications are available through the society including a catalog of Bloch's published works, a complete discography, etc. Membership dues are as follows: $3 for students, $10 for Annual Members, $25 for Contributing Members, $100 or more for Patrons. Officers of the society are: **Charles C. Cushing,** President; **George Wood,** Vice President; **L. B. Dimitoff,** Secretary-Treasurer; **Sita Milcev,** Assistant Secretary; **Ida Geary,** Editor.

BROADCAST MUSIC, INC. (BMI), 40 West 57th Street, New York, N.Y. 10019. Tel.: (212) 586–2000. Founded in 1939. BMI is a performing rights organization obtaining rights from the owners of copyrights (writers and publishers) to publicly perform their music for profit and, in turn, licensing these rights to users of music. Licensing operations for BMI began on February 15, 1940. Broadcast Music, Inc., like the American Society of Composers, Authors, and Publishers (ASCAP) is a major performing rights licensing agency in America. Both organizations can claim jointly to license the greatest percentage of performing rights of American composers and lyricists and those of foreign composers and lyricists licensed in America through foreign performing rights agencies having affiliations with ASCAP or BMI. Unlike ASCAP, BMI is not a membership organization of creators and publishers; instead, it is a corporation whose stock is owned by some 500 of America's 6,000 or so licensed broadcasters. Purchase of the stock was made only once, in the early stages of BMI's formation; no stock has been offered for sale since. The stock pays no dividend nor was payment predicted or expected, according to the original corporation prospectus. BMI claims that no special benefit accrues to its broadcaster-stockholders, whose rate of fee payment for the use of licensed music is the same as that of broadcasters who are not stockholders. BMI is competitive with ASCAP; indeed, it was organized to offset what was felt to be an unhealthy monopoly held by ASCAP. Its competitive stance and its user-oriented basis of operation have provided BMI with a markedly different image from that of ASCAP. However, in recent years, the distinctions between them have become somewhat blurred in so far as their service to writers is concerned; furthermore, there are some signs of cooperation between them. Of the two, BMI is by far the larger, having licensing agreements covering 20,000 writers (composers and lyricists—particularly of popular songs) and 10,000 publishers. Its repertory covers the broadest representation of music creation: popular music in all its variety—country and western, rhythm and blues, rock, jazz, folk music, the current song hits—theater and film music, concert music, Latin American music, etc. The comparative newness of BMI's catalogue gives it strength in the areas of current popular music trends. Industry tabulations (specifically those published by *Billboard* magazine) show dominance in recent years of BMI-licensed music in retail sales in such trade-identifying categories as "hot 100 singles," "easy listening singles," "country singles," "top-selling albums," etc. In American concert music, BMI's repertory includes the work of a good number of distinguished composers. From its inception, BMI invited into its licensing catalogue music that was popular in genre but not national in acceptance or dissemination. Such regional music as country music, or what is now called rhythm and blues, or gospel music, or other kinds of indigenous American music that were generally not found in national network programming (with some important exceptions), now enjoy national and international commercial exploitation—a state of affairs for which BMI claims much responsibility. It has looked upon this achievement as the "democratization of American music," a reference to the fact that much of the performing rights activity, prior to 1940, had been controlled from New York and Hollywood, which were outlets for a popular music that was comparatively urbane, sophisticated and reflective of the tastes and musical needs of Tin Pan Alley, Broadway, and the filmmaker. These marketing distinctions had greater delineation twenty or thirty years ago than at present when, as a result of two-and-a-half decades of great broadcast distribution growth, as well as certain social factors, regional markets in music consumption have approximately the same "mix" as the national market. In order to oversee the use of its licensed music, BMI receives daily logs of all music performed each quarter of the year from a representative cross section of its licensed stations. These logs indicate the number of broadcast performances of each piece of BMI music. With the aid of a computer system, this information is multiplied by a factor which represents the percentage of the number of stations logged in relation to the total number of stations licensed. The result is a projected total number of performances of BMI music, piece by piece, for the quarter. Television theme and cue music is logged with the aid of cue sheets which are prepared by the producer of each logged program. These forms are used also to determine the number of performances of BMI music in movies, film series, and the like. Performances of symphonic, operatic, chamber music and other forms of concert music are tallied from the printed programs of symphonic organizations, producers of concert series, etc. All logging is conducted by an independent accounting firm. Royalties payable to BMI affiliates from a given logging period are determined by a published schedule of performing rights royalties which is available to affiliated writers and publishers. Payments for broadcast performances in the United States and Canada are made four times a year; foreign royalty payments are made twice annually; live concert performance royalties are paid once a year. All royalty payments come from fees charged the users of BMI music. BMI returns the monies collected from the fees in the form of royalties after deducting operating expenses and a certain amount for capital reserve. In the case of BMI music performed outside the U.S. or Canada, foreign affiliated performing rights organizations (some 31 of them) collect the fees locally for BMI. These fees are subject to a 10 percent handling charge prior to remittance to either writer or publisher. Affiliated writers and publishers pay no dues or fees to BMI. Eligibility for affiliation with BMI for a writer is extended to anyone who has written a musical composition, alone, or in collaboration with other writers, that has been commercially recorded or published or is otherwise likely to be performed publicly for profit. BMI's licensees (users of music) include broadcasting stations, nightclubs, restaurants, ballrooms, hotels (all of these total many thousands in the U.S.). License fees for these users were structured through negotiations with broadcast industry groups and various trade organizations such as the American Hotel and Motel Association, the Arena Managers Association, the International Association of Amusement Parks, and the National Ballroom Operators Association. BMI's promotional and service activities include publication of *The Many Worlds of Music,* a magazine issued ten times a year covering news of BMI writers and publishers and containing articles on music and musicians; brochures on individual composers in the concert music field (these are small but valuable publications containing biographic sketches, lists of premieres and major performances, discography and bibliography, as well as portraits of composers); "Concert Music USA," an annual summary of the state of affairs in the concert world using statistics from BMI's own findings as well as those of the American Symphony Orchestra League, American Music Conference, *Opera News* of the Metropolitan Opera Guild, the *Schwann Catalog,* and other sources; the "BMI Orchestral Program Survey," an extensive computer print-out compilation of the kind of works performed, their composers, the number of performances found in the concert programs of American symphony orchestras, etc., during the concert year (its purpose, in part, is to reveal the extent of performance of works of the twentieth century vis-à-vis the standard orchestral repertory; however, following the survey of the 1969–70 orchestral season, BMI indicated that its future surveys would be restricted to determining the performance activity of works of the twentieth century only. The surveys have been conducted in conjunction with the American Symphony Orchestra League.) BMI supports a Musical Theater Workshop for writers interested in that field; it conducts two annual competitions: the Varsity Show Competition for the best college musical or varsity show written by undergraduates, and the Student Composers Awards, which make scholarship grants to winning young composers of concert music (see Contests). Offices other than the New York address are as follows: 9720 Wilshire Boulevard, Beverly Hills, California 90212; 680 Beach Street, San Francisco, California 94109; 150 S.E. Second Avenue, Miami, Florida 33131; 710 Sixteenth Avenue South, Nashville, Tennessee 37203; 217 Montgomery Street, Syracuse, New York 13202; 230 North Michigan Avenue, Chicago, Illinois 60601. Other offices are in Canada, in Toronto, Montreal, and Vancouver. BMI's officers are: **Sydney M. Kaye,** Chairman of the Board; **Edward M. Cramer,** President; **Mrs. Theodora Zavin,** Senior Vice President; the following Vice Presidents (their responsibilities are also listed): **Ronald M. Anton** (performing rights, Western U.S.A.), **Justin Bradshaw** (broadcaster relations), **Leo Cherniavsky** (performing rights, foreign), **Oliver Daniel** (performing rights, concert), **George Gabriel** (nonbroadcast licensing), **Robert J. Higgins** (general services—Secretary), **Richard L. Kirk** (California), **Edward J. Molinelli** (finance—Treasurer), **Mrs. Frances Preston** (Nashville), **Russell Sanjek** (public relations).

THE BROADCASTING FOUNDATION OF AMERICA (BFA), 52 Vanderbilt Avenue, New York, N.Y. 10017. Tel.: (212) MU 4–2505. Founded in 1955, BFA is a nonprofit educational nongovernmental organization dedicated to making available to American radio stations taped programs from around the world including the important annual music festivals, folk music, press commentary, programs on the arts, sciences, educational affairs, etc. Some 800 "master" hours of such programming is gathered and distributed by BFA each year from about 40 broadcasting systems (nations) throughout the world. These are offered to radio station members of BFA at extremely low rates and to nonmember stations at slightly higher cost. Member stations number over 300. (Membership is open to any commercial or educational station.) Radio stations carrying BFA distributed programs are in forty-six states, the District of Columbia, and Canada. The U.S. Armed Forces uses BFA weekly programs for worldwide broadcast. In addition, BFA is a United States member for the European Television and Radio Program Competition, the Prix Italia; a member of the European Broadcasting Union, the distributing agency in the United States for UNESCO and SEATO radio programs; and is the United States State Department designated agency for distributing radio programs from Russia under the intergovernmental East–West cultural exchange agreement. In 1966 and 1967, BFA began providing archival services to colleges and universities, special materials to schools of music and journalism, and increased its programming acquisitions of folk music from Asia, Africa, and the Middle East. Future activities of BFA include offering productions in television and film. BFA's music service is demonstrated at its best by the series of famous European music festivals taped live from such locations as Spoleto, Bergen, Budapest, Prague, Salzburg, Bayreuth, and elsewhere. These are available without payment of royalty and cost from about $5 to $6, depending on the duration of the tape. The festival programs have added a new dimension to radio broadcasting of fine music in the United States and, at a time when the percentage of cultural music programming is generally decreasing on the nation's radio time, they may represent, for some stations, the only form of taped live performances of concert music. "The World's Great Music," is the name of a two-hour program offered to stations each week and consists of live recordings of complete music concerts from around the world—Israel, Poland, Russia, Japan, Yugoslavia, Germany, Holland, Hungary, Brazil, etc. These are offered for $20 per weekly program. Another weekly music series is "The First Fifty Years," which originates from Chicago (as do several BFA-distributed domestic programs, specifically those produced by station WFMT) and is a 30-minute program of rare operatic recordings and other vocal performances of the first fifty years of the recording industry. The weekly cost of this program is $10. Officers of BFA are: **George E. Probst,** Chairman; **Seymour Siegel,** President; **Howard L. Kany,** Executive Director. Music Director is **Paul Snook.**

BRUCKNER SOCIETY OF AMERICA, INC., c/o President, **Charles L. Eble,** P.O. Box 1171, Iowa City, Iowa 52240. Tel.: (319) 338–0313. Founded in 1931. Its purpose is to encourage performances of the music of Bruckner and Mahler and to promote interest among musicians and scholars in the study and research of their music. An annual award is presented to an individual serving the aims set forth by the Society, in the form of a Medal of Honor and special citation in honor of either Bruckner or Mahler. Some recipients of the Bruckner Medal have been **Otto Klemperer,** Serge Koussevitzky, Arturo Toscanini, Bruno Walter, George Szell, **William Steinberg, Josef Krips,** Paul Hindemith, and radio stations WNYC (New York), WFMT and WEFM (both FM stations in Chicago), KWFM (Minneapolis), the Canadian Broadcasting Company, and others. The Mahler medal has been awarded to some of the foregoing as well as Fritz Reiner, **Leonard Bernstein, Dika Newlin, Rafael Kubelik, Leopold Stokowski, Antal Dorati, Jascha Horenstein, Deryck Cooke, Jack Diether, Benjamin Britten,** and many others. The citations have gone to radio stations, conductors, etc. Membership in the Bruckner Society is available to any interested person through specified types of contributions. Regular members are those contributing under $5; Founder members contribute $5 or more. The publication of the organization is *Chord and Discord* (see Periodicals). Officers (1969—last available confirmed date) other than president: **Harry Neyer** and **Dika Newlin,** Vice Presidents (the latter is also Executive Secretary). There is a committee of executive members and another of directors plus a host of honorary members who are conductors, scholars, writers, and musicians.

BUSINESS COMMITTEE FOR THE ARTS, INC. (BCA), Mezzanine Suite 7, 1270 Avenue of the Americas, New York, N.Y. 10020. Tel.: (212) 765–5980. Founded January, 1968. The Committee is composed of about 110 members, mostly top executives of America's largest corporations. Membership is by invitation only. The purpose of BCA is to stimulate support of the arts by the business community. It is a private, tax-exempt, national organization whose field of interest covers architecture, craft and folk arts, dance, films, graphic arts, industrial design, music of all kinds, painting, sculpture, drama, amalgams of electronic media, etc. Its concept of support for the arts involves gathering and publishing surveys, reports, statistics, etc., regarding financial support of the arts for use by the business community. It provides advisory services for business firms interested in making contributions to the arts for the first time or in expanding their current programs of support. In this regard, BCA attempts to keep corporations informed of existing opportunities for support of the arts and, at the same time, to inform the arts world of what corporations are doing in this area. Cultural organizations, on the other hand, may seek assistance from BCA in finding the most effective way to receive support from business sources. BCA makes clear what it will not do: raise funds for any specific art organizations, channel funds to any group, or guarantee the support of any particular arts group by any specific business source. It publishes a quarterly newsletter, *BCA News,* edited by **Peter M. Mesney,** which is issued free of charge to about 14,000 businessmen and arts groups and which covers organizational news, information about national arts support programs, reports of innovative arts programs throughout the country, etc. Other publications include the book, "Business and the Arts: An Answer to Tomorrow," by **Arnold Gingrich** (publisher of *Esquire Magazine*); "Business in the Arts '70" (1971), among others. The Committee's activities include meetings involving businessmen and representatives of the arts world, the maintenance of a speakers bureau, a publicity program for detailing industry's activities in the arts, and so on. In 1967, *Esquire Magazine* began to sponsor, in cooperation with BCA, an annual "Business in the Arts Award," which was extended to enterprising endeavors undertaken by business firms in assisting the arts. An indication of what BCA seeks to do, or, at least, what it may consider exemplary within the field of its interest, can be seen in the following business-supported programs which have been cited by the awards (restricted to those involving music only): Texaco's long-time sponsorship of the radio broadcast performances of the Metropolitan Opera; Jos. P. Schlitz Brewing Company's financial support of free New York Philharmonic concerts held outdoors; family concerts of the Rhode Island Philharmonic financed by the Columbus National Bank of Providence; the Detroit Edison Company's sponsorship of the free concerts "Symphony Under the Stars" with the Detroit Symphony; young people's concerts presented free by the Houston Symphony and financed by that city's Foley's Department Store; and The Air Preheater Company's initiative in organizing an annual series of live concerts in Wellsville, New York, a first experience for this remote community of 8,000. The first Chairman of BCA was **C. Douglas Dillon** who served until 1970; he was succeeded by **Robert O. Anderson** (Atlantic Richfield Co.). Current Chairman is **Frank Stanton** (Columbia Broadcasting System). President is **G. A. McLellan.** Secretary is **H. Bruce Palmer.**

CECCHETTI COUNCIL OF AMERICA, INC., c/o Corresponding Secretary, **Virgiline Simmons,** 1128 East Michigan Avenue, Lansing, Michigan 48912. The organization's purpose is to promote and cultivate the Enrico Cecchetti Method of dance instruction, whereby the student learns to dance "not by imitating the movements of the teacher only, but by studying and imbibing the basic principles which govern the art and which, when developed from within, give him the poise and self-reliance necessary to greatness in any artist." Membership is open to any teacher having a certificate in any of the grades; Junior members must have student certificates. Membership stands at about 600 including Junior members. Initiation fees and dues are $25 and $15 annually thereafter. Junior branch dues are $2. Activities of the Council include publishing a semiannual *Newsletter* sent free to members, and brochures regarding summer seminars and conferences. One refresher course and three training sessions are held annually by the Council. Officers are: **Virgiline Simmons,** Corresponding Secretary; **Jane Caryl Miller,** Recording Secretary and Registrar, 2302 St. Francis Drive, Ann Arbor, Michigan 48104; **Marjorie Hansard,** President.

CENTRAL OPERA SERVICE (COS), Lincoln Center Plaza, Metropolitan Opera, New York, N.Y. 10023. Tel.: (212) 799–3467. Founded in 1954. This organization is sponsored by the Metropolitan Opera National Council. Its membership of about 650 is composed of opera companies and opera workshops, persons professionally involved in the field of opera (musicians, directors, designers, producers, et al.) and other interested persons. Its stated purpose is "to foster a closer association among civic, community, college, and national opera companies throughout the country." Its major activity is that of a comprehensive information center covering the opera field and of acting, through its national and regional conferences, as an agency for bringing together disparate endeavors in the field of opera and for the discussion of common problems, and, finally, in reporting on these meetings through its publications. The information services provided by COS include general opera organizational counseling; advice regarding public relations techniques and suggestions for fund-raising (in this regard, its counterpart for the orchestral field, is the American Symphony Orchestra League) for established and incipient groups; information regarding opera music materials such as scores, parts, orchestrations, publishers, translations of foreign operas; sources for scenery, costumes, and props for rental, exchange, purchase, etc.; and information on opera repertory in general. Its main publication is the *Central Opera Service Bulletin,* a bimonthly issue without advertising or illustrative matter containing succinct news reports not only on the field of opera, but also a surprising amount of information on other aspects of the music field. It reports on new operas and premiere performances, translations, finances and grants in music, news from opera companies of all kinds—including foreign companies; vocal competitions, appointments (managerial, conductorial, etc.) in opera companies, symphony orchestras, schools, organizations; foundation news, obituaries, announcements and reviews of books and other new publications, listings of seasonally scheduled performances of opera companies and opera-producing groups throughout the United States, and so forth. Its content, therefore, is totally factual, making it an extremely useful publication. Editor is **Mrs. Maria F. Rich.** Its availability is restricted to members, but special classifications of COS membership permit the acquisition of the *Bulletin* at low cost (see dues structure below). Using, for the most part, the same format as the *Bulletin,* COS publishes the following references: "Directory of Sets and Costumes for Rent" (1970), which covers a total of 236 operas, $5; "Directory of Opera Producing Organizations" (most recent issue was published in December, 1971), part of the foregoing publication; "Directory of Foreign Contemporary Operas" (1969), which lists over 1,500 works by 581 composers from forty countries, $5; "Directory of American Contemporary Operas" (1967), containing over 1,000 opera listings, $3; "American Operatic Premieres: 1962–1968" issued dually with "Awards for Singers," $2; "English Translations of Foreign Language Operas" (1966, revised 1971), $2.50. COS members receive these publications as part of their membership privileges. Dues are $10 for individual members and libraries (the latter receive the *Bulletin* only); $25 for group membership; $50 for institutional membership. Privileges vary with each membership classification. Regional conferences are held annually; national conferences, biennially. Officers are: **Elihu M. Hyndman,** National Chairman; **Mrs. Norris Darrell** and **George Howerton,** National Co-Chairmen; **Robert L. B. Tobin,** Honorary National Chairman; **Mrs. Maria F. Rich,** Executive Secretary. There is a 6-member National Council Directors Committee and a 30-member Professional Committee made up of head administrators and artistic directors of opera groups from the professional and academic world. Chairman of the Professional Committee is **Julius Rudel.**

CHURCH MUSIC ASSOCIATION OF AMERICA, Boys Town, Nebraska 68010. Tel.: (402) 558–7279. Founded in 1964. Membership is 1,200. The organization consists of a merger of the two oldest church music societies in America: the American Society of Saint Caecilia (founded in 1874) and the Society of Saint Gregory (founded in 1914). It is affiliated with the Consociatio Internationalis Musicae Sacrae (Rome), founded by Pope Paul VI in 1963. Its purpose is "the advancement of Sacred Music in keeping with the norms established by competent ecclesiastical authority." Membership is open to all but consists mainly of organists, choirmasters and choirmembers, music teachers, etc. Annual dues and types of membership are: Voting Member, $12.50; Subscribing Member, $7.50; Student Member, $4. Publication (free to members) is *Sacred Music,* a quarterly periodical (which replaced the former *Caecilia* and the *Catholic Choirmaster*) edited by **Rev. Ralph S. March,** S.O. Cist. (see Periodicals). Membership meetings are biennial; meetings of Board of Directors are held at least once a year. In addition to its publication and national and regional meetings, professional assistance to members is provided by holding open forums on church music and liturgy, reviewing new music and books, commissioning new music for church use, and providing for workshops and seminars. Officers are: President, **Roger Wagner;** Vice President, **Noel Goemanne;** Secretary, **Rev. Robert A. Skeris;** Treasurer, **Frank D. Szynskie.**

CHURCH MUSIC PUBLISHERS ASSOCIATION, 5707 West Lake Street, Chicago, Illinois 60644. Founded in 1925. (Formerly the Church and Sunday School Music Publishers Association.) Membership (12) is open to sacred music publishers. President is **George H. Shorney, Jr.** Treasurer is **Floyd Hawkins.**

COLLEGE BAND DIRECTORS NATIONAL ASSOCIATION (CBDNA), c/o Secretary-Treasurer, **Acton Ostling, Jr.,** Iowa State University, Exhibit Hall, Ames, Iowa 50010. Tel.: (515) 294–2080. Founded in Chicago in 1941. Membership is about 600, made up of college band directors and representatives of the music industry. The CBDNA is devoted "to the College Band, which, as a serious and distinctive medium of musical expression, may be of vital service and importance to its members, its institution, and its art." It attempts to apply some basic standards to the profession of college band directing and the four-part role of musician, conductor, educator, and administrator that is required of its practitioners. Its activities include, in addition to biennial conferences, organizing conductors workshops, publishing music lists, commissioning new band works, etc. CBDNA's main publication is *Proceedings,* a summary of the national conferences, which is free to members ($5 to nonmembers). The organization is formed into six geographic divisions each with its own division president. National business is handled during the biennial conferences held in even years. Divisional meetings occur on alternate years. CBDNA is an Associate Member of the Music Educators National Conference. Dues for Active Members of the association are $18; Associate Members (music firms, etc.) are charged $35. Officers other than Secretary are: **William D. Revelli,** founder and Honorary Life President; **Richard Bowles,** President; **Karl Holvit,** Vice President; **Guy Duker,** Immediate Past President.

COLLEGE MUSIC SOCIETY (CMS), c/o various officers' addresses (see below). The Society is incorporated "for the philosophy and practice of music in higher education." Its membership is composed of "persons devoted to the interests of music and musicians in higher education." Its purpose is to provide an organization that will be a general forum for musicians in the academic world indiscriminate of their teaching specialties. Accordingly, members are music educators, composers, musicologists, administrators, applied music teachers. The schools with which they are associated may be colleges (state, private, or church-affiliated), conservatories, universities, and junior colleges. There are over 1,000 members in the Society. CMS holds local, regional, and annual national meetings. Its journal is the annual *College*

Music Symposium. Its most useful and perhaps unprecedented publication is the "Directory of Music Faculties in American Colleges and Universities," a computer-compiled listing of virtually all music faculty members in U.S. higher education. The 1st edition, published in 1967, contained nearly 9,000 names; the 2nd edition, published in 1968 (covering 1968 to 1970), contained 11,768 names from more than 900 institutions of higher education; the 3rd edition covers 1970 to 1972 and has over 15,000 names. It is available for $7.50 from CMS, Department of Music, Harpur College, State University of New York, Binghamton, New York 13901. In addition to the complete listing of faculty members arranged by states and institutions within states, the computerized listing yields cross indexes of the teaching area interest of faculty and a national alphabetical listing. The Executive Board of CMS (for 1972) included: **Walter S. Collins,** President, College of Music, University of Colorado, Boulder, Colorado 80302; **Harry B. Lincoln,** Department of Music, Harpur College, Binghamton, New York 13901; **Edna Parks,** Secretary, Department of Music, Wheaton College, Norton, Massachusetts 02766. There are also two vice-presidents and a treasurer, a Council of 30 members and 6 members-at-large representing composition, theory, musicology, performance, ethnomusicology, and music education.

THE ELIZABETH SPRAGUE COOLIDGE FOUNDATION IN THE LIBRARY OF CONGRESS, The Library of Congress, Washington, D.C. 20540. Founded in 1925 at the time the Coolidge Auditorium in the Library of Congress was completed with funds donated by Mrs. Coolidge. The auditorium is used for the presentation of chamber works. The Foundation supports the composition, dissemination, and development of chamber music. It is noted for its series of chamber music concerts performed by leading ensembles. Its commissions for new chamber works have gone out to many great composers; the manuscripts of these works are added to the holograph collection of the Library of Congress. The policies of the Foundation are determined by an administrative committee; the activities of the Foundation are governed by the Music Division of the Library of Congress, Chief, **Edward N. Waters.** (See also Library of Congress entry under Music Libraries.)

COMPOSERS AND LYRICISTS GUILD OF AMERICA (CLGA), 6565 Sunset Boulevard, Suite 419, Hollywood, California 90028. Tel.: (213) 462–6068. Also at 270 Madison Avenue, New York, N.Y. 10016. Tel.: (212) 683–5320. Organized in May, 1954 as a collective bargaining agency to represent composer and lyricist members in employment relationships. Has a membership of 400. CLGA represents all composers and lyricists employed by the Association of Motion Picture and Television Producers, Inc. It negotiated in 1960 a Minimum Basic Agreement of CLGA members in the motion picture and television industries. (Expiration date for that contract was June 30, 1969.) Officers are **David Raksin,** President; **Ted Cain,** Executive Director; **Alexander Courage,** Secretary-Treasurer.

COUNTRY DANCE AND SONG SOCIETY OF AMERICA (CDSS), 55 Christopher Street, New York, N.Y. 10014. Tel.: (212) AL 5–8895. Founded in 1915. Prior to June, 1967 it was known as the Country Dance Society of America. Its purpose is "to spread knowledge of the folk cultures of the people of America and England in music, dance and song." The fields of interest to the Society include English country, morris, and sword dances; American square and contra (country) dances; folk music and song; folklore and its historical background; and baroque chamber music. Membership (open to all interested in the goals of the Society) totals over 700 subscribing national members; with the membership of affiliated groups considered, the total is over 1,500. Dues are: $2 for Junior members (those under sixteen years of age); $5 for Educational members (libraries, schools, etc.); $8 Regular members; $12 Regular-Combined (married couples); $15 Contributing members; $25 Supporting members; $50 Sustaining members; $100 for Patrons. Activities include the creation of a service center at the CDSS headquarters, as well as a reference library and publications division. The Society engages in workshops, lectures, training programs, social programs, parties, festivals, and summer camp sessions. It answers questions about folk music and dance, provides films, dance instruction manuals, sheet music, records, and dance equipment. A main event sponsored by the Society is a four-week summer session (consisting of four one-week sessions) at Pinewoods Camp near Cape Cod, Massachusetts, attended by 400 to 500 people (about 100 to 145 each week). Local centers and affiliated groups hold similar sessions elsewhere. The main publication of CDSS is *Country Dance and Song* (see Periodicals), free to members. National Director is **May Gadd.** Other officers are: **Norman Singer,** President; **Mrs. Richard K. Conant,** Honorary President; **J. Michael Stimson,** Secretary; **Philip Merrill,** Music Director.

COUNTRY MUSIC ASSOCIATION, INC., 700 16th Avenue South, Nashville, Tennessee 37203. Tel.: (615) 244–2840. Founded in 1958. The purpose of the organization is to act as a trade association open to all who are involved in country music, its promotion, performance, composition, and commercial recording. It is active in promoting, publicizing, and expanding the acceptance and uses of country music. Total membership is about 3,000. It publishes a monthly magazine, *Close-Up,* edited by **Mrs. Jan Ray Garratt,** which is sent free to members. Dues are: $15 for individuals; $100 for individual Life Membership; $100 to $1,000 for organizations. The association is governed by a 23-member Board of Directors, which meets quarterly. President is **Bill Farr;** Executive Director is **Mrs. Jo Walker.**

DANCE NOTATION BUREAU, INC. (DNB), 8 East 12th Street, New York, N.Y. 10003. Tel.: (212) YU 9–5535. Founded in 1940. It is a nonprofit educational organization "dedicated to the advancement of the arts and sciences through the use of movement analysis and notation." The Bureau maintains a school and library and conducts research into dance movement and notation. Membership is open to anyone interested in the goals of the Bureau and those actively engaged in the field of notation and movement. Dues for membership run from $15 (Professional Membership) to $100 and upwards (Donors). Privileges for members include access to the DNB library, receipt of the *DNB Newsletter,* and reduced rates on the purchase of books and scores (dance scores) sold by the Bureau and supplies sold at certain New York City stores, etc. It publishes and distributes for sale a large number of publications, which are listed in annual catalogues and which cover all aspects of the dance, including notated choreography, periodicals, and score paper. DNB's school conducts instruction in Labanotation and related subjects, effort–shape movement studies, dance and movement classes for adults and children, correspondence courses in Labanotation, and training programs for teachers and notators. Its library contains over 1,500 items including scores of dances, ballets, sequences, etc.; over 150 tapes of music, over 100 manuscripts, articles, etc., on notation systems and the field of movement. The library also has some 60 notated major dance works including those of great choreographers (Balanchine, Petipa, Robbins, Tudor, et al.). DNB sponsors a biennial conference on movement analysis and notation, with lectures and seminars. It has more than 500 individual members. Officers: **Nancy Zeckendorf,** President; **Marjorie Isaac,** Treasurer; **Joyce Greenberg,** Secretary. Executive Director is **Herbert Kummel.** Director of Labanotation is **Muriel Topaz.**

DELTA OMICRON INTERNATIONAL MUSIC FRATERNITY, c/o Executive Secretary, 18518 Cherrylawn, Detroit, Michigan 48221. Founded in 1909 at the Cincinnati Conservatory of Music by three women students of music; it is the only organization of its kind founded by students for students. Membership is open to women only. Current membership is about 10,000 in over 100 alumnae chapters and some 75 collegiate chapters throughout the United States. In addition, there are collegiate chapters in four Korean universities. Its basic activity is to assist and encourage young women musicians as they prepare for entry into the music profession. Its formally declared purposes are: "To create and foster fellowship through music; to give music students an opportunity to meet with one another and, by personal contact and exchange of ideas, to broaden the individual outlook; to strengthen a devotion to loyalty to Alma Mater; to develop character and leadership; to encourage the highest possible scholastic attainment, excellence of individual performance and appreciation of good music; to give material aid to worthy students; to mainfest interest in young women entering the professional world." In line with these proposals, Delta Omicron has outlined specific objectives to work for, including the promotion of American music and musicians and the work of women composers, mutual understanding of Eastern and Western cultures, and bettering the appreciation of good music on the community level. Its national projects are supported by the Delta Omicron Foundation, Inc., established in 1958, whose funds are the donations and gifts of members and friends. The Foundation works on a broad philanthropic front dispensing funds for such projects in need of contributions as endowment seats for Lincoln Center in New York City and Kennedy Center in Washington, a building program for the Brevard Music Center in North Carolina, a Delta Omicron studio at the MacDowell Colony in New Hampshire and a studio at National Music Camp; scholarships and awards for high school music students attending the summer camps at Transylvania and the University of New Hampshire, Stephen Foster Collins Camp, National Music Camp, and the camp of the University of Cincinnati; the Roy L. Underwood fellowship in music therapy; gifts to organizations aiding the blind in the United States and in Korea; scholarships for Delta Omicron members including annual rotating scholarships for collegiate chapters; scholarships made available annually to Aspen School of Music, Berkshire Music Center, Brevard Music Center, etc. Membership in Delta Omicron is by invitation only extended to women having talent and possessing certain required qualities of character and scholarship. The invitations are offered by collegiate chapters which can be established in accredited schools only. The fraternity selects women musicians of professional achievement as National Honorary Members and men of national or international stature in the music field as National Patrons. Persons so honored have included composers, conductors, instrumental and vocal performers, music administrators, and others. Every three years, Delta Omicron sponsors a composition contest for women composers (1971 was the latest such event), which grants a cash award and a premier performance to coincide with the triennially held national conference. The fraternity also sponsors an annual Composer's Concert as part of the Festival of American Music held each year by radio station WNYC in New York City, which also broadcasts, either live or recorded, bimonthly music programs of Delta Omicron performers and composers. (The Delta Omicron participation in WNYC has been under the supervision of **Marion Morrey Richter,** Delta Omicron Music Advisor.) Elected officers of Delta Omicron are: **Adelaide L. Collyer,** President; **Alice Williams Stiner,** First Vice President; **Bernice Sheppard Tilton,** Second Vice President. (Elected officers are chosen every three years.) Appointed officers are: Treasurer, **Ray Calfee Wideman;** Executive Secretary, **Jane Wiley Kuckuk** (at address shown above). Delta Omicron Foundation President is **Roxine Beard Petzold;** Treasurer is **Anna Marie Gantner.** The organization's official publication is the quarterly, *The Wheel of Delta Omicron* (see Periodicals), sent to members and patrons. Editor is **Meredith Russell Dugan (Mrs. John).** Other fraternity publications are *The Whistle,* an annual newsletter; the Delta Omicron History; a Songbook, and various manuals.

ELECTRONIC INDUSTRIES ASSOCIATION (EIA), 2000 I Street, N.W., Washington, D.C. 20006. Tel.: (202) 659–2200. Founded in 1924. Previous names of the organization have been Radio Manufacturers Association (original name) and Radio-Electronics-Television Manufacturers Association. "Television" was added to the name in 1950;

"Electronics" in 1953. Members must be American manufacturers of such products as tape recording and playback equipment, raw or prerecorded tape, consumer electronic appliances, industrial electronic items, defense equipment and systems, electronic components, etc. Dues charged members are based on the gross annual sales of the member company. Total membership is over 300. Among the activities of the EIA are periodic surveys of the electronic industry, which include information of interest to the music field such as reports of sales and manufacture of recording playback equipment, tape sales, radio sales, and other items. Past statistics have shown such significant trends as the growth of prerecorded tape on the consumer level, cassettes, cartridges, automobile sound systems for music playback, FM radios, etc. Executive Vice President is **James D. Secrest.** President is **George D. Butler.**

FORD FOUNDATION, 320 East 43rd Street, New York, N.Y. 10017. Tel.: (212) 573–5000. The following is extracted from the Annual Report of the Foundation for the year 1971: "The Ford Foundation is a private, nonprofit institution dedicated to the public well-being. It seeks to identify, and contribute to the solution of certain problems of national or international importance. It works principally by granting funds to institutions and organizations for experimental, demonstration, and developmental efforts that give promise of producing significant advances in certain fields." Founded in 1936 by Henry and Edsel Ford; it was largely devoted to activities in Michigan until 1950, when it became a national organization. Including 1971 (fiscal year), the Foundation has made contributions and commitments totaling $3.9 billion including grants to 6,283 institutions and organizations throughout the fifty states and the District of Columbia and various foreign countries. A 16-member Board determines Foundation policy, supported by professional staffs that evaluate grant applications, make proposals for projects, etc. The Foundation requires that applications for grants outline the objectives of the project involved and provide detailed methods for their execution; these should be sent to the Secretary of the Foundation. The Foundation supports only charitable, educational, or scientific activities and only those that would somehow have an effect throughout the country; in this regard, it does not make grants for individual or local needs, the construction or maintenance of buildings, etc. Grants are made in four divisions: education and research, humanities and the arts, national affairs, and international. The Foundation is by far the largest charitable organization working in the field of music. It began its support of the creative and performing arts in 1957. It has assisted orchestras, opera companies, professional schools, and individual performers and composers. The work of the Foundation in the field of music is of such a dimension as to permit only the briefest description of it in this book. Its activities have ranged from a $80.2 million grant begun in 1966, partly on a matching basis, for 61 orchestras to develop their resources over a ten-year period, to the support of individual talent in various fields of music. The latter has included composers, singers, instrumentalists, choral directors, opera and orchestral administrators, musicologists; it has supported commissions, scholarships, subsidies for recordings and performances; it has reached into the areas of helping to develop the musical education of elementary and secondary school children by supporting programs of training offered by certain institutes and schools and by funding lecture-demonstration concerts; it has financed opportunities for young minority-group musicians; it moved to provide funds for three major private music conservatories so that they could develop their resources over a period of time (the Juilliard School, the New England Conservatory of Music, and the Cleveland Institute); it undertook a novel plan of support for living composers by allowing a partial subsidy to publishers and record companies for the costs of recording and publishing the work of certain composers (the three-year program allotted $375,000 for this purpose; the plan, the "Recording–Publication Program," permits subsidies of up to $7,500 per LP record; publishers may be permitted subsidies to an aggregate of $40,000 during the course of the Program; the Program accepted applications from publishers and collaborating recording companies from January 1, 1970 to December 31, 1972); it devised a program of matching grants to the nonprofit Affiliate Artists, Inc. ($235,000 in 1969) to help young singers, instrumentalists and dancers by setting up affiliations with academic institutions and organizations in communities for a period of in-residence performing. For its total humanities and the arts program of support, the Ford Foundation in the years 1969, 1970, and 1971 approved respectively grants of $19.1 million, $17.8 million, and $30.9 million. Due to the complexity of grants, the approved appropriations, the carry-over, refunds, endowment funds, and payments actually made for given years, it is not possible to provide a detailed breakdown of funds operating in the field of music alone within the limits of this entry. Some specific grants approved for given years, which may provide a sense of the Foundation's music commitments, are as follows: 1969: Council for Public Schools, Boston ($184,000 for developing a Kodaly music training center); Goldovsky Opera Institute ($175,000); Seattle Opera Association ($32,000); San Francisco Conservatory for the formation of a New Music Ensemble ($41,500). 1970: New York Committee for Young Audiences ($137,790); Roberson Memorial Center ($200,000 for concerts presented to school children); International Institute for Comparative Music Studies, Venice ($105,000 for preserving and disseminating non-Western music); Center Opera of Minneapolis ($89,750); Settlement Music School of Philadelphia ($41,980 for private instruction for poor school-age children); Symphony of the New World (an orchestra in New York) ($222,752 for training nonwhite musicians). 1971: to 15 opera companies including the Baltimore, Boston, Cincinnati Summer, Dallas Civic, Houston Grand, and Kansas City Lyric companies ($43.4 million); the Cleveland Institute of Music ($1 million); Juilliard School ($7.2 million); New England Conservatory of Music ($2.5 million); Mills College ($35,200 for the use of its electronics music studio by selected composers), etc. (Figures in preceding summation are in round numbers.) Over the years, the Foundation has provided funds for use by certain key organizations in the field of music to pursue various projects or to sustain their activities. Among them have been the Music Educators National Conference and the American Symphony Orchestra League. In 1971, the Foundation undertook three important projects: a national survey of the economics of nonprofit performing arts groups; a program of cash reserve grants to help performing arts groups to eliminate accumulated operating losses and to create a capital reserve fund; and a support of the long-range educational resources of major conservatories of music. Of the last two categories specific survey, have been made above. The economic survey, which will be published in 1972, covered the financial background and analysis of some 200 groups in opera, dance, symphony, and the theater. Officers of the Ford Foundation are: **Alexander Heard,** Chairman of the Board; **McGeorge Bundy,** President; **W. McNeil Lowry,** Vice President and head of the Division of Humanities and the Arts. The Division has some seven program officers and assistants. Secretary and General Counsel of the Foundation is **Howard R. Dressner.**

THE FRIDAY MORNING MUSIC CLUB, INC. 1649 K Street, N.W., Washington, D.C. 20006. Founded in 1885. It claims to be the second oldest women's club of its kind in the United States. Membership is between 600 and 700. In 1948, the Club established the Friday Morning Music Club Foundation to assist students of voice, piano, and strings in the furtherance of their careers (see Contests). To bring this about, the Foundation, since 1950, has held annual national auditions for the purpose of hearing talented young performers competing for one of three monetary prizes offered. The Foundation is supported through gifts and legacies and operates as a nonprofit organization.

FROMM MUSIC FOUNDATION AT HARVARD UNIVERSITY, 1028 West Van Buren Street, Chicago, Illinois 60607. Tel.: (312) CA 6–5502. Founded in 1952. The foundation is dedicated to the furtherance of contemporary music. It commissions new works, and arranges for publishing, recording, and performing contemporary music. It functions as an incorporated nonprofit organization, whose aims are quoted in full as follows: "The composer today occupies an anomalous position. His creativeness is the source of musical culture, but his status in the musical world is uncertain. Because of the deepening rift between artistic and commercial values, he is excluded from influencing and inspiring the direction of public taste. He is generally denied the recognition commensurate with the importance of his function. The Foundation, wishing to bring the living flow of musical creation closer to the public, aims to return the initiative to the composer and to strengthen the most vital source of a healthy musical culture: composition. Upon invitation by the Foundation, composers may submit unpublished works. When a composition is judged significant, funds are available to put into effect the following program: Performance: The Foundation will sponsor public performances of the composition in various parts of the country under the best concert or recital conditions. Publication: The Foundation has negotiated a contract with the publishing house of Boosey and Hawkes, New York, to print and distribute the compositions. Recording: The Foundation will have the composition recorded and released through regular channels. Cash award: The composer will receive a cash award from the Foundation." Certain general restrictions are imposed as conditions under this program, but the foundation acquires no musical property as its own and will protect the rights of the composer in each case. Composers who have received commissions from the foundation have numbered about 5 as an average annually; thus, in the twenty years of the foundation's existence, some 100 composers produced works under its sponsorship. The composers represent various age and aesthetic categories as well as levels of professional stature. Among them are historical figures in contemporary music (**Babbitt, Carter, Ginastera, Krenek,** Riegger, **Sessions,** et al.) and those who are hardly known beyond a small circle of composers and musicians. Some unknown at the time of their commissions have, since then, become established nationally. The extent to which assistance from the Foundation was important to the development of their careers can only be conjectured. Since 1963, the foundation has supported the Festival of Contemporary American Music held within the framework of the Berkshire Music Festival and the Berkshire Music Center (see Music Festivals). An annual event given much press, it features the music of composers from a wide range of aesthetic persuasions (many are not Americans) among whom are recipients of special commissions from the foundation. In conjunction with the Chicago Chapter of the International Society of Contemporary Music (q.v.) and the Contemporary Chamber Players of the University of Chicago, the Fromm Foundation helped to organize and make possible a number of important concerts of contemporary music in that city as well as in New York. Also receiving direct support from the foundation is the periodical, *Perspectives of New Music,* published twice a year by Princeton University Press. The publication is distinguished by its high level of scholarship and depth of coverage in the technical and aesthetic aspects of contemporary music. It is a highly regarded publication whose value goes beyond the topical, earning for itself a permanent place in the field of music literature (see Periodicals). The foundation's founder, president, and guiding force is **Paul Fromm.** The Foundation's affiliation with Harvard University is quite new (since September, 1972). The administration of the Foundation is continued from the Chicago headquarters, but policies and programs are directed by a committee of three: **Elliot Forbes,** Chairman of Harvard's music department, **Paul Fromm,** and **Gunther Schuller,** President of the New England Conservatory of Music and composer.

THE DANIEL AND FLORENCE GUGGENHEIM FOUNDATION, 120 Broadway, New York, N.Y. 10005. Founded in 1924. The Foundation has been an active supporter of the flight sciences, aeronautics, and medicine, and has contributed to hospitals and various civic and philanthropic organizations. In music, the Foundation sponsors New York's Guggenheim Memorial Concerts, which feature the Goldman Band (see Bands). For these series of annual summer concerts, the Foundation constructed at the Lincoln Center for the Performing Arts complex the Daniel and Florence Guggenheim Memorial Bandshell. The Foundation is administered by descendants of the founders.

JOHN SIMON GUGGENHEIM MEMORIAL FOUNDATION, 90 Park Avenue, New York, N.Y. 10016. Tel.: (212) MU 7–4470. Founded in 1925. The Foundation "offers fellowships to further the development of scholars and artists by assisting them to engage in any of the fine arts, including music, under the freest possible conditions and irrespective of race, creed, or color." In music the Foundation offers fellowships to composers or scholars who propose research projects in history or the theory of music. No awards are made available for the performing arts. (See Contests, Awards, etc., for more details.) The Foundation publishes "Reports of the President and of the Treasurer" which is sent free to all Fellows and a select list of libraries and universities. In addition, an annual brochure for each of the two competitions is published covering the year in question. These are available to applicants for fellowships. The Guggenheim music fellowships are considered a high honor among music scholars and composers. Past recipients of the fellowships include many well-known in their professions.

GUITAR AND ACCESSORY MANUFACTURERS ASSOCIATION OF AMERICA (GAMA), c/o Secretary-Treasurer, **Charles A. Rubovits,** 4800 Chicago Beach Drive, Chicago, Illinois 60615. Tel.: (312) 536–5004. Founded 1924. Has a membership of 38 firms. GAMA is one of the supporting organizations of the American Music Conference (q.v.). It holds two meetings annually. Its main interest is finding areas of cooperation among firms engaged in manufacturing guitars and accessory products. In recent years it has worked to promote, through the AMC, the use of the guitar in music education for teaching music fundamentals. Officers are: **Robert B. Johnson,** President (C. F. Martin & Co.); **Herbert N. Hagel,** Vice-President (National Music Strings); **James D. Webster,** Honorary Life Director. There is a 7-member Board of Directors.

HYMN SOCIETY OF AMERICA, 475 Riverside Drive, New York, N.Y. 10027. Tel.: (212) RI 9–2867. Founded in 1922 and incorporated in 1938. Among its purposes is the intent "to cultivate the use in worship of the better Christian hymns and tunes . . . to collect hymnic data and to encourage research and discussion in the field of hymnology. . ." Membership is open to any interested person. Total membership in the U.S., Canada and some twenty-seven countries is over 1,800. The society promotes hymn festivals throughout the country and maintains a library housed in the Union Theological Seminary in New York City. One of the Society's projects is a continuing search for new hymns reflecting modern developments in musical composition and for modern needs in the church. The project is open to all composers. The Society is especially interested in finding new tunes for the new hymn texts it publishes, which include the following: "Fifteen New Bible Hymns" (1966), "Ten New Hymns on the Ministry" (1966), "12 New Hymns for Children" (1965), "Seven New Social Welfare Hymns" (1961), also "Hymns of Hope," and "Hymns for Modern Youth." These and many other hymn publications are available through the society (a catalogue is available). Composers wishing to submit hymn tunes may do so (deadlines are sometimes imposed for tunes for specific texts). Published tunes are copyrighted by the Society. The Tunes Committee of the Society is under its chairman, **David Hugh Jones.** Other publications include the Society's official organ, *The Hymn,* a quarterly (see Periodicals), *Papers of the Society,* and a long list of hymnology literature. Members of the Society receive these publications. Annual dues are $6.50; students are charged $4. President is **J. Vincent Higginson;** President Emeritus is **Rev. Deane Edwards.**

INSTITUTE OF HIGH FIDELITY (IHF), 516 Fifth Avenue, New York, N.Y. 10036. Tel.: MU 2–5131. The Institute is made up of two membership classifications: General Members (manufacturers of high-fidelity components), and Associate Members (publishers of consumer and trade high-fidelity/FM magazines). There are some 50 members of IHF. The purpose of the Institute is to widen the consumer base for the high-fidelity component industry and to effect promotion to that end. It has sponsored an annual series of high-fidelity music shows which are open to the public and which serve to display and demonstrate the latest in high-fidelity components from manufacturers throughout the world. Attendance at these shows has been consistently very high. In 1972, the show was held in New York City for the first time. IHF also represents the interests of the high-fidelity industry and consumers of components in matters of rulings and standards emanating from the Federal Trade Commission and other government agencies. It has published a number of pamphlets, booklets, etc., which are available to the public. Among them: "IHF Standard Methods of Measurement for Audio Amplifiers" (IHF–A–201–1966, $2); "IHFM Standard Methods of Measurement for Tuners" (IHFM–T–100, December, 1958, $1); "An Introduction to Hi-Fi and Stereo," a guide for the layman which has sold some half million copies (50 cents); "Your Future in the High Fidelity Industry," by Bernard Newman ($4); "A His and Her Guide to Component High Fidelity," a flyer distributed free. The Institute is currently establishing a clearinghouse which will provide a source of information concerning high fidelity to consumers, journalists, publishers, and others. Materials and service provided by the clearinghouse will be without charge. Officers of IHF are: **Walter Goodman,** President and Chairman of the Board; **Bill Kasuga,** Secretary; **Walter O. Stanton,** Treasurer; **Gertrude Nelson Murphy,** Executive Secretary.

INTERNATIONAL BACH SOCIETY, INC. (IBS), 140 West 57th Street, New York, N.Y. 10019. Tel.: (212) 247–4788. Founded in 1966 at the University of California in San Diego and later incorporated in the State of New York. The aim of IBS is "to support Bach scholarship; to raise the standards of performance in all areas of Bach's music; to provide study grants for professional musicians and exceptionally gifted students for advanced studies in Bach style; to provide auditing opportunities for teachers, students, and laymen." Membership is open to anyone interested in the purposes of the Society. The Society attempts to bring together performers, scholars, teachers, and students in the course of exchanging knowledge and ideas about Bach and his music. This effort culminates in the annual International Congress of IBS, the advanced studies in Bach, held in the Auditorium of Lincoln Center's Library for the Performing Arts in New York. (The Sixth Congress was held in 1972.) For two hours each evening Monday through Thursday, during a period of three weeks, lectures, demonstrations, and performances are presented to IBS members and a general audience. Participants and audience are mainly American, but some have come from Canada and Europe. IBS awards performance opportunities to young artists seeking to participate in the congresses. Auditions for selecting the performers are held in April; in addition to playing or singing during some segment of the congress—that is, illustrating a lecture or master class, performing an open rehearsal, etc.—winners, some 30 in all (who include singers, keyboard performers, and string and wind players) also have the chance to attend all other congress meetings. Other participants are well-known scholars and performers, but the central figure throughout the congress and the hub of IBS activity in general is the noted **Rosalyn Tureck,** founder and director of the Society. During the congress, **Mme. Tureck** lectures, demonstrates, performs on the harpsichord, clavichord, and piano, and conducts instrumental and vocal groups. During the regular concert season, in addition to her own concert schedule, she performs various special concerts in the name of the Society. The Society has organized an orchestra, which appeared with **Mme. Tureck** in a special lecture-demonstration series at the

Metropolitan Museum of Art and in Carnegie Hall in New York City. The intent of the IBS is that it develop into a truly international organization with foreign branches throughout the world. The first such branch was established in The Hague, Holland, in 1970. The total membership of the Society is about 150. Dues are as follows: Student, $20; Affiliate, $30; Friend, $100; Donor, $300; Sponsor, $500; Benefactor, $1,000; Founder, $5,000. Various reports, newsletters, etc., are published by IBS. Officers are: **Rosalyn Tureck,** Director; **Max Abramovitz,** Vice President; **Alan Wallin,** Treasurer; **Alice H. Bonnell,** Executive Secretary. Among the Honorary Advisory Board and the Honorary Members are many well-known music patrons, musicians, and scholars.

INTERNATIONAL CONFERENCE OF SYMPHONY AND OPERA MUSICIANS (ICSOM), Addresses are c/o various officers. In 1972, they were: Chairman, **Ralph Mendelson,** 30 West 60th Street, Apt. 11, New York, N.Y. 10023; Tel.: (212) 257–8289; Secretary, **Robert Maisel,** 3317 West Main, Belleville, Illinois 62221; Tel.: (618) 277–3519. (Other officers are listed below.) ICSOM was founded in 1961. Its officers and general members are all working musicians of symphony orchestras, ballet orchestras, or opera orchestras. As of October, 1971, 36 major orchestras in the United States and Canada, totaling some 3,000 musicians, were members of ICSOM. Orchestra membership signifies that a majority of the musicians in an orchestra have voted for application to ICSOM and agree to abide by its by-laws, aims, and official policy of the organization. ICSOM functions as an "independent, self-organized group composed of delegates from its member-orchestras who meet at least once a year for the purpose of promoting the welfare of, and making the livelihood more rewarding for, the orchestral performer." ICSOM's formally declared purposes are: "to direct continuous cooperative efforts between representatives from symphony orchestras, the members of which are members of the American Federation of Musicians, within the framework and as a Conference of, in accordance with the By-Laws of the Federation, and thus to promote the welfare of, and make more rewarding the livelihood of the orchestral performer, and enrich the life of our society." Only orchestras whose players are members of the American Federation of Musicians (AFM—q.v.) can qualify for joining ICSOM. At present, 1 ballet orchestra, 4 opera orchestras, and 31 symphony orchestras constitute the variety of performing ensembles belonging to ICSOM. The government of the organization lies in the membership-sanctioned duties and acts of the officers and the delegates appointed by the orchestras to act in their behalf at national meetings. There are five geographical areas to the organization of ICSOM, each with its own area "head," who is automatically a second vice president of the national organization. (The areas are Southern, Eastern, Central, Western, and Canadian—covering such orchestras as the Atlanta Symphony, Boston Symphony, Metropolitan Opera Orchestra, New York Philharmonic, Chicago Symphony, Cleveland Orchestra, Denver Symphony, Los Angeles Philharmonic, Honolulu Symphony, Montreal Symphony, to mention a few from each respective area.) Dues for the musicians are charged according to the following scale: $6 for each member whose orchestral salary is less than $5,000 annually; $8 for those earning more than $5,000 but less than $10,000; $10 for players earning over $10,000 from their orchestras. The work of ICSOM is almost totally devoted to matters of players' orchestral income, working conditions, contract negotiations, and problems and strategy pertaining to members as a labor force—albeit a unique one. It was the singularity of the orchestra musician's life and profession that formed ICSOM in the first place, since it was believed by present members that no one existing organization had previously undertaken their special cause with any degree of effectiveness. High on the list of rights sought by orchestra musicians were (and are) such matters as direct collective bargaining over employment contracts with orchestra managements; the right to offer opinion and advice to management and orchestra associations regarding the selection of a permanent conductor; the review of problems that may arise during the season between personnel and management and the power to alleviate what may be determined as unfair practices, such as summary dismissal of individual musicians; stringent or impractical rulings covering personal or professional behavior or routine at rehearsals, in concert, and on tour. The winning of these rights has been a gradual accomplishment with individual orchestras, credit for which can be attributed in part to the growing power base of ICSOM and its developing sophistication in the skills needed in the labor field. ICSOM's official magazine, *Senza Sordino,* is an important instrument for enlarging the organization's power base. It is, like many labor or trade journals, strongly propagandistic—even militant. As a source of information about the struggles on the labor front of orchestras, it is unrivaled, just as it is indicative of much that lies below the surface of America's cultural ferment. To the layman, it comes as something of a shock to encounter the cream of America's highly trained instrumental musicians—all undisputed artists—speaking in the pages of *Senza Sordino* not of their art, the mastery of which is totally presumed among the officers and rank of ICSOM, but of contracts, fringe benefits and services, of run-outs, shop stewards, strikes, and arbitration, and a host of other appropriately mundane details that constitute the daily concerns of the men and women producing beautiful music. *Senza Sordino* (a musical term meaning "without mute") has played an important role also in bringing unity of action throughout the labor front of the major American orchestras. Orchestra strikes and the issues behind them are reported in detail, the unfair rulings or practices of any orchestra management are given notoriety (often with witty counterpoint), and there is constant exhortation to increase the enrollment of members, for greater vigilance against the erosion of rights won through contracts, and so forth. This is the style of ICSOM. Its accomplishments are several. It helped to achieve the right of orchestra members to ratify their contracts with management. Previously, contracts were negotiated privately between AFM union officials and management with very little, if any, liaison between union and musicians. Players also now figure prominently in actual contract negotiations, often with the help of ICSOM at large and its retained legal counsel. ICSOM's "Rapid Communications Center" keeps a file on all current contracts. This, special bulletins to members, and *Senza Sordino,* have preserved an active information exchange between orchestras so that a picture of mutual problems among them can be formed. Official recognition from the AFM of the special need for ICSOM (terminating some earlier misunderstandings) was achieved along with conference status within the AFM. Among the results of this collaboration are the establishment of a Strike Fund, symphony symposia (financed by AFM), and greater availability of AFM bargaining expertise in ICSOM contract negotiations. The Conference also has set up an Emergency Relief Fund from which striking orchestras may draw during prolonged work stoppages. ICSOM also draws up charts outlining all services, benefits, wages, and other matters accomplished by contract between member orchestras and their management. It shows in detail all monetary benefits and conditions. An imaginative idea of the organization is its Conductor Evaluation Chart. These are filled out by members of an orchestra for each conductor appearing before it and are kept on file by ICSOM. They are intended to be used for conductor recommendations by either orchestral personnel or management in the latter's search for guest or permanent conductors. The questions and criteria on the evaluation sheet are formulated and cover such conductorial skills as baton technique, knowledge of score, orchestra, musical style, and so forth. Some noted conductors (**William Steinberg,** for one) have indicated approval of the evaluation charts and endorsed the validity of the objective judgement of orchestra players. Officers of ICSOM are: **Ralph Mendelson,** Chairman (member of the New York Philharmonic); **David Smiley,** First Vice Chairman (San Francisco Symphony); **Robert Maisel,** Secretary (St. Louis Symphony); **Harry J. Barnoff,** Treasurer

(Cleveland Orchestra). Editor of *Senza Sordino* is **Vance Beach** (of the Los Angeles Philharmonic); editorial address is: 4161 Holly Knoll Drive, Los Angeles, California 90027.

THE INTERNATIONAL SOCIETY FOR CONTEMPORARY MUSIC—CHICAGO CHAPTER (ISCM), General Office: 33 West Jackson Boulevard, Suite 401, Chicago, Illinois 60604; Illinois Musical Register and Information Service: 60 West Walton Street (Newberry Library), Chicago, Illinois 60610. Tel.: (312) 922–8634 and (312) 664–4661. The ISCM was founded in Salzburg, Austria, in 1922. The Chicago Chapter, one of three United States branches of the ISCM, was founded in 1950. Approximate membership is 500. Its area of representation is the U.S. Midwest. The Chapter is incorporated not-for-profit under the laws of the State of Illinois and is endorsed by the so-called Mayor's Committee for Economic and Cultural Development of Chicago, which is to say, it is sanctioned as the central agency for coordinating activities concerned with contemporary music within the community. The Chapter's activities include more than just presenting concerts (which are by no means restricted to the music of composers in or from the Midwest); it organizes symposia, seminars, and lectures, and is responsible for The Illinois Musical Register and the Illinois Composers Register, a documentation and information center on Midwestern composers and musical activities maintained by the Chapter at Chicago's Newberry Library. It has also established a forum called "The Group for Mathematical and Automatic Music," the ISCM Bureau of Speakers and Lecturers, and the ISCM Concert Bureau, which presents performances of new and avant-garde music. Membership is open to anyone interested in contemporary music. The categories of membership permit both public and a professional participation in the Chapter. Dues are as follows: Student, $5; Professional, $10; Institutional (academic), $100; other categories such as Associate, Subscribing, Supporting, etc., range in dues from $15 to over $500. Larger dues are required for Sponsors and Patrons. Publications of the Chapter are: *The Bulletin of The Illinois Musical Register,* a quarterly (published at the Walton Street address shown above), available as an annual subscription for $5; the *ISCM Newsletter,* sent free to members; a *Calendar of New Music;* various technical reports, brochures, and scores of member composers; and research papers. President and General Director is **James Albert Hermes;** Secretary for Corporate Affairs is **Michael J. Sullivan;** Secretary for Musical Affairs is **Easley Blackwood.**

JEWISH MUSIC ALLIANCE, One Union Square, New York, N.Y. 10003. Tel.: (212) WA 4–8311. Founded in 1926. Membership: 2,000. The Alliance helps to perpetuate Jewish folklore by organizing concerts throughout the country, encouraging new musical compositions suitable to the tradition, organizing choruses, and supplying choruses and mandolin orchestras with conductors and music needs. Membership is open to anyone wishing to join a chorus or a mandolin orchestra. Dues are an average of $2 payable to the chorus or orchestra to which the members belong. The Alliance has published "Fifty Years of Jewish Music in America," a history, and "Yiddish Poets in Song," a collection of 70 songs (words and music) in Yiddish, Hebrew, and English. Every three or four years national conventions are held; smaller meetings are held each month. National Secretary is **Abraham Lechowitzky.**

KAPPA KAPPA PSI NATIONAL FRATERNITY, National Office, 122 Center for the Performing Arts, Oklahoma State University, Stillwater, Oklahoma 74074. Founded in 1919. An honorary fraternity for men who are members of college and university bands (for its sororal equivalent, see Tau Beta Sigma). Its purposes are akin to those of Tau Beta Sigma (q.v.). Membership strength is 39,570. Publication: *The Podium,* free to members, but available by subscription for $3 a year. The fraternity sponsors the National Intercollegiate Bands and a commissioning program for new band music. Grand Secretary-Treasurer is **Donald A. Stanley** (at the above address).

SERGE KOUSSEVITZKY MUSIC FOUNDATION IN THE LIBRARY OF CONGRESS, Washington, D.C. 20540. Founded in 1950 by Serge Koussevitzky, the Foundation carries on the work of the Koussevitzky Music Foundation Inc. (founded in 1942) by commissioning important scores and encouraging their dissemination. It has commissioned over 100 works since 1942 from composers throughout the world. Chairman of the Advisory Board: **Mrs. Olga Koussevitzky.**

KULAS FOUNDATION, 1750 Union Commerce Building, Cleveland, Ohio 44115. Incorporated in Ohio in 1937. The Foundation has made grants to nonprofit music organizations usually in the Greater Cleveland Area. In 1971, it donated $25,000 to the Library of Congress to establish a computer program for converting music notation into braille as prepared by the Library's Division for the Blind and Physically Handicapped and the American Printing House for the Blind of Louisville, Kentucky. Some 2,000 blind or visually handicapped musicians and music students will, as a result of the program, be able to borrow without charge music scores and music instruction books. The Foundation expends approximately $250,000 annually in grants. Donors are **F. H. Kulas** and **E. J. Kulas.** President and Treasurer is **J. W. Reavis.**

LEAGUE OF COMPOSERS—INTERNATIONAL SOCIETY FOR CONTEMPORARY MUSIC (League—ISCM), c/o the American Music Center, 2109 Broadway, Suite 1579, New York, N.Y. 10023. Tel.: (212) TR 3–7716. The International Society for Contemporary Music was founded in Austria in 1922; the U.S. section was established in 1923. (See also ISCM—Chicago, this section.) The organization is active in the New York area, presenting concerts of modern music with well-known performers. It is governed by a Board of Advisors, almost all of whom are composers in the New York area. Membership is open to anyone who wishes to attend the concerts.

THE LESCHETIZKY ASSOCIATION, INC., c/o The President, 105 West 72nd Street, New York, N.Y. 10023. Tel.: (212) EN 2–3912. Founded in 1942 "to perpetuate the principles of Theodor Leschetizky (1830–1915) in piano teaching and playing and to honor his memory." Membership is open to those who studied with Leschetizky, and their pupils and musical descendants of Leschetizky. Although the membership qualification may appear restrictive, there are about 350 members, internationally, including a number of prominent pianists and pedagogues. Among the so-called regional directors for example are **Guiomar Novaes** (Brazil), **Clifford Curzon** (England), **Richard Byk** (France); and among the Advisory Council: **Leonard Bernstein, Alexander Brailowsky,** and **Rudolf Firkusny.** The Association sponsors and organizes recitals by gifted students of members—which can mean children, teen-agers, and young, pre-professional adults—and young concert-artist members, as well as other musical affairs. It holds a biennial contest, the winner of which receives a New York debut recital opportunity. The contest is open to pupils of members of the Association or students whose last teacher was a musical descendant of Leschetizky. A reprint of the book, "Leschetizky As I Knew Him," by Ethel Newcomb (London, 1921) was endorsed by the Association, members of which contributed new introductory material for the reprint (issued by Da Capo Press, New York). Other publications are a list of Leschetizky's pupils (over 1,500), and the Association's official bulletin, which is sent free to members and is available to libraries. Through radio station WNYC (owned by the City of New York), the Association produced, beginning in 1970, two series of bimonthly broadcasts featuring, respectively, pupils of Association members and members themselves in recital. Dues in the Association are $8 for those within a radius of 50 miles of New York City (the organization's activities are mainly centered there), $4 to all others. A Sustaining membership is available to interested persons who would otherwise be ineligible to join. Officers are: **Genia Robinor,** President (address shown above); **Edwine Behre,** President Emeritus (served as president for twenty years until 1970); three Vice Presidents: **Ernesto Berumen, Henry Levine,** and **Luisa Stojowska;** Corresponding Secretary, **Freda Rosenblatt,** whose address is 2324 Morris Avenue, New York, N.Y. 10568; **Jane Mayer,** Recording Secretary; **Beatrice Peet,** Treasurer.

THE MACDOWELL COLONY OF THE EDWARD MACDOWELL ASSOCIATION, INC., Peterborough, New Hampshire. Tel.: (603) 924–645. Also: 1083 Fifth Avenue, New York, N.Y. 10028. Tel. (212) SA 2–8884. Founded in 1907 "to provide a place where the creative man or woman may find freedom to concentrate for long periods upon his work. . ." The Colony is established on the site of Edward MacDowell's summer home, which was deeded by his widow to the memorial association formed after his death. The 400-acre retreat for composers, painters, sculptors, writers, and poets is open to all with professional qualifications—from the United States and abroad. A committee for each of the art categories determines the proof of professional ability of each applicant. Artists who can afford it pay a modest residence fee of $25; others pay nothing. Each resident receives room, board, and the exclusive use of an isolated studio equipped for his work. His stay may last from one to three months in winter or for one to two months in summer depending on space availability. Application for summer residence is required before March 15; for winter, at least ten days before the beginning date of requested residence. A total of 1,654 Fellows have worked at the Colony from 1910 to June 14, 1971. Of these 873 were writers, 354 composers, and 427 painters and sculptors. From an average annual total of 100 or so residents, the number had gradually risen to about 140 in 1970. The Fellows of the Colony include some of the most distinguished artists of our time. Their time at the Colony figures importantly in their output, as significant works have been begun, continued, or completed there. The Association publishes an *Annual Report* and *The MacDowell Colony News.* Its Board of Directors meets four times annually. Annual meetings for the Corporation are held in January. An annual benefit dinner is held in New York in November; an annual awards ceremony (Edward MacDowell medal) takes place at Peterborough in August. There are 156 corporate members of the Association. General Director of the Colony is **George M. Kendall.** President is **Aaron Copland.** Vice President is **Russell Lynes. Mary C. Bass** is Associate Director with offices at the New York headquarters.

THE MARY LOUISE CURTIS BOK FOUNDATION, 1726 Locust Street, Philadelphia, Pennsylvania 19103. Tel.: (215) 735–2525. Founded in 1931. The Foundation's major activity is the support of the Curtis Institute of Music, an institution entirely made up of scholarship-supported students (q.v.). The Foundation consists of 7 members; meetings are held about six times a year or as needed. President is **Mary Curtis Zimbalist. Cary W. Bok** is Vice President. **J. H. Mattis** is Secretary and Treasurer.

METROPOLITAN OPERA GUILD, INC., 1865 Broadway, New York, N.Y. 10023. Tel.: (212) 582–7500. Founded in 1935; incorporated in 1936. Its purpose is "to develop and cultivate a wider public interest in opera and its allied arts, and to contribute to their support; to further musical education and appreciation; and to sponsor and give assistance to operatic, musical, and cultural programs and activities of an educational character." Total membership is about 70,000 in the U.S. and some sixty foreign countries. The Guild is closely allied with the Metropolitan Opera and since its founding has contributed to the Metropolitan over $5 million raised from income received for its various services and publications. Membership in the Guild is divided into three categories: Supporting, Educational, and National. Supporting membership, in turn, is made up of four divisions (with dues shown as effective rates for 1971–72): Sponsor, $200; Donor, $100; Contributing, $60; and Sustaining, $30. Supporting Members as a whole realize the most benefit from Guild membership, as their privileges are more numerous. Other categories of membership are: Educational, $20, and National, $10. Supporting Members are given the opportunity to attend the Met's working rehearsals, to avail themselves of special Met ticket services (block ticket purchases, ticket resale service, etc.), and to receive first announcements of all Guild-sponsored benefits at the Metropolitan Opera. Invitations are also extended to Supporting Members for annual luncheons, lecture-teas, etc. Educational Members receive various informative materials designed to enhance the appreciation of specific operas (these change annually) and opera in general. These include a "Teacher's Guide" to a given opera containing articles, piano-vocal scores of musical highlights for use by nonprofessional musicians, a 35mm filmstrip of the opera as staged at the Met, and a 35mm filmstrip of any other opera selected by the member from a catalogue of thirty other Met production filmstrips. All Guild members are qualified to take part in Met backstage tours, receive mail-order librettos for $1 each, and purchase other opera education materials at special prices. Guild members, from time to time, are invited to group flights to Europe to attend summer opera and other music festivals. These are subject to certain eligibility requirements. The group flights allow economy rates to be charged to participants. All Guild members receive the main publication of the Guild, *Opera News.* The foremost periodical in America devoted to opera, it is issued twenty-four times a year. Regular issues are published in the spring and fall, special issues are devoted to "saluting" opera companies in other cities, and 19 issues are published during the season of Metropolitan Opera Saturday afternoon broadcasts, for which the periodical has special issues, each one covering the forthcoming opera broadcast with special articles, plot synopsis, cast, background data, and illustrations. The magazine also reveiws music books, recordings, live opera performances all over the world; it contains interviews with leading people in the opera world, and in general provides news about opera activity throughout the professional and academic opera world. In conjunction with the Central Opera Service of the Metropolitan National Council (q.v.), it conducts an annual survey of the opera scene in the United States. *Opera News* carries commercial advertising and is, in respect to its editorial and production standard, a completely professional magazine. (See Periodicals for further details.) The educational work of the Guild extends to developing an interest in opera among the young. Through its educational program, some 750,000 students have witnessed fully staged opera productions at the Met at reduced prices. Some 80,000 additional young people have attended performances of the Metropolitan Opera Studio under the sponsorship of the Guild. The Guild distributes to teachers and other interested persons teaching aids which describe opera in text and illustrations in a "Teacher's Guide" series and a series of filmstrips. An average of 5,000 filmstrips and 1,500 guides are distributed each season to libraries and individual members. The Guild also conducts an In-Service course for teachers in New York City with a view to providing some fundamental knowledge for their use in the classroom. The Guild's Speakers Bureau is also part of the general education program whereby speakers on opera subjects are made available to any group requesting them. Officers of the Guild are: **Mrs. August Belmont,** Founder and Emeritus President; **Michael V. Forrestal,** Chairman of the Board; **Laurence D. Lovett,** President; **Dario Soria,** Managing Director.

MODERN MUSIC MASTERS SOCIETY, P.O. Box 347, Park Ridge, Illinois 60068. Tel.: (815) 823–7148. Founded in 1952, the Society, sometimes referred to as "Tri-M," is an international, nonprofit, honor society for young musicians in junior and senior high schools. Chapters of the Society are established in all fifty states and several foreign countries; chapters total about 1,200, and the collective membership is about 150,000. (Ten years ago, chapters numbered over 400, with a combined membership of about 18,000.) The chapters are organized within schools with the approval of school administrators. A faculty member of each school acts as sponsor, selecting students for membership on the basis of music talent, academic standing, character, leadership, etc. Activities of each chapter are programmed under the motto

"Service Through Music," and are guided toward church and the community as well as the school. Students of the Society are made life members, since the goal is to continue their music interests and activities beyond high school graduation. The Society publishes *Tri-M Notes Newsletter* (at the same address as above), which is sent to members only and is not available by subscription. Officers are: **O. D. Premo,** President; **Frances M. Harley,** Executive Secretary.

THE MORAVIAN MUSIC FOUNDATION, INC., 20 Cascade Avenue, Drawer Z, Salem Station, Winston-Salem, North Carolina 27108. Tel.: (919) 725 0651. Founded in 1956. Its purpose is "to develop and perpetuate research in the discovery, publication and distribution of Early American Moravian Music and other such music as is complimentary to it." Membership is open to any interested person. There are no fixed dues as such, but voluntary contributions are accepted. The Foundation's work stems from the substantial and important music archives it maintains, through the Moravian Church, in Winston-Salem; Bethlehem, Pennsylvania; and elsewhere (see Music Libraries). The archives contain much music of the early American Moravian community, research into which has shed new light on the musical life of certain areas of early America as well as on specific works of European composers of the time. The archives contain not only the music composed in America by the Moravians themselves but also copied-out parts of music brought from Europe. The projects of the Foundation include preparing catalogues of music in the archives of the American Moravian Church, preparing modern editions of the music for commercial publishers and lending libraries, preparing music materials and historical notes for the Early American Moravian Music Festivals (q.v.), advising scholars and advanced students in any research projects relative to Moravian music, and assisting in the issuance of recordings of music from the archives. The Foundation has published six historical studies: "The Moravian Contribution to American Music," by **Donald M. McCorkle;** "John Antes, 'American Dilettante'," by **McCorkle;** "The Collegium Musicum Salem: its Music, Musicians, and Importance," by **McCorkle;** "Historical Notes on Music in Bethlehem, Pa. from 1741 to 1871," by **Rufus A. Grider;** "Regiment Band of the Twenty-Sixth N.C.," by **Julius Leinbach;** "Musical Life in the Pennsylvania Settlements of the Unitas Fratrum," by Hans T. David. It has also issued "Catalog of the Johannes Herbst Collection," edited by **Marilyn Gombosi** (first in a series of catalogues as reference work for researchers). Recent music publications prepared from the archives include "Dawn of Glory," an oratorio by the English Moravian, Christian I. Latrobe (published by Brodt Music Co.), which was subsequently performed at the Ninth Early American Moravian Music Festival in New York under the conductor, **Thor Johnson,** and in the Concert Hall of the John F. Kennedy Center for the Performing Arts in Washington during its inaugural weeks (in fact, the opening two weeks programmed a festival dealing with music composed or performed in America during the late eighteenth and early nineteenth centuries; all of the music performed was found in the Moravian archives of Winston-Salem and Bethlehem, Pennsylvania). Several Sinfonias by J. C. F. Bach, son of Johann Sebastian, were reconstructed by **Ewald V. Nolte** from parts found in the Moravian collections. The parts, representing the only existing form of the works, had been copied out by the Moravian, J. F. Peter, and brought by him to America in 1770. Several other works have been prepared under the supervision of the Foundation and published by commercial publishers. The Foundation publishes the semiannual *Moravian Music Foundation Bulletin,* edited by **Karl Kroeger,** which is sent free to interested persons (circulation is about 2,000). The Trustees of the Foundation hold semiannual meetings. Chairman of the Foundation is **R. Arthur Spaugh;** Director, appointed in September, 1972, is **Karl Kroeger.** Cataloguer–Librarian of the Archives is **Miss Frances Cumnock.**

MU PHI EPSILON, International Professional Music Sorority. Address (changes with new officers): c/o **Madge Cathcart Gerke,**

National President, 5003 North Seville Drive, Indianapolis, Indiana 46208. Founded in Cincinnati in 1903. The purposes of the Mu Phi Epsilon is "the advancement of music in America and throughout the world; the promotion of musicianship and scholarship; loyalty to the Alma Mater; the development of a true sisterhood." Eligible for membership are young music majors or minors enrolled in schools where the Sorority has chapters. Currently there are some 118 collegiate chapters and about 87 alumnae chapters with a total of 30,000 initiated members. Dues vary for collegiate and alumnae members. The Sorority publishes its official periodical, *The Triangle,* four times a year ($2 annual subscription). Editor is **Pearl Peterson,** 220 Greenstone Drive, Reno, Nevada 89502. The sorority engages in a number of philanthropic and charitable activities. Among them: regular annual contributions to community music schools (settlement houses) in Detroit, St. Louis, and Los Angeles; scholarships to National Music Camp in Interlochen, Michigan, and the construction of a lodge there; awards to women in the field of music therapy; contributions for endowed seats at Lincoln Center, New York, the Washington J. F. Kennedy Center, and the Music Center in Los Angeles. Through its Memorial Foundation, founded in 1963, the Sorority organizes a special concert series to enable young musicians to perform publicly (they are selected through audition) and grants a continuing series of scholarships to such schools as Aspen, Brevard Music Center, Music Academy of the West, etc.; it also makes an annual contribution to the MacDowell Colony in New Hampshire. The Foundation also contributes music, books, instruments, and equipment to music schools in the Philippines. Collegiate and alumnae chapters support music scholarship programs in their respective areas. The organization has also been active in taping music and music books for the blind. These tapes are deposited in the Library of Congress, where duplicates are made for distribution throughout the country. National Executive Secretary-Treasurer is **Roberta W. O'Connell.**

MUSIC CRITICS ASSOCIATION, INC. (MCA), c/o President (1971–73 term) **Irving Lowens,** *Washington Evening Star,* Washington, D.C. 20003. Founded in 1958. Its purpose is "to promote higher standards of music criticism in all media; to engage in self-criticism and exchange of data and ideas; to enlarge the scope of music criticism; to increase general interest in music." Its current estimated membership is about 120 members. Eligible for membership in MCA is anyone who writes about music regularly for a newspaper or periodical. Officers for the 1971–1973 term are (see above for President): **John W. Dwyer** (*Buffalo Evening News*), **William Littler** (*Toronto Daily Star*), **Mrs. Betty Dietz Krebs** (*Dayton Daily News*), Vice Presidents; **Byron Belt** (*Newhouse Newspapers*), Treasurer; **Elliott Galkin** (*Baltimore Sun*), Secretary. In addition there are three directors at-large. Address of Treasurer for membership information is 50 West 67th Street, New York, N.Y. 10023. The MCA holds annual conferences and workshops for its members and engages from time to time in special projects. Under a grant from the National Endowment for the Arts it undertook to publish a unique periodical (on a nonprofit basis) which would contain digests, abstracts, and reprints of articles from a wide selection of published sources throughout the world. The first issue of the *American Music Digest* was the April, 1969 pre-publication issue. Volume 1, No. 1 was the issue of October, 1968; the periodical subsequently ceased publication with the issue of Volume 1, No. 6. Recent projects of MCA include an exchange-of-critics program involving Canadian and U.S. critics, which was launched with a matching grant from the National Endowment and the Canada Council; the program enabled critics to exchange posts for a specific period. In the summer of 1972, MCA administered a Music Critics Institute sponsored by the Kennedy Center for the Performing Arts in Washington, D.C., for which ten young critics were granted stipends to attend seminars with major critics and to report on musical activities in the area.

MUSIC EDUCATORS NATIONAL CONFERENCE (MENC), 1201 16th Street,

N.W., Washington, D.C. 20036. Tel.: (202) 833–4216. Founded in 1907 as Music Supervisors National Conference; present name since 1934; in 1940 became a department of the National Education Association (NEA), where it is now headquartered; cooperates with the United States Office of Education, the State Department, UNESCO, and the Pan American Union; it is the most important and largest music education organization in the United States. Among its purposes: to promote "and activate a useful and broad program of music education in the schools, and to serve all members of the music profession through maintenance of a general clearing house and publication program, so that music educators may be better prepared and informed in the discharge of their duties. . ." MENC operates six regional districts—Eastern, North Central, Northwest, Southern, Southwestern, and Western—representing the fifty states and the District of Columbia; each of the fifty states and the District has organized its own State Music Educators Association. MENC is governed by a National Board of Directors, which has as an advisory the so-called State Presidents National Assembly, made up of the 51 presidents of the federated music educators associations. This large organizational structure itself is affiliated with eight national auxiliary and associated organizations in the music field, such affiliation indicating to a significant degree the scope of MENC's field of interest in music and music education. These auxiliary and associated organizations are: Music Industry Council, National Interscholastic Music Activities Commission, American Choral Directors Association (q.v.), The American String Teachers Association (q.v.), College Band Directors National Association (q.v.), National Band Association (q.v.), The National School Orchestra Association (q.v.), The National Association of College Wind and Percussion Instructors (q.v.). Active membership in MENC is open to all those engaged in music teaching or other music education activities. Members belong to both the national organization and a state music educators organization and pay combined dues. Other categories of membership are special active membership, and student chapter membership, each having its set of MENC privileges. The current total membership of MENC is over 60,000; undergraduate members are about 20,000 of this total. MENC is one of the most highly organized groups in the field of education, to say nothing of music. It is an active organization in the extreme, moving on many fronts to improve and change the lot of music educators and give impetus to the profession which perennially attracts large numbers to its ranks, from elementary to college-level instructors, administrators of musical organizations and educational institutions to those having adjunctive interests in the field of music or music education, such as music publishers or other members of the music industries. The activities of MENC are, consequently, so multifaceted within its field of endeavor and so numerous, with some sustaining an almost amorphous quality to those not privy to the thought processes and concerns of the institutional music educator, that to attempt to enumerate them in any comprehensive manner here would not be possible. Through its commissions, study groups, administered projects, publications, conventions, meetings, pronouncements, etc., the organization has become the single most forceful protagonist for music education in the world. Its effectiveness cannot readily be calculated. Its prime areas of concern through the years still remain generally the same: the improvement of the music educator as a teacher; the spread of music instruction as a basic part of school training for the young and the influencing of school administrators toward that goal; the improvement of methods in training the professional music educator; and the music educator's adaptability to change in the music world at large. Toward these goals, MENC conducts surveys; acts for or against federal, state, and local legislation that affects music education; prepares and publishes seminars. It is extremely active as a publisher. Its most important publication is its official magazine, *Music Educators Journal* (see Periodicals), which is published under the supervision of an Editorial Board and is sent free to members as part of their membership privileges. It also publishes the scholarly *Journal of Research in Music Education,* issued four times a year. In addition, the organization has published accumulatively over the years a long list of publications covering all aspects of the music education field from studies on aesthetics and philosophic concepts, select lists of music for various education needs, to practical guides for the classroom teacher. These publications reach over a half million in distribution each year; all are available from organizational headquarters. Officers of MENC include **Jack E. Schaeffer,** President; **Charles L. Gary,** Executive Secretary.

MUSIC LIBRARY ASSOCIATION, INC. (MLA), c/o Executive Secretary, **William J. Weichlein,** School of Music, University of Michigan, Ann Arbor, Michigan 48105. Tel.: (313) 764–2528. Founded in 1931. The MLA is a national organization of music librarians, scholars, students, musicians, and institutions. Its formal statement of purpose is, in part: "To promote the establishment, growth, and use of music libraries and collections of music, instruments, musical literature, and audiovisual aids in the United States; to initiate and encourage projects aiming to improve the organization, administration, and contents of such libraries; to cooperate in the pursuit of these aims with other organizations in related fields." Membership in MLA is open to all persons or institutions actively engaged in library work as well as anyone interested in the overall objectives of the Association. Current membership of the MLA is approximately 1,500. The practical affairs of MLA involve: the development of standards within the profession, the clarification of the role of the music librarian as it exists in different institutions; the solving of technical problems attendant upon the music librarian's daily work, such as cataloguing, indexing, use of reference materials. (The complexity and diversity of music materials, including as they do recordings, text books, general books of music literature, bound music scores, music scores as sheet music, variant and unusual forms of published music, manuscripts and holographs, incunabula, reprints of music and music literature, collected editions of music, microforms of both music and music literature, miscellaneous collections and libraries [within libraries], letters, documents, clippings, iconographic materials, and so forth—these factors, in addition to the inevitable use of foreign languages throughout music materials and the general lack of standards employed currently in music publishing, pose significant technical problems to the profession.) Beyond these internal considerations, the work of the MLA and music librarians in general (not all are members of the Association), is of strong interest to many throughout the field of music, particularly musicologists and other music scholars and users of music research materials. Increasingly, through the years, the ranks of music librarians have become filled with those who are essentially practicing musicologists, writers on music subjects, general music researchers, teachers of a variety of musical subjects, performers, etc. This concentration of varied and specialized talents within the field has delineated the "new" music librarian as a markedly different professional from, for example, the "generalist" librarian or the librarian specialist in such other fields as technology, science, and law. MLA maintains a close liaison with such musical organizations as the American Musicological Society, the Society for Ethnomusicology, College Music Society, and others, to say nothing of other library associations. Apart from two general meetings a year (in winter and summer) when the problems of the profession are confronted, the MLA maintains throughout the year a constant contact with the membership by a series of publications, the most significant of which is its official journal, *NOTES, The Quarterly Journal of the Music Library Association.* (See Periodicals.) Issued in September, December, March, and June (those months in that order represent a volume year), it is sent to members as part of their membership privileges. It is one of the best organized and technically perfect publications in the field of music. Its contents are both objective (indexes, lists, bibliographies) and subjective (reviews, essays, etc.). Reviews are generally written by specialists and cover topics in depth. Of inestimable value are the

"Index to Record Reviews" and the "Music Received" sections, annual necrologies, and surveys of organ music, choral music, music for the young, "Books Recently Published" (English, German, French, Italian, Spanish, etc.), and other regularly appearing sections. The periodical has value for all in the music field. Editor of *NOTES* is **Frank Campbell,** Research Library of the Performing Arts, 111 Amsterdam Avenue, New York, New York 10023. (Back copies of *NOTES* have been reprinted by the AMS Reprint Company.) MLA also issues a *Newsletter* three times a year. Published in typescript, it covers mostly organizational matters. A *Music Cataloging Bulletin* is a monthly issue available on subscription. Other publications of MLA are the "MLA Index Series," a series of indexes to musical sources. "Rules for Brief Cataloging," "Checklist of Music Bibliographies and Indexes: In Process and Unpublished," and "Basic Music Collection." Several MLA standing and special committees work as study groups. Their areas of interest are apparent by the committee names: Publications Committee, Record Analytics Committee, Building and Equipment Committee, Automation Committee, Microforms and Photo Duplication Committee, etc. A special service to members is the Placement Service for job openings. MLA has seven regional chapters: Midwest, New England, Greater New York City, New York State, Northern California, Southern California, and Washington–Baltimore. Operating expenditures for the year ending December 31, 1971 were $75,000. Officers: President, **William M. McClellan,** University of Illinois; Vice-President, **James W. Pruett,** University of North Carolina, Chapel Hill; Recording Secretary, **Geraldine Ostrove,** Peabody Conservatory; Treasurer, **Ruth Hilton,** New York University. Executive Secretary is **William J. Weichlein** at the organizational address above. Dues are $6.50 (students), $12 (individual members), $15 (institution).

MUSIC PERFORMANCE TRUST FUNDS (MPTF), 1501 Broadway, New York, N.Y. 10036. Tel.: (212) 239–8550. The organization was created by "agreements entered into by producers of phonograph records, electrical transcriptions and television film in the United States and Canada" and the American Federation of Musicians (AFM). Founded in 1948. Trustees of the MPTF are appointed by the U.S. Secretary of Labor; the present Trustee is **Kenneth E. Raine;** The Trustee expends contributions based on the sale of records by the recording industries in order to give employment to musicians (See American Federation of Musicians). The Funds are supported by contributions from the recording industries on the basis of sales of recordings or film containing performances by members of the American Federation of Musicians. The contributions made to the Funds are not cumulative, but must be expended annually according to a fixed percentage of distribution covering 670 geographical areas of the United States, its Territories, and Canada. The expenditures consist of payments to instrumentalists only, whose performances must be offered free to the public in the interest of public enlightenment and music appreciation. The musicians paid may be union or nonunion (such as in civic symphony orchestras, which frequently mix professional, semiprofessional, and amateur players). In this way, many local performing groups are, in part, supported or encouraged to continue their community service. The MPTF does not permit grants-in-aid or contributions directly to any organization. It permits only wage payments at the local union scale to individual instrumental performers (both union and nonunion) for services actually rendered at a free public performance. Typical examples of such performances are those at schools, hospitals, parks, playgrounds, public ceremonies, band concerts, parades, and "performances of music of special artistic significance." Its overall engagement in this activity makes the MPTF the largest single sponsor of live music in the world. Performing groups have been, and can be, marching bands, symphony orchestras, rock groups performing for educational groups, professional groups playing to school children, chamber ensembles, etc. Annually the MPTF makes about 500,000 individual payments to more than 400,000 different musicians. In some areas of the U.S. and Canada the Funds-supported performances constitute the only form of live music presentation. The total number of people who have attended fund-sponsored events is impossible to know but has been generalized as "tens of millions." Since it must expend its funds, MPTF allows suggestions to come to the office of the Trustee, where some 30 persons, including the Trustee, constitute the staff. The Trustee also seeks co-sponsors of public music events for funding expenses other than musicians fees.) Organizations wanting to take part in the Fund program apply for grants under a fixed procedure. Generally suggestions for grants come from the union locals of the AFM. Applications must arrive at the Trustee's office at least thirty days before the proposed concert date. MPTF publishes certain pamphlets and other material which make suggestions about forming concerts, arranging for publicity, etc. From 1950 to 1971 (fiscal year ending June 30) MPTF paid out $99.9 million to musicians, including the first year's payment of $900,000 and the sum paid out in fiscal 1971: $7.25 million. Prior to 1950 a separate fund existed, the so-called 1948 Recording Fund, which was the first trust agreement. In 1948, this Fund allocated $85,000, contracted for expenditures of $83,166, and actually disbursed $83,166. As an example of the growth of the MPTF's activities the following funds were involved for the year ending December 31, 1971: $8 million allocated, $5.06 million contracted for expenditures, and $4.03 million actually disbursed. Total administrative expenses for 1971 were $749,000. Income for the Fund from all contract signatories amounted to $3.88 million during the six months ending December 31, 1971. Funds not in use are invested in guaranteed bonds and notes of the United States and Canadian governments.

MUSIC PUBLISHERS' ASSOCIATION OF THE UNITED STATES (MPA), 609 Fifth Avenue, New York, N.Y. 10017. Tel.: (212) PL 2-4300. Founded in 1895. Incorporated in 1907. Among its purposes: "To foster trade and commerce and the interest of those in the music publishing business; to reform abuses relative thereto . . . to protect musical works against piracies . . . to promote uniformity and certainty in the customs and uses of the trade; to settle differences . . . to promote friendly intercourse and action and cooperation between publishers. . ." Membership is open to publishers of "standard music, of good standing, having fixed places of business." The MPA makes an annual award, the Paul Revere Award, for excellence in music engraving and graphic design. The organization is governed by a 16-member Board of Directors—all representing various publishing firms—and the executive officers who serve for two years. The 1972–1974 officers were: **Arnold Broido,** President (Theodore Presser Company); **John Owen Ward,** First Vice President (Oxford University Press); **Sol Reiner,** Secretary (Warner Bros. Music); **Sam Snetiker,** Treasurer (MCA Music); **Philip B. Wattenberg** is Executive Director.

MUSIC TEACHERS NATIONAL ASSOCIATION, INC. (MTNA), 1831 Carew Tower, Cincinnati, Ohio 45202. Tel.: (513) 421–1420. Founded 1876 by Theodore Presser. Eligible for membership in the MTNA are private, college, university, and professional-school music teachers in applied music subjects; also persons, institutions, and organizations interested in music teaching. The total membership is about 13,000. For years, the MTNA has been a pioneering association for the benefit of Americans generally in the field of music and specifically for those teaching music. It has been a germinal organization which has inspired the founding of other important musical societies such as the Music Educators National Conference, National Association of Schools of Music, and others. It currently cooperates with these as well as other leading groups. Its services include teacher certification (an important aspect of the association, the program for which was first put into effect in 1967), professional publications, student activities, teacher group insurance for national members as well as retirement programs. It has local, state, divisional organizations, holds conventions on all these levels, and in general provides information and idea exchanges in pedagogy, technique, musicology, etc. The MTNA certification plan is an outgrowth of a recognized need by many professionals in the field of music for establishing music teaching standards, particularly for the private music teacher. One reason for the certification is to give assurance to the public that MTNA certified teachers have gained recognition by their colleagues by virtue of having met certain standards. Certification is granted for any applied music teacher and MTNA member in good standing who holds an earned degree in music, with a major in the performing medium he desires to teach, from a school approved by the MTNA National Certification Board (composed of one representative from each of the MTNA geographical regions). This follows after recommendation by the State Association for certification. The recognized degree-granting school is one published in the annual listing of the American Association of Collegiate Registrars and Admissions Officers. MTNA also grants certification to teachers not holding earned degrees after the applicant has successfully completed a series of oral, written, and performance examinations (in theory, music history, pedagogy, etc.). Currently there are some 2,500 full-time music teachers with MTNA certification. This certificate is valid for five years only. It is renewed when the teacher shows evidence of further in-service course work, public performance, etc. Membership in MTNA falls into the following classifications: Active, Associate, Provisional, Student, Sustaining, and Patron. Dues for Active members vary from $14 to $17 annually. One of the privileges of membership is free subscription to the MTNA's official journal, *American Music Teacher* (see Periodicals). Editor is **Homer Ulrich.** It is published six times a year and contains articles on piano, organ, voice, strings, theory, music and book reviews, etc. Officers of MTNA are: **Celia Mae Bryant,** President; **Allen I. McHose,** Treasurer; **Albert Huetteman,** Executive Secretary. Chairman of the Certification Board is **Sister M. Christian Rosner,** Saint Mary of the Plains College, Dodge City, Kansas 67801.

MUSICAL FUND SOCIETY OF PHILADELPHIA, c/o **Arthur Claffey,** 16 Booth Lane, Haverford, Pennsylvania 19041. Tel.: (215) HO 6–5137. Instituted on January 7, 1820; organized on February 3, 1820; incorporated on February 22, 1823. Its aim is the "cultivation of skill and diffusion of taste in music." It sponsors and contributes to musical projects and to the relief of widows and children of deceased members. New members are proposed and seconded by incumbent members of the Society, currently some 132. Board of Directors meets four times annually, and the general membership holds one yearly meeting. Dues are $10 a year. Among the projects of the Society is the sponsorship (through the Edward Garrett McCollin Fund for the Encouragement of Creative Work in the Higher Forms of Music) of an international competition for a new chamber orchestra composition in commemoration of the Society's 150th Anniversary. (See Competitions—McCollin Fund). The Musical Fund Society has no official publication; however, a history of the organization is being compiled by **Robert A. Gerson** of Philadelphia. There are several claimants to the distinction of being the oldest musical society in the United States: the Musical Fund Society is one of them. (For others, see Boston's Handel and Haydn Society, for example.) Officers of the Society are: **John Y. Mace,** President; **Edwin S. Henry, Jr.,** Vice President; **John R. Ott,** Treasurer; **H. Royer Smith, Jr.,** Assistant Treasurer; **Arthur Claffy,** Secretary; **Willem Ezerman,** Assistant Secretary.

MUSICIANS CLUB OF AMERICA, 303 Minorca Avenue, Coral Gables, Florida 33134. Founded in 1939 by the late Dr. Bertha Foster, who served as president for many years (Dr. Foster was an organist and choir director who founded the Miami Conservatory of Music in 1921, was one of the founders of the University of Miami, and subsequently served as dean of its School of Music.) Purpose of the Club is to provide "a residence for retired musicians with no distinction between those who can pay and those who cannot." Members who are not able to "sustain themselves physically or financially will be entitled to apply for residence in the Club." Plans have been recently formulated to expand the Club's present facilities into a proposed $4 million complex of apartments, recreation areas, galleries, music libraries, performance rooms, a 506-seat auditorium, gardens, and office and shop areas. As is presently the case, retired musicians and music lovers will be able to live in the new facility, called Music City. Professional and nonprofessional members will have the right to apply for the rental of a retirement apartment, the use of the Club facilities, travel at reduced rates, low-cost medical insurance, etc. Dues for professional musicians are $25 a year; nonprofessionals pay $30; a life membership can be secured with the payment of $1,000. The Musicians Club of America functions as a charitable, nonprofit organization for which contributions are always sought. Membership is over 2,600. An Advisory Board serving the Club includes many civic leaders and famous musicians. President is **Annafreddie Carstens.**

NATIONAL ASSOCIATION FOR THE ADVANCEMENT OF AMERICAN COMPOSERS AND MUSICIANS, (NAANACM), Box 473, P.O. Station, Richmond, Indiana 47374. Tel.: (317) 962–1356. Founded in 1961. The organization's purpose is to promote American music, musicians, and composers. Its support comes from voluntary contributions and professional assistance. Any American composer or musician, native born or naturalized, may belong to NAANACM. There are some 300 members. The activities of the association are mainly the presentation of live concerts and recorded broadcasts of music by American composers and performers, the latter particularly in the Ohio and Indiana area. Executive Director is **Karol Fahnestock,** pianist and teacher.

NATIONAL ASSOCIATION FOR AMERICAN COMPOSERS AND CONDUCTORS, INC. (NAACC), Lyra House, 133 West 69th Street, New York, N.Y. 10023. Tel.: (212) 874–3360. Founded in 1933 by composer Henry Hadley. It is the oldest organization of its kind in America. It is devoted exclusively to the promotion of American music. Its purpose: "To arrange and encourage performances of works by American composers, and to help develop understanding and friendly cooperation between composers and conductors." NAACC sponsors four free concerts each year in New York City; in the first thirty years of its existence, over 5,000 American works were performed under the aegis of NAACC. Membership is open to composers, conductors, and others interested in promoting American music. Total membership is over 1,200. NAACC publishes a yearly *Bulletin* and awards an annual Henry Hadley Medal to a worthy recipient who has performed outstanding services for American music. The Medal in the past has gone to Sigmund Spaeth, Deems Taylor, **Nadia Boulanger,** Charles Ives (1949), Edwin Hughes, **Leopold Stokowski,** ASCAP, **Aaron Copland, Morton Gould,** and others. (The first recipient was **Howard Hanson** in 1938.) Its annual series of New York concerts are broadcast over the Municipal radio station WNYC and include a variety of music by a large number of composers. Its chapters in Washington, D.C., Los Angeles, and Philadelphia also present concerts, seminars, etc. NAACC maintains the Henry Hadley Memorial Library, which is housed in the Music Division of the New York Public Library at Lincoln Center. The collection consists of scores contributed for deposit by member composers of NAACC. Membership dues are: $10 for Composers, Conductors, Professional, and Associate members; $15 for Cooperative members; $25 for Sustaining; $100 for Life members. President is **Paul Price.**

NATIONAL ASSOCIATION OF BAND INSTRUMENT MANUFACTURERS (NABIM), c/o Secretary-Treasurer, **John Morena,** Fibes Drum Div. of C. F. Martin Organization, 1500 New Highway, Farmingdale, Long Island, N.Y. 11735. Tel.: (215) 759–2837. Founded in 1945. Membership is open to any manufacturer of band instruments or closely related products. There are 27 members in NABIM (February, 1972). They are: W. T. Armstrong Co., Inc.; Artley,

Inc.; J. J. Babbitt Company; E. K. Blessing Co., Inc.; Chicago Music Instrument Co.; Coin Art, Inc.; C. G. Conn Corporation; E. L. DeFord of Elkhart, Inc.; DEG Music Products, Inc.; Evans Products, Inc.; Fibes Drum Div. of C. F. Martin Organization; Alfred Freistat Case Company, Inc.; K. G. Gemeinhardt Co., Inc.; The Getzen Company, Inc.; The Fred Gretsch Mfg. Company; Frank Holton and Company; King Musical Instruments; G. LeBlanc Corporation; Lesher Woodwind Company; Linton Manufacturing Co.; Ludwig Drum Company; Remo, Incorporated, F. A. Reynolds Band Instrument Co., Inc.; Rogers Drums; H. & A. Selmer, Inc.; Slingerland Drum Company; and Avedis Zildjian Co. The association holds annual meetings and conducts annual seminars for band instrument dealers in conjunction with the NAMM Trade Show (National Association of Music Merchants). President of NABIM is **Vito Pascucci** of LeBlanc Corporation; Vice President is **Al Brancae** of King Musical Instruments.

NATIONAL ASSOCIATION OF COLLEGE WIND AND PERCUSSION INSTRUCTORS (NACWPI), c/o Music Educators National Conference, 1201 16th Street, N.W., Washington, D.C. 20036. Founded in 1951, NACWPI is one of the associate organizations of the MENC (q.v.). It had a membership of 644 as of April, 1972. The purpose of the organization is the advancement of the performing and teaching of wind and percussion instruments in general and on the college level in particular. Active membership is open to anyone teaching woodwind, brass, or percussion instruments on the college level. Associate members are those interested in the aims of the organization. Students of wind and percussion instruments also may join. Dues for each category of membership range from $1 for students to $6 for active and associate members. NACWPI publishes a quarterly *Bulletin* sent free to members, which is available to nonmembers for $1 annually. National meetings are held in even-numbered years in conjunction with the national conventions of MENC; divisional meetings also coincide with those of MENC in odd-numbered years; state meetings are held yearly. The Association commissions some three compositions annually. It also provides its members with a "vacancy notice" service (information on job opportunities), a research library, etc. Officers for the national board are elected biennially, thus no positions are permanent. Secretary-Treasurer (1972): **Thomas Ayres,** School of Music, University of Iowa.

NATIONAL ASSOCIATION OF MUSIC MERCHANTS, INC. (NAMM), National Headquarters: 222 West Adams Street, Chicago, Illinois 60606. Tel.: (312) 263–0679. Founded in 1901. Its membership of approximately 1,300 includes merchants from the U.S. and possessions, Canada, the Caribbean, Central and South America, Europe, Africa, the Far East, and Australia. It engages in activities designed to benefit the retail and wholesale music industry. Its most important annual activity is its sponsorship and organization of the Music Industry Trade Show, the high point of the industry's year. This show is generally held in Chicago but has been held elsehwere from time to time. It publishes the *Prospective Monthly Bulletin* (circulation: about 2,750) and the *Member Monthly Bulletin* (circulation: about 2,730). Other publications: *Better Management Bulletin, Merchandising Bulletin,* etc. NAMM holds five regional meetings each year, one annual meeting and the Music Industry Convention (Trade Show). Membership dues are: $100 for each store and $50 for each branch or additional store a member may have. Officers: **Ray Hendricks,** President; **William R. Coyle,** Vice President; **George M. Lukas,** Secretary. Executive Vice President is **William R. Gard.**

NATIONAL ASSOCIATION OF MUSICAL MERCHANDISE WHOLESALERS (NAMMW), 111 East Wacker Drive, Chicago, Illinois 60601. Tel.: (312) 644–6610. Founded in 1933. The organization represents the interest of wholesalers in musical products and promotes their role in the music industry. About 49 firms belong to NAMMW. Any eligible wholesaler may join. Dues are assessed on a scale ranging from $300 to $600 per year for each member firm. The organization's official publication is the *NAMMW Quarterly,* first issued in fall, 1971 and distributed mainly to retailers. NAMMW holds two meetings annually; one coincides with the NAMM Trade Show. Executive Secretary (at the address above) is **William W. Carpenter.**

NATIONAL ASSOCIATION OF ORGAN TEACHERS (NAOT), 7938 Bertram Avenue, Hammond, Indiana 46324. Tel.: (219) TI 4–3395. Founded in November, 1963, it is fashioned somewhat after the National Guild of Piano Teachers (q.v.). Purposes of NAOT are, in part: ". . . to conduct a continuing program of teaching improvement in the home organ and related electronic organ field. To [develop the] use of improved teaching methods and materials. . . . To foster cooperation for advancement of the organ music field by the various elements concerned including instrument producers, music publishers, music merchants, organ clubs, individual organ owners and students, music composers, teachers and teacher training institutions." Basic to the organization's activities is the promotion of its "All Music/All Organs" teacher workshops' concept of organ playing and teaching, that is, an all-inclusive approach to the kind of music and the kind of organ that can be utilized for musical experiences for those of any age who wish to make their own music. Some of NAOT's activities include the National Organ Playing Auditions open to "any age, any stage, any organ" student of NAOT teacher-members; annual organ music composition evaluations, held each spring; sponsorship of the National Society of Student Organists, which admits students who have successfully completed annual auditions; a scholarship program for students achieving continued excellence in the annual auditions. The auditions are noncompetitive and are intended to reward meritorious effort by student and amateur performers of the organ and to encourage the use of home organs. By its nature, NAOT is oriented toward the mass electronic home organ field, since owners' interest in playing the instruments may sometimes flag after their purchase of them. To offset this likelihood and to give some kind of direction to the amateur organist is the general goal of NAOT. Since sales of organs have breached the 135,000-a-year level, and, since the estimated number of people playing the organ (according to the American Music Conference) is over 4 million, the field of activity for NAOT is quite vast. Pins and certificates of the NAOT are rewarded to those successfully completing the auditions. To establish standards of graded playing, the NAOT publishes recommended playing materials and holds teacher workshops for improving teaching methods in each grade of material. The official publication of NAOT is *Notes of NAOT,* sent free to members and issued bimonthly except July and August. Categories of membership are: Active (music teachers), Student (those learning to teach organ), and Associate (all others). Dues vary accordingly. Officers are: **Mrs. Dorothy S. Greig,** President; **Jack C. Greig,** Secretary-Treasurer. Both are founders of the organization. NAOT is incorporated not-for-profit.

NATIONAL ASSOCIATION OF RUDIMENTAL DRUMMERS (NARD), 1728 North Damen Avenue, Chicago, Illinois 60647. Tel.: (312) 276–3360. Founded in 1933. NARD established a system of standardized drumming patterns (rudiments) to enable the judging of all drummers and facilitate the teaching of drumming, particularly the snare drum. The need for the standardized rudiments was apparent in the early part of this century with the rapid growth of drum-and-bugle corps and civic marching groups. The method books in use at the time, originating from the mid-nineteenth century and earlier, were in conflict with each other on details. It is obvious that drummers playing en masse would have to employ the same stroke patterns and have the same understanding of rhythmic figures in order to play together and present a uniform appearance. Thus, left-hand and right-hand attacks and alternations had to be systematized. NARD was brought about at the National Convention in 1932 of the American Legion (which had been organizing a large number of drum-and-bugle corps as well as drumming contests throughout the country). Thirteen drummers prominent in professional, Legion, and civic musical groups met to establish the standard American drum rudiments. They included Bill Kieffer, drummer with the Marine Band; Bill Hammond, with the Pittsburgh Symphony; **Roy Knapp,** radio drummer and teacher; **William F. Ludwig,** now a well-known drum manufacturer, who was responsible for bringing the group together (**Ludwig** was also former snare drummer of the Chicago Symphony and the Chicago Grand Opera Company); and others. Of the 26 extant drum rudiments, 13 were chosen as the first essentials—those that would be required as the test of rudimentary drum playing and be required of each applicant to the newly formed association. (The remaining 13 rudiments are usually taken up subsequently by most drummers.) On the basis of that beginning and subsequent NARD educational efforts, nearly all drum contests today are judged by the NARD rudiments. The 13 essential rudiments are: the long roll, the 5-stroke roll, the 7-stroke roll, the flam, the flam accent, the flam paradiddle, the flamacue, the ruff, the single drag, the double drag, the double paradiddle, the single ratamacue, and the triple ratamacue. Any drummer, regardless of age, may apply for membership in NARD, acceptance of which follows after passing the examination of playing the 13 rudiments. Applicants may apply for a copy of the rudiments and, after he feels he has mastered them, may audition before a member judge in his area (members over twenty-one are qualified to examine new applicants). The examination also includes playing other test material. Those not passing the first test may apply again. There is no examination fee; annual membership dues are $1, which includes the *NARD Bulletin* contained in the semiannual publication, *The Ludwig Drummer,* published by the Ludwig Drum Co. There are about 4,000 members in NARD. Officers are: **Wm. F. Ludwig, Sr.,** President; **Frank Arsenault,** Vice President; **Wm. F. Ludwig, Jr.,** Secretary-Treasurer.

NATIONAL ASSOCIATION OF SCHOOLS OF MUSIC (NASM), One Dupont Circle, N.W., Suite 750, Washington, D.C. 20036. Founded in 1924. Its purposes are: "To exercise leadership in the training of musical performers, composers, and researchers. To encourage excellence in the preparation of teachers of music for collegiate institutions, public schools, and private studios. To further the understanding of music's importance as an essential element of liberal learning. To communicate to its members information on current developments in music in higher education. To provide a forum for the discussion of major issues relating to music in higher education." In general NASM works to establish a uniform system of granting credit and to set minimum standards for schools for granting music degrees. Toward this end, NASM is recognized by the National Commission on Accrediting as the accrediting agency for music in higher education. It is a member of the American Council on Education and other educational organizations. All types of schools are eligible to apply for membership in NASM: universities, colleges, conservatories, junior colleges, theological seminaries. Some of the requirements for school membership in NASM are: accreditation by the appropriate regional agency; at least one complete curriculum in music or music education, and at least one graduating class must have completed the curriculum prior to the school's application for membership; there must be at least 25 majors in the music department. In addition, there is an individual membership classification in NASM which is open to musicians of recognized standing. As of January, 1971, the last date of reported membership in the NASM annual "Directory," there were the following institutional members: 288 Full Members, 79 Associate Members, and 1 Preparatory School Member, to total 368 institutions; in addition there were 9 individual Honorary Members and 119 Individual Members. NASM cooperates with six regional accrediting associations and with the National Association for Music Therapy. It also maintains a close liaison with such large music education organizations as the Music Educators National Conference and the Music Teachers National Association. It maintains standing study committees for such areas as ethics, junior colleges, library, etc. Among the NASM publications are: the annual "Directory," which lists all member schools and gives details about their degrees, chairmen, etc.; "By-Laws and Regulations," which contains curriculum standards ($1); "Graduate Studies," a list of recommendations; "A Basic Music Library," a bibliography for schools offering undergraduate music degrees ($2); "The Proceedings of the Annual Meeting" ($1); and other publications, all of which are available directly from the office of the Executive Secretary. NASM is governed by the institutional members through the annual meetings of their representatives, held in November. The administration consists of a Board of Directors and an Executive Committee, Trustees, and Commissions on undergraduate and graduate studies. Total receipts of NASM for the fiscal year ending August 31, 1970 were $135,000. Total disbursements were $130,000. Officers of NASM are: **Carl Neumeyer,** President; **Everett Timm,** Vice President; **Charles H. Ball,** Treasurer; **Robert Briggs,** Recording Secretary; **Warner Imig,** Chairman of the Commission for Graduate Studies; **Robert Glidden** is Executive Secretary, at the address shown above.

NATIONAL ASSOCIATION OF TEACHERS OF SINGING (NATS), 250 West 57th Street, Suite 817, New York, N.Y. 10019. Tel.: (212) 582–4043. Founded and incorporated in Cincinnati in 1944. NATS is an organization of professional teachers of singing and others interested and involved in singing or vocal instruction in private schools, colleges, universities, etc. Its purposes include goals for establishing high standards of ethical principles and practices in the teaching of singing and to encourage cooperation among voice teachers. NATS publishes a "Code of Ethics" which outlines the professional practices sought. Membership is restricted to vocal teachers who can meet the standards set forth in the "Code." Specifically this includes the requirement that the teacher be a U.S. or Canadian citizen and that he has engaged in voice teaching for a minimum of five consecutive years, has had professional training, and that he devotes at least 50 percent of his time to voice teaching. Application for membership by prospective teachers is made with the sponsorship of two members of NATS. Among the activities of NATS are annual national conventions and regional and chapter meetings, summer workshops, conducting and sponsoring contests and auditions, and the support of the fellowship program of the American Institute of Vocal Pedagogy, which is the higher-level accrediting agency for NATS. One of the most publicized of the Association's activities is the "Singer of the Year Scholarship Auditions" established in 1955 for discovering new young vocal talent. It offers a cash award and auditions with leading opera companies and concert managers. The official publication of NATS is *The NATS Bulletin.* Editor is **Harvey Ringel,** 430 South Michigan Avenue, Chicago, Illinois 60605. (see Periodicals). There are about 2,700 members in the organization. Annual dues are $20. Officers (for 1972–74): **Jean Ludman,** President; **Margret Kommel,** Secretary; **Eugene Pence,** Treasurer. **Martha Baxter** is Executive Secretary, at the organizational address above.

NATIONAL CATHOLIC BANDMASTERS ASSOCIATION (NCBA), P.O. Box 523, Notre Dame, Indiana 46556. The address is that of the National Coordinator, **Robert O'Brien,** telephone (219) 284–7136. Founded August, 1953. Membership is open to all Catholic and non-Catholic bandmasters teaching in Catholic schools and Catholic bandmasters teaching in public schools. Membership for these bandmasters is referred to as "Active." An "Associate" membership is open to all other educators and bandmasters who may be interested in the work of NCBA. Students, institutions, and commercial firms may also join. Membership is about 300. Dues are: $7 for Active, Associate, and School members; $12 for Associate Retail; $25 for Commercial membership. The purpose of the association is to work towards the solution of problems peculiar to the Catholic band and to coordinate Catholic school band activities on a national level; to organize yearly conventions of Catholic band educators; to support the NCBA National Summer Band Camp; to develop music scholarships; commission new band compositions; to organize a composite band curriculum for presentation to Catholic educators and school administrators. The NCBA is also engaged in improving salary and tenure for the bandmaster and raising the standards of teacher qualification. The NCBA's official publication is the magazine *School Musician* (q.v.), sent to members as part of their membership dues. Officers are: **William Holcombe Pryor,** President; **Charles Winking,** Vice President; **Robert O'Brien,** National Secretary-Treasurer.

NATIONAL CATHOLIC MUSIC EDUCATORS ASSOCIATION, INC. (NCMEA), 4637 Eastern Avenue, N.E., Washington, D.C. 20018. Tel.: (301) 277–1577. Founded in 1942. It has a membership of nearly 4,900. Membership is open to anyone interested in music education in Catholic schools and churches. Its purposes are: "to advance the cause of high standards of music and music education at all levels in Catholic schools and churches, [to] promote a closer integration between the music taught in the schools and the life of worship in the church, [to] create and sustain a spirit of mutual cooperation and help among all interested in Catholic music and music education." Dues are respectively $8 for regular membership, $10 for contributing members, and $100 for life members. The NCMEA is organized into eight departments of special study and responsibility: elementary music education, secondary music education, college, instrumental music, vocal music, piano music, liturgical music, and student activities; each department is headed by a national department chairman. The official journal of NCMEA is *MUSART,* issued six times annually and sent to members as part of their dues. Other periodicals are *OVERTONES,* a research bulletin issued eight times a year with each issue devoted to one of the departments of NCMEA (see above), and *NOW!,* a quarterly bulletin with professional articles for teachers. NCMEA has also published a number of supplementary monographs, special reports, and reprints of selected articles from *MUSART.* These are all available for general distribution. To provide service for its members, NCMEA organizes a large-scale national convention each year (in April) which, since 1969, has been held in conjunction with the National Catholic Educational Association, with which the NCMEA is affiliated. (The NCMEA also has working contact with such secular educational music organizations as the Music Educators National Conference and the Music Teachers National Association.) The convention offers clinics, workshops, and other informative activities for members. NCMEA also advises and assists diocesan school superintendants and diocesan music commissions throughout the country in establishing or sustaining school music programs. Officers of NCMEA are: **Rev. William V. Volk, C. PP.S.,** President; **Rev. Eugene M. Lindusky, O.S.C.** and **Joseph M. Woods,** respectively first and second Vice Presidents; **Vincent P. Walter, Jr.,** Executive Secretary-Treasurer and Editor of *MUSART.*

NATIONAL ENDOWMENT FOR THE ARTS, 806 15th Street, N.W., Washington, D.C. 20506. Tel.: (202) 382–6085. Established September 29, 1965 as a federal government agency within the National Foundation on the Arts and the Humanities. Its purpose is to promote the arts, develop a broadening public support for them, and administer the grants allotted to the arts by public and private sources, as specified by the terms of Public Law 89–209 as amended (see National Foundation on the Arts and the Humanities). The arts categorized by the Endowment are: architecture and environmental arts (planning and design of the environment: cities, parks, landscape, etc.), dance, education (inclusion of the arts in the school experience), expansion arts (professionally directed, community-based arts organizations such as settlement houses, community centers, ethnic centers, etc.), literature, museums, music, public media (radio, TV, and film) and the visual arts. The chief activity of the Endowment is granting money to individuals and organizations under programs mandated by

Public Law 89–209 and those initiated by the Endowment. The administration of the Endowment is in the hands of a Chairman appointed by the President of the U.S. and confirmed by the U.S. Senate. A Deputy Chairman, a staff, and the National Council on the Arts complete the mechanism by which the Endowment functions (this structure is duplicated in the National Endowment for the Humanities, the sister Endowment within the National Foundation on the Arts and the Humanities). The Chairman of the Endowment also serves, by statute, as Chairman of the National Council, the essential advisory unit of the Endowment. Besides the Chairman, it is composed of 26 presidentially appointed private citizens "who are widely recognized for their broad knowledge of or experience in, or for their profound interest in the Arts." National Council members are nominally appointed for six-year terms. (Approximately one third of its appointments expire every two years.) The Council meets four times a year. Occupying the position of Chairman of the National Endowment for the Arts is **Miss Nancy Hanks,** who began her four-year term on October 6, 1969. Her only predecessor was **Roger L. Stevens.** Serving on the National Council on the Arts as of May, 1972 were: **Maurice Abravanel, Marian Anderson, Richard F. Brown, Jean Dalrymple, Kenneth N. Dayton, Charles Eames, Duke Ellington, O'Neil Ford, Virginia B. Gerity, Lawrence Halprin, Helen Hayes, Charlton Heston, Richard Hunt, James Earl Jones, Charles K. McWhorter, Jimilu Mason, Robert Merrill, Gregory Peck, Rudolf Serkin, Beverly Sills, Edward Villella, E. LeLand Webber, Donald Weismann, Anne Potter Wilson, Nancy White, Robert E. Wise.** Applications for grants within the scope of the Endowment's regular, continuing aid programs are not initially given the National Council's attention. Rather, they are referred first to various advisory panels of experts set up for each of the arts: music, (with a special panel for jazz), literature, theatre, public media, etc. Each panel has at least one chairman. Music Advisory Panel members for fiscal year 1972 were: **Donald Engle,** Co-Chairman, **Peter Mennin,** Co-Chairman, **A. Beverly Barksdale, Richard Cisek, Van Cliburn, Willis Conover, Roger Hall, R. Philip Hanes, Jr., Robert Mann, Gian-Carlo Menotti, Benjamin Patterson, Russell Patterson, David Rockefeller, Jr., Max Rudolf, William** Severns, Robert N. Sheets, Risë Stevens, **Howard Taubman, William Thomson,** Alfred Wallenstein. Jazz Advisory Panel: **Willis Conover,** Chairman, **John G. Gensel, Milton Hinton, Marian McPartland, Dan M. Morgenstern, Russell Sanjek.** Dance Advisory Panel: **Roger Englander,** Co-Chairman, **Deborah Jowitt,** Co-Chairman, **George Beiswanger, Jerry Bywaters Cochran, Merce Cunningham, Martha Hill Davies, Alexander Ewing, Cora Cahan Gersten, Kathleen Stanford Grant, Thelma Hill, C. Bernard Jackson, Joe Layton, Stella Moore, Frances Poteet, Judith Sagan, Allegra Fuller Snyder, Michael Steele.** Other Endowment staff members include Deputy Chairman **Michael Straight,** Director of Performing Arts and Public Media **Norman L. Fagan,** and the Program Director of each of the art categories. Music Program Director is **Walter Anderson;** Dance Program Director is **Don S. Anderson.** In addition, special consultants are hired by the Endowment. The law creating the Endowment intended that it develop programs of aid which would benefit arts activity nationally. Grants are directed to regional and local nonprofit arts organizations, many of which were brought into existence as a result of the establishment of the Endowment. Further dissemination of arts activity occurs from grants allotted to touring performing groups—orchestras, dance companies, opera companies, and theater groups, which make regional or national tours combining performances with educational work within the communities during their period of engagement. Another goal of the Endowment is to help already established performing groups, arts organizations, and art institutions such as schools, museums, and the like to improve their standard and to find ways to broaden their public support and appeal by increasing or improving their programs of public service. There is an educational motivation behind this goal, for the survival of the arts is dependant upon continuing generations of those who would make the arts part of their lives. Thus, Endowment funds are often extended to those arts groups capable of reaching out beyond the normal confines of the concert hall, dance studio, or art gallery to entertain, enlighten, or otherwise attract new audiences and participants. On the other hand, the individual artist's own vested interest in his art is recognized by the Endowment as a vital resource. To encourage gifted artists the Endowment grants fellowships and creates programs for commissions, residencies, and other forms of aid that strengthen the artist's ties to institutions which benefit from his work. Endowment funds are authorized by Congress in three categories: (1) National Program Funds: money is provided the Endowment to aid talented individuals and nonprofit, organizations throughout the country in a wide variety of cultural activity. (2) Federal–State Partnership Funds: money is made available for the specific use of official state arts councils. The councils are in each of the fifty states, the District of Columbia, American Samoa, Guam, Virgin Islands, and Puerto Rico. Money appropriated for the arts councils is divided equally, with the exception of American Samoa and Guam, whose grants cannot exceed $65,000 each. The arts councils are required to submit a year in advance details of their programs for which Endowment funds will be used. These programs are subject to review by the Endowment. The emphasis of the state arts councils' programs is on meeting the characteristic cultural needs of the people in the areas served by the councils. (State councils can also apply for grants under other Endowment programs which by their nature are best administered through state arts councils, such as the Artist-in-School Programs and the Coordinated Residency Touring Program.) (3) Treasury Fund: monies in this category become available only when private donations are received by the Endowment. The intent of this Fund is to stimulate and continue nonfederal sources of money for the arts. Such support, from individuals, business firms, and foundations, has been traditional in the U.S. To strengthen this tradition the government creates larger grants by matching dollar for dollar all private donations with Treasury Funds. This double amount is then made available to grantees, who must then match the double amount. Thus, the grantee will finally work with dollar amounts four times the original private donation. Gifts to the Endowment may be designated for specific grantees—a dance company, a symphony orchestra, opera company, theater, or for any of the Endowment programs—or may be contributed for unrestricted use for projects suggested to the Endowment by the National Council on the Arts. Gifts may be in the form of money, property, or bequests. Prospective donors should contact the Office of General Counsel at the Endowment's address shown above. To be eligible for grants from NEA, groups must be nonprofit, so that contributions made to them are tax-deductible as defined by the Internal Revenue Service (Section 170c, 1954 Internal Revenue Code). Proof of tax-exempt status must be supplied by any organization applying for a NEA grant. Grants to organizations must be matched at least dollar for dollar with funds from sources other than the federal government. Such sources may include funds contributed by private persons, business firms, foundations, state and local governments, etc. Further provisions for grants to organizations refer to compliance with Title VI of the 1964 Civil Rights Act and parity wage levels for hiring performers, staff, and laborers. Grants can only be made to individuals of exceptional talent. Normally, only U.S. citizens or permanent residents of the U.S. can receive grants from the Endowment. The Endowment does not extend grants for deficit funding, purchase of equipment, construction, travel or study abroad, tuition assistance for study in U.S. colleges or universities, or what it terms "general support." Since fiscal year 1966, funds actually appropriated for the National Foundation on the Arts and Humanities have been below the sums authorized (for both Endowments). Authorized and appropriated amounts, respectively, for the years 1966 to 1972 have been (appropriated amounts are shown in parentheses): 1966: $17,250,000

	1966	1967	1968
National Program Funds	$2,500,000	$4,000,000	$4,500,000
Federal–State Partnership	—	$2,000,000	$2,000,000
Treasury Funds	$ 34,308	$1,965,692	$ 674,291
Total Appropriated	$2,534,308	$7,965,692	$7,174,291
(Total Authorized)	($7,250,000)	($10,000,000)	($10,000,000)

* Final total is dependent on the amount of donations received.

($5,034,038); 1967: $20,000,000 ($10,071,-970); 1968: $20,000,000 ($10,999,548); 1969: $22,750,000 ($12,719,348); 1970: $24,750,000 ($16,300,000); 1971: $40,000,000 ($28,650,-000); 1972: $60,000,000 ($54,200,000). Funds appropriated and authorized for the National Endowment for the Arts alone and the disbursement to the three fund categories were as shown above for the years 1966 to 1972. The breakdown of the funds allotted to the Federal–State Partnership Program for remittance to the fifty state arts councils and the arts councils of District of Columbia, Puerto Rico, and the Virgin Islands were the following amounts to *each council:* 1968: $39,383; 1969: $30,909; 1970: $36,363; 1971: $75,377; 1972: $101,320. (The first year of funding for the Program was 1967, when varying amounts were granted.)

The final totals for fiscal years 1966 to 1972 (including the 1972 Treasury Fund figure of $3.5 million and similar matching amounts from private sources).

Total Funds appropriated for the National Endowment for the Arts	$78,521,166
Total Private Donations (to match Treasury Funds)	13,048,548
Total U.S. Office of Education Transfers as of January 15, 1972	1,000,000
Total Appropriated	$92,569,714
(Total Authorized)	($101,000,000)
Total Appropriated from Government Funds alone	$79,521,166

Funds obligated by the National Endowment for the Arts for the fiscal years 1970 and 1971 (July 1, 1969 to June 30, 1971) are shown below (the 1971 figures issued in January, 1972 are the latest available at the time of writing). Added programs were Expansion Arts, Museums, and Special Projects; the latter is a change in name from Coordinated Programs.

	1970	1971
Architecture and Environmental Arts	$ 347,750	$ 178,681
Dance	1,751,350	1,251,170
Education	1,240,000	571,831
Expansion Arts	—	307,600
Literature	513,121	407,450
Museums	—	926,957
Music	2,525,195	5,188,383
Public Media	195,000	1,264,455
Special Projects	—	538,529
Theatre	2,891,000	2,021,482
Visual Arts	970,244	552,141
Coordinated Programs	505,711	—
Federal–State Partnership Program	1,963,602	4,062,981
Program Development and Evaluation	74,644	305,475
Transferred to National Endowment for the Humanities	5,000	4,800
TOTAL	$12,982,667	$17,644,935

1969	1970	1971	1972
$3,700,000	$4,250,000	$ 8,465,000	$20,750,000
$1,700,000	$2,000,000	$ 4,125,000	$ 5,500,000
$2,356,875	$2,000,000	$ 2,500,000	*$ 3,500,000
$7,756,875	$8,250,000	$15,090,000	$29,750,000
($11,375,000)	($12,375,000)	($20,000,000)	($30,000,000)

At present music is the largest single program within the National Endowment for the Arts. Both music and dance (and the other arts) not only receive support from their own programs within the Endowment but also may be further supported in other program categories: Education (grants to musicians and dancers under the Artists-in-the-Schools Program), Expansion Arts (folk music and dance, musical theaters and other activities by urban cultural centers, ethnic groups, community music schools, etc.), Public Media Program (broadcast of music, dance films, and television dance workshops), Special Project Program (grants to regional organizations which sponsor tours of orchestras and ballet companies), and Theatre Program (may include opera performed by special theater groups). Music and dance are also aided in part by state arts councils with grants they receive under the Federal–State Partnership Program. Thus, monies granted to music and dance are even greater than the sums shown by the expenditure of their respective separate grant programs. The fiscal 1970 grants under the Music Program numbered 75 distributed to 55 organizations and 19 individuals in twenty-five states and the District of Columbia. In fiscal 1971 there were 169 grants to 126 organizations and 31 individuals in forty states. Recent Music Program aid includes matching grants to symphony orchestras for "artistic and administrative development, public service, touring and educational projects" (not more than $100,000 from program funds, or $200,000 from the Treasury Fund; most grants do not reach the maximum amount); matching grants to professional opera companies (with the same quoted purposes and monetary ceilings as for symphony orchestras); to the National Opera Institute for commissioning and performing new works, for productions of rarely staged operas, for hiring young American singers, etc.; grants to jazz musicians and organizations in the form of fellowships, residencies at academic institutions, jazz concerts in schools, experimental works, etc. (grant amounts currently do not exceed $2,500 each). The symphony orchestra aid program, among the largest undertaken by the Endowment, at the end of its second year (fiscal 1972) totaled $5,370,817 in private and federal funds for 93 groups (28 major orchestras, 48 metropolitan orchestras, 2 chamber orchestras, and 15 orchestras and other groups under the program's special category) located in forty states, the District of Columbia, and Puerto Rico. The opera program as of fiscal year 1972 extended to 28 opera companies in eighteen states aid totaling $924,610, exclusive of $600,000 in Treasury Funds for the National Opera Institute in 1970. Grants to jazz activities in 1971 totaled $50,325 to 50 recipients. Other recent Music Program grants include a Composer Assistance Program of $4,870 in 1970; Contemporary Music Performing Groups Program of $37,300; grants to the American Symphony Orchestra League (q.v.) in 1970 and 1971; the Carnegie Hall Corporation, 1971; Affiliate Artists, Inc. of New York; and the National Guild of Community Music Schools (q.v.). The Music Program does not extend grants for summer music camps; research, publication, or recording costs; sabbatical leaves; purchase of musical instruments or equipment; for festival or symposia participation abroad of youth or university music performing ensembles. Music aid under the Education Program includes grants in 1970 and 1971 totaling $51,000 to Affiliate Artists, Inc. of New York, for booking musicians to perform in schools under the Education Program's "Artist-in-the-Schools" plan. (Affiliate Artists received an additional $254,000 with $115,000 in private funds under the General Programs category of the Music Program). Expansion Arts grants to music in 1971 included $7,000 to the Community Music School of St. Louis; $17,500 to the National Guild of Community Music Schools; and $50,700 to the Harlem School of the Arts for the training of children in music and theater (the school is directed by former famed singer, **Dorothy Maynor**). Aid under the Endowment's Dance Program included $163,300 and $392,950 in fiscal years 1970 and 1971, respectively, for commissioning new works from well-known choreographers; $146,250 in fellowships to some 16 choreographers in 1971; $1,397,000 in 1970 and $693,480 in 1971 to help subsidize the cost of tours of such companies as the American Ballet Theatre, American Ballet Company, City Center Joffrey Ballet, Pacific Northwest Ballet Association, among others. The sums include grants to selected state arts councils for participation in the Endowment's Coordinated Residency Touring Program. This program is designed to facilitate regional or interstate tours of dance companies through a system of local sponsors coordinated by state arts councils. Each local sponsor is obligated to engage at least two dance companies for at least a half week each. In addition to performances, the companies give master classes, lecture demonstrations, workshops, etc. In 1971, the Endowment extended grants of $126,500 in support of various institutions such as the Association of American Dance Companies, the Dance Notation Bureau (q.v.), the José Limon Dance Company, etc. To apply for a grant under specific Endowment programs, applicants must write to the appropriate Program Director (for music, dance, theater, etc.) for application forms and other information relating to the assistance program in question. Completed forms are sent to the Grants Office of the NEA. Each program has its own set of stipulations regarding eligibility, application, procedure and deadlines. Deadlines are often many months in advance of the fiscal year covering the proffered grants. Applications received by the Endowment staff are reviewed and referred to an advisory panel. Recommendations of the panel and the staff are presented to the Chairman and the National Council for final action. A publication, issued by the Endowment, called "Our Programs" (May, 1972) is available from the Government Printing Office, Washington, D.C. 20402 ($1). All of the application procedures, eligibility requirements, and deadlines are listed in detail for all current programs.

NATIONAL FEDERATION OF MUSIC CLUBS (NFMC). National Headquarters: Suite 1215, 600 South Michigan Avenue, Chicago, Illinois 60605. Tel.: (312) HA 7–3683. Founded 1898. NFMC is the world's largest musical organization. It has approximately 600,000 members in over 5,000 organizations throughout the United States and Puerto Rico. Its purpose is "(1) To bring into working relation with one another musical organizations and individuals associated with musical activity, for the purpose of aiding and encouraging musical education. (2) To make music an integral part of the civic, industrial, educational, and social life of the state and nation. (3) To stimulate American creative musical art, and to promote American artists. (4) To make America truly musical." Its members are individuals and groups, formed within state-level Federations ("clubs"). Membership in a State Federation brings an automatic membership in the National Federation of Music Clubs. Membership classifications are as follows: Groups (active and associate), to include Senior, Student, and Junior members; Individual, to include Special, Contributing, Life Subscriber, Donor, Patron, and Cradle Roll (see below). A brief description of each category of membership reveals at the same time a glimpse of the working strength and extreme variety of potential talent at the service of the NFMC. Group Active Members, Senior Division, include (a) "organizations formed for the purpose of promoting the study or performance of music, such as adult music clubs, choral societies . . . festivals and orchestral associations . . . music teachers associations. . ."; (b) family groups and ensembles of 3 to 10 members. Student Division (ages 16 to 25) includes (a) student clubs, choirs, dance groups, orchestras, etc.; (b) music conservatories, schools of music, elementary or high schools "actively federated in mass enrollment;" (c) family groups and small ensembles. Junior Division (to age 18) includes junior music clubs, choirs, dance groups, orchestras, etc., and family groups and small ensembles. Associate Members, Senior Division: organizations, church choirs, orchestras and bands, amateur (not student) opera groups; Student Division: student organizations, music and dance groups; Junior: junior organizations, music and dance groups. A National Affiliate membership category permits other music service organizations to affiliate with the NFMC. This category has some 18 organizations including the American Music Center, American Symphony Orchestra League, International Bach Society, Music Teachers National Association, and music fraternities and sororities. Individual membership is open to music teachers in public schools and private classes, students, conductors and managers of orchestras, directors of vocal groups, music merchants, etc. Dues vary with the category of membership; most categories require dues for both state and national federations. Group memberships have per capita national dues ranging from 15 cents to 50 cents, with stipulated minimum total amounts required of the entire group. Affiliated membership is $25 annually. Individual Junior, Student, Senior Contributor (an individual or a business firm) and Senior Special have dues ranging from $1 to $12.50 a year. There are permanent member fees ranging from $100 to $5,000 for Life, Subscriber, Donor, and Patron. One final category of membership, the so-called Cradle Roll, reveals, perhaps as nothing else can, the extent of NFMC's desire to enlist every possible range of person in its ranks, for this classification allows a membership in the name of a child up to five years old (that is, from birth to five years old). Dues in this category are $5, paid once. The Federation is financed by membership dues, gifts for its Endowment Fund, income from special projects, publications, special funds and gifts for its extensive program of scholarships and other music awards. The most impressive of the Federation's many projects in active support of music is its abundance of scholarships and monetary awards (for details, see Contests). An important award held biennially is the Young Artist Auditions for pianists and violinists, age 18 to 30, and singers, age 23 to 35. This nationally held event, which carries significant supplementary awards (such as concert appearances with professional orchestras and at festivals), has launched the careers of 128 young performers since it began in 1915. The award program of NFMC encompasses performers, young composers, veterans whose musical careers have been interrupted by service in the Armed Forces, dancers, music therapists, and special categories of awards to young blind composers and instrumentalists. NFMC sponsors two nationally promoted annual events, the month-long Parade of American Music in February and National Music Week, held the first full week in May. The former emphasizes performance of music by United States composers; the latter, which in 1973 had its 50th observance, receives endorsement from civic groups, municipalities, radio stations and, at times, the President of the United States. Its purpose is to infuse a consciousness of music throughout the population. Essay contests on the subject of music are conducted for school grades 9 to 12; citations by NFMC are awarded to community boards, civic groups, and other organizations for the quality of their music week observance; proclamations for National Music Week are issued by governors and mayors; concerts and recitals are organized with the help of NFMC members in schools, hospitals, clubs, libraries, radio and television—all conducted with varying degrees of intensity depending upon the dedication and enthusiasm of Federation members in each locality. Other NFMC activities include efforts to raise the standards of church music, the promotion of opera sung in English, and "grass roots" opera. Active internationally, the Federation has a representation on the U.S. National Commission for UNESCO, as well as an accredited representative at the United Nations. It offers gifts of music scores, records, and instruments to foreign musicians and organizations and a $1,000 annual award to encourage performances abroad of American music. NFMC's publications are numerous. Its official magazines are *Music Clubs Magazine,* and *Junior Keynotes,* each issued respectively five and four times a year. A subscription to *Music Clubs Magazine* is required of every Active and Associate organization in the Senior and Student Division. *Junior Keynotes* covers the interest of the young musician and is a required subscription for every Junior organization of NFMC. The other publications of NFMC fall into the broad category of Federation educational materials: handbooks, charts, application blanks, rules and regulations for awards, bulletins, study aids, list of suggested music and music literature, monographs, posters, flyers, bibliographies, etc. Two of the larger publications are the "Who's Who in the National Federation of Music Clubs" (2nd Edition, 636 pages, $7.50); and "Directory of American Women Composers" ($1.50), which covers the work of over 600 composers. Composer **Julia Smith,** who compiled the Directory, is Chairman of NFMC's drive to stimulate more performances of the music of American women. In 1972, she organized a series of 13 thirty-minute radio programs of recorded music of American women composers, as well as another series of both men and women composers, which was broadcast by 72 radio stations in 34 states, the District of Columbia, and Okinawa. NFMC's organization consists of 9 National Officers; an Executive Committee of 18; a Board of Directors made up of all state representatives, members-at-large, designated members, past national presidents, and others; a National Council of District and State Presidents representing the four NFMC regions (Central, Northeastern, Southeastern, and Western) with their respective groups of states or "districts" (e.g. Southwest District of the Central Region represents the states of Arkansas, Kansas, and Missouri); National Chairmen of the various departments of activity, which affect all divisions of membership (American Music Department, Dance, Finance, Music Service in the Community, Opera, Scholarships, etc.); Chairman of the various departments of the Senior Division only; Standing Committees; Special Committees; and National Affiliate organizations. President of NFMC is **Merle Montgomery,** 222 East 80th Street, New York, N.Y. 10022. First Vice President: **Mrs. Frank A. Vought;** Treasurer: **J. Phillip Plank;** Recording Secretary: **Mrs. R. E. L. Freeman;** Corresponding Secretary: **Mrs. L. Gray Burdin;** Office Manager of the NFMC Headquarters Office in Chicago: **Mrs. John McDonald.** The Federation holds a biennial convention in odd-numbered years. National meetings are held annually.

NATIONAL FOUNDATION ON THE ARTS AND HUMANITIES, Washington, D.C. 20506. Established as an independent agency of the executive branch of the federal government by law, the National Foundation on the Arts and Humanities Act of 1965 (Public Law 89–209, as amended by Public Law 91–346 in 1970). The Foundation is made up of the National Endowment for the Arts (q.v.), the National Endowment for the Humanities, and the Federal Council on the Arts and Humanities. Each Endowment has its own National Council, made up of a chairman and 26 private citizens (appointed by the President), who have particular experience or knowledge of, respectively, the arts and the humanities. A joint administrative staff is utilized by both Endowments. The Federal Council lies between the two Endowments, in effect, coordinating their activities and policies, advising the Endowment chairmen of major problems, and developing coordination between the programs of the two Endowments and those of other federal agencies. The Council is composed of the Chairmen of the two Endowments, the United States Commissioner of Education, the Secretary of the Smithsonian Institution, the Director of the Science Foundation, the Librarian of Congress, the Director of the National Gallery of Art, the Chairman of the Commission of Fine Arts, the Archivist of the

United States, and a person selected by the Secretary of State. The purpose of the Foundation is to develop and promote a national policy of support for the arts and humanities. The creation of the Foundation and its operative constituents came about after many years of effort by individuals and arts organizations, as well as certain members of the Congress, to convince the federal government of its obligation in these areas of activity. The obligation involved the recognition of the government that the arts and humanities were beneficial to the country and ought to be kept vital and that funds ought to be made available from private and public sources to support them. The public law establishing the Foundation was therefore an historic one for the United States. The Foundation is authorized to continue its programs until fiscal year 1973 (July 1, 1972 to June 30, 1973). New authorization by Congress is necessary for subsequent years. The funds authorized by Congress to continue the Foundation for the years 1971, 1972, and 1973 were, respectively, $40 million, $60 million, and $80 million. The amounts actually appropriated for those years, however, have consistently fallen below these sums. The Arts and the Humanities Endowments receive equal allotments of funds.

NATIONAL GUILD OF COMMUNITY MUSIC SCHOOLS, INC., c/o Executive Director, 9214 Three Oaks Drive, Silver Spring, Maryland 20901. Tel.: (301) 585–1070. Founded in 1937, it is an association of over 40 nonprofit community music schools in the United States and Canada. Community music schools are found in a number of large cities in the nation, where they are sometimes organized in conjunction with so-called settlement schools—centers of instruction and educational activities for a wide age range of students (preschoolers to retirees). The Guild's purpose is "to unite, coordinate and extend the work of the several community music schools into a national movement." Membership is open to any nonprofit music school that meets the standards of the Guild's by-laws. The activities of community music schools are heightened during periods of social stress, the particular kind of condition that brought about their formation originally. Thus, in recent years, the role of the community music school has increased in value and scope to provide a special agency for children in particular, but adults as well, to participate in some kind of musical experience on a level which may not otherwise exist for them. Such schools as New York's Third Street Settlement, Turtle Bay Music School, Henry Street Settlement, St. James Community Center, and the community music schools or settlement houses of Boston, Cleveland, San Francisco, St. Louis, Detroit, Los Angeles, Chicago, Philadelphia, and other cities all provide services to community residents with an avowed disregard of their race, national origin, or religion. These services include individual instrumental and vocal instruction, ensemble playing or singing, courses in music theory, ballet, modern dance, etc. Instruction is by professionals. To maintain its national office, the Guild has received annual grants to $15,000 or more from the National Endowment of the Arts and Humanities and from the Rockefeller Foundation. It has engaged in special projects to establish new schools in urban and rural areas throughout the country. A so-called Arts for All Fund was established in 1968 to bring music experiences to urban and rural children, union cultural programs, etc. An example of its application was the Mobile Academy of the Performing Arts for Children of Southeast Arkansas, which provided resident professional artists to supplement the school music programs for six consolidated school districts in three Arkansas counties. The Fund was headed by a distinguished Board of Governors under the chairmanship of **Arnold Gingrich** (publisher of *Esquire* magazine). Other Guild projects have been directed to participation in public school music instruction programs where such programs were either inadequate or in jeopardy for lack of funds. In 1969, the Guild formed the Music Institute, a project for application in the Chicago public school system from kindergarten to the third grade. The project enabled primary school teachers to avail themselves of modern music teaching techniques (Orff,

Kodaly systems, etc.) for daily classroom use. Officers of the Guild: President, **Dorothy Maynor;** Vice President, East, **Sol Schoenbach;** Vice President, Midwest, **Robert Christensen;** Vice President, West, **Samuel Scarlett;** Secretary, **Kenneth Wendrich;** Treasurer, **Kalman Novak.** Executive Director is **Charles C. Mark.**

NATIONAL GUILD OF PIANO TEACHERS (NGPT), Box 1807, Austin, Texas 78767. Tel.: (512) GR 8–5775. Founded in 1929 by **Irl Allison.** Purposes: "To furnish suitable incentive for all piano students; to give sympathetic hearing; to supply dignified recognition on a national basis." Eligible for membership are piano teachers "capable of preparing pupils in a balanced repertoire . . . and who welcome the challenge and helpfulness of unprejudiced auditions." Total membership: over 7,000. Among the extensive and successful activities of the NGPT are the annual National Auditions held in the spring, which can involve the participation of 75,000 teachers and students in about 620 organized Guild centers throughout the U.S. The Guild provides a host of materials and incentives to both private teachers and students of the piano. These include plaques, medals, monetary awards (scholarships), etc. For the past fifteen years the Guild has dispensed some $120,000 in $100 scholarships. The NGPT sponsors composition contests and recording contests. It is highly organized and maintains extremely close liaison with its member teachers. Its publications include a *Yearbook* and a *National Directory,* and *Guild Notes.* Guild President is **Irl Allison, Jr.**

NATIONAL INSTITUTE OF ARTS AND LETTERS, 633 West 155th Street, New York, N.Y. 10032. Tel.: (212) AU 6–1480. Founded in 1898. Affiliated with the American Academy of Arts and Letters (q.v.). Purpose: "The furtherance of literature and the fine arts in the United States." Members must be U.S. citizens and must have made notable achievements in art, music, and literature. Total membership is limited to 250 at any time. The Institute makes grants of $2,500, which cannot be applied for, to nonmember young artists, composers, and writers. Other awards of the Institute are the Gold Medal and the Award for Distinguished Service to the Arts. Recipients of music grants have their works recorded by an arrangement between the American Academy and the National Institute and Composers Recordings, Inc. (CRI). Among musician-members of the Institute are: **Samuel Barber, Elliott Carter, Aaron Copland, Howard Hanson, Roy Harris, Walter Piston, Richard Rodgers, William Schuman, Roger Sessions,** and such appointees within the last few years as **Peter Mennin, Duke Ellington, Nicolas Nabokov, William Bergsma, Gunther Schuller, Robert Ward, Leon Kirchner,** and **Ben Weber.** The Institute is chartered by the United States Congress. President is **William Maxwell.**

NATIONAL JEWISH MUSIC COUNCIL (NJMC), 15 East 26th Street, New York, N.Y. 10010. Tel.: (212) 532–4949. Founded in 1949, under the sponsorship of the National Jewish Welfare Board. Since then, it has functioned under the Welfare Board as an alliance of 62 national Jewish organizations and some 10 local Jewish music committees throughout the country. The organizations affiliated with NJMC include B'nai Brith, Hebrew Arts Foundation, Jewish Liturgical Music Society of America, Jewish Music Alliance, Yeshiva University, and Hadassah, to name some. Local committees are in Brookline, Massachusetts; Buffalo, New York; Chicago; Hartford, Connecticut; Los Angeles; Lynn, Massachusetts; Miami; Philadelphia; Toledo, Ohio; and Washington, D.C. The Council's task is to promote "appreciation of Jewish music and [to stimulate] its performance, [raise] standards and [aid] groups to use Jewish music. . ." It seeks "to coordinate Jewish music activities nationally; to stimulate composition, production of recordings, research and publication; to offer information and advice concerning Jewish music; to plan programs for Jewish Music Festival and year-round musical activities." In the Jewish Welfare Board's publication, *JWB Circle,* the Council writes of new and old Jewish music and comments on activities in a supplement called *Jewish Music Notes.* NJMC publications (all of which are for sale and are listed in the Council's catalog) include: "The Contribution of Russian Jewry to Jewish Music," "The Cantorial Art," "The Life and Work of A. W. Binder," "Music of Ernest Bloch," "Music of Israel Today," "Jews in Music;" the bibliographies: "Jewish Vocal Music, 1958, 1967," "Instrumental Music, 1956," "Jewish Folk Song Resources, 1957," "Books and Articles of Jewish Interest, 1955"; also available are scripts of radio talks on musical themes, reviews of recordings of Jewish music, etc. In addition, NJMC makes available anthologies of music which were published by the Jewish Welfare Board. More than 100 new compositions have been added to the repertory of modern Jewish music as a result of the Council's encouragement to synagogues and local committees and its commissioning programs. A month-long series of musical programs held throughout the country each year, the so-called Jewish Music Festival, takes place in synagogues, in the programs of orchestras, choral groups, radio and TV stations, etc. Affiliated organizations of NJMC pay dues of $50 and up. Meetings of the Executive Board are held three times a year. Officers of the Council are: **Rabbi Avraham Soltes,** Chairman; **Manual G. Batshaw,** Director, National Services; **Irene Heskes,** Vice Chairman; **Julius Schatz,** Vice Chairman; **Robert Segal,** Vice Chairman; **Tamara Ryger,** Secretary.

NATIONAL MUSIC COUNCIL (NMC), 2109 Broadway, Suite 1579 New York, N.Y. 10023. Tel.: (212) 799–0100. Founded in 1940; issued a Congressional Charter in 1957 (Public Law 873) becoming the only music organization so chartered. NMC is an organization of organizations; its current 57 members (winter, 1972) are among the leading music organizations in America, most of which are described in this book under separate entries. The purpose of NMC is: "To provide member organizations with a forum for the free discussion of problems affecting the national music life of the country. To speak with one voice for music whenever an authoritative expression of opinion is desirable. To provide for the interchange of ideas between various member organizations. . . ." NMC does not engage in the separate activities of its member organizations nor interfere with their internal operation, since each member organization is a separate, autonomous unit. Its practical function is to bring member organizations together through their appointed representatives for regularly scheduled meetings and, through the NMC *Bulletin,* to publish the activities of the members and to make announcements of NMC activities. Its very modest operating budget (expenditures for fiscal year 1971: $23,000; total assets: $28,000) does not permit NMC to be as effective an organization as its stated purposes suggest. Nevertheless, NMC has moved on broad fronts: it advises the Federal Government and its agencies, on request, in matters pertaining to music; proposes Congressional legislation referring to music with suggestions for such proposals arising from the membership as well as the Board of Directors; it has suggested ways in which the members of NMC can act unitedly for or against legislation affecting music or any other proposition or problem it confronts. The Council was also responsible for the establishment of certain organizations, such as the National Opera Association and the American String Teachers Association; it is the only music organization selected by the State Department to be represented on the U.S. Commission for UNESCO and is the official U.S. representative in the International Music Council of UNESCO; and from time to time NMC acts as an administrator of special music projects funded from without. Its official publication, *National Music Council Bulletin* (sent free to members and available to anyone on subscription—see Periodicals) covers all important activities of NMC, reports in length on meetings, speeches and talks presented, etc. It also provides often detailed descriptions of its member organizations' activities as reported by the members themselves. It announces national and international events such as contests, conventions, and meetings and in general provides the only source of organizational information in depth. As of spring, 1972, the following organizations were members of NMC: (representing a reported total of over 1,500,000 persons): Amateur Chamber Music Players; American Academy of Teachers of Singing; American Choral Directors Association; American Composers Alliance; American Federation of Musicians; American Guild of Authors and Composers; American Guild of Musical Artists; American Harp Society; American Liszt Society; American Matthay Association; American Music Center; American Music Conference; American Society of Composers, Authors and Publishers; American Society of University Composers; American String Teachers Association; American Symphony Orchestra League; Broadcast Music, Inc.; Central Opera Service; College Band Directors National Association; Composers and Lyricists Guild of America; Delta Omicron; Hymn Society of America; Intercollegiate Musical Council; International Bach Society; Kappa Kappa Psi; League of Composers—International Society for Contemporary Music—U.S. Section; Leschetizky Association; Modern Music Masters; Moravian Music Foundation; Mu Phi Epsilon; Music Critics Association; Music Educators National Conference; Music Library Association; Music Publishers' Association of the United States; Music Teachers National Association; National Association for American Composers and Conductors; National Association for Music Therapy; National Association of Organ Teachers; National Association of Schools of Music; National Association of Teachers of Singing; National Federation of Music Clubs; National Guild of Community Music Schools; National Guild of Piano Teachers; National Music Camp—Interlochen Arts Academy; National Music Publishers' Association, Inc.; National Opera Association; National Piano Manufacturers Association of America, Inc.; National School Orchestra Association; People to People Music Committee, Inc.; Phi Beta; Phi Mu Alpha Sinfonia; Piano Technicians Guild; Pi Kappa Lambda; Recording Industry Association of America; Sigma Alpha Iota; Society for the Preservation and Encouragement of Barber Shop Quartet Singing in America; Violoncello Society, Inc. These organizations are assessed dues, which provide for the main funding of NMC; other funding sources are *Bulletin* sales and subscriptions and special contributions made by some of the above organizations, as well as by certain music publishers, manufacturers, concert managements, foundations, corporations and over forty individual donors. As of winter, 1973, officers of NMC were: **Peter Mennin,** Chairman of the Board; **Leonard Feist,** President; **Merle Montgomery, Edward M. Cramer,** and **Stanley Adams,** Vice Presidents; **Martin Bookspan,** Secretary; **Oliver Daniel,** Treasurer; **Mrs. Leslie Kallmann,** Executive Secretary. There is a members-at-large council of 11.

NATIONAL MUSIC PUBLISHERS' ASSOCIATION, INC. (NMPA), 110 East 59th Street, New York, N.Y. 10022. Tel.: (212) 751–1930. Founded in 1917; formerly called the Music Publishers' Protective Association. It is a trade association of publishers of popular music. There are 57 members. President is **Salvatore T. Chianti.** Executive Vice President is **Leonard Feist.**

NATIONAL OPERA ASSOCIATION, INC. (NOA), c/o **Constance Eberhart,** Secretary-Registrar, Hotel Wellington, Seventh Avenue and 55th Street, New York, N.Y. 10019. Founded under the auspices of the National Music Council in 1955. Purpose: to support all phases of opera production, composition, promotion, and appreciation in the United States, including the provision of forums, activities for coordinating members, etc. Membership is open to all engaged in or interested in opera, both individuals and groups. It publishes a *Journal.* President is **Arthur Schoep.**

NATIONAL PIANO TRAVELERS ASSOCIATION, c/o Executive Secretary, **Robert E. Johnson,** Schaff Piano Supply Co., 2009 Clybourne Avenue, Chicago, Illinois 60614. Tel.: (312) 549–3117. Founded in 1905, it is the oldest music industry association in the United States. Its purpose is to promote better relations between piano manufacturers and dealers. All traveling salesmen of pianos and piano supplies are eligible for membership. However, in 1971, the association voted to admit women into its ranks. Officers of the organization and the firms they represent are: **George Vigorito** (The Wurlitzer Co.), President; **Jack Strange** (Everett Piano Co.), Vice President; **Harry Kapreilian** (Chas. Ramsey Co.), Treasurer; **Robert E. Johnson** (see above), Executive Secretary.

NATIONAL RECREATION AND PARK ASSOCIATION (NRPA), 1700 Pennsylvania Avenue, N.W., Washington, D.C. 20006. Tel.: (202) 223–3030. Founded in January, 1966. The NRPA is a nonprofit service organization "dedicated to the wise use of free time, conservation of natural resources, and beautification of the total American Environment. It is actively concerned with improvement of park and recreational facilities and programs, and more wholesome and meaningful leisure time activities for everyone." Members total over 1,200 and are professional and lay leaders and public and private agencies in the parks and recreation field. Financial support comes from voluntary contributions, sales of NRPA publications, and from membership dues. It is included here because of NRPA's work with the American Music Conference (q.v.) in making use of community and national park facilities for some music activities as one way of providing outlets for amateur music making. Among its many publications, NRPA issues a monthly magazine, *Parks & Recreation.* Membership categories, and their respective dues structure, run from student to commercial membership.

NATIONAL SCHOOL ORCHESTRA ASSOCIATION (NSOA), c/o various officers. In 1972, the president of NSOA was **James H. Godfrey,** 330 Bellevue Drive, Bowling Green, Kentucky 42101. Tel.: (502) 842–7121. Founded in August of 1958. Founding President was **Traugott Rohner,** publisher of *The Instrumentalist* magazine, the publication which serves as the official journal of NSOA through its column, "NSOA Soundpost," and by its general content, which is aimed at the school orchestra (and band) director. The membership of NSOA stands at approximately 750 and is made up of directors of school orchestras at the elementary and secondary school and college levels, teachers of string instruments and other instruments of the orchestra, educators, and others interested in the goals and activities of the association. The formally stated purposes of NSOA can be summarized as follows: to improve orchestras on all levels of education as well as those in the community and in the professional field; to encourage orchestra students to continue their interest in music and orchestra playing beyond the limits of school; to generate appreciation of the school orchestra among school administrators and the public by better performance, rehearsals, programs, and musical selections; to recruit more young players for orchestras, especially for string instruments, for which there is a continuing lack; to act as one voice for school orchestra directors, etc. The activities of the NSOA are focused, generally speaking, on its various national convocations, at which its widespread membership can meet for a concentrated period of clinics, workshops, demonstrations, and performances. The most important of these gatherings is: the Midwest National Band and Orchestra Clinic, held in Chicago in December of each year. There, the NSOA takes part in demonstrations and clinics during the so-called Orchestra Days. Each year it forms an All-American Directors' Orchestra, which reads through new music for school orchestra under various guest conductors both in and out of the academic world. School orchestras selected by NSOA from several states perform for concerts and demonstrations. Similar clinics and demonstrations are sponsored by NSOA during the Mid-East Instrumental Conference held at Duquesne University in Pittsburgh in March of each year. The organization's largest effort is its Annual Summer Conference in August, held in various locations and open to members and their families and to school players who participate in the Summer Youth Orchestra Camp—the latter a part of the Conference. A Directors' Orchestra, a Reading Orchestra, and the Youth Orchestra are formed for various functions during the Conference. The Directors' Orchestra selects and performs new compositions submitted for the Roth Orchestra Composition Award (see Competitions). Both the Directors' Orchestra and the Youth Orchestra are given the opportunity to perform under guest conductors of stature including such recently engaged men as **Henry Mazer, Gibson Morrissey,** and **Frederick Fennell.** The Reading Orchestra has been known to read through as many as 175 pieces during the five-day conference. Other activities sponsored by the NSOA are the orchestra sessions held in conjunction with the six divisional conventions of the Music Educators National Conference of which NSOA is an affiliate organization. From time to time, the NSOA publishes surveys and teaching guides, research papers, and other publications to inform its members of developments in the school orchestra field. The NSOA is governed by its elected officers, board members, divisional chairmen, and associate members. A dues schedule is established for individual, institutional, and industrial memberships; respectively, $10, $15, and $35 annually. These dues are unified with those of the Music Educators National Conference (MENC) to which they are submitted.

THE NATIONAL SOCIETY OF ARTS AND LETTERS (NSAL). The national headquarters of this organization is that of the National President of NSAL, who changes every two years. There are no continuing office holders, since each national officer is limited to two years in each position. The NSAL is a nonprofit, tax-exempt organization founded in October, 1944 in Chevy Chase, Maryland and incorporated June, 1949 in Washington, D.C. The aims of the Society are: "to encourage and assist young artists; create opportunities for artistic endeavor and expression; give scholarships and awards to non-members after competition in any of the creative arts; conduct or assist with non-competitive exhibitions in the arts; promote a greater public interest in the arts." Members of NSAL are men and women "who are or have been engaged professionally in creative arts or who are sponsoring the work of young artists." A stipulation is that all members must be United States citizens. Members come from the fields of art, dance, drama, literature, and music. In the case of music, they may be composers, instrumentalists or singers, arrangers, teachers, or conductors. Proof of professional status is required for membership in NSAL. Besides professionals in the arts, the NSAL permits arts patrons to become active members. An associate membership is available to those qualifying as active members, but this membership category is devoid of voting and office-holding rights. Although open to both men and women, the NSAL membership is composed largely of women; national officers are virtually all women, as are nearly all chapter officers. The support NSAL gives to the arts is at both the local chapter level and on the national level. The 28 chapters of the Society each give scholarships and awards, both competitive and noncompetitive, while the National Career Award is the major award of the NSAL. It is a competitive award, candidates for which are selected through NSAL chapter contests according to fixed rules. Winners of the National Career Awards are given the opportunity to present concerts (or exhibitions, in the case of artists) as a professional debut. NSAL can point to several chapter and national winners of competitions and scholarships who have become artists and musicians of importance. Many NSAL chapters contribute directly to universities and colleges, galleries, societies, etc., instead of to individual artists. Special trust, endowment, memorial, and gift funds have been established by the organization for furthering its awards programs and through which contributions may be made by anyone. NSAL is governed by its elected officers: a president, six vice presidents, various other officers such as secretaries, treasurer, registrar, historian, etc., and numerous chairmen of national committees; it has a National Advisory Council of famous figures in the arts (**Faith Baldwin, John Ciardi, Risë Stevens, Victor Borge, Greer Garson, Helen Hayes,** et al.). Honorary members have been traditionally the wives of American presidents (Mrs. Eisenhower, Mrs. Kennedy, Mrs. Johnson, etc.).

THE WALTER W. NAUMBURG FOUNDATION, INC., 155 West 65th Street, New York, N.Y. Tel.: (212) 874–1150.

Founded in 1926. It sponsors young musicians through competitions, awards American composers by recording their works in conjunction with commercial recording firms, etc. President: **Robert Mann.** (See Contests—Part 8.)

ORGAN HISTORICAL SOCIETY, INC. (OHS). Headquarters is at the Historical Society of York County, 250 East Market Street, York, Pennsylvania 17404. Founded in 1956. Membership is about 400. The purpose of the society is to promote interest in the pipe organ and its builders in North America. It attempts to gather historical information about organs and organ builders in North America and to make this information known so that the significance of certain historical organs can be more generally understood. OHS is also eager to help preserve or restore important organs throughout North America. The Society operates as a nonprofit organization. It holds national conventions in different locations, usually where there are organs of historical or musical interest. Exhibits, recitals, and tours are organized for the conventions. Panel discussions, lectures, and illustrated talks are also held, along with business meetings. Other work of the OHS includes the publication of its official journal, *The Tracker,* which contains articles of scholarly research on organs, information about the restoration of old organs and recitals given upon them, and member activities (see Periodicals). OHS has produced a slide–tape program, "The History of the Organ in America from 1700 to 1900," which is available for rental for $25 plus postage; recordings of past conventions are also available on long-play records for $4.95 each. Membership is open to any interested person. Dues are $5 for regular members, $10 for contributing members, and $25 for sponsors. Membership includes a subscription to *The Tracker.* President: **Kenneth F. Simmons,** 17 Pleasant Street, Ware, Mass. 01082; Vice President: **Rev. Donald C. Taylor;** Treasurer: **Donald C. Rockwood;** Corresponding Secretary: **Mrs. Helen Harriman;** Editor of *The Tracker:* **Albert F. Robinson.**

ORGAN AND PIANO TEACHERS ASSOCIATION, INC. (OPTA), P.O. Box 1291, Gardena, California 90249. Tel.: (213) 324–3666. Founded in 1966; incorporated in 1967. Purposes: "to advance, promote, foster and benefit all those professionally connected with the teaching of organ and piano; to procure better conditions in our profession; to protect and secure the legal rights of our membership in all matters arising from professional relations; to advocate appropriate legislation on matters affecting the profession of our members. . . ." Membership categories are: Active Teacher, or one who has been actively engaged in teaching piano or organ, with at least two years experience and who is twenty-one or older; Affiliate Teacher, or one who can qualify as an Active Teacher within two years of date of application; Associate Membership is open to interested persons, commercial music firms, students, and others not qualified for either Active or Affiliate membership; Honorary Membership is granted to persons and organizations who have, in the opinion of OPTA's local and national executive committees, made a worthy contribution to the association, the keyboard teaching field, or the keyboard music industry. Dues vary according to classifications; an initiation fee is charged to new members. Although OPTA's purposes state generally its support of the teacher of piano and organ, its orientation is toward the teacher who is engaged in private instruction of what is termed "modern, contemporary, popular" music. New members are provided with various "prestige" accouterments—decals, certificates, business cards, code of ethics (for framing), all bearing the insignia of OPTA—plus a $1,000 insurance policy covering accidental death, dismemberment, or loss of sight. These are intended to give a sense of professionalism to that segment of the music teaching profession which, in the past, has often been ignored. The association opts for close cooperation with the music industry, permitting teacher-members to buy products at a discount, etc. Workshops, promotion, professional advice, and special projects are offered members of OPTA. News within the field and information of professional use are provided by the official publication, *OPTA-MIST,* sent free to members (available by subscription to nonmembers). Issued bimonthly, it prints news, advice, recommended reading and music lists, and progress reports on various association endeavors. (One project of particular interest to OPTA members, if not to all private music teachers, is the public stand OPTA has taken against certain community zoning and licensing laws which make it illegal for music teachers to teach in their homes.) In an attempt to upgrade the quality of teaching by its members, the association intends to institute and implement an evaluation program for judging the progress of the keyboard student, which at the same time might provide the public with certain standards it may expect from private instruction. **William Irwin** is President of the association; **Michael Evanko,** Vice President; Executive Secretary and Treasurer is **Phyllis MacFadden.** Membership is over 300.

PAN-AMERICAN UNION, MUSIC DIVISION, Organization of American States, Washington, D.C. 20006. Founded in 1941 with a grant from the Carnegie Corporation. Its purpose: the organization of musical resources and activities of the Western Hemisphere, and the promotion of musical goodwill and understanding among all North and South American nations; the dissemination of knowledge about the musical culture of each nation of the Hemisphere. Members are nations belonging to the Organization of American States (OAS). The Music Division's activities include sponsoring in the Pan-American Union concerts with United States and Latin American musicians which feature the work of indigenous composers; and organizing the Inter-American Music Festivals in Washington (see Festivals). It established the Inter-American Music Center; it arranges meetings and exchanges of musicians and has set up depositories for distributing the scores of new works. The Music Division is particularly active in publishing. Among its publications are: *Boletin Interamericano de Música,* and in English, the *Inter-American Music Bulletin,* which have totaled some 81 issues thus far, each, in effect, a monograph on some aspect of music of interest to musicians in the Western Hemisphere. Published by offset, of either typescript or set type, the issues may run from 8 to 10 pages to 40 or more. Whereas some of its earliest issues served as newsletters, its issues in recent years have emphasized both depth and range in covering Pan-American musical life. Increasingly, scholars have had their writings on the music and musicians of the Americas published in the *Bulletin.* Recent issues, by way of examples, have published the following monographs or reports: "Tribute to José Bernardo Alcedo (1788–1878)," by **Robert Stevenson** (Vol. 80, March–June, 1971); "Francisco Mignone: His Music For Piano," by **Sister Marion Verhaalen** (Vol. 79, November, 1970–February, 1971); "Latin American Music in the College Curriculum: Problems and Prospects," by **Charles Haywood** (Vol. 75/76, January–March, 1970); "Gottschalk in Buenos Aires," and "Gottschalk in Western South America," by **Robert Stevenson** (Vol. 74, November, 1969), etc. A "Listing of all Major Articles in the Inter-American Music Bulletin Volumes 1–72" was compiled by **Charles T. Brown** and published in Vol. 73 (September, 1969). The *Bulletin* is available to anyone free on request from the Sales and Promotion Division of the Pan-American Union. Also published by the Union is "Composers of the Americas" ("Compositores de America"), a series begun in 1955 and now totaling 14 volumes (1,937 pages). The series includes lists of works, year of composition, publisher, duration in minutes, biographical data, photograph, and a facsimile page of the music of a total of 225 composers. (Total cost $10; per volume: $1.) Text is in Spanish and English. Other Pan-American Union music publications are "Musical Directory of Latin America" (selected nations), "A Guide to the Music of Latin America," by Gilbert Chase, 2nd edition, 1962; various folk song monographs (Honduras, youth, Dominican Republic), and other music anthologies—all sold at low cost; music scores include piano works, works for solo voice, chamber music (scores and parts), choral works, and orchestral works. Orchestral rental material is available through Peer International (see Southern Music Publishing Co., Inc.). Chief of the

Music Division, since 1953, has been **Guillermo Espinosa** of Colombia.

PEOPLE-TO-PEOPLE MUSIC COMMITTEE, INC., John F. Kennedy Center for the Performing Arts, Room 5227, 726 Jackson Place, N.W., Washington, D.C. 20566. Tel.: (202) 343–8994. Established by President Eisenhower in 1956 as one of 42 People-to-People Committees of various commitments and areas of responsibility designed to bring more direct contact between Americans and peoples abroad. The Music Committee functions now as an independent philanthropic organization. Since 1962 it has had no federal government funding (most of the People-to-People Committees have dissolved into separate self-governing organizations similar to the Music Committee), and since 1967, it has been an incorporated organization with officers and directors drawn from a number of areas of the music world. Funding is from a small annual grant from Sigma Alpha Iota, the women's professional music fraternity. Volunteer service on the executive level and contributions of music materials from individuals and organizations in the United States interested in the work of the Music Committee, which dispenses such materials abroad, compose the balance of the Committee's critical resources. The objectives of the People-to-People Music Committee are, broadly, to increase the contact between America's musicians and those in America who support music, and their counterparts throughout the world; to assist music teachers and schools in developing countries; and to make American music more widely known in advanced nations. The Committee, rather than serve as a bureaucratic agency, acts instead as an instrumentality through which foreigners in need of help in a musical situation may receive help from Americans who are willing to give it. But the Music Committee may also initiate a plan of action or a service. In either case, the material resources and services proffered emanate from charitable individuals and groups. The Committee operates on several levels. It responds to specific requests for assistance both informational and material by offering what it may already have or by finding what is needed; it may provide material help for countries whose musical needs are chronic; it arranges for young American musicians to tour areas of the world not often, or rarely, visited by concert artists and by the same token, has brought musicians from Latin America, Asia, Africa, and Europe to take part in musical activities in the United States; it offers assistance to cultural officers of foreign embassies in Washington. Illustrating some of these activities at random are the following: in 1970, a gift of rhythm instruments was made to a school for retarded children in Hong Kong and a joint Sigma Alpha Iota-Music Committee gift, to a school in Haiti; joint gifts in 1969–70 included teaching materials in music for Guyana, recorders, harmonicas, and guitars for a youth group in Gabon, choral music for Ghana, music teaching materials for Brazil, and jazz records for groups in Niger and Sudan; musical instruments, hard to obtain in many places in the world, have been among the most important gifts from the Music Committee; recipients of instruments have been orchestras in Chile and Ecuador, as well as the National Orchestra of Bolivia; gifts, ranging from band and choral music for use as a revolving lending library to collections of records, books, magazines on music, etc. have been sent to the Dominican Republic, Singapore, Rumania, Soviet Union, Senegal, Brazil, and Barbados to name but a few countries. As the result of a request from the Dominican Republic, the Music Committee arranged for a tour through the Caribbean and Central America of the American sopranos, **Jessye Norman** and **Esther Hinds,** both performing in places generally not visited by professional musicians. Similarly, pianist **Emmanuel Ax,** in 1970, toured Latin America under the sponsorship of the Music Committee, the Epstein Foundation, and Boys' Club of America. For several years, People-to-People has arranged for Icelandic musicians to participate in the American Symphony Orchestra League's summer Orchestral Institute at Orkney Springs. The Committee readily responds to opportunities for promoting American music, particularly where interest is already manifest. Accordingly, study scores and recordings of American symphonic works have been dispatched to the Iraqi Symphony Orchestra in Baghdad; collections of American folk music and jazz to India's National Academy for Music, Dance, and Drama, for its incipient international music research collection; and a large selection of scores and recordings of the music of Edward MacDowell to a Soviet musicologist interested in the work of that composer. To maintain its supply of music materials and instruments, the Music Committee makes appeals to known sources for voluntary contributions. Potential donors are requested to contact the Committee's Executive Director first, rather than make a unilateral move to contribute something. President of the People-to-People Music Committee, Inc. is pianist, **Ann Schein;** Executive Director is **Mrs. Ruth Sickafus.**

PERCUSSIVE ARTS SOCIETY (PAS), 130 Carol Drive, Terre Haute, Indiana 47805. Tel.: (812) 466–2982. Founded in 1960, "to raise the level of musical percussion performance and teaching; to expand understanding of the needs and responsibilities of the percussion student, teacher, and performer; and to promote a greater communication between all areas of the percussion arts." Membership (currently about 1,500) is open to anyone. The Society seeks to enroll professional performers, private and academic teachers, and composers, as well as those in the music industry who are involved with percussion instruments. Dues are: $5 for a Regular membership; $5 for Student; $8 for Professional; $5 for libraries; $25 for publishers and dealers; $250 for manufacturers. The Society's publication is *Percussionist* (see Periodicals). President is **Saul Feldstein; Gary Olmstead** and **Ronald Fink** are Vice Presidents; Executive Secretary is **Neal Fluegel.**

PHI BETA FRATERNITY, Central Office, 4950 West Walton Street, Chicago, Illinois 60651. Tel.: (312) 287–6971. Founded May, 1912. A national professional fraternity of music and speech for women. Membership is over 15,500, allotted to over 70 collegiate and alumnae chapters. Its purpose is "to promote the best in music and speech; to foster service in these arts within the college and community; to advance the members intellectually and professionally; to develop the highest type of womanhood." The fraternity is composed of chapters whose members are bona fide students of music and speech in accredited schools or are women of professional ability in the music and speech fields. As with many fraternities, the alumnae membership is of great significance in Phi Beta, providing a perpetual basis of support. Artists of national reputation are selected from time to time for honorary membership. *The Baton* is the official publication of Phi Beta. Issued quarterly, it is sent only to members at an annual subscription rate of $1. Editor is **Mrs. James M. Auer,** 209 Linden Court, Neenah, Wisconsin 54956. Among the fraternity's projects and activities are its annual contribution to the MacDowell Colony (q.v.), technical assistance to the Veterans Administration, various programs of community service, an Armed Forces Professional Entertainment Project, and a project to supply musical instruments, reference materials, magazines and literature to foreign countries. National conventions are held triennially (1971, 1974, etc.); the National Council of Phi Beta meets annually. Officers (serving for 1968–71) are: **Mrs. Stanley H. Frohmader** (514 LeRoy Road, Madison, Wisconsin 53704), President; **Mrs. T. O. Siegmund,** First Vice President; **Mrs. Harold Taylor,** Second Vice President; **Mrs. Harry J. Lumby,** Executive Secretary-Treasurer.

PHI BETA MU (ΦBM), c/o Executive Secretary, **Jack H. Mahan,** 2019 Bradford Drive, Arlington, Texas 76010. Tel.: (817) CR 5–1856. Founded in 1938. It has 1,000 members in 31 state chapters. It is a "non-political, non-profiting fraternity organized; 1) to promote good fellowship among its members; 2) to encourage the building of better bands and the development of better musicians in American schools; and 3) to foster deeper appreciation of good music and more widespread interest in it on the part of the lay public." The fraternity honors outstanding bandmasters. Membership is by invitation only. It awards certificates of merit to bandmasters and bandsmen. Chapter meetings are held annually, as are the national convocations. The official publication of the organization is *The School Musician,* which publishes a Phi Beta Mu column in each issue. The magazine is sent free to fraternity members. Dues vary with each state chapter. There is a member installation fee of $10. President is **Milburn E. Carey;** Vice President is **Raymond F. Dvorak;** Honorary Life President is **D. O. Wiley.** Founder of the organization is the late Col. Earl D. Irons.

PHI MU ALPHA SINFONIA FRATERNITY OF AMERICA. National Offices: Lyrecrest, 10600 Old State Road, Evansville, Indiana 47711. Tel.: (812) 867–2433. A national fraternity founded in 1898; incorporated in 1904. Its purpose is "to advance the cause of music in America; to foster the mutual welfare and brotherhood of students of music. . . ." Membership is open to undergraduate and graduate students at colleges and universities who have a sincere interest in music. Current estimated membership is 7,500 in approximately 270 active chapters and 50,000 in about 35 alumni chapters throughout the United States. Dues: $10 (active) and $5 (alumni). The fraternity established the Sinfonia Foundation as a nonprofit organization to raise funds in support of selected fraternity projects in music. Among the projects is the annual Research Assistance Grant for music research projects deemed worthy by the Foundation's Scholarship Commission. The grants have increased in value from $500 in 1969 to $750 in 1970, and $1,000 was projected for 1972. Examples of research projects eliciting grants from the Foundation are the 1969 award to **James M. Burk** for a study, "Charles E. Ives: His Music for Winds," and the 1971 grant to **Charles E. Stevens** for his "Source Readings in Moravian Music," the Foundation-supported portion of which covers the works of Christian Latrobe. In addition, the fraternity grants an "American Man of Music" Award every three years coincident with its national convocation. This award, at the last convention in 1970, was extended to **Aaron Copland.** The activities of the fraternity and the Foundation are governed by the executive committee and the National Delegate Representative Assembly which meets triennially to elect officers, pass on resolutions, assess programs and projects, etc. Chapters of the Phi Mu Alpha are grouped into "provinces" each under the responsibility of a province governor of which there are some 37 in all. The fraternity publications are: *Sinfonian Newsletter,* issued six times a year and sent free to active and alumni members (available on subscription otherwise for $2.50 per year), the official songbook, various handbooks, pledge manuals, and brochures. Officers for the 1970–73 triennium are: **Robert C. Soule,** President; **J. Eugene Duncan,** First Vice President; **Carl M. Neumeyer,** Second Vice President and Past President; **Alan E. Adams,** Executive Secretary (at the national headquarters address) and Editor of the *Newsletter.* President of the Foundation is **J. Eugene Duncan.**

PI KAPPA LAMBDA NATIONAL MUSIC HONOR SOCIETY, P.O. Box 2886, University, Alabama 35486. Tel.: (205) 348–7110. Founded in 1918. An honorary national music fraternity accepting both men and women, Pi Kappa Lambda has as its purposes the furtherance of music education in institutions of high learning and the support and maintenance of acceptable curricula in music. It has about 13,000 members in some 82 chapters. New members are proposed and elected by each chapter. Among its national projects is the publication of a series of scholarly books covering lesser-known aspects of American music. The most recent book, issued in 1971, is "Music in the Cultured Generation," by **Joseph Mussulman,** published by Northwestern University Press. The fraternity publishes an annual *Newsletter.* National conventions are held biennially in even-numbered years. Officers (elected at the 1972 Biennial): **William J. Weichlein,** President; **Wilbur H. Rowand,** Secretary-Treasurer (at the organization's address above).

THE PIANO TECHNICIANS GUILD, INC. (PTG), Box 1813, Seattle, Washington 98109. Tel.: (206) 329–2237. Founded in 1958; incorporated in the State of Illinois. PTG is an international nonprofit organization of professional craftsmen engaged in tuning and servicing pianos. It was created out of the former American Society of Piano Technicians (founded 1940) and the National Association of Piano Tuners (founded 1908). Its purpose is "to achieve the highest possible service standards and to most effectively promote the technical, economic and social interests of piano technicians." It also seeks "to provide the nation's piano owners with an accredited service, readily available and thoroughly dependable." It registers its accredited piano technicians, who carry the PTG membership card with the organization's seal and signature. The membership of PTG (open to application) stands at approximately 1,750. The classifications of membership are: Craftsman (Registered Tuner-Technician), admitted by examination and election (dues: $50 per year as chapter member); Apprentice, admitted by examination and election (dues: $34 per year as chapter member); Allied Tradesman, admitted by election (dues $50 per year as a chapter member); Associate, admitted by election (dues: $50 for chapter membership. There is an entrance fee of $20 for all classes of membership. (Each member must subscribe to a Code of Ethics vis-à-vis his relationship with his customers, the Guild, and the music industry in general. (Errant members are subject to trial.) The organization and government of PTG consist of a council of delegates from member chapters and members-at-large who meet annually to conduct the business of the Guild and set its policies. The Executive Board is responsible for carrying out the orders of the Council; it is composed of 9 members (some of whom are listed below) elected annually, usually in July. The continuing business on a daily level is, in the manner of most organizations, conducted by the Executive Secretary as an employed administrator. Other administrative staff members are a field secretary and a project administrator, the former to help found new chapters, the latter to assist them in their activities. PTG publishes *The Piano Technicians Journal,* a monthly magazine sent free to members (see Periodicals). The activities of PTG are channelled in two main directions: toward its members, their competence and welfare, and toward the piano-owning public and its awareness of piano tuning and maintenance as a necessary adjunct to ownership. PTG has issued information sheets for public distribution on piano care with various "do's" and "don't's" described. For its members, PTG provides technical clinics, workshops, and the like and an informal clearing house for employment opportunities, as well as hard-to-get or rare repair parts and tools; it also provides a small monetary benefit to the families of deceased members or to members suffering crippling disability, etc. PTG publishes, in addition to the *Journal,* a *Bulletin* and an annual directory of members. It endorses piano tuning courses at nine schools (in 1972) including universities, correspondence schools, and schools for the visually handicapped. A film produced by the PTG, "The Music of Sound," won the Audio-Visual Achievement Award of the American Society of Association Executives. Officers of the PTG are: **James H. Burton,** Executive Secretary and Editor of the *Journal* (c/o the address shown above); **George R. Morgan,** President (for 1972 and 1973); **F. M. Ward,** Vice President.

POLISH SINGERS ALLIANCE OF AMERICA, 180 Second Avenue, New York, N.Y. 10003. Tel.: (212) AL 4–6642. An association of amateur Polish choral groups throughout the United States, organized in 1889. It has about 5,000 members. President is **Joseph F. Czechlewski.** General Secretary is **Walter Falencki.**

RECORDING INDUSTRY ASSOCIATION OF AMERICA, INC., (RIAA) One East 57th Street, New York, N.Y. 10022. Tel.: (212) MU 8–3778. Founded in 1952. Its purpose is to promote the interests of the industry and to foster good relations among all concerned with the recording industry and the music business in general. It is essentially a trade association representing phonograph record manufacturers. It has about 60 members. President is **Jarrell McCracken;** Executive Director is **Henry Brief.** Its publications, *On the Record,* and *News from R.I.A.A.* (news bulletins and industry reports) are issued to members; the latter goes also to the press. One of the annual reports of the RIAA, concerns the sales of discs, tapes, cassettes, and cartridges in the U.S. The Association is noted for its Gold Record Award certifications. Under RIAA certification rules, a single record must amass a minimum of one million copies sold in order to qualify for these industry-touted awards; a record album must sell for a minimum of $1 million in manufacturers' sales. Where formerly these awards had a certain distinction, they are now awarded in such great number that the honor has been somewhat eroded. For the year 1969, for example, 93 albums and 64 singles received the Gold Record Award. Virtually all belonged to the broad category of popular music. The number of awards bestowed for 1969 was an all-time high up to that time. RIAA has also been responsible for setting certain recording standards for manufacturers.

THE ROCKEFELLER FOUNDATION, 111 West 50th Street, New York, N.Y. 10020. Tel.: 265–8100. Cable: Rockfound, New York. Founded 1913. Officers: **Douglas Dillon,** Chairman of the Board of Trustees; **John H. Knowles,** President; **Allan C. Barnes, Kenneth W. Thompson, Kenneth Wernimont,** and **Sterling Wortman,** Vice Presidents; **J. Kellum Smith, Jr.,** Secretary; **Theodore R. Frye,** Treasurer. Various directors are responsible for program grants in five areas of broad inclusion. Director of Arts and Humanities is **Norman Lloyd.** The Foundation is established to "promote the well-being of mankind throughout the world." The Foundation has for years concentrated on supporting research and other activities in the agricultural sciences, biomedical sciences, social sciences, and other fields; in 1963, it began its first support program of the performing arts—music, dance, and theater. In general, the Foundation sought to aid composers through such programs as residencies for symphony orchestras, whereby they would perform as visitors on campus the music of lesser known composers (the music of some 280 composers was performed by 18 orchestras under this program); and created a program for selected composers to serve residencies with leading orchestras. Other programs were directed to help foundering conservatories experiencing financial hardships, to chamber ensembles performing contemporary music, etc. The thrust of most of the programs in music was to the creator of music and the awareness of his role in relationship to other musical institutions. To demonstrate in detail the scope of the Foundation's aid to the performing arts in general, but music and dance in particular, the following is a complete listing of grants and approved programs of aid for the years 1970 and 1971, published respectively in 1971 and 1972.

Grants approved, for U.S. only, in 1970 for music, dance and performing arts (which would include music and/or dance): Antioch College, Ohio: toward the costs of instituting a program of jazz workshops: $25,000; Atlanta Symphony Orchestra, Georgia: to enable **T. J. Anderson** to serve as composer-in-residence for an additional year: $7,500; Ballet Theatre Foundation, New York: toward the costs of establishing a permanent professional artistic staff for the American Ballet Theatre and for its development program for young choreographers: $150,000 for a three-year period; Boston College, Massachusetts: toward establishing a consortium of colleges and universities in the New England area to cooperate with and participate in the programs of the Opera Company of Boston: $24,600; Boston Philharmonia Society, Massachusetts: toward the costs of rehearsing contemporary music for performance in the Boston area: $15,000; Cleveland Institute of Music, Ohio: to enable it to provide financial assistance to talented students from the United States, in the form of Rockefeller Foundation Awards: $75,000 for a three-year period; Converse College, South Carolina: for use by the Brevard Music Center for a program of musical training in economically and culturally depressed areas of the Southeast: $20,600; Duke University, North Carolina: toward the costs of filming a series "Dance as an Art Form" by the Murray Louis Dance Company: $25,000; Juilliard School of Music, New York City: to enable it to provide financial assistance to exceptionally talented students from the

United States in the form of Rockefeller Foundation Awards: $265,000 for a three-year period; LaMama Experimental Theatre Club, New York City: toward the costs of developing an experimental workshop on the theatrical uses of music, dance, and cinema: $100,000; **Vera Brodsky Lawrence,** New York City: to research and prepare for re-publication historical American music of the eighteenth, nineteenth, and early twentieth centuries: $14,400; Manhattan School of Music, New York: to enable it to provide financial assistance to exceptionally talented students from the United States, in the form of Rockefeller Foundation Awards: $100,000 for a three-year period; Marlboro School of Music, Vermont: toward the continuation of its contemporary music program: $50,000; Martha Graham Center of Contemporary Dance, New York City: toward the costs of concerts and residencies of the Martha Graham Dance Company at colleges and universities throughout the United States: $25,000; National Guild of Community Music Schools, Illinois: toward the costs of operating the executive office of the Guild: $15,000; New England Conservatory of Music, Massachusetts: to enable it to provide financial assistance to exceptionally talented students from the United States, in the form of Rockefeller Foundation Awards: $200,000 for a three-year period; New Orleans Philharmonic Symphony Orchestra, Louisiana: toward the costs of a two-part program of instrumental and orchestral training for young people: $18,500; New York Public Library: for use by the Dance Collection for the notation of **Doris Humphrey's** dance work "Water Study": $500; North Carolina School of the Arts: to assist in the creation of a professional dance company to be known as Dance Theatre South: $24,300; Northeastern University, Massachusetts: toward the second phase of development of a cooperative and participative program involving colleges and universities in the New England area and the Opera Company of Boston: $24,500; Oakland Symphony Orchestra Association, California: additional support for **Edward Applebaum** as composer-in-residence: $236; Oberlin College, Ohio: for the continuation of its Teachers Performance Institute for school music teachers; $170,000 through August, 1971; Peabody Institute of the City of Baltimore, Maryland: to enable the Peabody Conservatory of Music to provide financial assistance to exceptionally talented students from the United States, in the form of Rockefeller Foundation Awards: $170,000 for a three-year period; Repertory Theatre, Louisiana: toward the costs of creative experimentation in musical theatre: $12,000; Rutgers, the State University, New Jersey: research project by **Gordon Myers** on early American solo songs: $4,056; San Francisco Conservatory of Music, California: to enable it to provide financial assistance to exceptionally talented students from the United States, in the form of Rockefeller Foundation Awards: $85,000 for a three-year period; Southeastern Academy of Theatre and Music, Georgia: toward the costs of development and expansion of its programs in theater: $175,000 for a three-year period; Southern Illinois University: toward the costs of developing a performing company under the direction of **Katherine Dunham** at the Performing Arts Training Center of the East Saint Louis Campus of the University: $23,020; Temple University, Pennsylvania: toward the salary of a full-time administrator for the teaching fellowship program operated by the University in conjunction with the Settlement Music School of Philadelphia: $8,000; University of California at Los Angeles: toward the costs of establishing a Graduate Dance Center: $12,000; University of Cincinnati, Ohio: toward the costs of establishing at the University the East Coast branch of the Congress of Strings: $30,000 through September, 1972; University of Michigan: toward the costs of continuing the Contemporary Performance Project of the School of Music: $36,225 for a two-year period; University of Iowa: toward the costs of expanding its Center of the New Performing Arts: $440,000 for a five-year period; University of New Mexico: to enable **John Donald Robb,** composer and dean emeritus of the College of Fine Arts, to complete a treatise on Hispanic folk music in New Mexico and the Southwest: $10,000; University of Southern California: toward the costs of continuing the West Coast branch of the Congress of Strings: $45,000 through September, 1972, and for the continuation by its School of Performing Arts of a training program for music critics: $34,000 through August, 1973. Total of the foregoing grants is $2,434,437.

Payments made in 1970 on programs for music, dance, and performing arts: Mills College, California: development of a center for the creative and performing arts: $37,000; Oakland Symphony Orchestra Association, California: composer-in-residence with the orchestra: $236; Performing Arts Society of Los Angeles, California: staff for its writing and performance workshops: $13,560; San Francisco Conservatory of Music, California: awards to talented students from the United States: $28,295; University of Southern California: establishment of a West Coast branch of the Congress of Strings: $30,000, and the university orchestra program with the Los Angeles Philharmonic Orchestra: $10,000; Music Associates of Aspen, Colorado: program of advanced teacher training: $35,000; Connecticut College: creative project in choreography: $3,000, and research project on a biography of **Doris Humphrey:** $4,450; Atlanta Symphony Orchestra, Georgia: composer-in-residence with the orchestra: $7,500; Southeastern Academy of Theatre and Music, Georgia: development and expansion of its program in theater: $75,000; National Guild of Community Music Schools, Illinois: toward costs of operating its executive office: $15,000; Southern Illinois University, Edwardsville: development of a performing arts company: $23,020; University of Chicago, Illinois: program to foster the composition and performance of contemporary music: $30,000; University of Iowa: establishment of a Center for the New Performing Arts: $61,000; New Orleans Philharmonic Symphony Orchestra, Louisiana: composer-in-residence with the orchestra: $6,000, and instrumental and orchestral youth training program: $18,500; Boston College, Massachusetts: establishment of a consortium of colleges and universities in cooperation with the Opera Company of Boston: $24,600; Boston Philharmonia Society, Massachusetts: rehearsals of contemporary music for performance in the Boston area: $15,000; Boston Symphony Orchestra: fellowship and scholarship program of the Berkshire Music Center: $35,000; Elma Lewis School of Fine Arts, Massachusetts: support of dance programs: $170,000; Williams College, Massachusetts: program in music education and performance: $4,000; University of Michigan: establishment of a performing group for contemporary music: $24,213; Rutgers, the State University, New Jersey: research on early American solo songs: $4,056; Association of American Dance Companies, New York City: toward operating expenses: $3,500; Ballet Theatre Foundation, New York City: development program for young choreographers: $12,000; Brooklyn Institute of Arts and Sciences, New York: toward activities of resident performing companies: $125,000; Columbia University, New York City: support of its Group for Contemporary Music: $15,000; LaMama Experimental Theatre Club, New York City: experimental workshop in music, dance, and cinema: $50,000; Martha Graham Center of Contemporary Dance, New York City: concerts and residencies at various New York colleges and universities: $25,000; New York Public Library: notation of a dance work: $500; Pro Arte Symphony Orchestra Association, New York: performance of new music: $15,000; Society for Strings: summer program for strings teachers: $7,590; State University of New York at Buffalo: expansion of the center for the Creative and Performing Arts: $24,000; Duke University, North Carolina: toward costs of filming a dance series: $25,000; North Carolina School of the Arts: creation of a professional dance company: $24,300; Cleveland Institute of Music, Ohio: awards to talented students from the United States: $25,000; Karamu Foundation, Ohio: consultants for community arts and humanities centers: $10,000; Oberlin College, Ohio: follow-up program for its summer school program for junior high school students: $30,000, and summer workshops for public school music teachers: $80,650; Temple University, Pennsylvania: teaching fellowships in music: $60,933; Converse College, South Carolina:

musical training in depressed areas of the Southeast: $20,600; University of Utah: support of the Children's Dance Theatre: $7,500, and modern dance repertory company: $24,000; Marlboro School of Music, Vermont: for a contemporary music program: $16,666. The total amount of the foregoing is: $1,276,690.

Grants and Programs for 1971 for music and dance in whole or in part are as follows: Agnes de Mille Dance Theatre, New York City: American heritage dance theater project: $25,000; American University, Washington, D.C.: for use by the Wolf Trap American University Academy for the Performing Arts to enable students to participate in the National Youth Orchestra: $20,000; Appalachian Research and Defense Fund, West Virginia: creation of an experimental series of workshops and festivals of Appalachian music: $20,350; Center for Modern Dance Education, New Jersey: resident professional companies: $14,500; Converse College, South Carolina: musical training for high school students at the Brevard Music Center, North Carolina: $100,000 for a three-year period; Edward MacDowell Association, New Hampshire: modernization and renovation of the MacDowell Colony facilities for year-round use: $25,000; Foundation for American Dance, New York City: City Center Joffrey Ballet to establish a choreographers' workshop: $25,000; Long Island University, New York: C. W. Post Center for restoration of musical manuscripts donated by Stefan Wolpe: $9,000; Manhattan School of Music, New York: experimental program of string training by the Preparatory Division of the School, in conjunction with Eleanor Roosevelt Junior High School 143, and of creating string exercises designed specifically for American children: $25,000; Middlebury College, Vermont: development of an innovative approach to music education: $14,850; Morehouse College, Georgia: to prepare the first performances of Scott Joplin's folk opera, "Treemonisha," in conjunction with the Atlanta Symphony Orchestra: $25,000; National Guild of Community Music Schools, Illinois: to operate the executive office of the Guild: $15,000; New York Public Library: to establish an Index of New Musical Notation at the Music Division of its Library of the Performing Arts at Lincoln Center: $55,000 for a three-year period, for use by the Dance Collection to catalogue materials for an eighteen-volume bibliography of its holdings: $24,000, and to enable **Vera Brodsky Lawrence** to research and prepare for republication historical American music of the eighteenth, nineteenth and early twentieth centuries: $15,000; North Carolina School of the Arts: to establish a resident dance company: $250,000 for a three-year period; Northeastern University, Boston: further development of a program involving colleges and universities in the New England area and the Opera Company of Boston: $24,500; State University of New York at Buffalo: to expand the work of the Center for the Creative and performing Arts into areas of theater, dance, and film: $18,600; University of California at San Diego: to establish a Center for Music Experiment and Related Research: $400,000 for a three-year period; Universal Christian Church, Maryland: for use by the Appalachian South Folklife Center, West Virginia, for a program of workshops and performances in indigenous performing arts: $14,200; University of Utah: to continue its Repertory Dance Theatre: $145,000 for a three-year period. The total amount of the foregoing is: $1,265,000.

Appropriations and payments for 1971 were as follows (where two figures are shown the first figure signifies 1971 approved grants and programs; the second signifies actual payments made): San Francisco Conservatory of Music, California: awards to talented students: $28,035 (payment); University of California at San Diego: center for music experiment and related research: $400,000 (grant); University of Southern California: training for music critics: $99,325 (payment), and West Coast branch of the Congress of Strings: $30,000 (payment); Music Associates of Aspen, Colorado: advanced teacher training: $30,000 (payment); American University, D.C.: scholarships to National Youth Orchestra: $20,000, $20,000; Morehouse College, Georgia: preparation of the first performance of the folk-opera "Treemonisha": $25,000, $25,000; National Guild of Community Music Schools, Illinois: operation of executive office: $15,000, $15,000; Indiana University Foundation: study of repertories of American symphony orchestras: $4,000 (payment); University of Iowa: center for the New Performing Arts: $172,500 (payment); Repertory Theatre, Louisiana: experimentation in musical theater: $12,000 (payment); Universal Christian Church, Maryland: workshops in performing arts in Pipestem, West Virginia: $14,200, $14,200; Elma Lewis School of Fine Arts, Massachusetts: dance programs: $70,000 (payment); New England Conservatory of Music, Massachusetts: awards to talented students: $67,000 (payment); Northeastern University, Massachusetts: cooperative program with Opera Company of Boston: $24,500, $49,000; University of Michigan: contemporary performance project of the School of Music: $19,950 (payment); Edward MacDowell Association, New Hampshire: renovation of MacDowell Colony facilities: $25,000, $25,000; Center for Modern Dance Education, New Jersey: resident professional companies: $14,500, $14,500; University of New Mexico: study of Hispanic folk music in the Southwest: $10,000 (payment); Agnes de Mille Dance Theatre, New York: American heritage project: $25,000 (grant); Ballet Theatre Foundation, New York: artistic staff: $75,000 (payment); Business Committee for the Arts, New York: development of support for the arts: $50,000 (payment); Foundation for American Dance, New York: choreographers workshop, City Center Joffrey Ballet: $25,000, $25,000; Juilliard School of Music, New York: American Opera Center for Advanced Training: $100,000 (payment), and awards to talented students: $84,500 (payment); LaMama Experimental Theatre Club, New York: experimental workshop in music, dance, and film: $50,000 (payment); **Vera Brodsky Lawrence,** New York: research on historical American music: $7,200 (payment); Long Island University, New York: restoration of musical manuscripts: $9,000, $9,000; Manhattan School of Music, New York: awards to talented students: $31,637 (payment), and program of strings training: $25,000 (grant); New York Public Library: cataloguing of dance collection: $24,000 (grant), index of new musical notation: $55,000, $17,978, and preparation for republication of historical American music: $15,000, $15,000; State University of New York at Buffalo: Center for the Creative and Performing Arts: $18,600, $18,600; North Carolina School of the Arts: resident professional dance company: $250,000, $78,000; Antioch College, Ohio: Jazz workshops: $25,000 (payment); Cleveland Institute of Music, Ohio: awards to talented students: $25,000 (payment); Oberlin College, Ohio: summer workshop for public school music teachers: $67,500 (payment); University of Cincinnati, Ohio: East Coast branch of the Congress of Strings: $20,000 (payment); Converse College, South Carolina: summer training for high school students: $100,000, $49,300; University of Utah: repertory dance theater: $145,000, $146,000; Marlboro School of Music, Vermont: contemporary music program: $16,666 (payment); Middlebury College, Vermont: music education project: $14,850 (grant). Total grants approved in 1971: $1,239,650; total payments made in 1971: $1,616,891. Total appropriations by the Foundation for all fields of endeavor for 1971 including the above as applicable was $41,934,380, of which $2.5 million was for New York Program expenses and $3.1 million for 1972 general administrative costs. Some grants are paid almost immediately upon approval by the Trustees of the Foundation, and others may be paid out over a number of years or at a future time when matched by other funds. Since its founding, and including the 1971 figures, the Foundation has appropriated, for all fields, a total of $1.130 billion. The Foundation assets as of December 31, 1971 were $388,895,643.

SCHUMANN MEMORIAL FOUNDATION, INC., 2904 East Lake Road, Livonia, New York 14487. Incorporated in September of 1949. Membership: 133. Begun as a private collection of books and memorabilia concerning Clara and Robert Schumann which was later extended to include all Romantic music. The Foundation is also engaged in the promotion of Casterbridge Village of Fine Arts in Conesus, N.Y., a retreat for creative artists in music, letters, painting, architecture, etc. The Foundation has published memoirs of Felix Mendelssohn and the reminiscences of Clara Schumann from letters of her grandson, Ferdinand Schumann, Jr. Publications of the Foundation are sent free to members. Membership is open to anyone. Dues are $10 a year; life memberships are $100, payable once. President: **Mrs. June M. Dickinson;** Executive-Secretary: **Edward Dickinson;** Treasurer: **Mrs. Esther M. McWade.** Meetings are held annually. There is an Advisory Council of well-known musical figures and descendants of Robert Schumann.

SOCIETY FOR ETHNOMUSICOLOGY, INC. (SEM), c/o the Treasurer, School of Music, University of Michigan, Ann Arbor, Michigan 48105. Tel.: (313) 764–6527. Founded in November, 1955. Membership is over 1,000. The Society's purpose is to aid in the advancement of research on the world's folk and popular music and dance as well as the art music and dances of non-Western cultures. Membership is open to all interested persons and includes anthropologists, musicologists, sociologists, and psychologists. Dues are: $7.50 for Student membership; $12.50 for Regular; $15 for Institutions. One annual meeting of the Society is held in the fall. The major publication of SEM is *Ethnomusicology,* a scholarly journal issued three times a year (see Periodicals). The *SEM Newsletter,* issued six times annually, covers news items of interest to the Society. Both of these publications are issued free to members as part of their membership dues. President is **Bruno Nettl,** University of Illinois School of Music; Vice President is **Nicholas England,** Columbia University; Treasurer is **William Malm,** University of Michigan (see above address); Secretary is **Theodore Grame,** Yale University.

SESAC, INC., 10 Columbus Circle, New York, N.Y. 10019. Tel.: (212) 586–3450. In Nashville: The SESAC Building, 1513 Hawkins Street, Nashville, Tennessee 37203. Founded in 1931 by **Paul Heinecke,** President of the organization. Initials of SESAC originally referred to Society of European Stage Authors and Composers; later designation was to mean Standard Editions of Select American Catalogs. At present, the initials have no significant meaning. SESAC is the third largest American music licensing organization. It is the smallest of the three which dominate the music scene in America (the other two are ASCAP and BMI—q.v.). Unlike ASCAP, which is a membership-governed organization of writers and publishers, or BMI, which is a stock company owned by broadcasting stations, SESAC is a privately held corporation organized for profit which represents primarily the interests of publishers and which increasingly of late has extended affiliation opportunities directly to composers and authors. It is the only performing rights organization in America which also represents the mechanical and synchronization rights of its affiliate publishers and writers. Its current catalogue contains over 120,000 copyrighted musical compositions, about 1 percent of which are of European copyright origin. SESAC has performance, mechanical, and synchronization rights agreements in most of the countries of the world and encourages foreign publishers to publish and record under sub-contract works from the SESAC catalogue for the purpose of increasing the income base for its publisher and writer affiliates. Internationally, SESAC is also active in placing SESAC repertory at the disposal of radio and television stations throughout the world. SESAC's central activity is the U.S. market, in which it has broadcast and non-broadcast licensees, the latter covering hotels, theaters, nightclubs, airlines, circuses, musical shows of all kinds, and athletic events. SESAC claims to have licenses with about 98 percent of the entire broadcast industry. In addition to acting as advisor to its affiliates for the purpose of increasing the exploitation of copyright property, SESAC's services include the establishment of various departments with specific areas of responsibility. SESAC's Station Relations Department handles all contacts with the broadcasting industry; its staff makes personal contacts each year with about 4,000 radio station personnel and managers. The Publisher Relations Department advises publishers on copyright and other legal matters. The Copyright Index Department organizes and tabulates copyright data and indexes all items in the SESAC catalogue; it also handles copyright clearances for users of SESAC's catalogue and maintains published catalogues of SESAC music titles and recordings having SESAC titles. The music titles are published in the "SESAC Repertory Index," last published in 1966 with subsequent annual supplements. The recordings index is the "SESAC Record-A-Ref," which is an annual issue. Both publications are made available without charge to SESAC licensees. SESAC also produces "packaged" music of recordings for use on air time by broadcasters. This transcribed library consists of short musical arrangements intended as fillers for commercials and other local station uses. SESAC also publishes a newsletter, *SESAC Music,* and its "Schedule A," which lists its affiliated publishers and writers. The latter is issued in January each year. Although the SESAC catalogue represents some publishers of concert music or educational music, it contains many publishers and composers and authors in country music, hymn and gospel music, and such popular music publishers as those publishing for accordion, band, etc. Officers: **Paul Heinecke,** President; **Alice Heinecke Prager,** Vice President and Managing Director; **Salvatore B. Candilora,** Vice President and Executive Director. Director of Public Relations is **Charles Scully.**

SOCIETY FOR THE PRESERVATION AND ENCOURAGEMENT OF BARBER SHOP QUARTET SINGING IN AMERICA, INC. (SPEBSQSA), 6315 Third Avenue, Kenosha, Wisconsin 53141. Tel.: (414) 654–9111. Founded in 1938. Its purpose is the preservation of "old fashioned vocal quartet harmony." It is a nonprofit, fraternal order founded in the state of Oklahoma. Barbershop quartet singing itself is a not-too-serious allusion to the old village barbershop of the America of the 1900's—a favorite male gathering place—where possibly some quartet singing took place. The style is distinguished by a special emphasis on close harmony and frequent harmonic changes (for both moving melody notes and under sustained melody notes), often chromatic and mildly dissonant. No accompaniment is used and tempered scale pitches are avoided. A wide variety of ballads and songs are used as the musical substance. The art is phenomenally popular; it is distinctly American and an important aspect of a developing American vernacular music. It has often been commercialized and even mocked, but it is irretrievably linked to good times, good fellowship, simple sentiment, and nostalgia. As of March 31, 1972 there were 33,456 Society members in 705 chapters throughout the United States and Canada. In addition, there were 27 licensed groups containing 727 men striving to achieve the necessary requirements for becoming chartered Society chapters. The Society has more than 1,100 registered quartets and at least 600 barbershop choruses. The latter are basic to the Society, for it is from the choruses that quartets are usually formed. In 1972, the Society, with the cooperation of the Music Educators National Conference, began a nationwide series of quartet competitions in high schools. This program, known as "Young Men in Harmony" is intended to interest the young in this form of music participation. Also, in 1972, several chapters were established in England. The Society holds midwinter meetings and summer annual conventions during which quartet competitions are held and winners accorded International Championships—the height of recognition for barbershop quartets. As a fraternal order, the Society engages in a number of social work projects. Among them: a service project with the Institute of Logopedics in Wichita, Kansas, which works with children and adults who have problems that inhibit normal speech; and a cooperative effort with the U.S.O. whereby the Society sends quartets to hospitals in the Far East and Mid-Pacific to entertain hospitalized servicemen. The Society's official magazine is the *Harmonizer* (issued from the organization's headquarters); editor is **Leo W. Fobart.** It is issued bimonthly (January–February, March–April, etc.). Dues for international membership are $15; in addition there are chapter and district dues. Officers are: **Barrie**

Best, Executive Director; **Richard H. de-Montmollin,** President.

SOCIETY OF AMERICAN MUSICIANS, 1014 South Michigan Avenue, Chicago, Illinois 60605. An organization of about 250 members whose purpose is "to raise standards of music education through sponsoring contests and to assist young artists through arranging performances." President is **Saul Dorfman;** Secretary-Treasurer is **Denis Moffat.** Director of competitions is **Richard Flewell.** Dues: $12 per year.

SOCIETY OF THE CLASSIC GUITAR, INC., 409 East 50th Street, New York, N.Y. 10022. Tel.: (212) MU 8–7586. Founded in 1936. The purpose of the society is to "foster the love and appreciation of the guitar as one of the greater instruments of musical arts. . ." Membership is about 400 and is composed of guitarists and interested nonplayers from the New York area, mostly, but some are located in other parts of the country and abroad. The society is a nonprofit organization. Its activities include promoting guitar recitals (already well over a hundred), lectures, and the publication of guitar music. Its official journal is *The Guitar Review* (see Periodicals). A smaller publication is the *SCG Bulletin.* President (for many years) is **Vladimir Bobri;** Vice President is **Gregory d'Alessio;** Secretary is **Martha Nelson;** Treasurer: **Louis Gill. Honorary President is Andrés Segovia.** Dues are: $15 a year for members within a 50-mile radius of New York City; $10 for out-of-town members.

TAU BETA SIGMA, HONORARY SORORITY FOR BAND WOMEN, National Office, 122 Center for the Performing Arts, Oklahoma State University, Stillwater, Oklahoma 74074. Tel.: (405) 372–2333. Founded in 1946. Its membership is over 24,000. The sorority is exclusively for women in college and university bands and is affiliated with Kappa Kappa Psi, the band fraternity. Its purposes are: "To promote the existence and welfare of the college and university bands and to cultivate at large a wholesome respect for their activities and achievements; to honor outstanding women in the band through privilege of membership extended as a reward for technical achievement and appreciation for the best in music; to stimulate campus leadership and promulgate an uncompromising respect, through the medium of the college band, for womanly conduct, good taste and unswerving loyalty; to foster close relationship between college bands . . . to cooperate with other musical organizations in any manner consistent with the purpose of the institution at which chapters are located." There are three classes of membership: Active (dues for which are $10 a year), Honorary, and Pledge. Tau Beta Sigma publishes *The Podium,* a quarterly journal published at the National Office and sent free to members (available to nonmembers on subscription). Both the Kappa Kappa Psi and Tau Beta Sigma are service organizations for collegiate band members, thus they function from a different point of perspective than those band associations whose members are primarily directors. Tau Beta Sigma's national conventions are held in odd-numbered years, district meetings in even-numbered years. Among its activities is a commissioning program for new band music. Grand Secretary-Treasurer is **Donald A. Stanley** (at above address). National President: **Sharon E. Lebsack;** National Secretary: **Nadine Dorschler;** National Treasurer: **Connie Gale.**

THORNE MUSIC FUND, INC., 116 East 66th Street, New York, N.Y. 10021. Founded in 1965. Like the Fromm Foundation (q.v.), the Fund is concerned with composers and is essentially the creation of one man, in this instance, **Francis Thorne,** composer and pianist. The Fund is dedicated to providing mature and accomplished composers (American) with a source of income for a limited period of time, during which they are free to spend all their time composing. In this respect, the Fund is unusual. It has granted sums of up to $15,300 for a three-year period, payable in monthly allotments. It has also extended commissions for new major works to a limited number of composers and has made honorary grants to distinctive musicians. Characteristic of the support programs have been the three-year fellowships granted to **Ben Weber,**

Stefan Wolpe, and **Lou Harrison;** commissions have gone to **David Diamond, Alexei Haieff, Elliott Carter,** and **Robert Helps;** honorary grants for "special contributions to our musical life" have been made to Edgard Varèse, Henry Cowell, **Duke Ellington,** and **Harry Partch.** In addition, there have been grants for extraordinary circumstances, such as the underwriting of a brain operation and hospitalization of a noted woman composer and a grant to assist **Howard Swanson** after his return to the United States from a period of ten years in Europe. The Fund receives its money from other foundations and, on at least one occasion, from the National Endowment for the Arts. Most of the income results from the efforts of Mr. Thorne. The Fund operates with a Board of Directors and an Advisory Committee consisting of well-known composers (Milton Babbitt, Copland, Gunther Schuller, et al.). **Francis Thorne** is President and Treasurer.

UNITED STATES INFORMATION AGENCY (USIA), MUSIC BRANCH, Washington, D.C. 20547. Tel.: (202) DU 3–3110. The USIA Music Branch is responsible for all music activities conducted under the Cultural Operations Division abroad, activities which, for the most part, are focused on promoting contemporary American music in some one hundred countries. It supplies music materials such as tapes and disc recordings, printed music, etc., for use by U.S. Information Centers overseas and by foreign musicians and conductors wanting to perform the music of American composers. Thus, music rental materials, performance rights clearances, and other preparatory matters are handled by the Music Branch, which also offers assistance to Cultural Affairs Officers overseas in preparing for festivals, exhibits, and other events that may feature American music. For the Department of State Cultural Presentations, under which program numerous musicians and musical groups from the professional and academic world have toured foreign countries, the Music Branch supplies various forms of publicity and information material. Apart from the work it does for other United States agencies and departments, the Music Branch works with some degree of independence (although it receives policy guidance, generally, from a specially constituted Music Advisory Panel appointed by the Director of USIA) to produce promotional pamphlets on American music for worldwide distribution and to cooperate with public and private cultural organizations interested in the furtherance of America's music. Head of the Music Branch is the Music Advisor, currently **Daryl D. Dayton,** who in addition to supervising the tasks and responsibilities of the Music Branch, represents the USIA on the music panels of the Department of State, the Advisory Council on the Arts, the National Music Council, and the Committee on Music for UNESCO.

VOICE OF AMERICA, 330 Independence Avenue, S.W., Washington, D.C. The International Broadcasting System of the United States Information Agency, the Voice broadcasts approximately 850 hours a week in 37 languages. Approximately 20 percent of this time is devoted to music. The first Voice broadcast was in German on February 24, 1942. Its original purpose was to broadcast news on the war to both Allied and Axis listeners. Among its present functions is the task of presenting abroad "those aspects of American life and culture which will promote understanding of United States policies and objectives." The Voice's music programming is of extreme importance to the overall objectives of the service; the Music Branch of the Voice of America produces about 1,000 hours of programming each year. Taped program packages are prepared for the 200 United States Information Service posts in 105 countries for broadcast locally. Tapes of live music performances are included along with commercial recordings. The music programming in general attempts to present as varied a picture of America's musical life and talent as possible, emphasizing broad cultural qualities. It is estimated that the weekly audience for the Voice broadcasts is about 43 million. The music programs are balanced to attract both the musically unsophisticated and the connoisseur. The following is a sampling of the programs: "Music U.S.A." is perhaps the most widely listened to Voice music broadcast. It is hosted by **Willis Conover,** who has worked for the Voice since 1954, when he first acted as a disc jockey for programs of jazz beamed to the Scandinavian countries. An offshoot of the program are the jazz clubs formed around the world (reportedly some 1,300 clubs in 89 countries, totaling about 20,000 listeners) as Friends of Music U.S.A. So strong has been the response to broadcasts of American jazz by means of this sustained programming, that it has been credited with helping to lay the groundwork for the now officially sanctioned place occupied by jazz in the Soviet Union, whose government previously had been displeased by its popularity. "Music from the World of Learning," and "Music in Industry," are programs respectively of music performances taken from tapings of concerts at universities and conservatories in America and programs showing the interest of the American worker in cultural activities. "Music from Interlochen" broadcasts the concerts performed at National Music Camp (q.v.) and, in the same manner, some selected American music festivals are taped for rebroadcast abroad. The concerts of the few major American orchestras that are on the air domestically are likewise acquired for the Voice of America. The concert series presented at the Library of Congress, the broadcast performances of the Metropolitan Opera Company, specially produced programs of the history of the American musical theater, American opera from 1800 to the present, interview programs including conversations with leading American musicians—are all further examples. One of the most novel musical ideas of the Voice of America is the series, "Musical Salutes," which has an American city and its symphony orchestra dedicate a concert to a city overseas. The concert is taped from a live performance with a script added in the language of the country of dedication. The city's mayor takes part in the program, extending greetings and presenting the key to the city to a diplomatic representative of the foreign country, etc. Over 120 such programs have been produced with the participation of 40 symphony orchestras—usually not major ensembles, since the point of the series is to exhibit the qualities of the lesser-known American symphonic ensembles. Of the foreign cities so "saluted," about 65 percent have staged reciprocal concerts for American listeners. The Voice's Music Director and Chief of the Music Branch is **Harold Boxer.**

GERTRUDE CLARKE WHITTALL FOUNDATION, Music Division, The Library of Congress, Washington, D.C. 20540. Established to ensure the use of five valuable Stradivari instruments (through a series of concerts presented in The Coolidge Auditorium) given to the Library in 1935 and 1936 by Mrs. Whittall (1867–1965). The Foundation is also responsible for a large number of very valuable autographs of music and letters including a large Brahms Collection. For twenty-three years the Budapest String Quartet (now disbanded) was engaged to play a series of concerts in the Library of Congress making use of the Stradivari instruments. In 1962, the quartet was succeeded by the Juilliard String Quartet, which now gives an annual series of approximately twenty chamber music concerts in The Coolidge Auditorium.

Part 2 | Instrumental Ensembles

Symphony Orchestras

The American Symphony Orchestra League (ASOL), which functions as caretaker to the symphony orchestra, is a membership organization composed (as of early 1972) of 355 U.S. orchestras of all kinds. This total includes 28 major orchestras, 72 metropolitan, 28 urban, 163 community, 31 college, and 26 college–community orchestras—all named according to the classification system adopted by the League (see Organizations).

Among its responsibilities as a service organization is the gathering of information concerning orchestras and (through surveys, projections, and estimates) the production of summaries which reflect the state of American symphonic ensembles. It is the only organization in America that performs these tasks. Its findings are therefore of some consequence.

The best estimate of the League is that there are in the United States 1,204 symphonic ensembles—28 major orchestras, 76 metropolitan orchestras, and 1,100 urban and community orchestras—whose annual expenditures range from zero to $6 million. Altogether, American orchestras expend some $100 million annually (ten years ago the amount was $25 million).

About 70,000 musicians play in the orchestras, 8,000 of whom earn most of their income from playing and teaching. The orchestras are backed up by a minimum of 100,000 civic and culturally minded men and women who volunteer their services in various active ways as members of orchestra boards, women's associations, and auxiliary organizations which establish forms of support for the orchestras. However, several times that number of people contribute to or hold membership in various symphony organizations.

Each year, throughout the country, between 12,000 and 13,000 orchestral concerts are given (about 33 each day); during fiscal year 1971–72 6,000 were performed by the major and metropolitan orchestras alone (104 orchestras).

Total attendance at concerts played by all 1,204 orchestras is about 18 million people a year. In addition, there are indeterminate numbers of people who listen to these orchestras through the broadcast services and through recordings.

The 28 major orchestras' annual operating costs for 1971 totaled $65.7 million, or 65 percent of the total estimated for all orchestras. The majors brought in $30.6 million in income for 1971 and received $26.7 million in private contributions from individuals, industry, foundations, etc., and $5.9 million in government support (local, state, and federal), leaving a total net deficit of over $2.4 million for the year.

Concerts performed in 1971 by the major groups totaled 4,501 (more than a third of the total played by all orchestras). Total live concert attendance was 10.5 million people.

The repertories of American symphony orchestras have been the subject of a series of annual surveys conducted jointly by ASOL and Broadcast Music, Inc. (BMI). The most recent survey covers the 1969–70 season and is a computerized summary of the music performed by 620 American orchestras (29 major orchestras, 63 metropolitan, 351 urban–community, and 177 school orchestras).

Of the over 3,200 works performed, representing 1,100 composers, over 59.6 percent were works of the twentieth century. Of the total, 42.7 percent were composed since 1940. Fifty-nine percent of the twentieth-century works were composed by Americans (Latin Americans, Canadians, and U.S. composers) and 40 percent by Europeans. Seventy-nine percent of all the composers were of the twentieth century. Sixty-five percent of all the twentieth-century composers whose music was performed by the 620 orchestras were American as defined above, 34 percent were European, and the remainder were Africans or Asians.

Of the over 3,200 works performed, 1,323 were of the standard literature (composed before 1900). Although this figure is over 40 percent of all the works performed, the pieces in this category received 53 percent of all the performances played by the orchestras.

Classical composers receiving the greatest number of performances were Beethoven (1,861), Mozart (1,576), Tchaikovsky (927), Brahms (811), Haydn (776), Wagner (572), Bach (523), Dvořák (503), Rossini (435), Handel (365), Berlioz (352), Verdi (336—concert versions of opera and excerpts, primarily), Mendelssohn (322), and Schubert (302), continuing decreasingly to 30 performances of Wieniawski.

The most frequently performed twentieth-century composers were Stravinsky (480), Prokofiev (474), Ravel (409), Richard Strauss (385), **Aaron Copland** (371), Debussy (268), Sibelius (267), Bartók (250), **Leroy Anderson** (220), George Gershwin (214), **Leonard Bernstein** (205), **Shostakovitch** (198), **Richard Rodgers** (193), etc., to **Henry Mancini's** 106 and **Frederick Loewe's** 100.

The performance frequency of composers of lighter music may be attributable to the fact that 528 of the 620 orchestras covered by the survey were either urban–community orchestras (351) or school training orchestras (177), which frequently mix lighter fare with other music to serve audiences in a broader way and, in the case of school groups, to permit variety in the training repertory.

The 166 orchestras included in the section that follows are those found in U.S. communities of about 75,000 or over in population. Not all cities falling within this population category are included. Most metropolitan areas are represented by at least one ensemble. Budgetary classifications are not used; rather the list relates population density to the establishment and maintenance of a symphonic ensemble. No school groups are shown except where they may be allied with a civic or community orchestra (the section on schools refers to more orchestras on campuses); no orchestras assembled specifically for festivals are included (for such, see Festivals). The number of performances of the orchestras included here range from 2 or 3 a year to 300. The quality of the ensembles is also variable from the finest of any in the world to the competent or merely adequate. Recording labels shown refer to recordings made within the last ten or twelve years which are believed to be commercially available.

Alabama

BIRMINGHAM SYMPHONY ASSOCIATION, 800 City Hall, Birmingham, Alabama 35203. Conductor: **Amerigo Marino** (1964). Assistant conductors: **John Owen, Douglas Igelsrud.** Concertmaster: **Harold Wolf.** 65 players; founded 1946. Auditorium: Temple Theater (capacity: 2,100). Season: October to March, 8 to 10 concerts. Summer season: May to August, 4 to 6 concerts. Budget: $330,000. In addition, the orchestra gives 8 or 10 tour concerts per year, and about 20 youth concerts.

Arizona

TUCSON SYMPHONY SOCIETY, INC., 2720 East Broadway, Tucson, Arizona 85716. Conductor: **Gregory Millar** (1966). 92 players. Founded 1928. Auditorium: Palo Verde High School Auditorium (capacity: 1,372). Season: Six months, six pairs of concerts. Budget: $150,000.

California

BURBANK SYMPHONY ORCHESTRA, 1506 Longview Drive, Fullerton, California 92631. Conductor: **Leo Arnaud** (1964). Concertmaster: **Elliot Fisher** (1967). 100 players. Auditoriums: winter, John Burroughs High School Auditorium, (capacity: 1,500); summer, Starlight Bowl (capacity 3,000). Season: September to June, four concerts. Summer season: three concerts. The orchestra charges no admission at its concerts. **Leo Arnaud,** the conductor, is also a composer and arranger for Hollywood. . . . COMPTON CIVIC SYMPHONY ORCHESTRA, Post Office Box 5283, Compton, California, 90221. Conductor: **Hans Lampl** (1964). Concertmistress: **Dorothy Wade** (1966). 70 players. Founded 1947. Auditorium: Compton College Gymnasium (capacity: 1,000). Season: four concerts. The orchestra sponsors the Compton Civic Youth Orchestra, which has a membership of 70. . . . FRESNO PHILHARMONIC ORCHESTRA, 1362 North Fresno Street, Fresno, California 93703. Conductor: **Guy Taylor** (1970). Assistant Conductor and Concertmaster: **Melvin Baddin** (1953). Founded: 1953. Players: 81. Auditorium: Fresno Convention Center Theatre (capacity: 2,359). Season: nine months, eight concerts. Concerts are rebroadcast over local radio station, KFRE–FM. Four young people's Saturday morning concerts yearly. . . . GLENDALE SYMPHONY ORCHESTRA, 121 West Lexington Drive, Glendale, California 91203. Conductor: **Carmen Dragon** (1963). Concertmaster: **James Getzoff** (1960). 80 players. Founded 1923. Auditorium: Dorothy Chandler Pavilion Music Center, Los Angeles (capacity: 3,250). Season: November to May, 6 to 10 concerts. Three locally televised programs annually, including an Emmy Award Christmas program which is syndicate-broadcast to about fifty cities. All concerts are broadcast on Armed-Forces Radio. Some programs are carried on local AM or FM stations. About three guest conductors are engaged each season. Beginning in 1972, the orchestra will play outside the Los Angeles area. . . . LONG BEACH SYMPHONY ASSOCIATION, 121 Linden Avenue, Long Beach, California 90802. Conductor: **Alberto Bolet** (1968). Concertmistress: **Edwina Smith.** Founded 1935; 60 players.

Auditorium: Long Beach City College Auditorium (capacity: 1,077). Season: seven months, 15 concerts. Summer season: five weeks, 3 concerts. Sponsors an annual Student Musicians Competition, winners of which perform as soloists with the orchestra. Sometimes plays special concerts away from home auditorium. Budget: $68,000. Support for the orchestra comes from the City of Long Beach, Los Angeles County Board of Supervisors, Los Angeles County Music and Performing Arts Commission; etc. . . . LOS ANGELES PHILHARMONIC ORCHESTRA, Southern California Symphony–Hollywood Bowl Association, 135 North Grand Avenue, Los Angeles, California 90012. Founded 1919. Musical Director and Conductor: **Zubin Mehta** (1962). Associate Conductor: **Gerhard Samuel** (1970). Concertmaster: **David Frisina** (1942). Players: 105. Auditorium: The Music Center (capacity: 3,250). The orchestra is contracted for a 52-week year. This includes a regular season of 43 weeks and 9 weeks for the summer season. It performs over 200 concerts a year. Its summer season is the series in Hollywood Bowl (some 3 concerts weekly). Apart from its regular subscription series, the orchestra plays youth concerts, in-school concerts, and a campus series in various colleges in Southern California. The orchestra undertook a world tour in fall, 1968 in the nations of Europe, the Middle East, and the Far East. It made a tour of the Eastern states in 1967 and 1968, and, in 1969, played a spring tour in the San Francisco Bay area. For the twenty-fifth anniversary observance of the founding of the United Nations in 1970, the orchestra was invited to perform a special concert in New York. Under the present conductor the orchestra has recorded for *London;* recordings under earlier conductors are on *Capitol, Pickwick, Victor,* and *Seraphim* labels. In 1971, it met the requirements for receiving the Ford Foundation matching grant of $2 million. For continuing its youth concerts and concerts in nearby communities as well as inner-city concert programs, the orchestra received $100,000 from the National Endowment in 1972, a figure matched through private fund raising. . . . OAKLAND SYMPHONY ORCHESTRA, 601 Latham Square Building, Oakland, California 94612. Music Director and Conductor: **Harold Farberman** (1971). Assistant Conductor: **Robert Hughes.** Concertmaster: **Nathan Rubin** (1962). Founded 1933; 87 players. Auditorium: Oakland Auditorium (capacity: 2,000). Season: October to May; 24 concerts. Annual budget: $450,000. In 1971, the orchestra received a $1 million matching grant from the Ford Foundation. The orchestra organizes Youth Concerts and sponsors a Young Artists Award Competition, the winner of which receives a cash prize of $1,000 and a solo appearance with the orchestra. . . . PASADENA SYMPHONY ORCHESTRA, 301 East Colorado Boulevard, Pasadena, California 91101. Conductor: **Richard Lert** (1936). Concertmistress: **Virginia Baker** (1964). Founded 1928. Players: 85. Auditorium: Pasadena Civic Auditorium (capacity: 3,000). Seasons: eight months, seven concerts. Budget: $100,000. (Conductor **Lert,** after the 1971–72 season, will limit his appearances with the orchestra to one or two concerts.) . . . RICHMOND SYMPHONY, Richmond Art Center, Richmond, California 94800. Conductor: **William Jackson** (1965). Concertmaster: **Willard Tressel** (1966). Founded 1950. Players: 90. Auditorium: Richmond Auditorium (capacity: 3,900). Season: twelve months, 16 concerts. The orchestra offers various special concerts such as school concerts, TV rehearsal program, and "family concerts" in school auditoriums. . . . RIVERSIDE SYMPHONY ORCHESTRA SOCIETY, Post Office Box 2342, Riverside, California 92506. Conductor: **James K. Guthrie** (1965). Concertmaster: **Clyda Yedinak** (1959). Founded 1959. Players: 65. Auditorium: Riverside Municipal Auditorium (capacity: 1,700). Season: October through April, six concerts. [Budget: $24,000. . . . SACRAMENTO SYMPHONY ORCHESTRA, Post Office Box 2249, Sacramento, California 95810. Conductor: **Harry Newstone.** Assistant Conductor: **Ross Shub.** Concertmaster: **Ward Fenley.** Founded 1912. Players: 81. Auditorium: Hiram Johnson High School (capacity: 1,464). Season: 32 weeks, 16 concerts. Budget: $205,000. Received a $500,000 matching grant from the Ford Foundation in 1971. In addition to its regular concerts, the orchestra gives 6 young people's concerts, 6 "connoisseur concerts," 125 instrumental demonstrations in schools, 16 broadcasts, 4 special concerts, and 3 youth orchestra concerts. . . . SAN BERNARDINO SYMPHONY ORCHESTRA, Post Office Box 2312, Uptown Station, San Bernardino, California 92406. Founded in 1961. Conductor: **Michel Perrière** (1968). Concertmaster: **Armen Turadian** (1961). Auditorium: Gibbs Auditorium (capacity: 1,000). Season: eight months, five concerts. Budget: $10,000. . . . SAN DIEGO SYMPHONY ORCHESTRA ASSOCIATION, Post Office Box, 3175, San Diego, California 92103. Founded in 1927. Music Director and Conductor: **Peter Erös** (1971). Assistant Conductor and Concertmaster: **Robert Emile** (1959). Auditorium: Civic Theatre (capacity: 2,945). Season: 20 weeks, 14 concerts. Summer season: five weeks, 5 concerts. Budget: $333,000. In 1971, the association qualified for a Ford Foundation matching grant of $500,000. . . . SAN FRANCISCO SYMPHONY ASSOCIATION, 107 War Memorial Veterans Building, San Francisco, California 94102. Founded in 1911. Conductor and Music Director: **Seiji Ozawa** (1969). Assistant Conductor: **Niklaus Wyss** (1970). Concertmaster: **Jacob Krachmalnick** (1964). Players: 100. Auditorium: War Memorial Opera House (capacity: 3,252). Performs 36 weeks, 60 Regular Subscription Series concerts, plus about 90 additional concerts including nonsubscription special concerts, broadcasts over radio station KKHI, a chamber orchestra series (featuring members of the San Francisco Symphony), a series of concerts in nearby cities, youth concerts, public school concerts and educational encounters, etc. Made its first overseas tour with a 16-day visit to Japan in 1968. Recordings: *CRI, RCA Victor* (under predecessor conductors **Enrique Jorda** and the late Pierre Monteux); in 1972, the orchestra signed a recording contract with *Deutsche Grammophon Gesellschaft*. . . . STOCKTON SYMPHONY ASSOCIATION, INC., Post Office Box 1126, Stockton, California 95201. Conductor: **Kyung-Soo Won** (1967). Concertmaster: **Warren Von Bronkhorst** (1967). Founded 1927. Players: 75. Auditorium: Stockton Junior High School Auditorium (capacity: 1,829). Season: nine months, six concerts. Budget: $50,000. Recordings: *Custom Records*, 7212 Rosewood Drive, Stockton, California 95207.

Colorado

DENVER SYMPHONY ORCHESTRA, 1615 California Street, Denver Colorado 80202. Founded 1934 (out of the Denver Civic Symphony, which was founded in 1922). Conductor: **Brian Priestman** (1970). Associate Conductor: **Alan Miller.** Players: 86. Auditorium: Denver Auditorium Theatre (capacity: 2,250). Season: 33 weeks, 140 concerts. Tours throughout the region. Awarded a $1 million Ford Foundation matching grant in 1971. . . . PUEBLO SYMPHONY ORCHESTRA, 1117 Lake Avenue, Pueblo, Colorado 81004. Founded 1966. Conductor: **Gerhard Track** (1966). Concertmistress: **Dorothea de Turk** (1970). Players: 85. Auditorium: Memorial Hall in Pueblo (capacity: 1,675). Season: October to May with five series of concerts. Budget: under $50,000. The orchestra supports a Youth Symphony which gives two concerts yearly. Additional concerts by the Pueblo Symphony are a "Hausmusik" Series of four chamber concerts at the Pueblo Metropolitan Museum, a concert with the Pueblo Symphony Chorale, and children's concerts.

Connecticut

BRIDGEPORT UNIVERSITY CIVIC SYMPHONY, University of Bridgeport, Bridgeport, Connecticut 06602. Founded 1947. Conductor: **Harry R. Valante.** Players: 55. Season: 32 weeks, three concerts. A semiprofessional ensemble. . . . SYMPHONY SOCIETY OF GREATER HARTFORD (HARTFORD SYMPHONY ORCHESTRA), 15 Lewis Street, Hartford, Connecticut, 04103. Conductor: **Arthur Winograd** (1964). Concertmaster: **Renato Bonacini** (1962). Players: 85. Auditorium: Bushnell Memorial Hall (capacity: 3,277). Season: 32

weeks, 46 concerts. Summer season: 6 weeks, 6 concerts. Budget: $500,000. Records: *Vanguard, Decca,* and *Spoken Arts.* Annual concert in Carnegie Hall, New York City. In 1971, the orchestra received a $1 million Ford Foundation matching grant. In 1972, the National Endowment for the Arts granted the orchestra $20,000 to expand its young peoples' and educational concerts. . . . NEW HAVEN SYMPHONY ORCHESTRA, 254 College Street, New Haven, Connecticut 06510. Conductor: **Frank Brieff** (1951). Assistant conductor: **John Ferritto.** Auditorium: Woolsey Hall (capacity: 2,695). Season: 40 or more concerts. Summer season: 5 weeks, 5 concerts. The orchestra also gives 12 Young People's concerts in school auditoriums, 14 high school concerts, 3 chamber player concerts, 100 quartet and quintet demonstrations in local schools. The orchestra commissions a major orchestral work each season; past commissions have gone to Quincy Porter, **Luigi Dallapiccola, Mel Powell,** et al. The orchestra gave the first performance in modern times of the complete version of Mahler's Symphony No. 1. In 1971 it received a $500,000 matching grant from the Ford Foundation and in 1972 a grant from the National Endowment for the Arts for expanded educational concerts. Recordings: *Odyssey* (Mahler Symphony No. 1 as cited).

Delaware

DELAWARE SYMPHONY ORCHESTRA, 2302 Concord Pike, Wilmington, Delaware 19803. Conductor: **Van Lier Lanning** (1955). Concertmaster: **Leo Ahramjian** (1963). Founded 1929. Players: 80. Auditorium: Salesianum Auditorium (capacity: 1,234). Season: Seven months, 5 to 11 concerts. Budget: $30,000.

District of Columbia

NATIONAL GALLERY ORCHESTRA, Sixth Street and Constitution Avenue, N.W. Washington, D.C. 20565. Conductor: **Richard Bales** (1943). Concertmaster: **Mark Ellsworth** (1953). Founded 1943. Players: 55. Auditorium: East Garden Court of National Gallery of Art (capacity: 650, plus standees). Season: 12 concerts. Records: *Columbia.* Additional concerts outside the museum, string orchestra concerts, annual televised concerts. On April 4 and 11, 1971, the orchestra performed the first U.S. performance of Bruckner's Symphony in D minor ("Nullte"). . . . WASHINGTON NATIONAL SYMPHONY, Kennedy Center for the Performing Arts, 17th and H, N.W., Washington, D.C. 20009. Founded 1930. Musical Director and Conductor: **Antal Dorati** (1970). Associate Conductor: **James De Priest** (1972). Concertmaster: **Werner Lywen.** Players: 95. Auditorium: Concert Hall of the Kennedy Center (capacity: 2,700). The orchestra plays a 45-week season and a total of nearly 300 concerts. Its subscription series during the regular winter season consists of 24 concerts, each performed three times. It performs many young people's concerts and concerts in schools. It also performs a summer series at Wolf Trap Farm for the Performing Arts in Virginia (see Music Festivals). Additional concerts are given on tour, notably for a series in New York City and in cities in Virginia and Maryland. Its major tours in the past have been a Latin American tour in 1959 (which offered 64 concerts in nineteen nations); a tour of Mexico in 1967 and in the same year, of Europe (three weeks, eight nations, 15 concerts); and the tour in 1968 to the West and Southwest of the United States. The orchestra plays at all presidential inauguration concerts. Recordings are on *RCA Victor* and *Westminster.* Arrangements were made in 1972 for recordings under the *London* label. The orchestra has received grants from the National Endowment and from the Ford Foundation's matching fund program for orchestras. In 1971 the latter's requirements were met by the orchestra, thereby earning the grant of $2 million.

Florida

FLORIDA SYMPHONY ORCHESTRA, Cherry Plaza, Post Office Box 782, Orlando, Florida 32802. Conductor: **Pavle Despalj** (1970). Concertmaster: **Alphonse Carlo** (1967). Founded 1950. Players: 70. Auditorium: Orlando Municipal Auditorium (capacity: 2,950). Season: 20 weeks, 75 concerts. Budget: $300,000. In addition, the orchestra sponsors a chamber group which gives 12 concerts in a four-week season. . . . FORT LAUDERDALE SYMPHONY ORCHESTRA ASSOCIATION, 450 East Las Olas Boulevard, Fort Lauderdale, Florida 33301. Conductor: **Emerson Buckley** (1963). Concertmaster: **Alexander Prilutchi** (1960). Founded: 1949. Players: 85. Auditorium: War Memorial Auditorium (capacity: 2,300). Season: October to April, 16 concerts. Budget: $110,000. . . . FLORIDA GULF COAST SYMPHONY, Post Office Box 449, Tampa, Florida 33601. Conductor: **Irwin Hoffman** (1969). Players: 80. Auditorium: Bayfront Center, Saint Petersburg (capacity: 2,119); McKay Auditorium, Tampa (capacity: 1,800). The orchestra is a merger, made in 1969, of the former Tampa Philharmonic and the St. Petersburg Symphony Society. Operating budget (1969–70): $350,000. . . . JACKSONVILLE SYMPHONY ASSOCIATION, 46 West Duval Street, Room 218, Jacksonville, Florida 32202. Conductor: **Willis Page** (1971). Concertmaster: **Aaron Krosnick.** Founded: 1949. Players: 70. Auditorium: Civic Auditorium (capacity: 3,200). Season: eight regular concerts, plus an increasing number of special concerts. Budget: $106,000 (1968). In 1971, the orchestra received a $250,000 Ford Foundation matching grant; in 1972, it received $15,000 from the National Endowment for the Arts for educational concerts.

Georgia

ATLANTA SYMPHONY ORCHESTRA, 1280 Peachtree Street, N.E., Atlanta, Georgia 30309. Conductor: **Robert Shaw** (1967). Assistant Conductors: **Michael Zearott** and **Michael Palmer.** Concertmaster: **Martin Sauser** (1957). Founded 1945. Players: 89. Auditorium: Symphony Hall, Atlanta Memorial Center (capacity: 1,850). Season: 40 weeks, including summer; 120 regular concerts. Budget: $800,000. In 1971, the orchestra completed its requirements to receive a Ford Foundation matching grant of $1 million; in 1972 received $100,000 in matching funds from the National Endowment for the Arts for expanded public service programs in the Southeast. . . . COLUMBUS SYMPHONY ORCHESTRA, Post Office Box 5361, Columbus, Georgia 31906. Conductor: **Harry Kruger** (1965). Concertmaster: **Arthur Cotruvo** (1967). Founded 1949. Players: 80. Auditorium: Three Arts Theatre (capacity: 1,900). Season: eight or nine months, four adult concerts, four children's concerts. . . . SAVANNAH SYMPHONY SOCIETY, INC., Post Office Box 217, Savannah, Georgia 31402. Conductor: **Ronald Stoffel** (1969). Concertmaster: **George Lapenson** (1967). Founded 1953. Players: 71. Auditorium: Savannah Civic Center (capacity: 2,600). Season: 20 weeks, 45 concerts; 35 of the orchestra's yearly concerts are Youth Concerts.

Hawaii

HONOLULU SYMPHONY SOCIETY, Suite 303, Bishop Trust Building, 1000 Bishop Street, Honolulu, Hawaii 96813. Conductor: **Robert LaMarchina** (1967). Associate Conductor: **Andrew C. Schenck** (1970). Concertmaster: **Fredric Balazs.** Auditorium: Honolulu Concert Hall (capacity: 2,157). Regular season: 30 weeks, 100 concerts. Summer season (Waikiki Shell): five weeks. Budget: $554,000 (1967–68). *Decca* records (availability uncertain). Sponsors Honolulu Symphony Opera Festival. Youth concerts played to audiences totaling 90,000. Ensemble demonstrations given for 50,000 school children. In 1971 received a $750,000 Ford Foundation matching grant and $84,000 from the National Endowment, the latter for expanded public service programs.

Illinois

CHICAGO BUSINESS MEN'S ORCHESTRA, 1207 Helen Court, Ingleside, Illinois 60041. Conductor: **Charles H. Schell.** Assistant Conductor: **James Bolle.** Concertmaster: **Al Duman.** Founded 1921. Players: 50. Auditorium: Francis Parker Auditorium (capacity 500 to 700). Season: nine months, four concerts. . . . CIVIC ORCHESTRA OF CHI-

CAGO, Orchestra Hall, Chicago, Illinois 60604. Coordinator: **Gordon Peters.** Players: 80. A training orchestra for the Chicago Symphony, performing seven concerts a year in Orchestra Hall (2,566 seats). . . . CHICAGO SYMPHONY ORCHESTRA, Orchestra Hall, 220 South Michigan Avenue, Chicago, Illinois 60604. Founded: 1891. Musical Director and Conductor: **Georg Solti** (1968). Associate Conductor: **Henry Mazer** (1970). Co-concertmasters: **Samuel Magad** and **Victor Aitay.** Players: 106. Auditorium: Orchestra Hall (capacity: 2,566). Recordings: *RCA Victor, Mercury, Angel, Columbia, Pickwick,* and *London.* Season: 52 weeks, including its summer engagement for the Ravinia Festival. Undertook its first European tour in fall, 1971, giving 25 concerts in fifteen cities of nine countries; has toured other cities in the United States. Has its own chorus, the Chicago Symphony Chorus, directed by **Margaret Hillis.** Celebrated its eightieth anniversary with special commissions to **Easley Blackwood, Alan Stout, Elliott Carter, Michael Tippett, Petrassi, Maderna, Henze,** and **Lygeti.** In 1971, the association created the Chicago Symphony Society, a membership organization ($20 a year dues), to provide an added source of income. Members receive certain privileges including special recordings and reduced-price tickets. Received in 1971 a $2 million Ford Foundation matching grant; in 1972, a grant of $100,000 from the National Endowment for the Arts to develop youth and college audiences. Principal guest conductor (since 1968) is **Carlo Maria Giulini.** Conductor of the orchestra for the Ravinia Festival is **Istvan Kertesz** (up to the 1972 season). . . . EVANSTON SYMPHONY, Post Office Box 778, Evanston, Illinois 60201. Conductor: **Frank Miller** (1962). Founded 1945. Players: 75. Season: four to six concerts. **Frank Miller** is principal cellist of the Chicago Symphony Orchestra. In commemoration of its twenty-fifth season in 1970–71, the orchestra commissioned a new work from Karel Husa. . . . PEORIA SYMPHONY ORCHESTRA, 1200 West Loucks Avenue, Peoria, Illinois 61604. Conductor: **Harold Bauer** (1967). Assistant Conductor: **Frederick Huber.** Concertmaster: **Allen Cannon** (1946). Founded 1898. Players: 75. Auditorium: Shrine Mosque (capacity: 1,835). Season: 25 weeks, 16 concerts. The orchestra also gives three student concerts to an audience of 10,000 school children, and summer pops concerts. Has received support from the Sears-Roebuck Foundation and the Illinois Arts Council. . . . ROCKFORD SYMPHONY ORCHESTRA, Box 655, Rockford Illinois 61105. Conductor: **Crawford Gates** (1970). Players: 85. Auditorium: Jefferson Junior High School Auditorium, capacity 1,000. Season: eight months, six concerts. Summer season: four months, six concerts. . . . SPRINGFIELD SYMPHONY ORCHESTRA ASSOCIATION, INC. 1537 South Douglas, Springfield, Illinois 62704. Conductor: **Harry Farbman** (1951). Players: 70. Auditorium: Springfield High School (capacity: 1,500). Season: September to May, five concerts. The orchestra also presents one children's concert. . . . THE YOUTH ORCHESTRA OF GREATER CHICAGO, 410 South Michigan Avenue, Chicago, Illinois 60605. Conductor: **Dudley Powers** (1958). Founded: 1946. Players: 117. Auditorium: Orchestra Hall (capacity: 2,566). Season: eight months, two concerts. Concertmaster and principals of each section are chosen by audition before each concert. The membership of the orchestra represents 56 schools in the Greater Chicago area. All administrative work is done by the parents of orchestra members, of former members, and orchestra alumni. The repertory played is from the standard orchestral literature.

Indiana

EVANSVILLE PHILHARMONIC ORCHESTRA, Post Office Box 84, Evansville, Indiana 47706. Conductor: **Minas Christian** (1953). Concertmaster: **Gerald Fischbach.** Founded: 1934. Players: 85. Auditorium: Vanderburgh Auditorium (capacity: 2,000). Season: 30 weeks, 14 subscription concerts. Budget: $105,000. In addition to regular subscription concerts, the orchestra gives 1 pops concert, 3 chamber quartet concerts, 4 youth concerts, and 75 to 100 quartet concerts in local schools. In 1972, the orchestra received

$10,000 from the National Endowment for the Arts to expand its youth programs. . . . FORT WAYNE PHILHARMONIC ORCHESTRA, 201 West Jefferson Street, Fort Wayne, Indiana 46802. Conductor: **Thomas Bricetti** (1970). Associate Conductor: **Eve Queler.** Concertmaster: **Paul Bizz.** Founded 1942. Players: 65. Auditorium: Scottish Rite Auditorium (capacity: 2,175). Season: 31 weeks, 34 concerts. Budget: $100,000. String and woodwind quartets made up of orchestra members give 40 in-school concerts yearly. Philharmonic chorus of 100. Received a $15,000 National Endowment grant in 1972 for expanding in-school lecture demonstrations and concerts; in 1971, received a Ford Foundation matching grant of $250,000. . . . INDIANAPOLIS SYMPHONY ORCHESTRA, 4600 Sunset Avenue, Indianapolis, Indiana 46207. Conductor: **Izler Solomon** (1956). Associate Conductor: **Thomas Briccetti.** Concertmaster: **Arthur Tabachnick** (1966). Founded 1930. Players: 85. Auditorium: Clowes Memorial Hall (capacity: 2,200). Season: 35 weeks, 150 concerts, approximately. Received a $2 million Ford Foundation matching grant in 1971 and in 1972, a $56,000 grant from the National Endowment for expanded youth concerts. . . . SOUTH BEND SYMPHONY ORCHESTRA, 215 West North Shore Drive, South Bend, Indiana 46617. Conductor: **Edwyn Hames** (1932). Concertmaster: **Gerald Lewis** (1962). Players: 85. Founded 1932. Auditorium: Morris Civic Auditorium (capacity: 2,500). Season: October to April, five concerts.

Iowa

CEDAR RAPIDS SYMPHONY ORCHESTRA ASSOCIATION, P.O. Box 1903, Cedar Rapids, Iowa 52406. Conductor: **Richard Williams** (1970). Assistant Conductor: **Robert Thayer** (1957). Concertmaster: **Marlis Windus** (1960). Founded: 1921. Players: 85. Auditoriums: Coe College Auditorium (capacity: 1,140); Sinclair Auditorium (capacity: 1,150); Paramount Theatre (capacity: 1,950); 10 to 18 concerts. Budget: $35,000. The orchestra gives scholarships to high school players of orchestral instruments yearly. . . . DES MOINES SYMPHONY ORCHESTRA, 210 Securities Building, Des Moines, Iowa 50309. Conductor: **Thomas Griswold** (1971). Concertmaster: **Wilfred Biel** (1967). Founded 1937. Players: 85. Auditorium: KRNT Theatre (capacity: 4,000). Season: September to May, six concerts. . . . SIOUX CITY SYMPHONY ORCHESTRA, 402 Commerce Building, Sioux City, Iowa 51101. Conductor: **Leo Kucinski.** Concertmaster: **Jayne Barnes.** Founded: 1917. Players: 75. Auditorium: Municipal Auditorium (capacity: 4,200). Season: five months, 19 concerts. Budget: $75,000. . . . TRI-CITY SYMPHONY, Office Box 3865, Davenport, Iowa 52801. Conductor: **James A. Dixon.** Founded 1915. Players: 85. Auditoriums: Centennial Hall, Rock Island (capacity: 1,670); Masonic Temple, Davenport (capacity: 2,760). Season: 12 concerts. Budget: $100,000. The orchestra gives three young people's concerts, and six concerts in schools.

Kansas

WICHITA SYMPHONY ORCHESTRA, 225 West Douglas, Room 207, Wichita, Kansas 67202. Conductor: **François Huybrechts** (1972). Concertmaster: **James Ceasar** (1950). (**James Robertson** had been conductor from 1950 to 1969.) Founded 1944. Players: 86. Auditorium: Wichita Civic Center (capacity: 2,200). Season: October to March, nine subscription pairs, plus youth concerts. The orchestra sponsors two 110-piece youth orchestras, the Naftzger Young Artist Auditions, and opera productions. In 1971, the orchestra received a $500,000 matching grant from the Ford Foundation; in 1972, $20,000 of National Endowment funds were granted to support the young people's concerts, the youth orchestras, and a string quartet drawn from the orchestra.

Kentucky

THE LOUISVILLE ORCHESTRA, 211 Brown Building, 321 West Broadway, Louisville, Kentucky 40202. Conductor: **Jorge Mester** (1967). Concertmaster: **Paul Kling**

(1959). Founded 1936. Players: 60. Auditorium: Brown Theatre (capacity: 1,453). Season: 32 weeks, 20 subscription concerts, 30 other concerts; 16 children's concerts, 30 programs for preschool children; tours by the orchestra's string quartet and woodwind quintet. The orchestra is active in the sponsorship of contemporary music, issuing six records yearly on its own label *Louisville Orchestra First Edition Records* (see Record Companies). The total number of records issued thus far is 112. In 1971, the orchestra qualified for a $500,000 matching grant from the Ford Foundation; in 1972, it received $16,000 from the National Endowment for the Arts to provide special rehearsals for in-school concert programs.

Louisiana

BATON ROUGE SYMPHONY, 3759 Perkins Road, Baton Rouge, Louisiana 70808. Conductor: **Peter Paul Fuchs** (1960). Associate Conductor: **Kenneth B. Klaus.** Concertmaster: **Dinos Constantinides** (1966). Founded: 1946. Players: 70. Auditorium: Louisiana State University Union Theater (capacity: 1,305). Season: October to March, nine concerts. . . . NEW ORLEANS PHILHARMONIC SYMPHONY ORCHESTRA, 333 St. Charles Avenue, Suite 207, New Orleans, Louisiana 70130. Founded in 1936. Conductor: **Werner Torkanowsky** (1963). Associate to the Conductor: **Robert K. Rohe.** Assistant Conductor and Concertmaster: **Carter Nice** (1967). Season: 33 weeks, 125 concerts. Auditorium: Municipal Auditorium (capacity: 2,750). The orchestra supports a Youth Training orchestra, directed by **Carter Nice.** In 1971, the orchestra received a $1 million matching grant from the Ford Foundation, and, in 1972, it matched a $100,000 National Endowment grant with a similar sum raised privately for expanding its city and touring programs and other projects. . . . SHREVEPORT SYMPHONY SOCIETY, Box 4057, Shreveport, Louisiana 71104. Conductor: **John Shenaut** (1948). Concertmaster: **Leonard Kacenjar.** Founded 1948. Players: 70. Auditorium: Shreveport Civic Theatre (capacity: 1,765). Season: 33 weeks, 12 regular pairs of concerts. Budget: $180,000. The orchestra premieres one major contemporary work yearly. In addition, the orchestra sponsors the Shreveport Symphony Society Repertory Opera Company (four productions, eight performances), Ballet Company (two productions), and Chorale (2 concerts); special soloist concerts; 28 children's concerts; and two youth orchestras. In 1971, the Society received $350,000 in matching grants from the Ford Foundation and in 1972, $9,500 from the National Endowment for the Arts.

Maine

PORTLAND SYMPHONY ORCHESTRA, City Hall, Portland, Maine 04111. Conductor: **Paul Vermel** (1967). Assistant Conductor: **Clinton Graffam.** Concertmaster: **Dezso Vaghy** (1966). Founded 1924. Players: 90. Auditorium: City Hall Auditorium (capacity: 2,873). Season: eight months, 26 concerts. Annual budget: $957,000. In 1970, the first year of aid extended to symphony orchestras, the National Endowment for the Arts granted the orchestra $12,700 for establishing concerts of broader appeal; in 1972, another grant of $20,000 was received for the purpose of hiring professional string players for the ensemble, and for continuing a concert series in Augusta, Maine.

Maryland

BALTIMORE SYMPHONY ORCHESTRA, 120 West Mount Royal Avenue, Baltimore, Maryland 21201. Founded in 1916 (first season). Conductor: **Sergiu Comissiona** (1968). Assistant Conductor: **Rainer Miedel.** Concertmaster: **Isidor Saslav.** Auditorium: Lyric Theater (capacity: 2,610). Season: 38 weeks, 240 concerts. Budget: $1,200,000. Players: 89. The orchestra tours widely through Maryland and the Eastern United States, and plays annually to some 100,000 children through its Music Education Program. Concerts are either free or at very low price tickets. In the summer of 1969 the orchestra initiated 11 free outdoor concerts at nine different locations in Baltimore (32,000 estimated total audience). The orchestra plays for all performances of the Baltimore Civic Opera Company. It receives a partial subsidy from the City of Baltimore in the amount of $120,000 a year. In 1971, the orchestra qualified for a $1 million Ford Foundation matching grant; in 1972, it received $100,000 from the National Endowment for the Arts for continuing its Maryland concerts (45 concerts in fifteen communities).

Massachusetts

BOSTON POPS ORCHESTRA, Symphony Hall, Boston, Massachusetts 02115. Conductor: **Arthur Fiedler** (1930). Season: nine weeks in the spring, 55 concerts. The Pops concerts are a tradition going back to the early years of the Boston Symphony (see Music Festivals). The orchestra consists of 95 players from the Boston Symphony Orchestra. The Boston Pops records for *RCA Victor* and *Polydor* (Deutsche Grammophon Gesellschaft). . . . BOSTON SYMPHONY ORCHESTRA, Symphony Hall, Boston, Massachusetts 02115. Musical Director and Conductor (beginning with the 1973 season): **Seiji Ozawa,** succeeding **William Steinberg** who served from 1969 to 1972. Associate Conductor: **Michael Tilson Thomas.** Concertmaster: **Joseph Silverstein** (1962). Founded in 1881. Players: 106. Season: 31 weeks for the regular season, 9 weeks of Pops concerts; 120 regular concerts, 55 Pops concerts. Additional post-season concerts are played for the Esplanade series. Its summer season of eight weeks and 26 concerts is at Tanglewood, Massachusetts (see Music Festivals for separate entries on these series). The orchestra's contract covers a 52-week year. Recordings: *Deutsche Grammophon* and *RCA Victor.* The latter recording company has installed some $75,000 worth of recording equipment in Symphony Hall on an intended permanent basis; the orchestra is the only one in the U.S. which is contracted to a specific annual output for a recording firm. In the spring of 1971, the orchestra toured Europe, its first such trip since 1956 and its first to include performances by the Boston Pops. It performs annual concerts in New York, Brooklyn, and elsewhere and has toured to other areas in the U.S. (e.g., Florida in 1969). In 1971, the orchestra met qualifications for receiving a $2 million Ford Foundation matching grant and in 1972, received from the National Endowment for the Arts $100,000 to be matched against privately raised funds, in support of its Berkshire Music Center activities in Tanglewood. The orchestra has certain of its principal chairs endowed through special contributions (concertmaster: $750,000; principal flute: $100,000; principal viola and cello). . . . NEW BEDFORD SYMPHONY ORCHESTRA ASSOCIATION, INC., Swift Road, South Dartmouth, Massachusetts 02748. Conductor: **John R. Pandolfi** (1967). Concertmaster: **Kenneth Park** (1967). Founded 1957. Players: 61. Auditorium: Keith Junior High School (capacity: 300). Season: fall to spring, three concerts. . . . QUINCY SYMPHONY ORCHESTRA, Post Office Box 492, Quincy, Massachusetts 02169. Conductor: **Robert E. Brown** (1967). Concertmistress: **Eleanor Nelson** (1962). Founded 1953. Players: 55. Auditorium: Quincy High School Auditorium (capacity: 1,200). Season: nine months, five or six concerts. Budget: $4,000. . . . SPRINGFIELD SYMPHONY ORCHESTRA, 49 Chestnut Street, Springfield, Massachusetts 01103. Permanent Conductor and Music Director: **Robert Gutter** (1969). Players: 78. Auditorium: Springfield Municipal Auditorium (3,140 seats). Season: fall to spring, about 15 concerts. In 1972, the orchestra received a National Endowment for the Arts grant of $15,000 for children's concerts, free ghetto concerts, and in-school concerts. . . . WORCESTER ORCHESTRA, 321 Main Street, Worcester, Massachusetts 01608. Music Director and Conductor: **Arthur Winograd** (1972). Auditorium: Worcester Memorial Auditorium (capacity: 3,000). Presents six concerts a year.

Michigan

DEARBORN ORCHESTRAL SOCIETY, Box 2084, Dearborn, Michigan 48124; or 750 North Elizabeth, Dearborn, Michigan 48128. Conductor: **Nathan Gordon** (1961). Associate Conductor: **James R. Irwin.** Concertmaster:

Edouard Kesner (1962). Founded 1961. Players: 75. Auditoriums: Ford Central Office Building (capacity: 650); Edsel Ford High School (capacity: 950). Season: eight months, six concerts. The orchestra gives an annual free school concert. **Nathan Gordon** is the principal violist of the Detroit Symphony. . . . DETROIT SYMPHONY ORCHESTRA, Ford Auditorium, 20 East Jefferson, Detroit, Michigan 48226. Founded in 1914. Music Director and Conductor: **Sixten Ehrling,** appointed in 1961; will conduct his last season in 1972–73. Beginning in 1973, Principal Conductor will be **Aldo Ceccato.** Associate Conductor: **Pierre Hétu** (1971); Conductor-in-residence: **Paul Freeman.** Concertmaster: **Gordon Staples** (1968), succeeding **Mischa Mischakoff** who served from 1952 to 1968. Auditorium: Ford Auditorium (capacity: 2,927). Number of players: 102. The orchestra plays a winter season of 33 weeks and a summer season of about 14 weeks. Altogether it performs about 223 concerts a year: 44 concerts in the regular series, 4 young people's concerts, 16 school concerts, 40 to 50 concerts on tour, 8 pops concerts, 32 concerts for the Meadow Brook Festival (summer), an annual series at the Worcester (Massachusetts) Festival, and the following free concerts: 15 at the Michigan State Fair Grounds, 10 for the Belle Isle series, and 44 in-school concerts for the young. About 22 of its regular series concerts are broadcast on the radio for local audiences only. The orchestra operates on a budget of over $2 million. Recordings: *Mercury* (with Paul Paray, Ehrling's predecessor). The orchestra is one of America's most dynamic, exhibiting unusual capacity for growth and innovation. It enjoys wide community support, which it reciprocates by creating new ways to attract audiences of all kinds. Through its support organizations and officers, it uses modern advertising and promotional techniques to enhance the prestige and value of the orchestra for Detroiters. Its concert series are designed to be accessible to all, with various "packages," price discounts, etc. Thus, its Thursday subscription series is available complete as 22 concerts ("Royal" series) or as two different 11-concert segments ("Laureate" and "Constellation" series); its Saturday evening series of 18 concerts ("Elite" series), too, is segmented into two different portions ("Impresario" and "Sampler" series), and so on. There are four Friday morning (10:45 A.M.) "Coffee Concerts" (with a complimentary continental breakfast). The Saturday Young People's Concerts (which include, besides the orchestra, ballet groups, puppet theater, and multi-media productions) are available at two different times on the same day ("Early-bird" Series in the morning and "Lazybird" in the afternoon). In the spring, the Cabaret Pops concerts are offered at East Eight Mile Light Guard Armory, where eating and drinking is featured along with special programs of light music. In recent seasons eight members of the orchestra—six of them occupying first chair posts—performing a variety of instruments, have presented themselves at regular concerts as The Symphonic Metamorphoses, a group synthesizing rock music and the classics. The group has had its own commercial success through its recordings on *London* Records. In 1970, with a grant from the National Endowment, a Youth Orchestra was formed; its 119 players are under the direction of **Paul Freeman.** A recently formed Detroit Symphony Chamber Orchestra is led by **Pierre Hétu.** The orchestra will take part in the residency programs in select colleges, presently Western Michigan University and Williams College (Massachusetts). The orchestra's board chairman, **John B. Ford,** was responsible for creating the so-called Detroit Plan, a plan calling for the widest possible civic financial support, with representatives of the various support groups—business, labor, foundations, the city, etc.—taking part in the symphony management. This plan is one now in general use throughout the nation in one form or another. In 1971, the orchestra met qualifications for receiving a $1 million Ford Foundation matching grant. In 1972, the National Endowment extended a grant of $100,000 for various community concerts and school residency programs. . . . (FLINT) MUSICAL PERFORMING ARTS ASSOCIATION, 812 Citizens Bank Building, Flint, Michigan 48502. This group sponsors the Flint Symphony Orchestra, an Opera Society, and Ballet Society. Conductor: **William Byrd** (1966). Concertmaster: **Mary Kozak** (1967). Founded 1964. Players: 80. Auditorium: Whiting Auditorium (capacity: 2,000). Season: September to May, 12 concerts. . . . GRAND RAPIDS SYMPHONY SOCIETY, Exhibitors Building, Grand Rapids, Michigan 49502. Conductor: **Gregory Millar** (1968). Concertmaster: **Charles Avsharian** (1963). Founded 1928. Players: 75. Auditorium: Civic Auditorium (capacity: 4,495). Season: seven months, 10 concerts. . . . KALAMAZOO SYMPHONY SOCIETY, 426 South Park Street, Kalamazoo, Michigan 49007. Conductor: **Pierre Hétu** (1968). Concertmaster: **Voldemars Rushevics** (1950). Founded 1921. Players: 85 to 90. Auditorium: Kalamazoo Central High School Auditorium (capacity: 2,576). Season: 30 weeks, 14 concerts. Summer season: month of July, 4 concerts. Budget: $150,000. The orchestra gives two or three out-of-town concerts, one contemporary chamber orchestra concert, eight school concerts, 30 ensemble programs in schools, sponsors a Young Artist Competition, and has eight concerts annually broadcast over the local university station, WMUK–FM. . . . LANSING SYMPHONY ORCHESTRA, 113½ West Michigan Avenue, Lansing, Michigan 48933. Conductor: **A. Clyde Roller** (1967). Concertmaster: **Thomas LeVeck.** Founded 1950. Players: 70 to 80. Auditorium: Everett High School Auditorium (capacity: 1,128). Season: October to April, five concerts. The orchestra gives four free concerts yearly for the upper elementary grades. . . . SAGINAW SYMPHONY ORCHESTRA, 227 South Washington, Saginaw, Michigan 48607. Conductor: **Gideon Grau** (1965). Concertmaster: **Loren Cady.** Founded 1934. Players: 60. Auditorium: Saginaw Auditorium (capacity: 2,700). Season: eight months, eight concerts. Budget: $40,000. Tours are sponsored by the Michigan Arts Council.

Minnesota

DULUTH SYMPHONY ORCHESTRA, 704 Alworth Building, Duluth, Minnesota 55802. Conductor: **Joseph Hawthorne** (1967). Concertmistress: **Diane Spognardi Balko.** Founded 1932. Players: 85. Auditorium: Duluth Auditorium (capacity: 2,403). Season: seven months, twelve concerts. Budget: $135,000. The orchestra sponsors the Duluth Junior Symphony which gives three concerts annually. The Duluth Symphony also gives one or two concerts out of town. . . . MINNESOTA ORCHESTRA, 807 Hennepin Avenue, Minneapolis, Minnesota 55403. Founded 1903. Music Director and Conductor: **Stanislaw Skrowaczewski** (1960). Associate Conductor: **George Trautwein.** Assistant Conductor: **Henry Charles Smith.** Concertmaster: **Lea Foli.** Number of players: 93. Auditoriums: Northrop Auditorium (capacity: 4,822) and, in Saint Paul, the O'Shaughnessy Auditorium (capacity: 1,800) on the campus of the College of St. Catherine. Season: 48 weeks with a 39-week winter season. About 175 concerts are performed each year. In recent years the orchestra has expanded its activity greatly by giving itself a regional identification. In 1968 the orchestra changed its name from the Minneapolis Symphony to its present one, extending its area of responsibility to include not only Minneapolis, but also Saint Paul and other cities in Minnesota. In 1970 it began a Saint Paul series of concerts which duplicate exactly the series for Minneapolis. During the summer the orchestra presents free concerts in the twin-cities area under the sponsorship of local businessmen, agencies, and individuals (the so-called Symphony for the Cities Project) and performs many young people's concerts (annual attendance over 84,000). It broadcasts through an 18-station Upper Midwest network. Recordings (as both the Minneapolis and the Minnesota orchestra): *Mercury* (mostly under Antal Dorati), *Pickwick, Philips,* and *CRI* (reissue). The orchestra has performed in New York and in other major cities. At the time of its reorganization, the orchestra raised a $10 million endowment fund; it has also been granted funds for endowing 10 first chairs, each for $250,000, and the concertmaster chair for $500,000. In 1971, the orchestra qualified for a Ford Foundation matching grant of $2 million; in 1972, $125,000 of both National Endowment and private funds were received for special concerts of contemporary music and the engagement of new young artists. . . . SAINT PAUL CHAMBER ORCHESTRA, 30 East Tenth, Saint Paul, Minnesota 55101. Music Director: **Dennis Russell Davies** (1972). Concertmaster: **Eugene Altschuler.** Founded 1959 and conducted from that year until 1971 by **Leopold Sipe.** Players: 23. Auditoriums: Crawford Livingston Theatre Arts and Science Center (capacity: 650); Janet Wallace Fine Arts Center (capacity: 450); Tyrone Guthrie Center (capacity: 1,400). Season: October to May, 24 concerts. Budget: $310,000. Records for the Saint Paul Recording Company, which is owned by members of the orchestra. The orchestra tours for eight weeks a year, and sponsors a Summer Youth Symphony in the Twin Cities area and a Philharmonic Summer Music Center at Wisconsin State University, at River Falls. The orchestra is unique in many ways. It is a teaching unit for beginning string programs in Ramsey County and a teaching and performing unit for five colleges; its members form two string quartets and a woodwind quintet, which are maintained on a full-time basis. In 1972 it received a $25,000 matching grant from the National Endowment for its college residencies, its tours, etc. . . . SAINT PAUL POP CONCERT ORCHESTRA, 143 West 4th Street, Saint Paul, Minnesota 55102. Conductor: **Leo Kopp.** Assistant Conductor: **Max Metzger.** Concertmaster: **Eli Barnett.** Founded 1957. Players: 30. Auditorium: (capacity: 8,000). Season: six weeks in the summer.

Mississippi

JACKSON SYMPHONY ORCHESTRA, P.O. Box 4584, Fondren Station, Jackson, Mississippi 39216. Conductor: **Lewis Dalvit** (1965). Concertmaster: **Milton Ryan** (1967). Founded 1944. Players: 90. Auditorium: City Auditorium (capacity: 2,500). Season: September to April including a week with the Mississippi Arts Festival. Summer season: summer pops concerts in June. Budget: nearly $200,000. In 1967, the orchestra received a matching grant from the Mississippi State Arts Council to tour five universities and colleges. In April 1968, the orchestra opened a new auditorium in Jackson, for which it commissioned Paul Creston to write a piece for contralto and orchestra. Its 50 annual concerts include many that are free; among them are the so-called brown bag concerts, which are held during the noon lunch-hour in one of Jackson's downtown parks. The orchestra sponsors a junior symphony and three youth string orchestras and is active in developing community interest in teaching string instruments to the young. In 1972, the orchestra received a grant from the National Endowment for developing this string instruction program, as well as for string quartet concerts, etc.

Missouri

INDEPENDENCE SYMPHONY ORCHESTRA, P.O. Box 103, Independence, Missouri 64051. Conductor: **Franklyn S. Weddle** (1946). Associate Conductors: **M. O. Johnson, Harold Neal.** Concertmaster: **Dorothy Rendina,** (1967). Founded 1946. Players: 65 to 70. Auditoriums: R.L.D.S. Auditorium (capacity: 5,800); William Chrisman High School Auditorium (capacity: 1,200). Season: September to May, five concerts. Budget: $20,000. . . . KANSAS CITY PHILHARMONIC ASSOCIATION, 210 West 10th Street, Kansas City, Missouri 64105. Founded 1933. Players: 90. Following the resignation of **Hans Schweiger,** who led the orchestra from 1948 to 1971, **Jorge Mester** was appointed Artistic Advisor (1971) and **John Covelli,** resident conductor (1971). Associate Conductor is **Charles Schneider.** Concertmaster: **Alfred Schencker.** Auditorium: Music Hall (capacity: 2,572). Performs a 30-week season of over 135 concerts. Budget: $850,000. Recordings: *Urania.* Received in 1972 a National Endowment grant of $75,000 for expanding its main concert series and concerts in other city locations plus a special series for outlying locations. . . . PHILHARMONIC SOCIETY OF SAINT LOUIS, P.O. Box 591, Saint Louis, Missouri 63188. Conductor: **Rudolf Alexis Hauser.** Founded 1860. Concertmaster: **Louisa**

Kellam. Players: 95. Auditorium: Kiel Auditorium (capacity: 3,500). Season: October to April, four concerts. Budget: $15,000. . . . SAINT JOSEPH SYMPHONY ORCHESTRA, 510 Francis Street, Saint Joseph, Missouri 64501. Conductor: **Russell T. Waite.** Concertmaster: **Louis Riemer** (1959). Founded 1959. Players: 65. Auditorium: Missouri Theatre (capacity: 1,200). Season: four subscription concerts, two pairs of children's concerts, one pops concert. The orchestra sponsors a youth symphony. . . . ST. LOUIS SYMPHONY ORCHESTRA, 718 North Grand Boulevard, St. Louis, Missouri 63103. Founded 1880. Music Director and Conductor: **Walter Susskind** (1968). Associate Conductor: **Leonard Slatkin** (1971). Players: 95. Auditorium: Powell Symphony Hall (capacity: 2,689). The orchestra plays a season of over 200 concerts which, in addition to its regular 47 weeks in the winter (24 subscription pairs of concerts, etc.), includes a nine-week summer season, part of which is for the Mississippi River Festival (see Festivals). Recent years have seen the role of the orchestra (like many others in the nation) grow from that of primarily a performing ensemble for subscribers to that of a cultural service organization also. In 1970, it participated in the so-called Missouri Project, which called for the sponsorship of a major orchestra by a community one. While in the community, the major orchestra (the St. Louis Symphony and the Kansas City Philharmonic both took part in the project) would perform but also would provide its services for teaching and coaching young musicians, local professionals, etc. The orchestra also has received from the City of St. Louis a sum of $50,000 for special convention concerts as a means of helping to build the city's image and to attract more conventions to the city. In 1970, the Symphony formed its first Youth Orchestra (125 members), consisting of musicians 12 to 21 years old; the orchestra is under the direction of **Leonard Slatkin** and is sponsored by the Women's Association of the Symphony. With a grant from the Martha Rockefeller Baird Fund for Music and the National Endowment, the orchestra sponsored the American Institute of Orchestra Conducting in 1970. This effort permitted eight young conductors to study under four major conductors including **Walter Susskind** and **Leonard Slatkin.** In 1972, the organization received from the National Endowment $100,000 in matching funds (and an equal amount from private sources), to expand its Mississippi River Festival. In 1971, the orchestra met its matching fund requirements for receiving a $2 million grant from the Ford Foundation. The orchestra's recordings are under the *Pickwick* and *Odyssey* labels (with earlier conductors Golschmann and Van Remoortel). . . . SPRINGFIELD SYMPHONY ORCHESTRA, 227 East Sunshine, Springfield, Missouri 65804. Conductor: **Charles R. Hall.** Founded 1934. Players: 75. Ten concerts annually in Central High School Auditorium (capacity: 1,480).

Nebraska

LINCOLN SYMPHONY ORCHESTRA, P.O. Box 1455, Lincoln, Nebraska 68502. Conductor: **Leo Kopp** (1942). Assistant Conductor: **Jack Snider.** Concertmaster: **Arnold Schatz** (1961). Auditorium: Stuart Theater (capacity: 1,858). Season: six months, eight concerts. . . . OMAHA SYMPHONY ORCHESTRA, 3929 Harney Street, Omaha, Nebraska 68132. Music Director and Conductor: **Yuri Krasnapolsky** (1971). Assistant Conductor: **Paul W. Whear.** Concertmaster: **Myron Cohen** (1949). Founded 1923. Players: 100. Auditorium: Joslyn Art Museum Concert Hall (capacity: 1,169). Season: seven months, 12 concerts. Summer season: seven weeks, seven concerts. Budget: $200,000. In addition to its regular concerts, the orchestra gives 6 to 9 concerts on tour in the Midwest, 2 one-hour television broadcasts, 24 chamber music concerts, 14 youth concerts, and 6 free public concerts. Received a $400,000 matching grant from the Ford Foundation in 1971.

New Jersey

ELIZABETH CIVIC ORCHESTRA, Jefferson High School, 27 East Scott Place, Elizabeth, N.J. 07083. Conductor (and founder):

Herman Toplansky (1955). Concertmaster: **Frederick Zomzely** (1955). Founded 1955. Players: 40. Auditorium: Thomas Jefferson High School (capacity: 960). Season: October to May, three to four concerts, all free. This orchestra is associated with the Elizabeth School of Adult Education. It has obtained the cooperation of the local chapter of the American Federation of Musicians to supplement the regular orchestra membership when needed. . . . GREATER TRENTON SYMPHONY ASSOCIATION, 28 West State Street, R–1410, Trenton Trust Building, Trenton, N.J. 08608. Conductor: **William Smith.** Concertmaster: **John Pintavalle** (1966). Founded 1921. Players: 75 to 80. Auditorium: War Memorial Building (capacity: 1,926). Season: ten months, five concerts. The orchestra also sponsors two operas and two children's concerts. . . . THE LITTLE SYMPHONY OF NEWARK, c/o Newark Public Library, 5 Washington Street, Newark, N.J. 07101. Conductor: **Ira Kraemer** (1966). Assistant Conductor: **James Buchanan.** Concertmaster: **Max Robbins** (1966). Auditorium: Newark Public Library Auditorium (capacity: 300). Season: September to June, three or four concerts. Summer season: one or two concerts. . . . NEW JERSEY SYMPHONY ORCHESTRA, 1020 Broad Street, Newark, N.J. 07102. Conductor: **Henry Lewis** (1968). Concertmaster and Associate conductor: **Frank Scocozza** (1961). Founded 1929. Players: 80. Auditoriums: Symphony Hall, Newark (capacity: 3,365); Montclair High School (capacity: 1,500); Millburn High School (capacity: 1,032), etc. Regular season: seven months, 40 concerts. Summer season: three months, 23 concerts at Waterloo Village and the Garden State Arts Center. The orchestra plays many concerts throughout a wide area in New Jersey and has performed in New York. In 1971, it received a $500,000 matching grant from the Ford Foundation. . . . NORTH JERSEY PHILHARMONIC ORCHESTRA, Box 1545, Patterson, N.J. 07509. (Formerly, the Paterson Philharmonic.) Conductor: **Walter Schoeder** (1947). Concertmaster: **Frank Levy** (1947). Founded 1947. Players: 65. Auditoriums: various high school auditoriums in northern New Jersey (capacities: 800 to 1,200). Season: eight concerts. Summer season: sponsored by Music Performance Trust Fund, three concerts. Budget: about $20,000.

New Mexico

ALBUQUERQUE SYMPHONY ORCHESTRA, 3017 Monte Vista Boulevard, N.E., Albuquerque, New Mexico 87106. Conductor: **Yoshimi Takeda** (1970). Players: 90. Auditorium: Popejoy Concert Hall (capacity: 2,000). Eight regular concerts; four young people's concerts.

New York

ALBANY SYMPHONY ORCHESTRA, INC., Suite 26, Delaware and Hudson Building, Albany, N.Y. 12605. Conductor: **Julius Hegyi** (1966). Founded 1931. Players: 65. Auditorium: Palace Theatre (capacity: 2,800). Season: seven months, 18 concerts. Budget: $110,000. The orchestra presents concerts in several communities in the Albany metropolitan area: Troy, Gloversville, Cohoes, Saratoga, Schenectady, etc. . . . AMERICAN SYMPHONY ORCHESTRA, 200 West 57th Street, New York, N.Y. 10019. Music Director and Conductor: **Leopold Stokowski.** The orchestra was founded by **Leopold Stokowski** in 1962. In the words of the conductor, it was founded "to afford opportunity to highly gifted musicians, regardless of age, sex, or racial origin, and to offer concerts of great music within the means of everyone." Associate Conductor: **Ainslee Cox.** Assistant Conductors: **Matthias Bamert** and **Isaiah Jackson.** Players: 100. Auditoriums: Philharmonic Hall and Carnegie Hall (capacities: 2,874 and 2,836 respectively). Season: October to May with 16 pairs of subscription concerts; half of them in each of the two halls. Many of the orchestra's concerts are sponsored by foundations and business firms. Recordings: *Columbia, Victor, Decca,* and *CRI.* . . . BINGHAMTON SYMPHONY, 2 Bellevue Heights, Binghamton, N.Y. 13905. Conductor: **Fritz Wallenberg** (1954). Concertmaster: **Ralph Wade** (1954). Founded 1954. Players: 80 to 100. Auditorium: West Junior High School (capacity: 1,500). Season: eight months, five pairs of concerts. The Binghamton Symphony tours the state, and gives a five-concert series in Owego (Free Academy—900 seats) under the auspices of the New York State Arts Council. The Binghamton Symphony, and the smaller Binghamton Symphonette, comprised of members of the orchestra, gives many school concerts under Title III Federal Grant. . . . BROOKLYN PHILHARMONIA, Brooklyn Academy of Music, 30 Lafayette Avenue, Brooklyn, N.Y. 11217. Conductor: **Lukas Foss** (1970). Concertmaster: **Dino Pintavelli** (1967). Founded 1954 by **Siegfried Landau,** conductor until 1970. Auditorium: Brooklyn Academy of Music (capacity: 2,205). Season: six regular concerts, 13 youth concerts. Concerts are broadcast over radio station WNYC. The 1971–72 season presented special "marathon" concerts, featuring works by one composer in a lengthy program (four and a half hours) and enabling listeners to come and go at will. . . . BUFFALO PHILHARMONIC ORCHESTRA, Kleinhans Music Hall, 370 Pennsylvania Street, Buffalo, N.Y. 14201. Musical Director and Conductor: **Michael Tilson Thomas** (1971). Associate Conductor: **Melvin Strauss.** Concertmaster: **Charles V. Haupt.** Auditorium: Kleinhans Music Hall (capacity: 2,900). Season: 37 weeks, 36 regular subscription concerts. Budget: $1,000,000. In addition to the regular subscription concerts the orchestra gives 16 pops concerts, 18 "run-out" concerts, 48 youth concerts, 3 special holiday productions, 1 children's concert, 12 tour concerts, 1 local telecast, and 6 concerts in the American Music in the University Series, etc. In 1971 the orchestra qualified to receive a matching grant of $1 million from the Ford Foundation; in 1972, it received $73,850 from the National Endowment for concerts performed in factories, union halls, a children's series, etc. Recordings: *Nonesuch* (under **Lukas Foss**). . . . THE CLARION MUSIC SOCIETY, 415 Lexington Avenue, New York, N.Y. 10017. Conductor and founder: **Newell Jenkins** (1957). Concertmaster: **Gerald Tarack.** Founded 1957. Players: 27–33. Auditorium: Alice Tully Hall (capacity: 1,100). Season: October to April, six concerts. Recordings: *Decca* and *Vanguard.* Concerts are broadcast locally (WNYC) and over the Voice of America. The orchestra performs frequently at colleges outside of New York and toured Eastern Europe in 1964. "The Clarion Series" of eighteenth-century music, edited by Newell Jenkins, has been published by G. Schirmer, Inc. The orchestra's repertory is one of rare music from the past and new music, often in premiere performances. . . . ESTERHAZY ORCHESTRA, P.O. Box 47, Manhasset, N.Y. 11030. Conductor: **David Blum** (1961). Concertmaster: **Isidore Cohen** (1961). Founded 1961. Players: 25. Auditorium: Town Hall, New York (capacity: 1,500). Season: eight months, 40 concerts, including tour. *Vanguard* records. The orchestra has given premieres of many rarely heard Haydn symphonies, some of which have been recorded. The orchestra has toured the Eastern United States. . . . THE LITTLE ORCHESTRA SOCIETY, 1860 Broadway, New York, N.Y. 10023. Founder and Conductor: **Thomas Scherman** (1947). Assistant Conductor: **Simeon Sargon.** Concertmaster: **Peter Dimitriades** (1963). Founded 1947. Auditoriums: Philharmonic Hall, Alice Tully Hall (capacities: 2,800 and 1,100). Season: seven months, 24 concerts. The orchestra has introduced a great deal of rarely heard music. It has performed in New York nearly 200 works never before heard there, many of them world premieres. Its Concerts for Young People have been heard by more than 400,000 young listeners since they began in 1948. Recordings: *Decca.* . . . THE MASTER VIRTUOSI OF NEW YORK, 157 West 57th Street, New York, N.Y. 10019. Conductor: **Gene Forrell** (1964). Concertmaster: **Isidore Cohen.** Founded 1964. Players: 38. Auditorium: Philharmonic Hall (capacity: 2,800). Season: October to April, five concerts. . . . MOZART FESTIVAL ORCHESTRA, Box 1396, New York, N.Y. 10017. Conductor: **Baird Hastings** (1960). Concertmaster: **Harold Kohon** (1963). Founded 1960. Players: 25. Auditorium: Town Hall (capacity: 1,500). Season: two concerts. Occasional summer concerts. *Vocarium* Records. This group grew out of the Mozart Chamber Players, founded in 1957. It has performed the works of 100 composers encompassing four centuries and including many American premieres. . . . MUSIC FOR WESTCHESTER SYMPHONY, 200 Bloomingdale Road, (Box 35—Gedney Station), White Plains, N.Y. 10605. Conductor: **Siegfried Landau.** (1962). Founded 1962. Players: 80. Auditorium: Highlands School, White Plains (capacity: 1,300). Season: November to March, five concerts. Recordings: *Turnabout*. . . . NATIONAL ORCHESTRAL ASSOCIATION, 111 West 57th Street, New York, N.Y. 10019. Conductor: **Leon Barzin** Founded 1930. Players: 75. Auditorium: Carnegie Hall (capacity: 2,900). Season: October to May, three to four concerts. *Vanguard* and *CRI* Records. The National Orchestral Association is a training orchestra giving internship training to musicians to equip them for work with professional orchestras. In 1970 the orchestra added the training of young conductors to its program. . . . NEW YORK ORCHESTRAL SOCIETY (THE EARTH SYMPHONY), 40 West 67th Street, New York, N.Y. 10023. Conductor: **Joseph Eger** (1961). Assistant Conductor: **Robert Rudolf.** Concertmaster: **Dixie Blackstone** (1963). Auditoriums: Town Hall, Carnegie Hall; performances also in schools, parks, etc. Season: four to twelve concerts. The orchestra initiated the Harlem Music project. . . . NEW YORK PHILHARMONIC, Philharmonic Hall, Broadway and 65th Street, Lincoln Center, New York, N.Y. 10023. Founded 1842. Music Director and Conductor: **Pierre Boulez** (1971). Laureate Conductor: **Leonard Bernstein.** Assistant conductors change annually. Concertmaster: **Rafael Druian** (1971). Associate Concertmaster: **Frank Gullino** (1971). Players: 106. The orchestra is contracted for a 52-week year. Its subscription series runs from September to May, lasts 33 weeks, and engages about nine guest conductors. The 1971–72 season offered, in addition to the subscription series, four avant-garde "Prospective Encounters" (in locations other than Philharmonic Hall), two "retrospective series" (concerts devoted to certain composers only), two special informal evenings, four half-hour pre-concert recitals during the subscription series, two Saturday night concerts under **André Kostelanetz.** Its summer season includes free concerts in city parks (see under Music Festivals) and the Lincoln Center Promenade Concerts. During the season there are four Young People's Concerts televised nationally on network CBS-TV formerly with **Leonard Bernstein** but beginning with the 1972–73 season, with **Michael Tilson Thomas** as conductor and master of ceremonies. The orchestra tours regularly, both in the U.S. and overseas. Currently it has no radio broadcast outlet, having canceled in 1967 the radio series it had carried since 1922. Its recordings, under a variety of conductors, are on *Columbia* and *Odyssey* labels. The total number of available recordings make the New York Philharmonic one of the major recording orchestras of the world. The orchestra employs perhaps the only full-time salaried president of a symphony society in the nation. For its 1967–68 season, its 125th anniversary, the orchestra extended 18 commissions for new works—the largest number in its history—many going to some of the world's best known composers. Recent grants to the organization have come from the National Endowment ($100,000 for the orchestra's free parks concerts and a series devoted to contemporary music), $1 million in 1971 from the Ford Foundation's matching grant program, and, in 1970, the sum of $336,940 from the New York State Council on the Arts. . . . NIAGARA FALLS PHILHARMONIC ORCHESTRA, 653 Orchard Parkway, Niagara Falls, N.Y. 14301. Conductor: **Milton Barnes** (1966). Concertmaster: **Frances Hull** (1960). Founded 1941. Players: 65. Auditorium: La Salle Senior High School (capacity: 1,300). Season: eight concerts. . . . THE ORCHESTRA OF AMERICA, 119 West 57th Street, New York, N.Y. 10019. Conductor: **Richard Korn** (1958). Concertmaster: **Harry Glickman** (1963). Founded: 1958. Players: 90. Auditorium: Carnegie Hall (capacity: 2,900). Season: six months, six concerts. Summer season: six concerts in New York City parks. In addition performs as an accompanying orchestra at many oratorio and choral concerts. . . . ROCHESTER PHILHARMONIC, 60 Gibbs Street, Rochester, N.Y. 14604. Conductor: **David Zinman**

(1973). Concertmaster: **Howard Weiss** (1967). Founded 1923. Players: 85. Auditorium: Eastman Theatre (capacity: 3,352). Season: 36 weeks, 90 concerts. Budget: $1,088,000. Records: *Everest, CRI.* In addition to its regular concerts, the orchestra performs concerts on educational television, high school concerts, pops concerts, and a Mozart series; participates in ballet and opera performances; and tours throughout New York State, etc. In 1972 a grant of $100,000 was made to the orchestra by the National Endowment to expand its television program "Shape of Music" and its service to colleges and universities. It earned a $1 million Ford Foundation matching grant in 1971. . . . SCHENECTADY SYMPHONY ORCHESTRA, 1113 Chrisler Avenue, Schenectady, N.Y. 12306. Conductor: **Anthony J. Pezzono** (1964). Assistant Conductors: **Edward Sprenger** and **Harold Weaver.** Concertmaster: **Earle Hummel** (1966). Auditorium: Linton High School (capacity: 1,200). Season: seven concerts. . . . SYRACUSE SYMPHONY ORCHESTRA, 113 East Onandaga Street, Syracuse, New York, N.Y. 13202. Founded 1941. Musical Director and Conductor: **Frederik Prausnitz** (1971). Associate Conductor: **Calvin Custer.** Players: 80. Auditorium: Henninger High School Auditorium (capacity: 1,046). The orchestra offers a variety of musical services over a wide region within the State of New York and often subdivides into smaller playing units for this purpose (wind quintet, string quartet, a sinfonietta, pops orchestra, etc.). These services include college residency programs of two days or more with lectures and workshops, as well as full orchestral concerts with soloists. As a result, the orchestra performs about 300 times a season (eight months long) and travels about 5,000 miles, performing either as a full ensemble or as smaller groups which are deployed often in several different communities in one day. The regular subscription series in Syracuse consists of ten pairs of concerts. The orchestra has received grants from the New York State Council on the Arts (in one season its grant was the highest per capita given any organization), the National Endowment ($20,000 in 1972 for its varied services), and, from the Ford Foundation, $750,000 in matching grants. . . . PHILHARMONIC SYMPHONY OF WESTCHESTER, 8 East Prospect Avenue, Mount Vernon, N.Y. 10550. Conductor: **Martin Rich.** Auditorium: Wood Auditorium (capacity: 1,879). Serves Mount Vernon. . . . UTICA SYMPHONY ORCHESTRA, 261 Genesee Street, Utica, N.Y. 13501. Conductor: **Thomas Michalak.** Assistant Conductor: **Murray Bernthal.** Concertmaster: **Anthony Milograno.** Auditorium: Stanley Theater (capacity: 3,000). Season: October to May, 12 concerts. Budget: $60,000.

North Carolina

CHARLOTTE SYMPHONY ORCHESTRA, 519 Fenton Place, Charlotte, North Carolina 28207. Founded 1931. Conductor: **Jacques Brourman** (1967). Concertmaster: **Elaine Richey** (1964). Auditorium: Ovens Auditorium (capacity: 2,512). Season: eight months, five concerts in Charlotte, five concerts out of town. The orchestra also gives 24 children's concerts, and sponsors an 85-member Youth Orchestra. . . . GREENSBORO SYMPHONY ORCHESTRA, 808 North Elm Street, Greensboro, North Carolina 27401. Conductor: **Sheldon Morgenstern** (1967). Concertmaster: **Don Hansen** (1961). Founded 1960. Players: 70. Auditorium: Greensboro Memorial Auditorium (capacity: 2,500). Season: six months, five concerts. Budget: $40,000. . . . NORTH CAROLINA SYMPHONY ORCHESTRA, Bingham X, University of North Carolina, Chapel Hill, North Carolina 27514. Founded 1932. Conductor: **John Gosling** (1972). Conductor Emeritus: **Benjamin Swalin.** Assistant Conductors: **Alfred Heller** and **Thomas Conlin.** Players: 65. This orchestra was the first state-sponsored symphony orchestra in the United States. In 1971, the orchestra received a Ford Foundation matching grant of $750,000; in 1972 the National Endowment granted $20,000 for continuing its public service program. . . . WINSTON–SALEM SYMPHONY ASSOCIATION, 610 Coliseum Drive, Winston-Salem, North Carolina 27106. Conductor: **John Iuele** (1955). Concertmaster: **Eugene Jacobowsky.** Founded 1957. Players: 70. Auditorium: Reynolds Auditorium (capacity: 2,000). Season: October to April, five concerts. Summer season: June and July, four concerts. Budget: $60,000.

North Dakota

FARGO-MOORHEAD SYMPHONY ORCHESTRAL ASSOCIATION, Box 1753, Fargo, North Dakota 58102. Conductor: **Sigvald Thompson** (1937). Concertmaster: **Isabelle Thompson** (1948). Founded 1931. Players: 70. Various auditoriums. Season: September to April, 24 concerts. Summer season: July, two to four concerts. Budget: $20,000. One recording issued under sponsorship of the Fargo Chamber of Commerce. The orchestra gives 5 regular concerts, 2 chamber concerts, 4 televised concerts, 3 children's concerts and 10 chamber concerts in schools annually. The orchestra has been playing in various halls since 1966, when its permanent home was destroyed by fire. Admission to all concerts is free.

Ohio

AKRON SYMPHONY ORCHESTRA, 572 West Market Street, Akron, Ohio 44303. Conductor: **Louis Lane** (1959). Assistant Conductor: **Vincent Frittelli.** Players: 80. Auditorium: Akron Civic Theatre (2,053). Season: October to May, seven concerts. . . . CINCINNATI SYMPHONY ORCHESTRA, 1313 Central Trust Tower, Cincinnati, Ohio 45202. Founded 1895. Musical Director and Conductor: **Thomas Schippers** (1970). Associate Conductor: **Erich Kunzel.** Assistant Conductor: **Carmon DeLeone.** Concertmaster: **Sigmund Effron** (1946). Players: 100. Auditorium: Music Hall (capacity: 3,718), a 100-year old structure renovated in 1970. Season: the orchestra is employed for a 52-week year; its regular season runs from September to May. Annually it performs nearly 300 concerts, making it the busiest American symphonic ensemble. Recordings: *Decca* and *CRI.* The orchestra is used for the Cincinnati Summer Opera productions and the Cincinnati May Festival (see Festivals for both). It performs a series of free open-air summer concerts with young winners of instrumental competitions; a summer pops concert series of three concerts each for twelve neighboring communities; with special funds from grants, the orchestra has given in-school concerts and special concerts for adults and young people in communities within a 75-mile radius of Cincinnati (a total of 13 concerts per community). In 1966, the orchestra made a 32,000-mile world tour under the auspices of the U.S. State Department (the first American orchestra to be so sponsored), giving some 43 concerts in fourteen nations in Europe, the Middle East, and the Orient. In 1969, it toured Europe and in 1971, made its first U.S. tour. It has received numerous grants from federal agencies, private funds, and foundations for various concert and orchestra community services. Six of the orchestra's chairs are endowed, each for $250,000 or more. In 1972, the National Endowment granted $100,000 in matching funds (the balance from private contributions) to provide an Area Artists series involving 146 concerts, an in-school series, and a program permitting young musicians to rehearse and perform with the orchestra. In 1971, the orchestra successfully met its requirement for a Ford Foundation grant of $2 million. . . . THE CLEVELAND ORCHESTRA, 11001 Euclid Avenue, Cleveland, Ohio 44106. Founded 1918. Music Director and Conductor: **Lorin Maazel** (1972). Principal guest conductor: **Pierre Boulez.** Resident Conductor: **Louis Lane.** Concertmaster: **Daniel Majeske** (1971). Players: 107. Auditorium: Severance Hall (capacity 1,980) for winter season. The orchestra also plays a summer season at the Blossom Music Center (see Music Festivals). The orchestra is contracted for a 52-week year: 38 weeks for its regular season and 14 for the summer. It performs about 230 concerts a year including the subscription series, from September to May, and such concerts as are played on tour (some 28 days each season), the summer series at Blossom, various educational concerts, etc. For its 1971–72 season (which may not be typical) 13 guest conductors—all of major rank—were engaged to conduct the subscription series. The orchestra has its own chorus, under the direction of **Robert Page.** Recordings: *Columbia* and *Angel* (under Szell and **Boulez**). Performances of the orchestra are broadcast nationally over select stations. It has toured both within the U.S. and overseas. In 1971 it met its fund-raising obligations for receiving a $1 million Ford Foundation matching grant. A National Endowment grant in 1972 of $100,000 (plus a matching sum raised privately) was used for continuing the orchestra's program of low-priced family concerts and free children's concerts in both Severance Hall and at the Blossom Center. . . . COLUMBUS SYMPHONY ORCHESTRA, 100 East Broad Street, Columbus Ohio 43215. Conductor: **Evan Whallon** (1956). Assistant Conductor and Concertmaster: **George Hardesty** (1953). Founded 1951. Players: 85. Auditorium: Ohio Theatre (capacity: 3,079). Season: October to April, 50 concerts. Budget: $300,000. In 1972, the orchestra received from the National Endowment a grant of $14,000 to expand in-school concerts and to present a special performance of Mahler's Eighth Symphony with Ohio University choruses. In 1971, it qualified for a Ford Foundation matching grant of $600,000. . . . DAYTON PHILHARMONIC ORCHESTRA ASSOCIATION, Sheraton-Dayton Hotel, Dayton, Ohio 45402. Conductor: **Paul Katz** (1933). Concertmaster: **Jaroslav Holesovsky.** Founded 1933. Players: 85. Auditorium: Memorial Hall (capacity: 2,500). Season: October to April, seven regular concerts. Summer season: June and July, five concerts. Recordings: *National Audubon Society, Coronet Recordings* (Dayton, Ohio). The orchestra gives 16 children's concerts and 2 concerts for elementary grades annually (annual audience: 45,000). Regular concerts are broadcast locally. . . . SPRINGFIELD SYMPHONY ORCHESTRA, Box 1374, Springfield, Ohio 45501. Conductor: **John E. Ferritto.** Concertmaster: **John Smarelli.** Founded 1943. Players: 80. Auditorium: Memorial Hall (capacity: 1,700). Season: five subscription concerts; four student concerts; Summer Arts Festival of two concerts. Budget: $50,000. . . . TOLEDO ORCHESTRA, 1 Stranahan Square, Toledo, Ohio 43604. Conductor: **Serge Fournier** (1964). Concertmaster: **Charles Everett.** Players: 80. Auditorium: Peristyle-Toledo Museum of Art (capacity: 1,752). Season: October to May, eight pairs of concerts. Recent grants to the orchestra have been: $500,000 Ford Foundation matching grant (1971) and a $25,000 grant from the National Endowment for a concert series in black neighborhoods and the expansion of young people's concerts. . . . YOUNGSTOWN SYMPHONY ORCHESTRA, 260 West Federal Street, Youngstown, Ohio 44503. Conductor: **Franz Bibo** (1967). Concertmaster: **Ivan Romanenko.** Auditorium: Stambaugh Auditorium (capacity: 2,700). Season: seven months, seven concerts; however, its total number of concerts exceed those of the regular season. The orchestra is sponsored by the Youngstown Symphony Society, which also sponsors a Ballet Guild, Philharmonic Chorus, Junior Symphony Orchestra, etc.

Oklahoma

OKLAHOMA CITY SYMPHONY ORCHESTRA, Civic Center Music Hall, Oklahoma City, Oklahoma 73102. Conductor: **Guy Fraser Harrison** (1951). Associate Conductor: **Ray Luke.** Concertmaster: **Kenji Kobayashi** (1967). Founded 1938. Players: 76. Auditorium: Civic Center Music Hall (capacity: 3,200). Season: 25 weeks, 100 concerts. Budget: $400,000. Outside grants to the orchestra have come from the National Endowment ($20,000 in 1972 for continuation of its school and young people's concerts) and the Ford Foundation ($600,000 in matching funds under the 1971 program). . . . TULSA PHILHARMONIC SOCIETY, Dowell Building, 1579 East 21st Street, Tulsa, Oklahoma 74144. Conductor: **Skitch Henderson** (1971). Assistant Conductor: **Dwight M. Dailey.** Concertmaster: **Francis E. Jones** (1953). Auditorium: Tulsa Municipal Theater (capacity: 2,800). Season: six months, 20 concerts. Summer season: 10 pops concerts. Budget: $270,000. The orchestra gives three concerts on tour annually (within a 200-mile radius), and two series of young people's concerts (included in the 20-concert figure). The orchestra met the 1971 qualifications for receiving a Ford Foundation matching grant of $500,000.

Oregon

OREGON SYMPHONY ORCHESTRA, 426 Park Building, Portland, Oregon 97205. (Formerly the Portland Symphony Orchestra.) Conductor: **Jacques Singer** (1962). Concertmaster: **Hugh Ewart** (1948). Founded 1911. Auditorium: Civic Auditorium (capacity: 2,990). Season: 25 weeks, 50 concerts. Budget: $365,000. The orchestra plays about 20 tour concerts annually. A National Endowment grant of $10,000 went to the orchestra in 1972 in support of its in-school concerts for high school students. In 1971, the orchestra met the fund-raising qualifications for receiving a $1 million Ford Foundation matching grant. . . . PORTLAND JUNIOR SYMPHONY ORCHESTRA, 617 Park Building, Portland, Oregon 97205. Conductor: **Jacob Avshalomov** (1954). Associate Conductor: **James Eoff.** Concertmaster: **Robin O'Brien.** Founded 1924. Players: 104. Auditorium: Portland Civic Auditorium (capacity: 2,900). Season: nine months, seven concerts. *CRI* records. In addition to its regular concerts the orchestra gives yearly several concerts out of town and two in local high schools. Its recordings are of pieces commissioned by the orchestra under a Rockefeller Foundation grant. The orchestra made its first European tour in 1970 and played in New York that same year.

Pennsylvania

ALLENTOWN SYMPHONY, Symphony Hall, 23 North Sixth Street, Allentown, Pennsylvania 18801. Founded 1951. Conductor: **Donald Voorhees** (1951). Assistant Conductors: **Donald P. Bryan, Henry G. Nebert.** Auditorium: Symphony Hall (capacity: 1,456). Season: Seven concerts. Summer season: two concerts. . . . ERIE PHILHARMONIC SOCIETY, 720 G. Daniel Baldwin Building, Erie, Pennsylvania 16501. Conductor: **John Gosling** (1967). Assistant Conductor: **Herbert Harp.** Concertmaster: **Ruthabeth Marsh** (1966). Founded 1930. Players: 75. Auditorium: Memorial Auditorium (capacity: 1,140). Season: October to April, six pairs of concerts. . . . HARRISBURG SYMPHONY ORCHESTRA, Room 506, Telegraph Building, 216 Locust Street, Harrisburg, Pennsylvania 17101. Conductor: **Edwin McArthur** (1950). Founded 1931. Players: 85 to 90. Auditorium: The Forum (capacity: 1,800). Season: five concerts. . . . THE PHILADELPHIA ORCHESTRA, 230 South 15th Street, Philadelphia, Pennsylvania 19102. Founded 1900. Musical Director and Conductor: **Eugene Ormandy** (1936). Assistant Conductor: **William Smith.** Concertmaster: **Norman Carol** (1966). Players: 105. Auditorium: Academy of Music (capacity: 2,929). The orchestra is contracted for a 52-week year and plays approximately 194 concerts annually. The subscription series runs from September to May. The orchestra has a maximum of six weeks of touring plus one week spent in Ann Arbor for the May Festival (see Music Festivals). Its summer season consists of performance series at Saratoga, New York and its Philadelphia Robin Hood Dell concerts (see Music Festivals for both series). The orchestra has for many years performed a series in New York and has toured overseas. Many of its performances are broadcast through selected stations. It is the most recorded orchestra in America, having made recordings early in the history of the industry. Labels: *RCA Victor* (present contract) and *Columbia.* Grants to the orchestra in recent years have come from the Ford Foundation (a matching grant of $2 million in 1971) and the National Endowment ($100,000), the latter for the expenses incurred in preparing youth concerts, etc. . . . PITTSBURGH SYMPHONY ORCHESTRA, 600 Pennsylvania Avenue, Pittsburgh, Pennsylvania 15222. Founded 1927. Musical Director and Conductor: **William Steinberg** (1952). Associate Conductor: **Donald Johanos** (1970). Concertmaster: **Fritz Siegal** (1966). Players: 100. Auditorium: Heinz Hall for the Performing Arts (capacity: 2,729). Season: 48 weeks totaling about 225 concerts. These include a regular winter subscription series, pops concerts in the summer, a New York series, and the in-resident series at the Temple University Music Festival and Institute (see Music Festivals) during the summer. The orchestra has toured (contract at present permits some 64 touring days): in 1964, the orchestra made a fourteen-nation tour of Europe and the Middle East (under the sponsorship of the State Department), and in 1968, it toured cities between Pittsburgh and the West Coast. Recordings: *Command, Capitol, Everest, Angel,* and *Pickwick.* It is the recipient of a Ford Foundation matching grant of $2 million and recently (1972) received from the National Endowment $100,000 in matching funds (the matching balance to come from private sources) for expanding its Temple University work, establishing a residency program at two colleges, and organizing performances in eight communities. . . . READING SYMPHONY ORCHESTRA, 219 North Fifth Street, Reading, Pennsylvania 19601. Conductor: **Louis Vyner** (1961). Founded 1912. Players: 80. Auditorium: Rajah Theater (capacity: 2,160). Season: October to April, five concerts. Budget: $35,000. . . . SCRANTON PHILHARMONIC ORCHESTRA, Chamber of Commerce Building, Scranton, Pennsylvania 18503. Conductor: **Beatrice Brown** (1962). Concertmistress: **Irene Palasyewskj** (1965). Founded 1937. Players: 70. Auditorium: Masonic Temple (capacity: 1,823). Season: October to May, eight concerts. Budget: $30,000.

Rhode Island

RHODE ISLAND PHILHARMONIC ORCHESTRA, 39 The Arcade, Providence, Rhode Island 02903. Founded 1945. Conductor: **Francis Madeira** (1945). Associate Conductor: **Jeff Cook.** Concertmaster: **Joseph Conte.** Auditorium: Veterans Memorial Auditorium (capacity: 2,200). Season: 8 series concerts, 16 children's concerts, 8 high school concerts, 4 junior high school concerts, 3 pops concerts, 3 family concerts, 4 contract concerts, 80 small ensemble programs. Budget: $217,000. The orchestra sponsors two Rhode Island Youth Orchestras. It has been the recipient of a Ford Foundation matching grant of $350,000 and a National Endowment grant of $25,000, the latter for continuing educational projects.

South Carolina

COLUMBIA PHILHARMONIC ORCHESTRA, 1527 Senate Street, Columbia, South Carolina 29201. Conductor: **Arthur M. Fraser** (1965). Concertmaster: **John A. Bauer** (1965). Founded 1965. Players: 58. Auditorium: Dreher High School Auditorium (capacity: 1,176). Season: six months, four concerts. Budget: $24,000.

Tennessee

CHATTANOOGA SYMPHONY ASSOCIATION, 730 Cherry Street, Chattanooga, Tennessee 37402. Conductor: **Richard Cormier** (1968). Concertmaster: **Ross Shub.** Founded 1935. Players: 75. Auditorium: Tivoli Theater (capacity: 1,788). Season: seven months, 18 concerts. Regular concerts are re-broadcast on Sunday following the concert. The Association sponsors a 55-member youth orchestra, which gives three concerts annually. The Symphony plays youth concerts to an estimated 32,000 children a year. To expand its educational concerts (in colleges and at neighborhood centers) the orchestra received a National Endowment grant of $100,000 in 1972. The orchestra's annual budget is $125,000. . . . KNOXVILLE SYMPHONY ORCHESTRA, Arcade Building, 618 Gay Street, Knoxville, Tennessee 37902. Conductor: **David Van Vactor** (1947). Players: 75. Auditorium: Knoxville Civic Auditorium (capacity: 2,534). Recordings: *CRI.* . . . MEMPHIS ORCHESTRAL SOCIETY (MEMPHIS SYMPHONY ORCHESTRA), P.O. Box 4682, 60 South Auburndale, Memphis, Tennessee 38104. Conductor: **Vincent de Frank** (1952). Associate Conductor: **Peter Loran Spurbeck** (1968). Concertmistress: **Joy Brown Wiener** (1952). Founded 1952 as the Memphis Sinfonietta. Players: 75. Auditorium: Auditorium Music Hall (capacity: 1,900). Season: October to April, six pairs of concerts. In addition, the orchestra gives three or four pops concerts and ten young people's concerts. The orchestra has a "Little Symphony" of 16 players for 25 informal school concerts during the year, and also supports a Youth Orchestra (founded in 1966) of 70 players. In 1971 the orchestra met the requirements for receiving a $400,000 matching grant from the Ford Foundation. Among the guest conductors for the orchestra has been **Pablo Casals**. . . . NASHVILLE SYMPHONY ORCHESTRA, 1805 West End Avenue, Nashville, Tennessee 37203. Conductor: **Thor Johnson** (1967). Assistant Conductor: **Harold Cruthirds.** Concertmaster: **Samuel Terranova.** Founded 1946. Players: 75. Auditorium: War Memorial Auditorium (capacity: 2,100). Season: 36 weeks, 55 concerts. Budget: $350,000. *Dot* Records. The orchestra sponsors the Nashville Little Symphony of 20 players, which tours extensively in Middle Tennessee and plays a series in Nashville and the surrounding area; it has also taped two programs for educational television (WDCN). The Nashville Symphony was the recipient of a $500,000 Ford Foundation matching grant in 1971 and has received a grant from the National Endowment.

Texas

ABILENE PHILHARMONIC ASSOCIATION, 310 North Willis, Abilene, Texas 79603. Conductor: **George Yaeger** (1966). Concertmaster: **Lino Bartoli.** Founded 1947. Players: 75. Auditorium: Abilene Civic Center (capacity: 2,162). Season: seven months, seven subscription concerts, eight youth concerts. . . . AMARILLO SYMPHONY, P.O. Box 2552, Amarillo, Texas 79105. Conductor: **Thomas Hohstadt** (1963). Assistant Conductor: **George Bledsoe.** Concertmaster: **Donald Todd** (1968). Founded 1924. Players: 85 to 100. Auditorium: Amarillo Civic Center (capacity: 2,400). Season: seven months, 20 concerts. Summer season: one month, 4 concerts. Budget: $100,000. Three recordings on orchestra's own label. Concerts are broadcast world wide on the Voice of America. The orchestra has an extensive youth program, with concerts and demonstrations in schools, a program of student symphony soloists, and sponsorship of scholarships at Amarillo College and West Texas State University. . . . AUSTIN SYMPHONY ORCHESTRA, 908-G West 12th Street, Austin, Texas 78703. Founded 1937. Conductor: **Maurice Peress** (1970). Assistant Conductor and Concertmaster: **Leopold La Fosse** (1958). Auditorium: Municipal Auditorium (capacity: 2,938). Season: October to April, 12 concerts. . . . BEAUMONT SYMPHONY SOCIETY: 321 Goodhue Building, Beaumont, Texas 77701. Conductor: **Joseph B. Carlucci** (1971). Concertmistress: **Barbara Meeker** (1965). Founded: 1952. Players: 50. Auditorium: Beaumont City Auditorium (capacity: 2,300). Season: six concerts. . . . CORPUS CHRISTI SYMPHONY, Box 495, Corpus Christi, Texas 78403. Founded 1945. Music Director and Conductor: **Maurice Peress** (1962). Players: 73. Season: 8 regular concerts and 11 children's concerts. Has received grants from the National Endowment for the development of audiences and for free public concerts. . . . DALLAS SYMPHONY ORCHESTRA, P.O. Box 8472, Dallas, Texas 75205. Music Director and Conductor: **Anshel Brusilow** (1970). Associate Conductor: **Earl Bernard Murray** (1971). Concertmaster: **Phillip Ruder.** Founded 1900. Players: 92. Auditorium: McFarlin Auditorium of Southern Methodist University (capacity: 2,400). Season: 35 weeks, 125 concerts. Budget: $1,000,000. *RCA* and *Turnabout* records (under previous conductors). Recent grants to the orchestra include the Ford Foundation matching grant of $2 million and the National Endowment grant in 1972 of $100,000 for youth and adult concerts within a 125-mile radius of Dallas and other educational services. . . . EL PASO SYMPHONY ORCHESTRA, 1401 Montana Avenue, El Paso, Texas 79902. Founded 1931. Conductor: **William Kirschke** (1971). Concertmaster: **Laurence A. Gibson.** Auditorium: Liberty Hall (capacity: 2,400). Season (regular subscription series): seven months, eight concerts. Summer season: five concerts. Other concerts include those for young people, out of town concerts, etc. A grant of $10,000 has been received from the National Endowment for strengthening these additional concerts plus those for ghetto areas, in-school concerts, etc. . . . FORT WORTH SYMPHONY ORCHESTRA, 3505 West Lancaster, Fort Worth, Texas 76107. Conductor: **Ralph R. Guenther.** Concertmaster: **Kenneth Schanewerk** (1957). Founded 1957. Auditorium: Tarrant County Convention Center (capacity: 3,066). Season: eight subscription concerts plus young people's concerts. . . . HOUSTON SYMPHONY ORCHESTRA, Jesse H. Jones Hall for the Performing Arts, 615 Louisiana, Houston, Texas 77002. Founded 1913. Musical Director and Conductor: **Lawrence Foster** (1971). Associate Conductor: **A. Clyde Roller.** Concertmaster: **Ronald Patterson** (1972). Players: 90 (or more as needed). Auditorium: Jesse H. Jones Hall for the Performing Arts (capacity: 3,001). Season: 41 weeks (35 for regular season and 6 for the summer season). This includes 18 pairs of subscription concerts, 18 student concerts, 3 concerts sponsored by the *Houston Chronicle,* a New Year's Eve special concert, a three-week tour, 8 regional concerts, 18 summer concerts, etc. The orchestra is used for some 25 performances of the Houston Grand Opera Company. Twenty-four of its concerts are broadcast over station KTRH. In 1963, the orchestra was taken on its first tour of the Eastern Seaboard cities, becoming the first orchestra from its region to perform in such cities as New York and Washington. It toured again in 1968 and subsequent years. The orchestra has recorded under previous conductors (**Stokowski** most recently) for *Everest, Seraphim, Capitol,* and *Golden Crest.* Its budget is over $1.2 million. In 1971 it completed its requirements for receiving a Ford Foundation grant of $2 million. . . . LUBBOCK SYMPHONY ORCHESTRA, 1416 Avenue Q, Lubbock, Texas 79401. Conductor: **William Harrod** (1946). Concertmaster and Assistant Conductor: **Mitchell J. Zablotny** (1950). Founded 1946. Players: 92. Auditorium: Municipal Auditorium (capacity: 3,000). Season: six months, five concerts. . . . MIDLAND–ODESSA SYMPHONY ORCHESTRA AND CHORALE, P.O. Box 6266, Terminal Station, Midland, Texas 79701. Conductor: **Phillip Spurgeon** (1971). Concertmaster: **James Gambino.** Founded: 1952. Players: 80. Auditorium: Bonham Junior High School and Lee High School Auditorium (capacity: 1,500 seats). Season: September to May, 10 concerts. Budget: over $100,000. The orchestra sponsors an annual young artists competition, the winners performing at one pair of concerts during the season. . . . SYMPHONY SOCIETY OF SAN ANTONIO, 600 Hemisfair Plaza Way, Suite 102, San Antonio, Texas 78205. Conductor: **Victor Alessandro** (1952). Assistant Conductor: **Harvey Garber.** Concertmaster: **John Corigliano** (1966). Founded 1939. Players: 92. Auditoriums: Theater for the Performing Arts (capacity: 2,800); Laurie Hall, Trinity University (2,750). Season: 34 weeks, 250 concerts. Budget: $1,000,000. *Mercury* and *Philips* Records. The orchestra participates in the San Antonio Grand Opera season, in a total of 12 performances. In 1971, it successfully met its fund-raising requirements for receiving the $1 million Ford Foundation matching grant and in 1972, received from the National Endowment $100,000 for expanded public service activities. . . . WICHITA FALLS SYMPHONY ORCHESTRA, 702 Hamilton Building, Wichita Falls, Texas 76301. Conductor: **William H. Boyer** (1964). Concertmaster: **Sheldon Goldsholl** Founded 1948. Players: 65. Auditorium: Memorial Auditorium, 2,718 seats. Season: six months, eleven concerts. Budget: $55,000.

Utah

UTAH SYMPHONY ORCHESTRA, 55 West First Street South, Salt Lake City, Utah 84101. Founded 1939. Conductor: **Maurice Abravanel** (1947). Associate Conductor: **Ardean Watts.** Players: 85. Auditorium: Salt Lake Mormon Tabernacle (capacity: 4,772). Season: 170 concerts. The orchestra is one of the few major ones in the U.S. enjoying extensive recording activity. It records on *Vanguard, Westminster, Bach Guild,* and *Music Guild* labels. In 1971, the orchestra undertook a tour of South and Central America, beginning first with appearances in Washington, New York, and the Carribbean. During its five-week trip it performed over 25 concerts. Among the grants recently received by the orchestra were the following: a 1970 grant from the National Endowment for a 36-day regional tour including concerts on Indian reservations; a Ford Foundation matching grant of $1 million effective in 1971.

Vermont

VERMONT STATE SYMPHONY ORCHESTRA, Box 548, Middlebury, Vermont 05753. Conductor: **Alan Carter** (1935). Assistant Conductor: **Anthony Pezzano.** Concertmaster: **Alvin Rogers** (1972). Founded 1935. Players: 60. Auditoriums: 18 different halls throughout the state (capacity: 700 to 1,500). Season: six months, 19 concerts. Summer season: one month, 2 concerts. Concerts are broadcast by 16 radio stations; three are televised during the season. Has made a recording on *Century* label.

Virginia

ALEXANDRIA SYMPHONY ORCHESTRA, P.O. Box 359, Alexandria, Virginia 22313. Conductor: **George Steiner** (1966). Concertmistress: **Mary Young.** Players: 65. Auditorium: T. C. Williams Auditorium (capacity: 1,400). Season: six concerts. . . . NORFOLK SYMPHONY ORCHESTRA, 302 Allard Building, 102 West Olney Road, Norfolk, Virginia 23510. Conductor: **Russell Stanger** (1966). Concertmistress: **Dora Short** (1966). Founded 1921. Players: 85. Auditorium: Chrysler Hall (capacity: 2,500). Season: November to April; 25 or 30 concerts. Summer season: 3 concerts. Budget: $145,000. . . . PENINSULA SYMPHONY ORCHESTRA, Box 437, Newport News, Virginia 23607. Conductor: **Cary McMurran** (1947). Concertmaster: **Ronald W. Marshall** (1968). Date founded: 1947. Players: 55 to 60. Auditorium: Newport News High School Auditorium (capacity: 1,400). Season: six to eight months, four concerts. Summer season: one or two concerts. The orchestra has commissioned several works and given first performances. Additionally, it gives about ten youth concerts per season. . . . RICHMOND SYMPHONY INC., 112 East Franklin Street, Richmond, Virginia 23219. Conductor: **Jacques Houtmann** (1971). Concertmistress: **Elizabeth Moore.** Founded 1957. Players: 87. Auditorium: The Mosque (capacity: 3,767). Season: 32 weeks, 40 concerts. Budget: $200,000. Received a $500,000 Ford Foundation matching grant in 1971. . . . ROANOKE SYMPHONY ORCHESTRA, Saint John's Parish House, Elm Avenue, Southwest, Roanoke, Virginia 24009. Founder and Conductor: **Gibson Morrissey** (1952). Concertmaster: **Alfred Lanegger** (1960). Founded 1951. Players: 84. Auditorium: American Theater (capacity: 1,800). Season: September to April, 4 subscription and 12 student concerts. Budget: over $50,000. Tours locally, concerts broadcast locally (WLRJ–FM). Sponsors the 54-member Roanoke Youth Orchestra. . . . VIRGINIA STATE SYMPHONY ORCHESTRA, 2003 Hanover Avenue, Richmond, Virginia 23220. Conductor: **William Häcker.** Season: 50 concerts. Players: 45.

Washington

SEATTLE SYMPHONY ORCHESTRA, 305 Harrison Street, Seattle, Washington 98109. Founded 1903. Music Director and Conductor: **Milton Katims** (1954). Associate Conductor: **Joseph Levine.** Concertmaster: **Henry Siegl** (1956). Players: 90. Auditorium: Seattle Opera House (capacity: 3,100). Season: 34 weeks, 184 concerts. The season consists of 12 pairs of subscription concerts, 27 tour concerts in the West and Northwest, 3 pops concerts, 112 school concerts, 6 "Stars of the Future" concerts (young musicians' concerts), and 12 family concerts. The orchestra was one of the first to consider itself a community service cultural organization and in this regard undertook a number of novel approaches for expanding concert audiences and for clarifying the role of an orchestra in a community. It was the first to present "family concerts"—concerts taken to neighborhoods and smaller communities outside the city where whole families are invited to attend at special prices. It was also the first orchestra in the country to perform school concerts under Federal Title III grants (which later were continued through funding by the state legislature). During the 1971–72 season, the orchestra, management, and musicians, concluded a highly unusual work contract involving musician participation in some affairs of the orchestra, the subdivision of the orchestra into smaller playing units as needed, etc. A feature of the contract permitted a residency period in Alaska of one week, during which some 46 separate concerts were performed (in 1972) in eighteen cities, using the full orchestra for six concerts and the smaller ensembles for the remainder. The orchestra has recorded for the *Victor* label as well as its own label, the *Seattle Symphony Recording Society.* Budget: $1,210,000. The orchestra qualified in 1971 for its Ford Foundation matching grant of $1 million; in 1972 it received National Endowment funds for its school concerts. . . . SPOKANE SYMPHONY SOCIETY, 301 Great Western Building, Spokane, Washington 99201. Conductor: **Donald Thulean** (1967). Founded 1924. Players: 75. Auditorium: Fox Theater (capacity: 2,296). Season: September to May, 45 concerts. Budget: $175,000. . . . TACOMA SYMPHONY ORCHESTRA, P.O. Box 905, Temple Theatre, Tacoma, Washington 98401. Conductor: **Edward Seferian.** Players: 84. Auditorium: Temple Theatre (capacity: 1,650). Season: four yearly subscription concerts.

West Virginia

CHARLESTON SYMPHONY ORCHESTRA, INC., P.O. Box 2292, 1104 Quarrier Street. Charleston, West Virginia 25328; Conductor: **Charles Schiff** (1965). Concertmaster: **L. John Lambros** (1952). Founded 1939. Players: 70. Auditorium: Charleston Municipal Auditorium (capacity: 3,500). Season: six regular concerts, three children's concerts. Summer season: two concerts. Orchestra members also give string instruction in local public schools.

Wisconsin

MADISON SYMPHONY ORCHESTRA, 211 North Carroll Street, Madison, Wisconsin 53703. Conductor: **Roland Johnson** (1961). Concertmistress: **Miriam Schneider** (1966). Founded 1926. Players: 75. Auditorium: Madison Area Technical College Auditorium (capacity: 1,070). Season: October to May, 11 concerts. Budget: $80,000. . . . MILWAUKEE SYMPHONY ORCHESTRA, 929 North Water Street, Milwaukee, Wisconsin 53202. Founded 1959. Musical Director and Conductor: **Kenneth Schermerhorn.** Concertmaster: **Edward Mumm** (1962). Auditorium: Performing Arts Center (capacity: 2,331). Season: 36 weeks, 120 concerts; includes a six-week summer session. Basic winter season is comprised of 15 pairs of subscription concerts. The orchestra has grown rapidly in recent years to major status. In 1971 it qualified for a $1 million matching fund grant and in 1972, received $83,000 from the National Endowment for expanding its concerts for young people and other educational activities.

Founding Dates of Selected Orchestras

1842

New York Philharmonic.

1860

The Philharmonic Society of St. Louis.

1880

St. Louis Symphony Orchestra.

1881

Boston Symphony Orchestra.

1891

Chicago Symphony Orchestra.

1895

Cincinnati Symphony Orchestra . . . Pittsburgh Symphony Orchestra.

1898

Peoria Symphony Orchestra.

1900

Dallas Symphony Orchestra . . . The Philadelphia Orchestra.

1903

Minneapolis (now Minnesota) Symphony Orchestra . . . Seattle Symphony Orchestra.

1911

Oregon Symphony Orchestra . . . San Francisco Symphony Assn.

1914

Detroit Symphony Orchestra.

1916

Baltimore Symphony Orchestra.

1918

The Cleveland Orchestra.

1919

Los Angeles Philharmonic Orchestra.

1921

Cedar Rapids Symphony Orchestra (Iowa) . . . Kalamazoo Symphony Society (Michigan) . . . Greater Trenton Symphony Assn. (N.J.) . . . Norfolk Symphony Assn. (Virginia).

1922

Denver Symphony Orchestra (as Denver Civic Symphony).

1923

Omaha Symphony Orchestra . . . Rochester Philharmonic Orchestra (N.Y.).

1924

The Amarillo Symphony . . . Portland Symphony Orchestra (Maine) . . . Portland Junior Symphony Orchestra (Oregon) . . . Spokane Symphony Orchestra (Washington).

1925

Lincoln Symphony Orchestra (Nebraska) . . . Youngstown Symphony Orchestra (Ohio).

1926

Madison Symphony Orchestra (Wisconsin).

1927

San Diego Symphony Orchestra . . . Stockton Symphony Assn. (California) . . . Pittsburgh Symphony Orchestra.

1928

Grand Rapids Symphony Society (Michigan) . . . Pasadena Symphony Orchestra.

1929

New Jersey Symphony Orchestra . . . Wilmington Symphony Orchestra (Delaware).

1930

Lansing Symphony Orchestra (Michigan) . . . National Orchestral Association (N.Y.) . . . Erie Philharmonic Society (Pennsylvania) . . . Indianapolis Symphony Orchestra . . . National Symphony Orchestra (Washington, D.C.).

1931

Charlotte Symphony Orchestra (North Carolina) . . . Fargo–Moorhead Symphony Orchestra Assn. (North Dakota) . . . El Paso Symphony Orchestra Assn.

1932

Duluth Symphony Orchestra (Minnesota) . . . South Bend Symphony Orchestra (Indiana).

1933

Oakland Symphony Orchestra . . . Dayton Philharmonic Orchestra . . . Schenectady Symphony Orchestra (N.Y.) . . . Kansas City Philharmonic Assn.

1934

Evansville Philharmonic Orchestra (Indiana).

1935

Chattanooga Symphony Assn. . . . Vermont State Symphony Orchestra.

1936

Buffalo Philharmonic Orchestra . . . Louisville Orchestra . . . New Orleans Philharmonic Symphony Orchestra.

1937

Scranton Philharmonic Orchestra (Pennsylvania) . . . Austin Symphony Orchestra (Texas) . . . Des Moines Symphony Orchestra (Iowa).

1938

Oklahoma City Symphony Orchestra.

1939

Charleston Symphony Orchestra (West Virginia) . . . Symphony Society of San Antonio.

1941

Niagara Falls Philharmonic Orchestra.

1942

Fort Wayne Philharmonic Orchestra (Indiana).

1943

National Gallery Orchestra (Washington, D.C.) . . . Springfield Symphony Orchestra (Ohio).

1944

Jackson Symphony Orchestra (Mississippi) . . . Wichita Symphony Orchestra (Kansas).

1945

Atlanta Symphony Orchestra.

1946

Baton Rouge Symphony Orchestra (Louisiana) . . . Birmingham Symphony Orchestra (Alabama) . . . Independence Symphony Orchestra (Missouri) . . . Nashville Symphony Orchestra . . . Lubbock Symphony Orchestra (Texas).

1947

Compton Civic Symphony Orchestra (California) . . . North Jersey Philharmonic Orchestra (formerly Patterson Philharmonic) . . . The Little Orchestra Society (N.Y.) . . . Peninsula Symphony Orchestra (Virginia).

1948

Shreveport Symphony Society . . . Wichita Falls Symphony Orchestra (Texas).

1949

Jacksonville Symphony Association (Florida) . . . Columbus Symphony Orchestra (Georgia) . . . Fort Lauderdale Symphony Orchestra.

1950

Florida Symphony Orchestra . . . Richmond Symphony Orchestra (California).

1951

Columbus Symphony Orchestra (Ohio) . . . Roanoke Symphony Orchestra (Virginia).

1952

Memphis Orchestral Society (Tennessee) . . . Beaumont Symphony Society (Texas).

1953

Quincy Symphony Orchestra (Massachusetts) . . . Savannah Symphony Society . . . Fresno Philharmonic Orchestra (California).

1954

Binghamton Symphony Orchestra (N.Y.) . . . Brooklyn Philharmonia, Inc.

1955

Elizabeth Civic Orchestra (N.J.).

1957

New Bedford Symphony Orchestra (Massachusetts) . . . Fort Worth Symphony Orchestra.

1958

The Orchestra of America (N.Y.).

1959

St. Paul Chamber Orchestra (Minnesota) . . . St. Joseph Symphony Orchestra (Missouri) . . . Milwaukee Symphony Orchestra . . . Riverside Symphony Orchestra (California).

1960

Mozart Festival Orchestra (N.Y.) . . . Greensboro Symphony Orchestra (North Carolina).

1961

Dearborn Symphony Orchestra (Michigan) . . . Esterhazy Orchestra (N.Y.) . . . New York Orchestral Society . . . San Bernardino Symphony Orchestra.

1964

Musical Performing Arts Assn. (Michigan).

1965

Columbia Philharmonic Orchestra (South Carolina).

Conductors

Maurice Abravanel (b. 1903, Salonika); in U.S. since 1936; U.S. citizen; Conductor of the Utah Symphony since 1947; Music Director, Music Academy of the West; formerly conducted at the Metropolitan Opera and on Broadway; in 1971, won Alice M. Ditson Award for conducting and encouraging performances of contemporary American music. Recordings: *Angel, Bach Guild, Music Guild, Odyssey, Vanguard, Westminster.* Mgt.: Hurok Concerts, Inc. . . . **Peter Herman Adler** (b. 1899, Czechoslovakia); in U.S. since 1940; U.S. citizen; conducted in Germany and Russia early in his career; co-founder of NBC–TV opera in 1949 and served as Music Director until 1960; led the Baltimore Symphony from 1959 to 1967; currently Artistic Director and Music Director of NET–TV Opera Theater; engaged as Conductor for the Metropolitan Opera for the 1972–73 season. Recordings: *RCA Victor.* . . . **Victor Alessandro** (b. 1915); Conductor of the San Antonio Symphony since 1952; conducted the Oklahoma Symphony from 1938 to 1951; has guest-conducted the New York City Opera Company and other ensembles. Recordings: *Mercury.* . . . **Franz Allers** (b. 1905, Czechoslovakia); prominent director of musical shows; toured U.S.S.R. in 1960 with "My Fair Lady." Mgt.: Thea Dispeker, Artists' Representative. . . . **Alfredo Antonini** (b. 1901, Italy); U.S. citizen; presently, Musical Director of CBS Broadcasting System; former Conductor of Tampa Philharmonic; now guest-conducts in Europe, Canada, South America and the U.S.; has recorded much contemporary American music for *CRI* label; Mgt.: Thea Dispeker, Artists' Representative. . . . **Franco Autori;** Conductor of the Tulsa (Oklahoma) Philharmonic Orchestra from 1961 to 1970; Recordings: *Bartók.* . . . **Theodore Avitahl;** Conductor of the Philharmonic Society of Saint Louis, Missouri, since 1963; Mgt.: Sheldon Soffer Management. . . . **Jacob Avshalomov** (b. 1919); Conductor of the Portland Junior Symphony Orchestra (Oregon) since 1954; recordings: *Columbia, CRI.*

Richard Bales (b. 1915); Conductor of National Gallery Orchestra since 1943; directs the A. W. Mellon concerts held in the Gallery. . . . **George Barati** (b. 1913, Hungary); in U.S. since 1938; Executive Director of the Montalvo Center for the Arts in Saratoga, California and Conductor of the Santa Cruz County (California) Symphony Orchestra since 1971; a composer; former cellist with the San Francisco Symphony and Opera during early career; conducted the Honolulu Symphony from 1950 to 1968. Recordings: *Lyrichord* and *CRI.* . . . **Orlando Barera;** Conductor of the El Paso (Texas) Symphony since 1951. . . . **Leon Barzin** (b. 1900, Brussels); Artistic Director and Conductor of the National Orchestral Association (N.Y.). Recordings: *Serenus, Angel.* . . . **Harold Bauer;** Conductor of the Peoria Symphony Orchestra since 1967; conducted first performance in Denmark of Ives's Second Symphony in 1971. . . . **Leonard Bernstein** (b. 1918); Laureate Conductor of the New York Philharmonic since his retirement as Musical Director and Conductor in 1969; served as the latter since 1958; composer and pianist and one of the world's most celebrated musicians;

has guest conducted many major ensembles in the U.S. and in Europe. Recordings: *Columbia, Decca, London.* . . . **Franz Bibo;** Conductor of the Youngstown (Ohio) Symphony Orchestra since 1967. . . . **David Blum;** Conductor of the Esterhazy Orchestra (Manhasset, N.Y.) since 1961. Recordings: *Vanguard, Bach Guild.* . . . **Alberto Bolet;** Conductor of the Long Beach Symphony Association since 1968; Mgt.: Marianne Marshall. . . . **Pierre Boulez** (b. 1925, France); Music Director and Conductor of the New York Philharmonic since 1971; faculty, Wolf Trap American University Academy for the Performing Arts (1971); guest conductor of great orchestras; noted composer, pianist, and musical polemicist. Recordings: *Columbia, Angel, Everest, Turnabout, Nonesuch, CBS.* Mgt.: Columbia Artists Management, Inc. . . . **William H. Boyer;** Conductor of the Wichita Falls (Texas) Symphony Orchestra since 1964. . . . **Thomas Briccetti;** Music Director of Fort Wayne Philharmonic Orchestra (Indiana) beginning 1970; Associate Conductor of Indianapolis Symphony since 1968. Mgt.: Tornay Management, Ltd. . . . **Frank Brieff** (b. 1912); Conductor of the New Haven Symphony since 1951; also conducts the Bach Aria Group; has conducted the Naumburg Concerts in New York, the Orchestras of Buffalo, Rochester, and San Antonio; does programming of educational radio station WSCR in Amherst. Recordings: *Decca, Lyrichord, Everest, Period, Desto,* and *Odyssey.* . . . **Jacques Brourman;** Conductor of the Charlotte (North Carolina) Symphony Orchestra since 1967. Guest conductor in Japan (1971) with the Japan Philharmonic and other orchestras. Recordings: *Regal.* Mgt.: Tornay Management, Ltd. . . . **Beatrice Brown;** Conductor of the Scranton (Pennsylvania) Philharmonic Orchestra since 1962. . . . **Robert E. Brown;** Conductor of the Quincy (Massachusetts) Symphony Orchestra since 1967. . . . **Anshel Brusilow;** Conductor of the Dallas Symphony since 1970; founder and Conductor of the Philadelphia Chamber Symphony; former Concertmaster of the Philadelphia Orchestra. Recordings: *RCA Victor;* Mgt.: Columbia Artists Management, Inc. . . . **Emerson Buckley;** Conductor of the Fort Lauderdale (Florida) Symphony Orchestra since 1963; much sought-after conductor of opera, having conducted many productions in New York, Miami, and Central City, Colorado. Recordings: *CRI*; Mgt.: Herbert Barrett Management, Inc. . . . **Igor Buketoff** (b. 1915); Conductor of the Fort Wayne Philharmonic from 1948 to 1970. Recordings: *CRI, RCA Victor;* Mgt.: Herbert Barrett Management, Inc. . . . **William Byrd;** Conductor of the Musical Performing Arts Association of Flint, Michigan, since 1966; also Artistic Director of Flint Institute of Music, appointed in 1971.

John Canarina (b. 1934); Conductor of Jacksonville (Florida) Symphony from 1961 to 1968; during his tenure, directed an annual Delius Festival; currently guest-conducting in Europe with such orchestras as London Philharmonic and Belgian Radio Orchestra; has conducted the orchestras of Edmonton and Calgary of Canada and the Baltimore and Chicago Civic Orchestras; served as Assistant Conductor under Bernstein with the New York Philharmonic, 1960–61; while in the service conducted 97 concerts in Europe with the U.S. Seventh Army Symphony. Mgt.: David Schiffmann, Mgr. . . . **Alan Carter;** Conductor of the Vermont State Symphony Orchestra since 1935. . . . **Michael Charry** (b. 1933); Musical Director and Conductor of Canton (Ohio) Symphony for the past several years; Assistant Conductor since 1965 and apprentice conductor from 1961 to 1965 of the Cleveland Orchestra; conducts all of that orchestra's Children's Concerts; appointed Principal Guest Conductor of the Kansas City Philharmonic for 1972–73; has guest-conducted the orchestras of Pittsburgh, Louisville, Akron, and the Oberlin Music Theater; was Assistant Conductor and pianist for the José Limon dance company on tours of Europe and South and Central America under U.S. State Department auspices (1957 and 1960). Mgt.: Tornay Management, Ltd. . . . **Minas Christian;** Conductor of the Evansville (Indiana) Philharmonic Orchestra since 1953. . . . **Sergiu Comissiona** (b. 1928, Rumania); Music Director and Conductor of the Baltimore Symphony Orchestra since 1968; began his first season in that post in

1969; formerly principal Conductor of the Rumanian State Opera and the Bucharest Philharmonic; other conducting with the London Philharmonic, Stockholm Philharmonic, the Berlin Radio Symphony, etc. Recordings: *Mace;* Mgt. (as conductor): Mariedi Anders Artists Management, Inc. . . . **Richard Cormier;** Conductor of the Chattanooga (Tennessee) Symphony since 1968. . . . **Robert Craft** (b. 1923); has guest-conducted orchestras in America and Europe for many years; achieved early fame with the recording of the complete works of Anton von Webern for Columbia Records; co-authored with Stravinsky six volumes (1959–1969) of conversations with the composer; supervised recordings by Stravinsky and remained the composer's companion, assistant, guide, collaborator, and intimate friend until the latter's death in 1971. Recordings: *Columbia, Argo, Everest, London, RCA Victor, Lyrichord, Odyssey,* and *Urania.*

Lewis Dalvit; Conductor of the Jackson, Mississippi Symphony Orchestra since 1965. . . . **James De Priest;** Associate Conductor of the National Symphony Orchestra since 1971; has guest-conducted the Philadelphia Orchestra, the New York Philharmonic Orchestra, the Chicago Symphony and the Minnesota Symphony; assistant to Bernstein for 1965–66 season; in 1964 won first prize in the Mitropoulos conductor's competition; in 1962 conducted and lectured in the Far and Near East under U.S. State Department auspices. . . . **Dean Dixon** (b. 1915); since 1949 has worked in Europe, where his career was primarily established; since 1961 has led the Hesse Radio Orchestra, Frankfurt; Conductor of the Göteborg Symphony (Sweden) and the Sydney Symphony of Australia (resigned in 1967); returned to the U.S. as conductor after twenty-one years in Europe, making his first American tour in 1971 leading the orchestras of Minnesota; Milwaukee; Chicago; Detroit; San Francisco; Washington, D.C.; etc.; early in his career he led the NBC Symphony (in 1941) and the orchestras of New York, Philadelphia, and Boston; first black American conductor. Recordings: *CRI, Everest, Desto;* Mgt.: Sherman Pitluck, Inc. . . . **James Dixon** (b. 1915) Conductor of the Tri City (Iowa) Symphony. Recordings: *Westminster.* . . . **Antal Dorati** (b. 1906, Hungary); U.S. citizen; American debut in 1937 with the National Symphony Orchestra (Washington, D.C.); former Conductor of the Minneapolis Symphony from 1949 to 1960; Conductor of London's BBC Orchestra from 1963 to 1966; Musical Director of the Stockholm Philharmonic from 1966 to the present; in 1970, was engaged as Musical Director and Conductor of the National Symphony (concurrent with the Stockholm position); recently completed a recording project involving the complete symphonies of Haydn (the first conductor to do so); altogether has made over 300 recordings. Recordings: *Mercury, Angel, Seraphim, Columbia, Pickwick, London, RCA Victor.* Mgt.: Hurok Concerts, Inc. . . . **Carmen Dragon** (b. 1914); Musical Director and Conductor of the Glendale Symphony Orchestra since 1963; for many years has conducted the Hollywood Bowl Orchestra and the Capitol (records) Symphony. Recordings: *Capitol;* Mgt.: Richard F. Perry, Glendale Symphony Association. . . . **Richard Dufallo** (b. 1933); clarinetist in his earlier career; has conducted the Dallas Symphony (1971), the Chicago Symphony, the Pittsburgh Symphony, the New York Philharmonic (on tour); was Associate Conductor of the Buffalo Philharmonic during the tenure of Lukas Foss. Recordings: *CRI, RCA Victor, Ars Nova;* Mgt.: Herbert Barrett Management, Inc.

Dean Eckertsen (b. 1928); early in his career was known for his recordings of the works of Corelli for Vox records; has conducted "I Musici" and other European ensembles. Recordings: *Vox, Dover.* . . . **Joseph Eger;** Conductor of the New York Orchestral Society since 1961 (The Earth Symphony). Regular Conductor with the American Symphony Orchestra. Mgt.: Hurok Concerts, Inc. . . . **Sixten Ehrling** (b. 1918, Sweden); Conductor of the Detroit Symphony since 1963 (debut with the orchestra in 1961); guest conductor of major orchestras in the U.S. Recordings: *London, Angel, Nonesuch.* Mgt.: Columbia Artists Management, Inc. . . . **Lehman Engel** (b. 1910); conductor of Broadway musicals, composer, author, and music editor. Recordings: *Odyssey, Decca, Columbia.*

Harry Farbman; Conductor of the Springfield (Illinois) Symphony Orchestra since 1951. . . . **Harold Farberman;** Conductor of the Oakland (California) Symphony since 1970; guest conductor of the Denver Symphony Orchestra and other ensembles; former percussionist. Recordings: *Cambridge, Serenus, Vanguard, Deutsche Grammophon;* Mgt.: Herbert Barrett Management, Inc. . . . **Frederick Fennell** (b. 1914); known as conductor of wind ensembles and for his recordings with the Eastman Wind Ensemble, of which he was formerly director; now on the faculty of the School of Music of the University of Miami and Wolf Trap–American University (1971). Recordings: *Mercury.* . . . **Arthur Fiedler** (b. 1894); Conductor of the Boston Pops since 1930; established the pops orchestra idea; one of the world's most popular and most recorded conductors. Records: *RCA Victor, Polydor.* . . . **Leon Fleisher** (b. 1928); formerly more active as concert pianist; made conducting debut in New York in 1970 at the Mozart Festival. Mgt.: Columbia Artists Management, Inc. . . . **Gene Forrell;** Conductor of the Master Virtuosi of New York since 1964; Mgt.: Helen Jensen Artists Management. . . . **Lukas Foss** (b. 1922, Germany); in the U.S. since childhood; also composer and pianist; since 1970, Music Advisor and Conductor of Brooklyn Philharmonia; appointed in 1972 as Chief Conductor and Musical Advisor of the Kol Israel Orchestra of Jerusalem (concurrent with the Brooklyn post); former Musical Director and Conductor of the Buffalo Philharmonic Orchestra (1963 to 1970); has conducted many major ensembles throughout the world. Recordings: *Nonesuch, Turnabout; Heliodor.* Mgt.: Thea Dispeker, Artists' Representative. . . . **Lawrence Foster** (b. 1941); conducting debut in Los Angeles in 1960; Assistant Conductor of the Los Angeles Philharmonic in 1965; in 1969 was appointed permanent Guest Conductor of the Royal Philharmonic Orchestra (London), and in 1970 was appointed Conductor-in-Chief of the Houston Symphony Orchestra then, beginning in 1972, as Musical Director. Recordings: *Desto, MGM.* Mgt.: Hurok Concerts, Inc. . . . **Serge Fournier;** Conductor of the Toledo (Ohio) Orchestra since 1964; Mgt.: Hurok Concerts, Inc. . . . **Vincent de Frank;** Conductor of the Memphis (Tennessee) Orchestra since 1952. . . . **Arthur M. Fraser;** Conductor of the Columbia (South Carolina) Philharmonic Orchestra since 1965. . . . **James Frazier;** first American to win the Guido Cantelli Competition for conductors; has conducted orchestras in Italy and was the youngest American to appear with the Leningrad Philharmonic; guest-conducted the Philadelphia Orchestra. Mgt.: Sherman Pitluck, Inc. . . . **Massimo Freccia** (b. 1906, Florence); U.S. citizen; Conductor of the New Orleans Philharmonic from 1944 to 1952; Baltimore Symphony from 1952 to 1958; since 1959, has guest-conducted in Europe. . . . **Paul Freeman;** Conductor-in-Residence of the Detroit Symphony; former Associate Conductor of the Dallas Symphony from 1968 to 1971; won second prize in the 1967 Mitropoulos conducting competition; early engagements include substituting for André Cluytens with the San Francisco Symphony, appearances at Spoleto (Festival of Two Worlds), and with the orchestras of Atlanta, New Orleans, Oklahoma City, Minneapolis, and Baltimore. . . . **Peter Paul Fuchs;** Conductor of the Baton Rouge, Louisiana, Symphony since 1960.

Nathan Gordon; Conductor of the Dearborn (Michigan) Orchestra since 1961; violist with the Detroit Symphony; Mgt.: Lee Jon Associates. . . . **John Gosling;** Conductor of the Erie (Pennsylvania) Philharmonic since 1967; succeeded Benjamin Swalin in 1972 as Conductor of the North Carolina Symphony. . . . **Morton Gould** (b. 1913); has conducted numerous broadcasting ensembles as well as his own group for recordings; guest conductor of many major U.S. orchestras; noted composer and arranger; of late, active in musical organizations (ASCAP, American Symphony Orchestra League, etc.) in addition to conducting. Recordings: *RCA Victor, Concert-Disc, Columbia, Everest.* . . . **Gideon Grau;** Conductor of the Saginaw (Michigan) Symphony Orchestra since 1965. . . . **Thomas Griswold;**

Conductor of the Fresno Philharmonic Orchestra from 1966 to 1971; in 1971 appointed Conductor of Des Moines Symphony (Iowa); also appointed professor at Drake University in Des Moines. . . . **James Guthrie;** Conductor of the Riverside (California) Symphony Orchestra Society since 1965; Mgt.: Concert Artists Management. . . . **Robert Gutter;** former Conductor of the Des Moines Symphony Orchestra and the Springfield (Ohio) Symphony; conducts (since 1969) Springfield (Massachusetts) Symphony Orchestra.

William Penny Häcker; Conductor of the New York State Symphony Orchestra since 1964; also Conductor of the Virginia State Symphony Orchestra in Richmond. . . . **Charles R. Hall;** Conductor of the Springfield (Missouri) Symphony Orchestra. . . . **Edwyn Hames;** Conductor of the South Bend (Indiana) Symphony Orchestra since 1932. . . . **Guy Fraser Harrison** (b. 1894, England); U.S. citizen; Conductor of the Oklahoma City Symphony since 1951; was Conductor of the Rochester Civic Orchestra from 1929 to 1951 and Associate Conductor of the Rochester Philharmonic from 1930 to 1951. Recordings: *CRI.* . . . **William Harrod;** Conductor of the Lubbock (Texas) Symphony Orchestra since 1946. . . . **Baird Hastings;** Conductor of the Mozart Festival Orchestra since 1960 (N.Y.). . . . **Joseph Hawthorne;** Conductor of the Duluth (Minnesota) Symphony Orchestra since 1967; recordings: *Listening Library;* Mgt.: Herbert Barrett Management, Inc. . . . **Julius Hegyi;** Conductor of the Albany Symphony Orchestra since 1966. . . . **Skitch Henderson** (b. 1918); appointed Music Director and Conductor of the Tulsa Philharmonic Orchestra in 1971; has guest-conducted the New York Philharmonic, the London Philharmonic, etc.; noted music director of popular music bands on TV; was accompanist to Judy Garland, musical director of the Bing Crosby radio show, etc.; also pianist, composer and arranger. Recordings: *London, RCA Victor.* Mgt.: Columbia Artists Management, Inc. . . . **Walter Hendl** (b. 1917); Director of Eastman School of Music from 1964 to 1972, when he was also Conductor of Eastman Philharmonia; Music Director of the Chautauqua Festival since 1952; former Associate Conductor of the Chicago Symphony Orchestra (1958 to 1964); former Music Director of Ravinia Festival; led the Dallas Symphony from 1949 to 1958. Recordings: *Desto, RCA Victor.* . . . **Pierre Hétu;** Canadian-born conductor of the Kalamazoo (Michigan) Symphony since 1958; Associate Conductor of the Detroit Symphony since 1971; former assistant to Zubin Mehta with the Montreal Symphony; in 1961, won the first prize in the Besançon International Competition for Young Conductors. Mgt.: Shaw Concerts, Inc. . . . **Irwin Hoffman;** Conductor of the Florida Gulf Coast Symphony; former Associate Conductor of the Chicago Symphony. . . . **Thomas Hohstadt;** Conductor of the Amarillo (Texas) Symphony since 1963.

Robert Irving; Musical Director and Principal Conductor of the New York City Ballet. Recordings: *Capitol, Angel, Decca, Everest;* Mgt.: Sheldon Soffer Management. . . . **John Iuele;** Conductor of the Winston-Salem (North Carolina) Symphony Association.

Newell Jenkins (b. 1915); conducts Clarion Concerts in New York; noted for his performances of rare music—new, old, and forgotten; has edited the 18th Century Music Series published by G. Schirmer, Inc.; has conducted various ensembles in Europe. Recordings: *Dover, Period, Decca, Everest,* and *Odyssey.* . . . **Donald Johanos** (b. 1928); Associate Conductor of the Pittsburgh Symphony; was Associate Conductor (1957) and then Resident Conductor (1961) of the Dallas Symphony; became Music Director in 1962; has conducted such major orchestras as the Philadelphia Orchestra, Minnesota Symphony, Amsterdam Concertgebouw. Records: *RCA Victor, Turnabout.* Mgt.: Columbia Artists Management, Inc. . . . **Roland Johnson;** Conductor of the Madison (Wisconsin) Symphony Orchestra since 1961. . . . **Thor Johnson** (b. 1913); Conductor of the Nashville (Tennessee) Symphony Orchestra since 1967; conducted the Cincinnati Symphony (1946–58), then became director of Northwestern University's orchestral department; former Conductor of the Chicago Little Symphony; Music Director of the Moravian Festival Orchestra, and the Peninsula Festival ensembles. Recordings: *CRI, Columbia, Odyssey, Westminster.*

Milton Katims (b. 1909); formerly conducted NBC Symphony and the Buffalo Philharmonic; innovative Conductor of the Seattle Symphony since 1954, enlarging the scope and raising the stature of the ensemble to make it one of America's best. Recordings: *RCA Victor;* Mgt.: Hurok Concerts, Inc. . . . **Paul Katz;** Conductor of the Dayton (Ohio) Philharmonic Orchestra since 1933; also chamber cellist with the Cleveland Quartet; Mgt.: Pacific World Artists, Inc. . . . **Christopher Keene** (b. 1946); has conducted for the New York City Opera, the Metropolitan Opera, the Santa Fe Opera, and at Spoleto (in 1968, 1969, and 1971); Musical Director of the American Ballet Company. . . . **Leo Kopp;** Conductor of the Saint Paul Pop Concert Orchestra; also Conductor of the Lincoln (Nebraska) Symphony Orchestra since 1942. . . . **Richard Korn** (b. 1908); Conductor of the Orchestra of America (since 1959); conducted the NBC Orchestra and orchestras in Japan. Recordings: *CRI.* . . . **André Kostelanetz** (b. 1901, Leningrad), U.S. citizen; has conducted his own ensembles (so-called "Kostelanetz Orchestras") for radio and recordings for many years; has appeared as guest conductor with major U.S. orchestras; regular Conductor of New York summer Promenade Concerts with the New York Philharmonic. For many years noted particularly as a conductor of light classics, sophisticated arrangements of popular standards, etc. Recordings: *Columbia.* . . . **Ira Kraemer;** Conductor of the Little Symphony of Newark, New Jersey, since 1966, and the South Orange Symphony (N.J.). . . . **Harry Kruger;** Conductor of the Columbus, Georgia, Symphony Orchestra since 1965. . . . **Leo Kucinski;** Conductor of the Sioux City (Iowa) Symphony Orchestra.

Robert La Marchina (b. 1928); since 1967, Conductor of the Honolulu Symphony; early in his career was cellist with the NBC Symphony under Toscanini and with the Los Angeles Philharmonic; was Music Director of the now-disbanded Metropolitan Opera National Company. Mgt.: Hurok Concerts, Inc. . . . **Hans Lampl;** Conductor of the Compton (California) Civic Symphony Orchestra since 1964. . . . **Siegfried Landau** (b. 1921, Berlin); in U.S. since 1940; founder and Conductor of Brooklyn Philharmonic from 1954 to 1970; Conductor of Music for Westchester (N.Y.) Symphony since its founding in 1962; Musical Director of the Chattanooga Opera Association since 1959. Recordings: *Turnabout.* . . . **Louis Lane** (b. 1923); former Assistant and now Resident Conductor of the Cleveland Orchestra; has been conducting that ensemble since 1956; Conductor of the Cleveland Pops since 1955; also conducts the Canton and Akron Orchestras (since 1959); was an apprentice conductor to George Szell early in his career (1947); in 1971 received the Mahler Medal of Honor from the Bruckner Society of America. Recordings: *Columbia.* . . . **Van Lier Lanning;** Conductor of the Delaware Symphony Orchestra (in Wilmington) since 1955. . . . **Erich Leinsdorf** (b. 1912, Vienna); U.S. citizen; Conductor of the Boston Symphony from 1962 to 1969; currently active as guest conductor with major orchestras and opera houses throughout the world; early career in America included conducting the Metropolitan Opera (1938 to 1943), the Cleveland Orchestra (1943 to 1944), and the Rochester Philharmonic (1947 to 1956). Recordings: *Capitol, RCA Victor,* and *Odyssey;* Mgt.: Hurok Concerts, Inc. . . . **Richard Lert** (b. 1885, Germany); U.S. citizen; has conducted the Pasadena (California) Symphony since 1936 (in 1972 began a reduced season of conducting with that orchestra); is musical advisor to the American Symphony Orchestra League's Eastern Institute of Orchestral Studies; head of New York Philharmonic's Orchestral Institute for minority musicians. . . . **James Levine;** made debut at ten conducting the Cincinnati Symphony; Principal Conductor of the Metropolitan Opera beginning with the 1973 season (first conductor to hold that title); served as assistant to George Szell until 1970; has led the Orchestras of Philadelphia, Chicago, Pittsburgh, San Francisco, etc. . . . **Joseph Levine** (b. 1910); Associate Conductor of the Seattle

Symphony; was Music Director and Conductor of the Omaha Symphony from 1958 to 1970; conducted the orchestra of the Ballet Theater from 1950 to 1958. Recordings: *Capitol.* Mgt.: Herbert Barrett Management, Inc. . . . **Henry Lewis** (b. 1932); Conductor of the New Jersey Symphony since 1968; appointed one of the conductors for the Metropolitan Opera Company beginning in 1972; has made guest appearances with the Symphony Orchestras of Boston, Chicago, and London and the San Francisco, Vancouver and Boston opera companies. Recordings: *London.* . . . **Alain Lombard;** Musical Director of the Greater Miami Philharmonic. Recordings: *Angel.*

Lorin Maazel (b. 1930); in 1971 received a five-year contract to become Musical Director of the Cleveland Orchestra; is Musical Director of the Berlin Radio Symphony Orchestra and Conductor of the New Philharmonia of London; former Director of Deutsche Oper, West Berlin; has guest-conducted many major U.S. orchestras. Recordings: *London, Deutsche Grammophon, Philips, Angel.* Mgt.: Hurok Concerts, Inc. . . . **Francis Madeira;** Conductor of the Rhode Island Philharmonic Orchestra since 1945. . . . **Fritz Mahler** (b. 1901, Vienna); U.S. citizen; former Conductor of the Hartford Symphony, from 1953 to 1964; previous conductorships were with the Erie Philharmonic, 1947 to 1952, and the Danish State Symphony, 1930 to 1935; in 1968, conducted orchestras in Japan, Korea, and in Manila. Recordings: *Decca, Vanguard, Spoken Arts.* . . . **Amerigo Marino;** Conductor of the Birmingham (Alabama) Symphony since 1964; has guest-conducted the Washington National Symphony in 1963, the New York Philharmonic in 1970. . . . **Henry Mazer;** Associate Conductor of the Chicago Symphony since 1970; has conducted the orchestras of Pittsburg, Wheeling, (West Virginia) and Orlando (Florida); starting in January, 1970 substituted for the ailing William Steinberg in New York and elsewhere; Associate Conductor of the Pittsburgh Symphony, 1966–1970. Mgt.: Hurok Concerts, Inc. . . . **Edwin McArthur** (b. 1907); Conductor of the Harrisburg (Pennsylvania) Symphony Orchestra since 1950; head of Opera Department at Eastman School. Recordings: *RCA Victor;* Mgt.: Herbert Barrett Management, Inc. . . . **Cary McMurran;** Conductor of the Peninsula Symphony Orchestra (Newport News, Virginia) since 1947. . . . **Zubin Mehta** (b. 1936, Bombay); Conductor of the Los Angeles Philharmonic since 1962; former Conductor of the Montreal Symphony; has conducted many of the world's great orchestras and is one of the most famous young conductors in music today. Recordings: *London, Angel, Turnabout.* Mgt.: Pacific World Artists, Inc.; Hurok Concerts, Inc. . . . **Jorge Mester** (b. 1935, Mexico City); in the U.S. most of his musical life; Conductor of the Louisville Orchestra since 1967; Music Director of Aspen Music Festival since 1972; in 1971 appointed Artistic Advisor of the Kansas City (Missouri) Philharmonic (concurrent with his other posts); early career included leading the St. Louis Philharmonic and the major orchestras of Boston, Cincinnati, Philadelphia, etc. Recordings: *CRI, Desto, Louisville, Vanguard, Columbia.* Mgt.: Hurok Concerts, Inc. . . . **Gregory Millar;** Conductor of the Tucson Symphony Society, Inc. since 1966; former conductor of the Kalamazoo Symphony Orchestra (1961–1967). Recordings: *Fantasy;* Mgt.: Pacific World Artists, Inc. . . . **Frank Miller;** Conductor of the Evanston (Illinois) Symphony since 1962; first cellist with the Chicago Symphony. . . . **Howard Mitchell** (b. 1911); Conductor of the National Symphony from 1949 to 1969 (former first cellist with that ensemble); now guest-conducts. Recordings: *RCA Victor.* . . . **Sheldon Morgenstern;** Conductor of the Greensboro (North Carolina) Symphony since 1967; also directs Eastern Music Festival; Mgt.: Albert Kay Associates, Inc. . . . **Gibson Morrissey;** Conductor of the Roanoke (Virginia) Symphony Orchestra since 1952.

Harry Newstone; Conductor of the Sacramento Symphony Orchestra; Recordings: *L'Oiseau Lyre, Artia, Vanguard.*

Eugene Ormandy (b. 1899, Hungary); in the U.S. since 1921; U.S. citizen; permanent Conductor of the Philadelphia Orchestra since 1938; conducting debut in New York in 1924; first conducted the Philadelphia Orchestra in 1931; conducted the Minneapolis Symphony from 1931 to 1936; winner of many honors and distinctions; in 1969 received the Presidential Medal of Freedom (highest U.S. civilian award) from President Nixon; one of the world's most extensively recorded musical artists. Recordings. *Columbia, RCA Victor.* Mgt.: Columbia Artists Management, Inc. . . . **Seiji Ozawa** (b. 1935, Japan); Musical Director and Conductor of the San Francisco Symphony beginning with the 1970 season (and contracted until the 1975–76 season); beginning with the 1973–74 season will bccomc Musical Director and Conductor of the Boston Symphony concurrent with his San Francisco post; Co-Artistic Director of the Berkshire Music Festival; has performed throughout the world with the major orchestras; early in his career was assistant to Bernstein (1960); made conducting debut in New York in 1961 at Carnegie Hall; guest-conducted the Chicago Symphony in 1964 and was Conductor of the Toronto Symphony in 1965. Records: *Angel, RCA Victor, Columbia.*

Willis Page (b. 1918); permanent Conductor of the Jacksonville (Florida) Symphony beginning in 1971; former conductor of the Nashville Symphony (for eight years) and the Des Moines Symphony; early conducting included leading the Boston Orchestral Society. Records: *Kapp.* . . . **Maurice Peress** (b. 1930); Conductor of the Austin (Texas) Symphony (since 1970) and the Corpus Christi Symphony (since 1962); was music director of Robert Joffrey Ballet; former assistant to Leonard Bernstein; acquired sudden national fame when, in 1971, he conducted the premiere of Bernstein's "Mass" at the opening of Kennedy Center in Washington, D.C. Mgt.: Colbert Artists Management, Inc. . . . **Anthony J. Pezzano;** Conductor of the Schenectady Symphony Orchestra since 1964. . . . **André Previn** (b. 1929, Berlin); in the U.S. since childhood; pianist and composer; active for many years in arranging and directing film music and was often involved in playing jazz; former Music Director of the Houston Symphony (1967–68); since 1968, has been Principal Conductor of the London Symphony; resides in England; guest-conducts many major U.S. and European orchestras. Recordings: *RCA Victor;* Mgt. (for U.S.): Columbia Artists Management, Inc. . . . **Brian Priestman;** English-born Conductor of the Denver Symphony (since 1970); was Conductor of the Baltimore Symphony from 1968 to 1969; is also Chief Conductor of the New Zealand Broadcasting Corp. Symphony Orchestra, appointed in 1971; was conductor of orchestras both in England and Canada. Records: *Westminster, RCA Victor.*

Eve Queler; Conductor of the Opera Orchestra of New York; Assistant Conductor of New York City Opera since 1965; Associate Conductor of the Fort Wayne Philharmonic concurrent with other positions; has conducted the Mozart Festival of Lincoln Center; was once assistant to Julius Rudel at the New York City Opera.

Martin Rich; Associate Conductor of Metropolitan Opera; Music Director and Conductor of Philharmonic Symphony of Westchester (N.Y.). . . . **A. Clyde Roller;** Conductor of the Lansing (Michigan) Symphony since 1967; former Conductor of the Eastman Wind Ensemble; was Musical Director of the Amarillo (Texas) orchestra for thirteen years; has conducted the New Zealand National Symphony, and, in 1960, was guest conductor for the Boston Esplanade Concerts; early in his career, he was principal oboist of the Tulsa Philharmonic and the Oklahoma City Symphony. Records: *Mercury.* . . . **Julius Rudel** (b. 1921, Vienna); in the U.S. since 1938; U.S. citizen since 1944; U.S. conducting debut was in 1943 with the New York City Opera; one of the most active of American conductors, holding top posts in several places; currently he is Artistic Director of the New York City Opera (has been at the helm of that company since 1957); Music Director of the Cincinnati May Festival, Music Director of the Caramoor Festival; Music Advisor and Conductor of Wolf Trap Farm Park; Musical Director of Kennedy Center for the Performing Arts; in opera, he has conducted many new works including premiere performances. Recordings: *RCA Victor, Westminster, Desto, Music Guild.* Mgt.: Thea Dispeker, Artists' Representative. . . . **Max Rudolf** (b. 1902, Germany); in the U.S. since 1940; U.S. citizen since 1946; currently head of the opera department at the Curtis Institute of Music (since 1970); was Conductor of the Cincinnati Symphony from 1958 to 1970; at the Metropolitan Opera from 1945 to 1958; has guest-conducted many of the world's great orchestras. Recordings: *Decca.* Mgt.: Hurok Concerts, Inc.

Gerhard Samuel (b. 1924, Germany); in the U.S. since childhood; Associate Conductor of the Los Angeles Philharmonic since 1970; was conductor of the Oakland Symphony from 1959 to 1970; is now also Director and Conductor of the Ojai (California) Festival; early in his career (1949–1959) was an Assistant Conductor with the Minneapolis Symphony; also a composer and violinist. Records: *CRI* (with Royal Philharmonic Orchestra of London). Mgt.: Sheldon Soffer Management. . . . **William Scheide** (b. 1914); Conductor-Founder of the Bach Aria Group; has conducted other chamber ensembles; recordings: *Decca;* Mgt.: Herbert Barrett Management, Inc. . . . **Thomas Scherman** (b. 1917); Founder-Conductor of the Little Orchestra Society in 1947; originated many concert-producing techniques in the U.S.; has conducted many American works, as well as infrequently heard classics. Records: *Decca, Desto.* Mgt.: Herbert Barrett Management, Inc. . . . **Kenneth Schermerhorn;** Conductor of the Milwaukee Symphony Orchestra. Former conductor of New Jersey Symphony (until 1968) and Robert Joffrey Ballet. Mgt.: Thea Dispeker, Artists' Representative; Herbert Barrett Management, Inc. (for Europe only). . . . **Charles Schiff;** Conductor of the Charleston (West Virginia) Symphony Orchestra since 1965. . . . **Thomas Schippers** (b. 1930); Conductor of the Cincinnati Symphony Orchestra since 1970; led the orchestra on its first American tour in 1971; is a guest conductor with many leading orchestras and opera companies throughout the U.S., Canada, and Europe; was a staff Conductor with the Metropolitan Opera (debut in 1955) and the New York City Opera; former Associate Conductor of the New York Philharmonic; is Music Director of Festival of Two Worlds in Spoleto, Italy. Recordings: *London, Columbia, RCA Victor, Angel.* Mgt.: Thea Dispeker, Artists' Representative (for South America and most European countries). . . . **Walter Schoeder;** Conductor of the North Jersey Philharmonic Orchestra since 1947. . . . **Hans Schweiger** (b. 1906, Cologne), U.S. citizen; Conductor of Kansas City Orchestra from 1948 to 1971; Conductor of the Fort Wayne Philharmonic from 1944 to 1948; now guest-conducts in Europe. Recordings: *Urania;* Mgt.: Hurok Concerts, Inc. . . . **Robert Shaw** (b. 1916); Conductor of the Atlanta Symphony since 1967; Music Director of the Alaska Music Festival in Anchorage; was Associate Conductor, under Szell, of the Cleveland Orchestra from 1956 to 1967; throughout his career has been known as a major conductor of choral groups. Recordings: *RCA Victor, CRI.* . . . **John Shenaut;** Conductor of the Shreveport (Louisiana) Symphony since 1948. . . . **Stephen Simon** (b. 1937); Music Director of the Handel Society of New York and the Orchestral Society of Westchester N.Y.; early in his career conducted the Symphony of the Air, the Liverpool Philharmonic, etc.; recorded with Lili Kraus the complete Mozart piano concertos in Vienna. Records: *RCA Victor, Epic* (Mozart concertos —perhaps out of print now). . . . **Jacques Singer;** Conductor of the Oregon Symphony Orchestra since 1962; Mgt.: Hurok Concerts, Inc. . . . **Leopold Sipe;** founded and conducted the Saint Paul Chamber Orchestra from 1959 to 1971; Recordings: *St. Paul.* . . . **Stanislaw Skrowaczewski** (b. 1923, Poland); Conductor of the Minnesota (former Minneapolis) Symphony since 1960; made U.S. conducting debut with the Cleveland Orchestra in 1958; has guest-conducted the Pittsburgh, the New York Philharmonic and other major U.S. ensembles. Recordings: *Mercury, Philips, RCA Victor, Angel.* Mgt.: Pacific World Artists, Inc. (for engagements abroad); and Shaw Concerts, Inc. (with the Minnesota Symphony). . . . **Felix Slatkin;** has conducted the Concert Arts Orchestra (Capitol record-studio orchestra) and the

Hollywood Bowl Orchestra. Recordings: *Capitol, Pickwick*. . . . **Izler Solomon** (b. 1910); Conductor of the Indianapolis Symphony since 1956; made conducting debut in 1932; has guest-conducted European orchestras and, with the Oslo Symphony, has recorded works by American composers. Records: *CRI, RCA Victor.* Mgt.: Herbert Barrett Management, Inc. . . . **Georg Solti** (b. 1912, Hungary); German, then English citizen; Musical Director and Conductor of the Chicago Symphony Orchestra since 1969; concurrently, Conductor of Orchestre Symphonique de Paris; American conducting debut in 1953 with the San Francisco Opera; conductor of Chicago's Opera Theater Association from 1956 to 1957; conducted the Metropolitan Opera in 1960; was Music Director of the Royal Opera at Covent Garden from 1961 to 1971; was Conductor of the Los Angeles Philharmonic for nearly one season: 1960 to early 1961; knighted by Queen Elizabeth in 1971. Recordings: *London, RCA Victor.* Mgt.: Colbert Artists Management. . . . **Johannes Somary** (b. 1935, Switzerland); advanced music education received in the U.S.; Musical Director of Amor Artis Chorale and Orchestra; choirmaster and organist of New York's Church of Our Savior, since 1959; Chairman, Music Department, Horace Mann School, since 1959; has conducted numerous premieres including the first U.S. performance of Handel's "Esther," "Theodora," and "Susanna"; has conducted for CBS–TV; Recordings: *Vanguard, Decca*. . . . **Laszlo Somogyi;** Conductor of the Rochester Philharmonic from 1964 to 1969. Recordings: *Music Guild, Westminster, Mercury*. . . . **Russell Stanger;** Conductor of the Norfolk (Virginia) Symphony Orchestra since 1966. Recordings: *CRI.* Mgt. Albert Kay Associates, Inc. . . . **William Steinberg** (b. 1899, Germany); in U.S. since 1937; U.S. citizen; Musical Director and Conductor of the Pittsburgh Symphony Orchestra since 1952; concurrently, held the same position with the Boston Symphony Orchestra from 1969 to 1972; conducted the Buffalo Philharmonic from 1945 to 1952; has conducted many of the world's great ensembles. Recordings: *RCA Victor, Command, Everest, Capitol, Angel, Pickwick.* Mgt.: Columbia Artists Management, Inc. (with the Pittsburgh orchestra). . . . **George Steiner;** Conductor of the Alexandria (Virginia) Symphony Orchestra since 1966. . . . **Jonathan Sternberg** (b. 1919); has conducted a great deal in Europe, where he has led important orchestras since 1947; has recorded with the Vienna Symphony Orchestra, the Vienna State Opera, and others; since 1968, has conducted the Atlanta Opera Company and the Atlanta Ballet. Recordings: *Dover, Turnabout, Urania, Bach Guild,* and *CRI*. . . . **Leopold Stokowski** (b. 1882, England); U.S. citizen; founder and Conductor of the American Symphony Orchestra since 1962; much honored and respected conductor whose career spans the history of music recording, to which his contributions are without equal among musicians; made his professional debut as conductor in the U.S. with the Cincinnati Orchestra in 1909. Recordings: *RCA Victor, Columbia, Decca, CRI, Vanguard, Everest, Seraphim, Capitol, London*. . . . **Walter Susskind** (b. 1913, Prague); Musical Director and Conductor of the St. Louis Symphony since the 1968–69 season; was Conductor of the Toronto Symphony from 1956 to 1965; previous conducting positions were held in Holland, England, Scotland, and Australia; was also Music Director of the Aspen Festival. Recordings: *Angel, Everest, Bartok, Pickwick, Capitol, Seraphim, Decca*. . . . **Benjamin Swalin** (b. 1901); Conductor Emeritus of the North Carolina Symphony; served as Conductor from 1939 to 1972; Mgt.: Alkahest Attractions (Atlanta, Georgia, with N.C. Symphony).

Michael Tilson Thomas (b. 1944); Conductor of the Buffalo Philharmonic Orchestra since 1971; Associate Conductor of the Boston Symphony, 1969 to present; has guest-conducted many major orchestras since 1969. Recordings: *Deutsche Grammophon.* Mgt.: Judd Concert Artist Bureau. . . . **Sigvald Thompson;** Conductor of the Fargo–Moorhead (North Dakota) Symphony Orchestral Association since 1967. . . . **Donald Thulean;** Conductor of the Spokane (Washington) Symphony. . . . **Herman Toplansky;** Conductor of the Elizabeth (N.J.) Civic Orchestra since 1955. . . . **Werner Torkanowsky** (b. 1926, Berlin); in U.S. since 1948; Conductor of the New Orleans Philharmonic Symphony Orchestra since 1963; has conducted the New York Philharmonic and the major orchestras of Philadelphia, Chicago, Houston, Minneapolis, Baltimore, Boston, etc.; early in his career he was a member of the Pittsburgh Symphony violin section. Recordings: *CRI, Columbia.*

David Van Vactor (b. 1906); Conductor of the Knoxville (Tennessee) Symphony since 1947; also a composer. Recordings: *CRI*. . . . **Paul Vermel;** Conductor of the Portland (Maine) Symphony Orchestra since 1967; formerly Conductor of the Fresno Philharmonic (California). . . . **Louis Vyner;** Conductor of the Reading (Pennsylvania) Symphony Orchestra since 1961.

Fritz Wallenberg; Conductor of the Binghamton (N.Y.) Symphony Orchestra since 1954. . . . **Franklyn S. Weddle;** Conductor of the Independence (Missouri) Symphony Orchestra since 1946. . . . **Evan Whallon;** Conductor of the Columbus Symphony (Ohio) Orchestra since 1956. . . . **Robert Whitney** (b. 1904, England, of U.S. parents); with Louisville Orchestra from 1937 to 1967; much honored for lengthy list of new music performances with that orchestra; now active at the University of Louisville. Recordings: *Louisville, Columbia*. . . . **Richard Williams;** 1970 appointed Music Director and Conductor of Cedar Rapids (Iowa) Symphony. In 1969, was Music Director and Conductor of Cabrillo Music Festival. . . . **Arthur Winograd** (b. 1920); was conductor of the MGM (studio) orchestra, Virtuoso Orchestra of London, and many chamber groups; Conductor of the Birmingham Symphony from 1960 to 1964. In 1964 became Conductor of the Symphony Society of Greater Hartford Orchestra and in 1972, Music Director and Conductor of the Worcester (Massachusetts) Orchestra. Early in his career he was cellist in Boston and NBC Symphony Orchestras, and with the Juilliard String Quartet. Recordings: *Audio Fidelity*. Mgt.: Shaw Concerts, Inc. . . . **Kyung-Soo Won;** Conductor of the Stockton Symphony Association, Inc. since 1967.

George Yaeger; Conductor of the Abilene (Texas) Philharmonic since 1966. . . . **James Yestadt;** Conductor of the Mobile Symphony Orchestra since 1963; former conductor of New Orleans Philharmonic.

Concertmasters of Selected Orchestras

(The year of appointment, when known, follows each name.)

Leo Ahramjian (1963), Wilmington Symphony Orchestra (Delaware)... **Victor Aitay** (co-Concertmaster), Chicago Symphony Orchestra ... **Eugene Altschuler,** St. Paul Chamber Orchestra ... **Charles Avsharian** (1963), Grand Rapids Symphony Society (Michigan).

Melvin Baddin (1953), Fresno Philharmonic Orchestra (California) ... **Virginia Baker** (1964), Pasadena Symphony Orchestra ... **Fredric Balazs** (1971), Honolulu Symphony Orchestra ... **Diane Spognardi Balko,** Duluth Symphony Orchestra ... **John A. Bauer,** (1965), Columbia Philharmonic Orchestra (South Carolina) ... **Wilfred Biel** (1967), Des Moines Symphony Orchestra ... **Paul Bizz** Fort Wayne Philharmonic Orchestra ... **Dixie Blackstone** (1963), New York Orchestral Society ... **Renato Bonacini** (1962), Hartford Symphony Orchestra ... **Warren Von Bronkhorst** (1967), Stockton Symphony Assn. (California).

Allen Cannon (1946), Peoria Symphony Orchestra (Illinois) ... **Alphonse Carlo** (1967), Florida Symphony Orchestra ... **Norman Carol** (1966), The Philadelphia Orchestra ... **James Ceasar** (1950), Wichita Symphony Orchestra (Kansas) ... **Isidore Cohen** (1961), Esterhazy Orchestra (N.Y.) ... **Myron Cohen** (1949), Omaha Symphony Orchestra (Nebraska) ... **Dinos Constantinides** (1966), Baton Rouge Symphony Orchestra ... **John Corigliano** (1966), Symphony Society of San Antonio ... **Arthur Cotruvo** (1967), Columbus Symphony Orchestra (Georgia).

Peter Dimitriades (1963), The Little Orchestra Society (N.Y.) ... **Rafael Druian** (1971), New York Philharmonic.

Sigmund Effron (1946), Cincinnati Symphony Orchestra... **Mark Ellsworth** (1953), National Gallery Orchestra (D.C.) ... **Robert Emile** (1959), San Diego Symphony Orchestra ... **Charles Everett,** Toledo Orchestra ... **Hugh Ewart** (1948), Oregon Symphony Orchestra.

Gerald Fischbach, Evansville Philharmonic Orchestra (Indiana) ... **Lea Foli,** Minnesota Orchestra ... **Leopold La Fosse** (1958), Austin Symphony Orchestra ... **David Frisina** (1942), Los Angeles Philharmonic.

James Getzoff (1960), Glendale Symphony Orchestra (California) ... **Laurence A. Gibson,** El Paso Symphony Orchestra Assn. ... **Harry Glickman** (1963), The Orchestra of America (N.Y.) ... **Sheldon Goldsholl,** Wichita Falls Symphony Orchestra (Texas).

Don Hansen (1961), Greensboro Symphony Orchestra (North Carolina) ... **George Hardesty** (1953), Columbus Symphony Orchestra (Ohio) ... **Charles V. Haupt,** Buffalo Philharmonic Orchestra ... **Jaroslav Holesovsky,** Dayton Philharmonic Orchestra ...

Frances Hull (1960), Niagara Falls Philharmonic Orchestra . . . **Earle Hummel** (1966), Schenectady Symphony Orchestra.

Frances E. Jones (1953), Tulsa Philharmonic Society.

Leonard Kacenjar, Shreveport Symphony Society . . . **Louisa Kellam,** The Philharmonic Society of St. Louis . . . **Edouard Kesner** (1962), Dearborn Symphony Orchestra (Michigan) . . . **Paul Kling** (1959), Louisville Orchestra . . . **Kenji Kobayashi** (1967), Oklahoma City Symphony Orchestra . . . **Harold Kohon** (1963), Mozart Festival Orchestra (N.Y.) . . . **Jacob Krachmalnick** (1964), San Francisco Symphony Assn. . . . **Aaron Krosnick,** Jacksonville Symphony Assn. (Florida).

L. John Lambros (1952), Charleston Symphony Orchestra (West Virginia) . . . **Alfred Lanegger** (1960), Roanoke Symphony Orchestra (Virginia) . . . **George Lapenson** (1967), Savannah Symphony Society . . . **Thomas LeVeck,** Lansing Symphony Orchestra (Michigan) . . . **Frank Levy** (1947), North Jersey Philharmonic Orchestra (formerly Patterson Philharmonic) . . . **Gerald Lewis** (1962), South Bend Symphony Orchestra.

Samuel Magad (1971) (co-Concertmaster), Chicago Symphony Orchestra . . . **Daniel Majeske** (1971), The Cleveland Orchestra . . . **Ruthabeth Marsh** (1966), Erie Philharmonic Society (Pa.) . . . **Ronald W. Marshall** (1968), Peninsula Symphony Orchestra (Virginia) . . . **Elizabeth Matesky** (1971), Syracuse Symphony Orchestra (N.Y.) . . . **Barbara Meeker** (1965), Beaumont Symphony Society (Texas) . . . **Elizabeth Moore,** Richmond Symphony Orchestra (Va.) . . . **Edward Mumm** (1962), Milwaukee Symphony Orchestra.

Eleanor Nelson (1962), Quincy Symphony Orchestra (Massachusetts) . . . **Carter Nice** (1967), New Orleans Philharmonic Symphony Orchestra.

Irene Palasyewskj (1965), Scranton Philharmonic Orchestra (Pennsylvania) . . . **Kenneth Park** (1967), New Bedford Symphony Orchestra (Massachusetts) . . . **Ronald Patterson** (1972), Houston Symphony Orchestra . . . **John Pintavalle** (1966), Greater Trenton Symphony Association . . . **Dino Pintavelli** (1967), Brooklyn Philharmonia, Inc. . . . **Alexander Prilutchi** (1960), Fort Lauderdale Symphony Orchestra.

Dorothy Rendina (1967), Independence Symphony Orchestra (Missouri) . . . **Elaine Richey** (1964), Charlotte Symphony Orchestra . . . **Louis Riemer** (1959) St. Joseph Symphony Orchestra (Missouri) . . . **Max Robbins** (1966), The Little Symphony of Newark . . . **Alvin Rogers** (1972) Vermont State Symphony Orchestra . . . **Ivan Romanenko,** Youngstown Symphony Orchestra (Ohio) . . . **Nathan Rubin** (1962), Oakland Symphony Orchestra (California) . . . **Phillip Ruder,** Dallas Symphony Orchestra . . . **Voldemars Rushevics** (1950), Kalamazoo Symphony Society . . . **Milton Ryan** (1967), Jackson Symphony Orchestra (Mississippi).

Isidor Saslav, Baltimore Symphony Orchestra . . . **Martin Sauser** (1957), Atlanta Symphony Orchestra . . . **Kenneth Schanewerk** (1957), Fort Worth Symphony Orchestra . . . **Arnold Schatz** (1961), Lincoln Symphony Orchestra (Nebraska) . . . **Alfred Schenker,** Kansas City Philharmonic Assn. (Missouri) . . . **Miriam Schneider** (1966), Madison Symphony Orchestra (Wisconsin) . . . **Frank Scocozza** (1961), New Jersey Symphony Orchestra . . . **Dora Short** (1966), Norfolk Symphony Assn. . . . **Ross Shub** (1971), Chattanooga Symphony Assn. . . . **Fritz Siegal** (1966), Pittsburgh Symphony Orchestra . . . **Henry Siegl** (1956), Seattle Symphony Orchestra . . . **Joseph Silverstein** (1962), Boston Symphony Orchestra . . . **John Smarelli,** Springfield Symphony Orchestra (Ohio) . . . **Gordon Staples** (1968), Detroit Symphony Orchestra.

Arthur Tabachnick (1966), Indianapolis Symphony Orchestra . . . **Samuel Terranova,** Nashville Symphony Orchestra . . . **Isabelle Thompson** (1948), Fargo–Moorhead Symphony Orchestra Assn. (North Dakota) . . . **Donald Todd** (1968), The Amarillo Symphony . . . **Armen Turadian** (1961), San Bernardino Symphony Orch.

Dezso Vaghy (1966), Portland Symphony Orchestra (Maine).

Dorothy Wade (1966), Compton Civic Symphony Orchestra (California) . . . **Ralph Wade** (1954), Binghamton Symphony Orchestra . . . **Howard Weiss** (1967), Rochester Philharmonic Orchestra . . . **Joy Brown Wiener** (1952), Memphis Orchestral Society . . . **Marlis Windus** (1960), Cedar Rapids Symphony Orchestra (Iowa) . . . **Harold Wolf** Birmingham Symphony Assn.

Clyda Yedinak (1959), Riverside Symphony Orchestra (California).

Mitchell J. Zablotny (1950), Lubbock Symphony Orchestra . . . **Frederick Zomzely** (1955), Elizabeth Civic Orchestra (N.J.).

Chamber Ensembles

(Violins in the string quartets are shown in order of first and second. Recording labels for all chamber ensembles refer to commercially available recordings. Concert managements were valid in spring, 1972 or for the season beginning 1972 and ending 1973.)

STRING QUARTETS

ALARD QUARTET. In residence since 1962 at Pennsylvania State University, University Park, Pennsylvania 16802. Founded 1954. Has been an "in-residence" ensemble at other schools. New York debut in 1965 and has appeared there (1967, and subsequently). Members: **Donald Hopkins,** violin; **Joanne Zagst,** violin; **Raymond Page,** viola; **Leonard Feldman,** cello.

BOWLING GREEN STRING QUARTET. In residence, Bowling Green State University School of Music, Bowling Green, Ohio. Founded 1962. Has toured England, European continent, Mexico, U.S. cities and campuses. New York debut was at Tully Hall, 1970. Members: **Paul Makara** and **Young Nam Kim,** violins; **Bernard Linden,** viola; **Peter Howard,** cello. Mgt.: Tornay Management.

CARNEGIE STRING QUARTET. In residence, Brooklyn College, Brooklyn, New York. Members: **Lamar Alsop** and **Alan Martin,** violins; **Julien Barber,** viola; and **Ruth Alsop,** cello.

CHICAGO SYMPHONY STRING QUARTET. In residence, University of Wisconsin at Milwaukee, summer, 1972. Players are all members of the Chicago Symphony Orchestra: **Victor Aitay** and **Edgar Muenzer,** violins; **Milton Preves,** viola; and **Frank Miller,** cello. Mgt.: Arthur Judson Management.

CLAREMONT STRING QUARTET. Founded in 1953. Named after Claremont Avenue, the former address of Juilliard from which Claremont's first violinist graduated. New York debut in 1954. Some of the players have been part of the "Music from Marlboro" series. Has performed at festivals, in major U.S. cities, etc. Toured Africa under State Department auspices. Members: **Marc Gottlieb** and **Vladimir Weisman,** violins; **Scott Nickrenz,** viola; **Irving Klein,** cello. Recordings: *CRI, Nonesuch,* and *Lyrichord.*

CLEVELAND STRING QUARTET. In residence, Cleveland Institute of Music. All players are members of the Cleveland Orchestra. Performing debut at the Marlboro Festival. New York debut made in 1970 at the New School Concerts. Some of the members have appeared previously in the "Music from Marlboro" series. Members: **Peter Salaff** and **Donald Weilerstein,** violins; **Paul Katz,** viola; **Martha S. Katz,** cello. Tours include two in the U.S., Europe, and South America. Presented a series at Hunter College in New York. Mgt.: Pacific World Artists, Inc.

COMPOSERS STRING QUARTET. In residence, New England Conservatory of

Music, Boston. The ensemble is known for outstanding concerts of contemporary music. Members: **Matthew Raimondi** and **Anahid Ajemian,** violins; **Jean Dupouy,** viola; **Michael Rudiakov,** cello. Labels recorded: *Nonesuch.* Mgt.: Pacific World Artists, Inc.

CURTIS STRING QUARTET. On the faculty of the New School of Music in Philadelphia. Founded in 1927. Has a distinguished history and has made many tours throughout Europe and the U.S.; has performed at the White House, etc. Members: **Jascha Brodsky** and **Geoffrey Michaels,** violins; **Max Aronoff,** viola; **Orlando Cole,** cello. **Mr. Aronoff** is also Director of New School. Recordings: *Westminster.* Mgt.: Sherman Pitluck, Inc.

DE PASQUALE STRING QUARTET. In residence, Haverford College, Haverford, Pennsylvania. The quartet is made up of brothers—all members of the Philadelphia Orchestra: **William De Pasquale** and **Robert De Pasquale,** violins; **Joseph De Pasquale,** viola; and **Francis De Pasquale,** cello. Mgt.: Columbia Artists Management, Inc.

FINE ARTS QUARTET. Artists-in-residence, University of Wisconsin, Milwaukee. A Chicago-based ensemble founded in 1946. One of the most famous and active of the world's string quartets, it has performed on radio and television, made extensive U.S. and world tours, and has commissioned new works; it has recorded the complete quartets of Beethoven and Bartók, many of those by Haydn, etc. The group's programs are often ambitious, such as performances of all 12 quartets of Haydn's opus 76 in a concert series, etc. Members: **Leonard Sorkin** and **Abram Loft,** violins; **Bernard Zaslav,** viola; **George Sopkin,** cello. Records: *Concert-disc, Columbia, Odyssey, Vox, Decca.* Mgt.: Melvin Kaplan, Inc.

GUARNERI STRING QUARTET. New York-based ensemble, organized at the Marlboro Music Festival. Made its New York debut in 1965 and has since become, in a relatively short time, one of the most famous of U.S. string quartets. Has toured nearly every state and has performed at many university and college campuses, festivals, concert series, etc. It has recorded and performed publicly with pianist **Arthur Rubinstein.** Members: **Arnold Steinhardt** and **John Dalley,** violins; **Michael Tree,** viola; **David Soyer,** cello. Labels: *RCA Victor.* Mgt.: Arthur Judson Management, Inc.

JUILLIARD STRING QUARTET. In residence, Juilliard School, New York. It is also the "resident" quartet in the Library of Congress (see Gertrude Clarke Whittall Foundation under Organizations). Founded in 1946, it is one of the best-known and most highly-regarded chamber groups in the world. It has recorded extensively and performs a large repertory (over 135) of many contemporary works, as well as the full range of classics. Members: **Robert Mann** and **Earl Carlyss,** violins; **Samuel Rhodes,** viola; **Claus Adam,** cello. Labels: *Columbia, RCA Victor.* Mgt.: Colbert Artists Management, Inc.

LA SALLE STRING QUARTET, Box 29090, Cincinnati, Ohio 45229. In residence, College-Conservatory of Cincinnati. An active touring group, its recent tours include Europe in 1969 (where, at the Vienna Festival, it played a cycle of works by Schoenberg, Berg and Webern), 1971, 1972, and 1973; United States and Canada in 1972–73; Israel and Scandinavia in 1969. Records: *Deutsche Grammophon.*

LENOX QUARTET. Artists-in-residence, Grinnell College in Iowa. One of the few quartets, if not the only one, which can transform from a string quartet into a piano quartet without a guest member. Has toured throughout the U.S. and Europe. Its New York debut was as a piano quartet in November of 1967. Members: **Peter Marsh** and **Delmar Pettys,** violins; **Paul Hersh,** viola and piano; **Donald McCall,** cello. Label: *Dover Records.* Mgt.: Herbert Barrett Management.

PHILADELPHIA STRING QUARTET. Has performed in New York, Philadelphia, London, Copenhagen, etc. European tours in 1964, 1965, 1969 (the latter under auspices of the U.S. State Department); South American tour in 1966 (State Department); and tour of India in 1968 (State Department).

Members: **Veda Reynolds** and **Irwin Eisenberg,** violins; **Alan Iglitzen,** viola; **Charles Brennand,** cello. Label: *CRI.* Mgt.: Pacific World Artists, Inc.

SAINT CLAIR STRING QUARTET. Comprised of members of the Detroit Symphony Orchestra: **Jerome Rosen** and **Haim Shtrum,** violins; **Philip Porbe,** viola; and **John Thurman,** cello.

STANLEY QUARTET. Resident quartet, University of Michigan. Founded in 1949. Toured South America under the federal government in 1958, giving some 20 concerts. Performs a series on campus each year and makes trips to other college campuses, the Library of Congress, etc. It has performed throughout Michigan and is particularly dedicated to making educational work in that state its first responsibility by appearing on television and in radio broadcasts. One third of the quartet's repertory is modern music. Members: **Gilbert Ross** and **Gustave Rosseels,** violins; **Robert Courte,** viola; and **Jerome Jelinek,** cello. Record labels: *CRI* and *Columbia.*

STRADIVARI QUARTET (formerly the Iowa String Quartet). In residence, University of Iowa. In 1967, four Stradivari instruments valued at $500,000 were lent to the Iowa String Quartet by the Corcoran Gallery of Art in Washington, D.C. The instruments were bequeathed to Corcoran by their late owner, Mrs. William Andrews Clark, who had previously lent them to the Paganini Quartet in California for many years. The group has performed in many U.S. cities and abroad in Berlin, Bergen, Heidelberg, Montreal, etc. Members: **Allen Ohmes** and **John Ferrell,** violins; **William Preucil,** viola; and **Charles Wendt,** cello. Personal management representative: Dodie Lefebre.

VERMEER STRING QUARTET. In residence, Northern Illinois University, Dekalb, Illinois. First formed and heard at the Marlboro Music Festival. New York debut in 1970 (New School Concerts). Members: **Shmuel Ashkenasi** and **Pierre Menard,** violins; **Scott Nickrenz,** viola; **Richard Sher,** cello. Mgt.: Columbia Artists Management, Inc.

WALDEN QUARTET. In residence, University of Illinois. Members: **Homer Schmitt** and **Bernard Goodman,** violins; **John Garvey,** viola; **Robert Swenson,** cello. Labels: *Columbia, Contemporary, Lyrichord, Desto,* and *Folkways.*

WOODSTOCK STRING QUARTET. Members: **Charles Libove** and **Alice Smiley,** violins; **Theodore Israel,** viola; **Charles McCracken,** cello. Mgt.: Herbert Barrett Management, Inc.

CHAMBER GROUPS: TRIOS, MISCELLANEOUS QUARTETS, QUINTETS, MIXED ENSEMBLES, ETC.

AEOLIAN CHAMBER PLAYERS. Members: **David Gilbert,** flute; **Jacob Maxim,** piano; **Lewis Kaplan,** violin; **Lloyd Greenberg,** clarinet; and **Michael Rudiakov,** cello. Mgt.: Sheldon Soffer Management, Inc.

ALMA TRIO, Members: **Andor Toth,** violin; **Gabor Rejto,** cello; **William Corbett Jones,** piano. Label: *Decca.* Mgt.: Mariedi Anders Artists Management, Inc.

AMERICAN ARTS TRIO. Members, all of whom are on the faculty of West Virginia University, are: **Arno Drucker,** piano; **Donald Portnoy,** violin; and **Jon Engberg,** cello. Mgt.: Anne J. O'Donnell Management.

AMERICAN BRASS QUINTET. In residence, Mannes College of Music, New York. Regarded by many as the foremost brass quintet in America. It has commissioned and premiered many new works. In spring, 1968 it made a nine-week tour of the Far East under State Department auspices and conducted a workshop for brass in Japan. Has performed with the National Orchestral Association in New York. Records: *CRI, Nonesuch, Desto, Folkways,* and *Serenus.* Mgt.: Melvin Kaplan, Inc.

AMERICAN STRING TRIO. Artists-in-residence, State University of New York at Albany. Members: **Marvin Morgenstern,** violin; **Karen Tuttle,** viola; **John Goberman,** cello. Record label: *Desto.*

BACH ARIA GROUP. This ensemble marked its 25th season in 1971. It is the only group devoted exclusively to the performance of the vocal chamber music (cantatas) of J. S. Bach. Its programs feature mostly selected arias from the large number of cantatas of Bach, but also include complete cantatas. The group is further distinguished by the fact that all members are well-known solo concert artists and chamber musicians. It has toured widely in the U.S. and has performed in South America and Europe. Director is **William H. Scheide.** Members are: **Samuel Baron,** flute; **Robert Bloom,** oboe; **Norman Farrow,** bass-baritone; **Maureen Forrester,** alto; **Bernard Greenhouse,** cello; **Richard Lewis,** tenor; **Lois Marshall,** soprano; **Oscar Shumsky,** violin; **Yehudi Wyner,** keyboard. Guest artists in recent years have been: **Lili Chookasian,** alto, and conductors **Mario Bernardi, Jorge Mester, Seymour Lipkin, Nicholas Harsanyi,** and **Brian Priestman.** Recordings: *Decca.* Mgt.: Herbert Barrett Management.

BALSAM-KNOLL-HEIFETZ TRIO. Two of the three members once formed the Albeneri Trio. Members: **Arthur Balsam,** piano; **William Kroll,** violin; and **Benar Heifetz,** cello. Mgt.: Colbert Artists Management.

BEAUX ARTS TRIO OF NEW YORK. In residence, Indiana University, School of Music. Formed in the early 1950's. Has performed well over a thousand concerts in North America, Europe, and Africa. Members: **Menahem Pressler,** piano; **Daniel Guilet,** violin; and **Bernard Greenhouse,** cello. Mgt.: Columbia Artists Management, Inc.

CHAMBER MUSIC SOCIETY OF LINCOLN CENTER, Lincoln Center for the Performing Arts, Alice Tully Hall, 1941 Broadway, New York, N.Y. 10023. Formed in 1969. Presents four subscription series of six concerts each from October to early May or late April. This group is in the forefront of the world's versatile chamber groups. The Society's concerts present performers in various instrumental sizes and combinations: duos, trios, quartets, chamber orchestra, etc. It has commissioned new works of outstanding composers. Its unhackneyed programming and the use of renowned guest performers has resulted in the ensemble playing to sold-out houses. In addition to the concert series at Tully Hall, the Society has established a series both in Washington, D.C. and Baltimore. Members of the ensemble are: **Charles Wadsworth,** Artistic Director and pianist; **Charles Treger,** violin; **Walter Trampler,** viola; **Leslie Parnas,** cello; **Paula Robison,** flute; **Leonard Arner,** oboe; **Gervase de Peyer,** clarinet; **Richard Goode,** piano and harpsichord. Guest performers have been **Pierre Boulez, Beverly Sills, Maureen Forrester, John Browning, Peter Serkin,** Guarneri String Quartet, Juilliard Quartet, et al.

CHICAGO UNIVERSITY CONTEMPORARY CHAMBER PLAYERS, University of Chicago. Director is composer **Ralph Shapey.** Founded in 1964 by the University with a grant from the Rockefeller Foundation. A number of its performances have been supported by the Fromm Foundation of Chicago. The ensemble consists of from about 13 to over 20 players in various instrumental combinations. In addition to performances in Chicago, the group has performed in New York City and elsewhere. Guest artists appearing with the ensemble have been **Bethany Beardslee** and **Neva Pilgrim,** vocalists, and violinist **Esther Glazer.** Record label: *CRI.*

THE CONTEMPORARY CHAMBER ENSEMBLE. A New York-based ensemble founded in 1960. Founder, Director (and bassoonist) is **Arthur Weisberg.** It is one of the most respected chamber ensembles in America. It is dedicated totally to modern music, having given countless premiere performances of new works in many styles. Presents an annual series in Carnegie Hall. Its 17 or so performers include those for strings, woodwinds, some brass, piano, and percussion. Labels: *CRI, Nonesuch,* Mgt.: Melvin Kaplan, Inc.

DORIAN WOODWIND QUINTET. In residence, Brooklyn College, Brooklyn N.Y. Founded in 1961 in Tanglewood, Massachusetts (Berkshire Music Center) under a Fromm Foundation grant (q.v.). The quintet has the unusual designation of "university-wide artists in residence" for the entire system of the State University of New York. Has played throughout the U.S., Europe (London, Vienna, Warsaw, etc.) and, under State Department sponsorship, in Africa. Members: **Karl Kraber,** flute; **Charles Kuskin,** oboe; **William Lewis,** clarinet; **Jane Taylor,** bassoon; **Barry Benjamin,** horn. Labels recorded: *Candide, Serenus.* Mgt.: Columbia Artists Management, Inc.

EASTMAN BRASS QUINTET, Eastman School of Music, Rochester, N.Y. Members: **Daniel Patrylak** and **Allen Vizzutti,** trumpets; **Verne Reynolds,** horn; **Donald Knaub,** trombone; and **Cherry Beauregard,** tuba. Mgt.: Arthur Judson Management, Inc.

EASTMAN QUARTET, Eastman School of Music, Rochester, N.Y. Members: **Frank Glazer,** piano; **Millard Taylor,** violin; **Francis Tursi,** viola; and **Ronald Leonard,** cello. Mgt.: Herbert Barrett Management, Inc.

GABRIELI TRIO. In residence, Boston Conservatory of Music. A string trio made up of members of the Boston Symphony Orchestra. Members: **Alfred Schneider,** violin; **Earl Hedburg,** viola; **Richard Kapuscinski,** cello. Mgt. Johanna Giwosky Management, Boston.

ISTOMIN–STERN–ROSE TRIO. **Eugene Istomin,** piano; **Isaac Stern,** violin; **Leonard Rose,** cello. Formed in 1961. A trio of famed virtuosi who perform the great trio literature whenever their own separate concert schedules can permit (usually about a month or two each year). In 1970, they performed a particularly noteworthy cycle of Beethoven (for the Beethoven year) in New York, London, Paris, Buenos Aires, and Tokyo. Recordings: *Columbia.* Mgt.: Hurok Concerts, Inc.

LOS ANGELES WOODWIND QUINTET. The quintet is particularly active in Southern California, giving school concerts in connection with Young Audiences of Greater Los Angeles, Inc. Members: **Karen Carrington,** flute; **John Ellis,** oboe; **Thomas Osborn,** clarinet; **Ralph Lee,** bassoon; and **Waldemar Linder,** horn.

MUSIC FROM MARLBORO. Established in 1965. (See Marlboro Music Festival.) A changing group of musicians, giving varied programs of chamber music on tour. A number of alumni of this series have gone on to form their own chamber ensembles. Mgt.: Columbia Artists Management, Inc.

THE NEW AMSTERDAM ENSEMBLE. Twelve instrumentalists and one singer performing concerts of chamber music for unusual combinations. Its programs contain modern and classical works for duos, trios, quartets, etc. Performs a series of concerts in New York. Mgt.: Thea Dispeker, Artists' Representative.

THE NEW PERCUSSION QUARTET, 63 Amsterdam Place, Buffalo, N.Y. 14222. Formed in 1966. Active in Western New York Chapter of Young Audiences, Inc., and annually performs concerts for thousands of young people. Repertory consists of works written originally for percussion and no transcriptions or arrangements. The quartet's programs offer solo works, duos, trio performances, etc. Members: **Edward Burnham, Lynn Harbold, John Rowland,** and **Jan Williams.**

NEW YORK BRASS QUINTET. In residence, Hartt College of Music, University of Hartford, Connecticut. Founded 1954. Members: **Robert Nagel** and **Alan Dean,** trumpets; **Paul Ingraham,** horn; **John Swallow,** trombone; and **Thompson Hanks,** tuba. European tours every other year; two tours under Department of State auspices; has conducted workshops and clinics and has performed throughout the U.S.; recipients of Rockefeller and Whittall Foundation grants; has made educational film for young people. Record labels: *RCA Victor, CRI, Serenus, Golden Crest,* and *Desto.* Mgt.: Columbia Artists Management, Inc.

NEW YORK CHAMBER ENSEMBLE. A group of ten players of winds, strings, and piano which has played at Lincoln Center Mozart Festivals in New York, Carnegie Hall,

Town Hall, etc. Sometimes uses guest artists. Since its founding, there have been personnel changes.

THE NEW YORK CHAMBER SOLOISTS. Members: **Stanley Ritchie, Gerald Tarack,** and **Isidore Cohen,** violins; **Ynez Lynch,** viola; **Fortunato Arico** and **Alexander Kougell,** cello; **Julius Levine,** double bass; **Thomas Nyfenger,** flute; **Melvin Kaplan,** oboe; **Harriet Wingreen,** piano and harpsichord; **Charles Bressler,** tenor. The ensemble's repertory covers music from the baroque to contemporary styles. Record labels: *Decca, Nonesuch, Project 3.* Mgt.: Melvin Kaplan, Inc.

NEW YORK HARP ENSEMBLE. Director is the noted harpist, **Aristid von Wurtzler.** Undertook its first European tour in 1972: Italy, Hungary, Austria, Germany, Holland. Members: **Rebecca Flannery, Martha Flannery, Ewa Jaslar,** and **Barbara Pniewska.** Mgt.: Albert Kay Associates, Inc.

NEW YORK PRO MUSICA, 300 West End Avenue, New York, N.Y. 10023. Tel.: (212) 874–7711. Founded in 1952 by Noah Greenberg, who was musical director until his death in 1966. The New York Pro Musica is both a performing ensemble and an educational institution with its own office, rehearsal studio, and research library. It is devoted to performing, instructing, and conducting research into the rare and unknown music of the Middle Ages, Renaissance, and early baroque periods. Its early fame was established by its reconstructed and fully staged performances of the medieval liturgical music dramas, "The Play of Daniel," first performed in 1957, and "The Play of Herod," first performed in 1963; both dramas premiered at The Cloisters of New York's Metropolitan Museum of Art. Since their first modern performances, the two music dramas have been performed on tour throughout the U.S. and Europe, taped for television, and recorded. The group is primarily a touring ensemble; its performances in general, but particularly those of the two "plays," have been seen by an average of about 100,000 people per season, many thousands more having heard and seen them through the recording and broadcasting media. The Pro Musica's most recent production, "An Entertainment for Elizabeth," premiered in 1969, is also now being performed throughout the U.S. each season. Other than these works, which are performed in costume with the instruments of the period but, more importantly, with an attempt at stylistic authenticity, the Pro Musica has performed live or recorded a wide-ranging repertory of vocal and instrumental music. The ensemble is generally thought to have established a standard by which other similar-minded ensembles may be appreciated. Its touring activity has included Europe in 1960, where performances took place in specially selected churches; in 1963, for appearances at summer festivals; and in 1964, for a tour of the Soviet Union under the auspices of the U.S. State Department. Its domestic tours include innumerable appearances at colleges and universities, as well as the major cities and festivals. The Pro Musica has received important grants from the Rockefeller and Ford Foundations for continuing its performance and educational work. In order to gain broader financial support, it has established the Friends of New York Pro Musica, through which contributions are accepted in exchange for certain membership privileges. Funds are used for needs that are unique among performing groups, such as purchase and repair of antique instruments and replicas used in performance, new costumes, the cost of transcribing music from old scores, etc. Musical Director is **George Houle,** who succeeded **Paul Maynard,** the director from 1970 to 1972. Current members of the performing ensemble are: **Daniel Collins,** countertenor; **Ray DeVoll,** tenor; **Brenda Fairaday,** soprano; **Rodney Godshall,** bass; **Judith Hubbell,** mezzo-soprano; **Lucy Cross,** lute, psaltery, recorder, and sackbut; **Shelley Gruskin,** flute, recorder, krummhorn, rauschpfeife; **Herb Meyers,** flute, recorder, krummhorn, shawm, vielle; **Frederick Renz,** organetto, regal; **Mary Springfels,** viols, vielle, and recorder. Guest artists are also engaged, which can augment the cast of players considerably. For example, "An Entertainment for Elizabeth," probably the most lavish production of Pro Musica to date, employs a cast of 24 including nine dancers, apart from production personnel. The educational work of Pro Musica includes a program, supported by a grant from the New York Council on the Arts, which provides instruction (chorus, viol consort, lute song, collegium musicum, etc.) at modest fees in the study and practice of the music within the range of interest of the organization. The New York Pro Musica library includes one of the largest playing collections of medieval, Renaissance, and baroque instrument replicas and antiques in the world. Begun in 1954, it was developed by collaboration between instrument builders and the instrumentalists of Pro Musica. (See Music Libraries.) Records: *Decca, Everest, Odyssey,* and *Esoteric.* (A recorded anthology, "Music for a Medieval Day," is distributed by Horizon Books.) Mgt.: Columbia Artists Management, Inc.

NEW YORK STRING SEXTET. Members: **Renato Bonacini** and **Kees Kooper,** violins; **Paul Doktor** and **Emile Simonel,** violas; **Janos Scholz** and **George Koutzen,** cellos. Mgt.: Colbert Artists Management, Inc.

NEW YORK WOODWIND QUINTET. In residence, Harpur College of the State University of New York at Binghamton. In existence for many years, the group has a distinguished history of having played many modern works and having recorded a large number of pieces. It has sometimes performed as a wind quartet and has also joined the Fine Arts Quartet (strings) in special performances. Members: **Thomas Nyfenger,** flute; **Ronald Roseman,** oboe; **David Glazer,** clarinet; **Ralph Froelich,** horn; **Arthur Weisberg,** bassoon. Labels recorded: *Concert-disc, Columbia, CRI, Washington University, Golden Crest, Esoteric, Nonesuch, Everest.* Mgt.: Herbert Barrett Management.

ORIGINAL PIANO QUARTET. Founded more than 30 years ago in Berlin. American debut, May, 1940. This is the first and only ensemble composed of pianists. It enjoyed a spectacular radio and concert career in the 1940's and 1950's, appearing on radio in its own weekly series on the NBC Network, later on television, in film shorts, etc. Current members: **Adam Garner, William Gunther Sprecher, Edward Edson,** and **David Poliakine.** Label: *Decca.*

PHILHARMONIA TRIO. Has performed at Town Hall, New York, in the Great Artist Series, etc. Members: **Charles Libove,** violin; **Aldo Parisot,** cello; **Nina Lugovoy,** piano. Label: *CRI.* Mgt.: Herbert Barrett Management.

PHILIDOR TRIO. Founded in 1965 by players who were then members of New York Pro Musica. Members: **Elizabeth Humes,** soprano; **Shelley Gruskin,** baroque flute or recorders; **Edward Smith,** harpsichord. All are on the graduate faculty of the University of Minnesota at Minneapolis and are in residence at the school's Summer Arts Study Center. The group has performed concerts of baroque music throughout the U.S. and Canada, in New York City, at the Library of Congress, on college campuses, etc. Mgt.: Russell & Volkening, Inc., 551 Fifth Avenue, New York, N.Y. 10017.

PHOENIX WOODWIND QUINTET. Members: **Margaret Schecter,** flute; **Andrejs Jansons,** oboe; **Francisco Donaruma,** French horn; **Aris Chavez,** clarinet; **Richard Vrotney,** bassoon. Mgt.: Thea Dispeker, Artists' Representative.

RICHARDS WOODWIND QUINTET. In residence, Michigan State University, East Lansing, Michigan. New York debut in 1968. Extensive U.S. and Canada concert tours. Has appeared in the NET–TV series, "Music of the 20th Century." Members: **Alexander Murray,** flute; **Daniel Stolper,** oboe; **Elsa Ludewig,** clarinet; **Edgar Kirk,** bassoon; **Douglas Campbell,** horn. Mgt.: Albert Kay Associates, Inc.

SONI VENTORUM. A woodwind quintet, in residence at the University of Washington. Members: **Felix Skowronek,** flute; **Laila Storch,** oboe; **William McColl,** clarinet; **Christopher Leuba,** horn; **Arthur Grossman,** bassoon. Records: *Lyrichord, Desto.*

SPECULUM MUSICAE. A New York-based ensemble specializing in contemporary music.

Made its debut in New York in January, 1972. All young musicians: **Richard Fitz,** percussion and conductor; **Paul Dunkel,** flute; **Joel Marangella,** oboe; **Virgil Blackwell,** clarinet; **Gerald Schwartz,** trumpet; **Karen Lindquist,** harp; **Ursula Oppens,** piano; **Rolf Schulte,** violin; **John Graham,** viola; **Fred Sherry,** cello; and **Donald Palma,** bass. Appeared its first year under the auspices of Young Concert Artists, Inc.

TRIO DA CAMERA. Members: **Rowland Sturges,** piano; **William Wrzesien,** clarinet; and **Endel Kalam,** viola. Mgt.: The Frothingham Management.

VIRTUOSA DA CAMERA TRIO. Presents programs of early music. Has performed in the U.S., South America, and Europe. Members: **Mordecai S. Rubin,** recorders, krummhorn, wooden flutes; **Genette Foster,** violin, viola, viols, medieval strings; **Kenneth Cooper,** harpsichord. Mgt.: Thea Dispeker, Artists' Representative.

WAVERLY CONSORT, 160 West 73rd Street, New York, N.Y. 10023. A group of five to six performers appearing in costume and playing a variety of medieval, Renaissance, and baroque instruments in concerts featuring the music of those eras. Members: **Kay Jaffee,** recorder, rauschpfeife, portative organ, psaltery, and organetto; **Sally Logemann,** baroque oboe, shawm, krummhorn, recorder, kortholt, nun's fiddle, and rackett; **Judith Davidoff,** medieval fiddles; **Bonney McDowell,** viola da gamba, cornetto; **Michael Jaffee,** the group's director, lute, theorbo, cornetto, psaltery, guitar, Moorish lute. The consort has performed with guest soloists including **Sarah Franklin,** soprano; **Constantine Cassolas,** tenor; and **Jan De Gaetani,** mezzo. A typical program may include court songs and dances of the fourteenth and fifteenth centuries or a program of medieval carols and dances. One of the most unusual concerts was performed by the group at Hunter College in April, 1971 when, in costume and in a production that was fully staged, it presented "Las Cantigas de Santa Maria," music and verse in the Court of Alfonso X, known as "el Sabio" (13th century). This concert received high critical praise. The group has toured with this work and has recorded it. Label: *Vanguard.* Mgt.: Shaw Concert, Inc.

WESTWOOD WIND QUINTET, 424 Mavis Drive, Los Angeles, California 90065. Formed in 1959, the quintet has been featured at Peter Britt Music Festival in Oregon (q.v.) and the Alaska Music Festival (q.v.). It has made tours to colleges and universities, played on radio and television, and has given over 300 children's concerts in the West. Members: **Gretel Shanley,** flute; **Peter Christ,** oboe, also founder of the ensemble; **David Atkins,** clarinet; **Kay Brightman,** bassoon; and **Robert Henderson,** horn. Records: *Columbia, Crystal.* Mgt.: Artists' Alliance.

ZELENKA WOODWIND QUINTET. Formed in 1968. Members: **William Barrett Brice,** flute; **Stephen Berkelhammer,** oboe; **Paul Orton,** clarinet; **Linda Lee Smith,** bassoon; **Verne Windham,** horn.

Bands in America

The total number of bands in America has never been determined. As is the case with choruses, band activity cuts across the boundaries of professionalism and amateurism and admits of hundreds of thousands of participants. As a result, hardly any community is without a band of some kind. Each town or school district indirectly subsidizes a local high school group and may also support a municipal band by providing uniforms and music, a bandstand, and sometimes, paying the musicians. If the town is very small, the municipal band may consist largely of high school and even grammar school students. Large and small cities, on the other hand, have a better opportunity to form bands from professional musicians who, perhaps, are also private or public school music teachers. These groups consist of members of the local musicians union and charge admission to their concerts or are available for hire. Some are privately organized; others are supported by nationality societies, veterans' groups, neighborhood clubs, industries, and even churches. There are few full-time bands outside the military. Professional bands of national fame have limited seasons but may augment their activities through tours, radio and television broadcasts, and recordings.

The largest single employer of performing instrumentalists in the United States is the Department of Defense, through its armed services, the Army, Navy, Air Force, and Marine Corps. Performers in these services number in the thousands. Only the top headquarters service bands are included among the military units described here.

The strongest segment of the band field is that of high school and college bands. Most schools have a band unit of some kind, even those where music may not be part of the credit-course curriculum.

In a survey published in 1970, based on projections of survey samplings, the American Music Conference estimated that about 1.5 million American students perform in 22,500 high school marching bands. Additionally, high schools sponsor some 25,000 concert bands (containing, undoubtedly, many of the same students who take part in the marching bands), and about 12,000 jazz or so-called stage bands.

The college and university bands described in this section, gathered from 60 schools in thirty-seven states, are among the many hundreds of bands found in higher education institutions throughout the country. Many universities have band training programs of considerable size, and several bands, serving different educational and functional purposes, can be formed from a single group of available students. These are all described under the major heading of the school in question. Some schools acknowledge one specific band among the several established on campus as the most exemplary, performing the most challenging band music, or having the highest playing standards. In such cases, only that band is described.

College bands are arranged alphabetically by states; professional and military bands alphabetically by name.

The references to record labels are for recordings made within the last ten to twelve years which are believed to be still obtainable commercially.

COLLEGE AND UNIVERSITY BANDS

Arkansas

UNIVERSITY OF ARKANSAS SYMPHONIC BAND, University of Arkansas, Fayetteville, Arkansas 72701. Conductor, since 1970, is **Eldon Janzen.** The 82-piece band plays three concerts during the school term and two during the summer session. Performances take place in Concert Hall (500 seats) in the Fine Arts Complex. The band makes biannual tours of public schools and makes special appearances at conventions during the year.

Arizona

ARIZONA STATE UNIVERSITY BANDS, Department of Music, College of Fine Arts, Arizona State University, Tempe, Arizona 85281. There are four bands—one a marching unit, and three concert bands. The Symphonic Winds, the most selective of the concert bands and the school's official touring band, is composed of 50 to 60 members and gives six concerts a year in Grady Gammage Auditorium (3,000 seats). Conductor (since 1970) of this group and director of the band program is **Kenneth Snapp.** Assistant Conductor is **Robert W. Miller.** A concert band of 75 players performs its own series of campus concerts. The Laboratory Band is open to any student in the school, sometimes augments other band groups, but is intended mainly to give advanced students a chance to study and perform special music materials under faculty supervision. The "Sun Devil" Marching Band is a 150-member unit used for home football games. It is led by **Robert Miller.** Off season its members play in one of the concert bands and other smaller ensembles.

California

SAN JOSE STATE COLLEGE BAND, San Jose State College, San Jose, California 95114. Conductor, since 1956, has been **Roger S. Muzzy.** Organized in 1928. One hundred and forty-four players are included in the total band program. Three concerts are performed during the school year in the school's Auditorium (520 seats). The Marching Band has recorded for *Fidelity Sound Recordings* (*FSR*). . . . TOURNAMENT OF ROSES BAND, Pasadena City College Lancer Band, 1570 East Colorado Boulevard, Pasadena, California 91106. Founded in 1930. Conductor since 1967: **Richard V. Coy.** An organization of 140 players, the band gives three concerts during its normal nine-month college season. It is noted primarily for its appearance at the annual Tournament of Roses Parade, seen on national television each New Year's Day. In addition to marching and playing in the parade, which it has done since 1930, the band has participated in a number of ceremonies, such as the opening of the Seattle World's Fair. . . . UCLA BANDS, University of California–Los Angeles, 405 Hilgard Avenue, Los Angeles, California 90024. Director of Bands: **Clarence E. Sawhill.** The basic band program at UCLA is composed of some 200 players, from whom are selected members for the Symphonic

Band, Marching Band, Wind Ensemble, and other units. The Symphonic Band spent four weeks touring Europe in 1961, playing in England, France, Switzerland, Austria, Germany, and Denmark. On campus, the bands play for formal concerts and "patio" concerts throughout the school session. Has recorded for Fidelity Sound Recordings. . . . UNIVERSITY OF CALIFORNIA BANDS, 53 Student Center, Berkeley, California 94720. Organized in 1891. Conductor is **James E. Berdahl** (1950). The bands perform throughout the three quarters of the Berkeley campus's school year. The Concert Band plays about three concerts annually. Performances take place in Hertz Hall (500 seats), Zellerback Auditorium (2,000), Sproul Plaza, and Greek Theater. The band has recorded for *FSR* label (*Fidelity Sound Recordings*). . . . UNIVERSITY OF SOUTHERN CALIFORNIA WIND ORCHESTRA, Booth Hall, University of Southern California, 820 West 34th Street, Los Angeles, California 90007. Founded in 1935 (?). The ensemble of 65 players is conducted by **William A. Schaefer** (1952); Associate Conductor is **Arthur C. Bartner** (1970). On campus the ensemble plays four concerts during the school year in Bovard Auditorium (2,000 seats). It undertakes a tour of about four high schools in southern California each year. The band's repertory consists of many standard symphonic works and other works outside the normal repertory of wind groups, transcribed by **Mr. Schaefer** and others. It has premiered many new works by both major and minor composers, including "Emblems" by **Aaron Copland.**

Colorado

COLORADO STATE UNIVERSITY BANDS, Colorado State University, Fort Collins, Colorado 80521. This band of 35 players was founded in 1902; since 1961 has been conducted by **Otto Werner.** Performances are held in the Student Center Theater (675 seats) and include four concerts during the school term and three in the summer session. On a seasonal basis, there is a marching, jazz, and pep band as well as the symphonic band. In addition to its local concerts, the symphonic band gives nine tour concerts a year. The bands work on an annual budget of $4,000.

Connecticut

UNIVERSITY OF CONNECTICUT BANDS, University of Connecticut, Storrs, Connecticut 06268. Organized in 1935. Conductor, since 1956, is **Allan E. Gillespie;** Assistant Conductor is **David M. Maker** (1966). The bands at the university consist of a marching band of 160 players, a concert band of 90, and a wind ensemble of 47. Campus concert performances take place in Albert N. Jorgensen Auditorium (3,600 seats). About six concert performances are played during the school year. The concert band undertakes an annual New England tour and performs numerous concerts throughout Connecticut. During the summer of 1970, it made a European tour. . . . YALE UNIVERSITY BAND, 2139 Yale Station, New Haven, Connecticut 06520. Conductor: **Keith Wilson.** Made European tours in summers of 1959, 1962, 1965, and 1968.

Delaware

(UNIVERSITY OF DELAWARE) UNIVERSITY SYMPHONIC BAND, Newark, Delaware 19711. Since its formation in 1946, the band has been conducted by **J. Robert King.** A unit of 55 players, it plays four concerts during the academic year in Mitchell Hall (850 seats) on campus. The ensemble has premiered or commissioned works from **Alfred Reed, Robert Hogensen** (faculty member), et al., and has presented four festivals of American music with **Dello Joio, Creston, Persichetti,** and **Schuman** as guest composers. The University also has a concert band of 85 players under the direction of **David P. Blackinton.**

Florida

UNIVERSITY OF FLORIDA "GATOR" BANDS, University of Florida, Gainesville, Florida 32601. Founded in 1883. Director of

Bands is **Richard W. Bowles,** who in 1958 succeeded the noted bandmaster, **Col. Harold B. Bachman.** The university band units are the "Gator" Marching Band, the Symphonic Band, the Concert Band, Pep Band, Basketball Band, the Variety Bands, and the Summer Band. The Gator Band, a unit of 240 members (204 of which are musicians, the rest being majorettes, drum majors, etc.) is featured at all of the university's football games. The prime performing ensemble is the Symphonic Band. It performs about five regularly scheduled concerts a year and plays some tours. Members of the Gator Band who are not members of the Symphonic Band when the football season ends automatically become members of the Concert Band. This ensemble generally plays programs of lighter music than does the Symphonic Band, and its members may come from any part of the university. The University Auditorium (1,100 seats) is used for concerts. Altogether 21 concerts are played by the bands during the regular school year; there are an additional three concerts in the summer session. Assistant Director of Bands is **Gary Langford.** A recording, "Echoes from Florida Field," was made by the band and is available from the University Bookstore. . . . UNIVERSITY OF MIAMI "BAND OF THE HOUR," School of Music, University of Miami, Coral Gables, Florida 33124. Founded in 1926, the band is a marching unit of 120 players which subdivides into a concert band of 85 musicians and other ensembles. The marching band plays for the football season, appearing in Orange Bowl (78,000 seats), on local and national television programs and various music conventions. It performs about eight concerts during a 14-week period. The performances of the concert band include six concerts over a 16-week season given in Dade County Auditorium (3,500 seats) and on campus (a hall of 600 seats), as well as tours of Florida. Director is **William B. Russell** (1971); Assistant Director is **William A. Gora.**

Georgia

UNIVERSITY OF GEORGIA CONCERT BAND, Department of Music, University of Georgia, Athens, Georgia 30601. An ensemble of 98 players founded in 1905. Conductor is **Roger L. Dancz** (1955). The band performs ten concerts a season in the 1,200-seat Fine Arts Auditorium on campus and, during the last complete weekend in April, undertakes an annual spring tour of Georgia. The band's performances are recorded on *Century* records.

Hawaii

UNIVERSITY OF HAWAII CONCERT BAND, University of Hawaii, 2411 Dole Street, Honolulu, Hawaii 96822. **Richard S. Lum** has been Director since 1960. The band consists of 101 players and was founded in 1946. There are two concerts during the school year, held in the Honolulu International Center (2,000 seats).

Illinois

NORTHERN ILLINOIS UNIVERSITY BAND, Northern Illinois University, Dekalb, Illinois 60115. Conductor is **Glen W. Riggin** (1971); Assistant Conductor is **James A. Paul.** Organized in 1960. Some six concerts are played during the regular school year and two during the summer session. Concerts take place in University Center Ballroom (2,200 seats). . . . NORTHWESTERN UNIVERSITY BANDS, School of Music, Northwestern University, Evanston Illinois 60201. Conductor, since 1953: **John P. Paynter.** . . . SOUTHERN ILLINOIS UNIVERSITY BANDS, Communications Building, Southern Illinois University, Edwardsville, Illinois 62025. All of the bands function within the Fine Arts Division of the University but, as is the case with many universities and colleges, they are open to students from all school departments. The bands altogether include: the Symphonic Band (founded 1958) of 70 players of advanced attainment who are selected through audition; it performs about 10 concerts during the school year in Communications Theater (500 seats); the University Band, open to any student who has played in a high school or college band, which often invites a professional musician of distinction to work with it as a soloist, clinician, or conductor; a stage band composed of students from the Symphonic Band and other qualified players; and various chamber woodwind, brass, and percussion ensembles all of which give regularly scheduled performances on campus. Instructors for certain of the instruments used in the bands are members of the St. Louis Symphony. **C. Dale Fjerstad** (1959) is Director of Bands and also conducts the Symphonic Band. Assistant Director is **Herbert Oberlag.** The Symphonic Band commissioned and premiered "Expansions" by **Hale Smith.** . . . UNIVERSITY OF ILLINOIS BANDS, 1103 South 6th Street, Champaign, Illinois 61820. Conductor, since 1948: **Mark H. Hindsley.** Bands were organized at the University shortly after that school's founding in 1868. Its most important band, the Concert Band, has been in existence since 1890. At present, four organizations are in the total school band program: the Concert Band, the First Regimental Band, and the Second Regimental Band (in two sections). A total of 400 students from both the undergraduate and graduate divisions participate in the bands; a significant number come from other than the university music school. The four bands further subdivide to create the Football Band ("Marching Illini" of 175 players) and smaller ensembles needed for other athletic events and for units in the school's ROTC program. The 119-member Concert Band undertakes tours, plays several on-campus concerts ("Twilight Concerts" in April and May, a Commencement Concert, and for the commencement exercises, concerts in January and March), performs for the inauguration ceremonies of the state governors, etc. It has recorded over 30 LP records on a nonprofit basis; these are available through the University of Illinois Bands for educational purposes. Assistant Director of Bands is **Everett Kisinger;** Assistant to the Director is **Guy Duker.**

Indiana

PURDUE UNIVERSITY BAND, Purdue University, Lafayette, Indiana 47907. Conductor, since 1954: **Al G. Wright.** Has recorded for *Fidelity Sound Recordings* label. . . . UNIVERSITY OF NOTRE DAME CONCERT BAND, P.O. Box 523, Notre Dame, Indiana 46556. Founded in 1845. Conductor: **Robert F. O'Brien** (1952); Assistant Conductor: **James S. Phillips** (1965). The founding date of the band refers to the founding of Notre Dame's bands as such. The total band activity at the University, as in most schools of higher education, includes other band units such as football and marching bands, etc. The University claims its band to be "one of the oldest, if not the oldest, university bands in the United States." The concert Band has from 55 to 60 players and performs about 15 concerts a season, which coincides with the school's second semester. Campus performances take place in the Athletic and Convocation Center (12,000 seats) and O'Laughlin Auditorium (1,500 seats). The band makes an annual tour of two weeks, covering in three-year cycles a section of the country—East, West, and South or Southwest. These concerts are sometimes televised or broadcast. The tour repertory usually includes one or more original pieces. A recording of the concert band is available on *FSR* label (Fidelity Sound Recordings).

Iowa

LUTHER COLLEGE CONCERT BAND, Luther College, Decorah, Iowa 52101. Founded in 1878. Director is **Weston H. Noble,** since 1948. The band consists of 72 players. It does considerable touring: five overseas tours, including three tours of Europe, and innumerable trips within the United States. In 1966, it became the first band to give a full concert in New York's Philharmonic Hall. Special conferences and meetings within the academic world have had the Luther College Band serve as the official band. . . . UNIVERSITY OF IOWA SYMPHONY BAND, University of Iowa. Conductor: **Frank A. Piersol.**

Kansas

KANSAS STATE UNIVERSITY BANDS, Department of Music, Kansas State University, Manhattan, Kansas 66502. Bands at the university consist of: the "Wildcat" Marching Band, a 200-player band (with 12 twirlers and a staff of 10 as additional members), which plays at all home games and two out-of-town games; the Concert Band, made up of 50 to 60 selected best campus performers, presents some 12 to 15 concerts annually, playing or reading from 75 to 100 separate works; its campus concerts take place in the auditorium (1,800 seats), but the tour concerts, performed during a three-day period each year, are generally given in Kansas high schools. The band engages nationally known soloists and usually premieres one new work each season. Other bands are the stage band, varsity, and pep bands, each giving their own series or individual concerts on campus. In all, about 400 students belong to the bands. Director of Bands and Conductor of the Concert Band is **Paul Shull** (1960). **Phil Hewitt** is Assistant Director and Director of Athletic Bands. . . . WIND ENSEMBLE AND SYMPHONY BAND, College of Fine Arts, Wichita State University, Box 53, Wichita, Kansas 67208. Director of Bands is **John Boyd** (1971). There are eight concerts during the school term and five in the summer; all are held at the Lewis & Selma Miller Concert Hall (600 seats) in the Duerksen Fine Arts Center.

Kentucky

"BIG RED" BAND OF WESTERN KENTUCKY UNIVERSITY, Western Kentucky University, Bowling Green, Kentucky 42101. A band of 125 members conducted by **Kent Campbell** (1970). The band was founded in 1907. In addition to six to eight concerts held on campus at Van Meter Auditorium (1,300 seats), the band plays at all football and basketball games.

Louisiana

SOUTHEASTERN LOUISIANA UNIVERSITY SYMPHONIC BAND, Southeastern Louisiana University, Hammond, Louisiana 70401. A band of 78 members, founded in 1927; conducted by **Robert Weatherly** since 1961. Three concerts are performed during the school year in the University Auditorium (700 seats). Recording: *Century Records* (1969), available from the Music Department of the University.

Maryland

UNIVERSITY OF MARYLAND BANDS, Department of Music, Tawes Fine Arts Building, University of Maryland, College Park, Maryland 20742. Director of Bands, since 1968, has been **John Wakefield;** Assistant Director is **Fred Heath.** The bands of the university are: the Symphony Band, an organization of 70 players (the best performers of winds and percussion on campus), which plays the significant works of the band literature in about four concerts a year in Tawes Fine Arts Theater (1,200 seats) and about six off-campus concerts in various high schools; the Marching Band, which plays at all home football games and one or more games out of town; the Varsity and Concert Bands; the Stage Band; and the Pep Band. There are about 200 students in all of the bands; many of them are majors in studies other than music who have had previous training in ensemble playing. The school's band budget is approximately $15,000.

Massachusetts

HARVARD UNIVERSITY CONCERT BAND, 9 Prescott Street, Cambridge, Massachusetts 02138. Founded in 1919. The concert band's 55 members are drawn from the 150-member marching band. The latter is known for its half-time show performances at football games and perhaps for certain extra-musical trademarks, such as having the "largest playable drum in existence" (drawn on a cart) and for its giant tuba. The concert band has been under the direction of **Thomas G. Everett** since 1971. It presents concerts, about ten during the school year, in the 1,100-seat Saunders Theater in Cambridge and tours, playing at colleges, high schools, and for civic groups. It has performed in Boston's Symphony Hall, Severance Hall in Cleveland, and in Carnegie Hall in New York. Two recordings made by the band, "Concert for Winds," and "The Ivy League

Album," are offered for sale by the band as a means of maintaining its financial independence. The band is organized independent from the school, has no administrative ties with Harvard's music department, and allows management of its affairs to be the responsibility of an all-student staff.

Michigan

UNIVERSITY OF MICHIGAN SYMPHONIC BAND, 1314 School of Music, Ann Arbor, Michigan 48195. Founded in 1878, the band has for years been considered one of the best of American collegiate bands and is probably best known to foreigners because of its world tours. Under the auspices of the U.S. Department of State and its Cultural Exchange Program, the band toured the Soviet Union and most nations of Europe. It has made frequent concert appearances in many cities in the United States. For over thirty years its reputation was parallel to that of its director, **William D. Revelli** (now retired), whose efforts to better American school bands set a standard still respected. The Symphony Band's present Director is **George Cavender,** appointed in 1971. **John Larkin** is Assistant Conductor. The band has 110 players and plays 15 concerts during its seven-month season. These are held in Hill Auditorium (4,000 seats). It has the following titled record albums recorded under the *Vanguard* label: "Kickoff U.S.A.," "Touchdown U.S.A.," "Hail Sousa," "On Tour with the Michigan Band," and "University of Michigan Band."

Missouri

UNIVERSITY OF MISSOURI BANDS, Band Department, University of Missouri, 46 Jesse Building, Columbia, Missouri 65201. Director of Bands is **Alexander L. Pickard,** appointed in 1966. Assistant Directors are **Ron Dyer** and **George DeFoe.** The major band at the university is the so-called Marching Mizzou, a 240–member ensemble best known for its appearances on national television during the football season. Originally established as an ROTC marching unit, it came under the supervision of the school's music department in 1946; its members, however, come from all departments of the university, since membership is not limited to music majors. After the football season, the band is subdivided (as is customary with many university marching bands) into other performing groups: wind ensemble, concert band, university band, brass ensemble, studio band, and stage band. The concert band gives some eight performances during a 16-week season in Jesse Auditorium and plays at several Missouri high schools during a spring tour. An album entitled ". . .And Away We Go," is recorded under the *Mark Educational Recordings* label featuring the Missouri bands. . . . UNIVERSITY OF MISSOURI AT KANSAS CITY BANDS, University of Missouri–Kansas City, Conservatory of Music, 4420 Warwick Boulevard, Kansas City, Missouri 64111. **Paul V. Backlund** has been Director of bands since 1970. **John R. Leisenring** is Assistant Director. The Symphonic Concert Band has 80 members, the Symphonic Wind Ensemble 43. Various-sized chamber ensembles of winds and percussion are organized from time to time according to the composition to be played. Four to eight concerts are played during the school year in Stover Auditorium (300 seats) and Pierson Hall (1,000 seats.)

New Jersey

PRINCETON UNIVERSITY BAND, Princeton University, Princeton, New Jersey 08540. The band was established in 1919 and currently has 70 players. **David Uber** (also first trombonist with the New York City Ballet) has led the band since 1970. Four concerts are presented during the school year on campus in Alexander Hall (1,000 seats) and in New York City in Philharmonic Hall. A private label recording has been made of Princeton University songs and is available through the band.

New Mexico

UNIVERSITY OF NEW MEXICO WIND ENSEMBLE, University of New Mexico, Albuquerque, New Mexico 87110. This band of 53 to 60 members was founded in 1935 (circa) and has been directed by **William E. Rhoads** since 1953. **Fred M. Dart** is Assistant Director and also conducts the university's marching band. The Wind Ensemble gives three or four concerts during the school year and the same number during the summer term. On campus the concerts are held in Popejoy Hall (2,400 seats.) Every three or four years, the band makes a statewide tour of high schools. It has performed at numerous national conventions in Chicago, St. Louis, Los Angeles, Santa Fe, and Tempe, Arizona. Nationally known wind instrumentalists have appeared as soloists with the ensemble.

New York

CORNELL UNIVERSITY BANDS, 821 Lincoln Hall, Cornell University, Ithaca, New York 14850. Director of Bands, since 1966; **Marice W. Stith.** Units consist of a "Big Red" Marching Band, 120 members; the Symphonic Band, 125 players; and the Wind Ensemble of 45 players. Performances take place on campus in Bailey Hall (2,500 seats). Has recorded for *Audio Recording* and *Fleetwood Records*. . . . EASTMAN WIND ENSEMBLE, Eastman School of Music, University of Rochester, Rochester, N.Y. 14640. Conductor (since 1964): **Donald Hunsberger.** Founded 1953. About 45 to 50 players. About six to eight performances are given during the regular school year, in either Kilbourn Hall (485 seats) or Eastman Theatre (3,385). In 1968, it made a tour of the West Coast. Under **Donald Hunsberger,** the group has recorded for *Decca;* previous conductors, **Frederick Fennell** and **A. Clyde Roller,** have recorded with the ensemble for *Mercury* Records. The ensemble has played the world premiere of many works written for wind groups.

North Carolina

DUKE UNIVERSITY WIND SYMPHONY, Department of Music, Duke University, Box 6695 College Station, Durham, North Carolina 27708. Founded in 1927, the ensemble of 75 has been conducted since 1951 by **Paul Bryan.** Associate Conductor is **James Henry.** The band gives ten concerts during the school year in Page Auditorium (1,200 seats). It makes an annual spring tour of four days playing from six to eight concerts at high schools and colleges. It has commissioned works from many contemporary composers including **Dello Joio,** Giannini, **Persichetti, Meyerowitz, Hamilton** and **Ward.** . . . EAST CAROLINA UNIVERSITY SYMPHONIC WIND ENSEMBLE, East Carolina University, Greenville, North Carolina 27834. **Herbert L. Carter** has been director of the 52-piece ensemble since its founding in 1946. It plays concerts on campus in Wright Auditorium (2,400 seats) and takes an annual tour through North Carolina and surrounding states. The Symphonic Wind Ensemble has performed at national music conferences. Recordings: *Crest, Century* labels.

North Dakota

UNIVERSITY OF NORTH DAKOTA WIND ENSEMBLE, University of North Dakota, Grand Forks, North Dakota 58201. **Michael Polovitz** has conducted this ensemble since its formation in 1954. The group has 40 players and presents six concerts during the normal school year and two during the summer session. Performances take place in Fritz Auditorium (2,400 seats) on campus. The ensemble has commissioned new works, subsequently published, by **Norman Dello Joio** ("From Every Horizon") and **David Ward-Steinman** ("Jazz Tangents").

Ohio

BALDWIN-WALLACE CONCERT BAND, Baldwin-Wallace College, Berea, Ohio 44017. Conductor: **Frank L. Battisti.** . . . KENT STATE UNIVERSITY SYMPHONY BAND AND WIND ENSEMBLE, School of Music, Kent State University, Kent, Ohio 44242. Conductor: **Richard H. Jacoby** (1967); Assistant Conductor: **William F. Curtin.** The band has 65 players; the number for the wind ensemble is variable. Four concerts are presented during the regular school year in Kent State University Auditorium (1,000 seats). The band makes an annual spring tour and has commissioned new works as well as administered composition contests for the symphonic band. An FM radio series, "Kent in Concert," broadcast over selected radio stations in the East and Midwest, has included performances of the Kent ensembles. Two recordings not available commercially have been produced with performances by the university's ensembles. They are respectively on *Century* and *Educational Record Reference Library* labels (see Franco Colombo, music publisher) and are available through the Band Office of the university. . . . OHIO NORTHERN UNIVERSITY CONCERT BAND, Ohio Northern University, Ada, Ohio 45810. Founded in 1882, the band has 87 players and is under the direction of **Alan H. Drake** (1969). Assistant Conductor is **George C. Miller** (1970). Six to ten concerts are presented each season of seven months' duration in Lehr Auditorium (1,300 seats). . . . THE OHIO STATE UNIVERSITY CONCERT BAND, 1899 North College Road, Columbus, Ohio 43210. An ensemble of 80 to 85 players founded in 1929. **Donald E. McGinnis** has been Conductor since 1952. Assistant Conductor is **Robert T. LeBlanc.** The band plays from 10 to 20 concerts a season in Mershon Auditorium (3,000 seats). It has recordings on *Coronet* and *Mark* labels.

Oklahoma

UNIVERSITY OF OKLAHOMA BAND, University of Oklahoma, Norman, Oklahoma 73069. Founded 1904. Conductor, since 1962: **Gene A. Braught.** The university bands include: the Marching Band, "The Pride of Oklahoma," and the Symphonic Band, both conducted by **Mr. Braught,** and the Concert Band, under Assistant Director, **Gary Stollsteimer.**

Oregon

OREGON STATE UNIVERSITY BANDS, Benton Hall, Oregon State University, Corvallis, Oregon 97330. Director of Bands at Oregon State since 1968 has been **James M. Douglass,** who also leads the performances of the school's Wind Ensemble, Symphonic Band (85 players) and Marching Band (150 players). Assistant Director of the Marching Band is **John Dilworth, Jr.** Other bands are the Varsity Band (over 70 players and open to all campus students), the Jazz Ensemble, and Basketball Band. The Symphonic Band represents the band department's most skilled endeavor, as does the smaller wind ensemble, which is made up of the first chair players of the larger band. In addition to formal concerts given on campus, the Symphonic Band performs at high school assembly concerts throughout the Northwest and has played for radio broadcasts. The Marching Band has played at football games televised either regionally or nationally. School concerts take place mainly in Gill Coliseum (12,000 seats). The band program at the university operates on a budget of $11,000. . . . UNIVERSITY OF OREGON SYMPHONIC WIND ENSEMBLE, The School of Music, University of Oregon, Eugene, Oregon 97403. Since 1950, the ensemble has been conducted by **Robert Vagner,** who is Director of University Bands and a concert clarinetist. Other band groups in the university include the Concert Band, Workshop Band, Football Band, Stage Band, Pep Band, and smaller ensembles including groups formed specifically for the purpose of studying and performing contemporary and avant-garde works. The Symphonic Wind Ensemble plays about five concerts a year in the School of Music Auditorium (600–700 seats). Its repertory includes all the major works for wind ensemble.

Pennsylvania

DUQUESNE UNIVERSITY SYMPHONY BAND, Duquesne University, Pittsburgh, Pennsylvania 15219. Founded in 1936. **George Cavanagh** is Director (1970). The ensemble has 68 players. Concerts are given in the Student Union Ballroom (1,400 seats) —from 10 to 15 during the school year.

South Dakota

SOUTH DAKOTA STATE UNIVERSITY SYMPHONIC WINDS, Music Department,

South Dakota State University, Brookings, South Dakota 57006. Founded in 1904. Conductor: **Warren G. Hatfield** (1961); Associate Conductor: **James A. Jarrell.** An ensemble of 80 players performing from five to ten concerts during the school year. Pugsley Union Building Christy Ballroom (seating 900) serves as the band's auditorium. The group undertook a tour of Western Europe during the summer of 1971. It played the premiere performances of works by **Paul Royer** and **Warren Benson,** whose "Mask at Night" was commissioned by the ensemble.

Tennessee

UNIVERSITY OF TENNESSEE AT CHATTANOOGA BAND, University of Tennessee at Chattanooga, Chattanooga, Tennessee 37403. A 135-piece band founded in 1940. Director of Bands since 1967: **Barry Jones;** Assistant Director: **Morris Bales** (1969). The university's bands work on a budget of $26,000. Two concerts are given during the school year. These are held in McCllyen Gym, (5,000 seats) or Tivsla Theater (1,800 seats).

Texas

BAYLOR UNIVERSITY "GOLDEN WAVE" BAND, Baylor University, Waco, Texas 76703. Founded 1903. Conductor, since 1948: **Donald I. Moore.** The band strength varies from 60 to 150 members. During the regular school year it performs from two to five concerts, presenting them in Waco Hall on campus (2,400-seat capacity). The band organized a European tour in 1968 and attended the Baptist Youth World Conference that year. Recordings include a collection entitled "Golden Wave Band in Concert," for *Word Records;* "Golden Favorites by the Golden Wave Band," for *Christian Home Music*. . . . MCMURRY COLLEGE CONCERT BAND, McMurry Station, Abilene, Texas 79605. Conductor, since 1946: **Raymond T. Bynum.** A 70-member ensemble. Undertook concert tour of Western Europe in 1955; some 15 tours in Mexico over the past twenty years, and over 30 tours in the U.S. Southwest. It has recorded a single disc for *RCA Victor* entitled "The McMurry Band Goes on Record." . . . TEXAS A & I UNIVERSITY SYMPHONIC BAND, Texas A & I University, Kingsville, Texas 78363. The band was founded in 1929 and is directed by **Joseph L. Bellamah** (since 1961). It presents 12 concerts on campus in Jones Auditorium (1,400 seats). It has won certain statewide awards and distinctions. Four recordings are available through the band (Educational Reference Library). . . . UNIVERSITY OF TEXAS AT AUSTIN SYMPHONIC BAND, Department of Music, College of Fine Arts, Austin, Texas 78712. An ensemble of 70 under the leadership of **William J. Moody** (1966). The band gives four concerts a season in Hogg Auditorium (1,200 seats).

Vermont

UNIVERSITY OF VERMONT CONCERT BAND, University of Vermont Music Department, Burlington, Vermont 05401. A 55-player ensemble founded circa 1926. Director is **Herbert L. Schultz** (1959). Three concerts are played each year in Ira Allen Chapel (1,100 seats). The band undertakes a three-day spring tour annually.

Virginia

VIRGINIA COMMONWEALTH UNIVERSITY SYMPHONIC BAND, 901 Franklin Street, Richmond, Virginia 23220. Founded in the 1930's. Since 1967, the conductor has been **Edwin C. Thayer.** The number of players in the band varies from 39 to 68 just as the location for performances does, due to the lack of a large campus auditorium. Thus far, the band has played in halls with a seating capacity of from 36 to 1,000. It performs four concerts during the normal school year and one during the summer months. The band plays much contemporary music as well as transcriptions of the music of all periods. In its repertory are works composed especially for the ensemble. It makes some tours to Virginia high schools and plays for charitable organizations in the area.

Washington

UNIVERSITY OF WASHINGTON BANDS, Graves Building, University of Washington, Seattle, Washington 98105. **William E. Bissell** is Director of the Concert Band (1970). **Bruce Caldwell** and **Garry Nakayama** are Co-Directors of the Marching Band. The bands were founded in the 1920's and have about 150 players. During the football season, the "Husky" Marching Band appears at half-time at the University of Washington Stadium and travels with the team for out-of-state games. The Concert Band gives two spring concerts in Kane Hall (800 seats). . . . WASHINGTON STATE UNIVERSITY BANDS, Washington State University, Kimbrough Music Building, Pullman, Washington 99163. Organized in 1893. There are three bands in the university making a total of 240 players. Director is **Randall Spicer** (1953). Assistant Director is **John Newman.** The bands have a regular season of 32 weeks, during which they perform about 14 concerts in all; two concerts are played during a six-week summer season. Performances take place in Kimbrough Music Hall (400 seats) and Compton Union Building (1,100 seats). Other performance activities include an annual tour through the State of Washington, radio programs via the Cougar Network (Washington, Idaho, Montana, Oregon, Northern California, and Canada), and NCAA television appearances at football and basketball games. Works by **Frank Erickson, James Niblock, Walter Skolnik, Kemble Stout,** and other composers have been premiered by the bands. Performances by the bands have been recorded on *Century* and *Crest* Records and are available through the University Music Department.

West Virginia

WEST VIRGINIA UNIVERSITY BANDS, Creative Arts Center, West Virginia University, Morgantown, West Virginia 26506. Director of Bands is **Don Wilcox** (1971), **C. Vernon Snyder** is Assistant Director. Bands were first established at the university in 1902. At present, the bands are a marching band, concert band, wind symphony, and a pep band— all totaling 150 players. Twelve band concerts are played in the auditorium of the Creative Arts Center (1,600 seats) each year. The Marching Band has played at football games and has been seen on national television.

Wisconsin

UNIVERSITY OF WISCONSIN WIND ENSEMBLE AND BANDS, School of Music, University of Wisconsin, Madison, Wisconsin 53706. There are six units in the university's band program: the Wind Ensemble of 45 to 48 players, which, along with the Symphonic Band (75 members), represents the school's best groups from the viewpoint of musicianship and the most challenging and perhaps most serious repertory; the Concert Band; the University Band; and members of the preceding ensembles make up the players of two additional groups, the Varsity Band and the Marching Band. There are about 400 players in all the bands; membership is not confined to music majors. **H. Robert Reynolds** (1968) is Director of Bands and Conductor of the Wind Ensemble and Symphonic Band. **Michael Lekrone** and **Stanley Schleuter** are assistant conductors. Band concerts total some eight to ten during the regular school year and one or two during the summer session. Performances are presented in Mills Concert Hall (850 seats).

Wyoming

UNIVERSITY OF WYOMING BANDS, University of Wyoming, Laramie, Wyoming 82070. **Charles P. Seltenrich** (1950) is Director of the Wind Ensemble, a select band of 48 members. **Ronald Kuhn,** appointed in 1968, is Director of the 110-member Symphonic Band and the Stage Band. Concerts were held in the Arts & Sciences Auditorium (2,300 seats) until the fall of 1972; they are now held in the Fine Arts Concert Hall (750 seats.)

PROFESSIONAL BANDS, MUNICIPAL BANDS, ETC.

THE ALLENTOWN BAND, Box 1142, Allentown, Pennsylvania 18105. A symphonic band of 65 players founded in 1828. Conductor since 1926 is **Albertus L. Meyers.** Associate Conductor is **Lucien Cailliet.** The band functions as an incorporated organization giving four concerts during the winter season and playing some 45 to 60 concerts (one day appearances) during the summer throughout Pennsylvania and New Jersey. In Allentown it performs in Symphony Hall (1,600 seats). Officials of the band believe historians rate it as the oldest civilian concert band in the nation, since it has played without interruption each year since its founding. The unit has toured, primarily along the cities of the Eastern Seaboard and Canada. It has recorded some six albums of band music for WFB Productions, Inc., 517 Cowpath Road, Lansdale, Pennsylvania 19446. . . . AMERICAN WIND SYMPHONY ORCHESTRA, Gateway Towers, Gateway Center, Pittsburgh, Pennsylvania 15222. The ensemble was founded in 1957 by its Music Director and Conductor, **Robert Boudreau.** This organization is unique—both in function and constitution— and might properly be considered outside the classification of "band." The orchestra consists of the regular percussion section of a symphony orchestra, the normal brass and woodwind sections of the symphony but of twice the usual strength (i.e., four flutes instead of two, six trombones instead of three, etc.), plus harp and piano. Altogether, the orchestra is made up of 43 musicians. It is well known for its summer series of concerts performed from its own concert river barge, which tours the cities and towns along such rivers as the Allegheny, Ohio, and Monongahela. The musicians of the orchestra are young professionals selected annually from American and foreign universities and music schools and symphony orchestras. More than 160 works have been commissioned by the orchestra, a number of which have been published by C. F. Peters Corporation in its American Wind Symphony Orchestra Editions. Its concert schedule during the summer totals from 35 to 50 engagements.

BANGOR BAND, 166 Union Street, Bangor, Maine 04401. Founded in 1859. Present Conductor (since 1963): **Harold O. Doe.** A 35-member band playing six concerts during the summer over a six-week period. Concerts are played in the 300-seat facility at Pierce Memorial in Bangor.

DAYTONA BEACH MUNICIPAL BAND, 84 Ponce DeLeon Drive, Ormond Beach, Florida 32074. Founded in 1935. Conductor since 1953 has been **William P. Schueler.** The band of 40 players performs a 12-week winter season of 12 concerts in Peabody Auditorium (2,560 seats) and a 10-week summer season of 52 concerts in Daytona's Band Shell (5,000 seats). The ensemble is sustained by a budget of $23,000 annually. It has made some 3,000 private recordings. . . . DENVER MUNICIPAL BAND, Parks and Recreation Department, 810 14th Street, Denver, Colorado 80202. Founded in 1893. Director since 1924 has been **Henry Everett Sachs.** The band uses 38 players and performs six times weekly for a season of six weeks. . . . DETROIT CONCERT BAND, 20962 Mack Avenue, Grosse Pointe Woods, Michigan 48236. Since its founding in 1946, the band has been led by its conductor, **Leonard B. Smith.** This unit of 54 musicians is sponsored by the City of Detroit and is well known for its summer concert series on Detroit's Belle Isle (see Detroit Concert Band Summer Series, under Festivals). The band's eight-week summer season offers six concerts per week in both Belle Isle and in the shell in Michigan State Fair Grounds (seating capacities, respectively 6,600 and 5,000). The ensemble tours and plays for private engagements. It has recorded for Bandland Records (information of availability obtainable through the band). During the summer season, the band performs from 800 to 850 works to large crowds attending the free concerts. Performances are broadcast one night a week over Station WJR (AM–FM).

ELKHART MUNICIPAL BAND, Box 641, Elkhart, Indiana 46514. Founded in 1938.

Conductor: **Arthur J. Singleton.** A tax-supported band playing a summer season.

FORT DODGE MUNICIPAL BAND, P.O. 702, Fort Dodge, Iowa 50501. Conductor, from its founding in 1920 until his death in 1971: Karl L. King. Assistant: **Ralph W. Peer.** (King's successor is not known at the time of writing.) The band has from 35 to 40 players and performs three concerts during the winter in the High School Auditorium (1,200 seats). During the summer, two concerts a week are performed for 10 weeks. The tenure of Karl L. King was a widely hailed phenomenon in the field of band music (see Grand Army Band). He was known also as a composer of hundreds of works for the band.

GOLDMAN BAND, 17 West 60th Street, New York, N.Y. 10023. Founded in 1911 by Edwin Franko Goldman. Conductor since 1956: **Richard Franko Goldman.** Associate Conductor is **Ainslee Cox.** One of America's most famous bands. Since 1918, the band has presented a yearly series of summer concerts, originally supported by public subscription. From 1924 on, financial support for the series has been underwritten by the Guggenheim family. The Goldman Band's summer series, now known as the Guggenheim Memorial Concerts (after Daniel and Florence Guggenheim), has been heard in New York's Central Park, Damrosch Park in Lincoln Center, and in Brooklyn's Prospect Park. The season consists of five concerts a week for eight weeks. The band's repertory is symphonically oriented to a large degree and includes works it has commissioned from many composers. Recordings of the band are on *Decca, Capitol, Vocalion,* and *Harmony* labels. . . . GRAND ARMY BAND, 55 Perryview Avenue, Pittsburgh, Pennsylvania 15214. Established in 1875. Bandmaster is **Alois Hrabak,** appointed in 1915, whose musical longevity may be unprecedented in the band world. The band has 40 players and plays a regular season and a summer season of eight concerts each.

HAGERSTOWN MUNICIPAL BAND, 1422 Potomac Avenue, Hagerstown, Maryland 21740. Founded in 1915. Conductor (since 1960): **Kenneth B. Slater.** Assistant Conductor: **Joseph M. Leptich.** The band plays a regular season of 16 concerts spread over a 31-week period; performances are held in South Hagerstown High School Auditorium (1,200 seats). Sixteen concerts are played during the 13-week summer season in City Park of Hagerstown (1,800 seats). In addition, the band plays for all official city functions and gives special concerts at hospitals. There are 48 musicians in the unit.

LONG BEACH MUNICIPAL BAND, 19 Cedar Avenue, Long Beach, California 90802. Founded in 1909. Conductor is **Charles Payne,** appointed in 1957. Assistant Conductor: **Manuel Vieira.** The band consists of 36 musicians and functions throughout the year—reportedly it is the only full-time municipally supported band in the United States. Each year, it presents over 600 concerts. Since 1930 it has broadcast over local radio station KGER. Its annual budget is $250,000.

NEVER'S SECOND REGIMENT BAND, 110 South State Street, Concord, New Hampshire 03301. A 25-player band founded in 1861. Since 1960 the conductor has been **Paul T. Giles.** The City of Concord sponsors Never's Band for a summer series of ten concerts. The State of New Hampshire sponsors another series of ten concerts presented at Mt. Sunapee State Park each summer. These two series plus other engagements throughout New Hampshire give the band the opportunity to play some 30 concerts a season. The band has performed annually since its founding, making it one of the oldest continuing musical organizations in America. One of its special program features is its performance of Civil War music using copies of the original editions and arrangements that are on file in the Library of Congress. The band was originally a National Guard unit; "Second Regiment" has been kept in the unit's name even though it no longer has any affiliation with the Guard.

OAKLAND MUNICIPAL BAND, Park Department, Oakland, California. Founded in 1914. Conductor: **Fred C. Rose.** The band, a 40-member ensemble, plays a city-sponsored season from June to October.

PEORIA MUNICIPAL BAND, c/o 800 North Swords Avenue, Peoria, Illinois 61604. Founded in 1937. Conductor is **Fred J. Huber.** Assistant Conductor: **Rudolph Jungst.** A 49-member band supported by a city band tax. Presents an 11-week season of 36 concerts scheduled from mid-June to Labor Day. All concerts take place in the 3,000-seat Glen Oak Park Band Reflector and Court House Plaza. Occasionally, the band presents a live television program during Christmas.

RACINE MUNICIPAL BAND (formerly the Park Board Band), c/o 1341 West Lawn Avenue, Racine, Wisconsin 53405. Founded in 1923. Conductor is **John T. Opferkuch.** A city-supported band of 35 players presenting about 20 concerts a year. . . . RINGGOLD BAND, P.O. Box 1232, Reading, Pennsylvania 19603. An incorporated band founded in 1852 (its predecessor, the Reading Band, was established in 1813). Since 1960, Conductor has been **Walter J. Gier.** Assistant Conductor is **John P. Talnack.** The band numbers from 30 to 35 players and plays engagements throughout the Reading area and in other towns in the state. Concerts for the City Park Band Shell, church picnics, civic events, and other public and some private engagements spread over the calendar year make up the band's concert activities.

SIOUX CITY MUNICIPAL BAND, 219 Cook Drive, Sioux City, Iowa 51104. Conductor: **Leo Kucinski.** Founded in 1920. Plays a summer season of 25 concerts in Grandview Park. . . . SIOUX FALLS MUNICIPAL BAND, 224 West 9th, Sioux Falls, South Dakota 57102. Founded in 1919. Conductor (since 1964): **Leland A. Lillehaug.** The 46-member band is supported through taxes as a department of the city. It plays a summer season of from 45 to 50 concerts in the parks of Sioux Falls. . . . SUNSHINE CITY BAND, P.O. Box 10548, St. Petersburg, Florida 33733. Founded in 1915. Conductor: **Joseph G. Lefter.** Twenty-four musicians form the band, which plays a regular season of 14 weeks (56 concerts) from mid-December to mid-March and a weekly series of special concerts from October to December. An annual budget of $18,000 is allotted the band.

MILITARY BANDS

MARINE SCHOOLS BAND, Quantico, Virginia 22134. Leader: **First Lt. B. F. Bequette.** . . . UNITED STATES AIR FORCE BAND, Bolling Air Force Base, Washington, D.C. 20332. Established in 1942. Leader is **Lt. Col. Arnald D. Gabriel,** appointed in 1964. Assistant Conductor is **Capt. Albert Bader.** Sixty-five players are in the band, which plays over 150 concerts a year. These include performances in Departmental Auditorium in Washington (1,800 seats) on Sunday afternoons during February and March, Tuesday evening concerts during June through August at the Capitol Plaza (unlimited audience capacity), and at the Watergate (5,000 seats) every Friday evening during June through August. In addition, the band undertakes two 28-day tours a year, either through sections of the United States or abroad. The band also yields further organizational subdivisions; among them: Airmen of Note (a dance–jazz group), the Strolling Strings, The U.S. Air Force String Orchestra, the U.S. Air Force Woodwind Quintet, the U.S. Air Force String Quartet, and the U.S. Air Force Pipe (Bagpipe) Band. **Capt. Gabriel** is also Director of the U.S. Air Force Symphony Orchestra. The U.S. Air Force Band has one recording issued on *RCA Victor* label and a private-issue recording available for promotional purposes. . . . UNITED STATES ARMY BAND, Washington, D.C. Founded in 1922 upon orders from General J. Pershing. Commanding Officer and Leader is **Lt. Col. Samuel Loboda,** appointed in 1964 (the highest-ranking officer ever appointed Leader). Associate Bandmaster: **Major Gilbert Mitchell,** appointed in 1960. The band performs many musical duties, which include the responsibility of leading the presidential inaugural parades (which it has done since the inauguration of Calvin Coolidge), performing as the official band for most diplomatic and state functions in the Capitol, and providing musical honors for the arrival of dignitaries in Washington, D.C. The band also plays public concerts at Watergate and the Capitol and for the radio. A recording of the band has been issued by *RCA Victor*. . . . UNITED STATES MARINE BAND, Marine Barracks, 8th and I Streets, S.E., Washington, D.C. 20390. Founded in 1798. Director is **Lt. Col. Albert Schoepper,** appointed in 1955. Associate Conductors are **Capt. Dale Harphan** and **Capt. James King.** A band of 135. Performs an 8-week spring season and a 12-week summer season and makes a 9-week annual fall tour. The band is recorded on *RCA Victor* label. . . . UNITED STATES MILITARY ACADEMY BAND, West Point, N.Y. 10996. Founded in 1817. Conductor: **Lt. Col. William H. Schempf.** Assistant Conductor: **Major Mario Petrelli.** The band is a unit of 185 players performing some 20 or 30 concerts during the regular season and about 10 concerts during the summer. Performs in Army Theatre and Trophy Point Amphitheatre (respectively, 1,700 and 5,000 seats). . . . THE UNITED STATES NAVY BAND, Washington Navy Yard, Washington, D.C. 20390. Founded March 4, 1925; formed out of its forerunner, the Washington Navy Yard Band, which had been assigned to the Navy Yard in 1916. Leader is **Lt. Donald W. Stauffer,** appointed 1969. The band has an authorized personnel strength of 134 enlisted men and 4 officers. Its concert appearances include regular Friday evening performances from January to March in Washington's Departmental Auditorium; in June, July, and August a Monday evening series on the steps of the Capitol, and a Thursday evening series at Potomac Watergate. In addition, the band goes on an annual tour lasting about ten weeks, performing two concerts each day. Other activities include two network radio shows weekly: "The Navy Hour" on ABC network and "The Navy Band Showcase," distributed to about 2,100 AM and FM stations weekly; so-called Lolli-Pops concerts for young people as part of the Washington summer season; and the Washington Area Soloist Festival, a competition organized by the band for high school musicians, winners of which perform with the band as guests. The band's total number of engagements yearly have reached as many as 1,700 and more. An album of marches has been recorded by the band for *RCA Victor.*

Part 3 | Vocal Ensembles

U.S. Choral Activity

The American Choral Foundation, Inc. conducted a survey of U.S. college, community, and church choruses in 1960. Findings based on reports from forty-six states and the District of Columbia were printed in the Foundation's Memo No. 19 dated December 15, 1960. The survey covered a total of 195 college, 193 community, and 130 church choruses from 1957 to 1960. There is no later survey. Although this report is now over twelve years old, it is not likely that the situation has changed very much in the intervening years; choruses have relatively stable organizational structures and traditions, to say nothing of their mode of activity.

Among the American Choral Foundation's findings: choral conductors are more often than not salaried, although they conduct nonprofessional groups; community choruses form the largest single group with unpaid conductors (however, 68.1 percent were paid in 1959–60); most conductors have a master's degree; most choruses were founded over twenty years ago; as a rule the oldest choruses belong to churches; the greater number of choruses of all types exceed 40 members (especially college groups); rehearsal time is usually about a two-hour period once a week; most community choirs give from five to ten concerts a year (college groups go beyond that figure); most church choirs perform at all services; the economics involved in choral activity are generally on a smaller scale than other professional musical ensembles within the community; most choral groups are managed with budgets under $5,000 (this may now be a higher ceiling), and groups exceeding this amount are more frequently church choirs; income for most groups stems from ticket sales, gifts, and endowments (ticket sales bring the most income to civic choruses); church choirs and school choruses are supported mainly by allotments from the general institutional budget; corporation support reveals no definite pattern, but the largest percentage went (in 1957–58) to colleges; understandably, no municipal support is given church choirs; in general, the purchase or rental of music constitutes a major expense for all choruses (however, this amount is exceeded in the case of college groups by transportation costs [for tours] and in the case of community and church groups by conductor's salary; beyond music purchase and transportation costs, school choruses expend little money; chorus salaries are more likely in community groups (10.6 percent) than church groups (2.4 percent); about 10 percent of the community choruses engage soloists through commerical artist management.

There is no standard use of the term "professional" in regard to choral groups. For its own purposes, however, the American Choral Foundation considers a chorus professional if its members belong to the American Guild of Musical Artists (AGMA) and are paid for their services. AGMA states that there are about 17 such choruses in America. Throughout the U.S. there is a general avoidance of use of the word "professional" in judging musical ability. An amateur chorus is still called that despite a possibly high level of musical accomplishment. The Foundation further estimates that, with or without pay, less than fifteen school choruses perform on a professional level, but this figure is arrived at with full appreciation of the lack of a universal method of judgment.

U.S. Male Choruses

Associated Male Choruses of America, Inc., reports that the total (exact or estimated) number of such choruses in America is unknown. Its own membership consists of 52 choruses (7 in Canada) totaling 2,000 members. However, it is able to say that industry-sponsored groups (which include such groups as the 3M Male Chorus of St. Paul, founded in 1947; The Delco Electronics of Milwaukee; and the IBM Men's Glee Club of Endicott, N.Y. founded 1929) have suffered cutbacks since 1960; this is even true of a number of choruses with long histories. In the past twenty years there has been a steady decline in the subsidy of plant choruses or instrumental ensembles. Some still exist but with reduced personnel. This may be the result of the lack of interest of both employees and employers. Some groups have maintained their numerical strength but receive only partial financial support from the company. However, unsponsored choruses in the Midwest continue to maintain their strength.

Barbershop Quartets

The Society for the Preservation and Encouragement of Barbershop Quartet Singing in America (SPEBSQSA) has a total membership of 33,456, with 705 chapters in the United States and Canada. Altogether there are more than 1,100 registered quartets and at least 600 barbershop choruses.

A few quartets, by their exceptional merit and achievement, gain professional status, but the majority of quartets willingly call themselves nonprofessional despite the possibility of their having gone beyond the average standard of barbershop singing. The ten top quartets of SPEBSQSA are determined by international quartet contests. The winners for 1971 were: The Gentlemen's Agreement, Detroit and Monroe, Michigan; The Golden Staters, Arcadia, California; The Pacificaires, Reseda, California; The Far Westerners, Whittier and Riverside, California; The Easternaires, Greater Jersey City and Livingston, New Jersey; The Roaring 20's, Cincinnati, Ohio; The Fan Fares, Waukesha, Wisconsin; The OK Four, Oklahoma City, Oklahoma; Grandma's Boys, Nashua, New Hampshire and Wilmette, Illinois; The Citations, Louisville, Kentucky.

| Academic Groups

ABILENE CHRISTIAN COLLEGE CHORUSES, Abilene Christian College, Department of Music, Abilene, Texas 79601. Conductor: **Jack Boyd** (1968). The choruses consist of the A Cappella Chorus, "Choralaires," and Chamber Singers, with 44, 60, and 12 voices respectively; groups founded 1937, 1955, 1968, respectively. Each group gives 20 to 40 performances a year. The ensembles perform on campus, and, in addition, each undertakes a one-week tour (mostly in the Southwest). . . . ASBURY COLLEGE CHORUSES, Asbury College, Wilmore, Kentucky 40390. Choruses conducted by **Jack A. Rains** (1958) are: Men's Glee Club (40 voices), 25 performances a year; Oratorio Chorus (150 voices), which gives 2 performances a year. The Women's Glee Club is directed by **Lisle M. Cameron** (1967), has 40 voices, and presents 20 performances a year. . . . AUSTIN COLLEGE A CAPPELLA CHOIR, Austin College, Sherman, Texas 75090. Conductor: **Bruce G. Lunkley** (1959). Number of voices: 60. Date founded: 1942. Number of performances a year: 20. Primarily a touring group. On-campus performances are held in Wynne Chapel. Basically *a cappella* repertory but occasionally large works by Brahms, Beethoven, Mozart, et al. have been performed with members of the Dallas Symphony.

THE BARNARD–COLUMBIA CHORUS, Columbia University, Department of Music, 703 Dodge, Columbia University, New York, N.Y. 10027. Conductor: **Daniel Paget** (1967). Number of voices: 80 to 100. Date founded: 1967 (was formerly the Columbia University Chorus). Number of performances a year: five. Performs in McMillin Theatre and St. Paul's Chapel on campus. Occasionally tours. Has appeared with the Little Orchestra Society and with the Mannes College of Music Orchestra as well as the Columbia University Orchestra. . . . BISON GLEE CLUB, c/o Oklahoma Baptist University, Shawnee, Oklahoma 74801. Conductor: **Warren M. Angell** (1936). An ensemble of 49 voices, founded 1938. Gives 50 concerts yearly, touring throughout Oklahoma and the South. Has recorded for *Word* records.

CADET GLEE CLUB, The United States Military Academy, West Point, N.Y. 10996. Conductor: **Major Hal J. Gibson** (1966). Number of voices: 120. Date founded: 1908; reorganized in 1928 after diminished activity. Number of performances annually: approximately 35. Primarily a touring group, having sung in Carnegie and Town Halls in New York City, Hollywood Bowl, Symphony Hall in Boston, and many other large cities in the United States. They have appeared on network and local television in New York City, Los Angeles, and Chicago. Much of the repertory consists of songs associated with the history of the Armed Forces; there are some concert pieces, popular song standards, and arrangements of folk songs. Has recorded for *Vox* and *RCA Victor*. . . . CATAWBA COLLEGE CONCERT CHOIR, Catawba College, Salisbury, North Carolina 28144. Conductor: **Gilbert C. Pirovano** (1966). Number of voices: 42. Number of performances annually: approximately 15. Performs in churches and schools, both local and on tour. . . . CENTENARY COLLEGE CHOIR, Shreveport, Louisiana 71104. Conductor: **Alvin C. Voran.** Date founded: 1941. Number of voices: 49. Tours in Far East at U.S. military stations. . . . COLUMBIA UNIVERSITY GLEE CLUB, Columbia University, 301 Ferris Booth Hall, New York, N.Y. 10027. Conductor: **Bailey Harvey** (1952). Date founded: 1872. Number of voices: 72. Number of performances annually: 25. Group performs at Wollman Auditorium, Columbia University, and at Town Hall in New York and at various women's colleges. Recorded on *Carillon*. . . . CORNELL UNIVERSITY CHORUSES, Cornell University, Ithaca, New York 14850. Conductor: **Thomas A. Sokol** (1957). Choruses consist of the Glee Club (founded 1868), which has 115 men, and the Chorus (founded 1906), which has 100 treble voices. The Glee Club performs on campus in Bailey Hall; approximately 30 performances a year are given. The Glee Club has recorded for *Fleetwood Recordings.* It has toured sixteen countries; in 1966, a 12-week tour of Southeast Asia was made under the auspices of the Office of Cultural Presentations of the Department of State. The Chorus also performs on campus in Bailey Hall, giving four performances a year. The Chorus has combined with the Glee Club to sing major works with the Philadelphia Orchestra, Rochester Philharmonic, Buffalo Philharmonic, and Cornell Symphony Orchestra.

DARTMOUTH COLLEGE GLEE CLUB, Dartmouth College, Hanover, New Hampshire 03755. Conductor: **Paul R. Zeller** (1947). Number of voices: 60 (almost all male). Date founded: 1869. Number of performances annually: 30. Group performs in various locations each season. Tours are sponsored by alumni. Occasional concerts with women's groups and with orchestras. Recorded on *United Artists* (may be out of print).

EASTMAN SCHOOL CHORUS, Eastman School of Music, Rochester, N.Y. 14604. Performs in Eastman Theatre, on campus. Concert Manager: **Mrs. Ruth Glazer,** Eastman School of Music. The Chorus has performed with the Rochester Philharmonic Orchestra and has recorded with *RCA Victor* and *Mercury* (out of print). . . . EMORY UNIVERSITY GLEE CLUB AND WOMEN'S CHORALE, Music Department, Emory University, Atlanta, Georgia 30322. The Glee Club was founded about 1920; the Women's Chorale in 1954. A third Emory ensemble, the Collegium Musicum, was founded in 1965 but includes persons from the Atlanta community and Emory faculty as well as students. The Glee Club and Chorale have from 80 to 100 voices. They have both toured throughout the South and East. The Club has toured Europe three times, has sung in Puerto Rico, Cuba, the Bahamas, and for three U.S. Presidents and, with the Chorale, has sung with the Atlanta Symphony under **Robert Shaw.** The groups are entirely student-managed. Director: **William W. Lemonds** (1963).

FATHER FLANAGAN'S BOYS TOWN CHOIR, Boys Town, Nebraska 68010. Conductor: **Msgr. Francis Schmitt** (1941). Date founded: 1941. Number of voices: 35. Annual concerts in the United States, Canada, and Japan. Concert Manager: **N. T. Letter,** Business Manager, Boys Town. . . . FLORIDA SOUTHERN COLLEGE CONCERT CHOIR, Florida Southern College, Lakeland, Florida 33802. Date founded: 1885. Conductor: **Jack Houts** (1962). Number of voices: 45. Number of performances annually: 25. Performs on campus at Branscomb Auditorium. Tours annually in Florida. Has toured New England, Ohio, and for Special Services, U.S. Army. Sacred and secular repertory. . . . FLORISSANT VALLEY COLLEGE CONCERT CHOIR, Florissant Valley College, 3400 Pershall Road, St. Louis, Missouri 63135. A choir of 38 voices founded in 1963. Director is **Henry Orland.** Presents about four concerts a year in the College Theatre and other halls in the St. Louis area. Has often performed with suburban symphonic groups.

GEORGIA COLLEGE CHORALE, Georgia College, Department of Music, Milledgeville, Georgia 31061. Date founded: 1935. Conductor: **Robert Wolfersteig** (1965). Number of voices: 80. Number of performances annually: 30 to 35. Tours within Georgia. Performed at Expo '67. Repertory includes large works by Bach, Britten, Debussy and Haydn. . . . GLENVILLE STATE COLLEGE CHOIRS, Glenville State College, Glenville, West Virginia 26351. Choirs consist of: Concert Choir, founded in 1965, which has 31 voices; Madrigal Singers, founded 1966, 12 voices. The Madrigal Singers give 15 performances annually. The Concert Choir is primarily a touring group and gives 20 performances a year. Both groups are conducted by **Robert H. Ellis** (1965). A 100-voice Choral Union, based at the College, includes students, faculty, and townspeople. It was founded in 1966 and gives two annual performances.

HARVARD GLEE CLUB, Harvard University, Cambridge, Massachusetts 02138. Conductor: **Elliot Forbes** (1958). Founded 1858. Sixty voices. Thirty performances annually. Performs in Sanders Theatre on campus. Appears annually with Boston Symphony Orchestra. Appearances also with Radcliffe Choral Society. North American and world tours (1964; 1961 and 1967, respectively). Recorded on *RCA Victor, Cambridge* and *Carillon* labels. . . . HEIDELBERG COLLEGE CONCERT CHOIR, Heidelberg College, Tiffin, Ohio 44883. Founded 1938. Conductor: **Ferris E. Ohl.** A choir of 90 voices. Performs about 45 concerts a year with a repertory of sacred and secular music, the latter including works from the classical literature as well as contemporary music in many styles. United States tours are made annually between school semesters; summer tours have been made in Europe. Fifteen members from the Choir (14 singers plus pianist) form the "Singing Collegians," who sing concerts on tour of popular music from musicals and movies.

INDIANA UNIVERSITY CHORAL ENSEMBLES, School of Music, Indiana University, Bloomington, Indiana 47401. Chairman of choral ensembles is **George F. Krueger.** The choral program at the University is an active one and consists of the following ensembles: The A Cappella Choir, 100 to 125 mixed voices, performs the larger choral works and gives concerts in the winter and spring. "Belles of Indiana," an ensemble of from 60 to 80 women's voices accompanied by four solo instruments and a rhythm section, tours the U.S. and overseas; its repertory consists of popular music arrangements and works from the classical literature. Chamber Singers, a group of 12 to 16 mixed voices, sings the music of all eras but emphasizes the music of 20th century composers. This group has sung in New York's Carnegie Hall and in the National Gallery of Art in Washington. The Collegium Musicum is a small ensemble (12 to 16 voices) devoted to singing the literature written before 1700. It performs with a variety of historical instruments. The University Chorale performs major choral works with orchestra. It has from 90 to 100 mixed voices and performs at least two major concerts a year. "Singing Hoosiers," 60 men and 60 women from throughout the University, sing sacred music and standard popular songs. They have toured Indiana and overseas. The University Singers, from 40 to 45 mixed voices, sing the *a cappella* works from all periods of music. The Women's Chorus (about 100 singers) performs several yearly concerts. The Opera Chorus of 40 to 50 voices is used for all opera performances on campus and is open to any qualifying student.

JOHN BROWN UNIVERSITY CATHEDRAL CHOIR, John Brown University, Siloam Springs, Arkansas 72761. Founder and Conductor: **Mabel Oiesen** (1942). Founded 1942. 60 voices. Number of performances annually: 30 to 40 off-campus appearances. Instrumental accompaniment is an 8-member brass and keyboard ensemble. Tours throughout United States and southern provinces of Canada. . . . JUILLIARD CHORUS, The Juilliard School, Lincoln Center Plaza, New York, N.Y. 10023. Conductor: **Abraham Kaplan** (1961). Founded 1926. Number of voices: 150 to 200. Two or three performances annually. Performs in Juilliard Theatre or Alice Tully Hall. Has appeared regularly in Philharmonic Hall with the New York Philharmonic, including the inaugural concert of Philharmonic Hall.

THE KAPELLE, Concordia Teachers College, River Forest, Illinois 60305. Conductor: **Thomas Gieschen** (1957). Founded 1957

(The Kapelle is a continuation of Concordia College Choir, founded in 1918). Number of voices: 65. Number of performances annually: 17. Gives concerts on campus but most concerts are sung on tour throughout the United States. In 1966, the choir sang for the Christmas-tree lighting ceremony at the White House with President Johnson present, an event which was televised nationally. The Choir undertook a worldwide mission tour in the summer of 1969.

LANDON SCHOOL CHORUSES, Landon School (for boys), Wilson Lane, Bethesda, Maryland. Conductor: **Jerry Holloway** (1966). Voices: 60 in Landon Lower School Chorus; 35 in Landon Men's Glee Club. Founded in 1937. Gives ten performances a year. The glee club appears in concert with nearby private girls' schools. It has sung at the Mellon Concerts, National Gallery, Washington, D.C. and has broadcast from station WGMS–FM. . . . LOUISIANA STATE UNIVERSITY A CAPPELLA CHOIR, Louisiana State University, School of Music, Baton Rouge, Louisiana 70803. Conductor: **Dallas Draper** (1947). Founded in 1947. Voices: 70. Eight performances given annually in L.S.U. Student Union. The choir undertakes an annual spring tour, has sung with the New Orleans Philharmonic, performs annual concerts of contemporary music and an annual Candlelight Christmas Concert. It also has been presented on nationwide television. . . . LUTHER COLLEGE CHOIR, Luther College, Decorah, Iowa 52101. Founded 1946. Conductor: **Weston Noble** (1948). 64 voices. Primarily a touring group with some performances on campus. Altogether it sings an average of 25 concerts annually. The group tours annually; in 1967 it toured Europe, giving concerts in Norway and East and West Germany. Other appearances of note include invitational concerts for the National Convention of Choral Directors and the North Central Music Educators National Conference; in the early 1960's, the choir sang on the NBC radio network series "Great Choirs of America" and "Voices of Easter" and the CBS program, "Church of the Air."

MANHATTANVILLE COLLEGE CHORUS (formerly known as Pius X Choir), Manhattanville College, Purchase, N.Y. 10577. Conductor: **Ralph Hunter** (1963). Voices: 50. Founded 1931. Organ accompaniment. Gives several performances annually and has appeared in New York at Town Hall, the Cloisters, Carnegie Hall, as well as its own Manhattanville Chapel. Originally the group was famous for the singing of Gregorian chant and classic polyphony; at the present time, it devotes its performances to music of the fifteenth and sixteenth centuries. The Manhattanville College Summer Session Choir has recorded for *Folkways* label under **Mother Josephine Morgan.** . . . MANNES COLLEGE CHORUS, Mannes College, 157 East 74th Street, New York, N.Y. 10021. Conductor: **Harold Aks** (1963). This is a 45-voice chorus which gives three or four performances annually. . . . MERCER UNIVERSITY CHOIR, Mercer University, Macon, Georgia 31207. Conductor: **Jack Jones** (1967). Number of voices: 80. Founded 1944. The choir gives 14 annual performances, and makes an annual spring tour which emphasizes performances of contemporary choral literature. . . . MOUNT UNION CHOIR, Mount Union College, Alliance, Ohio 44601. Founded 1932. Conductor: **Cecil Stewart** (1949). 52 voices. Since 1949 has toured annually, appearing in the major cities of the Midwest and the Eastern Seaboard. It has sung major choral works with the Canton Symphony Orchestra and the Youngstown Symphony. It has appeared for various convention concerts for the Methodist Church in America and sang at the Church's World Conference in Oslo, Norway, in 1961; subsequently it performed in England, Holland, France, etc. The Oslo concerts included a recording made for Ansgar Forleg (Scandinavian Grammophone Company). A worldwide tour in the summer of 1966 took the choir to fourteen countries. A total of 37 concerts were sung of a repertory that included texts in twelve languages.

THE NEW ENGLAND CONSERVATORY CHORUS, New England Conservatory, 290 Huntington Avenue, Boston, Massachusetts

02115. Conductor: **Lorna Cooke deVaron** (1947). Number of voices: 140. Date founded: 1947. The chorus gives more than 15 concerts annually, many of them in Jordan Hall in Boston. Has recorded for *RCA Victor* and *Columbia.* Appears each year in major concerts with the Boston Symphony Orchestra and makes one tour each year. In 1966, it was sponsored by the State Department for a tour of the Soviet Union as part of the Cultural Exchange Program. The chorus has probably given more premieres of new choral works in the last twenty years than any other Boston chorus. . . . NEWSCHOOL COMMUNITY CHORUS, 66 West 12th Street, New York, N.Y. 10011. Founded in the fall of 1970, Conductor and founder is **David Labovitz.** The ensemble has 50 singers and presents two to four performances annually. . . . NORTH PARK COLLEGE CHOIR, 5125 North Spaulding Avenue, Chicago, Illinois 60625. Conductor: **David Thorburn** (1966). A choir of 50 voices performing with ten instrumental musicians. Performs from 35 to 40 concerts annually. Concert manager is the North Park College Office of Development. Tours are made during alternate years on the West Coast, East Coast, and through the Midwest. Every spring the choir performs in Orchestra Hall, Chicago; in 1966 it went on a European tour. . . . NORTH TEXAS STATE UNIVERSITY GRAND CHORUS, School of Music, North Texas State University, Denton, Texas 76203. Conductor: **Frank McKinley** (1947). A chorus of 180 voices. Founded 1942. Performances take place in McFarlin and Municipal Auditoriums, in Dallas, and in the Main Auditorium at North Texas State. Annual performances total four to six. Recorded for *RCA Victor* with the Dallas Symphony (out of print). The Grand Chorus has sung 75 performances of major choral works including 50 performances with the Dallas Symphony. Other orchestras include the Houston, Fort Worth, and Corpus Christi orchestras. It has given premiere Southwestern performances of Beethoven's "Missa Solemnis," Verdi's Requiem, Honegger's "King David," Persichetti's Stabat Mater, Bach's B Minor Mass, and St. Matthew Passion, and other major choral works from the baroque to contemporary period. Among the conductors who have led the chorus in full performance of these major works have been: Antal Dorati, Walter Hendl, Donald Johanos, Paul Kletzki, Georg Solti, and Maurice Peress. . . . NORTHWESTERN COLLEGE A CAPPELLA CHOIR, Northwestern College, Orange City, Iowa 51041. Conductor: **Lawrence Van Wyck** (1954). A choir of 50 to 60 voices. Founded 1928. The choir is primarily a touring group which performs in churches, schools, and community auditoriums and gives about 25 performances a year. It undertakes annual tours to either coastal U.S. or in the central states and Canada. Tours are financed in the main by churches affiliated with the college. Its repertory is all sacred music, most of which is unaccompanied; however, each year the combined school choirs perform one major choral work accompanied by small local string groups. . . . NORTHWESTERN UNIVERSITY MEN'S GLEE CLUB, Northwestern University, Evanston, Illinois 60201. Conductor: **William Ballard.** Has made recordings for *Mercury.*

OAKLAND UNIVERSITY CHORUS, Oakland University, Rochester, Michigan 48063. The choruses are under the direction of **John Dovaras** (1966). They include the main chorus of 170 voices, founded in 1957, which performs three annual concerts on campus in Wilson Auditorium and which has sung with the Detroit, Pontiac, Mt. Clemens, Oak Park and Minnesota Symphony Orchestras. A smaller chorus of 35 singers, the Oakland Singers, performs about 12 concerts a year throughout the Detroit area and in neighboring states. This group was founded in 1963 and specializes in the smaller chamber vocal works. . . . OBERLIN COLLEGE CHOIR, Oberlin Conservatory of Music, Oberlin, Ohio 44074. Founded in 1929 as the Oberlin A Cappella Choir. (Another organization, the Oberlin Musical Union, was founded in 1837—as the Oberlin Music Association. Then, for a short time, it was called the Oberlin Choir, and ought not to be confused with the College choir. This group is made up of senior Oberlin students, faculty, and Oberlin townspeople.) Conductor: **Robert P. Fountain** (1948; has also conducted the Musical Union since 1954). The College Choir has 63 voices and sings some 14 performances a year. It makes an annual ten-day spring tour, alternately to the East and through the Midwest. In 1964, the chorus, under the sponsorship of the U.S. Department of State, made a nine-week tour of the Soviet Union and Rumania. Members of the College Choir are comprised equally of students from both the college and the Conservatory of Music. Each year a stereo recording is made of the choir; these are available from the College Business Manager.

PENNSYNGERS, Irvine Auditorium, University of Pennsylvania, 34th and Spruce Streets, Philadelphia, Pennsylvania 19104. Conductor: **E. Dennis Rittenhouse** (1966). A chorus of 64 women, founded in 1957. Presents 20 performances annually on campus and in the Philadelphia area. (The Pennsyngers is the new name for the former Pennsylvania Women's Chorus, which had once performed with the Philadelphia Orchestra.) . . . POMONA COLLEGE GLEE CLUBS, Bridges Hall of Music, Pomona College, Claremont, California 91711. Conductor: **William F. Russell** (1951). A combination of mens' and womens' glee clubs, totaling 60 voices. Approximately 30 concerts are performed annually, most of them on tour. The singers have appeared at the Ojai Festival in Stravinsky's "Les Noces" (under Boulez) and at the Monday Evening Concerts in Los Angeles. They have sung American premieres of works by Stravinsky and Lukas Foss. Each year a 16-voice polyphonic ensemble is chosen from the chorus and tours with a Renaissance mass for liturgical performances in Catholic and Episcopal churches and monasteries. Repertory in general runs from Gregorian chant to the works of the avant garde. Half of it is *a cappella*. . . . PRINCETON HIGH SCHOOL CHOIR, Princeton High School, Princeton, N.J. 08540. 55 singers. This is the first U.S. high school musical group to tour overseas on a State Department grant; in 1962 the chorus undertook a month-long 17-concert tour of Europe. The chorus specializes in modern music and has performed music by Schoenberg, Webern, Sessions, and Stravinsky, as well as works from the traditional choral repertory. . . . PRINCETON SEMINARY CHOIR, Princeton Theological Seminary, Princeton, N.J. 08540. Founded 1933. Conductor: **David Hugh Jones** (1934). 28 male voices. The chorus gives 150 to 175 performances annually, and has toured through all fifty states, Canada, Latin America, and Japan, singing most often in United Presbyterian churches. These tours schedule a basic program of singing for at least three churches a day, morning, afternoon, and evenings. Repertory is a wide range of sacred music. An organist is part of the ensemble.

RADCLIFFE CHORAL SOCIETY, Holden Chapel, Harvard University, Cambridge, Massachusetts 02138. Conductor: **Elliot Forbes** (1958). Founded in 1889. 60 voices. The chorus gives 10 performances annually, including an appearance with the Boston Symphony Orchestra. The group has toured North America as well as worldwide with the Harvard Glee Club. . . . ROCKEFELLER CHAPEL CHOIR, University of Chicago, 5810 South Woodlawn Avenue, Chicago, Illinois 60637. Conductor: **Richard Vikstrom** (1949). Founded 1937; 40 voices. Performs Sunday services when the University of Chicago is in session. Also gives an annual Oratorio Festival of six concerts accompanied by members of the Chicago Symphony Orchestra. . . . ROLLINS SINGERS, Rollins College, Box 160, Winter Park, Florida 32789. Conductor: **Ward Woodbury** (1966). 12 voices. An ensemble, reorganized in 1966, singing 15 to 20 performances annually, including tours. In 1969 the chorus, sponsored by the USO, toured Europe.

SAINT MARY'S SEMINARY SCHOLA, 9845 Memorial Drive, Houston, Texas 77024. Conductor: **Rev. John L. Sauerhage** (1967). 40 voices. Founded 1946. The choir's main work is preparing liturgical music for the seminary, but it does accept invitations to perform for outside secular and religious events. It has recorded for *Gregorian Institute* records. . . . ST. MARY'S SEMINARY AND UNIVERSITY CHOIR, Roland Park,

Baltimore, Maryland 21210. Conductor: **Rev. James M. Burns** (1960). 50 voices; founded 1791. Gives two to four concerts annually, as well as its weekly services in the Seminary Chapel. The chorus has performed the Berlioz Requiem in combination with the Goucher College choir and the Baltimore Symphony. . . . SAINT OLAF LUTHERAN CHOIR, Saint Olaf College, Northfield, Minnesota 55057. Conductor: **Kenneth L. Jennings** (1968). An *a cappella* chorus of about 60 founded in 1903. Founder F. Melius Christiansen led the chorus until 1941; he was succeeded by his son, Olaf, who served as director until 1968. The choir is one of the best known of college groups in America. Since 1920 it has sung in the cities of the Eastern Seaboard regularly. Currently, it tours some twenty American cities each year, singing in churches and concert halls. It has sung annual performances with the Minnesota Orchestra since 1927. Its tours in Europe were taken in the years 1913, 1930, 1955, 1957, 1970, and in 1972. A 25-day tour of Central Europe in 1970 included performances at the Heinrich Schütz Festival in Breda, Holland, and the International Strasbourg Music Festival in France; the latter extended an invitation for a repeat engagement for the 1972 festival. Of late, the chorus has sung with some instrumental accompaniment. Although its reputation for singing the great classics of the *a cappella* literature is well established, it has also performed with greater frequency music by contemporary composers. It is estimated that an average of 60,000 people attend the choir's concerts each year. . . . SAN JOSE STATE COLLEGE CHOIR, San Jose State College, San Jose, California 95114. Conductor: **William Erlendson** (1931). A choir of 80 voices founded 1931. Gives 6 to 10 concerts annually, including appearances with the San Jose Symphony, San Francisco Symphony, and the Santa Clara Philharmonic. Recordings: *Music Library Recordings* label. . . . SHRINE OF THE AGES CHOIR, Northern Arizona University, Flagstaff, Arizona 86001. Conductor: **Millard Kinney.** Founded 1933. A choir of 40 to 60 voices which is especially known for its annual concert for the Grand Canyon Easter Services. It tours through the Southwest region each year. . . . THE SEMINARY CHOIR, The Southern Baptist Theological Seminary, 2825 Lexington Road, Louisville, Kentucky 40206. Founded in 1945. Conductor: **Jay W. Wilkey** (1964). A choir of 40 voices. Campus performances are sung in Seminary Alumni Memorial Chapel. It sings some four local concerts plus those on tour. It has performed with the Louisville Orchestra and the Kentucky Opera Association. Its repertory includes, in addition to the church music of the past, avant-garde and other contemporary sacred works. Recordings have been made with the choir on *Columbia* and *Louisville* labels, in addition to private labels available from the Seminary. The Seminary's Male Chorale and the Oratorio Chorus both founded in 1952 are part of the choral program at the school. The Oratorio Chorus has some 125 voices and performs mostly standard oratorio literature with an orchestra of 40. It has performed with the Louisville Orchestra and has also recorded for *Columbia* and *Louisville* labels. . . . SOUTHERN METHODIST UNIVERSITY CHOIR, Southern Methodist University, Dallas, Texas 75222. Conductor: **Lloyd Pfautsch** (1958). A chorus of 48 voices presenting 25 performances annually in the Caruth Auditorium of Owen Fine Arts Center on campus and on annual tours throughout the country. . . . SOUTHWESTERN SINGERS, Southwestern at Memphis, Memphis, Tennessee 38112. Conductor: **Tony Lee Garner** (1967). 45 voices. Founded in 1937. Primarily a touring group singing about 25 concerts annually.

TEMPLE UNIVERSITY CHOIRS, College of Music, Temple University, Philadelphia, Pennsylvania 19122. Director of Choral Activities and Conductor: **Robert E. Page** (1956). The choral program was established at the university about 1930. The ensembles are: Temple University Choirs, the combined chorus of from 150 to 200 mixed voices; Temple University Concert Choir, 60 to 65 voices; and Temple University Women's Choir of 60 to 80 voices. The choruses are known for their many performances, live and recorded, with the Philadelphia Orchestra under **Eugene**

Ormandy; these are prepared by Mr. Page. They perform with the orchestra in Philadelphia's Academy of Music, on campus in Mitten Memorial Hall or Presser Music Hall, often in New York's Philharmonic Hall. Performances of the choruses are on *Columbia* records. The Concert Choir is the basic tour group of voices selected from the total available in the choral program. It has sung many premiere performances in Philadelphia and elsewhere of a wide range of works. Like the few other academic choral groups in the country that perform with established symphony orchestras on a regular basis, this chorus is highly regarded for its professionalism and artistic ability.

UNITED STATES AIR FORCE ACADEMY CADET CHOIRS, United States Air Force Academy, Colorado 80840. Conductor: **James Roger Boyd** (1957) (Director of Chapel Music). The vocal ensembles at the Academy are the Choir, founded in 1956 and composed of 100 voices, and the Chorale, a chorus of 100 voices first organized in 1958. Both choruses perform in the Academy Chapel; the Choir performs weekly; the Chorale is mainly a touring group. . . . UNITED STATES NAVAL ACADEMY CHORUSES, U.S. Navy Academy Chapel, Annapolis, Maryland 21402. The choral tradition at the academy began in 1884. Choral groups are the Academy Chapel Choir of 128 voices conducted by **Donald C. Gilley,** the Antiphonal Choir of 162 voices also under Gilley, and two groups led by **Joseph M. McCuen,** the Catholic Choir (140 voices) and the Academy Glee Club (100 voices). The three choirs perform in the Academy Chapel each Sunday of the academic year and give two concerts each outside of the Academy. The groups combine with visiting girls' groups for performances of mixed-voices literature. The Chapel Choir performs an annual concert of "Messiah" with Hood College. The Glee Club has sung on radio and television. . . . UNIVERSITY–CIVIC CHORALE, Department of Music, University of Utah, Salt Lake City, Utah 84112. Founded in 1950 as the University Chorale. Conductors: **Newell B. Weight** and **John Marlowe Nielson.** A chorus of 150 mixed voices, it performs in all the major choral works on the programs of the Utah Symphony under **Maurice Abravanel** and is the official chorus of the orchestra. It has its own concert series and performs in the series of other sponsors. It is not a touring group. Performances are mainly in Salt Lake Tabernacle and Kingsbury Hall on the University Campus. Its recordings are on *Westminster* and *Vanguard* labels. The chorus is made up of university students and townspeople. Other Utah University vocal groups are: University of Utah A Cappella Choir; 80 voices; founded 1962; Conductor: **Newell B. Weight;** performs 15 to 25 concerts a year on campus and on tour; has recorded in combination with the Civic Chorale on *Vanguard* records. University Chamber Choir; founded 1964; a group of 16 singers directed by **Bernell W. Hales;** has recorded on *Vanguard* label. University of Utah Men's chorus; founded 1912; Conductor: **John Marlowe Nielson;** 40 voices; performs on campus and on tour from 15 to 25 concerts a year. . . . UNIVERSITY OF ILLINOIS COLLEGIUM MUSICUM, School of Music, University of Illinois, Urbana, Illinois 61801. Founded 1949. Conductor: **George Hunter** (1949). A small vocal ensemble of two to five voices accompanied by three to five instrumentalists. Its repertory is essentially of medieval, Renaissance, and baroque music. Some 10 concerts are performed annually on tour, etc. Has recorded on *Westminster*. . . . UNIVERSITY OF MICHIGAN MEN'S GLEE CLUB, 3522 Administration Building, University of Michigan, Ann Arbor, Michigan 48104. First organized in 1859; the glee club claims to be the second oldest college glee club in America. It is an ensemble of 80 composed of graduate and undergraduate students from every college in the University. It sings some eight or ten performances in Michigan and from eight to twelve outside the state each year. On campus it performs in Hill Auditorium. Its annual tours take it throughout Michigan plus one major tour elsewhere in the U.S. Foreign tours include three made in Europe, in 1955, 1959, and 1963. The 1959 tour included the club's participation in the International Musical Eisteddfod in Llangollen,

Wales, in which it became the first American male choir to win in its category (a victory repeated during the 1963 tour). In 1967, the club undertook a world tour through seventeen countries. It was also among the groups invited to participate in the first International University Choral Festival held in New York in 1965. The group has sung for radio, television (national popular TV shows), and for a special movie short released by RKO–Pathe. The ensemble has made recordings for *Decca;* two special private recordings are available from the glee club. Director: **Phillip A. Duey** (1947), who has also published a series of choral arrangements through the Boston Music Company called "The Michigan Glee Club Series." . . . UNIVERSITY OF OKLAHOMA MEN'S GLEE CLUB, "THE SINGING SOONERS," University of Oklahoma, Norman, Oklahoma 73069. Conductor: **G. Russell Mathis** (1962). A glee club of 55 voices founded in 1901. It sings 50 to 60 concerts annually. It has performed on national television, at the New York World's Fair, Canada's Expo'67, and on tour in the South, Southwest, and Midwest. . . . UNIVERSITY OF SOUTHERN CALIFORNIA CHORUSES, School of Performing Arts, University Park, Los Angeles, California 90007. Conductor: **Charles C. Hirt.** Choruses are the USC Chamber Singers, USC Concert Choir, Trojan Chorale, Chapel Choir, and Opera Chorus. The USC Chamber Singers have toured Europe and Israel for the State Department, as well as touring in Mexico; they have sung occasional performances with the Los Angeles Philharmonic. . . . UNIVERSITY OF VERMONT MADRIGAL SINGERS, Music Department, University of Vermont, Burlington, Vermont 05401. Conductor: **Francis Weinrich** (1960). An ensemble of 12 voices founded in 1960. It sings two concerts locally and six on tour each year. Primarily, its repertory is of Renaissance and baroque music. Campus performances take place in Ira Allen Chapel.

ELIZABETH RODMAN VOORHEES CHAPEL CHOIR, Douglass College, Rutgers University, New Brunswick, New Jersey 08903. Conductor: **A. Kunrad Kvam** (1952). Founded in 1927. An *a cappella* group, which sometimes appears with organ or orchestra; has performed on radio and with men's groups from M.I.T., Lehigh, Haverford, and Williams Colleges.

THE WESTMINSTER CHOIRS, Westminster Choir College, Princeton, New Jersey 08540. The choirs organized by the college are the Westminster Symphonic Choir, the Westminster Choir, and the Chapel Choir. These were founded respectively in 1938, 1921, and 1932. The Westminster Choir and the Symphonic Choir are led by **Joseph Flummerfelt,** appointed Conductor in 1971. **Robert Simpson** has conducted the Chapel Choir since 1958. The 250-voiced Symphonic Choir performs about 15 concerts a year and has appeared in some of the notable halls in the country: Academy of Music, in Philadelphia, New York's Philharmonic Hall and Carnegie Hall, and the Kennedy Center in Washington, D.C. It has recorded on *Columbia* and *Columbia Masterworks* labels in performances with the New York Philharmonic and the Philadelphia Orchestra. As primarily a touring group, the Westminster Choir performs many concerts during its two annual tours. It has 48 voices, 36 of which form the touring group. The choir is chorus-in-residence at the Spoleto Festival in Italy. It has been managed by Hurok Concerts, Inc. but beginning in 1972, it contracted with the Arthur Judson Management. The Chapel Choir is also a touring ensemble singing in concerts in the churches and schools of the New Jersey area and, with 40 select students from the 125 members of the choir (all freshmen), makes an annual spring tour. The Westminster choirs, collectively, are among the most famous in America, enjoying a reputation from its performances with orchestras and conductors of high stature both on recordings and radio braodcasts. For years, the choirs were synonymous with their founder, John Finley Williamson, who also founded the Choir School—now College—in 1926. . . . WHEATON COLLEGE CHORUSES, Wheaton College, Wheaton, Illinois 60187. Wheaton College Concert Choir, Conductor: **Rex Hicks,** 65 voices; Wheaton College Men's

Glee Club, Conductor: **Clayton Halvorsen,** 70 members; Wheaton College Women's Glee Club, Conductor: **Ellen Thompson,** 65 members. Concerts are given in the college chapel and on tour. A recording has been made of the choir on *Word* records.

YALE DIVINITY SCHOOL CHOIR, 409 Prospect Street, New Haven, Connecticut 06511. Conductor: **Allen Birney** (1965). A choir of 24 voices. Makes a concert tour in New England every spring. It has been recorded on *Overtone* Records. . . . YALE GLEE CLUB, Box 1929 Yale Station, Yale University, New Haven, Connecticut 06520. Conductor: **Fenno Heath** (1953). A glee club of 80 voices founded in 1860. Gives about 20 performances annually. Annual concerts with Harvard and Princeton Glee Clubs. Takes a statewide Christmas tour each year and a foreign summer tour every three years. Each spring the chorus performs a major choral work with orchestra in a joint concert with voices from a girls school. When Yale University became coeducational, the glee club gained its own four-voice mixed choral structure. Has performed with Leopold Stokowski and the American Symphony Orchestra in New York. Recordings have been made on the *Carillon* label—an independent record company.

Independent and Professional Groups

AMERICAN CONCERT CHOIR, c/o American Choral Foundation, 130 West 56th Street, New York, N.Y. 10019. Conductor: **Margaret Hillis.** . . . THE AMOR ARTIS CHORALE, 23rd Floor, 777 Third Avenue, New York, N.Y. 10017. Conductor: **Johannes Somary** (1961). Founded 1961. A group of 33 singers; performs three or four concerts annually in New York, accompanied by the 30-member Amor Artis Orchestra, with guest soloists. An all-professional chorus (and orchestra) it has recorded for *Decca* and *Vanguard* records. The group publishes the *Amor Artis Bulletin,* which has a circulation of 5,300. The Chorale operates as a nonprofit organization sustained by income from concerts and recordings and voluntary contributions of members in Amor Artis, Inc. **Milton Goldin** is Administrative Director. . . . ANCHORAGE COMMUNITY CHORUS, INC. Box 325, Anchorage, Alaska 99501. Founded 1947. Conductor: **Elvera Voth** (1962). 95 voices. The chorus is an affiliate of the Anchorage Community College and is the performing chorus for the Alaska Festival of Music. Three to seven major performances are sung annually of mostly standard choral repertory. . . . BACH ARIA GROUP, c/o Herbert Barrett Management, 1860 Broadway, New York, N.Y. 10023. Director: **William H. Scheide.** Consists of nine vocalists and instrumentalists who are also well known as soloists. Founded in 1946. Performs arias and duets from Bach cantatas. (Further details are found under Instrumental Chamber Groups.) . . . THE APOLLO MUSICAL CLUB OF CHICAGO, 243 South Wabash Avenue, Chicago, Illinois 60604. Conductor: **William J. Peterman** (1963). Founded 1872; 175 voices. This is Chicago's oldest continuously functioning musical organization. The Club gives four concerts yearly, including performances of Handel's "Messiah" and an annual spring concert of a major choral work. Professional orchestral musicians as well as solo singers are engaged for most concerts. (A number of well-known concert singers made appearances early in their careers with the Apollo Musical Club. Generally they were those who began in the Chicago area. Among them are **Donald Gramm, Carol Smith,** and **Lili Chookasian.**) The chorus is self-supporting with funds coming from membership dues and the sale of concert tickets. The annual "Messiah" performance generally supports, through its ticket sales, the subsequent spring concert. No chorus member is paid; guest soloists receive fees. Performances are held in Orchestra Hall and St. Peter's church, both in Chicago's downtown area.

BERKSHIRE BOY CHOIR, 445 Park Avenue, New York, N.Y. 10022. Founded in 1967 by English organist and choirmaster, **George Guest.** It is a privately sponsored chorus of 38 boys and 17 men. The choir was formed at the Stockbridge School for Boys in Massachusetts during the summer of 1967 from singers drawn from choirs in other cities in the U.S. Special recordings of its performances are available from the choir's address above. Current director is **John Hoyt Stookey.** . . . BETHLEHEM BACH CHOIR, Main and Church Streets, Bethlehem, Pennsylvania 18018. Founded 1898. Conductor: **Alfred Mann** (since 1970). A choir of 150 voices which sings at the annual Bach Festival in Bethlehem (q.v.). Choir organist is **William Whitehead.** For the 1972 festival the choir performed, perhaps for the first time anywhere, all six masses of Bach.

CAMERATA SINGERS, 150 West End Avenue, New York, N.Y. 10023. Conductor: **Abraham Kaplan** (1960). A chorus of 26 to 100 voices founded in 1960. Five concerts are performed annually, plus a national tour. Records for *Columbia* Records, and collaborates frequently with the New York Philharmonic but has also sung with the American Symphony. The singers presented their first subscription series in 1969 with a specially formed Camerata Symphony Orchestra in programs of both choral and orchestral works. . . . THE CANBY SINGERS, c/o 152 West 42nd Street, Suite 911, New York, N.Y. 10036 (the address changes periodically). An ensemble of 20 or so singers under the direction of **Edward Tatnall Canby.** This chorus of serious amateur singers has presented some interesting concerts in New York, Connecticut, and New Jersey emphasizing a largely Renaissance and baroque repertory of *a cappella* works with some excursions into the classical and romantic choral literature. Its recordings are on the *Nonesuch* label. . . . CANTERBURY CHORAL SOCIETY, Church of the Heavenly Rest, 2 East 90th Street, New York, N.Y. 10028. Conductor: **Charles Dodsley Walker** (1952). A chorus of 100 voices, founded 1952. Performs with an orchestra of about 50 players in large choral works each season with noted concert soloists. It has sometimes performed in Philharmonic Hall. . . . CHICAGO SYMPHONY CHORUS, 220 South Michigan Avenue, Chicago, Illinois 60604. Conductor: **Margaret Hillis** (1957). A professional chorus of 160 voices, founded 1957. Between six and eight works are sung each season, with two or three performances of each work. Its recorded performances are on *Columbia* and *Victor* labels. It made its New York debut with the Chicago Symphony in 1967. . . . CHORAL SYMPHONY SOCIETY, INC., 945 West End Avenue, New York, N.Y. 10025. Founded in 1964, the Society is a nonprofit, tax-exempt organization dependent entirely on contributions from patrons. During the sixties the Society performed major choral works and opera in concert form; at present, for the purpose of fund raising, it concentrates on smaller concerts—some three or four a year —performed in various halls in the New York area. The Society has 16 to 30 voices depending on the performance needs and an orchestra of from 20 to 30 players. **David Labovitz** is Music Director. . . . THE COLLEGIATE CHORALE, INC., 130 West 56th Street, New York, N.Y. 10019. Conductor: **Abraham Kaplan** (1961). A chorus of 150 voices. Founded in 1941 by **Robert Shaw.** Two or three concerts are sung annually including concerts with the New York Philharmonic, *a cappella* concerts, or concerts with its own engaged orchestra. The Chorale maintains a lending library for use by other choruses. Because membership in the ensemble is not a full-time occupation, the singers are unpaid (as is the conductor) and are not free to tour. Members pay $30 dues per annum, which, along with sponsor donations and concert income, support the work of the chorus. The chorus is governed by a board of its own members. Its performances are held in Carnegie Hall and Philharmonic Hall. Within its repertory are many major choral works including Berlioz's Requiem (which was performed with the New York Philharmonic under Seiji Ozawa), Prokofiev's "Alexander Nevsky," Bach's B Minor Mass, etc. These and other works have been presented with leading solo artists. Recordings of the chorus are on the *Victor* and *Columbia* labels. . . . THE COLUMBUS BOYCHOIR, Box 350, Princeton, N.J. 08540. Founded 1939. Conductor: **Thomas Conlin** (1970). A concert choir of 30 voices performing 30 to 40 concerts each year. Sometimes performs with the accompaniment of two or three instruments. The ensemble is an active touring group. Each year it tours the United States and

Canada. Past foreign tours include South America in 1956 and again in 1968; Europe in 1965 and 1969; Japan in 1966. The choir performs frequently with great orchestras. It has sung in concerts with the New York Philharmonic, the Boston Symphony (at Tanglewood in the premiere performance of Britten's "War Requiem"), the Philadelphia Orchestra, the now defunct NBC Symphony, numerous college orchestras, community orchestras, and with the Bach Aria Group, etc. Its appearance on broadcasting networks include several appearances on the former Bell Telephone Hour, and other popular-style variety shows. It has also sung in shows in New York's Radio City Music Hall. Other notable appearances have been at the White House and for Pope Paul in Rome. Recordings of the choir are on *Columbia* Records. Concert management (in 1972): Tornay Management.

THE DE PAUR CHORUS, 746 Saint Nicholas Avenue, New York, N.Y. 10031. A professional touring chorus founded in 1946 by its conductor, **Leonard de Paur.** Comprised of 28 male singers. It has toured the United States and Canada each year and has made tours abroad to Africa, Europe, Latin America, and the Far East, altogether singing from 90 to 150 concerts a year. Its performances have been recorded on *Columbia* and *Mercury* labels. . . . DESSOFF CHOIRS, 244 East 52nd Street, New York, N.Y. 10022. Conductor: **Thomas A. Sokol** (1968). Has recorded for *Fantasy, Vox, Counterpoint,* and *Bach Guild.* The chorus (it is only a single ensemble, despite its name) had for 32 years been associated with its former conductor, **Paul Boepple** (now retired) who was responsible for many important New York choral premieres and for performing many neglected large-scale choral works, as well as the works of composers who were once much less performed than they are now (Palestrina, Lassus, Schütz, et al.). The chorus is essentially composed of amateur singers. Professional soloists are often engaged for concerts. . . . DON COSSACK CHORUS, 82 12th Avenue, Sea Cliff, N.Y. 11579. Founded 1921. Conductor: **Serge Jaroff** (1921). A chorus of 25 male voices. It presents about 180 to 220 concerts annually. Repertory consists mainly of Russian church songs, folk songs, and choruses from Russian operas. It has appeared in Europe during lengthy tours. Many anthologies of its repertory have been recorded. These are currently on *DGG, Decca,* and *London* labels.

GREGG SMITH SINGERS, c/o Arthur Judson Management, Inc., 119 West 57th Street, New York, N.Y. 10019. Founded in 1955 with first performances sung at the Los Angeles Japanese Methodist Church. Conductor: **Gregg Smith** (1955). A chorus of from 25 to 50 voices which performs some 75 to 100 concerts yearly. Its United States tours total about 50 concerts a season. From 1959 on, the chorus had collaborated often with Stravinsky, producing together some dozen or so recordings of the composer's music. Upon the composer's death, Gregg Smith was asked to prepare the orchestra and the chorus that performed for the funeral service in Venice. Since 1958, the chorus has toured Europe four times, performing at the Brussels World's Fair, the festivals of Salzburg and Edinburgh and others, and in Venice at St. Mark's Cathedral where it recorded some works of Gabrieli, a recording which later became the winner of the third Grammy Award for the chorus. The chorus claims other distinctions, such as that of being the most recorded classical music chorus, with over 25 albums (see labels below). Besides Stravinsky, the chorus has performed under Robert Craft and Leopold Stokowski, among others. Over 100 world premieres have been sung by the ensemble including five works by Stravinsky. Its recordings are on the *Columbia* label (for which it recorded the complete works of Charles Ives), *Everest, MGM,* and *Odyssey* labels. Concert management is under Arthur Judson Management, Inc.

HANDEL AND HAYDN SOCIETY, 416 Marlborough Street, Boston, Massachusetts 02115. Founded 1815. Conductor: **Thomas Dunn** (1967). A choral group of 90 voices which gives six subscription concerts a year in Boston's Jordan Hall and Symphony Hall. It performs with orchestra (for the 1971–72 season, one concert was entirely instrumental). Its current repertory includes the traditional choral literature as well as contemporary works. The Society claims the distinction of being the oldest musical society in America still engaged in presenting public concerts. A dominant force in America's cultured musical life for decades, this venerable society was active in organizing and presenting important concerts of choral, operatic, and orchestral music, music festivals in Boston and New York, and in publishing. It was often requested to perform at important public occasions. The history of the Society involves the names of many famous American and foreign musicians, composers, statesmen, intellectuals and other notables. The works first performed in Boston or in America by the Society are legion: Haydn's "Creation," Beethoven's 9th Symphony, Mendelssohn's "Elijah," Handel's "Messiah," "Samson," "Solomon," and "Israel in Egypt," Bach's B Minor Mass and St. Matthew Passion, to name some. In recent years, it made two recordings, both now out of print (Handel's "Messiah" on *Kapp* records and Brahm's Requiem on the *Boston* label), traveled to England, and appeared on educational television, etc. Its management is handled by Music Unlimited Associated at the address above. . . . HOLY VIRGIN PROTECTION CATHEDRAL CHOIR, c/o ABC–Westminster Records, 1330 Avenue of the Americas, New York, N.Y. 10019. Conductor: **Nicholas Afonsky.** *Westminster* Records. The recordings are mainly that of the Liturgy of St. John Chrysostom.

JANUS CHORALE OF NEW YORK, INC., 20 Sidney Place, Brooklyn, N.Y. 11201. Formed in 1969; incorporated as a nonprofit organization. Founder and Conductor is **Robert Hickok.** Members of the chorus are mostly music teachers and students—including graduate students in the New York area. The Chorale presents some five or six concerts annually, sometimes with an orchestra or other instrumental accompaniment in various New York City halls: Alice Tully Hall, Town Hall, the auditoriums of schools, etc. Its repertory is varied but generally restricted to smaller scale works from all periods. In 1972, it sang a concert devoted solely to the works of Purcell.

THE KARLSRUD CHORALE, THE MEN OF SONG, THE NEW YORK SEXTET, THE RONDOLIERS, THE CONCERTMEN AND EDMOND KARLSRUD, 948 The Parkway, Mamaroneck, N.Y. 10543 (Men of Song Enterprises, Inc.). Founding dates vary from 1947 onward. Ensembles have from 4 to 16 singers. These are professional groups which are brought together for the sole purpose of touring for limited periods of time and then are disbanded until the next season. From 70 to 90 concerts are sung yearly. Has recorded for *RCA Victor* and *Columbia.*

THE LEONARD MOORE CHORALE, 3008 East Laurelhurst Drive Northeast, Seattle, Washington 98105. Conductor: **Leonard Moore** (1953). Founded 1953; 25 voices. A touring group which sings about 15 performances annually, largely in the Northwest area. . . . LOS ANGELES MASTER CHORALE, The Music Center, 135 North Grand Avenue, Los Angeles, California 90012. Conductor: **Roger Wagner** (1964). An ensemble of 100 voices. Its first concert was sung in January, 1965. Sponsored by the Southern California Choral Music Association, an organization formed for the express purpose of founding and supporting a professional resident chorus for the Los Angeles area. The Chorale is the resident chorus in the Dorothy Chandler Pavilion of the Music Center and is under exclusive contract with the Center. It performs regularly with the Los Angeles Philharmonic and the Glendale Symphony and presents its own five-concert series each season. It is the only professional resident chorus in the United States. The Chorale participates in various educational projects in Los Angeles by sponsoring vocal quartets in the public schools and making itself available for civic groups, municipal programs, etc. School children are permitted to attend some of the Chorale's rehearsal sessions and the general public is offered free concert previews before performances. The Chorale has received unusually high critical acclaim from some of America's great conductors. Its recordings are on *Capitol* and *Angel* records. (See also the Roger Wagner Chorale.) . . . NORMAN LUBOFF CHOIR, c/o Kolmar–Luth Entertainment, Inc., 1776 Broadway, New York, N.Y. 10019. Conductor: **Norman Luboff.** A touring group of 30 singers and 4 instrumentalists. Recordings on *Victor* and *Columbia* are with groups from 7 to 100 members. Personnel varies from year to year. Altogether the choirs sing from 75 to 100 performances annually. Although their programs have a wide classical repertory, it is for their lighter fare that they are best known. The Luboff groups have appeared on radio, TV, and in motion pictures.

THE MADRIGAL GUILD, 868 Northampton Drive, Palo Alto, California 94303. Conductor and Founder: **Eileen Washington** (1943). A chorus of 10 voices (sometimes fewer) founded in 1943. The Guild performs in the Los Angeles and San Francisco areas, giving approximately 6 concerts annually. Its repertory emphasizes music of the late Renaissance; it performs with harpsichord and lute accompaniment. *Music Library* Recordings. . . . THE MASTERWORK CHORUS, c/o The Masterwork Music and Art Foundation, 300 Mendham Road, Morristown, N.J. 07960. Founded in 1955. Music Director of the Foundation and Conductor of the chorus is **David Randolph** (since 1955). The chorus has from 180 to 240 amateur singers and performs with instrumental accompaniment of from 28 to 68 professional musicians as needed. It performs in various halls in New York City and New Jersey but for its major concerts it appears in Carnegie Hall and Philharmonic Hall. An average of 8 to 10 concerts are presented each season. It has sung with the Philadelphia Orchestra under Eugene Ormandy and has appeared on New York's educational television station. The Chorus has performed the large-scale works of the standard choral repertory including an annual concert of Handel's "Messiah." Professional vocal soloists are always engaged for the regular concerts in New York. (An important aspect of the Foundation's activity are the so-called summer sings which are presented under its auspices. These eight or so sessions, held in the Foundation facilities, are open without audition to anyone who desires to participate in sightreading performances of great choral works.) The Masterwork Chorus has recorded for *Westminster* and *Design* Records. . . . THE MENDELSSOHN CHOIR OF PITTSBURGH, INC., P.O. Box 7333, Pittsburgh, Pennsylvania 15213. Founded in 1908 by Ernest Lunt, who directed it until 1950. A community chorus of about 180 voices; its members volunteer their time and services. It performs four or five concerts each season with the Pittsburgh Symphony; it has presented Handel's "Messiah" each year since 1919. Repertory includes over 50 major works and a number of commissioned works. Other orchestras it has sung with are the Cleveland Orchestra, the Minneapolis Symphony (now Minnesota), the Chautauqua Symphony, and the former New York Symphony. Among the conductors who have led the chorus are Robert Shaw, Hugh Ross, Walter Hendl, and William Steinberg. The choir is supported by members' dues ($10 per year), contributions through fund drives, and fees received for its performances. Recordings (with the Pittsburgh Symphony under Steinberg) are on *Everest* and *Command* labels (the latter Beethoven's 9th Symphony). . . . THE MITZELFELT CHORALE, 1951 Escarpa Drive, Los Angeles, California 90041. Founded in 1957 by its conductor **Dr. (M.D.) H. Vincent Mitzelfelt.** A chorus of 48 voices performing mainly in California and Nevada in such facilities as the Hollywood Bowl, Chandler Pavilion of the Los Angeles Music Center, Redlands Bowl, Los Angeles County Museum, in Royce and Schoenberg Halls on the campus of U.C.L.A., Las Vegas Convention Center, etc. It has sung on national radio and television broadcasts and has had its performances broadcast by Armed Forces Radio Broadcasting System. The Chorale's annual season consists of 8 to 10 concerts. Its repertory comprises over 70 works, most of which have been sung with orchestra; these include contemporary works by Zador, Rozsa, Hanson, John Vincent, Britten, Vaughn-Williams, Holst, et al. and the large-scale choral classics by Bach, Handel, Brahms, Mozart, Beethoven, Haydn, Palestrina, and so on. It has recorded an anthology, "Music of Faith and Inspiration," which was distributed through the Readers Digest Record Club, and has recorded for *Chapel* Records, *Christian Faith* Recordings, *Dorian* Records, and *Fiamma* Records. . . . MORMON TABERNACLE CHOIR OF SALT LAKE CITY, 19 West South Temple Street, Salt Lake City, Utah 84101. Founded 1847. Conductor: **Richard P. Condie.** A chorus of 375 voices. It performs in the Tabernacle in Salt Lake City, and has been heard by millions through recordings, and radio and television broadcasts. It has recorded many anthologies of choral music for *Columbia*. . . . MOUNT ANGEL ABBEY CHOIR, Mount Angel Abbey, Saint Benedict, Oregon 97373. Conductor: **Dom David Nicholson** (O.S.B.) (1950). The Abbey Choir has 40 voices; it performs daily for the liturgy. It is distinguished by its recordings of church chants for *Victor* and *World Library of Sacred Music;* earlier recordings, which may no longer be available, have been issued on *Gregorian Institute* and *Educo* labels. . . . MUSICA AETERNA, 375 Riverside Drive, New York, N.Y. 10025. **Frederic Waldman** has been conductor of the Musica Aeterna Orchestra and Chorus since its founding in October, 1961. The combined ensembles have up to 80 performers each; they give some 20 performances a season, 4 of which are vocal. These are part of the three series presented at the Metropolitan Museum of Art in New York City, one series at Lincoln Center's Alice Tully Hall, and two concerts at Carnegie Hall. The ensembles are recorded on *Decca* label. Concert managers are **Melvin Kaplan** and **Eleanor Morrison.**

THE NATIONAL SHRINE CHORALE, 4th and Michigan Avenue, N.E., Washington, D.C. 20017. Conductor: **Joseph Michaud** (1966). A choir of 40 voices founded in 1966. Performs two concerts in the Shrine and sings at all Shrine services. Concerts accompanied by some 19 members of the Washington National Symphony. . . . NEW YORK CHORAL SOCIETY, 165 West 57th Street, New York, N.Y. 10019. Music Director: **Robert DeCormier.** A choral ensemble of 100 voices founded in 1959. Three concerts annually, usually in Philharmonic Hall. In the summer informal reading sessions are held under various well-known choral conductors. Performances includes soloists and orchestras hired for the occasion. Guest conductors have been **Roger Wagner** and **John Motley.**

THE ORATORIO SOCIETY OF NEW JERSEY, Box 152, Montclair, N.J. 07043. Conductor: **Nixon S. Bicknell** (1967). Founded 1952. This group of 75 to 90 singers present two regularly scheduled concerts annually, accompanied by members of the New Jersey Symphony. It sponsors public sightsinging sessions during June. Its repertory covers the range from early music to contemporary. Most performances are of large-scale works—oratorios, passions, etc. To sustain its activities, the Society relies on patrons, dues from members, auctions and bazaars, etc. The Society is incorporated not-for-profit; prior to its incorporation, it made two commercial recordings for *Word* records (still available), under Founder–Conductor **Clarence Snyder,** of Stainer's "Crucifixion," and Dubois's "Seven Last Words." For these recordings the Society is incorrectly identified as the New Jersey Oratorio Choir. . . . ORATORIO SOCIETY OF NEW YORK, Room 504, Carnegie Hall, 881 Seventh Avenue, New York, N.Y. 10019. Conductor: **T. Charles Lee** (1959). The Oratorio Society, a group of 140 voices, was founded in 1873 by Leopold Damrosch and is New York City's second oldest musical organization. Dr. Damrosch's sons, Walter and Frank, followed him as Conductor for many years. Andrew Carnegie, president of the Society for more than 40 years, built Carnegie Hall in 1891 to house the Oratorio Society and the Symphony Society of New York. Although the chorus is the oldest tenant of the famous concert hall, it has performed throughout New York: in the old Metropolitan Opera House, Brick Presbyterian Church, Philharmonic Hall at Lincoln Center, and on the site of the New York World's Fair. Its Christmas performance of Handel's "Messiah" is a tradition which has been repeated over 145 times. The Society has given New York premieres of Bach's St. Matthew Passion and B Minor

Mass in their complete form, Wagner's "Parsifal," Berlioz's "Damnation of Faust," etc. Among the composers who have conducted the Society in performances of their own works are Gustav Mahler, Richard Strauss, and Tchaikovsky. Over the years the soloists have included Lilli Lehman, **William Warfield,** Louise Homer, Lillian Nordica, and **George Shirley.** . . . THE ORPHEON CHORALE, c/o Herbert Barrett Management, Inc., 1860 Broadway, New York, N.Y. 10023. Founded in 1968. Made its New York debut in 1969, after a period of touring the Eastern states. Founder and Conductor is **Dino Anagnost.** A professional chorus of 24 singers, many of whom are of solo capability. Its repertory consists of chamber choral music, both old and contemporary.

PAULIST CHOIR OF CHICAGO, 188 West Randolph Street, Chicago, Illinois 60601. Founded in 1904; the group gave its first concert in Chicago in 1907. In 1912, the choir won first prize in the International Competition of Choral Societies of the World, in Paris. The Paulist Choir records on its own label; *EFOM.* This label is an acronym for **Eugene F. O'Malley** (Reverend) who led the choir from 1928 until 1967. . . . PUEBLO SYMPHONY CHORALE, 1117 Lake Avenue, Pueblo, Colorado 81004. Founded in 1969, this ensemble of 100 voices is sponsored by the Pueblo Civic Symphony Association and appears in concert with the 85-member symphony orchestra. Conductor of both the Chorale and the orchestra is **Gerhard Track** (since 1969). **Mrs. Carmelita M. Keator** is Manager of the Association. The members of the Chorale are professional musicians, educators, students and citizens of Pueblo and nearby communities. Each year, a Christmas concert featuring both the Chorale and the orchestra is presented as a gift to the people of Pueblo. This program is delay-broadcast over station KVMN–FM. The chorus has also sung at the U.S. Air Force Academy, has had its 1971 spring concert replayed on the NBC network's "Great Choirs of America," in July, 1971, and has had its 1970 Christmas concert recorded (John Law Co., Colorado Springs). (See also PUEBLO SYMPHONY ORCHESTRA under Symphony Orchestras—Colorado.)

ST. THOMAS'S CHOIR, 830 Whitney Avenue, New Haven, Connecticut 06511. This group performs under various conductors and has recorded for *Overtone* records. In 1958, its recording of Alessandro Scarlatti's St. John Passion was awarded the Grand Prix du Disque. . . . SALT LAKE ORATORIO SOCIETY, 401 Medical Arts Building, Salt Lake City, Utah 84111. Conductor: **John Marlowe Nielson** (1962). Founded *circa* 1915, the group includes 375 singers and 50 instrumentalists. Each year the Society performs Handel's "Messiah" in the Salt Lake Tabernacle at Christmas time with full orchestra and about 400 singers. During the summer the Society chooses a group of 150 singers to perform a major work with the Aspen Music Festival Orchestra at Aspen, Colorado. . . . SALT LAKE SYMPHONIC CHOIR, P.O. Box 45, Salt Lake City, Utah 84110. Tel.: (801) 466–8701. Founded in 1949. Conductor since its inception has been **Armont Willardsen.** The choir has 100 voices and a staff accompanist. It is primarily a touring group and bills itself as the "largest independent traveling choir in America." In the more than twenty years of its existence it has sung over 600 concerts throughout the United States, in major cities, colleges and university campuses, for civic groups and cultural organizations. It has also performed in Canada and Mexico. Some seasons have taken the choir through more than 14,000 miles of travel. Its annual average number of performances is about 25 per season. The choir was first organized by a group of young people desiring to continue choral singing beyond their school years. Currently it is made up of people of a wide range of ages (from 17 to 55) from a variety of professions and occupations. The choir members receive no pay; when on tour, their transportation and lodging expenses are paid for out of choir funds. The Symphonic Choir's repertory ranges from Renaissance music to rock. It has performed with the Utah Symphony Orchestra and recently recorded with that ensemble Honegger's "Judith." The choir's financial base stems from all ticket sales and from foundation grants. Concert management for its tours is handled by the firm, Pryor-Menz Attractions. The choir's own concert manager is **Richard M. Taggart.** . . . THE SINGING BOYS OF ORLANDO, c/o **Mrs. Walter Rawlson,** 681 Emporia Avenue, Oviedo, Florida 32765. Formed in 1967 by its director, **Byron Swanson.** This group is a nonsectarian, unsponsored organization comprised of a concert choir and a training choir, each with 50 boys ranging in age from 9 to 14. Membership in the choir is based on vocal potential, personality, and school records. The choir has sung with the Florida Symphony in concert choral works and in concert presentations of opera. They have appeared at the Annual Bach Festival of Rollins College, and participated in the 12th International Congress of Pueri Cantores (Boy Singers) in Guadalajara, Mexico. Its repertory includes old and new music and arrangements for boys' choir of well-known works for solo voice, etc. The choir sang at Alice Tully Hall in New York in 1971. . . . SINGING CITY OF PHILADELPHIA, 35 South 9th Street, Philadelphia, Pennsylvania 19107. Founded in 1948 by its Director, **Elaine Brown.** Singing City is a complex of four choral ensembles as well as a nonprofit training and service organization offering workshops, seminars, clinics, and classes in choral training, singing, and literature. The choral groups are: Singing City Chorale, a group of 60 singers—all with formal musical training, some with music degrees—which performs choral masterworks as well as rarely performed contemporary works including those newly commissioned (it has sung the Philadelphia premieres of works by Britten, Persichetti, et al.). The Chorale serves the Philadelphia community but has also performed in Philharmonic Hall in New York, Constitution Hall in Washington, etc.; it has appeared with the Philadelphia Orchestra, the Bach Aria Group, the now-defunct Symphony of the Air, and under such conductors as Eugene Ormandy, Herman Scherchen, Nadia Boulanger, Lukas Foss, and others. In 1960, the Chorale's first recording, "The Peaceable Kingdom" by Randall Thompson, was released by *Fellowship* Records. Singing City Choir is Singing City's first and largest group. A chorus of 135 voices, it is made up of volunteer singers from a variety of ethnic and religious backgrounds. The chorus has a wide-ranging repertory from the early to modern classics, liturgical chants, folk music, etc., and has performed in churches, synagogues, schools, community centers, and in general is oriented toward community service. Among its national distinctions have been performances on national radio and television broadcasts and its invitation to sing for the Christmas-tree lighting ceremony at the White House (1964). In recognition of its services in the Philadelphia area, the choir received the annual Brotherhood Award from the local chapter of the National Conference of Christians and Jews. The Youth Choir of Singing City is led by Assistant Director, **Sonya Garfinkle.** A 50-voice unit, it is composed of students from over 20 schools in the Greater Philadelphia and Southern New Jersey areas. This group, in combination with other school choirs, has sung with the Philadelphia Orchestra as part of the orchestra's Youth Concert Series. The fourth and newest Singing City ensemble is the Chamber Choir. Its 16 members are mostly conductors being trained at the postgraduate level. It is often used as an experimental singing ensemble for the reading of unpublished music.

TEXAS BOYS CHOIR OF FORT WORTH, 1400 Hemphill, Fort Worth, Texas 76104. Founded in 1946 in Denton, Texas, by its Director, **George Bragg.** Altogether there are two concert choirs of 26 voices each (for touring and recording) plus preparatory and study choruses. To select, train, and conduct the choirs in performance there are three full-time directors and one part-time associate director. Thus, the touring groups may be traveling at the same time under different leadership. The boys are from the Fort Worth–Dallas area and are selected through auditions held twice each year. The concert choirs spend at least a year and a half in training. When they begin their choral studies, the boys are aged 8 to 12. They can remain with the choirs until voice change occurs. The choirs have performed more than

2,000 times in America and overseas. Tours have taken them to Westminster Abbey, Rome's St. Peter's Basilica, and the concert halls of major cities. They have appeared on leading popular television shows, at conventions, and in their own concert series in Fort Worth. Their first national tour took place in 1962, the first tour to Europe in 1959. They have performed and recorded with Igor Stravinsky in Hollywood. In concert, the boys appear in varying attire—choir vestments, Western garb, etc.—to suit the music being sung. Repertory includes both the full range of classics and modern light music. In 1966, the choirs were presented with the Grammy Award for their recording of "Charles Ives: Music for Chorus." Other recorded repertory includes Monteverdi's Vespers of 1610 and works by Soler and Gabrieli. Record labels are *Columbia* and *Decca.* Concert management (1972) is under Columbia Artists Management, Inc. . . . TUCSON ARIZONA BOYS CHORUS, P.O. Box 12034, Tucson, Arizona 85711. Founded in 1939 by Eduardo Caso, the chorus's Director until 1965; since that year the chorus has been directed by **Jeffrey R. Haskell.** The chorus is known mainly as a touring group. From a total number of about 80 available voices some 25 to 30 are chosen for the annual touring season, which can involve as many as 80 performances. The boys are aged 8 to 16 and all live and go to school in the Tucson area. They are selected for the chorus on the basis of musical aptitude and character; membership in the organization is conceived by its sponsors as an extension of general education for the boys. Since its earlier years, when support for the chorus came from various local organizations including radio station KVOA, the growth of community recognition of the chorus enabled it to become an incorporated, nonprofit, nonsectarian organization administered by a board of directors made up of citizens of Tucson. As an institutionalized performing ensemble, the chorus functions as a community asset; its activities and fame—now worldwide—are appreciated by its supporters on both a musical and civic level. The repertory of the chorus and its large number of touring engagements both at home and abroad make it unique. Basic to the repertory are its own original arrangements of songs from the American Southwest—folk songs, cowboy songs, Mexican carols and novelty songs—in addition to works from the classic choral literature. The boys sing their programs in choir vestments, modern cowboy outfits, and jeans and, in keeping with the showmanship aspect of their concerts, they utilize stage props and scenery. The chorus has been touring nationally since 1950, internationally since 1966. In 1944 it appeared for the first time on national TV (the NBC network) and has since then made guest appearances on a number of popular television shows. Highlights among tour performances for the chorus include its first performance outside the Southwest at the 1950 Chicago Fair; singing for 20,000 International Rotary Convention delegates in Atlantic City in 1951, which was a stop in a tour that included the boys' first concert in New York's Town Hall and an appearance on Ed Sullivan's television show, then called "Toast of the Town." In 1955 the chorus made its first trip to Europe, where it performed in England, Portugal, Spain, France, Germany, and Sweden. A trip to Australia was made in 1960 and, in 1962, the chorus sang before an audience of 60,000 at the now defunct Chicagoland Music Festival. Locally the chorus has sung with the Tucson Symphony Orchestra and the Tucson Civic Ballet, in various churches and halls. In summer, the members of the chorus are given the opportunity to spend several weeks on a ranch where rehearsals for the new season are held and where recreational training in horsemanship, leatherwork, camping, and general ranching is part of the daily schedule. Recordings by the chorus are available on *Capitol* and *United Artists* labels. Concert management is under Kolmar–Luth Entertainment, Inc.

UNITED NATIONS SINGERS, Post Office Box 20, Grand Central Station, New York, N.Y. 10017. Conductor: **Donald Read** (1955). The United Nations Singers is composed of 100 singers who are associated in some way with the United Nations. The ensemble's objective is to foster understanding between people of all nations by demonstrating teamwork among members of diverse nationalities and backgrounds. Members represent twenty-nine different countries. The group gives concerts in old peoples' homes, schools, hospitals, in foreign countries (Wales in 1963, Scandinavia in 1965), and cities in the U.S. (e.g., Boston, Philadelphia, Des Moines). The group performs with each member in national costume and has a repertory of over 100 folk songs and Christmas carols, sung in some thirty original languages and dialects.

ROGER WAGNER CHORALE, c/o Hurok Concerts, Inc., 1370 Avenue of the Americas, New York, N.Y. 10019. A touring group of from 24 to 28 singers, many of whom are drawn from the Los Angeles Master Chorale (q.v.). One of the best known choruses in America, it has a large repertory of choral music spanning the centuries. It has performed live or in recordings with many major instrumental ensembles including the Los Angeles Philharmonic, the London and Royal Philharmonic Orchestras, etc. Conductor is **Roger Wagner.** Recordings: *Capitol, Angel, Gregorian Institute, CRI,* and *Lyrichord*. . . . WASHINGTON CATHEDRAL CHOIR, Washington Cathedral, Washington, D.C. 20016. Conductor: **Paul Callaway** (1939). The Washington Cathedral Choir is a 50-voice choir, founded in 1909. Although it performs regularly in Washington Cathedral, in 1965 it sang daily services at Westminster Abbey in London for three weeks as part of the Abbey's 900th anniversary celebration. . . . THE WELCH CHORALE, 3025 Grand Concourse, Bronx, N.Y. 10468. Conductor: **James B. Welch** (1938). Twenty-five voices sing in the Welch Chorale, which performs in such places as Town Hall in New York and St. Philip Neri Church in The Bronx. The group gives 10 performances annually, has appeared on nationwide television, and has recorded for *Lyrichord* and *Gregorian Institute* records.

Part 4 | Music and the Stage

Opera in America

Opera groups in the United States number in the hundreds. *Opera News,* the magazine of the Metropolitan Opera Guild, in conjunction with Central Opera Service, publishes annually the results of a survey of all types of opera-producing groups in America. For the 1969–70 season, *Opera News* reported there were 648 opera organizations of all kinds. The survey ten years earlier showed there were 754 groups. The total number of performances taking place from 1969 to 1970 was 4,779, of which 3,011 were of the standard repertory and 1,768 were of modern works.

The number of operas performed were 341 for the season including 178 standard repertory operas and 163 contemporary works.

Twenty-six percent of all performances were by major companies performed before 2.5 million people at a cost of some $40 million.

The Central Opera Service published in its *Bulletin* of December 1971 a "Directory of Opera Companies and Workshops in the United States and Canada." Therein are listed 1,021 entries: 50 for Canada and 971 for the United States. The gap between that figure and the figure compiled for the *Opera News*/COS survey leaves open the question as to what constitutes an opera company and what does not.

The Directory contains major opera companies and other professional groups (which pay their singers and orchestra), touring groups, concert series that include opera, symphony societies, choral societies, festivals, school opera-producing groups and workshops, and a number of dubious entries.

From the Directory we learn there are some 39 companies with operating budgets of over $100,000 a year which are affiliated with the American Guild of Musical Artists (AGMA), meaning, among other things, that performers are paid. There are, in addition, some 30 companies with annual budgets of under $100,000 but which are also affiliated with AGMA. The latter group includes nine symphony societies.

The opera-producing groups in this book are divided between those on campus and those that are independent of academic affiliation whether or not they are professional in any accepted sense. They are described in detail, for the first time in any publication, so that an assessment can be made of how they function or, at least, what the scope of their activities is.

Both lists are arranged alphabetically by states. For many entries, space limitations prevented the inclusion of more detail. Such expansion would have given color and depth to the nature of a given group's activities but would not have altered basic facts.

Almost three out of five opera groups are on campus. (For additional references to school opera groups, see list of schools in Part 9.) In some states, school productions form the only source of resident live opera. Over 80 symphony societies produce opera in concert form—an increasingly popular feature of the regular symphony season. About 200 organizations are formed as independent opera companies, that is, nonacademic and not part of a symphony orchestra's subscription series, and these include a few which offer drama and dance as well. Roughly a fourth of these—about 50—may be said to be of some national consequence. A majority of professional opera groups are, in effect, impresarios, operating with national talent resources and tailoring their productions in accordance with the availability of this talent. Few have their own theaters, stage equipment, or permanent musical staff, and fewer still develop a repertory.

The largest concentration of opera groups in America, and perhaps in the world, is in New York City (all five boroughs), where there are at least 73. These range from the diminutive but eminently successful After Dinner Opera Company with its traveling cast and portable sets to the world famous Metropolitan with its multimillion-dollar combined assets and budget and its own tradition-laden house.

The activities of the major opera groups are well-known and self-explanatory. They are anchored, for the most part, to the star system and to the standard repertory. Recently the opera majors have expressed a desire to maintain closer ties with one another so that mutual practical matters may be more easily dealt with.

The outstanding feature of opera in America—setting apart U.S. activities in this art form from those of any other country—is the emergence, within the past twenty years, of school opera groups. These schools (143 of which are listed below)—universities, conservatories, and colleges—present opera performances varying in quality, number, and kind. Some are no more than dress rehearsals reflecting a kind of opera pedagogy, designed essentially as a climax to the voice student's semester. Others are sumptuously adorned, skillfully organized, boldly produced, and well performed—sufficiently so to warrant the presence and merit the attention of music critics, most of whom turn out reviews containing no patronizing attitudes or lowered critical standards. On the contrary, some school productions receive as much hard-eyed scrutiny and cupped-ear attention as professional groups. Only the matter of vocal polish and prowess is compromised or excused somewhat by professional critics, and this only because youth and inexperience figure unavoidably in student casting.

No school opera group has taken its place in the public's mind alongside those operatic institutions which symbolize the finest in America—the Metropolitan, the New York City Opera, the Chicago and San Francisco companies—nor has the attainment of this goal been the motivation behind the school opera movement; nevertheless, there are areas in which the most important school groups excel. Histrionic awareness, physical attractiveness, and the performing vigor and enthusiasm of the young singers are among their strengths. Were these all, they would make notable changes in future professional opera productions in proportion to the rate by which these young singers would be absorbed by the major repertory companies. However, the most remarkable accomplishments of the school groups lie in the field of contemporary opera—accomplishments which may have a profound effect upon the future of American opera.

The reasons are not hard to come by: first, a tradition is being established; second, training in the unique musical problems of contemporary opera is provided and in the best way—through practical experience; third, an audience for these operas is being developed. These are responsibilities which have been ignored by the major American opera companies. Another factor is the close collaboration between schools and opera composers, particularly those in residence, which lends authority and legitimacy to the schools' production efforts as well as to their right to serve as standard bearers for contemporary opera. Because schools work with little competition from professional companies, they move within the sphere of contemporary opera with apparent ease and little inhibition.

Not all schools are equally concerned with staging new works. Schools with very strong vocal departments are quite apt to stress training in the standard repertory, hoping to serve as links to the professional world where knowledge of the standard works is taken for granted. Other institutions not engaged in presenting modern opera have taken to producing little known operas by classical composers. Whether committed deliberately or perfunctorily to producing modern operas, it is the schools' collective attitude that is of paramount importance: they have not shunned or feared the association with new music. Furthermore, staging a premiere performance of a new opera is a matter of considerable prestige with certain schools. Composers have come to rely on them for first hearings.

Although the entire school opera movement is strong, its degree of intensity varies from school to school, sometimes with the size of the institution as the critical factor. Small colleges or music schools may work all semester or through the entire year on one opera; this may be presented with piano accompaniment. Large universities or conservatories usually present full-scale productions or "opera festivals" for a period of time. The large productions usually result from the collaboration of a number of school departments, such as drama and fine arts. Often faculty members engaged in the supervisory or performance end of the production may be musicians of high standing in the operatic world. Some schools engage famous opera stars as guest performers to give an added measure of professionalism while inspiring student singers, and, of course, to attract greater audiences and publicity. Instituted as they are, universities, particularly state-supported universities, avoid many of the purely economic problems of professional opera companies. This, of course, explains the flexibility shown in the choice of projects undertaken by certain school opera workshops.

To the promising singer in need of operatic experience, the schools' workshops are indispensable—they have become the United States equivalent of the European local opera house with its government subsidy. Yet, a widely recognized problem has arisen inevitably from all this: there are insufficient professional outlets in the United States capable of providing a livelihood for the growing number of talented young singers. Some have found opportunity in Europe; others simply find disappointment. A few are "discovered." Most of them broaden their singing activities to include concerts and recitals.

ACADEMIC OPERA-PRODUCING GROUPS

Alabama

UNIVERSITY OF ALABAMA OPERA, P.O. Box 2886, University, Alabama 35486. Founded in 1950. Conductors: **Michael Gattozzi, Emil Raab.** Administrative Head: **Sylvia Debenport.** Stages two productions totaling four performances each year. Singers are students. Orchestra consists of both students and faculty; at times only piano accompaniment is used. Performances are held in Morgan Hall (750 seats) on campus.

Alaska

UNIVERSITY OF ALASKA OPERA WORKSHOP, Music Department, College, Alaska 99701. Founded in 1964. Conductors: **Charles W. Davis** and **Klaus Karli.** Stages one production per semester in three performances. Singers are all students. The orchestra is composed of amateurs and students; piano accompaniment is often used in performance. Complete productions; no concert versions. Place of performance: Schaible Auditorium (300 seats).

Arizona

NORTHERN ARIZONA UNIVERSITY OPERA THEATRE, Flagstaff, Arizona 86001. Founded 1961. Musical Director: **Tom Kirshbaum.** Administrative Head: **Dennis Wakeling.** Functions from September to May producing four chamber operas and one larger work each in one performance. Singers are faculty, students, and occasionally guest professionals. The Flagstaff Symphony is used for the larger opera production, piano accompaniment for chamber operas; concert versions are sometimes presented. Places of performance: chamber works in Ashurt Music Hall (130 seats); full operas in University Auditorium (930 seats). . . . UNIVERSITY OF ARIZONA OPERA THEATRE, Tucson, Arizona 85721. Founded 1952. Music Director: **Henry Johnson.** Administrative Head: **Eugene T. Conley.** Other staff members include **James Singelis,** Artistic Director; **Elizabeth Chadwick** and **Elsie Comer,** Coaches. Season: September through July, five productions with three performances each. Singers and orchestra players are students. Piano accompaniment is used in three out of five performances. All are full productions. Place of performance is Crowder Hall (500 seats). All operas are sung in English.

Arkansas

UNIVERSITY OF ARKANSAS OPERA THEATRE, Music Department, Fayetteville, Arkansas 72701. Founded 1953. Musical Director: **Kenneth L. Ballenger.** Conductor: **Marx Pales.** Other staff members: **Max Worthley,** Director, Opera Workshop; **Preston Magruder,** Technical Director; **Paula Osborne,** Costumer. Produces two operas in six performances. Singers are students and faculty. The orchestra consists of students, but a two-piano accompaniment is used for some performances. All productions are fully staged. Performances take place in University Theatre (350 seats).

California

OPERA THEATER OF THE UNIVERSITY OF THE PACIFIC, University of the Pacific, Stockton, California 95204. Founded

1946. Musical Director: **Lucas Underwood.** Administrative Head: **Preston Stedman,** Dean of the Conservatory of Music. Operates during the school year giving one production per semester. Productions are college-produced, with no concert versions and only rarely a visiting production. The orchestra is composed of students occasionally reinforced by professionals (piano accompaniment is rarely used for public performance). Singers are students primarily. Pacific Auditorium (1,200 seats) is the location of the performances on campus. . . . SACRAMENTO STATE COLLEGE OPERA WORKSHOP, Sacramento, California 95819. Date founded 1950. Musical Director: **John M. Lewis.** Stages two productions in a total of 14 performances. Singers are students and faculty; the orchestra is composed of students. Piano accompaniment is occasionally used for performances. Performances are held in Little Theatre (456 seats). Many contemporary one-act works are in the repertory of the workshop. . . . SAN DIEGO STATE COLLEGE OPERA WORKSHOP, San Diego, California 92115. Musical Director: **Cleve K. Genzlinger.** Stage Director and Administrative Head: **Lyman C. Hurd, III.** Performances are staged in January and May, offering two productions in a total of 10 performances. Singers are students, occasionally faculty. The orchestra is composed of students; piano accompaniment has not been used recently. Productions are entirely college-produced. Two, in ten years, have been performed in concert version. Place of performance: Dramatic Arts Main Stage (530 seats) or Music Recital Hall (264 seats). . . . SAN FERNANDO VALLEY STATE COLLEGE OPERA THEATRE, 18111 Nordhoff Street, Northridge, California 91324. Founded 1963. Musical Director and Administrative Head: **David W. Scott.** Other staff members: **Maro Donabedian,** Head Coach; **Owen Smith,** Designer and Technical Director. A ten-month season with four productions, twenty-four performances. Singers include faculty; the orchestra is composed of students. Productions are entirely college-produced with no concert versions. Place of performance: Campus Theatre (400 seats). . . . SAN FRANCISCO STATE COLLEGE OPERA THEATRE, San Francisco State College, 1600 Holloway, San Francisco, California 94132. Musical Director: **Dewey Camp.** Stage Director: **Geoffrey Lardner.** One production, entirely college-produced, is staged with four performances. Singers and members of the orchestra are all students. Place of performance: Main Auditorium on campus (700 seats). Additional productions with piano accompaniment are presented by the Opera Workshop of the school but are separate from the major productions with orchestra which are presented as part of the school drama subscription series. . . . SONOMA STATE COLLEGE OPERA WORKSHOP, Sonoma State College, Music Department, Rohnert Park, California 94928. Founded in 1963. Musical Director and Administrative Head: **Peggy Donovan.** During the school year it presents two or three productions totaling about 10 performances. Singers are students, occasionally faculty or professionals. Orchestra, when used, is composed of faculty, students, amateurs, and some professionals, but the operas are sung with piano accompaniment usually. Performances take place in Charles Ives Hall (225 seats). . . . UNIVERSITY OF CALIFORNIA, SANTA BARBARA OPERA THEATRE, University of California at Santa Barbara, Santa Barbara, California 93106. Founded: 1953. Musical Director: **Carl Zytowski.** Conductor: **Ronald Ondrejka.** Season of seven months with three productions and three performances. Primarily student singers but some roles are sung by faculty and professionals. Orchestra is made up of professionals, students, and faculty. Place of performance: Music Theatre (480 seats). Repertory emphasizes chamber operas sung in English translation. In 1967, the school produced the first American performance of Haydn's "Paladino." . . . UNIVERSITY OF SOUTHERN CALIFORNIA OPERA THEATRE, University of Southern California, Los Angeles, California 90007. Formed in 1948. Musical Director: **Walter Ducloux.** Conductor is **Hans L. Beer.** Two productions are staged during the school year in three performances each. Singers include students, faculty, and some professionals. The orchestra consists of students. No concert versions of operas are produced by the group. Performances are held in Bovard Auditorium (1,600 seats). All performances are sung in English. The Opera Theatre has given some notable premieres. Among them: the first complete performance anywhere of Hindemith's "Mathis der Maler" (in 1966), the American premieres of Strauss's "Die Liebe der Danae" (1964) and "Friedenstag" (1967), and the West Coast premiere of Gluck's "Alcestis." Other important works in the repertory have been "Das Rheingold" (1964), "Wozzeck," "The Rake's Progress," etc. Beginning in 1958, the Theatre presented a five-year cycle of late Verdi operas. In recognition of this effort, the Theatre and its director were awarded the Bronze Medal of the Republic of Italy. In 1967 the Theatre was awarded the Order of Merit of the Federal Republic of Germany. . . . U.S. INTERNATIONAL UNIVERSITY OPERA WORKSHOP, (formerly California Western University) 3902 Lomaland Drive, San Diego, California 92106. Founded in 1955. Musical Director and Administrative Head: **Walter Teutsch.** Annual productions are three operas in 10 to 12 performances. Singers are students, as are members of the orchestra. Piano accompaniment is sometimes used for performance. All productions are fully staged. Performances take place in Salomon Little Theatre (200 seats).

Colorado

COLORADO UNIVERSITY OPERA WORKSHOP, Colorado University, Boulder, Colorado 80302. Founded 1957. Director: **Kuniaki Hata.** Two productions annually, one in spring, one in summer, totaling eight performances. Singers are students and faculty. The orchestra is composed of students. Piano accompaniment is sometimes used. Productions are primarily those of visiting companies. Performances are in Macky Auditorium (2,500 seats) or University Theatre (500 seats). . . . ROCKY RIDGE MUSIC CENTER VOICE AND OPERA WORKSHOP. Actual location is Estes Park, Colorado 80517. Admissions address is 123 South 13th Street, Lincoln, Nebraska 68508. Founded in 1967. Musical Director: **Joan Wall** (Texas Women's University). The season lasts for two and a half weeks in August. One opera is given one performance. Students of the Center sing all roles; however, Center students include some who may already be professional. Piano accompanies all performances. The productions are fully staged. Performances take place in Rocky Ridge Performance Hall (100 seats). . . . UNIVERSITY OF DENVER LAMONT SCHOOL OF MUSIC AND THE UNIVERSITY OF DENVER THEATRE, College of Arts and Sciences, University of Denver Opera Department, University Park, Denver 80210. Musical Director, Conductor and Stage Director: **Genevieve McGiffert.** One major opera production during the school year with six performances. Singers are students; faculty and star professionals are sometimes used. Orchestra is composed of professionals and students. No opera concert versions. Productions are entirely college-produced. Performances are staged in University of Denver Theatre (275 seats). . . . UNIVERSITY OF NORTHERN COLORADO OPERA GUILD, Greeley, Colorado 80631. Founded: 1954. Musical Director: **Howard Skinner.** Administrative Head: **Claude Schmitz.** Other staff heads: **John Willcoxon,** Stage Director; **Welby Wolfe,** Technical Director. Productions in March and August and Workshop in December. Two complete productions, four performances each. Opera excerpts are sung in Workshop. Singers are students, rarely faculty or professionals. The orchestra is composed of both students and faculty. Piano accompaniment is used in Workshop. Productions entirely college-produced; no concert versions are performed. Performances are held in Frasier Theatre (628 seats). The Guild made a telecast of complete Bizet's "Carmen" for educational TV.

Connecticut

HARTT OPERA–THEATRE, Hartt College of Music, University of Hartford, 200 Bloomfield Avenue, West Hartford, Connecticut

06117. Founded 1942. Musical Director: **Moshe Paranov.** Other staff heads: **Irene Kahn,** Coach and Accompanist; **Grayce Long,** consultant, opera representative. Season is from October to June with two major productions, three children's operas, altogether 39 performances. Singers and orchestra are college personnel. There are a few concert versions of operas. Performances are in Millard Auditorium (500 seats). The Company has given world premieres of William Schuman's "The Mighty Casey," Elie Siegmeister's "Miranda and the Dark Young Man," and others. American premieres include Rossini's "The Touchstone," Handel's "Deidamia," Egk's "Peer Gynt."

Florida

FLORIDA STATE UNIVERSITY SCHOOL OF MUSIC OPERA GUILD, School of Music, Florida State University, Tallahassee, Florida 32306. Founded 1950. Musical Director: **Harry Dunscombe.** Administrative Head: **Richard Collins. Karl Mohr** is Business Manager. During school year, the Guild produces three operas, with ten performances. Singers are students, occasionally faculty or professionals. The orchestra is a combination of students and professionals. Operas are entirely college-produced, no concert versions. Place of performance: Westcott Auditorium (1,600 seats). . . . STETSON UNIVERSITY OPERA WORKSHOP, Stetson University, Deland, Florida 32720. Founded 1937. Musical Director and Administrative Head: **L. Frederick Maraffie.** Two productions totaling eight performances are presented during the school year. Singers are students and some professional singers. Orchestra is composed of students and amateurs. Entirely school-produced; no concert versions. Performances are held in Elizabeth Hall and Stover Theatre (800 and 600 seats, respectively). Movies and slides are used in productions. . . . UNIVERSITY OF FLORIDA OPERA WORKSHOP, Music Department, Gainesville, Florida 32601. Founded 1968. Director of Opera: **Evelyn Taylor.** Administrative Head: **Reid Poole.** Operates during the school year, giving one full production and one of opera scenes—two performances in all. Singers are students and faculty. Orchestra is composed of amateurs, students, and professionals. Piano accompaniment is used with scenes. All operas are college-produced; there are no concert versions. Place of performance is University Auditorium (1,200 seats). . . . UNIVERSITY OF MIAMI OPERA THEATER, University of Miami, Coral Gables, Florida 33134. Founded 1967. Musical Director and Administrative Head: **Dorothy Ziegler.** Operates during school year, with one production, three performances. Singers are students only, as are members of the orchestra. Production is entirely college-produced; no concert versions are sung. Place of performance is Beaumont Hall (400 seats). . . . UNIVERSITY OF SOUTH FLORIDA OPERA WORKSHOP, University of South Florida, Tampa, Florida 33620. Founded 1964. Musical Director and Conductor: **Everett S. Anderson.** Operates during school year; one production, two performances. Singers are students, sometimes faculty members. Orchestra composed of students, amateurs, and professionals. Productions entirely college-produced; piano accompaniment occasionally used; only rarely are concert versions of operas sung. Place of performance: University Theatre (550 seats).

Idaho

UNIVERSITY OF IDAHO OPERA WORKSHOP, Music Department, University of Idaho, Moscow, Idaho 83843. Musical Director: **Charles Walton.** During the school year there are productions of scenes and chamber operas with a varying number of performances. Singers are students. Orchestra is composed of students; piano accompaniment is often used, however. Performances are held in University Auditorium (1,100 seats) or Recital Hall (335 seats).

Illinois

DEPAUL UNIVERSITY OPERA WORKSHOP, School of Music, 25 East Jackson Boulevard, Chicago, Illinois 60604. Founded

1945. Musical Director: **Annemarie Gerts.** All students in two performances each of two operas a year sung in English. . . . ILLINOIS WESLEYAN UNIVERSITY OPERA THEATRE, Illinois Wesleyan University, 210 East University, Bloomington, Illinois 61701. Founded: 1948. Director: **James Ascareggi.** Conductor and Musical Director: **Robert P. Donalson.** Productions in December and April, three performances each. Singers are students, occasionally faculty. Orchestra is composed of students and amateurs. Piano accompaniment is rarely used in performances. Productions are entirely college-produced; no concert versions. Place of performance: Westbrook Auditorium of Presser Hall (600 seats). . . . MILLIKIN OPERA GROUP, Millikin University, Decatur, Illinois 62522. Founded 1951. Musical Director: **W. Scobie.** Administrative Head: **H. Norville.** One production a year, four performances. Singers are students and sometimes faculty. Orchestra is composed of students. Productions are entirely college-produced; no concert versions performed; no piano accompaniment for public performances. Place of performance is Albert Taylor Hall (750 seats). . . . NORTHERN ILLINOIS UNIVERSITY DEPARTMENT OF MUSIC AND UNIVERSITY THEATRE, Northern Illinois University, DeKalb, Illinois 60115. Musical Director: **Elwood Smith.** Administrative Heads: **J. S. Ballinger** (Music Department); **John Ulrich** (University Theatre). Offers one production each semester to total eight performances for the year. The fall production is a chamber opera with piano presented in Studio Theatre (150 seats); the spring production is an opera or a musical (in Fine Arts Auditorium—500 seats) directed by the University Theatre staff. Singers are students; the orchestra is made up of students, faculty, and townspeople. Sets, costumes, etc., for all productions are supervised by the University Theatre staff. . . . NORTHWESTERN UNIVERSITY OPERA WORKSHOP, Northwestern University School of Music, Evanston, Illinois 60201. Director: **Robert Gay.** Two or three productions a year, two performances each. All singers are students, as are members of the orchestra. Scenes and one-act operas use piano accompaniment in performance. Productions are entirely college-produced; no concert versions are sung. Performances take place in Cahn Auditorium (1,200 seats) or Lutkin Hall (400 seats). The Workshop has produced some operas for television including Bernstein's "Trouble in Tahiti," and a shortened version of Verdi's "Falstaff." . . . SOUTHERN ILLINOIS UNIVERSITY OPERA WORKSHOP, Southern Illinois University, Carbondale, Illinois 62903. Founded 1956. Musical Director: **Marjorie Lawrence.** Administrative Head: **Burnett H. Shryock, Sr.** Conductor: **Herbert Levinson.** During the school year it presents three productions in a total of five performances. Singers are students, sometimes faculty or professionals. Orchestra is a combination of professionals, amateurs, and students. Productions entirely school-produced; no concert versions of operas are performed. Performances take place in Shryock Auditorium (1,500 seats). The Workshop has produced "The Marriage of Figaro" for educational television; has premiered Bottje's "Altgeld;" its productions of "Aida" and "The Medium" both included Marjorie Lawrence in leading roles. . . . UNIVERSITY OF ILLINOIS OPERA GROUP, School of Music, Urbana, Illinois 61801. Founded in 1948. Chairman, Opera Department: **David Lloyd.** Music Director: **R. Aslanian.** Produces three operas a year with about two performances each. Some of these are programs of operatic excerpts. Singers are students. The orchestra is the University of Illinois Symphony Orchestra. Productions are fully-staged and are sung in English. Performances take place on campus in Smith Music Hall (800 seats), but the Group has played to schools and other communities in Illinois. The Group has given the world premiere of Krenek's "The Bell Tower," Meyerowitz's "Esther," and Gaburo's "The Widow." It has produced the American premiere of Rieti's "Don Perlimplin," Blacher's "Romeo und Julia," and Petrassi's "Morte dell'aria." These and other operas presented at the University reflect an adventurous sense of selection: Britten's "The Rape of Lucretia," Chabrier's "An Incomplete Education," Debussy's "L'Enfant

Prodigue," Foss's "Introductions and Goodbyes," Galuppi's "Il Filosofo di Campagna," Holst's "Savitri," Schuller's "The Visitation," plus works by Gottlieb, Ibert, Martinu, Milhaud (four operas), Strauss, Stravinsky, Toch, Vaughn-Williams, et al.

Indiana

BALL STATE OPERA WORKSHOP, Music Division, Ball State University, Muncie, Indiana 47306. Founded 1946. Conductor: **John Campbell.** Administrative Head: **Robert Hargreaves.** Other staff: **George Irving,** set design; **Annette Albright,** costumes; **George Leedham,** orchestra preparation. Operates throughout the year; six productions, two to four performances each. Singers are students, occasionally younger faculty. Orchestra is composed of students, sometimes with faculty. Productions are entirely college-produced; no concert versions are performed, nor is piano accompaniment used in performances. Place of performance is Ball State Theatre (418 seats). The Workshop's emphasis is on variety in selecting operas: from Mozart to Verdi, Hindemith, Rorem, and some musicals. . . . DE PAUW UNIVERSITY OPERA THEATRE, De Pauw University, Greencastle, Indiana 46135. Founded 1964. Musical Director and Administrative Head: **Thomas Fitzpatrick.** Operates during four months of the school year; one production, four performances. All singers are students, as are orchestra members. Operas are entirely college-produced; no concert versions sung and no piano accompaniment used with performances. Place of performance is Speech Hall (390 seats). . . . INDIANA UNIVERSITY SCHOOL OF MUSIC OPERA THEATER, Bloomington, Indiana 47401. Founded in 1948 by **Wilfred C. Bain,** Dean of the School of Music. The opera "workshop" is the largest and one of the oldest in America. It is the world's largest school opera-producing organization. Its full-size productions, often spectacular, are superior to those of many companies in America that operate on a professional basis, that is, with paid performers and staff. Its season is composed of about eight productions given a total of 32 performances over a 10-month period. Opera is performed every Saturday night during the academic year. Bloomington, as a consequence, shares with New York City the longest season of continuous opera performances in America. Singers are primarily students, but some roles are sung by members of the faculty. All operas are completely staged; the orchestra is a full-size symphonic ensemble. Performances are held in the new (opened in 1971) Musical Arts Center (1,500 seats) and all are sung in English either in published translations or in translations made specifically for the Opera Theater. The productions are entirely under the supervision of a resident faculty, most of whom are from the professional world. These include voice teachers (some are former singers with the Metropolitan Opera), coaches, stage directors, designers, and costumers. The Opera Theater's staff consists of **Dean Wilfred C. Bain,** General Manager, and **Richard Snyder,** Assistant to the Manager; two scenic designers including head designer **C. Mario Cristini;** several coaches under principal coach, **Carl Fuerstner;** two conductors including **Wolfgang Vacano;** two stage directors, a chorus master, a choreographer and a technical director. The school produced the first collegiate production in the world of an opera by Wagner—"Parsifal." This work has been an annual tradition at the school for over twenty-two years (a tradition interrupted for the first time in 1970). Subsequent school first performances of Wagner operas have been "The Flying Dutchman" and "The Mastersingers of Nuremberg," and those of the "Ring" cycle. Since 1948, the University has produced over 110 different works for the musical theater in over 700 full-scale performances. These include operas from the Italian, German, French, and Russian repertories; contemporary works, some given their world premieres in Indiana; light opera; and American musical theater. . . . VALPARAISO UNIVERSITY OPERA COMPANY, Valparaiso University, Valparaiso, Indiana 46383. Founded 1960. Musical Director and Administrative Head: **Joseph F. McCall. Yoshihiro Obata** is Conductor; **Fred Sitton** is Stage Director. During one month of the school year, one production is prepared and given four performances. Singers are students, faculty, and occasionally professionals, as are members of the orchestra. Operas are entirely college-produced with no concert versions used and no piano accompaniment in public performances. Performances take place in Valparaiso Memorial Opera House (450 seats). Among the operas performed have been Mozart's "Idomeneo" and Britten's "Albert Herring."

Iowa

COE COLLEGE OPERA WORKSHOP, Coe College, Cedar Rapids, Iowa 52402. Founded 1966. Musical Director and Administrative Head: **Allan D. Kellar. Robert Harper** is Stage Director. Season, during three months of the school year, involves two productions with eight performances in all. Singers are students and sometimes faculty. The orchestra is composed of students, amateurs, and professionals. Piano accompaniment is sometimes used for performances. Daehler-Kitchin Auditorium (200 seats) or Coe Auditorium (1,000 seats) serve as the theaters. . . . DRAKE UNIVERSITY OPERA THEATRE, Drake University, Des Moines, Iowa 50311. Administrative Head: **Marion A. Hall.** Three productions during fall, spring, and summer are staged for a total of approximately eight performances. Singers are usually students, but occasionally faculty or professional singers. The orchestra's members are students and professionals. Operas are fully-staged, but piano accompaniment is sometimes used for performances, which take place in Drake University Auditorium (1,000 seats). . . . THE OPERA WORKSHOP, The School of Music, University of Iowa, Iowa City, Iowa 52240. Founded 1960. Musical Director and Administrative Head: **Herald Stark. Robert Eckert** is Associate Director. Yearly season is from September to June, and from June to August with three productions a year, two to four performances each. Singers are students, rarely faculty. Orchestra is composed of students. Piano accompaniment is used for opera scene productions. Entirely college-produced; no operas in concert versions. Theater is Macbride Auditorium (700 seats). First American performances by the Workshop include Haydn's "L'infedeltà delusa" and Henze's "The Miracle Theatre" (in the shortened version). The first performance outside New York of Ward's "Crucible" took place at the University. Much of the repertory has been of contemporary chamber operas. . . . SIMPSON COLLEGE OPERA WORKSHOP, Simpson College, Indianola, Iowa 50125. Founded in 1957. Musical Director and Administrative Head: **Robert L. Larsen. Janice Roche Hanson** is assistant and resident artist. During the school year, one full production, as well as two one-act operas and two scene recitals, each with two or three performances, are prepared. There are two resident singers and often faculty and professionals sing some roles. The orchestra is a combination of professionals, amateurs, and students. No concert versions are presented; occasionally piano accompaniment is used in performance. Operas are performed in Simpson College Little Theatre (250 seats). Operas are sung in English or in the original language and are from the traditional and contemporary repertory. . . . UNIVERSITY OF NORTHERN IOWA, MUSIC THEATRE, Department of Music, University of Northern Iowa, Cedar Falls, Iowa 50613. Founded in 1935. Musical Director: **Jane Birkhead.** Administrative Head: **Myron E. Russell.** Functions during academic year with two productions and six to eight performances. Singers are always students and the orchestra is composed entirely of students. Piano accompaniment is sometimes used for performances. Performances are held in Music Hall (606 seats).

Kansas

BETHANY COLLEGE OPERA WORKSHOP, Bethany College, Lindsborg, Kansas 67456. Founded in 1952. Director: **Elizabeth Patches.** During the school year one major work is produced with two or three performances. Student singers only. The orchestra is composed of students and faculty. Productions are fully-staged and performed in Presser Hall (1,700 seats). . . . FORT HAYS

KANSAS STATE COLLEGE, Division of Music, Fort Hays Kansas State College, Hays, Kansas 67601. Conductors: **Patrick Goeser, Lyle Dilley. Perry Schwartz** is Stage Director. **Robert Reinecke** is Technical Director and set designer. From October to January one opera is produced with three performances. Students fill all roles and the orchestra is composed of students and local musicians. The productions are fully staged and are performed in Felten-Start Theater (340 seats). . . . KANSAS STATE COLLEGE OPERA THEATRE, Kansas State College, Pittsburg, Kansas 66762. Conductor: **Walter Osadchuk.** Director of the Opera Theatre: **Laurence W. Siegle.** During the school year one or two operas are produced, with two performances each. In addition, there are productions of two musicals with about six performances. Students fill all roles. The orchestra is composed of faculty and students. The fully-staged productions are performed in Carney Hall Auditorium (2,000 seats). The Theatre provides special performances for schools and civic organizations. . . . KANSAS STATE UNIVERSITY OPERA THEATRE, Kansas State University, Manhattan, Kansas 66502. Director and Conductor: **Tommy Goleeke.** Administrative Head: **Luther Leavengood.** Technical Director is **Carl Hinrichs.** During the school year one or two operas are produced to total two performances. Roles are generally sung by students. The orchestra is made up of students and faculty. Productions are usually fully-staged, but occasionally a concert version is performed. Performances take place in Williams Auditorium (500 seats). . . . ST. MARY OF THE PLAINS OPERA THEATRE, St. Mary of the Plains College, Dodge City, Kansas 67801. Founded in 1960. Musical Director: **Mark Gruett.** Administrative Head: **Sister M. Christian Rosner. Lawrence Basile** is Technical Director. During the nine-month school term, two operas are produced, with five performances each. Students sing all roles. Piano accompaniment is used for the public performances, which take place in Plains Playhouse (100 seats). . . . WICHITA STATE UNIVERSITY OPERA THEATRE, School of Music, Wichita State University, P.O. Box 53, Wichita, Kansas 67208. Conductor: **James Robertson.** Director: **George Gibson.** During the school year two operas are produced with nine performances in all. Students sing all roles and make up the orchestra. In the spring production, piano accompaniment is used for performances. Performances, which are all staged, are held in the Duerksen Fine Arts Center (600 seats.)

Kentucky

UNIVERSITY OF KENTUCKY OPERA THEATRE, Department of Music, University of Kentucky, Lexington, Kentucky 40506. Director: **Sheila House.** Administrative Head: **Aimo Kiviniemi.** During the year, from September to July, three or four operas are produced, with, apparently, one performance each. The singers are both students and faculty. The orchestra, when used, is composed of students and faculty, but usually a piano accompanies performances. Some concert versions are performed. Performances are held either in Laboratory Theatre (150 seats) or the Guignol Theatre (455 seats). Works of resident or faculty composers are frequently produced. The Theatre provides performances for Community Colleges throughout the state.

Louisiana

LOUISIANA STATE UNIVERSITY OPERA THEATRE, Louisiana State University School of Music, Baton Rouge, Louisiana 70803. Founded circa 1935. Musical Director: **Peter Paul Fuchs.** Administrative Head: **Everett Timm.** Three operas are produced during the year for six to eight performances. Singers are usually students, rarely faculty. The orchestra is made up of students and faculty. All productions are fully-staged and are performed in the Louisiana State University Union Theatre (1,300 seats). Many American and world premieres of contemporary operas have been performed by the opera group, including Zador's "The Magic Chair," and Hermann Reutter's "The Widow of Ephesus." . . . LOUISIANA TECH OPERA WORKSHOP, Music Department,

Louisiana Polytechnic Institute, Ruston, Louisiana 71270. Founded in 1955. Director: **Daniel Pratt.** Administrative Head: **Jimmie Howard Reynolds. James Goodman** is Technical Director and Conductor. The season, of three productions and six performances, consists partially of visiting productions. Roles are occasionally sung by faculty or professional singers. The orchestra is a combination of professionals, amateurs, students. Performances take place in Howard Auditorium (2,000 seats). . . . LOYOLA COLLEGE OF MUSIC OPERA WORKSHOP, Loyola University, 6363 St. Charles Avenue, New Orleans, Louisiana 70118. Founded in 1957. Director: **Arthur Cosenza;** Administrative Head: **Michael Carubba.** Three productions a year, three performances. Piano accompaniment is used for public performances. Students fill all roles. Most performances are in concert version. Performances take place in Marquette Auditorium (200 seats). . . . SOUTHEASTERN LOUISIANA COLLEGE OPERA THEATER, Southeastern Louisiana College, Hammond, Louisiana 70401. Founded in 1962. Musical Director and Conductor: **Robert Weatherly.** Administrative Head: **James H. Wilcox.** During the school year two operas are produced with three performances each. Students fill all roles. The orchestra is made up of students, amateurs, and professionals. Productions are fully staged; piano accompaniment is never used for public performance. Performances take place in College Music Auditorium (700 seats). . . . TULANE–NEWCOMB OPERA WORKSHOP–TULANE SUMMER LYRIC THEATRE, Tulane University–Newcomb College, 1331 Louisiana Avenue, New Orleans, Louisiana 70115. Founded: 1968. Administrative Head: **Francis L. Monachino. George Hendrickson** is Chairman of the Department of Speech and Theatre. Season lasts all year with five operas produced in about twenty performances. Singers include faculty members. The orchestra is a combination of professional players, amateurs, and students. Piano accompaniment is sometimes used in productions and concert versions are sometimes performed. Performances take place in Dixon Hall (900 seats). . . . UNIVERSITY OF SOUTHWESTERN LOUISIANA OPERA GUILD, P.O. Box 1534, University of Southwestern Louisiana, Lafayette, Louisiana 70506. Founded in 1961. Producer-Director: **G. S. Beaman Griffin.** Conductors: **James Burke, John Turner. Mrs. Anne Simpson:** rehearsal accompanist. Administrative Head: **Willis Ducrest.** Singers are talented amateurs, faculty, and some professionals, as are members of the orchestra (in addition to student instrumentalists). Piano accompaniment is used for some workshop productions. Three or four major productions are given with from three to six performances in all. . . . XAVIER UNIVERSITY GRAND OPERA, Xavier University, Palmetto and Pine Streets, New Orleans, Louisiana 70125. Founded in 1934. Musical Director: **Gordon O. Brown.** Administrative Head: **Sister M. Elise. Don Dorr** is in charge of staging. In the spring, usually in March, one grand opera is produced with one performance. Roles are sung by students, occasionally by professional alumni. The orchestra is composed of students and professionals. All operas are fully staged and performed in Municipal Auditorium (2,500 seats). The school claims to have been the first small college in the South to undertake the production of grand opera with roles sung by students. It has trained many black singers in opera, some of whom are now in professional companies in America and Europe. The repertory covers the full range of standard works as well as contemporary operas.

Maryland

PEABODY OPERA COMPANY, Peabody Conservatory of Music, 1 East Mount Vernon Place, Baltimore, Maryland 21202. Musical Director: **Norman Johnson.** During the school year two operas are produced, three performances. All roles are filled by students; the orchestra is also a student ensemble. All productions are fully staged. Performances take place in Peabody Concert Hall (1,000 seats). . . . UNIVERSITY OF MARYLAND OPERA WORKSHOP, University of Maryland, College Park, Maryland 20742. Founded in 1966. Musical Director: **William**

Winden. Martin Katz is musical assistant and pianist. Two productions of opera scenes, in January and May. Students fill all singing roles. Piano is used for the performances, which take place in Recital Hall (Tawes Fine Arts Building) (500 seats).

Massachusetts

BOSTON CONSERVATORY OF MUSIC, OPERA DEPARTMENT, Boston Conservatory of Music, 8 The Fenway, Boston, Massachusetts 02215. Founded in 1867. Musical Director: **James Stewart.** During the academic year, one major production is given four performances, and three minor productions are given two performances. Students fill all roles, and compose the orchestra. Some concert versions of operas are performed, but most operas are fully staged. Performances take place in Conservatory Auditorium (500 seats). . . . BOSTON UNIVERSITY OPERA THEATRE, Boston University, School of Fine and Applied Arts, 855 Commonwealth Avenue, Boston, Massachusetts 02215. Founded in 1952. Conductor: **Ludwig Bergmann.** Administrative Head: **Wilbur D. Fullbright.** Stage Director: **Guus Hoekman.** During the school year, two operas are produced, fully staged, with three performances. Singers are usually students, occasionally faculty. The orchestra is composed of students, but piano accompaniment is sometimes used in public performances. The performances take place in Boston University Theatre (900 seats). . . . NEW ENGLAND CONSERVATORY OPERA THEATRE, New England Conservatory of Music, 290 Huntington Avenue, Boston, Massachusetts 02115. Musical Director: **Thomas Philips.** During the eight-month school year, three to four operas are produced and each is given two performances. Students fill all roles. The orchestra is composed entirely of students. All productions are fully staged, although piano accompaniment is occasionally used for performances. Performances take place in Jordan Hall (1,000 seats).

Michigan

EASTERN MICHIGAN UNIVERSITY OPERA WORKSHOP, Department of Music, Eastern Michigan University, Ypsilanti, Michigan 48197. Founded in 1967. Musical Director: **Charles Roe.** Administrative Head: **Howard Rarig.** During the school year one opera is produced with two performances. The students fill all roles and make up the orchestra. Piano accompaniment is used in opera scene programs. Otherwise, the productions are fully staged. Performances take place in Pease Auditorium Concert Hall (1,000). . . . MICHIGAN STATE UNIVERSITY OPERA WORKSHOP, Michigan State University, East Lansing, Michigan 48823. Founded in 1959. Musical Director and Administrative Head: **Dennis Burk.** Two operas are produced during the season (school year) for a total of six performances. Students (sometimes faculty or professional singers) fill the roles. The orchestra is composed of students. All operas are fully staged. All performances take place in the Music Auditorium, or University Auditorium (400 and 4,000 seats respectively). . . . UNIVERSITY OF MICHIGAN SCHOOL OF MUSIC OPERA CLASSES, University of Michigan, School of Music, Ann Arbor, Michigan 48105. Founded in 1952. Musical Director: **Josef Blatt.** Administrative Head: **James B. Wallace. Ralph Herbert** is Stage Director. From June to May three operas are produced; ten to twelve performances in all. Students fill the roles as well as the positions in the orchestra. All productions are fully staged and are performed in Lydia Mendelssohn Theatre (700 seats). Operas of ambitious dimensions performed include "Wozzeck" (1965), "Lohengrin" (1966), "Pelléas et Mélisande" (1961), "Das Rheingold" (1960). . . . WAYNE STATE UNIVERSITY THEATRE, Wayne State University, Detroit, Michigan 48202. Founded in 1929. Administrative Head: **Leonard Leone.** The theatre occasionally produces an opera, giving it about six performances. Singers are mainly undergraduate students, sometimes graduate students or local singers. The orchestra is a combination of students, amateurs, and professionals. Sometimes piano accompaniment is used for performances. The productions are fully staged and performed in the Bonstelle Theatre. (1,200 seats). . . . WESTERN MICHIGAN UNIVERSITY MUSIC DEPARTMENT, Western Michigan University, Kalamazoo, Michigan 49001. Full opera productions were first founded in 1967. Musical Director: **William C. Appel.** Administrative Head: **Robert Holmes.** During the school year one or two operas are produced, with three performances. Students fill all roles, as well as positions in orchestra (faculty added if needed). The productions are fully staged. Some visiting productions, such as Goldovsky Grand Opera Theater and the American Opera Company, are invited. Performances in Shaw Theatre (550 seats).

Minnesota

MANKATO STATE COLLEGE OPERA WORKSHOP, Mankato State College, Mankato, Minnesota 56001. Musical Director: **Daniel C. Nelson.** One production annually; six performances. Singers are mostly students, sometimes faculty members. The orchestra is composed of amateurs and students. All productions are fully staged. Visiting productions are sometimes presented. The performances take place in the Theatre of the Performing Arts Center (530 seats). . . . MOORHEAD STATE COLLEGE OPERA PRODUCTION, Moorhead State College, Moorhead, Minnesota 56560. Founded in 1965. Director and Administrative Head: **Loris Z. Tjeknavorian.** Two or three operas are produced and performed three or four times altogether. Singers are usually students, sometimes faculty members. The orchestra consists mainly of students and faculty. Sometimes opera stars are engaged. All productions are fully-staged. They are performed in the Moorhead State College Fine Arts Auditorium (900 seats). . . . UNIVERSITY OF MINNESOTA AT DULUTH OPERA WORKSHOP, University of Minnesota, Duluth, Minnesota 55812. Musical Director: **Loris Langdon.** Conductor: **Willard Oplinger.** Administrative Head: **James Murphy.** There is one production annually with three performances. Students fill all roles and make up the entire orchestra. All productions are fully staged and performed in Old Main Theatre (350 seats). Occasionally a musical or a chamber opera will be substituted for the regular opera production. . . . UNIVERSITY OF MINNESOTA OPERA WORKSHOP, University of Minnesota, 5 Wulling Hall, Minneapolis, Minnesota 55455. Founded in 1959. Director: **Paul Knowles.** Administrative Head: **Roy Schuessler.** Assistant Director: **Nancy Martin.** The season, from October to May, offers two productions for 8 to 10 performances. Students fill all roles and make up the orchestra; however, piano accompaniment is sometimes used for public performances. The productions are fully staged and are performed in Baroque Theatre (100 seats).

Mississippi

THE UNIVERSITY OF MISSISSIPPI OPERA THEATRE, University of Mississippi, University, Mississippi 38677. Musical Director and Conductor: **Leland S. Fox. Arthur Kreutz** and **James Ferguson,** conductors; **Miklos Bencze,** coach; **Wanda Nelson,** costumer. During the school year four or five operas are produced with three to four performances each. The singers are students (occasionally faculty) and the orchestra is composed of students. All productions are fully staged; piano accompaniment is rarely used. Visiting productions are sometimes engaged. Performances take place in Meek Hall (250 seats). . . . UNIVERSITY OF SOUTHERN MISSISSIPPI OPERA THEATRE, University of Southern Mississippi, Hattiesburg, Mississippi 39401. Founded in 1948. Musical Director: **William T. Gower.** General Director of Opera Theatre: **Clifton Ware. Marian Nowakowski** is Consultant. The season lasts eleven months; five full operas are produced and also one or two opera scenes. Performances number from 19 to 22. Singers are students and faculty. The orchestra is composed primarily of students with some faculty. Piano accompaniment is used with the productions of opera scenes. Productions are fully staged. There are some visiting productions.

Performances are in USM Main Auditorium during the regular school year (1,400 seats) and in Marsh Hall during the summer (350 seats).

Missouri

SOUTHWEST MISSOURI STATE COLLEGE OPERA WORKSHOP, Southwest Missouri State College, Springfield, Missouri 65802. Founded in 1962. Administrative Head: **Dawin Emanuel.** Two productions (one in the fall, one in the spring), five performances. Students sing all roles but the orchestra is composed of both students and faculty. All productions are fully staged and are performed in the School Theater (600 seats). Repertory includes, besides standard operas such as those by Verdi and Puccini, "Marriage of Figaro," "Tales of Hoffman," and Lee Hoiby's "The Scarf." . . . STEPHENS COLLEGE OPERA WORKSHOP, Opera Department, Stephens College, Columbia, Missouri 65201. Founded in 1951. Musical Director: **Val Patacchi.** Conductor **Martin–Beatus Meyer. Gertrude Ribla** is Instructor of Opera Workshop Class. **Edward Gallagher** is scenic designer. Three or four productions a year, some performed in concert version, with six to eight performances, either in Assembly Hall (3,000 seats) or Auditorium (600 seats). Male roles are sung by faculty, students from the University of Missouri, or by professional singers. (Stephens College is a college for women.) Some visiting productions are presented. Works performed are from the standard repertory and contemporary chamber operas. . . . UNIVERSITY OF MISSOURI OPERA WORKSHOP, Music Department, Missouri University, Columbia, Missouri 65201. Founded in 1960. Musical Director: **Harry S. Morrison, Jr.** During the school year two operas are produced with eight performances given. The students fill all roles, as well as all positions in the orchestra. The fall production uses piano accompaniment for performances. The spring production uses the orchestra. Both are fully staged and performed in the University Theatre (300 seats). . . . WASHINGTON UNIVERSITY OPERA STUDIO, Washington University, St. Louis, Missouri 63130. Founded in 1951. Musical Director and Administrative Head: **Harold Blumenfeld. Evelyn Mitchell** is Associate Music Director, **C. J. Zander,** Associate Stage Director, and **James Brooks** is Manager. Each school year three operas are produced, fully staged, and performed two to five times each. Singers are drawn from the entire three-state area (communities and universities). Stars are occasionally invited. The orchestra is composed of professionals (members of the St. Louis Symphony). Productions are performed on tour and in various halls on campus: Brown Hall Auditorium (300 seats); Steinberg Hall (500 seats). The Studio can be credited with many premiere performances and for its unhackneyed repertory. It performed the world premiere of Mark Bucci's "The Hero" (1968), and the U.S. premiere of Rimsky-Korsakov's "Kaschei" (1964). Premiere productions for St. Louis include Stravinsky's "Rossignol" (1968), Donizetti's "Rita" (1967), Monteverdi's "Coronation of Poppea" (1966), Pergolesi's "Livietta and Tracollo" (1963), etc. Former Studio singers are among the professional ranks of opera singers in the U.S. and abroad. All full opera productions are sung in English, often in the Studio's own translations.

Nebraska

UNIVERSITY OF NEBRASKA OPERA, University of Nebraska, Department of Music, Lincoln, Nebraska 68508. Founded: 1964. Musical Director: **Richard Grace.** Director of Opera: **John J. Zei.** Three productions during the year (January, February, May, and August), 13 performances. Singers are usually students, occasionally faculty. The orchestra is composed of a combination of amateurs, students, and professionals. All productions are fully staged and performed in Howell Theatre (800 seats). . . . UNIVERSITY OF NEBRASKA–OMAHA OPERA THEATRE, University of Nebraska, 60th and Dodge Streets, Omaha, Nebraska 68101. Founded in 1965. Musical Director: **Robert G. Ruetz;** Technical Director: **Donald Ferguson.** During the school year, two opera productions are prepared, one full-length production with orchestra, sets, costumes, etc., sung in English and one program of operatic scenes sung in the original language, staged (without sets), and accompanied by piano. Singers are students or members of the community, and the orchestra consists of students and members of the Omaha Symphony. Performances are held in University Auditorium (600 seats); however, the Opera Theatre often plays to audiences on tour in other locations in Omaha, in other communities in Nebraska, and occasionally out of state.

New Jersey

GLASSBORO STATE COLLEGE OPERA WORKSHOP, Glassboro State College, Glassboro, N.J. 08028. Musical Director: **James R. Shaw.** The season lasts during the school year. Seven operas are produced with 11 performances. Students fill all roles; the orchestra is composed of a combination of professionals, amateurs, and students. All productions are fully staged and take place in Tohill Auditorium (500 seats). . . . MONTCLAIR STATE COLLEGE OPERA WORKSHOP, Montclair State College, Upper Montclair, N.J. 07043. Musical Director and Administrative Head: **Jack Sacher.** Opera scenes rather than total productions are prepared. Students fill all singing roles. Piano accompaniment is used. Performances are for other students rather than for the paying public. The stress is on modification of acting to suit various operatic styles. . . . TRENTON STATE COLLEGE OPERA WORKSHOP, Trenton State College, Trenton, N.J. 08625. Founded in 1963. Musical Director: **Byron Steele.** During March, one opera is produced and given three performances. All roles are filled by students and the orchestra is composed of students and faculty. All productions are fully staged and performed in Kendall Auditorium (1,100 seats).

New Mexico

Eastern NEW MEXICO UNIVERSITY OPERA WORKSHOP, Eastern New Mexico University, Portales, New Mexico 88130. Director: **Don W. Moore.** Administrative Head (Dean): **Paul Strub.** During the academic year, three productions are given in nine performances. Singers are all students. The orchestra is composed of students, although the fall production uses only piano accompaniment. All productions are fully staged and performed in the University Theatre (460 seats). The usual agenda is opera excerpts in the fall; grand opera in the spring; a Broadway musical in the summer (with piano). . . . UNIVERSITY OF NEW MEXICO OPERA WORKSHOP, University of New Mexico, Albuquerque, New Mexico 87106. Founded in 1951. Director: **Jane Snow.** Conductor: **Kurt Frederick.** During three months of the school year, one opera is produced and performed four times. Students fill all roles as well as all positions in the orchestra. All productions are fully staged and performed in Recital Hall of the Fine Arts Center (325 seats). In 1968, the Workshop gave the first staged production of Menotti's "Bishop of Brindisi."

New York

ADELPHI UNIVERSITY OPERA WORKSHOP, Adelphi University, Garden City, N.Y. 11530. Founded in 1950. Musical Director and Conductor: **Lawrence Rasmussen.** Stage Director: **Dorothy Raedler.** During eight months of the school year, two operas are produced, with four performances of each. Singers are usually students, occasionally faculty or professionals. The orchestra is composed of students and amateurs, and a few professionals. All productions are fully staged and performed on campus in Little Theatre (300 seats). . . . BARNARD COLLEGE THEATRE COMPANY, Minor Latham Playhouse, 119th Street and Broadway, New York, N.Y. 10027. Founded in 1959. Administrative Head: **Kenneth Janes.** Assistants to the Director: **Ellen Terry, Donald Pace, Janet Soares.** Two operas and two Gilbert and Sullivan operettas are produced each year with 20 performances in all. Singers include students, faculty, and professionals. The orchestra is composed of professionals and students. Sometimes piano accompaniment is used. Productions are fully staged and performed at the Minor Latham Playhouse of Barnard College (197 seats). Opera repertory consists of new works whenever possible and rarely performed classics. . . . BROOKLYN COLLEGE OPERA THEATER, Brooklyn College, Brooklyn, N.Y. 11210. Founded in 1964. Conductor and Stage Director: **Károly Köpe. J. Challener** is Associate Director; **J. Cunningham** Resident Designer; **G. Rothman,** Technical Director; **M. Kroll** and **H. Kronroth,** musical assistants. During eight months of the school year, three operas are produced with nine performances. Singers include students, faculty, and professionals. The orchestra is composed of professionals. All productions are fully staged and performed in Whitman Auditorium (2,500 seats) or Gershwin Hall (500 seats). All performances are in English. The Theater attempts to perform one premiere each year. It staged the American premiere of Salieri's "Prima la Musica," among other works. . . . EASTMAN OPERA THEATRE, Eastman School of Music, Rochester University, 26 Gibbs Street, Rochester, N.Y. 14609. Founded in 1923. Conductors: **Edwin McArthur, Richard Pittman.** Artistic Director: **Leonard Treash.** Stage Directors: **Leonard Treash, Robert Murray.** During the academic year three operas are produced for a total of six performances. Students fill all roles. The Eastman School of Music Orchestra is used except for performances of operatic scenes. All productions are fully staged and performed either in the Eastman Theatre (3,300 seats) or the Cutter Union (300 seats). . . . HENRY STREET SETTLEMENT MUSIC SCHOOL OPERA THEATRE SCHOOL, Henry Street Settlement Music School, 504-D Grand Street, New York, N.Y. 10002. Founded in 1954. Musical Director: **Frank E. White.** Conductor: **Stelio Dubbiosi.** Administrative Head: **Robert F. Egan. Richard Jones** is Stage Director. The season lasts during the school year. Three operas are produced with a total of eight performances. The singers are ordinarily students; the orchestra is a combination of students, amateurs, and professionals. Piano accompaniment is used when separate opera scenes are performed. All complete productions are fully staged. Performances take place at the Henry Street Settlement Playhouse (350 seats). Although the Opera Theatre was established in 1954, opera has been presented at the school since its earliest days. In this regard, the school has had some notable achievements. A few ought to be cited here: Kurt Weill's "Der Jasager" received its American premiere at the school in 1933 with Lehman Engel conducting; Aaron Copland's "The Second Hurricane" was especially written for the School. In 1937 it was performed under Engel with Orson Welles as director. Haydn's "The Songstress" received its first U.S. performance in 1949 at Henry Street. Some of the unusual works performed by the Theatre are: Wolf-Ferrari's "School for Fathers" and "The Inquisitive Women," Weber's "Abu Hassan," and Donizetti's "The Night Bell." . . . HUNTER COLLEGE OPERA ASSOCIATION, 695 Park Avenue, New York, N.Y. 10021. Musical Director: **William Tarrasch.** During the school year, from September to June, one complete performance of a full opera plus two scene recitals are given. The workshop students sing all roles. The orchestra, when used, is composed of professional players; piano accompaniment is used with the scene recitals. The productions are fully staged and are performed in the Hunter Playhouse (68th and Lexington). . . . MANHATTAN SCHOOL OF MUSIC JOHN BROWNLEE OPERA THEATRE, 120 Claremont Avenue, New York, N.Y. 10027. Established in 1956; named in honor of the late Manhattan School president. Musical Director: **George Schick.** Conductors: **George Schick, Anton Coppola.** Manager: **William Miles.** Stage Directors: **James Lucas, Basil Langton.** From December to May, three operas are produced with a total of nine performances. All singing roles are filled by Manhattan School students and others admitted by audition. The orchestra is an all-student ensemble. Operas are fully staged and are performed in Borden Auditorium (1,000 seats). The Opera Theatre has produced some infrequently heard operas. Among them: Smetana's "The Kiss" (1971), Granados's "Goyescas" (1969), Dallapiccola's "Volo di notte." In addition, works from the

French repertory have been revived. . . . NEW SCHOOL OPERA WORKSHOP, New School for Social Research, 66 West 12th Street, New York, N.Y. 10011. Music Director: **Emanuel Levenson;** Stage Director: **Richard Flusser.** The Workshop is open to singers preparing to perform opera. It presents generally short operas and opera scenes from either the standard opera repertory or contemporary operas and music theater works. Full opera productions have been "Tales of Hoffmann," "The Medium," and such short works as Blitzstein's "Triple Sec." Rorem's "Last Day," etc. . . . SARAH LAWRENCE COLLEGE OPERA WORKSHOP, Music Department, Bronxville, N.Y. 10708. Directors: **Bessie Schoenberg** and **Paul Ukena.** Presents operettas, musicals, and scenes from operas. . . . SEAGLE COLONY OPERA GUILD, Schroon Lake, N.Y. 12870. Founded in 1939. Musical Director: **Thomas Booth.** Administrative Head: **John Seagle. Gunda Mordan** is Stage Director. During two months of the summer two operas are produced, with a total of seven performances. Most roles are filled by students, some by faculty members. Piano is used for accompaniment for performances. All productions are fully staged. Performances are in Oscar Seagle Memorial Theater (194 seats). The Colony is accredited by and affiliated with Trinity University, San Antonio, Texas. . . . STATE UNIVERSITY OF NEW YORK AT BUFFALO OPERA DEPARTMENT, Baird Hall, Buffalo, N.Y. 14214. Administrative Head: **Muriel Hebert Wolf. Heinz Rehfuss** is Artistic Director. During the academic year three to four operas are produced, totaling from 8 to 12 performances. Singers are usually students, sometimes faculty or professional singers. The orchestra is composed of professional players (collaboration with the Buffalo Philharmonic Orchestra). Sometimes a concert version is performed. There are some visiting productions. Performances take place in either Baird Hall, Albright Knox Gallery or Kleinhans Music Hall (from 400 to 2,000 seats). Premiered Henri Pousseur's "Votre Faust" in 1968. . . . STATE UNIVERSITY COLLEGE AT FREDONIA OPERA THEATRE, Fredonia, N.Y. 14063. Musical Director: **Mary Elaine Wallace.** Administrative Head: **Robert Marvel.** During the school year, there are three productions with a total of eight performances. Singers are usually students, but faculty sometimes fill in. The orchestra is composed of students and faculty; piano accompaniment is sometimes used for performances. The productions are fully staged. Occasionally the college has a visiting opera company on the concert series. Performances take place in Old Main Auditorium (750 seats). The Opera Theatre tours to area schools with one–act operas or opera scenes. . . . STATE UNIVERSITY COLLEGE OPERA WORKSHOP, Crane Department of Music, State University College, Potsdam, N.Y. 13676. Founded in 1949. Musical Director and Conductor: **Harry I. Phillips.** During three months of the school year three operas are produced, with a total of six performances. Roles are usually sung by students, occasionally by faculty. The orchestra, composed of students, is usually employed, although piano accompaniment is sometimes used in performances. All productions are fully staged and are performed either in College Theatre (820 seats) or Crane Recital Hall (350). There has been one visiting production and a commissioned opera, "Domestic Relations," by Arthur Frackenpohl, performed in 1963. . . . SYRACUSE UNIVERSITY OPERA WORKSHOP, School of Music, Syracuse University, Syracuse, N.Y. 13210. **Donald Miller,** Director. The school usually presents opera scenes without scenery or costume, but there is sometimes one full-scale production planned during the year. . . . VASSAR COLLEGE DEPARTMENT OF DRAMA, DEPARTMENT OF MUSIC, Vassar College, Poughkeepsie, N.Y. 12601. Musical Director: **Albert van Ackere.** Stage Director: **William F. Rothwell, Jr.** During the year, one full-length opera is produced, or two short ones, in four performances. Since Vassar is a women's college, only the female roles are sung by students; the male singers are hired. Small or chamber operas, rather than grand operas are usually presented. A small (five-piece) professional instrumental ensemble is sometimes used; otherwise, only piano accompaniment.

All productions are fully staged and performed in Avery Hall (500 seats). Generally, comic operas, all performed in English, are presented. In 1968, "La Molinara" ("Maid of the Mill") by Paisiello was given its American premiere.

North Carolina

NORTH CAROLINA SCHOOL OF THE ARTS, SCHOOL OF MUSIC, Winston-Salem, North Carolina 27107. Founded in 1965. Opera Director: **Norman Johnson.** Conductor: **John Iuele.** Administrative Head: **Robert Ward.** During four months of the year, three operas are produced, with two performances of each. Students fill all roles as well as all positions in the orchestra. All productions are fully staged and take place in the Main Auditorium (900 seats). . . . UNIVERSITY OF NORTH CAROLINA OPERA THEATRE, University of North Carolina, Hill Music Hall, Chapel Hill, North Carolina 27514. Musical and Artistic Director: **Wilton Mason.** Founded in 1945. Two fully staged operas are presented each year. Casts are made up of students, members of the community, and faculty. There are occasional extra performances of scenes and TV presentations. (The Drama Department, "The Carolina Playmakers," produces musical comedies.) . . . UNIVERSITY OF NORTH CAROLINA AT GREENSBORO OPERA THEATRE, University of North Carolina, Greensboro, North Carolina 27412. Founded in 1963. Director of Opera: **Rolf Sander.** Conductor: **Jack Jarrett.** During the school year one and "one-half" operas are produced, with a total of five performances. Students fill all roles (faculty used only if necessary) and make up the orchestra. Piano accompaniment is used for the opera "half." All productions are fully staged and performed in Taylor Theatre (550 seats).

North Dakota

UNIVERSITY OF NORTH DAKOTA OPERA COMPANY, Music Department, University of North Dakota, Grand Forks, North Dakota 58201. Founded in 1957. Musical Director and Administrative Head: **Philip D. Hisey.** Other staff members: **Paul Lundquist,** Accompanist and Assistant Musical Director; **Roger Wilhelm,** Chorus Master. Each year one opera is produced with a total of three performances. Roles are limited to students whenever possible. All productions are fully staged, but piano accompaniment is used in performances. The performances take place in Burtness Theatre (385 seats). All productions are sung in English; the policy is to alternate between traditional and contemporary operas.

Ohio

BALDWIN–WALLACE COLLEGE OPERA WORKSHOP, Baldwin–Wallace College, Berea, Ohio 44017. Musical Director: **James Wainner.** During the school year two operas are produced, each performed once. Singers are usually students. The orchestra is composed of students and faculty. For one production piano accompaniment is used. All productions are fully staged and performed in Concert Hall, Kulas Music Building (650 seats). . . . CLEVELAND INSTITUTE OF MUSIC OPERA THEATRE, Opera Theatre Department, Cleveland Institute of Music, 11021 East Boulevard, Ohio 44106. Director: **Anthony Addison.** Founded in 1964. During the school year and summer workshop, there are four to six productions, with two or more performances each. The singers are usually students, though sometimes faculty or professionals. The orchestra is composed of students and professionals. Some productions are accompanied by piano. All productions are fully staged and performed in Kulas Hall (540 seats). The Opera Theatre has toured in Ohio. . . . DENISON UNIVERSITY OPERA WORKSHOP, Denison University, Granville, Ohio 43023. Founded circa 1948. Administrative Head: **Herman Larson.** The number of productions varies each year, from one to three; the total performance number varies from two to four. Students fill all roles, whenever possible. The orchestra is a combination of professionals, amateurs, and students. All productions are fully staged and performed in either Ace Morgan Theatre (225 seats) or Recital Hall (240 seats). The usual productions are chamber operas with piano accompaniment; sometimes larger works with orchestra. . . . MIAMI UNIVERSITY OPERA WORKSHOP, Miami University, Oxford, Ohio 45056. Founded in 1957. Musical Director: **Otto Frohlich.** During the school year one or two operas are produced with a total of four performances. Students fill both the singing roles and the positions in the orchestra. Productions are usually fully staged, though sometimes a concert version is performed. Performances take place in Benton Hall (1,000 seats). . . . OBERLIN COLLEGE GILBERT AND SULLIVAN PLAYERS, Hall Auditorium, Oberlin, Ohio 44074. Founded in 1949. Musical Director: **Andrew Meltzer. W. Hayden Boyers,** Founder. **Richard Miller,** Faculty Advisor. During the winter there are one or two productions on campus. The total number of productions is 10 with a total of 50 performances. Students usually fill all singing roles as well as compose the orchestra. All productions are fully staged in Hall Auditorium (500 seats). Light opera exclusively is produced. The Players gave the U.S. premiere of Gilbert and Sullivan's "The Grand Duke" and have performed all the works of Gilbert and Sullivan in the original orchestration. . . . OBERLIN OPERA THEATRE, Oberlin College Conservatory, Oberlin, Ohio 44074. Founded in 1950. Musical Director: **Robert Baustian.** Administrative Head: **Daniel Harris.** During the school year two operas are produced, each performed twice. Students fill all roles and all orchestra positions. Piano accompaniment is used only in programs of opera exerpts. All large productions are fully staged and are performed in Hall Auditorium (500 seats). The world premiere of Walter Aschaffenburg's "Bartleby," was produced by the Theatre; other contemporary operas include Berio's "Passaggio" and Copland's "The Tender Land." . . . OHIO STATE UNIVERSITY OPERA THEATER, Ohio State University, School of Music, Columbus, Ohio 43210. Founded in 1957. Musical Director: **Paul Hickfang.** Administrative Head: **Lee Rigsby** (Dean). Conductor: **Evan Whallon** (Conductor, Columbus Symphony). During the academic year and the summer two to three operas are produced. Total number of performances are five or six. The singers are students, faculty, and professionals (sometimes imported from New York). The orchestra is made up of University members and professionals, but piano is sometimes used for public performances. All productions are fully staged and take place in Mershon Auditorium (3,000 seats). There are some visiting productions. . . . OHIO UNIVERSITY OPERA WORKSHOP, School of Music, Ohio University, Athens, Ohio 45701. One opera production is given one performance. Students usually sing the roles, although faculty members sometimes perform. The orchestra is composed of students and faculty; piano accompaniment is often employed for the public performances, which take place in Ewing Auditorium (700 seats).

Oklahoma

OKLAHOMA CITY UNIVERSITY THEATER, Oklahoma City University, Oklahoma City, Oklahoma 73106. Founded in 1952. Director: **Inez Lunsford Silberg.** Conductor: **Ray Luke.** Administrative Head: **Fred C. Mayer.** During the months of October and November, February and March, two full operas or four or five one-acts are produced, with a total of six performances. Students usually fill all roles, although occasionally faculty members are employed. The orchestra (48 pieces) is composed of students and faculty. All productions are fully staged and performed in Oklahoma City University Auditorium (1,300 seats). The Theatre has made local TV appearances of the one-act productions. . . . THE UNIVERSITY OF OKLAHOMA OPERA THEATRE, University of Oklahoma, Norman, Oklahoma 73069. Founded in 1960. Director of Opera Theatre: **Jack Harrold.** Administrative Head: **C. M. Stookey.** During the school year four operas are produced with four performances each. Except for Mr. Harrold, who is artist-in-residence, students sing all roles. The orchestra is an all-student ensemble. Piano accompaniment is used only for the opera concerts (excerpts). All major productions are fully staged. Performances take place in either Holmberg Hall (1,000 seats) or Rupel Jones Theatre (650 seats). . . . UNIVERSITY OF TULSA OPERA DEPARTMENT, School of Music, University of Tulsa, Tulsa, Oklahoma 74104. Founded in 1962. Director: **Daniel Wright;** Conductor: **William McKee.** During the school year there are three productions: one fully-staged work with orchestra, and two workshop productions with piano. The singers are usually students, but Tulsa Opera Members help out occasionally in solo and chorus roles. The orchestra is composed of students. Performances take place in Kendall Hall Auditorium (450 seats).

Oregon

UNIVERSITY OF OREGON OPERA WORKSHOP, University of Oregon, Eugene, Oregon 97403. Founded in 1949. Musical Director: **James Miller.** Administrative Head: **Robert Trotter.** During the school year two or three operas are produced and given a total of 8 to 10 performances. Singers are students, faculty, or local talent. The orchestra is made up of students and amateurs. Piano accompaniment is sometimes used for performances. Productions are usually fully staged, but concert versions are sometimes performed. Performances take place in the University Theater and School of Music Auditorium (450 seats). Emphasis is on chamber repertory. . . . WILLAMETTE OPERA THEATRE, Willamette University, Salem, Oregon 97301. Founded in 1967. Conductors: **Walter Farrier** and **Charles Heiden.** Administrative Head: **Julio Viamonte.** During the school year of eight months two operas are produced, each given two performances. The singers are usually students, sometimes faculty members. For one of the two productions piano accompaniment is used; otherwise, performance is with an orchestra composed of students and professionals. All productions are fully staged and are performed in Willamette Fine Arts Auditorium (1,250 seats).

Pennsylvania

THE ACADEMY OF VOCAL ARTS, 1920 Spruce Street, Philadelphia, Pennsylvania 19103. Director of the Academy: **Vernon Hammond.** Opera performances are fundamental to the Academy's work since it is open to singers, on a scholarship basis only, who are highly talented and who may fulfill professional engagements while pursuing the specialized studies at the Academy. Thus, opera performances are given throughout the academic year. These number about eight a year and are held in Philadelphia Civic Center and the Academy Auditorium as well as in other locations. Many alumni have gone on to professional work with opera houses in America and Europe. . . . CARNEGIE–MELLON UNIVERSITY OPERA WORKSHOP, Carnegie–Mellon University, Pittsburgh, Pennsylvania 15213. Founded in 1964. Musical Director: **Rudolph Fellner.** Stage Director: **Lee Cass.** During the school year one opera is produced with a total of three performances. Students fill all stage roles as well as all positions in the orchestra. All productions are fully staged and are performed in the Carnegie Theatre (350 seats). . . . THE CHATHAM COLLEGE OPERA WORKSHOP, Chatham College, Woodland Road, Pittsburgh, Pennsylvania 15232. Founded in 1949. Musical Director: **Richard Woitach.** Stage Director: **Richard Flusser.** During the month of August there are four performances. Students fill most roles, faculty are sometimes used. Piano is always used for accompaniment at public performances. The productions are fully staged. The performances take place (temporarily) at the Winchester-Thurston School. . . . CURTIS INSTITUTE OF MUSIC OPERA CLASS, Curtis Institute of Music, Locust Street at Rittenhouse Square, Philadelphia, Pennsylvania 19103. Founded in 1924. Director: **Max Rudolf.** Conductor: **William Smith.** Musical Coach: **Elizabeth Westmoreland.** During the school year one or two productions are given a total of six to eight performances. Students fill all roles as well as all positions in the orchestra. Sometimes piano accompaniment is used in performances. Regular performances are held at the Philadelphia Civic Center and at various colleges. . . . INDIANA UNIVERSITY OF PENNSYLVANIA OPERA THEATER, Indiana University of Pennsylvania, Indiana, Pennsylvania 15701. Founded in 1964. Director: **J. H. Wildeboor.** Conductor: **David Borst. Merle Lentz,** Technical Director. During the academic year two or three operas are produced with a total of six to nine performances. Students fill all singing roles. The orchestra is composed of students and townspeople. All productions are fully staged and are performed in Fisher Auditorium (1,600). Operas have included a number of major American works in the repertory: "The Crucible," "Susannah," "The Tender Land," etc. . . . MANSFIELD STATE COLLEGE OPERA WORKSHOP, Mansfield State College, Mansfield, Pennsylvania 16933. Founded in 1956. Director and Administrative Head: **Jack M. Wilcox.** During the school year and summer program there are three productions with a total of nine performances. Students fill all singing roles. The orchestra is composed of students and faculty. All productions are fully staged and performed in Straughn Auditorium (1,167 seats). . . . TEMPLE UNIVERSITY OPERA WORKSHOP, Temple University, Philadelphia, Pennsylvania 19122. Conductor: **Keith Brown.** During the school year one production is given with three performances. Students fill all singing roles; the orchestra is composed of amateurs. All productions are fully staged and performed in Mitten Hall (1,500 seats).

South Dakota
Dakota

THE UNIVERSITY OF SOUTH DAKOTA OPERA WORKSHOP, The University of South Dakota, Vermillion, South Dakota 57069. Musical Director and Administrative Head: **John Stenseth.** Stage Director: **Ronald Reed.** Every other year during the months of February and March an opera is produced and given four performances. Most roles are filled by students, some by faculty. The orchestra is composed of students and professionals. The production is fully staged and is performed either in Slagle Auditorium (2,254 seats) or Old Main Theatre (151 seats).

Tennessee

MEMPHIS STATE UNIVERSITY OPERA THEATER, Memphis State University, Memphis, Tennessee 38111. Founded in 1948. Conductors: **Paul Eaheart, George Osborne** (who is Artistic Director). During the school year four operas are produced. Each is performed from two to five times. Some roles are sung by faculty and professional stars; many by students. All productions are fully staged. The orchestra is composed of professional players and students. The performances take place in the University Auditorium (1,200 seats). The 1967–68 season, one of the most ambitious for this group, featured "Don Pasquale," "Hansel and Gretel," "The Merry Widow," and "Boris Godounov." Sets for "Boris" were by Andreas Nomikos; Metropolitan Opera soprano Karen Armstrong sang in "Don Pasquale."

Texas

BAYLOR UNIVERSITY OPERA WORKSHOP, School of Music, Baylor University, Waco, Texas 76703. Founded in 1947. Musical Director: **Daniel Sternberg.** Dramatic Director and Designer: **Felicitas Sternberg.** During the school year one full-scale opera is produced and given six performances, sung in English. Students fill all roles. The Workshop has performed Tchaikovsky's "Pique Dame," Smetana's "Bartered Bride," Verdi's "Don Carlo," Ward's "The Crucible," etc. . . . LAMAR STATE COLLEGE OF TECHNOLOGY OPERA WORKSHOP, Music Department, Lamar State College of Technology, Beaumont, Texas 77704. Musical Director: **Joseph Truncale.** Conductor: **Richard Burkart.** During the months from September to January one opera is produced. It is given two or three performances. The roles are filled by students, but sometimes by faculty or professionals. The orchestra is composed of students and faculty; piano is used for accompaniment on occasion. Although most of the productions are fully staged, some concert versions are performed. Performances take place in College Theatre (550 seats). Operas are mainly from the standard literature, sung in English or Italian . . . NORTH TEXAS STATE UNIVERSITY OPERA WORKSHOP, North Texas State University, Denton, Texas 76203. Founded in 1948. Director: **Arthur Schoep.** Musical Director and Conductor: **Donald Kerne.** Assistant: **Margaret Grubb.** During the school year two operas are produced. Each is given two performances. Students fill all singing roles as well as all the positions in the orchestra. Piano accompaniment is used for about one half the public performances. All productions are fully staged and are performed in either the Main Auditorium (2,000 seats) or Recital Hall (600 seats). Some productions have been taken to Dallas. Most of the operas thus far have been sung in Italian, French, and English. . . . SOUTHERN METHODIST UNIVERSITY DIVISION OF MUSIC LYRIC THEATRE, Southern Methodist University, Dallas, Texas 75222. Founded in 1950. Co-Directors: **Thomas Hayward, William Pickett.** Administrative Head: **Don Gillis.** During the school year two to four complete operas are produced, each given two performances. There are also 6 to 10 concert readings of American one-act operas. Ninety-five percent of the roles are filled by students. The orchestra is composed of students and some professionals. Piano accompaniment is used with the one-act operas only. Performances take place in either Caruth Auditorium or Bob Hope Theatre (450 seats each). The Lyric Theatre has a reciprocal arrangement with North Texas State University for some productions. . . . TEXAS CHRISTIAN UNIVERSITY OPERA WORKSHOP, Department of Music, Texas Christian University, Fort Worth, Texas 76129. Founded in 1950. Musical Director: **Fritz Berens.** Administrative Head: **Michael Winesanker.** During the academic year two or three operas are produced. Each is given two performances. Singers are mostly students, occasionally faculty. The Texas Christian University Symphony Orchestra is used; piano accompaniment is used for chamber operas only. All productions are fully staged and performed in Ed Landreth Auditorium (1,250). The production of "The Golden Cockerel" by Rimsky-Korsakov was taken to San Antonio to appear with the San Antonio Symphony under Victor Alessandro. . . . TEXAS WESLEYAN COLLEGE OPERA WORKSHOP, Texas Wesleyan College, Fort Worth, Texas 76105. Musical Director: **William Dailey.** Administrative Head: **Donald Bellah. Mason Johnson** is in charge of staging, **Cecil Cole,** lighting and sets. During November one opera is produced and given one performance. The singing is done entirely by students. Piano accompaniment is always used for public performances. Productions are fully staged and are performed in the Fine Arts Auditorium (1,200 seats). The repertory emphasis is on contemporary chamber operas. . . . TEXAS WOMEN'S UNIVERSITY OPERA WORKSHOP, Department of Music, Texas Women's University, Box 3865, TWU Station, Denton, Texas 76204. Founded in 1960. Musical and Stage Director: **Joan Wall.** Conductor: **J. Wilgus Eberly.** During the school year two operas are produced. All the female singers are from Texas Women's University. Male roles are filled by faculty or professionals. The orchestra is composed of students and professionals, but sometimes piano accompaniment is used for public performances. All productions are fully staged and are performed in the Main Auditorium (3,000 seats) or Redbud Auditorium (325 seats). The emphasis is on producing operas having an abundance of women's roles ("Hansel and Gretel," "Dido and Aeneas," etc.). . . . UNIVERSITY OF HOUSTON OPERA WORKSHOP, University of Houston, Cullen Boulevard, Houston, Texas 77004. **John Druary** and **Stephen Harbachick** are in charge of opera instruction. The season coincides with the school year. Students fill all roles. The orchestra is composed of a combination of students, amateurs, and professionals, but piano accompaniment is often used. All productions are fully staged and performances take place in Cullen Auditorium (1,500 seats). . . . THE UNIVERSITY OF TEXAS AT AUSTIN OPERA THEATRE, The College of Fine Arts, Department of Music, University of

Texas at Austin, Austin, Texas 78712. Musical Director: **Walter Ducloux.** Artistic Advisors: **Orville White, Jesse Walters.** During the school year the opera workshop prepares three productions and gives nine performances. The roles are usually filled by students, sometimes by faculty. The orchestra is composed of students; piano accompaniment is sometimes used for performances. Performances are given in Hogg Auditorium (1,200 seats). . . . UNIVERSITY OF TEXAS AT EL PASO OPERA, P.O. Box 12132, University of Texas, El Paso, Texas 79912. Founded in the 1940's. Musical Director: **Brian Swingle.** Administrative Head: **O. E. Eidbo. Danice Kress** is Assistant; **William Farlow** is Coach. The seasons consist of five days in February and three days in May. Two operas are produced with a total of eight performances. Most singers are students, but some roles are sung by faculty and professionals. The orchestra is a combination of students, amateurs, and professionals. Piano accompaniment is rarely used for public performances, which take place in Magoffin Auditorium (1,600 seats). Most productions are fully staged; a few are performed in concert version.

Utah

UNIVERSITY OF UTAH OPERA COMPANY, University of Utah, Salt Lake City, Utah 84112. Founded in the 1940's. Musical Director: **Ardean W. Watts.** Assistant musical director: **Shann Jacobsen.** Three operas are produced each year, one in December, one in February, and one in April. Each is given three performances. Most leading roles are sung by faculty or local professional singers. The orchestra is composed only of professionals. All productions are fully staged and performed in Kingsbury Hall (2,000 seats). One performance per year is strictly for television. Programs of operatic excerpts are performed with piano for junior high schools under the sponsorship of Young Audiences, Inc.

Vermont

UNIVERSITY OF VERMONT, Department of Music, 70 Williams Street, Burlington, Vermont 05401. Opera production at the university began in 1927. Director of productions (no formally organized workshop): **Frank W. Lidral.** Vocal Coach: **Francis Weinrich.** Stage Director: **Edward Feidner.** One or two operas are staged each season for a total of one to four performances. Normally only students make up the casts. The orchestra is composed of professionals and students. All productions are fully staged and performances are held in the University of Vermont Arena Theater (230 seats).

Virginia

LYNCHBURG COLLEGE OPERA WORKSHOP, Lynchburg College, Lynchburg, Virginia 24504. Founded in 1946. Musical Director: **Robert Ellinwood.** During the school year there are two productions; each is given three performances. Students usually perform the roles, occasionally faculty and professionals. The orchestra consists of a combination of amateurs, students, and professionals. Piano accompaniment is sometimes used for public performances. All productions are fully staged. The performances take place in Hopwood Hall (198 seats) or Snidow Chapel (400 seats). The repertory consists basically of chamber operas. . . . OLD DOMINION COLLEGE OPERA WORKSHOP, Old Dominion College, Norfolk, Virginia 23508. Founded in 1951. Conductors: **Harold G. Hawn** and **John MacCormack.** Other staff: **John Davye,** Chorus Master; **Mrs. John Wohner,** Choreographer; **Maynard Allen,** Lighting Director. The season lasts during the school year, in which four operas are produced for a total of ten performances. Singers include students, members of the staff and community. Occasionally professional opera singers are employed. The Old Dominion College Community Symphony Orchestra (composed of students, amateurs, and professionals) is used. Performances take place in the Center Theatre (1,800 seats). All productions are sung in

English and are prepared in conjunction with the Tidewater Arts Council and local television stations. Since 1951 over 60 productions have been staged, consisting of classic and contemporary operas, four world premieres, operettas, and musicals. In 1960, the Workshop received the Award of Merit commendation from the National Federation of Music Clubs for its performances of American opera.

Washington

FESTIVAL OPERA, University of Washington, Seattle, Washington, 98105. Founded in 1958. Musical Director and Conductor: **Stanley Chapple.** Coach: **Alex Kuchunas.** Stage Director: **Ralph Rosinbum.** During the school year there are four productions with a total number of twelve performances. Singers include students, faculty, and professionals. The orchestra is composed of students and faculty. All productions are fully staged and performed in Jane Addams Auditorium (1,200 seats). . . . WASHINGTON STATE UNIVERSITY OPERA THEATRE, Washington State University, Pullman, Washington 99163. Founded in 1952. Musical Director: **Barton Frank.** Administrative Head: **Margaret West Davis.** Assistant: **Allan Boyer.** The number of productions is two per year. Each is performed four to six times. Roles are filled by graduate and undergraduate music students. The orchestra is a student orchestra; piano accompaniment is very rarely used for public performances. All productions are fully staged and are performed in Kimbrough Concert Hall (400 seats). The University TV station films isolated opera scenes. Some touring is done within the state.

West Virginia

OGLEBAY INSTITUTE OPERA WORKSHOP, Oglebay Park, Wheeling, West Virginia 26003. (Held on the campus of West Liberty State College). Founded in 1952. Musical Director: **Boris Goldovsky.** Administrative Head: **Mrs. Chase Greer.** Other staff members (who sometimes vary): **Arthur Schoep,** Associate Director; **Fredric Popper, Anthony Addison, Paul Berl,** Senior Staff. The season lasts during the month of August. One full-scale opera is produced and given one performance, and approximately fifty scenes are prepared and performed in four or five scene recitals. Students (some of whom are already professionals) fill all roles. Piano accompaniment is used for public performances. The large-scale opera is fully staged and performed in Glessner Auditorium (800 seats). A grant from the Martha Baird Rockefeller Fund for Music, Inc. makes possible some Oglebay scholarships. The National Federation of Music Clubs offers one full scholarship for a student coach. . . . WEST VIRGINIA UNIVERSITY OPERA THEATRE, West Virginia University, Morgantown, West Virginia 26506. Founded in 1959. Conductor: **Donald Portnoy.** Administrative Head and Director of Theatre: **Joseph Golz.** During the school year two or three operas are produced. Each is given four performances. All roles are filled by students. The orchestra is composed of students; piano accompaniment is sometimes used for public performance. All productions are fully staged and are performed in the Creative Arts Center Theatre (1,600 seats).

Wisconsin

UNIVERSITY OF WISCONSIN OPERA THEATRE, The School of Music, University of Wisconsin, Madison, Wisconsin 53706. Founded in 1956. Musical Director: **Karlos Moser.** During the school year there are three productions with a total number of 15 performances. Students usually sing most roles; occasionally faculty and professionals are used. The orchestra is composed of students. Most productions are fully staged but a few are performed in concert version. All performances take place in Music Hall Auditorium (780 seats). Repertory consists of standard works, infrequently performed classics, and modern operas. An occasional production will be sung in both English and its original language. This was the case with productions of "Macbeth" and "La Bohème." . . . UNIVERSITY OF WISCONSIN–MILWAUKEE OPERA WORKSHOP, University of Wisconsin, Milwaukee, Wisconsin 53201. Founded in 1960. Music Director: **Edward Foreman.** Administrative Head: **LeRoy W. Daniels.** There are one or two productions during the academic year, each given several performances. Students sing most roles; some are sung by faculty and professional singers. University students form the orchestra; sometimes piano or harpsichord is used as accompaniment for performances. All productions are fully staged and performed either in Fine Arts Recital Hall (300 seats) or Fine Arts Theatre (600 seats).

INDEPENDENT, PROFESSIONAL OPERA COMPANIES

Alabama

BIRMINGHAM CIVIC OPERA ASSOCIATION, 86 Fairway Drive, Birmingham, Alabama 35213. Founded in 1955. Musical Director and Producer: **Martha Dick McClung.** Conductor: **Amerigo Marino.** President: **Cassell Stewart.** Stage Director: **Richard Collins.** During the opera season, two or three full-scale operas are produced in four to six total performances. Singers are brought in only when roles cannot be locally cast; otherwise they are resident performers. The orchestra used is the Birmingham Symphony Orchestra. All productions are fully staged and take place in Temple Theatre (2,200 seats). Major operas and chamber operas have been produced. . . . MOBILE OPERA GUILD, INC. (Mobile Opera Guild Workshop), Box 8366, Mobile, Alabama 36608. Founded in 1944 by the late Rose Palmai Tenser. Musical Director and General Manager: **James Yestadt.** One opera is produced and given two performances in March. The star system is employed for engaging singers for Guild performances. The orchestra is composed of professionals with some (10 percent) nonprofessionals. All productions are fully staged and take place in Mobile Municipal Auditorium (1,950 seats). The season also includes one visiting production. The Workshop performs mostly American operas; the Guild, mostly traditional.

California

EDUCATIONAL OPERA ASSOCIATION, INC., 609 Diablo Drive, Burbank, California 91711. Founded in 1951 to bring a new type of music education to school children and to create an outlet for local professional singers. The group has presented over 400 performances for over a half million students. Head: **John Arnold Ford.** Musical Director: **Curtis Stearns.** During the school year, one opera is produced and given 24 performances in various schools. The Association is composed of resident professional singers. Piano accompaniment is used, but the operas are fully staged. They consist of hour-long comic operas, sung in English and performed in school auditoriums throughout Southern California (1,000 seats average capacity). . . . GUILD OPERA COMPANY, INC., 427 West Fifth Street, Room 722, Los Angeles, California 90013. Founded 1949. Business Administrator: **John R. Moss.** General Director: **Carl Ebert.** Stage Director: **Peter Ebert.** The company's performing season lasts about three weeks. It produces four fully staged operas in a total of about 15 performances a year. Only resident young professional singers are used. The orchestra is also professional. The company performs in Shrine Auditorium (approximately 6,500 seats). The company has staged 163 performances of the four operas in its repertory. The Guild is established to provide opera primarily for children. More than 850,000 young people from many parts of Los Angeles have seen performances by the Guild Opera (approximately 65,000 a year). Operas are sung in English. . . . PASADENA OPERA COMPANY, P.O. Box 2496, Pasadena, California 91105. Founded in 1962. President: **Mrs. Don H. Rose.** The season lasts for two months during which three operas are produced with a total of six performances. The Company includes resident singers, but opera stars are also engaged. The orchestra is composed of professionals. All operas are fully staged and take place in the Pasadena Civic Auditorium (2,968 seats). . . . SAN DIEGO OPERA COMPANY, Box 988, San Diego, California 92112. Founded in 1965. Artistic Director: **Walter Herbert.**

Manager: **William L. Denton.** The season involves the months of November through April. Four fully staged operas are produced and are performed four times each including two youth performances. Some resident singers are used, but star singers are engaged for leading roles. The company does feature visiting productions. In 1968, the company presented the American premiere performance of Bizet's autographed score of "Carmen"; in 1966, Henze's "The Young Lord." . . . SAN FRANCISCO CHILDREN'S OPERA ASSOCIATION, INC., P.O. Box 18143, San Francisco, California 94118. Musical Director: **Norbert Gingold.** Stage Director: **Beth Van Dyke.** The season lasts from October through April. Six operas are produced with six performances. Local singers are used. The orchestra is composed of students (professionals for one performance). All operas are fully staged and take place at the Opera House (3,200 seats) or at two other theaters. All the operas performed by this company are written especially for children by **Heddy Gingold** (lyrics) and **Norbert Gingold** (music). . . . SAN FRANCISCO OPERA COMPANY, War Memorial Opera House, San Francisco, California 94102. Founded in 1923. General Director is **Kurt Herbert Adler.** Manager is **Edward Corn.** Its 11-week season runs from September to November. Twelve operas are staged and given, altogether, about 56 performances. Founder of the company was Gaetano Merola, who was General Director until his death in 1953; Mr. Adler has been General Director since. The company is one of the important opera-producing groups in America. Its history is intertwined with many of the great opera singers, conductors, stage directors, and designers of the century. Past singers include such names as Rethberg, Pinza, Melchior, Crooks, Bori, Jeritza, Flagstad, Warren and many more from the international world of opera. Since World War II, the company provided the U.S. opera debut of such well-known European singers as **Mario del Monaco, Elisabeth Schwarzkopf, Renata Tebaldi, Giulietta Simionato,** and others. Its U.S. premiere productions include "Les Troyens" (1966), in its first professional American performance, "Dialogues of the Carmelites" (1957), "Die Frau ohne Schatten" (1959), and "The Makropulos Case" (1966). The Association also operates as a subsidiary company the so-called Spring Opera Theater (q.v.) and the Western Opera Theater, a touring company (q.v.). The Merola Fund and the San Francisco Opera Guild are two important adjuncts to the company. The Fund sponsors an annual series of auditions for young professional singers from throughout the Western states and Canada and provides also a ten-week summer program of opera performances for young singers. The Guild, which is the second largest in the nation and is patterned after that of the Metropolitan Opera, raises funds for various opera needs, donates funds for new productions, and underwrites four student matinee performances each year. The company engages about six or seven conductors each season. It has its own chorus, chorus director, ballet corps, etc. Performances take place in the War Memorial Opera House (3,052 seats). . . . SAN FRANCISCO OPERA GUILD TALENT BANK, 2100 Green Street, San Francisco, California 94123. Founded in 1959. Chairman: **Mrs. Alfred Crapsey.** Musical Director: **Peggy Donovan.** Production Designer: **Richard Rose.** Management Assistant: **George Baker.** The season spans ten months, with an average of four productions and 24 performances. Resident singers are used. At least half the performances use two-piano accompaniment; otherwise a professional orchestra is used. All operas are fully staged and take place in various theaters (average of 900 seats). Has presented West Coast premieres of Mozart's "La Finta Giardiniera," Rossini's "La Scala di Seta," and "Turk in Italy." Recipient of Martha Baird Rockefeller Fund for Music grants for three years. . . . SANTA BARBARA CIVIC OPERA COMPANY, 1521 Dover Road, Santa Barbara, California 93103. Incorporated in 1940 to produce operas with the local WPA Symphony. President: **William Bell Collier III.** The Santa Barbara Civic Opera Association is a nonprofit educational organization incorporated for the purpose of training singers and other musicians and giving them experience in actual stage production. The repertory of the company includes "La Bohème," "Otello," "La Traviata," "Carmen," "Aida," "La Tosca," and "Madame Butterfly." Performances are held in various theaters in Santa Barbara. In the years from 1954 to 1967, the company staged several operas with professionals who were already established or who were to become better known subsequently in the national opera scene. **Marcella Reale** sang her first Cio-Cio-San with this company in 1954; other singers who sang certain first role performances in their careers include **Christopher Lachona, Norma Lynn, Alan Gilbert** (all in roles in "Otello" in 1963), and **Jean Fenn** as Mimi (sung in English, in 1964), etc. . . . SANTA MONICA CIVIC OPERA ASSOCIATION, 1322–10th Street, Santa Monica, California 90404. Founded in 1944. Musical Director: **Mario Lanza.** Production and Business Manager: **Joseph W. Garrotto.** During the year five operas are produced and five performances given. Resident singers are engaged. The orchestra is composed of students and professional players. All productions are fully staged and take place in Barnum Hall (1,400 seats). . . . SPRING OPERA THEATER, Alcoa Building, Suite 20, San Francisco, California 94111. Incorporated in 1960; had its first season in 1961. The company is an affiliate of the San Francisco Opera. Producer is **Kurt Herbert Adler.** President is **W. W. Godward.** Formerly, productions were staged in the War Memorial Opera House. Since 1971, performances have taken place in Curran Theater. Four to six operas are produced each spring, for a total of from 8 to 12 performances. The purpose of the company is to provide a professional performing opportunity to young singers and others involved in creating opera productions. All productions are fully staged, and feature many operas sung in English. Both contemporary works and classics are scheduled. In the former category, the Spring Opera presented the San Francisco premiere of "The Crucible," "The Turn of the Screw," the West Coast premiere of "Carry Nation," and others. Among the now well–established singers who received early performing opportunities with the company are **Ara Berberian, Patricia Brooks, Simon Estes, Marilyn Horne, Chester Ludgin, George Shirley,** and **Norman Treigle.** Tickets to the performances are sold at popular prices, thereby attracting out-of-town audiences and student groups. . . . STOCKTON OPERA ASSOCIATION, Suite 301, 305 North El Dorado, Stockton, California 95207. Founded in 1967. Musical Director: **Lucas Underwood.** From one to three operas are produced each season and are given two performances each. Mostly resident singers are used; singers are imported for some roles as needed. All operas are fully staged. The orchestra is made up of players from the Stockton Symphony and other professionals and students. Performances are held in different auditoriums ranging in seating capacity from about 400 to approximately 2,100. . . . VALLEY OPERA ASSOCIATION, P.O. Box 497, Livermore, California 94550. Founded in 1965. General Director: **Henry Holt.** The season lasts for ten months. Two operas are produced with piano accompaniment and one with an orchestra in concert version. The orchestra is composed of professionals and amateurs. The company gives a total of about nine performances each season. Performances are held in Livermore High School Auditorium (seats 900). . . . WESTERN OPERA THEATRE, War Memorial Opera House, San Francisco, California 94102. Founded in 1966. Musical Director: **Richard Woitach.** Administrative Head: **Kurt Herbert Adler.** The season lasts from September through June. Three or four fully staged operas are produced, and from 100 to 150 performances are given. Only resident singers are used. The orchestra is a combination of professionals and students. The company is a touring group of the San Francisco Opera and performs in schools and colleges throughout California, Oregon, and Arizona. It visited Alaska for the first time in 1970. The founding and initial operation of the Western Opera Theatre was funded by a grant of $105,000 from National Endowment for the Arts; subsequent grants from NEA were made in 1968 and 1971.

Colorado

CENTRAL CITY OPERA HOUSE ASSOCIATION, Suite 636, University Building, 910 16th Street, Denver, Colorado 80202. Founded in 1932. (see Music Festivals.) . . . COLORADO SPRINGS OPERA ASSOCIATION, 631 North Tejon Street, Colorado Springs, Colorado 80702. Founded in 1959. Musical Director and Conductor: **J. Julius Baird.** The opera season lasts from November through April. Three operas are produced and are given six performances; 24 resident singers are engaged. Piano accompaniment is used for chamber opera tours. Some performances are in concert version. The orchestra is professional. Performances are held in Palmer High School Auditorium (1,447 seats). Repertory is mostly traditional ("Romeo and Juliet" and "The Girl of the Golden West," etc.), sung in English, and some contemporary ("Susannah" in 1971). . . . DENVER LYRIC OPERA, 3855 South Monaco Parkway, Suite 159, Denver, Colorado 80237. Artistic Director and Conductor: **Norman Johnson.** Two or three operas (fully staged) are produced every season and are given one or two performances each. Resident singers are used and outside stars are engaged only when necessary. The orchestra is the Denver Symphony, which officially supports Denver Lyric Opera. Regular performances are held in Auditorium Theater (2,200 seats).

Connecticut

CONNECTICUT OPERA ASSOCIATION, 15 Lewis Street, Hartford, Connecticut 06103. Founded in 1942. Executive Director: **Frank Pandolfi.** Administrative Assistant: **Helen G. Silansky.** During a season, which spans from October to April, six operas are produced, with a total of 10 performances. The Association has no resident singers. Star soloists are engaged from the professional field. The orchestra is composed of professional players. All productions are fully staged and take place in Bushnell Memorial Hall (3,277 seats). The Association has staged Gounod's "Romeo and Juliet;" "Tosca," "Manon Lescaut," "Otello," "Tristan and Isolde," among others. Singers have been **Franco Corelli, Anna Moffo, Renata Tebaldi, Placido Domingo, Renata Scotto, Elinor Ross, Beverly Sills, Dorothy Kirsten, Richard Tucker,** et al. . . . NEW HAVEN OPERA SOCIETY, INC. P.O. Box 6144, Hamden, Connecticut 06517. Founded in 1963. Musical Directors: **Gustav Meier, Donald Comrie, Frank Brieff, Yehudi Wyner.** Artistic Director: **Herta Glaz–Redlich.** One or two operas not necessarily from the standard repertory are produced. Each is given two performances plus extensive school programs. There are resident and imported singers, but stars as such are not engaged. Piano accompaniment is used at times, otherwise New Haven Symphony Orchestra members make up the orchestra. Some performances are in concert version. Performances take place in school auditoriums (1,000 seats average). New Haven Foundation Grant given for workshops in local high schools. Other grants and sources of support have come from the Federal Government (Title III), and the boards of education of school districts benefiting from the touring school productions (Waterbury, Stamford, Meridian, etc.). Some of the unusual complete operas produced include: Bizet's "Dr. Miracle," Haydn's "The Songstress," Martinu's "Comedy on the Bridge," among others.

Delaware

WILMINGTON OPERA SOCIETY, 2029 Kynwyd Drive, Wilmington, Delaware 19803. Founded in 1944. Musical Director: **Powell Middleton.** Head: **Mrs. Elizabeth Ferris.** Each year two operas are produced and given a total of six performances. There are resident singers but outside singers are also engaged. The orchestra is composed of professional (union) musicians. All productions are done in concert version and take place in the Playhouse in Wilmington (1,250 seats).

Washington, D.C.

OPERA SOCIETY OF WASHINGTON, INC., 1028 Connecticut Avenue, N.W.,

Washington, D.C. 20036. Founded in 1957. President: **Lionel C. Epstein.** General Director: **Ian Strasfogel.** Conductors are engaged on an opera-to-opera basis. Over a period of six to nine months, 4 operas are produced and given altogether 15 performances. Resident singers and imported opera stars are engaged; the orchestra is entirely professional and all productions are fully staged and original with the company. Performances were formerly held in Lisner Auditorium, but since the opening of the John F. Kennedy Center for the Performing Arts, the Center's Opera House (2,200 seats) has served as the home auditorium for the Opera Society—the official opera company of the Center. For a company with such a limited season and young history, the Society has made an unusually strong reputation for itself. It has recorded for Columbia Records Stravinsky's "Le Rossignol," and "Oedipus Rex," under the composer's direction, Schoenberg's "Erwartung," under **Robert Craft,** and Menotti's "The Medium," under **Jorge Mester.** It has achieved greatest notoriety, perhaps, through its several premieres and commissions, most notably two commissioned operas by **Alberto Ginastera:** "Bomarzo" (performed in 1967 and later recorded for Columbia Records), and "Beatrix Cenci," (which was premiered during opening week at Kennedy Center in September, 1971). The company premiered Delius's "Koanga" in 1970. . . . SOKOL OPERA GROUP, 2071 Park Road, N.W., Washington, D.C. 20010. Founded in 1960. Musical Director: **Mrs. Lida Brodenova.** Administrative Head: **Matthew Neumann.** During the year one or two operas are produced, of which two performances are given in Washington and two in New York City. The Group consists of resident professional and near professional singers. Piano accompaniment is used for all performances, which in Washington take place at Mount Vernon Junior College (400 seats). The productions are fully staged. Premieres have included: Dvořák's "The Peasant Rogue," Blodek's "In the Well," and Smetana's "The Kiss." Scenes from the latter have been televised. . . . WASHINGTON CIVIC OPERA ASSOCIATION, c/o D.C. Department of Recreation, 3069 Mt. Pleasant Street, N.W., Washington, D.C. 20010. Musical Director: **Frederick Fall.** From September to June three operas are produced and given six performances. The orchestra is composed of professionals; piano accompaniment is sometimes used. The performances are in concert version and take place in Roosevelt High School Auditorium (1,078 seats). This is an amateur group with most lead parts filled by professional singers. Most of the funds are provided by a grant from the U.S. Congress and the balance from the Department of Recreation.

Florida

CIVIC OPERA OF THE PALM BEACHES, 760 South County Road, Palm Beach, Florida 33480. Founded in 1962. Musical Director: **Paul Csonka.** President: **Mrs. Carleton Dodge.** During the winter one to three operas are produced with a total of one to three performances. There are resident singers but the engagement of star singers is basic. The orchestra is composed of professional players. All productions are fully staged and take place in the Civic Auditorium (2,500 seats). Past productions include "La Traviata," "Manon," "La Bohème," "Carmen," "Tosca," etc., with such stars as **Licia Albanese, Frank Guarrera, Roberta Peters, Frank Campora,** et al. . . . OPERA GALA GUILD OF THE FLORIDA SYMPHONY SOCIETY, INC., The Florida Symphony Orchestra, Box 782, Orlando, Florida 32802. Founded in 1957. Executive Vice President: **Helen Ryan.** Presents within a week two performances of one opera in Orlando Municipal Auditorium (2,950 seats). The orchestra used is the Florida Symphony Orchestra. Singers from the Metropolitan and New York City Operas are engaged; resident singers perform only minor roles. . . . OPERA GUILD OF FORT LAUDERDALE, INC., 1040 Bayview Drive, Florida 33304. Founded in 1944. Administrative Head: **H. Charles Kersten.** Musical Director: **Emerson Buckley.** One performance each of two productions are offered in War Memorial Auditorium (2,500 seats). A professional orchestra is used. . . . OPERA GUILD OF GREATER

MIAMI, 1200 Coral Way, Miami, Florida 33145. Founded in 1941, it is the fifth oldest opera company in the United States. The late Founder, General Manager, and Artistic Director was Arturo Di Filippi (d. June, 1972) who had had the longest tenure of any opera impresario in the country. General Manager and Artistic Director is **Lorenzo Alvary.** Musical Director and Chief Conductor is **Emerson Buckley.** Other staff members: **Walter Palevoda,** Assistant Manager; **Paul Csonka,** Associate Conductor and Chorus Master. The Guild's season runs from November to May and offers five or six operas in about 16 performances. All productions are fully staged and are held in Miami Beach Auditorium (3,500 seats) and Dade County Auditorium (2,500 seats). The company plays two productions in Fort Lauderdale each season. The Guild is a major producer of opera, employing local professional singers and the star performers of the Metropolitan Opera, the New York City Opera, and of the opera houses of Europe. It has its own locally trained chorus. Until the spring of 1971, the Guild had staged 194 performances of 34 grand operas—mostly from the standard repertory. At the address above is the Guild's Educational Center, a building designed primarily for educational applications of opera for schoolchildren. It has a 175-seat auditorium for staging modest opera productions and presenting concerts. Over the years, the Guild has made a point of attracting young people to opera. Annually some 11,000 Miami school-age children attend opera previews as well as other special performances prepared for young people. In 1967, the company videotaped a 75-minute production of "Pagliacci" for Florida educational TV stations which subsequently was viewed by a reported half million people. The project received funding from the State of Florida and the National Endowment for the Arts. The Guild has also been the recipient of a five-year $20,000 annual Ford Foundation grant. The annual budget of the company exceeds $500,000. . . . OPERA REPERTORY GROUP, INC., 4227 Peachtree Circle East, Jacksonville, Florida 32207. Founded in 1961. Founder and Managing Director: **Amelia Smith.** Musical Directors in addition to **Amelia Smith** have included **Thomas Briccetti, C. Carter Nice,** and **Jack E. Rogers.** The Group's season lasts 10 months. Four to six operas are produced and given altogether about 12 performances. Most singers are resident, but occasionally stars from leading opera companies have been engaged. Piano accompaniment is used only seldom; the orchestra is made up of professional musicians. Some summer productions are presented in concert version; otherwise the productions are fully staged. Performances are held in Civic Auditorium (3,200 seats) and Civic Theatre (600 seats). The Group began in 1961 as the only professional opera company in the area, presenting mainly chamber opera, and as Florida's first professional television and touring opera company. The group was commercially sponsored on television. In 1966, it incorporated as a nonprofit, cultural organization and became North Florida's only resident professional opera group. The company attempts to encourage professional talent to remain in Florida. Its repertory includes modern chamber operas, sung in English: Argento's "The Boor," Carlisle Floyd's "Slow Dusk," Weisgall's "The Stronger," Moore's "Gallantry," etc. . . . SAN CARLO OPERA OF FLORIDA, INC., 103 Beach Place, Bayshore Gardens, Florida 33606. Founded in 1955. Musical Director: **Donald Thiem.** Conductor: **Alfredo Silipigni.** President: **Mrs. J. D. Rosenthal.** Manager and Artistic Director: **Norma Tina Russo.** The season lasts from November to May, during which time two performances are offered of two operas. Roles are taken primarily by the artists of the Metropolitan and La Scala. Resident singers are also used. The orchestra used is composed of both professionals and students. Performances are held in McKay Auditorium (1,882 seats).

Georgia

THE AUGUSTA OPERA COMPANY, Box 3865, Hill Station, Augusta, Georgia 30904. Executive Director: **Nancy Gleason.** Artistic Director: **Ian Strasfogel.** General Manager: **B. E. Evans.** One opera production is performed four times for the season. Repertory is traditional; star singers are engaged. . . . SOUTHERN REGIONAL OPERA COMPANY, Trust Company of Georgia Building, Atlanta, Georgia 30303. Founded 1969 by the current Managing Director, **Blanche Thebom,** after the demise of the Atlanta Opera. Its 1971 season consisted of performances in the parks of Atlanta in the months of July and August. One opera production was presented 15 times.

Hawaii

HAWAII OPERA THEATRE OF THE HONOLULU SYMPHONY SOCIETY, 328 Merchandise Mart Building, Honolulu, Hawaii 96813. Formed as an outgrowth of opera productions presented by the orchestra as opera festivals during the concert season. General Manager is **Roger R. Jones.** Music Director and Conductor is **Robert LaMarchina.** President of the Theatre is **Daniel C. Bonright.** It produces two operas from the standard repertory, each with three performances including one performance for children. Performances in Honolulu are in Honolulu Concert Hall (2,200 seats). Performances are also given in the islands of Kauai and Mauai. Singers are all stars from various opera houses in the U.S. and abroad. In 1971, the first performance in Hawaii of a Wagner opera ("The Flying Dutchman") was given.

Illinois

ALL CHILDREN'S GRAND OPERA, 1306 West Roscoe Street, Chicago, Illinois 60657. Founded in 1937. President: **Rolland Metzger.** Musical Director and Conductor: **Zerline M. Metzger.** Season is irregular, but three or four performances are usually given. Piano accompaniment is used. Performances are held in Curtiss Hall in the Chicago Fine Arts Building, as well as in libraries, churches and clubs. Preschool as well as adolescent children—ages 5 to 16—are featured in the operas. They sing in the original keys and the original languages such operas as "Carmen," "Lohengrin," "Aida," etc. (Two complete "Ring" cycles were once performed.) English is used where there is much dialogue, as in "The Magic Flute." Only grand opera is performed. The children in some seasons have been used in professional opera productions visiting Chicago (New York City, Metropolitan, etc.). . . . CHICAGO PARK DISTRICT OPERA GUILD, Park Department, 425 East 14th Boulevard, Chicago, Illinois 60605. Founded in 1945. Music Supervisor: **Ann M. Higgins.** Two all-amateur productions of standard opera repertory are given every season. Produced under the auspices of Chicago's Park District, Department of Recreation. . . . LYRIC OPERA OF CHICAGO, 20 North Wacker Drive, Chicago, Illinois 60606. Founded in 1954. General Manager: **Carol Fox** (also one of the original organizers of the first season). Artistic Directors: **Bruno Bartoletti** (Principal Conductor) and **Pino Donati.** The company presents a 12-week fall season of nine operas, some in new productions, in about 52 performances. These are offered in 13 subscription series. The Lyric is the longest continuously run opera company in Chicago's history and is one of the major companies in the United States. Its repertory is varied: Verdi, Puccini, Mozart, Wagner, Strauss, new works, contemporary works in the repertory, and some infrequently performed works of the past (see below). It engages about four conductors a season. The company has its own ballet corps, under the direction of **Ruth Page,** and its own chorus, directed by **Michael Lepore.** Singers are the great American and foreign stars of today's opera world—some making their U.S. debut or their debut in particular roles with the Lyric. Performances take place in the Chicago Opera House, whose capacity is 3,535 seats—reportedly the second largest theater in the country. Singers who have made their U.S. debuts with the Lyric include **Callas, Walter Berry, Christa Ludwig,** and **Anna Moffo.** The list of artists who have sung with the company is long. Among them: **Tito Gobbi, Richard Lewis, Birgit Nilsson, Patricia Brooks, Theodor Uppman, Renata Tebaldi, Boris Christoff, Regine Crespin,** Jussi Bjoerling, **Elisabeth Schwarzkopf, Joan Sutherland, Leontyne Price, Rita Streich,** and **Grace Bumbry.** Recent guest conductors have been **Christoph von Dohnanyi, Jean Fournet,** and **Nino Sanzogno.** Others in the past have included **Georg Solti,** Tullio Serafin, Artur Rodzinski, and Lovro von Matacic. Some of the infrequently performed operas produced anew by the Lyric include "Thaïs," "Pearl Fishers," "Prince Igor," "Khovanshtchina," "Taming of the Shrew," "Jenufa," and others. Britten's "Billy Budd" was given its first American professional performance by the Lyric in 1970; Chicago heard its first "Ring" cycle in 1971 with the Lyric productions. The first tour undertaken by the company was in 1970 to Ames, Iowa. A subscription ticket drive is conducted by the Lyric each spring, followed by a nonsubscription ticket campaign in the summer and box office sales during the season. In 1966 the receipts for the company were $1,163,236, or 97.4 percent of the total ticket capacity. Receipts for 1970 were $1,379,184. Attendance for the 1971–72 season was 99 percent—the highest on record for the company. Deficits, which tally well over a half million each season, are covered by special fund-raising campaigns. Business Manager is **R. H. Ball.** Production Director is **Michael Manuel.**

Kentucky

KENTUCKY OPERA ASSOCIATION OF LOUISVILLE, Gardencourt, Alta Vista Road, Louisville, Kentucky 40205. Founded in 1952. Musical Director: **Moritz Bomhard.** The season lasts seven months (October to April), during which five operas are produced and performed three times each. Some singers are imported, but there are resident singers as well. The orchestra is a professional one. Performances are held in Brown Theatre, which seats 1,453. The Kentucky Opera Association took part in an H.E.W. program of performances for more than 50,000 school children in 1967. It has also toured Kentucky under the sponsorship of the Kentucky Arts Commission. In conjunction with the Louisville Orchestra's Rockefeller grant (see Symphony Orchestras), the Kentucky Opera Association was called upon to record, under the *Louisville* label, a number of new operas, recordings of which are all still available: Peggy Glanville–Hick's "The Transposed Heads," Richard Mohaupt's "Double Trouble," George Antheil's "The Wish," Rolf Liebermann's "The School for Wives," Lee Hoiby's "Beatrice," and Nabokov's "The Holy Devil." This recording series credits the Kentucky Opera with an accomplishment that is unique among American opera companies.

Louisiana

NEW ORLEANS OPERA HOUSE ASSOCIATION, 420 Saint Charles Avenue, New Orleans, Louisiana 70130. Founded in 1943. President: **H. Lloyd Hawkins.** Musical Director and Conductor: **Knud Andersson.** General Director: **Arthur Cosenza.** The fall season lasts from October through December and the spring season from March through May. For the 1968–69 season, a total of sixteen performances were given of the eight operas produced; in 1970–71, six operas in 12 performances were staged. Resident singers are used, although stars are engaged for leading roles. The orchestra is a professional one. Performances are held in the Municipal Auditorium (3,000 seats). . . . NEW ORLEANS RECREATION DEPARTMENT OPERA WORKSHOP, 1–W–16, City Hall, New Orleans, Louisiana 70112. Founded in 1957. Sponsored by the City of New Orleans as part of its recreation program. Over 30 full-length standard repertory operas have been performed using all local casts chosen through citywide auditions. Costumes and scenery are created by the Costume and Art Departments of the Recreation Department. Two pianos are used for accompaniment. Performances take place in Dixon Hall (900 seats) on the campus of Tulane University. Director is **Arthur Cosenza.** . . . SHREVEPORT CIVIC OPERA ASSOCIATION INC., P.O. Box 1830, Shreveport, Louisiana 71102. Founded in 1949. Production Chairman: **E. P. Courtney.** Opera season lasts from November through March, during which period three operas are produced. Singers and the orchestra players are engaged from professional rosters. Some concert version performances are given. Performances are held in Shreveport Civic Theatre (1,900 seats). The Woman's Guild of the Association sponsors an annual TV opera. The Association also sponsors performances for local students, concerts for regional winners of Metropolitan National Council Auditions, and other activities.

Maryland

BALTIMORE OPERA COMPANY INC., 11 East Lexington Street, Baltimore, Maryland 21202. Incorporated in 1950. Artistic Director: **Rosa Ponselle.** Managing Director: **Robert J. Collinge.** The season lasts from October through April. Three fully staged operas are produced and are performed three times each. Leading opera singers are engaged for main roles but resident singers are also used. The Baltimore Symphony Orchestra accompanies the performances, which are held in the Lyric Theatre (2,500 seats). The repertory is traditional.

Massachusetts

AMHERST COMMUNITY OPERA, Amherst, Massachusetts 01002. Founded in 1952. President: **Richard R. Rescia.** One opera is produced every season and is given two or three performances. Only resident singers are used. The orchestra is made up of professionals and amateurs. Performances are held in Amherst Regional High School (1,000 seats). All services, except those of orchestra members and the musical director, are donated by participants. . . . THE CAMBRIDGE OPERA, 11 Garden Street, Cambridge, Massachusetts 02138. Founded in 1966. Sponsored by the First Church (Congregational). Administrative Head: **Campbell Johnson.** The opera season lasts eight months. Two to four operas are produced and are given 4 to 10 performances. Only resident young professional singers are engaged. Both professional and nonprofessional orchestras are used. Piano accompaniment is sometimes used for productions of the Children's Opera Theatre, ensemble, and workshop productions. Performances are held in colleges, high schools, churches, temples, theaters, and auditoriums. Repertory includes works of contemporary American composers as well as more traditional works. . . . GOLDOVSKY OPERA THEATRE, 183 Clinton Road, Brookline, Massachusetts 02146. Also: Studio 95, 154 West 57th Street, New York, N.Y. 10019. Founded in 1946. Musical Directors: **Boris Goldovsky** and **Edward Ailey.** Associate Director: **Fredric Popper.** The Theatre tours for three months. Its one production is given about 70 performances. Only resident singers are used. The orchestra is professional. Performances, during the tour, are usually held for audiences of about 1,000. . . . OPERA COMPANY OF BOSTON, INC., 172 Newbury Street, Boston, Massachusetts 02116. Founded in 1958. Formerly the Boston Opera Company. Artistic Director is **Sarah Caldwell** who is also Conductor. Managing Director is **Robert E. Reilly.** The company's season consists of three months rehearsal and a three-month period of five productions in 15 or more performances. Leading roles are taken by well-known singers from the Metropolitan, New York City Opera, and other companies. The chorus is made up of resident singers; the orchestra players are members of the Boston Symphony Orchestra. All productions are fully staged and are created by the company using its own designers, stage managers, and other personnel. Various theaters are used for performances. The kind of operas staged by the company run the full range, from the classics of all past periods to the contemporary, and include the infrequently performed works of all periods. The company is respected for its daring and ambition, often producing epic works in inadequate theaters and with restrictive budgets. The company has staged "The Trojans" in its first complete American performance, Berg's "Lulu," Schoenberg's "Moses and Aaron," Verdi's "Falstaff," and other difficult works. The company recently received a grant from the Ford Foundation for deficit aid and future development for the amount of $492,000. Past grants have been given by the Ford and Rockefeller Foundations and the National Endowment for the Arts.

Michigan

THE MUSICAL PERFORMING ARTS ASSOCIATION OF FLINT MICHIGAN, Dort Music Center, 1025 E. Kearsley, Flint, Michigan 48503. President: **Arthur E. Summerfield.** Artistic Director and Conductor: **William Byrd.** Founded in 1965. The concert season lasts from September through May, during which two operas—one, a chamber opera—are produced; the full-length opera is given two performances. Resident singers are used primarily. The orchestra is professional. Performances are held in Whiting Auditorium (1,850 seats) and in Flint College Lecture Hall (400). . . . OVERTURE TO OPERA (DETROIT GRAND OPERA ASSOCIATION), Ford Auditorium, 20 East Jefferson Avenue, Detroit, Michigan 48226. Founded in 1962. Administrative Head: **David DiChiera.** Musical Directors: **David DiChiera** and **William Byrd.** Two operas are produced in the period from January to April and are given about 20 performances. Resident singers are used and occasionally stars are engaged for leading roles. Piano accompaniment is used for performances during tours. The orchestra is professional. Regular performances are held in the Detroit Institute of Arts (1,200 seats). Special works produced include Cherubini's "The Portuguese Inn," the rock opera, "Joseph and His Technicolor Dreamcoat," Weill's "Der Jasager," etc. . . . PICCOLO OPERA COMPANY, 18662 Fairfield Avenue, Detroit, Michigan 48221. Founded in 1962. Artistic Director (also performer): **Marjorie Gordon.** Musical Director: **Nathan Gordon.** The company tours throughout the year. Piano accompaniment is used; some performances are in concert version. The company specializes in chamber opera sung in English. Productions are staged and in costume. About 12 works are presented in a season. The repertory includes operas for children as well as adults. On tour, the company is sometimes engaged to appear in performances with a local resident orchestra, choral group, or ballet company. Repertory includes Weber's "Abu Hassan," Pergolesi's "The Music Master," Barab's "Little Red Riding Hood," etc.

Minnesota

MINNESOTA OPERA COMPANY (formerly Center Opera Company of Walker Art Center), 1812 South 6th Street, Minneapolis, Minnesota 55404. Founded in January of 1963. General Manager: **John M. Ludwig.** Musical Director: **Philip Brunelle.** Stage Director: **H. Wesely Balk.** Designer: **Robert Israel.** The Minnesota Opera produces about four operas a season, giving altogether about 40 performances. The season runs from November to May, but this has varied in the past. The company is essentially a repertory company with its own regular casts selected on the basis of acting ability, voice, and other theatrical attributes. Performances take place mostly in Tyrone Guthrie Theatre (1,400 seats), and a few are performed in Cedar Village Theatre (500 seats). The group's instrumental accompaniment varies from orchestra to small chamber ensembles and solo instruments. All performers are professional. The company is devoted primarily to the presentation of contemporary opera, having produced over 20 works thus far, some as commissioned operas, others performed in their American premieres or as revivals. Among the new works, "Horspfal" by Eric Stokes, premiered in 1969; "Faust Counter Faust" by Gessner et al., premiered in 1971. U.S. premieres were given of Birtwistle's "Punch and Judy" (1970) and Egk's "Seventeen Days and Four Minutes" (1970), to name two operas. These and other productions have been taken on tour to New York and elsewhere; in fact, the Minnesota Opera is probably the first U.S. opera group to make guest appearances at summer festivals and as part of the season of other opera-producing groups. It has performed as part of the San Francisco Spring Opera season, the Ambler Festival, the Lake George Opera Festival, and at Wolf Trap Farm. Most of the newly commissioned works and those receiving American premieres have been avant-garde operas employing unconventional stage effects, music, mixed media devices, etc. Some more conventional contemporary works have also been performed, such as the operas of Britten, Kurka, Thomson, et al., and among the classics, works by Mozart, Haydn, and John Blow. The opera company is unusual in so far as it is part of the complex of a museum of modern art, the Walker Arts Center, and utilizes the Center's collaborating artists, designers, sculptors, and others who work in conjunction with stage and music directors. It has received grants from the Rockefeller Foundation, the McKnight Foundation, the National Endowment for the Arts, and others. Its budget is over a quarter of a million dollars. . . . SAINT PAUL OPERA ASSOCIATION, 143 West 4th Street, Saint Paul, Minnesota 55102. Founded in 1933. General Manager: **George M. Schaefer.** Music Director: **Igor Buketoff.** The company's season lasts from September to a summer season through the month of July. Seven operas are produced and presented in about 40 performances. Imported opera star singers are featured in fully staged productions, all of which are rehearsed and directed in Saint Paul. The full orchestra is a professional one. Performances take place in O'Shaughnessy Auditorium (1,500 seats) on the campus of the College of St. Catherine. The repertory consists of grand opera, infrequently performed works from the past, and modern operas; in addition, there is a season of musical comedy. In 1972, the company gave the American premiere of Nielsen's "Maskarade." Recent productions of contemporary opera include Hoiby's "Summer and Smoke," Floyd's "Of Mice and Men," and Antheil's "Venus in Africa."

Mississippi

MISSISSIPPI OPERA COMPANY, 4220 Eastover Place, Jackson, Mississippi 39211. (Formerly called Jackson Opera Guild.) Founded in 1945. Chairman: **Samuel Johnson.** President: **Mrs. John H. White, Jr.** Conductor: **Richard Alderson.** The season lasts three months. Two operas are produced and are given two performances each. Imported stars are engaged for leading roles, but resident singers are also used. The orchestra is composed of professional players. Regular performances are held in Jackson Municipal Auditorium (2,500 seats). Repertory is generally traditional.

Missouri

COLUMBIA LIGHT OPERA COMPANY, 110 Parkade Boulevard, Columbia, Missouri 65201. Founded in 1958. Administrative Head: **Kent Toalson.** Musical Director: **Harry Morrison.** Conductor: **Larry Sutherland.** One or two operas are produced and are usually given four or five performances during two months of the summer. Only resident singers are used. The orchestra is a combination of professionals and nonprofessionals. Regular performances are held in Stephens College Playhouse (300 seats). The company's repertory consists mostly of Gilbert and Sullivan and some contemporary light opera. . . . KANSAS CITY LYRIC THEATER, 823 Walnut, Suite 1200, Kansas City, Missouri 64106. Founded in 1958. General Director and Conductor since its inception has been **Russell Patterson.** Other conductors are: **George Lawner** and **Rudolph Fellner.** The Lyric's season is during the months of September and October. From 20 to 30 performances are staged of about five operas—mostly from the grand opera literature but including some contemporary works. Singing is in English. Casts are made up of young Americans who are selected by nationally held auditions. The singers are usually those who have some professional experience and who have sung with other opera groups in the country. Members of the orchestra are from the present and past ranks of the Kansas City Philharmonic. All productions are fully staged and originate with the company. The Lyric is credited with providing important stage experience to a number of opera singers who, since their appearances with the company, have become members of more well-known companies in the U.S. and abroad. The company has received grants from the Rockefeller Foundation, the Missouri State Council on the Arts and from other sources.

Nebraska

OMAHA OPERA COMPANY, INC., 4515 Military Avenue, Omaha, Nebraska 68104. Founded in 1958. President: **W. S. Matthews.** Musical Director: **Leo Kopp.** Performances are in January and May. Two operas are produced and are given five performances. Some resident singers are used; stars are engaged for leading roles. The orchestra used is professional. Regular performances are held in Omaha Civic Auditorium Music Hall (about 2,600 seats). . . . PINEWOOD BOWL OPERA, Nebraska Weslyan University, Lincoln, Nebraska 68504. Founded in 1950. Chairman: **Norma Carpenter.** Musical Director: **Oscar Bennett.** Orchestra Director: **Eugene Stoll.** Choral Director: **Hugh Rangeler.** During the opera season, one work from the light opera repertory is produced and is given four performances. Only resident singers are used. All performances are with orchestra. Performances are held in Pinewood Bowl (3,000 seats).

New Hampshire

HANOVER OPERA WORKSHOP, 2 Webster Terrace, Hanover, New Hampshire 03755. Founded in 1963. Musical Director: **Ruth Morton.** The workshop's season lasts for eight months, during which time two operas are produced. Four performances are given altogether. Only resident singers are used. Piano accompaniment is used for public performances. Some performances are in concert version. Regular performances are held in various locations including halls in Dartmouth College.

New Jersey

THE PATERSON LYRIC OPERA THEATRE, 309 Delaware Avenue, Paterson, N.J. 07503. Founded in 1958. Musical Director: **Armen Boyajian.** The opera season is nine months long; four operas are produced and eight performances are given. Only resident singers are used. The orchestra is composed of both amateurs and professionals. Piano accompaniment is used occasionally for public performances. In 1965–66 it performed Tchaikovsky's "Yolanta."

New Mexico

SANTA FE OPERA, c/o the Opera Association of New Mexico, P.O. Box 2408, Santa Fe, New Mexico 87501. Year round address: 156 East 52nd Street, New York, N.Y. 10022. Founded in 1957. General Director and Conductor: **John Crosby.** (For details on this opera company see Festivals.)

New York

AFTER DINNER OPERA COMPANY INC., 550 Fifth Avenue, New York, N.Y. 10036. Founded in 1949. General Manager and Stage Director: **Richard Flusser.** Musical Director: **Emanuel Levenson.** The season consists of 10 months of touring. About 17 operas are produced and given approximately 600 performances every year. No stars are engaged; but the resident singers are professionals. The company does not have its own orchestra, but performs with orchestras when it is engaged to participate in their series. Piano accompaniment is used most often for public performances. The company, chartered as a chamber opera organization to produce opera in English, has produced more than 20 world premieres. It has commissioned works and conducts research in order to choose suitable works for production. American operas have been introduced by the group to European audiences in Britain, Scotland, Germany, and Austria. Since 1963, the company has been so active it has created affiliate operatic groups: After Breakfast Opera, After Lunch Opera and After Supper Opera. For some time, the company had restricted itself to three singers. The roster now generally numbers about ten. After Dinner Opera Company was the first "off-Broadway" Company to perform at an international festival in Europe and the first to produce an omnibus evening of operas—seven short operas in a two-hour program—in New York City (1963). . . . AMATO OPERA THEATRE, INC., 319 Bowery, New York, N.Y. 10003. Founded in 1948. Director is **Anthony**

Amato. The company is a unique operatic venture. It presents intimate opera performances in its own theater, the 103-seat Amato Opera Showcase Theatre (above address), each Friday and Saturday evening from November to May. Piano is used for accompaniment. Singers are young, generally "unknowns" who are a sufficient number each season to provide for several cast changes; they also freely interchange roles. About 11 operas are produced, sung in the original language—all from the standard literature in any given season. The company also provides "Operas-in-Brief," a 90-minute presentation of opera made available for young audiences. . . . CHAUTAUQUA OPERA ASSOCIATION, Chautauqua Institution, Chautauqua, N.Y. 14722. (Opera has been presented at Chautauqua since the early 1920's.) Part of the Chautauqua Summer Music Programs (see Festivals). Director: **Leonard Treash.** Musical Director: **Evan Whallon.** Conductors: **Evan Whallon** and **Richard Voitaght.** The season lasts through the months of July and August. Six or seven operas are produced in a total of about 14 performances. Guest artists are engaged from the Metropolitan Opera and other companies. The orchestra used is a professional one. Regular performances are held in Norton Hall (1,200 seats). All operas are sung in English and are fully staged. Verdi's "Otello," Wagner's "The Flying Dutchman," Smetana's "The Bartered Bride," were among the operas presented in 1972. A Broadway musical is usually part of the schedule of productions. . . . CITY CENTER GILBERT & SULLIVAN COMPANY, c/o New York State Theater, Lincoln Center Plaza, New York, N.Y. 10023. Founded in 1961. General Director: **Felix Popper.** Conductors and Music Staff: **David Effron, Thomas Martin, Felix Popper, Byron Dean Ryan, Judith Somogi.** The season is four weeks long, lasting from April through May. During this time 29 performances are given of the five operas produced. Only resident singers are used. The orchestra is professional. Regular performances are held in City Center Theater, 131 West 55th Street, New York City (3,000 seats). . . . FBN OPERA WORKSHOP, (New York Opera Theatre and Workshop) c/o 42–55 Colden Street, Apartment 7H, Flushing, N.Y. 11355. Administrative Head: **Lee Fowler.** Conductor: **Mimi Stern-Wolfe.** The season lasts from September through June. About 12 performances are given of the three or four operas produced. Piano accompaniment is used in all performances. FBN teaches complete operatic roles to young professional singers. FBN has received grants from the New York State Council on the Arts and has received an award from the National Jewish Welfare Board. FBN performances are held in Educational Alliance–Isidor Strauss Theatre, 197 East Broadway, New York (500 seats). . . . FIFTH AVENUE OPERA ASSOCIATION, 1270 Fifth Avenue, Suite 75, New York, N.Y. 10029. Founded in August, 1961. General Manager and Musical Director is **Stanley L. Friedberg.** There are additional conductors, costume and set designers, and several stage directors. Five operas are presented during a season that runs from September to June of each year. Each opera, taken from the classic–romantic repertory, is prepared in a condensed, English version of about an hour's duration. About 100 performances are scheduled each year. Singers are engaged from the Metropolitan Opera, New York City Opera, the Goldovsky Opera Theater, and other companies and groups. There are no stars as such; an emphasis on ensemble work is basic to the productions, which are specially devised for presentation in elementary and high schools, music academies, cultural centers, colleges, and universities. Performances are sung to audiences ranging upwards from kindergarten level. Altogether, over one million students, parents, and teachers have had the opportunity to witness these special productions. Their goal, in addition to providing entertainment, is to develop imagination, a familiarity with the art form of opera, and to use opera as an educational tool for adding a new dimension to the teaching of history, spelling, human behavior, geography, etc. Generally, in the schools, pre- and post-performance educational projects are coordinated with the opera being presented. . . . FRIENDS OF FRENCH OPERA, 162 West

54th Street, Suite 5A, New York, N.Y. 10014. Founded in 1962. Administrative Head: **George Bassett Robert.** Musical Director: **Robert Lawrence.** Two or three performances are given every season. Stars are engaged for leading roles. The orchestra is professional. Performances are held in Carnegie Hall. . . . GREATER UTICA OPERA GUILD, 1153 Hammond Avenue, Utica, N.Y. 13501. Founded in 1965. Guild President: **George Betro.** Co-Artistic Directors: **Robert Murray** and **Pasquale Caputo.** Production Coordinator: **Charlotte Williams.** A spring and fall season respectively of three performances of one opera and one concert version or scene program. Only resident singers are used. Guest artists are only used in case of illness. The orchestra is a local one made up of both professionals and amateurs. Performances are held in Proctor High School Auditorium (1,350 seats). . . . THE INTERSTATE OPERA ASSOCIATION, INC., P.O. Box 3109, Grand Central Station, New York, N.Y. 10017. Founded 1968. Musical Director and Conductor is **Eugene Papay.** Artistic Director: **Gloria B. Grayson.** Administrative Head is **Rachelle Lazarre.** The company operates an eight-month season, presenting about eight productions from a repertory of about 18 operas, all of which are drawn from the standard repertory. It uses about 50 singers. Operas are usually staged, although some are performed in concert version. An orchestra made up of both professional players and students is used, but some performances have piano as accompaniment. The company functions as a nonprofit, tax-exempt organization. It claims to be the only opera company offering intermediate performance opportunities to professional-calibre singers between the singing and acting experience on the workshop/studio level and the larger professional houses, without requiring the singers to pay a fee. . . . INWOOD CHAMBER OPERA PLAYERS, 32 Orange Street, Brooklyn, N.Y. 11201. Founded in 1956. Musical Director: **Elizabeth Rodgers.** Administrative Head: **Susanne Edelman.** The Inwood Players hires itself out to organizations and schools or performs *gratis* in hospitals, nursing homes, etc. Repertory is performed only in English and consists only of chamber operas in staged productions. The Players have performed works by Mozart, Arne, Cimarosa, Galuppi, Offenbach, Pergolesi, and others. . . . ITHACA OPERA ASSOCIATION, INC., 208 Muriel Street, Ithaca, N.Y. 14850. Founded in 1950. Artistic Director: **Ken C. Baumann.** Musical Director: **Robert J. Prins.** The season covers 12 months a year. Two operas are produced and are given two performances each. Resident singers are used, although singers from other cities are sometimes engaged. The orchestra used is professional. Piano accompaniment is used in workshop only. Regular performances by the association are held in Statler Hall of Cornell University (about 900 seats). Repertory is of modern and standard works. . . . LAKE GEORGE OPERA FESTIVAL, Box 471, Glens Falls, N.Y. 12801. Founded in 1962. (see also Festivals.) General Director: **David Lloyd.** Musical Directors: **Paul Callaway, Rudolph Doblin, John Moriarity.** Opera is presented during the months of July and August. Five operas are produced and are given about 34 performances. Only residents are used. The orchestra is composed of professional players. During the 1968 season the world premiere of Amram's "Twelfth Night" was given. The festival received the New York State Award in 1967. Regular performances are held in Queensbury School Auditorium in Glens Falls (750 seats). . . . THE LITTLE ORCHESTRA SOCIETY, 1860 Broadway, New York, N.Y. 10023. Founded in 1947. Musical Director and Conductor: **Thomas K. Scherman.** Administrative Head: **Herbert Barrett.** The season spans six months of the year. Three operas are produced in concert version with The Little Orchestra and well-known singers. Regular performances are held in Philharmonic Hall of Lincoln Center (2,800 seats). The society has given the North American premiere of Orff's "Antigonae" and the New York premiere of Janáček's "The Makropulos Affair." Repertory includes such works as Strauss's "Egyptian Helen" and Janáček's "Jenufa." . . . LONG ISLAND OPERA SHOWCASE, INC., 699 Plato Street, Franklin Square, N.Y. 11010. Founded in 1961. President: **Walter Chmara.** Musical Director: **Bernard Hart.** The season lasts from September through May, plus summer performances. Ten to fifteen operas are produced, and about 25 to 30 performances are given. The orchestra, when used, is composed of both professionals and nonprofessionals, but most performances are with piano accompaniment. The Opera Showcase is hired often for fund-raising purposes. Regular performances are held in either of two high school auditoriums (each with about 500 seats). . . . THE LYRIC ARTS OPERA, INC., 160 West 73rd Street, New York, N.Y. 10023. Founded in 1959. Held in Port Jervis, New York. Administrative Head: **Grace Panvini.** Musical Director: **Curtis Rice.** Six operas are produced, in six performances during July and August. Some resident singers are used; stars are engaged for leading roles. Piano is the only accompaniment. Performances are held in Port Jervis (New York) High School (about 700 seats). . . . METROPOLITAN OPERA ASSOCIATION, Lincoln Center Plaza, New York, N.Y. 10023. Founded in 1883. It is the oldest continuously run opera company in the United States and the largest and most complex music performing organization in the world. Including post-season and pre-season activities, the Metropolitan is in operation 52 weeks of the year. Its performing facility, the Metropolitan Opera House on the Plaza in the Lincoln Center complex, is the largest opera house in the world, with a seating and standing capacity of 3,973. Among the world's opera-producing organizations, the artistic rank of the Metropolitan is exceedingly high. The text that follows is a statistical and logistical summary of the Met's operation with a brief reference to its past. The Metropolitan was established in its own house, erected on the corner of 39th Street and Broadway in New York. Its first production in 1883 was Gounod's "Faust." It occupied that site until its move to Lincoln Center for the 1966–67 season. Its earliest productions and seasons were under the artistic direction of several impresarios until 1908, when general manager Giulio Gatti-Casazza's record-setting tenure began, one that lasted until 1935. His successors and their dates in office were Herbert Witherspoon (1935; died shortly after his appointment); Edward Johnson (1935–1950); **Rudolf Bing** (1950–1972), who presided over the Met's most spectacular period of growth and change, Goeran Gentele, from Sweden, whose appointment began July 1, 1972, but ended with his death on July 18, 1972, and the current General Manager, **Schuyler G. Chapin.** Throughout its history, the Metropolitan has engaged the great singers and conductors of the day and staged many operas outside what is now termed the standard opera repertory. These have included new works, both American and foreign, and lesser-known works from the past. The Metropolitan Opera Association, Inc., established in the 1930's, is a nonprofit corporation governing the activities of the Met. Its policies are set forth by a Board of Directors of 42, elected by the Association, which is composed of some 55 additional members. The Board of Directors meets monthly; each member serves a three-year term. The Board elects its own officers. The general membership meets annually. All officers and directors serve without remuneration. The Met's General Manager and assistant managers are appointed by the Board. The Association has organized within its membership several Standing Committees for various functions as their names imply: nominating committee, production committee, development and finance committees, etc. Other committees are formed for certain long-range projects. Corporate officers for the 1971–72 season were as follows: **Lowell Wadmond,** Chairman of the Board; **Langdon Van Norden,** Vice Chairman; **George S. Moore,** President (the position is that of chief executive officer of the Association); **James F. Jaffray,** Treasurer; **Paul Hallingby, Jr.,** Secretary. Honorary Chairman of the Board is **G. Lauder Greenway;** Emeritus Director of the Board is **Mrs. August Belmont.** Of the Executive Committee (one of the Standing Committees), **William Rockefeller** is Chairman. Members of the Association are prominent in business, finance, law, the arts, etc. The General Manager is responsible for all artistic and production matters and the administrative organization; he is responsible, in turn, to the Metropolitan Opera Association, through its President. Serving under the General Manager in all artistic, technical, financial, and logistical departments are altogether some 1,000 employees, 90 percent of whom belong to some 14 trade unions (including the American Guild of Musical Artists, American Federation of Musicians, United Scenic Artists, Theatrical Stage Employees, and others covering stage crews, press agents, engineers, wardrobe aides, etc.). The musical staff for the 1970–71 season consisted of 136 solo singers including major artists and those singing supporting roles; half of the total number of singers are engaged for only a few performances during the season, and are paid by performance, and the remaining half are engaged throughout the year, with the singers in this group on weekly salary. (It is the policy of the Met to have three singers available for each part needed in performance, in order to meet emergencies.) There are 28 conductors and associate and assistant conductors; a 91-member orchestra playing five times a week and rehearsing some three or four days weekly; the chorus is made up of 78 regulars, and the ballet troupe of 37 regulars is sometimes augmented by additional dancers as needed. Both the chorus and the ballet corps are under a 52-week contract. Stage managers and directors, rehearsal pianists, prompters, and others make up the balance of the performing staff. The performing segment of the Met is backed up by various stage and shop technical personnel. Among them: a carpenter shop of 30 working in wood, metal, and plastics, constructing new scenery and repairing old; 7 property shop workers for making and repairing all props; a tailor shop of 32; 12 workers in a scenery department; some 9 wig and makeup artists; a wardrobe department of 14 handling, cleaning, and repairing all costumes, shoes, jewelry, etc.; an electric department of 48 technicians of all kinds; and 88 stage hands for scenery and props on stage and in rehearsal areas. The administrative staff consists of top management, subscription staff, and others handling press, financial matters, etc.—altogether about 120. Members of the administration are as follows: General Manager: **Schuyler G. Chapin;** Assistant Manager: **Francis Robinson;** Director of Finance: **William H. Hadley;** Executive Assistant: **Eva Popper;** House Manager: **James Heffernan;** Comptroller: **William H. Rahe;** Artistic Administrator: **Charles Riecker;** Technical Administrator: **Michael Bronson;** Company Manager and Musical Secretary: **Frank Paola;** Production Coordinators: **Charles Bonheur** and **Jay Rutherford;** Press Representative: **Ann Gordon;** Box Office Manager: **Alfred F. Hubay;** Budget Director: **John Zangara;** Director of Development: **Floyd Landis;** Box Office Treasurer: **Sol Wallace;** and others, including administrative assistants and staff. Beginning with 1973, the Met will have a full-fledged Music Director in the person of conductor, **Rafael Kubelik.** Of the performing artists, a random selection from the roster of the 1971–72 season yields the following names (sopranos, mezzos and contraltos, tenors, baritones, and basses): **Lucine Amara, Martina Arroyo, Grace Bumbry, Montserrat Caballé, Lili Chookasian, Regine Crespin, Rosalind Elias, Dorothy Kirsten, Evelyn Lear, Jean Madeira, Edith Mathis, Mildred Miller, Anna Moffo, Birgit Nilsson, Roberta Peters, Leontyne Price, Nell Rankin, Judith Raskin, Elinor Ross, Leonie Rysanek, Renata Scotto, Anja Silja, Teresa Stratas, Joan Sutherland, Renata Tebaldi, Shirley Verrett, Sandra Warfield; John Alexander, Lorenzo Alvary, Carlo Bergonzi, Walter Berry, Gene Boucher, Russell Christopher, Franco Corelli, Fernando Corena, Justino Díaz, Placido Domingo, William Dooley, Loren Driscoll, Ezio Flagello, Nicolai Gedda, Tito Gobbi, Robert Goodloe, Donald Gramm, Frank Guarrera, Jerome Hines, William Lewis, Cornell MacNeil, Rod MacWherter, James McCracken, Morley Meredith, Robert Merrill, Sherill Milnes, Barry Morell, Hermann Prey, John Reardon, Mario Sereni, George Shirley, Cesare Siepi, Thomas Stewart, Jess Thomas, Giorgio Tozzi, Richard Tucker, Theodor Uppman, Andrea Velis, Jon Vickers,** and **William Walker.** The Met's conducting staff varies each year but recent seasons have included among the chief conductors: **Kurt Adler, Franz Allers, Karl Böhm,**

Richard Bonynge, Josef Krips, James Levine, Alain Lombard, Zubin Mehta, Jean Morel, Thomas Schippers; Associate Conductors have been: **Jan Behr, Martin Rich, Ignace Strasfogel,** and **Walter Taussig.** Opera productions have been staged in recent seasons by **Jean-Louis Barrault, Henry Butler, Herbert Graf, Alfred Lunt, Nathaniel Merrill, Günther Rennert, Cyril Richard, Otto Schenk, Margherita Wallmann, Dino Yannopoulos,** and **Franco Zeffirelli.** Designers have been: **Boris Aronson, Cecil Beaton, Marc Chagall, Frederick Fox, Rolf Gerard, Rudolf Heinrich, Wolfgang Roth,** and others. The Met's Ballet group is directed by **Milko Sparemblek; Audrey Keane** is Ballet Mistress. Choreographers for the Metropolitan's opera dance sequences include **Thomas Andrew, William Burdick, John Butler, Lele de Triana, Katherine Dunham, Dame Alicia Markova,** and others for a total of from 6 to 10 choreographers on the annual roster. Three organizations are affiliated with the Metropolitan Opera Association; two, the Metropolitan Opera Studio and the Metropolitan Opera National Council, are part of the corporate structure, and the third, the Metropolitan Opera Guild, Inc., is a separate corporation. Both the Guild and the National Council were founded by **Mrs. August Belmont,** a figure probably unique in the annals of opera. They were founded respectively in 1935 and 1952. The Guild, a nonprofit membership organization, was set up to generate wide interest in opera and to help support the Metropolitan. Its 70,000 members are spread throughout the United States and in some sixty foreign countries. It is known to the opera public at large as the publisher of *Opera News* magazine, and for a wide variety of services geared toward promoting opera in general and improving the level of the understanding of it. Through membership contributions and with income realized from its services, the Guild has contributed over $5 million to the Metropolitan Opera Association. (For further details on the Guild, see Organizations.) Although the Guild works to promote all opera as a cultural force, the Metropolitan Opera National Council directs its efforts to developing nationwide support and participation not only in opera in general but in the Metropolitan Opera *per se* as a singular national institution. It underwrites and administers the well-known Regional Auditions Program of the Met, which finds new talent for the company and helps to establish their careers (see Contests, Awards); it sponsors the Central Opera Service (see Organizations); and it finances new opera productions at the Met as well as those adapted for the company's annual spring tour. Since 1952, the Council has underwritten the cost of 14 new Met productions. The Council's membership consists of about 650 men and women in civic affairs, business, the arts, etc., from throughout the U.S., Puerto Rico, Canada, the Bahamas, and Australia. Funds contributed by the members vary annually; during the 1970–71 season, some $100,000 was raised by the Council for the Met's spring tour. A large percentage of Council members provided additional financial support to the Met as Patrons of the Metropolitan Opera. Members of the Council are also active in support of opera companies and workshops in their localities. President of the National Council is **Alexander Saunderson** (of California). The Metropolitan Opera Studio functions as a junior opera ensemble. Founded by former Assistant Manager **John Gutman** in 1960, the Studio presents young singers, some of them winners of the Metropolitan Opera Auditions, in modest, scaled-down productions of operas, scenes from operas, and educational programs of opera called "Introduction to Opera." These programs are meant to provide young audiences in New York City, in other communities in New York State, and in other Eastern states, with a chance to hear and see opera—often for the first time—and to help young opera singers gain experience. More than 250 performances by the Studio have been given each year in over 140 cities and towns. Most of the performances are devised to fit school schedules, but the Studio has developed special concerts of opera and art songs and other entertainments for general audiences. Studio performers have appeared for the Newport (Rhode Island) Festival (q.v.) and have toured under separate concert management

(Sheldon Soffer Management, Inc.) as the Metropolitan Opera Studio Ensemble. (See separate entry on the Studio for further details.) The repertory of the Metropolitan Opera focuses on grand opera and all that its traditions imply. A typical season will have a mixture of standard works from the German, Italian, French, and sometimes Russian opera literature. These will include some new productions. Since moving to Lincoln Center, the Met has produced only two works new to opera, each in their world premieres and each written on commission in celebration of the new House. These were **Samuel Barber's** "Anthony and Cleopatra," and **Marvin David Levy's** "Mourning Becomes Electra," both staged during the 1966–67 season. Occasionally the Met will revive an opera from the past such as Weber's "Der Freischütz," which had not been heard at the Met since 1928–29. Beyond these novelties, there are few operas in the Met repertory that do not belong to the traditional fare. Operating within this concept of repertory, the Met strives to present productions of the standard literature in some new way—with a new dramatic approach or some novel aesthetic concept—with varying degrees of success. For the 1970–71 season, the most recent year for which a seasonal report is possible, the Metropolitan presented 26 operas in a total of 292 performances divided as follows: 202 subscription performances for the regular season running from September 14, 1970 to April 17, 1971 (31 weeks); 22 performances were offered outside the subscription series; the six-week tour to other cities ending on May 29, 1971 presented 42 performances; the tour was followed by the now-annual series, the June Festival, in New York City (see Festivals), when 14 performances are staged during two weeks; and the final offering before beginning rehearsals for the new season: three weeks of free concerts in New York City Parks (see Festivals), when 12 performances are produced. The 1970–71 season included four new productions, five benefit performances and seven student performances. Seasons previous to that of 1970 follow the same general ratio of total operas and new productions. The actual performing year for the Metropolitan is, therefore, a total of 42 weeks. That the Metropolitan Opera considers itself a national cultural institution rather than an opera company serving New York City is based on a number of activities without which its claim to a national following would be impossible. Most important, perhaps, are the annual tours and the annual season of Saturday afternoon broadcasts of live performances direct from the Met's stage. The work of the Met Studio and that of the Metropolitan Opera Guild are also directed to the nation at large, and of course, the roster of Metropolitan artists is one that is drawn upon by many professional opera companies in the United States. Singers, conductors, and others who formerly were associated with the Metropolitan are to be found in the leading music schools and music departments of colleges and universities throughout the country, where their influence on future opera lovers and performers is incalculable. The Met's tours have been a tradition with the company since its beginning and, with the exception of four years, have been undertaken annually. The tours involve the entire company—about 300 singers, musicians, dancers, etc. Lately, the tours have been to Boston, Cleveland, Atlanta, Memphis, Dallas, Minneapolis, and Detroit. Audience attendance for the six weeks of tours is about 200,000 annually. The Met receives a fee of $48,000 for each tour performance, which is paid by the host city's sponsoring organization (also responsible for the sale of tickets). Despite this fee, which may be increased in future seasons, the cost of the tours to the Met is more than its total receipts from all sources on tour. The weekly Saturday broadcasts are the strongest link the Met has to opera fans throughout the United States. They have been presented since 1931 and since 1940 have been carried by the same sponsor, Texaco, the longest commercial sponsorship of a coast-to-coast broadcast series in radio history. The opera performances are aired over a special network, the Texaco Metropolitan Opera Radio Network, which includes 218 stations in all fifty states, Puerto Rico, and in Canada through that country's broadcasting system. No count of the Saturday broadcast audience is possible, except to conjecture that the total is in the millions. In the field of recordings, the Metropolitan has been inactive for over a decade. [The opening opera for the 1972–73 season, "Carmen," was recorded by Deutsche Grammophon Gesellschaft (*DGG*). This recording, not yet issued at the time of this writing, is the first in 14 years for the Met.] Some of the recordings of the past are still available commercially (they include reissues of performances of considerable age) on *Columbia, Odyssey,* and *RCA Victor* labels. Operating expenses for the Metropolitan for the 1970–71 season (with some figures as estimates) totaled $20 million. Ticket and operating income was $15.7 million; this, plus $4.1 million in contributions, provided an income of $19.8 million. About 81 percent of the operating expenses went to payroll costs: $16.2 million. Of this amount, 43 percent paid the artistic staff and 18 percent went to stage personnel wages. Half of the artistic staff payroll, or $4 million, covered the cost of engaging principal singers. Orchestra costs were 10 percent of the whole operating expenses—or $2 million. Chorus and ballet costs together were 7 percent, or $1.5 million. Of the non-payroll costs of some $3.8 million, $600,000 was for the acquisition and maintenance of scenery and costumes; $1 million was for travel and transfer (the latter of sets and costumes from warehouses to the Opera House and costs on tour); $1 million for building maintenance and operations; and $1.2 million for administrative and other costs. Of the Met's income total of $19.8 million, 63 percent (or $12.8 million) was exclusively box office receipts. The Metropolitan could not operate without income raised from its many annual fund-raising drives. Contributory income comes from a number of sources. Approximately 38 percent of all contributions to the Met come from the so-called Patrons Program administered by the Association's Development Committee. Under the program some 800 individual patrons have agreed to an annual contribution of $1,000 or more, and over 100 business-firm patrons have agreed to contribute $2,500 or more each year. Voluntary contributions made by subscribers to the Met generally constitute about 16 or 18 percent. For the 1970–71 season this figure meant some $643,000 raised from 63 percent of the total number of subscribers. Other contributions come from the Metropolitan Opera Guild and the National Council. For the years 1969 and 1970, contributions from these two organizations were over $900,000. Outside income also comes from various gifts intended to underwrite specific opera productions, which, although they cover actual production costs, cause a general increase in expenditures needed to administer them. Some limited income comes from foundations and government sources. The City of New York contributes about one fourth the cost of the free summer concerts. In 1970, the New York State Council on the Arts made its first contribution to the Met, a sum of $328,000 to help with the cost of the free park concerts and the activities, largely educational, of the Met Studio. No government funds have ever been received for opera production during the regular season at Lincoln Center. The deficit situation of the Metropolitan Opera is often cited by arts organizations, arts lobbyists, and arts economic analysts as a classic example of the impossibility of supporting a high standard of opera in an inflationary economy without substantial outside support, despite realistic efforts to reduce costs of operation and maintain high performance attendance records. In the latter instance, the Metropolitan has a ten-year average of over 95 percent of capacity audience. Finally, some miscellaneous statistics regarding the Metropolitan Opera: a quarter to a half million different people attend the Met during the regular season; in addition, some 200,000 attend its performances on tour. Over 200,000 people, mostly students, attend performances of the Metropolitan Opera Studio; about 1,250,000 people visit the Opera House each year as part of tours, Guild-sponsored performances, and to see visiting ballet and opera companies. . . .

METROPOLITAN OPERA STUDIO, Lincoln Center Plaza, New York, N.Y. 10023. Founded in 1960. Director: **William Nix.** Music Director: **Marshall Williamson.** The season lasts from August through the end of May. Four operas in condensed version are produced and are given more than 250 performances. About 35 young resident singers are used; stars are not engaged. The orchestra, when used, is a professional one. Some performances are in concert version; piano accompaniment is most often used. Performances are usually held in college and high school auditoriums at the invitation of those schools. The Studio is an integral part of the Metropolitan Opera Association and receives operating funds from the Association and the Metropolitan Opera Guild. Deficits are covered by the Metropolitan Opera. The Studio receives $20,000 from Lincoln Center; it has also received over $100,000 from the New York Council on the Arts for a single season's activities. The Studio's large annual deficit (about $250,000) is in fact demonstrative of the Studio's high level of activity and the low rates for which it lends itself out for what are essentially educational performances of opera. . . . NEW YORK CITY OPERA, New York State Theater, Lincoln Center Plaza, New York, N.Y. 10023. Founded in 1944. Directors since its founding have been (in order): Laszlo Halasz, Joseph Rosenstock, **Erich Leinsdorf,** and since 1957, **Julius Rudel.** The New York City Opera is a constituent member of the City Center of Music and Drama, established by the City of New York. President: **Mayor John V. Lindsay** (and subsequent mayors); Chairman of the Board: **Richard M. Clurman;** and Executive Director: **Norman Singer.** (Other member performing-arts groups with the City Center are the New York City Ballet, at Lincoln Center, and, at City Center Theater, the City Center Joffrey Ballet and others.) Although statistically the City Opera is the second largest in the United States, many consider it to be second to none artistically. In originality, variety of repertory, staging, cast, etc., the company is often considered to be superior to any in the nation and is certainly one of the leading opera companies in the world. It presents two seasons in a calendar year, a fall season and a winter–spring season. Performances take place in the New York State Theater of Lincoln Center (2,729 seats). Following each season is an out-of-town series respectively in Washington, D.C. at the John F. Kennedy Center for the Performing Arts, and in the Los Angeles Music Center. From September 1971 to May 1972, the seasonal year, by way of example, was organized as follows. The company's 54th season ran from September to November for a period of 11 weeks, during which 17 operas were staged for a total of 86 performances. The repertory included three new productions, "Albert Herring," "Carmen," and "Susannah," and operas from the standard literature, as well as such infrequently performed works as Handel's "Giulio Cesare," Boito's "Mefistofele," and Donizetti's "Roberto Devereux." The season's tickets were available in 22 subscription series with performances every evening from Tuesday to Sunday plus matinees on Saturday and Sunday. The 54th season was followed by a three-week engagement in Los Angeles from November 17 to December 5, during which 10 operas were given a total of 21 performances. The 55th season ran from February 23 to April 30 (10 weeks) and offered 19 operas for a total of 79 performances. The repertory contained works from previous seasons as well as new productions, "Maria Stuarda," and the New York premiere of Lee Hoiby's "Summer and Smoke." These performances were also available in 22 subscription series. The 55th season was followed by a two-week stay at Kennedy Center in Washington, D.C., where five operas were presented for a total of 15 performances. Altogether the two seasons and the out-of-town engagements covered a period of 26 weeks, during which 201 performances were staged. Throughout its history, the company has been known for its ensemble work, youthful vigor, its emphasis on actor-singers and the dramatic qualities of opera. The veterans of the company are among the leading singers of opera in America. The repertory since 1944 has included not only the standard operas, some sung in English translation, but also many American operas, operas long neglected or only infrequently performed, and foreign contemporary works. Among the world premieres since 1944 have been Copland's "The Tender Land," (1954), Kurka's "Good Soldier Schweik" (1958), Weisgall's "Six Characters in Search of an Author" (1959), Moore's "The Wings of the Dove" (1961), Ward's

"The Crucible" (1961), Beeson's "Lizzie Borden" (1965), and Rorem's "Miss Julie" (1965). American premieres include Strauss's "Ariadne auf Naxos" (1946), Orff's "The Moon" (1956), Strauss's "The Silent Woman" (1958), Egk's "The Inspector General" (1960), Prokofiev's "The Flaming Angel," and others. Other operas have been those performed in New York for the first time or receiving their first staged production in America. Among the less familiar operatic fare staged by the company have been: "Love for Three Oranges," Kern's "Show Boat," "The Golden Slippers" of Tchaikovsky, Verdi's "Macbeth," Monteverdi's "Orfeo," "Porgy and Bess," and others. The spring 1972 roster of singers had 24 sopranos, 12 mezzos and contraltos, 16 tenors, and 23 baritones and basses. Among the well-known singers: **Judith Anthony, Patricia Brooks, Joy Clements, Carol Neblett, Maralin Niska, Nancy Shade, Beverly Sills, Frances Bible, Kay Creed, Joy Davidson, Muriel Greenspon, David Clatworthy, Dominic Cossa, Michael Devlin, Chester Ludgin, Spiro Malas, Louis Quilico, John Reardon, Norman Treigle, Michele Molese,** and **Salvador Novoa.** The conducting and music staff (altogether about 15) include **Julius Rudel, Christopher Keene, Thomas P. Martin, Giusseppe Morelli, Felix Popper, Judith Somogi, Walter Susskind,** and **Charles Wilson.** Among the directors and staging staff: **Tito Capobianco, Frank Corsaro, Theodore Mann. Thomas Andrews** is Director of Ballet; **Chris Nance** is Chorus Master. Among the company's administrative staff are: **John S. White,** Managing Director; **Felix Popper,** Music Administrator; **Daniel R. Rule,** Assistant Manager; **Hans Sondheimer,** Production Coordinator. Other personnel are administrative assistants, press representatives, librarian, costumers, wigmakers, et al. The company's budget is about $4 million. Income is from the sale of tickets; special gifts for production purposes; grants from foundations including the Rockefeller and Ford Foundations, the National Endowment for the Arts, the New York Arts Council; and private contributors. The company has its own fund-raising arm, the New York City Opera Guild. This organization, composed of volunteer help, is affiliated with The Friends of the City Center, which seeks funds for the total City Center community. Membership is open to anyone upon payment of annual fees ranging from $15 to $1,000 and above. As with other organizations of this type, membership is in exchange for certain privileges such as rehearsal attendance, seminars, and special events. President of the Guild is **Mrs. Martha Moore Sykes.** Director of the Executive Committee is **Richard Mealey.** Available recordings of productions of the New York City Opera are on *RCA Victor, Columbia, Desto,* and *CRI* labels. . . . NEW YORK STATE OPERA SOCIETY, INC., 2109 Broadway, New York, N.Y. 10023. Founded in 1959. Director: **Carl Yost.** Conductor: **Anthony Morales.** The season runs nine months, during which six to eight performances are given by the Society. The orchestra used is a combination of professional and nonprofessional players. The Society is an educational group which presents standard works in their original languages in fully staged productions with orchestra, chorus, and ballet. Regular performances are held in Palm Gardens (1,000 seats). . . . OPERA THEATRE OF NEW YORK, INC., 344 West 89th Street, New York, N.Y. 10024. Founded in 1963. Administrative Head: **Richard Barri.** Musical Directors: **James Howe** and **Thomas Nichols.** This is a touring company operating for ten months a year. Eleven operas have been produced, and each year the company gives about 130 performances. Its own roster of singers are used. Piano accompaniment is used for public performances. The company stresses the theatrical aspects in opera and specializes in Shakespeare-inspired operas. It tours universities and other schools primarily and has made three coast-to-coast tours. It has appeared at festivals, on television, at the New York World's Fair, and in park performances. . . . OPERA UNDER THE STARS, 18 Tuxford Road, Rochester, N.Y. 14534. Founded in 1953. Producer-Director: **Leonard Treash.** Conductor: **Herman Genhart.** A summer series held in June and July. Three operas are produced for a total of six performances. Resident singers, graduates of the Eastman School of Music, and artists from

New York and Europe are used. The orchestra is professional. Performances are held outdoors in Highland Park Bowl, Rochester (8,000 to 15,000 attendance per performance). Operas are all sung in English and are from the standard opera literature; an occasional modern work is performed ("Susannah," "The Crucible," "The Taming of the Shrew," etc.). . . . QUEENS OPERA ASSOCIATION, INC. P.O. Box 172, Jamaica, N.Y. 11435. Founded in 1961. (Formerly the Messina Opera Company.) Administrative Head: **Joseph Messina.** Musical Directors: **Richard Woitach** and **Kurt Saffir.** The season in the spring lasts from March through May and in the fall from October through November. About 8 to 10 operas are produced and 12 to 20 performances given. Both guest artists and resident singers are featured. The orchestra is professional. Regular performances are held in Francis Lewis Auditorium (about 1,000 seats). . . . TRI-CITIES OPERA, INC., 315 Clinton Street, Binghampton, N.Y. 13905. Founded in 1949. Executive Director: **Mrs. George Ainslie.** Artistic Directors: **Peyton M. Hibbitt** and **Carmen S. Savoca.** The season lasts from October through May. Two full-length operas, one chamber opera, and one choral concert are produced and are presented for a total of 23 performances. Resident singers are used. The orchestra is a combination of professionals and nonprofessionals—all paid. Regular performances are held in Binghampton Masonic Temple (600 seats) and Opera Center (300 seats) at the above address. The company received a grant from Martha Baird Rockefeller Fund for costumes and scenery in a production of "La Bohème." It holds weekly opera workshop classes and owns its own rehearsal hall with facilities for making scenery, costumes, and for presenting chamber opera. . . . TURNAU OPERA ASSOCIATION, INC., c/o National Music League, 130 West 56th Street, New York, N.Y. 10019. Founded in 1959. Administrative Head: **Ward J. Pinner.** Musical Director: **Warren G. Wilson.** The season includes six weeks during the summer, six weeks during the winter, and a three-month period of tours. Eight operas are produced during the season and are given 85 performances. Resident singers are featured. Piano accompaniment is used for regular performances. The company performs with orchestra when hired to do so. Regular performances are held in the Auditorium of S.U.N.Y. at New Paltz and Asolo Theatre in Sarasota, Florida. . . . VILLAGE LIGHT OPERA GROUP LTD., Box 143, Village Station, New York, N.Y. 10014. Founded in 1935. President: **Norman K. Keller.** Musical Director: **Ronald W. Noll.** Two operas are produced every season and are given usually four performances. The orchestra used is made up of professional players. Piano accompaniment is used on occasion. Some performances are given in concert version. The group is a nonprofit, nonprofessional Gilbert and Sullivan group performing all operas in the Gilbert and Sullivan repertory. Regular performances are held in Fashion Institute Theater (800 seats).

North Carolina

BREVARD MUSIC CENTER OPERA WORKSHOP, P.O. Box 592, Brevard, North Carolina 28712. Founded in 1965. General Director: **John R. McCrae.** Musical Director: **Henry Janiec.** Summer season in July and August. Six operas are produced and are given one performance each. Resident singers and guests for leading roles. The orchestra is composed of professionals and students. Performances are held in Brevard Music Center (1,500 seats). . . . CHARLOTTE OPERA ASSOCIATION, INC., 519 Fenton Place, Charlotte, North Carolina 28207. Founded in 1948. General Director: **John R. McCrae.** Musical Director: **Charles Rosekrans.** Three operas are produced and performed once; a free youth matinee is also given. Invited opera stars were used for the first time in the 1967–68 season. The orchestra is a combination of professional and nonprofessional players. Regular performances are held in Ovens Auditorium, Charlotte, North Carolina (2,500 seats). The Association owns its own Workshop–Rehearsal building. . . . NATIONAL OPERA COMPANY, Box 12000, Raleigh, North Carolina 27605. Founded

1948 as the Grass Roots Opera Company. President: **A. J. Fletcher.** Musical Director: **Robert Schaaf.** General Manager: **D. M. Witherspoon.** The season lasts from January through April. Three operas are produced and are given a total of 70 to 75 performances. Singers are selected from national auditions. Piano accompaniment is used. The company is a touring group, covering about 15 states annually. It has performed in numerous schools for children in North Carolina. An estimated 1 million school children have attended the National's performances. All operas are sung in English.

Ohio

AMERICAN NEW OPERA THEATRE SOCIETY, P.O. Box 5503, Cleveland, Ohio 44101. Founded in 1954. Artistic and Musical Director: **Leslie Kondorossy.** Several performances are given yearly with professional and amateur singers. Productions are either staged or in concert form. Repertory includes mainly one-act contemporary chamber works, a number of them having been written by **Leslie Kondorossy.** Some productions have been broadcast; the society is nonprofit and encourages the performance of new works. Performances are held in various Cleveland auditoriums. . . . CINCINNATI SUMMER OPERA ASSOCIATION, Suite 109, Vernon Manor Hotel, Oak and Burnet Avenue, Cincinnati, Ohio 45219. Founded in 1920. General Manager: **Styrk Orwoll.** President of the Association: **James M. E. Mixter.** Production Manager: **James de Blasis.** Among the conductors are **Anton Guadagno, Aldo Faldi,** and guest conductors including **Julius Rudel** (1972). From its inception until the summer of 1972, the Summer Opera was held in the Pavilion of the Zoological Gardens of Cincinnati and was always referred to as the Zoo Opera. In the summer of 1972, performances were offered for the first time in the newly restored, 3,634-seat Music Hall (first opera performance there on June 24, 1972) which, since 1970, had been the home of the Cincinnati Symphony Orchestra and the Cincinnati May Festival. (The restoration of the Hall began in 1969 and cost $6 million, half from the Corbett Foundation and half from the City of Cincinnati. It has full theater facilities for opera including orchestra lift, rehearsal rooms, workrooms for scenery and costume making, etc. It reportedly ranks high, acoustically, among U.S. music auditoriums.) Because the old Zoo sets could not be used in the new Hall, the first summer's operas were generally imported productions from New York, Seattle, Boston, etc. Eventually, the Association will present its own productions. The season in the new location in 1972 presented six operas in two performances each, plus a special Verdi concert, all over a four-week period. Well-known stars from the major companies and some local singers are on the roster of performers. The orchestra is composed of members of the Cincinnati Symphony Orchestra. (For more details see under Festivals.) . . . DAYTON OPERA ASSOCIATION, 15 East Second Street, Dayton, Ohio 45402. Founded in 1959. Musical Director: **Lester Freedman.** The season of this company extends from October to May. Three operas are produced and three performances are given. Stars are used for leading roles. The orchestra is a professional one. Regular performances are held in Memorial Hall (2,500 seats). . . . LAKE ERIE OPERA THEATRE, 11125 Magnolia Drive, Cleveland, Ohio 44106. Founded in 1964. Executive Producer: **Howard Whittaker.** Musical Director: **Louis Lane.** The opera season includes the months of May, June, July, and September. During these months, four operas are produced and 21 performances offered. Twenty resident singers are on the roster; some are on the faculty of local schools. The Cleveland Orchestra is used. The Theater received a grant from the Martha Baird Rockefeller Fund for costumes in the 1968 performance of "Bartered Bride." Regular performances are held in Severance Hall and in Cleveland Parks. . . . SPRINGFIELD CIVIC OPERA COMPANY, Box 432, Springfield, Ohio 45501. Founded in 1962. President: **Richard C. Farish.** Musical Director and Conductor: **Robert C. Delbeer.** The season lasts for eight months; two operas are produced and two performances are given. Resident singers only are used. The orchestra is made up of professional players and college students. Regular performances are held in Roosevelt Junior High School Auditorium (500 seats). . . . TOLEDO OPERA ASSOCIATION, 3301 West Central Avenue, Toledo, Ohio 43606. Musical Director: **Lester Freedman.** The company's season lasts from October to May. Three operas are produced and six performances are given. The orchestra is composed of professionals. The Association presents a free student performance for every operatic production. Regular performances are held in Museum of Art Peristyle (1,700 seats).

Oklahoma

TULSA OPERA, INC., 1610 South Boulder Avenue, Tulsa, Oklahoma 74119. Founded in 1948. Manager: **Jeannette Turner;** Conductor: **Carlo Moresco.** Two to three operas are produced and are given two performances each. Resident singers take minor roles, but stars of the Metropolitan opera and other composers are brought in for leading parts. Most of the members of the orchestra are from the Tulsa Philharmonic. Performances are held in Tulsa Municipal Theatre (2,682 seats).

Oregon

PORTLAND OPERA ASSOCIATION, INC., 1436 S.W. Montgomery Street, Portland, Oregon 97201. Founded in 1950; in 1957 a city ordinance established opera on a year-round basis through the Theatre Arts Opera Association, a name later changed to the present one. The Association is a nonprofit organization administered by a Board of Directors whose Executive Secretary is the Director of Recreation for the City of Portland. This office is part of the Bureau of Parks and Recreation of the City Government. The Musical Director of the Opera Association is the only member in the Association who receives monetary payment for his work; he is under contract to the City of Portland. He is assisted by a voluntary and paid cast (the latter includes star performers from the Metropolitan Opera, the New York and San Francisco companies, and others), a stage director, set designer, costumer, choreographer, and stage crew. General Director and Conductor: **Stefan Minde.** The season is year-round and features five or six operas in a total of 15 performances. Some performances are free. In addition to well-known opera stars, there are young resident singers, a chorus, and an orchestra made up mostly of professional musicians. There are piano-accompanied presentations of opera, mostly available as lecture demonstrations rather than regular public performances. Some concert versions of operas are performed for the purpose of lending experience and promotion to promising young singers. Civic Auditorium is the site of the regular season performances (3,000 seats). The opera company has had television coverage as a public service through TV stations KGW and KATU. These have been one-hour and half-hour presentations. The Association operates with a budget of about $300,000. Manager is **Richard C. Williams.** Director of Recreation, City of Portland, is **Dorothea M. Lensch.**

Pennsylvania

PHILADELPHIA GRAND OPERA COMPANY, 1422 Chestnut Street, Philadelphia, Pennsylvania 19102. Founded in 1955. Manager: **Max M. Leon.** The season lasts from October through April. Seven fully staged operas are produced and are given one performance each. The orchestra is composed of professional players. Performances are held in Academy of Music (3,000 seats). . . . PHILADELPHIA LYRIC OPERA COMPANY, 1518 Walnut Street, Philadelphia, Pennsylvania 19102. Founded in 1956. President and Business Manager: **William B. Warden.** Musical Director: **Anton Guadagno.** General Manager: **Aurelio Fabiani.** The season spans eight months out of the year; 8 to 10 fully staged operas are produced and are given a total of 15 performances. The orchestra is composed of professional instrumentalists. Performances are held in the Philadelphia Academy of Music (2,700 seats). Leading stars of the opera world are featured including singers from the Metropolitan Opera,

New York City Opera, and European companies. The repertory is all standard. . . . PITTSBURGH OPERA, INC., 209 Heinz Hall of the Performing Arts, 600 Pennsylvania Avenue, Pittsburgh, Pennsylvania 15222. Founded in 1938. President: **Gurdon F. Flagg.** Artistic Director: **Richard Karp.** The season usually lasts from October through March or April. Five operas are produced and ten performances are presented. Some local singers are used, but leading roles are filled by internationally known singers. The orchestra is composed of members of the Pittsburgh Symphony. Piano accompaniment is used in some public performances. The company holds its performances in Heinz Hall (2,729 seats). Such stars as **Gabriella Tucci, Claire Watson, Roberta Peters,** and **Beverly Sills** are among those recently engaged. . . . SUBURBAN OPERA COMPANY, 4201 Edgmont Avenue, Chester, Pennsylvania 19015. Founded in 1962. General Manager: **James Parkinson.** Musical Director and Conductor: **Chris Macatsoris.** The opera season is spread over six months. Six fully staged operas are produced and 12 performances are given. Only local singers are used. The orchestra includes some professional players from Philadelphia.

South Carolina

COLUMBIA LYRIC THEATRE, 1527 Senate Street, Columbia, South Carolina 29201. Founded in 1956. Manager: **Leon Harrelson.** Musical Director and Conductor: **Sidney J. Palmer.** Producer: **Frank Harris.** The Columbia produces one opera in the spring and one in the fall. Only resident singers are used. The orchestra is composed of both professional and amateur players. Piano accompaniment is used for some public performances. The company holds its regular performances in Dreher High School Auditorium (1,100 seats).

Tennessee

CHATTANOOGA OPERA ASSOCIATION, P.O. Box 1212, Chattanooga, Tennessee 37401. Founded in 1943. President: **Samuel Binder;** Musical Director and Conductor: **Siegfried Landau;** Choral Director: **Milton Allen;** Stage Director: **Dorothy Hackett Ward.** The season lasts from October to April. Two fully staged operas are produced and two to four performances are given. Some resident singers are used, but singers are imported as well. The orchestra is made up of both professionals and amateurs. Performances are held in Tivoli Theatre (1,700 seats). In October, 1967, the group, sponsored by the Tennessee Arts Commission, performed at University of the South. . . . MEMPHIS OPERA THEATRE, INC., 60 South Auburndale, Memphis, Tennessee 38104. Founded in 1956. Managing Director: **Marler Stone.** Conductors are hired by the Theatre for each production. Two or three operas are produced, usually standard repertory, and six to nine performances are given. There are usually two student performances. All productions are fully staged. The orchestra is composed of professionals, students, and amateurs. Performances are held in Ellis Auditorium (1,900 seats). The repertory is standard; operas are sung in English. The company produced the world stage premiere of Leonard Kastle's "Deseret." Past conductors have been: **Kurt Adler, Moritz Bomhard,** and **Fiora Contino.** Singers have included **Birgit Nilsson, Mignon Dunn, Justino Díaz,** and **Gail Robinson.**

Texas

BEAUMONT CIVIC OPERA, 5640 North Circuit, Beaumont, Texas 77706. Founded in 1962. Administrative Head: **Naaman J. Woodland.** Conductor and Stage Director: **Peter Paul Fuchs.** One opera is produced and performed twice (fully staged). Although resident singers are used, young, professional singers are engaged from outside for some roles. The orchestra is composed of professionals, a few students, and amateurs. Performances are held in Stephen J. Austin Junior High School Auditorium (1,000 seats). . . . DALLAS CIVIC OPERA ASSOCIATION, 505 N. Ervay, Dallas, Texas 75201. Founded in 1957. General Manager: **Lawrence Kelly.** Musical Director: **Nicola Rescigno.** The season lasts for three weeks in November. Three fully staged operas are produced and are given eight performances. Some resident singers are used, but leading artists of international opera are engaged for important roles. The orchestra is the Dallas Symphony. Performances are held in State Fair Music Hall (4,120 seats). The Dallas Civic Opera has produced 3 American premieres, 5 Dallas premieres, and 43 American debuts including **Franco Zeffirelli, Judith Raskin, Joan Sutherland, Teresa Berganza,** and **Jon Vickers.** . . . FORT WORTH OPERA ASSOCIATION, 3505 West Lancaster Street, Fort Worth, Texas 76107. Founded in 1946. Musical Director and General Manager: **Rudolf Kruger;** Assistant General Manager: **William Massad.** The season lasts from November through April. Resident singers are used for secondary roles, and leading roles are sung by guest stars. Four fully staged operas are produced and eight performances are given. The orchestra is composed of professional players. Performances are held in Will Rogers Memorial Auditorium (2,964 seats). The association received a five-year grant of $100,000 from the Ford Foundation in 1963. Recent leading roles have been sung by **Norman Treigle, Carol Neblett, John Alexander, Spiro Malas,** et al. . . . HOUSTON GRAND OPERA ASSOCIATION, Jones Hall, 615 Louisiana Street, Houston 77002. Founded in 1955. General Director: **David Gockley** (1972). Principal Conductor: **Charles Rosekrans.** The regular season lasts from November through May. Five fully staged operas are produced and 25 performances are given. In 1972, the company gave its first Spring Opera Festival with 10 free public open-air performances of three operas sung in English in the city's Hermann Park. Resident singers are used only in the chorus. The leading roles are sung by highest-level professionals. The Houston Symphony Orchestra is used for performances, which are held in Jones Hall for Performing Arts (3,000 seats). During the winter season the Houston produces more opera than that of any city in the Southwest or the entire South. It is one of the important American opera-producing companies. . . . SAN ANTONIO GRAND OPERA, 600 Hemisfair Plaza Way, San Antonio, Texas 78205. Founded in 1944 as part of the symphony season. Musical Director and Conductor: **Victor Alessandro.** The season lasts nine months during the year. Five to seven operas are produced (fully staged) and ten to twelve performances are given. Stars are engaged for leading roles. The orchestra is the San Antonio Symphony. Performances are held in Hemisfair Auditorium and on tours to surrounding cities.

Virginia

OPERA THEATRE OF NORTHERN VIRGINIA, 300 North Park Drive, Arlington, Virginia 22203. Founded in 1961. The Theatre is under the administration of Arlington's Department of Recreation and Parks. Musical Director and Conductor: **Richard Weilenmann.** Artistic Director: **Adelaide Bishop.** Three fully staged operas are produced and three performances are given. Resident singers are used; outside artists are engaged for leading roles. The orchestra is a combination of professional and nonprofessional players. Regular performances are held in Kenmore Auditorium (630 seats). Operas in the repertory are standard and contemporary works. . . . PENINSULA CIVIC OPERA, INC., P.O. Box 395, Newport News, Virginia 23607. Founded in 1934. Administrative Head: **Lewis Whitehouse.** President: **Richard Sawyer;** Musical Director: **Harold Chapman.** The season lasts from October or November to April or May. Three fully staged operas are produced and are performed two to three times each. Only resident singers are used. The orchestra is composed of professionals. Piano accompaniment is used only for a childrens' performance. Performances are held in a school auditorium with a capacity of 800 to 1,200.

Washington

SEATTLE OPERA ASSOCIATION, INC., 158 Thomas Street, Seattle, Washington 98109. Founded in 1964. General Director: **Glynn Ross;** Music Assistant: **Henry Holt.** The season lasts from September through

April. Five fully staged operas are produced for a total of 25 performances. The chorus is composed of from 36 to 54 resident singers. Internationally known artists are engaged for leading parts. The orchestra is composed of professional players. The company received a $100,000 grant from the Ford Foundation in 1966. In 1967 the Seattle Opera Association produced the world debut performance of Joan Sutherland as "Lakme." In 1967 Igor Stravinsky conducted his own "Story of a Soldier."

West Virginia

CLARKSBURG OPERA GUILD INC., 339 Washington Avenue, Clarksburg, West Virginia. Founded in 1951. Musical Directors: **Ruby M. Scott** and **Richard Karp.** Two operas are produced every year and are given a total of five performances. The orchestra is composed of professionals. Performances are held in Robinson Grand Theater (1,200 seats).

Wisconsin

FLORENTINE OPERA COMPANY OF MILWAUKEE, 750 N. Lincoln Memorial Drive, Milwaukee, Wisconsin 53202. Musical Director: **John Anello.** The company produces five fully staged operas and gives a total of ten performances during its regular season. Resident singers are used as well as singers engaged from the outside. The orchestra is composed of players of the Milwaukee Symphony. Regular performances are held in Performing Arts Center (2,200 seats).

Dance Companies

California

BALLET LA JEUNESSE OF LOS ANGELES, 10120 Riverside Drive, North Hollywood, California 91602. Founded in 1958. Artistic Director: **Natalia Clare.** Associate Director: **Michael Liotweizen.** Performances are given throughout the year (annual average is 10 to 12). The group has 15 productions in its repertory and is a resident organization that performs its classical and modern repertory in theaters in the Los Angeles area. It performs with recordings as well as orchestra. . . . DANCE WEST, THE JENNY HUNTER DANCE COMPANY, 330 Clement Street, San Francisco, California 94118. Founded 1957. Artistic Director: **Jenny Hunter.** The company is primarily a resident group performing mostly contemporary works by **Jenny Hunter** and commissioned works. The company, made up of from 3 to 10 performers with **Jenny Hunter** as the principal soloist, performs with accompaniment from piano, instrumental combos, rock bands, tapes, and without accompaniment. The group performed the West Coast premiere of Gian-Carlo Menotti's "The Unicorn, The Gorgon, and the Manticore." It has performed on television for KQED and ETV in San Francisco. Its performances take place in Legion of Honor Theatre and Fillmore Auditorium (300 seats). . . . DANCERS WORKSHOP COMPANY OF SAN FRANCISCO, 321 Divisadero Street, San Francisco, California 94123. Founded 1954. Administrative Head: **Robert Raymer.** Artistic Director: **Ann Halprin.** The company, made up of from 8 to 50 dancers, specializes in avant-garde repertory. They perform with drum or with tape recordings. The group has performed in the Hunter College series in New York. Its season is nine months long. . . . THE ETHNIC DANCE THEATRE, 2211 South Highland Avenue, Los Angeles, California 90016. Founded 1952. Artistic Directors: **Karoun Tootikian** and **Lonny Cothron** (1952). The company is composed of 12 *corps de ballet* members and 6 soloists who perform Hindu, Indonesian, South Pacific, and Middle Eastern dances. They are accompanied by piano, a small orchestra at times, and by tapes. The Ethnic Dance Theatre has made three films—of Armenian, European, and Japanese dance. **Karoun Tootikian** has appeared with her dancers from coast to coast and in Europe, Armenia, and the Soviet Union. . . . ELLE JOHNSON DANCE COMPANY, 1945 Westwood Boulevard, Los Angeles, California 90025. Founded in 1966. Artistic Director: **Elle Johnson.** Administrative Head: **Benn Howard.** This organization is primarily a resident one, although it does tour. Its six to eight dancers perform both solo and ensemble work. The group's season lasts from October through May, during which time three modern and Afro-Cuban productions are given 21 performances. Performances are held in Academy West Dance Theatre (approximately 70 seats). . . . BELLA LEWITZKY DANCE COMPANY, c/o Darlene Neel Management, 3594 Multiview Drive, Hollywood, California 90068. Founded in 1966. Director and Choreographer: **Bella Lewitzky.** Artistic Director: **Clifford Nelson.** The group performs primarily on tour throughout the year in concerts and lecture-demonstrations accompanied by tape recordings. The company is made up of nine dancers including **Bella Lewitzky;** no soloists or *corps* are billed. Repertory includes modern works and works choreographed by **Bella Lewitzky.** The company has toured in the Midwest. . . . LOLA MONTES AND HER SPANISH DANCERS, 1529 North Commonwealth Avenue, Los Angeles, California 90027. Administrative Head and Artistic Director: **Lola Montes;** Musical Director: **Virko Baley.** The troupe includes from 7 to 10 dancers who specialize in Spanish classical, regional, flamenco, and Mexican folk dances, and South American repertory. The group performs with piano, flamenco guitar, and sometimes with orchestral accompaniment. Their season lasts from about 12 to 16 weeks and includes 45 productions and about 60 performances. The company has toured the Pacific Coast as well as Canada and Mexico. . . . GLORIA NEWMAN DANCE COMPANY, 3845 East Fernwood Avenue, Orange, California 92667. Founded in 1957. Artistic Director: **Gloria Newman.** Musical Director: **Ami Aloni** (1968). Administrative Head: **C. M. Schoenberg.** The company is a touring group, primarily, composed of 10 dancers. They dance to accompaniment from piano, ensemble, and recordings; repertory is mainly contemporary. . . . PACIFIC BALLET, 2121 Market Street, San Francisco, California 94114. Founded in 1960. Founder and Artistic Director: **Alan Howard.** The company is made up of a base group of 10 dancers (**Alan Howard** as Principal Dancer) and 10 to 20 apprentices make up the *corps de ballet* for larger productions. A touring group, the company dances classical and contemporary works, usually with taped and sometimes with orchestral accompaniment. Its season lasts for two weeks in May or June; 12 works are produced and are performed eight times. The company is well known for its annual Christmas performance of "Nutcracker" in the Bay area. . . . PASADENA DANCE THEATRE, 25 South Sierra Madre Boulevard, Pasadena, California 91107. Founded in 1965. Artistic Director: **Eveleyn Le Mone** (1965). The company is composed of 18 dancers: 4 soloists and 14 *corps de ballet.* It is a local group and performs both modern and classical works to tape recordings. The company engages guest dancers. Its performances are held in Pasadena Civic Auditorium (2,900 seats) and has also toured out of state. . . . SAN FRANCISCO BALLET, 378 18th Avenue, San Francisco, California 94121. Founded in 1933. Artistic Director: **Lew Christensen** (1951); Executive Director: **Leon G. Kalimos.** The San Francisco Ballet, the oldest performing classical resident ballet company in America, consists of 36 dancers who perform mainly contemporary dance works. The company has toured thirty-six countries in the Far East, Central and South America, Africa, and the Middle East. It also has the distinction of being the only major cultural institution from San Francisco to have performed in New York's Lincoln Center. It performs with orchestral accompaniment in San Francisco Opera House (3,300 seats). It has performed for national television specials including the "Bell Telephone Hour," "Dupont Show," and the "Ed Sullivan Show" (all no longer programmed). . . . THEATRE FLAMENCO OF SAN FRANCISCO, 171 Liberty Street, San Francisco, California 94110. Founded in 1964. Artistic and Musical Directors: **Adela Clara** and **Juana Francesca.** The company, which features flamenco, classical, folklore, and original works combined with Spanish poetry and performed with guitar, piano, and flamenco song accompaniment, is composed of four solo dancers. Its season in San Francisco is the month of May, during which it presents one production at the University of San Francisco's Gill Theatre (300 seats). The company has appeared on NET–TV. . . . WEST VALLEY BALLET, 16 Lyndon Avenue, Los Gatos, California 95030. Founded in 1964. Administrative Head: **Paul E. Curtis, Jr.** Artistic Director: **Shawn Stuart** (1967). Musical Director: **John O'Neill** (1966). The company is made up of 2 female and 2 male soloists, 8 to 20 female and 4 male members of the *corps de ballet.* The company's repertory includes classical, ethnic, and modern works. It presents two 3-week seasons annually and plays at various theaters with accompaniment from piano or tapes or with the Los Gatos–Saratoga Symphony.

Connecticut

DANCERS OF FAITH, Box 286, Southport, Connecticut 06490. Founded in 1946. Artistic Director: **Louise Mattlage.** The company has 5 to 10 dancers (no soloists) who perform modern and contemporary idiom works only. It is a touring group and rarely hires guest artists. Its 25 or so annual performances are with musical accompaniment from organ, piano, trio, or voice. The group has lectured in Greece and has performed on national television. It operates throughout the year. . . . HARTFORD CONSERVATORY MODERN DANCE COMPANY, 834 Asylum Avenue, Hartford, Connecticut 06105. Founded 1940. Artistic Director: **Truna Kaschmann.** The company consists of from 8 to 16 dancers who perform modern dance, usually to live music. The season lasts from September through June and sometimes includes the summer. It gives special children's performances, lectures and demonstrations, and has appeared on educational TV.

Washington, D.C.

ETHEL BUTLER COMPANY, 5204B River Road, N.W., Washington, D.C. 20016. Founded in 1943. Artistic Director: **Ethel Butler.** The company, consisting of 10 dancers, performs modern dance to piano or taped accompaniment. During its 12-month season, the company performs in Washington and also tours. Guest dancers are also engaged. . . . DANCE THEATRE, INC., 2934 M Street, N.W., Washington, D.C. 20007. Founded in 1942. Incorporated 1966. Administrative Head and Artistic Director: **Erika Thimey.** The company's repertory consists of modern works for children and adults. Much of the music performed is commissioned and especially composed for the choreography, almost all of which is done by Erika Thimey. The group, a touring company, is composed of from 5 to 24 dancers who perform mostly to recordings. From 5 to 12 works are produced and given from 30 to 60 performances every year. The Company has appeared on local and network TV as well as educational TV. . . . NATIONAL BALLET, 2801 Connecticut Avenue, N.W., Washington, D.C. 20008. Founded in 1961. Co-Artistic Directors: **Frederic Franklin** and **Ben Stevenson.** The company is made up of 6 principals, 9 soloists, 12 *corps de ballet* and 6 apprentices. It is primarily a resident ballet and performs with symphony accompaniment in Lisner Auditorium in Washington (1,502 seats). Its season lasts from September through April. The company's repertory includes commissioned and adapted works as well as standard classical works. The company has performed "Swan Lake" at New York City Center and "Les Sylphides" at Brooklyn College in New York City. Its tours are under the management of Columbia Artists Management, Inc. . . . THE WASHINGTON MODERN DANCE SOCIETY, 4321 Wisconsin Avenue, N.W., Washington, D.C. 20016. Founded in 1964. Artistic Director: **Louis Tupler.** Administrative Head: **Richard Hellman.** The company is a resident group made up of from 8 to 12 dancers plus guest dancers. The group's repertory includes classical, modern, and newly commissioned works from young composers. The group performs to piano, orchestral, and recorded accompaniment.

Florida

CONTEMPORARY DANCE THEATRE, 910 East Buffalo Avenue, Tampa, Florida 33603. Founded in 1960. Artistic Director: **Frank Rey.** Administrative Head: **Richard Rader.** Made up of 10 dancers, this resident group performs contemporary dance, usually with taped accompaniment. It does not engage dancers from the outside for performances. The group's season lasts for 12 months, during which time one work is produced and given multiple performances. These are held in McKay Auditorium (1,500 seats) and Falk Theatre (1,200).

Illinois

GUS GIORDANO DANCE COMPANY, c/o Shirley Hamilton Inc., 360 N. Michigan Avenue, Chicago, Illinois. Founded in 1960. Artistic Director: **Gus Giordano.** The company is made up of seven dancers—five women and two men—all soloists, whose repertory includes modern dance and jazz works. The group, both a resident and touring one, gives 25 performances of 12 productions each season, which lasts from January through May. Performances are given at colleges and on NET television. . . . ILLINOIS BALLET COMPANY, 410 South Michigan Avenue, Chicago, Illinois 60605. Founded 1958. Artistic Directors: **Richard Ellis** and **Christine Du Boulay.** The company is composed of 12 dancers—3 principal female dancers, 2 principal male dancers and members of the *corps de ballet.* The company's repertory includes classical and contemporary works; it performs with recordings and occasionally with orchestra. It has toured high schools in the Chicago area and has given 15 television performances on Chicago's NET station. The company's season lasts from September through June; about 30 performances are given. The company performs in Chicago at Athenaeum Theatre (940 seats). It has received grants from the Illinois Arts Council, the Chicago Board of Education, and the Sears Roebuck Foundation. . . . RUTH PAGE INTERNATIONAL BALLET, 1100 Lake Shore Drive, Chicago, Illinois 60611. Founded in 1954. Artistic Director: **Ruth Page.** Musical Directors: **Neal Kayan** and **Isaac Van Grove.** The company, which consists of 6 regular stars, 2 guest stars, 4 soloists and 16 *corps de ballet,* specializes in commissioned and adapted works. Repertory includes some classical works. On tour the company performs with 12 musicians; performances of the "Nutcracker" are played with full orchestra. The company's season includes 10 weeks at Chicago's Lyric Opera and 60 to 80 performances on tour. . . . PHYLLIS SABOLD DANCE COMPANY, 442 Central Avenue, Highland Park, Illinois 60035. Founded 1966. Artistic Director: **Eric Braun.** Administrative Head: **Phyllis Sabold.** The company, a resident group made up of from 5 to 20 dancers, combines classical and modern works in its repertory. During its season, lasting about three months, the group performs with accompaniment from recordings, tapes, and on occasion, small orchestra. The group has performed on television and has given lecture demonstrations for Chicago's Board of Education. Regular performances are held at Drake Theatre (625 seats). . . . THE SYBIL SHEARER COMPANY, Lee Road, Northbrook, Illinois. Founded in 1961. Artistic Director: **Helen Morrison** (at above address). The company, made up of 10 dancers and 1 soloist, is a resident group, performing with tape and chamber accompaniment. Repertory includes only modern works. The company has performed on television and has been filmed. Performances, given once or twice a month, are usually held at the National College of Education (750 seats), in Evanston, Illinois.

Maryland

ROBERT DAVIS DANCE THEATRE, 2906 Taylor Avenue, Baltimore, Maryland 20002. Founded in 1965. Artistic Director: **Robert Davis.** Musical Director: **Margaret Barnwell.** The company is composed of two principals, four soloists and six to eight *corps de ballet.* The company is augmented when larger productions are performed; guest artists are engaged on occasion. It is a resident group whose repertory includes six to eight classical works each season. Tapes or orchestras are used as musical accompaniment. The group gives many performances for underprivileged groups and has performed on television. Regular performances are held in high school auditoriums.

Massachusetts

BOSTON BALLET COMPANY, 577 Washington Street, Boston, Massachusetts 02112. Founded in 1964. Artistic Director: **E. Virginia Williams.** Musical Director: **Harry Shapiro.** Administrative Head: **Ruth Harrington.** The company has 4 principal dancers, 6 soloists and 22 *corps de ballet.* It is a resident company that performs modern (Pearl Lang, Talley Beatty, John Butler) and classical works. The group's season is four months long, from January to April. Eight performances are given. The company engages guest ballet artists. Performances are given in Back Bay Theatre (3,200 seats). The company was established in 1964 with a $144,000 grant from the Ford Foundation. . . . DANCE CIRCLE COMPANY OF BOSTON, 367 Beach Avenue, Hull, Massachusetts 02045. Founded in 1964. Artistic Director: **Anne Tolbert.** Administrative Head: **Colin Godfry.** The company's 10 dancers perform modern works to tape or live music. The group is a resident organization but does some local touring. It produces two works a year and gives 8 to 10 performances. Dance artists are engaged from the outside. Performances are usually held at the Massachusetts Institute of Technology. . . . FESTIVAL DANCE COMPANY, 44 Atlantic Avenue, Swampscott, Massachusetts 01907. Founded in 1961. Artistic Director: **Noami Aleh–Leaf.** The company is composed of eight dancers (all teachers in the Boston area); its repertory includes modern dance, much of the inspiration for which comes from Biblical and Jewish themes. The group performs with accompaniment from string trios, voice, flute, and chorus. The group is a touring organization and has traveled through New England and Canada. It has performed on television.

Michigan

MUSICAL PERFORMING ARTS ASSOCIATION OF FLINT, 812 Citizens Bank Building, Flint, Michigan 48502. Founded in 1965. Artistic Director: **William Byrd** (1966). Ballet Master: **George Skibine** (1967). Administrative Head: **Arthur E. Summerfield, Jr.** The group, made up of 16 dancers, imported soloists and local extras, performs standard works with orchestral accompaniment. The group is resident with a season lasting from September through May. There are two productions in a season with two major performances and one chamber music performance. The ballet is part of a subscription series of eight programs.

Minnesota

CONTEMPORARY DANCE THEATRE, 404 13th Avenue, S.E., Minneapolis, Minnesota 55414. Founded in 1961. Artistic Director: **Loyce Houlton.** Musical Director: **David Voss.** The company includes 12 dancers who perform classical and modern works to the accompaniment of orchestra, piano, rock bands, etc. Every March, the company presents a full-scale dance production with the Minneapolis Symphony in Northrop Auditorium (5,000 seats). Other performances are in Guthrie Theatre (1,500 seats) and Contemporary Dance Playhouse (300 seats). The company is both a resident and touring group whose season lasts throughout the whole year. **Miss Houlton** has choreographed for ETV. In 1967 the company was awarded a grant by the Minnesota State Arts Council for the premiere of works by **Miss Houlton.** . . . DANCE GUILD THEATRE, 330 North Prior Avenue, Saint Paul, Minnesota 55104. Founded in 1961. Administrative Head and Artistic Director: **Nancy Hauser.** Musical Director: **Herb Pilhofer** (1962). During the September through June season, the company, made up of 12 dancers, gives approximately 20 performances. Its repertory consists of modern works. The company is resident and also tours; it performs at local theaters. It has received a grant from the Minnesota State Council on the Arts.

Missouri

SAINT LOUIS DANCE THEATRE, 7202 Delmar Boulevard, Saint Louis, Missouri 63130. Founded in 1967. Artistic Directors: **Nathalie Levine, Sally Duncan, Marjorie Mendolia, Michael Simms, Alexandra Zaharias,** and **Mary K. Perkins.** There are 20 members of the company, 6 soloists and 14 *corps de ballet,* and 20 junior members of the company. The group's repertory includes both classical and contemporary works performed to piano or taped accompaniment. Guest dancers are engaged from schools; the

Saint Louis is a resident company which performs in American Theater (200 seats) and Kiel Auditorium Opera House (3,000 seats).

New Jersey

STORY-TIME DANCE THEATRE, 100 High Street, Leonia, N.J. 07605. Founded in 1959. Producers: **Sheila Hellman** and **Louise Mazzolla.** The company is composed of seven dancers who perform modern works, ballet, adaptations of children's classics and works of writers, including Gertrude Stein. The group tours New York, New Jersey, and Connecticut, performing with taped recordings and giving about 35 performances a season (October–May). . . . THE JOAN WOLF BALLET ENSEMBLE, 286 Kinderkamack Road, Oradell, N.J. 07649. Founded in 1962. Artistic Director: **Joan Wolf.** The group, a resident company, is made up of about 40 dancers: 10 soloists, 20 *corps de ballet* and about 10 extras. They perform classical and character works to recorded accompaniment. The group performs at Beechwood Center for Performing Arts (2,000 seats) and River Dell High School (800).

New York

FRANCES ALENIKOFF AND COMPANY, c/o Judith Liegner, 33 Greenwich Avenue, New York, N.Y. 10014. Founded in 1960. Artistic Director: **Frances Alenikoff.** The company, a touring group, is made up of three or four soloists who perform traditional and modern works including multimedia works. During its dance season, which lasts from October through June, the group gives from 40 to 60 performances to accompaniment of tape recordings. In 1968 the company toured Israel. . . . AMERICAN BALLET THEATRE, 1619 Broadway, New York, N.Y. 10019. Founded in 1940. Artistic Directors: **Lucia Chase** and **Oliver Smith.** The company, among the most renowned in the U.S., has 10 principals, 15 soloists and 32 *corps de ballet.* The group is a touring company, performing a 12-month season. Performances are given with a 20-piece orchestra on tour and with an augmented orchestra in New York City. The American Ballet Theatre was the first American group to tour abroad after World War II, the first company to appear on American television and the first American ballet ensemble to dance in the Soviet Union. The company maintains its own school. Repertory is both classical ("Swan Lake," "Giselle," "La Sylphide," etc.) and modern ("Les Noces" by Robbins, "Undertow" by Tudor, etc.). Performances in New York are at the New York State Theater, Metropolitan Opera House at Lincoln Center, or City Center Theater. The American Ballet Theatre is the official company for dance at the John F. Kennedy Center for the Performing Arts in Washington, D.C. It functions under the sponsorship of the Ballet Theatre Foundation, Inc., 888 Seventh Avenue, New York, N.Y. 10019, and City Center of Music and Drama, Inc. Principal Conductor of the ABT orchestra is **Akira Endo.** Ballet Master is **Enrique Martinez.** Régisseur is **Dimitri Romanoff.** General Manager is **Daryl Dodson.** Among the company of dancers: **Paolo Bortoluzzi, Eleanor D'Antuono, Royes Fernandez, Carla Fracci, Natalia Makarova, Bruce Marks, Mimi Paul,** and **Gayle Young.** . . . MARY ANTHONY DANCE THEATRE, 736 Broadway, New York, N.Y. 10003. Founded in 1956. Artistic director: **Mary Anthony**. The company varies in size from 10 to 14 dancers, including **Mary Anthony**; no soloists or corps are billed. In addition to works by Mary Anthony, the company's repertory includes those by Anna Sokolow, Lester Horton, and others. Primarily a touring group performing to taped accompaniment at colleges and schools throughout the country, the company has summer and winter seasons in New York at the Riverside Church (c. 250 seats). It performs as part of the Coordinated Residency Touring Program funded by the National Endowment for the Arts. . . . JUKI ARKIN MIME THEATRE, 45 West 75th Street, New York, N.Y. 10023. Founded in 1966. Artistic Director: **Juki Arkin.** The company is a resident group of six dancers who perform classical and modern mime. They perform without music. The company has five productions and about 100 performances every season. . . . AYAKO & COMPANY, 957 1st Avenue, New York, N.Y. 10022. Founded in 1967. Artistic Director: **Ayako Uchiyama.** The company, made up of four dancers, performs contemporary, Japanese, and Kabuki dance. During its nine-month season, the group produces two works and gives four performances. It usually performs at civic centers in New York. . . . BALLET ARTS COMPANY, Carnegie Hall, 154 West 57th Street, New York, N.Y. 10019. Founded in 1960. Artistic Directors: **Dean Crane** and **Vladimir Dokoudovsky.** Administrative Head: **Virginia Lee.** The company is made up of four soloists and additions as required. Repertory consists of both classical and modern works. The group is both resident and touring. It has given special performances at the Metropolitan Museum of Art and has performed on television. . . . CHOREO-CONCERTS, Choreographers Theatre, Inc., c/o 66 West 12th Street, New York, N.Y. 10011. Founded in 1964. President: **John Watts;** Artistic Director: **Laura Foreman.** The company is composed of a nucleus group of 18 choreographers and their companies. ChoreoConcerts is the major performance project of Choreographers Theatre, Inc., a nonprofit organization. It presents a cross section of contemporary choreography from traditional style to avant garde. The group is in residence at The New School for Social Research in New York. Choreographers Theatre is the first organization of choreographers in the U.S. to establish its own academic dance department (the New School, in turn, was the first academic institution to offer modern dance courses). ChoreoConcerts has presented the works of 77 choreographers in 179 dances (116 premieres and 40 commissions), using a total of 350 dancers. . . . CITY CENTER JOFFREY BALLET, 130 West 56th Street, New York, N.Y. 10019. Artistic Director: **Robert Joffrey;** Assistant Director: **Gerald Arpino;** General Director: **Alexander C. Ewing;** Music Director: **Seymour Lipkin.** The company normally consists of 38 dancers. It is one of the great American dance companies. Its repertory consists of about 30 productions of classical and contemporary works. Among them: "Trinity," "Pineapple Poll," "The Clowns," "Astarte," "Cakewalk," "Petrouchka," and "The Green Table." Although it is a resident organization, it does tour. In New York City, performances are given with full orchestra at City Center Theater (3,000 seats). During its New York fall season of about six weeks it gives 42 performances of some 25 works; its spring season of about five weeks consists of 40 performances. The company has received grants from the Ford Foundation, National Endowment for the Arts, the Avalon Foundation, etc. . . . ALICE CONDODINA AND DANCE COMPANY, c/o Mary Spector Artists Management, Inc., 250 West 57th Street, New York, N.Y. 10019. Founded in 1967. Artistic Director: **Alice Condodina.** The company is made up of three soloists, nine assisting dancers, and one actor. Repertory includes modern works under the direction and choreography of **Alice Condodina.** The company, a touring group, performs with taped recordings; it sometimes engages guest dancers. It performed the world premiere of "Axion Esti" at Circle in the Square Theatre in New York City. In the spring of 1969 the group toured the East Coast. . . . MERCE CUNNINGHAM AND DANCE COMPANY, c/o Cunningham Dance Foundation, Brooklyn Academy of Music, 30 Lafayette Avenue, Brooklyn, N.Y. 11217. Founded in 1951. Artistic Director: **Merce Cunningham;** Musical Director: **John Cage;** Administrative Head: **Lewis L. Lloyd.** The company, composed of 11 dancers and 1 soloist, tours the United States and abroad. Repertory includes modern works with an avant-garde emphasis performed to contemporary music, with decor and costumes by such artists as Andy Warhol and Marcel Duchamp. The company has received commissions from The French–American Festival of the New York Philharmonic Society, the American Dance Festival, and the National Council on the Arts, and has performed on television in the United States, Sweden, Finland, Belgium, and Germany. It has given charity performances for the Cunningham Dance Foundation. Performances are accompanied by piano, orchestra, tapes, narrators, and electronic music. The season lasts 12 months; 12 to 18 works are produced and given 50 to 100 performances. . . . DANCE THEATER WORKSHOP COMPANY, 215 West 20th Street, New York, N.Y. 10019. Founded in 1965. Artistic Directors: **Jeff Duncan** and **Jack Moore;** Musical Director: **John Wilson.** The company is a dancer–choreographer cooperative, a pool of 25 to 30 modern dancers; a nucleus of 8 forms the touring contingent. Repertory consists of modern dance, experimental, multimedia and commissioned works. The group is a resident one whose season lasts from October through May and from July through August. Thirty to forty performances are given during the season. For four weeks **Jeff Duncan** and seven other members of the group were artists-in-residence at the University of Wisconsin in lecture–workshop and performance programs made possible by a Rockefeller Foundation grant. . . . DANSE GENERALE, 160 West 85th Street, New York, N.Y. 10024. Founded in 1966. Artistic Director: **C. Leo Quitman.** The company is made up of eight dancers whose repertory consists of classical and modern works. They perform to taped and live music. The company is both a resident and touring organization. It has toured colleges in the Southeast. The company's season lasts from June through October; two works are given 60 or more performances. . . . EGLEVSKY BALLET COMPANY OF LONG ISLAND, 20 Unqua Road, Massapequa, N.Y. 10011. Founded 1961. Artistic Director: **Andre Eglevsky;** Administrative Head: **Murray Farr.** The company includes 2 soloists, 2 principal dancers and 10 *corps de ballet.* Repertory consists of classical works: adaptations of "Swan Lake," "Sleeping Beauty," "Peter and the Wolf," and other works. The company is a touring group whose season lasts from September through June, during which time 15 or 20 performances are given. The company has appeared on television several times, has given lecture demonstrations for 60,000 Long Island public school students, and has given several premiere performances. . . . JEAN ERDMAN THEATER OF DANCE, c/o Kay Perper Management, 152 West 58th Street, New York, N.Y. 10019. Founded in 1945. Artistic Director: **Jean Erdman.** Modern repertory works and works by **Jean Erdman** are performed with her choreography. The group has received an Ingram Merrill Grant and a Vernon Rice Award (Drama Desk), among many other distinctions and honors. **Jean Erdman** has collaborated with a number of leading American composers, some of whom have composed music especially for her works. The composers include John Cage, Lou Harrison, Henry Cowell, Alan Hovhaness, and Ezra Laderman. She has toured Europe and Japan. . . . THE FIRST CHAMBER DANCE QUARTET, INC., 213 Park Avenue South, New York, N.Y. 10003. Founded in 1961. Artistic Directors: **Charles Bennett, Lois Bewley** and **William Carter.** The company is composed of five solo dancers. The quartet is a touring group that performs traditional, classical, and original works. The dancers perform the repertory of 25 works to taped music. . . . MARTHA GRAHAM DANCE COMPANY, 316 East 63rd Street, New York, N.Y. 10021. Founded in 1926. Artistic Director: **Martha Graham.** Musical Director: **Eugene Lester.** The company is made up of 22 to 24 dancers, of whom 8 to 10 are soloists. Repertory includes works by **Martha Graham** and works created with funds from the National Endowment for the Arts, foundations, and commissioned by individuals. The company, a resident and touring organization, performs with orchestra accompaniment. Season lasts from three weeks to three or four months. **Martha Graham** is ranked among the great figures in the history of American dance. . . . THE ERICK HAWKINS DANCE COMPANY, 100 Fifth Avenue, New York, N.Y. 10011. Founded in 1952. Artistic Director: **Erick Hawkins;** Musical Director: **Lucia Dlugoszewski;** Administrative Head: **Murray Farr.** The company, a touring organization, is composed of four to six dancers. Repertory includes modern and newly commissioned works. The group is accompanied by "timbre piano" (a piano performed with special techniques of bowing and muting the strings with varying materials—a conception of composer Dlugoszewski) percussion orchestra, and chamber orchestra. The season lasts 11 months a year, in which time three works are produced and 30 to 100 performances are given. In 1963, the company represented the United States in the Theatre of Nation's Festival in Paris. In 1966 it toured North America and in 1967 represented the United States at Expo '67. It also became the first modern dance company to perform at the Smithsonian. . . . HUNTINGTON DANCE ENSEMBLE, Box 465, Huntington, Long Island, N.Y. 11743. Founded in 1968. Director: **Richard Englund;** Administrative Head: Huntington Performing Arts Foundation. The company, a resident organization, is made up of from 14 to 16 dancers. Repertory is varied, including classical, traditional, and contemporary works. The season lasts 6 to 8 months; 12 to 14 ballets are produced and 100 to 120 performances are given. Choreographers and coaches are hired. The company has performed for high school students. . . . KAZUKO HIRABAYASHI & DANCE COMPANY, 302 Elizabeth Street, New York, N.Y. 10012. Founded in 1966. Artistic Director: **Kazuko Hirabayashi.** The company is composed of six to eight dancers; guest artists are engaged. Repertory consists of modern works. The dancers usually perform with recorded accompaniment. The company performed "In a Dark Grove," a No play, commissioned by Connecticut College School of Dance. . . . KATAYEN DANCE THEATRE, INC., Sag Harbor, N.Y. 11963. Founded in 1961. Artistic Director: **Lelia Katayen.** The group has six to nine dancers, depending on the program, and performs exclusively to tapes. The repertory of the company, a touring organization, consists of works which "combine the historical development of music and dance" in terms of modern dance. Guest dancers are engaged. The season lasts for eight months: two programs are produced and given about 20 to 30 performances. . . . HAVA KOHAV DANCE COMPANY, 118 Riverside Drive, New York, N.Y. 10024. Founded 1959. Artistic Director: **Hava Kohav.** This resident group has six dancers, who perform mostly with recorded accompaniment. It engages guest dancers. Repertory consists of modern works. . . . KATHERINE LITZ DANCE COMPANY, 62 Montague Street, Brooklyn, N.Y. 11201. Founded 1960. Artistic Directors: **Stuart** and **Richard Thomas.** Administrative Head: **Katherine Litz.** The group is composed of from two to six dancers. It is a resident and touring organization whose repertory consists of modern works. Guest artists are sometimes engaged. The company performs to accompaniment of piano or tape and gives from one to three performances in New York every season. It has received a Guggenheim Fellowship and a Walter Gutman and Lena Robbins grant. . . . MANHATTAN FESTIVAL BALLET, c/o Tornay Management, 250 West 57th Street, New York, N.Y. 10019. Founded in 1965. Artistic Director: **Ron Sequoio.** The company has six soloists and seven *corps de ballet.* Repertory is made up of both classical and modern ballets, performed to taped accompaniment. During its 12-month season, this resident group produces about 15 ballets and gives about 60 performances at 80 Saint Marks Place (199 seats). Since 1965, the group has premiered 35 works and toured throughout the U.S. . . . MERLE MARSICANO DANCE COMPANY, 23 West 16th Street, New York, N.Y. 10011. Founded in 1962. Artistic Director: **Merle Marsicano;** Musical Director: **Edwin Hymovitz.** The group, made up of six dancers, is a resident company and performs with accompaniment from string ensemble, piano, or tapes. Repertory includes contemporary works by composers Morton Feldman, John Cage, et al. The season lasts from September through May, during which time one to three performances are given. The company has received grants from the Walter Gutman Foundation, Ingram Merrill, etc. . . . MICHAEL MAULE'S DANCE VARIATIONS, 139 East 63rd Street, New York, N.Y. 10021. Founded 1967. Artistic Director: **Michael Maule.** The company, a touring group, is composed of four principal dancers who perform various types of ballet, with emphasis on classical ballet. During the three-month season, one program is produced and is given 55 performances. . . . METROPOLITAN OPERA BALLET, Metropolitan Opera, Lincoln Center Plaza, New York, N.Y. 10023. Founded in 1883. Artistic Director: **Milko**

Sparemblek. Administrative Head: **Schuyler G. Chapin.** The company is a resident organization composed of 9 soloists, 2 guest artists and 28 *corps de ballet.* It performs for the Metropolitan Opera productions (see Opera Companies). . . . NEW YORK CITY BALLET, New York State Theatre, Lincoln Center Plaza, New York, N.Y. 10023. Founded in 1949. Artistic Director: **George Balanchine.** President and Director: **Lincoln Kirstein.** The company has 74 dancers and is among the world's most honored. Its repertory includes the works of **Balanchine, Jerome Robbins,** and **John Taras** and has had an especially close association with the music of Stravinsky, in whose name a spectacular one-week festival of ballets was produced by the company in June, 1972. Its principal dancers include: **Jacques d'Amboise, Karin von Aroldingen, Anthony Blum, Jean-Pierre Bonnefous, Melissa Hayden, Allegra Kent, Gelsey Kirkland, Sara Leland, Conrad Ludlow, Patricia McBride, Nicholas Magallanes, Peter Martins, Kay Mazzo, Francisco Moncion, Helgi Tomasson, Violette Verdy,** and **Edward Villella.** Music Director and Principal Conductor of the NYC Ballet Orchestra is **Robert Irving;** Associate Conductor is **Hugo Fiorato;** Concertmaster of the 63-member orchestra is **Lamar Alsop.** The New York City Ballet is a constituent member of the Lincoln Center for the Performing Arts and is administered by the City Center of Music and Drama, Inc., **Norman Singer,** Executive Director. Its performances take place in the New York State Theater of Lincoln Center. Its New York seasons include a season from November to February and a season from May to July. Its summer home is the Saratoga Performing Arts Center in Saratoga, New York (see Festivals), where it performs through the month of July. As a touring company, it has performed in Europe, at Wolf Trap Farm, and has made regular appearances with the Chicago Symphony at Ravinia Festival. . . . ALWIN NIKOLAIS DANCE COMPANY, c/o Chimera Foundation, 344 West 36th Street, New York, N.Y. 10018. Founded 1956. Artistic Director: **Alwin Nikolais.** The company's three soloists and seven *corps de ballet* perform contemporary works to electronic tape accompaniment. A resident and touring group, it produces about two works and gives 100 performances during its year-long season. The company has performed on American and foreign television, has been filmed, and has toured Europe (in 1961 and 1968). Regular performances are held at the Henry Street Playhouse (360 seats). It has received two Guggenheim Grants and one from the National Council on the Arts, as well as the Dance Magazine Award. . . . THE NORTHERN WESTCHESTER DANCE COMPANY, Pinebrook Road, Bedford Village, N.Y. 10506. Founded in 1964. Artistic Director: **Elizabeth Rockwell.** Administrative Heads: **Claire Miller** and **Joan Faxon.** The company includes between six and eight dancers plus two to three soloists. Repertory includes modern and jazz works, choreographed mostly by **Elizabeth Rockwell.** Performances take place at Fox Lane Auditorium; they are accompanied by quartet and taped electronic music and are held throughout the year. The company produces two or three new works every season and gives between 8 and 20 performances. It has toured the West Coast, Carribean, Israel, and U.S. colleges. . . . MARIANO PARRA BALLET ESPAÑOL, c/o Musical Artists, 119 West 57th Street, New York, N.Y. 10019. Founded in 1961. Artistic Director: **Mariano Parra.** The group, made up of two soloists and three *corps de ballet,* performs Spanish eighteenth-century, neoclassical, and flamenco dance. Performances are given with piano or guitar accompaniment. The company is a touring organization working throughout the year. It has given educational programs (lectures and demonstrations) for children and adults. . . . ELEO POMARE DANCE COMPANY, c/o Pacific World Artists, 250 West 57th Street, New York, N.Y. 10019. Founded in 1958. Artistic Director: **Eleo Pomare.** Musical and Managing Director: **Michael E. Levy.** The company has 12 to 14 dancers, and performs modern works choreographed by **Eleo Pomare** to taped music. Performances are given throughout the year; repertory includes about 18 works. The company is resident but also tours. It has performed on New York NET television and has toured colleges from New York to Florida. . . . THE TINA RAMIREZ DANCERS, 65 West 55th Street, New York, N.Y. 10019. Founded in 1965. Artistic Director: **Tina Ramirez.** The company's six dancers perform Spanish classical and flamenco at various places throughout New York City. Performances are held with piano, orchestra, or flamenco guitar accompaniment. The company's season lasts all year, with touring in the summer. Thirty-five works have been produced and over 100 performances given. The company has performed on educational television. . . . ROD RODGERS DANCE COMPANY, Clark Center for the Performing Arts, YMCA, 8th Avenue and 51st Street, New York, N.Y. 10019. Founded in 1964. Artistic Director: **Rod A. Rodgers.** The company is a touring unit whose six dancers perform modern works throughout the year. The company engages guest dancers on occasion. Performances are given with accompaniment from percussion instruments or with tapes. The company has toured extensively throughout the United States. . . . PAUL SANASARDO DANCE COMPANY, 59 West 21st Street, New York, N.Y. 10010. Founded in 1958. Artistic Director: **Paul Sanasardo;** Musical Director: **Paul Knopf;** Administrative Head: **William H. Weaver.** The company varies in size from 10 to 12 dancers. Repertory includes 25 works of modern dance and commissioned pieces. The company, primarily a touring group, performs throughout the whole year to accompaniment from orchestra, piano, or taped music. It hires guest artists on occasion. . . . ANNA SOKOLOW DANCE COMPANY, 1801 East 26th Street, Brooklyn, N.Y. 11229. Founded 1964. Artistic Director: **Anna Sokolow;** Administrative Head: **A. J. Pischl.** The company's 12 dancers perform modern dance with accompaniment from tapes. It is a touring group whose season lasts for six months. During its season, 25 to 40 performances are given of eight productions. The group has also appeared on NET television. . . . EDITH STEPHEN DANCE THEATRE, c/o E. Kapel, 40 King Street, New York, N.Y. 10014. Founded in 1958. Artistic Director: **Edith Stephen.** Musical Director: **Richard Barri.** The group has from five to seven dancers who perform works choreographed in modern idiom by **Edith Stephen.** A touring organization; performs to tape accompaniment. Its season is from January through February, April, and October through November; six productions are given 65 performances. The group tours through the United States and has performed in Europe. It performed the premiere of "Homage to a Hotdog" at Lincoln Center in 1968 and has also appeared in films. . . . SYVILLA FORT WORKSHOP STUDIO OF THEATRE DANCE, 153 West 44th Street, New York, N.Y. 10036. Founded in 1954. Artistic Director and Administrative Head: **Syvilla Fort.** The company, a resident group that choreographs modern and Afro–Caribbean works, is made up of from 6 to 10 dancers including 2 soloists. Guest artists are sometimes hired. The company travels in the New York City area. . . . THE PAUL TAYLOR DANCE COMPANY, c/o **Judith E. Daykin,** General Manager, 550 Broadway, New York, N.Y. 10012. Artistic Director: **Paul Taylor.** A touring group made up of 10 dancers performing modern dance to orchestra and tape accompaniment. Seasons vary in length. . . . THE GLEN TETLEY DANCE COMPANY, 15 West 9th Street, New York, N.Y. 10011. Artistic Director: **Glen Tetley.** Founded in 1962. A touring company of about 12 dancers. Repertory includes modern dance. Performances are given with musical accompaniment by orchestra and tape. The company has appeared on the Hunter College series of modern dance in an American premiere, "The Mythical Hunters." . . . TWYLA THARP AND DANCERS, Spurr Street, New Berlin, N.Y. 13411. Founded in 1965. Artistic Director: **Lewis L. Lloyd.** A touring organization made up of five dancers. Repertory consists of modern dance. Performances are accompanied with drums, silence, and tape. The company gives 15 to 25 performances of its four to six productions during the year. It toured Europe in 1967 and performed Twyla Tharp's "Deuce Coupe" with the City Center Joffrey Ballet in March, 1973. . . . NORMAN WALKER AND DANCE COMPANY, c/o Herbert Barrett

Management, 1860 Broadway, New York, N.Y. 10023. Founded in 1960. Artistic Director: **Norman Walker.** The company has two lead dancers, three soloists and seven *corps de ballet.* Guest artists are engaged. Repertory of the group is of commissioned works and other works in modern idiom. Performances are given with accompaniment of taped music. Its season (three scattered months) features two or three productions in a total of 25 to 35 performances. The company has appeared on television many times and has performed at Jacob's Pillow Dance Festival. . . . RUTH WALTON DANCE COMPANY, 233 West 99th Street, New York, N.Y. 10025. Founded in 1940. Artistic Director: **Ruth Walton.** The groups vary in size from trios to about 13 dancers. Repertory is made up of modern dance and jazz works. The company is primarily a resident one. It has appeared on television. . . . ANNE WILSON DANCE COMPANY, 151 Central Park West, New York, N.Y. 10023. Founded 1960. Administrative Head: **Anne Wilson.** The company has from one to seven dancers (guest dancers are sometimes hired) who perform classical and modern dance on tour, during its 12-month season. They have performed in Israel and on NET television. . . . YOUNG PEOPLE'S DANCE OF LONG ISLAND, 1434 150th Street, Whitestone, N.Y. 11359. Founded in 1967. Artistic Director: **Ted Magnan.** Administrative Head: **Frances Landrim.** The company has 12 dancers whose repertory includes classical and modern works. The group is resident; its season lasts from September through June; two performances are given. . . . IGOR YOUSKEVITCH BALLET ROMANTIQUE, 846 Seventh Avenue, New York, N.Y. 10019. Founded 1964. Artistic Director: **Igor Youskevitch.** The company has 15 to 18 dancers who perform modern, contemporary and classical works (commissioned or adapted.) The company is a touring group and hires guest performers.

Ohio

CLEVELAND MODERN DANCE ASSOCIATION WEST, 28783 Windsor Drive, North Olmsted, Ohio 44070. Founded in 1962. Artistic Director: **Ellen Daiber.** Administrative Head: **Susan Beck.** The company has 10 dancers who perform modern dance and give lecture demonstrations for elementary and secondary school students. It is a resident group with a 12-month season.

Pennsylvania

ACADEMY DANCE THEATRE COMPANY OF THE PHILADELPHIA DANCE ACADEMY, 1035 Spruce Street, Philadelphia, Pennsylvania 19107. Artistic Director and Founder: **Nadia Chilkovsky Nahumck.** The company is a touring group of five female and two male dancers with a modern dance repertory. Performances are given with piano and recorded music. The group is mainly engaged in lecture-demonstrations (at institutions and colleges in the Philadelphia area) in order to further understanding of the dance. . . . THE PENNSYLVANIA BALLET, 102 South 13th Street, Philadelphia, Pennsylvania 19107. Founded 1963. Artistic Director: **Barbara Weisberger;** Musical Director: **Maurice Kaplow** (1964). Administrative Head: **Michael Freshwater.** The company, a resident and touring group, is made up of 9 principal dancers, 8 soloists, and 15 *corps de ballet.* Repertory includes both classical (Balanchine, Tudor, Robert Rodham, Francisco Moncion, William Dollar) and modern (John Butler, Anna Sokolow). During the year-long season 45 performances are given. Works are performed with orchestral accompaniment. Regular performances are held in Academy of Music (2,900 seats). . . . PITTSBURGH BALLET, Lawrence Hall, Wood Street and Blvd. of Allies, Pittsburgh, Pennsylvania 15222. Founded in 1967. Artistic Director: **Nicolas Petrov;** Artistic Advisor: **Leonide Massine;** Administrative Head: **Mark Lewis.** The company is a resident organization and has one couple as soloists and 30 dancers in the *corps de ballet,* of whom 10 to 12 are professionals; the rest are amateurs and students. Guest dancers are hired (Villella, Verdy, Martin–Viscount, et al.) The group's repertory includes classical, modern, and jazz works; operas, and children's ballet.

The company's season lasts nine months; 15 performances are given with orchestral, piano, or tape accompaniment. Regular performances of the Pittsburgh Ballet are held in Pittsburgh Playhouse (550 seats) and Pittsburgh Opera House (2,000 seats). The company has performed on television.

Texas

DISCOVERY DANCE GROUP, 5303 Holly Springs, Houston, Texas 77027. Founded 1963. Artistic Director: **Camille Long Hill.** The company has 15 *corps* dancers and 4 soloists and performs contemporary and jazz works. Performances are given with taped musical accompaniment. The company has performed on television.

Utah

UTAH CIVIC BALLET COMPANY, 145 South State Street, Salt Lake City, Utah 84111. Founded in 1963. Artistic Director: **William F. Christensen.** Administrative Head: **Alan Behunin.** The company has 10 principal dancers, 10 soloists, and 7 scholarship members. The *corps de ballet* is from the University of Utah. The season lasts 45 weeks from September through May and the month of July; altogether about 200 performances are given. The company performs classical works with the 75-member Utah Symphony and on tour with recordings. It engages well-known guest dancers. Regular performances, are given at Kingsbury Hall on the University of Utah campus (1,917 seats). It has toured the Southwest and performed in many high schools.

Washington

MARTHA NISHITANI MODERN DANCE COMPANY, 4203 University Way, N.E., Seattle, Washington 98105. Founded in 1951. Artistic Director: **Martha Nishitani.** Musical Director: **Beatrice Higman.** The company has 10 adult, 6 teen-age and 10 child dancers who perform modern works and children's theater. It sometimes engages guest dancers. During the season, lasting from September through June, one to eight performances are given, usually with piano or recorded musical accompaniment. The company has appeared on television many times and has been filmed. It tours regularly.

Wisconsin

FINE ARTS DANCE THEATRE, University of Wisconsin, Milwaukee, Wisconsin 53201. Founded in 1965. Artistic Director: **Myron Howard Nadel.** Administrative Head: **A. A. Suppan.** The company is composed of five principal dancers and is both a resident and touring group. It engages guest artists for dancing roles. The group's repertory is made up of modern and contemporary works, with some classical ballet. Musical accompaniment is supplied by taped and sometimes live music. The group's season lasts from September through May; about eight performances are given.

Music Tents and Summer Theaters

The extension of the regular musical theater season into the summer months is the purpose of over 250 music tents and summer theaters—the so-called strawhat circuit—located throughout the nation.

Because they present their own productions, or packaged shows and touring groups, of established repertory—musicals, variety shows, plays, operettas, etc.—the tents and summer theaters are more institutionalized than, for example, the cluster of theaters in New York City which are used by ever-changing syndicates of risk-assuming producers and creative writers hopeful of bringing new works into the musical theater repertory.

The tents and theaters are to the world of lighter musical fare what the institutionalized summer music festival is to the concert, recital, and opera world. Originally operated without famous stars, the summer theaters now feature singers, actors, and dancers from Hollywood, Broadway, and even the world of opera. The link to the great sources of talent and the undeniable popularity of the repertory presented assure the tents and theaters of continued success, particularly in those areas of the country where they may be the only source of live stage entertainment.

The theaters shown following are given their community location. Mailing addresses, when known, are added. In some instances, the mailing address and the theater location are identical.

California

MELODYLAND THEATRE, Anaheim, California. Mailing address: Box 3460, Anaheim, California 92803. . . . GREEK THEATRE, 2700 North Vermont Avenue, Los Angeles, California 90027. . . . SACRAMENTO MUSIC CIRCUS, 1419 H Street, Sacramento, California. CIRCLE STAR THEATRE, 1717 Industrial Road, San Carlos, California. . . . CAROUSEL, West Covina, California.

Colorado

CENTRAL CITY OPERA HOUSE, 910 16th Street, Denver, Colorado 80202. . . . ELITCH GARDENS, 4620 West 38th Avenue, Denver, Colorado 80212.

Connecticut

GOODSPEED OPERA HOUSE, Box A, East Haddam, Connecticut 06423. . . . CANDLEWOOD THEATRE, New Fairfield, Connecticut. Mailing address: 339 Flanders Road, East Lyme, Connecticut 06333. . . . IVORYTON PLAYHOUSE, Ivoryton, Connecticut. . . . SHARON PLAYHOUSE, Box 488, Sharon, Connecticut 06069. . . . OAKDALE MUSICAL THEATRE, Wallingford, Connecticut.

Georgia

THEATRE UNDER STARS, 710 Peachtree Street, Atlanta, Georgia 30308.

Illinois

CORN STOCK THEATRE, Box 412, Bradley Park, Peoria, Illinois. . . . THE LITTLE THEATRE ON THE SQUARE, Box 155, Sullivan, Illinois 61951.

Indiana

STARLIGHT MUSICALS, 2511 East 46th Street, Indianapolis, Indiana 46205. . . . WAGON WHEEL PLAYHOUSE, Route 30 East, Warsaw, Indiana 46580.

Maine

BRUNSWICK MUSIC THEATRE, Bowdoin College, Brunswick, Maine 04011. . . . KENNEBUNKPORT PLAYHOUSE, Kennebunkport, Maine. . . . OGUNQUIT PLAYHOUSE, Ogunquit, Maine.

Maryland

SHADY GROVE MUSIC FAIR, Gaithersburg, Maryland. . . . PAINTERS MILL MUSIC FAIR, Owings Mills, Maryland.

Massachusetts

NORTH SHORE MUSIC THEATRE, Box 62, Beverly, Massachusetts 01915. . . . SOUTH SHORE MUSIC CIRCUS, Cohasset, Massachusetts. . . . CAPE PLAYHOUSE, Dennis, Massachusetts. . . . FALMOUTH PLAYHOUSE, Falmouth, Massachusetts. . . . THE COLLEGE LIGHT OPERA COMPANY HIGHFIELD THEATRE, Box F., Falmouth, Massachusetts 02541 (See Festivals—Massachusetts: The College Players). . . . CAPE COD MELODY TENT, Hyannis, Massachusetts. . . . TUFTS ARENA THEATRE, Tufts University, Medford, Massachusetts 02155. . . . BERKSHIRE PLAYHOUSE, Stockbridge, Massachusetts.

Michigan

BARN THEATRE, Augusta, Michigan. . . . TIBBITS OPERA HOUSE, Coldwater, Michigan. . . . FLINT MUSIC TENT, Flint, Michigan. . . . LEDGE'S PLAYHOUSE, Fitzgerald Park, Grand Ledge, Michigan 48837. . . . RED BARN THEATRE, Saugatuck, Michigan 49453.

Missouri

STARLIGHT THEATRE, Kansas City, Missouri. . . . SAINT LOUIS MUNICIPAL OPERA, Saint Louis, Missouri.

Montana

OLD BREWERY THEATRE, 931 Knight Street, Helena, Montana 59601. . . . GOLDEN GARTER OPERA HOUSE, West Yellowstone, Montana.

New Hampshire

LAKE SUNAPEE PLAYHOUSE, George's Mills, New Hampshire. . . . HAMPTON PLAYHOUSE, Winnacunett Road, Hampton, New Hampshire 03842. . . . ROCHESTER MUSIC THEATRE, Rochester, New Hampshire. . . . WEATHERVANE THEATRE, Whitefield, New Hampshire.

New Jersey

SURFLIGHT SUMMER THEATRE, Beach Haven, N.J. . . . HALFPENNY PLAYHOUSE, 155 Midland Avenue, Kearney, N.J. 07032. . . . LAMBERTVILLE MUSIC CIRCUS, Lambertville, N.J.

New York

GATEWAY PLAYHOUSE, Bellport, Long Island. . . . JOHN DREW THEATRE, 158 Main Street, East Hampton, Long Island 11937. . . . JONES BEACH THEATRE, Jones Beach, Wantagh, Long Island, New York. . . . LAKE PLACID PLAYHOUSE, Lake Placid, N.Y. . . . COLONIE SUMMER THEATRE, Latham, N.Y. . . . FOREST-BURGH THEATRE, Monticello, N.Y. . . . MOUNTAINDALE PLAYHOUSE, Box 132, Mountaindale, N.Y. 12763. . . . MEL-ODY FAIR, Wurlitzer Park, North Tona-wanda, N.Y. . . . PLAYHOUSE ON THE HUDSON, 2 Idlewilde Street, Cornwall-on-The-Hudson, N.Y. 12520. . . . TAPPAN ZEE PLAYHOUSE, Nyack, N.Y. . . . WESTBURY MUSIC FAIR, Westbury, Long Island, N.Y. 11590. . . . WOOD-STOCK PLAYHOUSE, Box 268, Wood-stock, N.Y. 12498.

North Carolina

PARKWAY PLAYHOUSE, Brunsville, North Carolina. . . . EAST CAROLINA UNIVERSITY SUMMER THEATRE, Greenville, North Carolina. . . . WATER-SIDE THEATRE, Fort Raleigh National Historic Site, Roanoke Island, Manteo, North Carolina 27954. . . . FESTIVAL THEATRE, Box 4657, North Carolina School of the Arts, Winston-Salem, North Carolina 27107.

Ohio

CANAL FULTON SUMMER THEATRE, Canal Fulton, Ohio. . . . SHOWBOAT MAJESTIC, Foot of Broadway, Cincinnati, Ohio 45202.

Pennsylvania

ALLENBERRY PLAYHOUSE, Allenberry, Pennsylvania. . . . VALLEY FORGE MU-SIC FAIR, Devon, Pennsylvania. . . . EPHRATA STAR PLAYHOUSE, Box 334, Ephrata, Pennsylvania 17522. . . . TOTEM POLE PLAYHOUSE, Caledonia State Park, Fayetteville, Pennsylvania 17222. . . . GRETNA PLAYHOUSE, Mount Gretna, Pennsylvania. . . . MOUNTAIN PLAY-HOUSE, Jennerstown, Pennsylvania. . . . MILLBROOK PLAYHOUSE, Millhall, Pennsylvania. . . . POCONO PLAYHOUSE, Mountainhome, Pennsylvania. . . . LAND-ING PLAYHOUSE, Shamokin Dam, Penn-sylvania. . . . PENNSYLVANIA STATE FESTIVAL THEATRE, University Park, Pennsylvania 16802. . . . FAYETTE COUNTY PLAYHOUSE, Uniontown, Pennsylvania.

Rhode Island

THEATRE-BY-THE-SEA, Matunuck, Rhode Island 02880. . . . WARWICK MU-SICAL THEATRE, Warwick, Rhode Island.

Texas

CASA MAÑANA, Fort Worth, Texas. . . . DALLAS STATE FAIR PARK, Dallas, Texas.

Utah

VALLEY MUSIC HALL TENT, Salt Lake City, Utah.

Vermont

DORSET PLAYHOUSE, Dorset, Ver-mont. . . . STOWE PLAYHOUSE, Box 267, Stowe, Vermont 05672. . . . WESTON PLAYHOUSE, Weston, Vermont.

Virginia

BARTER THEATRE, Abingdon, Virginia 24210.

Wisconsin

ATTIC THEATRE, Box 41, Appleton, Wis-consin 54911.

Part 5 | Performers

The names of the musicians below are followed by brief, pertinent facts related to their careers and activities (concert managers, record labels, debuts, specializations, etc.). The list consists only of performers from the field of concert music. Special attention has been paid to new personalities. A number of young artists have made impressive careers for themselves in America and abroad within the last five or ten years; they were given preference whenever a choice arose between an older, well-established, but now less active performer, and a new musician with a growing reputation.

Singers are grouped by voice. Instrumentalists are classified by instrument.

Concert managers were valid for spring, 1972 or for the 1972–73 season. Some changes can be expected for subsequent seasons; however, some very famous artists have had the same concert manager for years.

Record labels refer to those recordings in which the performer appears as soloist or chamber musician, unless otherwise indicated. For orchestral recordings necessarily containing performances by section principals, the reader is referred to the record label identified with the orchestra (see Instrumental Ensembles).

Performers here are native-born Americans, naturalized citizens, citizens by marriage, long-time residents, or foreigners directing their careers from American headquarters and returning to a place of residence in the United States during off-season.

Instrumental

PIANO

Webster Aitken (b. 1908), concert pianist, recitalist and chamber musician; debut in Vienna, 1929; U.S. debut, 1935. Recordings: *Lyrichord.* . . . **Maro Ajemian** (b. 1924), concert artist, recitalist, chamber musician; performs much contemporary music; Town Hall debut, 1941. Recordings: *Columbia, Folkways, CRI.* . . . **Agustin Anievas,** American pianist of Mexican–Spanish descent; since 1961 has played throughout the U.S. with many of the major orchestras and has played 10 South American tours; since 1965, has given performances in most of the major cities of Europe (in London before Queen Elizabeth for a benefit concert, etc.); has toured the Middle East, the Far East, and Australia; was the first winner of the International Mitropoulos Competition (1961), and placed high or won other important contests in the U.S. and in Europe; was the first child ever to play in Mexico's Palace of Fine Arts; his orchestral debut was with the Little Orchestra Society (New York) at age 18; his repertory favors the Romantic composers. Recordings: *Angel, Seraphim.* Management: Colbert Artists Management, Inc. . . . **Pina Antonelli,** young pianist; at age ten she played with the Philadelphia Orchestra; played all of the sonatas of Mozart in a series of live concerts in Philadelphia at the age of fourteen; won first prize at the Washington International Bach Festival in 1959; has played in ensemble in New York, etc. Management: Bichurin Concerts Corp. . . . **Claudio Arrau** (b. 1903, Chile), concert pianist and recitalist; U.S. debut in 1923; has lived in the U.S. since 1941; performer of international stature. Recordings: *Philips, Angel, Vanguard, Everest, Decca, Seraphim.* Management: Columbia Artists Management, Inc. . . . **Edward Auer,** young pianist; prizewinner in major international competitions: Chopin International Competition, Warsaw, 1965; Tchaikovsky Competition, Moscow, 1966; Marguerite Long Concours, Paris, 1967; Queen Elizabeth Competition, Brussels, 1968, etc.; performed at Prague Spring Festival in 1971; performed in 1971 in U.S.S.R.; has played in France, Monaco, and Italy. Recorded in Europe for Pathé Marconi (*EMI*). Management: Hurok Concerts, Inc.

David Bean, recitalist, concert pianist; has emphasized performances of lesser known works of older master composers, as well as such composers as Busoni, Reger, Scriabin, Villa-Lobos. Recordings: *RCA Victor, Westminster.* Management: Tornay Management. . . . **Stephen Bishop** (b. 1940), concert pianist, recitalist; has had an active career in England since 1960; has performed throughout Europe and America; appearances with the Boston Symphony, the St. Louis Symphony, Chicago Symphony, Houston Symphony, Los Angeles Philharmonic, Stockholm Philharmonic, BBC Orchestra and orchestras in Holland, etc. Recordings: *Philips, Angel, Seraphim.* Management: Shaw Concerts, Inc. . . . **Roy Bogas,** concert pianist; was soloist with the San Francisco Symphony at six; accompanist to Yehudi Menuhin at nineteen; was Laureate winner of the Second Tchaikovsky Competition in Moscow and a prizewinner in the Queen Elizabeth of Belgium Contest; has played with the San Francisco Symphony on many occasions and has toured Alaska, Argentina, U.S., Canada, Europe, and the Soviet Union. Management: Rudolph Lisarelli Management. . . . **Jorge Bolet** (b. Cuba), artist-in-residence, University of Indiana; a pianist of international fame; has performed with the New York Philharmonic, American Symphony Orchestra, Boston Symphony, and other U.S. major orchestras; many foreign tours. A noted Liszt interpreter. Recordings: *Everest, Colpix.* Management: Columbia Artists Management, Inc. . . . **Alexander Brailowsky** (b. 1896); internationally known recitalist and concert artist; Chopin specialist. Recordings: *Columbia, Everest, RCA Victor.* . . . **John Browning** (b. 1933), one of America's major pianists; winner of the Leventritt Award, 1955, Queen Elizabeth Gold Medal, 1956, and the Steinway Centennial Award in 1954; New York debut in 1956 with the New York Philharmonic; debut at ten in Denver; has made over 20 European tours including 3 in the Soviet Union; toured Japan for the first time in 1972; a typical season will include appearances with some 20 U.S. orchestras, about 15 foreign ones, and many recitals; he has recorded all concertos by Prokofiev, the complete Chopin Études, etc.; in 1962, he premiered the Barber Piano Concerto and has performed it over 250 times. Recordings: *RCA Victor, Columbia, Capitol, Desto, Seraphim.* Management: Herbert Barrett Management, Inc.

Richard Cass (b. 1931); won the 1953 National Federation of Music Clubs Award, and took part in the Viotti International Contest; recitals in the U.S. (since 1957), in Europe (since 1954), and in Canada. . . . **Shura Cherkassky** (b. 1911), has maintained a career in Europe appearing in recitals and with major orchestras. Recordings: *DGG, Mercury.* . . . **Van Cliburn** (b. 1934), one of America's most famous native musicians; winner of the following awards: Kosciuszko Foundation Chopin Award, 1952; Leventritt Award, 1954; First Prize, Tchaikovsky International Competition, Moscow, 1958; concerts and recitals in the U.S. since 1954, in Europe since 1958; many U.S. appearances since 1958 on television, popular shows, benefits, festivals, and other special occasions; also appeared as conductor. Recordings: *RCA Victor.* Management: Hurok Concerts, Inc. . . . **Nicolas Constantinidis,** born in Egypt of Greek parents; blind since the age of six; early education in Egypt and Greece; began piano study as a teen-ager; made his debut in Egypt at age seventeen following, in the next two years, with some 75 recitals; in the 1950's, he toured Europe and, in order to raise the funds to come to America, concertized in Egypt for a year; came to the U.S. on a scholarship in 1957; despite the lack of a formal secondary school education, he earned his Bachelor degree in 1961, his Master's in 1962; has performed in New York, London, Amsterdam, Cleveland, Vienna, and with orchestras conducted by Serebrier, Abravanel, and Louis Lane; he is presently also Curator of Music of the Akron Art Institute. Management: Albert Kay Associates, Inc.

Ivan Davis (b. 1932, Texas), a leading pianist of his generation; winner of the National Federation of Music Clubs Award, 1955; Busoni Competition, Bolzano, Italy, 1957; Casella Competition, Naples, 1958; Franz Liszt International Competition, New York, 1960; artist-in-residence, University of Miami, Coral Gables; has performed with many front rank U.S. orchestras and in solo recitals throughout the U.S.; London debut in 1967–68 season. Recordings: *London, Columbia.* Management: Columbia Artists Management, Inc. . . . **Robert de Gaetano** (b. 1946, New York), "discovered" by Soviets Richter and Oistrakh when performing in Philadelphia in 1969; first musician to win Rotary International Scholarship; has performed and studied with Alexis Weissenberg; first major tour of U.S. in 1971–72. Management: Hurok Concerts, Inc. . . . **Anthony di Bonaventura,** recitalist and concert pianist; performed with the Philadelphia, New York Philharmonic, and Baltimore Orchestras, among other major groups; has toured Australia, New Zealand, Mexico, Scandinavia, Bulgaria, etc. Recordings: *Columbia.* Management: Columbia Artists Management, Inc. . . . **Misha Dichter,** (b. 1945, China); raised in U.S.;

prizewinner (2nd prize) in 1966 Tchaikovsky Competition, Moscow; performed with Boston Symphony and other major orchestras. Recordings: *RCA Victor.* Management: Hurok Concerts, Inc. . . . **James Dick,** concert pianist and recitalist; winner in several prestigious European and American piano prizes including the Tchaikovsky Competition, the Leventritt Award, and the Busoni Competition in Italy; has performed frequently in England, where he spent a period of study; has toured Russia, Canada, and the U.S. Management: Shaw Concerts, Inc. . . . **Raymond Dudley,** pianist-in-residence at University of Cincinnati; has toured with facsimile of 18th-century piano; in 1968, first pianist to perform all 52 Haydn Sonatas in a series of eight concerts in Purcell Room of London's Royal Festival Hall. Recordings: *Lyrichord.* Management: University of Cincinnati Concert Bureau.

Rudolf Firkusny (b. 1912, Czechoslovakia), internationally active concert artist and renowned recitalist; American debut in Town Hall, New York in 1938; since 1942 has played with most of the nation's major orchestras; festival engagements include Ravinia, Tanglewood, Saratoga, Aspen; has made 25 tours of Europe, 10 of South America, 12 through Mexico, plus tours to Australia and Israel. Recordings: *Westminster, DGG, Pickwick, Decca, Seraphim, RCA Victor.* Management: Columbia Artists Management, Inc.; for the Near East, Australia, New Zealand, etc.: Bichurin Concerts Corp. . . . **Eileen Flissler,** recitalist and chamber pianist; has undertaken world tours; first major orchestral concert with the Philadelphia Orchestra in 1941; wife of violinist Aaron Rosand, with whom she has recorded. Recordings: *Vox.* . . . **Sydney Foster,** faculty, University of Indiana; was first winner of the Leventritt Award in 1940; followed by an appearance with the New York Philharmonic; has subsequently toured Europe, the Soviet Union, Latin America, Japan, and throughout the U.S. Management: Herbert Barrett Management, Inc. . . . **Malcolm Frager** (b. 1935), winner of the following awards: Geneva Competition, 1955; Michaels Memorial Award, Chicago, 1956; Leventritt Award, 1959; Queen Elizabeth of Belgium Competition, 1960; has appeared with major U.S. orchestras and in recitals. Management: Columbia Artists Management, Inc. . . . **Vera Franceschi** (b. 1926), San Francisco-born; has pursued a career in both Europe and America; debut 1939 in Paris; U.S. debut in 1948; played in Venice and on Rome television in 1960. . . . **Claude Frank** (b. 1925) has performed in U.S. and Europe in concerts and recitals since 1950; performed with Boston, Chicago and other major orchestras; has recorded and performed in recital Beethoven's 32 piano sonatas; husband of pianist Lilian Kallir. Recordings: *RCA Victor.* Management: Columbia Artists Management, Inc. . . . **John Augustus Frusciante,** young pianist from Florida; recent graduate (1968) from Juilliard School; has played throughout Florida and other areas of the South, Pennsylvania, Ohio, etc.; has performed in Vienna and Salzburg; his teachers include Jacob Lateiner. Management: Bichurin Concerts Corp.

Frank Glazer, visiting Professor of Piano at Eastman School; artist-in-residence, Bennett College; member of Eastman Quartet; has played on tour in U.S., Near East and Israel, Europe, and Canada; Town Hall debut, 1936; concerts (first dates) with Boston (1939), New York Philharmonic (1950), and the Chicago (1950) Symphony Orchestras and such European orchestras as Lamoureux, The Hague, etc.; also television and radio performances. Recordings: *Concert-Disc, Vox, Candide, Everest* as soloist and chamber player. Management: Herbert Barrett Management, Inc. . . . **Robert Goldsand** (b. 1911, Vienna); U.S. debut in 1927; resident in the U.S. since 1939; recitalist and concert pianist; faculty, Manhattan School of Music; formerly on the staff of the Cincinnati Conservatory of Music; made debut at age ten in Vienna; his reputation is that of a performer with an exceedingly rich repertory, from the classic masters to much contemporary music, involving a variety of forms; he has a penchant for presenting historical cycles; his tours include concerts in America, South America, and Europe. Recordings: *Desto.* Management:

Albert Kay Associates, Inc. . . . **Richard Goode,** young chamber musician, solo pianist; member of the Chamber Music Society of Lincoln Center performing in a variety of chamber and solo recitals; has been performing in New York since 1961; since then has played in Alexander Schneider's Bach Series, with the Music from Marlboro group, in New York, and on tour, etc.; has performed in Canada, Mexico, England, the Festival of Two Worlds in Spoleto, and toured the Soviet Union with the Boston Chamber Players; elsewhere in the U.S. he has played with the National Symphony and the Baltimore Symphony and at Tanglewood. Recordings: *Columbia.* Management: Herbert Barrett Management, Inc. . . . **Gary Graffman** (b. 1928), concert pianist, recitalist, and sometime chamber music player; New York recital debut at age ten; appeared as soloist with orchestra under Fabian Sevitzky at age eight; winner of the Leventritt Award in 1949 and began appearances with major orchestras that year; first U.S. tour in 1951; first South American tour in 1955; first tour of Europe in 1956; first world tour in 1958; since these initial tours, he has repeated them on a regular basis, becoming one of the world's most traveled musicians; his U.S. engagements are seasonally extensive; altogether his annual performance commitments total over 100 a year; a pianist of virtuosic attainments, his repertory includes many of the large concertos and solo works of the Romantic school; he has recorded with virtually every front rank U.S. orchestra. Recordings: *RCA Victor, Columbia, London.* Management: Arthur Judson Management, Inc.; Bichurin Concerts Corp. (for U.S.S.R. and Latin America); Pacific World Artists, Inc. (for the Orient, etc.). . . . **Horatio Gutierrez** (b. Havana); in the U.S. since 1962; became an American citizen in 1967; at age eleven performed with the Havana Symphony; in the U.S., he played early in his career with the Los Angeles and Pasadena Orchestras, and the Springfield (Illinois) Symphony; appeared with the New York Philharmonic under Bernstein at a Young People's concert in 1966; was a 1970 prizewinner in Moscow of the Tchaikovsky Competition. Management: Hurok Concerts, Inc.

Leonid Hambro (b. 1920), concert pianist, recitalist, and accompanist; debut recital, Town Hall, 1946; winner of Naumburg Award in 1946. Recordings: *Lyrichord, Golden Crest, RCA Victor, Command.* . . . **Walter Hautzig** (b. 1921, Vienna), has been in the U.S. since 1939; Town Hall debut in 1943; has given recitals in U.S., Europe, Latin America, Asia, and the Middle East. Recordings: *Monitor, Vox, Turnabout.* . . . **Natalie Hinderas,** piano recitalist and concert artist; on the faculty of Temple University; debut with the Philadelphia Orchestra at regular subscription series in 1971; has appeared with the Cleveland Orchestra, the Baltimore Symphony, the Detroit Symphony, etc., and has performed in England, the Philippines, Germany, and elsewhere; has toured with lecture-recitals on the black musician in America. Recordings: *Desto.* Management: Joanne Rile, Artists' Representative. . . . **Lorin Hollander** (b. 1945), made debut at age eleven in Carnegie Hall; active recitalist and concert artist; has appeared on TV and recently has given free outdoor recitals in Harlem; made world tour with the Cincinnati Symphony; has performed on the Baldwin electronic piano and appeared at popular music haven, Fillmore East, in New York, etc. Recordings: *Angel, RCA Victor.* Management: Columbia Artists Management, Inc. . . . **Vladimir Horowitz** (b. 1904, Russia); U.S. citizen since 1944; one of the most celebrated pianists in modern times; made his debut at age seventeen; toured Europe in 1924; American debut early in 1928 with the New York Philharmonic; in the U.S. since 1940; after twelve years of retirement from public performance, he played a concert in Carnegie Hall on May 9, 1965 attended by much publicity; currently, still primarily a recording pianist. Recordings: *RCA Victor, Columbia, Seraphim.* . . . **Mieczyslaw Horszowski** (b. 1892, Poland), recitalist, chamber musician, and concert pianist in appearances throughout the U.S. and Europe; made formal debut at age nine with considerable notoriety; American debut in 1906; in the U.S. since 1940; one of the world's esteemed pianists; has performed with some of the great historical figures in music; has been a frequent chamber performer with Casals, Serkin, Schneider, et al. and has given a number of monumental recitals, e.g., the 1957 series devoted to all the works for piano solo by Beethoven; with Casals and Schneider, he has performed at the White House, before the United Nations, etc.; on the faculty of the Curtis Institute of Music, and has had a close association with the Marlboro Music Festival and the Casals Festival in Puerto Rico. Recordings: *Columbia, RCA Victor, Decca, Philips, Vox, Vanguard.* Management: Colbert Artists Management, Inc.

Eugene Istomin (b. 1925), internationally known as recitalist and concert pianist; also eminently established as a chamber artist: in U.S., Europe, Far East, and Australia; regular appearances at Casals Festival and with major orchestras everywhere; performs with Leonard Rose and Isaac Stern as a celebrated trio (q.v.). Recordings: *Columbia.* Management: Hurok Concerts, Inc. . . . **José Iturbi** (b. 1895, Spain), internationally known as soloist in recitals and concerts, and as conductor. Recordings: *Angel, RCA Victor;* also *Turia* (Turia Record Co., Box 1917, Beverly Hills, California 90210). Management: Robert M. Gewald.

Agi Jambor (b. 1915), made debut in Budapest, 1926; came to U.S. in 1947; active in concerts and recitals; teacher at Bryn Mawr College. Recordings: *Capitol.* . . . **Byron Janis** (b. 1928), has appeared as concert pianist and recitalist throughout the world since his debut in 1943 in Pittsburgh; one of the great pianists of his generation. Recordings: *RCA Victor, Mercury, Everest.* Management: Hurok Concerts, Inc. . . . **Grant Johannesen** (b. 1921), New York debut in 1944; has performed in Europe since 1947; has since traversed the world playing in the Soviet Union (1963, 1965, 1971), the major cities of France, England, Germany, the Far East, etc.; his season consists of concerts, recitals, recordings, and master classes; he is a frequent guest artist at U.S. festivals and regular concert series; in 1970, he played twice a complete cycle of Beethoven piano concertos (with the Atlanta Symphony) and is reputed to have played such a cycle the most often. Recordings: *Golden Crest, Columbia, Vox.* Management: Columbia Artists Management, Inc.; Bichurin Concerts Corp. (Latin America, East Europe); Thea Dispeker Artists' Representative (Europe). . . . **Gunnar Johansen** (b. 1906, Copenhagen); in the U.S. since 1929; artist-in-residence, University of Wisconsin at Madison; produces his own recordings (commercially available) on his own label, *Artist Direct,* for which he has recorded significant, large collections: the complete keyboard solo works of Bach (43 discs in 20 albums), the complete piano music of Liszt (24 discs in 23 albums; still in process), the complete piano works of Busoni (seven discs); performed in New York and at the University of Wisconsin in 1966 important works by Busoni; a pianist of virtuosic inclinations, he appears at the Romantic Festival held by Butler University in Indianapolis playing works of notorious difficulty and was especially in the national music news when, in 1969, he substituted for Peter Serkin on about 30 hours notice performing with the Philadelphia Orchestra under Ormandy a work he had never known before—Beethoven's transcription for piano of his violin concerto. Recordings: *Artist Direct* (see Record Companies).

Joseph Kalichstein (b. 1946, Tel Aviv), studied in New York and made debut in that city in 1967; in 1969, won the Leventritt Award; he has played with the New York Philharmonic, the Chicago, Cleveland, Pittsburgh, Detroit Symphonies, and orchestras in Denver, Buffalo, etc. Recordings: *RCA Victor.* Management: Hurok Concerts, Inc. . . . **Lilian Kallir** (b. 1931), chamber musician and solo recitalist; Town Hall debut in 1949; won National Music League Award in 1948; appeared in North Africa in 1953; made tours of U.S. and Europe, 1954–1955, and 1957. Recordings: *Columbia, RCA Victor.* Management: Columbia Artists Management, Inc. . . . **John Kirkpatrick** (b. 1905), made debut in Paris in 1931, and at Town Hall, New York, 1936; frequent performer of contemporary American piano music; on the faculty of Yale University School of Music;

has been closely associated with the music of Charles Ives for many years. Recordings: *Columbia.*

Ruth Laredo, concert pianist, chamber musician, and recitalist; performs often in joint recitals with her husband, violinist Jaime Laredo; has toured with the Music from Marlboro Series within the U.S. and overseas to Israel, Greece, etc., under State Department sponsorship; her close association with the Marlboro Festival has resulted in her performing with many of its luminaries on tour and for recordings; other performances include special appearances at the White House and the United Nations, with members of the Budapest and Guarneri quartets, at Tanglewood, with the Cleveland Orchestra, etc. Recordings: *Connoisseur Society, Columbia.* Management: Arthur Judson Management, Inc. . . . **Jacob Lateiner** (b. 1928), one of the important pianists of his generation; recitals and concerts in the U.S., Europe, and Australia, etc.; a specialist in the works of Beethoven. Recordings: *RCA Victor.* Management: Tornay Management. . . . **Theodore Lettvin** (b. 1926), American and European concerts and recitals since 1948; won Naumburg Award, 1958 and Michaels Memorial Award, 1950. Management: Thea Dispeker Artists' Representative. . . . **Raymond Lewenthal** (b. 1926), known particularly for his repertory of virtuoso Romantic works; has performed for the Newport and Butler University festivals (q.v.) and such major orchestras as the Boston Symphony and New York Philharmonic; has toured throughout the U.S. and abroad; recipient of France's Chevalier of the Order of Arts and Letters. Recordings: *RCA Victor, Westminster, Columbia.* Management: Columbia Artists Management, Inc. . . . **Seymour Lipkin** (b. 1927), primarily active as conductor at present; has given recitals and appeared at concerts since 1948; has made 11 American tours; early in his career he won the Rachmaninoff Competition. Recordings (as pianist): *Columbia.* . . . **Eugene List** (b. 1918), well-known recitalist and concert pianist with major orchestras since 1938; debut at the age of twelve with the Los Angeles Philharmonic; New York debut with the Philharmonic in 1935; has performed for all the post-war U.S. presidents at various official functions; sometimes appears in recital with his wife, violinist Carroll Glenn. Recordings: *Westminster, Mercury, Music Guild, Vanguard, Odyssey.* Management: Columbia Artists Management, Inc. . . . **Albert Lotto,** has performed with Pittsburgh Symphony and Tokyo Philharmonic; participated in 4th Tchaikovsky Competition; performed in five major cities of Japan in 1970; first European tour in 1968. Management: Anne O'Donnell Management. . . . **Jerome Lowenthal,** much-traveled piano virtuoso of the younger generation; debut with the Philadelphia Orchestra at age thirteen; in 1963 he played for the first time with the New York Philharmonic; has subsequently traveled to over forty countries in Europe, the Far East, South America, including Israel, the Soviet Union, etc.; makes annual cross-country tours of the U.S.; with the Pittsburgh Symphony and conductor, William Steinberg, he toured for 11 weeks in 1966 in Western and Eastern Europe; teaches at Music Academy of the West. Recordings: *Columbia, Vanguard.* Management: Hurok Concerts, Inc. . . . **Cecil Lytle,** first prize Franz Liszt International Piano Competition in Budapest in 1971; concert appearances with Boston Symphony, Madison, Wisconsin Summer Symphony, and others; also performs jazz. Management: Frothingham Management.

Alan Mandel, faculty, American University, Washington, D.C.; has given recitals of American Music; recently attracted attention by featuring ragtime piano works in a solo recital at Carnegie Recital Hall; recorded complete piano works of Charles Ives, as well as over 40 pieces by Gottschalk. Recordings: *Desto.* . . . **Stephen Manes,** made his New York debut in 1963; winner in several piano competitions and winner of the Harriet Cohen International Beethoven Prize; has performed with several leading orchestras including the New York Philharmonic, Boston Symphony, Buffalo Philharmonic, Detroit Symphony, etc. Management: Shaw Concerts, Inc. . . . **Ozan Marsh,** faculty, University of Arizona, Tucson; has played concerts and recitals since 1937; made U.S.–Canada tour in 1956 and 1959 and subsequently; toured with the Boston Pops Orchestra as soloist. Recordings: *RCA Victor*. . . . **Frederick Marvin** (b. 1923), debut at age sixteen; played in Europe in 1954 and 1958, etc.; discoverer, editor, and performer of the piano sonatas by Soler; on the faculty, Syracuse University. Recordings: *Decca*. . . . **William Masselos,** piano virtuoso with a particularly strong reputation for performing demanding recitals such as lengthy so-called marathon recitals (at Hunter College in New York, 1972, etc.); he has performed many contemporary works, a number of them in premiere hearings; orchestral concerts include performances with the New York Philharmonic and the London Symphony (in New York), and orchestras in Chicago, Washington, etc.; festival appearances have been at Aspen, Fish Creek, Cabrillo; his performances of the music of Charles Ives have been especially noteworthy; he is on the faculty of the Catholic University of America. Recordings: *Columbia, Odyssey, RCA Victor, CRI*. Management: Herbert Barrett Management, Inc. . . . **James Mathis,** Texas-born recitalist and concert artist; played piano in public as a child; graduated from Juilliard in 1955 (Master's degree); winner of many important prizes: Kosciuszko Foundation Chopin Award, 1954; First Prize Munich International Competition, 1956; Busoni Competition, 1960; New York debut in 1962; has been on the faculty of the University of Oklahoma in Norman since 1967; he has concertized throughout the U.S. (St. Louis, Houston, Dallas orchestras, etc.) and in Europe in Germany, Austria, Italy, England, and other countries. Management: Colbert Artists Management, Inc. . . . **Mack McCray,** won Silver Medal in the 1970 International Enesco Competition in Bucharest; won 2nd prize in International Liszt Competition; performed with the San Francisco Symphony and other orchestras; also performed in Switzerland. Management: Anne O'Donnell Management. . . . **Mayne Miller,** recitalist and accompanist; active in New York; has performed in Chicago, London, Geneva, etc. Management: Wayne Wilbur Management. . . . **Marjorie Mitchell,** has performed with the Zagreb Philharmonic, Berlin Philharmonic, and other European ensembles; appearances in the U.S. in recitals; frequently performs contemporary music in Pan American festival, Washington, D.C., etc. Recordings: *Decca, CRI, Vanguard*.

Marilyn Neeley, won Emmy Award with husband, Robert Gerle, for complete Beethoven piano and violin sonatas for ETV; with husband performs as Gerle–Neeley Duo; performed with Joanne de Keyser, cellist, as Neeley–de Keyser Duo; has performed with Boston Pops, Chicago Symphony, Pittsburgh Symphony, altogether over 75 orchestras; made two U.S. State Department tours: Mexico, 1961, Europe, 1966; performed at Berkshire, Marlboro and Carmel–Bach Festivals; won Michaels Memorial Music Award–Chicago; won unanimous medal in International Competition at Geneva; is on the faculty at Ohio State University. Management: Thea Dispeker Artists' Representative.

Garrick Ohlsson (b. 1948), came to prominence as winner of first prize of the 1970 Chopin Competition in Warsaw (first American to do so); he had also won the 1969 Busoni Competition in Italy and the Montreal Competition; subsequent rapid rise to front rank concert artist included performances with the Philadelphia Orchestra, New York Philharmonic and other major U.S. orchestras; appeared on popular TV shows as well as a special national telecast on CBS. Recordings: *Connoisseur*. Management: Shaw Concerts, Inc. . . . **Ludwig Olshansky,** young pianist, has made six European concert tours to date. Recordings: *Monitor*. Management: Robert M. Gewald Management. . . . **Ursula Oppens,** has performed in London, Munich, Berlin, Bolzano; toured Italy in 1971; winner of 1969 Busoni Competition, first prize; New York debut in 1961; member of chamber group, Speculum Musicae.

Dwight Peltzer, faculty, University of Massachusetts; performed at Carnegie Hall in 1971; has toured the U.S., Germany, Austria, France, Canada; has recorded for CBC (Canadian Broadcasting Corp.); has been active as an interpreter of avant-garde music. Recordings: *Washington University, Serenus*. . . . **Leonard Pennario** (b. 1924), performs with major American orchestras and has given recitals in the U.S. and Canada, Europe, and Africa; toured Australia and New Zealand in 1967; has had over 40 record releases; played with the Dallas and Los Angeles orchestras at ages twelve and fifteen, respectively. Recordings: *Capitol, Pickwick, RCA Victor*. Management: Columbia Artists Management, Inc. . . . **Murray Perahia,** performs often as chamber musician; has performed with Guarneri, Galimir, and former Budapest, quartets and at Marlboro Concerts at New York's Alice Tully Hall; played at Lincoln Center Mostly Mozart Festival; performed with Boston Philharmonia, St. Louis and Seattle Symphonies, and in recitals; on faculty Mannes College of Music; in 1972 he made his debut with the New York Philharmonic. Management: Frank E. Salomon Management. . . . **Michael Ponti** (b. 1937, Germany, of American parents); raised in the U.S., where he also began his piano training; in Germany since 1955; won various international competitions while in Europe including the Casella (Naples), the Busoni (Bolzano) prize in 1964, a prize in the Queen Elizabeth (Brussels) contest; between 1958 and 1964 he appeared more than 150 times in West Germany alone; his European career included recordings (for Vox); his reputation from these and his European concerts preceded his New York debut in 1972; first major appearance with an American orchestra was with the Detroit Symphony in 1972; known not only for a prodigious technique, but also for a wide, lengthy, and unusual repertory which includes many works of the neglected Romantics and virtuoso works of the twentieth century; this repertory permits him to offer his audiences at live performances encores from a long list of selections, a factor which accounts for the duration of his recitals; he has recorded over 30 LP's including the complete piano works of Tchaikovsky and Scriabin and a host of lesser-rank Romantics. Recordings: *Vox, Candide*. Management: Jacques Leiser. . . . **Menahem Pressler** (b. 1928, Israel), pianist with the Beaux Arts Trio of New York; professor at Indiana University; won first prize Debussy Competition, 1946; made American debut with the Philadelphia Orchestra in 1947; has also subsequently played with the Cleveland Orchestra, New York Philharmonic, Indianapolis Symphony, etc.; performs duo-recitals with Bernard Greenhouse, cellist. Recordings: *CRI, Monitor*. Management: Herbert Barrett Management, Inc.

Thomas Richner, pianist, organist; faculty, Douglass College of Rutgers, the State University (N.J.); equally proficient as pianist or organist, he has been known for many years as a prime specialist of the keyboard works of Mozart; he is author of "Orientation for Interpreting Mozart Sonatas"; his repertory includes the piano and organ works of all periods; has performed many times in New York City and elsewhere in the U.S.; undertook a Far East tour in 1969. Recordings: *Lyrichord*. Management: Bichurin Concerts Corp. . . . **Michael Rogers** (b. 1939, Missouri), on faculty Central Missouri State College; New York Town Hall debut in 1961; won the 1964 Michaels Award of Ravinia Festival; appearances with orchestra include the symphonies of Minneapolis, Knoxville, Pittsburgh, Baltimore, Chicago, Boston Pops, etc. . . . **Charles Rosen,** appeared first in concert in 1952; has given recitals and has played with major orchestras in the U.S. and Europe where he has played for the BBC, London, and Radio Basle; most recently authored a book, "The Classical Style, Haydn, Mozart, Beethoven," which won the 1971 National Book Award in its category. Recordings: *Odyssey, Columbia, Counterpoint/Esoteric, Epic*. Management: Columbia Artists Management, Inc. . . . **Joel Rosen,** concert pianist and recitalist; has performed nearly 500 concerts and lecture-recitals in Europe, Asia, and Latin America within a six-year period under the auspices of the U.S. State Department. Recordings: *Decca*. Management: Albert Kay Associates, Inc. . . . **Carol Rosenberger,** New York debut at Alice Tully Hall in 1970; Carnegie Hall debut in 1971; made first of five European tours in

1964; played with the Houston, Detroit, and Binghamton Symphonies; between 1955 and 1964 her career was interrupted by an attack of polio which made it necessary ultimately to relearn the piano. Management: Anne O'Donnell Management. . . . **Arthur Rubinstein** (b. 1886), one of the most famous pianists of all times; made his U.S. debut with Philadelphia Orchestra in 1906; became U.S. citizen in 1946. Recordings: *RCA Victor.* Management: Hurok Concerts, Inc. . . . **Roman Rudnytsky,** faculty of University of Cincinnati College–Conservatory of Music; has performed in U.S., Canada, and Europe since the age of ten; performed with major orchestras, e.g. Washington National Symphony, Detroit, Warsaw National Philharmonic, Toronto. . . . **Abbott Ruskin,** young concert pianist and recitalist; made his formal New York debut in 1971 after having played in public since childhood; subsequent concerts include one with the National Symphony in Washington of Kabalevsky's Third Piano Concerto with the composer conducting; performed with the Baltimore Symphony, Philadelphia Orchestra, the Boston Pops, the Chicago and Minnesota orchestras, among others. Management: Herbert Barrett Management, Inc.

György Sándor (b. 1912, Hungary), professor of piano, University of Michigan; made U.S. debut in 1939; undertakes annual U.S. and European tours; played in Australia in 1950; has made nine South American tours since 1939; has been a Bartók specialist (was a student of the composer); premiered Bartók's Piano Concerto No. 3 and performed at Bartók Memorial Concert, Carnegie Hall, September 26, 1970 as well as the Bartók festivals 1970–71 in Rio, Tokyo, and Lima; has recorded all the Bartók piano works and is the only artist thus far to have done so. Recordings: *Turnabout, Vox, Columbia.* Management: Pacific World Artists, Inc. . . . **Jesús María Sanromá** (b. 1902) appeared first in 1924 as pianist; was for many years the pianist with the Boston Symphony; has played throughout U.S., Europe, and Latin America. Recordings: *Everest.* . . . **Miklós Schwalb** (b. 1909, Budapest); made U.S. debut in 1942; on the faculty of the New England Conservatory of Music since 1947; plays solo recitals, appears with orchestras and is a chamber musician; he has played five concerts in Carnegie Hall, numerous performances in other New York halls and throughout the country; he made a series of 39 filmed concerts for television as well as four all-Brahms and four all-Chopin tapes for National Educational Television. . . . **Thomas Schumacher,** New York debut at Town Hall in 1963; premiered concerto by David Diamond in 1961; winner of various awards: Italy's Busoni Competition, Harold Bauer Award, Damrosch Award; performs in the U.S. and abroad. Management: Columbia Artists Management, Inc. . . . **Peter Serkin** (b. 1947), chamber musician, solo recitalist, concert artist, son of Rudolf Serkin; has appeared at Tanglewood, Ravinia, Meadowbrook, Lincoln Center's Mozart Festivals and others; performed in Europe and South America, with many U.S. major orchestras including the New York Philharmonic, Minnesota, San Francisco, etc.; in Europe he has performed in Italy, Germany, Switzerland, Iceland, and England; he has given many performances in Tokyo. Recordings: *Columbia, RCA Victor, Vanguard.* Management: Frank Salomon Management. . . . **Rudolf Serkin** (b. 1903), one of the great pianists of today; eminent as recitalist, concert artist, chamber musician, and teacher; made U.S. debut in 1933 and has undertaken annual American tour since 1934; Director of the Marlboro Festival; Director, Curtis Institute. Recordings: *Columbia, RCA Victor, Seraphim, Odyssey.* Management: Judd Concert Artist Bureau. . . . **Joel Shapiro,** faculty, University of Illinois; undertook his tenth European tour in 1972; performs throughout the U.S. . . . **Craig Sheppard,** young concert pianist and chamber musician; made his professional debut with the Philadelphia Orchestra at the Robin Hood Dell concerts in 1960; has since then repeated his appearances with that orchestra; played thereafter in Detroit, San Francisco, and Los Angeles; in 1968 he participated in the Busoni Competition in Italy and played at Tanglewood under Leinsdorf; he is winner of the William Kapell and Edward Steuermann

Awards; his debut recital in New York occurred in 1972. Management: Arthur Judson Management, Inc. . . . **Don Shirley,** Jamaica-born pianist of classical and popular music repertory; composer and arranger; has performed with the orchestras of Cleveland, Washington, Detroit, Chicago, La Scala, Milan; tours extensively with his concert format called "The Music of Don Shirley" (with cello and bass players), averaging about 70 concerts annually throughout the U.S.; these evenings of music feature his arrangements of a wide assortment of standard popular tunes, spirituals, melodies from musical theater, etc.; his recordings of this music have been very successful. Recordings: *Columbia.* Management: Columbia Artists Management, Inc.; Bichurin Concerts Corp. (for Central and South America and the Far East). . . . **Leonard Shure** (b. 1910), on faculty of University of Texas at Austin; performs concerts and recitals; debut in Berlin, 1927; U.S. debut, 1933; first pianist to play at Tanglewood in 1941; infrequent New York recital appearances of late—however, performed at New York's Alice Tully in January, 1971. Recordings: *Epic.* . . . **Jeffrey Siegel** (b. 1942, Chicago), concert pianist and recitalist; early in his youth won various opportunities to play in public including a concert with the Chicago Symphony in 1958 in its youth concert series; in 1960 made his first debut recital at Chicago's Art Institute; in 1962 played again with the Chicago Symphony and the orchestras of Grant Park, Chautauqua, and other summer ensembles; he played with the London Philharmonic in 1965 after having pursued studies at Marlboro and in England; he won first prize in the 1968 Queen Elizabeth of Belgium Contest, which enlarged his performance opportunities in America and Europe; he has since then performed with many major orchestras in the U.S. and abroad, has undertaken four European tours, etc.; his New York recital as soloist took place in 1969. Management: Arthur Judson Management, Inc. . . . **Abbey Simon,** recitalist and concert performer; faculty of University of Indiana; a Naumburg Award winner; New York debut in 1940. Recordings: *Turnabout, Capitol.* Management: Shaw Concerts, Inc. . . . **Ruth Slencyznska** (b. 1925), first debut as child prodigy in 1929, as adult, 1951; has given recitals and concerts with orchestra in the U.S., Europe, Latin America, South Africa, etc.; authoress of two books: one, of her tragic life as a child prodigy, the other, a book on piano technique published in 1970; she is artist-in-residence at Southern Illinois University; excels in performances of Chopin and has recorded much of his music; received Poland's Golden Cross of Merit. Recordings: *Decca.* Management: Bichurin Concerts Corp. . . . **Hilde Somer** (b. 1930, Vienna), in the U.S. since 1938; plays both the classics and much contemporary music; she has given world premieres of new concertos and has achieved special distinction in recent seasons as an outstanding interpreter of the piano music of Scriabin; has toured playing his music in a mixed media program with projected colored lights. Recordings: *Desto, Mercury, CRI.* Management: Tornay Management, Inc. . . . **Susan Starr,** young pianist; made her debut at six as the youngest soloist ever to appear with the Philadelphia Orchestra; winner of the 2nd prize in the 1962 International Tchaikovsky Competition in Moscow; subsequently performed in the Soviet Union on several occasions as well as throughout Europe and the U.S., on TV, etc.; appeared with such major orchestras as Chicago Symphony and the Philadelphia Orchestra; has made numerous cross-country tours. Recordings: *RCA Victor.* Management: Columbia Artists Management, Inc.

Rosalyn Tureck (b. 1914), pianist, organist, and sometimes performer on harpsichord and clavichord; also conductor; Bach specialist; solo debut in Chicago, 1924, with orchestra (Chicago Symphony) in 1926; Carnegie Hall debut, 1936 with the Philadelphia Orchestra; played annual Bach recitals in New York from 1944 to 1955; made European debut in London in 1947; European tours since 1957; founder and director of the International Bach Society (q.v. Musical Organizations). Recordings: *Decca.* Management: Columbia Artists Management, Inc. . . . **Ronald Turini,** has performed in Holland, U.S.S.R., and other European countries; performances with major orchestras: Chicago, Atlanta, Montreal, San Antonio, etc. Recordings: *RCA Victor.* Management: Columbia Artists Management, Inc.

Ralph Votapek (b. 1939, Milwaukee); won instant fame when, in 1962, he was awarded the first prize ($10,000—the most ever awarded a music contestant in the U.S.) of the first Van Cliburn International Competition in Fort Worth, Texas; gained much publicity (write-ups in national news magazines, etc.) and performing opportunity (substituting for the indisposed Emil Gilels in 1965 in Washington, D.C., as one example) following that triumph; he performs throughout the U.S. with orchestras, at festivals, in recital. Management: Hurok Concerts, Inc.

André Watts (b. 1946, Nuremberg, of American father); debut on television's Young People's Concert with Leonard Bernstein and the New York Philharmonic in 1963; innumerable European and American tours; debut in Germany in 1967; toured with the Los Angeles Philharmonic under U.S. State Department sponsorship in 1967; performed in Budapest, Hungary, in 1969; has performed with major orchestras throughout the world including the Berlin Philharmonic (at festivals), London Symphony, Philadelphia Orchestra, etc.; his New York recital debut was in the Great Performer Series at Philharmonic Hall in October, 1966. Recordings: *Columbia.* . . . **Beveridge Webster** (b. 1908), recitalist, concert artist, and teacher of renown; on the faculty of Juilliard School since 1946; artist-teacher at Aspen since 1961; first major concert appearance in the U.S. was with the New York Philharmonic in 1934, which marked his return to America after seven years of study in France as a young man—a period that included his winning the first prize in piano at the Paris Conservatoire (first American to do so) and a close association with Ravel; known for his performances of the works in the French repertory; in 1968, he performed a cycle, in three concerts in both New York and Chicago, of the complete piano music of Debussy, commemorating the 50th year of the composer's death; also has played much contemporary music by such composers as Sessions, Berg, Schoenberg, Carter; he has recorded a complete Stravinsky piano set for *Dover;* has appeared on radio and television. Recordings: *Dover, Desto, Columbia.* Management: Herbert Barrett Management, Inc. . . . **Alexis Weissenberg,** born in Bulgaria; came to the U.S. in 1946; studies in the U.S.; made his European debut in 1950; won the Leventritt Award in 1947; performed that year in Carnegie Hall with the New York Philharmonic under Szell; from about 1957 to 1966 he remained inactive as a public musical figure; since renewing his career, he has appeared with major orchestras in Europe and America and is an active recording artist; his tours cover Europe, Middle East, South Africa, and the U.S. Recordings: *Angel, RCA Victor.* Management: Hurok Concerts, Inc. . . . **Earl Wild,** major recitalist and concert artist; considered one of America's outstanding pianists; has performed with virtually all the front rank U.S. ensembles, and at such festivals as Ravinia, Tanglewood, Robin Hood Dell, Hollywood Bowl series, etc.; performs a repertory that contains music of all periods but has an emphasis on the virtuoso pieces of the Romantic era. Recordings: *RCA Victor, Vanguard, Columbia, Nonesuch;* also for *Reader's Digest Records.* Management: Sheldon Soffer Management, Inc.

DUO-PIANO

Bencini and Lee, Sara Bencini and Troy Lee; first appeared as a duo in 1958; both women are from North Carolina; repertory consists of arrangements of solo piano works, music for orchestra, songs, etc., as well as original piano duo music. Management: Albert Kay Associates, Inc. . . . **Ena Bronstein** and **Philip Lorenz,** husband-and-wife team who first pursued solo careers; as a duo have made one world tour, four tours of South America, and have performed throughout the U.S. and Europe; repertory includes two-piano works with orchestra; both were born abroad, he of an American mother; both have been in America for most of their professional lives; both on the faculty of Fresno State

College, California. Management: Bichurin Concerts Corp.

Richard and John Contiguglia (identical twins b. 1937, New York State); studied at Yale then in England; made their professional debut in London (Wigmore Hall) in 1962; have since performed in Europe and the U.S. playing mostly music written for two pianos from Bach to the moderns; they have acquired a reputation as outstanding performers of the music of Bartók. Recordings: *Connoisseur.* Management: Shaw Concerts, Inc.

Ferrante and Teicher, Arthur Ferrante and Louis Teicher, have played popular as well as classical music. Recordings: *Urania* (classical recording).

Gold and Fizdale, Arthur Gold and Robert Fizdale, have performed in the U.S. and in Europe with orchestras and in recitals; modern works and unknown classics their specialty. Recordings: *Columbia, Odyssey.* Management: Columbia Artists Management, Inc.

Hodgens and Howard, Dolores Hodgens and Samuel Howard; first performed on tour in Europe: London, Munich, Berlin, Geneva, etc.; tours in the U.S. in 1971–72. Management: Columbia Artists Management, Inc.

Markowski and Cedrone, husband-and-wife team of **Victoria Markowski** and **Frank Cedrone;** perform for concert series in various cities and campuses throughout North America; both are artists-in-residence at Southern Colorado State College in Pueblo. Management: Albert Kay Associates, Inc. . . . **The Marlowes, Ronald and Jeffry Marlowe;** tours in the U.S. Management: Columbia Artists Management, Inc.

Stecher and Horowitz, Melvin Stecher and Norman Horowitz; have been playing for some 20 seasons on tours throughout the U.S., Hawaii, and Canada; overseas they have played in Europe and Latin America; appearances are solo or with orchestra. Recordings: *Everest.* Management: Columbia Artists Management, Inc.

Jean and Kenneth Wentworth, duo, performing on one piano; husband and wife; have played in India and the Middle East, Europe, and Eastern U.S.; have performed programs of new, original works for piano four-hands as well as works from the past. . . . **Whittemore and Lowe, Arthur A. Whittemore and Jack Lowe;** New York debut in 1940; have given many first performances of new works; have played on U.S. tours and on television; one of the best known duo-piano teams in the world. Recordings: *Capitol, RCA Victor.* Management: Columbia Artists Management, Inc.

Yarbrough and Cowan, Joan Yarbrough and Robert Cowan; husband-and-wife team; toured throughout country, including college and community circuits; have performed with orchestra but are primarily recitalists; performed several premieres, including concerto for two pianos and orchestra by Paul Creston. Management: Bernard and Rubin.

VIOLIN

(see also Concertmasters, Symphony Orchestras)

Anahid Ajemian (b. 1927), debut, Town Hall in 1946; concert artist, recitalist and chamber musician (with sister Maro, pianist). Recordings: *CRI, Columbia.*

Walter Brewus, concert violinist and recitalist; has performed in New York, in a number of European cities, and in concert with several of the Scandinavian orchestras. Management: Bichurin Concerts Corp. . . . **Robert Brink** (b. 1924), recitalist, chamber musician, and concert artist; debut with the Boston Pops, 1940; Town Hall debut in 1947; is also a concert manager. Recordings: *CRI, Lyrichord.* . . . **Anshel Brusilow,** former concertmaster of the Philadelphia Orchestra; also chamber music performer and soloist in recitals; now Conductor of the Dallas Symphony Orchestra. Recordings (as performer): *Columbia.* . . . **James Oliver Buswell, IV,** performed in 1966 with the New York Philharmonic and Pittsburgh Symphony in New

York; gave debut recital at age twenty in New York in 1967 for the "Great Performers at Philharmonic Hall" series; at age seven he had played in a young people's concert with the New York Philharmonic; London debut in 1971; has appeared in major concert series and festivals throughout the U.S.; on faculty of the University of Arizona. Recordings: *RCA Victor, Vanguard.* Management: Columbia Artists Management.

Pina Carmirelli, concert violinist and solo recitalist; has performed with Rudolph Serkin the Beethoven violin and piano sonatas; appearances with major U.S. orchestras; has played in festivals in Vienna, Athens, and Israel; has performed with Rosalyn Tureck at the International Bach Society Congresses. Recordings: *Music Guild.* Management: Judd Concert Artist Bureau. . . . **Charles Castleman,** young concert violinist and recitalist; on the faculty of the Philadelphia Musical Academy; played with the Boston Pops at age six; gave Town Hall, New York recital at age ten, and appeared with the New York Philharmonic when he was twelve; winner of prizes in the Queen Elizabeth of Belgium Contest and the Tchaikovsky Competition in Moscow; while still a teen-ager he appeared on various popular TV shows; made first European tour in 1968; he was a recent recipient of the Ford Foundation Concert Artist Program grant for commissioning and premiering a new work for violin; he has prepared a college in-residency program which consists of a three-day period on campus giving lectures, recitals, demonstrations, coaching lessons, and "jamming" in jazz violin style; these residency programs have been presented at U.C.L.A., and other schools. Management: Colbert Artists Management, Inc. . . . **John Corigliano** (b. 1901), concertmaster, San Antonio Symphony; former concertmaster of the New York Philharmonic from 1943 to 1966; also solo concert artist, recitalist, and chamber player. Recordings: *Columbia, Mace, CRI* (all as soloist).

François D'Albert, concert violinist and recitalist; President of Chicago Conservatory; has performed in U.S., Canada, and Europe. Recordings: *B & F Gold Label.* Management: Rapsodia Concert Management, P.O. Box 3990, Merchandise Mart, Chicago, Illinois 60654. . . . **David Davis,** has appeared in concerts and recitals in Europe and the U.S.; debut at eight with the Chautauqua Symphony Orchestra; performed with the Chicago Symphony Orchestra, has toured U.S., Canada, Mexico; has composed and conducted. Management: Wayne Wilbur Management. . . . **Glenn Dicterow,** concert violinist and recitalist; made his debut in 1962 with the Los Angeles Philharmonic at age eleven; was among the top winners for the 1970 Tchaikovsky Competition in Moscow; his performances with orchestras include the New York Philharmonic, the San Francisco Symphony, the Seattle Symphony (on two national tours), etc.; he has participated in the festivals at Aspen and Marlboro. Management: Arthur Judson Management, Inc. . . . **Paul Doktor,** (b. 1919), gave his American debut at the Library of Congress chamber music concert in 1948; born and educated in Vienna; joined faculty of Juilliard School for 1971–72 academic year. . . . **Rafael Druian,** concertmaster of the New York Philharmonic; former concertmaster of the Cleveland Orchestra and former concertmaster of the Dallas and Minneapolis orchestras; soloist and chamber player. Recordings (as soloist): *Philips, Columbia.*

Erick Friedman (b. 1939), made his Carnegie Hall debut in 1957; faculty North Carolina School of the Arts; gave a season of 81 concerts in the U.S., Europe, and South America in 1969–70; performed with major conductors and orchestras throughout the world. Recordings: *RCA Victor.* Management: Columbia Artists Management, Inc. . . . **Joseph Fuchs** (b. 1900), has played with ranking American and European orchestras; also performs in recitals and as chamber player; faculty of Juilliard School; toured Europe in 1954, South America in 1957, Russia, 1965; annual recitals in New York: has appeared with pianist Arthur Balsam and with his sister, Lillian Fuchs, violist; performed over 75 works for Boston Station QGBD–TV during a three-year television series called "Sonata";

has an exceedingly large repertory of classical and contemporary works. Recordings: *Decca, Everest, CRI.* Management: Herbert Barrett Management, Inc.

Robert Gerle, concert violinist, recitalist; husband of pianist Marilyn Neeley; both won an Emmy Award for Educational Television Series of the complete Beethoven violin and piano sonatas; on faculty Mannes College of Music; also on faculty Ohio State University; performed with Orchestre National in Paris; recorded six Bach violin sonatas, Barber and Delius concertos, Berg Chamber Concerto, concertos by Joseph and Michael Haydn as well as complete Brahms Hungarian Dances. Recordings: *Decca, Westminster.* Management: Thea Dispeker Artists' Representative. . . . **Carroll Glenn,** made debut in New York in 1938; has appeared as soloist and concert artist in the U.S., Europe, Canada, and the Orient; appears with husband, Eugene List, in joint recitals. Recordings: *Columbia, Music Guild, Westminster, Odyssey, CRI.* . . . **Syzmon Goldberg** (b. 1909, Poland), in the U.S. since 1938; concert artist, recitalist, chamber musician; has played in the leading cities of the world. Recordings: *Decca, Philips.* Management: Columbia Artists Management, Inc.

Sidney Harth (b. 1925), former concertmaster of the Chicago Symphony; former concertmaster and assistant conductor of the Louisville Orchestra; presently Chairman, Music Department, Carnegie–Mellon University in Pittsburgh; won Laureate Prize, Wieniawski Competition, 1957; international tour in 1952, and thereafter, as soloist; in 1968 toured England, Poland, and Holland, and performed at Aspen Festival in Colorado; performs as chamber musician and recitalist. Recordings: *Louisville.* Management: Sheldon Soffer Management, Inc. . . . **Daniel Heifetz,** California-born young concert violinist and recitalist; winner of the Merriweather Post Competition in 1969; New York debut in 1970 at Philharmonic Hall with the visiting Washington National Symphony Orchestra. Management: Hurok Concerts, Inc. . . . **Jascha Heifetz** (b. 1901), one of the world's most famous musicians; made U.S. debut in 1917; active as teacher; on the faculty of University of Southern California since 1962; among the world's most recorded violinists. Recordings: *RCA Victor.*

Yong Uck Kim (b. 1947, Seoul, Korea); in the U.S. since 1961 when he began his more advanced studies; in 1963 he appeared on television with Eugene Ormandy and the Philadelphia Orchestra; subsequent early orchestra appearances were with the National Symphony (1965), the New York Philharmonic in a young people's concert under Bernstein (1966); in 1967, he performed more than 50 concerts in North America; European debut, which included radio and television performances, in 1969; he made his first recording with Deutsche Grammophon in 1970; he now concertizes regularly in the U.S. and Europe. Recordings: *DGG.* Management: Arthur Judson Management, Inc.

Fredell Lack, concert violinist, recitalist, teacher; artist-in-residence, University of Houston; made debut at age eleven with the Tulsa Symphony; professional debut at age seventeen with the St. Louis Symphony under Golschmann; for a while was concertmistress with the Little Orchestra Society; has toured extensively in the U.S., Canada, Central America, and Europe appearing in recital and with such orchestras as the Pittsburgh, Houston, BBC London, Utah, Halle, Royal Philharmonic and other orchestras; founder of the Houston-based Lyric Art Quartet. Recordings: *CRI.* Management: Albert Kay Associates, Inc. . . . **Jaime Laredo** (b. 1941 in Bolivia); in U.S. since childhood; in 1959 won the Queen Elizabeth of Belgium International Competition in Brussels, which began his career; often appears with his wife, Ruth Laredo, pianist, in joint recital. Recordings: *RCA Victor, Columbia, Monitor, Nonesuch.* Management: Columbia Artists Management, Inc. . . . **Isidor Lateiner,** commissioned original work from Milton Babbitt through Grant of Concert Artists Guild in 1968; toured Europe, where he appeared with the Munich Philharmonic Orchestra, and has performed at festivals, recitals, and concerts throughout the U.S. Management: Judith Liegner Artists Management. . . . **Evi Liivak** (b. Finland); American citizen; first public recital at age six; at age eleven played with the Helsinki Symphony as soloist; performs extensively in the U.S. and Canada; makes annual tours to Europe, where she has played from Copenhagen to Athens; a Far Eastern tour took her to Japan and Korea, where she played at the International Music Festival (Seoul). Management: Bichurin Concerts Corp. . . . **Guy Lumia,** native of New York; made his debut there in 1960; won recognition in various international competitions; has given three New York recitals and has performed in France, Germany, England, the Soviet Union, and elsewhere in Europe. Management: Hurok Concerts, Inc.

Yehudi Menuhin (b. 1916), internationally famed recitalist and concert artist, festival director, conductor, and teacher; made debut in 1923; currently resident in England; received in 1965 an honorary knighthood from Queen Elizabeth II of England; from France the Chevalier of the Order of Arts and Letters, and from Greece, the Order of the Phoenix; recipient of many honorary degrees; founder of the Yehudi Menuhin School at Stoke D'Abernon in England; artistic director of the Bath and Gstaad Festivals; one of the major musical figures of the times. Recordings: *Capitol, Angel, Seraphim, Mercury.* Management: Columbia Artists Management, Inc. . . . **Nathan Milstein** (b. 1904, Russia), world famous recitalist and concert violinist; in the U.S. since 1928; made U.S. debut in 1929. Recordings: *Pickwick, Angel.* Management: Hurok Concerts, Inc. . . . **Erica Morini** (b. 1904, Vienna); made U.S. debut in 1921; became U.S. citizen in 1943; New York resident; internationally known concert violinist and recitalist; one of the world's great musicians. Recordings: *Decca, Angel, Westminster.* Management: Arthur Judson Management, Inc.

Julian Olevsky (b. 1927, Berlin), soloist and concert violinist; Buenos Aires debut, 1937; U.S. debut in 1949; performed in South America 1937–1948 and in 1961; U.S. appearances since 1949; European concerts, 1951–1961; Far East tours in 1955 and 1961; faculty, University of Massachusetts. Recordings: *Westminster, Music Guild.*

Edith Peinemann, concert violinist; performs throughout Europe and America. Recordings: *DGG.* Management: Columbia Artists Management, Inc. . . . **Itzhak Perlman** (b. 1945, Tel Aviv); in the U.S. since 1958; winner of the 1964 Leventritt Award; a highly acclaimed performer appearing internationally with orchestras and in recitals in some 90 concerts a year; has performed with the front rank orchestras and conductors. Recordings: *RCA Victor.* Management: Hurok Concerts, Inc.

Ruggiero Ricci (b. 1918), a violinist of world fame with a prodigious repertory, whose concerts are often marked by the unusual; his repertory includes more than 40 concertos of all schools plus a great deal of unaccompanied violin literature including all of the Caprices of Paganini; his programs have featured chamber and small ensemble pieces with harp accompaniment, and duos with other violinists or other instrumentalists; such recordings as his "Glory of Cremona," where he plays upon 15 rare great violins, or his recording of Vivaldi's "Seasons," which involves his playing four Stradivarius instruments while accompanied by an ensemble of Stradivarii, are hallmarks of his sense of performance; he has been performing since the age of ten; made his New York debut in 1929; has performed with virtually every major orchestra in the world and in the music capitals on all continents; he has made three world tours, three in the Soviet Union and Australia, four to South Africa, and eight to South America; altogether he has played over 3,000 concerts and recitals; he has been on the faculty of the University of Indiana and the Shawnigan Lake Summer School of the Arts in Vancouver, Canada. Recordings: *Columbia, London, Decca.* Management: Herbert Barrett Management, Inc.; Bichurin Concerts Corp. (for Latin America); Pacific World Artists (for Orient, etc.). . . . **Aaron Rosand** (b. 1929), made debut appearance with the Chicago Symphony under Stock at the age of ten; has made annual American and European tours including performances with leading orchestras; performs as a duo with his wife, pianist Eileen Flissler. Recordings: *Vox, Turnabout.*

Isidor Saslav, concertmaster, Baltimore Symphony; former concertmaster of Minneapolis Symphony; former member of Buffalo Philharmonic and Detroit Symphony; solo recitalist and concert artist, not only with orchestra in which he was a member but also with other ensembles; has given joint recitals with his wife, pianist Ann Heiligman; has performed in Casals Festival Orchestra; appeared more than 30 times as soloist with the Buffalo Philharmonic. . . . **Alexander Schneider** (b. 1908, Russia); in U.S. since 1933; concert violinist, recitalist, chamber player, conductor, teacher; one of the concert world's most versatile musicians; musical activist; former member of the now dissolved Budapest String Quartet; frequently associated with Rudolf Serkin and Pablo Casals. Recordings: *Columbia, RCA Victor, Vanguard, Seraphim.* Management: Frank Salomon. . . . **Berl Senofsky,** concert violinist, recitalist, and teacher; on the faculty of the Peabody Conservatory and the Music Academy of the West; made his Town Hall New York debut in 1946 as winner of the Naumburg Award; in 1955, became the first American to win the Queen Elizabeth of Belgium Competition and to date is the only American violinist to have done so; he concertizes throughout the world: Western and Eastern Europe, New Zealand and Australia, the Far East, Latin America, Africa, the Soviet Union, etc.; he has performed with nearly all of the major U.S. orchestras. Management: Arthur Judson Management, Inc. . . . **Oscar Shumsky,** solo violinist, concert artist, and teacher; also violist, conductor of Empire Sinfonietta; member of Bach Aria Group (q.v.); faculty, Juilliard School since 1953. . . . **Tossy Spivakovsky** (b. 1907), concerts and recitals in the U.S., Canada, and Europe; U.S. debut, 1942. Recordings: *Everest.* . . . **Isaac Stern** (b. 1920, Russia—in the U.S. since infancy), internationally renowned violinist; U.S. debut in 1931 with San Francisco Symphony; New York debut in 1937; toured Australia 1947; first tour of Russia in 1956; one of world's foremost violinists; solo recitalist, concert performer, chamber musician; performed in virtually every major city of the world and with every major ensemble; received many awards and honors; performs with famed collaborators, Leonard Rose and Eugene Istomin, as a trio. Recordings: *Columbia.* Management: Hurok Concerts, Inc. . . . **Joseph Szigeti** (b. 1892, Budapest), American citizen since 1951; one of the world's most famous violinists; authored book in 1965, "A Violinist's Notebook"; in 1969, "Szigeti on the Violin: Improvisations on a Violinist's Themes"; has now retired from public life. Recordings: *Bach Guild, Vanguard, Columbia.*

Roman Totenberg (b. 1913, Poland); debut in Warsaw in 1925; U.S. debut in 1935; faculty, Boston University since 1961; has performed often at Tanglewood, where he is head of the string department of the Tanglewood Institute; performs in New York, and annually in Europe; he has a significant repertory of modern concertos. Recordings: *Vanguard.* Management: Eric Semon Associates, Inc. . . . **Charles Treger,** violinist with the Lincoln Center Chamber Ensemble; solo artist and recitalist; faculty New England Conservatory of Music; has performed at Aspen, Music at the Vineyards Festival in California, Peninsula Music Festival in Fishcreek, Wisconsin, Saratoga, New York, and at other festivals; toured fourteen countries of Europe and the Middle East with the Pittsburgh Symphony under Steinberg; won first prize in 1962 in the Wieniawski Competition in Poland; former member, Detroit Symphony and formerly taught at Iowa State University. Recordings: *Louisville Orchestra First Edition.* Management: Herbert Barrett Management, Inc.

Zvi Zeitlin, born in Russia; raised in Israel; received advanced training in New York; faculty, Eastman School of Music; has performed under Bernstein, Mehta, Dorati, Kubelik, Sawallisch, and other conductors in America and Europe; has toured South America eight times, Australia three times; he makes regular tours of the U.S. and Europe; he plays a number of large-scale contemporary works in the violin repertory, particularly those with orchestra. Management:

Thea Dispeker Artists' Representative. . . . **Marvin Ziporyn,** solo recitalist and concert artist; has toured Europe four times and has played three tours of India, Ceylon, the Orient. Management: Albert Kay Associates, Inc. . . . **Pinchas Zukerman** (b. 1948, Tel Aviv); in the U.S. since his teens; winner of 1967 Leventritt Award; has since become one of the most admired young violinists; has performed in Germany, Italy, Spain, England, etc., in recitals, concerts, important festivals. Recordings: *Columbia.* Management: Hurok Concerts, Inc. . . . **Paul Zukofsky** (b. 1943), concert violinist, recitalist; has made a singular reputation for himself as a foremost performer of contemporary works for the violin; made his professional debut at age eight with the New Haven Symphony; at thirteen he performed a recital in Carnegie Hall; in 1968 he organized a series of recitals under the name "Music for the 20th Century Violin"; his repertory includes some of the most difficult works for the instrument; has performed with the Boston Symphony, the Los Angeles Philharmonic and other ranking orchestras; played a series of taped telecasts for National Educational Television of the complete Beethoven sonatas; teaches at New England Conservatory. Recordings: *Vanguard, CRI, Columbia, Nonesuch, DGG, Folkways.* Management: Sheldon Soffer Management, Inc.

VIOLA

Paul Doktor (b. 1919, Vienna); in the U.S. since 1947; concert violist, recitalist, chamber player, teacher, and music editor; among the world's best known violists (originally played the violin); as a youth had an active career as a chamber musician; won first prize in viola at the International Music Competition in Geneva in 1942—the only such prize for viola ever awarded in the contest; he made his American debut in Washington, D.C. in 1948; toured extensively in Alaska in 1963; a propagandist for the viola, he has played many viola-perspective concerts of music from all eras; he has taught or lectured at a number of American universities and colleges; presently teaches at Mannes College of Music, New York University, and the Juilliard School; four videotapes have been made of his lecture demonstrations for national distribution. Recordings: *Louisville First Edition, Odyssey, Westminster, Telefunken.* Management: Colbert Artists Management, Inc.

Lillian Fuchs, concert violist, chamber player, recitalist, and teacher; well-known artist in the U.S. and Europe; teacher at Aspen in Colorado and at the Manhattan School of Music; has shared recitals with her brother, Joseph Fuchs, violinist; has made a recording with him and another brother, Harry, cellist with the Cleveland Orchestra (Decca 9574, Beethoven String Trio in C minor). Recordings: *Decca, CRI.* Management: Albert Kay Associates, Inc.

Robert Glazer, solo violist and chamber musician; performs as Glazer Duo with his wife Gilda Glazer, pianist; toured Europe in 1971 and 1972. Management: Wendel Artists Management, Inc. . . . **Nathan Gordon,** faculty of Wayne State University; solo violist with the Detroit Symphony, conductor of the Dearborn Orchestra Association; also concert soloist; has performed with his wife, soprano Marjorie Gordon; toured Israel and Greece in 1971 with his wife. Management: Lee Jon Associates.

Raphael Hillyer (b. Ithaca, New York), concert violist and recitalist; former orchestral musician as member of the Boston Symphony (under Koussevitsky), the NBC Symphony (under Toscanini), etc.; joined the Juilliard String Quartet as a founding member in 1946; on faculty of Juilliard since and has taught at other institutions; his performances with the Juilliard Quartet are well known; is presently appearing with orchestras and in solo recitals. Recordings (as soloist): *Louisville First Edition.* Management: Arthur Judson Management, Inc.

Karen Phillips, young soloist and chamber player; has performed at the Marlboro, Spoleto, and Aspen festivals; guest artist with the Lincoln Center Chamber Music Society; she is the wife of Walter Trampler. Management: Sheldon Soffer Management, Inc. . . . **William Primrose** (b. 1903), probably the world's most famous violist; was originally a violinist; as violist played first as chamber musician in 1935; has been known as concert soloist since 1942; on the faculty of Indiana University. Recordings: *RCA Victor, Columbia, Seraphim.* Management: Sherman Pitluck, Inc.

Walter Trampler, violist and player on the viola d'amore; considered by many to be the world's leading violist; born in Munich, he has been part of the American music scene since 1939; on the faculties of Yale University and the Juilliard School; has played as an orchestral musician, concert soloist and recitalist, and as a chamber musician (with the former Budapest Quartet as guest for quintet performances, etc.); he is a permanent member of the Chamber Music Society of Lincoln Center. Recordings: viola, *CRI, Mainstream, RCA Victor, Columbia, Music Guild;* the viola d'amore, *Music Guild, Odyssey.* Management: Sheldon Soffer Management, Inc.

CELLO

Vahe Berberian, faculty, Clarion State College in Pennsylvania; active recitalist: has performed in Ohio, Boston, Italy, the Near East, etc.

Marion Davies, faculty, North Carolina School of the Arts; has performed in New York, New Orleans, Atlanta, and in Portugal, Czechoslovakia; played a tour in 1971 of Yugoslavia, Rumania, Germany, Austria, and Switzerland. Management: Albert Kay Associates, Inc.

Lawrence Foster, young American, performed with orchestras of Chicago, Detroit, Houston, Memphis, Rochester, London Symphony, etc.; televised appearance with the New York Philharmonic Concert Series of Young Artists. Management: Columbia Artists Management, Inc.

Bernard Greenhouse, chamber cellist and solo artist; a member of the Beaux Arts Trio of New York and the Bach Aria Group; has performed for over 18 years as a duo with pianist, Menahem Pressler. Recordings: *Decca, Music Guild, Columbia, Desto, CRI, Philips, Mercury.* Management: Herbert Barrett Management, Inc.

Michael Haran, young cellist born in Israel; faculty, Temple University; won various awards including the 1967 Geneva Competition; has toured the U.S., Europe, Central America, and has appeared with the Pittsburgh Symphony, the National Orchestral Association, etc. Management: Sheldon Soffer Management, Inc. . . . **Lynn Harrell,** former principal cellist with the Cleveland Orchestra; has played solo with that orchestra as well as such orchestras as the New York Philharmonic, Chicago Symphony, American Symphony, etc.; on the faculty of the Cleveland Institute of Music; received a Ford Foundation Concert Artist Program grant to commission and premiere a new major work for cello and orchestra; his other awards earlier in his career include winning the Merriweather Post Contest and the Piatigorsky Award; New York debut in 1964 following latter award; he is the son of the late Metropolitan Opera baritone, Mack Harrell. Management: Herbert Barrett Management, Inc.

Stephen Kates, winner of the 1971 Ford Foundation Concert Artist Program for commissioning a new cello work by an American composer; winner in the third International Tchaikovsky Competition in Moscow; performed with the New York Philharmonic Young People's Concerts. Recordings: *RCA Victor.* Management: G. Turkisher, 838 West End Avenue, New York, N.Y. 10025. . . . **Ralph Kirshbaum** (b. 1946, Texas), concert cellist and recitalist; winner of many young musicians' awards; among them: Hendl Award, Dallas, 1961; Merriweather Post (second prize), 1963; first prize, Houston International Young Artists Competition, 1968; also won sixth prize in 1970 Tchaikovsky Competition in Moscow; made a tour of Europe in 1970 and again in 1971. Management: Colbert Artists Management, Inc. . . . **James Kreger** (b. 1947) has performed in New York's Carnegie Recital Hall and Alice Tully Hall in debuts there in 1971 and received outstanding favorable critical response. Management: Shaw Concerts, Inc. . . . **Joel Krosnick,** young solo cellist; has played in Europe,

Taiwan, etc. Recordings: *Nonesuch.* Management: Dodie Lefebre.

Laurence Lesser, concert cellist, chamber player, and solo recitalist; faculty, Peabody Conservatory; was student and assistant to Piatigorsky; a prizewinner in the 1966 Tchaikovsky Competition in Moscow; performed for the Los Angeles Monday Evening Concerts, with the London Philharmonic, Los Angeles Philharmonic, the Boston Symphony, and with orchestras in Europe; recorded in the U.S.S.R. (*Melodiya* label); has performed with Michael Tilson Thomas, the latter as pianist. Recordings: *Columbia, Desto.* Management: Bichurin Concerts Corp.; Arthur Judson Management, Inc.

Samuel Mayes, principal cellist, Boston Symphony since 1948; also chamber performer and soloist. Recordings: (as soloist) *RCA Victor.* . . . **Frank Miller,** principal cellist of the Chicago Symphony; conductor; former member of the NBC Symphony; frequently appears in chamber groups. Recordings: *RCA Victor.* . . . **Gilberto Munguia,** Texas-born cellist; winner of several student musician awards; has performed at the Yale Concerts in Norfolk, Kneisel Hall summer series in Maine, and with chamber groups in Italy; in 1972, he performed recitals in Oslo, Copenhagen, Vienna, and Zürich. Management: Bichurin Concerts Corp. . . . **Lorne Monroe,** (b. 1925), principal cellist with the Philadelphia Orchestra since 1951; former principal cellist of the Minnesota Orchestra; appears as chamber music player also. Recordings: *Columbia.*

Zara Nelsova, (b. Canada), educated in England, U.S. citizen; concert cellist, recitalist, and chamber musician; debut with the London Symphony at age twelve; she has performed in concert series, festivals, and for recordings in both the U.S. and Europe; first U.S. cellist to tour the Soviet Union; as a chamber musician, she performs in duo recitals with her husband, pianist, Grant Johannesen in the U.S., Canada, South America, and Europe. Recordings: *Vanguard, Golden Crest.* Management: Columbia Artists Management, Inc.; Bichurin Concerts Corp. (Latin America).

Paul Olefsky, has performed as soloist with major U.S. orchestras and has given recitals in Canada and the U.S.; winner of the 1948 Naumburg Award and the 1953 Michael Memorial Award. Recordings: *Monitor, Vox.* Management: Eric Semon Associates, Inc.

Aldo Parisot (b. 1918, Brazil), faculty, Yale University School of Music; active recitalist and chamber musician; since 1950 has performed as soloist with leading American orchestras including the New York Philharmonic, the Los Angeles Philharmonic, the Chicago Symphony, etc., the major orchestras of Paris, Vienna, London, Berlin, and others; he has performed much new music in addition to a wide range of classical works; works dedicated to him have been composed by Mel Powell, Claudio Santoro, Camargo Guarnieri, Quincy Porter, et al. Recordings: *Columbia, Counterpoint/Esoteric, Music Guild.* Management: Herbert Barrett Management, Inc. . . . **Leslie Parnas** (b. 1931, St. Louis); made his professional debut in 1946 with the St. Louis Little Symphony and in 1955 became principal cellist with the St. Louis Symphony; winner of the 1957 Pablo Casals Prize in Paris, which gained him over 40 concert engagements in Europe; in 1962 he won second prize in the Moscow Tchaikovsky Competition; he has since had a high-level career in both Europe and the U.S.; has been a frequent participant in the concerts given at the Marlboro Music Festival, where he has confirmed his ability as a chamber musician. Recordings: *Columbia.* Management: Arthur Judson Management, Inc. . . . **Gregor Piatigorsky** (b. 1903, Russia), world-famed cellist; soloist in recitals and concerts and as chamber player; a resident of California, he is presently exerting an enormous influence as teacher and mentor on a new generation of outstanding young virtuosos. Recordings: *RCA Victor.*

Gabor Rejto, faculty, University of Southern California and Music Academy of the West; member, Alma Trio; has appeared with orchestras or as soloist throughout the U.S. and in Australia, New Zealand, Israel, Hungary. Recordings: *Orion, CRI.* . . . **Leonard Rose** (b. 1918), eminent solo cellist, concert artist, and chamber player; appeared in debut in 1943 with the New York Philharmonic; has been soloist with numerous U.S. and European orchestras; former member of the NBC Symphony and former principal cellist with the New York Philharmonic; has performed exclusively as solo artist since 1951; member of the much heralded Istomin–Stern–Rose Trio. Recordings: *Columbia.*

Jeffrey Solow, young cellist from California, where he was the winner of the first Piatigorsky Award of the Young Musicians Foundation; student of Piatigorsky; made his debut in New York in 1970 to high critical praise. Management: Hurok Concerts, Inc. . . . **Janos Starker** (b. 1924, Budapest), in the U.S. since 1948; solo cellist in recitals and concerts throughout the world; former principal cellist with the Chicago, Dallas, and Metropolitan Opera orchestras and, in Hungary, with the Budapest Opera and Philharmonic; on the faculty of Indiana University since 1958; New York debut in 1960; in addition to performances as soloist with major orchestras everywhere, he has played recitals of unaccompanied cello works (Edinburgh, Chicago, Tokyo); his repertory covers the full range of history for cello music and includes much contemporary music; he sometimes conducts master classes and seminars; inventor of a cello tone-improvement device, the so-called Starker Bridge. Recordings: *London, DGG, Period, Mercury, Angel, Everest.* Management: Colbert Artists Management, Inc.

Christine Walevska, young cellist from Los Angeles, where she studied with Piatigorsky; her later training followed in Paris, where she graduated from the Conservatory with first place honors in cello and chamber music—the first time for an American; her career immediately thereafter was mainly European-based with performances in Germany, Holland, Spain, Poland, etc.; she has since toured the U.S. and some cities of South America. Recordings: *Philips.* Management: Hurok Concerts, Inc.

STRING BASS

Gary Karr, young virtuoso bassist in concerts with orchestras, and solo recitalist; teacher and clinician; appeared with the New York Philharmonic in 1962 under Bernstein in a Young People's concert, making also that year his recital debut in New York's Town Hall; has since appeared with over 75 orchestras and has played over 100 recitals in the U.S., Canada, Mexico, Europe, and on various TV and radio programs; is an effective propagandist for the aggrandizement of the bass; has organized a string bass institute and published a magazine devoted to the instrument; composers have written special works for his abilities; he is on the faculty of the New England Conservatory of Music; has held clinics in a number of campuses. Recordings: *Golden Crest, CRI, RCA Victor, Columbia, Odyssey.* Management: Sheldon Soffer Management, Inc.

Bertram Turetzky, solo bassist, chamber musician, music editor, and teacher; faculty University of California, San Diego and Claremont Music (Festival) Institute; was member of several ensembles including the Hartford Symphony; has performed and recorded a remarkable range of contemporary works involving the string bass on a high virtuosic level; his repertory contains much early music also; editor of "Music for Double Bass" series and other music publications. Recordings: *Ars Nova/Ars Antiqua, Advance, Medea, Nonesuch, CRI.*

HARPSICHORD

Ilsa Foerstel Bliss, German-born American harpsichordist; founder and director of the New Collegium Musicum of Long Island (New York); received her mature training in New York; has played in London, Berlin, Amsterdam, Vienna, etc. Management: Bichurin Concerts Corp. . . . **Edward Brewer,** served as music director of Judson Memorial Church (New York); founded the Trio da Camera; in 1971 in a concert at Tully Hall, he performed on a specially constructed facsimile harpsichord from the Baroque period. Management: David Schiffman; also National Music League.

Margaret Fabrizio, harpsichordist, active in California; has taught at Stanford University and other schools in San Francisco; has played at the Cabrillo Festival and on tours in the Western states; in 1966 she gave, in San Francisco, the first American performance on the harpsichord of Bach's "Art of the Fugue," performed it throughout the West and in New York for the first time in 1967, which also marked her debut in that city. . . . **Albert Fuller,** active chamber player and recital soloist; has toured Europe as chamber musician; has been artist-in-residence in colleges and universities throughout the country; editor of early works for harpsichord. Recordings: *Nonesuch, Decca, Project 3, Cambridge.* Management: Melvin Kaplan, Inc.

Igor Kipnis, American harpsichordist (b. 1930, Berlin), son of basso Alexander; on faculty, Fairfield University in Connecticut; debut as harpsichordist in 1959 over New York's municipal radio station, WNYC; solo recital debut in New York followed in 1961; became a performer and lecturer in Baroque harpsichord performance practices, teaching at Tanglewood and conducting his own radio show "The Age of the Baroque" for station WQXR in New York; has reviewed concerts and recordings for various newspapers and music publications; active touring performer with concerts coast-to-coast in the U.S.; has played under Leinsdorf, Munch, Ozawa, Stokowski, et al.; tours abroad include London, Amsterdam, Munich, Vienna, Bern, etc.—altogether has toured Europe three times; toured Australia in 1971; won the German recording prize, "Deutsche Schallplattenpreis"; undertook a recording project for *Epic* (unfinished) of the harpsichord music of various countries. Recordings (available): *Bach Guild, Golden Crest, Columbia, Odyssey.* Management: Albert Kay Associates, Inc. . . . **Ralph Kirkpatrick** (b. 1911); on the faculty of Yale University since 1940; performer on the harpsichord, clavichord, and modern piano; made debut as harpsichordist in 1930; performed in Berlin in 1933, in England in 1947; has toured extensively since 1947; editor of much music (Bach, Scarlatti, etc.) and author of an important biography of Domenico Scarlatti; an international performer in concerts and recitals, for festivals, concert series, etc., in all of the major cities of the U.S. and Europe; is noted for his recordings and performances of complete collections, e.g., Bach's "Well-Tempered Clavier" for Deutsche Grammophon; he recorded complete keyboard (clavier) works of Bach comprising 20 discs; he has also performed the music of Piston, Milhaud, Stravinsky, et al. Recordings: *DGG, Odyssey.* Management: Herbert Barrett Management, Inc.

Sylvia Marlowe, well-known solo recital and concert artist, chamber musician, and teacher (Mannes College of Music); in 1932 gave a radio recital (CBS Network) of Bach's complete "Well-Tempered Clavier"; has performed in Belgium, London, Paris, Naples, and other European cities; performs contemporary works as well as music of the past; has appeared as soloist, continuo player, and chamber musician; she has given lecture-recitals, and has conducted master classes; has recorded a wide range of music in many forms. Recordings: *Decca.*

Anthony Newman, young harpsichordist, pianist, organist and conductor; has performed in Town Hall, New York; as an organist, has performed all works of Bach in a series of concerts; he is considered by many to be a major new keyboard performer. Recordings: *Columbia, Turnabout.*

Daniel Pinkham (b. 1923), harpsichordist, organist, and well-known as a composer; has performed contemporary works as well as works from the traditional harpsichord repertory; faculty, New England Conservatory of Music. Recordings: *CRI, Cambridge, Lyrichord.*

Fernando Valenti, New York-born harpsichord recitalist, teacher, and chamber musician; was resident performer at 1950 Prades Bach Festival; has performed in the U.S., South America, and Europe; makes annual international tours; teacher at Juilliard since 1952; has recorded much Bach, Handel, and Scarlatti. Recordings: *Lyrichord, Westminster,*

Columbia, Vanguard, Music Guild. Management: Ann Summers.

FLUTE

Julius Baker, eminent flute soloist and chamber player; former member, Bach Aria Group; teacher, Juilliard School. Recordings: *Decca, Orpheus, Westminster, Vanguard, Columbia, Odyssey, Bach Guild.* Management: Pacific World Artists, Inc. . . . **Samuel Baron,** solo flutist, concert artist, and chamber musician; member of the Bach Aria Group and former member of the New York Woodwind Quintet; faculty, Mannes College of Music; has toured in the U.S. and overseas; one of America's major flutists. Recordings: *Dover, Decca, CRI, Concert–Disc, Nonesuch.* Management (as soloist): Sheldon Soffer Management, Inc.

Doriot A. Dwyer, has been principal flutist of the Boston Symphony since 1952; first woman to hold that position; frequent soloist with that orchestra. Recordings (as soloist): *RCA Victor.*

Claude Monteux, (b. 1920, Massachusetts); concert flutist, chamber musician, conductor, and teacher; Music Director and Conductor of the Hudson Valley Philharmonic Society in Poughkeepsie, New York; son of the late conductor; as a solo flutist, he has appeared in the major cities of Europe, performed at the White House, and has performed under renowned conductors, including his father; he is held in high regard as a conductor; on the faculty of Vassar College. Recordings: *London, L'Oiseau Lyre, Music Guild.* Management: Albert Kay Associates, Inc.

James Pappoutsakis, member of the Boston Symphony since 1937; also chamber player; faculty, Boston University. Recordings: *RCA Victor.*

Paula Robison, flute soloist; member of the Chamber Music Society of Lincoln Center (New York); New York debut in 1961; won first prize in flute at the 1964 International Munich Competition and the 1966 International Geneva Competition; has performed as soloist with the Suisse Romande Orchestra, the New York Philharmonic, and chamber orchestras under Alexander Schneider; she has played at Spoleto and at Marlboro and traveled with the Music from Marlboro series; recorded, with Rudolf Serkin, Schubert's "Introduction and Variations" for the Marlboro Recording Society; has performed many contemporary works in premieres. Recordings: *Connoisseur, Marlboro.* Management: Shaw Concerts, Inc.

Elaine Shaffer, made Town Hall debut in 1959 after playing in Europe for six years; born in Pennsylvania but a current resident of Switzerland; has performed as soloist with such orchestras as the (London) Philharmonia Orchestra, the Munich Philharmonic, the Colonne Orchestra in Paris, and the Orchestra of the Academy of Santa Cecilia in Rome; she recently toured the U.S. with pianist Hephzibah Menuhin; her husband is Efrem Kurtz, the conductor. Recordings: *Angel.* Management: Hurok Concerts, Inc.

John Wummer, orchestral and chamber musician and soloist; has performed with the ensembles of the Prades, Perpignan festivals, and Bethlehem Bach festivals; former solo flute with the Detroit and NBC orchestras and the New York Philharmonic; on the faculty of Teachers College (Columbia University) since 1955; Philadelphia Musical Academy since 1965; University of Hartford since 1966; Manhattan School of Music, since 1947; summer faculty Morehead University (Kentucky) since 1967. Recordings: *Odyssey, Westminster, Seraphim, Columbia.*

CLARINET

Clark Brody, principal clarinetist of the Chicago Symphony since 1951; was formerly with the CBS Symphony, 1941 to 1951; also active as chamber musician and solo artist, having performed with such groups as the Juilliard, Budapest, and Paganini string quartets. Recordings: *RCA Victor.*

Gino B. Cioffi, principal clarinetist with the Boston Symphony since 1950; former principal clarinetist with the following orchestras:

Pittsburgh, Cleveland, NBC, and the New York Philharmonic; faculty, Boston University.

Sidney Forrest, concert soloist and chamber musician; instructor at Peabody Conservatory of Music and George Washington University. Recordings: *Lyrichord.*

Anthony M. Gigliotti, principal with the Philadelphia Orchestra; also solo recitalist. Recordings: *Columbia.* . . . **David Glazer,** solo clarinetist and chamber musician; member of the New York Woodwind Quintet; also tours with soprano Camilla Williams in duo recitals; faculty, Mannes College of Music and the State University of New York at Binghamton. Recordings: *Vox, Turnabout, CRI, Concert Disc, Seraphim.*

Mitchell Lurie, faculty, University of Southern California; Music Academy of the West; former solo clarinetist with the Pittsburgh and Chicago Symphony Orchestras; has performed at the Casals Festival and has appeared in chamber recitals with the Paganini, Hungarian, and Fine Arts string quartets. Recordings (as soloist): *Capitol.*

Robert C. Marcellus, solo clarinetist of the Cleveland Orchestra; former member of the New York Philharmonic; faculty, Cleveland Institute of Music. Recordings: *Columbia.*

William Overton ("Bill") Smith (b. 1926, California), known as a clarinetist and composer in the fields of both jazz and concert music; performance in the latter is mainly, if not exclusively, contemporary music; performs sometimes mixed media and electronic pieces; former member of Brubeck combo (octet); has toured with the American Jazz Ensemble; hailed as a virtuoso in creating uncommon and unprecedented sounds from the clarinet and in the process devising an utterly new playing technique. Recordings (as classical performer or in his own works): *Contemporary.* Management: Sheldon Soffer Management, Inc.

HARP

Mildred Dilling (b. 1894); noted solo harpist; annual U.S. concert tours for several decades; annual tours also to Europe and to Canada; has performed in Australia, New Zealand, South America, and the Far East; conducts an annual workshop and master class at University of California, Los Angeles, each summer. Recordings (including one of a Town Hall recital): *Urania.* Personal Management: M. N. Thompson.

Susan McDonald, harpist; winner of Israel's International Harp Contest; has performed in annual tours of the U.S. including appearances in New York's Carnegie Hall; she regularly tours Europe and South America; has concertized in Canada and the Far East. Recordings: *Orion.* Management: William Felber Agency.

Aristid von Wurtzler (b. 1930, Budapest), concert harpist; U.S. citizen, residing in New York since 1958; Chairman, Harp Department, Hartt College of Music in Hartford; has played concerts with orchestras and has appeared on radio and television; his tours have included Europe and various U.S. cities; his repertory includes new works for harp, as well as works from throughout the past eras; he has appeared with such conductors as Dorati, von Karajan, Stokowski, Klemperer; he has authored several articles on the harp and has edited, composed, or arranged a number of harp works which have been published. Recordings: *Columbia, ASCO, Vox.* Management: Albert Kay Associates, Inc.

FRENCH HORN

Philip Farkas, former first horn, Chicago Symphony; faculty, Indiana University School of Music; soloist and chamber musician. Recordings (soloist): *Coronet.*

Mason Jones, principal horn with the Philadelphia Orchestra; soloist and chamber player. Recordings: *RCA Victor, Columbia.*

James Stagliano, first horn player, Boston Symphony, since 1946; was first horn in the orchestras of St. Louis, Chicago, Los Angeles and Cleveland; also was musical director of Boston Records; faculty, Boston University. Recordings (as soloist and chamber player): *Kapp.*

OBOE

Robert Bloom, orchestral and chamber musician, and soloist; member of the Bach Aria Group; faculty, Yale University School of Music. Recordings: *Decca, CRI.*

Peter Christ, chamber musician, solo oboist; member of the Westwood Woodwind Quintet; President of Crystal Records and President and Editor of the periodical, *Composium;* has performed with the Marlboro Festival Orchestra (recordings); active performer in Western states, particularly. Recordings: *Columbia, Crystal.*

John DeLancie, principal oboe of the Philadelphia Orchestra. Recordings (soloist): *RCA Victor, Columbia.*

Harold Gomberg, principal oboist of the New York Philharmonic, as well as chamber performer. Recordings: *Columbia, Counterpoint/ Esoteric, Vanguard, Decca.* . . . **Ralph Gomberg,** principal oboist of the Boston Symphony since 1949 and chamber player; faculty, Boston University. Recordings: *RCA Victor.*

Bert Lucarelli, solo recitalist and concert oboist; has performed in New York's Alice Tully Hall as guest artist with I Solisti Veneti, etc. Recordings: *Lyrichord.*

Ronald Roseman, oboe soloist, chamber player, teacher; on the faculties of Mannes College of Music and State University of New York at Binghamton and Stony Brook; artist-in-residence, University of Wisconsin in Milwaukee (summers); toured the Far East under U.S. State Department sponsorship; he has played with the New York Pro Musica and such chamber ensembles as the Alexander Schneider Chamber Orchestra, etc.; since 1961, he has been a member of the New York Woodwind Quintet; he tours offering special master classes. Recordings (as soloist): *Desto.* Management: Sheldon Soffer Management, Inc.

Ray Still, principal oboist of the Chicago Symphony since 1954; chamber player and teacher (Aspen Summer school and other institutions); was principal with the Baltimore, Buffalo, and Kansas City Orchestras; has recorded with the Juilliard, Fine Arts, and Lenox quartets. Recordings (as chamber musician): *Concert–Disc.*

ORGAN

Robert Anderson, head of organ department, Southern Methodist University, Dallas, Texas; concert organist and recitalist. Management: Lilian Murtagh Concert Management.

Robert Baker, organ recitalist; Dean of the School of Sacred Music, Union Theological Seminary in New York. Management: Lilian Murtagh Concert Management. . . . **E. Power Biggs** (b. 1906, England); U.S. citizen since 1938; internationally known performer in recitals, concerts, on television and radio; has recorded more than any other organist; the first organist to record on long-playing records; his repertory covers in great breadth and depth the organ music of the Baroque, Classical and Romantic eras; he has performed on many historical organs in Europe and America. Recordings: *Columbia.*

David Craighead (b. 1924), Head of Organ Department, Eastman School, since 1955; a church organist; also has performed on transcontinental U.S. tours. Management: Lilian Murtagh Concert Management. . . . **Catherine Crozier** (b. 1914), ensemble and recital performer in the U.S. and Europe; faculty, Rollins College. Management: Lilian Murtagh Concert Management.

Richard Ellsasser (b. 1926); New York debut in 1937; has given concerts and recitals in the U.S., Europe, Canada, Latin America. Recordings: *Nonesuch, Kapp, RCA Victor.* . . . **Robert Elmore** (b. 1913); Carnegie Hall debut in 1936; composer (see Composers) and church organist; teacher. Recordings: *Word.*

Heinrich Fleischer (b. 1912); faculty, University of Minnesota; former organist, University of Leipzig and St. Paul's University Church, Leipzig, as well as University of Chicago, Rockefeller Chapel; has been in the U.S. since 1949; toured Europe in 1956 and has given recitals in the U.S. and Canada. . . . **Virgil Fox** (b. 1912), well-known concert organist and recitalist; served as organist of New York's Riverside Church from 1946 to 1964; stands apart from most concert organists because of his flair for showmanship in his recitals; he is considered by many to be one of the great organists of today. Recordings: *RCA Victor, Command, Decca, Capitol.*

Clyde Holloway, organ recitalist; faculty, Indiana University; has toured in the U.S., Mexico. Management: Lilian Murtagh Concert Management.

Wilma Jensen, organ recitalist (touring) and teacher; faculty, Oklahoma City University and organist for the First Presbyterian Church there. Management: Lilian Murtagh Concert Management.

Joan Lippincott, organist performing recitals on tour; head of the organ department, Westminster Choir College in New Jersey; has performed in Connecticut, Washington, D.C., in Oklahoma City, and elsewhere. Management: Lilian Murtagh Concert Management.

Marilyn Mason (b. 1925), faculty, University of Michigan since 1947; has appeared in performance in the U.S., Canada, and Europe since 1946. Recordings: *Counterpoint/Esoteric, Columbia.* Management: Lilian Murtagh Concert Management. . . . **Lawrence Moe,** faculty, University of California at Berkeley. Recordings: *Cambridge.*

Robert Noehren (b. 1910), faculty, since 1949, University of Michigan; also an organ builder (see Manufacturers); performed on tour of the U.S., Canada, and Europe; has often performed Bach's complete organ works; he has recorded extensively, altogether some 30 LP discs representing 150 works from all periods. Recordings: *Lyrichord, Urania.*

David Pizarro, organ recitalist; has made six tours of Europe. Management: the Frothingham Management.

Alexander Schreiner (b. 1901, Germany); organist at Salt Lake City Tabernacle since 1924; made debut in Salt Lake City in 1921. Recordings: *Columbia, Music Guild.* . . . **Frederick Swann,** organist and director of music at Riverside Church in New York; has performed widely throughout the U.S. Recordings: *Westminster.*

MISCELLANEOUS INSTRUMENTS

Larry Adler (b. 1914), performer on the harmonica; classical and popular music virtuoso. Recordings: *RCA Victor.* . . . **Laurindo Almeida** (b. 1917, Brazil), guitarist; has been in the U.S. since 1946; classical and jazz player (formerly with Stan Kenton). Recordings: *Capitol.*

Martin Berinbaum, young virtuoso concert trumpet player; master of many kinds of trumpets including the piccolo trumpet and the baroque clarino trumpet; his repertory for appearances with orchestra includes a large representation of the concertos from the Baroque as well as modern trumpet pieces; has performed works for trumpet and organ with conductor-organist Johannes Somary; also active as trumpet clinician. Management: Sheldon Soffer Management, Inc.

John Eaton (b. 1935), performer on the Syn-Ket, pianist, and composer; tours in performances of his own music for Syn-Ket, an instrument specifically made for live performance of electronic music; performs as soloist, with orchestra, in lecture-recitals and with jazz groups. Recordings: *Decca, Turnabout.* Management: Sheldon Soffer Management, Inc.

Juan Mercadal, guitarist; born in Cuba; permanent U.S. residence established since 1960; faculty of University of Miami since 1965; early career included concerts as a classical guitarist touring South America; has performed with American orchestras in the

South and Southwest. Management: Arthur Judson Management, Inc.

Christopher Parkening, young classical guitarist from California; protégé of Segovia; has performed with symphony orchestras and in solo recital, as well as on popular television shows. Recordings: *Angel.* Management: Columbia Artists Management, Inc. . . . **Richard Pick** (b. 1915), classical guitarist, teacher (in Chicago), and composer. Recordings: *Music Library.*

Sigurd Rascher (b. 1907, Germany), concert saxophonist; since 1939 has been in the U.S., where he has appeared with major orchestras; performed in Europe and Australia. Recordings: *Columbia.*

John Sebastian, concert performer on the harmonica; has appeared at Grant Park Concerts, etc. Recordings: *Decca.* . . . **Thomas Stevens,** faculty, California Institute of the Arts; associate principal trumpet, Los Angeles Philharmonic; member, Los Angeles Brass Quintet. Recordings (as soloist): *Crystal.*

Roger Voisin, first trumpet player with the Boston Symphony (a member of the orchestra since 1935), concert artist and chamber musician. Recordings: *RCA Victor, Kapp.*

| Vocal

SOPRANOS

Adele Addison, singer in concerts, recitals; appearances with major U.S. orchestras including the New York Philharmonic; provided the voice of Bess for the sound track of the film "Porgy and Bess"; faculty, Aspen School; has also directed opera performances. Recordings: *Columbia, Decca, RCA Victor, Nonesuch.* . . . **Judith Alban–Wilk,** young soprano; for a while was a professional ballerina in Chicago; still a developing performer, she has sung at Chautauqua and in various Eastern cities in opera and concerts with orchestra; she appeared in "Il Trovatore" in Switzerland. Management: Eric Semon Associates. . . . **Karen Altman,** gained her early operatic training in the Metropolitan Opera Studio; she sang the soprano lead in world premiere of Leonard Bernstein's "Mass" at the Kennedy Center in 1971; she has appeared under Georg Solti with the Chicago Symphony in New York and Chicago; has sung with the Philadelphia Symphony, National Symphony, etc; made her European debut in 1970 with the Frankfurt Opera and has since sung with the Bordeaux Opera. Management: Thea Dispeker Artists' Representative. . . . **Lucine Amara,** soprano in opera and concert; debut recital in 1947; at the Metropolitan since 1950; has appeared with Glyndebourne and Stockholm opera companies and with major orchestras. Recordings: *Columbia, Angel, RCA Victor, Cambridge.* . . . **Karen Armstrong,** lyric coloratura with the New York City Opera; has sung with the opera companies of Santa Fe, Milwaukee, Lake George, Fort Worth, and San Francisco; also concert singer and recitalist. Management: Columbia Artists Management, Inc. . . . **Martina Arroyo** (b. 1940), leading soprano of Metropolitan Opera; opened the 1971–72 Met season as Queen Elisabeth in "Don Carlo"; performs in operas, concerts, and recitals all over the world; made Carnegie Hall debut in American premiere of Pizzetti's "Murder in the Cathedral"; in 1965 sang Aida at the Metropolitan as substitute; has since performed in almost every major opera house in the world; made her debut with New York Philharmonic in 1963, singing in the world premiere of Barber's "Andromache's Farewell." Recordings: *DGG, London, Desto, Columbia, Decca, EMI, Westminster.* Management: Thea Dispeker Artists' Representative.

Klara Barlow, soprano, active in Europe; has sung with the opera houses of Berlin, Vienna State, Hamburg, Trieste, Dresden, Munich, Stuttgart, etc.; in the U.S. with the Seattle, Houston, San Diego, and Portland opera companies; she has sung much Wagner, Strauss, and the dramatic soprano roles of Verdi. Management: Eric Semon Associates, Inc. . . . **Giulia Barrera,** Brooklyn-born dramatic soprano; has sung in Nuremburg, at Copenhagen's Royal Opera, the Gran Teatro Liceo in Barcelona, the New York City Opera, the San Francisco Opera and with orchestras in the U.S.; she has appeared with leading opera stars and conductors; her operatic repertory is mostly Italian. Management; Hurok Concerts, Inc. . . . **Bethany Beardslee** (b. 1927), soprano specializing for many years in the repertory of serial and avant-garde composers; appears in solo recital and with instrumental and orchestral ensembles; has sung under the direction of Leinsdorf, Boulez, Foss, Tilson Thomas, et al.; she is considered one of the leading interpreters of such composers as Berg, Babbitt, Schoenberg, Krenek, and Stravinsky; however, her repertory does include Baroque music, Debussy, etc. Recordings: *CRI, Columbia, Monitor.* Management: Sheldon Soffer Management, Inc. . . . **Susan Belling,** singer with the San Francisco Opera, St. Louis Opera, Santa Fe Opera, and Central City Opera; has sung with the Boston Symphony, Detroit, Buffalo and Oakland Symphonies; during second season with Santa Fe sang principal role in the American premiere of Riemann's "Melusine." Recordings: *Columbia.* Management: Thea Dispeker Artists' Representative. . . . **Judith Blegen,** opera singer and concert artist, made her debut with the Philadelphia Orchestra in 1963, subsequently appeared with Starlight Theatre in Kansas City, Santa Fe Opera, and the Berlin Festival; performed in Spoleto Festival chamber music series in 1963–64; became member of Nuremburg Opera in 1965; has since performed soubrette soprano roles in Vienna, at the Spoleto Festival, Salzburg Festival, etc.; she taped several operas for television under Georg Solti; made Metropolitan Opera debut in 1970. Recordings: *Columbia.* Management: Thea Dispeker Artists' Representative. . . . **Helen Boatright,** internationally known singer; began her musical training at Oberlin, made her operatic debut at Berkshire Music Center, under Herbert Graf and Boris Goldovsky; is well-known for oratorio performances of Brahms Requiem, Beethoven's Ninth Symphony and "Missa Solemnis," etc.; has sung in Bach festivals throughout the U.S.; also gives joint recitals with husband, Howard Boatright, violinist. Recordings: *Cambridge, Columbia, Vanguard, Urania, Decca.* Management: Arthur Judson Management, Inc. . . . **Carole Bogard,** mainly a recitalist and orchestral singer, began her studies and career on the West Coast, singing with the San Francisco Symphony, Spring Opera, and Oakland Symphony under such conductors as Pierre Monteux, Josef Krips, and Fiedler; at the University of California at Berkeley, she recorded Monteverdi's "Coronation of Poppea"; she also performed much contemporary music at Berkeley under Copland, Kirchner, Milhaud, and Lawrence Foster; has appeared at Carmel, New York's Philharmonic Hall, with the Boston Symphony, the Boston Opera, etc.; has also sung in Europe. Recordings: *Cambridge, Vox, Desto, New York Handel Society.* Management: Thea Dispeker Artists' Representative. . . . **Patricia Brooks,** well-known recitalist, opera singer, orchestral performer, began her career as dancer and actress; she is noted for portrayals of such roles as Violetta, Manon, and Mélisande at New York City Opera, as well as with opera houses of Covent Garden, Chicago Lyric, San Francisco, Santa Fe, etc.; has performed in almost every major festival in the U.S. and sung with such major orchestras as New York Philharmonic, Philadelphia Orchestra, Chicago Symphony. Recordings: *Decca, RCA Victor, CRI.* Management: Shaw Concerts, Inc. . . . **Joanna Bruno,** singer with the New York City Opera; sang in world premiere of Menotti's "Most Important Man in the World"; has appeared at the Holland Festival; made her Chicago Lyric Opera debut in 1972. Management: Columbia Artists Management, Inc. . . . **Grace Bumbry** (b. 1937), soprano, also has sung mezzo and contralto; member of the Metropolitan Opera; also engagements with the Royal Opera at Covent Garden, Teatro Colon in Buenos Aires, San Francisco, Chicago Lyric, and the great opera companies of Germany, Italy, France, etc.; one of the great singers before the public today; made her professional debut in London in 1959; achieved particular fame with her enactment of the role of Venus in "Tannhäuser" at Bayreuth in 1961—the first Negro to perform this role. Recordings: *Angel, Music Guild, DGG, Westminster, London, Philips.* Management: Hurok Concerts, Inc.

Maria Callas (b. 1923), legendary opera singer and concert artist; famed for Italian repertory; has performed in the major opera houses of Europe and America; had established European career before U.S. debut with Lyric Theatre of Chicago, 1954–55.

Recordings: *Angel, Seraphim, Everest/Cetra, Everest.* . . . **Barbara Smith Conrad.** Texas-born soprano; has sung with the New York City Center Opera, Harlem Opera Company of New York, Municipal Opera of St. Louis, Starlight Theatre of Missouri, etc.; appeared with Berkshire Chamber Orchestra at Tanglewood, Boston Symphony Orchestra at Tanglewood, Great Neck Chamber Orchestra, Long Island Little Orchestra, etc.; performed with numerous choral societies in New York, has given solo recitals, and has sung with contemporary music ensembles. Management: Bess Pruitt Associates, Inc. . . . **Mary Costa,** soprano, singing coloratura and spinto roles in opera; her operatic repertory consists of 47 roles which include not only the frequently heard operas of the standard Italian, German, and French repertory but also works by Orff, Boito, Britten, Floyd, et al.; her orchestral repertory includes most of the major solo–choral–orchestral works of Bach, Beethoven, Handel, as well as Mahler, Debussy, Duparc, Mozart, et al.; she has sung with the Metropolitan Opera since her debut in 1964 and has sung with many of the world's leading opera companies; she made a successful debut at the Bolshoi Opera, Moscow, in 1970 while touring the Soviet Union; she has also appeared on TV in the U.S. and abroad. Recordings: *RCA Victor.* Management: Hurok Concerts, Inc. . . . **Jeannine Crader,** made her operatic debut in San Francisco; after an engagement with San Francisco Opera she toured Europe three years, then returned to the U.S. and toured three years with the Metropolitan Opera Studio; she made her debut with New York City Opera in 1964 as Donna Elvira in "Don Giovanni"; with the opening of the New York State Theatre at Lincoln Center, she created the role of Florinda in the North American premiere of Ginastera's "Don Rodrigo"; she has appeared with leading opera companies in the U.S. and Europe including Baltimore Civic Opera, Fort Worth, Milan, etc.; she has sung with the New York Philharmonic, Boston Pops, Pittsburgh Symphony, and others. The soprano is artist-in-residence at North Texas State University. Recordings: *Desto.* Management: Arthur Judson Management, Inc. . . . **Gilda Cruz–Romo,** Mexican-born, young soprano; member of the Metropolitan Opera Company since 1970, the year she won the Metropolitan Opera auditions which led to an immediate contract; her debut with the New York City Opera was in 1969; in 1972 she appeared for the first time at Covent Garden; prior to her now mainly American career, she had appeared in opera in Mexico City; her roles are mostly in the operas by Verdi and Puccini. Management: Hurok Concerts, Inc. . . . **Phyllis Curtin** (b. 1922), soprano of international reputation; member of the Metropolitan Opera since 1961; she has sung with many of the great opera houses of the world and in concerts under prominent conductors. Recordings: *RCA Victor, Columbia, Bach Guild, Music Guild, Louisville, CRI.* Management: Columbia Artists Management, Inc.

Gloria V. Davy (b. 1931), concert and opera singer; concert debut in 1954; opera debut in Europe in 1957, in U.S. in 1958; has sung with the Metropolitan since her debut there in 1958; winner of the Marian Anderson Award in 1951 and 1952; in 1972, toured Israel with the Israel Philharmonic under Zubin Mehta. Management: Thea Dispeker Artists' Representative. . . . **Mattiwilda Dobbs,** (b. 1925), opera and concert singer; opera debut, La Scala, 1953; concert debut, The Hague, in 1951; U.S. opera debut, San Francisco, 1955; U.S. concert debut, 1954; first sang at the Metropolitan in 1956 and continued until 1964; undertakes annual U.S.–Europe tours; in 1955 toured Australia, Mexico, Central America; toured Russia in 1959; sang in New York, April, 1972 after an absence of eight years; she resides in Sweden. Management: Michael O'Daniel Artists' Representative. . . . **Helen Donath,** Texas-born soprano who established her career mainly in Europe; made her debut in 1962 in Cologne; later sang in Hanover, Salzburg Festival, Berlin, Frankfurt, Stuttgart, Stockholm, Paris, Madrid, etc.; is member of Munich Opera; in 1969 made her Vienna recital debut; debut with San Francisco Opera in 1971 as Sophie in "Der Rosenkavalier"; has also sung this role with the Vienna

State Opera in Moscow; has performed with Chicago Symphony under Solti. Recordings: *London, Angel, Eurodisc.* Management: Colbert Artists Management, Inc.

Carole Farley, young soprano from Iowa; leading soprano with the Cologne Opera, the youngest in the history of that opera company; her early years in music were as a pianist and clarinetist; she sang with the Indiana University Opera Theatre and later with the Metropolitan Opera Studio; her opera appearances and recitals have taken her to Spain, Austria, Israel, Germany, Scandinavia, and Great Britain; she performed the title role in the English premiere of "Lulu"; her appearances with orchestra include a performance of Boulez's "Pli selon pli" with the composer conducting the Cleveland Orchestra. Management: Hurok Concerts, Inc. . . . **Eileen Farrell** is considered one of the outstanding dramatic sopranos; known for performances in opera, concerts, recordings, TV appearances, and even popular music; career began on radio in 1940's, but not until 1955 did she decide to sing in opera; debut in Tampa, Florida, in "Cavalleria Rusticana"; 1958 she opened the San Francisco Opera season in "Medea," considered one of the most demanding roles in soprano repertory; Metropolitan Opera debut in 1960; appeared with almost every major opera company and symphony in the U.S.; appeared with the New York Philharmonic more often than any other singer; substituted for Louis Armstrong in 1959 at Spoleto and since then has made several recordings of popular music. Recordings: *Columbia, RCA Victor, Angel.* Management: Herbert Barrett Management.

Marisa Galvany, young American soprano; has sung leading roles in operas by Bellini, Donizetti, Mayr, Mozart, etc.; some of the less frequently heard roles she has assumed include the role of Yolanta in Tchaikovsky's opera of that name and Medea in Mayr's "Medea in Corinto"; she has sung with the Seattle, Central City Festival, and Kentucky opera companies. Recordings: *Scala, Eterna, Vanguard.* Management: Hurok Concerts, Inc. . . . **Reri Grist,** leading soprano with the Metropolitan Opera, Vienna Opera, Covent Garden, and the opera companies of San Francisco, Munich, and Salzburg; has appeared at major European festivals and with important orchestras in the U.S. and Europe; made her Teatro Colon (Buenos Aires) debut in 1970; her large operatic and concert repertory includes both traditional and contemporary works. Recordings: *Columbia, DGG, Angel, RCA Victor.* Management: Columbia Artists Management, Inc. . . . **Irene Gubrud,** young soprano from Minnesota; New York debut recital in 1970, presented by Concert Artists Guild; selected by Ford Foundation for Program for Concert Artists of 1971 to commission a new work by an American composer; recitals at New York Cultural Center and Phillips Gallery in Washington.

Janice Harsanyi, recitalist and soloist with orchestras throughout the country; has performed with Ormandy and the Philadelphia Orchestra, Atlanta Symphony Orchestra; soloist at the Bach Festival in Florida; recitals in San Francisco, Nashville, etc.; has taught at Interlochen National Music Camp, Michigan. Recordings: *Decca, Columbia, CRI.* Management: Anne O'Donnell Management. . . . **Marilyn Horne,** mezzo-soprano of international stature; star with the Metropolitan Opera, La Scala, Covent Garden, and the Chicago Lyric; her concert appearances include those with the Pittsburgh, New York, Washington, Boston, and Philadelphia Orchestras; she has also appeared in concert with her husband, conductor Henry Lewis, and the New Jersey Symphony both in New York and New Jersey; known for her bel canto interpretations; in recent years has sung as a soprano. Recordings: *London, Capitol.* Management: Columbia Artists Management, Inc.

Irene Jordan, faculty Manhattan School of Music since 1968; visiting Professor of Voice, Eastman School of Music, 1969–70; Metropolitan Opera debut, 1946; annual concert tours, 1950 to present. Recordings: *Columbia.* Management: Herbert Barrett Management. . . . **Doris Jung,** Illinois-born singer who first established her career in Europe; made her debut in Zürich; she has sung with the Hamburg State Opera; has performed in

"Fidelio" more than 80 times; appeared with the Vienna State Opera and Munich State Opera; she made her debut in the U.S. with the New York City Opera; has sung with the National Symphony of Washington, Cleveland Orchestra, and Minnesota Orchestra. Management: Thea Dispeker Artists' Representative.

Dorothy Kirsten, among the best known American singers since 1940; has sung in opera, concerts, recitals, and television; leading opera roles with Metropolitan and San Francisco opera companies. Recordings: *RCA Victor, Columbia,* and *Capitol.* Management: Columbia Artists Management, Inc.

Ella Lee, soprano singing in opera, recital, and concerts with orchestras in the U.S., Canada, and in Europe; she has sung with the Berlin Philharmonic, the Detroit Symphony, the Montreal Symphony, and other orchestras; her opera roles have been sung in Berlin and in Montreal. Recordings: *Command.* . . . **Evelyn Lear,** leading soprano, Metropolitan Opera and La Scala Opera; made her first impact in Europe beginning in 1958 with the Berlin Opera; sang "Lulu" in 1962; in "Wozzeck," with the Chicago Lyric Opera in 1966; these roles brought significant attention to her abilities and subsequently she became more active in the U.S.; made her Met debut in 1967; her modern repertory has been increasingly supplanted by works from the classic and romantic repertory; she has performed in concert and in recital; has appeared in joint recitals with her husband Thomas Stewart, baritone. Recordings: *DGG, Angel.* Management: Shaw Concerts, Inc.

Maxine Makas, Ohio-born, coloratura soprano; operatic debut in 1963 with the Philadelphia Lyric Opera; has sung with the American Opera Society, the Boston Opera Company, the Little Orchestra Society, the Kansas City Philharmonic, and the Omaha Symphony; contemporary works are in both her operatic and orchestral repertory; her single recording is of songs by Poulenc. Recordings: *Westminster.* Management: Hurok Concerts, Inc. . . . **Evelyn Mandac,** soprano; born in the Philippines, studied in the U.S.; has sung with the Seattle Opera Association, San Antonio Opera, San Francisco Opera, and St. Paul Opera, with the Boston Symphony, Philadelphia Orchestra (at Robin Hood Dell and in Philadelphia and New York), and the Pittsburgh, Chattanooga, Dallas Orchestras, etc.; toured with the Juilliard String Quartet in Schoenberg's Second String Quartet; appeared in American premiere of Berio's "Passaggio," then introduced the work to European audiences; also sang in Hans Werner Henze's "The Bassarids" at Santa Fe Opera; appeared in the NET–TV production of "The Queen of Spades." Recordings: *RCA.* Management: Columbia Artists Management, Inc. . . . **Jane Marsh,** soprano; became prominent in 1966 by winning first prize at the Tchaikovsky Competition becoming the second American to do so; recital and concert appearances in Russia followed soon after; debut in 1967–68 season of San Francisco Opera where she is now a leading soprano; also member of the Düsseldorf Opera; concert appearances have been with the orchestras of Boston, New York, Philadelphia; premiered Rorem's "Sun" with the New York Philharmonic in 1967. Recordings: *RCA Victor.* Management: Columbia Artists Management, Inc. . . . **Lois Marshall,** Canadian-born soprano; active performer in the U.S. in concerts, recitals, and opera; many concerts with major orchestras in Canada, the U.S., and Europe; toured Russia in 1958; has sung on Canadian television; member of the Bach Aria Group. Recordings: *RCA Victor, Angel.* Management: Columbia Artists Management, Inc. . . . **Zinka Milanov,** internationally known soprano; opera debut in 1927; Metropolitan debut in 1937; has sung in the opera houses of America, South America, and Europe and in concerts with major orchestras. Recordings: *RCA Victor.* Management: Sheldon Soffer Management, Inc. . . . **Anna Moffo** (b. 1932) leading operatic singer; has made appearances in opera and concerts in the U.S. and Europe at La Scala, Vienna State Opera, and Chicago; Chicago Lyric Opera debut in 1958; a member of the Metropolitan Opera since 1957; has appeared in films and television; one of the most famous of today's active opera performers. Recordings: *RCA Victor, Angel, Telefunken.* Management: Columbia Artists Management, Inc.

Carol Neblett, California-born soprano singing in opera and in concert; she has sung opera on a professional scale only since 1969, when she sang her debut with the New York City Opera; a regular singer with that company, she now has some 41 roles in 37 operas in her repertory including operas by American composers Menotti, Moore, Barber, and Floyd; her earlier career had been as an oratorio singer, primarily; her orchestral repertory is, accordingly, quite extensive, containing much Handel, Haydn, Bach, and such infrequently heard works as Schoenberg's "Gurre-Lieder," Bruckner's "Te Deum," Toch's "The Chinese Flute." Management: Hurok Concerts, Inc. . . . **Matilda Nickel,** dramatic soprano singing with the Seattle Opera, Honolulu Opera, Denver Lyric, San Diego Opera, and at Central City in Colorado. Management: William Felber Agency. . . . **Maralin Niska,** member of the New York City Opera; has performed with that company both in New York and in Washington, D.C.; has sung with the New York Philharmonic under Boulez, and with the Cleveland and Philadelphia Orchestras; her portrayals with the New York City Opera of leading roles in Janáček's "Makropulos Affair," Britten's "Turn of the Screw," and Floyd's "Susannah," have been particularly important in establishing her reputation in America. Management: Columbia Artists Management, Inc. . . . **Jessye Norman,** soprano, won the International Music Competition in Munich in 1968 and, as a result, began a three-year contract with Deutsche Oper in Berlin; performed at the Berlin Festival in 1970 with Fischer-Dieskau; sang at the Maggio Musicale in Florence, and made her debut at La Scala and Covent Garden; has given recitals throughout Europe and has sung at major festivals; in the U.S. has performed at the Hollywood Bowl with the Los Angeles Philharmonic, Wolf Trap Festival, at Tanglewood with the Boston Symphony, etc.; has performed many oratorio works. Recordings: *Philips, EMI* on *Odeon* label. Management: Arthur Judson Management, Inc.

Roberta Peters (b. 1930), member of the Metropolitan Opera, since 1950, singing leading roles; Covent Garden debut in 1952; a singer of international stature, she has sung in the major opera houses of the world and with many of the great orchestras; has also appeared on television; considered to be one of the brilliant coloratura voices of the day. Recordings: *RCA Victor, Command, DGG, Columbia.* Management: Hurok Concerts, Inc. . . . **Leontyne Price** (b. 1927), internationally known soprano in opera, concerts, recitals, and on television; member of the Metropolitan since her debut in 1961; Vienna State Opera performances debut in 1958–59, San Francisco Opera 1957, and others. Recordings: *RCA Victor.* Management: Columbia Artists Management, Inc.

Judith Raskin, star soprano with the Metropolitan Opera and concert singer and recitalist; frequent performer with the New York Philharmonic and other major orchestras; considered also to be one of the important lieder singers of today. Recordings: *RCA Victor, Decca, Columbia.* Management: Columbia Artists Management, Inc. . . . **Regina Resnik** (b. 1922), famed soprano singing lead roles with the Metropolitan Opera since 1944; sang at Bayreuth Festival, 1953 and Covent Garden in 1957, etc.; has also directed opera ("Carmen" with the Hamburg Opera and "Elektra" in Venice), singing in the productions as well; has also sung as a mezzo. Recordings: *Music Guild, London, Columbia, RCA Victor.* . . . **Faye Robinson,** has sung with Washington Civic Opera, San Francisco Symphony under Kurt Adler, Washington National Symphony, and Bayerischer Rundfunk in Munich; also toured with New York Camerata Singers. Management: Arthur Judson Management, Inc. . . . **Gail Robinson,** young Tennessee-born coloratura; with the Metropolitan Opera Studio in 1966 and that year with the Memphis Opera Theatre; on contract with the Metropolitan for the 1968–69 season, singing on stage first in 1970; made her leading role debut with the Metropolitan in "Lucia" as a substitute for ailing

Roberta Peters in a Met tour performance in Detroit, which brought about wider recognition; has sung also with the opera companies of Chicago, New Orleans, San Antonio, Cincinnati, Orlando, etc. Management: Columbia Artists Management, Inc. . . . **Elinor Ross,** made operatic debut with Cincinnati Summer Opera in 1958; appeared with Chicago Lyric Opera, San Francisco Opera, and the opera companies of Philadelphia, Pittsburgh, Houston, San Antonio, Fort Worth, Toronto, etc.; debut in Italy in 1965, which was followed by appearances in London, Zagreb, Vienna Staatsoper, Festival of Holland, etc.; her Metropolitan Opera debut came in 1970, singing five roles her first season; has sung in Latin America and is a frequent soloist with major orchestras in U.S. and Canada. Management: Herbert Barrett Management. . . . **Louise Russell** (former name Lois Crane), European debut with the State Opera in Stuttgart in 1970; New York City Opera debut in 1968; Vienna Opera debut in 1973; performed with Philadelphia Lyric Opera, Cincinnati Summer Opera, Wichita Opera, Lake George (N.Y.), and Aspen Music Festival; appeared with many orchestras in oratorios and orchestral repertory; in 1969, she won the Corbett Foundation Award first prize and the first prize at International Singing Contest in Vercelli, Italy. Management: Herbert Barrett Management.

Arlene Saunders, received her musical training in America but has had an active career in Europe; won American Opera Auditions in 1960, subsequently made her debut in Milan, Italy; in 1961 made her New York City Opera debut; also sang with companies in Houston, Fort Worth, Central City, Cincinnati, etc.; returned to Europe and became member of Hamburg State Opera, singing both traditional and contemporary soprano roles; has appeared in many of Hamburg Opera's film versions; in 1971 created title role in Ginastera's "Beatrix Cenci," the work commissioned to be the first opera given at John F. Kennedy Center in Washington. Recordings: *RCA Victor.* Management: Thea Dispeker Artists' Representative. . . . **Jacklyn Schneider** made her professional opera debut with the Connecticut Opera Association while still attending the Eastman School of Music; has sung with Rochester's Opera Under the Stars, Philadelphia Lyric Opera Company, Santa Fe Opera, and has appeared under Menotti's direction in "The Consul" for the San Francisco Spring Opera; made her New York recital debut in 1966 and her New York operatic debut in 1968 with the American Opera Society; has toured with the Metropolitan Opera Studio. Management: Colbert Artists Management, Inc. . . . **Barbara Shuttleworth,** Canadian-born soprano; received her formal training in New York at the Juilliard School; she appeared in opera productions at the Juilliard Opera Theater in Cavalli's "Ormindo," Bennett's "The Mines of Sulphur," and "La Voix Humaine" by Poulenc; with the Santa Fe Opera she sang Cherubino and the soprano lead in Luciano Berio's "Opera"; she has also sung in Canada for television including a production of Puccini's "Rondine"; she has performed with the New York Chamber Soloists and is a member of New York City Opera. Management: Colbert Artists Management, Inc. . . . **Beverly Sills** (b. 1929), member of the New York City Opera since 1955; world-renowned opera singer; her career has been one of the most spectacular in modern times; a singer since early childhood when she sang professionally; has sung for over thirty years, becoming one of the greatest coloraturas in the world and achieving international recognition as such only relatively recently; she made her New York recital debut in 1970; her debut with La Scala was in 1969; her first major opera company debut was with San Francisco Opera in 1953; she has appeared with orchestras and has recorded extensively. Recordings: *Westminster, RCA Victor, Vanguard.* Management: Ludwig Lustig and Florian, Ltd. . . . **Sylvia Stahlman;** has sung roles for the Chicago Lyric, San Francisco Opera, Frankfurt Opera, etc. and has appeared with important American and European orchestras. Recordings: *London, Vox, Argo, CRI.* . . . **Eleanor Steber** (b. 1916); internationally renowned opera and concert singer; winner of 1940 Metropolitan Auditions and made her opera debut at that house the same year; at the Metropolitan she sang some 50 roles and took part in the Met's first productions of a number of works from the standard repertory as well as the American premiere of Strauss's "Arabella," and the world premiere of Barber's "Vanessa." She was one of the first Americans to appear at such European festivals as those at Bayreuth, Salzburg, Edinburgh, Glyndebourne, Prades, Dubrovnik, and others; she is equally skilled in the great oratorio literature and other works for voice, chorus, and orchestra. Recordings: *Columbia, Viva, Odyssey, RCA Victor, Desto.* Management: Eric Semon Associates. . . . **Janet Steele,** soprano; studied at University of Iowa, Yale, and in Siena; joined Center for New Music at University of Iowa in 1966 for two years; performed at Summer Collegium in Early Music at Windham College (Vermont) for several summers; appeared with Speculum Musicae, Western Wind, and Trio Francesca Caccini, which gives summer concerts at the Cloisters in New York; has sung at Phillips Gallery in Washington and with Amor Artis Chorale (New York). . . . **Nancy Stokes,** soprano; world debut in "La Bohème" in Rome's Teatro Eliseo; opera and recitals throughout Italy; later toured with the Metropolitan Opera National Company and the Goldovsky Grand Opera Theater; has since sung with the Philadelphia Lyric Opera, Connecticut Opera Company, Toledo–Dayton Opera; performed in Santiago, Chile, during its special International Season; performed with Des Moines, Dayton, Atlanta, and Washington Orchestras; member of Affiliate Artists Program. Recordings: *RCA Victor.* Management: Herbert Barrett Management.

Veronica Tyler, leading soprano with the New York City Opera; concert singer and recitalist; was among the winners of the 1966 Tchaikovsky Competition in Moscow; frequent appearances with major orchestras such as the New York Philharmonic, Boston, Philadelphia, and Pittsburgh Orchestras, etc. Management: Columbia Artists Management, Inc.

Benita Valente, concert, recital, and operatic singer; she won the Metropolitan Opera Auditions in 1960; sang under Rudolf Serkin as artist-in-residence at the Marlboro Festival; in 1962 she made her European debut and has performed frequently with orchestras and opera houses there; she has appeared in the U.S. with the Boston Symphony, the Cleveland Orchestra, the Houston Symphony, San Francisco Symphony, and New York Philharmonic; she has sung Pamina in Mozart's "Magic Flute" in more than 20 productions but also performs such contemporary repertory as Britten's "The Turn of the Screw." Recordings: *Columbia, Candide, CRI.* Management: Thea Dispeker Artists' Representative. . . . **Lee Venora,** soprano, made her debut with New York City Opera in 1958 in the world premiere of Marc Bucci's "Tale for a Deaf Ear"; since then she has sung many contemporary as well as traditional soprano roles with that company, including the world premiere of Dello Joio's "The Triumph of St. Joan"; has also sung with San Francisco Opera, San Diego Civic Opera, Tulsa, New Orleans Opera, etc.; has appeared with New York Philharmonic, NBC's Television Opera Theatre, in a television production of "Carmen" under Bernstein, etc.; in Europe she has sung with the Deutsch Oper in Berlin for several seasons. Recordings: *Columbia.* Management: Arthur Judson Management, Inc.

Claire Watson, American soprano, member of the Vienna State Opera and performer in other important European opera houses; in America she has sung with the Chicago Lyric, the New Orleans Opera, and the San Francisco Opera; she has specialized in the roles of operas by Richard Strauss and Wagner. Recordings: *London, RCA Victor, Everest, Angel.* Management: Hurok Concerts, Inc. . . . **Felicia Weathers,** St. Louis-born soprano appearing in opera in the U.S. and Europe; made opera debut with the Zürich Municipal Opera, followed with engagements with the Munich State Opera and the Vienna State Opera; she appeared in the Hamburg Opera production of Schuller's "The Visitation" in performances in Hamburg and the visiting production in New York City; other opera engagements include the Chicago Lyric, the Stockholm State Opera, and Covent Garden; has sung with a number of major U.S. orchestras. Recordings: *London.* Management: Columbia Artists Management, Inc. . . . **Patricia Wells,** Louisiana-born soprano, appeared at Spoleto Festival in 1970 gaining first acclaim as Elaisa in Mercadante's "Il Giuramento"; won first prize in the Munich International Vocal Competition in 1971; has appeared at Aspen Festival and has sung with the Dallas Civic Opera, Opera Society of Washington, Cincinnati Symphony, St. Louis Symphony, Clarion Music Society and Chamber Music Society of Lincoln Center; made her debut with the New York City Opera in 1972. Recordings: *Vanguard.* Management: Shaw Concerts, Inc. . . . **Camilla Williams;** opera, concert, and recital appearances in the U.S., South America, and Europe; New York City Center debut in 1946; beginning in 1955 was with Vienna State Opera for several years; currently performing in duo recitals with clarinetist David Glazer. Recordings: *Odyssey.* Management: Pacific World Artists, Inc. . . . **Patricia Wise,** sang with Santa Fe Opera for four summer seasons before joining New York City Opera in 1968; performed in the New York premiere of Ginastera's "Bomarzo"; has sung in Covent Garden, at the Glyndebourne Festival, and made debuts in Geneva and Vienna in 1973; appeared at Ravinia Festival, New Orleans and Pittsburgh Operas in the U.S.; has also sung with leading orchestras throughout the U.S. Management: Herbert Barrett Management. . . . **Nadja Witkowska** has sung with New York City, Cincinnati, Central City Festival, Washington, Houston, Pittsburgh and Santa Fe Operas; also has appeared in musical comedy and on television with the former NBC Opera; symphonic engagements have included Detroit Symphony, Lindsborg Bach Festival, New York Philharmonic, Philadelphia Orchestra, Buffalo Philharmonic, and Lincoln Center Mozart Festival; Metropolitan Opera debut as Lucia in 1970–71 season. Management: Thea Dispeker Artists' Representative. . . . **Lou Ann Wyckoff** has performed widely in Europe since making her European debut in 1967 at the Spoleto Festival of Two Worlds as Donna Elvira in "Don Giovanni"; has since sung at La Scala, Genoa, Trieste, Hamburg, London, Düsseldorf, Cologne, Barcelona, and Zürich in concerts and operas; in 1969 she became a permanent member of the Berlin Opera; engagements in the U.S. have been with Chicago Symphony, Washington Symphony, Washington Opera Society, Philadelphia Lyric Opera, New York City Opera, New York Philharmonic, etc. Management: Thea Dispeker Artists' Representative.

MEZZO-SOPRANOS

Betty Allen, has sung in opera, recitals, and concerts throughout the U.S. and in Canada, England, Holland, Germany, and Norway, etc. Recordings: *Vox, Columbia, Decca, CRI.* Management: Columbia Artists Management, Inc.

Marcia Baldwin sang for two summers as apprentice artist with Santa Fe Opera, touring Europe in 1961 with the company; sang leading mezzo roles with the Metropolitan Opera Studio; also toured with Goldovsky Opera Theatre and appeared with San Francisco Spring Opera; made Metropolitan debut in 1963 and has sung more than 50 roles; has also appeared with Philadelphia Lyric, Cincinnati Summer Opera, Central City, etc.; has sung with Baltimore and Washington National Orchestras, Los Angeles Philharmonic, etc.; in 1969 created role of Viola in world premiere of Amram's "Twelfth Night" at Lake George Opera. Management: Arthur Judson Management, Inc. . . . **Cathy Berberian** (b. 1925), mezzo-soprano; resident of Italy since 1950; she is internationally known, having sung throughout Europe, the U.S., in Canada, and Japan, etc.; her reputation is solidly anchored to her interpretations of many works of the avant garde and to her remarkably unusual vocal recitals, wherein elements of showmanship are not without their importance; her voice has often been employed beyond the normal techniques of vocalization and, in this sense, is unclassifiable; however, her repertory does contain traditional music for the voice including Bach, Debussy, folk songs, and songs by the Beatles; composers who have written works specifically for her abilities are Berio (former husband), Cage, Bussotti. Recordings: *Telefunken, Mainstream, Turnabout, Columbia.* Management: Sheldon Soffer Management. . . . **Frances Bible,** leading mezzo with New York City Opera; debut with the New York City Opera in 1948; San Francisco Opera debut in 1955; guest artist with major opera companies in the U.S. and England: New Orleans, Houston, San Antonio, San Francisco, Glyndebourne; appearances at Caramoor and other festivals and with major orchestras. Recordings: *Angel, CRI.* Management: Columbia Artists Management, Inc. . . . **Elaine Bonazzi** made her professional debut in 1957 at Columbia University in New York in Chavez's "Panfilo and Lauretta"; subsequently she sang for 10 summer seasons with the Santa Fe Opera Company, performing many premieres including the U.S. premiere of "Lulu"; she has appeared with many major opera companies including Dallas, Seattle, and New York City opera companies; she has performed many works of Stravinsky and was chosen by him to sing several world premieres; has appeared with the Detroit Symphony, Philadelphia Orchestra, Cincinnati Symphony, etc., as soloist and has sung often in oratorio works; she sang the title role in Pasatieri's opera "The Trial of Mary Lincoln" for NET–TV. Recordings: *Columbia, Vox.* Management: Thea Dispeker Artists' Representative.

Joan Caplan, orchestral singer, recitalist, opera singer; on the faculty at State University at Fredonia, New York; she made her debut at the Caramoor Music Festival in Monteverdi's "L'incoronazione di Poppea"; has sung with the New York City Opera, the Opera Society of Washington, Miami Opera Guild, NBC–TV Opera, etc.; has appeared in Carnegie Hall and Lincoln Center and at the Bethlehem Bach Festival and New York's Mozart Festival; her symphony appearances include performances with the Philadelphia Orchestra, Chicago Symphony, Detroit Symphony, and Dallas Symphony. Management: Thea Dispeker Artists' Representative. . . . **Nedda Casei,** Baltimore-born, young mezzo-soprano; at the Metropolitan Opera since her debut there in 1964; opera debut in 1959 under Leopold Stokowski in Stravinsky's "Oedipus Rex" performed at the now-defunct Empire State Festival; she has trained both in the U.S. and Europe; her engagements are throughout Europe, South Africa, and South America; her orchestral-vocal repertory includes some masses, oratorios, etc.; her opera roles range from Orfeo to those in the operas of Wagner and Verdi. Recordings: *Nonesuch, Vanguard.* Management: Hurok Concerts, Inc. . . . **Corinne Curry,** mezzo-soprano, has appeared with Chicago Lyric Opera, Central City Opera, Boston Opera Group, etc.; has sung with Denver Symphony, Kol Israel Philharmonic, St. Louis Symphony, Boston Pops, and Milwaukee Symphony Orchestra; has premiered contemporary works at Tanglewood for Fromm Foundation-sponsored concerts; appeared at Marlboro under Rudolf Serkin and Alexander Schneider; performed for NET television in Bernstein's "Trouble in Tahiti." Recordings: *Cambridge.* Management: Herbert Barrett Management.

Irene Dalis (b. 1925); opera, recital, concert singer; opera debut in Germany in 1953; member of the Berlin State Opera since 1955 and the Metropolitan since 1957; San Francisco Opera debut in 1958; has sung also with Covent Garden, the Hamburg Opera, and at Bayreuth; often in Wagnerian roles. Recordings: *Philips.* . . . **Joy Davidson,** mezzo-soprano with the New York City Opera; winner of the first prize in the 1967 International Opera Contest in Sofia, Bulgaria; has sung with La Scala and the Maggio Musicale in Florence; noted for her performance as Carmen, which she has sung over 100 times; she has also sung with the orchestras of San Francisco and Pittsburgh. Management: Columbia Artists Management, Inc. . . . **Mignon Dunn,** mezzo-soprano who performs leading roles at the Metropolitan Opera; also appears regularly in Germany (Düsseldorf, Munich, Frankfurt, Hamburg), where she is noted for her portrayal of Carmen; performed first Wagnerian roles in Berlin, then in Chicago under Georg Solti; sang in Chile in 1970; performed with Philadelphia's Grand Opera, New Orleans, Connecticut Opera and Memphis Opera (her home town). Recordings: *DGG.* Management: Herbert Barrett Management.

Rosalind Elias, opera debut with Metropolitan Opera in 1954; orchestra appearances with major ensembles; has also sung on television; has sung 35 leading mezzo roles for the Metropolitan Opera, San Francisco Opera, Teatro Colon in Buenos Aires, Salzburg Festival, Scottish Opera, etc.; well-known for portrayals of Carmen, Dalila in "Samson et Dalila," etc.; the first mezzo to sing Zerlina in "Don Giovanni" (Metropolitan Opera); performed in opening night of new Metropolitan Opera House at Lincoln Center; in world premiere of Barber's "Vanessa"; has sung with leading orchestras throughout U.S. and Europe. Recordings: *RCA Victor, Columbia.* Management: Herbert Barrett Management.

Muriel Greenspon, member of the New York City Opera; has performed in both the standard opera repertory and much contemporary opera by such composers as Menotti, Weill, et al.; she has been particularly cited for her acting ability, notably as Madam Flora in the "Medium" and as Mrs. Begbick in "Mahagonny." Management: Eric Semon Associates. . . . **Joann Grillo** (b. 1939), member of the Metropolitan Opera; made her opera debut at the age of nineteen as Amneris in "Aida"; she has sung at least one role in the representative operas of nearly all the significant opera composers in the German, French, Italian, and Russian repertory; in America she has sung with the companies of Los Angeles, Cincinnati, Philadelphia, Hartford, Miami, the New York City Opera, and many more; her appearances in Europe have been with the Paris Opera and opera houses in Zürich, Barcelona, Geneva, etc.; she is also active as a recitalist. Management: Hurok Concerts, Inc.

Hilda Harris, mezzo-soprano, began her career on Broadway; subsequently, she toured Europe three times in as many years; appeared in recital and with orchestras in England, Holland, Luxembourg, and Switzerland; opera debut in 1971 as Carmen in Switzerland; upon return to U.S. made solo concert tour of Southern colleges; has sung with New York City Opera "Title III" Company and the St. Paul Opera. Management: Herbert Barrett Management. . . . **Grace Hoffman,** opera and concert singer; performed much in Europe from 1951 in such companies as La Scala, Covent Garden, and the Bayreuth Festival company; made Metropolitan debut in 1958. Recordings: *Vanguard, Nonesuch, Angel, Turnabout, London.*

Shirley Love, mezzo with the Metropolitan Opera; also in engagements with the opera companies of Santa Fe, Philadelphia, Cincinnati Summer Opera, the Kalamazoo and Carmel Bach Festivals, the major orchestras of Detroit, Cincinnati, and Chicago. Management: Ann Summers.

Nan Merriman, has sung at La Scala, Teatro Colon, and the Hollywood Bowl, etc. Recordings: *Music Guild, RCA Victor, DGG, Angel.* . . . **Mildred Miller,** mezzo with the Metropolitan Opera since her debut there in 1951; with the Stuttgart Opera from 1949 to 1950; member also of the San Francisco Opera; has sung with the Vienna Opera; performer in concerts and recitals. Recordings: *Westminster, Desto, Columbia.* Management: Columbia Artists Management, Inc.

Nell Rankin (b. 1926), active in opera, concerts, and recitals; opera debut in Zürich, 1949; the first American to win first prize in the Geneva International Concours (1950); member of the Metropolitan since 1951; has sung with other opera groups in the U.S. and Europe. Recordings: *Columbia, Richmond.* . . . **Susan Reid-Parsons,** mezzo-soprano, has sung operatic roles for the Goldovsky Opera Institute and the Opera Orchestra of New York (1968 to 1970) and with the Lake George Opera Festival in New York State, where she sang a leading role in Silverman's "Elephant Steps." Management: Eric Semon Associates. . . . **Carolyn Reyer,** known as an interpreter of contemporary American song; appeared throughout the eastern U.S. in recitals of traditional and contemporary music as well as oratorio; has given world premiere of works by David Diamond, Robert F. Baksa, Ned Rorem, Ben Weber; gives lecture-demonstrations at college campuses on interpreting American song. Recordings: *American Music Project,* c/o The West Virginia University Foundation, Morgantown, W. Virginia 26506. Management: c/o 1316 Fairfield Street, Morgantown, W. Virginia 26505.

Joanna Simon, opera singer, recitalist, and soloist with orchestras; has sung with the New York Philharmonic, the Boston Symphony, Philadelphia Orchestra, Cleveland Orchestra, the Pittsburgh and Chicago Symphonies and Los Angeles Philharmonic; has performed in the world and New York premieres of Ginastera's "Bomarzo"; sang in Berg's "Lulu" with American National Opera Company; toured with Mehta and the Israel Philharmonic in "Carmen"; appears in many summer festivals including Tanglewood, Saratoga, Ravinia, the Hollywood Bowl, etc.; has appeared on TV on popular talk shows. Recordings: *Command, Columbia.* Management: Thea Dispeker Artists' Representative.

Blanche Thebom (b. 1918), one of America's great mezzo-sopranos; recital debut in 1941; Town Hall debut in 1944; Metropolitan debut in 1944 and sang there for many years; she sang also at leading opera houses of the world; in a much-acclaimed trip in 1958, she became the first American singer to appear on the stage of the Bolshoi Theater in Moscow; in recent years she has served as Artistic Director of the (now deactivated) Atlanta Opera Company, the Southern Regional Opera, and other opera companies; she appears in duo recitals with soprano, Eleanor Steber. Recordings: *RCA Victor, Angel.* Management: Eric Semon Associates. . . . **Jennie Tourel** (b. 1910, Russia); educated in France; U.S. citizen since 1946; opera debut in Paris, 1933; U.S. engagements in 1941; Metropolitan debut in 1944; well-known soloist with major orchestras throughout the world, as well as recitalist; she has also sung at Covent Garden and the Opéra Comique in Paris; she was artist-in-residence at Aspen and at the Rubin Academy in Jerusalem; she has been on the faculty of the Juilliard School since 1963 and in 1967, conducted master classes on CBS–TV; recently she sang the role of the Countess for the NET–TV opera production of Tchaikovsky's "The Queen of Spades." Recordings: *Columbia, Decca, Odyssey.* Management: Sheldon Soffer Management, Inc. . . . **Tatiana Troyanos,** American-born mezzo-soprano whose career was first established in Europe, where she has performed with Hamburg State Opera, Covent Garden, Munich Opera, and the Berlin State Opera; sang title role in Handel's "Ariodante" during opening week of Kennedy Center in Washington, D.C.; performed with Chicago Lyric Opera and has sung at the Hollywood Bowl, with the Cincinnati Symphony Orchestra, etc.; with the New York Philharmonic Orchestra she sang in Stravinsky's "Oedipus Rex." Recordings: *DGG, Philips.* Management: Herbert Barrett Management. . . . **Claramae Turner** (b. 1920), opera debut with the San Francisco Opera in 1945; Metropolitan debut in 1946; has sung in Central America and throughout the U.S.; was a member of the New York City Opera. Recordings: *Columbia, RCA Victor.*

Helen Vanni, mezzo-soprano, concert singer and opera performer; appearances with Santa Fe Opera; orchestral concerts with the Little Orchestra Society and the St. Louis Symphony. Recordings: *Columbia, RCA Victor.* . . . **Shirley Verrett,** a leading mezzo-soprano on the roster of the Metropolitan Opera; an active concert singer and recitalist; she has sung with many of the world's great opera companies, symphony orchestras, and under the direction of major conductors; her orchestral and recital repertory consists of much Romantic music and she is well-known in opera for her portrayals of Carmen, Delilah, Azucena, and other important mezzo roles. Recordings: *Columbia, Everest, RCA Victor.* Management: Hurok Concerts, Inc. . . . **Frederica Von Stade,** young mezzo-soprano from New Jersey, made her Metropolitan Opera debut in 1970; left the company in 1972 to sing with other companies in the U.S. and Europe; a specialist in bel canto roles, the mezzo has sung with the San Francisco

Opera and Santa Fe Opera; European debut with the Paris Opera House in 1973 and performances with Hamburg Opera Company and Glyndebourne Festival later that season; has appeared as recital and orchestral singer under conductors Karl Böhm, Thomas Schippers, Alain Lombard, Solti, Bernstein, among others. Management: Shaw Concerts, Inc.

Sandra Warfield, mezzo-soprano with the Metropolitan Opera and other opera companies in the U.S.; has sung often with husband, tenor James McCracken, both of whom have also authored a revelatory book about the world of opera and singers, "A Star in the Family," which attracted much interest. Recordings: *London, RCA Victor.* Management: Columbia Artists Management, Inc. . . . **Beverly Wolff,** leading performer with the New York City Opera; created the title role in Moore's "Carrie Nation"; active recitalist and concert performer; European debut in 1970 at Spoleto; has sung in Rome, Florence, Venice, Mexico, and in innumerable U.S. cities. Recordings: *Westminster, RCA Victor, Desto, CRI, ABC.* Management: Columbia Artists Management, Inc.

CONTRALTOS

Eunice Alberts, contralto singing in opera, recitals, and with orchestra; she has sung with the opera companies of Boston, Chicago, New York City, San Francisco, New Orleans, and Washington; her appearances in concert have been under conductors Bernstein, Leinsdorf, Krips, Munch, and Steinberg; she has also performed with Hindemith and Copland; she performed under Leinsdorf in Mozart's Requiem, which was televised and recorded as a special memorial concert to the late President Kennedy. Recordings: *Westminster, Vanguard, CRI, RCA Victor, Music Guild.* Management: Eric Semon Associates, Inc.

Marvellee Cariaga, opera and concert contralto active in the Western states; has sung with the Los Angeles Guild Opera, the Pasadena, Seattle, Hollywood Bowl Orchestras, and at the Los Angeles Music Festival and the Ojai Festival. Management: Marianne Marshall. . . . **Lili Chookasian,** one of the leading contraltos in the concert and opera fields; member of the Metropolitan Opera and guest performer with other opera groups; particularly active as a concert singer, having sung in America with such orchestras as the New York Philharmonic (under many different conductors), The Philadelphia Orchestra, the Detroit Symphony, the Boston Symphony, the San Francisco and St. Louis orchestras and New York's Musica Aeterna orchestra. Recordings: *Decca, MGM, Columbia, RCA Victor.* Management: Columbia Artists Management, Inc.

Edna Garabedian-George, opera singer; has appeared with the major opera companies of San Francisco, San Diego, Houston, Chicago Lyric, New York City Opera, Baltimore, and the Kansas City Lyric. Management: Hans J. Hoffman Management. . . . **Batyah Godfrey,** opera singer and concert artist; was an apprentice artist with Santa Fe Opera for two summers; subsequently she was invited by Leinsdorf to sing with the Boston Symphony for two seasons at Tanglewood; she has appeared with the Philadelphia Orchestra at Saratoga and in Philadelphia, and at the Cincinnati May Festival; she has sung with the Geneva Opera; in 1969 she made her Metropolitan Opera debut. Management: Thea Dispeker Artists' Representative.

Florence Kopleff, many appearances at U.S. festivals and with major orchestras such as the Boston Symphony, etc. Recordings: *RCA Victor, Decca.* Management: Columbia Artists Management, Inc.

Louise Parker has appeared with the New York Philharmonic in such works as Hindemith's Requiem and Mozart's Requiem; soloist with the Vienna Philharmonic and at Carnegie Hall under Stokowski; has given recitals of lieder in North and South America and Australia; sang in American premiere of Henze's "The Young Lord" with the San Diego Opera. Recordings: *Bach Guild, Columbia, Cambridge.* Management: Arthur Judson Management, Inc.

Carol Smith, concert and opera contralto; has sung with the New York City Opera, San Carlo Opera Co., Bach Aria Group, and at Prades Festival. Recordings: *Decca, Columbia.* Management: Thea Dispeker Artists' Representative.

TENORS

John Alexander, Metropolitan Opera tenor; singer with the New York City Opera, San Francisco Opera, and other major U.S. opera companies; the Vienna State Opera; as a concert artist, he has sung with the New York Philharmonic, the Boston Symphony, the London Symphony, etc. Recordings: *Columbia, London.* Management: Columbia Artists Management, Inc.

Michael Best, young tenor who has sung at the Aspen and Tanglewood Festivals; has appeared with Washington Opera Society, American Opera Company of the Juilliard School, etc.; in 1971 sang with Eugene Ormandy and Philadelphia Orchestra in Britten's "Serenade for Tenor, Horn, and Strings"; has also performed oratorio widely. Management: Shaw Concerts, Inc. . . . **Charles Bressler,** one of America's most versatile concert tenors; member, New York Chamber Soloists; faculty, Mannes College of Music; his repertory is extremely broad, ranging from thirteenth-century to contemporary works; has specialized in much chamber vocal music with instrumental accompaniment, but has also sung major vocal-symphonic works with such orchestras as the Los Angeles Philharmonic, the New York Philharmonic, the Utah Symphony, etc. Recordings: *Decca, Columbia, Vanguard, Nonesuch, Urania, Cambridge, Odyssey, Project 3, CRI, Capitol.*

Walter Carringer; recitals and concerts throughout the U.S.; London debut in 1958; New York debut in 1959. Recordings: *RCA Victor.* Management: Beverly Hoffman Artists' Management. . . . **Richard Cassilly,** Maryland-born tenor with the New York City Opera; has sung with the San Francisco Opera, Chicago Lyric, the Philadelphia Lyric, and the opera companies of New Orleans, Santa Fe, Seattle, Boston, San Antonio, etc.; in 1965 made his European debut in Geneva, following which he has sung at La Scala, Covent Garden, and the opera houses of Germany (Berlin, Hamburg, Munich); his recordings (in contrast to his regular operatic and orchestral repertory) are all contemporary music (Copland, Schifrin, Weisgall). Recordings: *Columbia, MGM, CRI.* Management: Hurok Concerts, Inc. . . . **Nico Castel,** tenor with the Metropolitan and New York City Opera companies; has appeared with the opera companies of San Diego, Houston, Washington, D.C., the Philadelphia Lyric, New Orleans and Fort Worth Opera, and the Cincinnati Summer Opera; symphony appearances with the Boston, Richmond, and San Antonio orchestras. Recordings: *Westminster.* Management: Hans J. Hoffman Management. . . . **William Cochran** was offered a Metropolitan Opera contract during the semifinals of the Metropolitan Opera Auditions in 1968; in 1969 he became leading dramatic tenor of the Frankfurt and Munich Operas; he has made appearances in the U.S. with the San Francisco Opera, Houston Opera, Chicago's Grant Park and the symphonies of Rochester, Little Orchestra Society, Pittsburgh, Utah, etc; he has also appeared in oratorio with major European orchestras. Recordings: *DGG, Angel.* Management: Thea Dispeker Artists' Representative. . . . **Jean Cox,** American heldentenor with an active career primarily in Europe; has sung the complete "Ring" cycle at Bayreuth, Vienna, Munich, and Hamburg; also appeared in Naples, Geneva, and other music capitals abroad; in the U.S. he has sung in Chicago, New York, and Pittsburgh. Management: Columbia Artists Management, Inc.

Enrico DiGiuseppe, tenor with the Metropolitan, New York City Opera, the opera companies of Baltimore, Philadelphia Grand, etc.; early in the 1960's was a member of the Metropolitan Opera Studio; made his opera debut in Milan; his U.S. opera debut was with the New Orleans Experimental Opera Theater; made his Met debut in 1970; also has sung with major orchestras in the U.S.

Management: Columbia Artists Management, Inc. . . . **Nicholas di Virgilio** made his debut in 1963 at Tanglewood; sang the leading tenor role in Britten's "War Requiem" in its American premiere with the Boston Symphony Orchestra; first season with the New York City Opera in 1969, Metropolitan Opera debut in 1970; has sung with the San Francisco, Metropolitan Opera National, Baltimore, New Orleans, and St. Paul opera companies; European debut in 1968 in "Carmen" at Brussels' Théâtre de la Monnaie; has appeared with NBC Opera Company; has sung with major orchestras in the country. Recordings: *RCA Victor, Columbia.* Management: Herbert Barrett Management. . . . **Loren Driscoll,** opera singer; active in Europe; first important role was in "Rake's Progress" under Stravinsky with the Santa Fe Opera in 1957; his first European engagement was in 1962 with the Deutsche Oper in Berlin; he sang the title role in Henze's "The Young Lord" at its world premiere in 1965; he has sung for the Hamburg opera both in Hamburg and for its visit to the U.S. in 1967. Recordings: *DGG, Columbia.* Management: Thea Dispeker Artists' Representative.

Gary Glaze, tenor, member of the New York City Opera since 1970; his opera appearances have also been with the Santa Fe, the Kansas City Lyric, the Opera Gala of Orlando, and the Metropolitan Opera Studio; he has sung with the Miami Philharmonic, the Rhode Island Philharmonic, and other orchestras and choral groups in oratorio concerts; his repertory consists of leading tenor roles from the operas of Verdi, Mozart, Donizetti, et al. Management: Eric Semon Associates. . . . **Leo Goeke** has sung with the Metropolitan Opera, New York City Opera, Central City Opera; has a large concert repertory and has performed with the Cleveland Orchestra and Pittsburgh Symphony, at Carmel Bach and Chautauqua Festivals, and under such conductors as Karl Böhm, Emerson Buckley, Walter Hendl, Julius Rudel, Frederic Waldman, et al. Recordings: *Decca, RCA Victor.* Management: Herbert Barrett Management.

Grayson Hirst, made his New York debut with the American Opera Society; in 1971 he performed the main tenor role in the world premiere of Ginastera's "Beatrix Cenci" during the opening week of the Kennedy Center in Washington, D.C.; he has sung for the Boston Opera Company and in Bern, Switzerland; he sang in the TV production of Mozart's "Abduction"; both his operatic and orchestral repertories contain works less frequently performed; he has sung in operas by Cavalli, Floyd, Janáček, Pasatieri, and Searle; besides the well-known oratorios, masses, etc., he has sung Berlioz's "Lelio," Britten's "St. Nicolas Cantata," Dvořák's "Spectre's Bride" to name some works little known. Management: Hurok Concerts, Inc.

Vahan Khanzadian, made his debut with the San Francisco Opera as leading tenor in Puccini's "La Rondine"; appeared with Chautauqua Opera Company; on CBS television in Laderman's "Galileo" and in the NET–TV production of "The Queen of Spades"; soloist in performances with the Buffalo Philharmonic, the Collegiate Chorale, etc., in Carnegie Hall. Management: Herbert Barrett Management. . . . **James King,** Metropolitan Opera tenor and guest singer with other major U.S. opera companies; his roles are from the Italian, German, and French repertories; also a concert singer and recitalist; he has recorded with many foreign orchestras. Recordings: *Angel, London, DGG, RCA Victor.* Management: Thea Dispeker Artists' Representative.

William Lewis, tenor, singing leading operatic roles with the New York City Opera and the Metropolitan as well as other major companies in the U.S. and Europe; his orchestral appearances have been under the direction of such conductors as Bernstein, Beecham, Böhm, Leinsdorf, Schippers, and Stravinsky, to name some; he has sung on NBC–TV opera and for the BBC; his repertory is richly varied covering all periods and many vocal forms. Recordings: *Vanguard, Columbia.* Management: Eric Semon Associates.

John McCollum (b. 1922), active singer in concerts, recitals, opera, and festivals since his

Town Hall recital in 1952; has appeared in Spoleto, Tanglewood, and many other festival and concert series; a veteran performer of oratorios and other major vocal-symphonic pieces; faculty, University of Michigan. Recordings: *RCA Victor, Decca, Desto.* Management: Columbia Artists Management, Inc. . . . **Seth McCoy,** tenor from North Carolina, sang for several years with the Jubilee Singers; toured North America with Robert Shaw in 1963 and, under State Department sponsorship, toured South America the following year; appeared with the Philadelphia, Cleveland, Minnesota Orchestras, etc.; well-known for work in oratorio; sang during inaugural week of Kennedy Center in Washington, D.C.; appeared in the premiere of Joplin's "Treemonisha" in Atlanta; engaged five times in one season with the Philadelphia Orchestra; for 1969–70, was artist-in-residence in Atlanta. Recordings: *RCA Victor, Decca, CRI.* Management: Herbert Barrett Management. . . . **James McCracken,** dramatic tenor; on the roster of the Metropolitan Opera after an absence of some five years; known for his portrayal of Otello; has widely toured the opera companies of the U.S. and has frequently appeared with his wife, Sandra Warfield (q.v.), with whom he co-authored a book. Recordings: *London, Angel.* Management: Columbia Artists Management, Inc. . . . **William McDonald,** a lyric tenor, has sung with the New York City Opera, Kansas City Lyric Theater, Goldovsky Opera Theater, Houston Opera, etc., and also at the Kennedy Center during the inaugural season in Verdi's "Falstaff"; has performed with the St. Louis Symphony, National Symphony of Washington, Atlanta Symphony, Philadelphia Orchestra; has taught at Indiana University and currently an artist-in-residence at the Brevard Music Center in the summer; he is also with the Houston Affiliate Artist Series. Management: Arthur Judson Management, Inc. . . . **Michele Molese,** New York City-born tenor, studied in Italy and made his debut in Milan; has sung in major opera centers of Europe including Brussels, Amsterdam, Athens, Munich, Vienna, Paris, Marseilles, etc.; has performed leading roles with the New York City Opera since 1964, singing mainly the Italian and French roles; has sung throughout the country with leading orchestras, Boston Symphony at Tanglewood, opening of New York Philharmonic Promenade Concerts, etc.; recorded Stravinsky's "Persephone" under the composer. Recordings: *Columbia.* Management: Colbert Artists Management, Inc. . . . **Barry Morell,** leading tenor with the Metropolitan Opera; regularly engaged for such American companies as the Philadelphia Grand Opera, the San Francisco Opera, etc.; has sung at London's Covent Garden, in Berlin, Santiago, Chile. Recordings: *Westminster.* Management: Columbia Artists Management, Inc.

Russell Oberlin, countertenor, also a tenor, has sung in concerts and recitals in the U.S. and England; soloist with major orchestras since 1957; formerly sang with the New York Pro Musica; specializes in pre-Classical music; faculty, Hunter College in New York. Recordings: *Columbia, Urania, Decca, Odyssey, Counterpoint, EA.*

Jan Peerce (b. 1904); one of the great singers of modern times, he has enjoyed an undiminished international reputation for over three decades; made his opera debut in 1938 and with the Metropolitan Opera in 1941; has sung in many areas of the world and has appeared in every media: radio, television, films, in concerts, opera and recitals, and in musical theater; as an orchestral singer he has recorded and performed live many of the great works in the repertory under the leading conductors of the day; his recordings have long been a staple in the classical music catalogs. Recordings: *Vanguard, Decca, Westminster, RCA Victor, Everest, Desto, Bach Guild, United Artists, Columbia.* Management: Hurok Concerts, Inc.

Kenneth Riegel, made his professional debut in 1965 in the American premiere of Henze's "The Stag King" presented at Santa Fe Opera; he has since sung with Seattle, Houston, San Diego, Cincinnati, Miami, San Francisco, and New York City Operas in a variety of tenor roles; he is noted for portrayals in Benjamin Britten's works; has performed with major symphonies, including Boston, Pittsburgh, Philadelphia, New York Philharmonic, Chicago, etc.; he has also appeared at many festivals in the U.S. and the Spoleto Festival in Italy, marking his debut in Europe. Management: Thea Dispeker Artists' Representative. . . . **Robert Rounseville,** appeared in the English film "Tales of Hoffman" (1950) and the American film "Carousel" (1955); has also sung in Broadway musicals; (original cast "Man of La Mancha"); has appeared on television and radio, in recitals and orchestral concerts. Recordings: *Columbia, London.*

James Schwabacher, concert singer and operatic performer; music patron; has sung with the San Francisco Opera and in many concerts throughout the U.S.; recent cross-country tours were in 1969 and 1970; made a tour of Europe in 1969; is a frequent performer of oratorios and other major vocal-orchestral works; has appeared with orchestras such as the San Francisco Symphony, Musica Aeterna Orchestra (New York), Masterwork Chorus, Carmel Bach Festival and Spoleto Festival Orchestras, Bethlehem Bach Choir and Orchestra, RIAS (Berlin), etc. Management: Thea Dispeker Artists' Representative. . . . **George Shirley** (b. 1934), tenor with the Metropolitan Opera (since 1965) and Covent Garden, London; has sung also at the Teatro Colon, with the Scottish Opera Company, and in concert with many major orchestras including the New York Philharmonic, the London Symphony, Israel Philharmonic, etc. Recordings: *Decca, RCA Victor, Columbia, Angel.* Management: Shaw Concerts, Inc., and Ann Summers. . . . **Jerold Siena,** concert and opera tenor; has sung with the Boston and Cleveland Symphonies, the Canadian Opera Company, the Chattanooga Opera, and at the Stratford (Ontario) Shakespeare Festival. Management: Ludwig Lustig and Florian, Ltd. . . . **Paul Sperry,** tenor, singing mostly recitals; has made two European tours (1969 and 1970) and has given recitals in New York, Cleveland, and San Francisco; his repertory is unusual for its wide variety of solo vocal works, ranging from the Baroque to contemporary literature, in 10 languages. Management: Sheldon Soffer Management, Inc.

Harry Theyard, tenor with the New York City Opera, the San Francisco Opera, Chicago Lyric, Washington Opera Society, Opera Theatre of New Jersey, Boston Opera Company, and the Connecticut and Seattle Opera companies. Management: John B. Fisher. . . . **Jess Thomas,** recitalist as well as opera singer of Wagnerian roles; has performed Tristan all over the world, including Vienna, Moscow, Covent Garden in London, Paris, and at the Metropolitan in New York; made his debut with the San Francisco Opera after winning the 1957 auditions of that company; spent the next few years in Germany learning Wagnerian and Italian roles and sang in Karlsruhe, Munich, Berlin; has sung under von Karajan in the Salzburg Easter Festival; performs recitals and appears with orchestras in the U.S. and abroad. Recordings: *Angel, Philips, DGG, Eurodisc, RCA.* Management: Colbert Artists Management, Inc. . . . **William Toren,** tenor singing in opera, concerts, recitals; has sung in the Teatro Eliseo (Rome), in Germany, and in America with the Western Opera, the San Jose Opera, and with the Goldovsky Opera Theatre. Management: Helen Jensen Artists Management. . . . **Erik Townsend,** spinto tenor, member of the New York City Opera and the opera companies of Santa Fe, Seattle, and Toledo. Management: Ludwig Lustig and Florian, Ltd. . . . **Jack Trussel,** performances with the Chattanooga, St. Paul, Philadelphia Lyric, and Florentine (Milwaukee) opera companies; has also sung on NET–TV, New York, and with the Philadelphia Orchestra. Management: Hans J. Hoffman Management. . . . **Richard Tucker** (b. 1913), world renowned and much-honored tenor; leading tenor with the Metropolitan since debut there in 1945; has sung throughout the U.S., Europe, Israel, Far East, Mexico. Recordings: *Columbia, Odyssey, RCA Victor.*

Mallory Walker made his opera debut in "The Rake's Progress"; sang as tenor soloist in the Robert Shaw Chorale recording of Bach's B Minor Mass; has sung with the Metropolitan Opera Studio, San Francisco

Spring Opera, Houston Opera, etc.; appeared with Los Angeles Philharmonic at Ojai Festival, Cincinnati, Boston, etc.; has sung at Cologne Opera House and appeared as guest artist in Stuttgart, Basel, and with the Bayerische Rundfunk. Recordings: *RCA Victor.* Management: Thea Dispeker Artists' Representative.

BARITONES

Jerome Barry, lyric baritone, has sung over 150 performances in the U.S., Germany, Italy, Switzerland, and Israel; sings in opera, concerts, and recitals. Management: Helen Jensen Artists Management. . . . **James Billings,** baritone singing buffo roles with the Chicago Lyric, Philadelphia Lyric, Opera Guild of Miami, Boston, Chattanooga, and Dayton–Toledo opera companies; has sung with the Boston Symphony and at Spoleto. Management: Hans J. Hoffmann Management. . . . **McHenry R. Boatwright** (1928), made debut in 1956 and has been active in recital, opera, and concerts with major U.S. orchestras; Town Hall debut in 1958; winner of the Marian Anderson Award in 1953, and the National Federation of Music Clubs Award in 1957; orchestral debut in 1958 with Ormandy and the Philadelphia Orchestra; has toured Europe, Far East, and South America; created the role of Carter Jones in Schuller's "The Visitation" in Hamburg; he has been a soloist with most of the major American orchestras. Recordings: *RCA Victor, Columbia.*

Thomas Carey, baritone, member of Royal Covent Garden Opera in London; sang his debut in the premiere of Tippett's "The Knot Garden"; also appeared in the London revival of "Show Boat." Management: Anne O'Donnell Management. . . . **Walter Cassel,** member of the Metropolitan Opera; guest artist with the New York City, Chicago Lyric, San Francisco, Cleveland, Cincinnati, Fort Worth, New Orleans, San Antonio, Dayton–Toledo, and Pittsburgh opera companies; has sung in London, Palermo, etc.; portrays leading Wagnerian roles and the dramatic baritone roles of the Italian repertory, etc. Recordings: *Columbia.* . . . **David Clatworthy** became a member of the New York City Opera in 1962 and has performed many contemporary as well as traditional operatic roles; he has appeared with the opera companies of San Francisco, Houston, Fort Worth, Central City, and Chautauqua; has sung with the orchestras of Boston, Detroit, Chicago, Baltimore, Philadelphia, Dallas, and the New York Philharmonic. Recordings: *Vanguard, Mercury, RCA Victor.* Management: Thea Dispeker Artists' Representative. . . . **Dominic Cossa** made his debut at New York City Opera in 1961 at the age of 25; in 1970 the baritone gave his first performance with the Metropolitan Opera; also has appeared with Cincinnati Summer Opera, New Orleans Opera, Filene Center at Wolf Trap Farm Park for the Performing Arts in Virginia; has sung at London's Albert Hall with Joan Sutherland; performs orchestral-choral works in U.S. and Canada; former winner of the regional Metropolitan Opera Auditions. Recordings: *London.* Management: Colbert Artists Management, Inc.

John Darrenkamp, baritone; member of the New York City Opera; also performances with the opera groups of Baltimore, Connecticut, Fort Worth, Cincinnati Summer Opera, etc.; appearances as a recital artist and concert singer. Management: Columbia Artists Management, Inc. . . . **William Dooley,** baritone with the Metropolitan Opera; first established his career in Europe; received the honorary title of Kammersaenger with the Berlin Deutsche Oper; made his debut with the San Francisco Opera in 1970; has been particularly successful in Wagnerian roles. Recordings: *RCA Victor.* Management: Columbia Artists Management, Inc.

Ryan Edwards, young baritone, made his debut with the New York City Opera in "Makropulos Affair"; sang with American Opera Center at Juilliard School, Dallas Civic Opera, Fort Worth Opera Association, Florentine Opera of Milwaukee, etc.; appeared at Kennedy Center opening week under Julius Rudel; has performed with the Los Angeles Philharmonic, New York Philharmonic under Bernstein, Boston Symphony, Dallas and San Antonio Symphonies. Management: Herbert Barrett Management.

Adib Fazah, baritone, singing opera roles with the opera companies of San Francisco, Santa Fe, Chattanooga, Ithaca, and the Opera Society of Washington. Management: Hans J. Hoffmann Management. . . . **Richard Fredericks,** baritone, singing leading roles with the New York City Opera Company and the San Francisco Opera; he has sung exclusively for American opera groups including performances with the opera companies of Honolulu, Miami, New Orleans, Philadelphia, Fort Worth, etc.; his orchestral and operatic repertory is composed of both standard and modern works; the latter group includes operas by Copland, Beeson, Moore, and Menotti. Recordings: *Desto, Columbia.* Management: Hurok Concerts, Inc.

Robert Goodloe, baritone; Metropolitan debut in 1964; since then he has sung some 30 roles with that company; has sung with the opera companies of San Francisco (Spring Opera), Chautauqua, Lake George Festival, Toledo, and for the Grant Park concerts in Chicago; the majority of his operatic roles are in operas by Mozart, Puccini, and Donizetti. Management: Hurok Concerts, Inc. . . . **Frank Guarrera,** leading baritone at the Metropolitan (since 1948), where he has appeared more often than any other living baritone; has also sung with major U.S. orchestras, in recitals, and on television. Recordings: *RCA Victor.* Management: Columbia Artists Management, Inc. . . . **Leslie Guinn,** Texas-born baritone, appearing in recitals and with orchestras; has sung with the National Symphony, the Detroit Symphony, the Baltimore Symphony and the American Symphony Orchestras; his festival appearances include the Alaska Music Festival (1967), and the Tanglewood, Chautauqua, Marlboro, and Worcester (Massachusetts) festivals; he sang in the West Coast premiere of Britten's "War Requiem." Management: Sheldon Soffer Management, Inc.

Eugene Holmes, recitalist, opera singer, and teacher at the University of Miami and Tougaloo College in Mississippi; he sang the baritone lead in the American premiere of Delius's opera "Koanga" with the Washington Opera Society in 1970 and the world premiere of Menotti's "The Most Important Man in the World" with the New York City Opera in 1971; that year he also made his Vienna State Opera debut; he has toured with the Metropolitan Opera Company; appears often in recital and with leading symphony orchestras. Recordings: *Avant Garde.* Management: Sherman Pitluck (personal); Thea Dispeker Artists' Representative (opera appearances).

Cornell MacNeil, internationally known baritone; star singer with the Metropolitan Opera, La Scala, Covent Garden, Chicago Lyric, Teatro Colon, San Francisco Opera and other major opera companies in the U.S. and Europe. Recordings: *London, Angel.* Management: Columbia Artists Management, Inc. . . . **Morley Meredith,** Metropolitan Opera debut in 1962, singing all four baritone roles in "Tales of Hoffman"; national tours of major cities in the U.S. and Canada; European debut in Geneva; also has sung with Chicago Lyric Opera, San Francisco Opera, Philadelphia Lyric Opera, etc. Management: Herbert Barrett Management. . . . **Robert Merrill** (b. 1917), internationally acclaimed opera star; has sung at the Metropolitan since 1945; San Francisco Opera debut in 1957; film debut in 1951; has also sung in night clubs since 1953 and on popular TV shows; many concert tours of the U.S.; one of the most versatile singers on the scene today; has made a great number of recordings; he excels in Verdi operatic roles. Recordings: *London, RCA Victor, Columbia, Seraphim, Everest, Angel.* Management: Columbia Artists Management, Inc. . . . **William Metcalf** has performed many of Benjamin Britten's works including the "War Requiem" with the Kansas City Philharmonic, the American premieres of "Curlew River" and "Burning Fiery Furnace" at the Caramoor Festival, and "Prodigal Son" with the Little Orchestra Society; he is a member of New York City Opera and has appeared with the Fort Worth Opera, Opera Society of Washington, and the

Baltimore Opera; he sang the world premiere of Louise Talma's "The Tolling Bell" for baritone and orchestra with the Milwaukee Symphony and has sung with New York Philharmonic under Bernstein, and the Philadelphia Orchestra at the Saratoga Festival; also appears in recital. Recordings: *Columbia, Vanguard.* Management: Thea Dispeker Artists' Representative. . . . **Sherrill Milnes,** Illinois-born leading baritone of the Metropolitan Opera; important young performer in Verdian roles in the grand tradition; has sung for Royal Opera at Covent Garden, Vienna State Opera, and the Teatro Colon, Buenos Aires; also active concert artist with major orchestras in the U.S. and Europe; opera debut with the Baltimore Opera in 1961; former member of the New York City Opera; made his Met debut in 1965. Recordings: *RCA Victor, Angel,* and *London.* Management: Herbert Barrett Management. . . . **John Modenos,** a native of Cyprus, but a resident of the U.S. since 1948; made Town Hall debut in 1957; ninth winner of the American Theater Wing Concert Award; has appeared in U.S. and Canadian cities in opera, recitals, and with orchestras; has sung with Covent Garden, Vienna State Opera, San Francisco Opera, Cincinnati Summer Opera, and at the Athens Festival. Recordings: *CRI.* Management: Giorgio D'Andria.

Thomas Palmer, baritone, has sung with major symphonies and opera companies in the U.S. including the Chicago Symphony, Detroit Symphony, Kansas City Lyric Theatre, San Francisco Spring Opera, and for the Philharmonic Hall Mozart Festival; in 1967 he made his European debut at the Geneva Opera and since then has appeared at the Aix-en-Provence Festival and on television in Hamburg with the Norddeutscher Rundfunk; he has appeared in New York at Alice Tully Hall with the Clarion Concerts, Camerata Symphony at Philharmonic Hall, the New York Chamber Soloists and in concert at the Metropolitan Museum of Art. Management: Thea Dispeker Artists' Representative.

Louis Quilico, baritone with the New York City Opera Company; he has sung more than 30 roles in many opera houses including those of San Francisco, Pittsburgh, Philadelphia, New Orleans, Montreal, London's Covent Garden, Moscow's Bolshoi, and many others; Canadian-born, he sings many engagements in the U.S. each season. Recordings: *RCA Victor, London.* Management: Hurok Concerts, Inc.

John Reardon, versatile actor-singer performing since 1965 with the Metropolitan Opera and a large number of major opera companies, orchestras, and festivals in the U.S., Canada, and Europe; his experience ranges from TV opera and TV children's programs to Broadway musicals, grand opera, and contemporary opera; he has mastered over 100 roles, over 20 of which he created in premiere performances of operas by Henze, Hoiby, Levy, Menotti, Moore, Stravinsky, et al. Recordings: *Desto, Serenus, Columbia, Decca, Mercury.* Management: Hans J. Hoffmann Management.

Guillermo Sarabia (b. 1937 as a U.S. citizen in Mexico), baritone, appearing in opera and in concerts; his career has been pursued mostly in Germany, where he has sung with the opera companies of Munich, Stuttgart, Cologne, Bremen, Dortmund, and elsewhere; his opera roles include a number that have been translated into German from the original language ("Mourning Becomes Electra," "Les Contes D'Hoffman," "Pique Dame," etc.). Management: Hurok Concerts, Inc. . . . **Vern Shinall,** baritone, singing with a large number of opera companies throughout the U.S. including the New York City Opera, Kansas City Lyric, Brooklyn Opera, American Opera Society, Little Orchestra Society, Toledo Opera, Florentine Opera of Milwaukee, Opera Company of Boston, etc.; his roles range from those of Wagner operas and the standard French and Italian repertory to contemporary American operas such as "The Crucible," "Susannah," and "Ballad of Baby Doe." Management: John B. Fisher.

Jay Thompson, baritone, singing in opera, and concerts with orchestra; has sung with the Dallas Civic, the Kansas City Lyric Opera, Jacksonville (Florida) Opera, the Opera

Guild of Greater Miami, and other companies. Management: Eric Semon Associates. . . . **Thomas Tipton,** baritone, singing in the opera companies of Hamburg, Stuttgart, Vienna, Berlin (Deutsche Oper), Brussels, San Francisco, Houston, and Pittsburgh, as well as at Bayreuth and Salzburg. Management: Hans J. Hoffmann Management.

Theodor Uppman, made his debut with the San Francisco Symphony in 1947; New York City Opera debut in 1948; sang in the world premiere of "Billy Budd" at Covent Garden in 1951; debut with the Metropolitan in 1953; appearances with major orchestras, at festivals, and on television. Recordings: *RCA Victor.* Management: Columbia Artists Management, Inc.

William Warfield (b. 1920), has sung in concerts, recitals, opera, television, and films; made New York debut in 1950; undertook African tour in 1956, and two world tours in 1958; appeared with ranking European orchestras; has sung in "Porgy and Bess" in Vienna and in Weill's "Lost in the Stars" at Washington's Kennedy Center. Recordings: *Columbia, RCA Victor.* Management: Columbia Artists Management, Inc.

BASS-BARITONES

Herbert Beattie, bass, singing with the New York City Opera. Recordings: *Desto, Columbia, Cambridge.* Management: Ludwig Lustig and Florian, Ltd. . . . **Ara Berberian,** has sung more than 90 roles with San Francisco Opera, New York City Opera, New Orleans Opera, San Antonio Opera, etc.; performed oratorio works with leading orchestras in the U.S. and Canada; has sung at Marlboro, Casals, Tanglewood, Caramoor, Ann Arbor, Cincinnati, and other festivals in the U.S.; presented recitals under various auspices; toured Russia in series of concerts; performed with Israel Philharmonic in 1971; sings for major TV networks: appeared in 90-minute special of Berlioz's "L'Enfance du Christ." Recordings: *RCA Victor, Columbia, Poseidon Society.* Management: Herbert Barrett Management. . . . **Philip Booth,** bass concert and opera singer; in 1970 he won the Middle Atlantic Metropolitan Opera Regional Auditions and won several high awards on the national level; he has since sung with San Francisco Opera, Western Opera Theater, Baltimore Opera, etc., with an operatic repertory of more than 40 roles; he has appeared in several premiere performances including the American premiere of Pound's "Le Testament de Villon" and Von Einem's "The Visit"; also has large orchestral repertory. Management: Arthur Judson Management, Inc.

Lee Cass, bass-baritone; has sung roles with the opera companies of Philadelphia (the Lyric and the Grand), Tulsa, Fort Worth, Pittsburgh, Baltimore, Houston, Dayton–Toledo. Management: Hans J. Hoffmann Management. . . . **Richard Cross,** has been a leading basso of Frankfurt Opera in Germany since 1968; has performed with the opera companies of Vancouver, Santa Fe, Washington D.C., Seattle, San Francisco, etc.; also makes symphony appearances in the U.S. and Canada with leading orchestras; active recitalist as well as opera singer, he has made 10 tours throughout North America and has given joint recitals with his wife, Doris Yarick; has toured Australia with Joan Sutherland, singing leading bass roles in operas including "Eugene Onegin," "Faust," etc.; has performed at Festival of Two Worlds in Spoleto, Italy. Recordings: *RCA Victor, Westminster, Columbia, London.* Management: Thea Dispeker Artists' Representative.

Irwin Denson, bass-baritone with the New York City Opera; has sung also with the Philadelphia Grand Opera, the San Antonio, Connecticut, and the Tulsa opera companies. Management: Giorgio d'Andrea. . . . **Michael Devlin** made his debut with New York City Opera in 1965 in its opening night performance at Lincoln Center in Ginastera's "Don Rodrigo"; has since performed with the Houston, Santa Fe, San Diego, Fort Worth, and Cincinnati Summer opera companies; he has appeared with major symphony orchestras including New York Philharmonic, New Orleans Philharmonic, Philadelphia Orchestra, Chicago Symphony, etc. Recordings: *Columbia, RCA Victor.* Management: Thea Dispeker Artists' Representative. . . . **Justino Díaz,** born in Puerto Rico, made New York debut with American Opera Society; joined Metropolitan Opera roster the same year; has appeared in major opera houses of the world since then; chosen to sing the leading bass role in Ginastera's opera for the Kennedy Center opening; performs with major orchestras in U.S., Europe, and Canada; regular performer at Salzburg Festival, Festival of Two Worlds in Spoleto and has sung at Casals Festival in his native Puerto Rico; appeared in film of "Carmen" under von Karajan. Recordings: *London, Columbia, ABC, Vanguard.* Management: Herbert Barrett Management. . . . **Andrij Dobriansky,** born in the Ukraine; in the U.S. since 1956; bass-baritone with the Metropolitan Opera Company; early studies in New York followed by tours with the Ukrainian choir, Dumka, as soloist, to Chicago, Detroit, Philadelphia, Montreal, and elsewhere; operatic debut with Kirsten and Corelli in "The Girl of the Golden West," in 1964 with the Philadelphia Lyric; he was with the Metropolitan Opera Studio and the National Company; has sung with opera companies and orchestras throughout the country; his operatic repertory consists of 48 roles in 42 operas, many of them leading roles. Management: Hurok Concerts, Inc. . . . **Archie Drake,** bass-baritone, has sung with the Seattle Opera, San Francisco Opera, Chicago Lyric, Honolulu Opera, Portland Opera, and Edmonton (Canada) Opera. Management: William Felber Agency.

Simon Estes, Iowa-born bass-baritone; has sung with the Hamburg Opera, the San Francisco Opera (for both companies he sang different roles in Schuller's "The Visitation"), and the opera companies in Berlin, Lübeck, and elsewhere; his orchestra appearances include those in New York, San Francisco, Los Angeles, Chicago, Indianapolis, Philadelphia, etc.; he won awards in both the Munich and Tchaikovsky competitions. Recordings: *RCA Victor, Angel.* Management: Columbia Artists Management, Inc.

Norman Farrow (b. 1916), Canadian-born bass-baritone; U.S. trained; founding member of the Bach Aria Group; a seasoned vocalist, he has appeared with major orchestras and choral organizations, in opera and in concerts throughout North America and Europe. Recordings: *Decca, Columbia.* . . . **Ezio Flagello,** New York-born basso with the Metropolitan Opera since 1957; noted for his characterization of many of the leading bass and buffo roles in opera; his performances have for many years been with American companies including the San Francisco, Connecticut, Miami, and Dallas opera companies; in 1970 he made his debut with the La Scala Opera, followed by performances in Berlin, Florence and Vienna; he has made numerous recordings of opera, opera excerpts, and works for voice and orchestra. Recordings: *London, RCA Victor, DGG, Columbia.* Management: Hurok Concerts, Inc. . . . **Andrew Foldi** (b. 1926), has sung in concerts and recitals; active in opera; has sung with the Chicago Lyric from 1954; sang with the Zürich Opera during 1961–62 season; has performed with opera companies of Philadelphia, Santa Fe, Miami, Cincinnati, San Diego, and Palm Beach in the U.S.; in Europe he has appeared with companies in Munich, Geneva, Naples, Brussels and Amsterdam; he has made many concert appearances in Europe with orchestras of Munich, Amsterdam, Monte Carlo, etc., and in the U.S. with several orchestras. Has recorded in Europe. Management: Thea Dispeker Artists' Representative.

Donald Gramm (b. 1927), veteran performer in opera, concerts, and recitals; has made frequent appearances with the Boston Symphony, Cleveland Orchestra, New York Philharmonic and other major ensembles; extensive concert and recital engagements in the U.S.; as opera singer has had roles with the companies of New York City, NBC–TV, New Orleans, Chicago Lyric, and currently, the Metropolitan Opera; made New York debut in 1950; highly respected as an actor on the operatic stage; has sung a significant amount of contemporary music. Recordings: *RCA Victor, Columbia, London, CRI, Desto.* Management: Columbia Artists Management, Inc. . . . **Eugene Green,** has had roles with the Chicago Lyric Opera, Central City

Opera, Cincinnati Summer Opera, Dayton–Toledo Opera, the San Francisco Opera, the Goldovsky Opera Theater; he has also sung with the Hartford Symphony.

Robert Hale, bass-baritone with the New York City Opera, singing many leading roles with that company in Los Angeles as well as New York; native of Texas; made operatic debut in Frankfurt, Germany, as member of Armed Forces; has sung with major U.S. orchestras, including those of Boston, Minneapolis, Cincinnati, Philadelphia, Chicago, Milwaukee, etc.; appeared at Cincinnati May, Ravinia, Wolf Trap Farm, and Tanglewood Festivals; recitals throughout U.S. and Europe; appeared as soloist at United Nations in a special televised concert; sang under Aaron Copland his "Old American Songs." Management: Herbert Barrett Management. . . . **Jerome Hines** (b. 1921), one of America's great basses; made his debut with the Metropolitan Opera in 1946 and has sung with that company since; he is known throughout the world; in 1962, he sang the role of Boris Godunov at the Bolshoi Theater in Moscow, the first American to do so; has since sung this role in English and Italian; considered one of the best operatic actors; in recent seasons he has included in his recital tours a demonstration of how he prepares for his operatic roles, the use of makeup, costumes, etc.; he has an extensive orchestral repertory; he has also toured for several seasons with compositions of his own: "The 23rd Psalm" for solo singers, chorus, and orchestra, and "I Am the Way," an opera on the life of Jesus. Recordings: *Columbia, RCA Victor, Richmond, Angel.* Management: Hurok Concerts, Inc.

Douglas Lawrence, bass-baritone from Los Angeles; in Hollywood, he has sung more than 200 performances on network television and has dubbed the voices of famous actors in a number of movies; he toured Germany, Holland, France, Belgium, and other European countries under the sponsorship of the State Department; he is a frequently engaged artist at the Carmel Bach Festival in California; his operatic repertory is standard; his orchestral repertory includes works by Penderecki, Bloch, Stravinsky, Walton, Martin, Fauré, Bruckner, and others. Management: Hurok Concerts, Inc.

Spiro Malas, bass-baritone with the New York City Opera and singer with major orchestras; has sung at Covent Garden, Edinburgh Festival, Vienna Festival, and with the BBC and London Symphony Orchestras; made debut with the Chicago Lyric Opera in 1971 ("Semiramide"), and at Salzburg in 1970; known for buffo roles. Recordings: *London, CRI, RCA Victor.* Management: Shaw Concerts, Inc. . . . **Paul Matthen,** opera singer and recitalist; faculty, Indiana University. Recordings: *RCA Victor, Urania, Vanguard.* Management: Albert Kay Associates, Inc. . . . **James Morris,** bass singer (b. Maryland); on the roster of the Metropolitan Opera since 1971; he is one of the youngest singers ever to make a debut at the Metropolitan; he has sung 15 roles in 11 of the operas by Verdi; his appearances with other opera companies include the Baltimore Opera, the Dayton–Toledo company, the Philadelphia Lyric, the Santa Fe Festival, the Cincinnati Summer Opera (sang six operas during the summer of 1970) and abroad in Santiago, Chile, Barcelona (opposite Montserrat Caballé), etc. Management: Hurok Concerts, Inc.

Robert Oliver (b. 1923), is also a business executive; concert artist and recitalist; has sung on the West Coast and at the Vienna International Festival; has sung works of Stravinsky, Schoenberg, and other moderns. Recordings: *Columbia.*

Carl Palangi, has sung with the San Francisco Opera since 1954; engagements with other opera companies have included the St. Louis Municipal and the Cincinnati opera groups; made nine transcontinental tours of the U.S. and Canada; made debut in 1953 with the Boston Pops orchestra; has also sung on television. Management: Ludwig Lustig and Florian, Ltd. . . . **Thomas Paul,** made his debut at Carnegie Hall in 1961; also won first prize in the Liederkranz Foundation Contest that year; bass soloist with major symphonies in the U.S. and Canada; has given vocal recitals throughout the country; member of New York City Opera Company and has sung with San Francisco, New Orleans opera companies, among others. Recordings: *RCA Victor, Command, Columbia.* Management: Colbert Artists Management, Inc. . . . **Paul Plishka,** young member of the Metropolitan Opera; debut with the Met in 1967; as a character actor-singer he has prepared over 67 roles.

Will Roy, leading bass singer with the New York City Opera Company, performing such roles as Sarastro ("Magic Flute"), Osmin ("Abduction from the Seraglio"), Don Basilio ("Barber of Seville"), etc.; other opera companies with which he has sung include the Chautauqua Opera, the New Haven Opera Society, the Mozart Festival, etc.; he has sung on Broadway in "Hello Dolly," "Camelot," and in the stock productions of other shows in various parts of the country. Management: Eric Semon Associates.

Louis Sgarro, member of the Metropolitan Opera since winning Metropolitan auditions in 1954; sang at La Scala in 1951, and in Yugoslavia in 1959. . . . **David Rae Smith,** American trained bass-baritone, received Fulbright award for further study in Germany; made his European debut in Dortmund; has also appeared at Salzburg Festival, Vienna, etc.; in U.S. has sung with New York City Opera, American Symphony Orchestra, American Opera Society, and Concert Opera Society. Management: Arthur Judson Management, Inc. . . . **Malcolm Smith,** began his career in 1962 as bass soloist with the Robert Shaw Chorale tour through Russia; made his New York City Opera debut in 1965 in Prokofiev's "Flaming Angel"; has sung with San Francisco, Houston, Cincinnati, Central City, St. Louis opera companies; European operatic debut in 1968 at Spoleto Festival; he became leading bass of Düsseldorf Opera in 1971; performs oratorio as well as opera throughout Europe and America. Recordings: *Bach-Guild, Vanguard.* Management: Thea Dispeker Artists' Representative.

Giorgio Tozzi (b. 1923), leading bass with the Metropolitan Opera, debut at the Met in 1955; has sung with major European opera companies (Hamburg, State Opera, etc.); soloist with the Boston Symphony, Vienna Philharmonic, Orchestre de la Suisse Romande, etc.; joined faculty of Juilliard School in 1971, performed more than 100 roles in opera companies all over the world; has appeared in films, TV, and on Broadway. Recordings: *RCA Victor, Seraphim, London, Everest/Cetra, Odyssey.* Management: Columbia Artists Management, Inc. . . . **Norman Treigle** (b. 1927, New Orleans); leading male star with the New York City Opera; since 1953 has sung with that company, where he has appeared in over 50 roles; known particularly for his remarkable portrayal of Reverend Olin Blitch from the opera "Susannah," a role he created for the premiere in 1956, and for his roles as the devil in Boito's "Mefistofele" (revived at the New York City Opera in 1969) and in Gounod's "Faust"; has sung mostly in the U.S. with many major opera companies, festivals, orchestras; has also performed in Buenos Aires and in Santiago, Chile; considered one of the great actors in opera today. Recordings: *Columbia, RCA Victor, Westminster.* Management: Ludwig Lustig and Florian, Ltd.

Arnold Voketaitis, bass-baritone, singer with the Chicago Lyric Opera; has sung with Central City Opera, etc.; early in his career was a regular on the Arthur Godfrey Show. Management: Ludwig Lustig and Florian, Ltd.

Part 6 | Composers

General

There is no need here for a historical review of American composers and their music. What can be said is that in the last two decades America's composers have been more active than ever. They have continued to compose and have found that their earlier music—more discussed than heard—can now be presented under more favorable conditions of performance standards, audience receptiveness, and critical interest. Because of these factors, a new objective estimation of these men and women ought to be made. Such estimations can now be based on the reality of live performances, recordings, and the printed score, all of which are not so esoterically or so sparsely produced as formerly. There has been, of course, no lack of information about the accomplishments of a few famous composers, those who have had their music before the public for thirty years or so, but a number of important composers have had to wait that many years to see greater dissemination of their works. If for no other reason than this, it is necessary to reaffirm or reappraise the position and worth of American composers who have emerged since the thirties, particularly those who early were overshadowed by their more famous contemporaries. Although it is assumed that authors of the few critiques and histories of American composers so far published were familiar, to a reasonable and practical limit, with the work of the men they chose to write about, it has been largely a matter of their word against that of their readers. It is now quite possible to test those words. Towards that end, this section of the book on composers may be of some value. It was drawn up with the specific purpose of enabling anyone to avail himself of the music of over 200 composers.

The Status of the Composer

The most striking change seen in the professional affairs of the American composer is physical. The transformation, still taking place, was intensified in the 1950's, when America's musical institutions, organizations, and industries recognized to an unprecedented degree a responsibility to the composer. This recognition has since taken the form of more moral and financial support, that is, more opportunities for performance of new music and an increase in the number and kind of commissions, awards, and other forms of subsidy or payment.

Many composers have emerged from the academic umbra to enjoy the new light of publicity and concern emanating of late from such sources. Old names—some almost forgotten—have appeared like new; new ones have come forward less timorously. American composers have proved themselves to be a hardy breed and have shown that, with a little encouragement, their energy can be boundless—as witness their frantic crisscrossing of the musical scene giving lectures; appearing at forums, symposiums, festivals, competitions and performances; receiving awards and new commissions; and enjoying the benefits, however modest (and they are modest), of increased publishing and recording activities. The universities have taken the composer to heart and have sometimes built music departments around him. All this in no way should indicate that the composer has moved much beyond the restricted area imposed by the yet vital stigma of the term "contemporary music"; it merely shows that he is more active within this area and may even on occasion venture beyond its confines. One gets a mild shock when confronted with a news story of a living composer of concert music in a national magazine devoted to current affairs, literature, or home economics. But this has happened and without leaving a strong sensation that charity was in the making.

America still has no native composer of so-called serious music who, in relation to society in general, enjoys the status of Chávez of Mexico or Shostakovitch of Russia, or that held by the late composers, Sibelius and Villa-Lobos; that is, a status incorporating familiarity, respect, and even affection among musicians, intellectuals, laymen, and government officials. There has been no Grand Old Man of music, no man who has monopolized the musical history of America in his times. It is quite possible that in America's extremely diverse society of many preferences such a figure may never emerge, although many candidates are certainly available. Essentially, today's composer has written for and has been appreciated by select groups, large and small. This condition may be forever stabilized, creating not one dean of American music, but instead a number of figureheads for particular schools of style. The larger and more gracious concept of composer status previously mentioned is found in America, of course, but only among composers for the musical theater (or the exceptional figure of Duke Ellington, in the field of jazz). Their success is demonstrable in every conceivable way including, sometimes, the amassment of considerable fortunes. It is extremely unlikely that a similar status awaits the composer of string quartets, symphonies, and operas. Nevertheless, Roger Sessions was once moved to comment that there is such a thing as a career for the American composer of serious music. (Assuredly, it is a career within predictable limits, for few composers can either expect or receive such distinctions as that accorded Sessions himself in 1961 when Northwestern University and the Fromm Foundation presented a four-day festival of his music.)

Slowly, however, the American composer is being allied more consciously to the other cultural manifestations of his country. In 1960, for the first time, the name of a composer of serious music found its way to New York University's Hall of Fame for Great Americans, the concert hall's Edward MacDowell thus joining folklore's Stephen Foster—the only other musician so honored—in the company of Edison, Thoreau, and other household names.

The impetus given to contemporary music activities in America is due in no small way to the work done in behalf of composers by composers themselves. Since the imbroglios of the 1920's and 1930's American composers have had to fend for themselves and, through joint action, a number of lasting institutions have been created (see Organizations). One example is the American Composers Alliance with its extraordinary offshoot, Composers Recordings, Inc. There is little doubt, therefore, that composers will somehow survive.

Through books and articles and from influential positions in the music world, composers have had to present themselves largely as a cause, and among composers of not too dissimilar aesthetic bent, references to each other's music have had to be all too encomiastic. The drive toward preservation of the species still exists, but there is less need for it. Matters can now be more easily settled first hand: recordings, printed scores, and facsimile editions are readily available.

It is now apparent that many of the rather forbidding, or even obscure, names of the prewar era have achieved greater recognition today, not only from admiring colleagues, but also from conductors, performers, educators, musicologists and critics, students, and the responsible members of the recording and publishing industries.

Composers are still dissatisfied with the machinery of their profession (a major complaint is the reluctance of important orchestras to voluntarily program new works) and some have other contentions, one of which is preemption of the spotlight by New York (or Eastern) composers at the expense of those in other regions. Noble efforts have been made to destroy this real or imagined prejudice. Foundations interested in the work of composers have spread their largesse throughout the country, and beneficiaries are found everywhere. But the image of New York as *the* center of music publishing, recording, and important performing groups persists in the minds of composers resident elsewhere as an obstacle to overcome or a beneficence to court if one is to achieve widespread recognition. Where these beliefs are strong composers have felt it necessary to create their own outlets for performance and other modes of professional activity, which explains the cropping up of regional festivals, symposiums, and forums. Some of these events have assumed such magnitude that they have become cosmopolitan, losing whatever parochialism they might have begun with by inviting composers from all quarters of the country, including New York, to participate. Accusations of regionalism notwithstanding, the activities of composers in all parts of the nation receive notice in nationally distributed music periodicals, most of which originate in the East; and when an Eastern ensemble chooses to perform a contemporary American work, the work chosen is not always the product of an Easterner. It appears that the dissolution of regional prejudice may yet come about. The process has been hastened not only by improved communication and exchanges, but also by certain sociological factors such as the shift to the West of heavy population distribution. There, in the Midwest and Far West, great universities with ample resources have developed. Around them have grown pockets of musical and other cultural activity which have drawn attention to themselves and have helped to create greater national cultural balance. The American composer has never had a wider field of play.

Compositional Diversity and Productivity

The total picture of musical composition in America is vast and freewheeling. There are literally thousands of people writing music, the majority of whom write popular music in all its forms. They suffer no inconvenience if they are not called composers, for they occupy themselves enthusiastically and without inhibitions, turning out songs and the like and occasionally achieving success. Although the endeavors of most popular music writers are generally ignored by historians or academicians, except perhaps in a total general concept, their music is ubiquitous. From their collective pens, pianos, and guitars come a daily stream of folklike songs and ballads, dance tunes, sentimental love songs, march music, quasi-religious songs, occasional music, and so forth. The largest turnover in popular music types is that of fad music which readily expires in popularity and must be replaced, sometimes along with its creator, every other month or so. It is clear this larger definition of composer cannot be accommodated within the dimensions of this book.

Held more accountable for their work, but involuntarily omitted in the composer entries, are many worthy composers who specialize in one medium or style and who are important to the vitality and diversity of American music: jazz composers (usually also performers or arrangers), composers for television, sacred music composers, veteran songwriters, composers of concert or marching-band music, and composers of educational music. Many of the composers in the listing below have written in these genres, and even among specialists there is a certain amount of fence hopping. No record of American music can ever be complete until an attempt is someday made to weave a whole cloth of all areas of composition and performance, incorporating all patterns and styles. The patchwork quilt was an artistic utility of America's pioneer women; it should be the schema for considering the totality of America's composers.

Some idea of the scope of musical composition in America can be gained from the following figures: (From "Statistical Abstracts of the U.S.," editions of the years shown.)

Copyright Registration: 1940–1971 (with years ending June 30th). Issued to U.S. citizens and residents of foreign countries.

	1940	1945	1950	1955	1958	1959	1960
Dramatic or Dramatico-musical Compositions	6,450	4,714	4,427	3,493	2,754	2,669	2,445
Musical Compositions	37,975	57,835	52,309	57,527	66,515	70,707	65,558

1962	1963	1964	1965	1966	1967	1968	1969	1970	1971
2,813	2,730	3,039	3,343	3,215	3,371	3,214	3,213	3,352	3,553
67,612	72,583	75,256	80,881	76,805	79,291	80,479	83,608	88,949	95,202

Musical compositions constitute the largest single category of copyright registration and have accounted for an average of about 27 percent of all categories of copyright since 1940. In addition to musical compositions and dramatic and dramatico-musical compositions, the categories include such copyrighted works as periodicals and books of all kinds, lectures, maps, photographs, works of art, motion pictures, and photoplays.

Some selected years from 1940 show the following percentages of musical compositions to the total number of all categories of copyright registrations:

1940:22%	1955:26%	1960:26.8%	1969:28.7%
1945:32%	1958:28%	1965:27%	1970:28%
1950:25%	1959:29%	1968:26.5%	1971:28.9%

The overall decline in number of purely dramatico-musical works (a small percentage of the above figures) may be due, in the case of so-called musical theater, to rising theatrical production costs and the increasing risks of larger financial losses to investors and producers.

A more detailed breakdown of copyright registration is shown in the following figures from the "Music" volume of the "Catalogue of Copyright Entries." The figures, of course, include registration of published classics in addition to contemporary serious works and all popular music. Unpublished music includes a mass of popular music, mostly songs, and some serious works. Music compositions published outside the U.S. are defined in a more specific manner in 1965 and redefined in 1966.

Copyright Registrations for Music

	1965		1966	
	Jan–June	July–Dec	Jan–June	July–Dec
Music Compositions Published in U.S.	7,557	7,121	7,316	6,718
Music Compositions Published Outside U.S.	3,829	3,527*	3,967**	3,550**
Unpublished Music	30,928	27,913	27,178	27,160
Dramatico-musical Works	84	83	69	88
Music Registered in Books (class A)	495	459	444	512
TOTAL	42,893	39,103	38,974	38,028
Renewals	5,021	4,895	5,392	4,751

	1970	
	Jan–June***	July–Dec
Domestic Published Musical Compositions	7,647	6,859
Foreign Published Musical Compositions	4,228	4,091
Unpublished Music	35,832	34,299
Dramatico-musical Works (class D)	54	51
Music and Books about Music Registered in class A	635	600
TOTAL	48,396	45,900
Renewals	5,245	3,503

*Entry reading at this point: Musical compositions published abroad or the author of which is not a citizen or domiciliary of the U.S.

**Entry reading at this point: Musical compositions published outside the U.S., the authors of which are neither citizens nor domiciliaries of the U.S.

***Jan–June 1970 figures were incorrectly published in Catalog of Copyright Entries: Third Series (Music), Vol. 24, pt. 5, no. 1, section 1. The corrected figures shown here were furnished by the Chief, Cataloging Division, Copyright Office, Library of Congress.

Composers and Employment

American composers are employed in many ways; few can earn the substantial part of their living from composing. Most hold salaried posts in colleges, universities, and conservatories as teachers or administrators or both. The position of "composer-in-residence" is bestowed on composers in a growing number of private, religious, and state-run schools, as well as by symphonic ensembles. A number of America's most respected composers have been associated with the same schools for many years. By and large they have not led a sequestered life. In addition to influencing and giving impetus to the talents of new, younger composers, they have helped to make the university a true center of progressive contemporary musical activity.

The sum total of his activities as a professional man provides the composer a broad reputation within the music world. These activities often show him as a man of many careers; one pursuit may lead to an additional one. Thus, the composer-teacher can earn additional income within certain specializations serving the field of musical composition: conducting, criticism, research, performance, adjudication, and so on. Although these activities are engaged in for a number of reasons (including that of augmenting one's income) and admittedly take time away from composing, they occur inevitably, since they are proffered on the basis of the composer's reputation as a composer or teacher. Most extra-composing activities take place within academic circles but sometimes extend into the musical world at large. However, few American composers have conducted major symphony orchestras or have appeared extensively as performers on the concert circuits, even those who may have superior qualifications to do so. As conductors, they usually direct civic or campus ensembles; as performers, they usually appear in limited engagements as soloists or chamber musicians in the performance of their own music before festival audiences, at symposiums, or for recording sessions. The majority of composer-performers are pianists or string players, but there are, especially among younger composers, virtuosos of wind instruments and even percussion. A minority of composers are considered true concert artists by critics and public alike; they rank among the most active musicians in America.

Some composers are fully occupied in other than academic musical posts and only occasionally accept teaching positions, usually for a limited time. If they are not among the very few who can spend most of their time composing, they work as critics, editors of music periodicals or music columns of newspapers, or for music publishers. Some composers are full-time administrators of musical organizations or businesses. A few composers have gained excellent reputations as arrangers and orchestrators for television, films, and the musical theater.

There are, to be sure, composers in America who have been spared many of the vicissitudes of a contemporary composer's life, who have been able to devote most of their time to composing, who have ready publishers, and who may expect not only premieres, but also repeated performances of their works. Such men invariably belong to that much-maligned group called variously, and often obliquely, "traditional" or "conservative." But even these men have had to earn their keep. In a society where there are no pensions awaiting the successful and independent artist (he is called "self-employed"), this kind of composer must constantly replenish his source of royalties, particularly if he is a composer of symphonic music. As he does so, however, one still gets the impression (gathered from the frequency of appearances on concert programs and the duplication on records) that three or four well-known works—usually earlier compositions that originally established the reputation of the composer in question—supply the major source of royalties. In the meantime he is a prime choice for important commissions and prizes, all of which enable him to continue as a full-time composer. A career on this level is much helped by a great deal of free advertising in music-history books, biographies, dictionaries and encyclopedias, periodicals, record reviews, and other media having occasion to refer to contemporary music and which cannot help but keep alive the name of a front-rank composer. It would seem that industry or any other kind of enterprise would envy this pat system of production, free advertising, and propaganda. But industry does not readily manufacture that which it cannot sell. The composer may, often does, and sometimes must.

Pulitzer Prize Composers and Compositions

(For prize stipulations, see Competitions and Awards.)

The following list is arranged by years. No awards were granted in 1953, 1964, or 1965. 1943—**William Schuman:** Secular Cantata No. 2, "A Free Song." . . . 1944—**Howard Hanson:** Symphony No. 4, Opus 34. . . . 1945—**Aaron Copland:** "Appalachian Spring." . . . 1946—**Leo Sowerby:** "The Canticle of the Sun." . . . 1947—**Charles Ives:** Symphony No. 3. . . . 1948—**Walter Piston:** Symphony No. 3. . . . 1949—**Virgil Thomson:** "Louisiana Story." . . . 1950—**Gian-Carlo Menotti:** "The Consul." . . . 1951—**Douglas S. Moore:** "Giants in the Earth." . . . 1952—**Gail Kubik:** "Symphony Concertante." . . . 1954—**Quincy Porter:** Concerto for Two Pianos and Orchestra. . . . 1955—**Gian-Carlo Menotti:** "The Saint of Bleecker Street." . . . 1956—**Ernst Toch:** Symphony No. 3. . . . 1957—**Norman Dello Joio:** "Meditations on Ecclesiastes." . . . 1958—**Samuel Barber:** "Vanessa." . . . 1959—**John La Montaine:** Concerto for Piano and Orchestra. . . . 1960—**Elliott Carter:** Second String Quartet. . . . 1961—**Walter Piston:** Symphony No. 7. . . . 1962—**Robert Ward:** "The Crucible." . . . 1963—**Samuel Barber:** Piano Concerto No. 1. . . . 1966—**Leslie Bassett:** Variations for Orchestra. . . . 1967—**Leon Kirchner:** String Quartet No. 3. . . . 1968—**George Crumb:** "Echoes of Time and the River." . . . 1969—**Karel Husa:** String Quartet No. 3. . . . 1970—**Charles Wuorinen:** "Time's Encomium" (electronic score). . . . 1971—**Mario Davidovsky:** "Synchronisms No. 6" (piano and electronic sounds). . . . 1972—**Jacob Druckman:** "Windows."

A Special Citation was awarded in 1944 to **Richard Rodgers** and **Oscar Hammerstein,** 2nd, for the score and book of "Oklahoma."

Composer Listing

Composers are listed here alphabetically. Birth dates are included, along with institutions, schools, organizations, etc., with which the composer is now associated. (Foreign-born composers who are either United States citizens or long-time United States residents are included.) Other professional music activities of the composer are mentioned if he engages in them with some frequency.

Recorded works and publishers are listed so that each composer's music may be examined firsthand. The recordings listed are those available for purchase in the United States and which were in print during the period 1968–1972. The fullest information under recordings includes: title of the work, the date of composition, the record label, and serial number. A slash separates monaural from stereo numbers. If a composition is recorded as part of a collection, that fact is usually noted. The record company is listed with its address if the company is not placed in the main listing of record companies (Part 11). Included are some limited editions or foreign labels which may be difficult to obtain through normal retail outlets. For such cases, the address of the record company or its distributor in the United States is added wherever possible. "Out of print" (OP) recordings refer to those recorded during the ten-year period preceding 1968 and out of print sometime prior to 1968. Although its removal from record catalogues is the usual indicator of whether a recording is out of print, this does not preclude the recording's being available in record stores or specialized retail outlets. It will be seen that many of the recordings were made by Composers Recordings, Inc. Because of the frequency of their appearance, the label designation, "CRI" is used without additional identification.

Each composer's publishers are shown along with the categories of compositions published. Publisher's names are referred to by abbreviated designation in most cases (see Publishers section, Part 11, for full names and addresses). Selling agents, although included in the main listings of publishers, are often referred to in this section for the reader's convenience. A publisher-selling agent may be listed as publisher in lieu of the actual imprint name. This does not affect the availability of the music. Addresses are included when the publisher is not listed in the main listing. No mention is made of whether a composer's published works are still in print. Only publishers of the composer's music are listed; publishers of books, essays, etc., are generally omitted.

The composer–publisher information should be used with the following points in mind: (1) The bulk of a composer's work, or at least his published works, may be published by one firm; this is indicated, wherever possible, by the term "principal publisher." (2) The publishers listed have, in many cases, issued the scores of the recorded works. (3) A publisher's name does not necessarily suggest publication of a composer's major works (most composers still have major works in manuscript). (4) The number of publishers is no valid indication of a composer's productiveness, importance, or fame or of any other qualitative evaluation.

Unpublished musical compositions are often placed by composers in certain central libraries and depositories for examination by interested persons. The most important ones are mentioned in this section. They are:

American Composers Alliance
170 West 74th Street
New York, N.Y. 10023

American Music Center
2109 Broadway

Suite 1579
New York, N.Y. 10023

Edwin A. Fleisher Music Collection
The Free Library of Philadelphia
Logan Square
Philadelphia, Pennsylvania 19103

These have circulating libraries with their own specific regulations governing loans of scores, to which inquiries can be directed. It can be assumed that unpublished works are always available directly from most composers and that published works may also be filed with the three libraries mentioned. Important noncirculating collections, including manuscripts and holographs, of the music of contemporary American composers are found in the Americana Collection of the Library of the Performing Arts, Lincoln Center, New York City, and the Library of Congress, Music Division. (See Libraries, Part 9.)

It should be repeated that the information contained in this chapter on American composers is intended primarily as an aid to the study of the actual music of the composers. This chapter was organized in conjunction with the chapters on music publishers and recording companies so that references herein to publishers and recording firms will yield the specific information needed to acquire available music scores or recordings through those sources.

The core of the information about each composer was provided by the composer himself in virtually all cases. For some, the information was complete and sufficient as submitted; in most instances, however, much additional research was required to bring the information to a point of maximum utility and accuracy.

Samuel H. Adler (b. 1928, Germany; U.S. citizen); faculty, Eastman School of Music. Recordings: String Quartet No. 4 (1963), *Lyrichord* LL-203; "Capriccio" for Piano (1954) *RCA Victor* LM/LSC-7042 ("New Music for Piano"); "Recitation for Organ," *Lyrichord* 7191; "Mo-os Tzur" (1957). *Vanguard* 9237 ("Art of the Cantor"—Jan Peerce); "Southwestern Sketches," *Cornell University Record* 8; "Canto II" (1970), Four Concert Etudes for Bass Trombones, *Golden Crest* 7040. Principal publisher, beginning with 1966, is Oxford University Press (opera, orchestra, band, chamber, piano, organ, vocal, and choral). Other publishers: Associated Music Publishers (orchestral works); Abingdon Press (choral); C. F. Peters (orchestral); Chorister's Guild, 440 Northlake Center, Dallas, Texas 75218 (works for children's choir); Fine Arts Music Press, c/o Wayland College, Plainview, Texas (choral works); H. W. Gray (choral); G. Schirmer (chamber orchestra, choral); Lawson–Gould (piano solo, choral, organ); Robert King Music Co. (brass choir, chamber); Mercury Music Corp. (orchestra chamber); Mills Music (orchestra, chamber, piano solo, choral, children's vocal); Union of American Hebrew Cong., 838 Fifth Avenue, New York, N.Y. 10021 (children's vocal); Summy–Birchard (choral); Sacred Music Press, 40 West 68th Street, New York, N.Y. 10023 (children's vocal); Southern Music Publishing Co. (chamber, choral); Theodore Presser (chamber, string orchestra, choral with brass); Transcontinental (orchestra, organ, songs, choral); Alexander Broude (choral).

Hugh Aitken (b. 1924); Associate Dean, College of Arts & Sciences, William Paterson College, N.J. Publishers: Elkan–Vogel (chamber, piano solo, band); Oxford University Press (chamber, piano, band, string orchestra). Unpublished works are deposited with the American Music Center.

David Amram (b. 1930); also jazz performer; conductor. Recordings (all on *Washington Records/Orpheum* Productions): "Dirge and Variations" (1965), and Sonata for Violin and Piano (1965), both on *Washington* No. 469; Piano Sonata (1965), and "Shakespearean Concerto" (1964), both on *Washington* No. 470; "No More Walls," two records, *RCA Victor* VCS-7089. Principal publisher is C. F. Peters, which has published works for piano, voice, chorus, chamber orchestra, incidental music to the plays of Shakespeare, etc.

Leroy Anderson (b. 1908); active also as conductor. Recordings: "Irish Suite," *RCA Victor* and *Mercury;* his compositions have been recorded by the composer for *Decca* in several albums; other collections of his works have been recorded for *Victor, Mercury, London,* and *Vanguard;* a widely played composer, his short works are played in arrangements throughout the recording field. Works for string orchestra, orchestra, band, brass ensemble, and woodwind ensemble have been published by Mills Music and Woodbury Music Corporation, Woodbury, Connecticut.

Larry Austin (b. 1930); faculty, University of California at Davis. Recordings: "Improvisations for Orchestra and Jazz Soloists" (1963), *Columbia* ML-6133, stereo MS-6733; "Piano Set" (1964), and Piano Variations (1960), *Advance* S-10. Works are published by MJQ Music, and Composer/Performer Edition, 330 University Avenue, Davis, California 95616. These include works for orchestra, piano, chamber, works for jazz groups, etc., some using tapes and other electronic media.

Jacob Avshalomov (b. 1919), Conductor, Portland Junior Symphony. Recordings: "Taking of T'ung Kuan" for orchestra (1943, revised 1947 and 1953), *CRI*-117; "Phases of the Great Land" (1958) for orchestra, *CRI*-194 (composer conducting); "How Long, O Lord" (1949) for chorus and orchestra, *CRI*-210 (composer conducting); "Prophecy" for chorus, tenor, and organ (1947, revised 1952), *CRI*-191; Sinfonietta, for orchestra (1946, revised 1952), *Columbia* CSM-6089 (composer conducting). Publishers: American Composers Alliance (orchestral, including work for solo instrument and orchestra, works for small orchestra, work for chorus, narrator and orchestra without strings; choral works with instrumental accompaniment, choral with solo organ, male chorus *a cappella;* chamber music; and works for piano solo); Associated Music (work for flute and piano); E. B. Marks (chorus and orchestra); E. C. Schirmer (chorus with solo flute, chorus *a cappella,* chorus with three instruments); Highgate (choral, violin and piano); Merion (Presser) (small orchestra); Merrymount (Presser) (choral, clarinet and piano); Peer (Southern) (choral).

Milton Babbitt (b. 1916); faculty, Department of Music, Princeton University. Recordings: Composition for Four Instruments (1948), and Composition for Viola and Piano (1950), both *CRI*-138; "All Set" (1957), *Columbia* C2L-31, stereo: C2S-831. Partitions for Piano (1957), *RCA Victor;* Composition for Synthesizer (1961), *Columbia* MS-6566; Ensembles for Synthesizer (1964), *Columbia* MS-7051. The following out-of-print recordings: Composition for Twelve Instruments (1948), *Son-Nova;* "Du" for Piano and Soprano (1951), *Son-Nova.* Principal publisher is Associated Music. Other publishers: Boelke–Bomart (piano and vocal works); Theodore Presser (chamber and piano); E. B. Marks (piano and vocal); Lawson–Gould (piano); Princeton University Press, Princeton, New Jersey (choral work); Holt, Rinehart & Winston (educational works).

Richard Henry Horner Bales (b. 1915), Conductor, since 1943, of the National Gallery Orchestra and Music Director of the National Gallery of Art, both in Washington, D.C. Recordings (OP): "The Confederacy" (1953), *Columbia* LL-1003/LS-1004; "The Union"

(1956), *Columbia* LL-1005/LS-1006; "The American Revolution" (1955), *Columbia* LL-1001/LS-1002. Publishers: Southern Music Publishing (songs); H. W. Gray (choral); Kalmus (choral); Gregorian Institute (piano, violin and piano); Tetra (see A. Broude) (string orchestra, band); Theodore Presser (arr. for string orchestra); Rubank (orchestra). Unpublished works with the Fleisher Collection.

Esther Williamson Ballou (b. 1915), faculty, American University, Washington, D.C. Recording: "Prelude and Allegro for Piano and String Orchestra" (1949), *CRI*-115. Publishers: Mercury Music (piano solo, choral); American Composers Alliance (various works). Unpublished works on deposit with the American Music Center, Fleisher Collection, and American Composers Alliance.

George Barati (b. 1913, Hungary; U.S. citizen), professional orchestra conductor. Conductor of the Honolulu Symphony from 1950 to 1967. Director, Montalvo Center for the Arts (Saratoga, California). Recordings: Concerto for Violoncello and Orchestra (1953), *CRI*-184; Harpsichord Quartet (1964), *CRI*-S-226. Out of print: Chamber Concerto (1952), *Columbia* ML-5779/MS-6379; String Quartet No. 1 (1944), *Contemporary Records.* Publishers: C. F. Peters (orchestral and chamber); Peer International (orchestral and solo instrumental); Musikverlag Wilhelm Zimmerman (C. F. Peters, agent) (chamber music); Merion (solo instrumental); ACA Composer Facsimile Edition (orchestral, chamber, solo instrumental, choral). Unpublished works are deposited in the libraries of the American Music Center, the American Composers Alliance, and the Fleisher Collection.

Samuel Barber (b. 1910). Recordings: Adagio for Strings (from String Quartet No. 1), *Capitol* P-8542, P-8245, P-8444, and SP-8673, *Mercury* 50420/80420, *Mercury* 50148, *Vanguard* 2126, *Philips* 90001, *Columbia* ML-5624/MS-6224, *CBS*-32110005/32110006, *Pirouette* S-19024, and *Cook* 10683. "Andromache's Farewell," Op. 39 (1963) for soprano and orchestra, *Columbia* MS-6512; "Capricorn Concerto" (1944) for flute, oboe, trumpet, and strings, *Mercury* 90224; "Commando March," for band (1943), *Mercury* 50079, and *Victor* LSP-2687; Cello Concerto (1946), *Decca* 10132/710132; Piano Concerto (1962), *Columbia* MS-6638; Violin Concerto (1941), *Philips* WSS-9105, *Westminster* 19045/17045, *CRI*-137, and *Columbia* MS-6713; "Dover Beach," for voice and string quartet (1931), *Columbia* KS-7131; Essay No. 1 for Orchestra, Op. 12, *Mercury* 50148; Essay No. 2 for Orchestra, Op. 17, *CBS*-32110005/32110006, *Vanguard* 2083; "Hermit Songs" (1953) for voice and piano, *Columbia* CML-4988, and *Odyssey* 32160230 (Barber as pianist); "Knoxville: Summer of 1915" (1948) for soprano and chamber orchestra, *Columbia* ML-5843, *Odyssey* 32160230, *Victor* LSC-3062; "Medea," Op. 23, ballet suite (1946), *Everest* 3282 (composer conducting), *Mercury* 90224 and *Mercury* 90420; "Medea's Meditation and Dance of Vengeance," Op. 23A, *Victor* VICS-1391, and *CBS*-32110005/32110006; "Music for a Scene from Shelley" (1935) for orchestra, *Desto* 418/6418, *Vanguard* 2083; "Nuvoletta," Op. 25 (1947), *Lyrichord* 83, and *Desto* 411–2/6411–2; Overture to "The School for Scandal" (1933) for orchestra, *Mercury* 90420, *Mercury* 50148, *Desto* 418/6418, and *CBS*-3211005/32110006; String Quartet No. 1, Op. 11 (1936), *Stradivari* 602; and *MK*-1563 (foreign recording); Sonata for Cello and Piano, Op. 6 (1932), *Stradivari* 602, and *Golden Crest* 7026; Piano Sonata, Op. 26 (1949), 2-record collection *Victor* LD-7021, LSC-3229, *Decca* 10136/710136, and *Mace* S-9085; Songs (four selected songs), recorded on a 2-record set produced by *Duke University* (see record company listings); "Souvenirs," for orchestra, *Desto* 6433; "Summer Music," for woodwind quintet, Op. 31 (1956), *Concert-disc* 216, and *Columbia* CML-5441/CMS-6114; Symphony No. 1 in One Movement, Op. 9 (1936), *Mercury* 50148, *Mercury* 90420, and *CRI*-137; Symphony No. 2 (1944) *Everest* 3282 (composer conducting); "Three Reincarnations," Op. 16 (1936 and 1940) for chorus, *Everest* 3129, and *Cook* 11312; "Toccata Festiva," Op. 36 (1961) for organ and orchestra, *Columbia* MS-6398; "Vanessa" (1958) complete opera, 3-record set, *Victor* LSC-6138; "Antony and Cleopatra" (selections from the opera), *Victor*

LSC-3062. The composer's exclusive publisher in all categories is G. Schirmer.

Wayne Barlow (b. 1912), Chairman, Composition Department, Eastman School of Music. Recordings: Trio for Oboe, Viola, and Piano (1964); "Dynamisms" for Two Pianos (1967); Elegy for Viola and Piano (1967); all three works on *Mirrosonic* (S) 101. Out of print: "The Winter's Passed" (1938) for oboe and orchestra, *Mercury* MG 50299/SR 90299; "Night Song" (1938), *Mercury* MG 50277/SR 90277. Publishers: Concordia (organ solo); H. W. Gray (choral); Carl Fischer (orchestral, chamber); Presser (choral); Charles Scribners Sons (piano); J. Fischer (choral). Unpublished works at American Music Center.

Leslie Raymond Bassett (b. 1923), faculty, University of Michigan, Ann Arbor. Recordings: Trio for Viola, Clarinet and Piano (1953), *CRI*-148; Variations for Orchestra (1963), *CRI*-203; Five Pieces for String Quartet, *University of Illinois Custom Recordings* (c/o University of Illinois Bookstore, Urbana, Illinois). Publishers: C. F. Peters (orchestral, choral, band, chamber); Robert King Music Co. (brass music); Louisville House Autograph Editions (see Franco Colombo) (solo trombone); University Music Press (316 S. Thayer, Ann Arbor, Michigan) (clarinet duets); Abingdon Press (choral); Galaxy (chamber, vocal). Unpublished works with Fleisher Collection and American Composers Alliance.

John Alexander Bavicchi (b. 1922); faculty, Berklee School of Music, Boston; Conductor, Arlington (Mass.) Philharmonic Orchestra and Chorus, and Belmont (Mass.) Chorus. Recordings: Trio No. 4, Op. 33 (1958), and Sonata for Violin and Harpsichord, Op. 39 (1959), both on *CRI* -138; Sonata No. 1 for Violin and Piano, Op. 24 (1946), *Medea* 1002; Preludes for Unaccompanied Trombone, *Coronet* S-1407. Principal publisher is Oxford University Press (orchestral, chamber, and choral works). Chamber music for brass also published by Ensemble Publications, Inc. (see listings). Unpublished works are in the Fleisher Collection and the American Music Center.

Irwin Allen Bazelon (1922), active as composer for documentary films; occasional conductor. Recordings: Short Symphony ("Testment to a Big City") (1962), *Louisville* -664. Publishers: Boosey & Hawkes (principal publisher) (orchestral and chamber music); Southern Music Publishing (piano); Weintraub (through Music Sales Corp.) (chamber music). Some unpublished works obtainable through American Music Center.

Jack Hamilton Beeson (b. 1921), faculty, Music Department, Columbia University. Recordings: "Hello Out There" (opera) (1953), *Desto* 451/6451; "Lizzie Borden" (opera) (1965), *Desto* 3-discs: 455 to 457/6455 to 6457; Symphony No. 1 in A (1959), *CRI*-196; Three Rounds, *CRI* S-241. Publishers: Boosey & Hawkes (principal publisher) (operas, choral music, band music); MCA (orchestral); Mills Music (opera, choral, and vocal); Oxford (choral, chamber); Mercury (Presser) (chamber). Unpublished works on deposit at the American Music Center.

Warren Benson (b. 1924), faculty, Eastman School of Music. Recordings: "Polyphonies for Percussion," *Jubilee* records JGM 5011, and *Fidelity Stereo Recordings* FSR-1238; "Aeolian Song" (Concertino for Alto Saxophone and Piano) (1953), and "Farewell," (1964) for alto saxophone and piano, *Mark* MRS-22868; "Transylvania Fanfare," (concert march for band—1953), *Golden Crest* GC-4077, and *University of Illinois Band* Record No. 38; Three Pieces for Percussion Quartet, and "Variations on a Handmade Theme" (for eight handclappers), *Golden Crest* GC-4016 (composer conducting); "Recuerdo" for oboe and piano, *Mark* MRS-25726; "Marche-Encore" for woodwind quintet, *Golden Crest* GC-4075; "Helix" and "Star Edge" both respectively for tuba and alto saxophone with wind ensemble, *Golden Crest* GC-6001; "Arioso" for tuba and piano, *Mark* MRS-28437; "Gentle Song" for clarinet and piano, *Mark* MRS-32638. Out of print: Trio for Percussion, *Period* SPL-743; "Prologue," *Golden Crest* 7045. Principal publisher is MCA Music (works for orchestra, band, chorus, chamber ensembles, solo instruments, and concertos). Other publishers: Carl Fischer (orchestral); Interlochen

Press (orchestral); Shawnee Press (band, woodwind ensemble); Chappell (band); E. B. Marks (band, brass solo, percussion); C. F. Peters (wind orchestra); Plymouth (c/o Words & Music, 17 West 60th Street, New York, N.Y. 10023) (choral); Music for Percussion (percussion); G. Schirmer (percussion); Boosey & Hawkes (woodwind solo, piano solo, string solo). Unpublished works at MCA Music.

Arthur V. Berger (b. 1912), faculty, Brandeis University. Recordings: "Serenade Concertante" (1951) for violin, woodwind quintet, and small orchestra, *CRI*-143; Polyphony for Orchestra (1956), *Louisville* 584; String Quartet (1958), *CRI*-161; "Chamber Music for 13 Players" (1956) and Three Pieces for Two Pianos, *Columbia* MS-6959; Duo for Cello and Piano (1951), and Quartet for Woodwinds (1941), *Columbia* ML-4846; Bagatelle (1946), and Intermezzo (1947) for harpsichord, *Decca* 10021/710021 (in an album entitled "Six Americans"). Publishers: C. F. Peters (orchestral, chamber orchestra, solo instrumental, woodwind quartet); Associated Music (string orchestra); E. B. Marks (piano solo); New Music (Presser) (voice with solo instrument), among others. Unpublished scores with American Music Center.

William Bergsma (b. 1921), Chairman, School of Music, University of Washington, Seattle. Recordings: "Music on a Quiet Theme" for orchestra (1943), *CRI*-131; "Carol on Twelfth Night" for orchestra, *Louisville* 5410; "Chameleon Variations" for orchestra (1960), *CRI*-140; Concerto for Woodwind Quintet (1958), *Golden Crest* 4076; "Fortunate Islands" for string orchestra (1956 version), *CRI*-112; March with Trumpets (1957), *Decca* 8633/78633; String Quartet No. 2 (1944), *Desto* 425/6425; String Quartet No. 3, *Columbia* ML-5476; selections from the opera, "The Wife of Martin Guerre" (1956), *CRI*-105; Concerto for Violin, *Turnabout* 34428; Suite for Brass Quartet (1945), *Desto* 6474/7; "Tangents", *Golden Crest* CRS-4111. Publishers: Galaxy (orchestra, choral with orchestra, choral with brass and percussion, choral *a cappella,* band, woodwind quintet, viola solo, string quartet); C. Fischer (orchestral, string orchestra, choral, brass quartet, vocal); Hargail (orchestral, piano solo, string quartet), Boosey & Hawkes (orchestral); G. Schirmer (orchestral, string quartet).

Leonard Bernstein (b. 1918), conductor, pianist, author; Laureate Conductor, New York Philharmonic. Recordings (virtually all the recordings with orchestra on Columbia records are conducted by the composer): Symphony No. 1 ("Jeremiah") with voice (1943), *Columbia* ML-5703/MS-6303; Symphony No. 2 ("Age of Anxiety"), for piano and orchestra, *Columbia* M1-6285/MS-6885; Symphony No. 3 ("Kaddish") (1963), *Columbia* KS-6605; Serenade for Violin, Strings, and Percussion (1954), *Columbia* MS-7058; "Chichester Psalms" for chorus and orchestra (1965), *Columbia* MS-6792; "Mass" (1971), *Columbia* M2-31008; "Facsimile" (ballet suite) (1947), *Columbia* MS-6792 and *Capitol* HDR-21004; "Fancy Free" (1944) ballet score, *Columbia* MS-6677, selected dances: *Columbia* ML-6271/MS-6871, excerpts: *Victor* LSC-2747, and *Capitol* HDR-21004; "On the Town" (ballet), *Columbia* MS-6677 and *Epic* BC-1107; "On the Waterfront" (orchestral suite from the film score), *Columbia* MS-6251; "Prelude, Fugue, and Riffs" (1950), *Columbia* MS-6677 (composer as pianist), and *Columbia* MS-6805; "Trouble in Tahiti" (1952) chamber opera, *Heliodor* 25020; "West Side Story" (ballet music) *Columbia* MS-6251, and *Warner Brothers–Seven Arts* 1240; Overture to "Candide" on *Columbia* MS-6677, *Columbia* MS-6988, *Victor* LSC-2789, *Turnabout* 34459, *Austin* 6164, *Austin* 6240 (both for band), also part of a 2-record set of miscellany on *Columbia* M2X-795 and other multiple sets; recordings of music for musical shows and films are as follows: "On the Town" (1944), *Decca* 8030, and *Columbia* OL-5540/OS-2028; "Wonderful Town" (1952), *Decca* 9010/79010, and *Columbia* OL-5360/OS-2008; "Candide" on *Columbia* OS-2350; "Peter Pan," *Victor* LSO-1019 and *Columbia* OL-4312; "West Side Story," *Columbia* OS-2001, and the sound track from the film on *Columbia* OL-5670/OS-2070. Other recordings, such as arrangements found throughout the popular music and jazz field, of songs from the musical shows, are outside the scope of this listing. Principal publishers are G. Schirmer and Amberson Enterprises (G. Schirmer, selling agents), which have published most of the composer's works. Other publishers: Witmark (Warner Brothers–Seven Arts) (piano solo, piano and clarinet, violin with piano, orchestrations of works for the musical theater, choral with cantor and organ, soprano and piano); Harms–Remick (Warner Brothers), (Symphony No. 1 and ballet score); Boosey & Hawkes (piano solo arrangement of Copland's "El Salón México").

Philip Thomas Bezanson (b. 1916), Head, Music Department, University of Massachusetts, Amherst. Recordings: "Rondo–Prelude for Orchestra" (1953) *CRI*-159. Publishers: Presser (chamber); Interlochen Press (chamber); New Valley Music Press (chamber). Unpublished works on deposit with American Composers Alliance.

Gordon Binkerd (b. 1916), faculty, University of Illinois, Urbana. Recordings: Symphony No. 2 (1957), *CRI*-139; Sonata for Piano (1955), *CRI*-201; "Ad te levavi" (1959), *CRI*-191; "Aspects of Jesus" (1963), *Gregorian Institute.* Out of print: Symphony No. 1, *Columbia* ML-5691/MS6291. Publishers: Boosey & Hawkes (under exclusive contract since 1966), publisher of all the composer's music except works published prior to 1966 by Associated Music, Elkan–Vogel, Galaxy, H. W. Gray, and C. F. Peters (combined publications include choral music, works for organ, orchestra, and transcriptions for wind ensembles). Unpublished works with Fleisher Collection.

Easley Blackwood (b. 1933), faculty, University of Chicago; pianist. Recordings: Chamber Symphony for 14 Winds (1955), *CRI*-144; Concerto for Violin & Orchestra, Op. 21, *Louisville* S-685; Sonata for Flute and Harpsichord, *Desto* 7104. Out of print: Symphony No. 1, *RCA Victor.* Principal publisher: G. Schirmer. Others: Elkan–Vogel, Carl Fischer.

John Boda (b. 1922), faculty, Florida State University. Recordings: Sinfonia (1960), *CRI*-155; Prelude–Scherzo–Prelude (1959–1964), *Golden Crest* S-4084; Sonatina for Trombone, *Coronet* S-1506. Publishers: Franco Colombo (brass works); Robert King (brass); Kendor (clarinet and piano); Concordia (works for junior chorus—also recorded by Concordia).

Will Gay Bottje (b. 1925) faculty, and Director of Electronic Music Studio at Southern Illinois University. Publishers: Southern Music Publishers (band works); Robert King Music Co. (brass ensemble); Composer Facsimile Editions (principal publisher). Unpublished works on deposit with American Music Center, Fleisher Collection, but the majority at American Composers Alliance.

Henry Brant (b. 1913), faculty, Bennington College; Music Director, Bennington Community Orchestra; pianist, percussionist, and flutist. Recordings: Symphony No. 1 (1931), *Desto* 416/6416; "Angels and Devils" concerto for flute and flute orchestra (1931), *CRI*-106 (composer conducting); "Millennium II" for brass ensemble and percussion (1953), *Lehigh University Records* 1103 (Bethlehem, Pennsylvania) (composer conducting); "Millennium IV" for brass ensemble, *Advance Records* No. 2, *Nonesuch* 71222; "Signs and Alarms" (1953), and "Galaxy II" (1954) both for chamber groups, *Columbia* CML-4956 (composer conducting): "Hieroglyphics" (1966), *Advance* S-6; "Hieroglyphics 3," *CRI* S-260; "Music 1970," *Desto* 7108. Out of print: Saxophone Concerto (1940), *Remington Records.* MCA Music, Inc. is the composer's publisher under exclusive contract (works for chorus and orchestra, orchestra, and chamber music with and without voices including works for chamber orchestra.)

Alvin Brehm (b. 1925). Recordings: Dialogues for Bassoon and Percussion (1963), *Golden Crest*-7019; Quintet for Brass (1967), *Nonesuch* 71222. Publishers: MCA Music (educational pieces); Piedmont Press (E. B. Marks) (works for orchestra, chamber music). Unpublished works on file with American Composers Alliance.

Radie Britain (b. 1907). Recordings include releases by the U.S. Air Force of works recorded with the U.S. Air Force Symphony: "Prelude to a Drama," and "Lament." Publishers: Robert B. Brown Music Co. (orchestral, choral, piano); Ricordi and Sons, Brazil (orchestral); Carl Fischer (choral); Neil Kjos (choral, piano, violin, vocal); and others. Unpublished works on file with the American Music Center; Fleisher Collection; Los Angeles and New York City Libraries.

Earle Brown (b. 1926), composer-in-residence, Peabody Conservatory of Music. Recordings: "Four Systems" (1954), *Columbia* MS-7139; Music for Violin, Cello, and Piano (1952), Music for Cello and Piano (1954–55), and "Hodograph I" (1959), all on *Time*-8007; "Available Forms" (1961), *Victor* VIC 1239; "Corroboree," *Mainstream* 5000; String Quartet 1965, *Deutsche Grammophon* 2543002; "Times Five" (1963), *Editions Boîte à Musique* (France) 072; "Nine Rarebits" (1965), *Wergo Records* (Germany). Publishers: B. Schott, Mainz, and B. Schott, London (through Associated Music) (piano music, orchestral); Associated Music (solo instrumental, chamber, orchestral, electronic); Universal Edition (through Presser) (chamber and orchestral). Unpublished works with the American Music Center.

David Burge (b. 1930), faculty, University of Colorado, Boulder. Recordings: "Eclipse II" (1966) for solo piano, *Advance*-3. Publishers: Composer/Performer Edition; Bowdoin College Press; Alexander Broude.

John Cage (b. 1912). Recordings: "Amores" for Prepared Piano and Percussion (1943), *Time* 58000/8000, coupled with "Double Music for Percussion" (1941) (composed with Lou Harrison); "Atlas Eclipticalis" and "Winter Music," *Deutsche Grammophon* 137009; Concerto for Prepared Piano and Chamber Orchestra (1951), *Nonesuch* 71202; "Indeterminacy" for Narrator and Piano, 2-record set, *Folkways* 3704 (composer as narrator); "Solos for Voice 2" (1960), *Odyssey* 32160155/32160156; "Sonatas and Interludes for Prepared Piano" (1948), *CRI*-199; Sonata for Clarinet Solo (1933), *Advance* 4; "Variations II" (1961) (partly electronic), *Columbia* MS-7051; "Variations III," *Deutsche Grammophon* 139442; "Variations IV," *Everest* 3230 (with composer), and excerpts of the same work on *Everest* 3132; "Fontana Mix–Feed" (with electronic equipment), *Columbia* MS-7139; "Fontana Mix" (for magnetic tape alone), *Turnabout* 34046; "Cartridge Music," *Time* 8009 and *Deutsche Grammophon* 137009; "Hpschd" for harpsichords and 51 tape machines or any number (prepared with Lejaren Hiller), *Nonesuch* 71224 (an abridged version); Music for Keyboard (1935–48), *Columbia* M2S-819; a 3-record album produced by *Avakian Records* (see listing under record companies) contains the following works: Concerto for Piano and Orchestra (1958), Music for Carillon (1954), "Williams Mix" (1952), "She is Asleep" (1943), "Wonderful Widow of 18 Springs" (1942), "Imaginary Landscape No. 1" (1939), "Sonatas and Interludes" (1948), "Six Short Inventions for Seven Instruments" (1934), "Construction in Metal" (1937). Exclusive publisher is C. F. Peters (Henmar) for all works.

Elliott Cook Carter, Jr. (b. 1908), faculty, Juilliard School, professor-at-large, Cornell University, and composer-in-residence, American Academy in Rome. Recordings: Concerto for Piano (1965), *Victor* LM/LSC-3001; Double Concerto for Harpsichord, Piano, and Two Chamber Orchestras (1961), *Columbia* MS-7191, also on the English label *EMIALP*-2052/ASD-601; Eight Etudes and a Fantasy (1950), *Concert-Disc*-229, *Candide* 31016, and *CRI*-118; "Heart Not So Heavy as Mine" (1939) and "Musicians Wrestle Everywhere" (1945), both on *Nonesuch* 71115 (in a choral collection album entitled "Dove Descending"); String Quartet No. 1 (1951), *Columbia* CML-5104; String Quartets Nos. 1 and 2, *Nonesuch* H-71249; Sonata for Cello (1950), *Desto* 6419; Sonata for Flute, Oboe, Cello, and Harpsichord (1952), *Columbia* CML-5576/CMS 6176, and *Decca* 710108; Sonata for Piano (1946), *Desto* 6419, and *Dover* 5265/7265; Symphony No. 1 (1942), *Louisville* 611; "Tarantella" for male chorus (1936), *Carillon* 118 (*Carillon Records,* 520 Fifth Avenue, New York, N.Y. 10036); Variations for Orchestra (1955), *Columbia* MS-7191, and *Louisville* 583; Woodwind Quintet (1949), *Victor* LSC-6167, *Candide* 31016, Out of print recordings: Double Concerto, *Epic* LC-3830/

BC-1157; "The Minotaur" (1948), *Mercury* MG-50103; String Quartet No. 2 (1960), *Victor* LM-2481/LSC-2481; "Pocahontas"—Ballet Suite (1939), *Epic* LC-3850/BC-1250 (also containing Piano Sonata). Publishers: Associated Music Publishers (principal publisher) (orchestral, chamber, choral, vocal); Mercury, Merrymount, and New Music Edition (all available through Presser) (chamber and choral); Peer (Southern Music Publishing) (orchestral, chamber, choral, vocal). New Valley (solo voice).

Romeo Cascarino (b. 1922), faculty, Combs College of Music, Philadelphia. Recordings: Sonata for Bassoon and Piano (1950) (composer as pianist), *Columbia* CML-5821/6421. Out of print: "Pygmalion" (1955), *Stereo Fidelity/Somerset* 2900 (see Budget Sound, Inc.). Publishers: Arrow Music Press (see Boosey & Hawkes) (chamber music); Presser (band). Unpublished works available through composer.

Norman Cazden (b. 1914). Recordings: "Three Ballads from the Catskills" (1949), *CRI*-117; Piano Sonata, Op. 53, No. 3 (1963), *Victor* LM/LSC-7042. Out of print: "Catskill Mountain Folksongs," from Op. 58, *Stinson* SLP-72; "Merry Ditties", from Op. 59, *Riverside* RLP-12-603; "Puttin' on the Style," from Op. 59, *London* 45-1756, *Decca* 9-30409, *Mercury* 71181X45. Principal publisher is MCA Music (orchestral and band works). Other publishers are New Music Edition/Presser (piano, orchestral); Associated Music (orchestral, chamber); Boosey & Hawkes (piano); Lawson–Gould (piano); Jack Spratt (piano, orchestral, chamber). Unpublished works located at the American Music Center, Fleisher Collection, the New York Public Library, and the Music Library of Harvard University.

Barney Childs (b. 1926), Dean, Deep Springs College, California. Recordings: "Variations sur une chanson de canotier," *Advance* No. 2; "This is the praise of created things . . ." and "Heal me O Lord," on *Gregorian* EL-50; "Mr. T. His Fancy," for double bass, *Ars Nova* AN-1001 (*Ars Nova–Ars Antiqua Recordings,* 606 Raleigh Place, S.E., Washington, D.C. 20032), in a recorded collection called "The New World of Sound." Music for Two Flute Players, *CRI*-S-253. Publishers: Tritone Press (through Presser) (chamber); Composer/Performer Editions (chamber); M. M. Cole (tuba and piano); BMI–Canada (chamber), Ensemble Publications, Inc. (brass quintet). Unpublished music is on deposit with American Music Center; the majority of works are at American Composers Alliance.

Chou Wen-chung (b. 1923, China; U.S. citizen since 1958), faculty, Columbia University. Recordings: "Landscapes" for orchestra (1949), *CRI*-122; "All in the Spring Wind" for orchestra (1953), *Louisville* 614; "And the Fallen Petals" for orchestra (1954) *Louisville* 56-1; "Soliloquy of a Bhiksuni" (1958), *Louisville* 641; "Cursive" for flute and piano (1963), and "Yu Ko" for nine players (1965), Pien (1966), "Willows are New," *CRI*-251. Publishers: C. F. Peters (principal publisher) (orchestral, chamber, solo instrumental); Presser (vocal); Composer Facsimile Edition (vocal, orchestral, chamber). Unpublished works on deposit with American Composers Alliance.

Avery Claflin (b. 1898). Recordings: "Concerto Giocoso"—Concerto for Piano and Orchestra, *CRI*-178; "La Grande Bretèche" (1947), opera, *CRI*-108X; "Fishhouse Punch" (1947) for orchestra, *CRI*-107; three madrigals: "Lament for April 15," "Design for the Atomic Age," "Quangle Wangle's Hat" on *CRI*-102; "Teen Scenes" for string orchestra (1955), *CRI*-119. Publishers: Boosey & Hawkes (orchestral); Associated Music (vocal); H. W. Gray (organ); M. Senart, Paris (chamber). Unpublished works are mainly located in the library of the American Composers Alliance; some also with the Fleisher Collection.

Henry Leland Clarke (b. 1907), also musicologist, faculty, University of Washington School of Music, Seattle. Out of print recordings: "No Man is an Island," "L'Allegro and Il Penseroso," both institutional recordings. Principal publisher is Mercury Music (Presser) (choral music). Other publishers: MCA Music (choral, band); Colombo (choral); Western International Music, Inc. (2859 Holt Avenue, Los Angeles, California 90034) (chamber music). Unpublished works on file at American Music Center, American Composers Alliance, New York Public Library, and Harvard University Library.

Arthur Cohn (b. 1910), Director of Music, MCA Music, Inc., Conductor, Haddonfield (N.J.) Symphony Society and the Symphony Club of Philadelphia; member, editorial staff of *American Record Guide;* author. Former Director of the Fleisher Collection. Recording: "Kaddish," for orchestra, *CRI* S-259. Publishers: Elkan–Vogel (instrumental); Southern Music Publishing (brass chamber music); MCA (music text); Mills Music (percussion ensemble). Unpublished works with the Fleisher Collection, Mills Music Rental Library.

Aaron Copland (b. 1900), conductor, lecturer, author. Recordings of Copland's music are the most extensive of America's native contemporary composers. They include: "Appalachian Spring" complete ballet, *Columbia* ML-5157; "Appalachian Spring" Suite from the Ballet, *Victor* LSC-2401 (composer conducting), *Victor* LSC-3184, *Columbia* ML-5755/MS-6355, *Mercury* 90246, *Desto* 403/6403, *Westminster* 18284, *Command* 11038, *Everest* 3002. "Billy the Kid" Suite from the Ballet (1938), *Everest* 3015 (composer conducting), *Columbia* ML-5575/MS-6175, *Mercury* 90246, *Victor* LM-2195/LSC-2195, *Turnabout* 34169, *Capitol* HDR 21004/5-21004, *Westminster* 18284, *Columbia* ML-5157, *Command* 11038. Concerto for Clarinet and String Orchestra (1948), *Columbia* MS-6805 (composer conducting). Piano Concerto (1927), *Columbia* MS-6698 (composer as pianist), *Vanguard* 2094 (composer as conductor). "Connotations for Orchestra" (1962), part of a 2-record album on the first performance at the opening of Lincoln Center, *Columbia* L2L-1007/L2S-1008. "Dance Symphony" (1925), *Victor* LSC-2850, *CRI*-129, *Columbia* MS-7223 (Copland conducting), coupled with "Short Symphony" (1934). "Danzón Cubano" (1942), for orchestra, *Columbia* MS-6514 (also MS-6871), *Mercury* 90172, *Victor* VICS-1419. "Fanfare for the Common Man" (1944), *Columbia* MS-6684, *Turnabout* 34169, *Westminster* 18284. "In the Beginning" (1947), "Lark" (1939), "Twelve Poems of Emily Dickinson" (1950), "Las Agachadas" (1942), all choral or vocal works and all on *CBS* 32110017/32110018 with the composer. Other recordings of "In the Beginning" are on *Everest* 3129, *Lyrichord* 124/7124, and *Pfeiffer* No. 1 (see *Pfeiffer College* under Record Companies). "Letter from Home" (1944) for orchestra, *Westminster* 17131. "Lincoln Portrait" (1942), *Vanguard* 2115, *Columbia* MS-6684. "Music for a Great City" (1964), for orchestra, *CBS*-32110001/32110002 (composer conducting). "Music for the Theater" (1925), for orchestra, *Columbia* MS-6698, *Desto* 418/6418. "Old American Songs," *Columbia* MS-6497 (composer conducting). "Orchestral Variations" (1957), *Louisville* 59-1, *Vanguard* 2085. "Our Town" Suite (1940), *Vanguard* 2115. "Outdoor Overture" (1938), *Vanguard* 2115. Passacaglia for Piano (1922), *Lyrichord* 104. Piano Fantasy (1957), *Odyssey* 32160039/32160040. Piano Variations (1930), *Concert–Disc* 217, *Dover* 5265/7265, *Lyrichord* 104, *Odyssey* 32160039/32160040. Quartet for Piano and Strings (1950), composer as pianist, *CBS*-32110041/32110042. "Quiet City" (1940) for small orchestra, *Capitol* P-8245, *Everest* 3118, *Mercury* 90421, *Vanguard* 2115. "Red Pony" suite from the film (1948), *Columbia* MS-6583, *Decca* 3207/9616. "Rodeo" Ballet (1942), *Capitol* HDR-21004, *Columbia* ML-5575/MS-6175, *Mercury* 90172, *Turnabout* 34169, *Victor* LM2195/LSC-2195. "El Salón México" (1936) for orchestra, *Columbia* ML-5755/MS-6355 and ML-5841/MS-6441, *Mercury* 90172, *Westminster* 18284. "The Second Hurricane" (1937), play-opera for high school performance, *Columbia* MS-6181. "Short Symphony" (see listing for Dance Symphony). Sextet for clarinet, piano, and string quartet (1933), *CBS* 3211004/32110042 (composer as pianist). Sonata for Piano (1941), *Lyrichord* 104, *CRI*-171. Sonata for Violin and Piano (1943), *CRI*-171, *Decca* 8503. "Statements for Orchestra" (1935); both extant recordings are conducted by the composer: *Everest* 3015, *CBS*-32110001/32110002. Symphony for Organ and Orchestra (1924), *Columbia* MS-7058. Symphony No. 3 (1946), *Columbia* MS-6954, *Everest* 3018 (composer conducting), *Mercury* 90421. "The Tender Land" (1954), opera recorded in abridged version with the composer conducting on *Columbia* MS-6814; recorded as the orchestral suite, conducted by Copland, on *Victor* LM-2401/LSC-2401. "Vitebsk, Study on a Jewish Theme" (1929) for violin, cello, and piano, *CBS*-32110041/32110042 (composer as pianist) *CRI*-171, *Decca* 10126/710126, *University of Oklahoma*-1, *Victor* LM-6167/LSC-6167. Miscellaneous piano pieces: "Sunday Afternoon Music," "Young Pioneers" (1936), *Educo* 3021 (collection: "Masters of Our Day"). Recordings recently out of print: "Appalachian Spring" suite, *Vanguard* 439; "Billy the Kid" suite, *Westminster* 18840/14058; Clarinet Concerto, *Columbia* 4421; "Danzón Cubano," *Mercury* 50326/90326, *Victor* LM-2417/LSC-2417 (two-piano arrangement); "Four Piano Blues," *Dot*-3111; "Fanfare for the Common Man," *Vanguard* VRS-1067/VSD-2085. "In the Beginning," *Music Library* 7007; "Lincoln Portrait," *Columbia* ML-5347/MS-6040. "Outdoor Overture," *Epic* LC-3819/BC-1154; "Twelve Poems of Emily Dickinson," *Columbia* 5106 (composer as pianist); Quartet for Piano and Strings, *Columbia* ML-4421; "Rodeo" suite, *Westminster* XWN-18840/WST-14058; "El Salón México," *Columbia* CL-920, *Vanguard* VRS-439, *Victor* LM-1928, *Westminster* XWN-18840 and WST-14063; Piano Sonata, *Epic* LC-3862/BC-1262; Symphony No. 3, *Mercury* MG-50118. Principal publisher in all categories is Boosey & Hawkes. Other publishers: Durand & Cie., Paris; Carl Fischer; H. W. Gray; Editions Salabert, Paris (and New York); E. C. Schirmer Music.

John Corigliano, Jr. (b. 1938), Recordings: Sonata for Violin and Piano (1963), *CRI*-215; Concerto for Piano and Orchestra, *Mercury* 90517. Exclusive publisher: G. Schirmer.

Paul Creston (b. 1906), composer-in-residence and professor of music, Central Washington State College, Ellensburg, beginning school year 1968. Recordings: Symphony No. 2 (1945) and Symphony No. 3 (1950), *Westminster* 9708; "Invocation and Dance" (1953), *Louisville* 545-1; "Choric Dances" (1938), *Capitol* P-8245; "Dance Overture" (1954), *CRI*-111; "Corinthians: XIII," *Louisville* 655 (all of the foregoing are orchestral works); Partita for Flute, Violin, and Strings (1937), *Desto* 424/6424; Sonata for Saxophone and Piano (1939), *Columbia* ML-4989, *Award* 33-708, *Mark* MRS 22868; "Celebration Overture" (1955) for band, *Austin* 6104 and 6388; Concertina for Marimba and Orchestra (first movement) (1940), *Columbia* ML-6377/MS-6977; "Dedication" (1965), *Pfeiffer* No. 1; "Prelude and Dance," *Austin* 6226. Out of print records: "Walt Whitman," Symphonic Poem (1951) *Victor* LM-2426 coupled with "Lydian Ode"; String Quartet, *Capitol* P/8260. Publishers: G. Schirmer (orchestral, chamber, piano, songs, choral, and band); Franco Colombo (orchestral, chamber, piano, songs, choral, band, and textbook); Shawnee (orchestral, band, and choral); Mills Music (orchestral, piano). One unpublished work is deposited in the Fleisher Collection.

George Henry Crumb (b. 1929), music faculty, University of Pennsylvania, Philadelphia. Recordings: "Five Pieces for Piano" (1962), *Advance* 3; "Night Music I" for soprano, piano, celesta, and percussion (1963), *CRI*-218; "Eleven Echoes of Autumn" (1965), for violin, alto flute, clarinet, and piano, *CRI*-S-233; "Ancient Voices of Children," *Nonesuch* 71255; "Echoes of Time and the River," (1968) *Louisville* S-711; "Black Angels," for electric string quartet, *CRI*SD-283. Principal publisher: C. F. Peters; Mills Music (orchestral, piano, chamber, chamber ensembles with voice).

David Del Tredici (b. 1937), faculty, Harvard University. Recordings: "Syzygy" (1966) for soprano, horn, chimes, and 18 instruments, *Columbia* MS-7281; Fantasy Pieces, *Desto* 7110; "Night Conjure–Verse," *CRI* S-243.

Norman Dello Joio (b. 1913), Chairman, Policy Committee of the Contemporary Music Project (sponsored by the Ford Foundation); Acting Dean, Boston University, School of Fine and Applied Arts. Recordings: "Epigraph" (1953) for orchestra, *Desto* 416/6416; Fantasy and Variations for Piano and Orchestra (1962), *Victor* LSC-2667; "Meditations on Ecclesiastes" (1956), *CRI*-110 and *Decca* 10138/710138; "New York Profiles" (1949), for piano and orchestra, *CRI*-209/SD-209; "Serenade" (1948), *Desto* 413/4 & 6413/4;

Piano Sonata No. 3 (1947), *Music Library* MLR-7021, and *Concert–Disc* 217; "Triumph of Saint Joan Symphony" (from his opera) (1951), *Columbia* CML-4615; Variations and Capriccio for Violin and Piano (1948), *CML*-4845 (composer as pianist); "Nocturnes," *Golden Crest* CRS-4111. Out of print recordings are: "Air Power" (incidental music for TV) (1957) for orchestra, *Columbia* ML-5214/MS-6029; Concerto for Harp and Orchestra (1945), *Columbia;* Suite for Piano (1941), *Wardle* TW-63 (label discontinued); "To St. Cecilia" for chorus and instruments (1956), *Kapp;* "Variations, Chaconne, and Finale" (1946) for orchestra, *Columbia* ML-5263. Exclusive publisher from 1945 to 1962 was Carl Fischer (orchestral, chamber, choral, vocal, piano); from 1962 to present exclusive publisher has been Edward B. Marks Corp. (orchestral, chamber, choral, vocal, band, piano, organ). Other publishers include: G. Schirmer (orchestral, choral, piano); Hargail (chamber, piano); Merrymount (Presser) (choral); Franco Colombo (opera).

William D. Denny (b. 1910), faculty, University of California at Berkeley. Recording: Partita for Organ, *Fantasy* 5010. Publisher: Boosey & Hawkes (string quartet).

David Leo Diamond (b. 1915). Recordings (all for orchestra): "Music for Romeo and Juliet" (1947), *CRI*-216; "Rounds for String Orchestra" (1944), *Capitol* P-8245; "Timon of Athens" (1949), *Louisville* 605; Symphony No. 4 (1948), *Columbia* CML-5412/CMS-6089; "The World of Paul Klee" (1957), *CRI*-140. Out of print: String quartet No. 4 (1951), *Epic* LC-3907/BC-1307. Principal publisher and exclusive publisher until 1971: Southern Music Publishing (orchestral, chamber, piano concerto, violin concerto, cello concerto, choral, brass and percussion, piano). Other publishers: G. Schirmer; Boosey & Hawkes; Carl Fischer; Leeds (MCA); Presser; Elkan–Vogel. Unpublished works on file in the Fleisher Collection.

Marcel Dick (b. 1898, Hungary; U.S. citizen 1940), Chairman Theory and Composition Department, Cleveland Institute of Music; conductor. Recordings: Suite for Piano (1959), *CRI*-183. Publishers: Presser (orchestral); Composer's Autograph Publications (Redondo Beach, California) (chamber and solo); Henry Elkan (solo instrumental).

Charles Dodge, (b. 1942), faculty, Columbia University. Recordings: "Changes," (1970), *Nonesuch* 71245; "Earth's Magnetic Field," (1970), *Nonesuch* 71250 (both recordings are of electronic music). All publishing rights assigned to ACA (Composers Facsimile Editions).

Anthony Donato (b. 1909), faculty, Northwestern University, Evanston, Illinois. Publishers: Southern Music Co., San Antonio (orchestral, chamber, clarinet and piano); Southern Music Publishing Co., New York (orchestral, choral, piano); Edward B. Marks (orchestral, band); Boosey & Hawkes (band, choral); G. Schirmer (chamber); Composers Press (chamber); Presser (chamber, choral, organ, violin and piano); Interlochen Press (chamber music); Remick (chamber); Summy–Birchard (choral); Mills Music (choral); Frederick Charles (through Shawnee Press) (choral); H. T. FitzSimons (choral); Kjos (choral); Alphonse Leduc, Paris. Unpublished works on file with the Fleisher Collection.

Jacob Druckman (b. 1928), faculty Juilliard School; Columbia–Princeton Electronic Music Center. Recordings: "Dark Upon the Harp" (1962), *CRI*-167; "Animus I" (1966), *Turnabout* 34177; "Animus II," *CRI* S-255; "Animus III," and "Valentine," *Nonesuch* 71253; "Incenters," *Nonesuch* 71253. Publishers: Society for the Publication of American Music (through Presser) (vocal, chamber); Beekman (Presser) (choral); principal publisher is MCA Music. Unpublished works are deposited in American Music Center.

John C. Eaton (b. 1935), pianist and professional performer on the Synket. Recordings, all on *Decca* 10154/710154 and performed with the composer: "Microtonal Fantasy" (1965), "Songs for R. P. B." (1964), "Prelude to Myshkin" (1965), Piece for Solo Synket No. 3 (1966); Concert Piece for Synket and Symphony Orchestra, *Turnabout* 34428; "Electro–Vibrations," *Decca* 710165. The composer is exclusively published by Shawnee Press.

Jonathan Britton Elkus (b. 1931), faculty, Lehigh University. Recording: "After Their Kind" (1955), five lyrics by Flora J. Arnstein, *Fantasy* 5008. Publishers: H. W. Gray (musical plays for children and children's choruses); Charles K. Hansen (band transcriptions); E. B. Marks (band transcriptions); Mercury (band transcriptions, choral, organ); Presser (band); American Music Edition (chamber music); Peer International/Southern (band transcriptions). Unpublished works on file with American Music Center.

Merrill Ellis (b. 1916), faculty, North Texas State University, Denton; Director, Electronic Music Laboratory at North Texas State; Resident Composer, Rocky Ridge Music Center, Estes, Colorado. Recordings: "Tomorrow Texas" for chorus, piano, and percussion, and "7, A Numbers Game" for chorus, piano, bongos, and string bass, both on *Austin Records;* "Kaleidoscope" for Orchestra, Synthesizer, and Soprano, *Louisville* S-711; other works, including electronic music, have been taped by the North Texas State University Electronic Music Laboratory. Publishers: MCA Music (orchestral and electronic works); Summy–Birchard (choral); Carl Fischer (choral). Unpublished works are on deposit with American Music Center.

Robert Hall Elmore (b. 1913), Philadelphia Musical Academy, Tenth Presbyterian Church, Philadelphia; concert organist. Recordings; "One View" song, accompanied by composer, *Zondervan* (Singcord Corp.) in a collection called "Raymond McAfee Sings Religious Classics"; "Three Miniatures," *Word* 4026/9026 (played by the composer in a collection called "Sacred Classics"); "Fantasy on Nursery Tunes," *Mercury* ("Boardwalk Pipes"). Publishers (for mostly organ and choral music): J. Fischer; H. W. Gray; Galaxy; Harold Flammer; Sacred Songs; Lorenz; Elkan–Vogel.

Alvin Leonard Epstein (b. 1926), faculty, Hartt College of Music, University of Hartford (Conn.). Recording: "Dialogue for Double Bass and Percussion," (1965), *Medea Records* M/S-1001. Publishers: Mercury (chamber); World Library Publications (piano).

Donald Erb (b. 1927), faculty, Cleveland Institute of Music. Recordings: Sonata for Harpsichord and String Quartet (1962), *CRI*-183; "VII Miscellaneous" for flute and string bass (1964), *Medea* M/S 1001; "Phantasma" (1965), String Trio (1966), and "Diversion for Two" (1966) for trumpet and percussion, all on *Opus One* records No. 1 (*Opus One,* 212 Lafayette Street, New York, N.Y. 10012); "Summermusic" (1966), Trio for Two (1968), Kyrie (1967), *Ars Nova* S-1008; Symphony of Overtures, "The Seventh Trumpet" and Concerto for Percussion Solo and Orchestra, *Turnabout* 34433; "Reconnaissance," *Nonesuch* 71223. Publishers: Associated Music (vocal); Galaxy (orchestral, chamber); Apogee (chamber); Opus One (see address above) (chamber); Music for Percussion (percussion); Frank Music Corp., and Theodore Presser (brass choir).

Robert Erickson (b. 1917), faculty, University of California at San Diego. Recording: Chamber Concerto, for 17 players (1960), *CRI* S-218; Ricercar (1967), *Ars Nova* 1001. Publisher: Presser (violin and piano, piano). Other publications include lectures, reviews, articles, and a book. Unpublished works on deposit with American Composer Alliance.

Alvin Etler (b. 1913), faculty, Smith College, Northampton, Massachusetts. Recordings: Sonata for Bassoon and Piano (1952), *Columbia* CML-5821/CMS-6421; Quintet No. 1 for Woodwinds (1955), *Concert–Disc* 216; Concerto for Woodwind Quintet and Orchestra (1960), *Louisville* 651; "Triptych" for orchestra (1961), *Louisville* S-674; Quintet for Brass Instruments (1964), *CRI* 205/SD-205; Concerto for Brass Quintet, String Orchestra, and Percussion (1967) and "Sonic Sequence" for brass quintet (1967) both on *CRI*-229. Publishers: Alexander Broude (orchestral, chamber, choral); Associated Music Publishers (orchestral, chamber, choral); New Valley (chamber); Galaxy (recorder music). Unpublished works with American Music Center, the Fleisher Collection, and the Library of Congress.

Harold Farberman (b. 1930), conductor. Recordings: "Evolution" (1954), "Impressions" (1959), and "Progressions" (1960), all conducted by the composer on *Cambridge* 1805; "Then Silence" (1964) *Cambridge* 1820; Concerto for Saxophone and String Orchestra (1965), Trio for Violin, Piano, and Percussion (1963), "Elegy, Fanfare and March" (1965), "Three States of Mind" all performed with the composer on *Serenus* 1016/12016; "New York Times—August 30, 1964" (1964), "Five Images" for brass (1964), "Quintessence" (1963), "Greek Scene" (1957), all on *Serenus* 1011/12011. Out of print recordings include: "Evolution," "Music Inn Suite," and "Variations on a Familiar Theme" recorded for Mercury. Publishers: General Music Publishing (opera, percussion ensembles, wind and brass chamber groups, strings, etc.); Franco Colombo (opera, work for timpani); and Broude Brothers (orchestral, instrumental concertos, percussion ensembles alone or with voice or solo instruments).

Morton Feldman (b. 1926). Recordings: "Chorus and Instruments II" (1967) for tuba, chimes, and chorus, and "Christian Wolff in Cambridge" for *a cappella* chorus, both on *Odyssey* 32160156; "Out of Last Pieces" (1962) for orchestra, *Columbia* MS-6733; "Durations" for chamber groups (1960–61), *Time* 8007 (*Mainstream* 5007); "King of Denmark" for percussion and electronic equipment, *Columbia* MS-7139; "Viola in My Life," "False Relationships and the Extended Ending," *CRI* S-276. The following works are recorded in an album entitled "New Directions in Music 2: Morton Feldman" issued on *Odyssey* 32160302: "Structures" (1951) for string quartet, "Three Pieces" (1954–56) for string quartet, "Extensions I" (1951) for violin and piano, "Projection IV" (1951) for violin and piano, "Intersection III" (1953) for piano, "Two Pieces" (1954) for two pianos, "Extensions IV" (1953) for three pianos, and "Piece" (1957) for four pianos (composer as one of pianists). The composer's exclusive publisher is C. F. Peters.

Paul Fetler (b. 1920), faculty, University of Minnesota, Minneapolis. Recordings: "Nothing But Nature," comedy cantata (1961), on *St. Paul Records* (2-record set) 96585-6/96583-4 (*St. Paul Records,* Arts and Science Center, 30 East 10th Street, St. Paul, Minnesota 55101). Out of print: "Contrasts for Orchestra" (1958) *Mercury* MG-50282/SR/90282. Publishers: Associated Music (choral); B. Schott, Mainz, Germany (guitar); Lawson–Gould (choral); Augsburg (choral); Carl Fischer (orchestral, choral); American Music Edition (orchestral); Presser (Society for the Publication of American Music) (violin and piano); Concordia (organ).

Ross Lee Finney (b. 1906). Recordings: Symphony No. 1 (1942), *Louisville* 652; Symphony No. 2 (1959), *Louisville* 625; Symphony No. 3 (1960), *Louisville* S-672; String Quartet No. 6 (1950), *CRI*-116; Quintet for Piano and Strings (1953), *Columbia* ML-5477/CMS-6142; work for organ: "So Long as the Mind Keeps Silent" in organ collection, *Lyrichord* 191-7191. Publishers: Henmar Press (C. F. Peters) is principal publisher in all categories; others are Carl Fischer (choral, orchestral, chamber); G. Schirmer (chamber); New Valley Music Press (chamber); Bowdoin College Music Press and Boosey & Hawkes (chamber); Mercury (chamber).

Irwin Fischer (b. 1903), faculty, American Conservatory of Music, Chicago; Conductor, West Suburban Symphony, La Grange, Illinois. Recordings: "Hungarian Set," for orchestra (1937), *CRI*-122; "Overture on an Exuberant Tone Row" (1965) *Louisville* 676/S-767. Publishers: Witmark (organ); Highgate (organ); Deluxe Music (4063 North Milwaukee Avenue, Chicago, Illinois) (choral); Fitzsimons (choral); also has co-authored a textbook on modal counterpoint. Unpublished works located at American Music Center, Fleisher Collection, and American Composers Alliance.

Grant Fletcher (b. 1913), faculty, Arizona State University, Tempe; orchestra conductor. Publishers: Mills Music (orchestral); Neil Kjos (choral); Music Publishers Holding (choral); Byron–Douglas Publishing Co. (403 East Roosevelt, Phoenix, Arizona) (band music); Presser (piano); Sacred Music Press (through Lorenz Publishing Co.) (choral);

Interlochen Music Press (orchestral, opera); Summy–Birchard (choral); Carl Fischer (orchestral); Leuckhardt Verlag, Munich, Germany (through Associated Music) (choral); M. M. Cole (trumpet and piano). Autograph scores of the composer are available through Byron–Douglas. Unpublished works are deposited with American Music Center, Fleisher Collection, the Israel National Library, Belgian National Library, Brussels, and the Library of Arizona State University at Tempe.

Carlisle Floyd (b. 1926), faculty, Florida State University, Tallahassee. Recording: "The Mystery" (1960) ("Five Songs of Motherhood" for Soprano and Orchestra), *Louisville* 635; "Pilgrimage: Three Sacred Songs," *Orion* 7268. Publishers: Boosey & Hawkes (operas, vocal, piano, choral); Presser (orchestral).

Lukas Foss (b. 1922, Germany; U.S. citizen), Conductor, Brooklyn Philharmonia Orchestra; pianist. Recordings: "Baroque Variations" for orchestra, *Nonesuch* 71202 (composer conducting); "Echoi" (chamber work), *Epic* BC-1286; "Phorion" (1966—subtitled "Baroque Variation III"), *Columbia* ML-6452/MS-7052; "Time Cycle" (1960) for orchestra, *Columbia* MS-6280 (composer as pianist); "Time Cycle" (1963) for chamber ensemble, *Epic* BC-1286 (pianist is Foss); "Psalms" (1957), *CRI*-123; "Behold, I Build An House" (1950) for chorus, *CRI*-123; "Jumping Frog of Calaveras County" (1950) opera, *Lyrichord* 11; "Parable of Death" for narrator, tenor, chorus, and orchestra (1952), *Columbia* CML-4859; String Quartet No. 1 (1947), *Columbia* CML-5746; "Capriccio for Cello," *Victor* LSC-2940; "Geod" (composer conducting), *Candide* 31042; "Paradigm" (1968) (with composer), *Deutsche Grammophon* 2543005; in addition, on the *Wergo* label (*Wergo* is a German firm: Postfach 1103, Ludwig–Wilhelmstrasse 14, 7570 Baden–Baden, Germany): "Echoi," "Non-Improvisation," "Fragments of Archilochos," also on *Heliodor* 2549001. Out of print records are: Piano Concerto No. 2 (composer as pianist), *Decca* DL-9889. "Song of Songs" (1946), formerly *Columbia* ML-5451/MS-6123, now *CRI* S-284. Current exclusive publisher is Carl Fischer; publishers of earlier works have been Schirmer, Mercury, Southern, and Hargail.

Johan Franco (b. 1908, The Netherlands; U.S. citizen since 1942), occasional professional pianist. Recordings: "The Virgin Queen's Dream Monologue" (1947/1952) for dramatic soprano and orchestra, and "Fantasy" for cello and orchestra (1951), both on *CRI*-124; Symphony No. 5, "The Cosmos" (1958), *CRI*-135; "As the Prophets Foretold" (1955), cantata for soloists, mixed chorus, carillon, and brass (1955), *CRI*-222. Publishers: Presser (piano teaching pieces); Art Publication Society (Clayton Station, St. Louis, Missouri) (teaching pieces for piano); World Library Publications (choral). All other works are available in Composer Facsimile Edition at American Composers Alliance. Unpublished works are on deposit with American Music Center, Fleisher Collection, and American Composers Alliance.

Kenneth Gaburo (b. 1926), faculty, University of California at San Diego, La Jolla; Conductor, New Music Choral Ensemble. Recordings: "Line Studies" (1956), *Columbia* CML-5821/CMS-6421; two electronic music pieces, "Lemon Drops" (1965) and "For Harry" (1964), both on *Heliodor* (MGM) 25047; "Two" (1963), *Advance* No. 1; "Antiphony III (Pearl White Moments)" (1963), "Antiphony III (Poised)" (1967), "Exit Music I: The Wasting of Lucrecetzia" (1965), and "Exit Music II: Fat Millie's Lament" (1964), all four works on *Nonesuch* 71199, the first two conducted by the composer; two works on limited release recordings: "Psalm" and "Ave Maria" (1963 and 1957, respectively) on *Illinois Wesleyan Choral Recording Series,* Bloomington, Illinois. Publishers: Presser (chamber, orchestral); Carl Fischer (vocal, choral); World Library Publications (choral). Some unpublished works are on file at American Music Center.

Rudolph Ganz (b. 1877), President Emeritus and Professor Emeritus, Chicago Musical College of Roosevelt University. Recordings as pianist on *Welte Legacy of Piano Treasures* (see Recorded Treasures, Inc. under Record Companies) and *Veritas Records.* No recordings as composer except for a Ganz cadenza in a recording of the Haydn Piano Concerto in D, recorded for *Veritas.* Publishers: Carl Fischer (orchestral, piano concerto, piano solo); G. Schirmer (piano solo); Summy–Birchard; Edward B. Marks; Remick; Art Publication Society (Clayton Station, St. Louis, Missouri); Composers Press; Mills Music.

Edwin Gerschefski (b. 1909), retired Head, Music Department, University of Georgia, Athens (on the faculty). Recordings: "Saugatuck Suite" for orchestra, Op. 6, Nos. 2, 3, 4, 6 (1931), *CRI*-115; "Fanfare, Fugato, and Finale," Op. 24 (1937) for orchestra, *CRI*-228; "An Evening with Edwin Gerschefski," *Mark* UMC 2254. Publishers: Composers Facsimile Edition is principal publisher (orchestral, chamber, solo, piano, choral, vocal), Associated Music (choral, orchestral); Belwin (piano); Presser (Merion) (piano, choral, band); Witmark (band). Unpublished works and some tapes are deposited at American Music Center and American Composers Alliance; scores alone are in the Fleisher Collection.

Miriam Gideon (b. 1906), faculty, Manhattan School of Music and Jewish Theological Seminary. Recordings: "Lyric Piece for String Orchestra" (1941), *CRI*-170; "Symphonia Brevis" (1953), *CRI*-128; Piano Suite No. 3 (1951), *Victor* LSC-7042 (a collection called "New Music for Piano"); "Seasons of Time," *Desto* 7117. Out of print: "How Goodly Are Thy Tents" (1947), *Westminster* (collection: "Choral Masterworks of the Synagogue"); "Fantasy on a Javanese Motive" for cello and piano (1948), *Paradox* Records (collection: "New Music for Cello"). Publishers: New Music (Presser) (piano); Mercury (Presser) (two-piano music); Merrymount (Presser) (choral); Lawson–Gould (piano); E. B. Marks (piano); General Music (vocal chamber). Unpublished works are with Lincoln Center Library of the Performing Arts, Music Division (N.Y.), and the American Composers Alliance.

Peggy Glanville-Hicks (b. 1912, Australia; U.S. citizen since 1948). Recordings: "Nausicaa" (1961) (excerpts from the opera), *CRI*-175; Sonata for Harp, *Counterpoint/Esoteric* (*Everest*) 5523; "The Transposed Heads," opera (1954), *Louisville* 2-record set, 545-6. Out of print recordings: "Concertino da Camera," *Columbia* ML-4990; "Concerto Romantico," for viola and orchestra, *MGM* records; "Etruscan Concerto" (1956) for piano and orchestra, *MGM;* "Gymnopédie" Nos. 1, 2, and 3, *Remington* records and *MGM;* "Letters from Morocco," for tenor and orchestra, *MGM;* "Sinfonia da Pacifica," for orchestra (1956), *MGM;* Sonata for Piano and Percussion, *Columbia* ML-4990. (All of the foregoing dates are first performance dates; most works shown were performed in the year of composition.) Publishers: Associated Music (orchestral, concerted music, chamber, vocal, opera); C. F. Peters (orchestral, chamber, ballet music); Weintraub (through Music Sales Corp.) (chamber); Schott (through Associated) (chamber); Hargail (vocal); Colfrank (Franco Colombo) (opera). Unpublished works are on deposit with the Fleisher Collection and the Library of Congress.

Morton Gould (b. 1913), conductor, pianist. Recordings: "Fall River Legend," Ballet Suite for orchestra (1948), *Victor* LM/LSC-2532 (conducted by Gould), and on *Capitol* HDR-21004; "Interplay" for piano and orchestra (1944), with the composer as pianist and conductor, *Victor* LM/LSC-2532; "Latin American Symphonette" (1941), *Victor* LM/LSC-2532 (with composer as conductor), *Mercury* 90394, *Vanguard* 1103/2141, *Vanguard* S-275, *Victor* LM/LSC-2988, *Pickwick* S-4044; "Derivations" for clarinet and band (1957), *Columbia* MS-6805 (Gould conducting); "Spirituals" for orchestra (1940), *Victor* LSC-2850 (conducted by composer), *Everest* 3002; "West Point" Symphony No. 4 for Band (1952), *Mercury* 90220, and *Mark* MCBS 21360; "American Salute" for orchestra, *Columbia* ML-5874/MS-6474, *Victor* LM/LSC-2229; "Ballad" for band, *Mercury* 50079; "St. Lawrence Suite" for band, and "Jericho" for band, *Austin* 6016; "Night Watch," *Victor* LM/LSC-2542; "Venice, Vivaldi Gallery," *Victor* LSC-3079; "Formations," *Gallery Records* (609 Fifth Avenue, New York, N.Y. 10019); Marches: "Formations" (1964); "World War I: Revolutionary Prelude, Prologue"; "Santa

Fé Saga," "Battle Hymn of the Republic" (composer conducting) (for band), *Everest* 3253. Other recordings consist of excerpts from various works, arrangements, etc., and are found in collections recorded by bands and orchestras. Out of print records include "Jekyll and Hyde Variations," "Declaration Suite," "Dance Variations," all recorded for *Victor;* "Viola Concertette," *MGM* records; "World War I" incidental music: "Sarajevo Suite," "Wilson Suite," "Verdun Suite," etc., on *Victor* LM/LSC-2791; "Fall River Legend" on *Columbia* ML-4616 and *Mercury* MG-50263/SR-90263. Publishers: Chappell (exclusivc publisher at present); G. & C. (through Chappell), both for orchestral and band works, and works for miscellaneous ensembles; Mills Music (orchestral, band, two-piano works or arrangements, concertos, choral with orchestra, arrangements of popular music, spirituals, etc.); Carl Fischer (orchestral).

William Parks Grant (b. 1910), faculty, University of Mississippi, Oxford; author. Recordings: "Excursions" (1951), Opus 38, for two trumpets, horn, and trombone, *CRI*-222; Essay for Horn and Organ, *Coronet Records.* Publishers: Associated Music (vocal); J. Fisher (choral); Appleton-Century-Crofts (organ—two works published in "Method of Organ Playing" by Harold Gleason); Whitney Blake Publications (available from the Eastman School of Music) (orchestral, organ, chamber, vocal); Composer Facsimile Edition (the majority of the composer's works in all categories). Unpublished works are on file at American Music Center; Fleisher Collection; American Composers Alliance; Akademie für Musik, Vienna; Hebrew University, Jerusalem; Carl Venth Memorial Library at the University of Texas; Ohioana Library in Columbus, Ohio; New York Public Library; and the Free Library of Philadelphia. The composer is an active author and an editor of the music of Mahler.

Robert Arthur Gross (b. 1914), Chairman, Music Department, Occidental College, Los Angeles; active as concert violinist. Recording: "Epode" for solo cello (1955), *CRI*-208. Publisher: Composer Facsimile Editions (music of all categories). Unpublished works are located at American Music Center and the American Composers Alliance.

Gene Gutchë (b. 1907, Germany; U.S. resident since 1925). Recordings: Symphony No. 5, Opus 34 (1962), *CRI*-189; "Bongo Divertimento," Opus 35 (1962), *Saint Paul* (Arts and Science Center, 30th East 10th Street, St. Paul, Minnesota 55101) 96585/6 and S-06583/4. Exclusive and principal publisher is Galaxy Music (and its affiliates, Highgate and Galliard Limited). Unpublished works are located at American Music Center; Fleisher Collection; American Composers Alliance.

Edmund Haines (b. 1914), Chairman, Music Department, Sarah Lawrence College, Bronxville, N.Y. Recordings: Concertino for Seven Solo Instruments and Orchestra (1957), *CRI*-153; Quartet No. 4 for strings (1958), *CRI*-188; Toccata for Brass, *Golden Crest* CR-4023. Out of print: "Promenade, Air, and Toccata," on *Kendall Records.* Publishers: Carl Fischer (orchestral, choral); J. Fischer (organ); Music for Brass (Robert D. King) (brass ensemble); Alexander Broude (choral); Willis Music Co. (piano); Composer Facsimile Edition (in several categories). Unpublished works are filed with American Music Center and Fleisher Collection.

James Ray Hanna (b. 1922), faculty, University of Southwestern Louisiana, Lafayette. Publishers: Robert King Music (works for brass); Jack Spratt (woodwind); Music for Percussion (percussion); Carl Fischer (chamber orchestra).

Howard Hanson (b. 1896), conductor. Recordings (with the exception of the "Serenade" and "Chorale and Alleluia," all of the works following are conducted by Hanson): Symphony No. 2 ("Romantic") Opus 2 (1930), *Mercury* 90192; Symphony No. 3, Opus 33 (1937), *Mercury* 90449; "Mosaics" (1957), *Mercury* 90430; Suite from the Opera, "Merry Mount" (1937), *Mercury* 90423; "Songs from 'Drum Taps'" (after Whitman, for voices and orchestra—1935), *Mercury* 50073; Concerto for Piano and Orchestra (1948), *Mercury* 90430; Serenade for Flute,

Harp, and Strings (1946), *Epic* BC-1116, *Victor* VCM-6174, and *Victor* LM-2900; "Four Psalms" for baritone and string sextet, *Mercury* 90429; "Lament for Beowulf" (1925), for chorus and orchestra, *Mercury* 90192; "Chorale and Alleluia" for wind ensemble, Opus 42 (1954), *Mercury* 50084. Out of print recordings in recent years include: Symphony No. 1, "Nordic," Op. 21 (1923), *Mercury* 50165/90165; Symphony No. 4, Requiem, Op. 34 (1943), *Mercury* 50077; Symphony No. 5 "Sinfonia Sacra," Op. 43 (1955), *Mercury* 50087; "Song of Democracy" for chorus and orchestra, Op. 44 (1958), *Mercury* MG-50150/90150; Concerto for Organ, Harp, and Strings, Op. 2 (1941), *MGM Records;* "Elegy," Op. 44 (1955) for orchestra (composer conducting), *Mercury* MG-50150/90150; "Cherubic Hymn," Op. 37 (1950) for chorus and orchestra (composer conducting), *Mercury* MG-50087; "Fantasy Variations on a Theme of Youth," Op. 40 (1941) for piano and strings (composer conducting), *Mercury* MG-50114, and *Mercury* MG-50165/SR-90165; "For the First Time," for orchestra (1962), *Mercury* MG-50357/SR-90357 (composer as narrator and conductor); "March Carillon," for wind ensemble, *Mercury* MG-50080. Principal publisher is Carl Fischer. Others: J. Fischer; Summy–Birchard; Presser; Music Publishers Holding Corp. Unpublished works are in the Fleisher Collection.

Roy (Ellsworth Leroy) Harris (b. 1898), faculty, University of California, Los Angeles. Recordings: Symphony No. 1, *Columbia* CML-5095; "Symphony 1933," *Columbia* CML-5095; Symphony No. 3 (1938), *Columbia* ML-5703/MS-6303, *Mercury* 90421, and *Desto* 404/6404; Symphony No. 5 (1943), *Louisville* 655; Symphony No. 7 (1951), *Columbia* CML-5095; "Elegy and Dance" (1958) for orchestra, *CRI*-140; "Epilogue to Profile in Courage: J. F. K." (1964) for orchestra, *Louisville* 666; "Kentucky Spring" (1949), for orchestra, *Louisville* 602; Quintet for Piano and Strings (1936), *Contemporary* 6012/8012; Sonata for Violin and Piano (1941), *Contemporary* 6012/8012 and *Columbia* CML-4842; Trio (piano) 1934, *University of Oklahoma* #1; American Ballads, *Golden Crest* CRS-4411. Among out of print recordings: Symphony No. 4 (1940), *Vanguard* VRS-1064/VSD-2082. Publishers: G. Schirmer (piano solo, string orchestra, orchestral, piano and string quartet, string quartet, chorus and orchestra, chorus *a cappella,* piano and string orchestra); Associated Music (orchestral, voice with orchestra, chamber music, piano solo, organ with brass and timpani, voice with piano trio, piano with orchestra, clarinet and string quartet, etc.); Arrow (piano solo); Mills Music (orchestral, band, string quartet, flute with string quartet, piano with orchestra, organ with brass, piano, chorus with strings and two pianos); Carl Fischer (orchestral, choral, string orchestra, vocal, piano solo, two pianos and orchestra, accordion and orchestra, violin and orchestra, piano and orchestra); Harold Flammer (string orchestra); New Music Editions (Presser) (piano trio); Franco Colombo (orchestral).

Lou Harrison (b. 1917), faculty, San Jose State College. Recordings: "Canticle No. 1" for percussion (1940, *Time* 58000/8000; "Canticle No. 3" for percussion (1941), *Urania* 106/5106; "Four Strict Songs" for eight baritones and orchestra (1956), *Louisville* 582; Suite for Symphonic Strings, *Louisville* 621; Suite for Violin, Piano, and Small Orchestra (1951), *CRI*-114; Suite for Percussion, *CRI* S-252; Concerto for Violin and Percussion Orchestra, *Crystal* S-853; "Symphony on G" *CRI*-236; "Double Music for Percussion Quartet" (1941) (with John Cage) *Time* 58000/8000; "The Only Jealousy of Emer" (recitation of Yeat's poem with Harrison's music), *Counterpoint/Esoteric* ES-506; "Pacifika Rondo," Four Pieces for Harp, Two Pieces for Psaltery, Music for Violin with various instruments, all on *Desto* 6478. Out of print: "Song of Queztecoatl" for percussion orchestra, *Period* SPL-743/PRST 743; Mass for chorus, trumpet, harp and strings, *Epic* Records; Suite for Cello and Harp; Suite No. 2 for string quartet. Publishers: Peer (Southern) (orchestral, string orchestra, various chamber ensembles, vocal with instruments, opera, choral); C. F. Peters (orchestral, including transcriptions, string orchestra, chamber, choral with percussion, piano, violin with percussion orchestra, flute and percussion, choral, string trio); New Music Edition (Presser) (piano, orchestral); Merrymount (Presser) (string orchestra, string quartet); American Composers Alliance (orchestral, solo flute, chamber, piano solo); Associated Music (vocal with piano, violin with piano and small orchestra, vocal with orchestra, voice and piano); E. B. Marks (piano solo), Music for Percussion, Inc. (the "Canticles" shown under recordings and the "Song of Queztecoatl"). Unpublished scores are with American Music Center.

Walter S. Hartley (b. 1927), Chairman, Department of Music, Davis and Elkins College, Elkins, West Virginia; pianist. Recordings: Sonatina for Tuba and Piano (1957), *Mark Records* MRS-28437, coupled with Suite for Unaccompanied Tuba (1962); Two Pieces for Woodwind Quintet (1958), *Mark* MES-28486; Duo for Alto-Saxophone and Piano (1964), *Mark* MRS-22868; Divertissement for Brass Quintet (1965), *Mark* MES-32568; Sinfonia No. 4 for wind ensemble (1965), *Decca* 71063; Concerto for Alto-Saxophone and Band (1966), *Golden Crest* 4077; Poem for Tenor Saxophone, *Brewster* 1204; Caprice (1967), *Golden Crest* 7045. Out of print: Concerto for 32 Winds (1957), *Mercury* MG-50221/SR-90221. Publishers: Interlochen (main publisher) (orchestral, band, chamber, vocal, solo instrumental); Rochester Music Publishers, 358 Aldrich Road, Fairport, N.Y. 14450 (wind music); Tenuto (Presser) wind solo and ensemble); Elkan–Vogel (music for tuba); Ensemble Publications, Inc. (brass ensemble music); Galaxy (orchestral, chamber, and choral); MCA Music (wind ensemble and choral).

Charles Trowbridge Haubiel (b. 1892), Editor, founder of Composers Press; pianist, but no longer active as public performer. Recordings: "In the French Manner" for flute, cello, and piano (1942), *Dorian* 1007; "Pioneers" and "Portraits" (Capriccio–Idillio–Scherzo) for orchestra, both on *Dorian* 1008; "Three Portraits" for piano, *Dorian* 1006; "Solari," three pieces for piano, *Dorian* 1014; Sonata in C Minor for cello and piano (1944), *Dorian* 1009 (composer as pianist); "Gothic Variation" for violin and piano (1943) and "Nuances" for violin and piano, *Dorian* 1018 (composer as pianist). Each of the foregoing *Dorian* records is an anthology variously entitled "Contemporary American Piano Classics," "Contemporary American Cello Classics," etc. Publishers: Composers Press has published over 100 of the composer's compositions in all categories (see Southern Music, San Antonio) and thus is the principal publisher. Other publishers: J. Fischer (piano solo); Belwin (wind and brass ensemble music); Boston Music and H. W. Gray (choral); Henri Elkan (chamber music). Unpublished music is on deposit at American Music Center, Fleisher Collection, and the Ohioana Library Association, Columbus, Ohio.

Herbert Haufrecht (b. 1909), music arranger and editor. Recordings: "Square Set" for string orchestra (1941), *CRI*-111; Symphony for Brass and Timpani (1956), *CRI*-192; "Ferdinand the Bull" (1939), *ABC–Paramount* ABC-294 (composer conducting); recordings of music for children: "Peter Rabbit" (1948), *Harmony* (*Columbia*) HL-9527; the following recordings of music for children are on *Young Peoples Records* (100 Sixth Avenue, New York, N.Y. 10013): "Little Hawk" (1952), *YPR* 10518; "A Walk in the Forest" (1951), *YPR* 10013; "Robin Hood" (1952), *YPR* 45X-1010-11; "Whoa, Little Horses, Lie Down" (1950), *YPR* 714; "The Little Cowgirl" (1951), *YPR* 801. Publishers: Associated (orchestral, chamber music, piano solo); MCA (orchestral, band, vocal); Broude (Rongwen) (chamber, vocal); Bourne Music (Murbo) (wind ensemble, chamber); Boosey & Hawkes (brass ensemble); Peer International (choral, guitar); Presser (Merion) (instructional piano pieces); Franco Colombo (choral). Unpublished works are placed with American Music Center, Fleisher Collection, and American Composers Alliance.

Bernhard Heiden (b. 1910, Germany; U.S. citizen), faculty, Indiana University. Recordings: Sonata for Horn and Piano (1939), *Grand Award* 33-704; Sonata for Saxophone and Piano (1937), *Grand Award* 33-708 and *Mark* 22868; Sinfonia for Woodwind Quintet (1949), *Now Records* 9632 (Now Records, 3730

University, Muncie, Indiana); Five Short Pieces for Flute and Piano (1933), *Golden Crest* 7023. Principal publisher is Associated Music (vocal, orchestral, chamber). Other publishers: Alexander Broude (vocal, chamber, orchestral, opera); World Library (vocal). Unpublished works are in the Fleisher Collection and with the firm of Alexander Broude.

Robert Eugene Helps (b. 1928), pianist. Recordings: Symphony No. 1 (1955), *Columbia* MS-6801; "Image" (1957), short piano piece in a 2-record set called, "New Music for Piano," which represents a complete recording of the works found in the publication of the same name (containing music by 23 other composers) published by Lawson–Gould, *Victor* LSC-7042; entire recording played by Helps; "Portrait," *Desto* 7110. Publishers: C. F. Peters (principal publisher, works for piano solo and piano four-hands); E. B. Marks (publisher of Symphony No. 1); Lawson–Gould (see recording above). Unpublished works placed at American Music Center.

Lejaren Arthur Hiller, Jr. (b. 1924), faculty, University of Illinois, Urbana; State University of New York, Buffalo. Recordings: "Illiac Suite" for string quartet (1957), *Heliodor* HS-25053, coupled with "Computer Cantata" (1963); "Machine Music" for piano, percussion, and tape (1964), *Heliodor* HS-25047; "Algorithms I" (Versions I and IV) (1968), *Deutsche Grammophon* 2543005; "Avalanche," (for pitchman, prima donna, player piano, percussion, and tape), Suite for Two Pianos and Tape (1966), and Computer Music for Tape and Percussion, all on *Heliodor* 2549006. Principal publisher is Theodore Presser (New Music Edition); other publisher is C. F. Peters.

Lee Hoiby (b. 1926), pianist. Recordings: "Beatrice" (1959), opera in three acts, *Louisville* 2-record set 603; Piano Concerto (1957), *CRI*-214; "After Eden," *Desto* 6434. Publishers: G. Schirmer (vocal, instrumental, choral, chamber, operatic); Franco Colombo (choral); Boosey & Hawkes (orchestral, vocal, instrumental, operatic); Theodore Presser (choral, piano/organ).

Paul Wilson Holmes (b. 1923), faculty, Lamar State College of Technology, Beaumont, Texas. Recording: "Lento" for tuba and piano, *Coronet* 1259 (Coronet Recording Co., 375 East Broad, Columbus, Ohio 43215). Publishers: Shawnee Press (principal publisher); Summy–Birchard.

Alan Hovhaness (b. 1911). Recordings: Concerto No. 2 for violin and orchestra, coupled with "Lousadzak" for piano and strings, Op. 48 (1944), *Heliodor* 25040; Concerto No. 7 for Orchestra, Op. 116 (1953), *Louisville* 5454; Duet for Violin and Harpsichord (1954), *CRI*-109; "Fantasy on Japanese Woodprints" (1965), *Columbia* CL-2581/CS-9381; "Floating World-Ukiyo" for orchestra, *Columbia* MS-7162; "Khaldis," Concerto for piano, four trumpets, and percussion, Op. 91 (1951), *Heliodor* 25027; "Koke no niwa" ("Moss Garden"), Op. 181 (1960), *CRI*-186 (composer conducting); "Lousadzak" ("Coming of Light") for piano and strings, *Folkways* 3369 (composer as conductor); Magnificat, Op. 157 (1959), *Louisville* 614; "Meditation on Orpheus" (1957) for orchestra, *CRI*-134; "Mysterious Mountain," Op. 132, for orchestra, *Victor* LSC-2251; "October Mountain," for percussion, *Urania* 134/5134; Prelude and Quadruple Fugue, Op. 128 for orchestra, *Mercury* 90423; "Sharagan and Fugue" for brass ensemble, Op. 58, *Desto* 6401; Symphony No. 15 "Silver Pilgrimage," for orchestra, *Louisville* 662; Sonata for Solo Flute, Op. 118 (1964), *CRI* 212; Suite for Violin, Piano and Percussion, and "Upon Enchanted Ground" (1951), *Columbia* ML-5179; Symphony No. 4, Op. 165 for wind band, *Mercury* 50366/90366; Symphony No. 11, "All Men Are Brothers," *Poseidon* 1001; Symphony for Metal Orchestra (No. 17), *Mark* 1112; "Symphony Etchmiadzin," *Poseidon* 1004; Tryptych: "Ave Maria" (1956), "Christmas Ode" (1952), and "Easter Cantata" (1953), *CRI*-221; "In the Beginning Was the Word," oratorio, recorded for special event by *Methodist Student Movement* (q.v. under record company listings); Fantasy for Piano, Op. 16, *Poseidon* 2; "Fra Angelico," *Orion* 7268 and *Poseidon* 1002 (composer conducting); "And God Created Great Whales," *Columbia* M-30390;

"Holy City," *CRI* S-259; "Lady of Light," *Poseidon* 1006 (composer conducting); "Return and Rebuild the Desolate Places," *Mace* S-9099; Sonata for Trumpet and Organ, *Redwood* ES-2; Songs, *Poseidon* 1005. Out of print recordings (partial list): "Alleluia and Fugue," Op. 40B (1941), for string orchestra, *MGM* 3504; "Armenian Rhapsody," No. 2 Op. 51 coupled with "Celestial Fantasy," Op. 44 (1944), for string orchestra *MGM* E 3517; Concerto No. 1 ("Arevakal") for orchestra, Op. 88, *Mercury* 40005; "Saint Vartan" Symphony No. 9, Op. 180, *MGM* records; "Talin," Op. 93, concerto for viola and strings, *MGM* 3432; "Tzaikerk," Op. 53 (1945) for violin, flute, timpani, and strings, *Dial* Records 6, coupled with "Lousadzak," Op. 48; "The Flowering Peach," Op. 125, *MGM* 3164; piano music; "Mountain Idylls," "Slumber Song," "Siris Dance," all part of Op. 52 and recorded by *MGM*. Principal publisher by far is C. F. Peters. Other publishers: Associated Music (orchestral, choral, chamber, piano); Summy–Birchard (choral); E. B. Marks (choral); Edwin H. Morris (piano solo); Leeds (through MCA Music) (orchestral, piano solo); Lawson–Gould (piano solo); Mills (chamber); Peer International (Southern) (orchestral, chamber, piano solo); Robert King Music (orchestral, chamber music for brass); Rongwen (Broude Brothers) (orchestral, chamber).

Karel Husa (b. 1921, Czechoslovakia; U.S. citizen since 1959), faculty, Cornell University; conductor. Recordings: "Fantasies" for Orchestra (1957), recorded by *Cornell University* (number: N80P) and available through Cornell University Press, Ithaca, N.Y. 14850; "Mosaïques" for orchestra (1961), *CRI*-221 (both works conducted by the composer); Concerto for Saxophone, *Brewster* 1203; Quartets Nos. 2 (1959) and 3 (1968), *Everest* 3290; Symphony No. 1, Serenade for Woodwind Quintet with Strings, Harp and Xylophone; Fantasies for Orchestra, Nocturne, all on *CRI* S-261 (conducted by the composer). Principal publisher in B. Schott's Söhne of Mainz, Germany (available through Associated Music) (orchestral, chamber); Alphonse Leduc, Paris (orchestral, chamber, solo instrumental) (see Baron under Publishers); Galaxy (chorus and orchestra); Artia, Prague (Boosey & Hawkes) (instrumental music); some edited works of Lully published by Peters and Bärenreiter. Unpublished works with American Music Center; Fleisher Collection; Cornell University Music Library.

Andrew W. Imbrie (b. 1921), faculty, University of California, Berkeley. Recordings: Concerto for Violin and Orchestra (1954), *Columbia* CML-5997/CMS-6597; "Legend" for Orchestra (1959), *CRI*-152; String Quartet No. 1 (1942), *Columbia* CML-4844; String Quartets Nos. 2 and 3 (1953 and 1957), *Contemporary* 6003/7022; Sonata for Piano (1947), *Fantasy* 5009. Principal publisher is Malcolm Music, Ltd. (through Shawnee Press) (orchestral, chamber, choral, vocal); C. F. Peters (choral, opera); New Valley Music Press (piano solo).

Jean Eichelberger Ivey (b. 1923), summer faculty, Peabody Conservatory of Music; pianist. Recording: "Pinball" (1965), *Folkways* 33436 (collection entitled "Electronic Music") from a master tape created by the composer. Publishers: Lee Roberts (through G. Schirmer) (piano solo); McLaughlin & Reilly (piano, choral); Summy–Birchard (piano work in a collection called "Contemporary Collection 2"). Unpublished pieces on deposit at American Music Center.

Lockrem Harold Johnson (b. 1924). Publishers: Mercury Music (Presser) (piano); Dow Publishers (Box 176, Oyster Bay, N.Y.) (chamber, choral, vocal). Unpublished music on file at American Music Center; Fleisher Collection.

Benjamin Burwell Johnston, Jr. (b. 1926), faculty, University of Illinois, Urbana. Recordings: Duo for Flute and String Bass (1963), *Advance* 1; "Casta Bertram," *Nonesuch* 71237; "Ci-Git Satie" (1966), *Ars Nova* 1005; String Quartet No. 2, *Nonesuch* 71224. Out of print: "Dirge" for Piano and Percussion, *University of Illinois Custom Recordings*. Publishers: Josef Marx (see McGinnis & Marx) (chamber music); Composer-Performer Editions ("action" pieces, orchestral music). Unpublished works are on file at American Music Center.

Ulysses Kay (b. 1917), faculty, Herbert H. Lehman College of the City University of New York. Recordings: Brass Quartet (1950), *Folkways* 3651; Sinfonia in E (1950) for orchestra, *CRI*-139; two works for chamber singers: "What's in a Name?" (1954) and "How Stands the Glass Around?" *CRI*-102; Round Dance and Polka (1954) for orchestra, *CRI*-119; Serenade for Orchestra (1954), *Louisville* 5488; Fantasy Variations for Orchestra (1963), *CRI*-209/SD-209; "Choral Triptych" (1962), *Cambridge* 416/1416; "Umbrian Scene" (1964) for orchestra, *Louisville* 651; Short Overture (1947), *Desto* 7107. Out of print: Concerto for Orchestra (1948), *Remington* records. Publishers: MCA Music is principal publisher (orchestral, choral, chamber, instrumental, etc.). Other publishers: Associated Music (orchestral, choral, band); H. W. Gray (choral and organ); Franco Colombo (piano); C. F. Peters (orchestral, choral); Peer International (Southern) (choral, chamber).

Homer Keller (b. 1915), faculty, University of Oregon, Eugene; director of University Electronic Studio; summer faculty, National Music Camp. Recordings: Symphony No. 3 (1956), *CRI*-134. Out of print: Serenade for clarinet and strings, *Mercury* records. Publishers: Composer Facsimile Edition (American Composers Alliance) (orchestral, chamber music); Associated Music (instrumental); Carl Fischer (orchestral, instrumental). Unpublished works with American Composers Alliance.

Robert Kelly (b. 1916), faculty, University of Illinois, Urbana. Recordings: Symphony No. 2 (1958), *CRI*-132; "Patterns" for Soprano and Orchestra, *CRS*-4; Toccata for Marimba and Percussion, *CRS*-6 (*CRS:* University of Illinois *Custom Recording Series,* School of Music, University of Illinois, Urbana, Illinois 61801). Publishers: Highgate Press (Galaxy), Composer Facsimile Edition; Theodore Presser (trumpet and piano).

Kent Wheeler Kennan (b. 1913), faculty, University of Texas, Austin. Recordings: "Night Soliloquy" for flute and strings (1938), *Coronet* S-1724; Sonata for Trumpet and Piano, *Golden Crest* S-7042. Out of print: "Night Soliloquy" on *Mercury* MG-50299/SR/90299, and *Award Artists* 33-706; Three Pieces for Orchestra (1939), *Mercury;* Two Preludes for Piano (1951), *Victor.* Publishers: G. Schirmer (piano, chamber); Carl Fischer (orchestral, wind ensemble, choral); H. W. Gray (choral); Remick (chamber); Lawson–Gould (piano). Unpublished works are on deposit with the Fleisher Collection.

Harrison Kerr (b. 1897), Professor Emeritus of Music, University of Oklahoma. Recordings: Trio for Violin, Cello, and Piano (1938), *University Recordings* (see University of Oklahoma under Record Companies); Concerto for Violin and Orchestra (1951), *CRI*-142; "Sinfonietta da Camera" (1968) and Sonata for Violin and Piano (1955), *Century* 31380. Out of print: Trio for Clarinet, Cello, and Piano (1936), *New Music Recordings.* Publishers: Arrow Music Press (Boosey & Hawkes) (orchestral, piano, chamber); Merion Music (chamber); E. B. Marks (songs). Unpublished works are filed with Fleisher Collection and American Composers Alliance.

Nelson Keyes (b. 1928), faculty, University of Louisville, Kentucky. Recordings: "Music for Monday Evenings," Suite for Orchestra (1959), *Louisville* 631; "Abysses, Bridges, Chasms," *Louisville* S-712. Publisher is Elkan–Vogel (choral, band, etc.). Unpublished works are in Music Library, University of Louisville.

Leon Kirchner (b. 1919), faculty, Harvard University; pianist; occasional conductor. Recordings: Toccata for Strings, Winds, and Percussion (1956), *Louisville* 683; Quartet for Strings No. 1 (1949), *Columbia* CML-4843; Quartet No. 3 for Strings and Electronic Tape, *Columbia* MS-7284; Sonata for Piano, *Educo* 3081, Duo for Violin and Piano (1947), *Medea* 1002; Piano Concerto No. 1 (1953), *Columbia* CML-5185. Out of print: Concerto for Violin, Cello, 10 Winds, and Percussion (1960), *Epic* LC 3830 (composer conducting); Trio for Violin, Cello, and Piano (1954), Sonata Concertante for Violin and Piano (1952), both on *Epic* LC 3306. Publishers:

Associated Music (orchestral, chamber); Bomart (Boelke–Bomart) (piano solo); Mercury (orchestral, chamber, piano solo).

Ellis Bonoff Kohs (b. 1916), faculty, University of Southern California, Los Angeles; music administrator; author. Recordings: Chamber Concerto for Viola and String Nonet (or string orchestra) (1949), *Music Library Recording* 7004; "Psalm 23," (1958) *CRI*-191; "A Short Concert" for string quartet (1948), *CRI*-176; Symphony No. 1 (1950), *CRI*-104. Out of print: Chamber Concerto for Viola and String Nonet, *Columbia Records*. American Composers Alliance has published most of the composer's works (in most categories). Other publishers: Associated Music (orchestral, band); Cameo Music (1527½ North Vine Street, Los Angeles, California 90028) (chamber, piano); H. W. Gray (orchestral, organ); Merion (piano solo); Merrymount (orchestral, chamber, choral, keyboard); M. M. Cole (percussion and piano). Unpublished works (and recordings) are deposited at American Music Center; works are also in the Fleisher Collection, American Composers Alliance, Music Library of the University of Southern California, and the Music Library of Washington University in St. Louis.

Peter Jona Korn (b. 1922, Germany; U.S. citizen), Director, Richard–Strauss–Konservatorium der Stadt München in Munich, Germany. Recordings: Concertino for Horn and Double String Orchestra, Op. 15 (1952), and "In Medias Res," overture for orchestra, Op. 22 (1953), both on *Westminster* 17131; Variations on a Tune from "The Beggar's Opera," for orchestra, Op. 26 (1955), *Louisville* 58-2. Major publisher is N. Simrock of Hamburg, Germany (through Boosey & Hawkes by special arrangement) (orchestral, chamber, piano, vocal); Boosey & Hawkes itself is principal publisher (orchestral, chamber, vocal, piano, choral). Other publishers: Mercury (choral); Mills Music (orchestral); Bote & Bock, Berlin (opera); Carl Fischer. Unpublished pieces are in the Fleisher Collection.

Ernst Krenek (b. 1900, Austria; U.S. citizen). Recordings: Music for String Orchestra (1943), *Music Library* 7029; "Eleven Transparencies" for orchestra, Op. 142, *Louisville* 563; "Pentagram" for wind quintet (1957), *Lyrichord* S-158; "Lamentatio Jeremiae Prophetae," Op. 93 for mixed chorus *a cappella*, 2-record set *Bärenreiter–Musicaphon* BM-L-1303/4 (Heinrich–Schütz–Allee, Kassel/Wilhelmshöhe, Germany); Piano Sonata No. 3 (1943), *SPA*-4 (composer as pianist); Piano Sonata No. 4 (1948), and Four Bagatelles (1931) for piano 4-hands, *Music Library* 7014 (composer as one of the pianists); Piano Sonata No. 5 (1950), and Sonata for Violin and Piano (1948); *Music Library* 7029; "Monologue" for clarinet (1956), *Advance*-4; Organ Sonata (1941), *University of Oklahoma Recordings* No. 2; "Zwei geistliche Gesänge" (Two Sacred Songs) for soprano and piano, *Bärenreiter–Musicaphon* BM-30-L-1530; "Jonny spielt auf," opera (1927), *Mace* S-9094; "Sechs Vermessene," *Candide* 31015; Music for String Orchestra, *Music Library* 7029; Seasons, Op. 35, *Austin* 6224. Out of print: "Sestina" for solo soprano and chamber ensemble, *Epic* LC-3509 (Krenek conducting), "Lamentations of Jeremiah" ("Lamentatio Jeremiae Prophetae"), *Epic* LC-3509; Piano Sonata No. 3, *Columbia* ML-5336. Publishers: Universal Edition, Vienna (Presser) is a major publisher of the composer's works (orchestral including concerted works, voice with orchestra or chamber instrumental ensemble, winds with percussion, string orchestra, orchestral transcriptions, stage works including operas, ballet scores, scenic cantatas, etc., woodwind quintet, violin with piano, string quartets, various chamber works, piano solo including transcriptions and completion of Schubert's unfinished piano sonata D.840, choral with orchestra, songs and other vocal works with piano or other instrumental accompaniment or electronic songs). Universal Edition and Schott, Mainz, have jointly published some works (women's choral with orchestra, cello with chamber orchestra, violin concerto, chorus and string orchestra, orchestral, opera, songs). Bärenreiter–Verlag (see address above) is another important publisher of the composer's music (operas, orchestral including concerted music, chamber orchestra, woodwind quintet, voice with piano or solo instrument or orchestra, choral, two pianos 4-hands, piano solo, harp solo, string quartet and piano, and various chamber groups). Other publishers are: Rongwen (Broude Brothers) (clarinet and string orchestra, flute and string orchestra, orchestral, clarinet solo, oboe solo, various chamber groups, piano solo, works for children's choir); Boelke–Bomart (Associated Music) (piano solo, viola solo); Elkan–Vogel (string orchestra); G. Schirmer (piano solo); Doblinger Verlag (Associated Music) (guitar); E. B. Marks (violin, piano with orchestra, song); Peer (Southern) (piano solo).

Arthur R. Kreutz (b. 1906), faculty, University of Mississippi. Recordings: "Dance Concerto" for clarinet and orchestra, *Microfon Records,* Milan, Italy; "Scenes from Hamlet" and "Jazzonata"—both recorded on *University of Mississippi Recording.* Publishers: G. Ricordi (opera); Franco Colombo (opera); G. Schirmer (orchestral); Mercury (instrumental); Associated Music (vocal); World Library (choral). Unpublished works are filed with American Music Center, Fleisher Collection, and the Library of the University of Mississippi.

Gail Kubik (b. 1914), faculty, Scripps College, Claremont, California; conductor, lecturer. Recordings: Symphony No. 2 (1956), *Louisville* 58-5; Symphony Concertante (1952), *CRI* S-267; Sonata for Piano, and "Celebrations and Epilogue," for piano, *Contemporary* 6006/8006; American folk song, "Soon One Morning," *Victor* (Robert Shaw Chorale collection); Divertimento No. 1 for 13 players, Divertimento No. 2 for 8 players (conducted by the composer), Sonatina for clarinet and piano, and Sonatina for piano, all recorded on *Contemporary* 8013/6013; Choral Scherzo on a Well-known Tune: "Oh Dear What Can the Matter Be?" *Capitol* records (in a collection recorded by Roger Wagner Chorale). Out of print: Symphony Concertante for trumpet, viola, piano, and orchestra, *Victor* LM-2426 (conducted by Kubik); "Bennie the Beaver," a children's tale for narrator, percussion soloist, and nine instruments, *Columbia Records* (composer conducting). Publishers: MCA (the composer is under exclusive contract with the firm until 1973) (choral, orchestral, band, instrumental solo); Franco Colombo (choral, orchestral); Chappell (vocal, instrumental solo, orchestral, opera); Southern Music Publishing (choral, instrumental solo, orchestral, band, vocal); G. Schirmer (choral); H. W. Gray (choral, organ); Boosey & Hawkes (choral); Paramount (see Famous) (orchestral film scores). Unpublished works are in the Fleisher Collection and with MCA Music.

Meyer Kupferman (b. 1926), faculty, Sarah Lawrence College; clarinetist, conductor. Recordings: Symphony No. 4 (1956), *Louisville* 58-4; "Hallelujah the Hills," *Fontana Records* (see *Mercury*); "Lyric Symphony" (1956), Variations for Orchestra (1959), and "Ostinato Burlesco" for orchestra (1954), all on *Serenus* 1000/12000; Chamber Symphony (1950), Divertimento for Orchestra (1948), and Variations for solo piano (1948), on *Serenus* 1017/12017; "Sonata on Jazz Elements," for piano (1958), "Little Sonata," for piano (1948), and String Quartet No. 4 (1958), on *Serenus* 1001/12001; "Infinities Twenty-Two," for trumpet and piano, on *Serenus* records; "Evocation," for Cello and Piano (1952), *Opus One* 6; "Libretto" for Orchestra, and Concerto for Cello and Jazz Band, *Serenus* 12025; "Three Ideas," *Golden Crest* 7045. Recorded but not yet released: "Infinities Twelve," for nine instruments; "Infinities Jazz Concerto," for cello, three saxophones, woodwinds, and string bass; and Sonata for Two Pianos. Out of print: "Little Symphony," *Vanguard* records. Principal publisher is General Music Publishing; others: Mercury, Weintraub, and Sam Fox.

Ezra Laderman (b. 1924), faculty, State University of New York at Binghamton; President, American Music Center. Recordings: "Magic Prison," for two narrators and orchestra, *Louisville* S-712; String Quartet (1959), *CRI* 126; Quartet No. 2, *CRI* S-244; Theme Variations and Finale (1957), *CRI* 130; Duo for Violin and Piano, *Desto* 7125; Sonata for Flute and Piano, *Desto* 7104; "Songs for Eve," and "From the Psalms," *Desto* 7105. Principal publisher is Oxford University Press. Some unpublished works with the American Music Center and on rental from Oxford.

John La Montaine (b. 1920), pianist. Recordings: Concerto for Piano and Orchestra, Opus 9, *CRI* S-189 and *CRI*-166; "Birds of Paradise," for piano and orchestra, Opus 34, *Mercury* 90430 (composer as pianist); "Even Song," for organ (in an organ collection), *Wicks* S-V1S4 (see Organ Manufacturers: Wicks). Out of print: "Songs of the Rose of Sharon," Opus 6, for soprano and orchestra, *Stand Records* 420/7420; "Stopping by Woods on a Snowy Evening," *Stand Records* 411/2 (song collection album); Piano Sonata, Opus 3, "A Child's Picture Book," Opus 7, and Toccata for Piano, Opus 1, all on *Dorian Records* with composer as pianist. Principal publisher is Paul J. Sifler, 3947 Fredonia Drive, Hollywood, California 90028 (songs, piano solo, choral, orchestral, operas, song cycles with orchestra). Other publishers: G. Schirmer (orchestral, Christmas opera, piano, chamber); Galaxy (concerto for piano, songs); Carl Fischer (solo piano, piano and orchestra), Summy–Birchard (choral, piano-teaching pieces); H. W. Gray (organ works, choral, songs), Broude Brothers (piano, flute, voice with orchestra); Elkan–Vogel (cello, piano 4-hands); Oxford University Press (piano). Unpublished works are in the Fleisher Collection.

Richard Bamford Lane (b. 1933), pianist, accompanist. Out of print recording: Four Songs, for voice and orchestra, *Mercury* MG-50150/90150. Publishers: Boosey & Hawkes (chamber); Mills Music (choral); Carl Fischer (choral, instrumental, chamber, piano solo); CMP (Contemporary Music Project) (orchestral, choral, chamber). Unpublished works are filed with American Music Center and Contemporary Music Project. (CMP Library Editions available from University Microfilms, Ann Arbor, Michigan).

William Peters Latham (b. 1917), faculty, North Texas State University. Recordings: Three Chorale Preludes, for band (1956), *Austin Records* 6104; "Court Festival," for band (1957), *Austin* 6164; other limited edition recordings include works for band and choral work on labels issued by Summy–Birchard (publishers), Franco Colombo (the publisher's Educational Record Reference Library), *UCLA Concert Band Records* (serial number 20464), *University of Arkansas Schola Cantorum* (number CO763A), *University of Illinois Concert Band* (record number 24), and others. Publishers: Summy–Birchard (band, choral); Presser (chamber, choral); Carl Fischer (choral); Pro-Art Publications, Inc. (choral); Shawnee Press (band, choral); C. L. Barnhouse Company (110 B Avenue, East, Oskaloosa, Iowa 52577) (band), Jack Spratt (chamber, choral). Unpublished works are located in the Music Section, Main Library of North Texas State University.

Billy Jim Layton (b. 1924), Chairman, Department of Music, State University of New York at Stony Brook. Recordings: String Quartet in Two Movements, Opus 4 (1956), *CRI*-136; Five Studies for Violin and Piano, Opus 1, and Three Studies for Piano, Opus 5, *CRI* S-257. Exclusive publisher is G. Schirmer. Unpublished music is in the library of American Music Center.

Dai Keong Lee (b. 1915), Recordings: "Polynesian Suite" (1959), and Symphony No. 1 (1947), *CRI*-195. Publishers: G. Schirmer (instrumental); Mills Music (instrumental, band, orchestra); Chappell (vocal and orchestral); Boosey & Hawkes (instrumental).

Benjamin Lees (b. 1924). Recordings: "Prologue, Capriccio and Epilogue," for Orchestra (1958), *CRI*-140; Symphony No. 2 (1958), *Louisville* 595; Concerto for Orchestra (1959), *Louisville* S-665; Concerto for String Quartet and Orchestra (1964) *Victor* LSC-3095. Out of print: String Quartet No. 1 (1952), *Epic;* String Quartet No. 2 (1956), *Liberty Records.* Principal publisher is Boosey & Hawkes. Other publishers: Weintraub (Music Sales Corp.) (orchestral); Templeton (Shawnee Press) (piano solo). Unpublished pieces are with the firm of Boosey & Hawkes.

John Ayres Lessard (b. 1920), faculty, State University of New York at Stony Brook. Recordings: Concerto for Winds and Strings (1951), *CRI*-122; Sonata for Cello and Piano (1954), *CRI*-208; Octet for Winds (1953) and

Partita for Wind Quintet (1952), *Serenus Records* 1008/12008; Toccata for harpsichord (1955), *Decca* 10021/710021. Sinfonietta Concertante, Quodlibets for Two Trumpets and Trombone, and "Fragments from the Cantos of Ezra Pound," all on *Serenus* 12026. Principal publisher in all categories is General Music Publishing. Other publishers: Mercury (vocal, piano); Peer International (vocal). Unpublished works are on deposit with American Composers Alliance.

Merrills Lewis (b. 1908), faculty, University of Houston; choral director; Minister of Music, First Christian Church, Houston. Publishers: J. Fischer and Bro. (choral); Galaxy (choral, vocal); H. W. Gray (works for chorus and orchestra); Harold Flammer (works for chorus and orchestra). Unpublished music in the Fleisher Collection and the library of American Composers Alliance.

Normand Lockwood (b. 1906), faculty, University of Denver. Recording: "Praise the Lord" for chorus (1957), *Columbia* ML-6019. Among publishers: American Composers Alliance (orchestral, band, choral with soloists and orchestra, chorus *a cappella,* violin and piano, violin and instrumental accompaniment, various chamber ensembles, piano solo, opera); Associated Music (chorus with orchestra, chorus with piano, chorus *a cappella,* violin and piano, organ and brass); Augsburg (choral); Broude Brothers (chorus and band, chorus and orchestra); C. F. Peters (chorus *a cappella*); H. W. Gray (chorus with organ); Presser (as well as Merrymount and Mercury) (choral, chorus with flute and piano, violin and piano, piano solo, chamber); Westwood (choral); World Library (choral and instrumental).

Nikolai Lopatnikoff (b. 1903, Estonia; U.S. citizen), faculty, Carnegie–Mellon University, Pittsburgh. Recordings: Music for Orchestra, Op. 39 (1958), *Louisville* 596; "Variazioni Concertanti" for orchestra, *Louisville* S-654. Out of print: Concertino for Orchestra, Op. 30, *Columbia* ML-4996; "Variations and Epilogue" for cello and piano, *Columbia* ML-4990. Among publishers: Associated Music (violin concerto, orchestral works, works for two pianos and piano solo); Schott's Söhne (through Associated) (piano concerto, orchestra, violin and piano, piano solo); Leeds (MCA) (orchestral, two pianos and orchestra); C. F. Peters (Henmar) (wind ensemble, orchestral); Boosey & Hawkes (orchestral).

Otto Luening (b. 1900), former Chairman (now retired), Music Department, Columbia University. Recordings: Symphonic Fantasia No. 1 (1924) for orchestra, and "Kentucky Rondo" (1951), *CRI*-103; Two Symphonic Interludes (1935), and "Prelude to a Hymn Tune by William Billings," for piano and small orchestra (1937), *Desto* 429/6429; Fantasia for Organ (1929) and "Synthesis" for electronic sound and orchestra (1963), *CRI*-S-219; "Poem in Cycles and Bells" (1954) with Vladimir Ussachevsky), and "Music for King Lear" (1956 with Ussachevsky), *CRI*-112 ("Poem" is conducted by Luening); "Gargoyles" for Violin Solo and Electronic Sound (1961), *Columbia* MS-6566; "Rhapsodic Variations for Tape Recorder and Orchestra" 1954 with Ussachevsky), *Louisville* 5455; "Concerted Piece for Tape Recorder and Orchestra" (1960 with Ussachevsky), *CRI*-S-227; "Fantasy in Space" (1952), *Folkways* 6160 (in album entitled "Sounds of New Music"). Recordings not available through normal commercial record channels: "Fantasy in Space" (1952), Silver–Burdett Primary School Series, "Making Music Your Own" (see Publishers); "Moonflight" (1967), McGraw–Hill Secondary School Educational Series. Out of print recordings: "Andante and Variations" for violin and piano (1951), *Remington Records;* "Carlsbad Caverns" (1956), a sequence from "Wide, Wide World" television series, for orchestra, recorded by *Victor.* Recordings formerly out of print reissued on *Desto* 6466: "Invention in Twelve Tones (1952), "Low Speed" (1952), "Fantasy in Space" (1952), and "Incantations" (1955 with Ussachevsky)—all formerly recorded by *Innovation Records.* Recordings not yet released: "Legend" for Oboe and Strings, (1951), *Desto;* "Lyric Scene" for Flute and Strings (1958). Publishers: C. F. Peters (chamber music, solo instrumental, choral, orchestral and electronic); Merion Music (piano, choral); Pietro

Deiro (accordion); Presser (orchestral); Associated Music (chamber, vocal); Highgate Press (solo instrumental, choral, chamber, orchestral, electronic). Unpublished works are on file with American Music Center, Fleisher Collection, and American Composers Alliance.

Ray E. Luke (b. 1928), faculty, Oklahoma City University School of Music; Associate Conductor, Oklahoma City Symphony. Recordings: Symphony No. 2 (1961), *Louisville* S-634. Principal publisher is Oxford University Press (orchestral works). Unpublished works in Fleisher Collection.

Donald Lybbert (b. 1923), Chairman, Department of Music, Hunter College, New York. Recording: "Lines for the Fallen" (1967) for soprano and two pianos, *Odyssey* (Columbia) 32160161/32160162. Publishers: C. F. Peters (principal publisher) (chamber music); Mercury (vocal).

Donald James Martino (b. 1931), faculty, Yale University. Recordings: "Quodlibets" for flute (1954), *CRI*-212; "Cinque frammenti" for oboe and string bass (1961), *Advance* No. 1; "A Set for Clarinet" (1954), *Advance* No. 4; Concerto for Wind Quintet (1964), *CRI*-S-230; "Fantasy Variations" for Violin (1962), *Advance;* Trio for Violin, Clarinet, and Piano (1959), *CRI* 240. Publishers: McGinnis & Marx (woodwind solo and duo music); Apogee (woodwind solo); E. C. Schirmer and Ione Press (principal publishers) (vocal, choral, orchestra, chamber). Unpublished music is at American Music Center and American Composers Alliance.

Salvatore John Martirano (b. 1927), faculty, University of Illinois, Urbana. Recordings: "O,O,O,O That Shakespeherian Rag" (1958), *CRI*-164; "Cocktail Music" for piano (1962), *Advance* 3 (in album called "David Burge Plays New Piano Music"); "Underworld" (1965), *Heliodor* 25047 (album "Electronic Music from University of Illinois"); "L's GA"; "Ballad," and Octet, *Polydor* 245001. Publishers: Schott & Co., Ltd. of London (see Associated Music) (orchestral, choral, vocal, chamber music); MCA Music (chamber, music for theater, and vocal music).

William Mayer (b. 1925), writer on music for U.S.I.A., Chairman, Editorial Board, Composers Recordings, Inc. Recordings: "Overture for an American" (1958) for orchestra, "Essay" for Brass and Winds (1954), and "Country Fair" (1957) for two trumpets and trombone, all on *CRI*-185; Sonata for Piano (1960), *CRI*-198; Seven Songs (1952–1966), *Desto* 430/6430, coupled with "Brief Candle" (1964) (a "music drama in three acts and six minutes"); "Two Pastels" and Andante for Strings, *Desto* 7126; Concert Piece for Trumpet, *Golden Crest* 7045. Out of print: "Hello, World!" (A Musical Trip Around the World for Narrator, Orchestra, etc.) (1956), *Victor;* "The Greatest Sound Around" (1955), *Victor.* Publishers: Boosey & Hawkes (orchestral, brass and woodwinds, vocal, orchestral); MCA Music (orchestral, two-piano reduction of concerto, choral); Carl Fischer (vocal, piano); Galaxy (opera, choral), Presser (opera, instrumental solos, choral); G. Schirmer (choral, vocal). Unpublished works with American Music Center and Fleisher Collection.

Robert Guyn McBride (b. 1911), faculty, University of Arizona, Tucson. Recordings: Concerto for Violin (1954), *Desto* 417/6417; "Panorama of Mexico" (1960), and "March of the Be-Bops" (1948), *CRI* S-228; "Pumpkin Eater's Little Fugue" (1952), and "Workout for Small Orchestra" (1936), *CRI*-119; "Punch and Judy" (1941) for orchestra, *CRI*-107. Out of print: "Mexican Rhapsody" for orchestra, *Mercury* MG-50134/SR-90134; Concerto for Violin, *American Recording Society Records;* Quintet for Oboe and Strings, *Classic Recordings.* Publishers: Composer Facsimile Edition (principal publisher in all categories); Associated Music (orchestral); Carl Fischer (band, orchestral, choral); Mills Music (instrumental); Composers Press (woodwind quintet); Merion (piano); David Gornston (117 West 48th Street, New York, N.Y.) (orchestral, band, choral, piano, chamber).

George Frederick McKay (b. 1899). Publishers: Abingdon Press (organ); Allyn and Bacon (children's songs); American Book Co.

(children's songs); Associated Music (band, brass ensemble); Avant Music Publishing Co. (Los Angeles) (organ); C. L. Barnhouse Co. (110 B Avenue, East, Oskaloosa, Iowa 52577) (woodwind, brass ensemble music); Boosey & Hawkes (piano for elementary grades); Boston Music Co. (band, orchestra, instrumental solo, piano, choral); Robert B. Brown Music Co. (piano); Century (piano); Elkan–Vogel (string orchestra, choral); Carl Fischer (orchestral, instrumental solo, choral, brass ensemble, woodwind ensemble, organ); J. Fischer & Bro. (organ, orchestra, choral, piano); Frank Music (choral); FitzSimons (band, violin and piano, clarinet quartet); Sam Fox (piano); Galaxy (choral, organ, orchestral, string orchestra); H. W. Gray (choral, organ), The Horn Realm, Box 542, Far Hills, N.J. (brass ensemble); Leeds (see MCA) (piano); Lawson–Gould (choral); Hal Leonard (choral); McLaughlin & Reilly (organ); McGinnis & Marx (string bass with piano, violin and piano); Mills Music (piano); Mercury (clarinet and piano, piano); New Music Edition (piano); Oxford University Press (elementary piano); Presser (band, choral, instrumental solo, string ensemble, brass ensemble, woodwind ensemble, organ); Sacred Music Press (see Lorenz) (organ); G. Schirmer (instrumental solo, choral, orchestra, band); Shawnee Press (choral); G. Scott Publishing Co. (345 S. Citrus, Los Angeles, California) (clarinet quartet); Schmitt, Hall & McCreary (choral); Summy–Birchard (orchestra, string orchestra, choral), Southern Music Co. of San Antonio (flute quartet, brass chamber, string orchestra), Warner Bros.–Seven Arts (choral, piano, string orchestra, orchestra, band, trombone and piano); World Library (piano, choral); University Press, Ann Arbor, Michigan (tuba and piano); University of Washington Press, Seattle (orchestral, string quartet, organ). Unpublished works are in the Fleisher Collection, University of Washington Library (Special Collections), and Composers Autograph Publications, Redondo Beach, California.

Peter Mennin (b. 1923), President, Juilliard School, New York; music administrator in several national organizations. Recordings: "Canto and Toccata" from "Five Pieces for Piano" (1949), *Golden Crest* 4065; "Canto for Orchestra," *Decca* 710168; "Canzona" for band (1951), *Mercury* 50084; "Concertato" ("Moby Dick") for orchestra (1952), *Desto* 416/6416; String Quartet No. 2 (1951), *Columbia* ML-4844; Symphony No. 3 (1946), *CRI* S-278 (reissue of *Columbia* ML-4902); Symphony No. 5 (1950), *Mercury* SR-90379, and *Louisville* 613; Symphony No. 6 (1953), *Louisville* 545-3; Symphony No. 7 (1964), *Victor* LSC-3043; Concerto for Piano and Orchestra (1951), *Victor LSC*-3243; Concerto for Cello and Orchestra (1957), *Louisville* S-693. Current exclusive publisher is Carl Fischer, Inc.; however, some works for orchestra, string orchestra, and chamber ensemble have been published by Hargail Music.

Gian-Carlo Menotti (b. 1911, Italy; U.S. resident since 1927), author; founder–director, Festival of Two Worlds, Spoleto, Italy. Recordings: "Amahl and the Night Visitors," opera (1951), *Victor* LM/LSC-2762; Piano Concerto in F (1945), *Vanguard* 2094; "The Consul," opera (1950), with original cast on 2-record set, *Decca* DX-101; "The Medium," opera (1946), and "The Telephone," opera (1947), both on a 2-record set, *Columbia* OSL-154; "Old Maid and the Thief," (opera), *Mercury* 90521; "The Medium," (opera), *Columbia* MS-7387; "The Unicorn, the Gorgon, and the Manticore," a Madrigal Ballet, for chamber ensemble of mixed chorus and nine instruments, *Angel* 35447; "Sebastian" suite, *Desto* 6432. Out of print (among others): "Amelia Goes to the Ball," overture, in a collection entitled "Opera Overtures" on *Columbia* ML-5638/MS-6238; "Amahl and the Night Visitors," *Victor* LM-1701. Principal publisher is G. Schirmer. Franco Colombo (Ricordi) has published works for orchestra, band, chamber chorus and instrumental ensemble, piano solo, piano 4-hands, operas, piano with orchestra.

Jan Meyerowitz (b. 1913, Germany; U.S. citizen), lecturer, City College of New York. Publishers: Rongwen (Broude Bos.) (choral, orchestral, piano, woodwind quintet); Associated Music (orchestral, opera); E. B. Marks (opera, choral, organ, piano, orchestral).

Robert Walter Moevs (b. 1920), faculty, Rutgers, The State University, Brunswick, N.J. Recordings: Piano Sonata (1950), *CRI*-136; "Musica da Camera," (1965), and "Variazioni sopra una melodia," for viola and cello (1961), both on *CRI*-S-223; Brief Mass, *CRI* S-262. Not yet released: "Cantata Sacra" (1952), "Itaque Ut" for chorus (1961), "Et nunc, reges" for women's voices and solo instruments (1962), on *CRI Records.* Publishers: Max Eschig, Paris (through Associated Music) (songs, chamber music); Piedmont Music (through E. B. Marks), principal publisher (orchestral, vocal, chamber). Unpublished symphonic work in Fleisher Collection; one in the Library of Congress.

Lawrence Kenneth Moss (b. 1927), faculty, Yale University. Recordings: Sonata for Violin and Piano (1959), and "Four Scenes for Piano" both on *CRI*-186. Publishers: Presser is principal publisher (operas, chamber music, orchestral); Elkan–Vogel (piano 4-hands). Unpublished music with American Music Center.

Walter Mourant (b. 1910). Recordings: "Valley of the Moon" (1955), Air and Scherzo (1955), "Sleepy Hollow" (1955), all for orchestra, *CRI*-157; "Aria for Orchestra" ("Harper's Ferry, W.Va.") (1960), *CRI*-192. Publishers: Carl Fischer (orchestral); Associated Music (orchestral and chamber); Hendon Music Co. (43 West 61st Street, New York, N.Y.) (music for harp); G. Schirmer (choral); Shawnee Press (choral). Unpublished works on file at American Music Center, Fleisher Collection, American Composers Alliance, and the Library of Congress.

Ron Nelson (b. 1929), Chairman, Department of Music, Brown University, Providence. Recording: "Sarabande: For Katherine in April," *Mercury* 90337. Out of print: "Savannah River Holiday" *Mercury* MG-50134/90134; "Christmas Story," *Carillon Records* 123. Publishers: Boosey & Hawkes, principal publisher (orchestral, choral, band); Carl Fischer (orchestral, opera); Elkan–Vogel (choral); Shawnee Press (choral); Augsburg (choral).

Roger Nixon (b. 1921), faculty, San Francisco State College. Recordings: String Quartet No. 1, *Music Library Recordings* MLR-7005; "Six Moods of Love," (songs) *Fantasy* 5009 and *Music Library* MLR-7112; Movements from "The Wine of Astonishment" (Cantata from the Psalms), *Music Library* MLR-6997; "Fiesta del Pacifico," for band, *Decca* 710157 and *University of Illinois Records;* "Chinese Seasons," for voice and piano, *Music Library.* Publishers: Mills Music (string orchestra); Lawson–Gould (choral); Sam Fox (choral); Mercury (band, choral); Presser (orchestral, choral, chamber); Carl Fischer (band); Boosey & Hawkes (band); Galaxy (choral, band). Prentice-Hall has published some children's songs.

Paul Nordoff (b. 1909), Senior Music Therapy Consultant and Supervisor of Music Therapy Research, Child Study Center of Philadelphia. Recording: "Winter Symphony" (1954), *Louisville* 57-1. The following publishers have published songs by the composer: Associated Music; Schott (London); Mercury; and Presser (who has also published works for children). Unpublished music is deposited with American Music Center and Fleisher Collection.

Spencer Norton (b. 1909), faculty, University of Oklahoma, Norman; pianist, harpsichordist, and clavichordist. Recordings: Partita for Two Solo Pianos and Orchestra (1959), *CRI*-151. Unpublished works with American Music Center and American Music Edition.

Pauline Oliveros (b. 1932), faculty, University of California at San Diego. Recordings: "I of IV" (1966) (electronic work), *Odyssey* 32160160; "Sound Patterns" (1961), *Odyssey* 32160155/32160156, and *Ars Nova* 1005; "Outline for Flute, Percussion and String Bass," *Nonesuch* 71237. Publisher: Tonos Edition of Darmstadt, Germany (vocal music).

Hall Overton (b. 1920), faculty, Juilliard School, New York. Recordings: String Quartet No. 2 (1954), *CRI*-126; Sonata for Viola and Piano, and Sonata for Cello and Piano (1960), *E.M.S.* 403; Symphony No. 2 (1962), *Louisville* 633; "Polarities" for piano solo (1958), *Victor.* Out of print: "Sonorities" for orchestra, *Columbia Records.* Publishers: C. F.

Peters (orchestral); Lawson–Gould (chamber); Highgate (chamber); Marks Music (chamber); MJQ (orchestral). Unpublished works are with American Composers Alliance.

Robert Moffet Palmer (b. 1915), faculty, Cornell University. Recordings: Quartet for Piano and Strings (1947), *Columbia* CML-4842; "Memorial Music" for chamber orchestra (1957), *Cornell University Records* (Lincoln Hall, Cornell University, Ithaca, New York) N80P; "Nabuchodnosor" (1964), *Fleetwood Records* 6001 (*Fleetwood Records,* 321 Revere Street, Revere, Massachusetts 02151); "Choric Song and Toccata," *Cornell University*—2. Out of print: Chamber Concerto No. 1 for violin, oboe, and strings (1948), *Concert Hall Records;* Three Preludes for Piano (1941), *Allegro Records;* Toccata Ostinato for Piano, *Ficker* 41859. Publishers: Southern Music Publishers (principal publisher) (vocal, instrumental, orchestral, chamber music); C. F. Peters (chamber music); Presser (piano); Elkan–Vogel (piano); Society for the Publication of American Music (Presser). Unpublished works can be found in the Cornell University Music Library.

Harry Partch (b. 1901), builder of unique musical instruments, which are used in his compositions. Recordings: "And on the Seventh Day Petals Fell in Petaluma" (1964), *CRI*-213 (composer as director); "Daphne of the Dunes" (1958), "Barstow: Eight Hitchhiker Inscriptions from a Highway Railing at Barstow, California" (1941), "Plectra and Percussion Dances: Castor and Pollux" (1952), all on *Columbia* MS-7207; "Castor and Pollux" (from "Plectra and Percussion Dances"), "Wayward Letter" (1943), "Cloud Chamber Music" (1950), "Windsong" (film score—1958), and "The Bewitched"—Final Scene and Epilogue (1955), all on *CRI*-193 (the composer performing some of the pieces). "Delusion of the Fury," *Columbia* M2-30576 (2-record set).

George Perle (b. 1915), faculty, Queens College, Flushing, N.Y.; author. Recordings: "Monody I" for unaccompanied flute (1960), *CRI*-212; "Monody II" for unaccompanied string bass (1962), *Advance* No. 1; Quintet for Strings (1958), *CRI*-148; Rhapsody for Orchestra (1954), *Louisville* 545-9; Six Preludes for Piano (1946), in a *Victor* 2-record set, LSC-7042. Publishers: Presser (current exclusive publisher) (instrumental solo, chamber, orchestral); Lawson–Gould (piano: in the collection: "New Music for the Piano"—recorded on the *Victor* record above); E.C.I.C. (see Southern Music Publishing: Editorial Cooperativa) (solo piano, solo viola). Unpublished works: American Music Center.

Vincent Persichetti (b. 1915), faculty, Juilliard School; Director of Publications, Elkan–Vogel, Co. (since 1952); pianist and organist; author. Recordings: Symphony No. 5 for Strings (1953), *Louisville* 545-7; Serenade No. 5 for orchestra (1950), *Louisville* 606; Concerto for Piano, 4-Hands (alone) (1952), *Columbia* ML-4989 (composer and wife performing); Divertimento for Band (1950), *Mercury* MG-50079; Psalm for Band (1952), *Mercury* 50084; Pageant for Band (1953), *Austin Records* 6008; Serenade for Solo Tuba (1961), *Golden Crest* RE-7018; Serenade No. 11 for Band (1960), *Golden Crest* 6001; "Masquerade for Band," Opus 102, *Decca* 710163, and *Coronet* S-1247 (composer conducting); "Shimah b'Koli" (Psalm 130), Op. 89 (1962), (for organ), *Aeolian* S-327; "Sinfonia: Janiculum" (Symphony No. 9), *Victor* LSC-3212; Sonata for Solo Cello, Opus 54, *Opus One* 6; Symphony for Band, Psalm, Bagatelles, "So Pure the Star," all on *Coronet* S-1247 (composer conducting); Symphony No. 8, *Louisville* S-706, "Hollow Men," *Golden Crest* 7045. Out of print: Symphony No. 4, *Columbia* ML-5108; Symphony No. 6 for Band (1956), *Mercury* 50221; "The Hollow Men," for trumpet and string orchestra (1944), *MGM* E-3117; Little Piano Book (1953), *MGM* E-3147; "Pastoral" for Woodwind Quintet (1943), *Classic Editions* CE-2003-A and *Columbia* ML-5984. Principal publisher of the composer's music is Elkan–Vogel (orchestral, including concertos, chamber music for many combinations of instruments, solo piano, organ, harpsichord, flute, tuba, songs, band, choral, and a group of serenades written for various instruments from solo piano through duet and trio combinations to those for band or orchestra). Other publishers: Carl Fischer (orchestral, band, choral); Leeds (MCA Music) (two-piano music); Southern Music Publishing (chamber); G. Schirmer (chamber, choral); Mercury (piano, choral); Oliver Ditson (Presser) (band). Unpublished works: American Music Center, Fleisher Collection.

Wayne Turner Peterson (b. 1927), faculty, San Francisco State College. Out of print recording: "Free Variations for Orchestra," *Mercury* MG-50288/90288. Publishers: Boosey & Hawkes (choral and orchestral); Lawson–Gould (choral); Seesaw (wind and chamber). Unpublished music: American Music Center.

Burrill Phillips (b. 1907). Recordings: "Selections from McGuffey's Reader" (1934), *Desto* 423/6423; Sonata for Cello and Piano (1948), *S.P.A.* Records 54 (composer at the piano); Concerto for Piano and Orchestra (1942), and "The Return of Odysseus" (1957) both on *University of Illinois Recording Series* (Illini Union Bookstore, 715 South Wright Street, Champaign, Illinois); Sonata da Camera for organ (1964), and Sonata for Violin and Harpsichord (1966), both recorded on *Pleiades Records* P 101. Out of print: "Selections from McGuffey's Reader," *Mercury* MG-50136/90136; Concert Piece for Bassoon and Strings, (1940), *Columbia* ML-4629. Publishers: Elkan–Vogel (principal publisher) (piano, chamber music, choral); Carl Fischer (orchestral, choral); G. Schirmer (piano); Hargail (small orchestra); Interlochen Music Press (string orchestra); Presser (piano and chamber ensemble, choral); Southern Music Publishing (chamber music with piano); Robert King (brass ensemble); Summy–Birchard (choral); Galaxy (chorus and orchestra); Italy Hill Press (choral). Unpublished works: American Music Center, Fleisher Collection, Library of Congress Music Section.

Daniel Pinkham (b. 1923), faculty, New England Conservatory of Music; Music Director, King's Chapel, Boston; organist and harpsichordist. Recordings: *a cappella* choral works, "Piping Anne and Husky Paul," madrigal, and "Elegy" (1947), both recorded on *CRI*-102; Christmas Cantata (1957), *Angel* S-36016 (in an album called "Christmas Festival"); "Glory be to God" (1957) for double chorus, *CRI*-191; Partita for Harpsichord, *Cambridge Records* 412 (composer performing); Symphony No. 2 (1963), *Louisville* 652; "Signs of the Zodiac" for orchestra and · optional speaker, *Louisville* 673; Concerto for Celesta and Harpsichord Soli (1955) and Cantilena and Capriccio for Violin and Harpsichord (1956), both on *CRI*-109 (composer performing the harpsichord part); Concertante for Violin and Harpsichord Soli, String and Celesta (1954), *CRI*-143. Out of print: song, "Slow, slow fresh mount," on *Stand Records.* Publishers: E. C. Schirmer and its affiliate, Ione Press, Inc. (choral, vocal, organ solo and with other instruments, harpsichord, and other instrumental music); C. F. Peters (choral, vocal, organ, instrumental and orchestral); Associated Music; Highgate Press; Robert King Music Co.; and R. D. Row (Carl Fischer). Unpublished music is on file with American Composers Alliance.

Paul Amadeus Pisk (b. 1893, Austria; U.S. citizen since 1941), faculty, Washington University, St. Louis. Recordings: Passacaglia for Orchestra (1944), *CRI*-128; "Three Ceremonial Rites" for orchestra (1958), *CRI*-228; "Nocturnal Interlude" for piano, *Victor* LSC-7042 (2-record set called "New Music for Piano"); Sonata for Flute, Sonata for Clarinet (1947), Songs (after Joyce), Sonnets (after Shakespeare), all on a *Washington University* disc called "The Music of Paul Pisk" (see Record Companies). Publishers: Universal Edition (through Presser) (chamber music, piano, orchestral); Carl Fischer (piano, chamber); Associated Music (chamber); Presser (piano, chamber); Southern Music Publishing (choral, chamber); Mills Music (piano, choral); E. B. Marks (orchestral); Lawson–Gould (choral); Leeds (MCA Music) (choral, piano); Summy–Birchard (choral); C. F. Peters (chamber); Mercury (choral). Unpublished works are at American Music Center, American Composers Alliance, and the library of the University of Texas at Austin.

Walter Piston (b. 1894). Recordings: Symphony No. 2 (1943), *Desto* 410/6410; Symphony No. 4 (1950), *Columbia* CML-4992; Symphony No. 5 (1954), *Louisville* 653; Concertino for Piano and Chamber Orchestra (1937), *CRI*-180; Concerto for Viola and Orchestra (1957), *Louisville* 633; Concerto for Orchestra, *CRI* S-254; Concerto for Violin and Orchestra, *Mace* 9089; "Incredible Flutist" (ballet suite) for orchestra (1938), *Columbia* ML-6343/MS-6943, and *Mercury* 90423; "Serenata" for orchestra (1956), *Louisville* 58-6; "Tunbridge Fair" (1950), intermezzo for symphonic band, *Mercury* 50079; Divertimento for Nine Instruments (1946), part of a 3-record set *Victor* LSC-6167; Quintet for Piano and String Quartet (1949), *Heliodor* 25027; Sonata for Flute and Piano (1930), *Westminster* 19121/17121; Three Pieces for Flute, Clarinet, and Bassoon (1925), *Lyrichord* 158; Suite for Oboe and Piano, *Coronet* S-1409; "Carnival Song" (1938) for men's chorus and brass, *Fleetwood* 6001 (see address under Robert Palmer, this section); Chromatic Study on "B.A.C.H." for organ (1940), *University of Oklahoma Records* 2 (see under Record Companies), and *Lyrichord* 191/7191 (in a record album entitled "Twentieth Century American Music"). Out of print recordings: "Incredible Flutist" (ballet suite), *Epic* LC-3539/BC-1013; Quintet for Wind Instruments (1956) *Boston Records* 407/1005; Sonata for Flute and Piano (1930), *Claremont Records* 1205. Publishers: Associated Music Publishers is the principal publisher (orchestral, including concertos, chamber music for most combinations, choral); other publishers: Boosey & Hawkes (brass and percussion, orchestral, chamber music); MCA Music (one piano work in a collection "USA Vol. 1"); E. C. Schirmer (one work for oboe and piano), G. Schirmer (orchestral, string quartet), H. W. Gray (one organ work shown in record listings above), Mercury Music Corporation (one piano piece).

Mel Powell (b. 1923), Dean of Music, California Institute of the Arts; pianist. Recordings: Divertimento for Violin and Harp (1955), Divertimento for Five Winds (1956), Piano Trio (1956) on *CRI*-121; "Improvisation", "Two Prayer Settings" for tenor, oboe, violin, viola, and cello, "Piece for Tape Recorder," "Second Electronic Setting," "Events," all on *CRI*-227. Publishers: Franco Colombo (piano solo, orchestral); Society for the Publication of American Music (Presser) (wind chamber group); Carl Fischer (choral); G. Schirmer (orchestral, string quartet, clarinet with violin and piano, cello and orchestra, chamber music with and without voice); Templeton (Shawnee Press) (English horn and orchestra, orchestral).

John W. Pozdro (b. 1923), faculty, University of Kansas, Lawrence. Recordings: Symphony No. 3 (1960), *CRI*-151. Publishers: Boston Music Co. (vocal); Lawson–Gould (choral); Summy–Birchard (instrumental); Presser (orchestral); Choristers Guild, Dallas, Texas (music for children's chorus); Composers Autograph Publications (1908 Perry Avenue, Redondo Beach, California) (instrumental). Unpublished works: Fleisher Collection.

Gardner Read (b. 1913), faculty, Boston University; author. Recordings: "Toccata Giocosa" (1953), for orchestra, *Louisville* 545-5; "Night Flight" for orchestra (1961), *Louisville* 632. Out of print: "Three Preludes to Old Southern Hymns," *Mirrosonic Records* 1012. Publishers: Presser (choral, piano, chamber, orchestral); Galaxy (choral, vocal); J. Fischer (piano, choral); Carl Fischer (chamber, choral, orchestral); Associated Music (choral, vocal, orchestral); Summy–Birchard (choral, piano); H. W. Gray (choral, organ); Southern Music Publishing (choral, vocal, chamber); Leeds (MCA) (piano, organ); FitzSimons (choral); C. F. Peters (orchestral); Boosey & Hawkes (vocal, choral); Composers Press (vocal, orchestral); Witmark (organ, chamber); Abingdon (organ, choral); Lawson–Gould (band, choral); Robert King (brass ensemble); Volkwein (piano); M. M. Cole (percussion); Canyon Press (choral); McLaughlin–Reilly (organ). Unpublished works are on file with American Music Center, Fleisher Collection, Library of Congress Music Division, Boston Public Library, and the Library of Boston University.

Herbert Owen Reed (b. 1910), faculty, Michigan State University, East Lansing; author of music text books. Recordings: "La

Fiesta Mexicana" (1949), A Mexican Folk-Song Symphony, *Mercury* 50084, *Decca* 710157; Concerto for Cello and Orchestra (1949), *Dorian Records* 1009 (composer conducting); an arrangement of one of the composer's works, "El Muchacho," is found in the jazz album "Son Libre" of Cal Tjader, *Verve* 8531. Out of print: "El Toro March" and "Aztec Dance," from "La Fiesta Mexicana," *Mercury* (45rpm) 70678x. Other recordings are limited editions of noncommercial issue, such as Overture for Strings recorded for the A.F. of M. Congress of Strings, American Federation of Musicians, sponsor, "Spiritual for Band," recorded at the National Music Camp, and a recording of "La Fiesta Mexicana," recorded by the U.S. Air Force Band, etc. Publishers: Mills Music, principal publisher (orchestral, chamber music, opera, band, choral); Associated Music (band); Sam Fox (choral); Composers Press (see Southern Music, San Antonio) (orchestral). Also two pieces have been published by Allyn & Bacon in a collection called "Music for the High School Chorus." Unpublished works: American Music Center and Fleisher Collection.

Vittorio Rieti (b. 1898, Alexandria, Egypt; U.S. citizen). Recordings: "Introduzione e Gioco delle Ore" (1954) for orchestra, *Louisville* 545-11; "Capers," for orchestra, *Desto* 6434; Concerto for Harpsichord and Orchestra, and Partita for Flute, Oboe, String Quartet and Harpsichord (1945), both on *Decca* 10135/710135; Concerto No. 3 for Piano, *Serenus* 12033; Concertino for Five Instruments, "Medieval Variations" for Piano, Concerto for Cello, and Six Short Pieces ("Sei pezzi brevi"), all on *Serenus* SRE-1013/SRS 12013, an album entitled, "The Music of Vittorio Rieti—I"; "Sonata all' Antica" (1946) for harpsichord, *Decca* 10021/710021; "Quattro Liriche Italiane" (four Italian songs) on *Serenus* SRE 1019/SRS 12019, in an album called "John Reardon Sings Contemporary Art Songs"; Chorale, Variations and Finale, "Valse fugitive," "Three Vaudeville Marches" (for 2 Pianos), all on *Serenus* 12033; "La Fontaine" (1968), "Incisioni" (1967), Quartet No. 4 (1960), *Serenus* S-12023. Out of print recordings: "Madrigale" (1927), *MGM;* "Second Avenue Waltzes" (1941), *Columbia;* "Suite Champêtre" (1947), *Columbia;* Dance Variations (1956), *MGM* records. Publishers: Universal Edition (Presser) (orchestral, dramatic works, chamber music); Editions Salabert (Franco Colombo) (chamber); Editions Eschig (Associated Music) (orchestral); Broude Brothers (orchestral, chamber); Associated Music (orchestral, dramatic works, vocal, and chamber); General Music Publishing (orchestral, dramatic, vocal, chamber).

George Rochberg (b. 1918), faculty, University of Pennsylvania, Philadelphia; writer on music subjects. Recordings: "Night Music" for orchestra (1949), *Louisville* 623; Symphony No. 1 (1955), *Louisville* 634; Symphony No. 2 (1959), *Columbia* CML-5779/CMS-6379; String Quartet No. 2, with voice (1961), *CRI*-164; "Contra Mortem et Tempus" (1965), for flute, clarinet, violin, and piano, *CRI* S-231; Bagatelles for Piano (1952), *Advance* 3; "Serenata d'estate," *Nonesuch* 71220; "Bocca della Verita" (1958), *Ars Nova* S-1008; Duo Concertante for Violin and Cello, *Advance* S-6. Principal publisher is Theodore Presser (orchestral, chamber, wind ensemble, vocal, piano). Other publishers: MCA (orchestral, chamber); G. Schirmer (early songs); Society for the Publication of American Music (chamber work). Unpublished works are in the Fleisher Collection.

Ned Rorem (b. 1923). Recordings: "Design for Orchestra" (1955), *Louisville* 575; Symphony No. 3, *Turnabout* 34447; "Lions," *Orion* 7268; "Lovers" for Harpsichord and Chamber Ensemble (1963), *Decca* 10108/710108; Eleven Studies for Eleven Players (1963), *Louisville* 644; 32 Songs, *Odyssey* 32160274 (composer is pianist); "Poems of Love and the Rain" (1963) *CRI*-202, *Desto* 6480; "War Scenes," "Five Whitman Songs," "Four Dialogues," *Desto* 7101; "Some Trees" (songs), *CRI* S-238; Second Piano Sonata (1949), *CRI*-202; "Two Psalms and a Proverb" (1962), for chorus and strings, *Cambridge* 416/1416; Trio for Flute, Cello, and Piano (1960), *Westminster* 17147 (and on the following *Desto* record); "Water Music" for clarinet, violin, and chamber orchestra, and "Ideas for

Easy Orchestra" (four selections), both on *Desto* 6462; Four Madrigals, and "From an Unknown Past" (7 Madrigals), *Desto* 6480. Out of print recordings: "Barcarolles" for piano (three), *Epic* LC-3862/BC-1262; 32 Songs, *Columbia* ML-5961/MS-6561. Major publishers: Boosey & Hawkes (who currently have an exclusive contract with composer) and C. F. Peters. Other publishers: Southern Music Publishing; Hargail; Elkan–Vogel; E. C. Schirmer; Mercury, and Presser. Unpublished works; American Music Center and Fleisher Collection.

Jerome William Rosen (b. 1921), faculty, University of California, Davis. Recordings: Sonata for Clarinet and Cello (1950), *Fantasy* 5009 (composer is clarinetist). Out of print: String Quartet No. 1, *Epic* record. Publishers: Boosey & Hawkes (chamber and choral); Music for Percussion (percussion); LeBlanc Publications (chamber music for clarinets). Unpublished music: American Composers Alliance.

Robert L. Sanders (b. 1906), faculty, Brooklyn College of Music, New York. Recordings: "Little Symphony" No. 1 in G (1937), *Louisville* 635; "Little Symphony" No. 2 in B Flat (1953), *Louisville* 545-7; Quintet in B Flat (1942) for brass, *Kapp* records KL-1391, and *Golden Crest* GC-4003 (third movement only); Symphony in A (1955), *CRI*-156. Publishers: Associated Music (chamber); Broude Brothers (choral); Carl Fischer (orchestral, chamber, choral); Franco Colombo (orchestral); Galaxy (orchestral, trumpet and piano, songs, choral); H. W. Gray (choral); Mercury (chorus with orchestra, brass quintet, choral); Pro-Art Publications (choral); Remick (trombone and piano); Robert King (music for brass instruments); the *a cappella* choral work, "When Abraham Went Out of Ur," has been published by the composer and is available directly from him: 1011 East 37th Street, Brooklyn, New York.

A. Louis Scarmolin (b. 1890, Italy; U.S. citizen). Publishers: C. L. Barnhouse (110 B Avenue, East Oskaloosa, Iowa 52577) (woodwind, brass); Belwin, (band, instrumental solo, choral); Carl Fischer (orchestral, band, woodwind and brass chamber ensembles, instrumental solo, operetta, choral, educational piano pieces); Sam Fox Publishing (orchestral); Ludwig Music Co. (orchestral, band, woodwind ensembles, choral); Presser (piano, violin and piano); Pro-Art Publications (publisher of a significant number of the composer's works) (orchestral, band, woodwind and brass ensembles, instrumental solo, choral, piano, including arrangements for piano 4-hands); The Horn Realm, Far Hills, N.J. 07931 (ensemble music for French horns); Franco Colombo (opera, choral, elementary piano pieces); Summy–Birchard (piano, choral); Edizione Peri (Rome, Italy) (works for symphonic band); Edizione Nord-Sud (Rome, Italy) (songs with orchestral accompaniment); Composers Press (chamber, piano); Boosey & Hawkes (woodwind quintet, brass ensemble); G. Schirmer (operetta, piano studies); H. W. Gray (choral); Mills Music (choral); Arthur Schmidt (Summy–Birchard) (music for piano 6-hands). Many of the foregoing categories of music cover works for educational use. Unpublished music is on file at American Music Center; Fleisher Collection; Research Library of the Lincoln Center of the Performing Arts, New York; the Santa Cecilia Conservatory in Rome, Italy; and the Library of Conservatory San Pietro a Maiella in Naples, Italy.

Gunther A. Schuller (b. 1925), President, New England Conservatory of Music, Boston; conductor; author. Recordings: Concertino for Jazz Quartet and Orchestra (1959), *Atlantic* 1359; "Conversations" (1959), for jazz quartet, *Atlantic* 1345; "Densities No. 1" (1962), and "Night Music" (1962) for jazz chamber groups, both on *Cambridge* 1820; Fantasy Quartet for Four Cellos" (1958) and Music for Brass Quintet (1961), both on *CRI*-144; "Lines and Contrasts," *Angel* S-36036; "Seven Studies on Themes of Paul Klee" for orchestra (1959), *Victor* LSC-2879; "Transformations" (1957) for jazz orchestra, *Columbia* C2L-31/C2S-831; Woodwind Quintet (1958), *Concert Disc* 229; "Five Bagatelles" for orchestra, *Louisville* 686; "Dramatic Overture" for orchestra (1951), *Louisville* 666; "Triplum" for orchestra (1967), *Columbia*

ML-6452/MS-7052; "Abstraction" for chamber ensemble, *Atlantic* 1365; "Variants on a Theme of John Lewis" and "Variants on a Theme of Thelonius Monk," both on *Atlantic* label; "Journey into Jazz," for narrator, jazz quintet, and orchestra, *Columbia* CL/2247/CS-9047; Sonata for Oboe and Piano, *Desto* 7116; Symphony, and Quartet for four double-basses (1947), *Turnabout* 34412. Out of print: String Quartet No. 1, *University of Illinois Series;* "Seven Studies on Themes of Paul Klee," *Mercury* 50282/90282; Symphony for Brass and Percussion, *Columbia.* The composer is conductor for the recordings of the following: "Abstraction," "Concertino," "Journey," "Transformation," and the two "Variants." Publishers: Associated Music is principal publisher (orchestral, opera, band, chamber music including those works requiring a jazz ensemble, vocal); other publishers are Aldo Bruzzichelli (through Alexander Broude) (chamber); Schott (through Associated) (orchestral, chamber); Malcolm Music (Shawnee Press) (orchestral, brass and percussion, chamber); McGinnis & Marx (oboe and piano, woodwind quintet); Mentor Music (Room 141, Carnegie Hall, New York, N.Y. 10019) (brass quartet); MJQ Music (jazz ensembles with orchestra, chamber ensembles including jazz groups, orchestral transcriptions); Rongwen (Broude Brothers) (solo cello); Presser (orchestral transcription); Universal Edition (through Presser) (orchestral, chamber). A few unpublished works are in the Fleisher Collection and the Library of Congress.

William H. Schuman (b. 1910), Chairman, Videorecord Corp. of America. Recordings: "A Song of Orpheus" (1961) for cello and orchestra, *Columbia* ML-6028/MS-6638; "American Festival Overture" for orchestra (1939), *Desto* 404/6404; "Carols of Death," *Everest* 6129/3129; "Chester" (Overture for Band) (1956), *Decca* 8633/78633, and *Vanguard* 9114/2124; Concerto for Violin and Orchestra (1947), *Deutsche Grammophon* 25030103; Four Canonic Choruses (1933), *Concordia* S-1 (Concordia College, Moorhead, Minnesota 56560); "George Washington Bridge" (1950) for band, *Mercury* 50079; "In Praise of Shahn," *Columbia* 30112; "Judith" (Choreographic Poem for Dancer and Orchestra) (1949), *Louisville* 604; "New England Tryptych" (1956) for orchestra, *Mercury* 50379/90379, *Victor* LSC-3069, *Decca* 71068, and *Columbia* CSP91A02007; Prelude for Voice (1939), *Concordia* S-6 (see above); Symphony No. 3 (1941), *Columbia* ML-5645/MS-6245; Symphony No. 4 (1942), *Louisville* S-692; Symphony No. 5 (Symphony for Strings) (1943), *Columbia* MS-7442; Symphony No. 6 (1948), *Columbia* ML-4992; Symphony No. 7, *Turnabout* 34447; Symphony No. 8 (1962), *Columbia* ML-6512; Symphony No. 9 ("The Ardeatine Caves") (1969), *Victor* LSC 3212; "To Thee Old Cause," *Columbia* MS-7392; "Undertow" (1945—Choreographic Episodes for Orchestra), *Capitol* HDR-21004; "Voyage" (5 piece for piano) (1953), *Columbia* ML-4987; Variations on "America" from the organ work of Charles Ives, orchestrated by Schumann (1963), *Victor* LM/LSC-2893, and *Louisville* 651; "When Jesus Wept," *Cornell University* WE-9. Out of print: "Credendum" for orchestra, *Columbia* ML-5185; other out-of-print recordings are beyond the scope of this listing. Principal publishers are G. Schirmer and Presser (the latter since 1956) (orchestral, band, choral, chamber, vocal, piano solo). Other publishers: E. B. Marks (song, choral); Carl Fischer (choral); Arrow Music (Boosey & Hawkes) (string quartet); Boosey & Hawkes (choral with orchestra); Peer International (Southern Music Publishing) (music for four bassoons). The composer's unpublished Second Symphony (1937) is in the Fleisher Collection.

Paul Schwartz (b. 1907, Vienna), Chairman, Department of Music, Kenyon College, Gambier, Ohio; Musical Director, Knox County Symphony, Mount Vernon, Ohio. Recordings: Concertino for Chamber Orchestra (1947), *CRI*-128; Vienna Baroque Suite, *Coronet* S-1509. Publishers: Rongwen (Broude Brothers) (choral works); MCA Music (Duchess Music Corp.) (educational chamber works). Unpublished works: American Composers Alliance and on file with MCA.

Tibor Serly (b. 1901, Hungary; U.S. citizen since 1910), conductor; lecturer. Most recordings are issued by *Keyboard Records,* a new label, (157 West 57th Street, New York, N.Y. 10019) on two discs: K-101 ("The Music of Tibor Serly"), Four Songs (after "Chamber Music" by James Joyce) (1927), "Strange Story," and Concerto for Viola and Orchestra (1928); K-102 ("Music of Tibor Serly and Béla Bartók"), Concerto for Two Pianos and Orchestra (1958). The composer is conductor on both records. Other recordings include "Sonata in Modus Lascivus" for Solo Violin, *Bartok Records* 908, and works by the composer which involve compositions by Bartók completed or arranged by Serly (the former's "Mikrokosmos" for orchestra, the Viola Concerto, and the Third Piano Concerto, among others). Out of print: Concerto for Trombone and Orchestra and Miniature Suite for 12 Wind Instruments, on *Audio Fidelity* AFLP-1811. Publishers: Southern Music Publishing is principal publisher (orchestral, vocal, chamber, and instrumental solo). Other publishers: G. Schirmer (orchestral, vocal); Boosey & Hawkes (orchestra, chamber music, and completion or arrangements of the music of Bartók); MCA Music (orchestral, vocal, solo piano, and music for viola); Lyra Music (music for harp). Unpublished works are placed with Forrell & Thomas Associates, 157 West 57th Street, New York, N.Y. 10019, and in the Fleisher Collection.

Roger Sessions (b. 1896), faculty, Juilliard School. Recordings: Symphony No. 1 (1927), *CRI*-131; Symphony No. 2 (1946), *CRI* S-278; Symphony No. 3, *RCA Victor* LSC-3095; Concerto for Violin and Orchestra (1935), *CRI*-220; "Black Maskers Suite," *Mercury* 90423, and *Desto* 404/6404; "Idyll of Theocritus" for soprano and orchestra (1954), *Louisville* 574; String Quartet No. 2 (1951), *Columbia* ML-5105; Piano Sonata No. 1 (1930), *CRI*-198; Piano Sonata No. 2 (1946), *Dover* 5265/7265, and *Music Library* 7003; "From My Diary" (1940) for piano, *Music Library* 7003; Sonata for Violin Solo (1953), *Folkways* 3355; Chorale Prelude No. 1 for organ (1925) (from Three Chorale Preludes), *University of Oklahoma* (see under Record Companies); Chorale Preludes for Organ (complete), *Counterpoint* 5222. Out of print: "From My Diary" for piano, *Epic* LC-3862/BC-1262. Current exclusive publisher is E. B. Marks Music Corporation. Other publishers: New Music Edition (Presser) (violin and piano); Arrow (Boosey & Hawkes) (organ, orchestral); Edition Musicus; and G. Schirmer (orchestral).

Harold Samuel Shapero (b. 1920), faculty, Brandeis University, Waltham, Massachusetts. Recordings: "Credo for Orchestra" (1955), *Louisville* 56-5; "On Green Mountain" (Chaconne after Monteverdi), part of a *Columbia* 2-record set called "Outstanding Jazz Compositions of the 20th Century," *Columbia* C2L-31/C2S-831; Partita in C for Piano Solo and Small Orchestra (1960), *Louisville* 674; Quartet No. 1 (1940), for strings, *Columbia* CML-5576/CMS-6176; Sonata for Piano 4-Hands (1941), *Columbia* CML-4841 (with composer as one of the pianists); Three Piano Sonatas (1944), *Concert Disc* 1217/217, and *Decca* 10021/710021 (the latter contains the first sonata played on the harpsichord). Out of print: Symphony for Classical Orchestra (1948), *Columbia* 4889; Serenade in D for string orchestra (1945), *MGM Records.* Southern Music Publishing is principal publisher (symphonic, choral, chamber). Other publishers are G. Schirmer (piano works); Mills Music (piano 4-hands).

Ralph Shapey (b. 1921), faculty, University of Chicago; Music Director of the University's Contemporary Chamber Players; conductor. Recordings: "Evocation for Violin with Piano and Percussion" (1959), *CRI*-141; "Seven" for Piano 4-Hands, *Friends of Four Hand Music* 1027 (the recording label's address is: 1645 Edith Street, Berkeley, California 94703); "Songs of Ecstasy," *Desto* 7124; Rituals for Symphony Orchestra (1959) and Quartet No. 6 (1963) (composer conducting, *CRI* S-275; "Incantations" for Soprano and 10 Players (1961), *CRI* S-232. Out of print: Chamber Symphony for 10 Solo Players (1962), *Lexington Records.* Works are unpublished and are in the libraries of the American Music Center, Fleisher Collection, and the American Composers Alliance. The composer's works can be obtained from Independent Music Publishers, 215 East 42nd Street, New York, N.Y. 10017.

Seymour J. Shifrin (b. 1926), faculty, Brandeis University. Recordings: Serenade for Five Instruments (1954), *CRI*-123; Three Pieces for Orchestra (1958), *CRI* S-275; "Satires of Circumstance" (1964), *Nonesuch* 71220. Principal publisher is C. F. Peters. Other publisher: Bote & Bock, Berlin (Associated Music) (string quartet). Unpublished music is in the Library of Congress.

Elie Siegmeister (b. 1909), faculty, Hofstra University. Recordings: Symphony No. 3 (1957), *CRI*-185 (conducted by the composer); "Western Suite" (1945) for orchestra, *Turnabout* 34459; String Quartet No. 2 (1960), *CRI*-176; "Sing Out, Sweet Land!" (musical play) (1944), *Decca* DL-4304/74304 (composer conducting); "Sunday in Brooklyn" (1946) for orchestra, *SPA Records* 47 (see Society of Participating Artists under Record Companies); Sextet for Brass and Percussion, Sonata No. 3 for Violin, and Sonata No. 2 for Piano, all on *Desto* 6467; Sonata No. 2 for Violin and Piano, *Desto* 7125. Out of print: "Ozark Set" for orchestra, *MGM* record. Publishers: MCA Music, principal publisher (orchestral, instrumental, choral, opera, piano solo, etc.); Chappell (opera, orchestra); Carl Fischer (choral, band); E. B. Marks (orchestral, piano, choral, band, vocal); Henmar Press (C. F. Peters) (opera); Lawson–Gould (choral); Sam Fox (orchestral, instrumental); Shawnee Press (opera, orchestral); Presser (piano, choral, orchestral). Unpublished music is on file with American Music Center and Fleisher Collection.

Ezra Sims (b. 1928), staff member, Loeb Music Library, Harvard University. Recordings: Chamber Cantata on Chinese Poems (1954), *CRI*-186; String Quartet No. 3 (1962), *CRI* S-223. Unpublished music is in the library of American Composers Alliance.

Hale Smith (b. 1925), Editor, Sam Fox Publishing Co.; Advisor for Band Publications, C. F. Peters Corp. Recordings: "In Memoriam—Beryl Rubinstein" (1953) for choir and chamber orchestra, *CRI*-182; "Contours for Orchestra" (1962), *Louisville* 632; "Evocation," (for piano) *Desto* 7102/3. Publishers: E. B. Marks is current exclusive and principal publisher of the composer's works (band, orchestra, chamber music, vocal, etc.). Other publishers: Frank Music Corp. (band); Duchess Music (MCA Music) (band, piano); Highgate (choral). Unpublished music with American Composers Alliance.

Julia Smith (b. 1911), pianist and author. Recording: Quartet for Strings, *Desto* 7117. Publishers: Mowbray Music Publishers, principal publisher (see Presser) (piano solo, two pianos 4-hands, chamber music, including piano with strings, vocal, choral, band); Harold Flammer (choral with large orchestra, or small orchestra, or band); Carl Fischer (choral, orchestral); Presser (piano solo, band, string method, orchestral, operas, including some with tapes). Unpublished music is at American Music Center; Fleisher Collection; Presser Rental Library; Library of the Performing Arts, Music Division, Lincoln Center, New York City.

Leland Smith (b. 1925), faculty, Stanford University (both in the music department and as developer of the computer music program of the Stanford Artificial Intelligence Program); conductor, pianist, and woodwind player. Recording: String Trio (1953), *Fantasy* Records 5010. Carl Fischer and Merion Music are the composer's publishers. Unpublished music is filed with American Composers Alliance.

Russell Smith (b. 1927), faculty, University of Alabama. Recordings: "Tetrameron" (1957) for orchestra, *CRI* S-131; Second Piano Concerto, *CRI* S-214. Out of print: "Songs of Innocence" (1949), *New Editions* NE-2. Publishers: C. F. Peters (orchestral); G. Schirmer (opera); Franco Colombo (choral); Lawson–Gould (choral); H. W. Gray (vocal, organ). Unpublished music is with American Music Center.

Harvey Sollberger (b. 1938), faculty, Manhattan School of Music; flutist; conductor. Recording: Chamber Variations for Twelve Players and Conductor (1964), *CRI*-204. Publishers: McGinnis and Marx (chamber music) and American Composers Alliance (facsimile editions for rental or purchase).

Leon Stein (b. 1910), Dean, De Paul University School of Music, Chicago; conductor; author. Recordings: Quintet for Saxophone and String Quartet (1957), *Enchanté Records* 1001/2001 (Enchanté Records, 14 Brenda Lane, R. R. 7, Muncie, Indiana 47307); String Quartet No. 2 (1935), and Trio Concertante for Saxophone, Violin, and Piano (1961), *Music Library Recordings* 7118; Sonata for Violin and Piano (1932), and Sonata for Solo Violin (1960), *Music Library Recordings* 7115. Out of print: "Three Hassidic Dances" for orchestra (1941), *Remington Records.* Publishers: American Composers Alliance Facsimile Editions, principal publisher (orchestral including concerto, operas, chamber music, instrumental solo, piano solo, choral); Carl Fischer (orchestral including transcriptions); MCA Music (Leeds) (orchestral including transcriptions); Transcontinental Music (orchestral, organ); De Paul University Press (music for two violins); Presser (trumpet trio, piano solo); Summy–Birchard (piano solo); Southern Music, San Antonio (saxophone quartet); Cor Publications (67 Bell Place, Massapequa, Long Island, N.Y. 11768) (chamber music with saxophone); University of Miami Press (brass music). Unpublished music is in the Fleisher Collection and at American Composers Alliance.

Halsey Stevens (b. 1908), faculty, University of Southern California, Los Angeles; author. Recordings: Symphony No. 1 (1945), *CRI*-129; "Triskelion" for orchestra (1953), *Louisville* 545-1; "Sinfonia Breve" (1957), *Louisville* 593; Symphonic Dances (1958), *CRI*-166; Sonata for Solo Cello (1958), *CRI*-208; "Like as the Culver" (1954) for chamber singers, *CRI*-102; Psalm 98 (1955), *CRI*-191; Old Rhymes for Treble Voices, *Gregorian Institute Records;* Concerto for Clarinet and String Orchestra, *Crystal* S-851; Sonata for Trombone and Piano, *Golden Crest* S-7043; Sonata for Trumpet and Piano, *Golden Crest* S-7042; Sonatina for Bass Tuba (or Trombone) and Piano, *Golden Crest* 7040. Publishers: C. F. Peters (orchestral, chamber music, choral); Southern Music Publishing (Peer International) (orchestral, band, chamber, keyboard, choral); Associated Music (choral); Presser (keyboard works); Westwood Press (World Library) (choral, keyboard); Marko Music (see Mark Foster) (choral); Helios Music (Mark Foster) (choral, keyboard, chamber); Robert King (brass chamber); Cor Publications (67 Bell Place, Massapequa, Long Island, N.Y.) (chamber works); Highgate (choral, chamber); Mercury (chamber). Unpublished music is in the Fleisher Collection and the Library of American Composers Alliance.

Gerald Strang (b. 1908, Canada; U.S. citizen), faculty, California State College, Long Beach. Recordings: Concerto for Cello and Orchestra (1951), *CRI*-215; Percussion Music for Three Players (1935), *Period* (see *Everest*—Record Companies) SPL-743. Publishers: Presser (instrumental); Mills Music (solo instrumental, orchestral). Unpublished music with American Music Center, Fleisher Collection, and American Composers Alliance.

Morton Subotnick (b. 1933), faculty, California Institute of the Arts, Los Angeles. Recordings: "Silver Apples of the Moon" (1967) for electronic music synthesizer, *Nonesuch* 71174; "Wild Bull" (electronic pieces) (1967), *Nonesuch* 71208; "Electronic Prelude and Interludes from "2001: A Space Odyssey" (film), *Columbia* MS-7176; "Lamentations," (for orchestra), *Turnabout* 34428; "Touch," *Columbia* MS-7316; "Sidewinder," *Columbia* M-30683. Publishers: Bowdoin College Music Press (one work for flute, clarinet, violin, piano, and tape); MCA Music (piano and electronic sound, orchestra and electronic sound).

Richard Swift (b. 1927), Chairman, Department of Music, University of California, Davis. Publishers: University of California Press (piano and chamber ensemble); Presser (orchestral). Unpublished music is filed with American Music Center.

William J. Sydeman (b. 1928), faculty, Mannes College of Music. Recordings: Concerto da Camera for Violin (and six players) (1959), *CRI*-158; Concerto da Camera No. 2 for Violin (and four players) (1960), *CRI*-181; "For Double Bass Alone" (1957), *Advance Records* FGR-1; Seven Movements for Septet

(1958), *CRI*-158; Trio for Flute, Violin, and Bass (1957), *Medea Records* 1001; "Orchestral Abstractions" (1958), *Louisville* 644; Duo for Violin and Piano (1963), *Turnabout* 34429; Music for Flute and Piano, *Desto* 7104; Quartet for Oboe and Strings, *Desto* 7116. Publishers: Associated Music (orchestral, chamber, trumpet and piano); Ione Press (E. C. Schirmer) (piano 4-hands with orchestra, choral, piano solo, solo voice with instruments, solo voice with piano, solo instrument with piano); Leeds (MCA) (piano solo); E. B. Marks (piano solo, orchestral); McGinnis & Marx (solo string bass, woodwind quintet, chamber ensemble); Okra Music (brass quintet, woodwind quintet, and other chamber ensembles); Southern (Peer) (clarinet and piano, woodwind duo); C. F. Peters (chamber ensembles, orchestral, solo instrumental); University Society, Inc. (Cottage Street, Midland Park, N.J. 07432) (piano solo). Some unpublished works in the Library of the Performing Arts, Lincoln Center, New York City; all unpublished works are available through Okra Music Corporation (see under Music Publishers).

Louise Talma (b. 1906, France; U.S. citizen), faculty, Hunter College, New York City. Recordings: Toccata for Orchestra (1944), *CRI*-145; "La Corona"—Holy Sonnets of John Donne (1955), for chorus, *CRI*-187; Six Etudes for Piano, *Desto* 7117. Publishers: Carl Fischer, principal publisher; G. Schirmer; Edition Musicus; and Franco Colombo. Unpublished works are in the Library of the Performing Arts, Lincoln Center, New York City, and Library of Congress.

Alexander Tcherepnin (b. 1899, Russia; U.S. citizen), pianist, conductor, lecturer. Recordings (some of the recording labels designated as foreign may not be available in the United States): "Georgiana Suite," op. 92 (1940), *Lyrichord* 103/7103; Suite for Orchestra, op. 87 (1963), *Louisville* 545-2; Symphony No. 2 (1951), *Louisville* 645; Bagatelles, op. 5 (arranged for piano and orchestra), *DGG* (*Deutsche Grammophon*—see *MGM Records*) 138710 (foreign); Concerto for Harmonica and Orchestra, op. 86 (1956), *Heliodor* S-25064 (foreign—see *MGM*); Piano Concerto No. 2 and No. 5, *DGG*-139479 (composer performing); Piano Concerto No. 2, *Louisville* 615 (composer as pianist); "Sonatine Sportive," for saxophone and piano (1939), *Golden Crest* 7028, *Canadian Capitol* W-6066 (foreign), and *Fidelio* 34001 (foreign); Trio for Piano and Strings, op. 34 (1925), *Pro-Musica* 201 (Pro-Musica Records, 900 Lake Shore Drive, Chicago, Illinois 60611); "Nine Chinese Songs," for voice and piano, *IRAMAC* 6517 (foreign); an album of piano music: "Arabesques," op. 11 (1921), "Bagatelles," op. 5 (1918), Nocturnes, op. 2, No. 1, and "Sonatine Romantique," op. 4 (1918), played by the composer, *Music Library* 7043; 12 Preludes, op. 85 (1954) and "Expressions," op. 81, for piano, both on *Music Library* 7072; "Showcase" for piano, *Music Library* 7098; "Bagatelles" and Second Piano Sonata, *Columbia* EMI 80970 (foreign); an album entitled "Tcherepnin Plays Tcherepnin" containing: First Piano Sonata, Preludes, "Nostalgiques," "Bagatelles," Prelude, "Expression," Impromptu, Etude, "Burlesque," all on *Pathé Marconi HMV* (foreign); Introduction and Interlude from Suite for Harpsichord, on *WERGO* 60028 (foreign). Out of print recordings include: "Sonatine Sportive," *Decca* (London); "Ode" for cello and piano, *Columbia* 33CX 1700. (Other out-of-print records are outside the scope of this listing.) Publishers: Universal Edition (through Presser) (opera, ballet scores, chamber orchestra, solo cello and chamber orchestra, chamber music, including quartets, quintets, duos, piano solo); Durand, Paris (Elkan–Vogel in U.S.) (orchestral, cello and orchestra, chamber music, songs, piano solo including works for children and transcriptions); Benno Balan (Presser) (orchestral); Associated Music (ballet score, chamber orchestra, harmonica and orchestra or piano); Belaieff (through Boosey & Hawkes) (ballet, orchestral, piano concertos, narrator and chamber ensemble or piano, cantata, chamber music for solo instruments and accompaniment, flute ensembles, songs, works for piano including solo, two pianos 4-hands, transcriptions and pieces for children); Schott's Söhne, Mainz (through Associated) (chamber orchestra, piano concerto, miscellaneous concertos, small chamber ensembles, piano music including solo, two pianos 4-hands, and transcriptions for children); J. W. Chester, London (piano concerto, songs, two pianos 4-hands, piano transcriptions); Heugel & Cie, Paris (through Presser) (piano with orchestra, violin and piano, songs, piano solo, two pianos 4-hands, children's pieces for piano, and piano studies); Max Eschig, Paris (through Associated Music) (piano with string orchestra, solo piano, and two pianos 4-hands); Hinrichsen Edition, London (through C. F. Peters) (piano concerto, and two pianos 4-hands); Simrock (through Associated Music) (salon orchestra, violin and piano, piano solo, viola da gamba and chamber orchestra); C. F. Peters (ballet scores, works for orchestra, organ, piano solo, two pianos 4-hands, harpsichord, choral, piano studies); Hamelle, Paris (through Elkan–Vogel) (piano solo); Commercial Press, Shanghai (music availability doubtful) (piano studies); Boosey & Hawkes, London (through New York branch) (opera, orchestral, piano solo); Boosey & Hawkes, New York (timpani and orchestra or band, timpani and piano, brass and percussion); Ricordi, Paris (through Franco Colombo) (piano transcriptions); Leduc, Paris (saxophone and piano, songs); Lyche, Oslo (C. F. Peters) (piano solo); E. B. Marks (trumpet trio, piano solo); Bessel & Cie, Paris (Associated Music) (salon orchestra); G. Schirmer (orchestral); Leeds (MCA Music) (orchestral, band, piano solo); Templeton Publishing (through Shawnee Press) (ballet scores, orchestral, narrator with orchestra, narrator with piano and percussion, piano solo); Summy–Birchard (piano music for children including works for piano 4-hands); Ernst Eulenburg of London and Zürich (C. F. Peters) (orchestral, string orchestra); Pagani & Bro. (accordion solo); Bote & Bock (through Associated Music) (string duo); Hans Gerig, Cologne (MCA Music) (cantata, songs).

Randall Thompson (b. 1899). Recordings: "Alleluia" (1940), for chorus, *Victor* LSC-7043, *Gregorian Institute* EL-19, *Music Library* 6996, *Music Library* 7085, and *Cambridge* 403 (all choral anthology recordings); "Peaceable Kingdom," *Music Library* 7065 and *Lyrichord* 7124; "Last Words of David," for chorus, *Golden Crest* S-4032; Symphony No. 2 (1932), on *Columbia* MS-7392 and *Desto* 6406. Out of print: "Testament of Freedom" (1943), on *Mercury* 50073. Publishers: E. C. Schirmer (for large choral works with orchestra, and solo vocal works); Carl Fischer (orchestral works including symphonies).

Virgil Thomson (b. 1896), conductor, lecturer, author. Recordings: "Arcadian Songs and Dances" (1948) for orchestra, from the film "Louisiana Story," *Decca* 9616/3207; Concerto for Cello (1949) and "Mother of Us All," suite from the opera, for orchestra, *Columbia* CML-4468; Concerto for Flute, Strings, and Percussion (1954), *Louisville* 663; "Feast of Love," for voice and orchestra, *Mercury* 90429; "Four Saints in Three Acts," (1934) *Victor* LM-2756 (abridged version with composer conducting); Mass for Two-Part Chorus and Percussion (1934), *Cambridge* 412 (composer conducting); "Plow That Broke the Plains" (1939), suite from the music for film, *Vanguard* 2095; Psalms 123 and 126, for chorus, *Overtone* 2; "Scenes from Holy Infancy (Joseph and Angels)" (1937), *Gregorian Institute* EL-19 (in a collection called "Thirteen Centuries of Christian Choral Art—20th Century"); Sonata da Chiesa (1936) for five instruments, Violin Sonata (1930), "Praises and Prayers" (1963), all on *CRI*-207 (composer as pianist or conductor); Sonata No. 4 (1940), "Cantabile: Portrait of Nicolas de Chatelain" (1940), *Decca* DL 10021/710021 (an album called "Six Americans"—music for harpsichord); "A Solemn Music" (1949) for wind ensemble, *Mercury* 50084; String Quartet No. 2 (1932), *Columbia* CML-4987; Suite for Orchestra: "The River," from the film score, *Desto* 405/6405, *Vanguard* 2095; Symphony on a Hymn Tune (1928), *Mercury* 90429; Variations on Sunday School Tunes (1930) for organ, *Counterpoint* 5522. Out of print: "Arcadian Songs," *Epic* 3809/BC1147; "Filling Station," ballet suite, *Vox* PL-9050. Publishers: G. Schirmer (orchestral, choral, vocal, operas, and music for band); Elkan–Vogel (piano and chamber ensemble); Boosey & Hawkes (orchestral, chamber, vocal); Southern (orchestral, vocal); Franco Colombo (orchestra, chamber, choral, and vocal); Mercury (orchestra, chamber, choral, and piano); Carl Fischer (band, piano); American Music Edition (vocal); H. W. Gray (choral, vocal, chorus with orchestra); Leeds (MCA Music) (orchestral, choral, vocal); Weintraub (through Music Sales Corp.); New Music Edition (Presser) (vocal with piano); Arrow Music (Boosey & Hawkes) (soprano and string quartet); Santee (see Pietro Deiro) (solo accordion).

Francis Thorne (b. 1922), President–Founder, The Thorne Music Fund, Inc. (see Organizations); pianist. Recordings: "Burlesque Overture," for orchestra, and "Rhapsodic Variations," for piano and orchestra, both on *CRI*-216 (composer as pianist); Symphony in One Movement (1963), "Elegy" for Orchestra (1963), Fantasia for String Orchestra (1963), all on *Owl* ORLP-2; Songs (original popular songs played on the piano by the composer), *Owl* ORLP-4; "Liebesrock," *CRI*-S-258; Seven Set Pieces for 13 Players, *Owl* S-20. Publishers: A. Forlivesi (Franco Colombo) (songs, and work for piano); Mercurio (S.R.L. Via Stoppani 10, Rome, Italy) (orchestral, string orchestra); E. B. Marks (Piedmont) (orchestral, choral, piano music). Unpublished music is in the library of American Music Center and Fleisher Collection.

Lester Albert Trimble (b. 1923). Recordings: Symphony in Two Movements (1951) and "Five Episodes," for orchestra (1962), both on *CRI*-187; "Closing Piece" (1957) for orchestra, *CRI*-159; "Four Fragments from the Canterbury Tales," for solo voices, *Columbia* MS-6198. Publishers: C. F. Peters (orchestral, chamber orchestra, smaller chamber ensembles, vocal, choral); Duchess Music (MCA Music) (orchestral, piano solo). Unpublished works: American Music Center, Fleisher Collection, and American Composers Alliance.

Harry Gilbert Trythall (b. 1930), faculty, George Peabody College for Teachers, Nashville. Recordings: Symphony No. 1 (1958 and 1961 revised), *CRI*-155; "Entropy" for Stereo Bass, Improvisation Group, and Stereo Tapes, Op. 15 (1967), *Golden Crest* S-4085. Unpublished works in American Music Center.

Charles Turner (b. 1921), Dean, Arts and Music Department, Wykeham Rise School, Washington, Connecticut. Recordings: "Serenade for Icarus," for violin and piano (1957), *Golden Crest* 4072. Publisher is G. Schirmer (orchestral, ballet scores, vocal, chamber). Unpublished music: American Music Center.

Vladimir Alexis Ussachevsky (b. 1911, China; U.S. citizen), faculty, Columbia University; Chairman of Committee of Direction, Columbia–Princeton Electronic Music Center. Recordings: "Experimental Composition No. 1" (1952) and "Underwater Waltz," both electronic works (the latter is mislabeled as "Sonic Contours" on the record), *Folkways* FX6160; "A Piece for Tape Recorder" (1956), and, in conjunction with Otto Luening, "A Poem in Cycles and Bells" (1954) for tape recorder and orchestra, both on *CRI*-112; "Rhapsodic Variations for Tape Recorder and Orchestra" (1954) (Luening is collaborator), *Louisville* 545-5; three pieces: "Linear Contrasts" (1958), "Metamorphoses" (1957), and "Experiment 4711" (1958), all on *Orpheum* (*Son Nova*) SN-3; "Creation: Prologue" for recorded choruses and electronic accompaniment (1961), *Columbia* ML-5966/MS-6566; "Concerted Piece" for orchestra and electronic sounds (with Luening), and "Of Wood and Brass," and "Wireless Fantasy," *CRI*-227; "Tape Music–An Historic Concert" (with Luening), *Desto* 6466; all of the foregoing titles are productions of The Electronic Music Center. Out of print: "Sonic Contours" (1952) and, in conjunction with Luening, "Incantation" (1953), on *Innovations Records* (Gene Bruck Enterprises). Principal publisher is American Composers Alliance. Unpublished works are at the Columbia–Princeton Electronic Music Center, 632 West 125th Street, New York, N.Y. 10027.

David Van Vactor (b. 1906), faculty, University of Tennessee; Conductor, Knoxville Symphony Orchestra, Knoxville, Tennessee; guest conductor abroad. Recordings: Symphony No. 1 (1937), *CRI*-225 (composer as conductor); Symphony No. 2 (1958), *CRI*-169 (composer conducting); Fantasia, Chaconne and Allegro for orchestra (1957), *Louisville* 58-6; an album entitled "The Music of David Van

Vactor," *Everest* 3236 (composer conducting) contains: "Overture to a Comedy," No. 2 (1941), Bagatelles Nos. 3 and 5 (1938), Octet for Brass (1963), "Variazione Solenne" (1941—originally entitled "Gothic Impressions"), and Quintet for Flute and Strings (1932); "Concerto a quattro" for three flutes, harp and orchestra (1935) and Concerto for viola and orchestra (1940), *Orion* 7024; "Economy Band," *Golden Crest* S-4085; Music for Woodwinds: Solos, Duets, Trios, Quartets, Quintets, Double Quintets, 2- *Orion* 7025; Ode, Sarabande con Variazioni, Passacaglia, Chorale and Allegro, Prelude and March, Four Etudes for Winds and Percussion (composer conducting all), all on *Orion* 7029; Pastoral and Dance for Flute and Orchestra, Suite for Orchestra on Chilean Folk Tunes (1962), Recitative and Saltarello (1947), Introduction and Presto for Strings, Sinfonia Breve (1964) all on *Orion* 6910 (composer conducting). Publishers: American Music Edition (orchestral); G. Schirmer (string quartet with flute); New Music Edition (Presser) (vocal); Templeton (Shawnee) (string orchestra). Unpublished music is in the Fleisher Collection.

John Weedon Verrall (b. 1908), faculty, University of Washington, Seattle. Recording: String Quartet No. 4 (1949), *Music Library Recordings* MLR-7028. String Quartet No. 7, *CRI* S-270. Out of print: Prelude and Allegro for Strings (1948), *MGM* E-3771. Publishers: Oliver Ditson (Presser) (chamber, band, piano); Boston Music Co. (chamber, band, piano); Galaxy (orchestra, chamber); C. F. Peters (chamber, organ); New Valley (chamber, piano); Dow Publications (Box 176, Oyster Bay, N.Y. 11771) (chamber). Unpublished music at American Composers Alliance and Fleisher Collection.

John Vincent (b. 1902), occasional conductor, retired teacher. Recordings: String Quartet in G and "Consort" for Piano and String Quartet (1960), both on *Contemporary* 6009; Symphony in D, *Louisville* 572. Out of print: Symphony in D, *Columbia* ML-5263; and the same work coupled with "Symphonic Poem after Descartes," *Columbia* ML-5579/MS-6179. Mills Music was publisher of the composer's music prior to 1967 (theory workbooks and texts, string orchestra, orchestral, voice with orchestra, narrator with orchestra, ballet music, piano and string quartet, choral); publisher of all works since 1967 is MCA Music. Unpublished scores are in the Fleisher Collection.

Joseph Frederick Wagner (b. 1900), composer-in-residence, Pepperdine College, Los Angeles; conductor; author. Recordings: "Ballad of Brotherhood" for chorus (1947), *Harmony* (*Columbia*) 11273; "Missa Sacra" (1952) and "Liturgy" (1954), for chorus and organ and organ solo, respectively, *Dorian* 1023; "Fantasy Sonata" for harp (1963), *Boîte à Musique* (BAM) LD-092 (a foreign label distributed in the United States by Record & Tape Sales, 821 Broadway, New York, N.Y. 10003); "Sonata of Sonnets" (1961), Preludes and Toccata (1964), "Concert Piece" (1966) —all on *Orion* 7036. Publishers: Southern Music Publishing (principal publisher) (instrumental, vocal, chamber, opera, band, and organ); Boosey & Hawkes (instrumental, vocal, small orchestra); Robert B. Brown Music Co. (instrumental, orchestral, vocal, chamber, organ); Chappell (instrumental, vocal); Elkan–Vogel (vocal); Leeds (MCA) (band music); Lyra Music (harp and strings); Mills Music (piano, vocal with orchestra, band); R. D. Row (Carl Fischer) (organ solo); Franco Colombo (vocal with orchestra or organ); University of Miami Press (brass and percussion). Unpublished scores in Fleisher Collection.

Robert Eugene Ward (b. 1917), President, North Carolina School of the Arts, Winston-Salem; conductor. Recordings: "The Crucible" (1961) opera, *CRI* 2-record set, 168; Divertimento for orchestra, *CRI*-194; "Euphony" for orchestra (1954), *Louisville* 545-10; "Hush'd be the Camps Today" (1941) for chorus and orchestra, *CRI*-165; "Jubilation Overture" (1946) for orchestra, *CRI*-159; "Sorrow of Mydath," for voice and piano, contained in a 2-record set entitled "Songs of American Composers," *Desto* 411-2/6411-2; Symphony No. 1 (1941) *Desto* 405/6405; Symphony No. 2 (1947), *CRI*-127; Symphony No. 3 (1950) and "Songs for Pantheists,"

(1951) for soprano and orchestra, both on *CRI*-206; Concerto for Piano and Orchestra, *Desto* 7123. Publishers: principal publisher is Highgate Press, which has published virtually all of the composer's orchestral works as well as stage works, chamber music, choral, and vocal works; other publishers are H. W. Gray (choral); Merrymount Music (Presser) (choral, piano); Peer-Southern Music Publishing (chamber, orchestral, voice with piano).

David Ward-Steinman (b. 1936), faculty, San Diego State College, pianist. Recordings: Sonata for Piano (1957) and Three Songs for Clarinet and Piano (1957), both on *Contemporary Composers Guild* No. 1 (composer as pianist); "Fragments from Sappho" (1965) for soprano, flute, clarinet, and piano to be released by *Composers Recordings Inc. CRI* S-238 (composer as pianist). Publishers: Mercury Music Corp. (choral); Editions Salabert, Paris (Franco Colombo) (piano solo); MJQ Music (concert jazz works for band and orchestra); Lee Roberts Music (G. Schirmer) (piano, school orchestra); Highgate (piano); Holt, Rinehart & Winston, New York (vocal and choral works in "Exploring Music" series); San Diego State College Press (oratorio); American Composers Alliance Facsimile Editions has published the bulk of the composer's works and has on file a number of unpublished works.

Ben Weber (b. 1916). Recordings: "Concert-Aria after Solomon," Op. 29, for soprano and chamber ensemble, *Desto* 422/6422; Prelude and Passacaglia, Op. 42 (1955), for orchestra, *Louisville* 566; Serenade, Op. 39 (1953), for flute, oboe, cello, and harpsichord, *Decca* 1002/71002; "Symphony on Poems of William Blake," Op. 33 (1951), for baritone and orchestra, *CRI*-120; "Dolmen—An Elegy," for winds and strings (1964), *Louisville* 676. Out of print: Concertino, Op. 45 for flute, oboe, clarinet, and string quartet, Fantasia, Op. 25, for piano solo, and Serenade for Strings, Op. 46, all on *Epic* LC-3567/BC-1022; "Episodes" for piano, Op. 26a, *MGM Records;* Five Pieces, for cello and piano, Op. 13, on *Paradox Records;* Rapsodie Concertante for viola and small orchestra, Op. 47, *MGM Records.* Publishers: Composer Facsimile Edition of American Composers Alliance, principal publisher (orchestral, including concertos and vocal work with orchestra, chamber music, voice with piano or other instruments, choral, piano solo); Boosey & Hawkes (string orchestra, violin and piano); E. B. Marks (orchestral, vocal with piano, piano); Lawson–Gould (piano solo); Merion Music (Presser) (piano); New Music (Presser) (solo instrumental, chamber, vocal with solo cello, organ solo); Boelke–Bomart (piano solo). Unpublished music is on file with American Composers Alliance. All of the composer's works are deposited in the Library of Congress, including original manuscripts.

Hugo Weisgall (b. 1912, Czechoslovakia; U.S. citizen). Faculty, Queens College, New York; Chairman of Faculty, Jewish Theological Seminary (Cantor's Institute); guest conductor. Recording: "The Tenor," opera composed in 1950, *CRI* 2-record set 197; "Fancies and Inventions" (1970) and "The Stronger," (opera), *CRI* S-273. Out of print: "The Stronger," (opera) *Columbia* ML-5106. The composer has an exclusive publishing arrangement with Presser for all works (operas, orchestral, songs, chamber music, keyboard music and choral works.) Mercury Music (also Presser) has published a vocal work.

Charles Whittenberg (b. 1927), faculty, University of Connecticut, Storrs. Recordings: "Electronic Study II with Contrabass," (1962), *Advance Records* No. 1; Three Pieces for Clarinet Alone (1963), *Advance* No. 4; "Triptych" for Brass Quintet (1962), *Folkways* 3651 and *Desto* 6474/7; "Games of 5," for Woodwind Quintet, Op. 44 (1968), *Serenus* 12028; Quartet in one movement, *CRI* S-257. Publishers: C. F. Peters (chamber music); McGinnis and Marx (solo instrumental); other publishers are General Music, American Composers Alliance, and Murbo (Bourne). Some unpublished works are in the collection of the New York Public Library.

Frank Wigglesworth (b. 1918), Chairman, Music Department, New School, New York, N.Y. Recordings: Symphony No. 1 (1957), *CRI*-110; "Lake Music," for solo flute, *CRI*-212. Publishers: Merion Press (Presser) (chamber music); Composers Facsimile Edition (choral, orchestra, chamber). Unpublished music with American Composers Alliance.

Joseph Wood (b. 1915), faculty, Oberlin College, Ohio. Recording: "Poem for Orchestra" (1950), *CRI*-134. Publisher is Composer Facsimile Editions (orchestral, chamber, vocal). Unpublished works with American Music Center and American Composers Alliance.

Charles Wuorinen (b. 1938), faculty, Manhattan School of Music; pianist and conductor. Recordings: Symphony No. 3 (1959), *CRI*-149; Chamber Concerto for Cello and 10 Players (composer conducting), *Nonesuch* 71263; Chamber Concerto for Flute and 10 Players (1964), *CRI* S-230; Piano Concerto (1966) (composer as pianist), *CRI*-239; "Janissary Music," (1966) for percussion, *CRI*-231; "Ringing Changes" for percussion ensemble (composer conducting), *Nonesuch* 71263; Piano Variations (1963), *Advance*-3; Prelude and Fugue (percussion), *Golden Crest* 4004; "Time's Encomium," for synthesizer, *Nonesuch* 71225. Principal publisher: C. F. Peters (chamber music, instrumental solo music, solo instrument with orchestra, keyboard music). Some works on file with ACA.

Robert A. Wykes (b. 1926), faculty, Washington University, St. Louis. Recordings: "Four Studies for Piano" (1958), Flute and Piano Sonata (1955), Concerto for 11 Instruments (1956), and Four American Indian Lyrics (1957) for chorus, all recorded on *Washington University* label 1009. Principal publisher is Theodore Presser (choral, orchestral).

Yehudi Wyner (b. 1929, Canada; U.S. citizen), faculty, Yale University; pianist. Recordings: Concerto Duo for Violin and Piano (1957), *CRI*-161 (composer as pianist); Serenade for Seven Instruments (1958), *CRI*-141 (composer as pianist). Publishers: Merrymount (Presser) (vocal); Associated Music (principal) (vocal, chamber, orchestral). Unpublished music with American Composers Alliance.

Richard Yardumian (b. 1917). Recordings: Passacaglia, Recitatives and Fugue (Piano Concerto), *Victor* LSC-3243; "Come Creator Spirit," for solo voice, chorus and orchestra, *Victor* LSC-2979; Symphony No. 1 (1950), Symphony No. 2 for voice and orchestra (1965), and "Chorale," all on *Columbia* ML-6259/MS-6859. Out of print: "Cantus Animae et Cordis," for string orchestra, and "Chorale Prelude" for orchestra, on *Columbia* ML-5629/MS-6229; Concerto for Violin and Orchestra (1951) and Symphony No. 1, on *Columbia* ML-5862/MS-6462. Publishers: Elkan–Vogel (major publisher) (orchestral, piano with orchestra, violin and orchestra, solo violin, etc.); H. W. Gray (choral).

Eugene Zador (b. 1894, Hungary; U.S. citizen). Recordings: "Hungarian Caprice," "Dance," "Divertimento for Strings," and Variations on a Hungarian Folksong (1928), all recorded on *Music Library* 7099; "Lonely Wayfarer" and "Three Rondells," both works for women's voices, *Music Library* S-7095; "Csardas Rhapsodie" for orchestra (1939), *Fantasy* 9001. Publishers: C. F. Peters (orchestral); Mills Music (orchestral and choral); MCA Music (orchestral); Lawson–Gould (choral). European publishers are Eulenburg, London (Peters); Ries and Erler (Peters); and Universal Edition, Vienna (Presser).

Part 7 | Music Festivals

The term "music festival" has broad meaning in the United States. Sometimes it is used accurately to reflect all its implications. Often it is used because it has a good promotional ring or because there is no adequate substitute word for attracting audiences. It is sometimes an outright misnomer.

For the most part, American music festivals are musical events organized to extend the regular concert season into the summer months. The majority of such events occur between the months of March and September, the highest concentration taking place in July and August. Little or no change in music programming occurs during the summer. Prior to the advent of air-conditioned concert halls in some communities, however, given the continuity of traditional programming, the new attraction for the summer music listener was the change of venue—the invitation to hear music in the parks. Although parks are still popular places to hold concerts, the acoustically secure concert hall that provides the added benefit of controlled temperature is being used with increasing frequency, particularly in the cities, disrupting not at all the sense of a prolonged regular concert season.

Despite this trend, America remains enormously rich in the variety of its summer musical events.

The greatest number of festivals take place in West Coast and Eastern Seaboard states, with most of the regional activity in California and New York. Of the four extreme corners of the country, only Southern California and the New England states taken as a whole have concentrations of festival events. Florida, despite its favorable climate and tourist facilities, is noticeably lacking in important music festivals. In the Midwest, however, festivals are located in large cities, on the campuses of universities and colleges, and in newly constructed cultural complexes. Many of the music festivals in the Midwest have long and noteworthy histories; Illinois, Michigan, and Ohio can claim the greatest number.

Festivals are readily categorized. There are (1) free municipal concerts (Boston's Esplanade, Chicago's Grant Park, the New York Philharmonic and Metropolitan Opera concerts, Robin Hood Dell in Philadelphia, San Francisco's Stern Grove, etc.); (2) amphitheater concerts (Chicago's Ravinia, Garden State in New Jersey, Hollywood Bowl, Saratoga in New York); (3) festival–institutes (Tanglewood, Ambler, Blossom, Aspen, Wolf Trap, Chautauqua, Meadowbrook); (4) folk festivals (American Folksong Festival, Kentucky; annual Fiddlers' Convention, North Carolina; Old Fiddlers' Convention, Virginia); (5) youth-oriented festivals or summer camps (Interlochen, Chautauqua, Brevard, Sewanee); (6) pops orchestra concerts (in Boston, Detroit, and Cleveland); (7) intimate music presentations (Caramoor, Peter Britt, Masson Vineyards, Bach Carmel, Castle Hill, Red Fox, Peninsula); and (8) unique events (Marlboro, Santa Fe, Butler University's Romantic Festival, Jacob's Pillow, Newport Jazz).

American festivals presented in conjunction with special summer music schools have enjoyed considerable international attention. Schools, such as those at Aspen and Berkshire, maintain an international flavor with the presence of foreigners who come as students, teachers, or performers.

It can be seen that most festivals are organized to take advantage of some unusual physical or geographical factor or to assume direction from a central theme. The latter may be contemporary music, folk music, operetta, or an ensemble whose name has become synonymous with that of the festival. There are many examples of attractive festival settings from Santa Fe to Caramoor; but in crowded cities, even the simple expedient of an outdoor concert in a stadium or public park is enough of an advantage to attract audiences.

Many festivals make little attempt to draw any but local or statewide audiences. The large cities, however, receive countless vacationers, tourists, and conventioners who help to swell festival crowds. In this way events such as the Grant Park or the free outdoor Metropolitan Opera performances acquire national significance. The presence of well-known performers is still the all-important ingredient in a musical event if national or international interest is expected. Festival performances by great artists invariably receive reviews in the daily press and in music periodicals.

Some festivals are subsidized by municipalities and are free to the public. Concerts thus organized are not "festive occasions" in the real sense; however, informality abounds, particularly for open-air concerts, and audiences often may eat and drink while listening to the music.

The following list of festival events is necessarily representative and, despite its length, is certainly not all-inclusive. However, it is sufficient to demonstrate manifold examples of American festivals. (Other summertime events may be found in the lists of instrumental ensembles, opera companies, and music tents.)

Alabama

BIRMINGHAM FESTIVAL OF THE ARTS, c/o Chamber of Commerce, 1914 6th Avenue North, Birmingham, Alabama 35203. Founded in 1951, the Festival features both the performing and the visual arts: plays, ballets, musical concerts, lectures, and exhibitions. The events take place outdoors as well as in Temple Theater, Municipal Auditorium, college campus theaters and recital halls, and high school auditoriums. (By 1972, the Birmingham–Jefferson Civic Center, with a 3,000-seat Concert Hall and an 800-seat theater, will be completed for the use of the Festival.) Some events are free to the public. The Festival is sponsored by business groups and through private donations. It is held generally in the spring (in 1969, from March 14 to March 30). Each festival has thus far based its theme on a different country (Greece, in 1968; Italy, in 1969, etc.). Performers in the past have included **Gina Bachauer,** appearing with the Birmingham Symphony Orchestra, the Harkness Ballet, **Anna Moffo, Hal Holbrook,** and others. The Festival is under the direction of the Festival Chairman, who is selected each year.

Alaska

ALASKA FESTIVAL OF MUSIC, Box 325, Anchorage, Alaska 99501. Executive Director: **Frank W. Pinkerton,** former conductor of the Anchorage Symphony; Music Director and Conductor: **Robert Shaw** (since 1956). Founded in 1956. The Festival is sponsored by the Anchorage Symphony and the Anchorage Community Chorus (becoming the Festival Orchestra and Chorus with 64 and 79 members, respectively) and the Anchorage Community College of the University of Alaska. The Festival is organized to present more than a series of concerts. Visiting musicians are expected to work closely with Alaskans in study, rehearsals, and performances; in addition to musical performances, there are lectures and exhibitions. College credit is granted for participation in the workshops and for membership in the Festival Chorus or Orchestra. Also held within the framework of the Festival is the Alaska Native Arts Festival, consisting of exhibitions of native arts, crafts, games, and Eskimo music and dance. The Festival lasts for two weeks and is held in June. The events take place in Anchorage West High School; other locations are used for organ and recorder workshops, ballet performances, etc. Guest performers at the Festival in past years have been: **Donald Johanos** and **Thor Johnson,** conductors; Los Angeles String Quartet, Eastman Trio, UCLA Opera Theatre, **Adele Addison, John McCollum, Donald Gramm, John Celentano,** and **Raphael Druian,** among others.

Arkansas

INSPIRATION POINT FINE ARTS COLONY FESTIVAL, Eureka Springs, Arkansas 72632. Location of the Festival is at Inspiration Point, Route 62, seven miles west of Eureka Springs. Musical Director is **Isaac Van Grove,** appointed in 1954. The Colony is sponsored by the Federations of Music Clubs of Arkansas, Kansas, Missouri, and Oklahoma (however, see Phillips University under Schools). The Festival is some ten days of performances of operas presented by students, both singers and instrumentalists, who study at the colony's opera and orchestra workshops. The performances are usually held during the last two weeks in July. Four or five operas are performed along with concerts of orchestral and choral music.

OZARK FOLK FESTIVAL, Eureka Springs, Arkansas 72632. Mailing address is c/o Ozark Festival, Inc. Founded 1947. Held the third weekend in October in the City Auditorium and in the streets and parks of the town. Events feature folk music, square dancing, and performances on old-time musical instruments; impromptu performances along the sidewalks and in the parks are a tradition with the Festival. All events are free except the nightly performances in the Auditorium and Sunday afternoon special performance (which in 1968 consisted of a concert by the University of Arkansas Schola Cantorum). Folk performers have included **Boyce Davis,** folk singer; **Max Hunter,** singer of Ozark ballads; and **Jerry & Rhonda Hayes,** songs and banjo playing. Master of Ceremonies is **Donald "Red" Blanchard.** The Festival is claimed to be one of the oldest of its kind in the nation. Crowds estimated to number up to 15,000 are said to come into town each day of the Festival.

California

CABRILLO MUSIC FESTIVAL, 6500 Soquel Drive, Aptos, California 95003. All concerts take place in mid-August for ten days in the Cabrillo College Theatre (541 seats) in Aptos. Founded in 1963. Administrative Director is **Timothy Welch;** Musical Director and Conductor is **Richard Williams.** (From its inception to 1968, the Festival's Musical Director was **Gerhard Samuel.**) Sponsorship of the Festival is by the Cabrillo Guild of Music, Inc. The concerts consist of evening and afternoon performances of orchestral music (by the 60- to 65-member Festival Orchestra), concertos, works for dance and orchestra, staged opera, choral music, chamber music and solo recitals. Nonmusical events are the free art exhibits open before and after the concerts. A significant amount of new music is played, as well as rarely performed old works including U.S. and world premieres. Guest performers in past festivals have been: **Noel Lee, Charles Bressler, Isidor Lateiner, Ludwig Olshansky, Carlos Chavez,** and others.

CARMEL BACH FESTIVAL, Box 503, Carmel, California 93921. Carmel is located on the Monterey Peninsula in Southern California. Founded in 1935 by Dene Denny and Hazel Watrous (later both concert managers) as an outgrowth of a series of string quartet concerts begun in 1932. The quartet was supplanted by an amateur orchestra upon which was founded the Bach Festival at Carmel with the composer **Ernst Bacon** as first conductor. From the beginning, the Festival established some of its now quite well-known traditions including the use of the Carmel

Mission Basilica (built in 1771) for some of the performances. The Festival has taken place annually, with the exception of three years during World War II. Executive Secretary: **Mrs. Alastair MacKay;** President: **Arthur L. Dahl;** Music Director and Conductor (since 1956): **Sandor Salgo.** The Festival is organized as a nonprofit educational institution and exists entirely through voluntary contributions of both money and effort from a wide community and professional base. Although the focus is on the music of J. S. Bach—his major choral works, cantatas (including those infrequently performed), chamber music, organ works, and concertos —the music of other seventeenth- and eighteenth-century composers is an important aspect of the programming. Thus the music of Haydn, Mozart, Purcell, Monteverdi, J. C. Bach, and Beethoven (the latter in 1970 in celebration of the 200th anniversary of the composer's birth) is also performed. Notable single works performed in recent years have been Cavalli's "Messa Concertata" (first U.S. performance), Carissimi's "Judicium Salomonis," Handel's "Saul" and "Athaliah," and the "Play of Herod." Most of the concerts take place in the Sunset School Auditorium; other concerts, lectures, or recitals take place at Parish Hall of All Saints Episcopal Church, Bethlehem Lutheran Church in Monterey, and Community Church in Carmel Valley. Free events are the lectures and occasional symposiums. The Festival lasts for ten days beginning in mid-July. Performing groups appearing regularly are the Festival Orchestra (about 45 members) and the Chorus and Chorale (about 30 voices each). Performers over the years have included: **Carole Bogard, Joanna Simon, Fernando Valenti, James Schwabacher, Walter Trampler, Louise di Tullio, Istvan Nadas, LaNoue Davenport, David Abel, Lawrence Moe, Thomas Paul, Robert Oliver,** and **Joseph Schuster.** The harpsichordist, **Ralph Linsey,** has performed for many of the festivals as accompanist and as part of the basso continuo instrumentalists.

ISOMATA MUSIC FESTIVAL, Box 38, Idyllwild School of Music and the Arts (ISOMATA), Idyllwild, California 92349. The Festival is held in conjunction with the Idyllwild School, a summer school founded in 1950 and owned and operated by the University of Southern California since 1964. All aspects of ISOMATA are supported by the Idyllwild Arts Foundation and ISOMATA Associates. Director of the School and Festival is **Joseph G. Saetveit.** Idyllwild is located on 200 acres of valley near the San Jacinto Mountains west of Palm Springs (about 120 miles southeast of Los Angeles). Its main purpose is to offer an opportunity for study in music, art, drama, dance, and photography to both children (from age three) and adults for all levels of interest and participation. The summer session, lasting 11 weeks, has had enrollments totaling over 3,300 students, or about 300 students a week. Families can enroll as a group. The Festival, begun first in 1962, takes place during the final weeks of the summer schedule, from mid-August to September 1. Choral, orchestral, and chamber music is performed Friday and Saturday evenings and Sunday afternoon, totaling about eight concerts. **Daniel Lewis** is conductor of the ISOMATA Festival Orchestra; the 180-voice Festival Choir and the Madrigal Singers are under the direction of **Robert Holmes.**

JUNIOR BACH FESTIVAL, Box 590 (Junior Bach Festival Association), Berkeley, California 94701. Founded in 1953 by **Tirzah Mailkoff.** President (1972–1973) is **Mrs. Byron Seeburt;** Music Director is **William Duncan Allen.** The Festival comprises four days of performances exclusively of the music of Johann Sebastian Bach by musicians under the age of twenty-one. The performers are selected by a series of auditions usually held in February; those chosen are given dress rehearsals just prior to the Festival concerts in April. Every category of Bach's music is offered. Choral and instrumental groups are from secondary schools in the Berkeley area including the Berkeley High School String Orchestra, Modesto High School Concert Choir and Orchestra, California School for the Blind Glee Club and others. The performance standards during the Festival, which is believed to be the only one of its kind in existence, are often very near professional levels. Many former "alumni" are now professional musicians. The Festival is supported by volunteer help and financial contributions from organizations and individuals in the Bay area. Concerts take place in several locations: the San Francisco College for Women, Kaiser Auditorium in Oakland, Hertz Hall on the University of California campus in Berkeley, First Unitarian Church in Berkeley and others varying from year to year. Admission is charged for all concerts except the opening concert in Hertz Hall.

MUSIC AT THE VINEYARDS, P.O. Box 97, Saratoga, California 93306. Year round address is 1255 Post Street, Suite 505, San Francisco, California 94109. The location of the Festival is at the historic Paul Masson Mountain Winery on Pierce Road in Saratoga. The Festival was formed in 1958. The Managing Director is **Norman N. Fromm;** Musical Director is **Sandor Salgo,** who has directed the concerts since 1963. The Paul Masson Vineyards is the sole sponsor of the event. The concerts are held on three weekends during the summer (in 1970, from June 27 to August 30) with two performances, respectively on Saturday and Sunday afternoons at 3:30 PM, of each concert. The program content emphasizes music that is infrequently performed. In general, each concert features one performing group or solo artist. All net proceeds from the concerts are given to music scholarship funds at San Francisco State College and San Jose State College. The seating capacity for the performances is 900. Performers appearing at past concerts have been the Lenox Quartet, **Zvi Zeitlin,** the New York Woodwind Quintet, The Temianka Chamber Ensemble, Beaux Arts String Quartet, and others.

OJAI FESTIVAL, c/o Ojai Festivals, Ltd., P.O. Box 185, Ojai, California 93023. Ojai is located on Route 150 about 25 miles east of Santa Barbara. Concerts take place in Ojai Festival Bowl in Civic Center Park. Founded in 1947. Artistic Director is **Michael Tilson Thomas.** Concerts are spread over three consecutive days, in May or June, totaling about five performances in the morning, afternoon, and evening programs. Contemporary music has always remained an important part of the programs. Performers at the festivals have been: **Robert Craft, Pierre Boulez, Judith Raskin, Robert La Marchina, Karl Ulrich Schnabel,** the La Salle String Quartet, et al.

REDLANDS BOWL SUMMER MUSIC FESTIVAL, c/o Redlands Bowl, P.O. Box 466, Redlands, California 92373. Begun in 1924, the Festival is held in the Redlands Bowl, an outdoor amphitheater, from June through August, with programs similar to many outdoor bowl concerts. General Manager is **Charles D. Perlee; Harry Farbman** is Musical Director.

SAN FRANCISCO POPS CONCERTS, c/o Art Commission, 165 Grove Street, San Francisco, California 94102. A series of concerts founded in 1950 and held in the Civic Auditorium in San Francisco. The concerts are sponsored by the city of San Francisco and are organized by the Art Commission. The Pops Orchestra (drawn from the San Francisco Symphony) is conducted by **Arthur Fiedler.** The season lasts about one month, from July to August, with about nine concerts in all. Over 6,000 seats are available for each performance, but about 1,500 seats are arranged at tables on the main floor where refreshments are also served. As many as 48,000 people have attended the season's performances.

STANFORD SUMMER FESTIVALS OF THE ARTS, c/o Stanford Summer Festivals, P.O. Box 3006, Stanford, California 94305. Organized in 1963; the first festival was held in 1964. All events take place on the campus of Stanford University: Memorial Hall (1,700 seats), Frost Amphitheater (2,500 to 8,000), Dinkelspiel Auditorium (720), and other auditoriums and galleries. Conceived on a large scale, with some 125 events planned within a span of 49 days (in 1968, but perhaps typical of subsequent festivals), the Festival incorporates a wide variety of art forms in addition to music. Admission is charged for the performances by jazz groups and soloists, symphony orchestra, chamber music ensembles, opera companies, ballet and dance groups, and repertory theater companies, but there are a host of events, numbering from 25 to as many as 50, which are offered free during each festival. These free events serve the educational obligations expected of a university-sponsored festival; however, they are unique in breadth including, as they do, lectures, exhibitions, seminars, concerts, demonstrations, and audience briefings. Total attendance for all events has been estimated at 80,000. Some festivals have attempted to represent some unifying theme within the arts. In 1967, for example, the Festival was organized around the theme "Focus on America;" in 1966, the theme was "20th Century Innovations" (1900–1939). The Festival runs from mid-June to mid-August. Among the groups who have appeared at Stanford are City Center Robert Joffrey Ballet, New York Pro Musica, Philadelphia (string) Quartet, Stanford Chamber Players, Orchestre de la Suisse Romande, the Lenox and Parrenin String Quartets, Ravi Shankar's "Festival of India," New York City Opera, Preservation Hall Jazz Band, and the Count Basie Orchestra. Solo performers include: **Grant Johannesen, Bethany Beardslee,** Ernest Ansermet, **Carl Weinrich, Richard Dyer-Bennett,** and **Paul Badura-Skoda.** Executive Producer of the Festival is **Stephen A. Baffrey;** Director is **Virgil K. Whitaker.**

STARLIGHT BOWL, c/o Burbank Park and Recreation Department, 275 East Olive Avenue, Burbank, California 91503. The Bowl, built in 1951, is located in the Verdugo Mountains above Burbank and is operated by Burbank's Park and Recreation Department. Seating capacity is 2,930. Almost all the musical programs are played at night in a series of concerts usually running from mid-June to mid-September. The program content includes light opera, variety shows, ballet, pops concerts, and ice shows. Performing ensembles are the Burbank Symphony Orchestra, Burbank Choral Club, and the Civic Light Opera Chorus and Orchestra.

STERN GROVE FESTIVAL, c/o Stern Grove Festival Association, 2100 Pacific Avenue, San Francisco, California 94115. Stern Grove is a city park purchased in 1931 from private owners by Mrs. Sigmund Stern and given to San Francisco as a memorial to her husband. Famed for its natural beauty and acoustics, it comprises some 63 acres bounded on the South by Sloat Boulevard, Wawona Street on the North, 19th Avenue on the East, and 34 Avenue on the West. Eucalyptus trees, planted in 1871 by the son of the land's original settlers, firs and redwoods create a highly praised acoustical "shell" and also shelter the Grove from wind and fog. Although the Festival was first established in 1938, musical performances took place there as early as 1932. Founded in 1942, the Association functions as a nonprofit charitable trust, raising the funds for the concerts, but the care of the premises of the Grove is the responsibility of San Francisco's Recreation and Park Department. The Association's Executive Secretary is **Mrs. Elizabeth Eastlund Middione;** Concert Manager (since 1965) is **Albert White.** The Grove, as a city park, provides facilities throughout the season for a variety of recreational activities: parties, lawn bowling, tennis, horseshoe pits, barbecue pits, and tables for picnicking, etc. The Festival, placed in this environment, is meant to be enjoyed by individuals, groups, and families, who often make a visit to the park a day-long event. All of the Festival programs are offered free. They are held on 11 successive Sunday afternoons from mid-June to the end of August and consist of orchestral performances, ballet, musical theater, productions of entire operas, and jazz—the latter having been presented since 1966. Most of the groups appearing at the Festival are from the Bay area: The San Francisco Symphony, San Francisco Woodwind Quintet, University of California Symphony Orchestra, Merola Fund Opera, Western Opera Theatre, San Francisco Municipal Chorus, San Francisco Ballet, Lola Montes Spanish Dance Group, and others. Bruno Walter, Pierre Monteux, **Kurt Herbert Adler,** and **Enrique Jorda** are some of the conductors who have appeared at the Grove in the past. From its inception to 1967, some 403 programs were presented to an audience total of over four million. Average audience attendance is about 12,000.

(MUSIC ACADEMY OF THE WEST) SUMMER FESTIVAL SERIES, Music Academy of the West, 1070 Fairway Road, Santa Barbara, California 93103. The Lobero Theatre, 33 East Canon Perdido in Santa Barbara, and the Academy, situated on 10 acres near the ocean, are the actual locations for the special series of recitals, concerts, and opera performances given by the faculty and students attending the summer session of the Academy. (The school accepts only highly advanced students over sixteen years old in either its instrumental or vocal studies programs. Study is under well-known and active performer-teachers.) Orchestral concerts are conducted by **Maurice Abravanel,** Music Director of the Academy (since 1955) and Conductor of the Utah Symphony. Opera productions, usually limited to one opera sung in English, are under the direction of **Martial Singher,** head of the vocal department. Some seven weekly concerts are given in July and August. Admission is charged, although lectures and recitals are free to "Academy Friends," or supporters of the Academy. Artists performing at the Festival have been: **Gabor Reijto,** cellist; pianists **Leon Fleisher** and **James Fields, Reginald Stewart,** and **Jerome Lowenthal;** violinist **Berl Senofsky,** to name some. The Lobero Theatre holds 669 seats. The concerts were first begun in 1947. **Mrs. Virginia Cochran** is Executive Director.

UCLA CONTEMPORARY MUSIC FESTIVAL, c/o Music Department, University of California at Los Angeles, Los Angeles, California 90024. First festival held in 1968. Schoenberg Hall and Royce Hall on the campus of UCLA were the locations for the first event, which took place on four successive days in January. In addition to the concerts, a panel discussion and lectures about contemporary music were presented. Performers at the first festival were **Gerhard Samuel,** conductor, **Bethany Beardsley,** and the Philadelphia String Quartet. Sole sponsor is UCLA; **Walter Rubsamen** is administrative head; **Aleen Ashforth** is chairman of the Composers' Council.

Colorado

ASPEN MUSIC FESTIVAL AND MUSIC SCHOOL, P.O. Box AA, Aspen, Colorado 81611; New York address: 1860 Broadway, New York, N.Y. 10023. Aspen is located in western Colorado on State Route 82, approximately 200 miles west of Denver. It lies on a plateau along the Roaring Fork River and near Colorado's highest point, Mount Elbert. The spectacular setting for the Festival and the reputation of the summer Music School and its faculty combine to make the Aspen Festival one of America's most attractive summer musical events. The Festival and School consist of a nine-week season running from late June to the end of August. Approximately 400 American and foreign students attend lectures, master classes, and private lessons conducted by the artist-faculty, who teach as well as perform publicly in the large tent-amphitheater (1,500 seats). Festival performances run the gamut of orchestral concerts, chamber, solo, vocal, and instrumental recitals. Operas are performed in the Wheeler Opera House in Aspen. The Aspen Festival Orchestra (which consists of some specially selected students as well as professionals) is conducted by **Jorge Mester,** Festival Music Director, who succeeded **Walter Susskind** in 1970. Artist-faculty performances are three times a week. Over the years performers have been: **Szymon Goldberg, Walter Trampler, Eudice Shapiro, Sidney Harth, Rudolf Firkusny, Claude Frank, Vitya Vronsky,** and Victor Babin, **Jennie Tourel, Philip Farkas, William Masselos,** and many others. Guest conductors have been **Darius Milhaud,** on the composition faculty for many years, **Robert Shaw, Brian Priestman,** and **James Levine.** The Festival and Music School was founded in 1949 as an out-growth of the Goethe Bicentennial Convocation and Music Festival held that year. **Gordon Hardy** is Dean of the School and Executive Vice-President of Music Associates of Aspen, Inc., the sponsoring organization.

CENTRAL CITY FESTIVAL, c/o Central City Opera House Association, 910 Sixteenth Street, Suite 636, Denver, Colorado 80202. The Opera House in Central City (less than an hour's drive west of Denver) is the location for the performances of this festival. Built in 1878, nineteen years after Central City was first settled as a gold-mining frontier town, the structure is among several having historical interest in Central City. Its capacity is about 800 seats. The Central City Opera House Association administers the Festival which, until 1971, consisted of two major opera productions performed alternately for a total of about 40 performances. With the 1971 season, however, the opera productions were suspended in favor of more popular entertainment such as plays and other theatrical productions featuring well-known stars of Hollywood, the stage, and television. In 1972, opera production resumed, presenting that year two operas sung in English. Fifteen performances were offered over a 16-day period. Other programs included Chamber music and Gilbert and Sullivan operettas. Executive Director is **Carl Dahlgren.**

COLORADO PHILHARMONIC FESTIVAL, Box 975, Evergreen, Colorado 80439. Founded in 1966. The Colorado Philharmonic was founded in 1960 by its current Music Director and Conductor, **Walter Charles,** in the town of Estes Park. Its move to Evergreen in 1966 brought it into the Denver Metropolitan Area. The orchestra is primarily a training orchestra for advanced student-musicians from colleges and conservatories throughout the country. The Festival, like others organized by orchestras of this type, is simply a series of public performances of works prepared during a period of intensive rehearsals and practice. In the case of the Colorado Philharmonic, over 19 concerts containing over 57 works are scheduled for public hearing. No two programs are alike; nearly one half of the works performed are infrequently or hardly ever heard in the typical concert hall anywhere in the nation. (Additionally, four children's concerts are performed during the summer season.) The entire 19-program season is compressed within a period of six weeks (in 1971, from July 10 to August 21). Three concerts are given each week: on Wednesday and Sunday afternoons and Friday evening. Thus, the short Philharmonic season is the equivalent of a full fall–winter–spring season of many American symphony orchestras. The orchestra is made up of about 61 musicians, half of them women, drawn from some 800 applicants each year. (Colorado Philharmonic alumni are found in a number of professional American orchestras.) The orchestra has its own personnel residence, a former resort lodge; members are given free room and board plus a small educational grant. Public performances are held in Evergreen High School Auditorium.

Connecticut

AMERICAN DANCE FESTIVAL, c/o Connecticut College, New London, Connecticut 06320. Founded in 1948, the entire program of performances is held in Palmer Auditorium (1,334 seats) on the campus of Connecticut College. Director: **Theodora Wiesner;** Production Manager: **Michael Rabbitt;** Musical Director: **Simon Sadoff.** The Festival features productions of modern dance by visiting companies in about seven programs. Films and lectures round out the Festival to a total of about 10 events which run consecutively in mid-August. One free event is the performance by members of the student dance workshop of the Connecticut College School of Dance, the Festival's sponsor. Dancers, choreographers, and groups appearing at the Festival in recent years have been: **José Limon, Paul Taylor, James Cunningham, Martha Graham, Pauline Koner,** First Chamber Dance Quartet, **Lucas Hoving,** and others. Audience attendance varies from about 4,000 to 8,000, depending upon the number of programs.

CONCERTS ON THE GREEN, c/o 254 College Street, New Haven, Connecticut 06510. Free concerts by the New Haven Symphony under its Musical Director, **Frank Brieff.** The concerts, which take place on New Haven Green, are made possible by grants from the Music Performance Trust Fund. Founded in 1966.

HARTFORD FESTIVAL OF MUSIC, c/o Hartford Festival of Music, Inc., 834 Asylum Avenue, Hartford, Connecticut 06105. Founded 1957 by Musical Director and Conductor **Robert Brawley.** Manager is **Geraldine Douglass.** The essence of the Festival is the series of four Wednesday concerts of music for chamber orchestra held annually in July. Performances take place in the Auditorium (500 seats) of Hartford Tower in Hartford. Performing ensembles are the Hartford Festival Orchestra (35 players) and the Festival Chorus (25). Support for the Festival comes from contributions from individuals and business sources including the host company, the Hartford Insurance Group. Through the subsidies of the Music Performance Trust Funds, some concerts have been offered free to the public. Among the guest performers appearing at the Festival in recent years have been the Berkshire Boy Choir, conductor **Vytautas Marijosius,** violinist **Donald Weilerstein,** and soprano **Leslie Johnson,** among others.

INSTITUTE OF CONTEMPORARY AMERICAN MUSIC, c/o Hartt College of Music, University of Hartford, 200 Bloomfield Avenue, West Hartford, Connecticut 06117. An annual two-day event held in Millard Auditorium on the campus of Hartt College. Founded in 1948. Performances of contemporary music by the various ensembles of Hartt College and occasional guest artists are free to the public, as are the lectures and discussion sessions. Composers whose works are performed are always invited to attend, sometimes as guest conductors or performers. The festivals have no fixed date.

INTERNATIONAL HARP FESTIVAL, c/o Hartt College of Music, University of Hartford, 200 Bloomfield Avenue, West Hartford, Connecticut 06117. A week-long festival, founded in 1964, held during the summer session—usually for eight days in June—of the Hartt College of Music annual Harp Master Class. The festival is under the supervision of **Aristid von Wurtzler,** Chairman of the Harp Department at the College. Along with performances in the evening there are films, lectures, and the master classes themselves, which, although intended for harpists, are also open to observers for a fee. Well-known harpists are usually invited to participate in the master classes and the Festival. Among them: **Vera Dulova** (Soviet Union), **Pierre Jamet** (France), **Henrik Rohmann** (Hungary), **Tsutomu Mimura** (Japan), **Mildred Dilling** (United States), and **Hans J. Zingel** (Germany).

MUSIC MOUNTAIN CONCERTS, Falls Village, Connecticut 06031. Winter address: c/o **Urico Rossi,** Indiana University School of Music, Bloomington, Indiana 47401. The concerts at Music Mountain are among the oldest chamber music series in America; the forty-first season was held in 1971. Programs feature the Berkshire Quartet on 10 successive Saturday afternoons from early July to early September. Members of the ensemble are: **Urico Rossi** and **Julius Hegyi,** violins; **Richard Skerlong,** viola; and **Fritz Maag,** cello. Guest artists perform with the quartet so that works other than string quartets can be offered. Among guest performers in recent seasons have been: **Ward Davenny, Natasha Maag, Sidney Foster** and **Charlotte Hegyi,** pianists; **Zelda Manacher,** mezzo-soprano, **Albert Sprague Coolidge,** violist, **Kyril Maag,** flutist, and **Eric Barr,** oboist. Classical and contemporary works are programmed along with occasional premiere performances. In 1970, the Beethoven year was recognized at Music Mountain with the complete cycle of Beethoven's string quartets performed through the season. The Concert Hall atop Music Mountain is the location for all events. It lies southeast of Falls Village, below the intersection of State Routes 63 and 126.

NEW HAVEN FESTIVAL OF ARTS, c/o Box 104, New Haven, Connecticut 06513. The community-oriented festival, administered by the Greater New Haven Jaycees, consists of concerts, dance performances, plays, films, and exhibits of books, architecture, photography, and crafts. An Art Competition, offering prizes for winning works, daily sessions called "Art in Action," or live demonstrations of techniques by artists, exhibitions by invited artists and teen-age artists are all important aspects of the festival. Concerts take place in the open air on New Haven Green and have featured the New Haven

Symphony, New Haven Civic Ballet, New Haven Opera Society (in performances of duets, arias, ensembles, etc., from operas), Ballet Society of Connecticut, and solo performers.

NORFOLK CONCERTS, c/o Yale Summer School of Music and Art, Norfolk, Connecticut 06058. Founded in 1899, the concerts are sponsored by the Yale School of Music and the Ellen Battell Stoeckel Trust. It is held in conjunction with the Summer School at Norfolk, which accepts some fifty student performers of advanced attainment for an eight-week session of intensive training in ensemble playing. The School operates from the end of June to the end of August. Concerts are given in the Music Shed—a 1,200-seat theater on the Stoeckel estate built in 1908. These are scheduled on Friday evenings and feature performances by the resident faculty as soloists and in ensemble. Two or three admission-free recitals by the students of the Summer School are also presented each week. **Gustav Meier** is the permanent conductor of the orchestra. Performers have included the Yale String Quartet; **Keith Wilson,** clarinetist and artistic director of the concerts since 1960; oboist **Robert Bloom; Ward Davenny,** pianist; **Ralph Kirkpatrick,** harpsichordist; and others. The Litchfield County Choral Union frequently sings at these concerts; the Choral Union was the focal point of concerts held in the early part of this century on the estate of Carl Stoeckel, chief patron and sponsor of much important music activity in Norfolk. Great musicians (including a number of composers who received commissions for works to be performed at the concerts) are linked with the history of music at Norfolk. Rachmaninoff, Vaughan Williams, Samuel Coleridge-Taylor, Fritz Kreisler, Victor Herbert, and Jean Sibelius (whose visit to Norfolk in 1914 remained his only visit to the United States) are among the important men associated with Norfolk's musical past. Executive Officer is **Phillip T. Young.**

NORWICH ROSE–ARTS FESTIVAL, INC., 1 Constitution Plaza, Norwich, Connecticut 06360. This festival, held since 1964, is a community-oriented annual event offering mainly popular arts, entertainment, and sports. It receives its support from the City Government, the Chamber of Commerce, and other civic organizations in Norwich and operates on a nonprofit basis within a budget of about $37,000. Some events are free, such as operas for children, but admission is charged for the pops concert by the Eastern Connecticut Symphony Orchestra, the variety show, drum corps competition, band concerts, and plays. Popular music performers engaged are well-known bands, folk groups, and vocalists. A tent, erected on Norwich's Chelsea Parade, which holds 2,700 seats, serves as the main performance facility. The Festival is usually scheduled from the last days in June to a few days past July 4th. About 80,000 people attend during an average season.

SILVERMINE CHAMBER MUSIC FESTIVAL, c/o Silvermine Guild Chamber Music Center, Silvermine Ave., New Canaan, Connecticut 06840. Concerts are held in Gifford Auditorium of Silvermine Guild Chamber Music Center. Originally organized around a series of performances by the Silvermine String Quartet, beginning with the summer of 1959, the festival now also includes performances by the 15-member Silvermine String Orchestra conducted by **Paul Wolfe,** first violinist with the Quartet. Concerts are sponsored by the Silvermine Guild and private sponsors. Administrative head is **Edith R. Gruenwald.** Although small in scope (average attendance for each of the four concerts held in July and August is about 250 people), the festival maintains a distinctive level of sophistication in programming seldom-heard works by masters of the past and first performances of works by both American and European contemporary composers. Guest performers have been: **Julius Baker,** flutist; **Leonid Hambro,** pianist; **Stanley Drucker,** clarinetist; **Robert Bloom,** oboist; **Russell Oberlin,** counter-tenor. Composers and others who have given talks as part of the festival include: the late Quincy Porter and Wallingford Riegger, **Jay S. Harrison,** and **David Randolph.** Rehearsals are free to the public.

THE STARLIGHT FESTIVAL OF CHAMBER MUSIC, P.O. Box 6065, Hamden, Connecticut 06514. The Festival was founded in 1955; its musical director and chief administrator since 1956 has been **Julius E. Scheir,** violinist and conductor of the Festival's orchestra. The concerts, held in Yale University's Law School Courtyard (or indoors in case of rain), feature the Festival Quartet—**Julius Scheir** and **Ann Barak,** violins; **Sally Trembly,** viola; and **Nathan Stutch,** cello—and the Festival Orchestra in performances of chamber music varying widely in style, dimension, and the number of musicians. Guest performers in recent years have been **Robert Bloom, Aldo Parisot, William Kroll, Jesse Levine, Keith Wilson, Frank Brieff, Bruce Simonds,** and **Albert Fuller.** Yale University and its Law School contribute the facilities for the Festival, but many individual volunteers, patrons, and business firms assist in its organization and promotion. Average concert attendance ranges from 600 to 1,000. The Festival earns about 75 percent of its total operating budget of approximately $10,000; the balance is realized through contributions. It is held the last Tuesday in June and every Tuesday in July.

THE SUMMER CHAMBER MUSIC FESTIVAL, c/o Hartt College of Music, University of Hartford, 200 Bloomfield Avenue, West Hartford, Connecticut 06117. Founded in 1964. The Festival consists of eight Sunday evening concerts running from late June to August. Concerts are held in Hartt College's Millard Auditorium. (A similar series called the Winter Chamber Music Festival is held during the academic year.) Performances are by resident chamber ensembles, soloists, and guest artists. These have included the Hartt String Quartet; the Hartt Trio; **Robert Bloom,** oboist; **Kalmen Opperman,** clarinetist; **Paul Doktor,** violist; **Arthur Winograd,** cellist; **Bertram Turetzky,** string bassist and guitarist, and others.

District of Columbia

INTER-AMERICAN MUSIC FESTIVAL, Pan American Union, Washington, D.C. 20006. Founded in 1958 and held subsequently in late spring in 1961, 1965, 1968 and 1971. The support and organization of the event is derived from the Organization of American States and its General Secretariat, the Pan American Union, and the Inter-American Music Council (CIDEM). Patrons, sponsors, and contributors range from large corporations (Lorillard Co., Coca Cola Co., Standard Oil of New Jersey, etc.) and national governments to such well-known music supporters as the Fromm Music Foundation, The Serge Koussevitzy Music Foundation of the Library of Congress, The American Symphony Orchestra League, and the Elizabeth Sprague Coolidge Foundation. The music played is that of composers of North and South America and Spain. Specially commissioned works or works receiving world premieres are an important aspect of the festivals—indeed, the festivals are a dedication to new music. In 1968, in a series of 10 concerts, there were 18 world premieres (in 1965, there were 32, the greatest number thus far for any one festival in the series) and 28 first U.S. performances of works by some 57 composers. The concerts are mainly evening events taking place in halls and other performing facilities in and around Washington, such as the Department of Commerce Auditorium, Coolidge Auditorium in the Library of Congress, the Merriweather Post Pavilion at Columbia, Maryland, Hall of the Americas of the Pan American Union, and other locations. All concerts are offered without admission charge and are attended by invitation. They are held on consecutive days. Some of the orchestras playing at the festivals have been the Canadian Broadcasting Corporation Symphony Orchestra, Eastman Philharmonia of Rochester, Orquesta Sinfónica Nacional de Mexico, and the Washington National Symphony Orchestra. The last-named has been essentially the "host" orchestra and has played under such conductors as **Howard Mitchell,** its long-time director, **Julius Rudel, Antonio Tauriello, Walter Hendl, Efraim Guigui,**

Enrique Garcia-Asensio, and **Guillermo Espinosa.** Chamber ensembles have been the Claremont String Quartet, The Philadelphia Woodwind Quintet, Juilliard String Quartet, the Beaux-Arts String Quartet, the Lenox String Quartet, the Roberto de Regina choral ensemble of Rio de Janeiro, the Coro de Madrigalistas de Mexico, the Mozarteum Argentino of Buenos Aires, and others. Solo artists are engaged from throughout the Americas. Since its inception the festival's General Music Director has been **Guillermo Espinosa,** Chief of the Music Division of the Pan American Union. Honorary Chairmen are usually the incumbent President of the United States and his wife.

NATIONAL CHERRY BLOSSOM FESTIVAL, 1616 K Street, N.W., Washington, D.C. 20006. An annual event held in early April under the sponsorship of the Washington Convention and Visitors Bureau. Founded in 1934. Programs are held out of doors at the Washington Monument Grounds; the musical portion of the programs include performances by 53 high school bands and bands of the military service. Musical Director of the Festival since 1960 has been **Joel Margolis.**

NATIONAL GALLERY OF ART AMERICAN MUSIC FESTIVAL, c/o National Gallery of Art, Washington, D.C. 20565. Formed in 1944, the concerts are a series of free events held in May in the East Garden Court of the Gallery. Recitalists and chamber groups perform both old and contemporary music. The main ensemble is the National Gallery Orchestra. Its conductor and the festival's music director is **Richard Bales.**

NEW YORK OPERA FESTIVAL, c/o New York Opera Festival, Inc., 1860 Broadway, New York, N.Y. 10023. Founded in 1958. Despite its name, the festival takes place in Washington, D.C. for one week each summer at the outdoor facilities of Carter Barron Amphitheatre (5,000 seats). A specially formed professional company of singers and orchestra musicians present productions of the traditional Italian and French repertory in the original languages. The productions are fully staged, numbering about six, each with a single performance. Leading singers are engaged for the starring roles. General Manager is **Felix Salmaggi.** Conductors: **Anton Coppola, Anton Guadagno, Carlo Moresco, Alfredo Silipigni,** and **George Barati.**

Florida

BACH FESTIVAL OF WINTER PARK, Box 160, Rollins College, Winter Park, Florida 32789. A two-day festival in February or March devoted mainly to the music of Johann Sebastian Bach but sometimes presenting the large choral masterpieces of such composers as Beethoven, Haydn, Brahms, et al. Founded in 1936. All concerts are held in Knowles Memorial Chapel on the campus of Rollins College. Sponsorship is through the Bach Festival Society of Winter Park. **John Tiedtke** is Administrative Head; **Ward Woodbury** is Music Director and Conductor (since 1966). The performing ensembles are the Bach Festival Choir and the Bach Festival Orchestra consisting of instrumentalists drawn from the Florida Symphony Orchestra (of Orlando). Well-known vocal soloists have performed at the festival including **Louise Natale,** soprano; **Joanna Simon,** mezzo-soprano; **Stanley Kolk,** tenor; and **Thomas Paul,** bass. Program events include afternoon and evening concerts and a morning lecture. Talks have been presented by **Paul Henry Lang,** musicologist. There is an admissions fee to all events.

INTERCOLLEGIATE MUSIC FESTIVAL, P.O. Box 1275, Leesburg, Florida 32748. Originally a jazz competition-festival, founded in 1967, the event now includes, if not emphasizes, folk and popular music. (See details under Competitions.) The final climaxing event following the series of regional competitions in which college musicians compete is itself essentially a contest; however, the presence of a large audience, well-known popular musicians or critics as a jury, and press and broadcast facilities create a festive atmosphere throughout the three-day session. The location of the festival varies from year to year. President is **Robert E. Yde.** Sponsors are business firms such as Trans-World Airlines, Anheuser-Busch, Inc., and Shulton, Inc. The festival is taped and broadcast worldwide by the Voice of America.

NEW COLLEGE SUMMER MUSIC FESTIVAL, P.O. Box 1898, Sarasota, Florida 33578. Founded in 1965, the Festival is organized by New College; recently it has received additional support from the National Endowment for the Arts and the Florida Development Committee. Festival director is **Arthur R. Borden,** Dean of the Division of Humanities at New College. **Paul C. Wolfe,** violinist and conductor, has been Musical Director of the Festival since its beginning. Assistant Director is **Christopher von Baeyer.** The Festival concerts are a series of performances played by the guest artist-faculty, who conduct a series of master classes at New College for about two weeks in early summer. The stress is on chamber music, and various-sized groups are formed from the 10 or more faculty members. The New College String Quartet (**Paul Wolfe** and **Anita Brooker,** violins; **William Magers,** viola; and **Christopher von Baeyer,** cello) is the resident ensemble. Artist-faculty in recent years have included **Leonid Hambro,** pianist; **Robert Bloom,** oboist; **Walter Trampler,** violist; **Robert Marcellus,** clarinetist; **Julius Baker,** flutist; **Bernard Greenhouse,** cellist; **John Barrows,** French hornist; **Sol Schoenbach,** bassoonist; and others. Activities during the festival period consist of master classes, ensemble sessions, open rehearsals of faculty performances, and orchestra rehearsals. Students have the option of enrolling as participants or auditors. Admission charge is made for the five or more faculty concerts, but student recitals are offered free. About 120 students enroll each year. Performances take place in Hamilton Hall (500 seats) on the campus of New College and in Neal Auditorium (900 seats) at Manatee Junior College in Bradenton. Among the works performed are usually one or two new works commissioned for the Festival.

Hawaii

FESTIVAL OF THE ARTS OF THIS CENTURY, c/o Music Department, University of Hawaii 96822. Founded in 1957, and formerly called the Punahou Festival of Music and Art of this Century, the Festival is under the sponsorship of the University of Hawaii Summer Session and, variously, other supportive organizations, among them the East–West Center and the University of Hawaii Foundation. Through music, dance, drama, films, art exhibitions, and lectures the Festival focuses on contemporary Asian and Western arts. It is held in conjunction with the University Summer School and guest composers, artists, and dancers. Events take place in the evenings on the University campus in the Mae Zenke Orvis Auditorium (400 seats), the John Fitzgerald Kennedy Theatre (650 seats), and sometimes in Jefferson Hall of the East–West Center. Musical events are free of admissions charge. The programs are replete with world or Hawaii premiere performances with a concomitant emphasis on the composer and his music rather than on performers or ensembles; most of the program notes even are written by the composers. (The performers are generally those of the faculty or students of the University of Hawaii.) The programs are grouped into concerts of electronic music, solo and ensemble music, the music of young composers, and orchestra concerts. Guest composers have been: **Ernst Krenek, Chou Wen-Chung, José Maceda** (Philippines), **Yoshiro Irino** (Japan), **Bülent Arel, Joji Yuasa** (Japan), **Norman Dello Joio,** and others. Many of the compositions performed require unusual instrumental or vocal combinations, not to mention the use of Asian instruments, creating some of the most exotic sounds among music festivals devoted to modern music. Festival director is **Marian J. Kerr,** who has had the position since 1957.

Idaho

UNIVERSITY OF IDAHO FESTIVAL OF CONTEMPORARY ARTS, Moscow, Idaho 83843. Begun in 1959. The festival lasts about ten days and presents concerts of modern music and drama with an emphasis on American composers and playwrights. There are also exhibitions of art and architecture, lectures, and seminars.

Illinois

FESTIVAL OF CONTEMPORARY ARTS, University of Illinois, 110 Architecture Building, Urbana, Illinois 61801. Formed in 1948, the Festival is underwritten by the University and takes place on campus: musical events in Smith Music Hall and the Auditorium; exhibitions, lectures, dance concerts and the like, in Krannert Art Museum, Fine Arts Building, Urbana–Lincoln Hotel, Illini Union, Architecture Building, Mumford and Gregory Halls, and the Assembly Hall. In general, the Festival runs from late February to early April, but principally during March, and is an integral part of the school year. It is held every two years (1965, 1967, 1969, etc.) The contemporary arts encompassed by the Festival theme include music, dance, visual arts, drama, film, architecture, landscape architecture, literature, radio and television, and such categories as "design for communication" and home economics. Most of the programs are offered free. The music programs have a very large number of participants (soloists are either faculty or students, but outside performers are sometimes engaged): University of Illinois Opera Group under **Ludwig Zirner;** the Wind Ensemble; University of Illinois Percussion Ensemble; the Concert Choir, **Harold Decker,** Director; the New Music Choral Ensemble; Faculty Woodwind Quintet; the Chamber Orchestra and the Jazz Band, both under the leadership of **John Garvey;** the University Symphony Orchestra under **Bernard Goodman;** and the Chamber Choir. Concerts include full-length operas, and all varieties of ensemble and recital performances. Electronic music concerts in whole or in part are not uncommon. The musical events receive national critical attention, since composers of national and international repute are often invited to hear performances of their works and sometimes to lecture, conduct, perform, or otherwise supervise performances. Due to the nature of the programming, many American or world premieres are presented. Chief administrator of the Festival is **Allen S. Weller,** Dean, College of Fine and Applied Arts. **Duane Branigan,** Director of the School of Music, is the music committeeman on the Festival Committee Board.

GRANT PARK CONCERTS, Chicago Park District, 425 East 14th Boulevard, Chicago, Illinois 60605. A series of free outdoor summer concerts begun in 1935 and presented in Chicago's Grant Park on Lake Michigan. The concert facility is the Grant Park Music Shell located in the Park at the foot of 11th Street and the Outer Drive. The concerts are funded by the City of Chicago and administered through the Chicago Park District. General Manager, since 1968, is **Richard Bass.** The programs are spread over a nine-week period, from the end of June to the end of August, consisting of 35 evening concerts and 4 morning young people's concerts. The Grant Park Symphony, an orchestra first organized in 1944, is the featured ensemble, playing symphonic, operatic, and ballet music under a succession of well-known guest conductors. **Irwin Hoffman** is the principal Conductor, leading a third of all the scheduled performances. Other recent conductors: **Samuel Krachmalnick, Elakum Shapirra, Kenneth Schermerhorn, Giuseppe Patané, James DePriest, Julius Rudel, Antonio de Almeida, Brian Priestman, Jorge Mester, Paul Freeman,** and **Martin Rich.** Guest soloists have included: **Marian Anderson, Julius Katchen, David Bar-Illan, Itzhak Perlman, Young Uck Kim, Martina Arroyo, Jan Peerce, Sherril Milnes, Arnold Voketaitis, Alfred Brendel, Beverly Sills, Jorge Bolet, Janos Starker, Paul Olefsky, William Warfield, Bethany Beardslee,** dancers **Edward Villella** and **Patricia McBride,** and the Glen Tetley Dancers, to mention some. The Grant Park Symphony Chorus is under the direction of **Thomas Peck.** No other current municipally supported musical series in the United States equals or surpasses the length of season and the breadth and quality of programming offered in the Grant Park Concerts, which present not only works in the classic, romantic, and contemporary symphonic and concerto repertories, concert versions of Mozart and Verdi operas (or, as in 1970, complete concert versions of Gluck's "Orfée" and Dvořák's "Russalka"—the latter sung in Czech), large-scale choral works such as Brahms' Requiem, the Berlioz Requiem, and Beethoven's Mass in C, but also music infrequently programmed within the framework of the usual free outdoor concerts: Schoenberg's "Gurrelieder" and his "Erwartung," Prokofiev's "Alexander Nevsky," and Berg's Chamber Concerto, to cite some examples. A tradition of the Concerts is the use of a program commentator who speaks through an amplification system to the often widely dispersed audience sitting completely in the open.

Beginning in 1970, a Pops Concert Series was begun using the same Music Shell facilities sponsored by the city. The programs, totaling about 11, include gospel, rock, folk music, blues, and jazz and feature known pop musicians and groups: Duke Ellington Orchestra, New Lost City Ramblers, Cannonball Adderley Quintet, **Odetta,** et al. The concerts are scheduled variously in the morning, at noon, or in the late afternoon or evening. Admission is free.

MISSISSIPPI RIVER FESTIVAL, 718 North Grand Boulevard, St. Louis, Missouri 63103. First held in 1969. The festival takes place not in St. Louis but rather in Illinois —on the campus of Southern Illinois University in Edwardsville across the Mississippi River from St. Louis. Facilities there include the Festival Tent, which can hold 1,878 people, and the surrounding lawns, which can accommodate some 10,000 more. The St. Louis Symphony Orchestra under its conductor, **Walter Susskind,** is the permanent ensemble around which the festival is organized. Lasting six weeks, the festival presents the orchestra in six concerts with standard format featuring orchestral works and works for soloists and orchestra—these are scheduled for Saturday evenings—and six Sunday evening Pops concerts. In addition there are some 12 or so programs on weekday evenings bringing folk music, rock, and jazz groups to the Tent. Guest performers with the Symphony have been: **André Watts, Malcolm Frager,** and **Peter Serkin,** pianists; **Pinchas Zukerman** and **Max Rabinovitsj,** violinists, among others. **Dean Dixon** has appeared as guest conductor for the regular orchestral concerts, and **Franz Allers** and **Henry Mancini** have led the orchestra for the Pops series, the majority of whose programs are led by **Leonard Slatkin,** Assistant Conductor of the St. Louis Symphony Orchestra.

RAVINIA FESTIVAL, 22 West Monroe Street, Chicago, Illinois 60603. The location of the Festival is at Ravinia Park in the city of Highland Park, Illinois, approximately 25 miles from downtown Chicago on Chicago's North Shore. A major American summer festival, it is cast in the large proportions of festivals organized around ranking orchestral ensembles—in this case the Chicago Symphony Orchestra. Ravinia facilities include a Pavilion with 3,000 reserved seats, Murray Theatre, containing 900 seats, the Casino Art Gallery, and, spreading outward from the Pavilion, 36 acres of lawn space capable of holding audiences of 16,000 to 17,000 who can hear performances coming from within the Pavilion by means of special amplification systems. (For the "lawn audience," the lower price of admission to the Park is charged.) The grounds also contain free parking and picnic facilities and a restaurant. The Festival was established in 1936 by the Ravinia Festival Association (offices at 22 West Monroe Street, Chicago, Illinois 60603), a nonprofit organization. Ravinia Park, however, has been open since 1905, and between 1912 and 1931 opera and orchestral concerts took place there. The Ravinia schedule of summer events is one of the lengthiest in the nation, running over 13 full weeks (in 1970, from June 25 to September 27). The season is organized in three segments, as follows: (1) Seven consecutive weeks of musical concerts, with programs scheduled each night of the week. This, the largest segment of the Festival, is interspersed with isolated evenings of dance programs or special programs such as mime or puppet theater. The seven-week segment allocates Monday to performances in the Murray Theatre, where more intimate kinds of programs are likely to benefit from the smaller house; Tuesday, Thursday, and Saturday evenings are given over to symphonic programs, opera in concert version, and a few recitals. In recent seasons such conductors as the late Charles Munch, **Josef Krips, Rafael Kubelik, William Steinberg, Sixten Ehrling, Seiji Ozawa, Giuseppe Patané,** and **Michael Tilson Thomas** have appeared in this series with the Chicago Symphony Orchestra. Music Director, beginning in 1973, is **James Levine.** Soloists who have appeared with the orchestra include: **Byron Janis, Van Cliburn, Anna Moffo, Alexis Weissenberg, Elisabeth Schwarzkopf, John Browning, Misha Dichter, Leon Fleisher, Peter Serkin, Jacqueline du Pré, André Watts, Michael Block, Stephen Bishop, Eileen Farrell, Beverly Sills,** and many others. Wednesday and Friday concerts are devoted to jazz, rock, folk, blues, and other pop music categories. **Frank Zappa, Dionne Warwick, Al Hirt, Corky Siegel, Ramsey Lewis, Judy Collins, Ella Fitzgerald, Procol Harum,** the Modern Jazz Quartet, Crow, **Herbie Mann** and Quartet, **Peter Nero,** and **Leon Bibb** are among those who have performed in this series. (2) Following the seven week music series is a week of fully staged dance programs, in recent seasons featuring the New York City Ballet. Other dance groups engaged for the individual programs scheduled during the seven weeks dominated by musical evenings have been: **Merce Cunningham** and Company, **Carmen de Lavallade** and Company, **Sybil Shearer** and Her Ballet Company, and **José Greco** and Company, to mention some. (3) The week of dance is followed, after a few days' recess, by four or five weeks of theatrical productions held in Murray Theatre. In 1970, the entire series was devoted to performances by the Birmingham (England) Repertory Theatre. Other groups in the past have included the Chicago companies, Goodman Theatre, Second City productions, and the productions of Hull House. There is a low-priced Saturday morning series of Young People's Programs in July and August. To encompass as much variety as possible, no program is repeated. Thus, the series may contain one program each of orchestral concert, puppet theater, dance lecture-demonstrations, mime shows, and so forth. Attendance at the Ravinia events is about 270,000 a season. General Manager is **Edward Gordon** (appointed in 1968); Chairman of the Ravinia Association is **Stanley M. Freehling.**

Indiana

ANNUAL FESTIVAL OF CONTEMPORARY MUSIC, School of Music, DePauw University, Greencastle, Indiana 46135. Held on three consecutive days in April, with performances taking place in various concert halls in the School of Music. **Donald H. White,** composer and member of DePauw's music faculty, has been director of the Festival since its beginning in 1963. Each festival is centered around a guest composer or conductor, with the former usually engaged to conduct or perform his own works and to lecture and lead informal discussions of his music or modern music in general. The music of other composers is always included on the programs. Guest artists in the past have been **Robert Whitney,** former conductor of the Louisville Orchestra; **Vincent Persichetti,** composer; **Paul Creston,** composer; **Howard Hanson,** composer–conductor; **A. Clyde Roller,** conductor. Performing groups are the DePauw Symphony Orchestra, Wind Ensemble, and University Choir; students and faculty members appear as soloists. In addition to the School of Music, the Festival receives support from the fraternities Pi Kappa Lambda, Phi Mu Alpha, and Mu Phi Epsilon. All concerts are free; attendance ranges from 150 to 800 for each event.

COLLEGIATE JAZZ FESTIVAL, Box 115, Notre Dame, Indiana 46556. Formed in 1958, the first Festival occurred in the spring of 1959. Entirely the conception of undergraduate students at the University of Notre Dame, it is still run by students with the assistance of a faculty advisor and the partial sponsorship of the University of Notre Dame Student Union. Other support has come from *Downbeat* magazine and certain musical instrument manufacturers such as Selmer, Inc. The emphasis of the Festival is on the educational aspects of jazz and on providing the opportunity to college jazz soloists and groups to perform before those who are capable of rendering meaningful critical judgment regarding the fine points of jazz performance: style, originality, fluency, technical ability, quality of arrangements, and so on. Thus, judges are drawn from the fields of both professional jazz and jazz education. Over the years **Art Van Damme, Charles Suber** (one of the originators of the school stage-band movement), **Robert Share,** of the Berklee School of Music, **Stan Kenton, Willis Conover** of the Voice of America, **Quincy Jones, Leonard Feather, Henry Mancini, Billy Taylor, Clark Terry,** and others have served on the five- or six-member jury. The Festival is held in March on the campus of the University of Notre Dame.

FESTIVAL OF ROMANTIC MUSIC, Jordan College of Music, Butler University, 46th Street and Clarendon Road, Indianapolis, Indiana 46208. Founded in 1968 by **Frank Cooper,** pianist and faculty member of Jordan College. An eight-day event held in May. Concerts take place in Clowes Hall of Butler University. The Festival is unique among seasonal events. Its purpose is to present the forgotten or rarely performed repertory of nineteenth-century Romantic music with particular attention given to works of major proportions: symphonies, symphonic odes and poems, concertos, works for chorus and orchestra, etc. Curiosities, exotica, long-neglected and once-popular favorites, trivia, and music worthy of resurrection are performed in programs of considerable variety often involving touches of showmanship such as costumed performers and settings reminiscent of nineteenth-century salons. With such unusual fare and flair the Festival attempts to satisfy its double purpose of enlightenment and entertainment. Many of the works performed have never received performances in this century, some are given first American performances, and yet others have hardly been performed anywhere at all since their date of composition. Among the works performed which received some attention in the press have been: William Sterndale Bennett's "May Queen" Overture; "Le Désert" by Félicien David for chorus and orchestra, dancers, narrator, and two tenors; Offenbach's ballet, "Le Papillon"—never performed outside Paris; Charles-Valentin Alkan's "Funeral March on the Death of a Parakeet" (1859) for three oboes, one bassoon, and small chorus (performed in costume); and Jëno Hubay's Violin Concerto in G Minor. Other composers include: Benjamin Godard, Alfred Bruneau, J. Raff, A. Henselt, Marschner, Kalkbrenner, A. Dreyschock, Ole Bull, and Joseph Joachim, among others. The nature of many of the solo works and concertos of these composers calls for performers of unusual virtuosity. Pianists **Gunnar Johansen, Raymond Lewanthal, Malcolm Frager, Jorge Bolet,** and **Stephen Glover,** not to mention founder **Frank Cooper,** have played in recent festivals, as have violinists **Aaron Rosand, Eddy Brown,** and **Charles Treger** and cellist **Jascha Silberstein.** Conductors **Izler Solomon, Michael Semanitzky, Jackson Wiley, Jorge Mester,** and **Igor Buketoff** have led the concerts. Initially an orchestra consisting largely of Butler University students was used. Recent festivals have engaged the Indianapolis Symphony and the Louisville Orchestra.

FORT WAYNE FINE ARTS FESTIVAL, c/o Fort Wayne Fine Arts Foundation, 232½ West Wayne Street, Fort Wayne, Indiana 46802. Established in 1958; the Festival is held in Franke Park, one of Fort Wayne's municipal parks, the grounds of which contain an outdoor theater and several pavilions. The Fine Arts Foundation is sponsor and organizer of the Festival in its role advancing the cultural goals of the community. All the Festival events are offered free to the public and are presented over a period of five or six days. Some of the programs include concerts by the Fort Wayne Philharmonic under **James Sample** and performances of opera and ballet. Other events are exhibits of art and architecture, theater-in-the-round, historical exhibits, puppetry, public art classes and workshops, and jazz concerts. In 1967, the most recent year yielding statistics, some 80,000 attended the Festival.

Iowa

CORNELL COLLEGE MUSIC FESTIVAL, c/o Cornell College, Mount Vernon, Iowa 52314. Founded in 1899, and known as the "oldest music festival west of the Mississippi River," the Festival regularly features a major symphony orchestra, a chamber ensemble, and a soloist appearing on three successive evenings in April or May of each year. Sponsored by Cornell College and a number of individual patrons, the Festival is under the supervision of **Jesse G. Evans,** Chairman of the Music Department. All events take place in King Chapel on campus. The Chicago Symphony Orchestra has been the orchestra most frequently engaged for the Festival. Other orchestras and chamber ensembles which have appeared: the Kansas City Philharmonic Orchestra, the Beaux Arts Trio, New York String Sextet, Riverside Singers. Soloists recently appearing: **Susan Starr, Ralph Votapek,** pianists; **Richard Westenburg,** organist.

FALL FINE ARTS FESTIVAL, c/o Coe College, Cedar Rapids, Iowa 52402. Founded in 1952. The Festival consists of about 10 events within a period from late October to mid-November. In addition to music, there are lectures, poetry readings, dance concerts, dramatic plays, and exhibits. Musical programs take place in the Auditorium; the other programs usually in Daehler-Kitchin Auditorium of Marquis Hall. Soloists, in recital or concert, and chamber ensembles are generally the featured performers. These have included in the past: **Eileen Farrell, Maureen Forrester, Rudolf Firkusny, Kay Griffel, Eugene Istomin,** Bach Aria Group, José Molina Bailes Españoles, the Juilliard String Quartet, and others. The Cedar Rapids Symphony Orchestra is used to accompany soloists in concert. There is an admission charge, but some events, such as lectures and exhibits, are free. The Festival is supported by special college funds. In charge is **Eleanor Taylor,** Chairman, Public Events Committee.

Kansas

UNIVERSITY OF KANSAS FESTIVAL OF THE ARTS, c/o Student Union Activities, Kansas Union, University of Kansas, Lawrence, Kansas 66044. The Festival was conceived in 1966 as an outgrowth of the Centennial celebration, held that year, of the founding of the University of Kansas. The purpose of the Festival is to present a week's artistic events—such as films, poetry readings, music—and exchanges of ideas about the creative arts in the form of lectures, exhibitions, and discussions. Leading figures in the various art forms pertinent to the Festival are invited to participate. The emphasis is on contemporary American creators and performers—but those best recognized, in the public eye, as major proponents (and some experimentalists) of their respective generic fields. Thus, in music, this translates interestingly and logically enough into jazz and other associative pop music. Recent festivals have featured **Bill Evans** and his trio, **Count Basie, Oscar Peterson** and his trio, **Ella Fitzgerald,** and **Odetta.** Other participants, as lecturers or exhibitors: Edward Albee, Mark van Doren, Al Capp; filmmakers Lionel Rogosin, Chuck Jones, and Ed Emshwiller; and Henry Geldzahler, art scholar. The Festival is sponsored by Student Union Activities of the University, a new director being assigned for each Festival. Most programs are presented in Hoch Auditorium on campus (3,600 seats) and are scheduled in the spring. Admission charge is made for all programs.

Kentucky

AMERICAN FOLKSONG FESTIVAL, c/o 3201 Cogan Street, Ashland, Kentucky 41101. This annual event was founded in 1930 by its current director, **Jean Thomas,** an anthologist of Southern Appalachian songs. Her earlier travels as a court stenographer throughout the Kentucky hills permitted her to learn the region's traditions and culture and earned her the name, "The Traipsin' Woman." The Festival is her attempt to preserve and promote a lyric Anglo-Saxon culture which has its roots in the Elizabethan ballads brought to the hills by the earliest settlers. Participants in the Festival are of all ages and come with their homemade skills manifest: homespun costumes, musical instruments, and songs. No one pretends to professionalism. The music is played and sung in Carter Caves State Park, Cascade Area, in Olive Hill, Kentucky. The town is on U.S. Route 60 in the northwest corner of the state. The Festival lasts three days: two days of folk arts and crafts and dancing, and, on the final day, beginning at two in the afternoon, the singing and playing of music. The music continues until sunset, when the festival is brought to a close with all those present singing a folk version of "Down in the Valley." All the music is performed in natural surroundings on an open wooden stage set up before a log cabin, the door of which leads onto the stage. The musical program begins with a fox-horn call followed by a "Song of Welcome" sung in Cherokee by an Indian girl. The performers play such traditional instruments as the 3- or 54-string dulcimer, Irish harp, fiddle, recorder, pawpaw whistle, sixteenth-century lute, mouth harp, and cornstalk fiddle. Performances have been televised on national TV as well as by the U.S. Information Agency. A number of songs from the festivals and the region in general have been recorded by **Jean Thomas** and published in a number of anthologies. Such songs as "frolic and lonesome tunes, sea chanteys, gay ditties, play-game songs, courtin' songs, footwashin' and funeralizin' hymn tunes, flyting or scolding ballads, and answerin'-back ballads" are all included in the collections and represent the very essence of the Festival. The Festival is held in June, generally on the first weekend.

Louisiana

LOUISIANA STATE UNIVERSITY FESTIVAL OF CONTEMPORARY MUSIC, c/o School of Music, Louisiana State University, Baton Rouge, Louisiana 70803. Founded in 1944 and believed to be the oldest festival of its kind in the United States. The event is sponsored entirely by the University; a special faculty committee under the administration of **Everett Timm,** Dean of the School of Music, is responsible for running the Festival. **Kenneth Klaus** is committee chairman. All concerts are offered free and take place in either University or Union Theaters. The music performed is contemporary music with a special emphasis on music of quite recent origin. In general, the programs—some six in all—will alternately feature works for chamber groups, choral ensembles, symphonic band, symphony orchestra, and solo performers. The works of well-known composers are always included, but a special effort is made to perform works by newer—even student—American composers. Guests at the Festival in recent years have been the New Orleans Philharmonic Symphony Orchestra under **Werner Torkanowsky,** the Lenox String Quartet, and the composer, **Milton Babbitt,** who lectured and led a panel discussion. University ensembles, faculty, and students make up the regular performers. The Festival is held in either March or April.

NEW ORLEANS SUMMER POPS, c/o New Orleans Summer Pops, Inc., 203 Gallier Hall, 545 St. Charles Avenue, New Orleans, Louisiana 70130. Founded in 1953. Performances are held in Municipal Auditorium on Friday and Saturday nights from late June through the first weekend in August, totaling about seven weeks in all. The orchestra seats of the auditorium are removed, permitting the use of tables and chairs for groups of four and the serving of refreshments. A 55-piece orchestra performs the usual pops concert fare of light classics and popular music. Conductors are **Milton Bush** and **Peter Dombourian,** both appointed in 1960. Guest artists engaged for past seasons have been: **Norman Treigle, Marguerite Piazza,** and such pop musicians as **Frankie Laine, Carmen Cavallaro, Tito Guizar,** et al. Average concert attendance ranges from 2,600 to 3,000. **Mary N. McCann** is Manager of the series.

Maine

AMHERST SUMMER MUSIC CENTER CONCERTS, c/o Amherst Summer Music Center, Raymond, Maine 04071. Not a true festival, but a series of concerts presented by the young musicians who study at the Center and the faculty. The performances are offered free and include programs by the student band, orchestra, chorus, and solo performers. The town of Raymond is located off Exit 11 of Interstate Highway 95, some 20 miles north of Portland in the Sebago Lake region. **J. Clement Schuler** is founder and director of the Center.

BAR HARBOR FESTIVAL, c/o Bar Harbor Festival Corp., Bar Harbor, Maine 04609; New York address: 741 West End Avenue, Suite 4-B, New York, N.Y. 10025. The Festival's Artistic Director and the corporation's President is **Francis Fortier,** violinist. Programs, some offered free, consist of two weeks (generally in August) of concerts, films, lectures, and exhibits of painting, sculpture, and photography—all held in various locations throughout Bar Harbor, an important Maine coastal resort (for another summer music event in this area, see the Monteux Memorial Festival). Facilities include the Criterion Theatre (1,000 seats), Bar Harbor Club (300), and St. Saviour's Church (250). Plans for expansion, according to the corporation, include the use of additional auditorium facilities at Hulls Cove Festival Center, and those on Mt. Desert Island. The Criterion Theatre is usually used for orchestral concerts and dance programs. The leading ensemble is the Bar Harbor Festival Orchestra (some 26 players), under **William Hudson,** Conductor. Other groups are the eight-member Festival Ballet and the Acadia String Quartet **(James Carter, Thomas O'Donnell, Elliott Antokoletz,** and **Martin Dubow).** Artists appearing at the Festival: **Patricia Wilde** and **George Tomal,** choreographers; **Dorothy Fiore,** dancer; **Christopher Sager,** pianist; **Judith Olson,** pianist; **Francis Fortier; Stephen Adelstein,** oboist; and others. The Festival was founded in 1964. The Corporation oversees its organization and receives support or sponsorship from the Maine State Commission on the Arts and Humanities, the Bar Harbor Chamber of Commerce, and numerous other organizations and individuals.

BOWDOIN COLLEGE SUMMER MUSIC SERIES AND CONTEMPORARY MUSIC FESTIVAL, Bowdoin College, Brunswick, Maine 04011. These two events were begun respectively in 1959 and 1965 and have continued annually. The summer series take place in Smith Auditorium in Sills Hall and the Contemporary Music Festival in Wentworth Hall in Senior Center—both on the Bowdoin Campus. The summer series, under the direction of **Lewis Kaplan,** violinist, is held during July and August, when the College's Summer Music School is in session; it features the Aeolian Chamber Players, in most of the eight or so concerts, and well-known guest artists. The ability of the Aeolian Chamber Players to perform music ranging from solo works to those requiring up to five players and to offer a combination of piano, strings, and winds is largely responsible for concerts of considerable variety. The Contemporary Music Festival is under the supervision of **Elliott Schwartz,** composer and member of Bowdoin's faculty; once part of the Summer Series, the Festival is now scheduled during the academic year and lasts two or three days. The concerts feature works commissioned by Bowdoin and receiving their first performances, works established in the modern music repertory, and lesser known or unknown pieces. **Luciano Berio, George Rochberg, Morton Subotnick, Mario Davidovsky, George Crumb,** and **Elliott Carter** are among those who have been invited to the Festival to hear their works and to take part in discussions and other activities. Average attendance at each Bowdoin event is about 150. The prime sponsor is the College, but other support has come from ASCAP and the Maine State Commission on the Arts and Humanities.

MONTEUX MEMORIAL FESTIVAL, c/o Forest Studio 555, Hancock, Maine 04640. In 1942, the late conductor, Pierre Monteux, founded a school for conducting at his home in Hancock, Maine (a coastal town about 38 miles from Bangor). Since his death, the Pierre Monteux Memorial Foundation—an organization formed to perpetuate his work and to establish a memorial to his achievements—has sustained and developed the original idea. Under the direction of a number of Monteux's former pupils and other professional conductors of note, musicians are invited to play in training sessions and concerts during the month of August. Thus, the Festival consists of some four or five Sunday orchestral concerts and many chamber music performances, the latter under the direction of **William Kroll,** violinist. These festival concerts were begun in 1965 and have been given annually since. Among the musicians and conductors who have performed in recent festivals are: **Max Rudolf, Werner Torkanowsky, Claude Frank, Roland Hayes, Tossy Spivakovsky, Michael Charry, Siegfried Landau.** Admission is charged for all performances except the Thursday Tea Concerts. Proceeds go to the Foundation.

Maryland

MERRIWEATHER POST PAVILION, P.O. Box 937, Columbia, Maryland 21043. First season for summer concerts at the Pavilion was in 1967. The Merriweather Post Pavilion is located almost midway between Washington, D.C., and Baltimore, Maryland, on U.S. Highway 29 (Columbia Exit). The season lasts from late June to early September and is made up of two series, the "classical" subscription series and the "popular" series. Concerts by the National Symphony Orchestra are the main feature of the classical series, which consists of six Sunday evenings (not necessarily consecutive) with the orchestra and a guest soloist for the majority of the programs. Conductors for the series have included **Howard Mitchell, Jorge Mester, James Levine, Aldo Ceccato,** and **Donald Johanos.** Performers have included pianists **Van Cliburn, Vladimir Ashkenazy, Philippe Entremont, Stephen Bishop,** and **Garrick Ohlsson;** singers **Robert Merrill, Jan Peerce, Roberta Peters, Elisabeth Schwarzkopf;** and other solo instrumentalists, among them cellist **Jacqueline Du Pré** and guitarist **Christopher Parkening.** The popular section of the season offers seven events, each running on six successive nights, Monday through Saturday. This series is characterized by production-type entertainment such as a show starring **Red Skelton,** or six nights of **Sergio Mendes** and "Brasil '66" or **Harry Belafonte.** The organization of the programs is quite similar to that of the Garden State Arts Center in New Jersey, even to sharing most of the same popular performers during the same season. Like the Garden State series, the Merriweather Post Pavilion is under the program management of the Nederlander Organization, which refers to itself as promoters of "the best in family entertainment" and the "most exciting performers in show business."

Massachusetts

BERKSHIRE MUSIC FESTIVAL, Tanglewood, Lenox, Massachusetts 01240. Boston address: Symphony Hall, Boston, Massachusetts 02115. The Berkshire Music Festival, often referred to as just "Tanglewood," is among the most esteemed of the world's summertime musical events. Its rich history and pronouncedly high level of musical standards have few counterparts anywhere in the world and know no superior in America. In addition to accommodating a festival, Tanglewood also houses the Berkshire Music Center, founded in 1940 by the Boston Symphony Orchestra as a summer school for advanced musical training. The activities and musical offerings at Tanglewood are multifaceted: At the nucleus is the Berkshire Festival, an eight-week season of 24 concerts featuring the Boston Symphony Orchestra under the direction of some of the best-known conductors. These concerts are held on Friday and Saturday evenings and Sunday afternoon and offer programs as varied as those of the regular orchestral season, namely, works featuring vocal and instrumental soloists, works for chorus and orchestra, and opera in concert form. Interesting touches are the Friday evening "Weekend Preludes" which precede by two hours the regular concert program and are offered free to ticket holders of that evening's concert. The Preludes are short recitals performed by one or another soloist or ensemble engaged to appear at some time during the Festival. On Saturday mornings there are open rehearsals of the Boston Symphony

Orchestra. These are informal events: the seats are unreserved and the audience is more or less free to move about. The small fee charged for the rehearsals is for the benefit of the Orchestra's Pension Fund. On days other than the three days of the weekend devoted to the main festival programs, there are one or two concerts by the Boston Pops Orchestra under **Arthur Fiedler.** These performances, too, are for the benefit of the Pension Fund. Another annual tradition is the day-long "gala" called "Tanglewood-on-Parade," the event which involves all departments of the Berkshire Music Center and the Boston Symphony Orchestra, the Center's orchestra combining with the latter for the day's climaxing evening concert. The gala closes with a display of fireworks. The 24 Boston Symphony Orchestra concerts and the other mentioned activities take place in the Music Shed, whose seating capacity of 6,000 indicates a third or less of the audience potential of Tanglewood, since the Shed is constructed to project sound outward onto the surrounding grounds where a larger audience sits, stands, or lies. Thus, upwards from 15,000 people have been accommodated at a single concert. A special series at Tanglewood called "Contemporary Trends" features contemporary "nonclassical" music—a range including such performers as **Ravi Shankar,** Mahalia Jackson, the Modern Jazz Quartet, **Judy Collins,** The Jefferson Airplane, and others; these concerts are held on Tuesdays and have attracted audiences of over 20,000 people. A typical season's roster of performers gives the best indication of the Berkshire Festival's level of performance standards. In 1970, conductors were: **Leonard Bernstein, Aaron Copland, Antal Dorati, Rafael Frühbeck de Burgos, Alain Lombard, Charles Mackerras, Jorge Mester, Seiji Ozawa, Max Rudolf, Kenneth Schermerhorn, Gunther Schuller, William Steinberg,** and **Michael Tilson Thomas;** pianists: **Vladimir Ashkenazy, Christoph Eschenbach, Rudolf Firkusny, Claude Frank, Richard Goode, Gary Graffman, Lili Kraus, Jerome Lowenthal, Peter Serkin, Yuji Takahashi, André Watts,** and **Alexis Weissenberg;** other instrumentalists were: **Joseph Silverstein** and **Paul Zukofsky,** violinists, **Jules Eskin,** cellist, **James Stagliano,** hornist, and **Gervase de Peyer,** clarinetist. Singers were: **Eunice Alberts, John Alexander, Bethany Beardslee, William Cochran, Phillis Curtin, Rosalind Elias, Ezio Flagello, Lorna Haywood, Tom Krause, Christa Ludwig, Thomas Paul, George Shirley, Leopold Simoneau, Gwendolin Sims,** and **Teresa Stratas.** Choruses were: Berkshire Boy Choir, Chorus Pro Musica, Harvard Glee Club, Framingham Choral Society, M.I.T. Chorus, Radcliffe Choral Society, St. John's College Choir, and the Tanglewood Festival Chorus. More music is provided by the activities of the Berkshire Music Center, whose faculty and students give public performances almost daily. The majority of faculty are members of the Boston Symphony Orchestra, and the students, from throughout the United States and abroad, are young musicians of distinct ability. Together they form chamber groups of all kinds, since chamber music is emphasized within the Berkshire curriculum. A 90-member Berkshire Music Center Orchestra, composed of all members of the special Fellowship Program—a tuition-free opportunity granted to young musicians who are already active performers and who have completed formal studies, presents some seven full-length concerts each season under the conductorship of such as **Gunther Schuller, Aaron Copland,** and the Conducting Fellows at the Center (from the latter group have come many of today's top-ranking conductors). Most concerts of the Music Center are announced on a day-to-day basis; they are free to the so-called "Friends of Tanglewood," public-supporters who have paid a nominal membership fee for the season. On the other hand, those attending the Music Center's concerts on a random basis pay a small fee at a fixed rate for each event. The most publicized of the performances of the Music Center is the Festival of Contemporary Music, which is sponsored by the Center in conjunction with the Fromm Music Foundation of Chicago (see Musical Organizations). A four-day event, (scheduled so as not to conflict with the Berkshire Music Festival), it presents contemporary works, some of which are commissioned by the Center and the Fromm Foundation. With the exception of a few "repertory" pieces, most of the works scheduled receive their U.S. or world premieres at the Festival. American and foreign composers, both unknown and well-established, are represented. Frequently, participating composers are invited to take part in such adjunctive events as panel discussions, seminars, and the like. The performing facilities of the Berkshire Music Center include the Theatre (1,200 seats) for the Music Center's orchestra, the chamber music concerts, the Festival of Contemporary Music, and forums; a Chamber Music Hall (500 seats); the Rehearsal Stage; and numerous small studio buildings. As in the case of the Boston Symphony Orchestra, certain rehearsals of the Berkshire Music Center Orchestra are open to the public. Music performances have taken place at Tanglewood since 1934; in that year the "Berkshire Symphonic Festival" was established, using players from the then New York Philharmonic Symphony Society. When the Boston Symphony was invited to participate in the 1936 festival, the association between the orchestra and Tanglewood began and was subsequently perpetuated by the granting of the so-called Tanglewood estate to the orchestra by its private owners. The Tanglewood estate is some 210 acres of trees, lawns, and garden overlooking Lake Mahkeenac, between Lenox and Stockbridge in Berkshire County, western Massachusetts. In 1938, the Music Shed was constructed, and in 1940 the Berkshire Music Center was founded by Serge Koussevitzky along the lines of its present organization. The Berkshire Music Festival is America's oldest major music festival and the only one maintaining both a festival and a school under the direct control of a symphony orchestra. Artistic Directors of Tanglewood are **Seiji Ozawa** and **Gunther Schuller;** Advisor is **Leonard Bernstein;** Music Director of the Boston Symphony is **Seiji Ozawa,** appointed in 1973, following **William Steinberg.** The Music Center's Administrator is **Harry J. Kraut. Joseph Silverstein,** Concertmaster of the Boston Symphony, is Chairman of the Faculty; **Gunther Schuller** heads the Center's contemporary music activities; and **Charles Wilson,** Assistant Conductor of the Boston Symphony, is in charge of vocal music activities. Attendance at the Festival has grown steadily over the years. In 1958, attendance was 168,773; in 1961, it stood at 181,715; in 1970, attendance figures were 257,419, the Boston Symphony's 24 concerts and 8 rehearsals accounting for 186,190 persons. The programs are delay-broadcast by tape recording over a number of FM station outlets throughout the United States.

BOSTON POPS CONCERTS, Symphony Hall, Boston, Massachusetts 02115. Founded in 1885 as "The Music Hall Promenade Concerts," after the hall which served as the home of the Boston Symphony Orchestra until 1900. From the year 1930 the Boston Pops Orchestra has been inseparably associated with the name of its conductor, **Arthur Fiedler,** and has come to mean more than the nine-week season held in Symphony Hall each summer. The orchestra and the special kind of music programming it excels in are archetypical of the pops idea adapted in recent years by so many major and community symphonic organizations in the U.S. Made up of about 90 players from the Boston Symphony Orchestra, the Pops orchestra not only plays its regular season, but also has institutionalized the pops concept through concert tours and enormously successful recordings, thus becoming a pervasive phenomenon in American musical life. During the Pops season, which runs from late April to late June, Mondays through Saturdays, Symphony Hall is transformed into a music–dining–drinking hall where patrons enjoy light refreshments and a musical fare that is characteristically mixed: movements from symphonic works, light classics, current popular songs and medleys in arrangements, and a solo performer. Encores are an important feature of every Pops concert. Programs are announced approximately one week in advance. The Pops concerts are Boston's first "festival" following the close of the regular symphony season, but the city is one of the few in the U.S. that can offer yet another festival-like musical series immediately thereafter, and with the same orchestra, namely the Esplanade Concerts (q.v.).

CASTLE HILL FESTIVAL SERIES, c/o the New England Conservatory of Music Castle Hill Festival Series, Box 519, Ipswich, Massachusetts 01938. Established in 1950; Director: **Malcolm L. Creighton** (since 1968); Assistant Director: **Sara C. Walden.** The Festival is among a number in the United States whose most striking primary feature is its location—in this instance, a Georgian-style Great House built in 1927 after the general plan of two well-known original Houses in England. On the estate of Richard Teller Crane, Jr., the House contains such acquisitions as a complete library intact from the house of the Earl of Essex and paneled interiors from William Hogarth's London town house. After the death of Mrs. Crane in 1949 and the subsequent sale of books, furnishings, and other contents of the house, the Castle Hill Foundation was formed with a view to preserving the house's structure and grounds and to refurnishing it. For the first sixteen years of its existence, the Festival was sponsored by the Foundation. In 1967, sponsorship was passed to the New England Conservatory of Music, which maintains a summer school at Castle Hill, using the Great House, the Casino, the Castle Hill Farm, and adjoining grounds. The facilities are made available without charge by the Foundation and its Trustees. Castle Hill and the House dominate the coastline just above Crane Beach, an area made available to the public by the Trustees, and lie east of the town of Ipswich, itself some 25 miles northeast of Boston. A series of 10 or more concerts scheduled from late June or early July to mid-August, the Festival presents a variety of musical programs such as solo instrument and song recitals, choral programs, chamber music, jazz and folk music concerts, and staged operas. Performers have been: **Alfred Brendel, John Ogdon,** pianists; **Maria Stader,** soprano; **James Oliver Buswell IV,** violinist; Teddy Wilson's Quartet; Duke Ellington and Orchestra; Composers String Quartet; **Buffy Ste. Marie;** and the Berkshire Boy Choir. In addition concerts are presented by the faculty and students of the summer school. These are offered free. Faculty appearing in this series: **Daniel Pinkham, Allen Rogers, Victor Rosenbaum, Eric Rosenblith, Rudolf Kolisch, Russel Scherman, Miklos Schwalb,** and others.

ESPLANADE CONCERTS, 251 Huntington Avenue, Boston, Massachusetts 02115. Founded in 1929 by its conductor, **Arthur Fiedler.** This is a two-week series of free outdoor concerts beginning late in June a day or two after the end of the Boston Pops season. Like the orchestra for the Pops, the Esplanade orchestra is made up of members of the Boston Symphony Orchestra (about 85). Concerts are performed Monday through Saturday each evening at the Hatch Memorial Shell on the Charles River Esplanade. Audiences numbering 15,000 are not uncommon at these concerts.

JACOB'S PILLOW DANCE FESTIVAL, INC., Box 287, Lee, Massachusetts. Formed in 1941 by Ted Shawn (d. 1972), prominent figure in American dance. The Festival runs concurrently in the months of July and August with the University of the Dance, a course of dance instruction on the graduate level (and for professional training) given by a faculty well-known in the field of ballet, modern dance, ethnic dance, and other related studies; and a Dance Appreciation Course, actually a series of lecture-demonstrations, film-slide studies, and discussions offered by the Theatre staff and invited speakers and performers. All performances take place in the Ted Shawn Theatre (600 seats) built in 1942, the only theater in the U.S. made exclusively for dance performances. Annually 70 resident students and 24 scholarship students are registered; attendance figures per season for the dance programs total nearly 25,000. The dance programs are of the highest calibre, offering guest soloists and companies in premieres of new works and works in the repertory. Mimes and dance satirists are often featured. Past performers have included: **Patricia McBride, Edward Villella, Carmen de Lavallade, Toni Lander, Bruce Marks, Violette Verdy, Michael Maule, James Clouser, Mata and Hari, Olatunji** and Company, **Norman Walker** and

Company, Maria Alba's Spanish Dance Company, Murray Louis Dance Company, Boston Ballet Company, Pennsylvania Ballet. The number of performances weekly range from four to a typical schedule of six or seven; there are both evening and matinee events. Jacob's Pillow is in the Township of Becket, Massachusetts, off U.S. Route 20 a few miles east of the Lee-Pittsfield exit (Exit 2) on the Massachusetts Turnpike. Executive Director of the Festival is **John Christian.**

NEW MARLBORO MUSIC CENTER (Red Fox Music Barn), Star Route 70, Box 140, Great Barrington, Massachusetts 01230. Formed in 1958 by its current director, **Isabelle Sant Ambrogio,** pianist, the summer concert series is organized as part of the activities of the Red Fox Music Camp. The New Marlboro Chamber Players, the resident group, are 14 professional musicians who offer seven Saturday evening concerts of varied chamber music from mid-July to August. On Sundays, a series of free concerts is performed by students at the camp. The Camp is located in New Marlboro, southeast of Great Barrington on Route 57. About 1,000 people make up an average season's attendance. Among the members of the Chamber Players: **Patricia Parr,** pianist; **Michael Grebanier,** cellist; **Julian Olevsky,** violinist; **William Haroutounian,** violinist; and **Isabelle Sant Ambrogio.**

THE COLLEGE PLAYERS AT HIGHFIELD, Box F, Falmouth, Massachusetts 02541. Falmouth is on Route 28 in the southwest section of Cape Cod. College students, who until 1969 were mostly from Oberlin College in Ohio, are the members of this summer theater group. Formed in 1953, the group is primarily known for its highly professional performances of the operettas of Gilbert and Sullivan. Its present repertory, however, also includes light operas such as those by Offenbach and Lehár and short, frequently performed American operas. Performances take place in Highfield Theatre, off Depot Avenue in Falmouth. Once part of an estate, the Theatre is now owned by Highfield Associates, who offer Highfield as a center for developing young dramatic talent, a policy begun over twenty years ago by the estate's last private owners. Programs run for nine weeks each summer from July to late August or early September. The company consists of about 70 members and employs a full orchestra. The Theatre capacity is 300; average season attendance is about 14,000. General Manager is **Robert A. Haslun;** Artistic Director: **D. Thomas Tull.**

SOUTH MOUNTAIN CONCERTS, Box 23, Pittsfield, Massachusetts 01201. Established in 1918 as the Berkshire Festival of Chamber Music by Mrs. Elizabeth Sprague Coolidge and maintained, since 1935, by South Mountain Association, an organization founded that year also by Mrs. Coolidge. The earlier festivals were markedly significant events for the history of chamber music in America, insofar as some of the world's greatest performers were invited to participate and outstanding composers of the day were commissioned to write new works. At present, **Paul K. Fodder** is President of the Association and **Mrs. Willem Willeke** is Musical Director (since 1950). To sustain its activities, which also include many free "Young Audiences Concerts" for about 20,000 children in the Berkshire region, the Association depends entirely on voluntary contributions. Concerts take place in the Association's own concert hall, the Temple of Music (600 seats), an imposing hilltop structure off U.S. Route 7, south of Pittsfield. Chamber music and opera performances comprise the programs, which are scheduled on Saturday and Sunday afternoons from mid-July to mid-October. Among the soloists and groups who have performed in the series are: **Rudolf Serkin,** the late Myra Hess, **Leontyne Price, Gary Graffman,** Abbey Singers, Guarneri String Quartet, Budapest String Quartet, Juilliard String Quartet, New York Pro Musica, and the Metropolitan Opera Studio.

SUMMERTHING, 603 City Hall Annex, 23 Court Street, Boston, Massachusetts 02108. Dubbed "Boston's Neighborhood Festival," Summerthing was established in April, 1968 following the general idea set forth by Cleveland's Summer Arts Festival (q.v.) in 1967. The plan of Summerthing is to bring to each of Boston's distinct neighborhood communities free cultural entertainment in many categories and, at the same time, to encourage the neighborhoods to plan and develop their own cultural activities. The point of these two levels, other than the obvious one of making urban life a little more pleasant (particularly in city areas undergoing social change or severely lacking cultural and entertainment facilities) is to permit neighborhoods to recognize and support their local artists and performers and to provide opportunities for neighborhood residents, especially children and teen-agers, to develop their own creative skills under enjoyable conditions. Under the plan, each of the fourteen neighborhoods (East Boston, Charleston, North End, South Boston, Columbia Point, etc.) forms its own neighborhood arts council with a full-time coordinator, teachers, and volunteers. From this come workshops for art, music, drama, dance, photography, and film making. In addition, the councils select from lists gathered by the administrators of Summerthing various small-scale performances (professional, semi-professional, and amateur) of popular music, jazz, square or folk dancing, band competitions, and the like, to be presented in neighborhood parks and playgrounds. Summerthing's sponsorship of forty mass events, all free, offered in five major city parks, on a schedule of one per week for each park for eight weeks, best exemplifies the traditional festival idea. For these events, such groups as the Boston Ballet Company, Boston Philharmonia Promenade Orchestra, the Dance Circle of Boston, the African Heritage Ensemble, and performers **Pete Seeger, Joan Baez, Duke Ellington,** and many others have been engaged. It is estimated that the total reach of all the events in the Summerthing program of 1970 alone encompassed nearly one million people. The City of Boston contributes about $300,000 towards Summerthing's total operating budget of $420,000. The balance comes from Boston's business community, the Massachusetts Council on the Arts and Humanities, the National Endowment for the Arts, and individuals. **Katherine D. Kane,** special assistant for cultural affairs to the Mayor of Boston, is the Director of Summerthing.

WORCESTER MUSIC FESTIVAL, Memorial Auditorium, Worcester, Massachusetts 01608. Founded in 1858, it is the oldest annual music festival in America. A five-day event held in October, the Festival is sponsored by the Worcester County Musical Association, **H. Ladd Plumley,** President. Musical Director is **Alfred Nash Patterson,** who is leader of the 175-voice Worcester Chorus. The featured orchestral ensemble in the past has been the Philadelphia Orchestra; more recently, the Detroit Symphony under **Sixten Ehrling** has made regular appearances. The plan of the concert programs is such that works performed make use of solo instrumentalists and singers, as well as the chorus and orchestra. Thus, over the five-day period, there are concertos, oratorios and other large-scale choral works, operatic arias and songs, and symphonic works. Concerts are in the evening.

Michigan

ANN ARBOR MAY FESTIVAL, c/o University Musical Society, Burton Tower, University of Michigan, Ann Arbor, Michigan 48104. The May Festival was founded in 1894 by the University Musical Society (organized in 1879), which still remains its sole sponsor. Throughout the long history of the Festival, the structure of the musical programs has been a simple one, namely, music for orchestra shared with solo voice or instrument, and two choral programs also with orchestra. Each year since 1936, the only orchestra engaged for the Festival has been the Philadelphia Orchestra, succeeding the Chicago Symphony Orchestra, which performed at Ann Arbor from 1905 to 1935. The University Choral Union, a 300-voice chorus made up of Ann Arbor residents and students, has been the featured choral group since 1894. Principal conductors have been **Eugene Ormandy,** who has appeared with the Philadelphia Orchestra regularly since 1937, and **Thor Johnson,** from 1940 to 1942 and from 1947 to the present. Recent years have seen only one curious departure from the Festival's tradition-laden past: since 1967, the Festival has taken place either entirely or partly in April and in May; in 1972, it returned to May. The remarkable stability of this Festival provides an uninterrupted chronology of changing taste in concert music for a period of over seventy-five years, and at the same time yields a roster of those artists—American and foreign—who were in the forefront of their respective fields in any given decade. Among the well-known singers, for example, who performed at Ann Arbor are such names as: Lucrezia Bori (1921 and 1934), Anna Fitziu (1919), Kirsten Flagstad (1937), Alma Gluck (1912 and 1914), Marcella Sembrich (1899), Louise Homer (six appearances from 1902 to 1926), Ernestine Schumann-Heink (between 1900 and 1927), Edward Johnson (three performances), Giovanni Martinelli (nine appearances), Evan Williams (1896 to 1901), Richard Bonelli (from 1926 on), Emilio de Gogorza (five appearances beginning with 1902), Alexander Kipnis (1940 and 1943), Giuseppe de Luca (1917 and 1918), and other late greats such as Leonard Warren, Lawrence Tibbett, and Ezio Pinza. In more recent years Ann Arbor has presented singers **Adele Addison, Montserrat Caballé, Eileen Farrell, Lois Marshall, Birgit Nilsson, Leopold Simoneau, Donald Gramm, Cesare Siepi,** and **William Warfield,** to name a very few. Among pianists and violinists of the present century, the May Festival can boast of these participants: Harold Bauer, Arthur Friedheim, Ossip Gabrilowitsch, Rudolf Ganz, Josef Hofmann, Ernest Hutcheson, William Kapell, Ignace Paderewski, Sergei Rachmaninoff, Artur Schnabel, **John Browning, Van Cliburn, Glenn Gould, Sviatoslav Richter, Arthur Rubinstein, Rudolf Serkin,** Mischa Elman, Georges Enesco, Fritz Kreisler, **Jascha Heifetz,** and **Isaac Stern.** Conductors have included Frederick Stock, **Leopold Stokowski,** and others associated with the history of the Philadelphia Orchestra such as **Saul Caston, William Smith,** and guest conductors Gustav Holst (in 1923 and 1932), **Howard Hanson,** Percy Grainger (in 1928), **José Iturbi,** Georges Enesco, Igor Stravinsky, and others. Executive Director of the University Musical Society is **Gail W. Rector. Donald Bryant** is Director of the Choral Union. The Festival presents five concerts in four consecutive days in Hill Auditorium.

BELLE ISLE CONCERTS, c/o Detroit Symphony Orchestra, Ford Auditorium, Detroit, Michigan 48226, or: City of Detroit, Department of Parks and Recreation. A series of free summer evening concerts sponsored by the City of Detroit and featuring the Detroit Symphony Orchestra. The programs consist of symphonic music of the light and popular variety: overtures, suites, dances, orchestral transcriptions, and movements from larger works. Any soloists performing during the series are members of the orchestra. In all about 10 concerts are scheduled from the last weeks of August to September. Performances take place at the Jerome H. Remick Memorial Shell at Belle Isle on the mouth of the Detroit River.

DETROIT CONCERT BAND SUMMER SERIES, 20962 Mack Avenue, Grosse Pointe Woods, Michigan 48236. Established in 1946, the series features one of America's most famous professional bands under the leadership of **Leonard B. Smith.** The concerts are immensely popular, attracting over a quarter of a million people each season since their founding. Beginning early in June, the concerts run for eight weeks, nightly, except Monday and Tuesday, and offer a complete change of program for each concert. All concerts are free and are sponsored by the City of Detroit. Performances take place in the Band Shell on Belle Isle in the Detroit River (the series was once called the "Belle Isle Concerts") and in the Shell in the Michigan State Fairgrounds in the city's northern sector. The Band's repertory is unusually large and consists of works of symphonic nature, marches, waltzes, a multitude of transcriptions and arrangements of both popular and classical music, and works for solo instruments. **Leonard B. Smith** frequently performs as cornet soloist. Apart from the prepared programs, the Band always plays music on request.

SYMPHONY UNDER THE STARS, c/o Detroit Symphony Orchestra, Ford Auditorium, Detroit, Michigan 48226. Founded in 1949. This series of free public concerts is administered by the Detroit Symphony. Concerts take place in the Music Shell at Michigan State Fairgrounds in the northern section of the city. The generally light symphonic fare is presented on five evenings during a two-week period in June.

MEADOW BROOK MUSIC FESTIVAL, Oakland University, Rochester, Michigan 48063. Founded in 1964, the Festival was the first completed plan in the development of a performing arts center on the University's campus; subsequent projects were the construction of the Meadow Brook School of Music—completed in 1965—and the Meadow Brook Theatre. The Festival and the School of Music run concurrently, lasting respectively eight weeks and six weeks from June to August. The Detroit Symphony Orchestra is the central musical organization around which both the Festival and the School revolve and, in the tradition of other major orchestras with specially created facilities, is engaged in combined performance and teaching as a primary summertime obligation. The Orchestra's participation in the Meadow Brook School includes the use of first-desk men as faculty; for the Festival, the Orchestra plays some 34 major concerts in Baldwin Memorial Pavilion on the University Campus. The Pavilion, claimed to possess superior acoustics, has seating for 2,138 people with space on the surrounding lawn for an additional 6,200. The average concert attendance is 5,500. **Sixten Ehrling,** the Detroit Symphony's Music Director, conducts the majority of the concerts. Other conductors in the past have included **Charles Munch, Robert Shaw, Julius Rudel, Henry Lewis, Seiji Ozawa, Karel Ancerl,** and **Antal Dorati.** Performers have included: **Van Cliburn, Isaac Stern, Gregor Piatigorsky, Vladimir Ashkenazy, Gary Graffman, Eugene Istomin, Janos Starker, Peter Serkin, Anna Moffo, Beverly Sills, Judith Raskin.** Elliot Feld's American Ballet and the American Ballet Theatre have both performed at Meadow Brook with the Detroit Orchestra accompanying. The Festival's week begins on Thursday and ends on Sunday. All performances are scheduled for evenings. Additional concerts—about six each season—are organized by the Meadow Brook Music School orchestra and are offered free to Festival season subscribers. The Manager of the Meadow Brook Music Festival is **W. W. Kent.**

Missouri

STARLIGHT THEATRE SUMMER SERIES, c/o Starlight Theatre Association, P.O. Box 357, Kansas City, Missouri 64141. The Series consists of nightly programs of musicals and variety shows presented from mid-June to early September in Kansas City's 14-acre Swope Park. The Theatre, built in 1951 at a cost of $1,750,000, is owned by the City, which leases it to a nonprofit organization. There are 7,858 permanent seats. The Theatre claims to have one of the most modern and elaborate outdoor theater plants in the nation. Performers engaged for the Summer Series include some of the leading stars of Broadway.

ST. LOUIS MUNICIPAL OPERA, Municipal Theatre, Forest Park, St. Louis, Missouri 63112. Founded in 1919. The productions of the Municipal Opera once were operas, operettas, and ballets, followed by a period of mostly musical plays and a few operettas. These have yielded completely to a summer season of "packaged" productions of popular music-entertainment shows and musical plays. The Theatre has a 12,000 capacity, which prompts the official claim that it is the "largest and most complete summer outdoor theater in the world." Stars of Hollywood, Broadway, and television are often engaged for leading roles in the musical plays; these have included **Bob Hope, Eddie Albert, Ann Blyth, Kaye Stevens, Anna Maria Alberghetti, Sid Caesar, Ed Ames, Juliet Prowse, Milton Berle, Joel Grey,** Betty Grable, and **Barbara Eden.** Production shows have featured **Glen Campbell, Jim Nabors, Jimmy Durante, Robert Goulet,** et al. The stars are engaged weekly; the ensemble and technical staff are retained for the entire summer season. **William Zalken** is Manager; **Glenn Jordan** is Productions Director.

New Hampshire

NEW HAMPSHIRE MUSIC FESTIVAL, P.O. Box 147, Center Harbor, New Hampshire 03226. Founded in 1953; the Festival is incorporated and self-sustaining, receiving only a minimal amount of foundation assistance. It presents a series of tour concerts located in various communities in New Hampshire's Lake Region; its eight subscription concerts are apportioned for performances in such facilities as Interlakes Auditorium in Meredith, Kingswood Auditorium in Wolfeboro, Festival House in Center Harbor, Barnstormers' Theater in Tamworth, Belknap College Auditorium in Center Harbor, and other locations. Festival House, on the campus of Belknap College, is headquarters and residence for the Festival musicians and the Music Director and Conductor, **Thomas Nee.** The 30 or more musicians, apart from composing the Festival orchestra, offer private instruction for all keyboard and orchestral instruments during the six-week summer season, which begins the second week in July, and perform the weekly Sunday evening chamber music concerts held at Festival House. The musicians are drawn from major orchestras throughout the United States. Extra concerts outside the subscription series and Sunday chamber performances consist of special children concerts, Festival of New Music, choral concerts, and others directed towards special audiences. Average audience attendance for the basic eight-concert series is 450 to 500. Program content is remarkably varied and balanced. **Thomas Nee,** a member of the music faculty of the University of California at San Diego, has been associated with the Festival from 1960 to 1965 and again from 1968 to the present. **Elaine L. Colby** is President of the Festival corporation; Manager is **Frederick Halgedahl. Ann Stamps** is in charge of public relations.

WHITE MOUNTAINS FESTIVAL OF THE SEVEN ARTS, Pike, New Hampshire 03780. Founded in 1948. Held on the 5,500-acre White Mountain resort of Lake Tarleton Club (off State Route 25 near the Vermont State Line and Interstate Highway 91). The essence of the Festival is the outdoor discussion forum involving not only people in the performing, graphic, and literary arts, but also those well-known in politics, journalism, radio and television, and sciences. The forums are presented informally in an atmosphere of leisure and are an important part of the resort's attractions. Musical performances have featured singers from the Metropolitan Opera Company, **Lucine Amara** and **Robert Goodloe;** the finalists of the Metropolitan Opera Auditions; solo instrumentalists such as pianists **Claudette Sorel** and **Olegna Fuschi;** and folk singers and popular music vocalists. In addition, there have been performances by dancers from the Harkness Ballet, the Pennsylvania Ballet Company, and others. The programs are scheduled in July and August and are organized entirely by Lake Tarleton Club. **Jack Golbert** is Festival Director; Musical Director is **Hal Graham.**

New Jersey

GARDEN STATE ARTS CENTER, Box 116, Holmdel, N.J. 07733. Created in 1968 by the New Jersey Highway Authority, it is operated by the Authority through the direction of Nederlander Arts Associates, Inc. The Center is located at Telegraph Hill on the Garden State Parkway off Exit 116. This exit lies between New York and Philadelphia and leads only to the Arts Center—in fact, there are no other roads leading to the Center. Facilities there include a 5,000-seat amphitheater, surrounding lawns capable of accommodating an additional 9,000 people—to indicate the total that has thus far been reported. The programs are grouped into two series: "popular" subscription series and "classical" subscription series. The latter offers six events (reduced to three in 1973), each performed on two successive days, and the former offers seven programs, each scheduled to run nightly from Monday through Saturday. Thus the popular series will offer such production entertainments as six successive evenings of **Harry Belafonte,** or **Burt Bacharach** leading an orchestra, or a musical play current on Broadway. The classical series has offered **Henry Lewis** conducting the New Jersey Symphony; **Eugene Ormandy** and the Philadelphia Orchestra; **André Kostelanetz** and **Aldo Ceccato** conducting the New York Philharmonic Orchestra; singers **Beverly Sills** and **Marilyn Horne;** pianists **Gina Bachauer** and **Earl Wild;** the Alvin Ailey Dance Company; and the Stuttgart Ballet. The Center's activities are scheduled from early June to early September. Executive Director is **John P. Gallagher.**

New Mexico

SANTA FE OPERA, P.O. Box 2408, Santa Fe, New Mexico 87501. Year round address: 156 East 52nd Street, New York, N.Y. 10022. (See also under Opera Companies.) Founded in 1957 by its current General Director and Conductor, **John Crosby,** the Santa Fe Opera presents a season of opera productions from early July to late August in its own Opera Theatre (1,300 seats), located five miles north of the city of Santa Fe on U.S. Highway 64-84-285. The season generally consists of six or seven works totaling about 26 performances. The company mounts its own productions, employing internationally known stage directors, set and costumer designers, and guest conductors. In recent years conductors have been: **Robert Baustian, Gustav Meier, Stanislaw Skrowaczewski,** the German composer **Hans Werner Henze,** and **John Moriarty,** among others. Each season features important premieres and new productions. About half of the operas are sung in English including those in the standard opera repertory. In recent years, Santa Fe has presented the American premiere of Henze's "The Bassarids," Schoenberg's "Die Jacobsleiter," Menotti's "Help! Help! The Globolinks," Penderecki's "The Devils of Loudon" and the world premiere of "Opera" by Berio and "Yerma" by Villa-Lobos. In general, about half of the operas performed during any given season are works of this century. Singers include many who have sung with Santa Fe for a number of seasons as well as newcomers making their Santa Fe or American debuts. Some of the well-known artists have been: **John Alexander, Charles Bressler, Patricia Brooks, Donald Gramm, Jean Kraft, Judith Raskin, John Reardon, Regina Sarfaty, George Shirley, Benite Valente,** and **Felicia Weathers.**

New York

CARAMOOR FESTIVAL, c/o Walter and Lucie Rosen Foundation, Inc., Katonah, N.Y. 10536. Caramoor is the estate of the late Walter T. Rosen; until her death in 1968, his widow, Lucie Bigelow Rosen, remained President of the Foundation which was established to ensure the continuance of Caramoor as a musical series and to contribute to other activities in the arts. Located northeast of New York City in Westchester County (on Route 137, off State Route 22), Caramoor, with its Spanish Courtyard and outdoor Venetian Theater surrounded by wooded grounds, presents music in one of the most attractive settings in the East. The concerts begin in mid-June and spread over four or five weekends: Friday and Saturday evenings and Sunday afternoon. Also offered are four Wednesday afternoon lectures on music presented in the Music Room of Caramoor's main house. Despite its size and limited number of concerts (about 10 per season), Caramoor can be credited with a number of distinct musical achievements such as the American premieres of Benjamin Britten's church parables: "Curlew River," "The Burning Fiery Furnace," and "The Prodigal Son"; the Australian composer, Malcolm Williamson's "The Growing Castle"; and other productions of works rarely seen: Mozart's "Bastien and Bastienne," Monteverdi's "Incoronazione di Poppea," and a concert version of Handel's "Semele." **Julius Rudel** is the Musical Director and leads an orchestra organized especially for the Festival (although the orchestra in 1968 was the Philadelphia Orchestra, which made its Caramoor debut under his direction). In addition to operatic works, there are orchestral concerts, chamber music, and recitals. Soloists are invariably drawn from the first ranks in the active concert world: **Beverly Sills, William Metcalf, Peter Serkin, Antonio Janigro, Frances Bible,** and **Judith Raskin,** to name a few.

CHAUTAUQUA SUMMER MUSIC PROGRAMS, Chautauqua Institution, Chautauqua, N.Y. 14722. Chautauqua is both a community and an institution. The normally small population of the town increases to 8 or 10 thousand in the summer as people take up temporary residence there. Visitors and residents make up the more than 40,000 people who attend some part of the eight-week Chautauqua program of lectures, seminars, classes, religious services, theatrical and dance productions, and music concerts. Chautauqua is the original and single remaining vestige of an idea which began in 1874, when the first Chautauqua Assembly was established on the shores of Lake Chautauqua in Western New York State, not far from Lake Erie. The first Chautauqua was organized as a summer gathering for the training of Sunday School teachers (Methodist Episcopal). The use of summer vacation time for educational purposes was an important contribution to education in the United States; the idea expanded to become an original force in adult education by helping to develop home reading courses, correspondence and extension courses, and the like. Eventually, prominent lecturers from many fields—government officials, scientists, writers, critics, and religious leaders—were attracted to Chautauqua. In 1893 an amphitheater seating over 6,000 was built to accommodate the growing audiences. The success of the events soon spawned the era of the traveling Chautauqua, independent circuits offering a mixture of educational, political, and cultural lectures and meetings with religious services and other activities designed to bring people together for exposure to ideas not readily encountered in, for example, the rural communities of the Midwest, where the traveling Chautauqua became particularly popular. Today, Chautauqua is a 700-acre shoreline community complete with public halls, homes, hotels, clubs, parks, and recreational areas devoted to providing arts and music festivals, sports facilities, instructional opportunities (including credit courses), and nondenominational Christian study and worship—all within a sort of family-vacation atmosphere. After World War I, music assumed an increasingly important role in the offerings at Chautauqua. A season of orchestral concerts was initiated in 1920, followed a few years later by opera performances. Currently, the musical season at Chautauqua features the Chautauqua Symphony Orchestra under **Walter Hendl,** who has been Musical Director since 1953. The concerts are generally scheduled for Tuesday, Wednesday, and Saturday evenings and offer a broad range of programs with occasional instrumental and vocal soloists. Guest conductors have been **Arthur Fiedler, Howard Hanson, Skitch Henderson,** and **Morton Gould,** among others. Soloists appearing with the orchestra have included **Roberta Peters, José Iturbi, Masuko Ushioda, Ozan Marsh,** and **Van Cliburn,** who has performed as both soloist and conductor at Chautauqua. The Chautauqua Opera Association, under **Leonard Treash,** General Director, presents about six productions a season in two or three performances each. The performances are held in Norton Memorial Hall. The repertory includes light opera, operettas, and Broadway musical shows, as well as works from the standard repertory. **Evan Whallon,** who heads Chautauqua's Music School, is Musical Director and Conductor of the Opera Association. Other musical events include performances by the Chautauqua School of Music Symphony Orchestra under **James Walker,** Sunday afternoon organ recitals, evening recitals by well-known instrumentalists and vocalists, and performances each morning by the Chautauqua Choir under **William Wagner.** Jazz and popular music concerts have presented **Ella Fitzgerald, Al Hirt, George Shearing,** barbershop harmony ensembles, and some production shows. Foreign folk ensembles, United States service bands, and dance ensembles round out the typical season. Chautauqua is administered by the Chautauqua Institution (f. 1902) and the Chautauqua Foundation (f. 1937). **Oscar E. Remick** is President of the Institution and Program Director.

CONCERTS AT EIGHT, c/o Southampton College of Long Island University, Southampton, N.Y. 11968. A series of chamber music concerts, held in the Fine Arts Theater on the campus of Southampton College. The series is sponsored by the College and is under the direction of **Robert Shaughnessy,** Director of Music at the College, who has guided the programs since their inception in 1964. The concerts are held in conjunction with the summer school, running from the end of June to late August. (Some free events, such as lectures and recitals, are also presented during the summer season.) Among the ensembles have been the Kohon Quartet and the Gotham Chamber Orchestra under **Harold Kohon.**

JAZZ IN THE GARDEN, The Museum of Modern Art, 11 West 53 Street, New York, N.Y. 10019. First organized in the summer of 1960, "Jazz in the Garden" is a series of 10 Thursday evening concerts presented in the Museum's Sculpture Garden. The open-air garden has little in the way of seating and the audience stands or sits on the ground; beer and sandwiches are available. The Garden can accommodate some 3,000 people; average concert attendance is between 2,000 to 2,500. Admission to the concert is additional to the charge for admission to the Museum itself, which is open Thursday evenings throughout the summer for its other activities such as film showings and lectures. In recent years, the programs in the series have included performers who have attempted to merge the styles of jazz and rock. Such performers, and those known as essentially jazz or jazz-related musicians, have included **Clark Terry, Max Kaminsky,** the Pazant Brothers; the group, Earth Opera; **Richie Havens, Jimmy McGriff,** and **Gabor Szabo.** Program Director of the series, since 1968, has been **Ed Bland.** The series receives the cooperation of *Downbeat* magazine.

JULY MUSIC FESTIVAL, c/o Pawling Fine Arts Council, Taber Knolls, Pawling, N.Y. 12564. Founded in 1968. Concerts are held on three consecutive Thursday evenings in July in the Auditorium of Lathrop Memorial Building, Holiday Hills, in Pawling. **Claude Monteux,** Conductor of the Hudson Valley Philharmonic Society and flutist, is Artistic Director of the series as well as solo performer with the Monteux Quartet. Members of the quartet—**Claude** and **Marianne Monteux,** flutes; **Kenneth Fricker,** double bass; and **Silvia Suzousky,** harpsichord—perform mainly Baroque trio sonatas as well as other works using the Quartet's combination of instruments. The Monteux Chamber Players, an ensemble of 12 strings, is featured at one of the concerts. Both the Fine Arts Council and the Hudson Valley Philharmonic Society are sponsors of the Festival, which is but one of many cultural activities organized by the sponsors for the area residents. Pawling is located near the intersection of State Routes 55 and 22 in southeastern New York State.

LAKE GEORGE OPERA FESTIVAL, Box 471, Glen Falls, N.Y. 12801. A summer series of opera performances which take place in the festival theater located off Queensbury School, Exit 19 on the Adirondack Northway (about 20 minutes from Saratoga Springs). Founded in 1962. The performances are of operas from the standard and modern repertory sung in English. The season lasts from early July to late August. General Director is **David Lloyd.**

LAKE PLACID MUSIC FESTIVAL, Box 949, Lake Placid, N.Y. 12946. Established in 1963, the Festival is supported by the Lake Placid Music and Art Association and takes place in the Signal Hill Arts Center in Lake Placid. Artistic Director (from 1963 to 1969) was the late pianist José Echaniz, who was an active solo performer in the series and who, along with **Carol Sindell Domb** and **Daniel Domb,** was a member of the Lake Placid Festival Trio, the ensemble around which the Festival is organized. The series consists of seven Tuesday evening concerts from mid-July to late August. Other performers during the series have been **Brenda Lewis,** members of the Metropolitan Opera Studio Ensemble, and **José Iturbi.** The Arts Center Hall seats about 300. Annual attendance has usually been a capacity 2,100 people.

LINCOLN CENTER'S MID-SUMMER SERENADES, Philharmonic Hall, Lincoln Center, Broadway at 65th Street, New York, N.Y. 10023. Begun in 1966, this summer concert series has had several subnames: "Mozart Festival" (1966 and 1967), "A Mozart and Haydn Festival" (1968), and "A Mostly Mozart Festival" (1970 and 1971). Formerly sponsored by The Lincoln Center Fund in association with a concert management firm, the latest series (1971) was under the sponsorship of the Herman Goldman Foundation, Inc. Festival Director is **William Lockwood, Jr.** Festival Consultant is **George F. Schutz.** The festival is always held in August, filling the month completely with a concert every night from Monday through Saturday. All seats in Philharmonic Hall are offered at one price with special discount prices for purchases of 10 tickets. (Despite increases due to inflation, the tickets have been sold through the years at what might be termed "popular prices.") The programs offer orchestral works, chamber music, choral works, opera, and recitals, totaling 24 evenings of music altogether, primarily devoted to the music of Mozart (works by Haydn and Schubert were added to the 1971 series). An unusually large roster of conductors, soloists, and chamber groups, along with the great number and variety of works performed, have made the festival one of the most popular of all paid-admission concert series in New York City. Reportedly, about 200,000 people have attended the concerts since their inception. An important element in the festival is the display of new talent or old talent in new or unfamiliar guises. For example, among the 10 conductors engaged in 1971 to conduct the resident ensemble, the New York Chamber Orchestra, were pianists **Leon Fleisher** and **Philippe Entremont,** the latter making his U.S. conducting debut and appearing also as orchestral soloist and recitalist (the former made his New York conducting debut with this festival in 1970), and **Karl Richter,** appearing as both conductor and organist. Other conductors in recent festivals, some making their New York debuts, have been: **Sergiu Comissiona, Eve Queler** (the first woman to conduct at the festival), **Jorge Mester, Michael Tilson Thomas, Richard Dufallo, Neville Marriner, David Zinman, Brian Priestman, Seymour Lipkin, Werner Torkanowsky, Gerhard Samuel, John Nelson, Kenneth Schermerhorn, Boris Goldovsky, Alexander Schneider, Antonio Janigro, Peter Maag,** and **Lukas Foss.** Soloists are either new talent or those from the top echelon of available artists in the concert world. **Alfred Brendel, Alicia de Larrocha, Christoph Eschenbach, Claude Frank, Lili Kraus, Helen Schnabel, Karl Ulrich Schnabel, Elly Ameling, Nancy Shade, Marcia Baldwin, Carole Bogard, Veronica Tyler,** to name some, are representative of the caliber of soloists performing for the festivals. Chamber groups have been: the Boston Symphony Chamber Players, the Guarneri Quartet, Pro Arte Chamber Singers, the Amadeus Quartet, the Juilliard Quartet, the Galimir Quartet, and the Hungarian Quartet, among others.

MAVERICK SUNDAY CONCERTS, Box 655, Maverick Road, Woodstock, N.Y. 12498. Established in 1916. The Maverick Theater is the setting for this series. An unusual construction of raw timber, it is placed in a heavily wooded area providing a completely rustic atmosphere. Extraordinary acoustical qualities are attributed to the hall. Both indoor and outdoor seating is available at the concerts; the capacity of the hall is 300. About 10 to 15 concerts are scheduled annually in the series running from July 1 to Labor Day. Chamber music is the mainstay of the programs ranging from the traditional instrumental combinations for the performance of duos, trios, quartets, etc., to the mixed groups needed for contemporary music. Among the groups and performers have been the Beaux Arts Quartet; Curtis Quartet; Philharmonia Trio; the New York Chamber Soloists; **Zara Nelsova** and **Grant Johannesen, William Kroll** and **Arthur Balsam.** The concerts receive support from various business firms, as well as the New York State Council on the Arts. **Alexander Semmler,** pianist and composer, is Artistic Director. Woodstock is on Route 212 northwest of Exit 19 on the New York State Thruway in eastern New York.

METROPOLITAN OPERA FREE SUMMER CONCERTS, c/o Metropolitan Opera, Lincoln Center Plaza, New York, N.Y. 10023. The Metropolitan concerts are held in the parks of the five boroughs of New York City. Admission is free with no tickets required. Sponsored by the City of New York through its Administration of Parks, Recreation and Cultural Affairs and a number of business firms which, through the Metropolitan Opera, contribute to general costs or specific opera productions (among them are Pepsico, Inc., Glen Alden Co., and Frito–Lay), the operas are presented in concert form (no sets or costumes) and are performed by top Metropolitan artists supported by full chorus and orchestra. The Metropolitan's staff of conductors is drawn upon, and in recent years the concerts have been led by **Kurt Adler, Alain Lombard, Jean Morel, Jan Behr,** and **Ignace Strasfogel.** The outdoor concerts were first begun in the summer of 1967 following two summers of offering low-price admission to outdoor performances in Lewisohn Stadium (on the campus of City College of New York; its demolition is now being planned). The location of the concerts in the five boroughs is as follows: Sheep Meadow in Central Park for Manhattan; Nether Mead in Brooklyn's Prospect Park; Daffodil Hill in the Botanical Gardens, The Bronx; Queen's Crocheron Park in Bayside; and, in Staten Island, the concerts take place in Clove Lakes Park. Three operas provide the entire repertory in a total of about 12 performances; all three are performed in Queens and Manhattan and in the remaining boroughs two of the three are offered. The Metropolitan uses a specially designed outdoor acoustical shell and a loudspeaker system. The concerts are attended by huge crowds. The first concert in 1967 was estimated to have drawn over 35,000 people—the largest audience up to that time ever to hear a single performance of the opera company. Subsequent years, however, have brought crowds estimated to be over 50,000 for a single performance. Annual attendance is estimated to be 300,000. All performances are scheduled in the evening. The series begins in June and is under the direction of **Charles Riecker,** Artistic Administrator.

METROPOLITAN OPERA JUNE FESTIVAL, Metropolitan Opera, Lincoln Center Plaza, New York, N.Y. 10023. The June Festival is, in effect, an extension of the regular Metropolitan season. Performances are held in the Metropolitan Opera House. In 1969 seven performances were scheduled, whereas in 1970 the June schedule grew from an originally planned two weeks to four weeks as a result of the labor strike during the first half of the 1969–1970 season. In 1971, seven operas were each performed twice in 14 consecutive days.

NAUMBURG ORCHESTRAL CONCERTS, c/o 175 West 93rd Street, New York, N.Y. 10025. Since 1905, the Naumburg Concerts have been presented in Central Park, on the Mall, through the auspices of founder Elkan Naumburg and his successors, currently **Edward Naumburg, Jr.** and **George W. Naumburg.** The facility used for the concerts, the Naumburg bandshell, was donated to New York City by Naumburg in 1923 and has been used since to present many forms of outdoor entertainment. The Naumburg Concerts are offered on Memorial Day, Independence Day, July 31, and Labor Day of each year and are free to the public. The featured ensemble is a 48-piece symphony orchestra which plays under guest conductors, among whom have been **Samuel Krachmalnick, Emerson Buckley, Richard Burgin,** and **Boyd Neel.** Instrumental and vocal soloists who have performed with the orchestra include **Lorne Monroe, Aldo Parisot,** and **Leslie Parnas,** cellists; **Ruth Posselt,** violinist; **Lois Marshall** and **Laurel Hurley,** sopranos. The programs include concertos and orchestral works, opera in concert form, and generally a work by a contemporary American composer. Concert attendance ranges from 2,000 to 7,000 people.

NEW YORK PHILHARMONIC PARK CONCERTS, New York City Parks, Recreation and Cultural Affairs Administration, 830 Fifth Avenue, New York, N.Y. 10021. This is a series of free concerts offered in the parks of the five boroughs of New York City (see also Metropolitan Opera Free Summer Concerts under Festivals). The series is sponsored jointly by the Jos. Schlitz Brewing Company, the Parks Administration shown above, and the New York Philharmonic Orchestra. Additional aid in the form of grants have come from the New York State Council on the Arts and the National Endowment for the Arts. Begun in 1965, the concerts are played in a total of eight parks (the 1971 series increased both the number of parks and the number of concerts). Three programs of music are played for a total of 15 concerts. The programs have a balance of orchestral works and music requiring instrumental soloists with orchestra—usually concertos. Recent conductors have been **Dean Dixon, Istvan Kertesz, Aldo Ceccato,** and **James De Priest.** Soloists have included **James Oliver Buswell, IV,** and **Ruggiero Ricci,** violinists; and pianists **Lorin Hollander** and **Gina Bachauer,** to name a few. The performance sites, which are announced in advance and which have alternate dates scheduled in case of rain are: North Meadow in Central Park, Sheep Meadow in Central Park (both in Manhattan), Van Cortland Park and the Botanical Garden (The Bronx), Cunningham Park and Crocheron Park (both in Queens), Clove Lakes Park (Staten Island), and Prospect Park (Brooklyn). The 1971 season ran for four weeks, from early August to early September.

PORT JERVIS SUMMER OPERA FESTIVAL, c/o Lyric Arts Opera, Box 323, Milford, Pennsylvania 18337. The Lyric Arts Opera, under the direction of **Grace Panvini** and **Curtis E. Rice,** produces the Festival in the town of Port Jervis, New York, which is located some eight miles northwest of Milford, Pennsylvania, at a point where the states of New York, New Jersey, and Pennsylvania meet. The summer festival was founded in 1966 and is held during the months of July and August. The season consists of five or six Saturday nights of fully staged opera performances held in the auditorium of the Port Jervis High School. The operas are those from the standard French, German, and Italian repertory. The performances are sung to piano accompaniment.

SARATOGA PERFORMING ARTS CENTER, Saratoga Springs, N.Y. 12866. The Performing Arts Center was opened on June 16, 1966 and represents a major effort toward establishing a permanent summer performing arts event in New York State. The Center is located in the 1,500-acre Saratoga Spa State Park (opened in 1962) and occupies its space (150,000 square feet) on the basis of a rent-free agreement with New York State. Funded by private capital, it is administered as a nonprofit educational institution. The Center is in fact the 5,103-seat Amphitheater, an imposing structure of impressive dimensions built at a cost of four million dollars. Equivalent to the height of a 10-story building at its tallest point, the Amphitheater has both orchestral and balcony level seating, with the lower level constructed at 30-feet below surrounding ground. Access to the upper level is by means of four outside ramps which give the Amphitheater its unique appearance. The lawn sloping downward to the theater's orchestra level can accommodate 7,000 to 10,000 people, permitting the Center to play to audiences of 15,000 at a single event. The backstage housing is on three levels and contains a total of 87 rooms including two large ballet rehearsal rooms (one has the same size as the performing stage). With such facilities the Center has been able to provide a summer home for two of America's major performing groups: the Philadelphia Orchestra and the New York City Ballet. Public concerts are the prime activity of the Center, but educational programs such as choreographers' workshops, seminars for teachers, and special student and teacher matinee orchestra and ballet performances, have become increasingly important to the Center's program, as have the recent attempts to provide more forms of popular entertainment. The Saratoga season consists of eight weeks: four weeks each respectively to the New York City Ballet and the Philadelphia Orchestra. Since both organizations perform usually from Tuesday through Sunday, Monday evenings are given over to the so-called Connoisseur Series of chamber music, which are held in Canfield Casino in Saratoga Springs. The Amphitheater, often on the same evenings, schedules special performances by popular music groups. Two additional weeks of performances are the Pre-Season and Post-Season series, which feature primarily popular music groups and soloists. All guest performers, conductors, and groups are drawn invariably from the highest levels of the popular and classical music fields. Guest conductors of the Philadelphia Orchestra have included: **William Steinberg, Arthur Fiedler,** Charles Munch, **Julius Rudel, Seiji Ozawa,** and **Stanislaw Skrowaczewski. Eugene Ormandy,** Music Director of the Orchestra, conducts about half of the 16 scheduled orchestral concerts. Soloists at Saratoga have been, among others, **Van Cliburn, Rudolf Firkusny, Earl Wild, Benny Goodman, Martina Arroyo, John Browning, Rudolf Serkin, Isaac Stern, Veronica Tyler, Shirley Love, Joanna Simon, John McCollum, McHenry Boatwright** and **Placido Domingo.** Groups that have been engaged, in addition to those mentioned previously, include: the Mormon Tabernacle Choir, Capitol Hill Choral Society, Berkshire Boy Choir, the Philadelphia Woodwind Quintet, De Pasquale String Quartet and the Philadelphia Brass Ensemble, McGill (Montreal) Chamber Orchestra, Cardiff (Wales) Polyphonic Choir, and **Ravi Shankar** and his Festival from India. The New York City Ballet presents a full season, offering 24 performances of 10 or more different programs, matinees and evenings. **Robert Irving** is Conductor of the Ballet Orchestra. **George Balanchine** and **Lincoln Kirstein** are Directors of the company. A Film Festival under the direction of **Raymond Rizzo** offers two showings a night in the Spa Summer Theater during the Saratoga season and is devoted to important American and foreign classics and modern films. Saratoga Performing Arts Center is located south of Saratoga Springs between Routes 9 and 50 some 30 miles north of Albany. The Spa State Park is known for its health pavilions and mineral baths and is provided with swimming pools, golf courses, tennis courts, picnic areas, restaurants, and a hotel. The Saratoga Race Track and Raceway is also located in the vicinity. The Center's Executive Director is **Richard P. Leach;** General Manager is **E. Craig Hankenson.** Chairman of the Board of Directors is **Mrs. Nelson A. Rockefeller.** President is **Newman E. Wait, Jr.**

SCHAEFER MUSIC FESTIVAL IN CENTRAL PARK, 27 East 67th Street, New York, N.Y. 10016. Begun in 1966. Producer is **Ron Delsener.** This is a summer event featuring many categories of popular music. It is sponsored entirely by the F. & M. Schaefer Brewing Company. Wollman Memorial Skating Rink Theater in Central Park (with a capacity of about 5,000 a concert) is the location for the series, which is scheduled from the end of June to the end of August, four nights a week. Among the performers who have helped to draw the average annual attendance of 300,000 have been: **Count Basie, Sarah Vaughan, Benny Goodman, Lionel Hampton, Nina Simone, Ray Charles, Pete Seeger, Phil Ochs, Janis Ian, The Who, Richie Havens, Arlo Guthrie, Mothers of Invention,** and so on. An important aspect of the popularity of this series is that all tickets are priced at $1.00.

SPRING FESTIVAL OF THE ARTS, State University College at Potsdam, N.Y. 13676. Established in 1931, when the first spring concert was presented by the school's Crane Chorus, **Helen Hosmer,** founder. The Festival is sponsored by the College and the Student Government Association. Co-chairmen of the Festival Committee are: **Ralph J. Wakefield** and **Marvin P. Garner,** appointed respectively in 1952 and 1967. In addition to music, the Festival includes drama, dance, films, poetry readings, photography ("Portraits of Festival Personalities") and graphic arts ("National Print Exhibition"). Resident performing groups: the Crane Chorus, the Crane Symphony Orchestra, College Jazz Ensemble, the College Modern Dance Club, are engaged along with well-known guest artists. Conductors who have appeared at the Festival since its inception include: **Nadia Boulanger, Robert Shaw** (the most frequent), **Thor Johnson, Leopold Stokowski, Stanley Chapple, Lukas Foss,** and composers **Vincent**

Persichetti and **Virgil Thomson,** to name some. The Lucas Hoving Dance Company, and the Alvin Ailey Dance Theater are among the professional groups that have been featured at the Festival in recent years. The events are scheduled between March and May and although the musical programs are relatively few in number they attempt to reach for a very high level of interest and variety.

STONY BROOK MUSIC FESTIVAL, Stony Brook, Long Island, N.Y. 11790. Established in 1953, the festival is supported by the Stony Brook Community Fund. All events are held in Dogwood Hollow Amphitheatre. The series consists of six concerts on Saturday evenings beginning with the first Saturday in July. Performers who have appeared in the past are: **Yehudi Menuhin** and the Bath Chamber Orchestra, **Jan Peerce, Count Basie,** the duo-pianists **Ferrante and Teicher,** Louis Armstrong, and the José Greco Dance Group. Artistic Director (since 1964) is **Phil Schapiro.** Annual attendance is about 18,000.

STORM KING CHAMBER MUSIC SERIES, Box 99, Cornwall, N.Y. 12518. Established in 1959 and currently sponsored by the Storm King Chamber Music Committee of the Hudson Valley Philharmonic. **Claude Monteux,** conductor of the Hudson Valley Philharmonic Society, is Artistic Director of the Storm King series; Committee Chairman is **Katharine Assante.** The Series consists of four concerts (the second and fourth Sundays in July and August) presented in the Storm King Art Center (once a private home). The Center is located on Pleasant Hill Road (Route 79) near the New York State Thruway at a point midway between Exits 16 and 17. Concerts are played in the drawing room of the Center with sound amplification for those seated in the garden. Total seating capacity is about 250. In addition to **Claude Monteux,** who often performs as flutist, the series has included pianist **Robert Guralnik; Marion Davies,** cellist; **Karen Ranung,** soprano; members of the Hudson Valley String Quartet; the Monteux Chamber Players (string orchestra); **Luis Garcia-Renart,** guitarist and cellist; among others. The works featured in the programs represent a wide stylistic literature. Annual attendance ranges from 800 to 1,000.

WEST DOOR CONCERTS, Cathedral of St. John the Divine, 1047 Amsterdam Avenue, New York, N.Y. 10025. The concerts were begun in 1965 and are under the direction of **Alec Wyton,** who has been organist and choirmaster at the Cathedral since 1954. The concerts are entirely free of charge. Coinciding with Columbia University's Summer School, the concerts take place in the Cathedral on Sunday afternoons from the first of July to mid-August. The programs feature solo performers and chamber groups in performances of a wide range of music. Among the groups having performed for the West Door Series are: The Lyric Chamber Ensemble (string quartet plus horn and clarinet); The Premier Wind Quintet; The Brass Arts Quintet; **Eugenia Earle,** harpsichordist; **Dennis Russell Davies,** pianist; and others. The series is sponsored by the Cathedral.

North Carolina

ANNUAL OLD TIME FIDDLERS' CONVENTION, P.O. Box 38, Union Grove, North Carolina 28689. The Fiddlers' Convention was first organized in 1924 by **H. P. Van Hoy,** school teacher and champion old time fiddler, who is President of the corporation presently formed to maintain the Convention. Vice President and Program Director is **J. Pierce Van Hoy.** The original purpose of the event was to provide a popular form of entertainment and at the same time to raise money for the Union Grove School. The tradition remains the same annually when, during the two-day event (Friday and Saturday before Easter Sunday) performers compete in old time, blue grass, and country music groups for trophies, ribbons, and cash prizes. Fifty percent of the net gate receipts (in 1968: $60,000) is divided equally between the musicians and the School. The musical emphasis is on authentic "old time" country music. Events are held in a circus tent, school gymnasium, and auditorium. A general admissions charge covers all events. Union Grove is approximately 45 miles west of Winston-Salem and 100 miles east of Asheville on route 901 in the Brushy Mountains area. Union Grove has a population of 200. During the Convention, it grows to about 14,000.

BREVARD MUSIC FESTIVAL, winter address: Box 349 Converse Station, Spartanburg, South Carolina 29301; summer address: Box 592, Brevard, North Carolina 28712. Brevard is located in Transylvania County at the intersection of U.S. Routes 64 and 276, about 30 miles south of Asheville. The Festival is an important part of the summer activities of the Brevard Music Center which, in addition to the Festival, organizes and administers the Transylvania Music Camp and other summer study programs at Brevard. The Center was established in 1936 by James Christian Pfohl, who directed its musical activities for many years, making the Festival and music camp important to the musical growth of the South. Present Artistic Director and Conductor (since 1964) is **Henry Janiec,** Conductor also of the Spartanburg (South Carolina) Symphony and dean of the School of Music at Converse College. The concept of the Brevard Music Center is largely educational and, like most summer institutes for training in musical performance, youth-oriented. However, the Festival engages a significant number of professional performers for its programs. These are either members of the Brevard Music Center faculty (teachers of musical instruments, for example, are often members of professional ensembles during the regular season) or are concert artists drawn from the rosters of concert managers operating on a national scale. Artists who have performed at Brevard in recent seasons include singers **Jan Peerce, Richard Tucker, Licia Albanese, John Alexander, James McCracken, William Warfield, Rosalind Elias, William McDonald, Beverly Wolff,** and **Morley Meredith;** pianists **Lee Luvisi, Thomas Brockman,** and **Leonard Pennario;** and other instrumental performers such as **Tossy Spivakovsky, Emil Raab** and **James Caesar,** violinists, and harpist **Edward Vito.** Young, new professionals are often engaged. There are numerous performing ensembles at Brevard, one or the other performing throughout the season of 43 almost daily concerts spanning the seven weeks from early July to mid-August. In addition to the main performing group, the Brevard Music Center Orchestra, under **Henry Janiec,** there are the various groups of the Transylvania Music Camp: the Youth Orchestra, Wind Ensemble, Symphony Orchestra, Concert Band, and Chorus; opera productions are staged by the Brevard Opera Workshop. Programs, which are scheduled for both evenings and afternoons, are generally published in advance with the exception of student recitals.

EARLY AMERICAN MORAVIAN MUSIC FESTIVAL. The address for the 1972 event was: P.O. Box 10387, Winston-Salem, North Carolina 27108. Founded in 1950 by conductor **Thor Johnson,** who remains its Music Director. The festivals are held biennially, thus the festivals in 1966, 1969, and 1972 were, respectively the eighth, ninth, and tenth events. Festival locations vary: the 1966 and 1972 festivals were both in Winston-Salem on the campus of Salem College; the 1969 event was held in New York City at several churches including the First Moravian Church and Riverside Church. Other festivals have been held in Bethlehem, Pennsylvania, and elsewhere. The festivals are all under the auspices of the Moravian Music Foundation (q.v. under Organizations) and have as their fundamental theme the presentation, often as first modern performances, of the music of the early American Moravians (eighteenth and early nineteenth centuries) which lies in the music archives of the Foundation and the Southern and Northern Provinces of the American Moravian Church. (See also Library of the Moravian Foundation.) Bringing this music to light, and supporting and engaging in research concerning it, along with preparing modern editions for its publication, performance, and recording, is the main function of the Foundation. The festivals are among the important outlets for bringing this music to the public. Up through the ninth festival, 50 compositions from the Moravian archives have been prepared for their first twentieth-century performance at the festivals. The works are not only those written by such Moravians as John Antes (1740–1811), Johannes Herbst (1735–1812), David Moritz Michael (1751–1827), and Johann Friedrich Peter (1746–1813) but also the music of non-Moravians—many well-known eighteenth-century European composers—which had been copied by hand by Moravian musicians and brought to America. The latter music includes works by J. S. Bach, Johann Christoph Friedrich Bach (whose Sinfonia in D minor received its first modern performance at the ninth festival), Franz Joseph Haydn, et al. The festival programs combine chamber music with evenings of works in larger forms, organ recitals, concerts for chorus and orchestra, and seminars. By their nature, the programs are remarkably unhackneyed. Occasionally a work by a contemporary composer is included. The press has generally accorded the festivals careful critical attention. The festivals use an orchestra of nearly 40 players and a large amateur chorus. Soloists who have performed at the eighth and ninth events include **Mayne Miller,** pianist who also appeared with the Fine Arts Quartet for chamber programs; singers **Mary Beth Peil, Marlena Kleinman, Waldie Anderson, Andrew White, Lorna Haywood** and **Charles Bressler;** organist **Frederick Swann,** et al. The festivals are usually scheduled for a week in mid-June and are offered free to the public.

EASTERN MUSIC FESTIVAL, 712 Summit Avenue, Greensboro, North Carolina 27405. Established in 1962, the Festival is organized by the Guilford Musical Arts Center, the home of Eastern Music Camp, a summer-study facility for young musicians. The Eastern Philharmonic Orchestra is the prime performing ensemble of the Festival. Its 60 or more members are professional musicians drawn mainly from major symphonic units across the country as well as from leading music institutions. As faculty or staff members, the orchestral players are responsible for the instruction program provided for the 175 or so students who are enrolled each summer. The Eastern Philharmonic Orchestra is under the leadership of **Sheldon Morgenstern,** Musical Director of the Festival; he is also Conductor of the Greensboro Symphony Orchestra during the regular season. Concerts for the Eastern Music Festival are held in various locations. In Elon, programs are given in Whitley Auditorium on the campus of Elon College; in Greensboro, performances are scheduled for Page High School Auditorium; Fisher Park; University of Carolina, Greensboro Campus; and Guilford College. In addition to the Eastern Philharmonic, which performs in about 13 of the 29 or so programs offered by the Festival, there are other ensembles organized by the Arts Center. These include the Guilford Chamber Players, made up of faculty or staff members of the Center, and three student groups: the Eastern Symphony Orchestra, Eastern Chamber Orchestra, and the Guilford Musical Arts Center Orchestra. Professional soloists who have played at the Festival include pianists **David Bar-Illan, Joann Freeman, Robert Goldsand, Warren Rich, Veronica Jochum von Moltke,** and violinists **Charles Castleman** and Michael Rabin, among other instrumentalists. The Festival lasts about six and one half weeks and is generally scheduled from June to July. With the exception of the Sunday afternoon performances, all concerts are scheduled for the evening. The Arts Center is governed by a Board of Directors and receives its support from individual and organizational contributors. Executive Director is **Molly Coe.**

HUBERT HAYES MOUNTAIN YOUTH JAMBOREE, 30 Maney Avenue, Asheville, North Carolina 28804. Hubert H. Hayes, a locally based playwright, director of drama, and folklorist, and his wife founded the Jamboree in 1948. Since 1964, when Mr. Hayes died, his wife, **Leona Trantham Hayes,** has been Director and chief promoter of this annual event. The Jamboree's prime purpose is to present pure folk music and dancing by means of competition among young participants, generally those in school grades one to twelve, and noncompetitive exhibitions. Since its inception, an average of more than 1,000 boys and girls a year have performed at the Jamboree for the honor of receiving one of the 43 trophies awarded by the panel of local people who serve as judges. Under the program theme of "Folklore, Dancing, Singing, Music Makin'–Pickin'," the young performers, who over the years have come from nine states, compete for the various championships in smooth square dance, Western square, clog dance, and the dances of other countries. The Jamboree occurs in late April, usually for four days from Wednesday to Saturday. The contests are held in the evening for three or four hours. Asheville City Auditorium serves as the location of the Jamboree. Since 1949, thc cvent has been under the sponsorship of the Asheville Junior Chamber of Commerce.

Ohio

BACH FESTIVAL, Baldwin–Wallace College, Berea, Ohio 44017. Organized by the Baldwin-College Conservatory of Music, the Festival is a two-day event held in Fanny Nast Gamble Auditorium in the college's Kulas Musical Arts Building. The Festival was established in 1933 by Albert Riemenschneider (1878–1950), organist and Bach scholar. **Warren A. Scharf,** Director of the Conservatory (since 1967), is the administrative head; Musical Director is **George Poinar.** Although the music of Bach is the focal point of this annual event, works by composers contemporary to Bach are sometimes performed. Beyond that, very little non-Baroque music is presented. The Festival is always scheduled for the Friday and Saturday before Memorial Day and in general has at least one major afternoon and evening concert for each day. Often both the afternoon and evening concerts of the final day are devoted to one of Bach's larger choral works performed in two segments, permitting an intermission. With some exceptions, many of the larger choral works are performed at four- or five-year intervals (the Magnificat received 11 performances from the period 1933–1968, the B Minor Mass received nine, the St. John Passion, eight) and well over 70 cantatas have received at least one performance at the Festival, which has tried to cover every category of Bach's output as thoroughly as possible. Approximately 45 minutes prior to each concert, the Festival Brass Choir, under **Kenneth Snapp,** performs a group of chorales from the tower of the college's Marting Hall. The Festival Orchestra consists of faculty (in first-chair positions) and students. A large chorus is under the direction of **Maurice Casey.** Vocal soloists are usually professionals. **Betty Allen, Helen Boatwright, Henry Nason, Thomas Paul, Yi-Kwei Sze, Lois Marshall, Lili Chookasian,** and **Jane Hobson** have been among those who have appeared. All concerts are free; reserved seats are permitted the "guarantors," those who contribute a fixed minimum sum or more to the college. Berea is on Route 237 about two miles west of U.S. Route 42 and is three miles from Cleveland's Airport.

BLOSSOM MUSIC FESTIVAL, 1145 West Steel's Corner Road, Northampton Township, Cuyahoga Falls, Ohio 44223. Year round address: 1037 National City Bank Building, Cleveland, Ohio 44114. Founded in 1968. Blossom lies between Akron and Cleveland, some 15 miles from the latter. Manager of the festival is **Marshall Turkin.** Music Director is **Lorin Maazel.** Resident Conductor is **Louis Lane.** Blossom is the summer home of the Cleveland Orchestra and, although currently the location of only the public concerts of the Cleveland Orchestra, it is intended to serve a much broader purpose. Eventually, Blossom Music Center will house the Blossom Festival School of the Cleveland Orchestra—a school supported by both the orchestra through its parent organization, the Musical Arts Association, and Kent University. At present (1973), the Festival School is located on the campus of Kent University, about 14 miles from Blossom. (The orchestra–festival–summer school idea is common to a number of festivals. Major examples are the Berkshire Music Center and Temple University Music Festival and Institute, since they are associated with first-rank orchestras; other institutions would include those at Chautauqua, Sewanee, National Music Camp, and

Brevard, q.v.) The Blossom Festival School provides a faculty consisting of members of the Cleveland Orchestra, teachers on the staff of Kent University School of Music and guest composers, and professional artists or teachers from other institutions. Dean of the School is **John A. Flower.** Co-directors are **Louis Lane** and **Lindsey Merrill.** Concerts at Blossom take place in a pavilion of unusual design capable of seating over 4,600 people. It opens to the sloping lawn outside, where an additional 10 to 12 thousand listeners can be accommodated. In the general shape of an inverted half-shell, the pavilion is the dominant structure of the Music Center's 500 acres. The Center was financed with $4 million in private donations and $2 million from the Ford Foundation. More than 25 percent of the private funds came from the Blossom family of Cleveland, hence the name of the Center. The festival runs from late June to the first week in September, the concerts by the Cleveland Orchestra taking place for a six-week period, from early July to mid-August. The concerts are held on Friday and Saturday at 8:30 PM and Sunday at 7:00 PM and offer programs typical of major orchestras. Since the death of George Szell in 1970, guest conductors have been featured for most of the concerts. Among the conductors who have appeared at Blossom are: **Pierre Boulez,** who for a time was Musical Advisor, Charles Munch, **Robert Shaw, Karel Ancerl, William Steinberg, Aaron Copland, Leonard Bernstein, André Previn, Sixten Ehrling, Stanislaw Skrowaczewski, Bernard Haitink, Morton Gould, Rafael Frübeck de Burgos, Walter Susskind, Lorin Maazel, Michael Charry,** and **Daniel Barenboim.** Soloists are engaged for each concert and include well-known instrumental and vocal stars. Among the pianists have been: **John Browning, Jerome Lowenthal, Van Cliburn, Maurizio Pollini, Byron Janis, Philippe Entremont, Gary Graffman, Eugene Istomin, Christoph Eschenbach, Mischa Dichter,** and many others—indeed pianists seem to constitute the majority of solo artists engaged. Other instrumentalists include: violinists **Edith Peinemann, Itzhak Perlman,** and **Pinchas Zukerman;** cellists **Pierre Fournier, Zara Nelsova,** and **Lynn Harrell.** Singers include **John Mitchinson, Anastasios Vrenios, Theodore Uppman, Morley Meredith, Ernst Haefliger, Thomas Paul, Marilyn Horne,** and **Phyllis Curtin.** Most of the singers perform in symphonic works requiring vocal soloists rather than such "evenings of opera" as are common to many summer festivals throughout the country. The Festival Chorus, under the direction of **Clayton H. Krehbiel,** is drawn from the Choral-Vocal Institute of the Blossom Festival School and joins with the Cleveland Orchestra Chorus in major orchestral-choral performances. Aside from an occasional work by either a contemporary or past composer that is not often or rarely heard anywhere and the fact that all concerts maintain the expected high level of performance standards, there is nothing distinctive about the programs thus far offered at Blossom. The programs are heavily larded with concertos and the standard titles from the classical and romantic symphonic literature. The traditionally styled programs give way to a series of pops concerts and ballet performances on certain evenings, the former bringing in such conductors as **Arthur Fiedler, André Kostelanetz, Franz Allers,** and **Michael Charry** and the latter series the New York City Ballet and the Vienna State Opera Ballet. Additional festival activities include children's matinees, a jazz–folk series, outdoor art exhibitions, and art lectures.

CINCINNATI MAY FESTIVAL, Suite 109, Vernon Manor Hotel, 400 Oak Street, Cincinnati, Ohio 45219. Founded in 1873 by Theodore Thomas. The Festival is held usually the last two Fridays and Saturdays in May in Cincinnati's Music Hall. The essence of the Festival lies in performances of large works for chorus and orchestra. The Cincinnati Symphony Orchestra under major guest conductors shares the Festival with the May Festival Chorus, a basic unit of about 220 voices led by **Robert Knauf** which often combines with adult and children voices from a variety of nearby colleges, seminaries, and junior and senior high schools. These forces can reach large numbers as in 1968, when they totaled more than a thousand. Prominent among these are the children's choruses for which works are frequently commissioned. Menotti's "The Death of the Bishop of Brindisi" (1963), Franz Waxman's "The Song of Terezin" (1965), and Henze's "Moralities" (1968), all received their world premieres at the May Festival. Honorary Musical Director is Leonard Bernstein (1973). Among the guest conductors at the Festival have been: **Robert Shaw,** George Szell, and **Eugene Ormandy.** Vocal soloists have been: **Birgit Nilsson, Lili Chookasian, Phyllis Curtin, Sherrill Milnes, Eleanor Steber, Theodor Uppman, Richard Lewis, John McCollum, Judith Raskin,** and **Montserrat Caballé.** All concerts are scheduled for the evening.

CINCINNATI SUMMER OPERA FESTIVAL, 1241 Elm Street, Cincinnati, Ohio 45210. Founded in 1920, this summer series of professional opera performances was often referred to as the "Zoo Opera," when its productions were staged in the Pavilion of the Cincinnati Zoo. In 1972, for the first time, the festival used Cincinnati's newly restored Music Hall as its home. The emphasis is on performances of the well-known works in the operatic repertory ("Otello," "Madama Butterfly," "Tosca," "Carmen," "La Traviata," etc.). In general, the season lasts from four to five weeks from June to July and consists of 7 to 10 operas, each receiving two performances. The productions are fully staged and feature singers from the front ranks of the operatic world. Some past seasons have featured **Martina Arroyo, Mignon Dunn, Jean Fenn, Anna Moffo, Felicia Weathers, Elisabeth Schwarzkopf, Beverly Sills, Roberta Peters, Mary Costa, John Alexander, Frank Guarrera, Sherrill Milnes, Norman Treigle, Richard Tucker, Louis Quilico** and **Placido Domingo,** to name a few singers. Each season brings new casts, new conductors, directors, etc., although some performers and members of the directorial staff are engaged repeatedly by the Festival. Cincinnati's Summer Opera company is the first such organization to be established in America and is the second oldest continuing opera company in the nation. From the outset, the orchestra has consisted of members of the Cincinnati Symphony Orchestra; although its chorus formerly was made up of members of the Metropolitan Opera and the Lyric Opera of Chicago choruses, it is at present mostly locally recruited. Many famous careers, particularly among singers, were either begun at Cincinnati or were greatly aided by the opportunity to perform there. A number of leading opera singers sang their first performances of important roles at the Zoo: James Melton (Lt. Pinkerton), Gladys Swarthout and **Risë Stevens** (both as Carmen) are examples, and **Mary Costa, Jan Peerce,** Robert Weede, and **John Alexander** all made their operatic debuts with the Summer Opera. General Manager is **Styrk Orwoll;** President of the Cincinnati Summer Opera Association (founded in 1934) is **James M. E. Mixter.**

CLEVELAND SUMMER ARTS FESTIVAL, 11125 Magnolia Drive, Cleveland, Ohio 44106. Established May, 1967. The Cleveland Summer Arts Festival is a pioneering attempt by a major city to provide free widespread entertainment and participation activities in the arts for both the young and adults. Inspired in part by summer entertainment activities organized in the mid-1960's by New York City's Parks Recreation and Cultural Affairs Administration, the more precisely organized Cleveland idea in turn has spawned at least one similar event: Boston's "Summerthing" (q.v.). At the core of the program is the need for cities such as Cleveland, which experienced racial and social unrest—particularly during summer months—in part brought on by the lack of recreational and self-development facilities, to devise specific means of permitting the widest possible exposure of combined educational–cultural–entertainment offerings to neighborhoods or other population units within the city proper. The result of the Cleveland plan is an Arts Festival in the broadest sense of the word, guided by professionals in the arts for lay interest and participation, located throughout the city, and funded by a large number of foundations, businesses, individuals, and government agencies. The first Arts Festival—providing the model for subsequent years—was established with a budget of over a half million dollars ($190,000 consisted of contributed services by Cleveland's Departments of Recreation, Parks, and Public Safety; $234,000 came from 122 foundations, businesses, and individual contributors; and the balance from Cleveland's Board of Education, Museum of Art, Neighborhood Centers Association and the federal government's Council of Economic Opportunity). The funds were expended on a total of 103 mass-audience outdoor performances spread over a period of 68 days from mid-June to late August, including 36 indoor performances given by children enrolled in workshops for art, drama, dance and music; funds were also spent on the workshops themselves, which were conducted throughout the period of the Arts Festival. The mass-audience events were held in 12 city recreational areas; the workshops in 17 neighborhood centers. The former included repeat performances of one opera staged by the Lake Erie Opera Theatre accompanied by the Cleveland Orchestra under **Louis Lane** and **Michael Charry;** a staged drama by Shakespeare produced by the Cleveland Play House; performances by the Cleveland Ballet Guild and Ballet Russe of Cleveland; and a host of popular music programs featuring leading musicians and ensembles. Among them were: **Duke Ellington, Lionel Hampton, Chico Hamilton, Carmen McRae, Woody Herman, Sonny Terry, Brownie McGhee,** and the Mitchell Ruff Trio. Participating organizations, in addition to those performing groups and contributors already mentioned, were the Cleveland Music School Settlement, Karamu House (a nationally known interracial cultural arts center), and the individual neighborhood centers. Total attendance for all mass-audience events was over 153,000. Workshop exhibitions and performances drew a total attendance of over 44,000. **Howard Whittaker,** Director of the Cleveland Music School Settlement, is Director of the Summer Arts Festival. **Lester G. Glick** is President.

CLEVELAND SUMMER POPS CONCERTS, c/o The Cleveland Orchestra, Severance Hall, Cleveland, Ohio 44106. Held in the 8,100-seat Public Auditorium in Cleveland and features the Cleveland Orchestra under the direction of **Louis Lane.** The season is spread over a period of four weeks from June to July and consists of about 14 concerts programming classical music, show tunes, and some jazz.

FESTIVAL OF CONTEMPORARY MUSIC, Oberlin Conservatory of Music, Oberlin College, Oberlin, Ohio 44074. Begun in 1951. The Festival is a series of concerts devoted to music of the last decade with the goal of increasing the number and improving the quality of new music performances on Oberlin's campus, to the degree that a special festival designation will no longer be necessary for presenting new music. Thus, over a period of time, the concerts in this series will be spread increasingly throughout the school year rather than presented consecutively within a few days. At present, the Festival is in two parts, taking place in the fall and spring, each part consisting of four consecutive days of performances. These are held on campus in Warner Hall (667 seats) and Finney Memorial Chapel (1,300 seats). All events are free, with the exception of opera productions. Forums, lectures, and other talk formats are an integral part of the Festival. Generally, a composer whose works are featured during a segment of the Festival is present as lecturer. In recent years, guest composers have been Igor Stravinsky, **Aaron Copland,** Edgard Varèse, **Milton Babbitt, Leonard Stein, Luigi Dallapiccola, Elliott Carter, Ernst Krenek, Roger Sessions,** and others.

GREAT COMPOSERS FESTIVAL, c/o Lakeside Summer Symphony Orchestra, Lakeside, Ohio. New York address: 316 Second Avenue, New York, N.Y. 10003. **William Penny Häcker** is Conductor and Artistic Director of this Festival, which was begun in 1963. It is held in the 3,000-seat Hoover Auditorium in Lakeside, Ohio (on the peninsula northwest of Sandusky), and lasts for six weeks beginning in midsummer. Programs consist of symphony concerts, chamber music, opera, and choral works.

MAY FESTIVAL OF CONTEMPORARY MUSIC, The Cleveland Museum of Art, 11150 East Boulevard, Cleveland, Ohio 44106. Founded 1959. The May Festival is only one of many musical events sponsored by the Cleveland Museum of Art through its Department of Musical Arts, founded in 1922, reportedly the first such institution established anywhere in the world. Although the Department of Musical Arts lends support to the Festival by acting as host and providing the use of the Museum's 425-seat auditorium, the concerts of the Festival are completely underwritten by a federation of Cleveland area music institutions so that all concerts may be presented to the public free of charge. Each institution participates on a rotating basis. They are, in addition to the Department of Musical Arts: The Cleveland Orchestra, the Cleveland Philharmonic Orchestra, Western Reserve University, The Cleveland Music School Settlement, The Cleveland Institute of Music, Baldwin–Wallace College Conservatory of Music, the Cleveland Chamber Music Society, the Composers' Guild of The Fortnightly Musical Club, and the Musart Society of the Cleveland Museum of Art. The contemporary music presented in the four-day event—which days are not necessarily consecutive—is of great variety, offering works by composers throughout the world and calling for ensembles and soloists of all kinds. Each Festival contains a program of music by Cleveland area composers. Chairman of the Festival is the Museum's Curator of Musical Arts, **Walter Blodgett.** Among the conductors who have appeared at the Festival have been George Szell, **Robert Shaw, Louis Lane, George Poinar, Zoltan Rozsnyai,** and **Kenneth Moore;** performers have been: Victor Babin, **Miriam Molin,** pianists; **Antonia Lavane,** soprano; and various instrumental and vocal groups of the participating schools.

Oklahoma

AUTUMN FESTIVAL OF THE ARTS; SPRING FESTIVAL OF THE ARTS, Oklahoma State University, Stillwater, Oklahoma 74074. Established in 1944, the annual event alternated between summer and autumn scheduling until 1967, when two festivals a year were instituted. The theaters, auditoriums, and other buildings on campus serve as the locations of the musical events, which are only part of a larger festival program of drama, lectures, films, poetry readings, exhibits, and other events familiar to academic arts festivals. Past guest artists include: **Jan Peerce, Julian Bream,** conductors **Arthur Fiedler** and **Guy Fraser Harrison.**

TRI-STATE MUSIC FESTIVAL, Box 2068 University Station, Enid, Oklahoma 73701. Begun in 1933. Since 1933 the Managing Director of the Festival has been **Milburn Carey.** The event is sponsored by Phillips University and the citizens of Enid, Oklahoma, and takes place the first weekend in May in as many as 70 to 75 locations throughout Enid: churches, auditoriums, public halls, schools, and other facilities. It is primarily a competitive festival for high school solo musicians and musical groups and is one of the largest of its kind in the United States and the largest in the Southwest. In recent years, over 12,000 high school students have participated in each festival. Professional musicians, composers, arrangers, conductors, adjudicators, and music educators are engaged to direct the various activities including rehearsals, clinics, concerts, and so forth.

Oregon

MUSIC IN MAY, Pacific University School of Music, Forest Grove, Oregon 97116. This is a competition–festival begun in 1947 as a means of encouraging musical accomplishment in the public schools of the Pacific Northwest. Students, numbering 550, from Oregon, Washington, Idaho, and California, are drawn from the top 5 percent of the total membership of the public school music organizations applying for representation at the Festival. The selected performing groups—band, chorus, and orchestra—rehearse from Thursday of the week of the Festival (the first in May) until Saturday, when a final public concert is presented in the evening. This takes place in the Forest Grove Union High School gymnasium. Three guest conductors are invited to conduct the concert, each assigned to lead respectively the orchestra, chorus, or band. Conductors invited to past concerts have been: **Carmen Dragon, Jacob Avshalomov** (orchestra); **Frank Holman, William Scales** (chorus); **Don Gillis** and **Vaclav Nelhybel** (band). Director of the Festival is **Albert M. Freedman** of the music faculty of Pacific University.

PETER BRITT GARDENS MUSIC AND ART FESTIVAL, Box 669, Jacksonville, Oregon 97530. Jacksonville is in southwest Oregon off U.S. Interstate Route 5, five miles west of Medford in Jackson County. The Peter Britt Music Festival is held on the original land claim of Peter Britt (1819–1905) and in the ballroom of the restored United States Hotel in Jacksonville. (Britt, although Swiss-born, was an Oregon "original." He was an established photographer and portrait-painter—with the only photo studio west of the Rockies—a pack-train operator, wine producer, and horticulturist, being credited with having grown the first pear and apple trees in the region and the first palm tree in Oregon. Britt's pictorial record of early Oregon and, by implication, the Northwest, is considered a highly significant one and is currently preserved in the Jacksonville Museum. His gardens are in what is now a restored landmark under the ownership of Southern Oregon College.) **John Trudeau,** of the faculty of Portland State College, founded the Festival in 1963 and is the Music Director and Conductor. The Festival is held daily for a two-week period in August and is remarkably rich and varied in musical programming, with a conscious attempt to avoid the hackneyed. In a typical season's programming, 1968 in this example, some 35 orchestral and chamber works were presented in the two weeks of the Festival, exclusive of those concerts by the Peter Britt Chorale, and in the Youth Concerts and solo recitals. The music was by 24 composers including, besides the masters, Biggs, Block, Boyce, Dahl, Damase, Locke, Surinach, and Toch. Although works by the great composers played each summer at the Festival include the familiar, there is a good representation of the lesser-known works: Haydn's 6th, 8th, and 60th symphonies, for example; Dvořák's "Czech Suite"; Mozart's 27th Symphony; and so on. The outdoor Pavilion located in the gardens is the site for the orchestral concerts, youth concerts, and open rehearsals; the United States Hotel is used for the afternoon "Connoisseur Concerts" and "Artist Series" and concerts by the Peter Britt Chorale, under **Lynn Sjolund.** The Festival Orchestra is a "pick-up" orchestra of about 50 musicians, primarily from the Western states. The Festival functions as a nonprofit organization administered by its association officers and staff. The town of Jacksonville has been designated a National Historical Site and is full of homes and public buildings built during the height of the gold boom in the West. These are authentically restored and many are open to tourists. Nearby is the town of Ashland, where the Oregon Shakespearean Festival has taken place since 1941 in an outdoor Elizabethan-style theater. This event and the general tourist activity in the Rogue Valley area are among some of the important reasons for the founding and subsequent maintenance of the Peter Britt Festival.

Pennsylvania

BETHLEHEM BACH FESTIVAL, Main and Church Streets, Bethlehem, Pennsylvania 18018. The Bach Choir, the mainstay of this festival, was founded in 1898 by J. Fred (John Frederick) Wolle (1863–1933). A native of Bethlehem and an organist, Wolle is credited with conducting, in 1900, the first performance of the B Minor Mass sung in its entirety in the United States. The man most responsible for the growth and stability of the Bach Festival is **Ifor Jones,** who served as Director of the festival and its choir from 1938 (first performing in 1939) to 1969. Under Jones, the festival performed many times the larger Bach choral works. Of the 145 cantatas he conducted at the Bethlehem concerts, thirty were sung for the first time in the United States. Beginning with the 1970 festival, Musical Conductor and Director has been **Alfred**

Mann. The program format includes both choral and instrumental works of Johann Sebastian Bach, always with a performance of the B Minor Mass (the 1973 Festival presented the 101st and 102nd performance of this work at Bethlehem). The festival takes place the second and third weekends in May offering a total of eight programs, all of which are performed in Packer Memorial Chapel on the campus of Lehigh University in Bethlehem. Noted solo singers are engaged for the festival; past performers have been: **Lois Marshall, Jennifer Vyvyan, John McCollum,** Mack Harrell, **Kenneth Smith, Helen Boatwright, Elaine Bonazzi, Thomas Paul,** and **Robert White,** among others. Organist is **William Whitehead.** The Bach Choir is made up largely of nonprofessional musicians. The choir and festival is governed by an Executive Board. President is **Kenneth L. Houck.**

ROBIN HOOD DELL CONCERTS, INC. (concerts are billed as: "Robin Hood Dell Concerts Presents the Philadelphia Orchestra"), 1617 John F. Kennedy Boulevard, Philadelphia, Pennsylvania 19103. Founded in 1930, the concerts are a series of free evening performances supported by a special grant from the City of Philadelphia and funds provided by private contributors. **Fredric R. Mann** is President of the supportive corporation; **Mrs. David C. Martin** is Manager of the concerts. The Philadelphia Orchestra is the heart of these concerts and performs under a number of well-known guest conductors as well as Music Director, **Eugene Ormandy.** Among those who have led the orchestra at the Dell have been: **Arthur Fiedler, Lorin Maazel, Zubin Mehta, Sixten Ehrling,** and Charles Munch. **William Smith,** the Orchestra's Assistant Conductor, conducts three morning children's concerts, in addition to one or more of the regular evening concerts. The programs consist primarily of symphonic music, works for solo instrument and orchestra and solo voice with orchestra; the latter are usually operatic arias sung by famous guest singers from major opera companies. Instrumental and vocal artists of international fame featured at the Dell in recent seasons have included: **Van Cliburn, Isaac Stern, André Watts, Henryk Szeryng, Gary Graffman, Nicole Henriot-Schweitzer, John Browning, Anna Moffo, Roberta Peters, Ingrid Bjoner, Phyllis Curtin, Jan Peerce, Richard Tucker,** and **Robert Merrill.** It is obvious that with rosters of "star" conductors and soloists, the Dell concerts, not only in recent seasons but throughout its more than forty years, have endeavored to attract the widest possible audience —an attainment readily confirmed by attendance figures reaching about 425,000 annually. Altogether there are six weeks of concerts three nights a week, scheduled from mid-June to July. Although admission is free to the public, tickets are needed. Robin Hood Dell is in Philadelphia's Fairmount Park.

TEMPLE UNIVERSITY MUSIC FESTIVAL AND INSTITUTE, 1949 North Broad Street, Philadelphia, Pennsylvania 19122. First held in 1968. The University's 180-acre Ambler campus is the site of the festival and institute. Located in Upper Dublin Township about 18 miles north of Philadelphia, the campus is at the intersection of Meetinghouse Road and Butler Pike. The festival–institute idea bears resemblance to the organization of the Berkshire Music Festival, the Blossom Festival, Aspen and others and, like them, attempts to offer the highest possible level of combined instruction and performance. Temple's major ensemble in-residence is the Pittsburgh Symphony Orchestra under **William Steinberg** which, along with the Philadelphia Orchestra, provides many of the artist-faculty for the Institute. Over 200 students are enrolled each summer for the six-week session. Most are young professionals or quasi-professionals coming from about half the states in the nation and some foreign countries. Studies offered include voice, piano, orchestral instruments, chamber music, opera coaching, and composition. Some courses offer academic credit through Temple University's College of Music; however, the emphasis is not on a traditional framework of study but rather on having Ambler provide nearly limitless performance and practice opportunity for the student and the additional education derived from the student hearing a great variety of artists throughout the run of the Festival. While the Institute is in session there are student performances every night and on Saturday afternoon. The evening concerts are performed just prior to the scheduled events for the Festival. Chamber groups, solo recitalists, and the open rehearsals of the opera class all figure in these programs. Major performances featuring student soloists are sometimes offered by the Institute. In 1971, for example, "The Medium," by Menotti was staged by the composer and performed with members of the Pittsburgh Symphony and student singers. The Institute's chorus is also available for performances with the orchestra. Faculty performances are also an important part of the music making at Ambler. These take place in Campus Theatre and range from solo recitals to mixed ensemble chamber music. Faculty performing (in 1971) include pianists **Robert Goldsand, Alexander Fiorillo, Adele Marcus,** and **Natalie Hinderas;** Curtis String Quartet; **Eleanor Steber,** soprano; cellists **Lorne Monroe** and **Michael Grebanier;** clarinetist **Anthony Gigliotti.** The Festival itself constitutes 45 consecutive days of concerts including, besides the faculty recitals and the orchestral concerts of the Pittsburgh Symphony, pops concerts with the orchestra and such conductors as **Arthur Fiedler** and **Henry Mancini;** the Pennsylvania Ballet Company (in 1971 the company gave six performances); the Pittsburgh Chamber Orchestra; and other guest ensembles such as the Minnesota Opera Company, Preservation Hall Jazz Band, First Moog Quartet, and evenings featuring performers from the world of jazz or popular music. Among some of the artists who have appeared are: **Van Cliburn, Itzhak Perlman, André Watts, Virgil Fox, Sherrill Milnes, Edith Peinemann, Beverly Sills, Jerome Lowenthal, Duke Ellington, Ella Fitzgerald, Dave Brubeck, Gerry Mulligan, Ray Charles, José Greco,** and **Victor Borge.** Conductors include **William Steinberg, Roberto Benzi, Donald Johanos, Max Rudolf, Maurice Kaplow, William Smith, Lukas Foss, Emerson Buckley, Martin Rich, Dean Dixon, Morton Gould, Henry Mazer,** and **James DePriest.** Artistic Director of the Institute and Festival is **David L. Stone,** Dean of the College of Music of Temple University. Director of the Institute is **Harvey Wedeen,** and Managing Director of the Festival is **David Kanter.** Festival Music Coordinator is **Ling Tung.** In 1971, the Institute was scheduled from June 21 to August 2; the Festival lasted from June 25 to August 8.

Rhode Island

DIAMOND HILL MUSIC FESTIVAL, 33 Summer Street, Pawtucket, Rhode Island 02860. Founded in 1962. A series of free Sunday afternoon musical entertainment programs held in Diamond Hill State Park. The Park, in the Blackstone Valley region of the northeast corner of the state, is located in Cumberland. Founder and sponsor of the event is the Pawtucket–Blackstone Valley Chamber of Commerce. About 50,000 people attend the concerts each season. The program emphasis is on entertainment and to this end local popular music groups, concert bands, and some outside professional artists are engaged to provide music of the broadest possible appeal. The 88th Army Band, Rhode Island Youth Orchestra, the State Ballet of Rhode Island, and the Rhode Island Philharmonic are among the groups presented at Diamond Hill.

NEWPORT FOLK FESTIVAL, Newport, Rhode Island 02840. Founded in 1959 and run by a nonprofit organization called the Newport Folk Foundation. Chairman of the Board is **George Wein** (see Newport Jazz Festival). This festival follows the Newport Jazz Festival and also takes place in July, usually the last weekend. Leading folk-music singers such as **Joan Baez, Pete Seeger, Bill Monroe,** and **Arlo Guthrie** have appeared at Newport, along with performers from the ranks of commercial country and western music, rhythm and blues, and folk-inspired rock music. The brief festival has gathered total audiences of about 70,000.

NEWPORT JAZZ FESTIVAL, Box 329, Newport, Rhode Island 02840. Founded 1954. **George Wein,** well-known jazz impresario, is producer. The festival is held on three or four consecutive days in July (usually on the weekend of July 4th, although the 1970 festival was scheduled one week later). Probably the most famous jazz event anywhere in the world, the festival is noted for its annual array of great jazz talent: instrumental and vocal soloists, combos, big bands —names encompassing all areas of jazz and jazz-inspired music, from the most venerated to newly arrived professionals. Thus, a roster of those who have appeared at Newport under the aegis of jazz would be, in effect, a retelling of the history of that art and its offshoots within the last two decades and beyond. Performances by such musicians as **Duke Ellington, Count Basie,** Louis Armstrong, **Pee Wee Russell, Joe Venuti, Ella Fitzgerald, Dizzy Gillespie, Woody Herman,** and others mean more than the sum of their separate appearances, since they embody both the source as well as the changing forms of jazz over a significant period of time. In recent years, some attempts have been made to include other forms of popular music in the programs, such as rock, only to revert once more to jazz as the primary musical attraction. All events take place in Festival Field. Attendance may average about 55,000 for the entire festival.

(Author's Note: As a result of the calamitous disruption by youths of the 1971 festival, the 1972 Festival was held instead in New York City from July 1 to 9 in Carnegie Hall, Philharmonic Hall, and Yankee Stadium. In 1973, New York was again the site with concerts throughout the city.)

NEWPORT MUSIC FESTIVAL, 23 Bridge Street, Newport, Rhode Island 02840. Organized by the Rhode Island Arts Foundation at Newport. This festival contains many unusual elements. Three of Newport's famed mansions are made available for musical performances by The Preservation Society of Newport County: The Elms (the room used has a capacity of 200 seats), The Breakers–Vanderbilt House (400 seats), and Marble House (200 seats)—all providing sumptuous settings for musical programs consisting exclusively of works from the Romantic era (indeed, the festival is promoted as "a Romantic revival in Newport's fabled mansions"). An average of three concerts a day for 17 days (July 27 to August 12, in 1972) are given. The 11:00 AM series, called "Morning Music," offers chamber music, song recitals, and mixed vocal and instrumental music; the "Sundown Series," held at 5:30 PM, presents chamber music and some opera performances; the evening "Connoisseur Concerts" features the festival's opening-night opera gala, a costume concert, ballet, etc. In addition to the series programs there are band concerts; an event called "grand balloon regatta and ascension" held in the garden of The Elms, where huge balloons and their passengers are sent aloft in the manner of the spectacles of the nineteenth century; and a cruise concert held aboard *M/V Mount Hope,* or other boats, while it sails Narragansett Bay. Other musical events take place in the Spanish Courtyard of Portsmouth Abbey and in St. George's Chapel. A film series, offering large-scale films such as the 13-part "Civilisation" and the six-hour Russian film, "War and Peace," is an important part of the festival. The festival successfully skirts the familiar in its musical programming. The 1970 and 1971 festivals produced such works as Pauline Viardot's opera "Cendrillon" (written as a private entertainment by the singer–composer–pianist and presented at Newport in the same spirit); the one-act pastoral opera, "Il était une bergère," by Lattés; grand-style chamber works (septets, nonets, works for piano for one hand up to eight hands, etc.) by such rarely played composers of the nineteenth century as Hummel, Moscheles, Reinecke, Czerny, Joachim, Raff, Stiebelt; to say nothing of infrequently performed pieces by major composers. Some 50 artists participate in the festival including members of the Metropolitan Opera Studio, guest dancers, and instrumentalists who form various chamber groups. Recent performers include: violinists **Emanuel Vardi, Toni Rapport, Anthony Posk;** violists **Robert Maximoff, Hugh Loughran;** cellists **George Ricci, Leshek Zavistovski, Jesse Levy;** pianists **Peter Basquin, Flavio Varani, Raymond Lewenthal, Marshall Williamson;** and wind players

Margaret Schecter (flute), **Umberto Lucarelli** (oboe), **Arthur Bloom** (clarinet), **Howard Howard** (horn), and **Leonard Hindell** (bassoon). Director of the festival is **Glen Sauls.**

RHODE ISLAND BACH FESTIVAL, 93 Eddy Street, Providence, Rhode Island 02903. Founded in 1963 by the festival's current Director, **Louis Pichierri,** Conductor of the Rhode Island Civic Chorale and Orchestra (also founded by **Pichierri**), the ensemble around which the festival is organized. The festival takes place in Providence on a Thursday, Saturday, and Sunday early in May. Alumnae Hall on the campus of Pembroke College and Veterans Memorial Auditorium are the facilities used. Both instrumental and vocal music of Bach are performed with each annual event, attempting a balance of one large choral work with orchestra and vocal soloists, two or three cantatas, one or two instrumental concertos, and an orchestral suite. No chamber music is offered. Among the soloists having sung with the festival orchestra are: **Uta Graf, Helen Boatwright,** sopranos; **Corinne Curry,** contralto; **Charles Bressler, Henry Nason,** tenors; **Chester Watson** and **David Laurent,** bassos. **William Dinneen** of Brown University is harpsichordist and organist.

South Carolina

SPARTANBURG MUSIC FESTIVAL, c/o The Music Foundation of Spartanburg, Inc., Box 1274, Spartanburg, South Carolina 29301. Held in Twichell Auditorium at Converse College in Spartanburg. The Spartanburg Symphony under **Henry Janiec** performs with featured soloists; the Converse College Opera Workshop under **John Richards McCrae,** Producer–Director, usually performs one opera in English. Soloist with the orchestra in 1971 was the late Jean Casadesus, pianist. Concerts are held in late April and early May.

Tennessee

SEWANEE SUMMER MUSIC CENTER FESTIVAL, Sewanee Summer Music Center, Sewanee, Tennessee 37375. The Music Center is on the campus of the University of the South, an all-men's school which becomes coeducational in the summer when a number of camps, schools, and institutes covering various fields of study are in session. Sewanee itself is on U.S. Route 41/64, about 50 miles west of Chattanooga in southern Tennessee. The University's campus is on a 10,000-acre tract of land particularly known for its scenic beauty. The Center's music festival was established in 1957; since 1963, its Director has been **Martha McCrory.** The Center's curriculum is devoted primarily to instrumental music instruction, and the festival draws on the talents of both faculty and students for its programs, which climax the summer courses. Eight concerts are presented on four successive days the last week in July. However, throughout the five-week instruction period at least two public performances involving faculty and students are given at the Center each week. The Festival's concerts are most often held in Guerry Hall (1,000 seats); other locations are Convocation Hall and the outdoors Guerry Garth. Six of the eight concerts are free to the public. Guest conductors, who lead one or more of the concerts each season, in recent years include: **Thor Johnson, Frederick Fennell,** and **Lewis Dalvit.** The Center maintains three orchestral ensembles: the Sewanee Symphony, consisting of advanced students; the Concerto Orchestra, whose members are faculty, staff, and selected advanced students; and the Cumberland Orchestra, an ensemble for the training of students with more limited previous experience in orchestral playing. The Festival's final concert generally presents the combined orchestras performing one of the selections on the program. Artists on the faculty are nearly all drawn from professional sources, mainly from symphony orchestras throughout the country.

Texas

ANNUAL FINE ARTS FESTIVAL, School of Fine Arts, Texas Christian University, Fort Worth, Texas 76129. Begun about 1940. Its Director is the Chairman of the university's music department, **Michael Winesanker.** The Festival lasts for three weeks from mid-April to mid-May. Music events take place in Ed Landreth Auditorium and the University Theatre and consist of six to eight programs including performances by the University Symphony Orchestra and University Chorus (an oratorio usually closes the festival); faculty piano, organ, or voice recitals; chamber music programs; and often the staging of an opera. In general, the music programs are based on some unifying theme—a programming technique common to university festivals of this kind. Art exhibitions and dramatic plays are also part of the Festival. Admission to all events, with the exception of the opera and dramatic plays, is free.

MUSIC IN OUR TIME, School of Music, Hardin–Simmons University, Abilene, Texas 79601. A series of concerts founded in 1957 and devoted to contemporary music. The event is entirely sponsored by the School of Music and is held during the school year, normally in the spring. Students and faculty are the performers; guest performers and composers are invited to participate. Lectures complement the concerts. All events are free.

ANNUAL FINE ARTS FESTIVAL, University of Texas, College of Fine Arts, P.O. Box 7547, University Station, Austin, Texas 78712. Founded in 1942, the festival is considered one of the important academic arts festivals in the Southwest. It is held the first through the third week in November and embraces fine arts, drama, music, and architecture. The festival began as a dedication to the then new music building and, following the tradition, the 1962 festival was dedicated to the new drama building and the 1963 event to the new art building. Musicians engaged from outside the faculty are of international stature and have included **Geza Anda, Rudolf Firkusny, Van Cliburn, Ali Akbar Khan, Shirley Verrett, Jean-Pierre Rampal** and **Robert Veyron-Lacroix** and such groups as Little Orchestra Society, New York Brass Quintet, Smetana String Quartet, Alma Trio, and Guarneri String Quartet. Besides concerts there are lectures, art exhibitions of works by about 30 faculty artists (which are shown beyond the completion of other festival events), and six performances of dramatic productions. The University Symphony Orchestra under **Andor Toth** (who is violinist with the Alma Trio) is the main instrumental ensemble. Festival locations on campus include Hogg Auditorium, Recital Hall, Drama Building, Theatre Room, and University Art Museum. About one half to three fourths of the events are free to the public. Attendance has been estimated to include from 18,000 to 20,000 people for all events in a given festival season.

OCTOBER HOUSTON ARTS FESTIVAL, Houston Chamber of Commerce, P.O. Box 53600, Houston, Texas 77052. Founded in 1966. The month-long event covers all areas of the fine arts and performing arts and is sponsored and organized by the Chamber of Commerce, through a festival committee. Houston has impressive cultural and educational resources, and the broadest possible use is made of them, so that throughout the month of October there is an event of some kind each day either in a concert hall, church, school, college campus, art gallery, theater, museum, public building, or place of business. The last-named could mean the lobby of a bank or a shopping center or department store. Concerning musical events, the following organizations took part in the 1970 festival: Society for the Performing Arts, Houston Symphony Orchestra under conductor **Lawrence Foster,** Houston Grand Opera Association under **Walter Herbert,** Southwest Concerts, Inc., (Houston) *Chronicle* Concert Series, Young Audiences Inc. of Houston, Houston Allegro Ballet, Rice University School of Music, University of Houston School of Music, University of St. Thomas, San Jacinto College, Houston Friends of Music, among others. Some of these groups, for example, the Houston Symphony Orchestra, made their offerings as part of their normal seasonal activity and in this way well-known performing artists can be found in the October calendar of events outlined by the festival committee. Some of the musicians included in the 1970 schedule of concerts were: **John Ogdon,**

Misha Dichter, and **Alexander Slobodyanik,** pianists; singers **William Dooley, William Cochran,** and **Charles Aznavour; Carlos Montoya,** guitarist; **Robert Jones,** organist; **Burt Bacharach** as leader of a specially formed orchestra; conductor **Percy Faith;** and the Janáček String Quartet. Some school groups were: University of Houston Symphony Orchestra under **A. Clyde Roller,** the Pasadena Chamber Orchestra (San Jacinto College), Rice Chamber Orchestra. Facilities used reflect the gamut of participating organizations: Jesse H. Jones Hall (Houston's main concert hall), Sam Houston Coliseum, Rice University Chapel, Hamman Hall of Rice University, Arnold Hall on the campus of the University of Houston, Jones Hall of the University of St. Thomas, San Jacinto College Auditorium, Garden Center in Hermann Park, etc. The nonmusical aspects of the October Festival include dramatic plays, some lectures, but a particularly strong emphasis on gallery exhibitions of works of art.

Utah

BRIGHAM YOUNG UNIVERSITY SUMMER FESTIVAL, Music Department, Brigham Young University, Provo, Utah 84601. Founded in 1939. Takes place on campus from June to August. Musical programs are scheduled for weekdays only and offer chamber music, recitals, opera, orchestral, band, and choral concerts.

UNIVERSITY OF UTAH FESTIVAL OF CONTEMPORARY MUSIC, Music Department, University of Utah, Salt Lake City, Utah 84110. Established in 1959. The University of Utah, in cooperation with the Utah Symphony, presents this series of twentieth-century music in November and February. The orchestra, whose Musical Director and Conductor, **Maurice Abravanel,** is also on the faculty of the university, sometimes plays under a guest conductor–composer, e.g., **Aaron Copland, Lukas Foss,** among others. Local vocal soloists and nationally known pianists have performed at the concerts, which are held both in Kingsbury Hall (2,000 seats) on campus or in Mormon Tabernacle (6,000 seats) in Salt Lake City. Annual attendance averages about 6,000 persons. Lectures and symposia are held in conjunction with the musical programs. Chairman of the Festival Committee is **Lowell M. Durham.**

Vermont

BENNINGTON CHAMBER MUSIC AND COMPOSERS CONFERENCE, Bennington College, Bennington, Vermont 05201. The Conference was begun in 1946 at Middlebury College in Middlebury, Vermont, moving after five years to its present host institution. Founder-Director is **Alan Carter.** The Composers Conference is a two-week session scheduled in mid-August and devoted to performances of new music. Twenty-five composers are invited to participate in the Conference on the basis of scores submitted (from 75 to 100 composers reportedly apply each year for admittance to the Conference). Over the years participants have come from throughout the United States, South America, and a few European countries representing a variety of musical aesthetics and age groups. The "conference" nature of the gathering is manifest in the many hearings and discussions of the music at hand performed by some 27 instrumentalists provided by the Conference. The sessions are recorded on tape. Concurrent with the Conference is the Chamber Music Center which, in general, is engaged in the study and performance of the standard chamber repertory. Financial support for the Conference is partially derived from the Chamber Music Center on the one hand and on the other from a number of important organizations, among them the National Endowment for the Arts, Music Performance Trust Funds of the Recording Industries, Vermont Arts Council, Broadcast Music Inc., and American Society of Composers and Authors.

CONTEMPORARY MUSIC SYMPOSIUM, Music Department, University of Vermont, Burlington, Vermont 05401. Founded in 1968. A three-day event presented in Ira Allen Chapel on the university's campus, usually in April. The format is to present two lecture-demonstrations by two guest composers whose works—along with those of other composers—are performed at a free public concert on the third day. **T. Lawrence Read** is Musical Director.

FESTIVAL OF THE ARTS, Southern Vermont Art Center, Manchester, Vermont 05254. Held from May to November under the auspices of Southern Vermont Artists, Inc. (incorporated in 1929), which held its first show in 1927. The Center, on the slopes of Mt. Equinox, was once a private estate of 375 acres and was purchased by the Southern Vermont Artists in 1950 to serve as location of the festival. In 1967, the year of the last available figures, more than 15,000 people from all the states and thirty-two foreign countries visited the art exhibitions. The works are offered for sale; some $40,000 worth were sold in 1967. Musical programs consist of five evening concerts and four afternoon chamber recitals. These take place in the Music Pavilion (built in 1956 and seating 500 people). Admission is charged. Musical events have included concerts by the Vermont Symphony Orchestra under **Alan Carter; Eugene List** and **Carroll Glenn** in joint piano–violin recital; Pacific Trio; the Lake George Opera Festival; **Marilyn Costello,** harpist; the First Chamber Dance Quartet; and Olatunji and His Company of African Dancers, Singers and Drummers. The Center, which also offers classes in art, dance, and a children's theatre workshop, is administered by a board of trustees. President is **Carleton Howe.**

MARLBORO MUSIC FESTIVAL, Marlboro, Vermont 05344. Winter address: 1430 Spruce Street, Philadelphia, Pennsylvania 19102. Artistic Director: **Rudolf Serkin.** Manager: **Anthony Checchia.** Coordinator: **Frank Salomon.** Founded in the summer of 1950. The Marlboro Festival and related activities take place on the campus of Marlboro College, which leases its facilities to the festival for the summer. Marlboro is off Route 9, 10 miles west of Brattleboro. Not a festival in a formal sense, Marlboro functions as a community or workshop of professional musicians who come by invitation each summer from all over the world to study and perform the classical and contemporary chamber music repertory. About 85 such musicians participate each summer, remaining in residence at Marlboro for eight weeks. The participants represent a wide cross-section of professional performers: concert artists, members of leading chamber ensembles, first-chair players in major symphony orchestras, faculty members of conservatories and universities, etc., embodying virtually all categories of instruments and the singing voice. Out of this reservoir of talent all kinds of instrumental and vocal ensembles are formed—from duets to chamber orchestra. Participants pay for the opportunity to work in this environment, the sum of money being a fixed amount to meet Marlboro's expenses. From 80 to 100 works are rehearsed each week; when the musicians are ready to perform publicly a given program of works, the pieces are announced the day of the performance. Thus, no programs are known in advance of the day of performance. Despite that fact, the sixteen or so concerts to which the public is admitted are usually all sold out—many far in advance. These are scheduled for Friday and Saturday evening or Sunday afternoon and take place in the Marlboro College Auditorium (about 650 seats). Public performances are not the goal of the convocation of musicians at Marlboro but rather an added dimension. However, so rich is the mixture of talent assembling in this community each summer, three by-products have emerged which have enabled many more than those who have actually traveled to Marlboro to hear the kind of music making that is the hallmark there of a typical summer's activity. One is the series of recordings made at Marlboro and issued through Columbia Masterworks. These cover a wide range of chamber music masterpieces and include such performers as **Alexander** and **Mischa Schneider, Rudolf** and **Peter Serkin, Leon Fleisher, Leslie Parnas, Jaime Laredo, Mieczlslaw Horszowski, Marcel Moyse, Pablo Casals,** to name some of the more prominent artists. The second is "Music from Marlboro," formed in 1965, which offers Marlboro's high-quality chamber music playing on tour throughout the country during the regular concert season with a changing roster of musicians (the first season covered more than twenty U.S. cities). The third offshoot from Marlboro is a collection of tape recordings of concerts available for distribution to classical-music radio stations throughout the country. To mention that the 85 or so musicians coming to Marlboro each year for the past twenty years and more represent the best of professionals everywhere is to preclude listing them even selectively. Nevertheless, certain long-standing associates and intimates of founder **Serkin** are central to the success of Marlboro. These include **Marcel Moyse, Blanche Honegger-Moyse, Pablo Casals** (who is a guest each summer), **Alexander Schneider, Felix Galimir, Mischa Schneider, Herman Busch,** and **Mieczyslaw Horszowski.** Marlboro is administered by a Board of Trustees—**Rudolf Serkin,** President; **Frank E. Taplin,** Chairman of the Board—and has the assistance of a Music Advisory Committee consisting of a select number of world-famous musicians, composers, and conductors.

Virginia

FESTIVAL OF ARTS, Department of Recreation and Parks, The Mosque, Laurel and Main Streets, Richmond, Virginia 23220. A municipally supported series presented since 1957 and offered free to the public. The Federated Arts of Richmond, Inc. (founded in 1953) presents its participating member groups in the series; among them are such performing organizations as the Richmond Symphony, Richmond Ballet, Richmond Civic Opera Association, Richmond Choral Society, and others. The Richmond Musicians Association lends its support with band and orchestra concerts through grants from the Recording Trust Funds. Concerts, children's plays, plays by Shakespeare, carillon concerts, ballet, and poetry readings compose the programs for this six-week festival, which offers four evening events each week from late June to early August. All performances are held in Dogwood Dell in Richmond's Byrd Park. Annual attendance is about 60,000.

NORFOLK ARTS FESTIVAL. Tidewater Arts Council, Inc. produces this festival; public relations is handled through The Matthews Agency, Inc., 610 West 25th Street, Norfolk, Virginia 23517. **Mrs. Marcia Lindemann** is Publicity Director; **Robert D. Randolph** is Festival Director. The Norfolk Arts Festival is a major annual project of the Tidewater Arts Council, an organization founded in 1961 and made up of the area's primary cultural organizations. The festival dates from the founding of the T.A.C. Held in the month of July in Norfolk's Lafayette Park Amphitheatre, the festival offers four weeks of almost daily events of music, art shows, plays, and dance—all offered free to the public. The City of Norfolk renders virtually all financial support for these events, which depend heavily on local or state talent, apart from the performances of the military service bands (more than half of the music programming consists of concerts by the military units). Annual attendance is estimated to be about 65,000.

OLD FIDDLERS' CONVENTION, Box 655, Galax, Virginia 24333. Galax is more than 60 miles southwest of Roanoke on U.S. Route 58/221, not far from the North Carolina border. This event has been held annually since 1935—with the exception of one year during World War II—and offers an opportunity for folk musicians and dancers to demonstrate their skill and to compete for modest monetary prizes (some 20 or so totaling about $1,000). Categories of performances and contests include folk song, guitar, banjo-clawhammer, banjo-bluegrass, fiddle, clog or flatfoot dance, and band. No electrical instruments are permitted, and only those songs that are judged to be authentic folk songs are considered in the competitions. The Convention is entirely sponsored by Galax Moose Lodge No. 733 and is held the second week of August on a Thursday and Friday evening and Saturday afternoon and evening. Felts Park in Galax serves as the location of the event; its parking lot is frequently the scene of more music making, and audiences will gather there since the musicians and dancers often rehearse there, tune their instruments, and try out new steps and song renditions prior to going on stage. The event is dubbed "the oldest and largest old-time fiddlers' convention in the world." Long-playing recordings of the performances are available from the convention headquarters.

SHENANDOAH VALLEY MUSIC FESTIVAL, P.O. Box 12, Woodstock, Virginia 22664. Established in 1963, the festival is sponsored by Shenandoah Valley Music Festival Committee in association with American Symphony Orchestra League (q.v.). Program events are held in Orkney Springs Hotel Pavilion, Orkney Springs, Virginia, and at Massanutten Military Academy in Woodstock, in conjunction with the League's Eastern Summer Institute of Orchestral Studies. The Institute, begun in 1956, is essentially a study program enabling young conductors (10 to 12 each year) to work with a full-strength symphony orchestra in generously allotted rehearsal time under the observation of a master conductor. The Shenandoah Valley Music Festival thus takes advantage of the convocation of orchestral musicians and conductors at the Institute to present a series of public concerts. These total six during a two-week period and are organized as pops concerts, symphony concerts, chamber music concerts, and a youth concert. Artistic Director is **Richard Lert,** recent former permanent Conductor of the Pasadena (California) Symphony, who leads all conductor activities at the League Institute. The festival concerts take place approximately the same time each year early in August.

THE SOUTHEASTERN BAND FESTIVAL, P.O. Box 1039, Bristol, Virginia 24201. Bristol lies astride the Virginia–Tennessee border on Interstate Route 81, placing the city in both states. This event is a one-day competition for high school marching bands mainly from the states of Virginia and Tennessee, with some representation from Georgia, North Carolina, South Carolina, West Virginia, and Kentucky. It takes place on the first Saturday in October. About 70 bands with over 5,000 members have sometimes taken part in the competition. The day's programming consists of an early morning parade through Bristol, the afternoon competition at the town stadium (open to the public for an admissions charge), and an evening massed-band performance. The festival has been held since 1951.

VIRGINIA FOLK MUSIC ASSOCIATION FESTIVAL, P.O. Box 108, Crewe, Virginia 23930. Founded in 1946 and organized by the Virginia Folk Music Association under the sponsorship of the Crewe Kiwanis Club. Crewe is on State Route 46, about 42 miles west of Petersburg in Nottoway County, and is the location of one aspect of the festival only, namely, the competition of so-called regular bands. Chase City, a nearby town, is host to the bluegrass music competition, and a third town (which has not been decided on at the time of writing) is the location of the "Sacred Music Sing-A-Long." It can be seen that this festival is one of many in the South devoted to folk music or folk-style music that features competitions offering usually modest prizes as encouragement for participation by local musicians and singers. State championships are conferred on winners in various categories within the regular band or "country swing band," bluegrass, and sacred music events. These include best male and female singers, best instrumentalists (electric guitar and steel guitar for the bands division and best dobro player, mandolinist, banjoist, or fiddler in bluegrass), and best soloists, duets, quartets, and choirs in sacred music Winners in these categories have often gone on to professional careers in country music. Participation is restricted to residents of Virginia only. The V.F.M.A. has issued some six recordings of performers who have taken part in the festivals. Admission is charged for all programs. The Chase City segment of the festival is sponsored by that town's Jaycees. The festival is held in September.

WOLF TRAP FARM FOR THE PERFORMING ARTS, Vienna, Virginia 22180. Opened in 1971, the Park is the only performing arts center in the United States under the jurisdiction of the National Park Service, Department of the Interior. The Park Service administers the land, but all artistic and educational aspects of Wolf Park are run by privately organized administrational structures. Most of the Park grounds are a gift from **Mrs. Jouett Shouse,** prominent Washington, D.C., patroness of the arts. In 1961 she donated 36 acres of her land to the American Symphony Orchestra League for its national headquarters (see Organizations) and followed, in 1966, with the remaining land, some 59 acres, as a gift to the Park Service. The Service itself added some land of its own, bringing the total acreage of the Park to 140. In order to construct a central facility for concert performances of all kinds, the Park received from Mrs. Shouse over two million dollars toward the building of what is now Filene Center, an amphitheater seating 3,500 with additional provision for lawn audiences of about 3,000. Wolf Trap is located in the foothills of the Blue Ridge Mountains, in Virginia's Fairfax County, some 14 miles southwest of Washington, D.C. The first season scheduled performances by the National Symphony Orchestra under **Julius Rudel,** Artistic Director of Wolf Trap; the Cleveland Orchestra under **Pierre Boulez;** the New Jersey Symphony under **Henry Lewis;** the New York City Opera Company; Minnesota Opera Company; the City Center Joffrey Ballet; the Stuttgart Ballet; and the Alvin Ailey Dance Company, among other performing groups. A complement of well-known solo performers appeared. The season for the concerts runs from early July to early September. The Wolf Trap American University Academy for the Performing Arts is a summer institute created in conjunction with The American University, Washington, D.C., and Wolf Trap Park. It provides intensive summer study and performance opportunities for about 800 high school, college, and postgraduate music students during an eight-week session (late June to late August). **William Yarborough** is Director of the Academy.

Washington

GREATER SPOKANE MUSIC AND ALLIED ARTS FESTIVAL, E. 1321–27th, Spokane, Washington 99203. Founded in 1945. The Festival Association is incorporated as a civic nonprofit organization working to encourage the study and performance of music and allied arts among young people. The festival is, in effect, a competition open to any amateur from any state or country and is conducted the first week in May. Special music and art events are organized in conjunction with the festival: concerts and recitals by professional or university groups. Past years have featured Seattle and Spokane Symphony Orchestras under **Milton Katims** and **Donald Thulean,** respectively; University of Ohio Band; Spokane Choral Society; duo-pianists **Phyllis Schuldt** and **Boris Roubakine;** and others. There is an admissions charge for these special concerts, which are held in various locations in the area: Whitworth College, Gonzaga University, Fort Wright College, and Ferris High School, to name some. **Howard C. Mahan** is President of the Association.

Wisconsin

FESTIVAL OF THE ARTS, Marathon County Historical Society, 403 McIndoe Street, Wausau, Wisconsin 54401. Founded in 1965. This festival, presented the weekend after Labor Day, offers all its events free to the public. It is held in Wausau's Yawkey Park, with an average annual attendance of between eight and nine thousand. The prime emphasis of this festival, from its inception, has been on exhibitions of paintings, works of sculpture, and the crafts. Prizes are offered exhibiting artists whose works are also offered for sale. Other events have been added to the festival with a view to attracting more interest: poetry recitations, Indian dances, jazz, barbershop singing, brief musical concerts such as a performance by a concert band, an opera scene, etc. **Edward T. Schoenberger** is Executive Director of the Historical Society and founder of the festival.

MADISON SUMMER SYMPHONY ORCHESTRA CONCERTS, 731 State Street, Madison, Wisconsin 53703. This is a summer orchestra series in existence since 1960, when the ensemble was founded by its first conductor, **Gordon Wright.** The present conductor is **David Crosby.** The orchestra is composed of some 40 members, many of whom are players in other orchestras in the United States. The concerts take place on the campus of Edgewood College on Sunday evening throughout July. A varied programming is maintained; local guest instrumentalists are engaged as soloists. A number of Midwest premieres have been played by the ensemble, as well as works specially commissioned.

MUSIC UNDER THE STARS, Milwaukee County Park Commission, 4420 West Vliet Street, Milwaukee, Wisconsin 53233. An all-free public events series sponsored by the Milwaukee County Park Commission and The Journal Company. Scheduled from June through August and generally offering a concert with two performances on consecutive nights each week, the series presents orchestral music, opera scenes or arias, fully staged opera and operettas, ballet, and evenings of mixed musical entertainment. The series is a major summer music and dance event for the Milwaukee area, attracting up to 366,000 and more in seasonal attendance. The Milwaukee Symphony Orchestra under **John-David Anello** (who is also Director of Cultural Activities for the Park Commission) and the Milwaukee Florentine Opera Company, under **Anello** as music director and **Robert Simpson,** stage director and choreographer, are the main performing groups. To these are added numerous guest performers of national and international renown. Among them: singers **Barry Morrell, Theodor Uppman, William Walker, William Lewis, Rosalind Elias, Henri Noel, Raquel Montalvo, Nicholas di Virgilio,** and **Renate Holm.** Thus, stars from the Metropolitan Opera Company, La Scala, Vienna State Opera, Chicago Lyric, and other opera companies are an important ingredient to "Music Under the Stars," since programming leans heavily toward operatic music. Orchestral music tends to be shorter works or selected movements from symphonies and other larger works. Performances are distributed over the entire county area, using such public parks as Washington Park, Humboldt Park, Sheridan Park, Nathan Hale Athletic Field, Lincoln Park, Lake Park, the County Zoo, and Walker Square. **Howard Gregg** is the General Manager of the series. "Music Under the Stars" was first established in 1938.

PENINSULA MUSIC FESTIVAL, Pioneer School House, Ephraim, Wisconsin 54211. Winter address: 2400 West Acacia Road, Milwaukee, Wisconsin 53209. Location of the actual festival events is in Gibraltar Auditorium in Fish Creek, Wisconsin (54212). Fish Creek is in Door County on the peninsula that divides the waters of Lake Michigan and Green Bay. The festival is sponsored entirely by the Peninsula Arts Association (founded 1938). Festival Chairman is **Mrs. Carl T. Wilson;** Association President is **George H. Norton, Jr.** The Festival was founded in 1953, by **Thor Johnson,** who remains Music Director and Conductor. Always held in August, the Festival presents nine concerts—the majority of them held on Saturday evening and Sunday afternoon, with one or two offered in mid-week. The programs are richly varied. Each offers performances by the Chamber Symphony Orchestra and guest soloists or group. Works performed cover a wide range of composers—in nationality, historical period, and style. Artists engaged are uniformly of first rank. Among them have been pianists **Claude Frank, Gary Graffman, Ralph Votapek, Grant Johannesen, Mary Sauer, Arthur Fenimore, Gyorgy Sandor, Richard Cass,** and **John Browning;** violinists **Norman Paulu, James Oliver Buswell, IV, Sidney Harth;** cellist **Zara Nelsova;** singers, **Lois Marshall, Helen Boatwright, Martha Lipton,** and **Carol Smith.** The Don Redlich Dance Group and the woodwind quintet, Soni Ventorum, have been among the ensembles appearing in recent seasons. The capacity of the Auditorium is only 750 seats, with about two thirds of them subscribed to for the season, leaving the balance open to single seat purchasers. Capacity audiences, therefore, are the rule at Fish Creek.

Part 8 U.S. Musical Contests, Awards, Grants, Fellowships, and Honors

The opportunities and honors in this chapter fall into many categories. They cover all types of instrumental performers and singers, students, professionals and near-professionals, composers, conductors, music educators, theorists, musicologists, and scholars. Most are competitive, particularly in performing fields; some are highly distinguished honors for which no one can apply (e.g., the Pulitzer Prize).

At stake in the contests are cash prizes, debut recitals, publication or recording awards, scholarships to any school, scholarships to a specific school or schools within a certain region of the country, opportunities to perform with a professional group, travel, study, research, lectures—all in various combinations and subject to various degrees of restriction (such as for women only, or for residents of a particular state). Altogether, they are supported by foundations, schools, private endowments, the federal government, sororities and fraternities, publishers, festival associations, opera companies and symphony orchestras, and musical organizations of many kinds.

Applicants may be U.S. citizens, native-born or naturalized, foreigners residing or studying in America, or any person whatever. Scholarships and fellowships usually carry age limitations within their qualifications. Most very high honors do not.

The amount of money involved is not the criterion of worth or distinction in certain contests. Some competitions are judged completely anonymously; others are open to the public and are widely publicized. There are prizes to open the doors of a career; others will crown a lifelong dedication to music.

The following list consists mainly of opportunities that are presented at regular intervals; however, some special temporary events are included as examples of their kind. Since most schools offer scholarships and other tuition grants, these are necessarily omitted here, but are identified, in a general way, for each school offering them in the chapter, Music and Education.

Dates for application, audition, and the like are shown to guide readers desiring to take advantage of an opportunity. Whenever possible, dates are referred to both in a general way and in an exact manner using a random year, usually within the last five years, as a case in point.

Many awards increased their monetary prize amounts in 1972 and 1973, but not all such increases were possible to discover and report here.

The competitions and awards are arranged alphabetically by identifying name, e.g., The Friends of Harvey Gaul Composition Contest is under "g"; Minna Kaufmann-Ruud Foundation award is under "k." A cross index, which summarizes the events by category, precedes the detailed listing of contests.

U.S. MUSICAL CONTESTS, AWARDS, GRANTS, FELLOWSHIPS, AND HONORS BY CLASSIFICATION

Performance

AFM Congress of Strings Scholarships

Amarillo National Artist Auditions

American Opera Auditions

Marian Anderson Scholarships

Artists Advisory Council Awards

Johann Sebastian Bach International Competition

Baltimore Opera Company Award

Brevard Music Center Scholarships and Awards

Concert Artists Guild Award

Corbett Foundation Fellowship Program

G. B. Dealey Awards

Elizabeth Hodges Donovan Memorial Award

Emma Feldman Memorial Competition

Kirsten Flagstad Memorial Award

Friday Morning Music Club Foundation National Audition

Fulbright–Hays Awards for Graduate Study Abroad

Fulbright–Hays Awards for University Lecturing and Advanced Research Abroad

Grinnel–Detroit Grand Opera Scholarship

Houston Symphony Young Artists Competition

Illinois Opera Guild Auditions of the Air (see WGN–Illinois Opera Guild)

Intercollegiate Music Festival National Championships

International Louis Moreau Gottschalk Competition

International Harp Competition

Joske Scholarship Award of the San Antonio Symphony Orchestra

Minna Kaufmann-Ruud Foundation Distinguished Performance Awards

Kate Neal Kinley Memorial Fellowship

Kosciuszko Foundation Chopin Scholarship

Edgar M. Leventritt Foundation International Competition

Liederkranz Foundation Scholarship Fund Contest

Lauritz Melchior Heldentenor Foundation

Merriweather Post Contest for Violinists and Cellists

Metropolitan Opera Auditions

Michaels Award of Ravinia Festival

Dimitri Mitropoulos Piano Awards

Musicians Club of New York Young Artists Award

Naftzger Young Artists Audition

National Association of Teachers of Singing Artist Awards

National Federation of Music Clubs Scholarships and Awards:

See: **Biennial**

NFMC Young Artists Auditions

Biennial Student Auditions

Chatham College Opera Workshop Scholarship

NFMC Annual:

Vera Wardner Dougan Award

Anne M. Gannett Scholarship

Annual Student:

College–Conservatory of Music Scholarship in Violoncello

Eastman School of Music Scholarship

Marie Morrisey Keith Scholarship

Manhattan School of Music Scholarship

Millikin University Scholarship

New School of Music Scholarship

Oklahoma College of Liberal Arts Scholarship

Peabody Conservatory of Music Scholarship

Shreveport Symphony–Centenary College Scholarship

Annual Junior Awards:

Junior Festival Awards

Stillman Kelley Scholarship

Frances Rogers Scholarship

NFMC Summer Music Scholarships:

Arizona All State High School Fine Arts Camp

Aspen Music School

Berkshire Music Center Ada Holding Miller Scholarship

Chatham College Opera Workshop

Chautauqua Music School

Stephen Collins Foster Music Camp

Inspiration Point Hazel Post Gillette Scholarship

International Music Camp Agnes Jardine Scholarships

Kneisel Hall

Meadow Brook Summer School of Music

Meadowmount Camp

Music Academy of the West

National Music Camp

Oglebay Opera Workshop

Rocky Ridge Music Center

Sewanee Music Center

Transylvania Music Camp Hinda Honigman Scholarship

Pacific Northwest Music Camp

National Music League Auditions

Walter W. Naumburg Foundation Awards

Gregor Piatigorsky Triennial Artist Award

San Francisco Opera Auditions

Marcella Sembrich Scholarship in Voice

Sterling Staff Concerts International Competition

William Matheus Sullivan Musical Foundation Inc. Awards

Van Cliburn International Quadrennial Piano Competition

WGN–Illinois Opera Guild "Auditions of the Air"

Wieniawski Scholarships for Violinists

Young Artist Auditions (Oklahoma City Symphony Society)

Young Artist Competition (Denver Symphony Society)

Young Artist Competition (Fort Collins Symphony Society)

Young Musicians Foundation Competition

Musical Composition

American Academy in Rome Fellowships

Joseph H. Bearns Prize

Ernst Bloch Award Competition

BMI Student Composers Award (see Student Composers Award)

BMI Varsity Show Competition

Children's Opera Composition Contest

Choral Composition Competition

Composer's Prize

Creative Arts Award (Brandeis University)

Dartmouth Arts Council Prize

Delta Omicron Composition Competition

Fulbright–Hays Awards for Graduate Study Abroad

Fulbright–Hays Awards for University Lecturing and Advanced Research Abroad

Fromm Music Foundation Commissions

Friends of Harvey Gaul Composition Contest

International Louis Moreau Gottschalk Competition

Greenwood Choral Award

John Simon Guggenheim Memorial Fellowship

International Tuba Ensemble Composition Contest

Kate Neal Kinley Memorial Fellowship

Koussevitzky International Recording Award

Lado Composition Commission

MacDowell Colony Fellowships

Edward Garrett McCollin Fund Competition (Musical Fund Society)

NFMC Young Composers Awards (see NFMC Annual Student Awards)

NFMC Annual Junior Awards:

- Junior Composers Scholarship
- Junior Composers Awards
- Junior Conservatory Camp Scholarship
- Charles Ives Scholarship
- Fred Waring Award
- Laura K. Wilson Memorial Award

(Ohio State University School of Music) National Composition Award

Composition Contest for Percussion Quartet

Philadelphia A.G.O. Composition Contest

Pulitzer Prize in Music

Rochester Festival of Religious Arts Music Competition

Roth Orchestra Composition Award

Arthur Shepherd Composition Contest

(Sigma Alpha Iota) Inter-American Music Awards

Society for the Publication of American Music Award (SPAM)

Rheta A. Sosland Chamber Music Award

Sounds of Young America

Leo Sowerby Memorial Composition Awards

Student Composers Awards (BMI)

Thorne Music Fund Grants and Fellowships

Young Composers of America Competition

Young Musicians Foundation Competition

Miscellaneous

ASCAP–Deems Taylor Award (writings on music)

BMI–Varsity Show Competition (lyricists—also composers, q.v.)

Alice M. Ditson Fund of Columbia University (to organizations for performances of American music)

Alfred Einstein Award (musicology)

Fulbright–Hays Awards for Graduate Study Abroad (in any area of music, in addition to composition and performance)

Fulbright–Hays Awards for University Lecturing and Advanced Research Abroad (any area of music)

John Simon Guggenheim Memorial Fellowship (music history, theory, research, etc.)

Otto Kinkeldy Award (musicology)

Kate Neal Kinley Memorial Fellowship (music scholarship)

Dimitri Mitropoulos International Music Competition (orchestral conducting)

NFMC Annual Junior Award: Junior Dance Scholarship

NFMC Dorothy Dann Bullock Scholarship (music therapy)

Oklahoma College of Liberal Arts Scholarship (music education—see under NFMC Annual Student Awards)

Olds Scholarship in Music Competition (writings about instrumental music)

Singing City Conducting Fellowship (choral conducting)

John Hay Whitney Foundation Opportunity Fellowship (academic music career)

Harriet Hale Wooley Scholarship in Music and Art

AMARILLO NATIONAL ARTIST AUDITIONS, c/o Chairman, Auditions Committee, Mary Elizabeth Wilson, 903 Sunset Terrace, Amarillo, Texas 79106; or, Amarillo Symphony, Box 2552, Amarillo, Texas 79105. Co-sponsored by the Amarillo Symphony, Inc. and the Amarillo Music Teachers Association. Awards are granted to a pianist and a vocalist: an appearance each with the Amarillo Symphony and a cash $1,000 Blackburn Brothers · Award (pianist) and $1,000 Ray C. Johnson, Jr. Award (vocalist). (No secondary prizes are awarded.) No age limitations for candidates. An entrance fee of $10 is required of each applicant. In 1968 the competition was held on November 16 at Amarillo College. Permanent date for auditions is the third Saturday in November. Applications cannot be postmarked later than midnight, October 26. Winners' concerts take place the following January. Contestants are judged on the basis of artistic ability and selection of repertory. Required repertory and other rules are available from Auditions Committee Chairman.

AMERICAN ACADEMY IN ROME FELLOWSHIPS, c/o American Academy in Rome, 101 Park Avenue, New York, N.Y. 10017. A fellowship of $3,650 a year including stipend, round trip cost, European travel, studio supplies, and a free studio and residence at the Academy (Via Angelo Masina 5, 00153 Rome, Italy). Renewable for an additional year. Areas of study and creative work are: architecture, landscape architecture, musical composition, painting, sculpture, history of art, and classical and post-classical studies. The fellow is allowed free use of creative time; no instruction is offered at the Academy. Applicants must be U.S. citizens and capable of independent work. Fellowships are granted on the basis of ability and achievement. There is no age limit, but young candiates of unusual promise are a particular aim of the Academy. Funds are meant for the expenses of the fellow only. Compositions must be submitted by each composer candidate for examination. The Academy was established in 1894 and was chartered by the U.S. Congress in 1905. The music department was added in 1921. The Academy is supported by various gifts including those from American colleges and universities. Deadline for application is before January 1st of the year of application; the fellowship begins the following October 1st.

A.F. OF M. (AMERICAN FEDERATION OF MUSICIANS) CONGRESS OF STRINGS SCHOLARSHIP. Sponsored by the American Federation of Musicians, 220 Mt. Pleasant Avenue, Newark, N.J. 07104. The Scholarships were established in 1959 to further the musical education of competent young string players (violin, viola, cello, and string bass) for possible future positions in symphony orchestras. The program was instigated by many concerned figures in the symphonic music field after what was surmised to be a serious shortage of string-instrument performers. Each year 120 national winners are selected after local competitions.

Scholarship includes free transportation to special summer music camp sites, eight weeks free tuition, and room and board. Deadline for application is May 1.

AMERICAN OPERA AUDITIONS, 3609 Carew Tower, Cincinnati, Ohio 45202. Sponsored by Associazione Lirica e Concertistica Italiana, Milan, Italy; Associazione Italiana diffusione Educazione Musicale, Florence, Italy; College–Conservatory of Music, Cincinnati; and Radio Cincinnati, Inc. Founded in 1957. A vocal award encompassing nine weeks of study in Italy—all expenses paid—and subsequent debut in Milan. Age limits are: for sopranos, tenors, and baritones—32; mezzo sopranos, contraltos, and bassos—34. Applicants must be of professional calibre. Deadline for application is generally January 30. (In 1972, it was March 4.) Preliminary regional auditions are held in Cincinnati, New York, Chicago, and Denver. Winners in 1969: **Ana Riera,** soprano; **Gwynn Cornell,** mezzo; **Michael Cousins,** tenor; and **Leslie Guin,** baritone. In 1971 winners were: **Karin Kimble,** soprano; **Bess Arlene,** soprano; **Rafael LeBron,** tenor; **John Pflieger,** baritone; **Tom Fox,** bass.

MARIAN ANDERSON SCHOLARSHIP, 762 South Martin Street, Philadelphia, Pennsylvania 19146. Sponsored by Marian Anderson Scholarship Fund at the same address. Founded in 1941 by the singer **Marian Anderson** and awarded annually to assist "gifted young singers in the furtherance of their careers." The awards consist of $1,000 and two smaller amounts for use only for the study of voice in the United States. Applications are available March 1 of each year; deadline for applications is May 31. Auditions are held in October in Philadelphia before anonymous judges. Singers must be between the ages of 16 and 30. Notification of eligibility is sent to candidates on August 15. Other rules are available from the Fund. An important award; previous winners include: **Camilla Williams, Sara Mae Endich, Betty Allen, Judith Raskin, McHenry Boatwright, Grace Bumbry,** to name some who have achieved worldwide performing reputations. In 1971, winners were **Judith Farris,** contralto; and **Rebecca Sydnor,** soprano.

ARTISTS' ADVISORY COUNCIL AWARDS, 55 East Washington Street, Chicago, Illinois 60602. Open to singers and pianists from 16 to 35. The awards are international in scope and offer prizes totaling $10,000. Auditions are required.

ASCAP–DEEMS TAYLOR AWARDS, c/o ASCAP, One Lincoln Plaza, New York, N.Y. 10023. Established in 1967 to award excellent writing in the categories of books, magazines or newspaper articles, or any nonfiction prose concerning music. Eligible are writings published anywhere in the United States during the calendar year preceding the year of the award. Writers, editors, or publishers may send material for consideration. Prizes are $1,000, $500, and $300. The 1971 prizes for works published in 1970 were the books: "Legal Protection for the Creative Musician," by **Lee Eliot Berk** (Berklee Press publication), first prize; "Critical Affairs—A Composer's Journal," by **Ned Rorem** (Braziller), second prize; "The Singer and His Art," by **Aksel Schiøtz** (Harper & Row), third prize. Articles: articles published in *Toledo Blade* by critic, **Boris E. Nelson,** first prize; "A Hiatus in American Music History," by **Paul Glass** (*Afro-American Studies*), second prize; "Mozart: His Tragic Life and Controversial Death," by **Louis Carp** (*Bulletin of N.Y. Academy of Medicine*), third prize. Deadline for 1971 publications was April 30, 1972. Five copies of each submission are required.

JOHANN SEBASTIAN BACH INTERNATIONAL COMPETITION, c/o **Raissa Tselentis,** 1211 Potomac Street, N.W., Washington, D.C. 20007. An annual contest devoted to perpetuating the music of Bach and honoring the efforts of young pianists willing to develop the necessary discipline and artistry for performance of Bach's keyboard works. Open to pianists from 17 to 32 (those who reach their 33rd birthday before the opening day of the trials are ineligible; those younger than 17 may enter provided they secure a letter of recommendation from their teachers and submit a list of works in their repertory). First prize is $1,000, plus a year's scholarship for music study in Germany with expenses paid and a solo recital opportunity in Washington, D.C. Second and third prizes are respectively $500 and $250. Deadline for applications vary. In 1969, contestants had to file before May 15 (a $7.50 application fee is required). Preliminary, semifinal, and final auditions followed in September for three days beginning with September 26. In 1971, the auditions were held in mid-June. **Mari-Elizabeth Morgen** of Canada won first prize in 1968. **Judith Marilyn Engle,** also of Canada, won in 1969. Winner in 1971 was **Peter Vinograde.**

BALTIMORE OPERA COMPANY AWARD. Applications are obtainable from the Baltimore Opera Company, 11 East Lexington Street, Baltimore, Maryland 21202; applicants should mail completed forms to Auditions Chairman, 5005 St. Alban's Way, Baltimore, Maryland 21212. The award was founded in 1963 and is sponsored by the Carling Brewing Company of Baltimore. An annual vocal award with a top prize of $1,000 is given. Other awards in the name of the opera company are the $750 Baltimore Opera Guild prize, the $500 Clementine and Duane Peterson Award in honor of **Rosa Ponselle,** and the Sherman Laboratories Award of $250, respectively awarded as second, third, and fourth prizes. Applicants must be between the ages of 20 and 32 and must have "promising operatic voices." In 1969, auditions began June 2 with finals held June 11 at the Auditorium of the College of Notre Dame. Deadline for application was May 25th. The prize money is expected to be applied by the winners toward some aspect of voice training. Recent winners of Carling Prize: **James Morris** (1967) and **Elizabeth Volkman** (1968). Judges are headed by artistic director of the Baltimore Opera, **Rosa Ponselle.** In 1969, they included **Licia Albanese, Peter Herman Adler, John Gutman, Robert Lawrence,** and **Max de Schauensee.**

JOSEPH H. BEARNS PRIZE, c/o Bearns Prize Committee, 703 Dodge Building, Columbia University, New York, N.Y. 10027. An annual award open to U.S. composers between the ages of 18 and 25. The composition submitted may be in any form or media. Prizes for 1972 were two: $1,200 and $900, respectively for works in large and smaller media. Deadline is early in March, with winners announced the following June. The award was first presented in 1928. Although the award has been won by many who have since passed into musical oblivion or who are not now known as composers, it has been taken by a number of men and women who have achieved distinction as composers; among them: **Samuel Barber** (1929 and 1933), **Hugo Weisgall** (1931), **Louise Talma** (1932), **Milton Babbitt** (1941), **William Bergsma** (1943), **Peter Mennin** (1945), **Harold Shapero** (1946), **Seymour Shifrin** (1950), **Charles Wuorinen** (1958, 1959, and 1961), **Harvey Sollberger** (1963), **Charles Dodge** (1964 and 1967).

ERNST BLOCH AWARD COMPETITION, Box 73, Cedarhurst, N.Y. 11516. Sponsored by the United Choral Society (formerly United Temple Chorus). A composition prize first awarded in 1944. Not held every year. The 1967 competition was the seventeenth with previous recent contests held in 1959, 1960, 1962, 1963 (no award granted), 1964, 1965, and 1967 (none held for 1968–69). The prize consists of $350, publication of the composition by Mercury Music Corporation, and an option of a premiere performance of the winning work by the United Choral Society. The composition submitted must be a new work for mixed chorus of 8 to 15 minutes in length either with secular text or text based on or related to the Old Testament. No age or nationality restriction for composers. Some ten or eleven judges review the submitted works (1967 judges included **Leonard DePaur, Joseph Eger, Herbert Haufrecht,** and **David Randolph**). The deadline is usually October.

BMI VARSITY SHOW COMPETITION, c/o **Allan Becker,** Broadcast Music Inc., 40 West 57th Street, New York, N.Y. 10019. An award of $1,000 is offered by Broadcast Music Inc. (BMI) for the best musical written by collegiate composers and lyricists in the United States and Canada. The sponsoring collegiate organization wins $500. It is offered annually. Deadline for the 1972–73 competition was June 30.

BREVARD MUSIC CENTER SCHOLARSHIPS AND AWARDS, c/o **Henry Janiec,** Brevard Music Center, P.O. Box 349, Brevard, North Carolina 29301. Over 50 awards are available for qualified student band and orchestra players between the ages of 12 and 18, for study at the Transylvania Music Camp. Other awards are available for student players over 18 years old for study opportunities at the Brevard Music Center under the sponsorship of Southern businesses and other organizations (see also NFMC Summer Music Scholarships).

CHILDREN'S OPERA COMPOSITION CONTEST, c/o Music Department, Arizona State University, Tempe, Arizona 85281. A prize of $1,000 is awarded the best opera composed specifically for young audiences between the ages of five and 16. The opera desired is one that can be performed by college opera workshops and professional companies using a cast of three to six and an orchestra of 15 or less (no chorus), and lasting from 45 to 60 minutes. Competing composers must submit new and unperformed works in the form of a full score as well as a piano–vocal score. The selected opera will have its vocal and orchestral parts copied for performance at the expense of the contest's sponsor. The deadline in 1970 was March 1.

CHORAL COMPOSITION COMPETITION, c/o Executive Secretary, Southern California Vocal Association, Box 5522, Pasadena, California 91107. An annual contest established in 1968 and sponsored by the Association. The contest offers $250 for a new choral work. In 1969 the work required was one suitable for high school girls chorus. The winning composer also receives royalties from the sale of his work after publication by Shawnee Press. The work is also performed at special festivals by choruses belonging to the Association.

COMPOSER'S PRIZE, c/o **True Sackrison,** School of Music, University of Puget Sound, Tacoma, Washington 98416. Sponsored by the Northwest Chamber Music Workshop of the School of Music. First established in 1968; held annually. The purpose of the award is to encourage composers to write chamber music of moderate difficulty suitable for student performers and amateurs. The chamber work may be composed for strings alone or in any combination with woodwinds and piano. Deadline for entries for the 1968 competition was August 1 (no fees required). Manuscripts should be accompanied by instrumental parts for performance. Winning prize is $100.

CONCERT ARTISTS GUILD AWARD, Concert Artists Guild, 154 West 57th Street, New York, N.Y. 10019. A national competition for singers, pianists, and string instrumentalists. First prize is $1,000, second prize is $500; in addition, the winners receive a debut recital opportunity in New York and are booked for at least five paying engagements. Instrumentalists must be under 30; singers under 35. Applicants must be of professional quality, as the purpose of the competitions and awards is to promote the careers of "potentially great" young performers. Deadline in 1972 was March 15. Auditions were in May. Since first established in 1951, the Guild has presented over 500 young artists including such presently well-known performers as **Martina Arroyo, Gene Boucher, Erick Friedman, Evelyn Lear, Judith Raskin,** and **Ralph Votapek.** Judges have included: **Robert Goldsand, Lotte Lehmann, Rosina Lhevinne, Eugene List, George London, Yehudi Menuhin, Isaac Stern,** and **Blanche Thebom.**

CORBETT FOUNDATION FELLOWSHIP PROGRAM, c/o Corbett Foundation, 1501 Madison Road, Cincinnati, Ohio 45206. The first year of the scholarship was 1969; regional auditions for it began in 1968. The fellowships cover the field of opera and are organized in two categories: for those who are already professional singers but who require specialized training and practical experience in opera, and for those who are not yet professionals but whose technique and general musicianship are of sufficient promise to benefit from intensive training for a career in opera. The qualifications for singers applying for fellowships in the first group are thorough vocal technique, a performance background consisting of a reasonable number of professional engagements, a working knowledge of the German language, and that they must be between 25 and 30. The second category of applicants must have some solo singing experience, a working knowledge of German, suitable vocal technique (winners in this category may receive additional vocal instruction, if needed, as part of the fellowship benefits), and must be unmarried and be between 22 and 24. Applicants in both categories who pass regional hearings will receive intensive German lessons prior to the final auditions. The prize for singers with professional backgrounds is the opportunity to gain contracts with the Hamburg or West Berlin Opera companies in Germany. These opportunities are granted to winners selected after a series of auditions, the first of which consists of a tape recording of two opera arias (one in German) sung by the applicant and submitted to the audition jury. Singers chosen as a result of these hearings compete in regional auditions in New York, Atlanta, Cincinnati, Chicago, Denver, Dallas, Los Angeles, or San Francisco. Winners of the regionals proceed to Cincinnati, all expenses paid, for the final U.S. auditions (in 1969, the finals were held in May). The nonprofessional candiates for the fellowships compete in stages of auditions, the finals being held in February. Winners in this category may receive as prize a two-year training program at Munich Opera Studio (Munich, Germany). In 1969, the combined auditions produced 23 singers chosen out of 43 applicants to travel to Europe, all expenses paid, for the purpose of further study or auditions. Judges were: **Rolf Liebermann** (then with the Hamburg Opera), **Egon Seefehlner** (Berlin), and **Robert Schulz,** German agent for opera singers.

(BRANDEIS UNIVERSITY) CREATIVE ARTS AWARD, Brandeis University, Waltham, Massachusetts 02154. Creative Arts Awards Commission Office is located at 60 East 42nd Street, New York, N.Y. 10017. The Commission was established in 1956 and the first awards were granted in 1957. In music, the award covers only the field of composition (the other arts coming within the scope of the awards are the fine arts, literature, and theater). The purpose of the award is to support "beyond the campus" the artistic and cultural life of America. Two awards are granted, each accompanied by a $1,000 honorarium: The Creative Arts Medal Award to an established artist of lifetime distinction in his field, and the Creative Arts Citation Award, granted generally to younger artists already displaying notable talent. The awards are not open to application. The Awards Commission is responsible for selecting jurors who, in the case of the music awards, consist of one member of the Brandeis University Music Department and other individuals active in the profession. Musicians on the 36-member Commission are: **Arthur Berger, Leonard Bernstein, Aaron Copland, Carleton Sprague Smith,** and **Virgil Thomson.** Recent jurors have been: **Leon Kirchner, John Perkins, Roger Sessions, Seymour Shifrin,** and **Harold Shapero.** Recent award winners in music, respectively Medal and Citation recipients, have been: **Milton Babbitt** and **Charles Wuorinen** (1970), **Ernst Krenek** and **Henry Weinberg** (1969), and **Virgil Thomson** and **Easley Blackwood** (1968).

DARTMOUTH ARTS COUNCIL PRIZE, Department of Music, Dartmouth College, Hanover, New Hampshire 03755. A composition prize sponsored by the Department of Music of Dartmouth and the Griffith Electronic Music Studio of the College; first established in 1968. Compositions for consideration must be electronic music produced by tape studio, computer, or synthesizer. Winning composer receives $500 and a possible recording of his work. Deadline for the third event was April 1, 1970. General rules for the length of composition, kind of tape, form of entry, etc., are available from the director of the Griffith Electronic Studio. Winner of the 1968 competition was **Olly W. Wilson** (U.S.A.). The competition was held in 1969, 1971, 1973, and thereafter will be every other year. Judges for the first event were **Milton**

Babbitt, George B. Wilson and **Vladimir Ussachevsky.**

G. B. DEALEY AWARDS, c/o Audition Committee, P.O. Box 8171, Dallas, Texas 75205. A vocal and instrumental competition sponsored by the *Dallas Morning News* in cooperation with the Dallas Symphony and the Dallas Civic Opera Company. First prize in the vocal contest is $1,000 and a contract with the Dallas Civic Opera Company. This prize also carries with it the possibility of an appearance with the Dallas Symphony and in a production of the Dallas Summer Musicals. First prize for instrumentalists is $1,500 and an appearance with the Dallas Symphony. Second prizes are also offered. To be eligible, contestants must be between 17 and 28 (with time allowed for service in the armed forces) and be United States citizens or foreigners studying in the United States. Deadline for application and auditions has previously been in December of the year of the award. For the 1970 award, however, the deadline was March 1. The semifinal and final contests take place at Southern Methodist University. In 1969, the first prize winner was violinist **Arturo Delmoni.**

DELTA OMICRON COMPOSITION COMPETITION, c/o Chairman, **Marie Ezerman Drake,** Philadelphia Musical Academy, 1617 Spruce Street, Philadelphia, Pennsylvania 19103. Sponsored by Delta Omicron International Music Fraternity (for women). A triennial award in composition open to women composers only; established in 1919. The 1968 Competition was for a string quartet. The 1971 event was for a song cycle. Prize varies with each event (in 1968 the prize was $200; 1971: $300). The award also includes a world premiere at the fraternity's triennial international conference. A fee is required of all applicants, who must submit their compositions by a required deadline date (for the 1971 event: August 1, 1970). Rules are available from the competition chairman. Judges are usually well-known composers. Winner of the 1971 competition: **Elizabeth Gould;** for the 1968 competition: **Przemyslawa Rzucidlo** of Poland; 1965: **Jacqueline Fontyn,** of Belgium.

ALICE M. DITSON FUND OF COLUMBIA UNIVERSITY, 703 Dodge Building, Columbia University, New York, N.Y. 10027. A noncompetitive award granted for "the aid and encouragement of musicians." In effect, the award has been granted primarily to encourage performance of American music. First established in 1940. The monetary amount of the award varies with the nature of the grant, as do stipulations in each case and qualifications of the recipient. The annual Ditson Conductors Award is $1,000. The members of the Fund's Advisory Committee act as judges; recipients of the Ditson Awards have been mainly organizations rather than individuals.

ELIZABETH HODGES DONOVAN MEMORIAL AWARD, Detroit Grand Opera Association, Ford Auditorium, Detroit, Michigan 48226. An award of $1,000 established in 1968 for the encouragement of qualified singers toward the advancement of operatic careers. Offered as part of the Metropolitan Opera Regional Auditions programs (see also Grinnel Scholarship for rules and other stipulations).

THE ALFRED EINSTEIN AWARD, c/o the American Musicological Society (see Organizations). Established in 1967 to award outstanding music scholarship. The award of $400 is granted to the author of the best article in the field of music scholarship published in either the *Journal of the American Musicological Society* or *The Musical Quarterly.* Participants may be of any nationality but must be not more than 40 at the time of submitting the article. Judges are appointed yearly by the Executive Board of the Society. Winner for the first award in 1967: **Richard L. Crocker.** Winner in 1970 (for a 1969 publication) was **Lawrence Gushee.**

EMMA FELDMAN MEMORIAL COMPETITION, c/o Philadelphia All-Star Forum Series, 1718 Locust Street, Philadelphia, Pennsylvania 19103. First established in 1967 and is open to violinists, violists, and cellists who are residents of the United States and between 16 and 29. First prize is $1,000 and a recital at the Philadelphia Academy of Music under the auspices of the Philadelphia All-Star Forum Series. Second prize: $400; third prize: $200. There are three additional prizes of $100 each. In 1970 the deadline for applications was in April (a $10 fee was required); the contest took place the following May.

KIRSTEN FLAGSTAD MEMORIAL AWARD, c/o **Edwin McArthur,** 1400 East Avenue, Rochester, N.Y. 14610. One thousand dollars or more is granted at the discretion of the advisors to a promising aspirant who intends to make a career in the field of opera. In addition to singers, the award may be granted to pianists, coaches, conductors, and others. Names of likely candidates are considered by recommendation only—no applications are accepted. Advisors are **Edwin McArthur** and **Reginald Allen.** Winners of the 1968–69 awards were: **Patricia Guthrie,** soprano ($1,000); **Donna Roll,** soprano ($500); and **David Stone,** pianist–coach–conductor ($500). In 1970–71, winners were sopranos **Patricia Guthrie** and **Kirsten Huehn,** and tenor **Daniel Nelson.**

FRIDAY MORNING MUSIC CLUB FOUNDATION NATIONAL AUDITION, c/o Auditions Chairman, 3530 N. Dickerson, Arlington, Virginia 22207. Sponsored by the Friday Morning Music Club Foundation, YWCA Building, 17th and "K", N.W., Washington, D.C. 20006. Established in 1950. An annual award alternately offered for pianists, string instrument players (violin, viola, and cello), and singers (in 1969 and 1972, the contest was for pianists; in 1970 and 1973, for string players). First prize: $1,000, with second and third prizes respectively $750 and $500. First prize also includes a recital at the Phillips Collection in Washington. A registration fee of $5 is required of all applicants. The performer's application plus a tape recording of the repertory required must be received by the Foundation by March 15 (in 1973). Applicants must be between 18 to 25 and must not have given a professional performance in a large city and must not be under professional concert management. Semifinalists are chosen from the tape recordings and must agree to audition in person on a given date (in 1973, the auditions were held May 11). The cash awards are intended only for the use of pursuing concert careers. Judges have included such major musicians as: **Martial Singher, Eleanor Steber,** Victor Babin, **Leon Fleisher,** Boris Kroyt, and **William Masselos.** Winners in recent years have been: cellist, **Toby Saks;** violinist, **Elaine Skorodin;** soprano, **Esther Hinds;** pianists, **Bonnie Kellert** and **Nina Louise Tichman.**

FROMM MUSIC FOUNDATION COMMISSIONS, 1028 West Van Buren Street, Chicago, Illinois 60607. The Foundation has sponsored composer commissions and other composition awards since 1952. Over 100 commissions have been awarded since that date. Composers do not apply for awards; instead, the Foundation invites composers to submit unpublished works for judgment by a jury of composers. A selected composition is then given public performances, an opportunity for publication by the firm of Boosey & Hawkes, and an opportunity for recording. In addition, certain cash awards are made to the composer.

FULBRIGHT–HAYS AWARDS FOR GRADUATE STUDY ABROAD. The screening agency is the Institute of International Education, offices of which are located throughout the country as follows: Information and Reference Services Division, Institute of International Education, 809 United Nations Plaza, New York, N.Y. 10017; 65 East South Water Street, Chicago, Illinois 60601 (Midwest office serving Illinois, Indiana, Iowa, Kentucky, Michigan, Minnesota, Missouri, North Dakota, Ohio, South Dakota, and Wisconsin); Capitol Life Center, East 16th Avenue at Grant Street, Denver, Colorado 80203 (Rocky Mountain regional office serving Arizona, Colorado, Idaho, Kansas, Montana, Nebraska, New Mexico, Utah, and Wyoming); Suite 1411, Peachtree Center, 230 Peachtree Street, N.W., Atlanta, Georgia 30303 (Southeast office serving Alabama, Florida, Georgia, North Carolina, South Carolina, and Tennessee); Suite 1-A, World Trade Center, 1520 Texas Avenue, Houston, Texas 77002 (Southern office covering Arkansas, Louisiana, Mississippi, Oklahoma, and Texas); 1212 Wilshire Boulevard, Los Angeles, California 90017 (Southern California office for Imperial, Kern, Los Angeles, Orange, Riverside, San Bernardino, San Diego, San Luis Obispo, Santa Barbara, and Ventura counties); 1530 P Street, N.W., Washington, D.C. 20005 (Washington office serving Delaware, District of Columbia, Maryland, Puerto Rico, Virginia, and West Virginia); and 291 Geary Street, San Francisco, California 94102 (West Coast office for Alaska, California—excepting those counties served by the Southern California office—Hawaii, Nevada, Oregon, and Washington).

The grants are the result of Congressional legislation (Public Law 87–256, the Mutual Educational and Cultural Exchange Act of 1961, known as the Fulbright–Hays Act, an act superseding the Fulbright Act of 1946) and are financed by U.S. Government appropriations and foreign currencies, as well as universities and private donors. The Fulbright–Hays Act is part of the general education exchange program of the U.S. Department of State and was created to increase understanding between the people of the United States and those of other nations. The awards are made in the currency of the country visited by the scholar. The grants cover all fields of learning. In music, the applicant may be a student or a professional musician in any area of music.

Among requirements, other than the necessary educational background or experience, are U.S. citizenship and qualities of good citizenship, good personal character, good health, and knowledge of the language of the country to be visited.

There are two categories of grants: Full Grants and Travel Grants. Full Grants cover round-trip transportation, language or orientation course (when necessary), tuition, books, normal expenses sufficient to provide for one person within the frame of living costs in the host country, and health and accident insurance. Increased stipends are available to those who have received doctoral degrees between applying and receiving a full grant. Travel Grants in general are given to supplement funds for personal expenses and tuition scholarship when the latter do not cover transportation costs. The Travel Grants are therefore meant to augment the funds received by a student from universities, private donors, and foreign governments. The Travel Grants provide for round-trip transportation to the country where the student will study and cover the cost of an orientation course if one is needed.

It should be mentioned that the Institute of International Education is also the information agency for certain so-called Foreign Grants, or grants offered by foreign governments and universities which often cover only a small part of the expenses incurred during the time of study abroad. The recipients of such grants are expected to pay all remaining costs. Some of these foreign grants (the countries offering them are listed below) may be supplemented by (Fulbright–Hays) Travel Grants. It is understood that not all of the grants are related to music.

Countries participating in the awards exchange program for the Fulbright–Hays Full Grant in the American Republics Area are: Argentina, Brazil, Chile, Colombia, Ecuador, Peru, and Uruguay. Other countries for Full Grants are: Australia, Austria, Belgium–Luxembourg, Republic of China, Denmark, Finland, France, Federal Republic of Germany, Greece, Iceland, India, Iran, Ireland, Italy, Japan, Korea, Malaysia, Netherlands, New Zealand, Norway, Philippines, Portugal, Spain, Sweden, Thailand, Turkey, and the United Kingdom.

Countries included for the Fulbright–Hays Travel Grant are: France, Federal Republic of Germany, Israel, Italy, Poland, Romania, Spain, Sweden, Turkey, and Yugoslavia.

Foreign Grants are awarded by Austria, France, Germany, Iceland, Israel, Italy, Mexico, Poland, Romania, Sweden, Switzerland, Tunisia, Turkey, and Yugoslavia. All of the foregoing nations are participating in the exchange as of 1970–1971. Subsequent years may have changes.

Applicants for the Fulbright-Hays Full and Travel Grants may be either students currently enrolled at a school or so-called at-large applicants. Student candidates apply for the awards through their campus Fulbright Awards advisor; at-large applicants apply directly to the New York office of I.I.E.

Deadlines for application vary. Enrolled students may enter the competitions after May 1 of the academic year preceding the academic year applied for. They must submit completed applications by the date set by their campus advisor. At-large candidates must submit their applications to the New York office of the I.I.E. by November 1 of the year preceding the academic year applied for. Travel Grant deadline is February 1 for the following academic year (e.g., February 1, 1970 for the 1970–71 year).

Fulbright-Hays applicants are expected to submit study plans or projects in their respective fields. Applicants in the "creative" or "performing arts" must submit projects along with specific reasons for selecting a particular country, the results expected to be obtained, and examples of their work. It should be noted that the creative and performing arts are not recommended as fields of study for the American Republics Area under the Full Grants. Under the stipulations for the Full Grant, music or certain areas of music study are specifically not recommended as a field of study for: Denmark (except for organ study), Greece (study of Byzantine music is accepted), Italy (opera direction and production not recommended), Japan, Netherlands (music therapy not recommended), and Sweden (limited only to study with a specific music teacher which must be arranged beforehand).

FULBRIGHT-HAYS AWARDS FOR UNIVERSITY LECTURING AND ADVANCED RESEARCH ABROAD, Committee on International Exchange of Persons, Conference Board of Associated Research Councils, 2101 Constitution Avenue, N.W., Washington, D.C. 20418. The Committee is the agency for the Department of State which funds the program through its Bureau of Educational and Cultural Affairs. The Board of Foreign Scholarships, consisting of 12 members appointed by the President from educational, cultural, and other groups, supervises the program and selects participating individuals and institutions. However, the prime agency for the Lecturing and Advanced Research awards is the Committee on International Exchange of Persons of the Conference Board of Associated Research Councils, a private agency. The committee consists of 12 members appointed by the Conference Board. Its major task is publicity, the screening of applicants, and recommending candidates. For music, there is the Advisory Screening Committee in Music. According to the Committee, some 550 lecturing and 150 research awards are made annually involving about 75 nations; only a small portion of these awards cover music.

The University Lecturing awards have the following requirements. Applicant must be a U.S. citizen with college or university teaching experience (or Ph.D.) at the level for which application is made. Proficiency in a foreign language is sometimes required. Application is made before June 1 of the year preceding the academic year covered by the award. Screening begins after June 1. The duration of the lectureship is one academic year beginning with various months depending on the hemisphere to which the applicant's assignment takes him. The award covers a lectureship to only one country and pays for round-trip travel, books, services, small expenses essential to the assignment, and maintenance allowance for normal living costs for the grantee and his dependents accompanying him. (A grantee may receive a supplement in U.S. dollars for dependents accompanying him to certain of the available countries.) As examples of awards in music offered under the program, the following are listed for 1969–1970: Australia (for ethnomusicology), Colombia (music education and choral music), Germany (any area of music), Korea (music or art). Certain countries (Brazil, Greece, Iran, and others) accept applications for any field for combined lecturing and research assignments. The Committee maintains a Register, essentially a resource file, which informs scholars of lecturing and consultant assignments that are additional to those made in the annual announcements.

For Advanced Research awards, the requirements are basically the same as the lecturing awards except that, in the absence of a doctoral degree, the candidate must have recognized professional standing as shown by faculty rank, publications, compositions, concerts, etc. The grant period has a minimum of six months; there are no grants offered for the summer months only. The grant covers approximately the same expenses as those outlined for the lecturing award. Although Germany is specifically mentioned as permitting a research grant in music for 1969–1970, the following countries have awards that are open to applications in any field which may include music: Argentina, Austria, Belgium–Luxembourg, Denmark, France, Italy, Japan, Malaysia, Portugal, Romania, Spain, Turkey, United Kingdom, and Yugoslavia.

THE FRIENDS OF HARVEY GAUL COMPOSITION CONTEST, c/o The Friends of Harvey Gaul, Inc., 5914 Wellesley Avenue, Pittsburgh, Pennsylvania 15206. Founded in 1946, following the death of Harvey Gaul (1881–1945), a prominent figure in the musical and civic life of Pittsburgh by virtue of his career there as church organist, choral conductor, composer, teacher, and music critic. A composition contest offered annually with varying requirements as to musical media, general form, and length (1967: one-act opera; 1968: two categories, an art song, or a work for two harps and organ; 1969: a duo for organ and another instrument; 1970: choral work for women's voices; 1971: oboe work; 1972: song cycle; 1973: string quintet). Usually one prize ranging from $300 to $500 is offered. An application fee of $5 is required; deadline in 1972 was December 31. Open only to U.S. citizens. Only unpublished works accepted. Recent judges have been **Elie Siegmeister, Vincent Persichetti,** and **Philip James.**

GREENWOOD CHORAL AWARD, 2145 Central Parkway, Cincinnati, Ohio 45214. Sponsored by World Library Publications (see Music Publishers). Begun in 1967 and held irregularly. A contest for a new choral composition with first, second, and third prizes respectively $100, $50, and $25. Deadline is in February. The staff of World Library Publications act as judges in selecting the winning compositions.

GRINNEL–DETROIT GRAND OPERA SCHOLARSHIP, Detroit Grand Opera, Ford Auditorium, Detroit, Michigan 48226. The Grinnel Foundation of Music offers a $2,500 opera scholarship through the administration of the Detroit Grand Opera Association. It is offered in conjunction with the Metropolitan Opera National Council Regional Auditions programs with the same rules and regulations of those programs. Preliminary auditions are held (in 1969, they took place in the Ford Auditorium January 12; final auditions followed two weeks later); finalists are eligible for the Metropolitan Opera Regional Auditions. Age restrictions for applicants are as follows: sopranos, 19 to 30; altos, 19 to 32; tenors, 20 to 32; baritones, 20 to 32; basses, 20 to 35. Deadline for application varies but is generally in December. The Grinnel scholarship is for advanced study in voice and opera training under the supervision of the Scholarship Committee of the Detroit Opera. (See also Elizabeth Hodges Donovan Memorial Award.) Specific regional residency and nonresidency requirements are outlined by the Scholarship Committee and are available by writing to that organization.

JOHN SIMON GUGGENHEIM MEMORIAL FELLOWSHIPS, John Simon Guggenheim Memorial Foundation, 90 Park Avenue, New York, N.Y. 10016. An award for music composition or music theory or history research first established in 1925 (the Foundation also makes grants in other fields of art and research—see also under Organizations). The awards are monetary and vary with the need of each Fellow. The fellowships are awarded to "men and women of high intellectual and personal qualifications who have already demonstrated unusual capacity for productive scholarship or unusual creative ability in the fine arts." Fellows are generally between 30 and 45. The fellowships are granted usually for one year, during which time the Fellow may complete his work in any country. The fellowships are presented in two series; one for U.S. citizens and permanent residents of the United States and Canada, and the other for citizens and permanent residents of all other American states, the Caribbean, the French, Dutch, and British possessions in the Western Hemisphere, and the Philippines. Deadlines for applicants are: October 15 for U.S. and Canadian applicants; December 1 for the Western Hemisphere and Philippines applicants. Final selection of Fellows is made the following spring or summer. All appointments are made by a special Committee of Selection.

HOUSTON SYMPHONY YOUNG ARTISTS COMPETITION, Houston Symphony Orchestra, Jones Hall, Houston, Texas 77002. A competition open to student pianists, violinists, and cellists who are not yet 26 and who are American citizens or foreign citizens in the United States on student visas. Prizes are $1,500, $1,000, and $500 each and include an appearance with the Houston Symphony Orchestra. Sponsor of the contest is Pennzoil United, Inc. For the 1969 contest, the deadline for contestants' applications was October 15, 1968. The competitions were held November 26 and 27, the winners' performances taking place May 16, 1969 in Jones Hall. Judges for the 1969 event were **Vladimir Ashkenazy, Gary Graffman, Sidney Harth, Roy Harris,** and **André Previn.**

ILLINOIS OPERA GUILD AUDITIONS OF THE AIR (see WGN–ILLINOIS OPERA GUILD).

INTERCOLLEGIATE MUSIC FESTIVAL NATIONAL CHAMPIONSHIPS, P.O. Box 1275, Leesburg, Florida 32748. Sponsored by the Intercollegiate Music Festival (see also Festivals) at the same address with the financial support of TWA Airlines, Shulton, Inc., and Anheuser-Busch, Inc. Founded 1967. A competition in the field of popular music open to big bands, combos, vocal groups, composers and arrangers, and instrumental soloists who are college students and who must be taking six semester or nine quarter hours of courses at an American college or university at the time of applying for the championship. The purpose of the events is to provide recognition to the nation's best jazz–pop musicians and vocalists ("folk" music was added in 1969). The National Championship is awarded to the winning band, combo, or vocal group; scholarships are granted to the winning composer–arranger and 10 musicians. Deadlines for applicants is January 15; a small applicant's fee is required in some regional events. The regional competitions are held from February to April and comprise a series of Intercollegiate Jazz "Festivals." In 1970, the regionals took place in University of South Florida in Tampa; Villanova University at Villanova, Pennsylvania; University of Colorado at Boulder; Southern Illinois University at Edwardsville, Austin, Texas; and UCLA in Los Angeles. In 1969 some 10,000 students from 1,000 schools participated, from which 18 finalists were chosen for the National Championship Competition later held in St. Louis (May 22 to 24). The final event is also taped for broadcast over the channels of Voice of America. A National Advisory Board of some 36 figures in the music world supervise the Championships. Judges were: **Paul Horn, Oliver Nelson, Johnny Smith, Clark Terry,** and **M. E. Hall.** Recent winners have been: University of Illinois Jazz Band, Jac Murphy Trio of Southern Methodist University, Burgundy Street Singers of Kansas State University.

INTERNATIONAL HARP COMPETITION, c/o Director, **Aristid von Wurtzler,** International Harp Competition, Hartt College of Music, University of Hartford, 200 Bloomfield Avenue, West Hartford, Connecticut 06117. First held in 1969. Open to harpists of all nationalities who cannot be older than 34 on the opening day of the competition. The 1969 contest was held June 6 to 20 at Hartt College; deadline for contestant application was January 1. A fee of $10 is required for registration. The auditions consist of three stages of elimination; the third stage is limited to six finalists. First prize: $3,500; second prize: $2,000; third prize: $1,000. In addition, three gold medals, three silver medals, and three diplomas are awarded. Some travel grants are available to those contestants who may require them. The participants have the option of using their own instrument or one made available by the

College. Details regarding required compositions and other rules are available from the competition director. Judges consist of world-famous composers, conductors, harpists, et al.

INTERNATIONAL LOUIS MOREAU GOTTSCHALK COMPETITION, c/o Competition Secretariat, Pan-American Association for the Festival of the New World, 1028 Connecticut Avenue, Washington, D.C. 20036. Begun in 1969 under the sponsorship of the Organization of American States (OAS) in commemoration of the first centennial of the death of Gottschalk, a figure of importance in the music history of the Americas. The first competition was held in San Juan, Puerto Rico, from December 8 to 16, 1969. The competition is open to pianists and composers of all nations. There is no age restriction. Pianists may select their own programs, and composers are completely free to submit any type of composition. Prizes awarded are: one Gottschalk Gold Medal to the best pianist, gold medals to three composers in three age groups, and silver medals to two other composers. Cash awards include $4,500 to be shared by the winning pianist and two additional pianists selected as runners-up; each winning composer receives $1,000. Other benefits include a concert-tour offer to the best pianist and publication of the winning composers' works and their inclusion in the programs of future Festivals of the New World. Deadline for applications for the first event was October 1. A $10 entry fee was required of all applicants. The panel of judges was under the honorary chairmanship of **Pablo Casals.**

INTERNATIONAL TUBA ENSEMBLE COMPOSITION CONTEST, c/o University of Miami, School of Music, Coral Gables, Florida 33124. The sponsors of this contest offer three prizes, respectively for $200, $100, and $50, for the best original works composed for tuba ensembles exclusively. The compositions may be written for tuba trios, quartets, quintets, sextets, or octets. The 1969 competition's deadline date was April 1.

JOSKE SCHOLARSHIP AWARD OF THE SAN ANTONIO SYMPHONY ORCHESTRA. Sponsored by the Symphony Society of San Antonio (600 Hemisfair Plaza, San Antonio, Texas 78205) and the firm of Joske's of Texas (Alamo Plaza, San Antonio). Established in 1959 and offered annually. Categories of the contest include piano and orchestral instruments. Applicants must be of high school age or younger and residents of the San Antonio area (Bexar County). Two winners are selected, one in piano and one in an orchestral instrument, each receiving $200 and the opportunity for concert appearances with the San Antonio Symphony during the current season. Deadline for application is November 1. Auditions are held early the following year.

MINNA KAUFMANN-RUUD FOUNDATION DISTINGUISHED PERFORMANCE AWARDS, c/o Chatham College, Box 735, Pittsburgh, Pennsylvania 15232. Established in 1967 and open only to women singers who are between 18 and 29 and who have "professional promise, ability, and personal commitment." Three prizes of $1,000 each and two of $500 are awarded. Deadline for application is in February of each year. A review committee screens all applicants, who are then invited to compete in auditions in New York City. All audition expenses are borne by the applicant–candidate (accompanists are provided). The audition does not exceed ten minutes. The repertory presented by each singer should include a Mozart aria, a French or German art song, and a contemporary aria or song in English. The Kaufmann-Ruud Foundation also offers a $1,000 scholarship to women singers applicable toward study at Chatham College.

OTTO KINKELDY AWARD, c/o American Musicological Society, **Louise E. Cuyler,** School of Music, University of Michigan, Ann Arbor, Michigan 48105. Established in 1967 by the Society. Offers $400 for the "most distinguished work of musicological scholarship during one calendar year by an American or Canadian scholar." Award is granted in any given year to the winning work published two years earlier. Winner of the first award in 1967: **William W. Austin.** Winner in 1970 (for a 1969 publication): **Nino Pirotta.**

KATE NEAL KINLEY MEMORIAL FELLOWSHIP, c/o Dean **Allen S. Weller,** College of Fine and Applied Arts, Room 110, Architecture Building, University of Illinois, Urbana, Illinois 61801. Established in 1931 and offered annually. The Fellowship consists of the sum of $2,400 to be used by the recipient, during one academic year, in his area of study or work in the fine arts in America or abroad. Open to graduates of the above school or similar institutions of equal standing. Eligible are applicants who will not have reached their 25th birthday by June 1 of the year of application. Deadline for filing application is April 15. All branches of music are covered (the Fellowship also covers all branches of art and design or history in the field of architecture). Musician performers must submit to an examination; music scholars must submit completed projects as well as outlines for proposed work; composers should submit manuscripts of their works and tapes, if available.

KOSCIUSZKO FOUNDATION CHOPIN SCHOLARSHIPS, Kosciuszko Foundation, 15 East 65th Street, New York, N.Y. 10021. An annual award of $1,000 to a pianist, age 15 to 21, for study in the United States. Open only to unmarried U.S. citizens. Auditions take place in June. Deadline for application is March 1. Winner in 1967 was **Justin Blasdale.** First prize in 1971 was won by **Myung-Whun Chung.**

KOUSSEVITZKY INTERNATIONAL RECORDING AWARD, American International Music Fund, Inc. (sponsor), 30 West 60th Street, New York, N.Y. 10023. Founded in 1963, the award is a prize of $1,000 given in the name of the late conductor for the purposes of honoring living composers throughout the world by making recordings of their works in the symphonic genre widely available. The award is granted annually and is given to the work adjudged "best" which has been released for the first time on a commercial recording. In addition to the monetary award, the recording is given the widest possible distribution to education institutions, broadcasting stations, libraries, and so forth. In 1969, the judges, **Raymond Erickson, Alfred V. Frankenstein,** and **Alexander Goehr,** chose "Concerto for Orchestra," by **Roberto Gerhard** (Argo Records RG 553) out of 82 recorded works submitted. In 1970, judges **Alfred Frankenstein, Mario Davidovsky,** and **Ross Lee Finney** selected Stefan Wolpe's "Chamber Piece No. 1" and **Seymour Shifrin's** "Satires of Circumstance," both recorded on Nonesuch Records (H-71220). The 1971 prize went to **George Crumb** for his "Ancient Voices of Children," Nonesuch Records (H-71255).

LADO COMPOSITION COMMISSION, Lado, Inc., 745 Fifth Avenue, New York, N.Y. 10022. The Lado prizes were established in 1948; originally a competition, it is now a commission award to composers. A commission of $1,000 is granted biennially. Lado selects a musical group which in turn commissions a young composer to write a new work. The work is guaranteed a performance. Recent commissioned composers have been **David Amram, Jacob Druckman,** and **Robert Hall Lewis.** Judges and advisors have been: **Paul Creston, Norman Dello Joio, Herman Neuman,** et al.

EDGAR M. LEVENTRITT FOUNDATION INTERNATIONAL COMPETITION, 1 Passaic Street, Wood-Ridge, N.Y. 07075. A competition founded in 1940 open alternately to pianists and violinists (the 1973 event was for violinists). The Foundation is the sponsor. Contestants must be between 17 and 28; time is allowed for military service. Deadline for application is February 28, the final contest events taking place in late May. Winner receives a $1,000 honorarium plus an offer of an RCA Victor recording contract and appearances as soloist with such American orchestras as the New York Philharmonic, Chicago Symphony, Detroit Symphony, Cleveland Orchestra, Pittsburgh Symphony, and others. Finalist contestants not winning the first prize receive $500 and career management for a three-year period, with approximately 35 U.S. recital and orchestral engagements yearly. The latter contestants may compete at future Leventritt competitions. Winners are not chosen automatically. Each must, in the opinion of the jury, be of exceptional musical ability and be prepared to begin a high-level professional career immediately. (In 1967, for the first time, there were two winners.) Among the rules is the stipulation that a candidate's previous professional public performances be of sufficient number and importance in relation to his age. All hearings are in New York. The performer is expected to pay his own transportation and accommodations for the purpose of the contest. There is an application fee of $10. Past winners include pianists **Eugene Istomin, Alexis Weissenberg, Gary Graffman, Van Cliburn, John Browning,** and **Anton Kuerti** and violinists **David Nadien, Betty Jean Hagen,** and **Itzhak Perlman.** Recent winners have been: in 1971, **Alberto Reyes, James Fields, Verda Erman,** and **Kun-Woo Paik,** all pianists; **Joseph Kalichstein,** pianist (1969); and the double winners, **Kyung Wha Chung** and **Pinchas Zuckerman** (1967), both violinists. Judges serving are selected from the highest level of the music profession and in the past have included Sir John Barbirolli, **Leonard Bernstein, Lukas Foss, Zino Francescatti, Robert Goldsand, Nathan Milstein, Erica Morini,** George Szell, and Arturo Toscanini.

LIEDERKRANZ FOUNDATION SCHOLARSHIP FUND CONTEST, 6 East 87th Street, New York, N.Y. 10028. An annual vocal award consisting of $1,000 first prize, two $500 prizes, and three $250 prizes. Applicants must be between the ages of 18 and 35. Winners perform for the Liederkranz Opera and Concert Showcase. Contestants are expected to be students of promising ability who will use the award money to further their training. Advisory Board and judges have been: **Risë Stevens,** Lauritz Melchior, **Milton Cross, Thomas Martin, Gerhard Pechner,** et al. Deadline for applicants is January 15.

MACDOWELL COLONY FELLOWSHIPS, c/o Edward MacDowell Association, 1083 Fifth Avenue, New York, N.Y. 10028 or Peterborough, New Hampshire 03458. Grants are extended to writers, painters, sculptors, and composers for residence periods of one to three months in winter, or one to two months in summer, at the MacDowell Colony in Peterborough, New Hampshire (see under Organizations). The grant covers food, lodging, and studio at the Colony. A residence fee of $25 is required. Artists unable to pay this fee may apply for fellowship aid. Applications for summer residence should be filed before March 15; for winter, they should be filed at least 10 weeks before the initial date requested.

EDWARD GARRETT MCCOLLIN FUND COMPETITION, c/o **John H. Arnett,** 2116 Pine Street, Philadelphia, Pennsylvania 19103. Sponsored by the Musical Fund Society, 16 Booth Lane, Haverford, Pennsylvania 19041 (q.v.). The frequency of offering the competition is at the discretion of the Musical Fund Society. First established in 1925. In 1969, the event was a composition competition for the best work for chamber orchestra, with a prize of $2,500. The work had to be between 18 and 45 minutes long and neither published nor previously performed in public. Deadline for the submission of scores was March 1. Previous winners have been Bernard Rogers (1955), **Theodore Newman** (1964), among others.

LAURITZ MELCHIOR HELDENTENOR FOUNDATION, 111 West 57th Street, New York, N.Y. 10019. Founded in 1969 to encourage professional singers to undertake careers in opera as heldentenors. The first competition in 1969 resulted in the winners receiving a cash grant plus funds for living expenses during the planned period of training. There are no age restrictions for this award. Winners in 1969 were **William Cochran** and **John Russell.**

MERRIWEATHER POST CONTEST FOR VIOLINISTS AND CELLISTS, c/o Washington National Symphony, John F. Kennedy Center for the Performing Arts, Washington, D.C. 20566. Sponsored by the Washington National Symphony in honor of **Mrs. Merriweather Post May,** the sponsor of that orchestra's free concerts for school children visiting Washington. Established in 1956, it is held in conjunction with those concerts. First prize is $1,500 and a guest appearance with the Washington National Symphony; second prize: $750; third prize: $350. Deadline varies: sometime in March or April. Eligible are those cellists and violinists who have not yet reached their 20th birthday at the time of deadline. Contestants are required to play from memory a concerto and an unaccompanied work by Bach for which music may be used. Each contestant must be recommended by his music teacher, school principal, or a conductor. Competition events are usually held in May. Previous winners have been: **Susan Starr** (1957), **Shmuel Ashkenasi** (1958), **Lynn Harrell, James Oliver Buswell, IV** (1962), **Denis Brott** (1968), **Daniel Heifetz** (1969); 1971 winners were three violinists, **Dong-Suk Kang, Inez Hassman,** and **Ronald Copes,** winning respectively first, second, and third prize.

METROPOLITAN OPERA AUDITIONS, c/o Metropolitan Opera National Council, Lincoln Center Plaza, New York, N.Y. 10023. The Council is the sponsor of the Auditions. Established in 1953–54 to aid the careers of young singers of operatic potential. The competition is open to Americans, Canadians, and Australians under 32. However, the specific age restriction for each voice category is as follows: sopranos, 17 to 28; mezzo-sopranos and contraltos, 19 to 30; tenors, 20 to 30; baritones, 20 to 30; and basses, 20 to 32. Applicants need not have professional singing experience but must have voices with operatic potential as well as general musical and artistic ability. Each candidate must have the sponsorship of a school, music club, or voice teacher. Other regulations are published and available from the National Council. Auditions proceed upward from regional auditions to national semifinals and finals. Deadlines for application for the regionals vary; there is an application fee of $5 for all regions except the Eastern Region. The 16 regions and the cities representing them for the purpose of the auditions are as follows: Southwest (San Antonio), Central (Chicago), Southeast (Atlanta), Midwest (Kansas City), Tri-state (Bloomington, Indiana), Midsouth (Memphis), Mid-Atlantic (Washington, D.C.), Western (Los Angeles), New England (Boston), Upper Midwest (Minneapolis), Great Lakes (Cleveland), Northwest (Seattle), Rocky Mountain (Denver), Gulf Coast (New Orleans), Eastern (New York), Pan-Pacific (Honolulu). The dates of the auditions in 1969 ranged from the early part of February to the end of March. National semifinals and the national final are held respectively in November and April at the Metropolitan Opera House in New York. For each of the 16 regions, there are three prizes: $300, $200, and $100. (In 1973, 23 regional winners were chosen for the national semifinals.) The national awards consist of study grants of $2,000 each; about 12 are awarded annually. In addition, there is the possibility of a contract with the Metropolitan Opera (or the Metropolitan's Opera Studio) and the opportunity to study under a special training program established by the Kathryn Long Trust. A new precedent was formed in 1968 when two semifinalists were given Met contracts. Former first-place regional winners are eligible for grants (after auditions, but not as part of the contests) under the National Council's Educational Fund. This fund totals some $45,000. Judges at the final event are the Met's General Manager and his artistic staff. Past finalists include now well-known performers: **George Shirley, Grace Bumbry, Justino Díaz, William Walker, Shirley Verrett,** et al.

DIMITRI MITROPOULOS INTERNATIONAL MUSIC COMPETITION, c/o Federation of Jewish Philanthropies, 130 East 59th Street, New York, N.Y. 10022. Established in 1961 and sponsored by the Women's Division of the Federation of Jewish Philanthropies. The competition is in orchestral conducting and is open to any conductor between the ages of 20 and 33. It is considered an important contest in its category, with high standards and rigorous preliminary examinations. In 1971 32 participants from twenty nations moved through the various stages of the competition over a period of 14 days. The conductors lead the Orchestra of

America, the official orchestra of the competition. All stages of the examinations are held in New York. Prizes include four first prizes of $5,000 each; winners of the first prize also receive gold medals and appointments as assistant conductors with orchestras such as the New York Philharmonic, Washington National Symphony, the National Orchestra of the Monte Carlo Opera, and others (the appointment for each winner is determined by the committee of judges). Second, third, and fourth prizes are cash amounts of $2,500, $1,000, and $750, respectively. Deadline for application is usually in December (a registration fee of $10 is charged), the actual trials beginning the following January. Winners in 1968 were: **Boris Brott** (Canada), **Gaetano Delogu** (Italy), **François Huybrechts** (Belgium), **Farhad Mechkat** (Iran). Winners in 1969: **Alfredo Bonavera** (Italy), **Mesru Mehmedov** (Bulgaria), **Uri Segal** (Israel), **Michael Zearott** (United States). In 1970 first prizes went to **Phillippe Bender** (France), **Mario Benzecry** (Argentina), **David Gilbert** (United States). In 1971 winners were: **Jacques Delacote** (France), first prize; **Wolfgang Balzer** (Germany), second prize; **Timothy Reynish** (England), third prize. Recent judges have been: **Leon Barzin, Frank Brieff, Richard Burgin,** Vladimir Golschmann, **Antal Dorati,** Fausto Cleva, and others.

DIMITRI MITROPOULOS PIANO AWARDS, c/o Director, Mitropoulos Awards, Stephens College, Columbia, Missouri. Sponsored by the Helis Foundation, the awards are a first prize of $6,000, a second prize of $4,500, and a third prize of $3,750. These are given to selected women pianists who intend to enroll at Stephens College. Regional auditions are held in Minneapolis, Chicago, New York, San Francisco, Atlanta, and Columbia and are spread over a period of several months.

MICHAELS AWARD OF RAVINIA FESTIVAL, 108 North State Street, Chicago, Illinois 60602. Sponsored by the Ravinia Festival Association (see Music Festivals—Illinois). Founded in 1949. Held every two years (1967, 1969, 1971, etc.). Open to pianists or string instrumentalists from 18 to 29. Contestants must be American citizens or those who intend to become citizens. Deadline is generally in February of the contest year. Preliminary auditions are held during April and May in New York, Chicago, and San Francisco. Dates for these auditions are announced to the selected candidates. A maximum of seven candidates are selected from the preliminary auditions. The simifinal auditions consist of up to three candidates who perform a few days prior to the finals with the Chicago Symphony Orchestra on a regular program of the Ravinia Festival. Winner of first prize receives $1,500 to further his career and to cover subsequent travel expenses incurred in appearances with certain American symphony orchestras such as the Boston Pops, Chicago Symphony, Pittsburgh Symphony, San Francisco Symphony, and other major ensembles. Second and third prizes are $300 and $200, respectively. Well-known musicians are chosen to judge the events. Recent winners are: **Daniel Domb,** cellist (1965), **Michael Rogers,** pianist (1964), **Tong Il Han,** pianist (1962), **Marilyn Neeley,** pianist (1960). No winner was chosen for 1967.

MUSICIANS CLUB OF NEW YORK YOUNG ARTISTS AWARD, c/o Chairman, **Ruth Bowen,** 207 West 106th Street, New York, N.Y. 10023. Sponsored by the Musicians Club of New York, Inc., 30 West 60th Street, New York, N.Y. 10023. Established in 1956. Covers many categories of instrumental and vocal performance with a different category for each annual event (1966: woodwinds; 1967: harp; 1968: soprano and tenor; etc.) Contestants must be American-born. Age restrictions vary each year with the limits generally between 17 and 30 over the period of several contests. Prize amounts usually are for $500 and $300 as first and second prizes, respectively. (The 1968 event, however, granted two prizes of $400). Deadline for applications vary between early March or April. A $3 application fee is required. Auditions are in late April. Past winners include: **Jean Kraft,** soprano; **Armenta Adams,** pianist; **Augustin Anievas,** pianist; **Judith Raskin,** soprano; and others.

NAFTZGER YOUNG ARTISTS AUDITION, c/o Wichita Symphony Society, Inc., 105 West Second Street, Wichita, Kansas 67202. Sponsored by the Naftzger Fund for Fine Arts administered by the Wichita Symphony Society. A vocal and instrumental contest founded in 1940. Open to performers residing or attending school in Kansas or Oklahoma. Limited to those under 23 (restrictive date announced with each contest). Contestant must provide his own accompanist and appear at the auditions at his own expense. Musical works are performed by memory. Deadline for application is usually March 15. Preliminary and final auditions are generally held in late April. A minimum of six contestants are selected for the final audition. Exact performance requirements are available from the address above. Prizes: Naftzger Young Artist Award of $500 plus an appearance with the Wichita Symphony, Naftzger Instrumental Award of $250, and Naftzger Vocal Award of $250. In addition, there are two Naftzger Honorarium Awards of $100 each granted at the discretion of the judges. Some winners: **Nancy Border** (1967), **Patricia Wise** (1966).

NATIONAL ASSOCIATION OF TEACHERS OF SINGING ARTIST AWARDS, c/o NATS Executive Secretary, 250 West 57th Street, Room 725, New York, N.Y. 10019. (See Organizations.) Application can also be made to the Regional Governors of NATS. The award was formerly known as "Singer of the Year Award"; founded in 1954. The award is open to singers who have studied with NATS teachers (the exact length of study requirements and other details concerning eligibility, or for that matter, other aspects of the contest, are available from the Association). The contestant must have passed his 21st birthday but not have reached his 31st at the time of his regional audition. Allowance is made for the time any contestant might have spent in active military service. Application, along with a fee of $15, must be filed no later than October 15. The application must be sent to the Regional Governor of NATS. Auditions proceed from the state level to the regional to the National Convention (usually held after Christmas). The first-place winner is presented in recital at the following NATS National Convention. Winners are nominated by their degree of readiness for immediately undertaking a professional singing career. Monetary prizes are: $1,000 for first place, $600 for second, and $400 for third. (Most regional auditions offer also certain cash prizes and scholarship awards.)

NATIONAL FEDERATION OF MUSIC CLUBS SCHOLARSHIPS AND AWARDS, c/o Suite 1215, 600 South Michigan Avenue, Chicago, Illinois 60605. The NFMC dispenses an unusual number (over 40 in this listing) of awards and scholarship programs in music through competition. The awards and scholarship programs are categorized by the NFMC as follows: Biennial (3), Annual (2), Annual Student (11), Annual Junior (10), and Summer Music Scholarships (18). All of the award programs are under special chairmanships, and information about them is available from NFMC Headquarters (a published Scholarship Chart is available for a small charge). Except for the Young Artist Auditions (see below), applicants must be members of the NFMC either by group affiliation or individual membership. The following information, pertinent to 1968–1969, should serve as a guide for future awards.

Biennial NFMC: YOUNG ARTISTS AUDITIONS are held through state federations in odd-numbered years. They are open to pianists, violinists, and the vocal categories of man's voice, woman's voice, and oratorio singing. Candidates for the Auditions are expected to be ready for national concert careers. Age limits: instrumentalists, 18 to 30, vocalists, 23 to 35, with additional allowances for any time spent in the military services. The Auditions are open to citizens of the U.S. and Puerto Rico and foreigners residing and studying in the U.S. First prize consists of $1,500 in each category with such supplementary awards as paid solo appearances with orchestras. Winners perform at the NFMC Biennial Convention. (Prizes can be withheld if no one is accepted as winner.) Only one winner is permitted in each performing category. Auditions proceed from state, district, to national stages, the last consisting of semifinal and final competitions. Deadline for applicants is February 15. An entrance fee of $10 is charged for each of the three audition stages. The Young Artists Awards claim many past winners who have subsequently made important musical careers for themselves, among them: **Margaret Harshaw, Leonard Treash, Joseph Knitzer,** and **Rosalyn Tureck** (all winners in 1935), **Martha Lipton** (1939), **William Masselos** (1947), **Ivan Davis** (1955), and **Shirley Verrett** (1961). In 1969, winners of first prize, selected from 27 entrants, were **Henry Criz,** violinist; **Wojcieck Matuszewski,** pianist; **Bennie Middaugh,** baritone; and **Daniel Doig,** lyric tenor. . . . BIENNIAL STUDENT AUDITIONS, held in odd-numbered years through state federations; includes the categories of piano, organ, man's voice, woman's voice, violin, cello, orchestral winds (flute, oboe, clarinet, bassoon, French horn); participants must be between the ages of 16 and 25; time spent in military service is allowed against the age limits. A $200 award is made in each category. The winners perform at the Biennial Convention of the NFMC. Deadline is February 15. A $5 audition fee is charged. . . . CHATHAM COLLEGE OPERA WORKSHOP SCHOLARSHIP, a summer scholarship applicable at Chatham College (in Pittsburgh) Summer Opera Workshop. Open to operatic voices, male or female, but preference is given to male singers ages 21 to 25. Candidates for the awards must be able to sing in at least two foreign languages. There are 14 scholarships of $300 supported by the Workshop and two others of the same amount supported by the NFMC and its Pennsylvania federation. The scholarships are offered in odd-numbered years; deadline for application is February 15.

NFMC Annual Awards: VERA WARDNER DOUGAN AWARD, given to an NFMC winner who has attained professional excellence. The $500 award is presented at the Peninsula Music Festival, Fish Creek, Wisconsin. . . . ANNE M. GANNETT SCHOLARSHIP, grants to military veterans whose musical training has been interrupted; two $500 scholarships; deadline: March 15.

NFMC Annual Student Awards: COLLEGE–CONSERVATORY OF MUSIC SCHOLARSHIP IN VIOLONCELLO (University of Cincinnati), is a scholarship of $2,000 covering tuition, room, and board offered to a high school senior who has won in the State Annual Student Auditions; it is renewable for an additional three years. Deadline for application is February 15; an audition fee of $5 is charged each applicant. . . . EASTMAN SCHOOL OF MUSIC SCHOLARSHIPS (Rochester, New York); one available to performers on the violin, viola, cello, or bass and one to harpists who are state winners of student auditions for these instruments. The scholarships are full four-year tuition scholarships ranging in value from $100 to $1,500. Applicants must send tape recordings of their performing ability directly to Eastman School of Music; deadline is February 15. An audition fee of $5 is charged. . . . MARIE MORRISEY KEITH SCHOLARSHIP, an award made available to the various NFMC regions in rotating order (1969, Central Region; 1970, Western; 1971, Northeastern; etc.). Applicants must be between 16 and 25. Open to performers on piano, strings, orchestral winds, or singers. The award is $250 and is renewable for a second year. Deadline: February 15. The Guy Maier Memorial Award is a $50 supplementary grant to a pianist within this scholarship program. A $5 fee is required of all contestants. . . . MANHATTAN SCHOOL OF MUSIC SCHOLARSHIP (New York City), open to students aged 16 to 25 who are singers or performers on piano or string instruments. Offered are three full-tuition scholarships of $1,500 each, renewable for three years. Deadline: February 15. A fee of $5 is payable. . . . MILLIKIN UNIVERSITY SCHOLARSHIP (Decatur, Illinois), consists of four four-year scholarships of a total of $1,500 each; open to pianists, singers, string players, and performers on orchestral wind instruments, between the ages of 16 and 25. Deadline for application is February 15. Applicants must pay a $5 fee. . . . NEW SCHOOL OF MUSIC SCHOLARSHIP

(Philadelphia) grants five $1,000 scholarships each renewable for three to four years. Open only to string instrument players ages 16 to 25. Deadline is February. Applicants are required to submit tape recordings. A fee of $5 is charged each applicant. . . . OKLAHOMA COLLEGE OF LIBERAL ARTS SCHOLARSHIP (Chickasha, Oklahoma), a scholarship in organ, piano, violin, viola, voice, or music education open to high school graduates or transfer students from another college. The amount of $250 is awarded, with a limit of $125 applicable for any one semester. The grant is renewable for a second year. A $5 audition fee is charged. Deadline: February 15. . . . PEABODY CONSERVATORY OF MUSIC SCHOLARSHIP (Baltimore, Maryland), available to string players ages 16 to 25 who are high school graduates or who are in a high school graduating class. The award is for the amount of $1,200 and is renewable to four years. Deadline is February 15. A $5 fee is charged. . . . SHREVEPORT SYMPHONY-CENTENARY COLLEGE SCHOLARSHIP (Shreveport, Louisiana), open to students ages 16 to 25 (string players only). The awards are four $850-a-year scholarships, which may be renewed up to the B.A. degree. Room and board are included in the scholarships. A fee of $5 is charged to all applicants; deadline is February 15. . . . MUSIC THERAPY, DOROTHY DANN BULLOCK SCHOLARSHIP is granted to a high school senior or college freshman or sophomore for the study of music therapy at an accredited school; the $250 scholarship is renewable for a second year. Deadline is March 15. . . . YOUNG COMPOSERS AWARDS grants two cash prizes in each of three classes of composition, namely, sonata for various instrumental combinations, choral work, or vocal or piano solo piece. Awards range from $75 to $250 (supported by ASCAP). The age limits for the composers are 18 and 26. Deadline is April 1. An additional $150 Devora Nadworney Award is given for the best composition submitted in any of the categories.

NFMC Annual Junior Awards: JUNIOR COMPOSERS SCHOLARSHIP, open to compositions for strings, solo or ensemble, by students of high school age; the award of $350 is applicable toward the $800 tuition at the National Music Camp in Interlochen, Michigan (summer session); deadline: March 15. . . . JUNIOR COMPOSERS AWARDS for students through age 18 vary from $35 to $15 plus a performance of the winning work at the NFMC Biennial Convention; deadline is March 15. . . . JUNIOR CONSERVATORY CAMP SCHOLARSHIP (East Burke, Vermont) awards two half scholarships of $350 each towards tuition, room, and board for a seven-week summer term; open to student composers ages 12 to 15; deadline is April 1. Also available for students ages 15 to 18 is the Dorothy Burrell Scholarship of $700 to the same summer school; deadline for this scholarship is April 1. . . . JUNIOR FESTIVALS AWARDS are a number of prizes available to students up to age 18; details are obtainable from the NFMC. . . . CHARLES IVES SCHOLARSHIP (summers at Indian Hill Workshop, Stockbridge, Massachusetts), open to student composers ages 16 to 18; the award is $750 covering room, board, tuition, and private lessons; deadline: April 1. . . . STILLMAN KELLEY SCHOLARSHIP, annually available in rotating order to the four NFMC regions; grants a $250 yearly scholarship (there is also a second-place award of $200) renewable to four years, to instrumentalists up to the age of 17; deadline: February 15. . . . FRANCES ROGERS SCHOLARSHIP (Indian Hill Workshop, Stockbridge, Massachusetts), is a summer study scholarship of $750 covering room, board, tuition and is available to a boy singer aged 16 to 18; deadline is April 1. . . . FRED WARING AWARD grants $50 and a performance at the NFMC Biennial Convention to a winning composition written for vocal solo or ensemble (an instrumental work is acceptable if no outstanding vocal work is submitted); open to student composers up to the age of 18 inclusively; deadline is April 1. . . . LAURA K. WILSON MEMORIAL AWARD, granted for a piano composition; $50 award and a performance at the Biennial Convention of the NFMC; open to composers between the ages of 16 and 18; deadline for application is April 1. . . . JUNIOR DANCE SCHOLARSHIP (Indian Hill Workshop, Stockbridge, Massachusetts), is available to a male dancer age 16 to 18 for summer study at the Workshop. The award totals $750. Deadline is March 15.

NFMC Summer Music Scholarships: Additional information about the following summer school scholarships may be had by writing directly to the addresses and administrators included with each school. ARIZONA ALL STATE HIGH SCHOOL FINE ARTS CAMP (in Tempe, Arizona), c/o **Mrs. Miles A. Dresskell,** Music Department, Arizona State University, Tempe, Arizona; open to voice or instrumental students of high school age; awards two $95 scholarships toward tuition and board during the two weeks (June to July) of the summer camp; deadline for application is May 15. . . . ASPEN MUSIC SCHOOL (Aspen, Colorado), c/o Music Associates of Aspen, Inc., 111 West 57th Street, New York, N.Y. 10019; an award of $400 toward tuition is granted students of strings who are not older than 25 as of March 15. The summer school lasts for nine weeks, July to August. Deadline for application is April 15. . . . BERKSHIRE MUSIC CENTER (Tanglewood, Massachusetts) offers the ADA HOLDING MILLER SCHOLARSHIP of $500 toward tuition (matched by the Camp) during the eight-week summer school session at the Center; the scholarship is available to students working in choral or instrumental music, or opera. Students must be between 18 and 25 as of March 15. Address: c/o **Harry Kraut,** Symphony Hall, Boston, Massachusetts; deadline: April 15. . . . CHATHAM COLLEGE OPERA WORKSHOP SCHOLARSHIP (Pittsburgh, Pennsylvania) offers an NFMC scholarship in opera singing to young singers aged 21 to 25; the amount is $300 and is offered biennially in the odd-numbered years. The scholarship applies to four weeks of study in July. Address: **Mrs. Louis A. Dunlap,** 918 N. Jefferson Avenue, Pulaski, Virginia 24301. Deadline: February 15. . . . CHAUTAUQUA MUSIC SCHOOL (Chautauqua, New York), c/o **Joseph C. Clarke,** Director of Education, Chautauqua Summer School, Chautauqua, New York 17422; offers six scholarships of $150 each for full tuition in each category of voice, piano, violin, organ, and flute. Maximum age limit for applicants is 25 in all categories. Minimum age is 16 except for violinists, who have no minimum age requirements. The summer school lasts eight weeks, from July to August. Deadline for applicants is June 1. . . . STEPHEN COLLINS FOSTER MUSIC CAMP (Richmond, Kentucky), c/o **Nick Koenigstein,** Eastern Kentucky University, Richmond, Kentucky 40475. String players of junior and senior high school age may apply before March 15 for the $150 scholarship, which covers tuition, room, and board during the four weeks of summer camp. . . . INSPIRATION POINT (Eureka Springs, Arkansas) HAZEL POST GILLETTE SCHOLARSHIP, c/o **Mrs. Harry A. Spradling,** 1410 Grand Avenue, Carthage, Missouri 64836. The award of $295 covers tuition, room, and board for a student of high school or college age desiring to study opera at Inspiration Point for six weeks in the summer; deadline: April 15. . . . INTERNATIONAL MUSIC CAMP (Peace Gardens, North Dakota) offers the AGNES JARDINE SCHOLARSHIPS for high school students of band, orchestra, twirling, music drama; information address: International Music Camp, University Station, Grand Forks, North Dakota, attention: **Dr. Utgard.** Partial scholarships ($500) for room, board, and tuition are available; deadline: March 15. . . . KNEISEL HALL (Blue Hill, Maine), c/o **Miss Marianne Kneisel,** 190 Riverside Drive, New York, N.Y. 10024; offers a $350 tuition scholarship (matched by the camp) to string players for eight weeks of summer study. Age limitations are 10 and 22; deadline (personal auditions or recordings): end of March. . . . MEADOWBROOK SUMMER SCHOOL OF MUSIC (Rochester, Michigan), c/o **Mrs. Vernon L. Venman,** 499 N. Eton Road, Birmingham, Michigan 48008. Offers a $200 tuition scholarship to string players (11th graders to age 25) for summer study. Deadline: March 1. . . . MEADOWMOUNT CAMP (Westport, New York), c/o **Ivan Galamian,** Director, 170 West 73rd Street, New York, N.Y. The scholarships available are three partial scholarships of $100 each for tuition, room, and board; the student must pay the balance of the costs. Open to string students only, ages 10 to 25. The Camp is held for eight weeks from the last week in June. Deadline for application is March 15. . . . MUSIC ACADEMY OF THE WEST (Santa Barbara, California) offers scholarships in the study of opera and voice technique. Information about the scholarships may be had by writing to **Martial Singher** (who directs the summer opera department at the Academy), 1821 Delancey Place, Philadelphia, Pennsylvania 19103. There are no age restrictions for applicants, but an audition is necessary. A partial scholarship of $200 is offered. Deadline: March 15. . . . NATIONAL MUSIC CAMP (Interlochen, Michigan) offers two scholarships of $400 each for high school students who either play piano or an orchestral instrument or who sing; the Reader's Digest Foundation at the Camp has established $1,600 for partial scholarships in the same categories. Deadline: February 15. Information about either scholarship division may be had from **Mrs. M. Cedric Dowling,** 1223 Loeser, Jackson, Michigan 49203. The National Music Camp is scheduled for eight weeks from July to August. . . . OGLEBAY OPERA WORKSHOP (Wheeling, West Virginia) offers, through the NFMC, a $230 full scholarship in operatic coaching to a proficient pianist (no age restriction) who already has experience in accompanying singers. The applicant must know a foreign language and have a working knowledge of at least six operas; the study sessions last four weeks in July. Deadline for application is June 1. Information address: **Boris Goldovsky,** New England Conservatory of Music, Boston, Massachusetts. . . . ROCKY RIDGE MUSIC CENTER (Estes Park, Colorado) gives a scholarship opportunity (the sum is $125) to junior or senior high school music students; information may be had from **Hilda Aspinall,** Executive Secretary, 132 South 13th Street, Suite 201, Lincoln, Nebraska. Requests for scholarship aid should be sent to the Foundation Office, 9600 West 11th Avenue, Lakewood, Colorado. The summer session at the Center lasts seven weeks. Deadline: March 15. . . . SEWANEE MUSIC CENTER (Sewanee, Tennessee), c/o **Martha McCrory,** Director, Sewanee Summer Music Center, University of the South, Sewanee, Tennessee. Available are two partial scholarships of $150 each applicable toward tuition, room, and board. Students may be of high school or college age. The summer session lasts five weeks; deadline is April 15. . . . TRANSYLVANIA MUSIC CAMP (Brevard, North Carolina) offers through the NFMC the HINDA HONIGMAN SCHOLARSHIP. Address: c/o **Mrs. Louise Young Workman,** 2245 Crescent Avenue, Charlotte, North Carolina 28207. The scholarship is open to a band or orchestra instrumentalist between the ages of 12 and 18. The $350 award covers partial tuition, room, and board for the six-week session. Deadline: April 1. . . . PACIFIC NORTHWEST MUSIC CAMP (Seattle, Washington). Orchestral instrumentalists (percussionists excepted) ages 13 to 21 are eligible for a $120 full scholarship for three weeks study in August. Application (deadline is March 15) is to: Seattle Youth Symphony Office, 416 Shafer Building, 523 Pine Street, Seattle, Washington 98101.

NATIONAL MUSIC LEAGUE (AUDITIONS), c/o National Music League, Inc., 130 West 56th Street, New York, N.Y. 10019. (See Concert Managements.) The League is a nonprofit concert management. It offers auditions to singers and instrumentalists who are permanent U.S. residents under 32 and who are without career management, toward obtaining a League contract for concert management. After the artist's reputation is established, he is released to commercial management. Maximum management service time is five years. The performer may terminate his contract at will by giving prior notice. The management service of the League consists of preparing publicity materials, advertising and programming advice, etc. Bookings are with symphony orchestras, choral groups, colleges, clubs, regional managers throughout the country and certain areas abroad. Former League artists include: **William Masselos, Carroll Glenn, Sidney Harth,**

Berl Senofsky, Betty Allen, Grace Hoffman, to mention a very few. Audition judges over the years have been: **Alexander Brailowsky, John Browning, Claude Frank, Walter Hendl, Eugene Istomin, Max Rudolf, Norman Scott,** et al.

WALTER W. NAUMBURG FOUNDATION AWARDS, c/o The Walter W. Naumburg Foundation, Inc., 155 West 65th Street, New York, N.Y. 10023. Periodically, the Foundation provides awards to performers of promising ability by financing debut recitals and granting funds for career development. Beyond these general facts, few details are readily available from the Foundation. Undoubtedly, they are provided when award events are actually scheduled. Also, since 1949, the Foundation has selected annually a composition by an American composer to be recorded on Columbia Records. These selections are not made competitively but are chosen by a jury composed mainly of music critics and writers, the majority of whom are from the area of New York City.

NATIONAL COMPOSITION AWARD, THE OHIO STATE UNIVERSITY SCHOOL OF MUSIC, 1899 North College Road, Columbus, Ohio 43210. Founded in 1967 and sponsored by the Ohio State University School of Music. The award is given to winning compositions, the category of which changes annually: 1967—work for brass ensemble, 1968—a work for men's glee club, 1969—a solo organ composition, etc. First, second, and third prizes are $200, $100, and $50, respectively. Applicants pay a fee of $2. Deadline varies (in 1969 it was April 1st), as well as the limitation on the length of the works to be submitted. The works must not have been published or publicly performed previously. Manuscripts are submitted anonymously with a *nom de plume* assigned to the work. More than one work may be submitted by a composer. Open only to American composers. The winning works are chosen within about two months after deadline date and performed shortly after announcement of winners. Judges are not members of the faculty of Ohio State University.

OLDS SCHOLARSHIP IN MUSIC COMPETITION, c/o Chicago Musical Instrument Co., 7373 North Cicero Avenue, Lincolnwood, Illinois 60646. Sponsored by F. E. Olds & Son, Inc., a subsidiary of Chicago Musical Instrument Co. (q.v. under manufacturers of brass and woodwind instruments). Founded in 1957, the contest is open to all juniors, seniors, and graduate students in accredited schools or departments of music at the college level. The prizes of $500, $350, and $200 are awarded to the best three theses, term papers, or articles written during the academic year of the date of the contest on the subject of instrumental music. The jury of four music educators, in deciding on winners, seek those papers that "show the greatest evidence of original thinking, sound research and intelligent objectives and which are prepared and presented in a readable and publishable form." The prize amounts are applicable toward tuition in an accredited music school at any one time during a three-year period after the date of the award. Under certain conditions, the awards are payable in cash. Details of other conditions, such as publishing rights accrued to F. E. Olds & Son, Inc. and the authors, are available from the contest committee. Entries must be mailed between April 15 and June 30 of the year of the contest. Winners are announced no later than October 15.

GREGOR PIATIGORSKY TRIENNIAL ARTIST AWARD, c/o Secretary, Violoncello Society, Inc., 119 West 57th Street, New York, N.Y. 10019. Established in 1961, the latest award covers the period 1968 to 1971. The award consists of a grant of $2,000 to an American-born cellist (or a naturalized citizen) who will apply the award toward his professional advancement with the guidance of the Violoncello Society. No age limit. Application deadlines vary, but generally the closing date takes place in the first year of the three-year period covered by the award. Each applicant must play a complete recital, which must include one of the unaccompanied suites by Bach. In addition, he is expected to play two complete concertos, one taken from the standard literature and one contemporary work. This audition takes place in New York City before a panel of well-known cellists. The award winner receives the sponsorship of the Violoncello Society, which may entail a New York recital, an appearance with an orchestra, and other performance opportunities. Past winners: **Douglas Davis, Lynn Harrell,** and **Stephen Kates.** Winner for the triennial ending in 1971 was **Nathaniel Rosen.**

COMPOSITION CONTEST FOR PERCUSSION QUARTET, Center of the Creative and Performing Arts, State University of New York at Buffalo, Music Department, Baird Hall, Buffalo, N.Y. 14214. Sponsored by the above school and The New Percussion Quartet. The award was first established in September, 1967. Deadline for submitting compositions was May 1, 1969. Subsequent contests have not been planned. Prize: $1,000 and publication by Music for Percussion, Inc. (see Publishers). No age or nationality restrictions for composers. Compositions had to be scored for percussion quartet with a duration of from 10 to 15 minutes. Judges for the first event were: **Lukas Foss, Paul Price,** and **Allen Sapp.**

PHILADELPHIA A.G.O. COMPOSITION CONTEST, c/o **Henry Cook,** 22 East Chestnut Hill Avenue, Philadelphia, Pennsylvania 19118. Sponsored by the Philadelphia Chapter of the American Guild of Organists, the contest is for a new composition for organ and brass ensemble not exceeding five instruments and lasting about 10 minutes. The work must be suitable for church festival or concert use. A $1,000 cash award goes to the winning composer; the prize composition is given its premiere in a special concert under the auspices of the Philadelphia Chapter. Deadline for submitting works in 1969 was May 1.

PULITZER PRIZE IN MUSIC, c/o Advisory Board on the Pulitzer Prizes, Graduate School of Journalism, Columbia University, New York, N.Y. 10027. An annual award of $1,000 "for distinguished musical composition in the larger forms of chamber, orchestra or choral music, or for an operatic work (including ballet), by a composer of established residence in the United States which has had its first American performance during the year." Works are nominated for consideration for the award generally by performing groups, publishers, etc. Qualified works are those which received their American premieres during the year from the previous April 1 to March 31 of the year of the award. The nomination (placed before March 1, generally) is made by submitting a completed nomination form, information concerning place and date of performance, a copy of the score and a recording of the piece when required, and an agreement from the performing group to allow the Advisory Board, at its discretion, to purchase tickets for reviewing a live performance of the nominated work. The winning work and composer is announced on the first Monday in May. A composer may receive the award more than once. The Prize has had widespread recognition in the United States (for past winners, see Composers).

ROCHESTER FESTIVAL OF RELIGIOUS ARTS MUSIC COMPETITION, c/o Rochester Festival of Religious Arts, 50 Plymouth Avenue, North, Rochester, N.Y. 14614. The contest has been offered since 1959. Prizes are awarded to three winning compositions written according to the specifications of each year's competition (in 1969, the contest was for a hymn from one to four parts with organ or brass ensemble accompaniment). Prize amounts vary. In 1969, the first, second, and third prizes were $100, $75, and $50 and possible publication. Compositions are expected to be suitable for performance during church service. In 1969, the deadline for entries was March 1. The Festival assumes the right to perform the work for a few months without financial profit.

ROTH ORCHESTRA COMPOSITION AWARD, c/o Chairman, 1702 Rangely Avenue, Dayton, Ohio 45403. Established in 1961 and sponsored by the National School Orchestra Association. (Prize and expenses are supported by a gift from **Heinrich Roth** and the NSOA.) A prize of $1,000 is awarded the best composition written for the average junior or senior high school orchestra in any genre: full orchestra, string orchestra, solo or ensemble with orchestra, etc. Compositions must not be longer than seven minutes. Deadline is usually at the end of May. Composers must submit a set of instrumental parts as well as score. Entries are performed at the annual NSOA convention, where they are judged by the contest chairman, board members of the NSOA, and others. An attempt is made to have the winning composition published by interested publishers.

SAN FRANCISCO OPERA AUDITIONS, c/o San Francisco Opera Association, Opera House, San Francisco, California 94102. An annual event begun in 1954 to encourage young professional opera singers. Sponsored by the Merola Fund, San Francisco Opera Guild chapters, and other organizations in each audition region. Open only to residents of western United States and western Canada. Age limitations are 20 and 32 for women, and 22 and 34 for men, inclusive (proof by birth certificate required). Auditions move upward from preliminary auditions to regional finals to San Francisco Opera finals. Preliminary and regional auditions are held in San Diego, Los Angeles, San Francisco, Sacramento, Portland, Seattle, Vancouver, Phoenix, Denver, Salt Lake City, Dallas, Honolulu, and other cities during March and April of each year. (Many regionals have their own awards.) Audition finals take place in the Opera House in San Francisco in June. The Opera orchestra is used at these auditions and the public is invited. Two winners are chosen. First prize is the James H. Schwabacher Memorial Award of $1,500 and the second prize is the Florence Bruce Award of $1,000. A special award, the William Kent, Jr. Memorial Award of $500 is given to a deserving contestant singing in the finals. The two winners sing in an orchestral concert with members of the San Francisco Symphony during its summer concert season at Sigmund Stern Grove in San Francisco and may be given the opportunity to sing with the San Francisco Opera (during the year of the contest), the Spring Opera, and the touring Western Opera Theater (see Opera Companies). Additional opportunities are the Merola Opera Program, which is a summer training program open to all qualifying contestants; a $1,000 Gropper Memorial Award, given to a selected participant in the Program on the basis of merit and financial need; and a $250 "Il Cenacolo" Award in memory of Gaetano Merola. All candidates in all levels of the Auditions are judged by professional standards. Deadline for applications is approximately March 1 of each year.

MARCELLA SEMBRICH SCHOLARSHIP IN VOICE, administered by The Kosciusko Foundation, 15 East 65th Street, New York, N.Y. 10021. Established in 1968 and offered every two years (even-numbered years). Open to American singers from 19 to 25 as of March 1 in the year of the contest. The winning contestant receives a $1,000 award applicable toward further study of singing either privately or in school. Deadline for application is March 1. Auditions begin the following May. The applicant is required to submit a tape recording of his singing. An invitation to appear for audition is based on a hearing of the tape. The repertory to be sung must include one or more Polish songs.

ARTHUR SHEPHERD COMPOSITION CONTEST, c/o Case Western Reserve University Music House, 11115 Bellflower Road, Cleveland, Ohio 44106. Sponsored by the Ohio Music Teachers Association, Cuyahoga Section. Founded in 1960 as a memorial to Arthur Shepherd, composer and former Chairman of the Music Department of Western Reserve University. Presented annually, but the award has been withheld in some years. Contest is open to composers who are residents of Ohio or have had an established residence in the state for at least three consecutive years. The award is in two parts: a Senior Award of $200 and a Student Award of $50, the latter open only to students in Ohio. Age limits are 23 years or older for the Senior Award and under 23 for the Student Award as of January 1, the annual deadline date for applicants. Entry fees are necessary for all applicants. The category of composition required for each contest varies according to a fixed rotating pattern consisting of four categories, each one applicable every four years. Precise details, rules, and regulations are all available from the contest chairman. Past winners include **Klaus G. Roy, Noel Lee,** and **Raymond Wilding-White.** Judges have been: **Walter Piston, Halsey Stevens, Peter Mennin, Daniel Pinkham, Vincent Persichetti,** among aothers.

SIGMA ALPHA IOTA INTER-AMERICAN MUSIC AWARDS, sponsored by Sigma Alpha Iota fraternity and its Foundation. Address: SAI American Music Awards, Director, 3201 Rowland Place, N.W., Washington 20008. Founded in 1948 and formerly known as the American Music Awards. A composition contest offering two awards in three-year cycles (1965–1968, 1969–1971, 1972–1974, etc.). Categories of compositions vary. The 1971 award required a choral composition for women's voices and one for mixed chorus, each offering a $300 award. The 1974 awards are for instrumental trio and a work for women's voices. The contest is open to any composer from North, Central, or South America between the ages of 18 and 40. Only previously unpublished or unperformed works are permitted in the contest. A composer may compete for both prizes as well as enter more than one work for both categories. Entry fee is $3. Compositions are submitted anonymously according to fixed rules; deadline is approximately March 1 in the final year of the three-year period. Winners are announced at the National Convention of Sigma Iota following the close of the contest. In addition to the cash prizes, the winners receive the benefit of publication in either of two series, the *Sigma Alpha Iota Modern Music Series* (published by Carl Fischer, Inc.) or the *American Music Awards Series* (published by C. F. Peters Corp.), both sponsored by the fraternity. The winning compositions are actively promoted throughout the 260 or more chapters of the fraternity by performances, study, gifts of the series to libraries, etc. All royalties remain with the composers. A unique feature of the contest are the "gift-compositions" written by the contest's judges, who are well-known composers. These works are also published in either of the two series, thereby linking the names of established composers with those of the contestants. Past winners have been: **Mel Powell, Kenneth Gaburo, Richard Willis.** Composer-judges include: **Alan Hovhaness, Ulysses Kay, Howard Hanson, Roy Harris, Ross Lee Finney,** and others.

SINGING CITY CONDUCTING FELLOWSHIP, Fellowship and Apprenticeship, Singing City, Inc., 35 South 9th Street, Philadelphia, Pennsylvania 19107. Supported by a grant from the Samuel S. Fels Fund of Philadelphia and administered by Singing City, Inc. and its complex of choral groups (see under Choral Groups). Established in 1966, the award is an opportunity for postgraduate study in choral conducting, with the support of a complete scholarship plus $250 monthly subsistence allowance for one year. Fellowship candidates must have a minimum of a year's teaching and/or conducting experience, must have been undergraduate and graduate music majors with good vocal and conducting technique and the ability to play a keyboard instrument. Also available is an Apprenticeship Program offering a full year's scholarship to a selected candidate with undergraduate music major training and talent in conducting and vocal and keyboard performance. The programs emphasize choral music with its attendant formal and in-service studies (score reading, conducting various choral groups, administrative procedures, workshops) and community service, the latter including opportunities to work with social, religious, and educational agencies. Deadline for applicants is February 1 for scholarships covering the following academic year. Judges and advisors are **Elaine Brown,** founder and director of Singing City, and her staff. The Fellowship program is offered annually.

SOCIETY FOR THE PUBLICATION OF AMERICAN MUSIC AWARD. A composition award offered since 1919. With the dissolution of the Society in 1969, the award has been discontinued. (The in print compositions published by the Society are distributed by Theodore Presser Company—see Music Publishers.)

RHETA A. SOSLAND CHAMBER MUSIC AWARD, c/o Conservatory of Music, University of Missouri at Kansas City, 4420 Warwick Boulevard, Kansas City, Missouri 64111. Founded in 1960 and sponsored by the Conservatory. An award of $1,000 is given to the composer of the winning original composition for string quartet. Open to all residents of the United States, Canada, and Mexico. No limitations are placed on the form, style, or length of the work submitted. The work must not have been publicly performed or published and the composer must be prepared to supply instrumental parts upon request. Other details are available from the contest headquarters. A $2 entry fee is required. Once held annually, the award is now biennial (the years involved are 1965, 1967, 1969, etc.). Deadline is usually August 1. The winning work is performed publicly at a special concert a few months after the close of the contest. Additional performance rights are retained by the University for non-profit concert or recording purposes for a period of six months after the final judging. The composer retains all other rights to royalties, however. Judges have been Quincy Porter and **Otto Luening.** Past winners include **David Diamond, John La Montaine,** and **Carolyn Conyers.**

SOUNDS OF YOUNG AMERICA, c/o Room 458, Union Pacific Building Annex, Salt Lake City, Utah 84111. A contest open to "collegiate" composers and writers. The musical categories are popular music, "folk" music, and jazz. A three-day performance event presents all entries performed by well-known pop music figures. Winning composers receive scholarships and national titles. Applicants can apply to the above address.

LEO SOWERBY MEMORIAL COMPOSITION AWARD, c/o John Walker, F.A.G.O., 410 South Michigan Avenue, Chicago, Illinois 60605. The Award was founded in 1969 by the Chicago Chapter of the American Guild of Organists to honor the memory of the late composer, Leo Sowerby, who was long associated with the musical life of Chicago and was a composer of many works for church use. The prize is $500 plus publication by H. W. Gray, Inc. of New York for the best sacred cantata for mixed voices and organ (plus optional small orchestra) suitable for performance by a moderate size chorus (30 to 40 voices) and lasting between 20 and 30 minutes. The contest is open to any composer. All works must be submitted under a *nom de plume;* a fee of $2 is charged each contestant. Deadline for the first contest was October 1, 1969.

STERLING STAFF CONCERTS INTERNATIONAL COMPETITION, c/o Chairman, **Claudette Sorel,** 333 West End Avenue, New York, N.Y. 10023. Sponsored by Mu Phi Epsilon Memorial Foundation, 560 North First Street, San Jose, California 95112 and founded in 1964 (see Organizations also). An award open every two years (1968, 1970, etc.) to singers, pianists, organists, accompanists, and performers on woodwind and string instruments. Only initiated members in good standing of Mu Phi Epsilon, an international professional music sorority, can apply. Instrumentalists must be between 18 and 25; singers: between 18 and 28. Deadline for entrant application is January 1 for each year of the contest. By March 15, the entrant must have submitted a number of materials to the Contest Chairman including tape recordings, programs of concert appearances, recommendations, entrance fee ($5), and other items. The applicant is informed by June 15 whether or not he is to appear at the National Final Auditions. The Final Auditions are held just prior to the sorority's biennial convention in the summer during which the final winners perform. Prizes are unique: The winners receive two-year concert tours of the United States giving some 60 concerts and receiving $25 gratuity for each concert performed. The concerts are sponsored and presented by local chapters of Mu Phi Epsilon. They are intended to provide concert experience to the winners who are moving between musical studies and a professional career. Winners in 1968: pianists, **Marian Buck-Lew** and **Miyaka Nakaya,** and organist **Karen Laycock.** Judges have been: **Adele Addison, Paul Creston, Brooks Smith, Martin Bookspan,** and others. Complete details concerning required repertory and rules are available from contest chairman.

STUDENT COMPOSERS AWARDS, c/o Director, SCA Project, Broadcast Music, Inc. (BMI), 40 West 57th Street, New York, N.Y. 10019. Established in 1951 and supported by BMI. Prizes are offered annually to composers under 26 residing and studying music anywhere in the Western Hemisphere. Prizes, granted at the discretion of judges who are professional composers, range from $250 to $2,000. The total amount of prizes granted annually varies to as much as $15,000. BMI donates $7,500 annually, but the full amount is not necessarily expended for each annual contest. Any unexpended sums are added to the following year's contest. The number of prizes varies each year (14, 19, etc.). Up to the 1971 awards, 173 student composers have won the prizes. Deadline for applications is February 15. Award announcements take place the following June. The purpose of the awards is to "encourage the creation of concert music by student composers." No limitation is imposed on submitted compositions regarding length of work, style, genre, or instrumentation. Composers may enter up to three works (but no composer can be granted more than one prize), which need not have been composed during the year of the award. All compositions are submitted anonymously according to a specific procedure, details of which are available from the SCA Director. Permanent chairman of the judging panel is **William Schuman.** Past judges have been: **Ernst Krenek, Boyd Neel, Chou Wen-Chung, Daniel Pinkham, Leon Kirchner,** and others. Names selected from the roster of past winners are the following established composers: **Ramiro Cortes, George Crumb, Mario Davidovsky, Teo Macero, José Serèbrier, David Ward Steinman, Charles Wuorinen,** among others.

WILLIAM MATHEUS SULLIVAN MUSICAL FOUNDATION, INC. AWARDS, c/o the Foundation located at 36 West 44th St., New York, N.Y. 10036. Noncompetitive grants "to aid and assist individual advanced vocalists who require financial assistance in furtherance of their careers." Cash amounts vary depending upon the qualifications and needs of the recipient. Recommendations from established musicians and subsequent auditions are required.

THORNE MUSIC FUND GRANTS AND FELLOWSHIPS, c/o Thorne Music Fund, Inc., 116 East 66th Street, New York, N.Y. 10021. Founded in 1965 (see Organizations). Only composers are considered for grants by the Thorne Music Fund. The grants or fellowships cannot be applied for; instead they are awarded on the decision of a committee of advisors. They are intended to assist "mature American composers of recognized accomplishment." The award amounts vary. In 1968, three composers, **Kenneth Gaburo, John Cage,** and **Lester Trimble,** each received $5,000 a year for a two-year fellowship; **Harry Partch** and **Howard Swanson** received special grants of $6,000 each; **Mario Davidovsky** received a $3,000 commission for a new work. Past recipients include **Ben Weber, Stefan Wolpe, Lou Harrison,** and **Peggy Glanville-Hicks.** The Fund's advisory committee has included **Milton Babbitt, Leonard Bernstein, Aaron Copland, Peter Mennin, Gunther Schuller, Virgil Thomson,** and others.

VAN CLIBURN INTERNATIONAL QUADRENNIAL PIANO COMPETITION, P.O. Box 17421, Fort Worth, Texas 76102. Founded in 1962 (the idea was formed in 1958) by **Irl Allison** and the late Grace Lankford in honor of the pianist, **Van Cliburn.** Sponsored by the National Guild of Piano Teachers, Austin, Texas; Fort Worth Piano Teachers Forum; Texas Christian University, Fort Worth; the Fort Worth Chamber of Commerce; and the Junior League of Fort Worth. The first contest was held in 1962, the second in 1966, the third, after only a three-year interim, in 1969 from September 29 to October 12, and the fourth from September 17 to September 30, 1973. Subsequent contests will take place every four years. Contestants may be from any nation and must be between 17 and 28. The purpose of the contest is to advance the careers of highly talented young performers. The scope, pace, and standards of the contest are such that only those contestants who are ready to embark upon professional careers immediately can hope to enter. Deadline for application to the 1969 event was April 1; for the 1973 event: June 15. A $20 fee is required. The first prize is $10,000 (payable in four yearly installments); the winner of this prize also receives a concert engagement in Carnegie Hall in New York plus other engagements throughout the United States, and a possible management contract with the firm of Hurok Concerts, Inc., New York, for performances in Latin America, Canada, the United States and possessions. Second prize is $6,000 (payable in three annual installments). The third to sixth prizes are respectively: $2,000, $1,500, $1,000, and $750. Other awards beyond the six major prizes are: $600 donated by **Van Cliburn** for the best chamber music performance; $500 gold watch given to the best performer of the piece especially commissioned for the contest; a Pan-American Union prize of $500 and a recital in Hall of Americas in Washington, D.C. to the highest-rated contestant from the Americas; a series of recitals called the "Pan-American Piano Festival" is granted to the most outstanding semifinalist from the Americas. All contest playing events are public. The preliminary, semifinal and winner's performances are held in Landreth Auditorium at Texas Christian University. The Final examination–concert with orchestra is held in Will Rogers Auditorium in Fort Worth (for 1973, in the Tarrant County Convention Center Theater). From the preliminary events, 12 contestants are chosen for the semifinals. From these, six players are selected for the final event (hence the six prizes). Judges are required to use a point system in rating players in all stages. Complete rules, required repertory, and other details are specifically listed in publications available from the contest headquarters. The 1962 winner was **Ralph Votapek** from Milwaukee; the 1966 winner was **Radu Lupu** of Rumania; in 1969: **Cristina Ortiz** of Brazil, who also won the Pan-American Union prize.

WGN–ILLINOIS OPERA GUILD "AUDITIONS OF THE AIR," c/o WGN Continental Broadcasting Company, 2501 Bradley Place, Chicago, Illinois 60618. Sponsored by the Illinois Opera Guild in collaboration with WGN. The contest is unique: it is the only national vocal competition in the field of opera that is presented in a series of broadcasts by a major broadcasting company. The first of such broadcasts was given on November 9, 1958. Two awards are given yearly to the most accomplished of the contestants: first prize is $3,000 and the second $2,000. The auditions are open to male and female U.S. citizens between 20 and 34 who reside in the U.S. or its possessions. It is expected that only those singers who are currently working to complete their musical training for opera will apply. The awards are granted specifically for the purpose of furthering such training. Prior to October 15 of each year, all applicants must submit their applications along with a recording of their voice in an operatic selection not exceeding 10 minutes and sung in the original language and key. By November 1 all applicants are notified whether or not they have been chosen to sing in live auditions (semifinals) held in Chicago, New York, Los Angeles, or San Francisco (and Dallas, in 1972). From these auditions, only 26 singers are selected for the third round, the "Auditions of the Air" series broadcast by WGN. The broadcasts run for 13 weeks beginning in December until all 26 singers are heard. All singers appearing in the broadcasts participate in the final competition held in the Chicago Civic Opera House the following February. The winners of the finals appear in a formal special "Awards Presentation" program on WGN Radio and Television. The first award winner is also given the opportunity to perform at one of the concerts of Chicago's summer outdoor series, Grant Park Concerts, the following summer season. Judges participating in the "Auditions" are taken from the field of opera, concert management, conducting, etc. and have included Sıch figures as **Walter Hendl,** Deems Taylor, **Majorie Lawrence, Lawrence Kelly, John Crosby, Aksel Schiøtz, Carol Fox, Eugene Conley, Rose Bampton, Blanche Thebom,** Brian Sullivan, and others. Recent winners have been **William Cochran,** tenor, and **Andrew Poulimenos,** baritone.

JOHN HAY WHITNEY FOUNDATION OPPORTUNITY FELLOWSHIPS, c/o the Foundation at 111 West 50th Street, New York, N.Y. 10020. Fellowship awards were once available for advanced or special study in music. Now, the Foundation accepts fellowship applications in music only if the candidate is working for a degree with the final goal of pursuing an academic career. Music is only one of the fields covered by the fellowship opportunities. The competition is open to United States citizens with the following racial or cultural backgrounds or regional origins: Negroes, Spanish-Americans, American Indians, and residents of Southern Appalachian and Ozark Mountains areas, Guam, Puerto Rico, Samoa, the Pacific Trust Territory and the Virgin Islands. Candidates under 35 are given preference. They must be college seniors who plan to go beyond a Bachelor's degree. Graduate students may also apply. Non-degree programs of study can be considered under certain qualifications, details of which are available from the Foundation. The fellowship awards are for a full year of work, with the amounts granted reaching a maximum of $3,000, depending on the nature of the study and the financial need of the candidate. Applications, on special forms provided by the Foundation, must be filed no later than November 30. Award announcements are made the following April.

WIENIAWSKI SCHOLARSHIPS FOR VIOLINISTS, c/o (the sponsor) The Kosciuszko Foundation, 15 East 65th Street, New York, N.Y. 10021. Established in 1969 and offered every two years in odd-numbered years. An award of $1,000 is given the winning violinist for furtherance of his training. Deadline for applications is March 1.

HARRIET HALE WOOLEY SCHOLARSHIPS IN MUSIC AND ART, c/o Director, Fondation des Etats-Unis, 15 boulevard Jourdan, 75 Paris 15, France. Open to unmarried American citizens between 21 and 34 having a Bachelor of Arts degree or its equivalent or, lacking these, having equivalent training. A knowledge of French is required. Four scholarships of $1,550 each are granted each academic year for study in Paris. Deadline for application is January 31.

YOUNG ARTIST AUDITIONS, sponsored by the Women's Committee of the Oklahoma City Symphony Society. Address for the Society is Civic Center Music Hall, Oklahoma City, Oklahoma 73102. Application forms for the audition and other information may be requested from the Chairman of the Auditions Committee, **Mrs. R. Drake Keith,** 2908 Drakestone, Oklahoma City, Oklahoma 73120. Open only to students and residents of Oklahoma, Arkansas, Kansas, Texas, and Missouri and covers the performance areas of piano, strings, and voice. Instrumentalists over 26 or vocalists over 28 are ineligible, as are any performers who are already engaged in a professional music career. The first prize in the instrumental category is the $300 Bloch Young Artist Award, which is awarded to the winner of either the $200 Holtzschue String Award or the $200 Johnson Piano Award. Other prizes are the Wilson Voice Award ($300) and the Rabstejnek Voice Award ($100). Deadline for application in 1973 was January 20. Final auditions take place in February in the auditorium of Oklahoma City University, where the instrumental contestants perform their required concertos with the Oklahoma City Symphony (details regarding the complete required repertory are available from the contest Chairman). An entry fee of $5 is required.

YOUNG ARTIST COMPETITION, c/o Denver Symphony Society, 1615 California Street, Denver, Colorado 80202. A competition for pianists founded in 1966 and sponsored by the Denver Symphony Guild and Colorado Federal Savings and Loan Bank. Held annually, the contest is open to any pianist residing or attending school in any state west of the Mississippi River who is not over 29 at the time of the actual contest. Awards are $1,000, $400, and $300, plus a special award of $500 given to the winner of the first prize at the discretion of the jury. The first-place winner is also given the opportunity to perform with the Denver Symphony during its regular season. Entrance fee is $20.

In 1969 the deadline for applicants was in February; in 1972 it was September 20.

YOUNG ARTIST COMPETITION, c/o Fort Collins Symphony Society, 801 East Elizabeth Street, Fort Collins, Colorado 80521. Established in 1956. Open only to high school juniors and seniors. Two categories of performers are covered by the contest: pianists, for the first; and singers and performers on the violin, viola, cello, flute, oboe, clarinet, bassoon, French horn, and trumpet for the second. One winner is selected from each of the categories and is awarded a $100 prize plus an appearance as soloist with the Fort Collins Symphony Orchestra during its regular season. In addition, both winners may be considered for a four-year scholarship at Colorado State University or a Symphony Society scholarship. Students entering the competition must be recommended by their high school or private music teacher and must be prepared to perform a concert piece or one movement of a concerto or, in the case of vocalists, three arias from the opera or oratorio repertory, preferably in the original language. Application deadline is in February (a $5 fee is required), with auditions and winners' concert following in March and May, respectively.

YOUNG COMPOSERS OF AMERICA COMPETITION, c/o Musical Director, Center for Inter-American Relations, 680 Park Avenue, New York, N.Y. 10021. This contest is open to any composer between 22 and 35 who is a citizen of any country in the Americas. It is sponsored by the Di Tella Foundation, Buenos Aires, and the Center for Inter-American Relations. Of the compositions submitted for judgment, two will be selected. Their composers receive a 20-month fellowship to study at the Buenos Aires Centro Latinamericano de Altos Estudios Musicales, with air travel paid and a $200 monthly allowance. The winning works are guaranteed publication and public performances. In 1969, the deadline for submitting scores was May 1. The composition submitted has to be a chamber work for one to seven players. Winners in 1969 were **Norman Dinerstein** (U.S.) and **Bruno D'Astoli** (Argentina).

YOUNG MUSICIANS FOUNDATION COMPETITION, c/o the Foundation, 434 South San Vicente Boulevard, Los Angeles, California 90048. Established in 1955, it is a competition in piano, violin and viola, cello, voice, and composition, with a $1,000 award for the winner of each of the five categories. Held annually. Age limit for all contestants is 25. Deadline for applications and the submission of scores is June 1 (this date may vary). The contest proceeds from preliminary, semifinal, to final competitions over a ten-day period. The final event takes place before an audience in the Ahmanson Theatre of the Music Center of Los Angeles, and the two earlier series of contests are held in Schoenberg Hall on the campus of UCLA. In addition to the cash awards, finalists are presented as soloists in recital or in a concert with the Young Musicians Foundation Orchestra during the season commencing in the year of the contest. The repertories for the performance categories require major works to be played from memory. The stipulations for composers require that the submitted works not be of excessive difficulty or length and be composed for the standard instrumentation of orchestra or chamber orchestra. Judges for the competition are chosen from the Music Council of the Young Musicians Foundation, most of whom are musicians of national or international reputation. Past winners of the competitions include **James Fields, Stephen Kates, Edward Auer,** and **Shirley Verrett.**

Part 9 | Music and Education

Schools Offering Music Instruction

The section that follows lists 863 schools in the United States (including one in Guam) that offer music instruction in some form. They include four-year colleges, junior and community colleges, universities, music conservatories, schools of the arts, and a few special institutions not in the category of higher education, such as settlement schools. The information follows approximately this order: (1) School name and address. (2) The kind of institution in which music is taught, that is, a department within a college, a college within a university, a conservatory, and so on. Member schools of the National Association of Schools of Music (q.v.) are shown parenthetically as: (Member, NASM); no distinction is shown for full members or associate members of the NASM in this listing. (3) The name of the administrative head of the music school or department and the year of his or her appointment to that post. (In some cases, as in a music division within a college of a university, the administrators of both the division and the college are shown.) When the specific title of the administrator is known, it is indicated; otherwise, the term "Head" signifies the administrator responsible for the music curriculum. (4) Dates of founding of the music school or division and the parent school, when applicable. It should be added that music instruction could have existed in a given school prior to the formal establishment of its music department. (5) Music degrees offered, if any, or academic degrees with a major or emphasis in music. Unusual degree initials are explained. (For a complete listing of academic degrees involving music, see Music Degrees Available.) (6) Number and dollar amount of music scholarships and fellowships. The statement "no music scholarships" does not preclude the possiblity that general scholarship aid or free tuition is open to the music student. (7) Average annual enrollment of all music students. Additional breakdown may show the number of music majors and non-majors enrolled in music courses. (8) Estimated number of volumes in the music library. Further details on a certain few academic music libraries can be found in Music Libraries. (Any discrepancy in the figures for library holdings between this section and the section on music libraries should be resolved in favor of the latter, for which a more exacting questionnaire supplied the information.) (9) School music ensembles officially supported by the school. (Additional information can be found in Part 2: School Bands; Part 3: Vocal Ensembles; Part 4: Academic Opera-producing Groups.) (10) Reference to any music instruction offered by the school during the summer. (11) Reference to any unique, unusual, or highly specialized music courses taught in depth (e.g., music administration, ethnomusicology, music editing, computer technology and music, music librarianship, and music therapy).

For the academic year 1971–72, there were 2,626 U.S. higher-education institutions including one each for the Canal Zone, Guam, and the Virgin Islands and five for Puerto Rico ("Education Directory, 1971–72, Part 3, Higher Education." U.S. Office of Education, U.S. Department of Health, Education and Welfare).

With the possible exception of highly specialized technical and professional schools (e.g., independent law, economics, business, and medical colleges) and the branch colleges on separate campuses of state, private, and religious universities—all included in the Government total—where specialized curricula do not allow for music courses, it can be presumed that most, if not all, of the remaining schools offer some kind of musical activity and instruction. These offerings may range from full music curricula leading to degrees to various minimum electives: marching bands, choirs or glee clubs, jazz combos, and music appreciation courses.

The latest tally by the College Music Society (q.v.) of music faculties yielded 14,500 names of teachers of music in 1,300 different colleges, universities, conservatories, schools of music, and community colleges ("Directory of Music Faculties in College and Universities of the U.S., 1970–72." Third Edition, Binghamton, N.Y., 1970). The figures include 430 Canadian faculty in 21 institutions. The remainder are U.S. schools. Thus, approximately half the number of institutions in the U.S. are represented by the CMS tally which may consist of the maximum likely number of institutions having music teachers. The 863 schools placed in this section constitute, therefore, a significant representation—two thirds —of the likely schools in the nation with music programs.

ALABAMA

ALABAMA CHRISTIAN COLLEGE, Atlanta Highway, Montgomery, Alabama 36109. Department of Music within College. Head: **Don Darby** (1969). College founded: 1942. Degrees: A.A. Scholarships: totaling $5,000. Music enrollment: 10. Volumes in music library: 100. Official school ensembles: chorus, chamber vocal ensemble, marching band, concert band, jazz ensemble, rock ensemble, other smaller chamber groups. Limited summer instruction. . . . ALEXANDER CITY STATE JUNIOR COLLEGE, Alexander City, Alabama 35010. Music Department within the Fine Arts Division. Head: **Miss Sarah E. Scott** (1966). College founded: 1965. Department founded: 1966. Degrees: A.S. No scholarships. Music students enrolled: 225. Volumes in music library: 255. Official school ensembles: chorus. No summer school. . . . BIRMINGHAM-SOUTHERN COLLEGE, Birmingham, Alabama 35204. (Member, NASM.) Department of Music within a college. Head: **Hugh Thomas** (1953). Music department founded: 1953. School founded: 1936. Degrees: B.M., B.M.E., B.A. Scholarships: nine, totaling $3,250. Music enrollment: 95. Music library: 1,930 volumes, 31 reels of microfilm. Ensembles: chorus, glee club, opera workshop. . . . JAMES H. FAULKNER STATE JUNIOR COLLEGE,

Box 880, Bay Minette, Alabama 36507. Department of Music within a college. Chairman: **Ronnie L. James** (1969). College founded: 1965. Music Department founded: 1966. Degree: two-year degree toward a four-year B.M.E. Music enrollment: 150. Music volumes: 75. Ensembles: chorus, chamber vocal ensemble, concert band, jazz ensemble. Summer courses offered. . . . JOHN C. CALHOUN STATE JUNIOR COLLEGE, Bee Line Highway (P.O. Box 548), Decatur, Alabama 35601. Music Department within the Fine Arts Division of the College. Head: **Robert E. Stevens** (1967), College and Department founded: 1965. Degrees: A.S. Scholarships: 10, totaling $1,200. Music enrollment: 35. Volumes in music library: 1,000. Official school ensembles: chorus, chamber vocal ensemble, concert band, jazz ensemble, community band and chorus. Summer instruction offered. . . . JUDSON COLLEGE, Marion, Alabama 36756 (Member, NASM.) Music Department within the College, supported by the Baptist church. Head: **Jack Coman** (1968). College and department founded in 1838. Degrees: B.A. in performance, B.S. in Music Education. Scholarships: three, totaling $1,500. Music enrollment: 26. Volumes in music library: 900. Official school ensembles: chorus, chamber vocal ensemble, opera workshop. Summer music courses offered. . . . MOBILE COLLEGE, P.O. Box 13220, Mobile, Alabama 36613. Department of Music within the college. Head: **Kenneth Bergdolt** (1970). College founded: 1961. Department founded: 1963. Degrees: B.A. Scholarships: four, totaling $1,600. Music students enrolled: 30. Volumes in music library: 1,000. Official school ensembles: chorus, chamber vocal ensemble. No summer music school. . . . SAMFORD UNIVERSITY, 800 Lakeshore Drive, Birmingham, Alabama 35209. (Member, NASM.) School of Music is one of seven schools within the university. Dean: **Claude H. Rhea** (1969). School of Music founded: 1970. Degrees: B.M. in church music, M.M.Ed., M.M. with emphasis in church music. Scholarships: 110 totaling $35,000. Music enrollment: 200. No summer music school. . . . TALLADEGA COLLEGE, Talladega, Alabama 35160. Music Department within the College. Head: **Roland Braithwaite** (1969). College founded: 1867. Degrees: B.A. Scholarships: three tuition scholarships ($1,145 maximum). Music students enrolled: 18. No separate music library. College has over 58,000 volumes for all departments. Official school ensemble: chorus. No summer music school. . . . UNIVERSITY OF ALABAMA IN HUNTSVILLE, P.O. Box 1247, Huntsville, Alabama 35807. Music discipline within Division of Humanities. Head: **D. Royce Boyer** (1966). University and division founded: 1966. Degrees: B.A. expected. Scholarships: three, totaling $150. Music students enrolled: 18. Volumes in music library: 1,851. Official school ensembles: chorus, chamber vocal ensemble, concert band, symphony orchestra. Limited summer instruction. . . . UNIVERSITY OF ALABAMA, University, Alabama 35486. (Member, NASM.) A department of a state-supported university. Head: **Wilbur H. Rowand.** Degrees: B.M. in performance, theory–composition; B.A. in performance, theory, music history; B.S. in education, music major; M.M. in education; M.A. in music education. Music Majors: 200. Music library: about 5,000 volumes. . . . UNIVERSITY OF MONTEVALLO, Montevallo, Alabama 35115. (Member, NASM.) A department in the College of Liberal Arts in a state-supported university. Chairman: **John W. Stewart.** Degrees: B.M. in applied music, composition, B.M.Ed. in general music, instrumental music. Music Majors: 100. . . . UNIVERSITY OF SOUTH ALABAMA, 309 Gaillard Drive, Mobile, Alabama 36608. (Member, NASM.) Department within College of Arts and Sciences of the university (state-supported). Chairman: **William J. Jones** (1965). University founded 1964. Music Department founded 1965. Degrees offered: B.A., B.M., B.S.Ed. Scholarships: 75, totaling $39,000. Music students enrolled: 100. Volumes in music library: 1,700. Official ensembles: choir, chorus, chamber vocal ensemble, concert band, chamber orchestra, string quartet, jazz ensemble, and other small student ensembles. Has a summer music school.

ALASKA

SHELDON JACKSON COLLEGE, Box 479, Sitka, Alaska 99835. Music Department is a one-man (one-faculty) department and a part-time teaching position. **Mrs. Marsha Buck** has had this position since 1968. College established in 1878. Music Department founded: early 1900's. Two-year school. Degree: A.A. for music majors. No scholarships available. Music students annually enrolled: 32. Volumes in music library: 50, plus an unspecified quantity of old music (piano, choir, and instrumental). School ensembles: chorus and athletic pep band. No summer school offered. . . . UNIVERSITY OF ALASKA, College, Alaska 99701. Music Department within the University. Head: **Duane J. Mikow** (1969). University founded: 1922. Degrees: B.A., B.M., M.A.T. Scholarships: 15 totaling $3,200. No fellowships. Annual enrollment: 50 music majors. Volumes in the music library: 3,750. Ensembles include: chorus, chamber vocal ensemble, concert band, opera workshop, symphony orchestra, chamber orchestra, jazz ensemble. Summer music instruction is available.

ARIZONA

ARIZONA STATE UNIVERSITY, Tempe, Arizona 85281. (Member, NASM.) A department in the College of Fine Arts of a state-supported university. Head: **Andrew J. Broekema** (1968). University and Music Department founded: 1885. Degrees: B.M., B.A., B.A. in Education, M.M., M.A. in education, Ed.D. Scholarships: 100, totaling $50,000; 10 fellowships totaling $35,000. Music students enrolled: 450. Volumes in music library: 25,000. On campus ensembles: chorus, chamber vocal ensemble, marching band, concert band, opera workshop, symphony orchestra, chamber orchestra, in-residence string quartet and woodwind quartet, jazz ensemble. Has a summer music school. . . . CENTRAL ARIZONA COLLEGE, Coolidge, Arizona 85228. Department of Music within the college. Head: **James Hamilton Johnson** (1969). College and department founded: 1969. Degrees: A.A. Scholarships: 25, totaling $6,250. Music students enrolled: 45. Volumes in library: 150. Official school ensembles: chorus, chamber vocal ensemble, pep band, concert band, Mariachi band. Special courses: music manuscript copying as a vocation. No summer music school. . . . EASTERN ARIZONA COLLEGE, Thatcher, Arizona 85552. Music Department within the college. Head: **William E. Purdy** (1963). College and department founded: 1890. Degrees: A.A. Scholarships: 20, totaling $1,520. Music students enrolled: 210. Volumes in music library: 225. Official school music ensembles: chorus, chamber vocal ensemble, marching band, concert band, symphony orchestra, jazz ensemble. . . . NORTHERN ARIZONA UNIVERSITY, Flagstaff, Arizona 86001. (Member, NASM.) A Department of Music in a state-supported university. Dean, College of Creative Arts: **William E. Whybrew.** Degrees: B.A. in music; B.M. in applied music, music education; M.M. in applied music, music education. . . . THE UNIVERSITY OF ARIZONA, Tucson, Arizona 85721. (Member, NASM.) School of Music within a College of Fine Arts of a state-supported university. Director: **Andrew W. Buchhauser** (1957). University established: 1885. Music school added: 1930. Degrees: B.M., B.A., M.M., and A.Mus.D. Scholarships and fellowships: vary annually both in number and monetary amounts. Music students enrolled: 375 majors. Music ensembles: chorus, glee club, chamber vocal ensemble, marching band, concert band, opera workshop, symphony orchestra, chamber orchestra, jazz ensemble, and smaller instrumental groups. Summer music school is offered.

ARKANSAS

ARKANSAS POLYTECHNIC COLLEGE, Russellville, Arkansas 72801 (Member, NASM.) A department in the Fine Arts Division of the college. Chairman: **Gene Witherspoon.** Degrees: B.A. with music education major. Music students enrolled: 126 majors. . . . ARKANSAS STATE UNIVERSITY, State University, Arkansas 72467.

(Member, NASM.) A division of a School of Fine Arts in a state-supported institution. Dean, School of Fine Arts: **Harold Copenhaver.** Chairman, Division of Music: **Donald R. Minx.** Degrees: B.M.Ed.; B.F.A. in music; M.S. in education, major in music. Music students enrolled: 150 majors. . . . HENDERSON STATE COLLEGE, Arkadelphia, Arkansas 71923. (Member, NASM.) A Department of Music in the School of Fine Arts of a state-supported college. Dean: **Robert R. Bruner.** Chairman: **James R. Harris.** Degrees: B.M.Ed., B.M. Music majors: 97. . . . HENDRIX COLLEGE, Conway, Arkansas 72032. (Member, NASM.) Department of Music within a Liberal Arts college. Head: **Ashley R. Coffman** (1943). College founded: 1884. Degrees: B.A. with a music major. Scholarships: 15, totaling $4,500. Music enrollment: 25 to 30. Ensembles: chorus, choir, chamber vocal ensemble, concert band, opera workshop, jazz ensemble, brass choir. No summer music session. . . . OUACHITA BAPTIST UNIVERSITY, Arkadelphia, Arkansas 71923. (Member, NASM.) A School of Music within a university affiliated with the Baptist Convention of Arkansas. Dean: **William Trantham.** University founded: 1886. School of Music founded: 1968. Degrees: B.A., B.M., B.M.Ed., M.M.E. Scholarships: 50, totaling $8,500. Fellowships: three, totaling $4,000. Music enrollment: 125. Volumes in music library: 2,000. On campus ensembles: chorus, glee club, chamber vocal ensemble, marching band, concert band, opera workshop, jazz ensemble, and other instrumental groups. Summer music school is offered. . . . PHILLIPS COUNTY COMMUNITY COLLEGE, Helena, Arkansas 72342. Music courses in Department of English and Fine Arts. Head: **Jean Knowlton** (1968). College founded: 1966. Music students enrolled: 10. Official school ensembles: chorus, pep band. No summer music courses. . . . SOUTHERN STATE COLLEGE, Magnolia, Arkansas 71753. Music Department within college. Head: **Robert Campbell** (1965). School founded: 1909. Department founded: 1951. Degrees: B.M.Ed. Scholarships: 60, totaling $18,000. Music students enrolled: 40 majors, 200 non-majors. Music library: 5,000 books and scores, 5,000 records. Official school ensembles: chorus, chamber vocal ensemble, marching band, concert ensemble, jazz ensemble. Summer music workshops offered. . . . STATE COLLEGE OF ARKANSAS, Conway, Arkansas 72032. (Member, NASM.) Music Department within a college. Head: **Carl E. Forsberg** (1970). College founded: 1908. Degrees: B.M., B.M.E. Scholarships: 50, totaling $7,500. Music students enrolled: 90. Volumes in music library: 4,500. Official school ensembles: chorus, chamber vocal ensemble, marching band, concert band, opera workshop, chamber orchestra, jazz ensemble, other smaller chamber groups. Limited summer instruction. . . . UNIVERSITY OF ARKANSAS, Fayetteville, Arkansas 72701. (Member, NASM.) Department of Music within a state university. Chairman: **John R. Cowell** (1966). University founded: 1871. Music Department founded: 1927. Degrees: B.M., B.A., B.S.Ed., M.M., M.Ed. Scholarships: 60, totaling $25,000. Fellowships: eight, totaling $21,000. Music enrollment: 225. Music library: 10,000 volumes. Ensembles: four choruses, glee club, chamber vocal ensemble, marching band, concert band, opera workshop, symphony orchestra, chamber orchestra, four smaller chamber groups. Summer music school offered. Special courses in class piano (electronic), pedagogy. . . . UNIVERSITY OF ARKANSAS AT LITTLE ROCK, 33rd and University, Little Rock, Arkansas 72204. Music Department within the Fine Arts Division of a university. Head: **John Hughes** (1968). University founded: 1929. Department founded: 1927. Degrees: B.A., B.M., B.M.E. Scholarships: total $6,000. Music enrollment: 60 majors. Volumes in library: 1,500 plus periodicals. Official ensembles: chorus, chamber vocal ensemble, concert band, opera workshop, jazz ensemble, woodwind, brass, and handbell ensembles. Summer music school offered. . . . UNIVERSITY OF ARKANSAS AT MONTICELLO, University of Arkansas, Monticello, Arkansas 71655. Music discipline is within Fine Arts Department. Head: **John W. Dougherty, Jr.** (1969). University founded: 1909. Department founded: 1940. Degree:

B.A. Scholarships: total $27,000. Music students enrolled: 50 majors, 20 minors. Volumes in music library: 2,000. Official school ensembles: chorus, glee club, chamber vocal ensemble, marching band, concert band, opera workshop, jazz ensemble. Summer music school offered. . . . WESTARK JUNIOR COLLEGE, Fort Smith, Arkansas 72901. Music taught within the Fine Arts Department. Chairman: **Logan A. Green** (1968). College founded: 1927. Degree: A.A. Scholarships: six, totaling $625. Music majors enrolled: 18. Volumes in music library: 750. Music ensembles: chorus, chamber vocal ensemble, symphony orchestra, and other instrumental ensembles. A few courses in music are offered in the summer school.

CALIFORNIA

AMERICAN RIVER COMMUNITY COLLEGE, 4700 College Oak Drive, Sacramento, California 95841. Music Department within college. Head: **Ivan Olson** (1971). Degree: A.A. Scholarships: 20, totaling $3,000. Music students enrolled: 65. Volumes in music library: 500. Official school ensembles: chorus, glee club, chamber vocal ensemble, marching band, concert band, chamber orchestra, string quartet, jazz ensemble, pep band. . . . ANTELOPE VALLEY COLLEGE, 3041 West Avenue K, Lancaster, California 93534. Music Department part of Fine Arts Division within college. Chairman: **Charles Costarella.** No music degrees offered, but there are 25 music majors. School ensembles include: chorus, marching band, concert band, community orchestra, woodwind ensemble, and brass ensemble. Music courses also offered in the summer. . . . BIOLA COLLEGE, 13800 Biola Avenue, La Mirada, California 90638. (Member, NASM.) Music Department within the Division of Fine Arts of the college. Acting chairman: **Jack W. Schwarz** (1971). College founded: 1908. Degrees: B.A., B.M. Scholarships: 30, totaling $25,000. Music students enrolled: 70. Volumes in music library: 2,888. Official school ensembles: chorus, chamber vocal ensemble, concert band, chamber orchestra. No summer music school. . . . BUTTE COLLEGE, P.O. Box 566, Durham, California 95938. Music Department within the college. College founded: 1968. Degree: A.A. No scholarships. Music students enrolled: 40. Volumes in music library: 200. Official school ensembles: chorus, chamber vocal ensemble, marching band, concert band, jazz ensemble. Summer music instruction. . . . CALIFORNIA INSTITUTE OF THE ARTS, 24700 McBean Parkway, Valencia, California 91355. A School of Music, one of six schools within an institute of arts, supported by tuition, gifts, and grants. Dean: **Mel Powell** (1968). School and institute opened: 1970. The institute is the result of a merger of the Los Angeles Conservatory of Music (founded 1888) and the Chouinard Art Institute (founded 1921), brought about by Walt Disney in 1961. The institute has received some funding from the Disney Foundation and will receive annual support from Walt Disney Associates for California Institute of the Arts. Degrees: B.F.A., M.F.A. Scholarships: 74, each for $1,300. No fellowships. Music school enrollment: 120. Volumes in music library: 1,360; 4,000 scores; 2,000 recordings. Official music ensembles: chorus, chamber vocal ensemble, opera workshop, symphony orchestra, chamber orchestra, and other smaller chamber groups. Summer instruction is offered. The curriculum of the Music School and its relationship with the Institute is unusual from the viewpoint of courses, mode of instruction, and educational goals. Special programs as such, therefore, abound. Among them: facilities for eye–ear (films and tapes) laboratory, extensive exposure to "world music" featuring instruction in the musical arts of other cultures, etc. . . . CALIFORNIA LUTHERAN COLLEGE, Thousand Oaks, California 91360. Music Department within college. Head: **C. Robert Zimmerman** (1961). College and department founded: 1961. Degree: B.A. Scholarships: 20, totaling $5,000; 2 undergraduate assistantships totaling $1,000. Music students enrolled: 200 (45 majors). Official school ensembles: concert choir, freshman choir, chamber vocal groups, concert band, opera workshop, symphony orchestra, chamber orchestra, other smaller chamber groups. Limited music instruction in summer school. . . . CALIFORNIA STATE COLLEGE AT DOMINGUEZ HILLS, 1000 East Victoria, Dominguez Hills, California 90246. Music Department within the college. Head: **Marshall Bialosky** (1964). College and department founded: 1965. Degree: B.A. No music scholarships as yet. Music students enrolled: 55. Volumes in music library: 2,200. Official school ensembles: chorus, chamber orchestra. Some summer instruction. Unusual courses: American Music, Afro-American Music, Latin-American Music, Folk Songs of Mexico, Music of China and Japan. . . . CALIFORNIA STATE COLLEGE AT FULLERTON, 800 North State College Boulevard, Fullerton, California 92631. (Member, NASM.) Department of Music in a state-supported college. Chairman: **Leo Kreter.** College and department founded: 1960. Degrees: B.A., B.M. Limited number of scholarships. Music students enrolled: 250. Music library within main college library. Official school ensembles: chorus, chamber vocal ensemble, concert band, opera workshop, symphony orchestra, chamber orchestra, jazz ensemble, and other smaller chamber groups. No summer music school. . . . CALIFORNIA STATE COLLEGE, LONG BEACH, 6101 East 7th Street, Long Beach, California 90801. (Member, NASM.) Music Department within a state college system. Department chairman: **Gerald Daniel** (1968). Department founded: 1949. Degrees: B.A., B.M., M.A. Scholarships: five, totaling $475. No fellowships. Music students enrolled: 295. Official school ensembles: chorus, chamber vocal ensemble, marching band, concert band, opera workshop, symphony orchestra, jazz ensemble, smaller chamber groups. Summer music school. . . . CALIFORNIA STATE COLLEGE, Hayward, 25800 Hillary Street, Hayward, California 94542. (Member, NASM.) A Department of Music in a state-supported college. Chairman: **Frederick A. Fox.** Degrees: B.A. in music, M.A. in music. . . . CALIFORNIA STATE COLLEGE AT LOS ANGELES, 5151 State College Drive, Los Angeles, California 90032. Department of Music with the School of Fine and Applied Arts. Head: **Hugh Mullins** (1968). College and Department founded: 1948. Degrees: B.A., M.A. Scholarships: 15, totaling $750. No fellowships. Music students enrolled: 400. No separate music library; incorporated in main library. Official school ensembles: chorus, glee club, chamber vocal ensemble, marching band, concert band, opera workshop, symphony orchestra, chamber orchestra, jazz ensemble, contemporary music ensemble, Collegium Musicum. Special courses: music administration, ethnomusicology. No summer music school. . . . CALIFORNIA STATE COLLEGE, SAN BERNARDINO, 5500 State College Parkway, San Bernardino, California 92407. Music Department within the college. Head: **Richard Saylor** (1968). Department founded: 1965. Degree: B.A. Music students enrolled: 35. Music library is part of main library. Official school ensembles: chorus, chamber vocal ensemble, chamber orchestra, opera workshop, other smaller chamber groups. Limited summer instruction. Special courses: electronic music and ethnomusicology. . . . CALIFORNIA STATE POLYTECHNIC COLLEGE, San Luis Obispo, California 93401. Music Department within the college. Head: **Harold P. Davidson** (1936). Department founded: 1936. There is no music major, but a strong music minor, with 1,000 music students annually enrolled. Volumes in music library: 3,000. On campus: glee clubs, chamber vocal ensemble, marching band, concert band, symphony orchestra, chamber orchestra, jazz ensemble. There is a summer session and a summer string quartet. Special courses offered: Ethnic Music, Contemporary Jazz. . . . CHABOT COLLEGE, 25555 Hesperian Boulevard, Hayward, California 94545. Music is considered a discipline within the Humanities Division. Music Coordinator: **Otto E. Mielenz** (1970). Both the college and division were established in 1963. Degree: A.A. in music. Scholarships: vary annually. Students enrolled in music: 120. Volumes in music library: 1,400. School music ensembles: chorus, chamber vocal ensemble, concert band, chamber orchestra, jazz ensemble, and other smaller chamber groups. There is no summer music school. . . . CHICO STATE COLLEGE, Chico, California 95926. (Member, NASM.) A Department of Music in a state-supported college. Chairman: **Walter O. Dahlin.** Degrees: B.A. in music, secondary teaching credential, elementary teaching credential; M.A. in music, music education, music theory and composition, music history and literature, performance, diversified program. . . . CITRUS COLLEGE, 18824 East Foothill, Azusa, California 91702. A Department within the college. Head: **Frank Magliocco** (1967). The college was established in 1915; the music department added in 1950. The A.A. degree is offered. Scholarships: 25, amounting to $1,250. Music students annually enrolled: 600. Volumes in music library: 3,000. Music ensembles: chorus, chamber vocal ensemble, marching band, concert band, opera workshop, symphony orchestra, and other chamber ensembles. Summer music instruction is offered. . . . CLAREMONT GRADUATE SCHOOL, 900 North College Avenue, Claremont, California 91711. Music Department within the college (school is a cluster of six colleges). Head: **Roland Jackson** (1970). Department founded: 1934. Degrees: M.A. (possibly a D.A. degree in 1971). Fellowships: three, totaling $3,600. Music students enrolled: 15 to 20. Volumes in music library: 7,000. Official school ensembles: chorus, glee club, concert band, opera workshop, chamber orchestra, other smaller chamber groups. Summer music festival and opera workshop, and music instruction. . . . COLLEGE OF THE HOLY NAMES, 3500 Mountain Boulevard, Oakland, California 94619. (Member, NASM.) A Department of Music in a liberal arts college. Chairman: **Sister Therese Cecile Murphy.** Degrees: B.M. in applied music; B.A. in history, literature and theory combined. Music majors: 70. . . . COLLEGE OF NOTRE DAME, 1500 Ralston Avenue, Belmont, California 94002. Music Department within the college. Chairman: **Sister Anthony Marie Herzo** (1955). Degrees: B.A., B.Mus. with majors in piano, voice, string instruments. Music enrollment: 35. Music library is part of main library. Official music ensembles: chorus, glee club, chamber vocal ensemble, chamber orchestra. Summer music school. . . . DE ANZA COLLEGE, 21250 Stevens Creek Boulevard, Cupertino, California 95014. Department of Music within the college. Head: **Royal Stanton.** College and department founded: 1967. Degree: A.A. Scholarships: four, totaling $750. Music students enrolled: 250. Official school ensembles: chorus, chamber vocal ensemble, concert band, symphony orchestra, chamber orchestra, jazz ensemble. No summer music school. . . . DIABLO VALLEY COLLEGE, Golf Club Road, Pleasant Hill, California 94523. The Music Department within a college. Head: **Allen A. Scholl** (1965). College founded: 1949. Department founded: 1950. Degree: A.A. Scholarships: one, for $150. Students enrolled annually: 150. Volumes in music library: 400. School ensembles: chorus, glee club, chamber vocal ensemble, concert band, opera workshop, chamber orchestra, jazz ensemble, and other smaller chamber instrumental groups. No summer instruction in music is offered. Special course: America's music. . . . EL CAMINO COLLEGE, 16007 Crenshaw Boulevard, Via Torrance, California 90506. Department of Music within the Fine Arts Division. Head: **Harold Wennstrom** (1960). College and division established: 1947. Degree: A.A. Scholarships: one, for $200. Volumes in music library: 500. Music students enrolled annually: 1,000. School ensembles: chorus, glee club, chamber vocal ensemble, marching band, concert band, symphony orchestra, and jazz ensemble. Summer music courses are taught. . . . FRESNO STATE COLLEGE, Fresno, California 93710. (Member, NASM.) Department of Music in the Division of Speech and Music in a state-supported college. Chairman: **Wilson W. Coker.** Degrees: B.A. with major in music; M.A. with major in music. . . . GRADUATE THEOLOGICAL UNION, 2465 Le Conte Avenue, Berkeley, California 94709. Music in Area VII: Theology and the Arts. Chairman: **Norman Mealy** (1971). Union founded: 1963. Music added: 1968. Degrees: M.A., PhD., both in work connecting music and theology. Scholarships: competitive for all students. Volumes in music library: 1,500. Summer music school: Institute of Liturgical Music. Special courses: Music and Liturgy. . . . HARTNELL COLLEGE, 156 Homestead

Avenue, Salinas, California 93901. A Music Department within the college. Head: **Vahe' Aslanian** (1950). The college established: 1920. Scholarships: $1,000. Music students enrolled annually: 300. School ensembles: chorus, chamber vocal ensemble, marching band, concert band, and jazz ensemble. Music courses offered in the summer session. . . . IMMACULATE HEART COLLEGE, 2021 North Western Avenue, Los Angeles, California 90027. (Member, NASM.) A Department of Music in a liberal arts college conducted by the Sisters of the Immaculate Heart. Dean: **Theresa Di Rocco.** Degrees: B.M. in applied music, composition; B.A. in applied music, theory, music history and literature. Music majors: 45. . . . LANZY COMMUNITY COLLEGE, 900 Fallon Street, Oakland, California 94607. Music Department within a college. Chairman: **E. D'Amante** (1965). Department founded: 1963. Degree: A.A. No music scholarships. Music students enrolled: 2,000. Music library: 2,000 volumes. Official school ensembles: chorus, chamber vocal ensemble, concert band, chamber orchestra, chamber groups, jazz ensemble. Summer music school offered. . . . LONE MOUNTAIN COLLEGE, 2800 Turk Boulevard, San Francisco, California 94118. Music Department within the college. Head: **Wyatt Insko.** College and department founded: 1932 (formerly San Francisco College for Women). Degrees: B.A.; B.F.A.; Elementary, Secondary, and Early Childhood Credential; M.A., M.S. Scholarships and Fellowships through college: amounting to $33,800 and $22,000 in tuition grants. Music students enrolled: 40. Volumes in music library: 3,500. Official school ensembles: chorus, opera workshop, chamber orchestra, jazz ensemble, rock band, other smaller chamber groups. Summer music instruction. Special courses: student-designed study courses. . . . LOS ANGELES VALLEY COLLEGE, 5800 Fulton Avenue, Van Nuys, California 91401. Music is a department within the two-year college. Head: **Richard Carlson** (1971). Both college and department established: 1949. Degree: A.A. Scholarships: nine, totaling $250. Music students enrolled annually: 500. Volumes in music library: 1,000. Music ensembles: chorus, chamber vocal ensemble, marching band, concert band, opera workshop, symphony orchestra, chamber orchestra, jazz ensemble, and other instrumental groups. There is limited summer instruction and a special course in music editing. . . . MARYMOUNT COLLEGE AT LOYOLA UNIVERSITY, Loyola Boulevard at 80th Street, Los Angeles, California 90045. Head of Music Department: **Walter Arlen** (1968). College established: 1936. Music Department founded: 1968. Degrees: B.S., B.A. in music. Scholarships: four, totaling $2,000. Music students enrolled annually: 20 majors. School ensembles: chorus, chamber vocal ensemble, symphony orchestra, gamelan ensemble. No music school during the summer. Special courses include ethnomusicology, harpsichord construction, and music criticism. . . . MENLO COLLEGE, Menlo Park, California 94025. Menlo College is a 2-year transfer college. The Music Department offers only a small number of courses for beginning music students. Head: **John Walker** (1971). College established: 1927. No degrees in music; no music scholarships offered. Volumes in music library: 200. School ensembles: chorus, glee club. No music courses are offered in summer. . . . MILLS COLLEGE, Oakland, California 94613. Music Department within college. Head: **Margaret E. Lyon** (1955). School founded: 1852. Degrees: B.A.; M.A. (music literature, composition); M.F.A. (performance and literature, electronic music, and the recording media). Scholarships: from $200 to full fees. Fellowships: two in music department; two in electronic music studio, up to full tuition. Music enrollment: 50 majors. Volumes in library: 10,387. Official music ensembles: chorus, chamber orchestra. Highly specialized courses: electronic music studio (Center for Contemporary Music). . . . MODESTO JUNIOR COLLEGE, College Avenue, Modesto, California 95350. Music Department within college. Head: **Robert H. Wing** (1970). Department founded: 1921. Degree: A.A. Scholarships: four, totaling $350. Students enrolled in music: 400 (75 majors). Official school ensembles: chorus, chamber vocal ensemble, concert band, opera workshop, symphony orchestra, jazz ensemble, other smaller chamber groups. Summer music courses are offered. . . . MT. SAN ANTONIO COLLEGE, 1100 Grand Avenue, Walnut, California 91789. Music Department within the college. Head: **Lewis E. Forney** (1968). College founded: 1946. Degree: A.A. Scholarships: five to seven, totaling $250 to $350. Music students enrolled: 110 majors. Volumes in music library: 500. Official school ensembles: chorus, glee club, chamber vocal ensemble, marching band, concert band, opera workshop, jazz ensemble, other smaller chamber groups. No summer music school. . . . MUSIC & ARTS INSTITUTE OF SAN FRANCISCO, 2622 Jackson Street, San Francisco, California 94115. Director: **Ross McKee.** Music majors: 84. . . . MOUNT ST. MARY'S COLLEGE, 12001 Chalon Road, Los Angeles, California 90049. (Member, NASM.) A Department of Music in a liberal arts college supported by the Sisters of St. Joseph Carondelet. Chairman: **Sister Miriam Joseph.** Degrees: B.M. in applied music; B.A. with music major. Students enrolled: 45 music majors. . . . PACIFIC COLLEGE, 1717 South Chestnut Avenue, Fresno, California 93702. Head: **Larry Warkentin** (1965). College founded: 1944. Music Department added: 1962. Degree: B.A. in music. Scholarships: eight, totaling $3,000. Music students enrolled: 20. Volumes in music library: 2,000. Music ensembles include: chorus, chamber vocal ensemble, concert band, and stage band. There is no summer music school. . . . PACIFIC UNION COLLEGE, Angwin, California 94508. (Member, NASM.) A Department of Music in a liberal arts college of the Seventh-Day Adventist Church. Chairman: **Melvin S. Hill.** Degrees: B.A. in music; B.M. with concentration in music education, performance; M.M. with concentration in music education, performance. . . . PASADENA COLLEGE, 1539 East Howard Street, Pasadena, California 91104. Music Department within the college. Head: **Chester C. Crill** (1947). College founded: 1902. Department founded: 1912. Degree: B.A. in various music concentration: applied, music education, church music, etc. Scholarships: 20, totaling $10,800. Music students enrolled: 175 (75 majors). Volumes in music library: 2,500, plus music scores, recordings, choral and instrument music. Official school ensembles: *a cappella* choir, chorus, two glee clubs, chamber vocal ensemble, concert band, chamber orchestra, stage band, other smaller chamber groups. No summer music school. . . . PEPPERDINE UNIVERSITY, 1121 West 79th Street, Los Angeles, California 90044. (Member, NASM.) A Music Department within the university. Head: **Clarence R. Haflinger** (1959). University and department established: 1937. Degree: B.A. with various forms of graduate studies toward a credential. Scholarships: 50, totaling $10,000. The Department gives "Achievement Awards." Music students enrolled: 150. The school music ensembles include: chorus, opera workshop, symphony orchestra, madrigals and choraliers groups, and smaller instrumental ensembles. Summer courses in music are offered. . . . POMONA COLLEGE, Claremont, California 91711. Department of Music within the college. Head: **William F. Russell** (1953). College and department founded: 1887. Degree: B.A. with a major in music. General college scholarships only. Music enrollment: 650. Volumes in music library: 5,000. Official school ensembles: chorus, glee club, chamber vocal ensemble, pep band, concert band, symphony orchestra, stage band. Summer activities include the Claremont Music Festival at Pomona College. . . . SAN DIEGO STATE COLLEGE, 5402 College Avenue, San Diego, California 92115. (Member, NASM.) Department within a college. Head: **J. Dayton Smith** (1955). School founded: 1898. Department founded: 1937. Degrees: A.B., B.M., M.A. Scholarships: 15, totaling $4,000. Music enrollment: 350. Volumes in music library: 8,350. Official music ensembles: chorus, glee club, chamber vocal ensemble, marching band, concert band, opera workshop, symphony orchestra, chamber orchestra, trio, jazz ensemble, Collegium Musicum. Summer music school offered. . . . SAN FERNANDO VALLEY STATE COLLEGE, 18111 Nordhoff Street, Northridge, California 91324. (Member, NASM.) A Department of Music within the School of Fine Arts and Professional Studies. Chairman: **Clarence Wiggins.**

Degrees: B.A. in music; B.M.; M.A. in performance, composition, musicology, music education. . . . SAN FRANCISCO CONSERVATORY OF MUSIC, 1201 Ortega, San Francisco, California 94122. (Member, NASM.) An independent, unendowed music conservatory. Head: **Milton Salkind** (1967). School founded: 1917. Degrees: B.M., M.M., Music Diploma, Artist Diploma. Enrollment: 135. Official ensembles: chorus, chamber vocal ensemble, opera workshop, symphony orchestra, instrumental chamber groups, jazz ensemble, improvisation ensemble, new music ensemble. Summer music school. Special courses: electronic music and technology. . . . SAN FRANCISCO STATE COLLEGE, 1600 Holloway, San Francisco, California 94132. (Member, NASM.) Department of Music within a college. Chairman: **Warren Rasmussen** (1969). School founded: 1899. Music department founded: 1921. Degrees: B.A., B.M., M.A. Scholarships: 40, totaling $6,000. Music enrollment: 350. Music library: 10,000 volumes. Ensembles: chorus, chamber vocal ensemble, concert band, opera workshop, string chamber groups, symphony orchestra, jazz ensemble. Summer music school offered. Special courses in electronic music and performance practice. . . . SAN JOSE CITY COLLEGE, 2100 Moorpark Avenue, San Jose, California 95114. Music Department within a college. Head: **Clifford Hansen** (1960). Department founded: 1953. School founded: 1921. Degree: A.A. Scholarships: four, totaling $100. Music students enrolled: 1,000. Official school ensembles: chorus, chamber vocal ensemble, concert band, chamber orchestra, jazz ensemble. Summer music courses offered. . . . SAN JOSE STATE COLLEGE, 125 South 7th, San Jose, California 95114. (Member, NASM.) Department of Music within a college. Head: **W. Gibson Walters** (1964). School and department founded: 1857. Degrees: B.A., M.A. (will offer B.M. in 1973 and M.M. in 1976). Scholarships: 50 tuition and fees granted. Music enrollment: 467. Music ensembles: chorus, glee club, chamber vocal ensemble, marching band, concert band, opera workshop, symphony orchestra, chamber orchestra, smaller chamber groups, jazz ensemble, improvisation ensemble. Summer music school offered. . . . SHASTA COLLEGE, Old Oregon Trail at 299E, Redding, California 96001. Music Department within a college. Head: **Ulando Tognozzi** (1964). Department and school both founded: 1950. Degree: A.A. Scholarships: no set amount, average $100 each. Music students enrolled: 30 to 40 majors and minors. Music library: about 1,000 books and some collections. Official school ensembles: chorus, chamber vocal ensemble, marching band, concert band, opera workshop, symphony orchestra, jazz ensemble. No summer music school. . . . SIMPSON COLLEGE, 801 Silver Avenue, San Francisco, California 94134. A Music Department set up within the college. Acting Chairman: **Miss Sandra Soderlund** (1970). College and department founded: 1920. Degree: B.A. in music theory, applied music (organ, piano, voice), and in Sacred Music. Scholarships: one or two of $45 each. Music enrollment: 12. There are 2,500 volumes in the music library. Ensembles include a chorus, glee club, and smaller instrumental chamber groups. No summer music instruction is offered. . . . SOLANO COMMUNITY COLLEGE, Box 246, Suisun City, California 94585. Music is a department within the college. Head: **David Froehlich** (1954). Department and college founded: 1944. Degree: A.A. (two-year college). Scholarships: one for $200. Music enrollment: 200. Music ensembles include: chorus chamber vocal ensemble, concert band, symphony orchestra, jazz ensemble. Music instruction is offered during the summer. . . . SONOMA STATE COLLEGE, 1801 East Cotati Avenue, Rohnert Park, California 94928. Music is a department within the college. Head: **Peggy Donovan-Jeffry** (1970). College established: 1961. Music Department added: 1963. Degree: B.A. Music majors enrolled: 75. No scholarships are available in music. Volumes in music library: 2,500 to 3,000. Music ensembles include: chorus, chamber vocal ensemble, opera workshop, symphony orchestra, jazz ensemble, and other small instrumental ensembles. Some instruction in music is offered in the summer. Special course: ethnomusicology. . . . STANISLAUS STATE

COLLEGE, 9800 Monte Vista Avenue, Turlock, California 95380. Music Department within a School of Fine Arts and Humanities. Head: **Scott Coulter** (1970). Degree: B.A. Scholarships: indefinite number totaling $300. Music students enrolled: 50 majors. Volumes in music library: 3,000. Official music ensembles: chorus, chamber vocal ensemble, concert band, chamber orchestra, other smaller chamber groups. Summer music instruction. . . . UNIVERSITY OF CALIFORNIA AT BERKELEY, Berkeley, California 94720. A Music Department within the College of Liberal Arts of the university. Chairman: **Daniel Heartz** (1969). University founded: 1869. Department founded: 1901. Degrees: A.B., M.A., Ph.D. Scholarships: about 15, totaling about $10,000. Graduate fellowships: about 30, totaling about $50,000. Music enrollment: 100 undergraduates; 50 graduates. Music library: 90,000 volumes (see Music Libraries). Music ensembles: chorus, chamber vocal ensemble, concert band, symphony orchestra, chamber orchestra, contemporary music ensemble, Collegium Musicum. The Department offers a summer school. Special courses: electronic studio; performance practice relative to the Department's several collections of rare, old instruments. . . . UNIVERSITY OF CALIFORNIA AT DAVIS, Davis, California 95616. Music Department within a College of Letters and Science. Head: **Theodore C. Karp** (1971). University founded: 1918. Department founded: 1958. Degrees: B.A., M.A. Scholarships and fellowships: those offered through the general university programs. Music students enrolled: 60. Volumes in music library: 24,000. Official school ensembles: chorus, chamber vocal ensemble, marching band, concert band, symphony orchestra, other student chamber ensembles. No summer music school. Special courses: electronic music. . . . UNIVERSITY OF CALIFORNIA, LOS ANGELES, 405 Hilgard Avenue, Los Angeles, California 90024. The Music Department is within the College of Fine Arts and College of Letters and Sciences. Chairman: **Walter H. Rubsamen** (1965). University founded: 1868. Department founded: 1919. Degrees: B.A., M.A., and Ph.D. Scholarships: 58 prizes totaling $30,700; 2 fellowships of $2,400 each; 25 to 30 teaching assistantships of $1,800 each. Music students enrolled: 450. Music library: 20,000 books; 22,000 records; 34,000 scores; 5,000 tapes; 2,000 microfilms and microprints (see Music Libraries). School music ensembles: chorus, glee glub, marching band, concert band, opera workshop, symphony orchestra, chamber orchestra, jazz ensembles, other instrumental chamber groups. Courses in music are offered in the regular summer session. Special music courses include: ethnomusicology, electronic music, and folk music. . . . UNIVERSITY OF CALIFORNIA AT RIVERSIDE, Riverside, California 92502. The Music Department is part of the College of Humanities. Chairman: **Donald C. Johns.** University established: 1954. Degrees: B.A., M.A. in music. Scholarships: none. Fellowships: two, totaling $5,000. Students enrolled: 600. Volumes in music library: 6,000. School ensembles include: chorus, chamber vocal ensemble, concert band, symphony orchestra, jazz ensemble, other smaller instrumental groups. No summer music school. . . . UNIVERSITY OF CALIFORNIA AT SAN DIEGO, Box 109, La Jolla, California 92037. Music Department within the university. Head: **John Silber** (1971). University founded: 1964. Music department founded: 1966. Degrees: B.A., M.A., Ph.D. No music scholarships. Music students enrolled: 150. Official school ensembles: chorus, chamber vocal ensemble, symphony orchestra, chamber orchestra, jazz ensemble, other smaller chamber groups. No summer music school. Special courses: acoustics, electronic music, new instrumental resources, audio circuitry. . . . UNIVERSITY OF CALIFORNIA AT SANTA BARBARA, Santa Barbara, California 93106. Department of Music within the College of Letters and Science. Chairman: **Peter Racine Fricker** (1970). University founded 1868. Department founded: 1944. Degrees: B.A., M.A., Ph.D. Music students enrolled: 165. Volumes in music library: 12,500. Official school ensembles: chorus, glee club, chamber vocal ensemble, concert band, opera workshop, symphony orchestra, chamber orchestra, jazz ensemble. No summer music school. . . . UNIVERSITY OF THE PACIFIC, 3501 Pacific Avenue, Stockton, California 95204. (Member, NASM.) Conservatory of Music connected with the endowed university. Dean: **Preston Stedman** (1966). University founded: 1851. Conservatory founded: 1878. Degrees offered: B.A., B.M., M.M., M.A., Ed.D. Scholarships: 49, totaling $53,110. Fellowships: four, totaling $13,450. Music students enrolled: 225. Volumes in music library: 10,000. Official school ensembles: chorus, glee club, chamber vocal ensemble, marching band, concert band, opera workshop, symphony orchestra, chamber orchestra, jazz ensemble, among others. Summer music school. . . . UNIVERSITY OF SAN DIEGO, Alcala Park, San Diego, California 92110. Music Department within university. Head: **Henry Kolar** (1970). University and music department founded: 1950. Degree: B.A. Scholarships: two, totaling $1,000. Music students enrolled: 55. Volumes in music library: 350. Official school ensembles: chorus, chamber vocal ensemble, opera workshop, symphony orchestra, chamber orchestra, in-residence chamber trio. Summer courses offered. Unique course: "The Romance of the Violin," an in-depth historical view of the violin with lectures by guest violin makers, performers, etc. . . . UNIVERSITY OF REDLANDS, Redlands, California 92373. School of Music in the university, affiliated with the Baptist Church. (Member, NASM.) Director: **Wayne R. Bohrnstedt** (1968). University founded: 1910. Degrees: B.M., B.A., M.M., M.A. Scholarships: no special music scholarships. Music students enrolled: 100. Volumes in music library: 8,528. Official school ensembles: two choruses, two chamber vocal ensembles, marching band, concert band, opera workshop, symphony orchestra, chamber orchestra, jazz ensemble. Summer school. Special courses: electronic music, Black music. . . . UNIVERSITY OF SOUTHERN CALIFORNIA, University Park, Los Angeles, California 90007. (Member, NASM.) School of Music within the School of Performing Arts. Dean: **Grant Beglarian.** University founded: 1880. Music School founded: 1884. Degrees: B.M., M.M., D.M.A., B.A., M.A., Ph.D. Scholarships: usually 50 to 60, totaling about $100,000. Fellowships: 20, totaling $40,000. Music students enrolled: 500. Volumes in music library: 40,000 (see Music Libraries). Official school ensembles: chorus, chamber vocal ensemble, marching band, concert band, opera workshop, symphony orchestra, chamber orchestra, and smaller chamber groups. Summer music school. Master classes with **Heifetz, Lhevinne** and **Piatigorsky.** . . . VENTURA COLLEGE, 4667 Telegraph Road, Ventura, California 93003. Music discipline within the Department of Performing Arts within a community college. Head: **Alfred Wilkinson** (1970). College and Department founded: 1952. No music scholarships. Music students enrolled: 100. Volumes in music library: 800. Official school ensembles: two choruses, chamber vocal ensemble, concert band, symphony orchestra, other smaller chamber groups. Summer courses. Also a Midsummer Music Festival.

COLORADO

ADAMS STATE COLLEGE, Alamosa, Colorado 81101. (Member, NASM.) Department within college. Music coordinator: **Gordon B. Childs** (1968). Chairman, Division of Fine Arts: **Glen A. Yarberry.** College and department founded: 1925. Degrees: B.A., M.A., either in music education or performance. Scholarships: 60, totaling $18,000. Fellowships: four assistantships totaling $9,000. Music students enrolled: 300 (100 majors). Volumes in music library: 1,200. Official school ensembles: chorus, chamber vocal ensemble, marching band, concert band, opera workshop, chamber orchestra, jazz ensemble, Collegium Musicum, other smaller chamber groups. Summer music school. Special courses: major on viola d'amore. . . . COLORADO COLLEGE, Colorado Springs, Colorado 80903. (Member, NASM.) Music Department within an endowed college. Head: **Albert Seay** (1966). College founded: 1875. Degrees: B.A., M.A., M.A.T. Scholarships: five, totaling $5,000. Fellowships: none. Music students enrolled: 50. Volumes in music library: 6,000. Official school ensembles: chorus, chamber vocal ensemble, concert band, opera workshop, symphony orchestra, chamber orchestra. Summer music instruction. . . . COLORADO STATE UNIVERSITY, Fort Collins, Colorado 80521. Department of Music in the College of Humanities and Social Sciences. Head: **Robert L. Garretson** (1968). Music department founded: 1884. University founded: 1870. Degrees: B.M. in performance, music education; B.A. in music; M.A. for teachers; M.M. in performance, conducting, music education, music history and literature, theory, and composition. Music enrollment: 250 (including summer). Music library: 6,000 volumes. Ensembles: chorus, chamber vocal ensembles, marching band, concert band, opera workshop, symphony orchestra, chamber orchestra, jazz ensemble, opera orchestra, symphonic wind ensemble, brass choir, woodwind choir, percussion ensemble, men's chorus, women's chorus. Two five-week summer sessions offered. . . . LAMAR COMMUNITY COLLEGE, Lamar, Colorado 81052. Music Department within college. Head: **Fritz K. Kramer.** Degree: A.A. in Mus. Ed. Scholarships: 10, totaling $2,500. Music students enrolled: 10. Music Library: 200 volumes and 200 records. Official school ensembles: chorus, chamber vocal ensemble, marching band, concert band, opera workshop. . . . METROPOLITAN STATE COLLEGE, 250 West 14th Avenue, Denver, Colorado 80204. Music Department within the college. Head: **Lloyd K. Herren** (1966). College founded: 1965. Department founded: 1966. Degree: B.A. Scholarships: 25 tuition waivers. Music courses enrollment: 900. Volumes in music library: 1,500. Official school ensembles: chorus, glee club, chamber vocal ensemble, concert band, opera workshop, symphony orchestra, jazz ensemble, other smaller chamber groups. Unusual courses: Afro-American Music. Summer music courses are offered. . . . MESA COLLEGE, Grand Junction, Colorado 81501. Department of Music within the college. Chairman: **Darrell Blackburn** (1963). College and music department founded: 1925. Degree: A.A. Scholarships: 10 to 15, totaling $1,700. Music students enrolled: 200. Volumes in music library: 1,000. Official school ensembles: chorus, modern choir, chamber vocal ensemble, marching band, concert band, symphony orchestra, jazz ensemble, brass quintet. No summer music instruction. . . . SOUTHERN COLORADO STATE COLLEGE, Pueblo, Colorado 81005. (Member, NASM.) A Department in the Division of Humanities in a state-supported college. Head: **James L. Duncan.** Degrees: B.A. in music history–literature, music education; B.S. in theory–composition, music performance. . . . UNIVERSITY OF DENVER, 2370 East Evans Avenue, Denver, Colorado 80210. (Member, NASM.) Lamont School of Music, a department of an endowed university. Head: **Roger Dexter Fee** (1953). University founded: 1864. School of Music founded: 1880. Degrees: B.A., B.M., B.M.E., M.A. Scholarships: 63, totaling $24,775.75. Fellowships: none. Music students enrolled: 150. Volumes in music library: 10,000. Official school ensembles: chorus, glee club, concert band, opera workshop, symphony orchestra, chamber orchestra, jazz ensemble. Summer music courses. . . . UNIVERSITY OF NORTHERN COLORADO, Greeley, Colorado 80631. Independent School of Music within a state-supported university. Dean: **James E. Miller** (1965). University founded: 1889. School founded: 1904. Degrees: B.A., B.M., M.A., Ed.S., Ed.D. Scholarships: number varies; total $20,000. Fellowships: number varies; total $30,000. Music students enrolled: 370. Music library: 4,500 books, 4,000 scores, 4,000 discs, 450 tapes. Official music ensembles: chorus, glee club, chamber vocal ensemble, marching band, concert band, opera workshop, symphony orchestra, chamber orchestra, string, brass, and woodwind ensembles, jazz ensemble. Summer music school. . . . WESTERN STATE COLLEGE, Gunnison, Colorado 81230. Music Division within the college. Chairman: **Rodney Ash** (1968). College and division founded: 1920. Degrees: M.A., B.A. Music students enrolled: 75. Official school music ensembles: chorus, chamber vocal ensemble, marching band, concert band, opera workshop, symphony orchestra, jazz ensemble, other smaller chamber groups. Summer instruction.

CONNECTICUT

ANNHURST COLLEGE, Woodstock, R.R. #2, Connecticut 06281. Music Department within the college. Head: **Sister Gertrude Bonin** (1969). College founded: 1941. Music department founded: 1969. At present no music degrees except for minor study. Scholarships: none. Music students enrolled: 50. Music library: 300 books, 475 records. Official school ensembles: glee club, chamber vocal ensemble. Summer courses in music. . . . CENTRAL CONNECTICUT STATE COLLEGE, 1615 Stanley Street, New Britain, Connecticut 06050. Music Department within college. Head: **Robert C. Soule** (1966). College founded: 1849. Degrees: B.A. in Mus. Ed. implemented in 1971. Scholarships: three, totaling $300. Music students enrolled: 50. Volumes in music library: 3,800. Official school ensembles: chorus, marching band, concert band, chamber orchestra, jazz ensemble. Summer music courses. . . . THE HARTFORD CONSERVATORY, 834–846 Asylum Avenue, Hartford, Connecticut 06105. A conservatory of music. Head: **Geraldine Douglass** (1971). Founded: 1890. Degrees: diploma (two-year program) in piano, voice, orchestra instrument, theory, jazz and popular music, modern dance, ballet, musical theatre. Scholarships: 40, totaling $6,400. Enrollment: 1,500. Music library: 10,000 volumes. Ensembles: symphony orchestra, small chamber groups, jazz and percussion ensembles, modern dance ensemble, Connecticut Valley Regional Ballet Company (affiliate). Summer courses offered, also a dance workshop. . . . HARTT COLLEGE OF MUSIC OF THE UNIVERSITY OF HARTFORD, 200 Bloomfield Avenue, West Hartford, Connecticut 06117. (Member, NASM.) College of Music of a privately supported and endowed university. Head: **Donald Mattran** (1972), successor to **Moshe Paranov** who served from 1920 to 1972. University founded: 1957. College founded: 1920. Degrees: B.Mus., B.Mus.Ed., M.Mus., M.Mus.Ed. Scholarships: 55, totaling $87,000. Fellowships: none. Music students enrolled: 600. Volumes in music library: 32,000. Official school ensembles: chorus, chamber vocal ensemble, concert band, opera workshop, symphony orchestra, chamber orchestra, jazz ensemble. Collegium Musicum, other smaller chamber groups. Summer music school. . . . NEIGHBORHOOD MUSIC SCHOOL, 100 Audubon Street, New Haven, Connecticut 06511. A community music school. Head: **Kenneth A. Wendrich** (1967). Founded: 1911. Scholarships: 101, totaling $20,000. Music enrollment: 900. Music library: 500 volumes. Ensembles: chorus, chamber vocal ensemble, symphony orchestra, chamber orchestra. Summer music school. . . . UNIVERSITY OF CONNECTICUT, Storrs, Connecticut 06268. (Member, NASM.) Music Department in a School of Fine Arts of a state university. Head: **Louis L. Crowder** (1965). Degrees: B.M., B.S. in music education, M.A. in music and music education. Scholarships: none through the music department; only available through the university. Fellowships: six graduate assistantships totaling $18,000. Music enrollment: 160 undergraduate, 60 graduate. Music library: 15,000 volumes. Ensembles: chorus, concert choir, chamber vocal ensemble, marching band, concert band, symphony orchestra, chamber orchestra, string quartet, jazz ensemble, woodwind quintet. Summer music school offered. . . . YALE UNIVERSITY SCHOOL OF MUSIC, New Haven, Connecticut 06520. (Member, NASM.) Graduate professional school, part of an endowed university. Dean: **Philip F. Nelson** (1970). University founded: 1701. School of Music founded: 1894. Degrees: M.M., M.M.A., D.M.A. Scholarships: available on basis of need. Music enrollment: 130. Official music ensembles: glee club, marching band, concert band, opera workshop, symphony orchestra, chamber orchestra, smaller chamber groups, jazz ensemble. Summer music school.

DELAWARE

UNIVERSITY OF DELAWARE, Newark, Delaware 19711. Chairman: **Anthony J. Loudis.** Music majors: 93. . . . WESLEY COLLEGE, Dover, Delaware 19901. Music

Department within a two-year college. Chairman: **Robert W. Bailey** (1957). College founded: 1873. Degree: A.A. Scholarships: five, totaling $1,000. Music students enrolled: 25. Volumes in music library: 650. Official school music ensembles: chorus, chamber vocal ensemble, concert band, chamber orchestra, jazz ensemble. No summer music school. . . . WILMINGTON MUSIC SCHOOL INC., 4101 Washington Street, Wilmington, Delaware 19802. Director: **Orlando Otey.**

WASHINGTON, D.C.

THE AMERICAN UNIVERSITY, Washington, D.C. 20016. (Member, NASM.) Department of Music within a college of arts and sciences of a university affiliated with the Methodist Church. Chairman: **Lloyd Ultan** (1962). University founded: 1893. Music department founded: circa 1940. Degrees: B.A., B.Mus.Ed., B.M., M.A. Scholarships: six, totaling approximately $5,000. Fellowships: six, totaling $26,088. Music enrollment: 175 to 200. Music library: 4,000 recordings; 4,000 scores; estimated 6,000 books and periodicals. Ensembles: chorus, chamber vocal ensemble, concert band, smaller chamber groups, jazz ensemble. Summer program with Wolf Trap American University Academy (see Festivals). Special work done with Moog synthesizer, historical approach to music theory for all undergraduates. . . . CATHOLIC UNIVERSITY OF AMERICA, Washington, D.C. 20017. (Member, NASM.) School of Music founded: 1950. Degrees: B.A., B.M., M.M., M.A., D.M.A., Ph.D. Scholarships: 75, totaling $55,000. Fellowships: six, totaling $27,000. Music students enrolled: 450. Volumes in music library: 20,000 Official school ensembles: chorus, chamber vocal ensemble, concert band, opera workshop, symphony orchestra, chamber orchestra, jazz ensemble, brass choir, string orchestra, trombone choir. Summer music school. Special facility: electronic music laboratory. . . . THE GEORGE WASHINGTON UNIVERSITY, Washington, D.C. 20006. Music Department within the College of Liberal Arts. Head: **George Steiner** (1961). University founded: 1820. Degrees: B.A., M.A., M.M. Official school ensembles: chorus, chamber vocal ensemble, symphony orchestra, jazz ensemble, other smaller chamber groups. Summer music courses. . . . HOWARD UNIVERSITY SCHOOL OF MUSIC, Washington, D.C. 20001. (Member, NASM.) A university school supported by the federal government. Dean: **Warner Lawson.** Degrees: B.M. in applied music, theory and composition, history, and literature; B.M.Ed.; M.M. in applied music, composition, history, and musicology. Music majors: 182. Music library: about 5,000 volumes.

FLORIDA

BREVARD COMMUNITY COLLEGE, Clearlake Road, Cocoa, Florida 32922. Music Department within the Division of Fine Arts of the college. Department chairman: **N. P. Baggarly** (1969). College founded: 1960. Department founded: 1964. Degree: A.A. Scholarships: 28, totaling $4,200. Music students enrolled: 60. Volumes in music library: 200. Official school ensembles: chorus, glee club, concert band, opera workshop, jazz ensemble. No summer music instruction. . . . FLORIDA AGRICULTURAL AND MECHANICAL UNIVERSITY (A & M), Tallahassee, Florida 32307. Music Department within a college of arts and sciences. Chairman: **William P. Foster** (1949). University founded: 1887. Music Department founded: 1893. Music enrollment: 186. Official school ensembles: chorus, marching band, symphonic band, wind ensemble, brass ensemble, percussion ensemble, jazz ensemble. Summer music courses. . . . FLORIDA ATLANTIC UNIVERSITY, West 20th Street, Boca Raton, Florida 33432. Music Department in the College of Humanities. Head: **Eugene N. Crabb** (1967). University and department founded: 1964. Degrees: B.A., B.F.A. Scholarships: 10 totaling $2,500. Music students enrolled: 65. Volumes in music library: 3,500. Official school ensembles: chorus, chamber vocal ensemble, concert band, opera workshop, symphony orchestra, chamber orchestra, jazz ensemble. Limited summer instruction. . . . FLORIDA INSTITUTE OF TECHNOLOGY, Country Club Road, Melbourne, Florida 32901. Music is an extra-curricular, school-supported activity. College founded: 1958. Music instituted: 1971. Official school ensemble: concert band. No summer music instruction. . . . FLORIDA PRESBYTERIAN COLLEGE, Box 12560, St. Petersburg, Florida 33733. Music Department within the college. Head: **William E. Waters** (1968). College and department founded: 1960. Degrees: B.A. Scholarships: number varies within a budget of $5,000. Music students enrolled: 100. Volumes in music library: 2,000. Official school ensembles: chorus, chamber vocal ensemble, brass ensemble, woodwind ensemble. No summer music instruction. . . . FLORIDA STATE UNIVERSITY, Tallahassee, Florida 32306. (Member, NASM.) School of Music within a university. Dean: **Wiley E. Housewright.** School of Music founded: 1911. Degrees: B.M., B.A., B.M.E., M.M., M.M.E., Ph.D., D.M., Ed.D. Scholarships: 60, totaling $40,000. Fellowships: 40, totaling $65,000. Music enrollment: 800. Music library: 36,000 volumes (see Music Libraries). Ensembles: chorus, men and women's glee club, chamber vocal ensemble, marching band, two concert bands, opera workshop, symphony orchestra, chamber orchestra, string quartet, wind quintet, jazz ensemble, dance theater, dance studio. Summer music school offered. Special dance and music therapy courses taught. . . . JACKSONVILLE UNIVERSITY, College of Fine Arts, Jacksonville, Florida 32211. (Member, NASM.) Music is a division within the College of Fine Arts within the university. Chairman, Division of Music: **James Hoffren** (1969). University and music division founded: 1934. Degrees: B.M.E., B.M., B.F.A., B.A. with major in music. Scholarships: many part- and full-tuition scholarships. Music enrollment: 140 majors, many minors. Music library, 20,000 volumes. Ensembles: chorus, glee club, chamber vocal ensemble, concert band, opera workshop, symphony orchestra, chamber orchestra, smaller chamber groups, jazz ensemble. Summer music school. Special courses in composition with Moog synthesizer; opportunity to perform with local symphony orchestra for $1,000 income. . . . LAKE CITY COMMUNITY COLLEGE, U.S. Highway 90, Lake City, Florida 32055. Music courses within Humanities Department including studies in art and philosophy. Head: **William L. Poplin, Jr.** (1968). College founded: 1962. Degree: A.A. No music majors. Volumes in music library: 300. Official school ensembles: chorus, chamber vocal ensemble, jazz ensemble, and other chamber groups. No summer music instruction. . . . PALM BEACH JUNIOR COLLEGE, 4200 South Congress, Lake Worth, Florida 33460. Music Department within the college. Chairman: **Letha Madge Royce** (1949). Degrees: A.A., A.S. Number and amount of scholarships varies. Students enrolled in music: 80. Official school ensembles: chorus, pop vocal ensemble, concert band, jazz ensemble. Summer music instruction. . . . ROLLINS COLLEGE, Winter Park, Florida 32789. (Member, NASM.) A Department of Music in an endowed college. Chairman: **Ross Rosazza.** Degree: B.A. with major in music. Music majors: 25. . . . ST. PETERSBURG JUNIOR COLLEGE, 6605 Fifth Avenue North, St. Petersburg, Florida 33710. Music Department within a two-year college. Head: **Charles M. Carroll** (1964). College and department founded: 1927. Degree: A.A. Scholarships: five for a total of $1,000. Music students enrolled: 100. Volumes in music library: 1,000. Official school ensembles: chorus, chamber vocal ensemble, concert band, opera workshop, chamber orchestra, jazz ensemble, and other smaller chamber groups. Summer music courses. . . . STETSON UNIVERSITY SCHOOL OF MUSIC, Deland, Florida 32720. (Member, NASM.) School of Music within a university. Dean: **Paul T. Langston** (1963). University founded: 1883. Music school founded: 1893. Degrees: B.M., B.M.E., A.B. in music. Scholarships: approximately $15,000. Music enrollment: 150. Music library: 2,400 volumes, 4,000 scores, 2,300 records. Music ensembles: chorus, chamber vocal ensemble (Collegium), concert band, opera workshop, chamber orchestra, symphony orchestra, faculty trio and quartet. Summer music school offered; also a four-week summer orchestral institute. Special courses in acoustics and audio electronics. . . . UNIVERSITY OF FLORIDA, Gainesville, Florida 32601. (Member, NASM.) Department of Music in the College of Architecture and Fine Arts of a state-supported university. Chairman: **Reid Poole** (1961). University founded: 1853. Department founded: 1948. Degrees: B.A., B.M., B.Mus.Ed., M.Mus.Ed. Scholarships: 40, totaling $6,000. Music students enrolled: 180. Volumes in music library: 20,000. Official school ensembles: university choir, glee clubs, chamber vocal ensemble, marching band, concert band, opera workshop, symphony orchestra, chamber orchestra, jazz ensemble, Collegium Musicum, many other small instrumental chamber groups. Summer music school. . . . UNIVERSITY OF MIAMI, SCHOOL OF MUSIC, Coral Gables, Florida 33124. (Member, NASM.) An independent school within an endowed university. Dean: **William F. Lee.** Degrees: B.M. in applied music, theory–composition; B.A. in applied music, theory–composition; M.M. in applied music, music education, theory–composition, conducting. Music majors: 430. Music library: about 10,000 volumes. . . . UNIVERSITY OF SOUTH FLORIDA, Tampa, Florida 33620. Department of Music within a college. Head: **Gale Sperry** (1960). University and department founded: 1960. Degrees: B.A., M.A., M.M. Scholarships: 23, each for $825. Fellowships: 11, each for $2,700. Music students enrolled: 375. Volumes in music library: 4,000. Official school ensembles: chorus, chamber vocal ensemble, two concert bands, opera workshop, symphony orchestra, chamber orchestra, jazz ensemble, other smaller chamber groups. Summer music school. . . . THE UNIVERSITY OF WEST FLORIDA, Pensacola, Florida 32504. Music Department within Gamma College of the University. Chairman: **Grier M. Williams** (1968). University and department founded: 1967. Degrees: B.A., major in music education. Scholarships: number varies but total approximately $2,000. Music students enrolled: 25. Volumes in music library: 7,500. Official school ensembles: chorus, chamber vocal ensemble, concert band, brass ensemble. Music courses in summer school.

GEORGIA

ALBANY STATE COLLEGE, Holley Boulevard, Albany, Georgia 31705. Music Department within the college. Head: **James Marquis** (1965). College founded: 1902. Music Department founded: 1961. Degrees: B.S., B.A. Scholarships: 25, totaling $4,000. Music students enrolled: 40. Volumes in music library: 3,000. Official school ensembles: chorus, chamber vocal ensemble, marching band, concert band, wind and percussion ensembles, jazz ensemble. Summer music courses. . . . ARMSTRONG STATE COLLEGE, 11935 Abercorn Street, Savannah, Georgia 31406. Music within the Fine Arts Department. Head: **James H. Persse** (1965). Department founded: 1965. Degree: B.A. No music scholarships. Music students enrolled: 25. Volumes in music library: 600. Official school ensembles: chorus, concert band, stage band. No summer music courses. . . . AUGUSTA COLLEGE, Augusta, Georgia 30904. (Member, NASM.) A Department of Music in the Division of Fine Arts of a state-supported college. Chairman: **Eloy Fominaya.** Degrees: B.A. in music; B.A. in music (prospective teacher). . . . BERRY COLLEGE, Mt. Berry, Georgia 30149. Department of Music within a liberal arts college. Head: **Darwin G. White** (1968). College and department founded: 1902. Degrees: B.A., B.M. Students enrolled in music: 50. Volumes in music library: 3,000. Official school ensembles: chorus, chamber vocal ensemble, concert band, opera workshop, jazz ensemble, smaller chamber groups. Summer instruction. . . . BREWTON PARKER COLLEGE, Mt. Vernon, Georgia 30445. Music Department within a two-year college. Head: **Hildegard Jo Stanley** (1966). Degree: A.A. Scholarships: 64 general scholarships totaling $26,500. Music students enrolled: 70. Volumes in music library: 1,000. Official school ensembles: choir, vocal ensemble, concert band, Dixieland band, stage band, brass ensemble, woodwind ensemble. No summer music courses. . . . BRUNSWICK JUNIOR COLLEGE, Altama at 4th Street, Brunswick, Georgia 31520. Music part of Humanities Division within a college in the university system of Georgia. Head: **Mrs. Neil Nilsson** (1970). College founded 1960. Division founded: 1968. No specific music degree. Music students enrolled: 5. Official school ensembles: chorus, jazz ensemble. No summer music program. . . . EMORY UNIVERSITY, Atlanta, Georgia 30322. Department of Music within a college of the university. Head: **William W. Lemonds** (1967). University founded: 1836. Department founded: 1963. Degree: B.A. with a major in music. Music students enrolled: 10. Volumes in music library: 7,000. Official school ensembles: chorus, glee club, chamber vocal ensemble, concert band, opera workshop, other smaller chamber groups. The department programs an annual Summer Workshop for Historical Instruments. . . . GAINESVILLE JUNIOR COLLEGE, Gainesville, Georgia 30501. Music Department within Humanities Division. Chairman: **Mary Ann Hickman** (1968). College founded: 1966. Department founded: 1968. Degree: A.A. in applied music or music education. Scholarships: eight, totaling $250. Music students enrolled: 13 majors. Volumes in music library: 350. Official school ensembles: choir, chamber vocal ensemble, band, jazz ensemble. No summer music courses. . . . GEORGIA SOUTHERN COLLEGE, Box 8052, Landrum Center, Statesboro, Georgia 30458. Department of Music in the School of Arts and Sciences. Head: **Jack W. Broucek** (1970). College founded: 1908. Department founded: 1937. Degrees: B.M., B.S. in Ed., B.A., M.S. for teachers, M.Ed., Sixth-Year Certificate for Ed.S. Scholarships: six, totaling $875. No fellowships. Music students enrolled: 115. Volumes in music library: 6,000. Official school ensembles: chorus, glee club, chamber vocal ensemble, concert band, opera workshop, symphony orchestra, jazz ensemble, other chamber groups. Summer music school. . . . GEORGIA SOUTHWESTERN COLLEGE, Wheatley Street, Americus, Georgia 31709. Music Department within Humanities Division. Head: **Donald W. Forrester** (1969). College founded: 1908. Department founded: 1970. Degree: B.S. in Education with music major. Scholarships: none presently. Music students enrolled: 24 (first year). Volumes in music library: 1,000. Official school ensembles: chorus, concert band. No summer music instruction. . . . GEORGIA STATE UNIVERSITY, 33 Gilmer Street, Atlanta, Georgia 30303. (Member, NASM.) Department of Music within a university. Head: **Thomas M. Brumby** (1950). University founded: 1914. Music department founded: 1947. Degrees: B.M., M.M. Music enrollment: 884. Music library: 5,000 volumes. Ensembles: chorus, chamber vocal ensemble, concert band, symphony orchestra, smaller chamber groups. Summer music school offered. . . . MERCER UNIVERSITY, Macon, Georgia 31207. Music Department within the Liberal Arts College. Head: **Arthur L. Rich** (1944). University and department founded: 1833. Degree: B.A. in music. Scholarships: 20, totaling $4,000. Music students enrolled: 150 (35 majors). Volumes in music library: 5,000. Official school ensembles: chorus, chamber vocal ensemble, piano ensemble. Summer courses in music. . . . MIDDLE GEORGIA COLLEGE, Cochran, Georgia 31014. Music Department within a junior college. Head: **Nat E. Frazer** (1967). College founded: 1884. Department founded: 1943. Degree: A.A. in music. Scholarships: work–study programs (10 for $480 a year). No separate music library; holdings in main library. Music students enrolled: 24. Official school ensembles: chorus, chamber vocal ensemble, jazz ensemble, community chorus. No summer music courses. . . . SHORTER COLLEGE, Rome, Georgia 30161. (Member, NASM.) A Department of Music in an endowed college. Head: **John Ramsaur.** Degrees: B.M. in theory–composition, applied music; B.A., B.M.Ed. Music majors: 90. . . . TIFT COLLEGE, Forsyth, Georgia 31029. Department of Music within a liberal arts college for women. Head: **James R. Davidson** (1971). College founded: 1849. Department founded: 1859. Degree: B.A. in music and music education. Scholarships: number varies; total $450. Music students enrolled: 24. Volumes in music library: 1,023 books, 256 scores, 1,038 recordings. Official school ensembles: chorus, wind ensemble. Summer courses in music. . . . TRUETT McCONNELL COLLEGE, Cleveland, Georgia 30528. (Member, NASM.) A Department of Music in a private junior college. Chairman: **David L. Johnson.** Degree: Associate in music. . . . UNIVERSITY OF GEORGIA, Athens, Georgia 30601. (Member, NASM.) A Department of Music in the Division of Fine Arts of the College of Arts and Sciences of a state-supported university. Head: **David A. Ledet** (1972). Degrees: B.M. in applied music, music education, composition, music therapy; B.F.A. in music theory, music literature; B.A. major in music; M.A. in musicology; M.F.A. in composition, music literature, applied music; M.Mus.Ed. Music majors: 240. Music Library: 1,000 volumes. . . . VALDOSTA STATE COLLEGE, Valdosta, Georgia 31601. Music Department within a college. Head: **Webster Teague** (1960). College and department founded: 1913. Degrees: B.A. in music, B.S. in music education. Scholarships: three, totaling $375. Music students enrolled: 40 majors. Volumes in music library: 3,000. Official school ensembles: chorus, chamber vocal ensemble, concert band, opera workshop, chamber orchestra, jazz ensemble, brass ensemble. Music courses in summer. . . . WESLEYAN COLLEGE, Macon, Georgia 31201. (Member, NASM.) A Department of Music in an endowed and church-related college. Chairman: **Leon Jacques Villard.** Degrees: B.M. in applied music, school music, church music; B.A. in applied music. Music majors: 80.

GUAM

THE UNIVERSITY OF GUAM, Box EK, Agana, Guam 96910. Music Department in the Fine Arts Division within a university. Head: **Daniel H. MacDonald** (1968). Degree: A.A. Scholarships: for first two years free tuition for all students who are residents. Volumes in music library: 1,800. Official music ensembles: chorus, chamber vocal ensemble, concert band, opera workshops, symphony orchestra, jazz ensemble. Summer music instruction. Special courses: Micronesian music.

HAWAII

CHURCH COLLEGE OF HAWAII, 55–220 Kulanui, Laie, Hawaii 96762. Music Department within a liberal arts college. Head: **M. L. Tew** (1969). College founded: 1954. Department founded: 1958. Degrees: B.A. in various music areas such as instrumental and choral education, etc. Scholarships: 15, totaling $7,700. Fellowships: three, totaling $3,000. Music students enrolled: 100. Volumes in music library: 500. Official school ensembles: two choruses, concert band, opera workshop, jazz ensemble, and other smaller chamber groups. Limited summer instruction based on demand. . . . UNIVERSITY OF HAWAII, 2411 Dole Street, Honolulu, Hawaii 96822. Department of Music within the College of Arts and Sciences. Head: **Allen R. Trubitt** (1971). School founded: 1907. Degrees: B.A., B.M., B.Ed. in music, M.A., M.M. Scholarships: (1970–71) 9, totaling $620; (1971–72) 17, totaling $3,000. Music enrollment: 230. Music library: 11,400 volumes. Official school ensembles: chorus, chamber vocal ensemble, marching band, concert band, opera workshop, symphony orchestra, stage band, ethnic ensembles. Summer music school is offered and "The Festival of the Arts of This Century." Special course in ethnomusicology.

IDAHO

THE COLLEGE OF IDAHO, Cleveland Boulevard, Caldwell, Idaho 83605. Music Department within a liberal arts college. Head: **Richard D. Skyrm** (1957). College founded: 1891. Department founded: 1912. Degree: B.A. in various music applications. Scholarships: vary in number and amount. Music students enrolled: 200 (30 majors). College library has over 150,000 volumes with no separate breakdown of music holdings. Official school ensembles: chorus, chamber vocal ensemble, concert band, symphony orchestra, chamber orchestra, jazz ensemble, wind ensemble, other smaller chamber groups. No summer music session. . . . RICKS COLLEGE, Rexburg, Idaho 83440. (Member, NASM.) A junior college supported by the Church of Latter Day Saints. Head: **Chester W. Hill.** Degrees: Associate Degree (Transfer Degree), Junior College Diploma (Terminal Certificate). Music majors: 86. . . . UNIVERSITY OF IDAHO, Moscow, Idaho 83843. (Member, NASM.) A school of Music in a state-supported university and land-grant college. Director: **Floyd Peterson.** Degrees: B.M. in music education, performance, composition: B.A. in music; M.M. in performance, composition–theory, music literature, music education; M.A. in music history and literature. Music majors: 150.

ILLINOIS

AMERICAN CONSERVATORY OF MUSIC, 410 South Michigan Avenue, Chicago, Illinois 60605. (Member, NASM.) An independent, unendowed conservatory. Dean: **Leo E. Heim** (1957). Conservatory founded: 1886. Degrees: B.M., M.M., B.M.E., D.M.A. Scholarships: 30, totaling $6,000. Fellowships: none. Music students enrolled: 400. Volumes in music library: 1,500. Official school ensembles: chorus, opera workshop, symphony orchestra, jazz ensemble. Summer music school. . . . AUGUSTANA COLLEGE, Rock Island, Illinois 61201. (Member, NASM.) A Department of Music in the Fine Arts Division of a college, endowed and supported by the Lutheran Church. Chairman, Division of Fine Arts: **Ronald F. Jesson.** Degrees: B.M. in applied music, composition, church music; B.A. in music, history and literature; B.M.Ed. Music majors: 85. . . . BLACKBURN COLLEGE, 700 College Avenue, Carlinville, Illinois 62626. Music Department within the college. Head: **Harold S. Lowe** (1947). College founded: 1857. Department founded: 1970. Degree: B.A. Official school ensembles: chorus, chamber vocal ensemble, concert band. No summer music instruction. . . . BLACK HAWK COLLEGE, 6600–34 Avenue, Moline, Illinois 61265. Music Department within a two-year college. Head: **Roger A. Perley** (1968). College and department founded: 1963. Degree: A.A. Scholarships: three, totaling $250. Music students enrolled: 50. Volumes in music library: 1,100 books; 1,200 records. Official school ensembles: chorus, chamber vocal ensemble, concert band, opera workshop, jazz ensemble, other smaller chamber groups. Summer instruction. . . . BRADLEY UNIVERSITY, Peoria, Illinois 61606. (Member, NASM.) A School of Music within a university. Head: **Allen Cannon** (1957). University founded: 1897. School of music founded: 1925. Degrees: B.M., B.M.E., B.S. in music-business, B.A. with major in music. Scholarships: five, totaling $10,000, plus financial aid beyond this as determined by need. Music enrollment: 75. Music library: 3,000 volumes, 5,000 recordings, 5,000 scores, 100 tapes. Ensembles: chorus, chamber vocal ensemble, concert band, opera workshop, symphony orchestra (arrangement with Peoria Symphony), chamber orchestra, jazz ensemble. Summer music school offered. Special courses: electronic music synthesizer, combination music and business degree. . . . CHICAGO CITY COLLEGE, KENNEDY–KING CAMPUS, 7047 South Stewart Street, Chicago, Illinois 60621. Music Department within a college. Chairman: **Otto T. Jelinek** (1966). College and department founded: 1933. Degree A.A. Scholarships: four, totaling $400. Music students enrolled: 450. Official school ensembles: chorus, chamber vocal ensemble, concert band, chamber orchestra, jazz ensemble, other smaller chamber groups. Special courses: commercial music workshop. Summer music school. . . . CHICAGO CONSERVATORY COLLEGE, 410 South Michigan Avenue, Chicago, Illinois 60605. (Member, NASM.) An independent, unendowed music conservatory. Head: **François D'Albert,** President (1959). Founded: 1857. Degrees: B.M., M.M., B.M.E., M.M.E. No scholarships or fellowships. Music students enrolled: 275 (college level). Volumes in music library: 7,000. Official school ensembles: chorus, chamber vocal ensemble, opera workshop, chamber orchestra. Summer music school. . . . CHICAGO MUSICAL COLLEGE OF ROOSEVELT UNIVERSITY, 430 South Michigan Avenue, Chicago, Illinois 60605. (Member, NASM.) A college within a university. Dean: **Felix Ganz** (1970). University founded: 1945. College of Music founded: 1867 (formerly an independent music college). Degrees: B.M., M.M., B.A., all in performance, music history, composition, theory, music education. Graduate fellowships: maximum of two totaling $2,000, plus full tuition. Music enrollment: 300 undergraduate, 70 graduate. Music library: 18,000 music books; 7,000 recordings. Ensembles: chorus, concert choir, concert band, opera workshop, symphony orchestra, baroque chamber orchestra, string quartet, jazz ensemble, woodwind, brass, percussion and contemporary music ensembles, duo piano ensemble. Summer music school offered plus additional special courses: electronic composition and a comprehensive music education curriculum. In 1970–71 the college won ASCAP/NFMC award for performing the most U.S. music among all private universities. . . . CHICAGO STATE UNIVERSITY, 6800 South Stewart Avenue, Chicago, Illinois 60621. Music Department within a university. Head: **Sylvan D. Ward.** University founded: 1869. Degrees: B.S. in education; B.A.—both with music majors. Scholarships: 10 totaling $1,800 per semester. Music students enrolled: 48. Volumes in music library: 950 in addition to music scores. Official school ensembles: chorus, glee club, chamber vocal ensemble, concert band, jazz ensemble, other smaller chamber groups. Summer music courses. . . . DEPAUL UNIVERSITY, 25 East Jackson Boulevard, Chicago, Illinois 60604. (Member, NASM.) A School of Music within a university supported by the Catholic Church. Dean: **Leon Stein** (1966). University founded: 1898. School of Music founded: 1919. Degrees: B.M. for all branches of applied music, composition, music education; B.A. with a major in music theory; M.M. in applied music, composition, music education, theory, and church music. Scholarships: 5 special competitive tuition awards of $1,000 each; 1 full-tuition at $1,740; 20 at $980 each (disbursed over four years for each recipient); various grants and loans from State of Illinois, DePaul School of Music, etc. Fellowships: amounts totaling $18,000. Music enrollment: 325 undergraduates, 65 graduates, and 90 in the Preparatory Division. Music library: 6,000 volumes. Music ensembles: chorus, glee club, chamber vocal ensemble, concert band, opera workshop, symphony orchestra, smaller chamber groups, jazz ensemble. Summer music school. Special course in electronic music. . . . EASTERN ILLINOIS UNIVERSITY, Charleston, Illinois 61920. (Member, NASM.) School of Music within a university. Dean: **Robert Y. Hare** (1965). University founded: 1895. School of Music founded: 1960. Degrees: B.M., B.A., B.S. in education, M.S., M.A. Scholarships: 20 tuition waivers totaling $10,000 (undergraduate). Assistantships: five totaling $12,150, plus tuition waiver. Music enrollment: 200. Music ensembles: chorus, chamber vocal ensemble, marching band, concert band, opera workshop, symphony orchestra, chamber orchestra, smaller chamber groups, jazz ensemble. Summer music school offered. Special courses include a master's degree program in class piano pedagogy. . . . ELMHURST COLLEGE, 190 Prospect Street, Elmhurst, Illinois 60126. Music Department within a college. Head: **T. Howard Krueger** (1950). College founded: 1871. Degrees: B.A. with a major in music. Students enrolled in music: 100. Volumes in music library: 2,000. Official school ensembles: chorus, marching band, jazz ensemble. Summer instruction. . . . HARPER COLLEGE, Algonquin and Roselle Roads, Palatine, Illinois 60062. Department of Music within a junior college. Head: **George Makas.** College and department founded: 1967. Degree: A. A. Music students enrolled: 76 majors. Volumes in music library: 3,000 Official school ensembles: chorus, chamber vocal ensemble, concert band, chamber orchestra, jazz ensemble, other smaller chamber groups. Summer instruction is limited. . . . ILLINOIS STATE UNIVERSITY, Normal, Illinois 61761. Music Department in the College of Fine Arts. Head: **James L. Roderick** (1970). University founded: 1857. Department founded: 1934.

Degrees: B.M., B.M.E., B.S., B.A., M.M., M.M.E., M.S., M.A. Scholarships: $40,000 annually. Fellowships: $25,000 annually. Music students enrolled: 350. Volumes in music library: 30,000. School ensembles: four choruses, glee club, chamber vocal ensemble, marching band, concert band, opera workshop, symphony orchestra, chamber orchestra, jazz ensemble, and many others. Summer music school. . . . ILLINOIS WESLEYAN UNIVERSITY, 210 University, Bloomington, Illinois 61701. (Member, NASM.) An unendowed School of Music within the university. University founded: 1853. School of Music founded: 1879. Degrees: B.A., B.M., B.Mus.Ed., M.M., M.Mus.Ed. Scholarships: 40 to 50 financial aid awards. Fellowships: four to five. Music students enrolled: 180 majors, 175 non-majors. Volumes in music library: 10,000 books, scores, and films. Official school music ensembles: chorus, glee club, chamber vocal ensemble, marching band, concert band, opera workshop, symphony orchestra, chamber orchestra, and other instrumental chamber ensembles. Summer music session. . . . KASKASKIA COLLEGE, Shattuc Road, Centralia, Illinois 62801. Music Department in the Fine Arts Division. Chairman: **Don W. Schroeder.** College founded: 1965. Department founded: 1970. Degree: A.A. in music. Scholarships: five at $100 each. Music students enrolled: 30. Volumes in music library: 150. Official school ensembles: chorus, chamber vocal ensemble, concert band, symphony orchestra, jazz ensemble. Summer music courses. . . . KISHWAUKEE COLLEGE, Malta, Illinois 60150. Music Department within the Humanities Division. Division chairman: **Betsy Harfst.** College and division founded: 1968. Degree: A.A. with a music major. No scholarships. Music students enrolled: 100. Volumes in music library: 250. Official school ensembles: chorus, chamber vocal ensemble, concert band, jazz ensemble, music theatre. Summer music courses. . . . KNOX COLLEGE, Galesburg, Illinois 61401. (Member, NASM.) Music Department within the college. Head: **H. Murray Baylor** (1969). Degree: B.A. in various areas of music. Music students enrolled: 80. Volumes in music library: 2,000. Official school ensembles: chorus, chamber vocal ensemble, symphony orchestra. No summer music school. . . . LEWIS & CLARK COMMUNITY COLLEGE (formerly Monticello College), Godfrey, Illinois 62035. Music discipline part of the Division of Fine and Performing Arts. Head: **Robert Oldham** (1954). College founded: 1838. Degrees: A.A., A.S. No music scholarships. Music students enrolled: 200. Volumes in music library: 500. Official school ensembles: jazz ensemble, stage band, Alton Civic Orchestra. No summer music school. . . . LINCOLN CHRISTIAN COLLEGE, Box 178, Lincoln, Illinois 62656. Music Department within the college. Chairman: **K. David Hargrove** (1968). College and department founded: 1944. Degree: Bachelor of Sacred Music, A.B. No music scholarships. Music students enrolled: 75 to 80. Volumes in music library: 1,000. Official school ensembles: three choruses, concert band. No summer music instruction. . . . McKENDREE COLLEGE, College Street, Lebanon, Illinois 62254. Music discipline within the Fine Arts Division. Chairman: **Glenn H. Freiner** (1953). College founded: 1828. Degrees: B.A. in Church Music; B.A. in music education; B.A. in Fine Arts. Scholarships: 50, totaling $33,000. Music students enrolled: 20. Volumes in music library: 1,500 (includes 400 records); separate record library contains 1,000 records and 400 tapes. Official school ensembles: chorus, chamber vocal ensemble, concert band, occasional opera workshop. Special course: Music and the Theatre in England. Summer music courses. . . . MACMURRAY COLLEGE, Jacksonville, Illinois 62650. (Member, NASM.) Department of Music within the college. Head: **Charles M. Fisher** (1965). College founded: 1834. Degrees: B.M., B.A. in music. Scholarships: 15, totaling $8,000. Music students enrolled: 35. Official school ensembles: chorus, glee club, chamber vocal ensemble, concert band, opera workshop, symphony orchestra, jazz ensemble. No summer music courses. . . . MILLIKIN UNIVERSITY, SCHOOL OF MUSIC, Decatur, Illinois 62522. (Member, NASM.) A school of Millikin University, an endowed institution. Dean: **Ronald D. Gregory.** Degrees:

B.M. in applied music, church music, music education; B.A. in music. Music majors: 190. . . . MU PHI EPSILON SCHOOL OF MUSIC, 1919 W. Cullerton Street, Chicago, Illinois 60608. Director: **Winnifrid R. Erickson.** . . . NORTH CENTRAL COLLEGE, Naperville, Illinois 60540. (Member, NASM.) Music is a discipline within the Creative Arts Division. Chairman: **Ann McKinley** (1971). College founded: 1861. Music division founded: 1862. Degree: B.A. with music major. Scholarships: no special sums set aside; help is offered to the disciplines in rotation. Music enrollment: 35. Music volumes in library: 2,100. Ensembles: chorus, chamber vocal ensemble, small chamber groups, jazz ensemble. Only applied music is offered in summer. . . . NORTH PARK COLLEGE, 5125 North Spaulding, Chicago, Illinois 60625. (Member, NASM.) A Division of Fine Arts in a liberal arts college sponsored by the Evangelical Covenant Church. Chairman: **Herbert R. Pankratz.** Degrees: B.M. in music education, applied music; B.A. in music. Music majors: 60. . . . NORTHEASTERN ILLINOIS STATE COLLEGE, Bryn Mawr at St. Louis, Chicago, Illinois 60625. Music Department within the college. Head: **R. D. Wenzlaff** (1968). College founded: 1961. Department founded: 1967. Degree: B.A. in secondary music, applied music, theory. Scholarships: 56, at $175 per semester each. Music students enrolled: 110 majors. Volumes in music library: 4,500. Official school ensembles: chorus, chamber vocal ensemble, concert band, opera workshop, chamber orchestra, jazz ensemble, percussion ensemble, other smaller chamber groups. Summer music school (three full semesters per year). . . . NORTHERN ILLINOIS UNIVERSITY, Fine Arts 216, DeKalb, Illinois 60115. A Department of Music within the college of Fine and Applied Arts. Head: **James Stanley Ballinger.** University founded: 1895. Department founded: 1903. Degrees: B.M., B.S.E., B.A., M.M.; a Certificate of Advanced Study (C.A.S.) in music is also offered, certifying 30 hours of academic credit beyond a Master's degree. Scholarships: 58, totaling $12,000. Fellowships: seven, totaling $13,500. Music enrollment: 315. Volumes in music library: 12,795. School music ensembles: chorus, marching band, concert band, opera workshop, symphony orchestra, jazz ensemble, and other smaller chamber groups. Music courses are offered in the summer. . . . NORTHWESTERN UNIVERSITY, Evanston, Illinois 60201. (Member, NASM.) School of Music within an endowed university. Dean: **Thomas W. Miller** (1971). University founded: 1851. School of Music founded: 1895. Degrees: B.M., B.M.E., M.M., Mus.D., Ph.D. Scholarships: 210, totaling $272,000. Fellowships: 11 teaching assistantships totaling $46,000. Music students enrolled: 489. Official school ensembles: three choruses, glee club, two chamber vocal ensembles, marching band, three concert bands, opera workshop, symphony orchestra, chamber orchestra, 18 smaller chamber groups, jazz ensemble. Summer music school. Special courses: ethnomusicology, computer technology and music, electronic music. . . . PRINCIPIA COLLEGE, Elsah, Illinois 62068. Music Department within the college. Head: **Reinhart S. Ross** (1966). Department founded: 1966. Degree: B.A. No scholarships. Music students enrolled: 25. Volumes in music library: 3,000 books, 3,000 records, 1,700 tapes. Official school ensembles: chorus, chamber vocal ensemble, other smaller chamber ensembles. No summer music courses. . . . QUINCY COLLEGE, 18th Street and College Avenue, Quincy, Illinois 62301. Music Department within the college. Chairman: **Lavern Wagner** (1958). College founded: 1860. Department founded: 1948. Degrees: B.A. in music; B.S. in music education. Scholarships: 10, totaling $17,000. Music students enrolled: 35. Volumes in music library: 5,000. Official school ensembles: chorus, glee club, chamber vocal ensemble, concert band, opera workshop, symphony orchestra (with community), jazz ensemble, Collegium Musicum. No summer music instruction. . . . REND LAKE COLLEGE, Ina, Illinois 62846. Music Department within a two-year college. Head: **Larry D. Phifer** (1971). College founded: 1967. Degree: A.A. Music scholarships: none. Music students enrolled: 15 majors. Volumes in music library: 500 books, 250 scores, 400 recordings. Official school ensembles: chorus, chamber vocal ensemble, concert band, symphony orchestra affiliated with the community orchestra, stage band. Private summer instruction. . . . ROSARY COLLEGE, River Forest, Illinois 60305. (Member, NASM.) A Department of Music in a liberal arts college. Chairman: **Sister Anne Schnoebelen.** Degrees: B.M. in applied music; B.A. in applied music, music history; B.M.Ed. Music majors: 30. . . . SHERWOOD MUSIC SCHOOL, 1014 South Michigan, Chicago, Illinois 60605. (Member, NASM.) A music conservatory. Musical Director: **Arthur Wildman** (1941). School founded: 1895. Degrees: B.M., B.M.E. Scholarships: 18, totaling $18,000. Music enrollment: 60. Music library: 5,000. Ensembles: chorus, opera workshop, symphony orchestra, wind ensemble. No summer session. . . . SOUTHERN ILLINOIS UNIVERSITY, Carbondale, Illinois 62901. (Member, NASM.) School of Music within a College of Communications and Fine Arts within a state university. Director: **Robert W. House** (1967). University and school founded: 1874. Degrees: B.M., M.M., M.Mus.Ed. Scholarships: 40, totaling $40,000. Fellowships: two, totaling $2,000. Music students enrolled: 300. Volumes in music library: 5,000. Official music ensembles: chorus, glee club, chamber vocal ensemble, marching band, concert band, opera workshop, symphony orchestra, chamber orchestra, jazz ensemble, other smaller chamber groups. Summer music school. . . . SOUTHERN ILLINOIS UNIVERSITY AT EDWARDSVILLE, Edwardsville, Illinois 62025. (Member, NASM.) Music Department within Fine Arts Division. Chairman: **William H. Tarwater** (1970). University and department founded: 1958. Degrees: B.A., B.M., M.M. Scholarships: 40, totaling $19,860. Fellowships: four, totaling $11,000. Music students enrolled: 280. Volumes in music library: 13,000. Official school ensembles: chorus, glee club, chamber vocal ensemble, concert band, opera workshop, symphony orchestra, chamber orchestra, Lincoln String Quartet, jazz ensemble. Special course: Suzuki Talent Education, String Development Program. Summer music school. . . . SPRINGFIELD COLLEGE IN ILLINOIS, Springfield, Illinois 62702. (Member, NASM.) A Department of Music within the unit of a fine arts division of a two-year college. Chairman: **Sister Mary Annunciata Horan.** Degree: A.A. . . . THORNTON COMMUNITY COLLEGE, 50 West 162nd Street, South Holland, Illinois 60473. Music Department within a two-year college. Head: **J. Albert Kindig** (1966). College founded: 1927. Department founded: 1965. Degree: A.A. Music students enrolled: 50. Volumes in music library: 700. Official school ensembles: chorus, chamber vocal ensemble, concert band, opera workshop, jazz ensemble. Summer instruction. . . . TOLENTINE COLLEGE, Box 747, Olympia Fields, Illinois 60461. Music appreciation courses within the Fine Arts Division. Head: **Rev. John M. Molnar** (1965). College and division founded: 1958. Music enrollment: 15. Volumes in music library: 300. Official school ensembles: chorus, glee club, jazz ensemble, other smaller chamber groups. . . . TRINITY COLLEGE, 2045 Half Day Road, Deerfield, Illinois 60015. Music Department within the college. Head: **Morris Faugerstrom** (1956). College founded: 1897. Department founded: 1956. Degree: B.A. in music or music in secondary education. Scholarships: six, totaling $2,000. Students enrolled in music: 40 majors, and about 400 non-majors. Volumes in music library: 1,500. Official school ensembles: chorus, two glee clubs, concert band, symphony orchestra, other smaller chamber groups. Limited summer instruction. . . . UNIVERSITY OF CHICAGO, 5835 University Avenue, Chicago, Illinois 60637. Music Department within the university. Chairman: **Howard M. Brown** (1970). University founded: 1893. Degrees: B.A., M.A., Ph.D. Scholarships: indefinite number and amounts. Music students enrolled: 40. Volumes in music library: 50,000 (see Music Libraries). Official school ensembles: chorus, chamber vocal ensemble, concert band, symphony orchestra, chamber orchestra, other smaller chamber groups. No summer music instruction. . . . UNIVERSITY OF ILLINOIS AT URBANA–CHAMPAIGN, 100 Smith Music Hall, Urbana, Illinois 61801. (Member, NASM.) A School of Music in the

College of Fine and Applied Arts. Director: **Thomas Fredrickson** (1971). University founded: 1867. School of Music established: 1895. Degrees: B.M., B.S. in music education; B.A. (in music granted by the College of Liberal Arts and Science); M.M., M.S. in music education; Advanced Certificate in music education; Ed.D., Ph.D., D.M.A. Variable number and amounts of scholarships and fellowships available (details undisclosed). Music enrollment: 750 majors. Music library: 139,000 volumes (see Music Libraries). Ensembles: chorus, glee club, chamber vocal ensemble, marching band, concert band, opera workshop, symphony orchestra, chamber orchestra, smaller chamber groups, jazz ensemble, and others. Summer music school is offered. Special courses: ethnomusicology, computer technology and music. . . . WAUBONSEE COMMUNITY COLLEGE, Illinois Route 47 at Harter Road, P.O. Box 508, Sugar Grove, Illinois 60554. Music Department within a two-year college (Humanities Division). Chairman, Humanities Division: **Robert Gregory** (1970). College and division founded: 1966. Degree: A.A. No music scholarships. Music students enrolled: 25. Volumes in music library: 375. Official school ensembles: chorus, glee club, chamber vocal ensemble, concert band, jazz ensemble. Summer music instruction. . . . WESTERN ILLINOIS UNIVERSITY, Macomb, Illinois 61455. (Member, NASM.) Music Department in the College of Fine Arts within a state-supported university. Head: **Glenn R. Wiesner** (1970). University founded: 1899. Degrees: B.A., B.M.E. Scholarships: 75, totaling $23,000. Music students enrolled: 150 majors, 50 minors. Volumes in music library: 4,000. Official school ensembles: chorus, glee club, chamber vocal ensemble, marching band, concert band, opera workshop, symphony orchestra, jazz ensemble, other smaller chamber groups. Summer music school (workshops and music camp). . . . WHEATON COLLEGE, Wheaton, Illinois 60187. (Member, NASM.) Conservatory of Music within the college. Head: **Harold M. Best** (1970). College founded: 1860. Degrees: B.A., B.M., B.M.E. Scholarships: number varies; total $50,000. Music students enrolled: 125. Official school music ensembles: chorus, glee club, chamber vocal ensemble, concert band, opera workshop, symphony orchestra, chamber orchestra. Summer music school. Special course: Suzuki Violin Method.

INDIANA

ANDERSON COLLEGE, Anderson, Indiana 46011. Music Department within a college. Head: **F. Dale Bengtson** (1969). College founded: 1917. Department added: 1928. Degrees: B.A., B.Mus.Ed. Scholarships: work grants based on need and ability. Official school ensembles: chorus, chamber vocal ensemble, marching band, concert band, opera workshop, symphony orchestra, jazz ensemble, other smaller chamber groups. Limited summer instruction. . . . BALL STATE UNIVERSITY, Muncie, Indiana 47306. (Member, NASM.) A Division of Music in a state-supported institution. Head: **Robert Hargreaves.** Degrees: B.A. in music, music education; B.S. in music, music education; M.A. in education; M.A. in performance, history and literature, theory–composition, music education; M.M. in performance, history and literature, theory–composition, music education. . . . CHRISTIAN THEOLOGICAL SEMINARY, Box 88267, Indianapolis, Indiana 46208. Music Department within a graduate theological school. Head: **James Carley** (1952). Seminary founded: 1924. Department added: 1952. Degree: Master of Ministry, received with a Master of Music from Butler University (two-year course). Scholarships: two, totaling $2,300. Music students enrolled: four. Volumes in music library: 1,400. Official school ensembles: glee club, chamber vocal ensemble, recorder group, hand-bells ensemble. Summer music instruction. . . . DePAUW UNIVERSITY, Greencastle, Indiana 56135. (Member, NASM.) School of Music within the university. Head: **Milton S. Trusler** (1956). University founded: 1837. School of Music founded: 1884. Degrees: B.M. in various areas; B.A. in music; M.M. Scholarships: number varies; total about $60,000 (for the 1971–72 school year). Music students enrolled: 120 B.M. students. Volumes in music library: 3,000. Official school ensembles: two choirs, male glee club, string, brass, woodwind, and percussion ensembles, marching band, concert band, wind ensemble, opera workshop, symphony orchestra, chamber orchestra, piano trio in residence, Collegians Madrigals. No summer music school. . . . EARLHAM COLLEGE, Richmond, Indiana 47374. Music Department within the college. Head: **Manfred Blum** (1970). College founded: 1847. Degree: B.A. Scholarships: general scholarships not limited to music. Music students enrolled: 250. Official school music ensembles: chorus, chamber vocal ensemble, symphony orchestra, chamber orchestra, jazz ensemble, other smaller chamber groups. Special courses: Japanese arts including music. No summer music instruction. . . . FORT WAYNE BIBLE COLLEGE, 1025 Rudisill Boulevard, Fort Wayne, Indiana 46807. Department of Music and Fine Arts. Head: **Lowell E. Weitz** (1970). College and department founded: 1904. Degree: B.M. in performance and music education. Music students enrolled: 40 to 50. Volumes in music library: about 1,000. Official school ensembles: chorus, concert band, chamber orchestra, other smaller chamber groups. Limited instruction in summer. . . . GRACE COLLEGE, Winoma Lake, Indiana 46590. Music Department within the college. Head: **Donald E. Ogden** (1950). College founded: 1937. Department founded: 1950. Degrees: B.A. in church music; B.M.E. Music students enrolled: 40 majors, 150 non-majors. Volumes in music library: 1,000. Official school ensembles: chorus, chamber vocal ensemble, concert band, chamber orchestra, other smaller chamber groups. No summer music courses. . . . HANOVER COLLEGE, Hanover, Indiana 47243. Department of Music within the college. Head: **J. David Wagner** (1968). College founded: 1820. Degree: B.A. with major in music. Music students enrolled: 60 to 70. Volumes in music library: 2,000. Official school ensembles: chorus, glee club, chamber vocal ensemble, concert band, jazz ensemble. No summer music instruction. . . . INDIANA STATE UNIVERSITY, Terre Haute, Indiana 47809. Department of Music within a university. Chairman: **James W. Barnes** (1964). Music department founded: circa 1910. Degrees: B.A. and B.S. in music and music education. Scholarships: 60 to 70, totaling $16,000 to $20,000. Fellowships: assistantships totaling $14,400. Music enrollment: about 350, not including general education classes. Music library: 2,500 books and/or monographs; 6,000 scores; 6,000 recordings. Ensembles: chorus; two glee clubs; chamber vocal ensemble; marching band; concert band; opera workshop; symphony orchestra; faculty woodwind and string quartet; brass, woodwind, and string ensembles. Summer music school offered. . . . INDIANA UNIVERSITY, Bloomington, Indiana 47401. (Member, NASM.) School of Music within a university. It is the largest music school in the world. Dean: **Charles H. Webb, Jr.,** successor to **Wilfred C. Bain,** who served from 1947 to 1972. University founded: 1820. Degrees: B.M., B.M.E., B.S., B.A., M.M., M.M.E., M.A., M.S., D.M., D.M.E., Ph.D. Music enrollment: 1,700. Music library: 273,439 (includes recordings and other library items; see Music Libraries). Ensembles: chorus, chamber vocal ensemble, marching band, concert band, opera workshop, symphony orchestra, chamber orchestra, smaller chamber groups, jazz ensemble. Summer music school offered. . . . INDIANA UNIVERSITY AT FORT WAYNE, 2101 Coliseum Boulevard East, Fort Wayne, Indiana 46805. Division of Music within the university. Chairman: **Andrew Harper** (1967). University founded: 1917. Division founded: 1967. Degrees: B.M., B.M.E., B.S. Scholarships: nine, of varying amounts. Music students enrolled: 35. Official school ensembles: chorus, chamber vocal ensemble, concert band, opera workshop, chamber orchestra, jazz ensemble, other smaller chamber groups. Special course is one dealing with the music education of children. Summer courses in music. . . . JORDAN COLLEGE OF MUSIC OF BUTLER UNIVERSITY, 46th Street and Clarendon Road, Indianapolis, Indiana 46208. (Member, NASM.) A college within the university. Dean: **J. K. Ehlert** (1952). University founded: 1855. Jordan College founded: 1895. Degrees: B.M., B.A.,

M.M., M.S.—all in music; B.S. in radio–TV; B.A. and M.A. in dance. Scholarships: variable from $180 (budget for scholarships in 1970–71 was $130,000). Fellowships: tuition exemption plus $1,000. Enrollment: 500 including dance, radio, and drama majors. Volumes in music library: 4,000 to 6,000. School music ensembles: chorus, glee club, chamber vocal group, marching band, concert band, opera workshop, symphony orchestra, chamber orchestra, jazz ensemble, and other groups. Summer school. . . . MANCHESTER COLLEGE, North Manchester, Indiana 46962. (Member, NASM.) A Department of Music in a liberal arts college related to the Church of the Brethren. Head: **Clyde W. Holsinger.** Degrees: B.S. in music education, B.S. with a major in music, B.A. with a major in music. . . . MARIAN COLLEGE, 3200 Cold Spring Road, Indianapolis, Indiana, 46222. Music Department within the college. Chairman: **Sister Vivian Rose Morshauser** (1960). College and department founded: 1937. Degree: B.A. with music major. Scholarships: 10, each for $200. Music students enrolled: 110. Volumes in music library: 1,200. Official school ensembles: chorus, chamber vocal ensemble, drum and bugle corps, concert band. Summer music instruction. . . . ST. JOSEPH'S COLLEGE, Rensselaer, Indiana 47978. Music Department within the college. Head: **Lawrence Heiman** (1970). College founded: 1889. Department founded: 1960. Degrees: B.A., B.S., both in music applications; M.M. in Church Music (in affiliation with DePaul University). Scholarships: 70, totaling $14,000. Music students enrolled: 35 majors. Official school ensembles: chorus, glee club, chamber vocal ensemble, marching band, concert band, stage band. Summer music school. Special courses: church music, the only area of study in which graduate work is done. . . . SAINT MARY-OF-THE-WOODS COLLEGE, Saint Mary-of-the-Woods, Indiana 47876. (Member, NASM.) Music Department in a liberal arts college under the auspices of the Sisters of Providence. Head: **Sister Laurette Bellamy** (1968). College and department founded: 1840. Degree: B.A. in music and music education. Scholarships: total $2,000. Music students enrolled: 30. Volumes in music library: 2,000 books, 1,050 scores. Official school ensembles: chorus, chamber vocal ensemble, other smaller chamber groups. No summer music school. . . . TAYLOR UNIVERSITY, Upland, Indiana 46989. (Member, NASM.) A Department of Music of an endowed, independent, interdenominational liberal arts college. Chairman: **Edward H. Hermanson.** Degrees: B.A. in applied music, theory; B.S. in music education. . . . UNIVERSITY OF EVANSVILLE, P.O. Box 329, Evansville, Indiana 47701. (Member, NASM.) Department of Music within the College of Fine Arts. Head: **Donald D. Colton** (1971). University founded: 1854. Degrees: B.M.E., B.A., B.M. Scholarships: 64, totaling $29,580. Music enrollment: 114. Ensembles: chorus, chamber vocal ensemble, marching band, concert band, opera workshop, chamber orchestra, smaller chamber groups, jazz ensemble. Summer school offered. . . . UNIVERSITY OF NOTRE DAME, Box 531, Notre Dame, Indiana 46556. Music Department of the College of Arts and Letters within the university. Head: **Reverend Carl Hager** (1955). University founded: 1842. Degrees: B.A., M.M., M.M.E. Scholarships: three, totaling $3,000. Fellowships: three, totaling $12,000. Music students enrolled: 12. Volumes in music library: 1,200. Official school ensembles: chorus, glee club, marching band, concert band. Summer music instruction. . . . VALPARAISO UNIVERSITY, University Place, Valparaiso, Indiana 46383. (Member, NASM.) Music Department within the College of Arts and Sciences. Head: **Frederick H. Telschow** (1970). School founded: 1859. Music degrees: B.M., B.M.E., B.A., M.A. in Liberal Studies. Scholarships: 46, totaling $27,150 (offered to those with concentration in music; no specific music scholarships). Music students enrolled: 80 majors, 30 minors. Music library: 10,000 volumes. Official school ensembles: chorus, chamber vocal ensemble, marching band, concert band, opera workshop, symphony orchestra, chamber orchestra, smaller chamber groups. Summer music term. Special courses offered in chamber music.

IOWA

CENTRAL COLLEGE, Pella, Iowa 50219. Music Department within a college. Chairman: **Davis Folkerts** (1969). College founded: 1853. Degree: B.A. with music major. Scholarships: 5 to 10, totaling $3,000. Music students enrolled: 30. Volumes in music library: 3,000. Official school ensembles: chorus, chamber vocal ensemble, marching band, concert band, symphony orchestra, jazz ensemble, other smaller chamber groups, Collegium Musicum. Limited summer instruction. . . . COE COLLEGE, 1220 First Avenue, N.E., Cedar Rapids, Iowa 52402. (Member, NASM.) Music Department in a liberal arts college related to the Presbyterian Church. Chairman: **Allan D. Kellar** (1965). College founded: 1851. Degrees: B.A. with a music major, B.M. with a major in music education. Scholarships: seven, totaling $6,000. Music students enrolled: 65. Volumes in music library: 1,000. Official school ensembles: chorus, glee club, chamber vocal ensemble, concert band, opera workshop, symphony orchestra, chamber orchestra, jazz ensemble. No summer music school. . . . CORNELL COLLEGE, Mount Vernon, Iowa 52314. (Member, NASM.) Music Department within an endowed college. Chairman: **Jesse G. Evans** (1965). College and department founded: 1853. Degrees: B.A., B.M. Music students enrolled: 55 music majors. Official school ensembles: chorus, chamber vocal ensemble, concert band, opera workshop, symphony orchestra, jazz ensemble, Japanese ensemble, other smaller chamber groups. . . . DORDT COLLEGE, Sioux Center, Iowa 51250. Music Department within the college. Head: **Dale Grotenhuis** (1960). College and department founded: 1958. Degree: B.A. in music education. Scholarships: eight, from $75 to $100. Music students enrolled: 200. Volumes in music library: 1,650. Official school ensembles: chorus, glee club, chamber vocal ensemble, concert band, opera workshop, other smaller chamber groups. No summer music school. . . . DRAKE UNIVERSITY, COLLEGE OF FINE ARTS, Des Moines, Iowa 50311. (Member, NASM.) One of the nine colleges which constitute Drake University, sharing in its endowment. Dean, College of Fine Arts: **Paul J. Jackson.** Degrees: B.M. in applied music, church music; B.M.Ed., M.M. in applied music, composition; M.M.Ed. Music majors: 250. . . . IOWA STATE UNIVERSITY, Ames, Iowa 50010. (Member, NASM.) A Department of Music in a state-supported university. Head: **N. L. Burkhalter.** Degrees: B.A. in music. B.M. . . . IOWA WESLEYAN COLLEGE, Mt. Pleasant, Iowa 52641. Music Department within the college. Head: **Burton P. Mahle** (1963). College founded: 1842. Degrees: B.A., B.M.E. in applied music or church music. Scholarships: one, for $400. Music students enrolled: 25 to 30. Volumes in music library: 3,000 plus 800 recordings. Official school ensembles: chorus, chamber vocal ensemble, concert band, opera workshop, symphony orchestra, wind quintet. No summer music instruction. . . . IOWA WESTERN COMMUNITY COLLEGE (CLARINDA CAMPUS), 923 East Washington, Clarinda, Iowa 51632. Division of Music within the Department of Fine Arts. Head: **Nelson E. Crow** (1967). College founded: 1923. Division founded: 1967. No music degrees offered. Scholarships: two, each $250. Music students enrolled: eight. Official school ensembles: chorus, chamber vocal ensemble, concert band, symphony orchestra. No summer music instruction. . . . LUTHER COLLEGE, Decorah, Iowa 52101. (Member, NASM.) A Department of Music in a liberal arts college endowed and supported by the Lutheran Church. Chairman: **Weston H. Noble.** Degree: B.A. in music, music education. . . . MARSHALLTOWN COMMUNITY COLLEGE, 113 North 1st Avenue, Marshalltown, Iowa 50158. Music Department within the Division of Fine Arts. Head: **Max S. Barker** (1968). College founded: 1927. Department founded: 1968. Degree: A.A. Scholarships: three, totaling $300. Music students enrolled: 200. Volumes in music library: 200. Official music ensembles: chorus, madrigal group, concert band. Summer music instruction limited to applied music only. . . . MORNINGSIDE COLLEGE, Sioux City, Iowa 51106. (Member, NASM.) Department of Music within a college supported by the Methodist

Church. Head: **Lawrence DeWitt** (1970). School founded: 1894. Degrees: A.B., B.M.E., B.M. Scholarships: 47, totaling $16,600. Music enrollment: 110. Music library: 2,800. Ensembles: chorus, chamber vocal ensemble, marching band, concert band, chamber orchestra, chamber trio, jazz ensemble. Limited summer courses. . . . NORTH IOWA AREA COMMUNITY COLLEGE, 220 East State Street, Mason City, Iowa 50401. Music Department within a two-year college. Head: **Henry T. Paine** (1968). College founded: 1918. Department founded: 1967. Degree: A.A. No specific music scholarships. Music students enrolled: 30 majors. Volumes in music library: 300. Official school ensembles: chorus, chamber vocal ensemble, concert band, symphony orchestra. Limited summer music instruction. . . . OTTUMWA HEIGHTS COLLEGE, Ottumwa, Iowa 52501. Music Department within a junior college. Head: **Sister Jane O'Donnell** (1964). College and department founded: 1925. Degree: A.A. Scholarships: two to four, from $100 to $500. Music students enrolled: seven to ten. Volumes in music library: 100. Official school ensembles: chorus, chamber vocal ensemble, chamber orchestra, 60-piece string ensemble. No summer music school. . . . PARSONS COLLEGE, Fairfield, Iowa 52556. Music Department within the college. Head: **William R. Medley** (1963). College and department founded: 1875. Degrees: B.A. in fine arts; B.M.E. Scholarships: number varies (15 to 24). Music students enrolled: 30 majors, 50 minors. Volumes in music library: 2,400. Official school ensembles: chorus, chamber vocal ensemble, concert band, jazz ensemble, other smaller chamber groups. Summer music courses. . . . SIMPSON COLLEGE, Indianola, Iowa 50125. (Member, NASM.) Music Department within a college affiliated with the Methodist Church. Head: **Robert L. Larsen** (1965). School founded: 1860. Music department founded: 1890. Degrees: B.M., performance and music education; B.A. in music. Scholarships: six half-tuition to freshmen. Fellowships: 18, totaling $18,000. Music enrollment: 70. Music library: 1,850 volumes. Ensembles: chorus, chamber vocal ensemble, concert band, opera workshop, chamber orchestra, jazz ensemble, wind and percussion ensemble, opera orchestra, Collegium Musicum. . . . ST. AMBROSE COLLEGE, 518 West Locust Street, Davenport, Iowa 52803. Music Department within a college. Head: **J. E. Greene** (1964). Degree: B.A. College founded: 1882. Scholarships: 15 full, totaling $150,000. Music students enrolled: 24 majors, eight minors. Official school ensembles: chorus, chamber vocal ensemble, concert band, brass and woodwind ensembles. Summer music courses. . . . UNIVERSITY OF IOWA, SCHOOL OF MUSIC, Iowa City, Iowa 52240. (Member, NASM.) Department of Music in a college. Head: **Himie Voxman** (1954). University founded: 1847. Degrees: B.A., B.M., M.A., M.F.A., Ph.D., D.M.A. Enrollment in music: 500. Music library: 40,000 volumes (see Music Libraries). Ensembles: chorus, chamber vocal ensemble, marching band, concert band, opera workshop, symphony orchestra, chamber orchestra, smaller chamber groups, jazz ensemble. Summer music school offered. . . . UNIVERSITY OF NORTHERN IOWA, Cedar Falls, Iowa 50613. (Member, NASM.) Department of Music in the College of Fine Arts and Humanities of a state university. Head: **Myron E. Russell** (1951). School founded: 1876. Music Department founded: circa 1900. Degrees: B.A., B.M., M.A. Scholarships: six, totaling $1,200. Fellowships: three, totaling $5,400 (each $1,800). Music enrollment: 260. Music library: 13,400 volumes. Ensembles: three choruses, men's glee club, chamber vocal ensemble, marching band, two concert bands, opera workshop, symphony orchestra, chamber orchestra, smaller chamber groups, three jazz bands. Eight-week summer school offered. . . . WARTBURG COLLEGE, Waverly, Iowa 50677. (Member, NASM.) Department of Music within a college. Head: **Franklin E. Williams** (1971). School founded: 1852. Music Department founded: circa 1853. Degrees: B.M.E., B.M., and B.A. with a major in music. Scholarships: eight, totaling $875. Music enrollment: 75 to 80. Ensembles: chorus, Castle Singers, concert band, symphony orchestra, chamber orchestra, smaller chamber groups, jazz ensemble, varsity band.

Summer music courses offered. . . . WESTMAR COLLEGE, 10th and Third Avenue S.E., LeMars, Iowa 51031. Music Department within a college. Chairman: **Frank Summerside** (1966). Department and school founded: 1890. Music degrees offered: B.A. in music; B.Mus.Ed. Scholarships: total about $11,300. Music students enrolled: 60 majors and minors. Music library: 300 volumes. Official school ensembles: two choruses, chamber vocal ensemble, marching band, concert band, jazz ensemble. Summer workshops in music offered. Special course: new music laboratory for exploration of sound concepts.

KANSAS

BAKER UNIVERSITY, Baldwin City, Kansas 66006. Music Department within a college of the university. Head: **William C. Rice** (1939). University founded: 1858. Department founded: 1860. Degrees: B.A. in music, B.M.E. (also in church music). Scholarships: 30, totaling $15,000. Music enrollment: 55. Volumes in music library: 2,000. Official school ensembles: chorus, chamber vocal ensemble, marching band, concert band, opera workshop, chamber orchestra, jazz ensemble. Summer music school. . . . BENEDICTINE COLLEGE, Atchison, Kansas 66002. Music Department within a college. Head: **Sister Joachim Holthaus** (1971). School founded in 1863 (became four-year college in 1933). Degrees: A.B., B.M., B.M.Ed. Scholarships: amount varies ($5,175 in 1971). Music students enrolled: 32 majors, 200 in service courses. Music library: 1,545 books, 11,470 scores, 8,000 recordings; 3,580 uncatalogued items. Official school ensembles: chorus, chamber vocal ensemble, symphony orchestra, chamber orchestra, chamber groups; also Schola Cantorum. No summer music school. . . . BETHANY COLLEGE, Lindsborg, Kansas 67456. (Member, NASM.) A Department of Music in a liberal arts college, endowed and supported by the Lutheran Church. Chairman: **Elmer Copley** (1969). College founded: 1881. Degree: B.A. Scholarships: three or four totaling $900. Music students enrolled: 75. Volumes in music library: 1,500. Official school ensembles: two choruses, chamber vocal ensemble, concert band, symphony orchestra, chamber orchestra, jazz ensemble, other smaller chamber groups. Limited summer music instruction. . . . CLOUD COUNTY COMMUNITY COLLEGE, Campus Drive, Concordia, Kansas 66901. Music Department within the college. Head: **Everett Miller** (1968). School founded in 1965. Music department established in 1968. Degree: A.A. Scholarships: 10 totaling $2,000. Official school ensembles: chorus, concert band, jazz ensemble, folk ensemble. Limited summer instruction. . . . THE COLLEGE OF EMPORIA, Emporia, Kansas 66801. Department of Music within the college. Head: **Roger H. Johnson** (1962). Department founded: 1901. Degrees: B.A., B.M., B.M.Ed. Music scholarships: total $5,000. Music students enrolled: 55. Official school ensembles: chorus, chamber vocal ensemble, concert band, opera workshop, jazz ensemble. No summer music school. . . . FORT HAYS KANSAS STATE COLLEGE, Hays, Kansas 67601. (Member, NASM.) Department of Music within the Humanities Division of a state college. Head: **Leland Bartholomew** (1966). School founded: 1902. Music Department founded: 1913. Degrees: B.A., B.M., M.M.Ed. Scholarships: 15, totaling $2,500. Fellowships: two. Music enrollment: 160. No separate music library. Ensembles: chorus, glee club, chamber vocal ensemble, marching band, concert band, opera workshop, symphony orchestra, chamber orchestra, smaller chamber groups, jazz ensemble. Summer music school offered. . . . FRIENDS UNIVERSITY, Wichita, Kansas 67213. (Member, NASM.) Department of Music in a college supported by the Society of Friends. Chairman, Division of Fine Arts: **Cecil J. Riney.** Degrees: B.M. in applied music, music education; B.A. in applied music, theory. Music majors: 100. . . . KANSAS STATE COLLEGE OF PITTSBURG, Pittsburg, Kansas 66762. (Member, NASM.) A Department of Music of a state-supported college. Chairman: **Millard M. Laing.** Degrees: B.M. in applied music; B.M.Ed.; M.M. in applied music, music theory and composition, music history and literature, music education.

Music majors: 120. . . . KANSAS STATE UNIVERSITY, Manhattan, Kansas 66502. (Member, NASM.) Department of Music within the university. Head: **Robert A. Steinbauer** (1970). University founded: 1863. Department founded: 1880. Degrees: B.Mus., B.S. in music education, B.A., M.M., M.A. Scholarships: 30, totaling $9,000. Fellowships: seven, totaling $16,000. Music students enrolled: 150. Volumes in music library: 7,000. Official school ensembles: chorus, glee club, chamber vocal ensemble, marching band, concert band, opera workshop, symphony orchestra, chamber orchestra, resident string quartet, jazz ensemble, pep band, New Arts Consort, and others. Summer music school. Special course: electronic music (synthesizer) for public schools. . . . MARYMOUNT COLLEGE OF KANSAS, East Iron Avenue and Marymount Road, Salina, Kansas 67401. (Member, NASM.) Department of Music within a college. Head: **Eric Stein** (1971). School and Music Department founded: 1922. Degrees: B.M., B.A. in music, B.M.Ed. Scholarships: 14, totaling $5,400. Music enrollment: 30. Music library: 3,423 volumes. Ensembles: chorus, glee club, concert band, symphony orchestra. . . . McPHERSON COLLEGE, 1600 Euclid Street, McPherson, Kansas 67460. Department of Music within the college. Head: **Paul V. Sollenberger** (1963). College founded: 1887. Degree: B.A. Scholarships (called awards): totaling $5,000. Music students enrolled: 125. Official school ensembles: chorus, chamber vocal ensemble, marching band, concert band, symphony orchestra. No summer music school. . . . MID-AMERICA NAZARENE COLLEGE, Box 1776, Olathe, Kansas 66061. Music discipline is a part of the division of "Artistic Service," which includes all music and art. Chairman: **N. James Main.** College and division founded: 1968. Degree: B.M.E. Scholarships: 15, at $100 to $250 each. Music students enrolled: 75 to 80. Music volumes: 1,000. Official school ensembles: chorus, two glee clubs, chamber vocal ensemble, concert band, chamber orchestra. Limited summer instruction. . . . MOUNT ST. SCHOLASTICA COLLEGE, Atchison, Kansas 66002. (Member, NASM.) A Department of Music of a college operated by the Benedictine Sisters. Chairman: **Sister M. Joachim Holthaus.** Degrees: B.M. in applied music; B.M.Ed.; B.A. in applied music, theory. Music majors: 3C. . . . SACRED HEART COLLEGE, 3100 McCormick, Wichita, Kansas 67213. Music Department within the college. Head: **Sister Mary Xavier Lampe** (1963). College founded: 1933. Degree: B.A. Scholarships: eight, totaling $3,300. Music students enrolled: 16 majors. Official school ensembles: chamber vocal ensemble, opera workshop, other smaller chamber groups. Summer instruction. . . . SAINT MARY COLLEGE, Xavier, Kansas 66098. (Member, NASM.) Department of Music in a liberal arts college owned and operated by the Sisters of Charity of Leavenworth. Chairman: **Sister Rose Tomlin.** Degrees: B.M., B.M.Ed., A.B. Scholarships: 10, totaling $8,000. Music students enrolled: 30. Volumes in music library: 800 books plus scores and music on microfiche. Official school ensembles: chorus, touring choir, madrigal group, opera workshop, chamber orchestra, Schola Cantorum, and other smaller instrumental ensembles. Limited summer instruction. . . . SOUTHWESTERN COLLEGE, Winfield, Kansas 67156. (Member, NASM.) Music is in the Division of Fine Arts in a college supported by the Methodist church. Head: **Warren B. Wooldridge** (1961). School and music division founded: 1885. Degrees: B.M. in applied music and school music; B.A. in music. Scholarships: 20, totaling $7,000. Music enrollment: 54. Music library: 600. Ensembles: chorus, chamber vocal ensemble, concert band, opera workshop, symphony orchestra, chamber groups, jazz ensemble. No summer session. . . . ST. MARY OF THE PLAINS COLLEGE, Dodge City, Kansas 67801. Music Department within Division of Fine Arts. Head: **Sister Christian Rosner** (1957). University founded: 1952. Music Department founded: 1957. Degrees: B.Mus.Ed., B.A. with music major. Amount of scholarships offered: $2,000. Music students enrolled: 30. Volumes in music library: 1,200 books, 1,375 records, 752 scores, 5 microfiche collections, 61 periodicals. Official school ensembles: chorus, chamber vocal ensemble, concert band, opera workshop, jazz ensemble. No summer music school. . . . STERLING COLLEGE, North Broadway, Sterling, Kansas 67579. Music Department within college. Head: **Robert W. Gordon** (1969). College founded: 1887. Degrees: B.A. with emphasis in Music Education, piano, voice, or instrumental instruction. Scholarships: 12, amounting to $6,000. Music students enrolled: 20 majors of 125 total participants. Music library: 660 volumes. Official school ensembles: chorus, chamber vocal ensemble, marching band, concert band. No summer music instruction. . . . TABOR COLLEGE, 400 South Adams, Hillsboro, Kansas 67063. (Member, NASM.) Music Department within a private college (Mennonite Brethren). Chairman: **Paul W. Wohlgemuth.** Department founded: 1908. Degree: B.A. Scholarships: 20, totaling $6,000. Music students enrolled: 32. Volumes in music library: 2,000. Official school ensembles: chorus, chamber vocal ensemble, concert band, chamber orchestra, opera workshop. No summer music school. . . . UNIVERSITY OF KANSAS, SCHOOL OF FINE ARTS, Lawrence, Kansas 66044. (Member, NASM.) A university school, state supported. Dean: **Thomas Gorton.** Degrees: B.M. in applied music, composition, theory; B.M.Ed. in music education, music therapy; B.A. in music; M.M. in applied music, composition; M.M.Ed., M.A. in musicology. Music majors: 456. Music library: about 10,000 volumes. . . . WASHBURN UNIVERSITY, Topeka, Kansas 66621. (Member, NASM.) A Department of Music in the Division of Humanities in a municipal university, tax-supported and endowed. Head: **Everett Fetter.** Degrees: B.A., B.M. in applied music, music education. Music majors: 80. . . . WICHITA STATE UNIVERSITY, COLLEGE OF FINE ARTS, Wichita, Kansas 67208. (Member, NASM.) School of Music within the College of Fine Arts of a municipally supported university. Dean: **Charles L. Spohn** (1970). University founded: 1895. School founded: 1896. Degrees: B.M., B.Mus.Ed., M.M., M.Mus.Ed. Scholarships: 159, totaling $32,750. Fellowships: 14, totaling $23,180. Music students enrolled: 480. Volumes in music library: 80,000; 5,000 records. Official ensembles: chorus, chamber vocal ensemble, marching and concert bands, opera workshop, symphony orchestra, chamber orchestra, jazz ensemble, other smaller chamber groups. Summer music school.

KENTUCKY

BRESCIA COLLEGE, 120 West 7th Street, Owensboro, Kentucky 42301. Music Department within the college. Head: **Sister Mary Cecilia Payne** (1970). College and department founded: 1949. Degrees: B.M., B.M.Ed. Scholarships: four, totaling $1,700. Fellowships: two (full tuition). Music students enrolled: 50. Volumes in music library: 1,000. Official school ensembles: chorus, chamber vocal ensemble, symphony orchestra, wind ensemble. Summer music school. . . . CUMBERLAND COLLEGE, Williamsburg, Kentucky 40769. (Member, NASM.) Music Department within the college. Head: **Harold R. Wortman** (1966). College founded: 1889. Degrees: B.A. in music, B.S. in music education. Scholarships: number varies; total $6,000. Music students enrolled: 120 (45 majors). Official school ensembles: two choruses, chamber vocal ensemble, marching band, concert band, jazz ensemble, other smaller chamber groups. Limited summer instruction. . . . EASTERN KENTUCKY UNIVERSITY, Richmond, Kentucky 40475. (Member, NASM.) College within a university. Head: **George Muns** (1969). School and Music Department founded: 1906. Degrees: B.M.Ed.; B.M.; B.A. with major in music; M.A. in education, music major; M.M.Ed., M.M. (pending). Scholarships: 119, totaling $28,000. Fellowships: five and a half, totaling $2,200 yearly, out-of-state fee waived. Music enrollment: 275. Music library: 5,000 volumes. Ensembles: chorus, chamber vocal ensemble, marching band, two concert bands, opera workshop, symphony orchestra, chamber orchestra, jazz ensemble. Summer courses offered. . . . GEORGETOWN COLLEGE, Georgetown, Kentucky 40324. Music Department within the college. Head: **Daniel B. Tilford** (1970). College founded: 1829. Degrees: A.B., B.M.Ed. Scholarships: 20, totaling $5,000. Music students enrolled: 100. Official school ensembles: chorus, chamber vocal ensemble, marching band, concert band, opera workshop, jazz ensemble. No summer music school. . . . KENTUCKY STATE COLLEGE, East Main Street, Frankfort, Kentucky 40601. Music Department within the college. Head: **Warren C. Swindell** (1970). College founded: 1887. Degree: B.S. in music education. Scholarships: 80, totaling $31,000. Music enrollment: 50. Volumes in music library: 1,000. Official school ensembles: chorus, chamber vocal ensemble, marching band, concert band, opera workshop, chamber orchestra, jazz ensemble. Summer music instruction. Special course: jazz improvisation. . . . KENTUCKY WESLEYAN COLLEGE, Owensboro, Kentucky 42301. Music Department within the college. Head: **Emil Ahnell** (1958). College founded: 1859. Degree: B.A. Scholarships: amounting to $8,000. Music students enrolled: 25. Music library: 3,100 volumes. Official school ensembles: chorus, chamber vocal ensemble, concert band, opera workshop. No summer music school. . . . MIDWAY JUNIOR COLLEGE, Midway, Kentucky 40347. Music Department within a college for women. Head: **Sue Tremble Henry** (1969). School founded 1847. Music degree: A.A. All students on scholarship and work–study programs. Music students enrolled: five. Music library: 405 volumes, 409 records. Official school ensembles: glee club. No summer music school. . . . MOREHEAD STATE UNIVERSITY, Morehead, Kentucky 40351. (Member, NASM.) A Music Department in the School of Humanities in a state-supported institution. Head: **E. G. Fulbright** (1964). School founded: 1922. Degrees: B.A. with music major, B.M., B.M.Ed., M.A. (music emphasis), M.M.Ed. Scholarships: 80, amounting to $11,500. Fellowships: seven, amounting to $15,400. Music students enrolled: 275. Official school ensembles: chorus, glee club, chamber vocal ensemble, marching band, concert band, opera workshop, symphony orchestra, chamber orchestra, in-residence chamber ensemble, jazz ensemble, percussion ensemble. Has a summer music camp (Daniel Boone Forest Music Camp). . . . MURRAY STATE UNIVERSITY, University Station, Murray, Kentucky 42071. (Member, NASM.) A Department in the School of Fine Arts of the university, state supported. Head: **Richard W. Farrell** (1957). Music Department founded: 1930. School founded: 1922. Degrees: B.M.Ed., B.M., M.M.Ed. Scholarships: totaling $24,000. Music students enrolled: 200. Music library: 7,500 volumes. Official school ensembles: chorus, chamber vocal ensemble, marching band, concert band, opera workshop, symphony orchestra, chamber orchestra, in-residence chamber ensemble, jazz ensemble, wind ensemble. Summer music school. . . . SOUTHERN BAPTIST THEOLOGICAL SEMINARY, Louisville, Kentucky 40206. (Member, NASM.) The School of Church Music in a theological seminary is supported by the Southern Baptist Convention. Dean: **Forrest H. Heeren.** Degree: Master of Church Music. Library: (see Music Libraries). . . . UNION COLLEGE, College Street, Barbourville, Kentucky 40906. Music Department within the college. Head: **Allen E. Green** (1970). Music Department founded: 1963. School founded: 1879. Degrees: B.M., B.M.Ed. No music scholarships. Music students enrolled: 30. Music library: 5,000 volumes. Official school ensembles: chorus, chamber vocal ensemble, concert band, opera workshop, in-residence chamber ensemble. No summer music instruction. . . . UNIVERSITY OF KENTUCKY, Lexington, Kentucky 40506. (Member, NASM.) Department of Music in a College of Arts and Sciences within the university. Head: **Wesley K. Morgan** (1970). University founded: 1869. Music Department founded: 1916. Degrees: B.M., B.A., M.M., M.A., D.M.A., Ph.D. Scholarships: 144 undergraduate, 16 graduate. Fellowships: number varies. Music enrollment: 236 undergraduates, 60 graduates. Ensembles: chorus, chamber vocal ensemble, marching band, concert band, symphony orchestra, chamber orchestra, trio, string quartet, jazz ensemble, Collegium Musicum. Limited summer session. . . . UNIVERSITY OF LOUISVILLE, SCHOOL OF MUSIC, 9001 Shelbyville Road, Louisville, Kentucky 40222. (Member, NASM.) School of Music, one of nine divisions of a municipal university. Head: **Jerry W. Ball** (1971). University founded: 1798. School of Music founded: 1932. Degrees: B.M., B.M.Ed., M.M., M.M.Ed. Scholarships: 65, totaling $30,000. Fellowships: seven, totaling $10,000. Music students enrolled: 170. Volumes in music library: 25,000 (see Music Libraries). Official school ensembles: chorus, chamber vocal ensemble, marching band, concert band, opera workshop, symphony orchestra, jazz ensemble, other smaller chamber groups. Summer music school. . . . WESTERN KENTUCKY UNIVERSITY, Bowling Green, Kentucky 42101. (Member, NASM.) Department of Music within the Potter College of Arts and Humanities. Head: **Howard Carpenter** (1965). School and Music Department founded: 1906. Degrees: B.M. in performance and music education; B.A. in music literature or theory; M.M. in performance; M.A. in education with major in music. Scholarships: approximately 110. Fellowships: two to four, totaling $4,200. Music enrollment: 150. Music library: 4,350 volumes. Ensembles: chorus, two glee clubs, chamber vocal ensemble, marching band, concert band, opera workshop, symphony orchestra, small chamber groups, jazz ensemble. Summer music school offered.

LOUISIANA

CENTENARY COLLEGE SCHOOL OF MUSIC, Shreveport, Louisiana 71104. (Member, NASM.) School of Music in an endowed college supported by the Methodist Church. Director: **Frank M. Carroll** (1969). College founded: 1825. Degrees: B.M., B.A. Scholarships: number varies; total $20,000. Music students enrolled: 50 majors. Official school ensembles: chorus, chamber vocal ensemble, concert band, opera workshop, other smaller chamber groups. No summer music school. . . . LOUISIANA POLYTECHNIC INSTITUTE, Ruston, Louisiana 71270. (Member, NASM.) A Department of Music in the School of Arts and Sciences. Head: **Jimmie Howard Reynolds** Degrees: B.A. in music, music education; B.M. in applied music, sacred music; M.A. in education, major in music; M.A. in music. Music majors: 200. . . . LOUISIANA STATE UNIVERSITY, Baton Rouge, Louisiana 70803. School of Music within a state-supported university. (Member, NASM.) Head: **Everett Timm** (1955). University founded: 1865. Music Department founded: 1915 (became school in 1943). Degrees: B.M., B.A., B.Mus.Ed., M.M., M.Mus.Ed., M.A., D.M.A., Ph.D. Scholarships and fellowships: vary from year to year. Music students enrolled: 320. Music library: 26,000 volumes. Official school ensembles: chorus, women's glee club, chamber vocal ensemble, marching band, concert band, opera workshop, symphony orchestra, chamber groups, jazz ensemble. Summer music school offered. . . . LOUISIANA STATE UNIVERSITY IN NEW ORLEANS, Lakefront, New Orleans, Louisiana 70122. Music Department within the College of Liberal Arts in the university. Head: **William S. Chute** (1968). College founded: 1958. Music Department founded: 1968. Degree: B.A. in music. Scholarships: 60 band scholarships, totaling $6,000. Music students enrolled: 50. Music library: 2,000 volumes. Official school ensembles: chorus, chamber vocal ensemble, marching band, concert band, jazz ensemble. Summer music courses on beginning level are offered. . . . LOYOLA UNIVERSITY, 6363 St. Charles, New Orleans, Louisiana 70118. College of Music within a university. (Member, NASM.) Head: **Joe B. Buttram** (1969). University founded: 1912. College founded: 1932. Degrees: B.M. in applied music, composition, music therapy; B.M.Ed., M.M.Ed., M.M.T. (music therapy). Scholarships: 80, totaling $35,167. Music enrollment: 155. Music Library: 3,000 volumes. Ensembles: chorus, chamber vocal ensemble, concert band, opera workshop, symphony orchestra, chamber orchestra, smaller chamber groups, jazz ensemble. Summer music courses: high school music institute. . . . McNEESE STATE UNIVERSITY, Lake Charles, Louisiana 70601. (Member, NASM.) A Department of Music in the School of the Arts of a state-supported university. Dean, School of the Arts, and Head, Department of Music: **Francis G. Bul-**

ber. Degrees: B.M. in applied music, theory and composition; B.M.Ed.; B.A. in music; M.M. in applied music; M.M.Ed. Music majors: 125. . . . NEW ORLEANS BAPTIST THEOLOGICAL SEMINARY, 3939 Gentilly Boulevard, New Orleans, Louisiana 70126. (Member, NASM.) A School of Church Music in a theological seminary of the Southern Baptist Convention. Head: **William L. Hooper** (1964). Department and school founded: 1918. Degrees: Master of Church Music, Ed.S., Ed.D. Music students enrolled: 50. Music library: 10,000 volumes. Official school ensembles: chorus, chamber vocal ensemble. Summer music school. Special course: church music education. . . . NORTHEAST LOUISIANA UNIVERSITY, Monroe, Louisiana 71201. A School of Music within a university. (Member, NASM.) University and music school founded: 1933. Degrees: B.M. in applied music, history and literature, theory and composition, music education; M.M. in music education, history and literature, theory and composition, applied music; A.B. in music. Scholarships and fellowships: number varies. Music enrollment: 180. Music library: 10,000 volumes. Ensembles: chorus, glee club, marching band, concert band, opera workshop, symphony orchestra, small chamber groups, jazz ensemble. Summer music school offered. . . . NORTHWESTERN STATE UNIVERSITY OF LOUISIANA, Natchitoches, Louisiana 71457. A Department of Music in the College of Liberal Arts, state supported. (Member, NASM.) Dean: **George A. Stokes,** Degrees: B.A. in applied music; B.M. in applied music; B.M.Ed.; M.M.Ed. Music majors: 130. . . . SOUTHEASTERN LOUISIANA UNIVERSITY, Hammond, Louisiana 70401. A Department of Music within the School of Humanities of the university. (Member, NASM.) Head: **David C. McCormick** (1970). Music department founded: 1934. School founded: 1925. Degrees: B.A., B.M., M.M., M.Mus.Ed. Music students enrolled: 150. Music library: 3,500 volumes. Official school ensembles: chorus, glee club, marching band, concert band, opera workshop, chamber orchestra, trombone trio, jazz ensemble. Summer music courses are offered. . . . SOUTHERN UNIVERSITY, Baton Rouge, Louisiana 70813. (Member, NASM.) A Division of Music in a state university. Dean: **H. D. Perkins.** Degree: B.S. in music education. Music majors: 171. . . . TULANE UNIVERSITY, New Orleans, Louisiana 70118. Music Department of an endowed college (Newcomb College) of the university. (Member, NASM.) Head: **Peter S. Hansen** (1957). University founded: 1884. Department founded: 1909. Degrees: B.A., B.F.A., M.A., M.F.A., M.A.T. Music students enrolled: 670. Volumes in music library: 16,000 (see Music Libraries). Official school ensembles: chorus, chamber vocal ensemble, concert band, opera workshop, chamber orchestra, in-residence string quartet. Summer music term. . . . UNIVERSITY OF SOUTHWESTERN LOUISIANA SCHOOL OF MUSIC, USL Box 100, Lafayette, Louisiana 70501. A School of Music in the College of Liberal Arts, tax supported. (Member, NASM.) Head: **Willis F. Ducrest** (1946). College founded: 1898. Music school founded: 1938. Degrees: B.M.Ed.; B.A. in applied music; B.M. in applied music, theory and composition; B.A. in music, history and literature. Scholarships: 50 to 100, totaling $100 to $300. Fellowships: two, each $2,000 plus fees. Music students enrolled: 175. Music library: 10,000 volumes. Official school ensembles: chorus, chamber vocal ensemble, marching band, concert band, opera workshop, symphony orchestra, chamber orchestra, jazz ensemble. Summer music school. . . . XAVIER UNIVERSITY OF LOUISIANA, 7325 Palmetto Street, New Orleans, Louisiana 70125. Music Department within a college. Head: **Malcolm J. Breda** (1970). School founded: 1915. Degrees: B.M., B.M.Ed. Scholarships: five full and many partial, totaling $12,000. Music students enrolled: 75. Music library: 8,500 volumes. Official school ensembles: chorus, glee club, chamber vocal ensemble, concert band, opera workshop, chamber ensemble in residence, jazz ensemble. Summer music school. Special course: Afro-American music.

MAINE

BOWDOIN COLLEGE, Brunswick, Maine 04011. Music Department within the college. Chairman: **Robert K. Beckwith** (1964). College founded: 1794. Degree: B.A. Scholarships: two, totaling $1,000. Music Students enrolled: 100 (three to four majors). Volumes in music library: 5,000 to 8,000. Official school ensembles: glee club, chamber vocal ensemble, marching band, chamber orchestra, other smaller chamber groups. Summer school of music. . . . NORTHERN CONSERVATORY OF MUSIC, 166 Union Street, Bangor, Maine 04401. Conservatory. Director: **William R. Mague** (1969). Degree: Bachelor of Music Education. Scholarships: eight, totaling $1,700. Music students enrolled: 75. Music library: 2,500 volumes. Official music ensembles: chorus, concert band, in-residence chamber ensemble. No summer session. . . . UNIVERSITY OF MAINE, Orono, Maine 04473. A department in the Arts and Sciences College of a state-supported university. (Member, NASM.) Chairman: **Robert Godwin.** Degrees: B.A., major in music; B.S. in music education.

MARYLAND

BOWIE STATE COLLEGE, Bowie, Maryland 20715. Music Department within a college. Chairman: **Eugene T. Simpson** (1970). College founded: 1895. No music degrees or scholarships. Fellowships: one, for $750. Music students enrolled: 10. Volumes in music library: 1,009. Official school ensembles: chorus, concert band. Summer instruction. . . . COLUMBIA UNION COLLEGE, Takoma Park, Maryland 20012. Music Department within a college. Head: **Charles L. Pierce** (1964). School and department founded: 1904. Degrees: B.A., B.S. No music scholarships. Music students enrolled: 25. Music library: 1,000 volumes. Official school ensembles: chorus, chamber vocal ensemble, concert band, symphony orchestra. Summer music school. . . . ESSEX COMMUNITY COLLEGE, Baltimore, Maryland 21237. Music Department in the Division of Humanities and Arts. Head: **Arno P. Drucker** (1970). School founded: 1959. Degree: Associate of Arts. Music enrollment: 25. Volumes in music library: 6,000. Official music ensembles: chorus. Summer music school. . . . MONTGOMERY COLLEGE, Takoma Park, Maryland 20012. Music program within Department of Creative Arts within Division of Humanities and Social Sciences of the college. Head: **Miss Gloria Monteiro** (1964). College founded: 1946. No music degree. Music students enrolled: 60. Official school ensembles: chorus, chamber vocal ensemble, percussion ensemble, jazz ensemble, other smaller chamber groups. Summer instruction. . . . PEABODY CONSERVATORY OF MUSIC, 17 East Mount Vernon Place, Baltimore, Maryland 21202. Conservatory. (Member, NASM.) Head: **Richard Franko Goldman** (1969). School founded: 1857. Degrees: Certificate, B.M., M.M., D.M.A., Artist Diploma. Scholarships: 142, totaling $150,000. Fellowships: 14, totaling $30,800. Music students enrolled: 400. Music library: 51,000 volumes (see Music Libraries). Official school ensembles: chorus, chamber vocal ensemble, concert band, opera workshop, symphony orchestra, chamber orchestra, contemporary music ensemble. Summer Music school. Special courses: electronic music, Bachelor's study program in classical guitar. . . . SAINT JOSEPH COLLEGE FOR WOMEN, Emmitsburg, Maryland 21727. Part of the Fine Arts Department, which is joined with that of Mt. St. Mary's College for men in the same city. Head, Fine Arts Coordinator: **Sister Jane Marie Perrot.** School founded: 1809. Degree: B.A. with major in fine arts. No music scholarships. Fine arts majors with some emphasizing music: 20. Music section of main library: 500 volumes. Official music ensembles: chorus and glee club. No summer music school. . . . ST. MARY'S COLLEGE OF MARYLAND, St. Mary's City, Maryland 20686. Music Department within Humanities Division. Head: **Ralph Baxter.** School founded: 1839. No music degrees nor music scholarships. Music students enrolled: 50. Music library: 1,500 volumes. Official music ensembles: chorus, marching band, jazz ensemble. No summer music school. . . . UNIVERSITY OF MARYLAND, BALTIMORE COUNTY. 5401 Wilkens Avenue, Baltimore, Maryland 21228. Music is an area of study within the university. Co-ordinator of Music: **Arthur R. Tollefson** (1970). Music studies and school founded: 1966. No music degrees, music scholarships or fellowships. Music students enrolled: 700. Music library: 4,000 volumes. Official school ensembles: chorus, in-residence chamber ensembles. Summer music courses taught. . . . UNIVERSITY OF MARYLAND, College Park, Maryland 20142. A Music Department in the College of Arts and Sciences. Head: **Eugene Troth** (1971). School founded: 1920. Music Department founded: 1953. Degrees: B.A., B.Mus., B.S. in music education, M.Mus., M.A. and M.S. in music education, Ph.D., D.M.A., Ed.D. in music education. Scholarships: 4, totaling $2,400. Fellowships: 11, totaling $27,000. Music students enrolled: 525. Music library: 18,000 volumes. Official school ensembles: three choruses, two glee clubs, chamber vocal ensemble, two marching bands, two concert bands, opera workshop, two symphony orchestras, chamber orchestra, eleven resident chamber ensembles. Summer music session. . . . WASHINGTON COLLEGE, Chestertown, Maryland 21620. Music Department within the college. Head: **Garry E. Clarke** (1968). College founded: 1782. Department founded: 1967. Degree: B.A. Scholarships: general college scholarship only. Music students enrolled: 100. Volumes in music library: 6,000 to 7,000. Official school ensembles: chorus, chamber vocal ensemble, concert band, other smaller chamber groups. No summer music instruction. . . . WESTERN MARYLAND COLLEGE, Westminster, Maryland 21157. (Member, NASM.) Department of Music in a liberal arts college related to the Methodist Church. Chairman: **Gerald E. Cole** (1955). College founded: 1868. Department founded: 1926. Degrees: B.A., B.S. Scholarships: 23, totaling $12,825. Music students enrolled: 554. Volumes in music library: 2,100. Official school ensembles: chorus, glee club, chamber vocal ensemble, marching band, concert band, chamber orchestra, jazz ensemble. No summer music school.

MASSACHUSETTS

AMHERST COLLEGE, Amherst, Massachusetts 00102. Music Department in a liberal arts college. Head: **Henry G. Mishkin** (1965). College founded: 1821. Degrees: B.A., M.A. No music scholarship. Fellowships: two, each $1,200. Music students enrolled: 250. Volumes in music library; 10,000. Official school ensembles: glee club, chamber vocal ensemble, symphony orchestra, chamber orchestra, jazz ensemble, brass ensemble, other smaller chamber groups. No summer music school. . . . ANNA MARIA COLLEGE, Sunset Lane, Paxton, Massachusetts 01605. A Department of Music within a college of liberal arts affiliated with the Catholic University of America (Associate Member, NASM.) Head: **Maureen E. Egan** (1968). Both the parent school and the Music Department were founded in 1946. Degrees: B.M., B.A. with a music major. Enrollment in music: 35 to 40 average. Ensembles: glee club, chamber vocal ensemble. A limited number of music courses are offered in summer. . . . BERKLEE SCHOOL OF MUSIC, 1140 Boylston Street, Boston, Massachusetts 02215. Administrator: **Robert Share.** School offering primarily studies in jazz, ensemble playing, theory, arranging, etc. Enrollment: 900. . . . BOSTON CONSERVATORY OF MUSIC, 8 The Fenway, Boston, Massachusetts 02215. A Conservatory of music, independent and unendowed. (Member, NASM.) Founded in 1867. President: **George A. Brambilla** (1967). Degrees: B.M. and M.M. Enrollment: 285. Music library: 24,000. Ensembles: chorus, chamber vocal ensemble, concert band, opera workshop, symphony orchestra, chamber orchestra, smaller chamber groups, jazz ensemble. Offers a summer music school. . . . BOSTON SCHOOL OF MUSIC INC., 686 Massachusetts Avenue, Cambridge, Massachusetts 02139. Supervisor: **Herman Vaun Binns.** . . . BOSTON STATE COLLEGE, 625 Huntington Avenue, Boston, Massachusetts 02115. Music Department within the college. Chairman: **Elizabeth A. O'Brien.** School founded: 1852. Degree: none in music. Students enrolled in music courses: 1,450. Official music ensembles: chorus, concert band. Music courses in summer school. . . . BOSTON UNIVERSITY SCHOOL OF FINE AND APPLIED ARTS, 855 Commonwealth Avenue, Boston, Massachusetts 02215. One of fifteen colleges constituting Boston University and sharing in its endowment. (Member, NASM.) Dean: **Norman Dello Joio.** Chairman, Division of Music: **Wilbur D. Fullbright.** Degrees: B.M. in applied music, theory and composition, music history and literature, music education, church music; M.M. in applied music, composition, theory, music history and literature, music education, church music; B.A. (through College of Liberal Arts); M.A. (through College of Liberal Arts). Music majors: 500. Music Library: about 10,000 titles (see Music Libraries). . . . BRADFORD JUNIOR COLLEGE, Bradford, Massachusetts 01830. Music Department within a college. Head: **Charles W. Ludington** (1960). College founded: 1804. Degrees: no music degrees. Music students enrolled: 100. Volumes in music library: 10,000. Official school ensembles: glee club, chamber vocal ensemble, opera workshop. No summer music instruction. . . . BRANDEIS UNIVERSITY, 415 South Street, Waltham, Massachusetts 02154. Music Department within the University. Head: **Paul Brainard** (1969). School founded: 1948. Music Department founded: 1949. Degrees: B.A. in Music; Master of Fine Arts in Music History, Theory, Composition; Ph.D. in Music History, Theory, Composition. Scholarships and fellowships: numbers and amounts vary. Music students enrolled: 45. **Music library: 14,000 volumes exclusive** of recordings (see Music Libraries). Official school ensembles: chorus, chamber vocal ensembles, symphony orhcestra, chamber orchestra, in-residence chamber ensembles, early music ensemble. No summer music school. There is a special course in electronic music. . . . CURRY COLLEGE, Milton, Massachusetts 02186. Music Department within the college. Head: **Kenton F. Steward** (1969). School founded: 1848. No music scholarships. Music enrollment: 25 to 35. Music library: 3,000 volumes. Official school ensembles: chorus, glee club, chamber vocal ensemble, concert band, jazz ensemble. No summer music school. . . . HARVARD UNIVERSITY, Cambridge, Massachusetts 02138. Music is taught within the Music Department of a College of Arts and Sciences. Chairman: **Elliot Forbes** (1972). Music Department founded: ca. 1865. University founded: 1636. Degrees: A.B., A.M., Ph.D., all in music. Scholarships: 27, totaling $79,000; no information available for undergraduate aid. Music enrollment: 50 undergraduate concentrators; 48 graduate students. Music library (as of June, 1971): 70,490. Music ensembles: chorus, glee club, marching band, concert band, symphony orchestra, smaller chamber groups. The department has summer music instruction. . . . HOLYOKE COMMUNITY COLLEGE, 165 Sargeant Street, Holyoke, Massachusetts 01040. Music Department within the college. Director: **Sidney B. Smith** (1966). College founded: 1946. Department founded: 1967. Degree: A.A. in music education. Scholarships: one for $100. Music students enrolled: 45 to 50. Volumes in music library: 700. Official school ensembles: chorus, chamber vocal ensemble, concert band, symphony orchestra, jazz ensemble. Limited summer instruction. . . . LONGY SCHOOL OF MUSIC, 1 Follen Street, Cambridge, Massachusetts 02138. Department of Music within a college. Head: **Nicholas Van Slyck** (1962). Music Department founded: 1915. Degree: B.M. Music scholarships: about 15, totaling $8,000. Music enrollment: 500. Music library: 20,000 volumes. School ensembles: chorus, chamber vocal ensemble, chamber orchestra, opera workshop. Summer music school offered. . . . NEW ENGLAND CONSERVATORY OF MUSIC, 290 Huntington Avenue, Boston, Massachusetts 02115. An independent conservatory of music. (Member, NASM.) President; **Gunther Schuller** (1967). Founded: 1867. Degrees: B.M.; Diploma (four-year undergraduate degree in applied music); M.M.; Artist's Diploma (graduate degree in applied music). Scholarships: 320, totaling $260,000. Fellowships: 24, totaling $20,000. Enrollment: 525. Music Library: 13,250 books; 30,942 scores; 14,000 recordings. Ensembles: chorus, chamber vocal ensemble, wind ensemble, opera workshop, symphony orchestra, chamber orchestra, smaller chamber groups, jazz ensemble. Summer music school offered. Special course: Performance of Early Music. . . . NORTH SHORE COMMUNITY COLLEGE, 3 Essex Street, Beverly, Massachusetts 01915. Music is a division of the Humanities Department. Head: **Helen N. Morgan** (1970). Founded: 1870 (as a branch of the New England Conservatory of Music). Degree: Associate in Arts. Scholarships: five partial, totaling $1,200. Music enrollment: 200 to 215. Music library: 500 volumes. Official music ensemble: children's chorus, wind, string and brass ensembles, piano ensemble. Summer music school. . . . PINE MANOR JUNIOR COLLEGE, 400 Heath Street, Chestnut Hill, Massachusetts 02167. Music instruction is offered within the Department of Performing Arts. School and music instruction both established in 1911. An Associate of Arts degree is offered, as the school is a two-year liberal arts college. Ensemble: chorus. . . . ST. HYACINTH COLLEGE AND SEMINARY, 66 School Road, Granby, Massachusetts 01033. Music Department within college. Head: **Rev. Jeremy Chodacki.** Music Department founded: 1968. Music students enrolled: 50. Official school ensembles: chorus, glee club. Summer music classes. . . . STATE COLLEGE AT BRIDGEWATER, Bridgewater, Massachusetts 02324. Music Department is part of the Division of Creative Arts. Head: **Kenneth W. Falkner** (1969). School founded: 1840. Degrees: no music majors; minor offered in B.A. and B.S. in Elementary Education. Music library: 482 volumes. Official school ensembles: chorus, glee club, chamber vocal ensemble, jazz ensemble. No summer music school. . . . UNIVERSITY OF MASSACHUSETTS, Amherst, Massachusetts 01003. A department in the College of Arts and Sciences of a state university. (Member, NASM.) Head: **Philip Bezanson.** Degrees: B.A. in performance, music history, theory and composition; B.M. in performance, theory and composition, music education; M.M. in performance, musicology, theory and composition, music education. . . . WILLIAMS COLLEGE, Williamstown, Massachusetts 01267. Music Department within a liberal arts college. Chairman: **Robert G. Barrow** (1949). Department founded: 1940. School founded: 1793. Degree: B.A. with emphasis in music. No music scholarships. Music students enrolled: 250. Official school ensembles: choral society; chamber vocal ensemble; marching band; symphony orchestra; brass, string, and woodwind chamber groups. No summer music school. . . . WORCESTER STATE COLLEGE, Worcester, Massachusetts 01602. Music Department within college. Head: **Abram Kaminsky** (1968). No music degrees. No music scholarships. Music library: 1,100 volumes. Official school ensembles: chorus, glee club, concert band, symphony orchestra, chamber groups. Limited summer music instruction.

MICHIGAN

ALBION COLLEGE, Albion, Michigan 49224. A Department of Music in a liberal arts college, endowed. (Member, NASM.) Chairman: **David L. Strickler.** Degree: B.A. in applied music, history and literature. Music majors: 25. . . . ADRIAN COLLEGE, Madison Avenue, Adrian, Michigan 49221. Music Department within a college. Head: **Arthur J. Jones** (1969). Department and school founded: 1845. Degree: B.A. in music and in music education. Scholarships: total $2,100. Music students enrolled: 45. Music library: 1,000 volumes. Official school ensembles: chorus, chamber vocal ensemble, madrigal singers, marching band, concert band, symphony orchestra, three instrumental chamber ensembles. Summer music school. . . . ALMA COLLEGE, Alma, Michigan 48801. Music Department within the college. Head: **Ernest G. Sullivan** (1953). College founded: 1886. Degree: B.A. Scholarships: two, totaling $700. Music students enrolled: 75. Volumes in music library: 2,500 volumes, 350 records. Official school ensembles: chorus, chamber vocal ensemble, marching band, concert band, opera workshop. No summer music school. . . . ALPENA COMMUNITY COLLEGE, Johnson Street, Alpena, Michigan 49707. Music Division within the Department of Fine Arts. Department Chairman: **Terry Hall.** No music degrees; basic music instruction is offered with credits transferable to major schools. Music enrollment: 90. Official music ensembles: chorus, concert band, symphony orchestra, adult choral society. No summer music school. . . . ANDREWS UNIVERSITY, Berrien Springs, Michigan 49108. Music Department in an undergraduate college of a university supported by the Lake Union Conference of Seventh-Day Adventists. (Member, NASM.) Head of Music Department: **Paul Hamel** (1955). University and music instruction both begun in 1875. Degrees: B.A., B.Mus., M.A., M.Mus. Total amount of scholarships available: $6,500. Average enrollment: 80. Volumes in music library: 7,000. Ensembles: chorus, glee club, chamber vocal ensemble, concert band, symphony orchestra, chamber orchestra, smaller chamber groups. Summer instruction is offered. . . . CALVIN COLLEGE, 1801 East Beltline, South East, Grand Rapids, Michigan 49506. Music Department within the college. Chairman: **John Hamersma** (1964). College founded: 1876. Degrees: A.B. Scholarships: eight, totaling $1,600. Music students enrolled: 70 to 80. Volumes in music library: 6,000. Official school ensembles: chorus, chamber vocal ensemble, concert band, chamber orchestra, Collegium Musicum, other smaller ensembles. Summer music instruction and summer workshops (church music, music camp, strings). . . . CENTRAL MICHIGAN UNIVERSITY, Mt. Pleasant, Michigan 48858. Music Department within the School of Fine and Applied Arts of a state-supported institution. (Member, NASM.) Chairman: **Rex Hewelett** (1968). Degrees: B.M., B.A., B.M.Ed., B.S., M.M., M.A. No specific fellowships in music. Scholarships vary. Music students enrolled: 300 majors, 400 minors, 5,100 total music enrollment. Official school ensembles: two choruses, two glee clubs, chamber vocal ensemble, marching band, concert band, opera workshop, symphony orchestra, jazz ensemble, symphonic wind ensemble, other smaller chamber groups. Summer music school. . . . DETROIT INSTITUTE OF MUSICAL ART, 5330-50 John R. Avenue, Detroit, Michigan 48202. Dean Emeritus: **Alle D. Zuidema.** . . . DUNS SCOTUS COLLEGE, 20000 West Nine Mile Road, Southfield, Michigan 48075. Music is part of the Division of Humanities. Head: **Rev. Peter A. Ricke** (1962). School founded: 1929. No music degrees or scholarships. Music enrollment: 40, no major. Music library: 2,000 volumes. No music ensembles. . . . EASTERN MICHIGAN UNIVERSITY, Ypsilanti, Michigan 48197. Music Department within the College of Arts and Sciences of a state university. (Member, NASM.) Head: **James B. Hause** (1971). University founded: 1849. Music Department founded: 1854. Degrees: B.A., B.S., B.M.Ed., M.A. Scholarships: 137, totaling $40,000. Fellowships: 10, totaling $25,000. Music enrollment: 260. Ensembles: chorus, glee club, chamber vocal ensemble, marching band, concert band, opera workshop, piano trio, woodwind quintet, chamber orchestra, symphony orchestra. Summer music school offered. . . . FERRIS STATE COLLEGE, Big Rapids, Michigan 49307. School was founded in 1884; music instruction has been taught since 1907. Music is offered in a "Music Activities Center." Director: **Dacho Dachoff** (1955). No music degrees or scholarships. Music enrollment: 1,200. Volumes in the music library: 550. Ensembles: chorus, men and women's glee club, chamber vocal ensemble, marching band, concert band, symphony orchestra, chamber orchestra, smaller chamber groups, jazz group, and a Choral Union. Summer music courses taught. . . . GLEN OAKS COMMUNITY COLLEGE, Centreville, Michigan 49032. Music Department within the college. Head: **Robert L. Gray** (1966). School founded: 1965. Degree: A.A. Scholarships: totaling $2,400. Music students enrolled: 30. Music library: 300 volumes. Official school ensembles: chorus, chamber vocal ensemble, brass, woodwind and percussion ensembles. No summer school. . . . GRAND VALLEY STATE COLLEGE, Allendale, Michigan 49401. Music Department within the College of Arts and Sciences. Head:

Wayne Dunlap (1971). College founded: 1960. Department founded: 1964. Degrees: B.A., B.S. in music. Music students enrolled: 45. Volumes in music library: 1,000. Official School ensembles: chorus, chamber vocal ensemble, concert band, chamber orchestra, jazz ensemble. Limited summer instruction. . . . HOPE COLLEGE, Holland, Michigan 49423. Music Department of the college. (Member, NASM.) Chairman: **Robert A. Ritsema** (1969). School founded: 1862. Degrees: B.A. in music theory, music history; B.M. in vocal and instrumental music education; B.M. in performance. Scholarships: 14, totaling $1,400. Music students enrolled: 90 majors, 600 participating in courses. Official music ensembles: chorus, chamber vocal ensemble, concert band, symphony orchestra, chamber orchestra, chamber groups, jazz ensemble. No summer music school. . . . JACKSON COMMUNITY COLLEGE, Jackson, Michigan 49201. Music Department within the college. Chairman: **David Zielinski** (1969). College and Department founded: 1938. Degree: A.A. No music scholarships. Music students enrolled: 100. Official school ensembles: chorus, chamber vocal ensemble, concert band, chamber orchestra, jazz ensemble. Limited summer instruction. . . . KALAMAZOO COLLEGE, Kalamazoo, Michigan 49001. A Music Department within a college of liberal arts. Chairman: **Russell A. Hammar.** College founded 1833. Degree: B.A. in music. Undetermined minimum number of scholarships available in amounts varying according to student need. One senior fellowship is available for each quarter of the four quarters of the school year. Enrollment in music: 40. Volumes in music library: 4,000. Ensembles: chorus, motet choir, chamber vocal ensemble, symphony orchestra, chamber orchestra, woodwind quintet and string quartet, jazz ensemble, a Bach Festival Chorus and Orchestra. The College offers instruction throughout the year; it is open for four equal quarters of eleven weeks each. Has developed (since 1964) an in-depth curriculum of "literature and style along with vocabulary and materials" as a core of study in music. . . . KALAMAZOO VALLEY COMMUNITY COLLEGE, 6767 West "O," Kalamazoo, Michigan 49001. Music program within a division of the college. Head: **Peter D. Rush** (1969). School and music program founded: 1967. Music enrollment: 300. Official school music ensembles: chorus, glee club, chamber vocal ensemble, concert band, jazz ensemble. Summer music courses. . . . MICHIGAN STATE UNIVERSITY, East Lansing, Michigan 48823. A Music Department within the College of Arts and Letters of a state-supported university. (Member, NASM.) Chairman: **James Niblock** (1963). School founded: 1855. Music instruction added: 1920. Degrees: B.M., B.A., M.M., M.A., Ph.D. Scholarships: 120, totaling $36,000. Fellowships: two, totaling $1,000. Enrollment in music: 525. Volumes in music library: 22,000. Official school ensembles: chorus, two glee clubs, chamber vocal ensemble, marching band, concert band, opera workshop, symphony orchestra, chamber orchestra, jazz ensemble. Summer music school. . . . MONROE COUNTY COMMUNITY COLLEGE, 1555 Raisinville Road, Monroe, Michigan 48161. Music is part of the Humanities Division. Head: **Robert P. Merkel** (1967). Music courses begun in 1967. School founded: 1964. Scholarships: two, totaling $200. Music students enrolled: 10. Music library: 1,000 volumes. Official school ensembles: chorus, jazz ensemble. No summer music courses. . . . NORTHERN MICHIGAN UNIVERSITY, Marquette, Michigan 49855. Department of Music within a School of Arts and Sciences. (Member, NASM.) Head: **Harold E. Wright** (1962). Music Department founded: 1920. School founded: 1899. Degrees: B.M.Ed.; B.A. (music major); M.A. in Education. Scholarships: 10, totaling $4,500. Fellowships: 10, totaling $1,000. Music students enrolled: 160. Official school ensembles: chorus, glee club, marching band, concert band, opera workshop, symphony orchestra, chamber orchestra, woodwind trio, string ensemble, brass ensemble, jazz ensemble. Summer music school. . . . NORTHWESTERN MICHIGAN COLLEGE, East Front Street, Traverse City, Michigan 49684. Music Department within a Humanities Division of a two-year college. Chairman of Humanities: **Walter Beardsley.** Head of Music Faculty: **George**

W. Mulder. The college and music studies established: 1951. Degree: A.A. No separate music scholarships; only the general college scholarship offerings. Music student enrollment: 200. Volumes in music library: 1,000. Ensembles: chorus, chamber vocal ensemble, chamber orchestra, smaller chamber groups. Summer instruction available. There is cooperation between the college and the National Music Camp at Interlochen. . . . OAKLAND COMMUNITY COLLEGE—HIGHLAND LAKES CAMPUS, 7350 Cooley Lake Road, Union Lake, Michigan 48085. Music discipline part of Communications and Humanities Department (English, Speech, Art, Music). Head: **John Cook** (1970). College and department founded: 1965. No music degrees given. Music students enrolled: 125. Volumes in music library: 600. No summer music school. . . . OAKLAND UNIVERSITY, Rochester, Michigan 48063. Department of Music within the university. Chairman: **David DiChiera.** University founded: 1957. Degrees: B.A. Scholarships: four (two half-tuition and two full-tuition). Music students enrolled: 125. Official school ensembles: chorus, concert band, opera workshop, symphony orchestra, Collegium Musicum. Summer music instruction. . . . SPRING ARBOR COLLEGE, Spring Arbor, Michigan 49283. Music is an area of study within the Humanities Division. School founded: 1863. Scholarships: 12, each from $100 to $500. Degree: B.A. Music students enrolled: 30. Music library: 1,500 volumes. Official school ensembles: chorus, chamber vocal ensemble, concert band, opera workshop, chamber orchestra. Summer music school. . . . UNIVERSITY OF MICHIGAN SCHOOL OF MUSIC, Ann Arbor, Michigan 48105. A School of Music in a state-supported university. (Member, NASM.) Dean: **Allen P. Britton** (1970). University founded: 1817. School of Music founded: 1880. Degrees: B.M., M.M., D.M.A., Ed.D., Ph.D. Scholarships: 95, totaling $57,000. Fellowships: 90, totaling $130,000. Music enrollment: 850. Music library: 48,000 volumes (see Music Libraries). Music ensembles: three choruses, glee club, chamber vocal ensemble, marching band, three concert bands, opera workshop, two symphony orchestras, smaller chamber groups, jazz ensemble. Summer music school. . . . WAYNE STATE UNIVERSITY, Room 210, Music Wing, Detroit, Michigan 48202. Chairman, Music Department: **Robert Lawson.** Music majors: 400. Music library: about 10,000 volumes. . . . WESTERN MICHIGAN UNIVERSITY, West Michigan Avenue, Kalamazoo, Michigan 49001. Music Department in the School of Liberal Arts and Sciences of a state-supported university. (Member, NASM.) Head: **Robert Holmes** (1966). University founded: 1903. Department founded: 1904. Degrees: B.A., B.S., B.M., M.M., M.A. Scholarships: 91, totaling $23,000. Fellowships: nine graduate assistantships totaling $25,200. Music students enrolled: 400. Volumes in music library: 8,644 music scores. Official school ensembles: chorus, glee club, chamber vocal ensemble, marching band, concert band, opera workshop, symphony orchestra, jazz ensemble, other smaller chamber groups. Summer music shcool. Special courses in music therapy.

MINNESOTA

ANOKA RAMSEY STATE JUNIOR COLLEGE, 11200 Mississippi Boulevard, Coon Rapids, Minnesota 55433. Music Department within the college. College founded: 1965. No music majors. Degree: A.A. Volumes in music library: 200. Official school ensembles: chorus, chamber vocal ensemble, concert band. Limited summer instruction. . . . BEMIDJI STATE COLLEGE, Bemidji, Minnesota 56601. A music Department within a college. School founded: 1919. Music Department founded: 1937. Head: **Fulton Gallagher** (1971). Degrees: B.S., B.A., M.S. Scholarships: 12, totaling $2,400. Enrollment in music: 150. Ensembles: chorus, glee club, chamber vocal ensemble, concert band, opera workshop, symphony orchestra. Two five-week sessions of instruction are offered in summer. . . . BETHEL COLLEGE AND SEMINARY, 1480 North Snelling, St. Paul, Minnesota 55101. Music Department within the college. Head: **Julius Whitinger** (1959).

College founded: 1890. Department added: 1950. Degrees: B.A. Scholarships: total $15,000. Music students enrolled: 100. Official school ensembles: chorus, glee clubs, concert band, opera workshop, chamber orchestra, brass and woodwind ensembles. No summer music school. Special courses: Black Culture. . . . COLLEGE OF SAINT TERESA, Winona, Minnesota 55987. A Music Department within a four-year liberal arts college. Chairman: **Elizabeth L. Hollway.** College founded: 1907. Music Department founded: 1907. Degrees: B.A. in Music Education; B.A. in Performance Studies. Scholarships: 8 to 10, totaling $4,800, renewable annually. Enrollment in music: over 100 with 40 to 50 music majors. Volumes in music library: 3,500. Ensembles: chorus; chamber vocal ensemble; chamber orchestra; string quartet; various brass, woodwind, and recorder ensembles. Music is offered in the summer. Special courses include "Music in Black America" and electronic music. . . . COLLEGE OF SAINT THOMAS, St. Paul, Minnesota 55101. Music Department within college. Head: **Anthony Chiuminatto** (1946). Department founded: 1946. School founded: 1885. Degrees: B.A., B.Mus.Ed., Master of Arts in Teaching. No music scholarships or fellowships. Music students enrolled: 25. Music library: 2,000 volumes. Official school ensembles: chorus, glee club, chamber vocal ensemble, concert band, opera workshop, chamber orchestra, resident chamber ensembles. Summer session occasionally. . . . COLLEGE OF SAINT SCHOLASTICA, Kenwood Avenue, Duluth, Minnesota 55811. Music Department within the college. Chairman: **Monica Laughlin OSB** (1954). College and department founded: 1924. Degrees: B.A. in Music Education, B.A. in Music Literature. Scholarships: 11, totaling $3,300. Music students enrolled: 18 majors, four minors. Volumes in music library: 1,000. Official school ensembles: glee club, chamber vocal ensemble, symphony orchestra, in-residence flute trio, early-music consort. No summer music school. . . . CONCORDIA COLLEGE, 7th Street South, Moorhead, Minnesota 56560. Department of Music within a college. (Member, NASM.) Head: **Paul J. Christiansen** (1937). College founded: 1891. Degrees: B.A.; B.M. in performance, theory, music education. Scholarships: 22, totaling $4,400. Music enrollment: 200 to 210 majors, 40 to 50 minors. Music library: 2,550. Ensembles: concert choir, chorus, concert band, symphony orchestra, chamber orchestra, jazz ensemble. Limited summer offering. . . . FERGUS FALLS STATE JUNIOR COLLEGE, Fergus Falls, Minnesota 56537. A Music Department within the college. Head: **Frank Hedlund** (1960). Department founded in 1960. One scholarship in music offered: $50. Enrollment: 10. Music volumes in library: 500. Ensembles: chorus, chamber vocal ensemble, pep band, and smaller instrumental groups. No music courses in the summer. . . . GUSTAVUS ADOLPHUS COLLEGE, Saint Peter, Minnesota 56082. Department of Music in a private liberal arts college supported by the Lutheran Church. (Member, NASM.) Chairman: **Myron R. Falck** (1967). School founded: 1862. Degrees: B.A. in Applied Music, Church Music, School Music. Scholarships are based on need. Music enrollment: 50 majors. Volumes in music library: 3,541. Official music ensembles: chorus, chamber vocal ensemble, concert band, chamber orchestra, smaller chamber groups, jazz ensemble. No summer music instruction. . . . HAMLINE UNIVERSITY, St. Paul, Minnesota 55101. A Department of Music in a liberal arts college affiliated with the Methodist Church. (Member, NASM.) Chairman: **Russell G. Harris.** Degrees: B.A. in music; B.A. in music education. Music majors: 50. . . . MANKATO STATE COLLEGE, Mankato, Minnesota 56001. Music Department within a college. Head: **Herbert E. Owen** (1964). Department founded: 1921. Degrees: B.S. (in teaching), B.S. (nonteaching), B.M., B.A., M.S., M.A., M.M. Scholarships: one for $300. Fellowships: three, at $2,100 each. Music students enrolled: 240. Music library: 5,150 volumes. Official school ensembles: chorus, two glee clubs, chamber vocal ensemble, marching band, two concert bands, opera workshop, symphony orchestra, chamber orchestra, chamber groups, jazz ensemble. Summer music school. . . . MESABI STATE JUNIOR COLLEGE, Virginia,

Minnesota 55792. Music Department within the college. Head: **Jay H. Carlsgaard** (1967). Department founded: 1967. School founded: 1964. Degree: A.A. Music students enrolled: 400. Music library: 900 volumes. Official school ensembles: chorus, chamber vocal ensemble, concert band, brass ensemble. No summer music school. . . . MOORHEAD STATE COLLEGE, Moorhead, Minnesota 56560. A Department of Music in a state college. (Member, NASM.) Chairman: **Earnest N. Harris.** Degrees: B.S. in music education (instrumental and/or vocal); B.A. in winds, strings, piano, theory, vocal music; M.S. in music education; M.M. in voice, orchestral and band instruments. . . . NORMANDALE STATE JUNIOR COLLEGE, 9700 France Avenue, Bloomington, Minnesota 55431. A Music Department within a two-year college. Head: **Carlo Minnetti** (1968). School and department founded in 1968. Degree: A.A. Music enrollment: 600. Number of volumes in library: 10,000. Ensembles: chorus, chamber vocal ensembles, concert band, smaller instrumental chamber groups. . . . NORTHLAND STATE JUNIOR COLLEGE, Highway One East, Thief River Falls, Minnesota 56701. A Music Department within a two-year college. Head of department: **Sverre G. Solheim.** Music department founded: 1965. A Degree: A.A. No music scholarships. Music enrollment: 50. Music volumes in library: 75. Ensembles: chorus, concert band, and jazz group. Music instruction is offered in the summer. . . . SAINT OLAF COLLEGE, Northfield, Minnesota 55057. A Department of Music within a liberal arts college endowed and supported by the Lutheran Church. (Member, NASM.) Department Chairman: **Adolf White** (1967). College founded in 1874. Music department founded in 1903. Degrees: B.A. in music and music education; B.Mus. in applied music, theory and composition and church music. Scholarships: 20, totaling $2,200. Music enrollment: 170. Ensembles: three choruses, two glee clubs, chamber vocal ensemble, two concert bands, and a symphony orchestra. No summer music courses. . . . SOUTHWEST MINNESOTA STATE COLLEGE, Marshall, Minnesota 56258. Music Department within the college. Head: **John L. Rezatto** (1967). Department and school founded: 1967. Degree: B.A. with concentration in music. No music scholarships. Music enrollment: 65 majors; 300 in music activities and courses. Music library: 5,000 volumes. Official school ensembles: chorus, glee club, chamber vocal ensemble, marching band, concert band, opera workshop, symphony orchestra, chamber orchestra, chamber groups in residence, jazz ensemble. Summer band camp and string ensemble. . . . UNIVERSITY OF MINNESOTA AT DULUTH, Duluth, Minnesota 55812. Department of Music in the Division of Humanities of a university. (Member, NASM.) Head: **Phillip H. Coffman** (1971). University founded 1869. Music department founded: 1942. Degrees: B.A., B.S. Scholarships: unspecified. Music enrollment: 50 to 60 majors. Ensembles: chorus, chamber vocal ensemble, marching band, concert band, opera workshop, symphony orchestra, chamber orchestra, smaller chamber groups, jazz ensemble. Summer music courses offered. . . . UNIVERSITY OF MINNESOTA, Minneapolis, Minnesota 55455. Music Department within the College of Liberal Arts of a state-supported university. (Member, NASM.) Head: **Roy A. Schuessler** (1965). University founded: 1869. Degrees: B.A., B.F.A., B.S. in music education, M.A., M.F.A., M.Ed., Ph.D. Music students enrolled: 650. Library: (see Music Libraries). Official school ensembles: chorus, glee club, chamber vocal ensemble, marching band, concert band, opera workshop, symphony orchestra, chamber orchestra, jazz ensemble, other smaller chamber groups. Summer music school. Special courses: ethnomusicology. . . . UNIVERSITY OF MINNESOTA, Morris, Minnesota 56267. Music is a discipline within the Division of Humanities. Head: **Clyde E. Johnson** (1961). University and division founded: 1960. Degree: B.A. with music major. No music scholarships. Music students enrolled: 25. Volumes in music library: 1,500 to 2,000. Official school ensembles: chorus, chamber vocal ensemble, concert band, symphony orchestra, faculty trio, men's chorus. No summer music school.

MISSISSIPPI

BELHAVEN COLLEGE, Jackson, Mississippi 39202. A Department of Music of an endowed college (Member, NASM.) Chairman: **Virginia Hoogenakker.** Degree: B.M. in applied music. Music majors: 50. . . . BLUE MOUNTAIN COLLEGE, Blue Mountain, Mississippi 38610. Music Department within the college. Head: **John Butler** (1969). School founded: 1873. Degrees: B.A., B.M. Music students enrolled: 25. Official school ensemble: chorus. Summer music school. . . . HOLMES JUNIOR COLLEGE, Goodman, Mississippi, 39079. Music Department within the college. Chairman: **David W. Young** (1970). College and department founded: 1925. Degree: A.A. Scholarships: 36, at $144 each. Music students enrolled: 30 majors. Volumes in music library: 275. Official school ensembles: chorus; chamber vocal ensemble; marching band; concert band; jazz ensemble; percussion, brass, and woodwind ensembles. Summer music workshop camp. . . . MISSISSIPPI INDUSTRIAL COLLEGE, Memphis Street, Holly Springs, Mississippi 38635. Music Department within the college. Chairman: **B. J. Irving** (Division of Humanities). College and department founded: 1905. Degrees: B.A. with various fields of music majors. Scholarships: 100, totaling $40,000. Music students enrolled: 125. Volumes in music library: 4,000. Official school ensembles: chorus, glee club, chamber vocal ensemble, concert band, opera workshop. Summer instruction. . . . MISSISSIPPI STATE COLLEGE FOR WOMEN, Columbus, Mississippi 39701. Music Department within a college. (Member, NASM.) Head: **Sigfred Matson** (1949). School and Music Department founded: 1884. Degrees: B.M., B.M.E., A.B. Scholarships: 30, totaling $8,000. Music enrollment: 50 majors; 150 students. Music library: 3,700 volumes. Ensembles: glee club, symphony orchestra, small chamber groups, jazz ensemble. . . . SOUTHWEST MISSISSIPPI JUNIOR COLLEGE, Summit, Mississippi 39666. Music Department within a college. Head: **Steven A. Jones** (1961). School founded: 1929. Department founded: 1934. Degree: A.A. Scholarships: 30, totaling $8,000. Music students enrolled: 20. Music library: 225 volumes. Official school ensembles: chorus, marching band, concert band, jazz ensemble, brass ensemble. No summer music school. . . . TOUGALOO COLLEGE, Tougaloo, Mississippi 39174. Department within a liberal arts college. Head: **Ben E. Bailey** (1967). School founded: 1869. Degrees: B.A. in piano or voice. Scholarships: five, totaling $3,000. Music students enrolled: 30. Music library: 500 volumes. Official school ensembles: chorus, chamber vocal ensemble. No summer music school. . . . UNIVERSITY OF MISSISSIPPI, University, Mississippi 38677. Department of Music within the College of Liberal Arts of a state university. (Member, NASM.) Head: **James Coleman** (1966). University founded: 1848. Music Department founded: 1890. Degrees: B.M., B.M.E., B.A., M.M., M.M.Ed., Ph.D., Ed.D. Scholarships: 220, totaling $20,000. Fellowships: 12, totaling $15,000. Music enrollment: 160. Music Library: 20,000 volumes. Official ensembles: chorus, chamber vocal ensemble, marching band, concert band, opera workshop, symphony orchestra, chamber orchestra, smaller chamber groups, jazz ensemble. Summer music school offered. . . . UNIVERSITY OF SOUTHERN MISSISSIPPI, Hattiesburg, Mississippi 39401. A Department of Music in the School of Fine Arts of a state-supported university. (Member, NASM.) Dean, School of Fine Arts: **Raymond Mannoni;** Chairman, Department of Music: **David Foltz.** Degrees: B.M. in applied music, theory and composition, church music, music history and literature; B.M.Ed.; M.M. in applied music, theory and composition; M.M.Ed. Music majors: 350. . . . WILLIAM CAREY COLLEGE, Tuscan Avenue, Hattiesburg, Mississippi 39401. A School of Music in a liberal arts college related to and supported by the Mississippi Baptist Convention. (Member, NASM.) Dean: **Donald Winters.** Degrees: B.M. in applied music, music education, church music; B.A. in music, applied music, music theory, church music history and literature, music history and literature. Music majors: 90.

MISSOURI

CENTRAL METHODIST COLLEGE, Fayette, Missouri 65248. The Swinney Conservatory of Music, a department of the college endowed and supported by the Methodist Church in Missouri. (Member, NASM.) Dean of the Conservatory: **Luther T. Spayde** (1952). Department founded: 1925. School founded: 1854. Degrees: Mus.B., B.M.Ed., A.B. Scholarships: 18, totaling $3,600. Music students enrolled: 100. Music library: 2,500 volumes. Official school ensembles: *a cappella* choir, chapel choir, brass choir, woodwind ensemble, stage band. No summer music school. . . . COLUMBIA COLLEGE, 8th and Rogers, Columbia, Missouri 65201. Conservatory of Music within a junior college. (Member, NASM.) Head: **Don M. Lester** (1969). School and conservatory founded: 1851. Degree: A.A. Scholarships: 15, totaling $13,150. Music enrollment: 70. Music library: 1,800 volumes. Ensembles: chorus, vocal ensemble, woodwind ensemble, stage band. No summer music courses. . . . CONSERVATORY OF MUSIC, UNIVERSITY OF MISSOURI–KANSAS CITY, 4420 Warwick Boulevard, Kansas City, Missouri 64111. A conservatory of music within a university. (Member, NASM.) Dean: **Joseph Blankenship** (1969). University founded: 1933. Conservatory founded: 1906. Degrees: B.A., B.M., B.M.E., M.A., M.M., M.M.E., D.M.A. (Programs in music and dance). Scholarships and fellowships: number varies annually. Music enrollment: 450. Music library: 25,000 volumes. Ensembles: chorus, glee club, chamber vocal ensemble, concert band, opera workshop, symphony orchestra, chamber orchestra, smaller chamber groups, jazz ensemble. Summer music school offered. Special courses: high school accelerated program for Bachelor's Degree in Music. . . . COTTEY COLLEGE, 1000 West Austin, Nevada, Missouri 64772. Music Department within a junior college for women owned by the P.E.O. Sisterhood. (Member, NASM.) Head: **Ronald Dawson** (1968). Department and school founded: 1884. Degree: A.A. (music department offers first two years' work leading to music major). Financial aid obtainable through Registrar. Music students enrolled: 15. Music library: 1,000 volumes. Official school ensembles: chorus, chamber vocal ensemble, chamber groups. No summer music school. . . . EVANGEL COLLEGE, 1111 North Glenstone, Springfield, Missouri 65802. Music area within the Fine Arts Department. Head: **Joseph Nicholson** (1966). Department founded: 1955. School founded: 1955. Degrees: B.M.Ed., B.A. Scholarships: 30, totaling $10,000. Music students enrolled: 72. Music library: 3,500 volumes. Official school ensembles: chorus and a touring choir, chamber vocal ensemble, bands, symphony orchestra, chamber ensembles. Summer music courses in general education courses. . . . FLORISSANT VALLEY COMMUNITY COLLEGE, 3400 Pershall Road, Saint Louis, Missouri 63135. Music Department within the college. Head: **Kenneth G. Schuller** (1969). Degree: A.A. in music. Music students enrolled: 50. Music library: 1,000 volumes. Official school ensembles: chorus, concert band, symphony orchestra, jazz ensemble. No summer music school. . . . FONTBONNE COLLEGE, Wydown at Big Bend Boulevards, Clayton, Missouri 63105. A private (Roman Catholic) liberal arts college for women. (Member, NASM.) Chairman, Department of Music: **Relford Patterson.** Degrees: B.M. in music education, applied music (piano, organ, voice), music literature; B.A. in elementary music. . . . FOREST PARK COMMUNITY COLLEGE, 5600 Oakland, St. Louis, Missouri 63110. Music Department within a college. College founded: 1965. Department added: 1967. Degree: A.A. Music students enrolled: 100. Volumes in music library: 235. Official school ensembles: chorus, concert band. Limited summer instruction. . . . LINCOLN UNIVERSITY, Jefferson City, Missouri 65101. The Department of Music in the Division of Humanities and Fine Arts in a university supported by the State of Missouri. (Member, NASM.) Head: **O. Anderson Fuller.** Degrees: B.M.Ed.; B.M. Therapy; B.M. in applied music, theory and composition. Music majors: 91. . . . MARYVILLE COLLEGE OF THE SACRED HEART, 13550 Conway Road, St. Louis, Missouri 63141. Music is a division within the

Humanities Area of the Liberal Arts College in cooperation with St. Louis Institute of Music, which is on campus. Head: **H. A. Padberg** (1958). School founded: 1870. Degree: B.A. with music major. Official music ensembles: chorus, glee club, concert band, smaller chamber groups. Summer courses offered by St. Louis Institute of Music on campus; teachers' workshop offered. Special courses: music therapy, piano-teacher training by the St. Louis Institute of Music. . . . MISSOURI WESTERN COLLEGE, 4525 Downs Drive, Saint Joseph, Missouri 64507. Music Department within the Division of Liberal Arts and Sciences. Head: **Oren R. Duvall** (1970). School founded: 1926. Department founded: 1968. Degree: B.S. in music education (elementary or secondary instrumental and vocal specialization). Scholarships: 40, totaling $8,000. Music students enrolled: 80. Music library: 5,500 volumes. Official school ensembles: chorus, chamber vocal ensemble, marching band, concert band, symphony orchestra, chamber orchestra, jazz ensemble. Summer music school. . . . NORTHEAST MISSOURI STATE TEACHERS COLLEGE, Kirksville, Missouri 63501. A Department of Music in the Division of Fine Arts of a state-supported teachers college. (Member, NASM.) Head, Division of Fine Arts: **Dale A. Jorgenson.** School founded: 1867. Degrees: B.A., B.M.Ed., M.A. Scholarships: 63, totaling $12,600. Fellowships: eight, totaling $10,500. Music students enrolled: 125. Official school ensembles: chorus, marching band, concert band, opera workshop, symphony orchestra, piano trio. Summer music school. . . . NORTHWEST MISSOURI STATE COLLEGE, Maryville, Missouri 64468. A professional department within the Division of Arts and Sciences. (Member, NASM.) Chairman: **John L. Smay.** Degrees: B.S. in education, music major (vocal and instrumental certification, vocal only certification, instrumental only certification); B.A. in music; M.S. in education with major in music. . . . PARK COLLEGE, Parkville, Kansas City, Missouri 64152. A Department of Music in a liberal arts college, endowed. (Member, NASM.) Chairman: **Robert C. Anderson.** Degrees: B.A. in music; B.A. in music education. . . . SAINT LOUIS INSTITUTE OF MUSIC, 13550 Conway Road, Saint Louis, Missouri 63141. An independent school privately supported. (Member, NASM.) Head: **Kenneth G. Schuller** (1965). School founded: 1929. Degrees: B.M., M.M. Scholarships: 22, totaling $8,500. Music students enrolled: 125. Music library: 3,000 volumes. Official school ensembles: chorus, glee club, concert band, two chamber ensembles. Summer music school. Special course taught toward Bachelor and Masters Degrees in piano pedagogy. . . . SAINT LOUIS UNIVERSITY, 221 North Grand, Saint Louis, Missouri 63103. Music Department within the university. Head: **Francis J. Guentner** (1969). School founded: 1818. Department founded: 1969. Degree: B.A. (in music education, performance, theory and composition). Scholarships (general): total $5,500. Students enrolled in music: 12 majors, 150 non-majors. Library: see Music Libraries. Official school ensembles: chorus, concert band, chamber vocal ensemble, pop vocal group, recorder consort. No summer music school. . . . SCHOOL OF THE OZARKS, Point Lookout, Missouri 65726. Music Department within the college. Head: **John Mizell** (1967). School founded: 1907. Department founded: 1967. Degrees: B.A. or B.S. with music major. Scholarships: all students are on a full scholarship covering tuition, room and board, and including private lessons. Music students enrolled: 145. Music library: not separate from college library, which contains 100,000 volumes. Official school ensembles: chorus, concert band, opera workshop, chamber vocal and instrumental ensembles, jazz ensemble. Summer music school. Special course: qualified undergraduates are trained and supervised in teaching applied music at the college level. . . . SOUTHWEST BAPTIST COLLEGE, Bolivar, Missouri 65613. Music Department within a four-year college. Chairman: **Harold Jackson** (1967). Degrees: B.A. with major in music; B.M. with major in music education or performance. Scholarships: total $5,000. Music students enrolled: 90. Official school ensembles: two choruses, two chamber vocal ensembles, concert band, jazz ensemble, two quartets and trio. Summer music school. . . . SOUTHWEST MISSOURI STATE COLLEGE, Springfield, Missouri 65802. A Department of Music in the Division of Arts and Humanities of a state-supported college. (Member, NASM.) Head: **Lloyd G. Blakely.** Degrees: B.A., major in music; B.M. in applied music; B.S. in education, comprehensive major in music. . . . STEPHENS COLLEGE, Broadway and College Avenue, Columbia, Missouri 65201. A department of a junior college partially endowed (Member, NASM.) Chairman: **Richard S. Johnson** (1946). School founded: 1833. Degrees: Bachelor of Fine Arts degree in Music; B.A. in music education. Scholarships: two, totaling $19,250. Music students enrolled: 500. Music library: 1,800 volumes. Official school ensembles: chorus, opera workshop, symphony orchestra, chamber orchestra, chamber ensembles. Summer music school. . . . UNIVERSITY OF MISSOURI, 140 Fine Arts Building, Columbia, Missouri 65201. Music Department within the College of Arts and Science. (Member, NASM.) Chairman: **Charles L. Emmons** (1966). School founded: 1827. Degrees: B.S. in music education, B.A., B.M., M.E., M.A., M.M. Scholarships: 89, totaling $22,620. Fellowships: four, totaling $4,000. Music enrollment: 282. Ensembles: chorus, glee club, chamber vocal ensemble, marching band, concert band, opera workshop, symphony orchestra, chamber orchestra, smaller chamber groups, jazz ensemble, Collegium Musicum. Summer music school offered. (See also Music Libraries). . . . UNIVERSITY OF MISSOURI AT ROLLA, Rolla, Missouri 65401. Music Section is in the Department of Humanities. School founded: 1870. No music degree. Official school ensembles: chorus, glee club, chamber vocal ensemble, marching band, concert band, symphony orchestra, jazz ensemble, chamber winds. No summer music school. . . . WASHINGTON UNIVERSITY, St. Louis, Missouri 63130. Music Department in a privately controlled university. (Member, NASM.) Chairman: **John MacIvor Perkins** (1970). University founded: 1853. Degrees: B.A., M.A., M.M., M.A.T., Ph.D., Ed. D. Scholarships: 16, totaling $29,400. Fellowships: five totaling $9,300. Music students enrolled: 90. Volumes in music library: 45,000 (see Music Libraries). Official school ensembles: chorus, concert band, opera workshop, symphony orchestra, in-residence string quartet. Summer music school. . . . WEBSTER COLLEGE, 470 East Lockwood, St. Louis, Missouri 63119. Music Department in a privately owned liberal arts college. (Member, NASM.) Head: **Eloise Jarvis** (1960). College and music department founded: 1925. Degrees: B.A. in music, B.M. in applied music, B.M.Ed. Music enrollment: 85. Music library: 4,000 volumes. Ensembles: chorus, chamber vocal ensemble, opera workshop, symphony orchestra, small chamber groups. Summer music school. Special courses in music criticism, black music, classical guitar, classical accordion. . . . WILLIAM WOODS COLLEGE, Fulton, Missouri 65251. Jameson Conservatory of Music, a department of an endowed college. (Member, NASM.) Director: **Eugene B. Addams.** Degree: B.A. in music.

MONTANA

COLLEGE OF GREAT FALLS, Great Falls, Montana 59401. Department of Music within the college. Head: **John Cubbage** (1970). Department founded: 1932. Degrees: B.A., B.S. Scholarships: six, totaling $3,460. Music students enrolled: 30. Official school ensembles: chorus, chamber vocal ensemble, concert band, opera workshop, chamber orchestra, jazz ensemble, brass choir. Summer music courses. . . . MONTANA STATE UNIVERSITY, Bozeman, Montana 59715. Department of Music in the College of Professional Schools of the university. Head: **H. Creech Reynolds** (1966). University founded: 1896. Degrees: B.M.Ed., M.Ed. Scholarships: 117, totaling $13,000. Fellowships: six totaling $12,600. Music students enrolled: 70 majors, 25 minors, 25 graduate students. Volumes in music library: 3,000. Official school ensembles: four choruses, chamber vocal ensemble, marching band, concert band, opera workshop, symphony orchestra, chamber orchestra, string ensembles, recorder ensemble, jazz ensemble, wind ensemble.

Summer music school. . . . ROCKY MOUNTAIN COLLEGE, 1511 Poly Drive, Billings, Montana 59102. Music Department within a college. Head: **Donald F. Pihlaja** (1969). School founded: 1883. Degrees: B.A. in music; B.S. in music education. Scholarships: 75, totaling $15,000. Music enrollment: 120. Volumes in library: 2,500. Official ensembles: chorus, chamber vocal ensemble, marching band, concert band, opera workshop, chamber orchestra, smaller chamber groups, jazz ensemble. No summer instruction. . . . UNIVERSITY OF MONTANA, Missoula, Montana 59801. Department of Music in the School of Fine Arts of a state university. (Member, NASM.) Chairman: **Lawrence Perry** (1965). School founded: 1893. Department founded: 1913. Degrees: B.M., B.M.Ed., B.A., M.M., M.M.Ed., M.A., Ed.D. Scholarships: 60, totaling $14,000. Fellowships: seven, totaling $14,000. Music students enrolled: 200. Official school ensembles: two choruses, chamber vocal ensemble, marching band, concert band, trio, string quartet, woodwind quintet, jazz ensemble. Summer music school.

NEBRASKA

CHADRON STATE COLLEGE, Chadron, Nebraska 69337. Department of Music within the Division of Fine Arts of the college. Division Chairman: **Harry E. Holmberg** (1960). College founded: 1911. Degrees: B.A., B.S.Ed. Music students enrolled: 50 majors. Official school ensembles: chorus, chamber vocal ensemble, marching band, concert band, symphony orchestra, jazz ensemble. Summer Music Week for High School Students plus regular summer music courses. . . . COLLEGE OF SAINT MARY, 72nd and Mercy Road, Omaha, Nebraska 68124. Music Department within the college. Head: **Sister Catherine Marie Franey** (1960). College founded: 1955. Department founded: 1957. Degrees: B.A. in applied music; B.A. in music education. Scholarships: three, totaling $600. Music students enrolled: 20 to 25. Volumes in music library: 800. Official school ensembles: chorus, glee club, chamber vocal ensemble. Summer music courses. . . . CONCORDIA TEACHERS COLLEGE, 800 North Columbia Avenue, Seward, Nebraska 68434. Music Department within a teachers college. Head: **Harry Giesselman** (1968). Department and school founded: 1894. Degree: B.S. Scholarships: limited. Music students enrolled: 200 taking music concentration. Music library: 15,600 volumes. School ensembles: chorus, glee club, marching band, concert band, symphony orchestra, jazz ensemble, brass choir. Summer music instruction. . . . HASTINGS COLLEGE, Hastings, Nebraska 68901. A Department of Music, part of a liberal arts college supported by the Presbyterian Church. (Member, NASM.) Head: **Millard H. Cates.** Degrees: B.M. in applied music, history and literature, music education; B.A. in music. Music majors: 80. . . . NEBRASKA WESLEYAN UNIVERSITY, 50th and Huntington, Lincoln, Nebraska 68504. Music Department in a liberal arts college supported by the Methodist Church. (Member, NASM.) Head: **Dennis Jackson** (1970). University founded: 1887. Department founded: 1915. Degrees: B.A., B.M., B.M.Ed. Scholarships: number varies; total $2,000 to $3,000. Music students enrolled: 85 to 100. Official school ensembles: chorus, chamber vocal ensemble, marching band, concert band, opera workshop, symphony orchestra, jazz ensemble. Summer music instruction. . . . NORTHEASTERN NEBRASKA COLLEGE, Fifth and Philip Avenue, Norfolk, Nebraska 68701. Music Department within a college. Head: **Charles A. Miller** (1969). School founded: 1928. Music Department founded: 1969. Degrees: Associate of Arts, Associate of Science. Scholarships: 12 full tuition scholarships ranging from $180 to $300. Music enrollment: 10 to 15. Volumes in music library: 150. Official music ensembles: chorus, chamber vocal ensemble, small chamber groups, jazz ensemble. No summer school. . . . PERU STATE COLLEGE, Peru, Nebraska 68421. Department of Music within a college. Head: **Gavin L. Doughty** (1969). College and department founded: 1867. Degrees: B.A. in education; B.F.A. Scholarships: five each $330. Music students enrolled: 30. Volumes in music library: 600. Official music ensembles: chorus, chamber vocal ensemble, concert band, chamber orchestra, jazz ensemble. Summer music instruction. . . . UNION COLLEGE, Lincoln, Nebraska 68506. A Department of Fine Arts in a liberal arts college supported by the Seventh-Day Adventist Church. (Member, NASM.) Chairman: **Robert A. Murray.** Degrees: B.A. in music; B.S. in music education. Music majors: 40. . . . UNIVERSITY OF NEBRASKA, SCHOOL OF MUSIC, Lincoln, Nebraska 68508. A School of Music in a College of Arts and Sciences in a state-supported university. (Member, NASM.) Director, School of Music: **Emanuel Wishnow.** Degrees: B.M.; B.M.Ed.; B.A. with major in music; B.A. in education with major in music; B.S. in education with major in music; M.M. in performance, music education, composition. Music majors: 350. Music library: about 7,000 volumes.

NEVADA

UNIVERSITY OF NEVADA AT RENO, Reno, Nevada 89507. Music Department in College of Arts and Sciences. Head: **M. E. Puffer.** School founded: 1874. Degrees: B.A. in music; M.M.; M.A. Scholarships: 100, totaling $50,000. Fellowships: three, totaling $7,500. Music students enrolled: 150. Official school ensembles: chorus, chamber vocal ensemble, concert band, opera workshop, symphony orchestra, chamber orchestra, trio, jazz ensemble, brass choir, woodwind choir. Summer music school.

NEW HAMPSHIRE

DARTMOUTH COLLEGE, Box 477, Hanover, New Hampshire 03755. Chairman, Music Department: **Donald Wendlandt.** Music majors: 12. Music library: about 10,000 titles. . . . KEENE STATE COLLEGE, Main Street, Keene, New Hampshire 03431. Music Department within a college. Head: **William D. Pardus** (1966). College founded: 1909. Department added: 1966. Degrees: B.A. in theory; B.M. in music education. Scholarships: two, totaling $1,200. Music students enrolled: 80. Official school ensembles: chorus, chamber vocal ensemble, concert band, symphony orchestra, chamber orchestra, jazz ensemble, brass ensemble, Collegium Musicum. No summer music school. . . . NOTRE DAME COLLEGE, 2321 Elm Street, Manchester, New Hampshire 03104. Music Department within a college. Head: **Sister Anita Marchesseault** (1952). Department founded: 1950. Degree: B.M. Scholarships: six, totaling $1,200. Music students enrolled: 75. Music Library: 400 volumes. Official school ensembles: chorus, glee club, chamber vocal ensemble, chamber ensembles, recorder consort. Summer music school. . . . PLYMOUTH STATE COLLEGE, Plymouth, New Hampshire 03264. Department of Music within college. Head: **Walter P. Smith** (1958). School founded: 1871. Music Department founded: 1963. Degrees: B.S. in music education; B.A. in music. Scholarships: total $5,000. Music students enrolled: 75 to 90 majors. Music library: 2,000 volumes. Official school ensembles: chorus, glee club, chamber vocal ensemble, concert band, chamber orchestra, chamber ensembles, jazz ensemble. Occasional summer music school. . . . RIVIER COLLEGE, 429 Main Street, Nashua, New Hampshire 03060. Music Department within the college. Chairman: **Sister Cecile Bibaud** (1955). College founded: 1933. Degrees: B.Mus., B.A. Scholarships: number varies according to students' needs. Music students enrolled: three to six. Official school ensembles: glee club. Limited summer instruction. . . . UNIVERSITY OF NEW HAMPSHIRE, Durham, New Hampshire 03824. Department of Music of a College of Liberal Arts in a state university. (Member, NASM.) Chairman: **Keith Polk** (1971). University founded: 1866. Music Department founded: 1923. Degrees: B.S. in music education, B.A., B.M., M.S. in music education, M.A. Scholarships: four to six, totaling $1,000. Music enrollment: 125. Music library: 2,613 books; 1,975 scores; 1,235 tapes; 4,317 recordings; 30 periodicals; 15 titles on microcards; 10 titles on microfilm. Ensembles: chorus, men's glee club, chamber vocal ensemble, marching band, wind ensemble, opera workshop, symphony orchestra. Summer youth music school—25th year, 1971 (see Summer Music Camps and School). The department is developing an electronic lab.

NEW JERSEY

ATLANTIC COMMUNITY COLLEGE, Mays Landing, N.J. 08330. Music Department within a college. Head: **Wilhelm A. A. Goetze** (1967). College founded: 1966. Degrees: A.A., A.S. Scholarships: two, totaling $1,000. Music students enrolled: 50. Volumes in music library: 600. Official school ensembles: chorus, chamber vocal ensemble, symphony orchestra, other smaller chamber groups, jazz ensemble, community chorus. No summer music school. . . . CENTENARY COLLEGE FOR WOMEN, Hackettstown, N.J. 07840. Music Department within a college. Head: **Richard D. Seidel** (1967). College founded: 1867. Degree: A.A. Scholarships: two, totaling $2,600. Music students enrolled: 375. Volumes in music library: 1,500. Official school ensembles: chorus, chamber vocal ensemble, chamber orchestra. No summer music school. . . . COLLEGE OF SAINT ELIZABETH, Convent Station, N.J. 07961. Music Department within the college. Head: **Sister Mary Elise Kabis** (1960). College founded: 1899. Department added: 1933. Degree: B.A. No music scholarships. Music students enrolled: four to five. Volumes in music library: 900. Official school ensembles: chorus. No summer music school. . . . COLUMBUS BOYCHOIR SCHOOL, Galbreath Drive, Princeton, N.J. 08540. A privately funded school for musically gifted boys from grades 4 through 9. Head: **Donald Hanson** (1970). School founded: 1940. Scholarships: school's capacity is 50 boys: grants-in-aid totaling $50,000 are available to needy, qualified boys. Enrollment: 50. Music library: 1,000. Ensembles: chorus. Summer music camp in July for candidates for the school. . . . DOUGLASS COLLEGE, New Brunswick, N.J. 08903. Music is a department in a liberal arts college of Rutgers, the State University of New Jersey. (Member, NASM.) Head: **A. Kunrad Kvam** (1952). College and Music Department founded: 1918. Degree: B.A. in performance and music education. Scholarships: 34, totaling $4,495. Fellowships: one for $3,200. Music enrollment: all classes, 750; majors, 85. Music library: 30,000 volumes. Ensembles: chorus, chamber vocal ensemble, symphony orchestra, chamber orchestra, smaller chamber groups. Summer courses in general history, theory, and some performance study. . . . FAIRLEIGH DICKINSON UNIVERSITY, 1000 River Road, Teaneck, N.J. 07666. Music concentration within the Fine Arts Department of a liberal arts college of a university. Chairman, Fine Arts Department: **A. W. Clark** (1970). School founded: 1941. Degree: B.A. Music students enrolled: 30. Music library: 100 volumes. Official school ensembles: chorus, concert band, opera workshop. No summer music school. . . . GLASSBORO STATE COLLEGE, Glassboro, N.J. 08028. Music Department within the college. Head: **W. Clarke Pfleger** (1947). Department founded: 1958. School founded: 1924. Degrees: B.A. in music education, B.A. in liberal arts. Scholarships: six, totaling $900. Fellowship: one for $2,000. Music students enrolled: 170. Official school ensembles: chorus, glee club, chamber vocal ensembles, marching band, concert band, opera workshop, symphony orchestra, chamber ensembles, jazz ensemble. Summer music school. . . . MERCER COUNTY COMMUNITY COLLEGE, 101 West State Street, Trenton, N.J. 08618. Foreign Language and Music Department within the college. Head: **Paul Scheid** (1967). College founded: 1967. Music students enrolled: 210. Volumes in music library: 170. Official school ensembles: chorus, concert band, dance band. Limited summer instruction. . . . MONTCLAIR STATE COLLEGE, Upper Montclair, N.J. 07043. A Department of Music within a School of Fine and Performing Arts in a state-supported institution. (Member, NASM.) Chairman: **Ward Moore.** Degrees: B.A. with major in music education, performance, sacred music, theory/composition, music therapy, music history/literature; M.A. with major in music education. . .

NEWARK STATE COLLEGE, Morris Avenue, Union, N.J. 07083. Music Department within the college. Head: **Fedor Kabalin** (1969). College founded: 1855. Department founded: 1913. Degrees: B.A. in music and music education. Music students enrolled: 1,200 (80 majors). Official school ensembles: chorus, chamber vocal ensembles, concert band, opera workshop, symphony orchestra, faculty trio. No summer music school. . . . THE NEW SCHOOL FOR MUSIC STUDY, Box 407, Princeton, N.J. 08540. A music conservatory. Head: **Louise L. Goss** (1968). School founded: 1960. Degree: Certificate in piano pedagogy, postgraduate only. Scholarships: four at $500 each. Fellowships: three at $1,000 each. Enrollment: 125 grade and high school piano students; 5 postgraduate professional students in pedagogy. Summer music courses offered. Highly specialized course: piano pedagogy. . . . PRINCETON UNIVERSITY, Princeton, N.J. 08540. Music Department within the university. Head: **Lewis Lockwood** (1970). Department founded: 1946. Degrees: B.A., M.F.A., Ph.D. Music students enrolled: 18 to 20 undergraduates, 30 graduates. Volumes in music library: 12,300 books; 10,750 scores (see Music Libraries). Official school ensembles: chorus, glee club, chamber orchestra. No summer music school. . . . RUTGERS UNIVERSITY, Newark, New Jersey 07102. Department of Music within the Newark College of Arts and Sciences of Rutgers University. Head: **Chester Fanning Smith** (1966). University founded: 1766. Music Department founded: 1966. Degree: B.A. in music or music education. Music enrollment: 300. Ensembles: chorus, concert band, chamber vocal ensemble, jazz ensemble. Only two courses offered in summer. . . . RUTGERS UNIVERSITY GRADUATE SCHOOL AT NEW BRUNSWICK, Van Dyck Hall, Room 111, New Brunswick, N.J. 08903. Chairman, Department of Music: **Henry Bullow.** Music majors: 40. (See Music Libraries.) . . . WESTMINSTER CHOIR COLLEGE, Princeton, N.J. 08540. An independent, unendowed school. (Member, NASM.) President: **Ray E. Robinson.** Dean: **Edward F. J. Eicher.** Degrees: B.M., B.M.Ed. Music majors: 370.

NEW MEXICO

THE COLLEGE OF ARTESIA, Artesia, New Mexico 88210. Department of Music within the Fine Arts Division of the college. Head: **David Ward** (1969). School and department founded: 1966. Degree: B.Mus.Ed. Music enrollment: 80 including 10 majors. Music library: 350 volumes. Official school ensembles: chorus, jazz ensemble. Summer music instruction available according to demand. . . . EASTERN NEW MEXICO UNIVERSITY, Portales, New Mexico 88130. School of Music within the state-supported university. (Member, NASM.) Dean: **Paul Strub** (1962). University founded: 1934. Degrees: B.M., B.Mus.Ed., M.M., M.A., M.Mus.Ed. Scholarships: 155, totaling $39,000. Fellowships: five, totaling $12,500. Music students enrolled: 155. Volumes in music library: 4,000. Official school ensembles: chorus, chamber vocal ensemble, marching band, concert band, opera workshop, symphony orchestra, jazz ensemble. Summer music school. Special course: music therapy. . . . NEW MEXICO HIGHLANDS UNIVERSITY, Las Vegas, New Mexico 87701. Music Department within the university. Head: **Champ B. Tyrone** (1951). School founded: 1893. Degrees: B.A., M.A. Scholarships: 43, totaling $11,127. Fellowships: two, totaling $4,600. Music students enrolled: 90. Music library: 1,200 volumes. Official school ensembles: chorus, glee club, chamber vocal ensemble, concert band, chamber orchestra. Summer music school. . . . NEW MEXICO STATE UNIVERSITY, Box 3F, Las Cruces, New Mexico 88001. Music Department within the College of Arts and Sciences. (Member, NASM.) Head: **John M. Glowacki** (1961). University founded: 1888. Music Department founded: 1934. Degrees: B.A., B.M., B.M.Ed., M.M., M.M.Ed. Scholarships: 160, totaling $32,000. Fellowships: four, totaling $11,200. Music enrollment: 175. Music library: 35,000. Ensembles: chorus, chamber vocal ensemble, marching band, concert band, opera workshop, symphony orchestra, chamber orchestra, smaller chamber groups, jazz ensemble. Summer music school offered. . . . UNIVERSITY OF NEW MEXICO, Albuquerque, New Mexico 87106. A Department of Music in the College of Fine Arts of a state-supported university. (Member, NASM.) Dean, College of Fine Arts: **Clinton Adams.** Degrees: B.M. in applied music, theory and composition, applied music pedagogy, music literature; B.M.Ed., M.A. in musicology; M.M. in applied music, theory and composition; M.M.Ed. Music majors: 150.

NEW YORK

ADIRONDACK COMMUNITY COLLEGE, Bay Road, Glens Falls, N.Y. 12801. Music Department within a two-year college. Head: **Frank J. Prindl** (1961). Department and school founded: 1961. Degree: A.A. Music students enrolled: 15. Music library: 1,500 volumes. Official school ensembles: chorus, concert band, chamber vocal ensemble, brass quartet. No summer music school. . . . BRONX COMMUNITY COLLEGE, 120 East 184th Street, Bronx, N.Y. 10468. Music and Art Department of a free-tuition community college. Head: **Marvin Salzberg.** Degree: A.A.S. Music students enrolled: 60. Official school ensemble: chorus, chamber vocal ensemble, symphony orchestra, chamber orchestra, small ensembles. No summer music school. . . . BROOKLYN COLLEGE, Bedford Avenue and Avenue H, Brooklyn, N.Y. 11210. Department of Music within a college. Chairman: **Dorothy Klotzman.** Degrees: B.A., M.A., M.M.Ed. Music enrollment: 200. Official music ensembles: chorus, concert band, opera workshop, symphony orchestra, small chamber groups including resident groups, the Dorian Quintet and Carnegie String Quartet. No summer instruction. The department houses the Institute for American Music (founded 1971). (See Music Libraries.) . . . CITY COLLEGE OF NEW YORK, West 138th Street and Convent Avenue, New York, N.Y. 10031. Music Department within a college supported by the City of New York. Chairman: **Jack M. Shapiro** (1969). School founded: 1847. Music Department founded (in its present form): 1946. Degrees: B.A., B.S., M.A., Ph.D. (as part of the City University Program). School is tuition-free. Fellowships: seven for graduate students, totaling $40,000. Music enrollment: 180 graduate and undergraduate music majors. Volumes in music library: 10,000. Music ensembles: chorus, chamber vocal ensemble, concert band, symphony orchestra, smaller chamber groups, jazz ensemble, Collegium Musicum. No summer school in music. . . . THE CITY UNIVERSITY OF NEW YORK GRADUATE CENTER, 33 West 42nd Street, New York, N.Y. 10036. Music is a discipline within the Graduate Center of the City University of New York. Head (Executive Officer): **Barry S. Brook** (1967). The Center is a convergent institution for graduate study for the City University system, which includes City College, Hunter College, Brooklyn College, and Queens College. Music discipline founded in 1968. Degree: Ph.D. in music. Scholarships and fellowships awarded by the University: stipends for tuition totaling $2,500 per year; research assistantships from $240 to $260 per month for ten months, plus tuition and dependency allowance; teaching assistantships of $4,000 per year plus tuition. In addition, there are various government and New York State awards. Music enrollment; 40 Ph.D.; 200 M.A. Music library: 3,000 volumes in the Graduate Center Library, 111,000 in the total music libraries of the sister city colleges. Special courses: music iconography, computer synthesis of electronic music, organology, musical systems and speculative theory, and the specialized courses of advanced musicological study such as Renaissance and medieval notation, etc. No summer session. . . . THE COLLEGE OF SAINT ROSE, 432 Western Avenue, Albany, N.Y. 12203. Music Department within a college. Head: **Dorothy A. Flood** (1970). Department and school founded: 1920. Degree: B.S. in music education. No music scholarships. Music students enrolled: 55. Music library consists of holdings in main library, number unavailable. Official school ensembles: glee club, madrigal group, chamber ensembles, wind ensemble. Occasional special summer workshops. . . . COLUMBIA UNIVERSITY IN THE CITY OF NEW YORK, Morningside Heights, New York, N.Y. 10027. Music Department within a university. Chairman: **Howard Shanet.** School founded: 1754. Music Department founded: 1896. Degrees: B.A., B.S., M.A., Ph.D., D.M.A.C. (Doctor of Musical Arts in Composition). Scholarship and fellowship figures unavailable. Music majors: 150. Music library: 46,000 books, scores, records (see Music Libraries). Ensembles: chorus, glee club, chamber vocal ensemble, marching band, concert band, symphony orchestra, informal jazz ensemble, African drum ensemble. Limited summer music courses offered. Special courses: ethnomusicology, computer technology and music, music librarianship (in the School of Library Science), electronic music lab. . . . CORNELL UNIVERSITY, Ithaca, N.Y. 14850. Department of Music within the College of Arts and Sciences. Department founded: 1903. Degrees: B.A., M.A. (in musicology, theory and composition), MFA (in composition), DMA (composition), Ph.D. (musicology). Scholarships and fellowships are administered by the university at large. Music students enrolled: 40. Music library: 55,000 volumes (see Music Libraries). Official school ensembles: chorus, glee club, chamber vocal ensemble, marching band, concert band, opera workshop, symphony orchestra, chamber orchestra, chamber ensembles. Summer music school. . . . DALCROZE SCHOOL OF MUSIC, 161 East 73rd Street, New York, N.Y. 10021. Teachers Training School and Conservatory with a large preparatory department emphasizing the Dalcroze system. Director: **Hilda M. Schuster** (1943). School founded: 1915. Degree: internationally recognized Dalcroze Teachers Certificate. Scholarships: 25, totaling $13,747. Enrollment: 750. Music library: 4,289 volumes. Ensembles: chorus, chamber vocal ensemble, chamber orchestra, wind ensemble, piano ensemble. Summer music school offered (six weeks). Special courses: Dalcroze eurhythmics, improvisation for movement. . . . DILLER-QUAILE SCHOOL OF MUSIC, INC., 24 East 95th Street, New York N.Y. 10028. An independent music school. Music Director: **Dorothy Weed.** Founded: 1920. No degrees. Scholarships: $5,000, mostly partial scholarships. Enrollment: 250 to 300. Music library: 1,000 volumes. Special teacher-training course, Renaissance instruments and consorts. (In 1972, or later, the school will move to larger quarters, permitting a minimum of 600 students.) The school's primary interest is to provide a musical education to children and to train teachers. . . . DUTCHESS COMMUNITY COLLEGE, Pendel Road, Poughkeepsie, N.Y. 12601. Music is a branch of the Humanities Department. Head: **Helen Baldwin** (1959). No music degrees. Music students enrolled: 200. Volumes in library: 300. Music ensembles: chorus, concert band, jazz ensemble, brass choir. No summer music courses. . . . EASTMAN SCHOOL OF MUSIC, UNIVERSITY OF ROCHESTER, 26 Gibbs Street, Rochester, N.Y. 14604. A university school with separate endowment. (Member, NASM.) Director: **Robert Freeman.** Founded: 1921. Degrees: B.M. in applied music, music education, composition, theory, history of music; B.A. with music concentration; M.M. in performance and literature, church music, composition, music education; M.A. in musicology, theory, music education; Ph.D. in music education, composition, musicology, theory; A.Mus.D. in performance and teaching. Scholarships: student aid is available from 24 endowed funds, 5 national scholarship funds, 8 annual funds, 5 cash or tuition prizes, plus various school and New York State loan funds. Graduate aid is in the form of service scholarships and graduate assistantships plus New York State fellowships and fellowships available under the National Defense Education Act, Title IV. Music enrollment: from 625 to 650 music majors of all kinds; about 200 other majors taking music electives; about 1,000 preparatory and special students. Music library: about 170,000 volumes (see Music Libraries). School ensembles: Eastman Philharmonia, school symphony orchestra, two choruses, chamber vocal group, wind ensemble and symphony band, smaller chamber groups. Offers a summer session. . . . EISENHOWER COLLEGE, Seneca Falls,

N.Y. 13148. Music is a discipline within the Division of Humanities. Division Director: **David Murdoch** (1968). Degree: B.A. No music scholarships. Music students enrolled: 20 majors, 250 in elective music courses. Music library: 500 volumes. Official school ensembles: chorus, chamber vocal ensemble, concert band, chamber orchestra. No summer music school. . . . ERIE COMMUNITY COLLEGE, Main Street at Youngs Road, Amherst, N.Y. 14221. Music Department within a two-year junior college offering five music courses. Head: **Alan G. Schmidt** (1962). School founded: 1946. Music library: 800 books, 1,300 recordings, 150 scores, 50 cassettes. Official school ensembles: chorus, concert band, jazz ensemble. No summer school. . . . HAMILTON COLLEGE, College Hill Road, Clinton, N.Y. 13323. Music Department within a college. Head: **Stephen Bonta** (1961). School founded: 1812. Degrees: B.A. with music major. No music scholarships. Music students enrolled: 10 majors, 120 in courses. Music library: 5,000 volumes. Official school ensembles: male chorus, chamber vocal ensemble, chamber orchestra, brass ensemble, woodwind ensemble. No summer music courses. . . . HARLEM SCHOOL OF THE ARTS, INC. 409 West 141 Street, New York, N.Y. 10031. Director: **Dorothy Maynor.** . . . HARPUR COLLEGE, STATE UNIVERSITY OF NEW YORK/BINGHAMTON, Vestal Parkway, Binghamton, N.Y. 13901. Department of Music within a college. Chairman: **Seymour Fink** (1971). College founded: 1946. Music department founded: 1951. Degrees: B.A. in music, M.A., M.M., M.S.T. Fellowships: 10 to 12 graduate assistantships. Music enrollment: approximately 100. Music library: approximately 30,000 books, records, scores, periodicals. Ensembles: chorus, glee club, chamber vocal ensemble, concert band, opera workshop, symphony orchestra, chamber orchestra, smaller chamber groups, jazz ensemble. Limited summer courses. Special courses in computer technology and music, quartet chamber program, ethnomusicology. . . . HENRY STREET SETTLEMENT MUSIC SCHOOL, 500A Grand Street, New York, N.Y. 10002. Chairman: **Andrew Frierson.** . . . HOBART AND WILLIAM SMITH COLLEGES, Geneva, N.Y. 14456. Music Department within the college. Head: **Nicholas V. D'Angelo** (1955). College founded: 1822. Department founded: 1951. Degree: B.A. General scholarships are available through the college. Music students enrolled: 30 music majors. Official school ensembles: chorus, glee club, chamber vocal ensemble, concert band, opera workshop, chamber orchestra, jazz ensemble, brass choir, other smaller chamber groups. Special course: Black Music. Summer music instruction. . . . HOFSTRA UNIVERSITY, 1000 Fulton Avenue, Hempstead, N.Y. 11550. Music Department in the College of Arts and Sciences. Chairman: **Albert Tepper** (1967). University founded: 1935. Department added: 1948[?]. Degrees: B.A. in music; B.S. in education and music education. Scholarships: 30, totaling $50,000. Music students enrolled: 215. Volumes in music library: 8,000. Official school ensembles: chorus, concert band, opera workshop, symphony orchestra, jazz ensemble, Collegium Musicum, other smaller chamber groups. Limited summer instruction including a two-week luthier course (making and repairing string instruments). . . . HOUGHTON COLLEGE, Houghton, N.Y. 14744. Department of Music within a college supported by the Wesleyan Church. (Member, NASM.) Head: **Charles H. Finney** (1946). School founded: 1883. Degrees: B.M. in music education. Scholarships: offered to freshmen. Music enrollment: 125. Music library: 2,650 volumes. Ensembles: two choruses, chamber vocal ensemble, concert band, symphony orchestra, two smaller chamber groups. Summer music school offered. . . . HUNTER COLLEGE, 695 Park Avenue, New York, N.Y. 10021. Department of Music within a college of the City University of New York. Head: **Bruce Prince-Joseph** (1970). School and Music Department founded: 1870. Degrees: B.A. in music; B.S. in music; M.A. in music, composition, historical musicology, theory, ethnomusicology, teaching; Ph.D. in historical musicology. Scholarships: three to five full-tuition scholarships. Music enrollment: 2,750 to 3,000. Ensembles: chorus, glee club, chamber vocal ensemble, concert band, opera workshop, smaller chamber groups, jazz ensemble. Special courses in ethnomusicology, electronic studio. . . . SCHOOL OF MUSIC, ITHACA COLLEGE, Ithaca, N.Y. 14850. (Member, NASM.) School of Music within an independent college. Dean: **Craig McHenry** (1957). College and School of Music founded: 1892. Degrees: B.M. in applied music, music education, composition; B.F.A. with major in music and minor in art or drama. Scholarships: $45,000 per freshman class. Fellowships: $30,000. Music enrollment: 450. Ensembles: choir, madrigal ensemble, three concert bands, opera workshop, symphony orchestra, chamber orchestra, jazz ensemble, woodwind and brass quintets (faculty). Summer music school offered. Special courses: piano technology, classical guitar. . . . THE JUILLIARD SCHOOL, Lincoln Center Plaza, New York, N.Y. 10023. A conservatory of music and other performing arts with an academic department. Founded in 1905. President: **Peter Mennin** (1961). Degrees: B.M., M.M., D.M.A. Scholarships: over half of the enrollment is on scholarship; total amount in excess of $350,000. Fellowships: 25. Enrollment: 640. Music library: see Music Libraries. School ensembles: chorus, chamber vocal ensemble, opera workshop, three symphony orchestras, chamber orchestra, 45 chamber groups, jazz ensemble. The school has no summer session. . . . MANHATTAN SCHOOL OF MUSIC, 120 Claremont Avenue, New York, N.Y. 10027. A conservatory–college, founded in 1917. (Member, NASM.) President: **George Schick** (1969). Dean: **David Simon.** Degrees: B.M. and M.M. Scholarships and fellowships are available (disclosure of amount not permitted by policy). Music enrollment: 800. Music library: 75,000. Official music ensembles: chorus, concert band, opera workshop, opera theater, symphony orchestra, chamber orchestra, smaller chamber groups, jazz ensemble. Summer music school. Special course taught: music administration. . . . MANHATTANVILLE COLLEGE, Purchase, N.Y. 10577. A Department of Music of the college. (Member, NASM.) Chairman: **Peguy S. Lyder.** Degrees: B.M., B.A. in music, B. Sacred Music. Music majors: 60. . . . MANNES COLLEGE OF MUSIC, 157 East 74th Street, New York, N.Y. 10021. President: **John Goldmark.** Enrollment: about 190. . . . MERCY COLLEGE, 555 Broadway, Dobbs Ferry, N.Y. 10522. Department of Fine Arts. Head: **John Rayburn** (1961). School founded: 1961. Degree: B.A. with music major, to begin in fall of 1972. Music library: 4,000 volumes. Official school ensembles: chorus, glee club, chamber vocal ensemble. No summer music school. . . . MOHAWK VALLEY COMMUNITY COLLEGE, 1101 Sherman Drive, Utica, N.Y. 13501. Music Department within the college. Head: **Albert Johnson** (1970). College founded: 1946. Department founded: 1970. Official school ensemble: chorus. No summer music school. . . . MOUNT SAINT ALPHONSUS SEMINARY, Route 9W, Esopus, N.Y. 12429. No music courses or faculty. Music library: 200 volumes of sacred music and church documents on music. Official school ensemble is the student-administered choir for sacred services. . . . NASSAU COMMUNITY COLLEGE, Garden City, N.Y. 11530. Music Department within the college. Head: **Ralph V. Ritchie** (1963). College founded: 1959. Department founded: 1963. Degrees: A.A., A.A.S. (Associate in Applied Science). Music enrollment: 1,200. Official school ensembles: chorus, chamber vocal ensemble, concert band, jazz ensemble, other smaller chamber groups. Limited summer instruction. . . . NEW SCHOOL FOR SOCIAL RESEARCH, 66 West 12th Street, New York, N.Y. 10014. Department of Music within a college. Head: **Frank Wigglesworth.** School and music department founded: 1918. Music enrollment: 300. Ensembles: chorus, chamber vocal ensemble, opera workshop. Summer music courses offered. . . . NEW YORK UNIVERSITY, Washington Square, New York, N.Y. 10003. A Division of Music and Music Education within the school of education in an independent institution, privately supported. (Member, NASM.) Head: **Jerrold Ross.** Degrees: B.S. in music education, music, music therapy; M.A. in music, music education, music therapy. . . . 92ND STREET SCHOOL OF MUSIC, 1395 Lexington Avenue, New York, N.Y. 10021. A Department of Music within a community center, the 92nd Street YM and YWHA. Head: **Mrs. Hadassah B. Markson** (1969). Founded: 1917. Undergraduate school, no degrees. "Y" certificate for Teacher Training Course in Eurythmics and Creative Movement. Scholarships: about 35, totaling $3,500. Enrollment: 650. Music library: approximately 350 volumes. Ensembles: chorus, children's chorale, opera workshop, symphony orchestra, chamber orchestra, smaller chamber groups, jazz ensemble. Summer music school offered. . . . NORTH COUNTRY COMMUNITY COLLEGE, 20 Winona Avenue, Saranac Lake, N.Y. 12983. Music Department of the college. Chairman, Division of the Humanities: **George F. Reynolds** (1971). School founded: 1967. Degree: Associate in Arts with music major. No music scholarships. Music students enrolled: 200. Music library: 275 books, 300 records. Official school ensembles: chorus, symphony orchestra, chamber ensembles. Summer music school. Special course: piano technology. . . . NYACK COLLEGE, Nyack, N.Y. 10960. (Formerly Nyack Missionary College.) Department of Music within a college, church-supported. (Member, NASM.) Chairman: **Paul F. Liljestrand** (1971). School founded: 1882. Music Department founded: 1937. Degrees: B.M., B. of Sacred Music, B.M. (music education). Scholarships: two, totaling approximately $360. Music enrollment: 70. Music library: 2,045 volumes; 1,100 recordings. Ensembles: chorus, glee club, madrigal singers, chamber orchestra, smaller chamber groups, brass ensemble. No summer session. . . . ONONDAGA COMMUNITY COLLEGE, Hill Campus, Syracuse, N.Y. 13215. Music Department within the Creative and Performing Arts Division of the college. Division Chairman: **C. Richard Rhoades** (1963). Department founded: 1963. School founded: 1962. Degree: Associate in Applied Science–Music. Scholarships: 10 for string players. Music students enrolled: 150. Music library: unknown number of scores plus 600 volumes in main library. Official school ensembles: chorus, choir, chamber vocal ensemble, concert band, brass, woodwind and percussion ensembles, jazz ensemble, brass sinfonia. Summer music school. . . . ORANGE COUNTY COMMUNITY COLLEGE, 115 South Street, Middletown, N.Y. 10940. Music Department within the college. Head: **Marvin K. Feman** (1951). Department founded: 1951. School founded: 1950. Degree: two-year Associate Degree with a major emphasis in music. Music students enrolled: 65 majors, 426 in all courses. Music library: 600 volumes. Official school ensembles: chorus, chamber vocal ensemble, concert band, chamber ensembles, jazz ensemble. Summer music school. . . . QUEENS COLLEGE OF THE CITY UNIVERSITY OF NEW YORK, Flushing, N.Y. 11367. Music Department within the college of a city-supported university. Head: **Lawrence Eisman** (1971). Department and school founded: 1937. Degrees: B.A., B.M., M.A., M.S., M.M., Ph.D. (through City University of New York). A tuition-free school to New York City residents on undergraduate level. Fellowships: 12 to 15, totaling $4,000. Music students enrolled: 300. Music library: 40,000 volumes (see Music Libraries). Official school ensembles: chorus, glee club, chamber vocal ensemble, concert band, opera workshop, symphony orchestra, chamber orchestra, chamber ensembles, jazz ensembles, Renaissance band. Summer music school. Special courses: electronic and computer music. . . . RENSSELAER POLYTECHNIC INSTITUTE, Troy, N.Y. 12181. Music is offered only as a service department in this essentially technological university. Head: **Ernest Livingstone** (1970). School founded: 1824. No music degrees, scholarships, or fellowships. Music enrollment: 275 participating in ensembles. Music library: 1,000 books, 200 scores. School ensembles: chorus, glee club, chamber vocal ensemble, marching band, concert band, chamber orchestra, jazz ensemble. No summer music instruction. . . . RICHMOND COLLEGE OF THE CITY UNIVERSITY OF NEW YORK, 130 Stuyvesant Place, Staten Island, N.Y. 10301. Music Department within the college. Head: **Victor H. Mattfeld** (1967). College founded: 1966. Department founded: 1967. Degrees: B.A. in music. Music students enrolled: 20.

Volumes in music library: 1,550. Official school ensembles: chamber vocal ensemble, Collegium Musicum, other smaller chamber groups. No summer music school. Special course: electronic music. . . . SAINT LAWRENCE UNIVERSITY, Canton, N.Y. 12617. Music Department within a college. Head: **Kenneth Munson** (1955). School founded: 1856. Degree: B.A. with music major. No music scholarships or fellowships. Music students enrolled: 5 majors, 200 in courses. Music library: 2,000 volumes. Official school ensembles: chorus, chamber vocal ensemble, chamber ensembles, early music ensemble. No summer music school. . . . SARAH LAWRENCE COLLEGE, Bronxville, N.Y. 10708. Music Department of a college. Head: **Joel Spiegelman** (1970). Department and school founded: 1928. Degrees: B.A., M.A., M.F.A. in electronic music, composition, theory, chamber music performance, early-music performance. No music scholarships or fellowships. Music students enrolled: 380. Music library: 9,250 records, 4,250 pieces of sheet music, 2,250 books, and 7,000 choral items. Official school ensembles: chorus, chamber vocal ensemble, symphony orchestra, chamber orchestra, chamber ensembles, Collegium Musicum. Summer Institute in early music. Special courses: chamber music performance, electronic music and intermedia, improvisation ensemble, early-music performance. . . . STATE UNIVERSITY OF NEW YORK, AGRICULTURAL AND TECHNICAL COLLEGE (DELHI STATE COLLEGE), Delhi, N.Y. 13753. Music Department within a college. Head: **Donald O. Shaver** (1964). College founded: 1948. Department founded: 1960. No music degrees or music scholarships. Music students enrolled: 85. Volumes in music library: 200. Official school ensembles: chorus, glee club, chamber vocal ensemble, jazz ensemble. No summer music courses. . . . STATE UNIVERSITY OF NEW YORK AGRICULTURAL AND TECHNICAL COLLEGE, Cobbleskill, N.Y. 12043. Music is part of the Humanities Department. School founded: 1948. Music library: 200 volumes. Official school ensembles: chorus, chamber vocal ensemble, jazz ensemble, chamber ensembles. No summer music instruction. . . . STATE UNIVERSITY OF NEW YORK AT ALBANY, 1400 Washington Avenue, Albany, N.Y. 12203. Music Department within a university. Chairman: **Nathan Gottschalk** (1970). Degree: B.A. with a music major. No music scholarships and fellowships. Music students enrolled: 60 majors. Official school ensembles: chorus, concert band, opera workshop, symphony orchestra, chamber ensembles. Summer music school. . . . STATE UNIVERSITY COLLEGE, Fredonia, N.Y. 14063. A Department of Music of the State University of New York. (Member, NASM.) Dean, Fine and Performing Arts: **Robert W. Marvel.** Degrees: B.A. in applied music, music theory; B.M. in music education: M.M. in music education. Music majors: 560. . . . STATE UNIVERSITY COLLEGE OF ARTS AND SCIENCE, Geneseo, N.Y. 14454. Department within a college. Head: **Robert M. Isgro** (1969). School founded: 1871. Degree: B.A. Music enrollment: 75. Official music ensembles: chorus, glee club, chamber vocal ensemble, concert band, opera workshop, chamber orchestra, string quartet. . . . STATE UNIVERSITY COLLEGE AT BUFFALO, 1300 Elmwood Avenue, Buffalo, N.Y. 14222. Department within the college, which is part of the State University of New York: Head: **Peter B. Yates** (1968). School founded: 1871. Degree: B.A. No special music scholarships. Music enrollment: 1,400. Official music ensembles: chorus, glee club, chamber vocal ensemble, concert band, symphony orchestra, jazz ensemble, chamber orchestra, gospel choir, small chamber groups. Summer music school. Special courses in American music. . . . STATE UNIVERSITY COLLEGE OF NEW YORK AT BROCKPORT, Holley Street, Brockport, N.Y. 14420. Music Department within the college. Head: **Ira Schwarz** (1970). Department founded: 1966. School founded: 1846. No music degrees. No music scholarships or fellowships. Music students enrolled: 75. Music library: 6,400 volumes. Official school ensembles: chorus, glee club, chamber vocal ensemble, concert band, symphony orchestra. Summer music school. . . . STATE UNIVERSITY COLLEGE OF NEW YORK AT NEW

PALTZ, New Paltz, N.Y. 12561. Music Department within a college. Head: **C. Thomas Barr** (1964). Department founded: 1964. Degrees: B.A., B.S. No music scholarships and fellowships. Music students enrolled: 65. Official school ensembles: chorus, glee club, chamber vocal ensemble, concert band, symphony orchestra. Limited summer music instruction. . . . STATE UNIVERSITY OF NEW YORK COLLEGE AT POTSDAM, Potsdam, N.Y. 13676. The Crane School of Music within a college of a state-supported university. (Member, NASM.) Dean: **Ralph J. Wakefield** (1965). Music Department founded: 1971. School founded: 1886. Degrees: B.M. in applied performance, theory–composition, music education, church music; B.A. in theory, music literature; M.S. in music education; M.A. in theory, music history and literature. Scholarships and fellowships: number varies from year to year. Music students enrolled: 550. Music library: 12,000 scores, 6,500 books, 7,000 recordings. Official school ensembles: chorus, glee club, chamber vocal ensemble, marching band, concert band, opera workshop, symphony orchestra, chamber ensembles, jazz ensemble. Summer music school. Special courses: CAI Instruction in Music, Music Administration, Music in Special Education, Computer Technology and Music. . . . STATE UNIVERSITY OF NEW YORK AT STONY BROOK, c/o Department of Music, Stony Brook, N.Y. 11790. Music Department within the university. Head: **Billy Jim Layton** (1966). University founded: 1957. Department founded: 1966. Degrees: B.A., M.A., M.M. Scholarships: traineeships. Fellowships: stipends of $2,600 or more, plus tuition exemption. Music students enrolled: 120 majors. Volumes in music library: 25,000. Official school ensembles: chorus, chamber vocal ensemble, concert band, symphony orchestra, other smaller chamber groups. No summer music school. Special instructional emphasis in the school is on the music of the twentieth century. . . . SYRACUSE UNIVERSITY SCHOOL OF MUSIC, 200 Crouse College, Syracuse, N.Y. 13210. Separate school within a university. (Member, NASM.) Dean: **Howard Boatwright** (1964). School founded: 1873. Music school established: 1877. Degrees: B.M. (performance, music education, theory and composition); A.B. (music); M.M. (performance, theory, composition, music education, music history and literature). Music enrollment: 160. Music ensembles: chorus, marching band, concert band, opera workshop, small chamber groups, jazz ensemble, wind ensemble. Summer music school. School has an electronic music studio. . . . THIRD STREET MUSIC SCHOOL SETTLEMENT, 55 East 3rd Street, New York, N.Y. 10003. A community music school. Director: **Harris Danziger** (1956). School founded: 1894. Scholarships: 200, totaling $40,000. Fellowships: 10 apprentice-teachers' totaling $12,000. Enrollment: 1,000. Music library: 5,000. Ensembles: chorus, symphony orchestra, chamber orchestra, jazz ensemble, rock group. Summer music school. . . . TURTLE BAY MUSIC SCHOOL, 244 East 52nd Street, New York, N.Y. 10022. A community music school, member of the National Guild of Community Music Schools. Head: **Clyde H. Keutzer** (1969). School founded: 1925. Scholarships: approximately 20, totaling $5,000, plus grants-in-aid. Music enrollment: 500. Ensembles: chamber orchestra, smaller chamber groups, jazz ensemble, brass ensembles. Summer music school offered. . . . UNION THEOLOGICAL SEMINARY, New York, N.Y. 10027. A school of sacred music. (Member, NASM.) Dean, School of Sacred Music: **Robert S. Baker.** Degree: Master of Sacred Music. . . . UNIVERSITY COLLEGE OF NEW YORK UNIVERSITY, University Heights, Bronx, N.Y. 10453. Music Department within a university. Head: **Elaine Brody** (1966). University founded: 1840's. Degree: B.A. with a major in music. Music enrollment: 400. Music library: 1,500 volumes. Ensembles: glee club, symphony orchestra. No applied music taught, only musicological subjects. . . . VASSAR COLLEGE, Poughkeepsie, N.Y. 12601. Music Department within the college. Chairman: **Albert Van Ackere** (1970). Degrees: B.A. Scholarships: 18 to 22, totaling $4,500. Music students enrolled: 200. Volumes in music library: 33,000 (see Music Libraries). Official school ensembles: chorus, choir, chamber vocal ensemble, opera workshop, chamber orchestra, Festival Winds (in residence). No summer music school. . . . YESHIVA UNIVERSITY, Amsterdam Avenue and 186th Street, New York, N.Y. 10033. Music is offered in the Cantorial Training Institute, an affiliate of Yeshiva University. Director: **Macy Nulman** (1966). Department founded: 1954. School founded: 1886. Degrees: Cantorial Diploma and Associate Cantor's Certificate. No scholarships or fellowships. Music students enrolled: 165. Music library: 7,000 records. Official school ensemble: chorus. No summer music courses.

NORTH CAROLINA

APPALACHIAN STATE UNIVERSITY, Boone, North Carolina 28607. A Department of Music of a state-supported college. (Member, NASM.) Chairman: **William G. Spencer.** Degree: B.S. in music education. Music majors: 150. . . . ATLANTIC CHRISTIAN COLLEGE, Wilson, North Carolina 27893. Music Department within a liberal arts college. Head: **James V. Cobb, Jr.** College founded: 1902. Department founded: 1961. Degrees: B.A., B.S. Scholarships: 20, totaling $3,400. Music students enrolled: 35 majors. Official school ensembles: chorus, chamber vocal ensemble, marching band, concert band, in-residence string quartet, percussion ensemble, woodwind ensemble, brass ensemble, recorder ensemble, string ensemble. Summer music school. . . . BENNETT COLLEGE, Greensboro, North Carolina 27420. Music Department within the college. Head: **Helen R. Trobian** (1970). College founded: 1873. Department founded: 1926. Degree. B.A. (music education). Music students enrolled: 25. Volumes in music library: 2,000. Official school ensembles: chorus, glee club, concert band, opera workshop (opportunity to audition for Greensboro Symphony). Special courses: African and Afro-American Music. No summer music school. . . . BREVARD COLLEGE, Brevard, North Carolina 28712. Department of Music within a two-year liberal arts college. (Member, NASM.) Chairman, Division of Fine Arts: **Nelson F. Adams** (1953). School and Music Department founded: 1934. Degree: Junior College Diploma leading toward A.B., B.M.Ed., or performance degree. Scholarships: 25, totaling $6,500. Music enrollment: approximately 45. Music library: 850. Ensembles: chorus, glee club, chamber vocal ensemble, concert band, small chamber groups. Limited summer music courses. . . . CAMPBELL COLLEGE, Buies Creek, North Carolina 27506. Music Department within the college. Head: **Paul M. Yoder** (1961). Department founded: 1961. School founded: 1888. Degrees: Bachelor of Music Education; B.A. with music major. Scholarships: 18, totaling $4,000. Music students enrolled: 60. Music library: 3,000 volumes. Official school ensembles: four choruses, chamber vocal ensemble, concert band, two jazz ensembles. No summer music school. . . . CATAWBA COLLEGE, Salisbury, North Carolina 28144. Music Department within college. Head: **Marvin D. Wigginton** (1949). School founded: 1926. Degree: A.B. with music major. Scholarships: 25 totaling $8,000. Music students enrolled: 25 majors, 200 nonmajors. Music library: 1,000 volumes. Official school ensembles: chorus, glee club, chamber vocal ensemble, marching band, concert band, opera workshop, symphony orchestra, brass quartet. Summer music school. . . . CHOWAN JUNIOR COLLEGE, Murfreesboro, North Carolina 27855. Daniel School of Music within the Department of Fine Arts. Head: **James M. Chamblee** (1959). Music Department founded 1850. College founded: 1848. Daniel School founded: 1955. Degrees: Associate of Arts, Associate of Science (music education), Associate of Music (all associate degrees are applicable to music degrees, senior college). Scholarships: nine, totaling $1,850. Music students enrolled: 30. Music library: 200 scores, 700 books, 1,100 recordings. Official school ensembles: chorus, chamber vocal ensemble, chamber ensembles, jazz ensemble. No summer music school. . . . COLLEGE OF THE ALBEMARLE, Elizabeth City, North Carolina 27909. A branch of the Fine Arts Department within the college Transfer Division. Head of Music branch: **Clifford Bair,** Director, Fine Arts Department. School founded: 1961. Music Department founded: 1964. Degree: Associate in Arts. Scholarships: number varies; $100 to $200. Music students: 40; extensions enrollees, 60. Music library: 129 books; 181 recordings. Ensembles: chorus, chamber vocal ensemble, extension division choral society. . . . DUKE UNIVERSITY, Duke Station, Durham, North Carolina 27706. Music Department within college. Head: **Julia W. Mueller** (1967). Music Department founded: 1933. School founded: 1859. Degree: B.A. Scholarships: four, totaling $6,500. No fellowships. Music students enrolled: 250. Music library: part of university library; about 50,000 volumes. Official school ensembles: chorus, chamber vocal ensemble, marching band, concert band, opera workshop, symphony orchestra, chamber orchestra, chamber ensembles. No summer music school. . . . EAST CAROLINA UNIVERSITY, P.O. Box 2517, Greenville, North Carolina 27834. A School of Music in a state-supported college. (Member, NASM.) Head: **Everett Pittman** (1971). University founded: 1907. Degrees: B.A., B.M., M.A., M.M. Scholarships: 26, totaling $6,765. Fellowships: 13, totaling $25,500. Music students enrolled: 300. Music library: 6,500 volumes. Official school ensembles: chorus, glee club, chamber vocal ensemble, marching band, concert band, opera workshop, symphony orchestra, chamber orchestra, chamber ensembles, jazz ensemble, wind ensemble, Collegium Musicum. Summer music school. Special courses: ethnomusicology, music therapy. . . . ELIZABETH CITY STATE UNIVERSITY, Parkview Drive, Elizabeth City, North Carolina 27909. Department of Music within a university. Chairman: **Edna L. Davis** (1965). University founded: 1891. Music Department founded: 1961. Degree: B.S. with major in music education. Music enrollment: 30 majors; 270 non-majors. Music library: 2,000 volumes. Ensembles: chorus, chamber vocal ensemble, marching band, concert band, jazz ensemble, brass and woodwind ensembles, Swingers (pop singing group). No summer music program. . . . ELON COLLEGE, Elon College, North Carolina 27244. Music Department within the college. Chairman: **C. Fletcher Moore.** College founded: 1889. Degrees: A.B. in music, B.S. in music education. Scholarships: number varies. Music students enrolled: 110. Volumes in music library: 3,000, including scores. Official school ensembles: chorus, chamber vocal ensemble, marching band, concert band, opera workshop, symphony orchestra, jazz ensemble, other smaller chamber groups. Special summer institutes and clinics. Special course: History and Performance of Jazz. . . . GARDNER–WEBB COLLEGE, Boiling Springs, North Carolina 28017. Division of Music within the Department of Fine Arts. Head: **George R. Cribb** (1969). Department founded: 1950. School founded: 1905. Degree: B.A. No music scholarships or fellowships. Music students enrolled: 35. Music library: 1,000 volumes in main library. Official school ensembles: chorus, chamber vocal ensemble, concert band, opera workshop. No summer music school. . . . GREENSBORO COLLEGE, Greensboro, North Carolina 27402. A School of Music connected with an endowed college. (Member, NASM.) Chairman: **Don W. Hansen.** Degrees: B.M. in applied music, B.M.Ed., B.A. in music. Music majors: 82. . . . GUILFORD COLLEGE, Friendly Avenue, Greensboro, North Carolina 27410. Music Department within a liberal arts college. Chairman: **George Gansz** (1969). College founded: 1837. Degree: B.A. Scholarships: five, totaling $3,300. Music students enrolled: 16. Official school ensembles: chorus, chamber vocal ensemble, chamber orchestra, jazz ensemble, pep band, other smaller chamber groups. No summer music school. . . . MARS HILL COLLEGE, Mars Hill, North Carolina 28754. A Music Department in a college of liberal arts, endowed and supported by the Baptist State Convention of North Carolina. (Member, NASM.) Head: **Joel R. Stegall** (1968). Department founded: 1920. School founded: 1856. Degrees: B.A., B.M. Scholarships: 20, totaling $5,400. Music students enrolled: 135. Music library: 11,000 volumes. Official school ensembles: chorus, chamber vocal ensemble, marching band, concert band, opera workshop, chamber orchestra, jazz ensemble. Summer music school. . . . MEREDITH COLLEGE, Raleigh, North Carolina 27611. Music Department within a liberal arts college supported by the Baptist Church. (Member, NASM.) Head: **W. David Lynch** (1969). School founded: 1891. Music department founded: 1891. Degrees: B.M. in performance or music education; B.A. Music scholarships: 19, totaling $7,025. Music majors: 110. Music library: 1,000 volumes. School ensembles: chorus, chamber vocal ensemble, other vocal ensembles, chamber orchestra. Limited summer music school. . . . METHODIST COLLEGE, Raleigh Road, Fayetteville, North Carolina 28301. Music Department within the college. Head: **Willis C. Gates** (1960). College and department founded: 1960. Degrees: A.B. Music students enrolled: 30 music majors. Official school ensembles: chorus, concert band, community orchestra. No summer music school. . . . NORTH CAROLINA CENTRAL UNIVERSITY, Durham, North Carolina 27707. Music Department within the university. Head: **Paul Gene Strassler** (1966). University founded: 1910. Degrees: B.A., M.A., certification on both levels. No music scholarships or fellowships. Music students enrolled: 40 to 60. Volumes in music library: 4,000. Official school ensembles: chorus, concert band, marching band, in-residence piano trio, jazz ensemble. Summer music instruction. . . . NORTH CAROLINA SCHOOL OF THE ARTS, P.O. Box 4657, Winston-Salem, North Carolina 27107. A school of the performing arts. Founded: 1965. President: **Robert Ward.** Dean of the School of Music: **Nicholas Harsanyi** (1971). Degrees: B.M.; also a High School Diploma with a concentration in music; Certificate in Arts. Scholarships: 14, totaling $9,250. Fellowships: 10, totaling $30,000. Music enrollment: 260. Music ensembles: chorus, chamber vocal ensemble, opera workshop, symphony orchestra, chamber orchestra, smaller chamber groups, jazz ensemble. Summer instruction on campus and abroad through a special program (in Siena, Italy). . . . NORTH CAROLINA WESLEYAN COLLEGE, Rocky Mount, North Carolina 27801. Department of Music within the Humanities Division of the college. Head: **William G. Sasser** (1966). Department and school founded: 1960. Degree: B.A. Scholarships: four, totaling $400; general scholarships also available. Music students enrolled: 25. Music library: 5,000 records, 4,200 scores. Official school music ensembles: chorus, concert band, chamber vocal ensemble, jazz ensemble. Summer music school. Special courses: one-month May term with changing courses in jazz history, opera workshop, history of singers and singing, musical comedy production. . . . PFEIFFER COLLEGE, Misenheimer, North Carolina 28109. Music Department in a private liberal arts college. Head: **Richard H. Brewer** (1962). Department founded: 1962. School founded: 1885. Degree: B.A. with emphasis in music education or church music. Scholarship: one for $400. Music students enrolled: 30. Official school ensembles: five choirs, concert band. . . . ROCKINGHAM COMMUNITY COLLEGE, Wentworth, North Carolina 27375. Music Department within the college. Head: **Richard Burts** (1968). College founded: 1966 (first year of instruction chartered in 1963). Department founded: 1967. Degree: A.A. Music students enrolled: 20. Volumes in music library: 250. Official school ensemble: chorus. No summer music courses. . . . SAINT ANDREWS PRESBYTERIAN COLLEGE, Laurinburg, North Carolina 28352. A Department of Music, part of the college's Division of Art, Music and Theatre, supported by endowment and the Synod of North Carolina of the Presbyterian Church. (Member, NASM.) Department founded: 1903. Head: **Thomas Somerville** (1969). Degrees: B.M., B.A. No music scholarships and fellowships. Music students enrolled: 35. Music library: 1,700 scores, 1,680 records, 1,600 books. Official school ensembles: two choruses, chamber vocal ensemble, concert band, pep band. Music summer camp for high school students. . . . ST. AUGUSTINE'S COLLEGE, Tarboro and Oakwood, Raleigh, North Carolina 27611. Department of Music in a college. Head: **Albert W. Grauer** (1960). School founded: 1867. Music Department founded: 1943. Degrees: B.A. in music, music education. Scholarships: $8,000 in the form of grants and work-aid. Music enrollment: 30 majors, 60 non-music majors. Music library: 1,200 books, 500 scores, 300 recordings. Ensembles: chorus, chamber vocal ensemble, concert band, jazz ensemble. No summer music courses. . . . SALEM COLLEGE, Winston-Salem, North Carolina 27108. A School of Music, sponsored by the Moravian Church. (Member, NASM.) Head: **Clemens Sandresky** (1952). College founded: 1772. Department founded: 1925. Degrees: B.A., B.M. in performance and music education. Music scholarships: not separate from general college aid (approximately $100,000 in available funds). Music students enrolled: 45 majors. Volumes in music library: 3,500. Official school ensembles: chorus, chamber vocal ensemble, community orchestra, other smaller chamber groups. No summer music school. . . . SANDHILLS COMMUNITY COLLEGE, Airport Road, Southern Pines, North Carolina 28387. Music Department within the college. Head: **Marion J. Rogers** (1968). Degrees: general education degree and Associate in Arts. Scholarships: three, totaling $1,335. Music students enrolled: 20. No special music library. Official school ensembles: chorus, chamber vocal ensemble, concert band, chamber orchestra, jazz ensemble. No summer music school. . . . UNIVERSITY OF NORTH CAROLINA AT CHAPEL HILL, 105 Hill Hall, Chapel Hill, North Carolina 27514. Music Department Chairman: **Edgar Alden.** Music enrollment: about 200. . . . UNIVERSITY OF NORTH CAROLINA SCHOOL OF MUSIC, Greensboro, North Carolina 27412. A School of Music of the university, state supported. (Member, NASM.) Dean: **Lawrence Hart.** Degrees: B.M. in applied music, music education, theory; B.A. in applied music; M.M. in applied music, music education. Music majors: 250. . . . UNIVERSITY OF NORTH CAROLINA AT WILMINGTON, Post Office Box 3725, Wilmington, North Carolina 28401. Music Department of the university. Head: **Richard Deas** (1971). Music Department founded: 1956. School founded: 1947. Degree: A.B. with a concentration in music. Scholarships: 12, totaling $2,700. No fellowships. Music students enrolled: 20 to 25. Music library: 450 volumes. Official school ensembles: chorus, concert band, small ensembles. Summer music courses. . . . WAKE FOREST UNIVERSITY, Box 7345, R.S., Winston-Salem, North Carolina 27109. Department of Music in a university. Head: **Calvin R. Huber** (1970). School founded: 1834. Degree: B.A. Scholarships: 15, totaling $1,500. No fellowships. Music students enrolled: 250. Music library: 8,000 volumes. Official school ensembles: chorus, chamber vocal ensemble, marching band, two concert bands, symphony orchestra, chamber orchestra, jazz ensemble, woodwind ensemble, brass ensemble, percussion ensemble. No summer music school. . . . WARREN WILSON COLLEGE, Swannanoa, North Carolina 28778. Music Department within the college. Head: **Robert P. Keener** (1964). College founded: 1894. Degree: A.B. with a major in music. Scholarships: 25 for applied music students. General financial aid available through Aid Office. Music enrollment: 50. Music library: 1,500 volumes. School ensembles: chorus, string quartet, community choir. No summer music courses. . . . WINGATE COLLEGE, Wingate, North Carolina 28174. Music Department within a college. Head: **James Blackwelder** (1965). Music degrees offered: A.A. with major in music. No music scholarships. Music students enrolled: 25. Music library: 1,500 volumes. Official school ensembles: chorus, two glee clubs, chamber vocal ensemble, concert band, chamber orchestra, chamber groups.

NORTH DAKOTA

DICKINSON STATE COLLEGE, Dickinson, North Dakota 58601. Division of Music within a state-supported college. Chairman: **Frank C. Pearson** (1963). College founded: 1918. Division added: 1931. Degrees: B.S., B.A. Scholarships: 10 to 20, totaling $2,000 to $3,000. Music students enrolled: 120. Volumes in music library: 1,400. Official school ensembles: two choruses, three chamber vocal ensembles; marching band, two concert bands, opera workshop, woodwind and brass chamber groups, jazz ensemble. Summer music school. . . . MINOT STATE COL-

LEGE, Minot, North Dakota 58701. Division of Music within the college. Division Chairman: **John A. Strohm** (1961). Music Department founded: 1927. School founded: 1913. Degrees: B.S. in music education; B.A. in music. Scholarships: seven, totaling $1,000. No fellowships. Music students enrolled: 103 majors, 34 minors, 350 total participating. Music library: 3,786 volumes. Official school ensembles: three choruses, glee club, chamber vocal ensemble, marching band, two concert bands, two opera workshops, symphony orchestra, jazz ensemble. Summer music school. . . . NORTH DAKOTA STATE UNIVERSITY, Fargo, North Dakota 58102. A Department of Music in a state-supported university. (Member, NASM.) Chairman: **Edwin R. Fissinger.** Degrees: B.S. in music education; B.A. in applied music. . . . UNIVERSITY OF NORTH DAKOTA, Grand Forks, North Dakota 58201. Department of Music within the university. Head: **William Boehle** (1960). University founded: 1883. Department founded: 1912. Degrees: B.A., B.S.Ed., M.A., M.Ed., Ed.D. Scholarships: total $2,500. Graduate teaching assistantships totaling $7,000. Music students enrolled: 100. Volumes in music library: 3,000. Official school ensembles: chorus, glee club, chamber vocal ensemble, concert band, opera workshop, chamber orchestra, jazz ensemble, Collegium Musicum. Summer music school. . . . UNIVERSITY OF NORTH DAKOTA AT WILLISTON, Williston, North Dakota 58801. Music Department of a college. Head: **Otto Muecke.** Department founded: 1966. School founded: 1960. Degrees: none; transfer music credit only. Official school ensembles: chorus, chamber vocal ensemble, chamber ensembles. No summer music courses.

OHIO

ASHLAND COLLEGE, Ashland, Ohio 44805. Department of Music in a liberal arts college related to the Brethren Church. (Member, NASM.) Head: **Calvin Y. Rogers** (1947). College and department founded: 1878. Degrees: A.B., Mus.B. Scholarships: 29, totaling $18,210. Music students enrolled: 110 (50 majors). Volumes in music library: 1,000. Official school ensembles: chorus, chamber vocal ensemble, marching band, concert band, opera workshop, symphony orchestra, jazz ensemble. No summer music school. . . . BALDWIN–WALLACE COLLEGE, Berea, Ohio 44017. A conservatory, one of the six divisions of a Methodist-affiliated college. (Member, NASM.) Director: **Warren A. Scharf.** Degrees: B.M. in applied music, theory, church music; B.M.Ed.; B.A. with music major. Music majors: 232. Music library: about 5,000 titles. . . . BLUFFTON COLLEGE, Bluffton, Ohio 45817. A Department of Music in a liberal arts college affiliated with the Mennonite Church. (Member, NASM.) Chairman: **Earl W. Lehman.** Degrees: B.A. in music; B.A. in music education. . . . BOWLING GREEN STATE UNIVERSITY, Bowling Green, Ohio 43403. A School of Music in a state-supported university. Director: **James Paul Kennedy.** Degrees: B.M. in music education, performance, history–literature, theory–composition; B.A. in music; M.M. Music majors: 500. Music library: about 5,000 volumes. . . . CAPITAL UNIVERSITY, CONSERVATORY OF MUSIC, Main Street, Columbus, Ohio 43209. A Department of an endowed university, supported by the American Lutheran Church. (Member, NASM.) Dean: **Marceau C. Myers** (1970). University founded: 1850. Conservatory founded: 1919. Degrees: B.M., B.A. Scholarships: total $30,000. Music students enrolled: 200. Official school ensembles: chorus, glee club, chamber vocal ensemble, concert band, opera workshop, symphony orchestra, chamber orchestra, jazz ensemble, other smaller chamber groups. Summer music school. . . . CENTRAL STATE UNIVERSITY, Wilberforce, Ohio 45384. Department of Music within the College of Arts and Sciences. Head: **Stanley D. Kirton** (1970). School founded: 1887. Music Department founded: 1941. Degrees: B.A. and B.S. in education. Scholarships: 30, totaling $20,000. Music enrollment: 70. Ensembles: chorus, marching band, opera workshop. . . . CHILLICOTHE CAMPUS OF OHIO UNIVERSITY, University Drive, Chillicothe, Ohio 45601. Branch campus of

Ohio University at Athens, Ohio, offering only freshman year courses. Head: **Peggy M. Boggs.** Music enrollment: 100. Official music ensemble: chorus. Summer music courses are offered. . . . THE CLEVELAND INSTITUTE OF MUSIC, 11021 East Boulevard, Cleveland, Ohio 44106. Independent, endowed and privately supported institution affiliated with Western Reserve University. (Member, NASM.) School founded: 1920. Degrees: B.M., M.M., D.M.A., Diploma and Artist Diploma; B.S., Mus. Ed., M.A., Ph.D. (the latter three in joint program with Western Reserve University). Scholarships and fellowships: 109, totaling $145,000. Music library: 30,000 volumes. Official school ensembles: chorus, glee club, chamber vocal ensemble, marching band, concert band, opera workshop, symphony orchestra, chamber orchestra, string quartet, jazz ensemble (bands and jazz ensemble in association with Western Reserve University). Summer music school. Special course: electronic music. . . . COLLEGE OF WOOSTER, Wooster, Ohio 44691. A Department of Music in a liberal arts college supported by the Presbyterian Church. (Member, NASM.) Chairman: **Richard T. Gore.** Degrees: B.M. in applied music; B.M.Ed.; B.A. in applied music. Music majors: 60. . . . DENISON UNIVERSITY, Granville, Ohio 43023. A Department of Music in an endowed college. (Member, NASM.) Chairman: **R. Lee Bostian.** Degrees: B.M. in applied music, music education; B.A. in music. Music majors: 35. . . . FINDLAY COLLEGE, Findlay, Ohio 45840. A Division of Fine Arts in a liberal arts college related to the Churches of God. (Member, NASM.) Chairman, Division of Fine Arts: **Roland E. Anfinson.** Degree: B.A. in applied music, history and literature, music theory and composition, music education. . . . HEIDELBERG COLLEGE, East Perry Street, Tiffin, Ohio 44883. Department of Music within a college partially supported by the United Church of Christ. (Member, NASM.) Head: **Ferris E. Ohl** (1964). School and Music Department founded: 1850. Degrees: B.M. (performance), B.M. in education; music major on A.B. degree. Scholarships: 50, totaling $12,000. Music enrollment: 135. Music library: 9,470, excluding records and tapes. Ensembles: chorus, chamber vocal ensemble, marching band, concert band, opera workshop, symphony orchestra, chamber orchestra, jazz ensemble. Summer courses occasionally taught. . . . HIRAM COLLEGE, Hiram, Ohio 44234. A Department of Music in a liberal arts college. Chairman: **Ben Gibson.** Degree: B.A. in performance, music theory, music history and literature, music education. . . . KENT STATE UNIVERSITY, Kent, Ohio 44242. School of Music within a university, state supported. (Member, NASM.) Director: **Lindsey Merrill** (1967). University founded: 1910. School of Music founded: 1946. Degrees: B.A., B.M., M.A., M.M., M.S.Ed., Ph.D. (in music education). Scholarships: 80; 18 assistantships. Music enrollment: 450 per quarter. Music library: 16,000 books and scores. Ensembles: chorus, glee club, chamber vocal ensemble, marching band, concert band, opera workshop, symphony orchestra, chamber orchestra, smaller chamber groups, jazz ensemble, recorder ensemble, baroque ensemble. Summer program with the Blossom Festival School of Kent State University and the Cleveland Symphony Orchestra (see Festivals). Special courses: ethnomusicology and music librarianship. . . . KENYON COLLEGE, Gambier, Ohio 43022. Department of Music within the college. Head: **Paul Schwartz** (1947). College founded: 1824. Department founded: 1947. Degrees: B.A. Music students enrolled: 150. Volumes in music library: 1,600. Official school ensembles: chorus, chamber vocal ensemble, symphony orchestra, string orchestra, Baroque ensemble, woodwind quintet. No summer music school. . . . LAKELAND COMMUNITY COLLEGE, Mentor, Ohio 44060. Music is taught within the Department of Humanities. Chairman: **John C. Vitale** (1968). School founded: 1967. No music degrees and music scholarships. Music courses enrollment: 215, including part-time students. Music library: 325 volumes. Official music ensembles: chorus, chamber vocal ensemble, jazz ensemble. One or two music classes in summer session. . . . LOURDES JUNIOR COLLEGE, 6832 Convent Boulevard, Sylvania, Ohio 43560. Music Department in a college. Head: **Sister M. Siena** (1961). School founded: 1957. Only preparation music courses taught. Music students enrolled: 15. Music library: 500 volumes. Official school ensembles: glee club, chamber vocal ensemble. No summer music courses. . . . MARIETTA COLLEGE, Marietta, Ohio 45750. The Edward E. MacTaggart Department of Music of Marietta College. Head: **Harold Mueller** (1967). College founded: 1835. Degree: B.A. No scholarships but prizes for achievement ($50 per semester). Music students enrolled: 15 to 20 majors, 200 to 300 minors. Volumes in music library: 4,000. Official school ensembles: chorus, chamber vocal ensemble, concert band, symphony orchestra. No summer music school. . . . MIAMI UNIVERSITY, Oxford, Ohio 45056. Music Department within a university. (Member, NASM.) Head: **Everett P. Nelson** (1959). University founded: 1809. Music Department founded: 1929. Degrees: B.M., M.M., Ph.D., and M.A. in cooperation with the University of Cincinnati. Scholarships and fellowships: 40, totaling $30,000. Music enrollment: 350. Music library: 15,000 volumes. Ensembles: chorus, glee club, chamber vocal ensemble, marching band, concert band, opera workshop, symphony orchestra, chamber orchestra, smaller chamber groups, jazz ensemble. Summer music school offered. . . . MOUNT UNION COLLEGE, Alliance, Ohio 44601. A Department of Music in an endowed college. (Member, NASM.) Head: **Cecil Stewart** (1946). Department founded: 1865. School founded: 1846. Degrees: B.M., B.M.Ed., A.B. with music major. Scholarships: 20, totaling $12,500. Music students enrolled: 85 majors. Music library: 9,000 scores, 1,500 books, 2,000 records. Official school ensembles: three choruses, chamber vocal ensemble, marching band, concert band, opera workshop, student quartets. Summer music school. . . . MOUNT VERNON NAZARENE COLLEGE, Martinsburg Road, Mount Vernon, Ohio 43050. Music Department within the college. Head: **Reuben E. Rodeheaver** (1968). Department founded: 1968. Scholarships: eight, totaling $2,400. Fellowships: three, totaling $900. Music students enrolled: 100 per term—three terms a year. Volumes in music library: 500. Official school ensembles: chorus, glee club, chamber vocal ensemble, concert band, jazz ensemble. Summer music instruction. . . . MUSKINGUM COLLEGE, New Concord, Ohio 43762. Music Department of an endowed college. (Member, NASM.) Head: **Charles Joseph** (1966). Degrees: B.A., B.M. Music enrollment: 50. Official school ensembles: chorus, concert band, symphony orchestra, in-resident trio, jazz ensemble. Limited summer instruction. . . . NOTRE DAME COLLEGE, 4545 College Road, Cleveland, Ohio 44121. Music Department within a college. Head: **Sister Mary Electa** (1963). Degrees: B.A. Scholarships are included in general financial aid. Music students enrolled: five. Volumes in music library: 1,000. Official school ensembles: chorus, chamber vocal ensemble. No summer music instruction. . . . OBERLIN COLLEGE CONSERVATORY OF MUSIC, Oberlin, Ohio 44074. A conservatory within a college. (Member, NASM.) Dean: **Emil Danenberg** (1971). College founded: 1833. Conservatory founded: 1867. Degrees: B.M. in applied music, composition, music history, music education; M.M.Ed., M.M. in teaching, conducting, music theater. Scholarships awarded by college according to need. No music fellowships. Music enrollment: 425. Music library: 50,000 books and scores; 8,000 records. Music ensembles: chorus, chamber vocal ensemble, wind ensemble, opera workshop, symphony orchestra, chamber orchestra, smaller chamber groups, brass ensemble. Summer courses in applied music. Special courses in ethnomusicology, electronic music. . . . OHIO NORTHERN UNIVERSITY, Ada, Ohio 45810. Department of Music within a college of liberal arts. Head: **Alan H. Drake** (1969). Department founded: 1875. School founded: 1871. Degree: A.B. in music, with or without teacher certification. Scholarships: three to six, totaling $900 plus federal allocations. Music students enrolled: 35 to 40. Music library: 400 volumes. Official school ensembles: chorus, glee club, chamber vocal ensemble, concert band, chamber ensembles, jazz ensemble. Summer camp for high school students, and a few music summer courses. . . . THE OHIO STATE UNIVERSITY, 1899 North College Road, Columbus, Ohio 43210. School of Music within a College of the Arts of a state-supported university. (Member, NASM.) Director: **Harold Luce** (1968). University founded: 1870. School founded: 1925. Degrees: B.M., B.M.Ed., B.A., M.M., M.A., Ph.D., D.M.A. Scholarships: 100, totaling $40,000 annually. Fellowships: 12, totaling $28,000 annually. Music students enrolled: 625. Volumes in music library: 35,000. Official school ensembles: chorus, glee club, chamber vocal ensemble, marching band, concert band, opera workshop, symphony orchestra, chamber orchestra, jazz ensemble, Collegium Musicum, other chamber groups. Summer music school. . . . THE OHIO STATE UNIVERSITY—MANSFIELD CAMPUS, University Drive, Mansfield, Ohio 44906. Department at this campus is a Division of the Ohio State University School of Music. School founded: 1870. Department founded: 1966. No degree offered. Music enrollment: 300 to 400. Music volumes in library: 200 to 300. Music ensembles: chorus, concert band, chamber vocal ensemble, opera workshop. No summer school in music. . . . OHIO UNIVERSITY, Athens, Ohio 45701. School of Music in the College of Fine Arts of a state-supported university. (Member, NASM.) Director: **Clyde Thompson** (1968). School founded: 1804. Music school founded: 1902. Degrees: B.Mus., M.Mus., B.S. in music education, M.Ed. in music education. Scholarships: 55, totaling $19,450. Fellowships: 11, totaling $31,840. Music enrollment: 280. Volumes in library: 10,081. Music ensembles: chorus, glee club, chamber vocal ensemble, marching band, concert band, opera workshop, symphony orchestra, chamber orchestra, jazz ensemble, Baroque trio. Summer school. Music therapy is taught as a special course. . . . OHIO UNIVERSITY AT ZANESVILLE, 1425 Newark Road, Zanesville, Ohio 43701. Music is an extension of a department within a college of the university. Head: **Marcia Herman** (1967). Music curriculum founded: 1967. School founded: 1803. Music degrees: none from Zanesville campus. Music scholarships and fellowships: none. Music students enrolled: 40. Official school ensemble: chorus. No summer music school. . . . OHIO WESLEYAN UNIVERSITY, Sanborn Hall, Delaware, Ohio 43015. Department of Music within a university supported by the United Methodist Church. (Member, NASM.) Chairman: **Charles E. Thompson** (1969). School founded: 1842. Music department founded: circa 1876. Degrees: B.M. in music education, instrumental, theory and composition. Scholarships: two for music; others from general funds. Music enrollment: 65 majors; 600 enrolled for music courses each term. Music library: 4,000 books, 4,000 records. School ensembles: chorus, glee club, chamber vocal ensemble, athletics band, concert band, opera workshop, symphony orchestra, trio, various instrumental ensembles. No summer music instruction. . . . OTTERBEIN COLLEGE, Westerville, Ohio 43081. Music Department within a college supported by the United Methodist Church. (Member, NASM.) Head: **Albert Huetteman** (1967). College founded: 1847. Music Department founded: 1890. Degrees: B.A. with major in music; B.M.Ed. Scholarships: 12, totaling $2,800. Music enrollment: 66. Ensembles: chorus, chamber vocal ensemble, marching band, concert band, opera workshop, symphony orchestra, jazz ensemble. No summer music school. . . . UNIVERSITY OF CINCINNATI, COLLEGE–CONSERVATORY OF MUSIC, Cincinnati, Ohio 45221. College within a university. (Member, NASM.) A municipal institution. Dean: **Jack M. Watson** (1962). University founded: 1819. Conservatory founded: 1867. Degrees: B.M., B.A., B.F.A. (in broadcasting, musical theater, and dance), M.M., M.A. (in broadcasting and arts management), D.M.A., Ph.D. Scholarships: 224. Music students enrolled: 950. Volumes in music library: 9,000 books, 8,300 scores, 4,000 records, 300 microfilm, 1,000 microcards (see Music Libraries). Official school ensembles: eight choruses, two glee clubs, chamber vocal ensemble, marching band, concert band, opera workshop, symphony orchestra, chamber orchestra, jazz ensemble, other smaller chamber groups, Collegium Musicum. Summer music school. . . . UNIVERSITY OF DAYTON,

300 College Park Drive, Dayton, Ohio 45409. Music is a division in the Performing and Visual Arts Department in the College of Arts and Sciences. (Member, NASM.) Head of Division: **Lawrence E. Tagg** (1970). Division founded: 1938. School founded: 1850. Degrees: B.M., B.A. with music major; B.S. in music education. Scholarships: 10, totaling $5,000. Music students enrolled: 65 majors, 300 in courses. Official school ensembles: chorus, chamber vocal ensemble, marching band, concert band, symphony orchestra, chamber ensembles, jazz ensemble. Summer music courses. . . . URBANA COLLEGE, College Way, Urbana, Ohio 43078. Music is a part of the Humanities Division of the college. Head: **Janet W. Ebert** (1962). School founded: 1850. Department founded: 1962. No degree offered in music. Music enrollment: 200. Music volumes in library: 2,000. Music ensembles: chorus, concert band. Summer courses offered. . . . WITTENBERG UNIVERSITY, Springfield, Ohio 45501. A School of Music within a university. (Member, NASM.) Dean: **L. David Miller** (1955). University founded: 1845. School of Music founded: 1887. Degrees: B.M., B.M.Ed., A.B. with music major, M.S.M (Master of Sacred Music). Scholarships: 50, totaling $45,000. Fellowship: one for $1,700. Music enrollment: 145 majors; 500 including liberal arts students receiving elective music instruction. Music library: 12,000 volumes. Ensembles: four choirs, chamber vocal ensemble, concert band, opera workshop, symphony orchestra, chamber orchestra, smaller chamber groups, jazz ensemble. Summer music school offered. Special courses: music printing in conjunction with Chantry Music Press at Wittenberg; "Fundamentals of Piano Technology" and "Piano Tuning"; Church Music with junior year in Berlin, Kirchenmusikschule. . . . WRIGHT STATE UNIVERSITY, Dayton, Ohio 45431. A department within the Division of Liberal Arts in a state university. (Member, NASM.) Chairman: **William C. Fenton.** Degree: B.M. in music education. . . . YOUNGSTOWN STATE UNIVERSITY, DANA SCHOOL OF MUSIC, Wick Avenue, Youngstown, Ohio 44503. A School of Music within a university. (Member, NASM.) Head: **Charles H. Aurand.** University founded: 1928. School of Music founded: 1869. Degrees: B.M., B.A., M.M. Scholarships: 35, totaling $16,500. Fellowships: seven graduate assistantships totaling $18,200. Music enrollment: 360. Music library: 5,000 volumes. Ensembles: chorus, glee club, chamber vocal ensemble, marching band, concert band, opera workshop, symphony orchestra, approximately 12 smaller chamber groups, jazz ensemble. Summer music school offered.

OKLAHOMA

CAMERON COLLEGE, Lawton, Oklahoma 73501. Music is a department within the college. Head: **George F. Smith** (1969). Department founded: 1927. School founded: 1909. Degree: B.A. in Music (major in voice, keyboard, and instruments). Teacher certification is optional. Scholarships: $15,000 total. Music students enrolled: 100. Music library: 2,000 volumes. Official school ensembles: chorus, marching band, concert band, opera workshop, chamber ensembles, jazz ensemble. Summer music school. . . . CONNORS STATE COLLEGE, Warner, Oklahoma 74469. Music Division of the Fine Arts Department. Chairman: **Tom Webb** (1968). College founded: 1908. No music degrees or scholarships. Music students enrolled: 30. Volumes in music library: 150. Official school ensemble: chorus. No summer music instruction. . . . LANGSTON UNIVERSITY, Langston, Oklahoma 73050. Music Department within the university. Acting Chairman: **John L. Smith** (1970). University and department founded: 1897. Degrees: B.A. in education. No music scholarships. Music students enrolled: 40. Official school ensembles: chorus, glee club, chamber vocal ensemble, marching band, concert band, chamber orchestra, jazz ensemble. No summer music school. . . . OKLAHOMA COLLEGE OF LIBERAL ARTS, Chickasha, Oklahoma 73019. A Department of Music in a state-supported liberal arts college. (Member, NASM.) Chairman: **Louise Waldorf.** Degree: B.A. in applied music, music education. Music majors: 40. . . . OKLAHOMA BAPTIST UNIVERSITY, Shawnee, Oklahoma 74801. A college within a university. (Member, NASM.) Head: **Warren M. Angell** (1936). University founded: 1910. College of Music founded: 1918. Degrees: B.M., B.M.Ed. Scholarships: total $12,000. Music enrollment: 275. Music library: 1,000 volumes. Ensembles: chorus, glee club, chamber vocal ensemble, concert band, opera workshop, chamber orchestra string quartet, jazz ensemble. Limited summer music school. . . . OKLAHOMA CITY UNIVERSITY, 2501 North Blackwelder, Oklahoma City, Oklahoma 73106. School of Music within an endowed university. (Member, NASM.) Dean: **Fred C. Mayer** (1962). School of Music founded: 1922. University founded: 1904. Music degrees offered: B.M., B.A. (music major). Music students enrolled: 210. Music library: 5,000 volumes. Official school ensembles: chorus, chamber vocal ensemble, concert band, opera workshop, symphony orchestra, trio, jazz ensemble. Summer music school offered. . . . OKLAHOMA STATE UNIVERSITY, Stillwater, Oklahoma 74074. A Music Department of the College of Arts and Sciences, state supported. (Member, NASM.) Head: **Max A. Mitchell** (1943). Department founded: 1901. School founded: 1891. Degrees: B.A., B.M., B.M.Ed. Scholarships: 75, totaling $10,000. No fellowships. Music students enrolled: 125. Music library: part of university library. Official school ensembles: chorus, glee club, chamber vocal ensemble, marching band, concert band, opera workshop, symphony orchestra, jazz ensemble. Week-long summer workshops in several fields. . . . PHILLIPS UNIVERSITY, University Station, Enid, Oklahoma 73701. A Department of Music in the School of Fine Arts and Sciences, supported by the Christian Church. (Member, NASM.) Head: **E. J. Ulrich** (1970). Department and school founded: 1906. Degrees: B.M.Ed., B.M. Scholarships: number varies. Music students enrolled: 45 full-time music majors. Music library: 10,000 volumes. Official school ensembles: chorus, chamber vocal ensemble, concert band, symphony orchestra, jazz ensemble. Summer opera workshop (Inspiration Point, Arkansas, Fine Arts Colony—partly sponsored by Phillips University; see Music Festivals). . . . SOUTHEASTERN STATE COLLEGE, Durant, Oklahoma 74701. Music Department within the college. Head: **Paul M. Mansur** (1965). College founded: 1909. Degrees: B.A., B.A.Ed., M.Ed. Music students enrolled: 80. Scholarships: 60, totaling $6,000. Volumes in music library: 1,000. Official school ensembles: chorus, chamber vocal ensemble, marching band, concert band, opera workshop, popular music entertainment group. Summer music instruction. . . . SOUTHWESTERN STATE COLLEGE, Weatherford, Oklahoma 73096. Music Department of the college. Head: **James Jurrens.** Department and school founded: 1901. Degrees: B.M.Ed., B.A., M.Ed. Scholarships: 35, totaling $4,000. Music students enrolled: 150. Music library: 3,000 volumes. Official school ensembles: chorus, glee club, chamber vocal ensemble, marching band, concert band, opera workshop, chamber ensembles, jazz ensemble. Summer music school. . . . UNIVERSITY OF OKLAHOMA, Norman, Oklahoma 73069. A university school, state supported. (Member, NASM.) Dean, College of Fine Arts: **F. Donald Clark.** Director, School of Music: **Arthur Corra.** Degrees: B.M. in performance, composition, music history, theory; B.M.Ed.; B.F.A. in music; M.M. in performance, composition, music history, theory; M.M.Ed. Music majors: 400. . . . UNIVERSITY OF TULSA, Tulsa, Oklahoma 74104. A School of Music in the College of Fine Arts and Professional Studies in a university, endowed. (Member, NASM.) Director, School of Music: **William E. McKee.** Degrees: B.M. in applied music, composition, B.M.Ed., M.M. in composition, applied music; M.M.Ed. Music majors: 165.

OREGON

CENTRAL OREGON COMMUNITY COLLEGE, Bend, Oregon 97701. Division within the Department of Social Science and Fine Arts. Head: **Orde Pinckney** (1967). School and Department of Music founded: 1949. Degree: Associate of Arts in Music.

Scholarships: seven, totaling $975. Music enrollment: seven to eight majors. Volumes in music library: 250. Music ensembles: chorus, chamber vocal ensemble, concert band, symphony orchestra, chamber orchestra, small chamber groups, jazz ensemble. Summer courses in music. . . . CLACKAMAS COMMUNITY COLLEGE, 16900 South Molalla Avenue, Oregon City, Oregon 97045. A Music Department within a two-year college. Head of Department: **LeRoy Anderson** (1969). School founded in 1965. Music Department founded in 1967. No degrees; the school offers a two-year transfer curriculum. Scholarships: five one-year scholarships totaling $400. Music enrollment: 100. Volumes in music library: 280. Ensembles: chorus, contemporary vocal ensemble, concert band, chamber instrumental groups, and jazz ensemble. No summer music instruction. . . . CLATSOP COLLEGE, 16th and Jerome Streets, Astoria, Oregon 97103. Music is a department of the college. Head: **Arthur C. Vaughn, Jr.** (1969). Department founded: 1969. School founded: 1960. Degree: A.A. with music major. Scholarships: two full scholarships. Music students enrolled: 150. Music library: 500 volumes. Official school ensembles: chorus, chamber vocal ensemble, concert band, symphony orchestra, chamber ensembles, jazz ensemble, Baroque ensemble. No summer music school. . . . LEWIS AND CLARK COLLEGE, Portland, Oregon 97219. Music Department within a college. (Member, NASM.) Head: **Reinhard G. Pauly** (1968). School founded: 1867. Music Department founded: 1946. Degrees: B.M. in applied music, theory, composition, music education; B.A. in music; B.S. in music; M.M. in applied music, composition and theory; M.M.Ed. Scholarships: 19, totaling $7,225 (fall, 1971). Music enrollment: 117 (fall, 1971). Music library: 4,050 titles. Ensembles: chorus, chamber vocal ensemble, concert band, opera workshop, symphony orchestra, jazz ensemble, Collegium Musicum. Summer music school. . . . LINFIELD COLLEGE, McMinnville, Oregon 97128. The Music Department of a liberal arts college. (Member, NASM.) Chairman: **Milo Wold.** Degree: B.A. in applied music, theory, music education. Music majors: 38. . . . MARYLHURST COLLEGE, Marylhurst, Oregon 97036. A Department of Music in a liberal arts college for women, conducted by Sisters of the Holy Names of Jesus and Mary. (Member, NASM.) Chairman: **Sister M. Anne Cecile.** Degrees: B.M. in applied music, theory and composition, music education, history and literature; B.A. in applied music, music theory, music history and literature. Music majors: 35. . . . MOUNT ANGEL SEMINARY, Saint Benedict, Oregon 97373. No music department; some music courses, introductory ensembles, and orchestra. Chairman, Division of Arts and Letters: **Donald Kelley.** School founded: 1887. Music students enrolled: 50. Music library: 5,000 volumes. Official school ensemble: symphony orchestra. No summer courses. . . . MULTNOMAH SCHOOL OF THE BIBLE, 8435 North East Glisan, Portland, Oregon 97220. Department within a Bible Institute. Head: **Brian W. Gerards** (1963). School and department founded: 1936. Degrees: B.A. in Biblical literature; B.S. in Biblical education. Music students enrolled: 40 majors, 200 in some courses. Music library: 2,000 volumes. Official school ensembles: chorus, chamber vocal ensemble, chamber orchestra, chamber ensembles. No summer music school. Special course: church music. . . . NORTHWEST CHRISTIAN COLLEGE, Eleventh and Alder, Eugene, Oregon 97401. Music is taught as a minor emphasis within a college offering a single major or core curriculum on the Bible and religion. School and music courses founded: 1895. Degrees: B.A., B.S. in Bible and Religion with emphasis in music. Scholarships: three, totaling $600. Music students enrolled: 3 "emphasis"; 90 in courses. Music library: 500 volumes. Official school ensembles: chorus, chamber vocal ensembles. No summer music school. . . . OREGON STATE UNIVERSITY, Corvallis, Oregon 97331. Music Department within a School of Humanities and Social Sciences. Head: **William A. Campbell** (1966). Department founded: 1900. University founded: 1868. Degrees: B.A., B.S. in music; B.S. in music education. No tuition scholarships (state school). Music students enrolled: 80.

Music library: 7,500 volumes. Official ensembles: chorus, chamber vocal ensemble, marching band, concert band, opera workshop, symphony orchestra, Baroque ensemble, trio, jazz ensemble. Summer music school. . . .PACIFIC UNIVERSITY SCHOOL OF MUSIC, Forest Grove, Oregon 97116. College of Music within a university. (Member, NASM.) Dean: **Albert C. Shaw** (1963). College of Music founded: 1884. School founded: 1849. Degrees: B.M.Ed., B.M., B.A. with music major. Scholarships: number varies; includes talent awards and grants based on need. Music students enrolled: 40 majors, 40 minors, 260 in courses. Music library: 8,000 volumes. Official school ensembles: chorus, glee club, chamber vocal ensemble, concert band, symphony orchestra, chamber orchestra, string quartet, jazz ensemble. Summer music school. . . . UNIVERSITY OF OREGON, School of Music, Eugene, Oregon 97403. Music School within the state-supported university. (Member, NASM.) Dean: **Robert M. Trotter** (1963). University founded: 1879. School of Music added: 1903. Degrees: B.A., B.S., B.M., M.A., M.S., M.M., D.Ed., Ph.D. (music education), D.M.A. Scholarships: number varies; totaling $24,000. Fellowships: four to six, totaling $12,000 to $14,000. Music students enrolled: 350. Volumes in music library: 25,000 (see Music Libraries). Official school ensembles: three choruses, chamber vocal ensemble, marching band, concert band, opera workshop, symphony orchestra, chamber orchestra, jazz ensemble, other smaller chamber groups. Summer music school. . . . PORTLAND COMMUNITY COLLEGE, 12000 S.W. 49th Avenue, Portland, Oregon 97219. Music is taught within a Visual, Audio, and Performing Arts Department. Head: **Robert A. Hughitt** (1969). Music Department founded in 1964. Degree: Associate of Arts (or Science). Music enrollment: 90. Ensembles: chorus, and chamber vocal groups. No summer music instruction. . . . SOUTHWESTERN OREGON COMMUNITY COLLEGE, Coos Bay, Oregon 97420. A Music Department within a two-year college. Head: **Frank Leuck** (1964). College founded in 1961; Music Department founded in 1964. Degree: Associate in Arts. The school offers six talent grants totaling $1,620. In addition, there are general funds available to qualified students. Music enrollment: 125, with 10 music majors. Volumes in music library: 700. Ensembles: chorus, concert band, opera workshop, chamber orchestra, and jazz ensemble. Some limited amount of music instruction offered in summer. A special jazz-oriented theory course is offered emphasizing improvisation. . . . WILLAMETTE UNIVERSITY, 900 State Street, Salem, Oregon 97301. A College of Music of an endowed university. (Member, NASM.) Acting Dean: **Richard Stewart** (1971). College of Music founded: 1870. University founded: 1842. Degrees: B.M., B.M.Ed., B.A. in Music. Scholarships: 50, totaling $35,000. Music students enrolled: 90. Music library: 2,238 volumes. Official school ensembles: chorus, glee club, chamber vocal ensemble, marching band, concert band, opera workshop, symphony orchestra, chamber ensemble, jazz ensemble. No summer music school.

PENNSYLVANIA

ACADEMY OF VOCAL ARTS, 1920 Spruce Street, Philadelphia, Pennsylvania 19103. A private music school. Head: **Vernon Hammond** (1941). School founded: 1935. Scholarships: full tuition scholarship for all students. Enrollment: 25. Music library: 2,000. Ensembles: opera workshop. No summer program. The school offers complete training in opera. . . . ALLIANCE COLLEGE, Fullerton Avenue, Cambridge Springs, Pennsylvania 16403. Music Department within the college. Department Chairman: **Judith A. Eckelmeyer** (1968). School founded: 1912. No music degrees offered as there is no music major program. Music students enrolled: 200 in courses. Music library: 300 books and scores; 1,000 records. Official school ensemble: chorus. No summer music instruction. Unique course: a history of Polish music. . . . ALLEGHENY COLLEGE, Meadville, Pennsylvania 16335. Music Department of the college. Head: **Jerome L. Landsman** (1969). Department founded:

1930. School founded: 1815. Degree: B.A. with major in music. Scholarships: 12, totaling $2,000. Music library: 600 volumes. Official school ensembles: chorus, chamber vocal ensemble, concert band, symphony orchestra, chamber ensembles. Summer music school. . . . ALLEGHENY CAMPUS (COMMUNITY COLLEGE OF ALLEGHENY COUNTY), 808 Ridge Avenue, Pittsburgh, Pennsylvania 15212. Department of Music within the college. Head: **Christopher R. Pignoli** (1968). Music Department founded: 1969. School founded: 1966. Degree: Associate of Science degree in music. No music scholarships and fellowships. Music students enrolled: 25. Music library: 650 volumes. Official school ensembles: chorus, concert band, symphony orchestra. Summer music school. . . . BUCKNELL UNIVERSITY, Lewisburg, Pennsylvania 17837. A Department within a privately supported and endowed university. (Member, NASM.) Chairman: **Thomas E. Warner.** School founded: 1846. Degrees: B.A., B.M. (applied), B.M. (music education). Scholarships: three, totaling $2,600. Music students enrolled: 40. Music library: 6,000 volumes. Official school ensembles: chorus, chamber vocal ensemble, Collegium Musicum. No summer music courses. Special courses: oriental music, folk music of the world. . . . BUCKS COUNTY COMMUNITY COLLEGE, Swamp Road, Newtown, Pennsylvania 18940. Music Department within the college. Head: **Richard E. Averre** (1968). Department founded: 1965. Degrees: A.A. Scholarships: three, totaling $1,000. Music students enrolled: 50. Volumes in music library: 900. Official school ensembles: chorus, concert choir, concert band, jazz ensemble, other smaller chamber groups. Summer music instruction. . . . CARNEGIE-MELLON UNIVERSITY, Schenley Park, Pittsburgh, Pennsylvania 15213. A Music Department within a College of Fine Arts. (Member, NASM.) The university is endowed. Head of Department: **Sidney Harth** (1962). Music has been taught since the founding of the university in 1900. Degrees: B.F.A. in music; B.F.A. in music education, composition; M.F.A. in music; M.F.A. in music education, opera; D.A. in music. Scholarships: $30,000. Fellowships: $20,000. Music enrollment: 200. Volumes in music library: 15,000. Ensembles: chorus, chamber vocal ensemble, concert band, opera workshop, symphony orchestra, chamber orchestra, instrumental chamber groups. Summer music courses are offered. . . . COLLEGE MISERICORDIA, Dallas, Pennsylvania 18612. A music department within a college. (Member, NASM.) Head of department: **Sister Mary Carmel** (1967). College founded in 1926; Music Department in 1935. Degrees: B.A. with a major in music; B.M. in music education. Performance scholarships available on the basis of student scores. Music enrollment: 55. Music volumes in library: 1,500. Ensembles: glee club, chamber vocal ensemble, chamber orchestra, string quartet. Music courses are offered in summer. . . . THE CURTIS INSTITUTE OF MUSIC, 1726 Locust Street, Philadelphia, Pennsylvania 19103. A conservatory of music. Director: **Rudolf Serkin** (1968). Founded: 1924. Degrees: B.M., Diploma, M.M. in composition only. Scholarships: full-tuition scholarship school. Enrollment: 180. Music library: 50,000. Ensembles: opera workshop, symphony orchestra. No summer session. . . . DICKINSON COLLEGE, Carlisle, Pennsylvania 17013. Music Department of a college. Head: **Truman Bullard** (1965). School founded: 1773. Degree: A.B. No music scholarships or fellowships. Music students enrolled: 190. Official school ensembles: chorus, two chamber vocal ensembles, symphony orchestra. Summer music school. . . . DUQUESNE UNIVERSITY, Pittsburgh, Pennsylvania 15219. A School of Music in a university. (Member, NASM.) Dean: **Gerald Keenan** (1954). University founded: 1878. School of Music founded: 1926. Degrees: B.M., B.S. in music education, M.M., Master of Music Education. Scholarships: 83, totaling $50,000. Fellowships: 12, totaling $17,000. Music students enrolled: 485. Official school ensembles: two choruses, chamber vocal ensemble, concert band, symphonic band, symphony orchestra, chamber orchestra, smaller chamber ensembles, jazz ensemble. Summer music school. . . . EAST STROUDSBURG STATE COLLEGE, East

Stroudsburg, Pennsylvania 18301. Music Department of a college. Head: **Raymond Vanderslice, Jr.** (1967). School founded: 1893. No music degrees. No music scholarships or fellowships. No music majors. Official school ensembles: chorus, chamber vocal ensemble, marching band, concert band. No summer music classes. . . . EDINBORO STATE COLLEGE, Edinboro, Pennsylvania 16412. Department of Music within the School of Arts and Humanities. Head: **William Alexander** (1962). College founded: 1858. Department founded: 1962. Degrees: B.S. in music education; B.A. in music. Scholarships: through general college aids. Music students enrolled: 180. Volumes in music library: 7,100. Official school music ensembles: chorus, glee club, chamber vocal ensemble, marching band, concert band, opera workshop, symphony orchestra, chamber orchestra, percussion ensemble, jazz ensemble, other smaller chamber groups. Summer music school. . . . HAVERFORD COLLEGE, Haverford, Pennsylvania 19041. Music Department within college. Head: **John Davison** (1969). College founded: 1833. Department founded: 1926. Degree: B.A. with music major. Scholarships: through general college aid. Music students enrolled: five majors average. Volumes in music library: 4,000. Official school ensembles: chorus, chamber vocal ensemble, symphony orchestra, other smaller chamber groups. No summer music school. Additional music courses are available to Haverford students at Bryn Mawr, Swarthmore College, and the University of Pennsylvania. . . . INDIANA UNIVERSITY OF PENNSYLVANIA, Indiana, Pennsylvania 15701. A Department of Music in a state-supported university. (Member, NASM.) Chairman: **Hugh B. Johnson.** Degrees: B.A. in music; B.F.A. in music; B.S. in music education; M.Ed. in music education. . . . JENKINTOWN MUSIC SCHOOL, 473 Old York Road, Jenkintown, Pennsylvania 19046. Co-Directors: **Monroe Levin, Cameron McGraw.** . . . LEBANON VALLEY COLLEGE, Annville, Pennsylvania 17003. A Music Department within a college. (Member, NASM.) Head of Department: **Robert W. Smith** (1956). College and Music Department founded in 1866. Degrees: B.A. in applied music; B.S. in music education. Various competitive scholarships for the college in general are available. Music enrollment: 150. Number of volumes in music library: 4,500. Ensembles: chorus, glee club, marching band, concert band, symphony orchestra, smaller chamber groups, jazz ensemble. Private instruction and clinics are offered in the summer. . . . LOCK HAVEN STATE COLLEGE, Lock Haven, Pennsylvania 17745. Music Department within the college. Head: **R. C. Nelson** (1968). College founded: 1870. No degrees in music as yet. No music majors. Volumes in music library: 3,500. Official school ensembles: chorus, chamber vocal ensemble, marching band, concert band, symphony orchestra. No summer music school. . . . MANSFIELD STATE COLLEGE, Mansfield, Pennsylvania 16933. A music department within a state-supported college. (Member, NASM.) Chairman: **John H. Baynes** (1966). College founded in 1857. Degrees: B.S. (in education), B.A., B.M., M.Ed. No music scholarships or fellowships. Music enrollment: 230. Volumes in music library: 6,000. Ensembles: chorus, chamber vocal ensemble, marching band, concert band, opera workshop, symphony orchestra, jazz ensemble. Music courses are taught in summer. . . . MARYWOOD COLLEGE, Scranton, Pennsylvania 18509. A Department of Music of a college operated by the Congregation of the Sisters, Servants of the Immaculate Heart of Mary. (Member, NASM.) Chairman: **Sister Mary Judith.** Degree: B.M. in applied music, music education, church music. Music majors: 70. . . . MESSIAH COLLEGE, Grantham, Pennsylvania 17027. Music Department within college. Head: **Ronald R. Sider** (1964). College founded: 1909. Department founded: 1950. Degree: B.A. Scholarships: two, totaling $1,000. Music enrollment: 55. Volumes in music library: 60,000. Official school ensembles: chorus, glee club, chamber vocal ensemble, concert band, chamber orchestra, jazz ensemble, other smaller chamber groups. No summer music school. . . . MILLERSVILLE STATE COLLEGE, Millersville, Pennsylvania 17551. A Music Department within a state-supported college. School founded in 1852; Music Department founded in 1971. Degree: B.S. Music enrollment: 100. Volumes in music library: 10,000. Ensembles: chorus, chamber vocal ensembles, marching band, concert band, symphony orchestra, chamber orchestra, jazz ensemble. Summer music courses are available. . . . MUHLENBERG COLLEGE, Chew Street, Allentown, Pennsylvania 18105. Music Department within the college. Head: **C. S. McClain** (1970). College founded: 1867. Degrees: B.A. Music students enrolled: eight majors. Volumes in library: over 5,000. Official school ensembles: chorus, concert band, opera workshop. Special course: Oriental Music. . . . NEUPAUER CONSERVATORY OF MUSIC, 250 South Broad Street, Philadelphia, Pennsylvania 19107. Trimester conservatory. Director: **Jacob C. Neupauer.** School founded: 1952. Degrees: Diploma (performance, teaching, arranging, composition); Certificate (applied music and musicianship). Music library: 9,000 items. Ensembles: chorus, jazz ensemble, concert orchestra. Summer music school. Special courses in accordion for concert and jazz work, arranging, repair of instrument, jazz workshop. . . . THE NEW SCHOOL OF MUSIC, 301 South 21 Street, Philadelphia, Pennsylvania 19103. A music conservatory. President and Director: **Max Aronoff.** School founded: 1943. Degree: B.M. Scholarships: 30, totaling approximately $45,000. Enrollment: 200 (including degree, diploma, and preparatory students). A small music library. Ensembles: symphony orchestra, small chamber groups. The school participates in Temple University Ambler Summer Festival. . . . NORTHAMPTON COUNTY AREA COMMUNITY COLLEGE, 3835 Green Pond Road, Bethlehem, Pennsylvania 18017. Music Department within the college. Head: **Robert E. Schanck** (1968). Volumes in music library: 400. Official school ensemble: chorus. No summer music classes. . . . PENNSYLVANIA STATE UNIVERSITY, COLLEGE OF ARTS AND ARCHITECTURE, University Park, State College, Pennsylvania 16802. A Music Department within the college. Head of Department: **Robert W. Baisley** (1965). Music Department founded in 1855. Degrees: B.A., B.F.A., M.A., M.F.A. Number and amount of scholarships and fellowships in music varies indeterminately. Music enrollment: 90 majors, 80 minors; a total of 2,000 in all music courses. Volumes in music library: 12,000. Ensembles: chorus, glee club, chamber vocal group, concert band, opera workshop, symphony orchestra, chamber orchestra, smaller instrumental chamber groups, and jazz ensemble. Music is taught in summer. . . . PHILADELPHIA COLLEGE OF BIBLE, 1800 Arch Street, Philadelphia, Pennsylvania 19401. Music Department within the college. Head: **Alfred E. Lunde** (1959). College founded: 1913. Department founded: 1958. Degree: B.M. Scholarships: 22, totaling $6,200. Music students enrolled: 50. Volumes in music library: 4,300. Official music ensembles: chorus, glee club, chamber vocal ensemble, brass ensemble. No summer school. Special course: Church Music. . . . PHILADELPHIA MUSICAL ACADEMY, 313 South Broad Street, Philadelphia, Pennsylvania 19107. An independent college of music. (Member, NASM.) President: **Joseph Castaldo** (1966). Academy founded: 1870. Degrees: B. Music, B. Music plus B. Mus.Ed., M.M. Scholarships: 91, totaling $51,000. Music students enrolled: 260. Volumes in music library: 6,000. Official school ensembles: chorus, concert band, opera workshop, symphony orchestra, jazz ensemble, other smaller chamber groups. Special course: electronic music. Summer music school. . . . POINT PARK COLLEGE, Wood Street and Boulevard of the Allies, Pittsburgh, Pennsylvania 15222. Music discipline in Philosophy and Fine Arts Department. Two faculty members in music, one full-time, one part-time. No music majors, no applied music, no band or chorus. . . . SETON HILL COLLEGE, Greensburg, Pennsylvania 15601. A Department of Music in a college supported by the Catholic Church. (Member, NASM.) Chairman: **Sister Miriam David Volker.** Degree: B.M. in music education. Music majors: 30. . . . ST. FRANCIS COLLEGE, Loretto, Pennsylvania 15940. Music is taught within the Department of Fine Arts. Department Chairman: **Father Warren L. Murphy**

(1968). No degrees offered in music. No scholarships. Music ensembles: chorus, concert band, and pep band. No summer music instruction. . . . SUSQUEHANNA UNIVERSITY, Selinsgrove, Pennsylvania 17870. Music Department within a university. (Member, NASM.) Head: **James Steffy** (1966). University founded: 1857. Music Department founded: 1930. Degrees: B.M. in music education, applied music, and church music. Scholarships: $3,900 annually. Music enrollment: 130. Ensembles: chorus, chamber vocal ensemble, marching band, concert band, opera workshop, symphony orchestra, chamber orchestra, smaller chamber groups. Summer music school offered. . . . SWARTHMORE COLLEGE, Swarthmore, Pennsylvania 19081. Music Department within the college. Chairman: **Peter Gram Swing.** College founded: 1864. Degree: A.B. in music. Scholarships: through the general college aid funds. Music students enrolled: 20. Official ensembles, chorus, chamber vocal ensemble, chamber orchestra, jazz ensemble, other smaller chamber groups. No summer music school. . . . UNIVERSITY OF PENNSYLVANIA, 201 South 34th Street, Philadelphia, Pennsylvania 19104. Chairman: **Richard Wernick.** Music enrollment about 50. . . . UNIVERSITY OF PITTSBURGH, Fifth and Bigelow Streets, Pittsburgh, Pennsylvania 15213. Department of Music within the university. Head: **Robert J. Snow** (1968). University founded: 1787. Department founded: 1936. Degrees: B.A., M.A., Ph.D. Scholarships: none exclusively for music. Fellowships: 10, totaling $2,700. Music students enrolled: 85 undergraduates, 30 graduate. Volumes in music library: 35,000 (see Music Libraries). Official school ensembles: chorus, glee club, chamber vocal ensemble, marching band, concert band, symphony orchestra, jazz ensemble, other chamber groups. Special courses: jazz, electronic music. . . . UNIVERSITY OF PITTSBURGH AT JOHNSTOWN, Johnstown Campus, Johnstown, Pennsylvania 15904. A university music department. Head: **Thomas O. Furlong** (1970). No degree program on this campus. No music major. Official school ensembles: chorus, glee club, concert band. . . . WEST CHESTER STATE COLLEGE, West Chester, Pennsylvania 19380. School of Music within a college. (Member, NASM.) Dean: **Charles A. Sprenkle** (1971). College founded: 1871. Music as a department founded: 1921; Music School established: 1967. Degrees: B.S., B.M., B.A., M.Ed., M.A., M.M. Scholarships: 23 totaling $2,800 plus seven of varying amounts. Fellowships: six assistantships totaling $16,000. Music enrollment: 650. Music library: 10,000 records, 10,000 scores, 3,500 texts, plus tapes, etc. Ensembles: chorus, glee club, chamber vocal ensemble, marching band, concert band, opera workshop, symphony orchestra, chamber orchestra, two smaller chamber groups, jazz ensemble. Summer music school plus string and high school workshops. Special courses in electronic and computer music. . . . WESTMINSTER COLLEGE, New Wilmington, Pennsylvania 16142. Department of Music within a college. (Member, NASM.) Head: **Clarence J. Martin** (1961). School and Music Department founded: 1852. Degrees: B.M. in music education, applied music, church music; A.B. Scholarships: five, totaling $3,000. Enrollment of music students: 100. Music library: 8,000. Ensembles: chorus, glee club, marching band, concert band, opera workshop, chamber orchestra, smaller chamber groups, jazz ensemble. No summer music school. . . . WILKES COLLEGE, Wilkes-Barre, Pennsylvania 18703. Music Department within a college. Head: **William R. Gasbarro** (1964). College founded: 1933. Department founded: 1948. Degrees: B.A. in performance; B.S. in music education. Scholarships: eight, totaling $12,000. Music students enrolled: 125. Volumes in music library: 1,700; 36 periodicals. Official school ensembles: chorus, two glee clubs, chamber vocal ensemble, concert band, opera workshop, community symphony orchestra, woodwind, brass, percussion ensembles. Summer instruction. . . . WILSON COLLEGE, Chambersberg, Pennsylvania 17201. Music Department within the college. Chairman: **Glen H. Gould** (1966). College and department founded: 1869. Degree: B.A. in music. Scholarships: one of $850; two of $250. Music students enrolled: 75 to 100 including members of ensembles. Volumes in music library: 880 books; 2,330 scores. Official school ensembles: two choruses. No summer music school. . . . YORK COLLEGE OF PENNSYLVANIA, Country Club Road, York, Pennsylvania 17405. Music discipline within the Department of Humanities and Fine Arts. Head: **George A. Papacostas.** Department founded: 1968. Degree: B.A. in music. Scholarships: total $10,000 to $15,000. Music students enrolled: 30 majors. Volumes in music library: 1,000 books, 2,000 records. Official school ensembles: chorus, chamber vocal ensemble, concert band, jazz ensemble. Limited summer instruction.

RHODE ISLAND

BARRINGTON COLLEGE, Barrington, Rhode Island 02806. (Member, NASM.) A School of Music within a division of Fine Arts. Chairman, Division of Fine Arts and Director of the School of Music: **Donald E. Brown.** Degrees: B.M. in performance, church music, music education; B.A. in music. . . . BROWN UNIVERSITY, Box 1872, Providence, Rhode Island 02912. Chairman: **Ron Nelson.** Music majors: 17. . . . RHODE ISLAND JUNIOR COLLEGE, 199 Promenade Street, Providence, Rhode Island 02908. Music Department within the college. Chairman: **Arthur E. Chatfield** (1964). College and department founded: 1964. Degree: A.A. Music students enrolled: 700. Volumes in music library: 800. Official school ensembles: chorus, chamber vocal ensemble, concert band, jazz ensemble, string and woodwind ensembles. No summer music school. . . . RHODE ISLAND SCHOOL OF DESIGN, 2 College Street, Providence, Rhode Island 02903. Five or six courses in music (music history, composition, etc.) are taught each year. A music course has been part of the curriculum since 1959. Credit is allowed courses in music toward a degree in the fine arts. Music enrollment: 100 to 150 a year. No ensembles. No summer music courses. Some special courses in the comparative studies of art and music and courses in the study of sound. . . . UNIVERSITY OF RHODE ISLAND, Kingston, Rhode Island 02881. A Music Department within the university. Chairman: **Albert C. Giebler** (1968). University founded: 1888. Music Department founded: 1933. Degrees: B.M. in applied music, music education, theory, etc.; B.A. in music. Scholarships: four for $400 each. One teaching fellowship is offered for $2,300. Enrollment: 75 music majors. Music library: 5,000 volumes. Ensembles: chorus, chamber vocal ensemble, marching band, concert band, opera workshop, symphony orchestra, smaller instrumental chamber groups, and jazz ensemble.

SOUTH CAROLINA

ANDERSON COLLEGE, Anderson, South Carolina 29621. Music Department within the college. Head: **William M. Bridges** (1964). College and department founded: 1911. Degree: A.A. Scholarships: six. Music students enrolled: 25. Volumes in music library: 500. Official school ensembles: chorus, chamber vocal ensemble, bell choir. No summer music instruction. . . . BAPTIST COLLEGE AT CHARLESTON, P.O. Box 10087, Charleston, South Carolina 29411. Music Department within college. Chairman: **Oliver J. Yost** (1969). College and department founded: 1960. Degree: B.A. in music. Scholarships: $1,400. Music students enrolled: 20. Volumes in music library: 1,000. Official school music ensembles: chorus, concert band, jazz ensemble, violin and piano in-residence duo. No summer music school. Special course: music therapy. . . . BOB JONES UNIVERSITY, Greenville, South Carolina 29614. Division of Music within the School of Fine Arts within the university. Division Chairman: **Gail Gingery** (1956). University and Division founded: 1927. Degrees: B.A., B.S., M.A., all in music. Scholarships: work scholarships available; free applied music lessons. Fellowships: four to five assistantships. Music students enrolled: 200 music majors, 500 non-majors taking applied music. Volumes in music library: 2,250 plus large choral and orchestral library; 4,000 records. Official school ensembles: chorus, chamber vocal ensemble, concert band, opera workshop, symphony orchestra, chamber orchestra, other smaller chamber groups. No summer music school. . . . CENTRAL WESLEYAN COLLEGE, Central, South Carolina 29630. Music Department within the college. Head: **Mary E. Budensiek** (1968). College founded: 1906. Department founded: 1968. Scholarships: seven, totaling $350. No music degree. Music students enrolled: 20. Official school ensembles: chamber vocal ensemble, chamber orchestra. Summer music instruction. . . . CLEMSON UNIVERSITY, Clemson, South Carolina 29631. Department of Music within the College of Liberal Arts within the university. Department Chairman: **John H. Butler** (1969). University founded: 1893. Department founded: 1969. No music degrees. No majors. Volumes in music library: 3,000. Official school ensembles: chorus, marching band, concert band. No summer music school. . . . COASTAL CAROLINA REGIONAL CAMPUS OF THE UNIVERSITY OF SOUTH CAROLINA. Conway, South Carolina 29526. A Music Department within the university. Head: **J. T. H. Mize** (1964). Music instruction limited to courses in music appreciation, introduction to music, and music education. Enrollment: 140 (in music appreciation). Ensemble: chorus. Two six-week summer sessions are taught. . . . COKER COLLEGE, Hartsville, South Carolina 29550. Music Department of an endowed liberal arts college. (Member, NASM.) Chairman: **Virgil Smith** (1935). College founded: 1908. Department founded: 1909. Degree: B.A. in applied music. No music scholarships. Music students enrolled: 40. Volumes in music library: 1,200. Official school ensembles: chorus, glee club, chamber vocal ensemble. Summer music instruction. . . . COLUMBIA BIBLE COLLEGE, Box 1322, Columbia, South Carolina 29203. Music Department within the college. Head: **G. William Supplee** (1949). School and Music Department founded: 1923. No music degree offered. Music enrollment: 550 (all students are required to take music courses). Music volumes in library: 1,000. Music ensembles: chorus, concert band, small vocal groups. No summer music courses. Specialization in teaching future missionaries how to incorporate ethnic music in worship. . . . COLUMBIA COLLEGE, Columbia College Drive, Columbia, South Carolina 29203. Chairman, Music Department: **James L. Caldwell.** Music majors: 47. . . . CONVERSE COLLEGE, East Main Street, Spartanburg, South Carolina 29301. School of Music within an endowed liberal arts college. (Member, NASM.) Dean: **Henry Janiec** (1967). College and school founded: 1889. Degrees: B.M., B.A., M.M. Scholarships and fellowships: vary according to annual need. Music students enrolled: 125. Volumes in music library: 8,000. Official school ensembles: chorus, concert band, opera workshop, symphony orchestra, chamber orchestra, other smaller chamber groups. Summer music school. . . . FURMAN UNIVERSITY, Greenville, South Carolina 29613. Music Department of an endowed college. (Member, NASM.) Chairman: **W. Lindsay Smith** (1961). University founded: 1826. Degrees: B.M., B.A. in music. Scholarships: vary in number; total $10,000. Music students enrolled: 140. Volumes in music library: 7,000. Official school ensembles: choir, chamber vocal ensemble, marching band, concert band, opera workshop, symphony orchestra, chamber groups, jazz ensemble. Limited summer instruction. . . . LIMESTONE COLLEGE, Gaffney, South Carolina 29340. Music Department within the Division of Fine Arts of an endowed college. (Member, NASM.) Head: **Douglas R. Nelson** (1968). College and department founded: 1845. Degree: B.A. in music education, applied music. Scholarships: 30 fine arts scholarships totaling $15,000. Music students enrolled: 25. Volumes in music library: 2,600 (1,500 records). Official school ensembles: chorus, chamber vocal ensemble. Limited summer instruction. . . . PRESBYTERIAN COLLEGE, Clinton, South Carolina 29325. Music is offered as an area of study within the Department of Fine Arts. Head: **Charles T. Gaines** (1965). School founded in 1880. Music first taught in 1965. Degree: B.A. with a major in fine arts. Scholarships: four to six, amounting to about $1,000. Music enrollment: four. Music library: 400 to 600 items. Ensembles:

chorus, chamber vocal ensemble. . . . UNIVERSITY OF SOUTH CAROLINA, Columbia, South Carolina 29208. Music Department within the College of Arts and Sciences of a state university. (Member, NASM.) Head: **Arthur M. Fraser** (1963). Music Department founded: 1942. Degrees: B.A., B.S. in music education; B.A. in music; B.M.; M.Mus.Ed; M.M. Scholarships: 40 to 50, totaling $25,000. No music fellowships. Music enrollment: 205 undergraduate, 35 graduate. Music library: 2,000 volumes. Ensembles: chorus, glee club, chamber vocal ensemble, marching band, concert band, opera workshop, symphony orchestra, smaller chamber groups, jazz ensembles, wind ensembles. Summer music school offered. . . . WINTHROP COLLEGE, Rock Hill, South Carolina 29730. A School of Music of a state-supported college. (Member NASM.) Dean: **Jess T. Casey.** Degrees: B.A. in music; B.S. in applied music, music education. Music majors: 95. . . . WOFFORD COLLEGE, North Church Street, Spartanburg, South Carolina 29301. A Music Department within the college. Head: **C. Roland Smith** (1970). School founded in 1863. Music Department established in 1894. No music degrees. Scholarships: seven, totaling $1,300. Enrollment in music (in courses and performing groups combined): 145. Ensembles: glee club and stage band. Music appreciation taught in summer.

SOUTH DAKOTA

DAKOTA STATE COLLEGE, Madison, South Dakota 57042. A Music Department in the college. Head: **Merrill Brown** (1967). School founded in 1881. Degree: B.S. in education. No specific number and amount of scholarships. Music enrollment: 25. Music library: 6,000 volumes. Ensembles: chorus, chamber vocal ensemble, marching band, concert band, and stage band. Music is taught in summer. . . . MOUNT MARTY COLLEGE, 1100 West Fifth Street, Yankton, South Dakota 57078. Department of Music within the college. Head: **John A. Lyons** (1968). College and department founded: 1936. Degree: B.A. Scholarships: three, totaling $1,800. Music students enrolled: 20. Volumes in music library: 825. Official school ensembles: chorus, glee club, chamber vocal ensemble. No summer music school. College has a Sacred Music Center (rare book and manuscript materials). . . . NORTHERN STATE COLLEGE, South Jay Street, Aberdeen, South Dakota 57401. (Member, NASM.) Music Department within the Division of Fine Arts. Chairman, Division of Fine Arts: **John R. Berggren** (1958). School founded: 1902. Music Department founded: 1910. Degrees: B.S. in music; B.A. in music. Scholarships: 25, totaling $3,000. Music enrollment: 115. Music library: 3,500 volumes. Ensembles: chorus, chamber vocal ensemble, marching band, concert band, opera workshop, symphony orchestra, chamber orchestra, smaller chamber groups, jazz ensemble. Summer music school offered. . . . SIOUX FALLS COLLEGE, Sioux Falls, South Dakota 57101. Music Department within a college. Chairman: **Maynard H. Berk** (1968). College founded: 1883. Degree: B.A. in music. Scholarships: total $8,500. Music students enrolled: 50 to 60. Volumes in music library: 75 to 150. Official school ensembles: concert choir, concert band, chamber orchestra, jazz ensemble, madrigal singers. Occasional summer workshops. . . . SOUTHERN STATE COLLEGE, Springfield, South Dakota 57062. Music Department in the Division of Fine Arts within the College. Division Chairman: **Paul R. Swanson** (1969). College founded: 1897. Department founded: 1947. Degree: B.S.Ed. Scholarships: 10, each $100. Music students enrolled: 45. Volumes in music library: 300. Official school ensembles: chorus, chamber vocal ensemble, marching band, concert band, opera workshops, jazz ensemble. Summer music instruction. . . . UNIVERSITY OF SOUTH DAKOTA, Vermillion, South Dakota 57069. Music Department within College of Fine Arts in a state-supported university. (Member, NASM.) Head: **Mrs. Beatrice Chaffee** (1971). University founded: 1862. Department founded: 1931. Degrees: B.F.A., M.M. Scholarships: 20, totaling $5,000. Fellowships: one for $1,800. Music students enrolled: 106. Volumes in music library: 3,500. Official school ensembles: chorus, chamber vocal ensemble, marching band, concert band, opera workshop, symphony orchestra, jazz ensemble, madrigal group, other smaller chamber groups. Special course: history of musical instruments. Summer music school. . . . YANKTON COLLEGE, Yankton, South Dakota 57078. A Conservatory of Music, part of an endowed liberal arts college, affiliated with the United Church of Christ. (Member, NASM.) Head: **J. Laiten Weed** (1947). College founded: 1881. Conservatory founded: 1888. Degrees: B.M., B.A. Scholarships: 18, totaling $9,450. Music students enrolled: 48. Volumes in music library: 5,000. Official school ensembles: chorus, chamber vocal ensemble, concert band, opera workshop, chamber orchestra, jazz ensemble, smaller chamber groups. Summer music school.

TENNESSEE

AUSTIN PEAY STATE UNIVERSITY, Clarksville, Tennessee 37040. Department of Music in a state-supported university. (Member, NASM.) Chairman: **Thomas W. Cowan** (1958). University and department founded: 1929. Degrees: B.A., B.S. in music education, M.M.Ed. Scholarships: 55, totaling $13,500. Fellowships: four, totaling $6,000. Music students enrolled: 100 to 120. Volumes in library: 5,000. Official school ensembles: chorus, chamber vocal ensemble, marching band, concert band, opera workshop, symphony orchestra, jazz ensemble. Summer music semester. . . . BELMONT COLLEGE, Nashville, Tennessee 37203. Music Department of a college. Head: **Jerry Warren** (1969). Department founded: 1951. Parent school founded: 1951. Degrees: B.M., B.A. Scholarships: 25, totaling $7,000. Music students enrolled: 80. Music library: more than 2,000 volumes. Official school ensembles: three choruses, concert band, jazz ensemble. Summer music school. . . . CARSON–NEWMAN COLLEGE, Jefferson City, Tennessee 37760. Music Department in a college. (Member, NASM.) Chairman: **Louis Ball** (1963). School founded: 1851. Music Department founded: circa 1900. Degrees: B.M. in music education, church music, applied music; B.A. Scholarships: 100, totaling $19,000 (including band). Music enrollment: 125. Music library: 1,500. Ensembles: chorus, two glee clubs, chamber vocal ensemble, marching band, concert band, opera workshop. Summer music school. . . . CHRISTIAN BROTHERS COLLEGE, 650 E. Parkway South, Memphis, Tennessee 38104. Music Department of a college. Head: **Brother Vincent Malham.** Department founded: 1969. School founded: 1871. No music degrees offered. No music scholarships and fellowships. Music students enrolled: 50. Music library: 150 volumes. Official school ensembles: chorus, chamber vocal ensemble, faculty–staff chorus. No summer music school. . . . COVENANT COLLEGE, Lookout Mountain, Tennessee 37350. A Music Department within a college. Head: **John Canfield** (1970). School and Music Department founded in 1955. Degrees: B.M.Ed., B.M., B.A. Scholarships: six, totaling up to $1,000. Music enrollment: 35 to 40. Music library: 2,000 volumes; 3,000 recordings, 2,000 scores. Ensembles: chorus, glee club, chamber vocal ensemble, bagpipe marching band, symphony orchestra, chamber orchestra, faculty string quartet and trio. There is a summer music camp. The Music Department specializes in chamber music, claiming one of the finest chamber music libraries in the South (over 4,000 chamber works). . . . EAST TENNESSEE STATE UNIVERSITY, Johnson City, Tennessee 37601. Music Department of a college. Head: **Virgil C. Self** (1960). Department and school founded: 1911. Degrees: B.S. in music education; B.A. with major in music. Scholarships: 50 (tuition). Fellowships: two, totaling $3,600. Music students enrolled: 150 majors, 20 minors. Music library: 10,000 volumes. Official school ensembles: chorus, glee club, chamber vocal ensemble, marching band, concert band, opera workshop, jazz ensemble. Summer music school. . . . FISK UNIVERSITY, 17th Avenue North, Nashville, Tennessee 32703. Department of Music within a college. (Member, NASM.) Head: **F. Bernard Hunter**

(1971). School founded: 1866. Music Department founded: 1885. Degrees: B.A., B.S. in music education, B.M. Scholarships: five, totaling $7,400. Fellowships: one for $20,000. Music enrollment: 20. Music library: 2,355 volumes. Ensembles: chorus, chamber vocal ensemble, marching band, concert band, chamber orchestra, smaller chamber groups, jazz ensemble, and gospel choir. There is summer music instruction. Special courses include: ethnomusicology, gospel and jazz, seminars in African and Afro-American music. . . . GEORGE PEABODY COLLEGE FOR TEACHERS, Nashville, Tennessee 37203. School of Music in a college. (Member, NASM.) Head: **Charles Ball** (1969). School founded: 1916. Parent school founded: 1875 (present name since 1909). Degrees offered: B.A., B.M., B.M.Ed., M.M., M.M.Ed., Specialist in Education (Ed.S.), Ed.D., Ph.D. Scholarships and fellowships: 82, totaling $79,500. Music students enrolled: 200 majors; 1,200 others in music classes. Music library: 25,000 volumes. Official school ensembles: chorus, chamber vocal ensemble, marching band, concert band, symphony orchestra, chamber groups, jazz ensemble. Summer music school. Special courses: electronic music, commercial music, music librarianship. . . . JACKSON STATE COMMUNITY COLLEGE, Highway 70 East, Jackson, Tennessee 38301. Music Department of a college. Head: **Donnie J. Adams** (1967). Department and school founded: 1967. Degree: A.A. with major in music. Scholarships: six, totaling $1,000. Music students enrolled: 12. Music library: 300 volumes. Official school ensembles: chorus, chamber vocal ensemble. No summer music instruction. . . . KNOXVILLE COLLEGE, 901 College Street, Knoxville, Tennessee 37921. Music Department within a private liberal arts college. Chairman: **B. M. Downing** (1968). Department and school founded: 1875. Music degrees: B.A. in music, B.S. in music education. Scholarships: 15 (totaling $1,700 in performance and $5,000 in special awards). Music students enrolled: 50 majors and 500 in music courses. Music library: 800 volumes. Official school ensembles: chorus, glee club, chamber vocal ensemble, marching band, concert band, jazz ensemble. No summer music school. Special course: Afro-American Music. . . . LINCOLN MEMORIAL UNIVERSITY, Harrogate, Tennessee 37752. Music Department of a university. Head: **Ronnie L. Smith** (1969). Department founded: 1966. School founded: 1897. Degrees: B.A. or B.S. with music major. No music scholarships and fellowships. Music students enrolled: 10. Music library: 300 volumes. Official school ensemble: chorus. No summer music school. . . . MARYVILLE COLLEGE, Maryville, Tennessee 37801. (Member, NASM.) Music is a part of the Department of Fine Arts. Department Chairman: **Harry H. Harter** (1964). School founded 1819. Music Department founded: 1936. Degrees: B.A. with major in music; B.M. with major in music education and applied music. Scholarships: none, but competition awards of $7,200 annually. Music enrollment: 153. Music library: 2,300 volumes. Ensembles: chorus, chamber vocal ensemble, marching band, concert band, opera workshop, symphony orchestra, jazz ensemble. Limited summer courses offered. . . . MEMPHIS STATE UNIVERSITY, Memphis, Tennessee 38111. Music Department of a college within a university. Head: **Robert Snyder** (1965). University founded 1908. Degrees: B.A., B.M., B.M.Ed., M.M., M.A., M.Ed. Scholarships: 200, totaling $42,000. Assistantships: 10 totaling $20,000. Music students enrolled: 350. Music library: 5,000 volumes and 4,000 records. Official school ensembles: chorus, glee club, chamber vocal ensemble, marching band, chamber groups, jazz ensemble. Summer music school. . . . MIDDLE TENNESSEE STATE UNIVERSITY, Murfreesboro, Tennessee 37130. A Department of Music in a state-supported institution. (Member, NASM.) Head: **Neil H. Wright.** Degrees: B.S. with music education major; B.S. with instrumental music education major; B.A. with music major; B.S. with music major. . . . SOUTHERN MISSIONARY COLLEGE, Collegedale, Tennessee 37315. Music Department of a college. Chairman: **Marvin Robertson** (1966). School founded: 1892. Degrees: B.A., B.M.Ed. Scholarships: two, totaling $400. Music students enrolled: 250. Music library: 2,000 volumes. Official school ensembles: chorus, concert band, symphony orchestra. No summer music classes. . . . SOUTHWESTERN AT MEMPHIS, 2000 North Parkway, Memphis, Tennessee 38112. Music Department within a College of Liberal Arts and Sciences of a university supported by the Presbyterian Church. (Member, NASM.) Head: **Charles Mosby** (1969). School founded: 1933. Music Department founded: 1943. Degrees: B.A., B.M. Scholarships: three, totaling $1,600. Music enrollment: 50. Music library: 3,500 volumes. Ensembles: chorus, chamber vocal ensemble, marching band, woodwind quintet, string quartet. Only applied music taught in summer. . . . TENNESSEE WESLEYAN COLLEGE, P.O. Box 40, Athens, Tennessee 37303. Department of Music in the college. Chairman: **Ronald Manley** (1967). School founded: 1857. Degrees: B.A. with major in music; B.S. with major in music education. Scholarships: four at $250 each. Fellowships: six work opportunities. Music students enrolled: 25. Official school ensembles: chorus, glee club, chamber vocal ensemble, concert band. . . . TENNESSEE STATE UNIVERSITY, Nashville, Tennessee 37203. Department of Music within a university. (Member, NASM.) Head: **Edward C. Lewis, Jr.** (1953). University founded: 1912. Music Department founded: 1948. Degrees: B.S. in music education, A.B. Scholarships: 120, totaling $75,000. Fellowships: three, totaling $2,280. Music enrollment: 120. Music library: 8,000. Ensembles: chorus, glee club, marching band, concert band, chamber orchestra, jazz ensemble. Summer music school offered. . . . TENNESSEE TECHNOLOGICAL UNIVERSITY, Cookeville, Tennessee 38501. A Department of Music in the college of education of a state-supported university. (Member, NASM.) Chairman: **James A. Wattenbarger.** Degree: B.S. in music education. . . . TUSCULUM COLLEGE, Greensville, Tennessee 37743. Music Department of a college. Head: **Arnold Thomas** (1962). Music instruction and school founded: 1784. Degree: B.A. with concentration in music. Scholarships: 10 for $3,200 each ($800 per year). Fellowships: 10 for $1,600 each ($400 per year). Music students enrolled: 12. Music library: 900 volumes. Official school ensembles: chorus, glee club, chamber vocal ensemble. Summer school music courses. . . . UNION UNIVERSITY, Jackson, Tennessee 38301. A Department of Music in a liberal arts college related to the Baptist Church. (Member, NASM.) Head, Department of Music: **Kenneth R. Hartley.** Degrees: B.M. in applied music, sacred music, music education; B.A. in music literature. . . . UNIVERSITY OF TENNESSEE AT CHATTANOOGA, Chattanooga, Tennessee 37401. (Member, NASM.) Department of Music within the College of Arts and Sciences. Head: **Peter E. Gerschefski** (1971). School founded: 1886. Music Department founded: 1935. Degrees: B.A., B.M., B.S. (music education). Scholarships: six, totaling $4,168. Music enrollment: 105. Music library: 3,500. Music ensembles: chorus, chamber vocal ensemble, marching band, concert band, chamber orchestra, smaller chamber groups, jazz ensemble. No summer music school. . . . UNIVERSITY OF TENNESSEE, Knoxville Campus, Knoxville, Tennessee 37916. Department of Music in the College of Liberal Arts. (Member, NASM.) Head: **Alfred L. Schmied** (1953). University founded: 1794. Music Department founded: 1947. Degrees: B.M., A.B. with a major in music, M.M., M.A. Scholarships: 366, totaling $35,248. Fellowships: 11, totaling $14,000. Music enrollment: 322 majors. Music library: 11,400 volumes. Ensembles: three choruses, men and women's glee club, chamber vocal ensemble, marching band, concert band, opera workshop, symphony orchestra, woodwind quintet, brass quintet, jazz ensemble, percussion ensemble, University of Tennessee singers. Summer music school; also high school summer camp. Special course in Suzuki Violin Method.

TEXAS

ALVIN JUNIOR COLLEGE, 3110 South Mustang, Alvin, Texas 77511. Music Department of the college. Head: **R. G. Bethke** (1968). School founded: 1949. Scholarships:

16 full for $2,500 a year. Music students enrolled: 250. Music library: 100 volumes. Official school ensembles: chorus, chamber vocal ensemble. No summer music classes. . . . AMARILLO COLLEGE, Box 447, Amarillo, Texas 79105. Department of Music within a junior college. Head: **Robert E. Hoffman.** School founded: 1929. Degrees: A.A., A.S. Scholarships: $3,000. Music enrollment: 35. Music volumes in library: 4,500. Music ensembles: chorus, chamber vocal ensemble, concert band, opera workshop, chamber orchestra, smaller chamber groups. No summer music courses. . . . AUSTIN COLLEGE, Sherman, Texas 75090. Music Department of a college. Head: **Bruce G. Lunkley** (1970). Department founded: 1940. School founded: 1849. Degree: B.A. Scholarships: 10, totaling $4,000. Music students enrolled: 20 majors but about 400 participants in groups, lessons, etc. Music library: 3,500 volumes. Official school ensembles: chorus, concert band, opera workshop, symphony orchestra, also wind/brass ensembles. Summer music school offered periodically. . . . BAYLOR UNIVERSITY, Waco, Texas 76703. Music college within a university supported by the Baptist Convention of Texas. (Member, NASM.) Dean: **Daniel Sternberg.** University founded: 1845. Music College founded: 1900. Degrees: B.M., B.M.E., M.M., B.A. Scholarships and fellowships: figures not available. Music enrollment: 360. Music library: 35,000 volumes. Ensembles: chorus, three glee clubs, chamber vocal ensemble, marching band, concert band, opera workshop, symphony orchestra, chamber orchestra, smaller chamber groups, jazz ensemble. Summer music school offered. . . . BEE COUNTY COLLEGE, Route 1, Beeville, Texas 78102. Music Department of a college. Head: **Everett McAulay** (1967). Department and school founded: 1965. No music degrees offered. Scholarships: 20, totaling $2,000. Music students enrolled: 15 to 20. Music library: 150 volumes (excluding scores and records). Official school ensembles: chorus, chamber vocal ensemble, jazz ensemble. No summer music school. . . . DALLAS BAPTIST COLLEGE, P.O. 21206, Dallas, Texas 75211. A Music Department within the college. Head: **Wesley S. Coffman** (1969). College founded in 1891; Music Department in 1965. Degrees: B.A., B.S. Scholarships: 50, totaling $20,000. Music enrollment: 130. Music library: 10,000 volumes. Ensembles: chorus, chamber orchestra, and jazz ensemble. Music instruction is offered in the summer. . . . DEL MAR COLLEGE, Baldwin and Ayers, Corpus Christi, Texas 78404. Department of Music in the Division of Fine Arts of a public community college. (Member, NASM.) Dean, Division of Fine Arts: **L. W. Chidester.** College founded: 1938. Music Department founded: 1945. Degree: A.A. Music enrollment: 290. Music library: 2,000 volumes. Ensembles: chorus, chamber vocal ensemble, concert band, opera workshop, chamber orchestra, smaller chamber groups. . . . DOMINICAN COLLEGE, 2401 East Holcombe, Houston, Texas 77021. Music Department within the college. Head: **Sister M. Ernest Schwerdtfeger** (1962). College and department founded: 1946. Degrees: B.A. Scholarships: eight, totaling $8,000. Music students enrolled: 25. Volumes in music library: 3,000. Official school ensembles: chorus, chamber vocal ensemble, opera workshop, other smaller chamber groups. Summer music instruction. . . . EAST TEXAS STATE UNIVERSITY, East Texas Station, Commerce, Texas 75428. Music Department of the College of Arts and Sciences. Head: **James Richards.** School founded: 1918. Degrees offered: B.S., B.M.Ed., B.A., B.M., M.S., M.A., M.M., Ed.M. Scholarships: number varies each year ($10,500 to $15,000). Fellowships: 14, for $2,700 each. Music students enrolled: 200. Official school ensembles: three choruses, chamber vocal ensemble, marching band, concert band, opera workshop, symphony orchestra, jazz ensemble. Summer music school. Special course: electronic music. . . . GULF COAST BIBLE COLLEGE, 911 West 11th, Houston, Texas 77008. Music Department of the college. Head: **Robert Adams** (1957). Department founded: 1957. School founded: 1953. Degrees: B.A. with major in voice, piano, organ; Bachelor of Sacred Music. Scholarships: indeterminate number. Music students enrolled: about 25 majors but over 100 involved in some music studies. Music library: 425

volumes. Official school ensembles: *a cappella* choir, oratorio chorus, chamber vocal ensemble. No summer music school at present. . . . HARDIN–SIMMONS UNIVERSITY, Abilene, Texas 79601. A university school, part of an endowed university. (Member, NASM.) Dean: **Talmage W. Dean.** Degrees: B.M. in applied music, theory and composition, music education, church music; B.A. in applied music; M.M. in theory and composition, applied literature, music education. Music majors: 115. . . . HILL JUNIOR COLLEGE, P.O. Box 619, Hillsboro, Texas 76645. Music is in the Department of Music and Fine Arts. Head: **Walt Paul** (1969). Department and school founded: 1961. Degrees: A.A., certificate of completion. Scholarships: 30, totaling approximately $6,000 a year. Music students enrolled: 50. Music library: 500 volumes. Official school ensembles: chorus, chamber vocal ensemble, concert band, jazz ensemble, stage band. No summer music instruction. . . . HOWARD COUNTY JUNIOR COLLEGE, Birdwell Lane and 11th Place, Big Spring, Texas 79720. A Music Department within a two-year college. Head: **Ralph D. Dowden** (1970). Music has been offered since the school's founding in 1946. Degree: A.A. Scholarships: about 50, totaling $2,800. Music enrollment: 62. Volumes in music library: 650. Ensembles: chorus, jazz ensemble. . . . HOUSTON BAPTIST COLLEGE, 7502 Fondren Road, Houston, Texas 77036. A Music Department within the college. Head: **R. Paul Green** (1967). School and Music Department founded in 1963. Degree: B.A. with a major in music or music education. Scholarships: 100, totaling $45,000. Music enrollment: 100. Volumes in music library: 2,132 catalogued; 340 uncatalogued; 1,622 recordings. Ensembles: chorus, chamber vocal ensemble, concert band, opera workshop, chamber orchestra, chamber groups, jazz group. No summer music school. . . . INCARNATE WORD COLLEGE, San Antonio, Texas 78209. A Department of Music of a college supported by the Catholic Church. (Member, NASM.) Chairman: **Sister Patricia O'Donnell.** Degree: B.M. in applied music, music education. Music majors: 20. . . . LAMAR STATE COLLEGE OF TECHNOLOGY, Beaumont, Texas 77705. A Department of Music in a state-supported college. (Member, NASM.) Chairman: **George L. Parks.** Degree: B.S. in music education and performance. . . . LUBBOCK CHRISTIAN COLLEGE, 5601-19th Street, Lubbock, Texas 79407. A Music Department within the college. Head: **B. Wayne Hinds** (1957). School and Music Department founded in 1957. Degrees: B.A. in music; B.S. in music education. Scholarships: 45, totaling $5,000. Enrollment: 35 music majors. Music library: 800. Ensembles: three choruses, concert band, jazz ensemble, and a piano ensemble. Summer instruction is the Lubbock Christian College Music Camp. . . . MARY HARDIN-BAYLOR COLLEGE, Mary Hardin-Baylor Station, Belton, Texas 76513. Department of Music within a college. (Member, NASM.) Head: **Roy W. Hedges** (1967). School and Music Department founded: 1845. Degrees: B.A., B.M.Ed. Scholarships: total $2,000. Music enrollment: 25. Music library: 500. Ensembles: chorus, chamber vocal ensemble. Limited summer school. . . . MIDWESTERN UNIVERSITY, Wichita Falls, Texas 76302. Department of Music, part of the School of Humanities and Social Sciences in a state-supported university. (Member, NASM.) Head: **Gene Brooks** (1969). University founded: 1922. Music Department founded: 1936. Degrees: B.M., B.M.Ed., M.M., M.M.Ed. Scholarships: 20, totaling $4,000. Fellowships: six for $2,700 each. Music enrollment: 125. Music library: 2,000 volumes. Ensembles: two choruses, chamber vocal ensemble, marching band, concert band, opera workshop, symphony orchestra, chamber orchestra, jazz ensemble. Summer music school offered. . . . NORTH TEXAS STATE UNIVERSITY, Denton, Texas 76203. School of Music within a university. (Member, NASM.) Dean: **Kenneth N. Cuthbert** (1958). University and School of Music founded: 1890. Degrees: B.M., B.A. with major in music, M.M., M.M.Ed., M.A. with major in music, Ph.D., D.M.A., Ed.D. Scholarships: 168, totaling $36,000. Fellowships: 70, totaling $227,548. Music enrollment: 1,176. Music library: 50,000 volumes. Ensembles: five choruses; chamber vocal ensemble; marching band; concert band; opera workshop; symphony orchestra; chamber orchestra; smaller chamber groups; jazz ensemble; wind, percussion, and brass ensembles; Collegium Musicum. Summer music school. Special courses in electronic music, dance band, radio–TV, film music. . . . ODESSA COLLEGE, P.O. Box 3752, Odessa, Texas 79760. Music Department in the Fine Arts Division of a state-supported junior college. (Member, NASM.) Chairman: **Jack W. Hendrix** (1965). College founded: 1946. Department founded: 1964. Degree: A.A. Scholarships: 20, totaling $2,400. Music students enrolled: 75. Volumes in music library: 300. Official school ensembles: chorus, chamber vocal ensemble, concert band, opera workshop, jazz ensemble, other smaller chamber groups. Summer music school. . . . OUR LADY OF THE LAKE COLLEGE, San Antonio, Texas 78207. A Department of Music in a liberal arts college conducted by the Sisters of Divine Providence. (Member, NASM.) Chairman: **Sister Lucy Marie.** Degrees: B.M. in applied music; B.A. in music; B.M.Ed. Music majors: 30. . . . PAN AMERICAN UNIVERSITY, 1201 West Harriman, Edinburg, Texas 78539. Music Department within the university. Head: **John D. Anderson** (1965). School founded: 1927. Degree: B.A. Scholarships: 126 (including work–study aids), totaling $18,000. Music students enrolled: 100. Music library: 950 volumes. Official school ensembles: two choruses, three chamber vocal ensembles, concert band, opera workshop, symphony orchestra, chamber orchestra. Summer music school. . . . SAM HOUSTON STATE UNIVERSITY, Huntsville, Texas 77340. Music Department of the university. (Member, NASM.) Director: **Fisher A. Tull** (1965). Department founded: 1939. School founded: 1879. Degrees: B.M.Ed., B.M., M.A. in music. Scholarships: about 150, totaling $25,000 per year. Fellowships: about eight, totaling $19,000 per year. Music students enrolled: 280. Music library: 16,000 volumes. Official school ensembles: five choruses, chamber vocal ensemble, marching band, two concert bands, opera workshop, symphony orchestra, chamber orchestra, chamber groups, jazz ensemble. Summer music school. . . . SAN ANTONIO COLLEGE, 1300 San Pedro Avenue, San Antonio, Texas 78212. A Music Department within a two-year community college. Head: **Marjorie T. Walthall** (1951). College founded in 1926. Music Department founded in 1951. Degree: A.A. Scholarships: 10, totaling $3,000 and covering all instruction costs for students. Enrollment in music: 600 (majors, minors, and music elective course students). Ensembles: three choruses, glee club, chamber vocal ensemble, concert band, opera workshop, Baroque ensemble, and recorder consort. Music courses are taught in the summer. . . . SOUTH TEXAS JUNIOR COLLEGE, One Main Street, Houston, Texas 77002. Music Department within the Division of Fine Arts. Head: **David A. Knickel** (1971). College founded: 1948. Department founded: 1971. Degree: A.A. Scholarships: two, totaling $1,000. Volumes in music library: 5,000. Official school ensembles: chorus, chamber vocal ensemble, pit orchestra, jazz ensemble. No summer music school. . . . SOUTHERN METHODIST UNIVERSITY, Dallas, Texas 75222. Music is a division within The Meadows School of the Arts of the university. (Member, NASM.) Chairman: **Eugene Bonelli** (1969). University founded: 1915. Music School founded: 1963. Degrees: B.M., M.M., B.A. in music. Scholarships: 80 to 100, totaling $75,000. Fellowships: 15 to 20, totaling $35,000. Music enrollment: 250. Music library: 15,000 volumes. Ensembles: chorus, marching band, concert band, opera workshop, symphony orchestra, chamber orchestra, smaller chamber groups, jazz ensemble, percussion ensemble. Summer music school offered. Special courses in arts administration and classical guitar. . . . SOUTHWEST TEXAS STATE UNIVERSITY, San Marcos, Texas 78666. Music Department within a college of the university. Head: **Arlis Hiebert** (1971). University founded: 1903. Degrees: B.M.Ed., M.Ed. Scholarships: 80, totaling $12,000. Music students enrolled: 100 majors, 125 minors. Volumes in music library: 4,600 books and scores; 1,500 records. Official school ensembles: chorus, chamber vocal ensemble, marching band, concert band, opera workshop. Summer music instruction. . . . SOUTHWESTERN BAPTIST THEOLOGICAL SEMINARY, Box 22,000, Fort Worth, Texas 76122. School of Music within a theological seminary supported by the Southern Baptist Convention. (Member, NASM.) Dean: **James C. McKinney** (1956). School of Music founded: 1915. Seminary founded: 1908. Music degrees: Bachelor of Church Music, Master of Church Music, Doctor of Musical Arts. Scholarships: 20, totaling $9,000. Music library: 11,000 books, 12,000 scores, 5,000 records, 15,000 anthems. Official school ensembles: chorus, glee club, chamber vocal ensemble, opera workshop, brass ensemble. Summer music school offered. Special courses: music in Missions course, and extensive church music offerings. . . . SOUTHWESTERN UNIVERSITY, Georgetown, Texas 78626. A School of Fine Arts in a college supported by the Texas Conferences of the Methodist Church. (Member, NASM.) Dean: **John D. Richards.** Degrees: B.M. in applied music, church music, B.M.Ed. Music majors: 49. . . . STEPHEN F. AUSTIN STATE UNIVERSITY, Nacogdoches, Texas 75961. A Music Department within the School of Fine Arts of the university. Head: **M. E. Hall** (1967). University and Music Department founded in 1923. Degrees: B.F.A. with a major in music; B.M. Scholarships: 80 to 100, totaling $12,000. Fellowships: six to nine, totaling $10,500. Music enrollment: 1,300 plus 800 music majors and minors. Music library: 3,600 volumes exclusive of music periodicals. Ensembles: chorus, chamber vocal ensemble, marching band, concert band, opera workshop, chamber orchestra, jazz ensemble, brass and percussion ensembles. Summer music courses are offered. . . . TARRANT COUNTY JUNIOR COLLEGE, 5301 Campus Drive, Fort Worth, Texas 76119. Music Department within a college. Head: **Leonard McCormick** (1969). Department and school founded: 1967. Has a two-year program. Scholarships: limited number for tuition. Music students enrolled: 70 music majors, 350 to 400 taking music courses. Music library: 4,900 volumes. Official school ensembles: chorus, glee club, chamber vocal ensemble, concert band, jazz ensemble. Summer music school offered. . . . TEMPLE JUNIOR COLLEGE, 2601 South First, Temple, Texas 76501. Music Department of college. Head: **Mary Alice Marshall** (1955). Department and school founded: 1926. Scholarships: 25, totaling $2,000. Music students enrolled: 150. Music library: 500 volumes and 456 records. Official school ensembles: chorus, chamber vocal ensemble, concert band, jazz ensemble. No summer music instruction. . . . TEXAS ARTS AND INDUSTRIES UNIVERSITY, Kingsville, Texas 68363. Music Department of a state-supported university. (Member, NASM.) Head: **Thomas C. Pierson** (1966). Department founded: 1928. School founded: 1925. Degrees: B.M., B.A., M.M., M.A. Scholarships: undetermined. Fellowships: undetermined. Music students enrolled: 135 music majors. Official school ensembles: chorus, chamber vocal ensemble, marching band, concert band, opera workshop, symphony orchestra. Summer music school. . . . TEXAS CHRISTIAN UNIVERSITY, Fort Worth, Texas 76129. A Department of Music in a School of Fine Arts of a church-supported university. (Member, NASM.) Head: **Michael Winesanker** (1956). University founded in 1873. Degrees: B.A., B.M., B.M.Ed., M.A., M.M., M.M.Ed., M.A.T. (Master of Arts in Teaching). Enrollment: 175 music majors. Ensembles: chorus, chamber vocal ensemble, marching band, concert band, opera workshop, symphony orchestra, chamber orchestra, jazz ensemble. Music is taught in summer. . . . TEXAS SOUTHERN UNIVERSITY, 3201 Wheeler, Houston, Texas 77004. A Music Department within the university. Head: **Jack C. Bradley** (1967). Degrees: B.M., B.M.Ed., M.M.Ed., M.Mus. Music enrollment: 130. Ensembles: chorus, chamber vocal ensemble, marching band, concert band, opera workshop, small jazz ensemble, large stage band. Summer music courses offered. . . . TEXAS TECHNOLOGICAL UNIVERSITY, Lubbock, Texas 79409. Department of Music within the College of Arts and Sciences in a state university. (Member, NASM.) Chairman: **Gene Hemmle** (1949). School and Music Department founded: 1923. Degrees:

B.M., B.M.Ed., M.M., M.M.Ed. Scholarships and fellowships: variable amounts. Music enrollment: 1,500. Music library: 12,500 volumes approximately. Ensembles: chorus, chamber vocal ensemble, marching band, concert band, opera workshop symphony orchestra, chamber orchestra, smaller chamber groups, jazz ensemble, Collegium Musicum. Summer music school offered. . . . TEXAS WOMAN'S UNIVERSITY, Box 23865, TWU Station, Denton, Texas 76204. A Department of Music in a College of Fine Arts in a state-supported university. (Member, NASM.) Dean of Fine Arts: **J. Wilgus Eberly** (1969). The university and the Music Department were founded in 1902. Degrees: B.A., B.S., M.A., in applied music, music education, music therapy, church music, and theory. Scholarships: 30, ranging in value from $100 to $500 each. Fellowships: seven for $2,500 each. Music enrollment: 1,000, with 125 music majors. Music library: 5,000 volumes. Ensembles: chorus, choir, concert band, opera workshop, chamber orchestra, jazz ensemble, and a popular vocal group. Music is offered in summer. Special course in music therapy is offered. . . . TEXAS WESLEYAN COLLEGE, P.O. Box 3277, Fort Worth, Texas 76105. Music Department of the Division of Fine Arts of a liberal arts college, supported by the Methodist Church. (Member, NASM.) Head: **Donald W. Bellah** (1940). School founded: 1891. Degree: B.M. in music education. Scholarships: various. Ensembles: chorus, *a cappella* vocal choir, concert band, opera workshop, chamber orchestra, lab band. No summer school. . . . TRINITY UNIVERSITY, 715 Stadium Drive, San Antonio, Texas 78212. A Music Department within a college of the university. Head: **William Thornton** (1961). University founded in 1869. Degrees: B.A. in music, B.M., M.A. in music. Scholarships include work grants and general scholarships only. No fellowships. Music enrollment: 575; 60 music majors. Music library: 4,500 volumes. Ensembles: chorus, chamber vocal ensembles, marching band, concert band, opera workshop, symphony orchestra, Collegium Musicum. Summer music courses are taught. . . . UNIVERSITY OF CORPUS CHRISTI, P.O. Box 6010, Corpus Christi, Texas 78411. Music Department of a college within the university. Head: **Melton B. James** (1964). Department founded: 1950. School founded: 1947. Degrees offered: B.A. in music. Scholarships: number varies—about 20, totaling $5,000. No music fellowships. Music library: 1,000 volumes. Official school ensembles: chamber vocal ensemble, chamber groups, jazz ensemble. Summer music school. . . . UNIVERSITY OF HOUSTON, Cullen Boulevard, Houston, Texas 77004. A School of Music in a college of arts and sciences of a state university. (Member, NASM.) Director: **Robert L. Briggs** (1969). School of Music and university founded: 1927. Degrees: B.M. (performance, theory, composition, literature, music education); A.B., major in music; M.M. (theory, performance, composition, music literature). Scholarships: 180, totaling $20,822. Fellowships: five, totaling $12,150. Music enrollment: 371. Music library: 3,000 books; 7,500 scores, 80 periodicals. Ensembles: two choruses, marching band, two concert bands, opera workshop, symphony orchestra, chamber orchestra, 20 to 25 smaller chamber groups. Summer music school offered. . . . UNIVERSITY OF ST. THOMAS, 3812 Montrose Boulevard, Houston, Texas 77006. Music Department within the university. Chairman: **Carl R. Cunningham** (1971). University founded: 1947. Music Department founded: 1966. Degree: B.A. with major in music. Scholarships: number varies. Music library: 3,200 records; 400 tapes; 675 books; 1,000 scores. Official school ensembles: chorus, chamber vocal ensemble, jazz ensemble, Collegium Musicum, madrigal singers. Summer music instruction. . . . THE UNIVERSITY OF TEXAS AT AUSTIN, Austin, Texas 78712. Music Department within the College of Fine Arts within the University of Texas system. (Member, NASM.) Head: **Robert E. Bays** (1969). University founded: 1881. Department founded: 1938. Degrees: B.A., B.Mus., M.Mus., D.M.A., Ph.D. Scholarships: 65, totaling $16,000. Fellowships: 50, totaling $102,000. Music students enrolled: 600. Volumes in music library: 27,000 (see Music Libraries). Official school ensembles: chorus, glee club, concert band, opera workshop, symphony orchestra, jazz ensemble. Summer music instruction. Special courses: Fine Arts Administration, Composition in Electronic Media, Piano and Organ Technology. . . . UNIVERSITY OF TEXAS AT EL PASO, El Paso, Texas 79968. Music Department of the university. Head: **Olav Elling Eidbo** (1965). Department founded: 1949. School founded: 1915. Degrees offered: B.M. in applied music, theory, music education. Scholarships: 150, totaling $30,000. No music fellowships. Music students enrolled: 160 majors (numerous non-majors). Music library: 3,168 volumes. Official school ensembles: chorus, glee club, marching band, concert band, opera workshop, symphony orchestra, chamber groups, jazz ensemble. Summer music school. Special courses: voice building, opera production. . . . WEST TEXAS STATE UNIVERSITY, Canyon, Texas 79015. A Department of Music in a School of Fine Arts in a state-supported university. (Member, NASM.) Dean: **John E. Green.** Degrees: B.M.Ed., B.M. in applied music, M.A., M.A. in music education. Music majors: 250. . . . WHARTON COUNTY JUNIOR COLLEGE, Boling Highway, Wharton, Texas 77488. A Music Department within the college. Head: **Robert O. Cody** (1968), Chairman of Fine Arts Division. Music Department founded in 1946. Degrees: Associate in Arts, Associate in Science. General scholarships: 80, totaling $8,000. Music enrollment: 200. Library: 20,000 volumes. Ensembles: chorus, chamber vocal ensemble, marching band, concert band. No summer music instruction.

UTAH

BRIGHAM YOUNG UNIVERSITY, Provo, Utah 84601. A department of the College of Fine Arts in a university supported by the Church of Jesus Christ of Latter-Day Saints. (Member, NASM.) Chairman: **A. Harold Goodman.** Degrees: B.A. in applied music, music education, theory; B.M. in music education; M.M. in applied music; M.A. in music education, music theory, musicology. Music majors: 500. . . . COLLEGE OF EASTERN UTAH, 857 North 6th East, Price, Utah 84501. Music Department within a college. Head: **Derral L. Siggard** (1970). Degrees: A.A., A.S. Scholarships: 10. Music enrollment: 300. Volumes in music library: 2,000. Official school ensembles: chorus, chamber vocal ensemble, marching band, concert band, small chamber groups, jazz ensemble. No summer music school. . . . SOUTHERN UTAH STATE COLLEGE, Cedar City, Utah 84720. Music Department within a college. Head: **Blaine Johnson** (1970). Department founded: 1925. School founded: 1897. Music degrees: B.A., B.S. Music scholarships: 20, totaling $5,500. Fellowships: three, totaling $3,000. Music students enrolled: 115 to 150. Music library: 650 volumes. Official school ensembles: chorus, chamber vocal ensemble, marching band, concert band, opera workshop, symphony orchestra, chamber groups, chamber orchestra, jazz ensemble. Summer music school offered. . . . UNIVERSITY OF UTAH, Salt Lake City, Utah 84112. Department of Music within the College of Fine Arts. (Member, NASM.) Head: **Newell B. Weight** (1968). University founded: 1850. Music Department founded: 1888. Degrees: B.M., M.S., M.A., M.M., Ph.D. (musicology, composition, music education). Scholarships: 20, totaling $5,000. Fellowships: 10, totaling $15,000. Ensembles: chorus, glee club, chamber vocal ensemble, marching band, concert band, opera workshop, symphony orchestra, chamber orchestra, smaller chamber groups, and jazz ensemble. Summer music workshops. . . . WESTMINSTER COLLEGE, 1840 South 13th East Street, Salt Lake City, Utah, 84105. Music Department of a college. Head: **Kenneth Kuchler** (1954). School founded: 1875. Degrees offered: B.S. and B.A. in music; B.S. and B.A. in music education. Scholarships: varying amounts. Official school ensembles: chorus, chamber vocal ensemble, concert band, symphony orchestra, jazz ensemble, chamber groups, Baroque ensembles. Occasional summer music courses.

VERMONT

LYNDON STATE COLLEGE, Lyndonville, Vermont 05851. A Music Department within the college. Head: **Peter M. Brown** (1960). College founded in 1911. Degree: B.S. in music education. No scholarships in music. Music enrollment: 45. Volumes in music library: 5,000. Official ensembles: chorus, chamber vocal ensemble, concert band, symphony orchestra, chamber orchestra, smaller instrumental groups. . . . UNIVERSITY OF VERMONT, Burlington, Vermont 05401. A Department of Music in the College of Arts and Sciences of a state-supported institution. (Member, NASM.) Chairman: **Frank W. Lidral.** Degrees: B.A. in music; B.S. in music education; M.A. in music; M.A. in teaching. Music majors: 60.

VIRGINIA

BLUE RIDGE COMMUNITY COLLEGE, Box 80, Weyers Cave, Virginia 22486. Music is taught within the Humanities Department. Music library: 100 volumes. Summer courses in music appreciation. . . . BRIDGEWATER COLLEGE, Bridgewater, Virginia 22812. Music Department within the college. Head: **Philip E. Trout** (1965). College founded: 1880. Department founded: 1890. Degrees: B.A. in music or music education. No scholarships. Music students enrolled: 30. Volumes in music library: 4,000. Official school ensembles: chorus, glee club, chamber vocal ensemble, concert band, chamber orchestra, jazz ensemble. Summer music school for high school students. . . . CLINCH VALLEY COLLEGE OF THE UNIVERSITY OF VIRGINIA, Wise, Virginia 24293. Music is taught as an area of study in the Humanities Department. Head of Humanities: **Judd Lewis** (1969). Head, Music Area: **Diedre Brantley** (1969). College founded in 1954. No scholarships in music offered. Music enrollment: 40. Music library: 250 volumes. Ensembles: chorus. No summer music instruction. . . . THE COLLEGE OF WILLIAM AND MARY IN VIRGINIA, Williamsburg, Virginia 23185. A Department of Music in the college. Chairman: **F. Donald Truesdell** (1960). The college was founded in 1693. Degrees: B.A. in music, B.A. in music education. No music scholarships. Music enrollment: 20 to 25. Music library: 4,500. Ensembles: chorus, choir, marching band, concert band, chamber orchestra, jazz ensemble. Summer music courses are offered. . . . EASTERN MENNONITE COLLEGE, Harrisonburg, Virginia 22801. Music Department of the college. Head: **Ira Zook** (1971). Department founded: 1951. School founded: 1917. Degrees offered: B.A. and B.A. in music education. No music scholarships or fellowships. Music students enrolled: 19 music majors. Music library: 400 volumes. Official school ensembles: five choruses, chamber orchestra. No summer music courses. . . . HOLLINS COLLEGE, Hollins College, Virginia 24020. A Department of Music of an endowed college. (Member, NASM.) Chairman: **John Diercks.** Degree: B.A. in applied music, history and literature, theory and composition. Music majors: 25. Music library: about 5,000 volumes. . . . LYNCHBURG COLLEGE, Lynchburg, Virginia 24504. A Music Department within the college. Head: **Robert Ellinwood** (1970). College founded: 1903; Music Department founded: 1946. Degrees: B.A. in music. Current fellowships: five, totaling $3,000. Music enrollment: 30 majors; 200 music students in all. Music library: 3,000 volumes. Ensembles: chorus, chamber vocal ensembles, concert band, opera workshop. No summer music courses. . . . MADISON COLLEGE, Harrisonburg, Virginia 22801. A Department of Music in a state-supported college. (Member, NASM.) Head: **Gordon L. Ohlsson.** Degrees: B.A., B.M.Ed., M.A. in education. . . . MARY WASHINGTON COLLEGE OF THE UNIVERSITY OF VIRGINIA, University of Virginia, Fredericksburg, Virginia 22401. A Music Department in the woman's college of the university, a state-supported institution. (Member, NASM.) Chairman: **George E. Luntz** (1957). University and college founded: 1908. Degree: B.A. Music students enrolled: 225. Official school ensembles: chorus, concert band. . . . OLD DOMINION UNIVERSITY, Norfolk, Virginia 23508.

Music Department of a college of the university. Head: **Harold Hawn** (1964). Department founded: 1931. School founded: 1930. Degrees offered: A.B., B.S. in music; B.S. in secondary education with concentration in secondary vocal or instrumental or elementary vocal. Scholarships: eight, totaling $3,400. Music students enrolled: 90. Music library: 2,508 volumes. Official school ensembles: chorus, chamber vocal ensemble, concert band, opera workshop, chamber orchestra, jazz ensemble. Summer music school. . . . RADFORD COLLEGE, Radford, Virginia 24141. A Music Department within the college. Head: **Norman Todenhoft** (1968). College founded in 1913; Music Department in 1914. Degrees: B.S., B.A., M.S., M.A., all with majors in theory, music history, applied music, etc. No scholarships in music. Music enrollment: 125. Music library: 5,000 books; 3,000 recordings. Ensembles: chorus, glee club, marching band, concert band, chamber orchestra, jazz ensemble, woodwind chamber groups. Summer courses are offered in music. . . . SHENANDOAH CONSERVATORY OF MUSIC, Millwood Avenue, Winchester, Virginia, 22601. Conservatory with an affiliation with Shenandoah Junior College. (Member, NASM.) Dean: **Verne E. Collins.** School founded: 1875. Degrees offered: B.M., B.M.Ed., B.M. in church music. Scholarships: 35, totaling $12,000. Fellowships: 15, totaling $7,000. Music students enrolled: 260. Official school ensembles: two choruses, glee club, chamber vocal ensemble, two concert bands, opera workshop, symphony orchestra, chamber orchestra, smaller chamber groups, two jazz ensembles. Summer music school. . . . SOUTHERN SEMINARY JUNIOR COLLEGE, Buena Vista, Virginia 24416. Music Department of the Fine Arts Division of the college. Head: **H. Grady Deas** (1970). School founded: 1867. No music degrees. Scholarship: one, amount unspecified. Music students enrolled: 80. Music library: 100 volumes. Official school ensembles: glee club. No summer music school. . . . STRATFORD COLLEGE, Danville, Virginia 24541. Music Department within the college. Head: **John C. Atwood** (1968). College founded: 1852. Degrees: B.A. in music, major in piano or voice. Scholarships: $2,000 total. Music students enrolled: 15. Volumes in music library: 500 to 1,000. Official school ensembles: chorus, chamber vocal ensemble. Summer instruction in applied music. . . . UNIVERSITY OF RICHMOND, Richmond, Virginia 23173. Music Department within the University. Head: **Suzanne Kidd** (1970). University founded: 1830. Degree: B.A. Scholarships: one for $300. Music students enrolled: 400. Volumes in music library: 2,000 scores, 800 books. Official school ensembles: chorus, glee club, marching band, concert band, chamber orchestra. No summer music school. . . . VIRGINIA COMMONWEALTH UNIVERSITY, 901 W. Franklin Street, Richmond, Virginia 23220. (Member, NASM.) A Music Division in the School of the Arts. Head: **Charles J. Campbell** (1970). University founded: 1926. Music Department founded: 1970. Degrees: B.M., M.M., M.M.Ed. Music scholarships: 18. Assistantships: seven. Music enrollment 225. Music library: 2,500 volumes. Music ensembles: chorus, chamber vocal ensemble, concert band, opera workshop, chamber orchestra, jazz ensemble. Summer music school. . . . VIRGINIA INTERMONT COLLEGE, Bristol, Virginia 24201. Department of Music within the Fine Arts Division of a college. (Member, NASM.) Chairman of Fine Arts Division: **Charles G. Tedford** (1970). School founded: 1884. Degrees: B.A. in music (with applied majors in voice, piano, organ, harpsichord); Teacher Certificate in elementary and secondary vocal music. Scholarships: seven, totaling $2,200. Music enrollment: 25 majors. Music library: 1,000 volumes. Ensembles: chorus, three chamber vocal ensembles. Special courses in music education for the elementary classroom teacher. . . . VIRGINIA STATE COLLEGE, Petersburg, Virginia 23803. Music Department within the School of Education of the college. (Member, NASM.) Head: **F. Nathaniel Gatlin** (1954). College founded: 1882. Department of Music founded: 1921. Degrees: B.S., B.M., M.S., M.Ed. Scholarships: 50, totaling $20,000. Fellowships: one for $1,800. Music library: 1,705 volumes in main library; 200 in department library. Ensembles: chorus, glee club, marching band, concert band, opera workshop, symphony orchestra, small chamber groups, jazz ensemble, woodwind quintet, brass ensemble. Summer music school offered. . . . VIRGINIA WESTERN COMMUNITY COLLEGE, 3095 Colonial Avenue S.W., Roanoke, Virginia 24015. Music Department of the college. Head: **Robert G. Banks** (1970). Department founded: 1970. School founded: 1966. Degrees offered: A.A. No music scholarships. Music students enrolled: 25. Music library: 600 volumes. Official school ensembles: chorus, chamber vocal ensemble, chamber groups, jazz ensemble. No summer music school. . . . WASHINGTON AND LEE UNIVERSITY, Lexington, Virginia 24450. Music and Drama Department of the college. Head: **Robert Stewart** (1970). School founded: 1749. No music degrees offered. Music students enrolled: 100. Music library: 3,000 volumes. Official school ensembles: glee club, brass choir. No summer music courses.

WASHINGTON

BELLEVUE COMMUNITY COLLEGE, 3000 145th Place, South East, Bellevue, Washington 98007. Music Department within the Humanities Division, within the college. Head: **Kae Hutchison** (1968). College and department founded: 1966. Degree: A.A. No music scholarships; some general aid available. Music students enrolled: 15 majors, 175 non-majors. Volumes in music library: 400. Official school ensembles: chorus, chamber vocal ensembles, other small instrumental ensembles. No summer music school. . . . CENTRAL WASHINGTON STATE COLLEGE, Ellensburg, Washington 98926. A Department of Music in a state college. (Member, NASM.) Chairman: **Wayne S. Hertz.** Degrees: B.A. in education, major in music education; B.A. in arts and science, major in music; M.A. in arts and science, major in music; M.M.Ed., major in music education. . . . CLARK COLLEGE, 1800 McLoughlin Boulevard, Vancouver, Washington 98663. Music Department within a college. Head: **W. Lee Mack** (1960). Degree: A.A. Scholarships: six for $50 each. Music students enrolled: 250 (45 majors). Volumes in music library: 2,500. Official school ensembles: chorus, chamber vocal ensemble, concert band, jazz ensemble, other smaller chamber groups. Summer music instruction. . . . CORNISH SCHOOL OF ALLIED ARTS, 710 East Roy Street, Seattle, Washington 98102. A school of music, art, and design. President: **Fred Patterson.** School founded in 1914. It offers diploma courses in music, art, and design. Scholarships: five, totaling $1,000. Music enrollment: 400 part-time, 25 full-time. Music library: 500 volumes. Ensembles: chorus, opera workshop, chamber orchestra, smaller chamber groups, jazz ensemble. Summer music school is offered, in particular a chamber music workshop. . . . EASTERN WASHINGTON STATE COLLEGE, Cheney, Washington 99004. Department of Music within the Division of Creative Arts in a state-supported institution. (Member, NASM.) Head: **George W. Lotzenhiser** (1960). School founded: 1885. Music department founded: 1900. Degrees: B.A. in music, music education; M.A. in music, theory, performance, composition, music education; M.Ed. in music education. Scholarships: 10, totaling $800. Fellowships: seven, totaling $18,900. Music enrollment: 225. Music library: 5,254. Ensembles: two choruses, three chamber vocal ensembles, concert band, opera workshop, symphony orchestra, chamber orchestra, string quartet, woodwind quintet, jazz ensemble. High school creative arts summer series. . . . EVERETT COMMUNITY COLLEGE, 801 Wetmore Avenue, Everett, Washington 98201. Music Department within a college. Head: **John D. Shawger.** Department founded: 1941. Degree: A.A. No music scholarships. Music students enrolled: 60. Volumes in music library: 1,500. Official school ensembles: chorus, chamber vocal ensemble, concert band, symphony orchestra, jazz ensemble. Limited summer instruction. . . . FORT WRIGHT COLLEGE OF THE HOLY NAMES, West 4000 Randolph Road, Spokane, Washington 99204. Department within a liberal arts college. Head: **Sister Flavia Bauer** (1965). School and department founded: 1938. Degrees: B.A., B.F.A. Scholarships: total $1,500. Music students enrolled: 20 majors. Volumes in music library: 34,000. Official school ensembles: chorus, chamber vocal ensemble, other smaller chamber groups. Limited summer instruction. . . . GREEN RIVER COMMUNITY COLLEGE, 12401 South East 320th, Auburn, Washington 98002. Department within a college. Head: **Bernard Bleha** (1968). Scholarships: number varies; total $1,700. Music students enrolled: 250. Official school ensembles: chorus, chamber vocal ensemble, concert band, opera workshop, chamber orchestra, jazz ensemble. Special courses: advanced jazz composition and arranging. No summer music school. . . . HIGHLINE COMMUNITY COLLEGE, Midway, Washington 98031. Music Department within a college. Department founded: 1963. No music degrees. Scholarships: four. Music students enrolled: 12. Volumes in music library: 200. Official school ensembles: chorus, chamber vocal ensemble, concert band, jazz ensemble, other smaller groups. No summer music courses. . . . SEATTLE PACIFIC COLLEGE, Seattle, Washington 98119. School of Music functions as one of 22 departments within the college. Director: **Wayne H. Balch** (1966). College founded: 1891. Degree: B.A. with music major. Scholarships: 15 to 20, totaling $8,000. Music students enrolled: 80 majors; 700 to 800 enrolled in some music courses. Volumes in music library: 3,000. Official school ensembles: chorus, glee club, chamber vocal ensemble, concert band, symphony orchestra, other smaller chamber groups. Limited summer instruction. . . . UNIVERSITY OF PUGET SOUND, Tacoma, Washington 98416. A School of Music, part of an endowed university. (Member, NASM.) Director: **Bruce Rodgers.** Degrees: B.A. in applied music; B.M. in applied music, theory and composition, school music, church music; M.M. in music education, applied music, theory composition, church music. Music majors: 115. . . . UNIVERSITY OF WASHINGTON, Seattle, Washington 98105. A School of Music in a College of Arts and Sciences in a state-supported university. (Member, NASM.) Director: **William Bergsma.** Degrees: B.M. in applied music; B.A. with a nonprofessional major in music; B.A. and B.M. (five-year) in music education, applied music, music history, composition. Music majors: 398. Music library: about 10,000 volumes (see Music Libraries). . . . WALLA WALLA COLLEGE, College Place, Washington 99324. A Department of Music in a liberal arts college affiliated with the Seventh-Day Adventist Church. (Member, NASM.) Chairman: **Melvin West.** Degrees: B.M. in music education, performance; B.A. in applied music, music theory, music history and literature. Music majors: 28. . . . WASHINGTON STATE UNIVERSITY, Pullman, Washington 99163. Department of Music within the College of Sciences and Arts of a state-supported university. (Member, NASM.) Chairman: **Howard Deming** (1970). Degrees: B.A., B.M., M.A. Music students enrolled: 225. Official school ensembles: chorus, glee club, chamber vocal ensemble, marching band, concert band, opera workshop, symphony orchestra, chamber orchestra, jazz ensemble, in-residence string quartet and trio. Summer music school. . . . WHITMAN COLLEGE, Walla Walla, Washington 99362. Department of Music within a college. (Member, NASM.) Head: **Stanley Plummer** (1969). School and Music Department founded: 1870. Degree: B.A. Scholarships: aid based on need. Fellowships: 15, totaling $3,000. Music enrollment: 200. Music library: 3,000 volumes. Ensembles: chorus, chamber vocal ensemble, concert band, opera workshop, symphony orchestra, smaller chamber groups. No summer music instruction. . . . YAKIMA VALLEY COMMUNITY COLLEGE, 16th and Nob Hill Boulevard, Yakima, Washington 98902. Music Department within the Creative Arts Division. Head: **Brooke C. Creswell** (1968). College founded: 1927. Music students enrolled: 30. Volumes in music library: 300. Official school ensembles: chorus, concert band, symphony orchestra, jazz ensemble, madrigal group, other smaller chamber groups. Some summer instruction.

WEST VIRGINIA

DAVIS AND ELKINS COLLEGE, Elkins, West Virginia 26241. Music Department within the college. Head: **John Russell Wilson** (1969). College founded: 1904. Department founded: 1920. Degree: B.A. with music major. No music scholarships. Music students enrolled: four to five majors, 200 non-majors. Volumes in music library: 1,300 books and scores; 1,600 recordings. Official school ensembles: chorus. Limited summer instruction. . . . FAIRMONT STATE COLLEGE, Locust Avenue, Fairmont, West Virginia 26554. Music Department within the Fine Arts Division of the college. Head: **Richard P. Wellock** (1960). College founded: 1867. Degree: B.A. in music and music education. Scholarships: six to eight, totaling $2,000 to $3,200. Music students enrolled: 130. Volumes in music library: 2,000. Official music ensembles: chorus, chamber vocal ensemble, marching band, concert band, symphony orchestra, jazz ensemble, faculty brass quintet. Summer instruction, workshops, festivals. . . . GLENVILLE STATE COLLEGE, Glenville, West Virginia 26351. Music Department within the Division of Fine Arts of the College. Head (Division): **David E. Harry** (1968). College founded: 1872. Department founded: 1937. Degree: B.A. in music education. Scholarships: number varies; total $150 to $500. Music students enrolled: 50. Volumes in music library: 700. Official school music ensembles: chorus, glee club, chamber vocal ensemble, marching band, concert band, jazz ensemble, other smaller chamber groups. Summer instruction. . . . SALEM COLLEGE, West Main Street, Salem, West Virginia 26426. Music Department within the college. Head: **C. Ray Martin** (1958). College founded: 1888. Degree: B.A. Scholarships: 50, totaling $21,200. Music students enrolled: 45. Volumes in music library: 1,000. Official school ensembles: chorus, chamber vocal ensemble, marching band, concert band, jazz ensemble. No summer music school. . . . WEST LIBERTY STATE COLLEGE, West Liberty, West Virginia 26074. Music Department within the college. Head: **Edward C. Wolf** (1963). College founded: 1837. Degrees: B.A., B.M. Scholarships: number varies. Music students enrolled: 80 majors. Volumes in music library: 5,000 (includes records). Official school ensembles: chorus, chamber vocal ensemble, marching band, concert band, chamber orchestra, jazz ensemble. Summer music school. . . . WEST VIRGINIA INSTITUTE OF TECHNOLOGY, Montgomery, West Virginia 25136. Music Department within the college. Head: **Donald J. Riggio** (1959). Institute founded: 1895. Degrees: B.S., B.A., in music education. No music scholarships. Music students enrolled: 90. Volumes in music library: 6,000. Official school ensembles: chorus, marching band, jazz ensemble. Summer music instruction. . . . WEST VIRGINIA UNIVERSITY, Morgantown, West Virginia 26505. Division of Music within the Creative Arts Center of a state-supported university. (Member, NASM.) Chairman: **Jon E. Engberg** (1969). University founded: 1867. Division founded: 1897. Degrees: B.M., M.M., Ph.D., D.M.A., Ed.D. Scholarships: 129, totaling $47,680. Fellowships: 26, totaling $57,500. Music students enrolled: 364. Volumes in music library: 12,000 books and scores; 5,000 records. Official ensembles: chorus, chamber vocal ensemble, marching and concert band, opera workshop, symphony orchestra, chamber orchestra, jazz ensemble, other smaller chamber groups. Summer music school. Special courses: African music, electronic music. . . . WEST VIRGINIA WESLEYAN COLLEGE, Buckhannon, West Virginia 26201. A professional department within a liberal arts college supported by the Methodist Church. (Member, NASM.) Chairman: **C. Buell Agey.** Degrees: B.M.Ed., B.A. in music, church music, applied music, theory. Music majors: 62.

WISCONSIN

ALVERNO COLLEGE, 3401 South 39th Street, Milwaukee, Wisconsin 53215. Department of Music in a liberal arts college for women supported and operated by the Congregation of School Sisters of St. Francis of St. Joseph Convent. (Member, NASM.)

Chairman: **Sister Mary Hueller** (1969). College founded: 1949 (Alverno Teachers College: 1936). Department founded: 1949 (Alverno College of Music: 1937). Degrees: B.A., B.M. Scholarships: four, totaling $1,700. Music students enrolled: 120. Volumes in music library: 2,500. Official ensembles: chorus, chamber vocal ensemble, chamber orchestra, Pro Musica Consort. Summer music school. . . . CARROLL COLLEGE, Waukesha, Wisconsin 53186. Music Department within a college. Head: **Cardon V. Burnham** (1961). College founded: 1846. Department founded: 1900. Degree: B.A. in music. Scholarships: $10,000 in music grants. Music students enrolled: 35. Volumes in music library: 1,000. Official ensembles: chorus, chamber vocal ensemble, marching band, concert band, chamber orchestra, jazz ensemble. Special offering: music–business major. No summer music school. . . . CONCORDIA JUNIOR COLLEGE, 3126 West Kilbourn Avenue, Milwaukee, Wisconsin 53210. Music Department within a college. Head: **James Engel** (1957). College founded: 1881. Department founded: 1957. No music degrees. Scholarships: 5 to 10, totaling $1,000. No music major. Volumes in music library: 500. Official school ensembles: chorus, chamber vocal ensemble, brass choir, jazz ensemble. No summer music session. . . . LAWRENCE UNIVERSITY, CONSERVATORY OF MUSIC, Appleton, Wisconsin 54911. A conservatory of music within a university. (Member, NASM.) Associate Dean, pro tem: **James W. Ming.** School and conservatory founded: 1887. Degrees: B.M., B.A. with major in music. Scholarships: 68, totaling $71,105 (1970). Music enrollment: 158. Music library: 4,000 volumes. Ensembles: chorus, women's glee club, chamber vocal ensemble, concert band, opera workshop, symphony orchestra, chamber orchestra, jazz ensemble, choral society. No summer session. . . . MADISON AREA TECHNICAL COLLEGE, 211 North Carroll Street, Madison, Wisconsin 53703. Music Department within a college. Head: **Roland A. Johnson** (1961). No music degree. Music students enrolled: 300. Official school ensembles: chorus, concert band, community orchestra, co-sponsor of civic chorus, civic opera, and Madison Symphony Orchestra. No summer music school. . . . MOUNT MARY COLLEGE, 2900 North Menomenee River Parkway, Milwaukee, Wisconsin 53222. Music Department within the college. Chairman: **Sister Julia Ann Sadowski** (1970). College founded: 1913. Degrees: B.A. in music or music education. Scholarships: Wisconsin Tuition Grants, Teresa Ross Memorial. Music students enrolled: 20. Volumes in music library: 1,500. Official school ensembles: chamber vocal ensemble, chamber orchestra, in-residence string quartet. Summer music instruction. . . . MOUNT SENARIO COLLEGE, Ladysmith, Wisconsin 54848. Music Department within the college. Head: **Max M. Waits** (1971). College founded: 1962. Department founded: 1969. Degrees: B.A., B.S. Official school ensembles: chorus, chamber vocal ensemble, stage band. Special courses: electronic music. Summer music instruction. . . . NORTHLAND COLLEGE, Ashland, Wisconsin 54806. Music Department within the college. Head: **Donald Jackson** (1965). College founded: 1892. Department founded: 1906. Degree: B.A. Scholarships: 10, totaling $5,000. Music students enrolled: 35. Volumes in music library: 1,500. Official school ensembles: chorus, chamber vocal ensemble, concert band, symphony orchestra, jazz ensemble. Summer music session. . . . RIPON COLLEGE, Ripon, Wisconsin 54971. Music Department within the college. Head: **Raymond Stahura** (1968). College and department founded: 1867. Degrees: B.A. in music. Scholarships: through main college fund. Music students enrolled: 20 to 25. Volumes in music library: 8,000[?]. Official school ensembles: chorus, chamber vocal ensemble, concert band, chamber orchestra, woodwind quintet, brass quintet, Collegium Musicum. Special offering: self-designed major. No summer music school. . . . ST. NORBERT COLLEGE, West de Pere, Wisconsin 54178. Music Department within the college. Head: **Reverend Xavier G. Colavechio.** College founded: 1898. Department founded: 1937. Degrees: B.M., B.A. Scholarships: total $15,000. Music students enrolled: 65. Official school ensembles: chorus, chamber vocal ensemble, concert band, opera workshop. Limited summer instruction (music theory for high school students). . . . SYMPHONY SCHOOL OF NEW MUSIC, Box 454, La Crosse, Wisconsin 54601. Music Director: **Francesco Italiano.** Music majors: 85. . . . UNIVERSITY OF WISCONSIN AT MADISON, Madison, Wisconsin 53706. School of Music, part of College of Letters and Science within the university. (Member, NASM.) Head: **Bruce Benward** (1970). University founded: 1849. School of Music founded: 1896. Degrees: B.A., B.M., M.A., M.M., M.S., Ph.D., D.M.A. Scholarships: total $52,000. Fellowships: total $150,000. Music students enrolled: 400. Volumes in music library: 80,000. Official school ensembles: chorus, glee club, chamber vocal ensemble, marching band, concert band, opera workshop, symphony orchestra, chamber orchestra, jazz ensemble, other smaller chamber groups. Summer music school. . . . UNIVERSITY OF WISCONSIN, MARATHON COUNTY CAMPUS, 518 South 7th Avenue, Wausau, Wisconsin 54401. This is a freshman–sophomore branch of the University of Wisconsin at Madison, Wisconsin. Music Department within a college. Chairman: **John A. Fitzgerald** (1969). Main university founded: 1849. Department founded: 1962. Sophomore and freshmen courses only. No degrees; no scholarships. Music students enrolled: seven. Volumes in music library: 500. Official school ensembles: chorus, chamber vocal ensemble, concert band, jazz ensemble, symphony orchestra. Limited number of summer courses. . . . UNIVERSITY OF WISCONSIN AT MARSHFIELD, Marshfield–Wood County Campus, 2000 West Fifth Street, Marshfield, Wisconsin 54449. Music Department within the university. Head: **Robert Biederwolf** (1967). Department founded: 1963. No degrees. Music students enrolled: 50. Volumes in music library: 20,000[?]. Official school ensembles: chorus, glee club, chamber vocal ensemble, concert band, symphony orchestra, chamber orchestra, jazz ensemble, other smaller chamber groups. Summer instruction. . . . UNIVERSITY OF WISCONSIN AT MILWAUKEE, 3200 North Downer Avenue, Milwaukee, Wisconsin 53201. Music Department within the School of Fine Arts of a state-supported university. (Member, NASM.) Head: **Emanuel Rubin** (1969). Department founded: 1910. Degrees: B.S., B.F.A., M.M. Scholarships: through university. Fellowships: three to five teaching assistantships. Music students enrolled: 480. Volumes in music library: 3,500. Official ensembles: five choruses, glee club, chamber vocal ensemble, marching band, concert band, opera workshop, symphony orchestra, chamber orchestra, jazz ensemble, in-residence Fine Arts Quartet, Woodwind Arts Quintet, brass choir, contemporary chamber ensemble, Collegium Musicum. Summer music school. Special courses: music therapy, chamber music playing. . . . UNIVERSITY OF WISCONSIN–PARKSIDE, Kenosha, Wisconsin 53140. Music Department within the university. Coordinator, Music Discipline: **Darrell R. Douglas.** University founded: 1848[?]. Department founded: 1966. Degree: B.A. in music. Scholarships: total $450. Music students enrolled: 130. Volumes in music library: 300. Official school ensembles: chorus, chamber vocal ensemble, concert band, chamber orchestra, jazz ensemble, other smaller chamber groups. Special majors: guitar–lute major. Summer music school. . . . UNIVERSITY OF WISCONSIN, ROCK COUNTY CAMPUS, Kellogg Avenue, Jonesville, Wisconsin 53545. Department of Music. Head: **Theodore Kinnaman** (on Rock County Campus); **John Fitzgerald** for Music Department of the Center System. No degrees offered (two-year campus). Music enrollment: 10. Music volumes in library: 500. Music ensembles: chorus, chamber vocal ensemble, concert band. Organizes a junior high school Summer Music Clinic. . . . VITERBO COLLEGE, 815 South 9th Street, LaCrosse, Wisconsin 54601. Music Department in a liberal arts college owned and operated by the Franciscan Sisters of Perpetual Adoration. (Member, NASM.) Chairman: **Sister Cyrilla Barr** (1966). College and department founded: 1933. Degrees: B.A., B.M.Ed. Scholarships: about 17, totaling $2,750. Music students enrolled: 32. Volumes in music library: 6,315 plus 1,206 recordings. Official school ensembles: chorus, chamber vocal ensemble, chamber orchestra, other smaller chamber groups. Summer music school. . . . WISCONSIN COLLEGE–CONSERVATORY OF MUSIC, 1584 North Prospect Avenue, Milwaukee, Wisconsin 53202. (Member, NASM.) Independent, unendowed conservatory (with a college and a school of dance). Head: **Stephen Jay** (1971). Conservatory founded: 1898. Degrees: B.M., M.M. Scholarships: 35, totaling $12,500. Fellowships: 10, totaling $7,600 (work–study). Music students enrolled: 150 (college), 950 (conservatory). Volumes in music library: 8,000. Official school ensembles: chorus, chamber vocal ensemble, opera workshop, chamber orchestra, piano quintet, jazz ensemble. Special courses: electronic music, East Indian music, classical guitar major, jazz major. Summer music school. . . . WISCONSIN STATE UNIVERSITY—EAU CLAIRE, Wisconsin 54701. Music Department within the college. (Member, NASM.) Head: **L. Rhodes Lewis** (1963). School and Music Department founded: 1916. Degrees: B.M.Ed., B.M. in applied music and music therapy; B.A. in music; M.S. in teaching-music; M.A. in teaching-music. Music enrollment: 425. Music ensembles: chorus, glee club, marching band, concert band, opera workshop, symphony orchestra, small chamber groups, jazz ensemble. . . . WISCONSIN STATE UNIVERSITY—LACROSSE, LaCrosse, Wisconsin 54601. Music Department within the College of Letters and Science. Head: **David Mewaldt** (1971). University founded: 1909. Degrees: B.A., B.S. Music students enrolled: 200. Official school ensembles: chorus, glee club, chamber vocal ensemble, marching band, concert band, symphony orchestra, jazz ensemble. Summer music school. . . . WISCONSIN STATE UNIVERSITY—OSHKOSH, 800 Algoma Boulevard, Oshkosh, Wisconsin 54901. Music Department within the School of Letters and Science in the university. Head: **Roger P. Dennis** (1952). University founded: 1871. Music major founded: 1953. Degrees: B.M., B.M.Ed., B.A., B.S., M.S.T. Scholarships: 15 to 20, totaling $3,000. Fellowships: two to three, totaling $4,600. Music students enrolled: 220 majors. Volumes in music library: 3,500. Official school ensembles: chorus, two glee clubs, chamber vocal ensemble, marching band, two concert bands, opera workshop, symphony orchestra, jazz ensemble, percussion ensemble, brass ensemble, other smaller chamber groups. Summer music instruction. . . . WISCONSIN STATE UNIVERSITY—STEVENS POINT, Stevens Point, Wisconsin 54481. Music Department within the College of Fine Arts of the university. Chairman: **Donald E. Greene** (1968). University founded: 1894. Department founded: 1950. Degrees: B.M., M.S. Scholarships: 10 for $100 each. Fellowships: one for $2,450. Music students enrolled: 200. Volumes in music library: 2,500. Official school ensembles: chorus, chamber vocal ensemble, marching band, concert band, opera workshop, symphony orchestra, jazz ensemble, wind ensemble, other smaller chamber groups. Summer music instruction. . . . WISCONSIN STATE UNIVERSITY, Whitewater, Wisconsin 53190. Music Department within the College of the Arts. Head: **Franklin F. Bushman** (1949). University founded: 1868. Department founded: 1949. Degrees: B.A., B.S. in music education. Instrumental scholarships: total $300. Vocal scholarships: $300. Music students enrolled: 190. Official school ensembles: chorus, glee club, chamber vocal ensemble, marching band, opera workshop, chamber orchestra, in-residence string trio. Summer music instruction.

WYOMING

UNIVERSITY OF WYOMING, Division of Music, Laramie, Wyoming 82070. Division of Music in the College of Arts and Sciences in a state-supported university. (Member, NASM.) Chairman: **Allan A. Willman** (1941). University founded: 1886. Division founded: 1895. Degrees: B.M., B.A., B.S., M.A. Scholarships: 85, totaling $35,000. Fellowships: seven assistantships totaling $20,300. Music students enrolled: 200. Volumes in music library: 5,000. Official school ensembles: chorus, glee club, chamber vocal ensemble, marching band, concert band, opera workshop, symphony orchestra, chamber orchestra, jazz ensemble, other smaller chamber groups. Summer music school.

Music Degrees Available

A study of degrees offered by schools in Part 9 shows that degrees granted vary from school to school, and although the degree titles vary, they tend to mean the same thing within fields of application. Some schools offer one or two music degrees only; others a multitude. Many specializations which differ in nomenclature contain the same curriculum substance. For example, History and Literature in some schools is tantamount to Musicology in others; Performance and Applied Music are likewise synonymous.

Degree Title	Initials	Field of Concentration (a composite list from many schools)
Bachelor of Arts	B.A. or A.B.	Applied Music; Music (general); History and Literature; Theory; Music Education; Music History; Theory and Composition; Church Music; Music Business; Music Literature; Church Music History and Literature; Secondary Music; Normal Piano (rare).
Bachelor of Music (sometimes stands alone without the major study indicated)	B.M.	Applied Music; Composition; Liturgical Music (or Church Music); Music Education; Theory; Music Therapy; School Music; Musicology (not common); History and Literature; Gregorian Chant (rare).
Bachelor of Music Education	B.M.E.	Applied Music; School Music; Music Therapy.
Bachelor of Science	B.S.	Music Business; Music Education; Instrumental Music; Music (general); Applied Music; History and Literature.
Bachelor of Fine Arts	B.F.A.	Music; Applied Music; Composition; Music Education; Music Literature; Theory; Music Theater; Dance–Ballet; Broadcasting.
Bachelor of Sacred Music (offered in some church-supported schools)	B.S.M.	
Bachelor of Church Music	B.C.M.	

Master of Arts	M.A.	Music (general); Music Education; Composition; Theory; Musicology; Historical Musicology (rare); Ethnomusicology (rare); Psychology of Music (rare); Historical and Critical Research (not common); Music Literature; Music Therapy (rare); Church Music (rare); Arts Management (relatively new); Broadcasting.
Master of Arts of Teaching	M.A.T. (uncommon)	Music Application.
Master of Music	M.M.	Applied Music; Composition and/or Theory; Conducting; Music Education; Music Theory and Literature; Musicology; Church Music; History and Literature; Historical and Critical Research (rare); Performance; Music Theater; Opera Theater; Voice and Opera (rare); Instrumental and Vocal Accompanying (rare); Public School Music (rare); Choral Conducting; Early Music Performance Practice (rare).
Master of Musical Arts	M.M.A.	Performance, Composition.
Master of Music Education	M.M.E. or M.Mus.Ed.	
Master of Sacred Music	M.S.M.	
Master of Music Therapy	M.M.T.	
Master of Fine Arts	M.F.A.	Applied Music; Composition; Music Education.
Master of Science	M.S.	Music Education.
Master of Science in Teaching	M.S.T.	Music Application.
Master of Church Music	M.C.M. (rare)	
Master of Philosophy	M.Ph.	History of Music; Theory of Music.
Doctor of Philosophy	Ph.D.	Music; Musicology; Music Education; Theory and/or Composition; Music History and Literature (sometimes designated separately); History of Music; Ethnomusicology; Music Theory; Theory of Music; Education (with emphasis on music); Secondary Education; Performance; Performance Practices; History; Piano Literature–Pedagogy; Research and Pedagogy of Music at the College Level (rare); Applied Music in combination with Theory and Literature; Music Composition.
Doctor of Musical Arts	D.M.A.	Composition; Music Education and Performance; Pedagogy and Musical Literature; Pedagogy and Performance; Applied Music (sometimes with specific instruments or voice indicated with the degree);

		Conducting; Chamber Music; Church Music (rare); Performance Practices; Composition and Choral Music (rare); Literature and Performance; Music Education; Performance and Church Music; Liturgical Music; Performance; Orchestral and Choral Conducting; History and Literature of Music; Pedagogy of Performance; Pedagogy of Music Education; Music Teaching.
Doctor of Musical Arts	D.Mus.A.	Composition and Performance; Choral Conducting and Literature; Pedagogy and Literature.
Doctor of Education	Ed.D.	Music Education; Education and Music Education; Music Minor; Advanced Certificate in Music Education; Education with Minor in Music.
Doctor of Music Education	D.M.Ed.	Music Education.
Doctor of Musical Arts	Mus.A.D.	Composition; Performance; Music Education.
Doctor of Music	Mus.D.	Music Literature and Performance, Piano/Organ, Strings, Woodwinds; Music Literature and Pedagogy in Piano, Brass, or Voice; Composition; Coaching, Conducting, Performance and Literature; Church Music; Performance (Piano, Organ, Voice, Strings); Piano Literature; Vocal Literature; Violin Literature; Violoncello Literature; Choral Conducting, Performance and Literature; Instrumental Conducting.
Doctor of Musical Science	S.M.D.	Performance; Composition; Musicology.
Associate of Arts	A.A.	Granted by two-year colleges as preliminary recognition.
Associate of Science	A.S.	It is awarded with some major emphasis on occasion (in music).

Music Degree Statistics

The following table indicates bachelor's and higher degrees conferred by level of degree and the sex of the student for "aggregate" United States for the years 1965–66 through 1968–69, the latest years for which complete figures are available. The data for the four years surveyed come from the following number of institutions: 1965–66: 1,549; 1966–67: 1,565; 1967–68: 1,567; 1968–69: 1,595. All statistics are from "Earned Degrees Conferred 1968–69. Part B—Institutional Data," Department of Health, Education, and Welfare, Office of Education, Washington, D.C., 1971.

	Number of Degrees Granted			
Level of Degree	**1968-69**	**1967-68**	**1966-67**	**1965-66**
Bachelor's degrees requiring 4 or 5 years	734,002	636,863	562,369	524,117
Men	412,864	359,747	324,236	301,051
Women	321,138	277,116	238,133	223,066
First professional degrees requiring at least 6 years	35,681	34,728	32,493	31,496
Men	34,069	33,083	31,064	30,071
Women	1,612	1,645	1,429	1,425
Master's degrees	194,414	177,150	157,892	140,772
Men	121,881	113,749	103,179	93,184
Women	72,533	63,401	54,713	47,588
Doctor's degrees	26,189	23,091	20,621	18,239
Men	22,753	20,185	18,164	16,121
Women	3,436	2,906	2,457	2,118
All levels—bachelor's and higher	990,286	871,832	773,375	714,624
Men	591,567	526,764	476,643	440,427
Women	398,719	345,068	296,732	274,197

For the school year 1968–69, there were 16,190 graduates receiving degrees from bachelor's to doctor's in the combined fields of music, music education, and sacred music. This represents 1.63 percent of the 990,286 total graduates for all degrees for that academic year. Bachelor's degrees received in music were 1.81 percent of all bachelor's degrees; 1.91 percent of all master's degrees were in music; 1.39 percent of all doctorates were music degrees. (These and other figures that follow which show comparisons between music and other fields of study are compiled from the publication cited above.)

Of the 16,190 music degrees, 8,620 were granted to women, 7,570 to men.

Music Education: 1968-69.

Bachelor's (Requiring 4-5 years)		Master's		Doctor's	
Men	Women	Men	Women	Men	Women
3,052	4,048	953	729	81	11

Music, Sacred Music, 1968-69.

Bachelor's		Master's		Doctor's	
Men	Women	Men	Women	Men	Women
2,145	2,876	1,123	917	216	39

Combined Music Education, Music (General), and Sacred Music, 1968-69.

Bachelor's		Master's		Doctor's	
Men	Women	Men	Women	Men	Women
5,197	6,924	2,076	1,646	297	50

Music Education and Education in General: Degrees granted in Music Education as compared with all degrees granted in Education (which includes music education, art education, administration of special education, education of various categories of the handicapped, etc.)

	Bachelor's (4-5 years)		Master's		Doctor's	
	Men	Women	Men	Women	Men	Women
Degrees in Music Education, 1968-69	3,052	4,048	953	729	81	11
Education (all fields), 1968-69	36,562	116,686	33,430	37,993	3,859	970

Fine and Applied Arts (Including Music) Compared with Other Broad Categories of Study, 1968-69.

	Bachelor's		Master's		Doctor's	
	Men	Women	Men	Women	Men	Women
Fine & Applied Arts (including music, sacred music, art—general, speech and dramatic arts, etc.)	12,950	18,690	4,094	3,320	565	119
Biological Sciences (general biology, botany, premedical, veterinary sciences, anatomy, bacteriology, biochemistry, biophysics, nutrition, physiology, etc.)	25,590	9,966	4,096	1,669	2,582	469
Physical Sciences (general studies, astronomy, chemistry, physics, geology, etc.)	18,639	2,952	5,243	668	3,653	206
Business & Commerce (general studies, accounting, finance, banking, marketing, real estate and insurance, secretarial studies, etc.)	85,972	8,644	18,727	671	560	13
Foreign Language and Literature (linguistics, philology, modern languages [more than two], and all specific languages—French, Italian, etc.)	5,915	10,070	2,130	2,920	492	257
Social Sciences (American studies, civilization and culture, anthropology, area and regional studies, economics, history, political science. Also applied social sciences: industrial relations, social work and administration, etc.)	89,027	52,941	15,396	7,344	2,749	401

Music Degrees Granted (Combined Music Education, Music—General, Sacred Music) Compared with the Number of Degrees in Other Specific Fields of Study, Academic Year 1968-69.

	Bachelor's		Master's		Doctor's	
	Men	Women	Men	Women	Men	Women
Combined Music Degrees, Granted Academic Year 1968-69:	5,197	6,924	2,076	1,646	297	50
Other Specific Fields of Study: Architecture	3,188	143	542	37	6	1
Physiology	73	22	137	44	191	31
Accounting	18,561	1,622	1,254	79	38	2
Aerospace, Aeronautical, Astronautical Engineering	2,606	19	828	7	207	—
Electrical Engineering, Electronics	11,629	66	4,011	22	858	4
Mech. Engineering	8,474	40	2,295	4	425	—
English & Literature	17,539	36,820	3,617	4,910	799	352
Journalism	3,003	2,194	553	232	20	2
Modern Languages (more than 2)	137	302	6	18	6	2
Nursing and Public Health Nursing	132	10,248	10	1,380	—	3
Pharmacy	3,429	692	199	33	70	4
Home Economics, General	29	4,541	11	414	1	9
Law	383	32	786	44	18	—
Library Science	64	936	1,136	4,796	12	5
Mathematics	16,862	10,153	3,806	1,421	897	59
Philosophy	3,620	1,039	495	119	233	34
Chemistry	9,641	2,154	1,655	377	1,751	144
Physics	5,213	322	2,139	120	1,264	32
General Psychology	16,314	12,283	1,941	850	836	247
Religious Educ., Bible	1,899	896	571	436	37	4
Theology	521	98	1,297	183	176	7
Economics	15,108	1,799	1,871	242	591	43
History	26,592	14,487	3,650	1,626	716	110
Sociology	10,342	16,213	1,125	531	344	86

First Professional Degrees Conferred in Higher Learning Institutions (requiring at least 6 years).

	Men	Women
Dentistry	3,400	37
Medicine	7,463	619
Law	16,585	723
Theology	4,227	111

Music Libraries

This section provides in detail the music holdings of 83 libraries in the United States. The information is current as of the period from February through April, 1972. Any information correct to an earlier date is indicated as such, when known.

The libraries are arranged alphabetically by states.

The guide to the information is as follows: (1) The name shown is a specific music library, a music department within a general library, or a general library making no reference in its name to a music division but which has music holdings. (2) The date in parentheses following the name of the librarian is the year of his appointment to that post. (3) Dates of founding refer to the date of the music library or department and the date of its parent library if such exists. Sometimes only one or the other date is shown. Qualifying information about founding dates is included when known. (The founding date does not necessarily indicate that no music collection existed in a given library prior to the official establishment of a music library or division.) (4) Total numbers of items are identified as volumes or titles whenever possible, volumes to mean bound units containing one or more titles including books and music scores. The word "item" is used otherwise. (5) A breakdown of totals shows books, music scores (collected editions, sheet music, choral folios, instrumental parts, anthologies), recordings (discs, tapes, etc.), microforms (film reels, opaque microcards, and microfiche [transparent film cards]), periodicals (excluding those in microform), and uncatalogued items. (6) If music is only part of a general parent library, the total holdings of the main library is shown. (7) Additional information is intended to describe any special characteristics of the library's music collection, its rare items, unique collections, special areas of emphasis, etc.

Although there are many thousands of libraries in the United States, most of which have books on music, music scores, or recordings, the libraries included here have value as research libraries generally on the higher levels of scholarship. Included are both large and small public, private, and academic libraries that own important, unique, extensive, highly specialized, or otherwise interesting holdings of music and music literature.

CALIFORNIA

OAKLAND PUBLIC LIBRARY, 125–14th Street, Oakland, California 94612. Founded in 1868. Music librarian is **Richard M. Colvig** (1961). The music collection consists of 5,000 volumes of books, 10,000 volumes of scores plus 30,000 choral octavo copies, 8,000 recording discs, 100 recording cassettes, 66 periodical titles, and about 5,000 uncatalogued items. The main library holds a total of one million volumes. The music collection is strong in opera scores, chamber and solo instrumental music, multiple copies of choral octavos, songs, and reference service.

SAN FRANCISCO PUBLIC LIBRARY, ART AND MUSIC DEPARTMENT, Civic Center, San Francisco, California 94102. Library founded: 1880; music department in 1917. Librarian in charge of music: **Mary Ashe** (1966). The music collection is composed of 7,000 titles of books, 17,000 titles of scores, 4,200 titles of recordings, 6 titles of microfilm reels, 1 title on microcards, 230 periodicals including 181 currently subscribed to. Uncatalogued items include concert programs and clippings and other ephemera. As of June 30, 1971 (last count available) the Main Library had 374,811 titles of general publications totaling 753,344 volumes. Branch libraries have additional holdings. The music collection of the Art and Music Department contains collected musical works, monuments, and historical sets; San Francisco music imprints; songs and music descriptive of San Francisco and California; and popular sheet music of the United States, 1800–1950.

UNIVERSITY OF CALIFORNIA, BERKELEY, MUSIC LIBRARY, Berkeley, California 94720. Music library established in 1947. Music librarian: **Vincent Duckles** (1947). As of July, 1971 the holdings of the music library were as follows: 28,491 music books, 49,421 volumes of scores, 21,987 recordings, 2,778 titles on microfilm reels, 693 titles on microcards, and 219 periodicals (titles). Some details of the holdings above are such items as 700 sets of choral music, 900 portfolios of orchestral parts, 700 sets of parts for concert band; 10,000 opera scores (including the Cortot opera collection) of which many are first editions and rare scores; 5,000 opera librettos; the musicological libraries of Alfred Einstein and Manfred Bukofzer. The record collection contains many foreign and out-of-print discs.

UNIVERSITY OF CALIFORNIA, MUSIC LIBRARY, Schoenberg Hall, 405 Hilgard Avenue, Los Angeles, California 90024. The music library was established in 1942. Music librarian is **Richard Hudson** (1967). A collection of 58,037 volumes (21,203 books, 36,834 volumes of music scores); 28,628 of all modes of recordings (discs, tapes, etc.); 870 microfilm reels; 2,236 microcards (number of titles covered by micro reels and cards not available); 647 periodical titles currently received. The number of uncatalogued items is not yet known. As of June, 1971, the total holdings of the entire university library numbered 3,038,828. Special features and collections within the music library and in other library resources at UCLA are: Manuscripts of Ernst Toch (Ernst Toch Archives), Rudolf Friml (Rudolf Friml Library of Music), **Henry Mancini, Alex North,** and **Eugene Zador;** special collections of guitar music, Japanese contemporary music, 17th- and 18th-century Dutch song and psalm books, 17th- and 18th-century Venetian opera librettos, 18th- and 19th-century opera scores, 18th- and early 19th-century French and German opera librettos, folk songs and dances of the British Isles; the Meredith Willson Library Stanley Ring Collection of popular American sheet music (about 150,000 items uncatalogued); Alfred Newman Collection of film score recordings. Attached to the music library is the Institute of Ethnomusicology Archive, **Ann Briegleb,** librarian, which has areas of emphasis in Oriental music and music history; the collection includes clippings, pamphlets, microfilms, slides, field recordings, etc. The Department of Special Collections of the University Research Library contains the George Pullen Jackson Collection of 19th-century American hymnals, the Joseph C. Stone Collection of early American psalm books, the Lionel Barrymore Music Collection of his own music manuscripts; the collection also includes American, Irish, and English ballad texts, 17th- to 19th-century dance, etc. Other libraries and collections at UCLA are the William Andrews Clark Memorial Library, **William Conway,** Librarian, containing among other items early editions of English music (1640–1750); the University's Folklore, Mythology Center (John Edwards Memorial Foundation), which houses a white country music and blues collection of sheet music (items from the 1920's to the present), recordings, and microfilm.

UNIVERSITY OF SOUTHERN CALIFORNIA, SCHOOL OF MUSIC LIBRARY, Los Angeles, California 90007. University library founded: 1880. Music library founded in 1930's; first music librarian appointed in 1948 but did not become a branch library until 1956 when books on music were added to music and recordings. Music librarian: **Joan M. Meggett** (1955). There are 1,300 books in the music library, 25,000 volumes of scores, 13,000 discs, 104 book titles on microfilm reels, 95 titles on microcards, 120 titles of current periodicals. Uncatalogued items include 250 subject headings in the Vertical File, publishers', dealers' catalogues; music on microfilm, opera librettos, multiple copies of children's song-books; and music school bulletins and catalogues. Areas of emphasis include material in music history, especially medieval, Renaissance, contemporary composers, chamber music. There are special areas with first editions of French opéra comique and 19th-century Russian operas, and also autographs of composers including Stravinsky's "Rake's Progress" and works by Ingolf Dahl.

COLORADO

DENVER PUBLIC LIBRARY, ART AND MUSIC DEPARTMENT, 1357 Broadway, Denver, Colorado 80203. Library founded 1889. Fine Arts Department founded in 1926, renamed the Art and Music Department in 1939 and separately housed until 1956 (but always under the administration of main library). **Kurtz Myers** has been music librarian since 1971. There are an estimated 12,000 music books, approximately 7,000 scores, 7,910 recordings, 1 title on microfilm reel, and 107 periodicals in the Music Department. The general library has a total of 1,281,454 volumes (1971). A special collection of folk music with emphasis on Anglo-American tradition includes 1,500 volumes (not included above) with books and scores interfiled.

UNIVERSITY OF COLORADO, MUSIC LIBRARY, NORLIN LIBRARY, Boulder, Colorado 80302. Music librarian: **Kent Hirst** (1968). The music collection has 9,100 titles of books and about 17,690 score titles. There are also approximately 14,100 recordings, 774 microfilm reels, 650 titles on microcards, 12 collections on microfiche, 400 titles of periodicals and about 12,000 uncatalogued 78rpm records in the sound archives.

CONNECTICUT

HARTFORD SEMINARY FOUNDATION, CASE MEMORIAL LIBRARY, 55 Elizabeth Street, Hartford, Connecticut 06105. The library was founded in 1834 and contains 6,600 music volumes. There are 243,000 volumes in the total library. Music consists of special collections of hymnals for all groups of people, i.e., church, Sunday school, gospel meetings, and temperance meetings. There are some psalms in manuscript.

UNIVERSITY OF HARTFORD, ALLEN MEMORIAL LIBRARY, 200 Bloomfield Avenue, West Hartford, Connecticut 06117. The music library was founded in 1920. Music librarian: **Ethel Bacon** (1960). The library has 7,500 books (including bound periodicals), 16,000 scores, 9,300 recordings, 65 titles on microfilm reels, 24 titles on microcards. The library subscribes to 125 current periodicals (included in the number of books). The total of volumes in the parent library is 180,000. Special collections include the Robert E. Smith Record Library containing early 78's, many operas; the Kalmen Opperman Collection of clarinet music; and Hartt School of Music concerts on tape.

YALE UNIVERSITY, JOHN HERRICK JACKSON MUSIC LIBRARY, 98 Wall Street, New Haven, Connecticut 06520. The music library was founded in 1917. Music librarian: **Harold E. Samuel** (1971). There are 30,000 books and 72,500 scores in the music library. Also 15,000 recordings, 1,900 titles on microfilm reels, 35 titles on microcards, 10,000 volumes of periodicals and 15,000 uncatalogued items. Features include special collections of original and early editions and manuscripts of the Bach family, Lowell Mason Library, Ives's manuscripts, 18th-century opera, and thcorctical treatises of the 17th and 18th centuries.

DISTRICT OF COLUMBIA

SMITHSONIAN INSTITUTION, The National Museum of History and Technology, Division of Musical Instruments, Washington, D.C. 20560. Curator of the Division of Musical Instruments is **John T. Fesperman.** Basic reference works are in the music section. For publications acquisitions in the division the prime emphasis is on increasing its collection of treatises on instrument manufacture and performance practices. There are also extensive collections of photographs of musical instruments. The musical instrument holdings number about 4,000.

LIBRARY OF CONGRESS, MUSIC DIVISION, Washington, D.C. 20540. The Library of Congress was founded in 1800. The Music Division was established in 1897. Chief of the Music Division is **Edward N. Waters** (1972) following **Harold Spivacke,** who served as Chief of the Division from 1937 to 1972. Head of the Music Division's Reference Section is **William Lichtenwanger.** The Music Division of the Library of Congress is one of the supreme music libraries of all time, in many respects unequaled by any in the world today. Currently it has a total of about 4,000,000 items, of which less than half are catalogued. Of the total, 3,500,000 is music; about 300,000 items are books and periodicals. Recordings total about 300,000. No statistics are available for its holdings in microforms, but the Library is a central source of microfilming, servicing individuals and institutions throughout the world; its master negatives, therefore, must exist in large number. The Music Division's annual acquisitions—in the tens of thousands of items of all kinds of publications—come mostly from copyright deposits, since the U.S. Copyright Office is part of the Library of Congress, but material other than that currently published is acquired through purchase, gift, and exchange. Through such means, rare and early publications have been acquired. The holdings in some areas of study are claimed by the Division to be probably unequaled anywhere. One area cited is the field of opera: orchestral scores, piano–vocal scores, librettos, and related histories, treatises, etc. The manuscript collections contain the holographs of all the great and many lesser-known composers. This includes both letters, documents, and music. The collection of Brahms holographs, for example, is the world's largest. Autograph scores of many significant contemporary composers are also to be found. The Division is understandably strong in all that relates to American music: manuscripts of both old and contemporary works, first printings and editions, rare publications, and unique items. The Division is an unrivaled depository of America's vernacular music: popular song sheets from Colonial times to the present, dance music, theater music, band music, folk music, ragtime music, jazz, etc. It is equally strong in American concert music. Early and original source materials for scholarly research include incunabula and 16th- and 17th-century manuscripts and books. The periodicals collection is in many languages, the quantity of which is undetermined. The library maintains an Archive of Folk Song with its own reading and listening and reference facilities, a Recording Laboratory with recording and duplicating equipment, a soundproof room equipped with record playback units and a piano. The library is involved in several adjunctive activities as a result of the establishment of musical foundations and funds placed under the administration of the Library of Congress. These are the Elizabeth Sprague Coolidge Foundation and the Gertrude Clarke Whittall Foundation (see both under Music Organizations), both of which provide for public concerts of chamber music; the Serge Koussevitsky Music Foundation in the Library of Congress, which has commissioned outstanding contemporary composers to compose works the manuscripts of which are added to the Division's holograph collections; the Louis Charles Elson Fund, for annual lectures in music; the Nicholas Longworth Foundation (for chamber music concerts); the Charles Martin Loeffler Fund; the Sonneck Memorial Fund (for the publication of studies in American music history); and the Dayton C. Miller Fund, which is used to maintain and increase the flute collection of Dayton C. Miller (over 1,600 flutes and flutelike instruments plus several thousand publications related to the flute and the flute family).

FLORIDA

FLORIDA STATE UNIVERSITY, WARREN D. ALLEN MUSIC LIBRARY, Tallahassee, Florida 32306. The university library was founded circa 1867, the music library in 1950. Music librarian: **Frank L. Hutchison** (1971). The Allen Library has some 1,442 reserve and reference books; the main library has about 14,000 music books. In the music library are 22,000 scores, 10,556 recordings, 66 titles on microfilm reels, 3 titles on opaque microcards (no main library microforms figures are available) and about 135 periodical titles. Uncatalogued items include about 4,500 tapes and discs (the Helwig collection) and 3,500 reference choral works. Music books and back issues of periodicals are housed in the main library. The Allen Library holds the record and tape library of Carl Helwig, an independent recording engineer who recorded many performances of radio broadcasts, speeches, and particularly Hungarian-American celebrations of unevaluated ethnomusicological worth. Helwig's card files are included, but no attempt to sort or reorganize the material has been made. Helwig's own numbering code for the tapes and discs has been utilized, for the present, on the catalogue cards.

ILLINOIS

THE NEWBERRY LIBRARY, 60 West Walton, Chicago, Illinois 60610. The library was founded in 1887. The music collection consists of (all 1969 figures—the latest available): 45,000 volumes of books, 55,000 scores, and 100,000 pieces of sheet music. There are also about 25 titles on microfilm reels and, in 1970, 400 periodical subscriptions were being received. The general library contains a total of 900,000 volumes. Special holdings on "primary and secondary materials for the study of Western European music from the Middle Ages through the 19th century, and of American music from its beginnings." Strongest holdings are in early theory, music literature, and music scores of the Renaissance and baroque periods (the libraries of Count Pio Reese and Alfred Cortot); opera scores and librettos; early American psalmody and religious music (library of Hubert Platt Main); music periodicals, monumental editions, and monographs; sheet music (library of J. Francis Driscoll); and music manuscripts.

UNIVERSITY OF CHICAGO, MUSIC COLLECTION, JOSEPH REGENSTEIN LIBRARY, Chicago, Illinois 60637. The library and music division were both founded in 1892. **Hans Lenneberg** has been the music librarian since 1963. There are about 30,000 books and 20,000 scores in the music collection and approximately 1,500 titles on microfilm reels, 500 microcards, about 200 microfiche, and approximately 100 periodicals. The library contains chiefly material on the history of Western music, with an emphasis on Renaissance and contemporary music.

UNIVERSITY OF ILLINOIS AT URBANA-CHAMPAIGN, MUSIC LIBRARY, Urbana, Illinois 61801. The library was founded in 1944. Music librarian: **William M. McClellan** (1965). There are 18,000 books in the music library plus 14,000 volumes in Main Library stacks. There are 90,000 volumes of scores, 12,000 recording discs, 6,600 microforms (5,000 microfilm reels, 1,600 microcards), and 800 titles of currently subscribed to periodicals. There are also 73,000 uncatalogued items. The general library has a total collection of 4,600,000 volumes. Special areas of music include about 2,000 pre-1800 music manuscripts and editions of music on microfilm, 1,500 graduate music theses on microfilm, a collection of 30,000 titles of American sheet music (1830–1950), the Rafael Joseffy collection of about 2,000 pieces of piano music, the Joseph Szigeti collection of violin music, 17,000 78-rpm records of classical music and jazz, WGN (Chicago) radio station collection of orchestrations (2,900 titles). A separate collection of choral folios and instrumental parts is maintained, including 112,000 pieces of choral music, 6,500 orchestral items, and 3,400 items for wind ensemble.

INDIANA

FORT WAYNE PUBLIC LIBRARY, ART AND MUSIC DEPARTMENT, 900 Webster Street, Fort Wayne, Indiana 46802. Library founded: 1894. Music library founded as part of the Art and Music Department: 1968. Music librarian since 1967, **Richard M. Elmer.** Music area consists of 847 titles of books, 2,800 (titles) scores (excluding sheet music), 31,619 recordings, 1 title on microfilm reel, 64 active titles of periodicals and about 1,700 items of uncatalogued sheet music. The main library has a total of 1,600,000 volumes (approximately). The Art Department has musical instruments in its collection of 15,000 color slides. Music book collection is entirely reference. Circulating books on music are handled by the circulations department. Scores circulate from the music department. Circulating music titles number about 5,000.

INDIANA UNIVERSITY SCHOOL OF MUSIC LIBRARY, Bloomington, Indiana 47401. The music library was founded in 1924. **Dominique-René de Lerma** has been music librarian since 1963. Calculated by volumes, the library has 68,828 music books (including scores), 154,839 performing editions of scores, 36,116 recordings, 2,087 microfilm reels, 513 microcards, 29 microfiche, 1,116 periodicals (by title), and an estimated 10,000 uncatalogued items. There are special collections of black music, Latin-American music, early keyboard music, opera, piano pedagogy, early violin music, and related literature and Americana (including sheet music).

IOWA

UNIVERSITY OF IOWA, MUSIC LIBRARY, School of Music, Iowa City, Iowa 52240. Established as a separate library within the university library system in 1957. Music librarian: **Rita Benton.** The music library has approximately 50,000 volumes of books and scores, 5,000 recordings, 3,000 microfilm reels, about 300 titles on microcards; periodicals include 150 current titles plus many older titles. There is a collection of uncatalogued 78 rpm recordings numbering in the thousands and comprising historical vocal recordings. The university library system has total holdings of 1.5 million volumes.

KENTUCKY

SOUTHERN BAPTIST THEOLOGICAL SEMINARY, THE JAMES P. BOYCE CENTENNIAL LIBRARY, 2825 Lexington Road, Louisville, Kentucky 40206. The library was founded in 1859; the music library was established in 1943. Music librarian: **Miss Martha C. Powell** (1969). There are almost 100,000 volumes in the music library including 13,801 volumes, 7,509 titles (collected editions included), and 85,560 scores including 62,000 anthems in multiple copies; 5,028 records and tapes, 156 titles on microfilm reels and 14 titles on microcards, plus subscription to 94 periodicals and 9,600 uncatalogued sample anthems, make up the remainder of the music collection. In addition to the music there are 196,473 volumes in the general library. The music library specializes in the area of church music. It has a small collection of early American hymnals. In 1962, the library purchased the working library of musicologist **Everett Helm,** who had emphasized Latin American materials and early editions of 18th- and 19th-century European composers.

UNIVERSITY OF LOUISVILLE, DWIGHT ANDERSON MEMORIAL MUSIC LIBRARY, 9001 Shelbyville Road, Louisville, Kentucky 40222. The library was founded in 1947; **Miss Marion Korda** has been music librarian since that time. There are 7,000 volumes, 13,100 volumes of scores, 5,000 record albums, 500 tapes, 182 titles on microfilm, 400 titles on microcards, 3 titles on microfiche (periodicals only), 91 titles of periodicals (excludes yearbooks, reports, proceedings), and 21,150 volumes of items uncatalogued. In addition there are 1,375 titles of music books (no music) in the general library (about 125 form a separate Afro-American collection). The collection is exclusively musical, supporting the school's preparatory, undergraduate, and graduate programs. There is a special collection of early American sheet music, a good portion of which are Louisville imprints; an archival collection of early Louisville music programs dating back over 100 years; letters of composers; and works and manuscripts of Kentucky composers.

LOUISIANA

TULANE UNIVERSITY, MAXWELL MUSIC LIBRARY, New Orleans, Louisiana 70118. The music library was founded in 1909. Music librarian: **Liselotte Andersson** (1962). The 16,351-volume collection of the music library consists of 7,345 volumes of books, 9,006 volumes of scores. Recordings on discs and tapes are an estimated 6,250. One hundred titles of material are on microfilm. There are 60 periodicals. In addition, there is an unknown quantity of uncatalogued material. The university's main library has 1,071,638 volumes. In 1958, the music library established the Archives of New Orleans Jazz.

MAINE

BOWDOIN COLLEGE, HAWTHORNE-LONGFELLOW LIBRARY, Brunswick, Maine 04011. The music collection consists of 2,300 book titles, 3,539 titles of music scores (includes 564 choral and 500 unbound scores), 3,000 recordings, 35 titles of music periodicals. There are 445,000 volumes in the total general library. Areas of emphasis in the music library are contemporary music and opera.

MARYLAND

ENOCH PRATT FREE LIBRARY, 400 Cathedral Street, Baltimore, Maryland 21201. The library was founded in 1886, the Fine Arts Department in 1921. Music librarian: **Ruth E. Witmer** (1969). The music library contains approximately 37,000 volumes, 18,500 discs, 11 titles on microfilm reels, 82 periodicals and a reserve collection of approximately 7,000 items of American popular sheet music. Uncatalogued items are: 3,000 opera libretti, approximately 8,000 pieces of sheet music (popular and classic), 185 gospel hymnals, and 20 vertical file drawers of material. The general library has 2,250,000 volumes and serves the general public as well as the Peabody Conservatory.

MARYLAND HISTORICAL SOCIETY LIBRARY, 201 W. Monument Street, Baltimore, Maryland 21201. The library was founded in 1844, the music library in the 1880's. **P. William Filby** has been the music librarian since 1965. The library has about 8,500 pieces of sheet music and 150 song books on music in addition to its main holdings of about 80,000 books on general subjects. Special items include many rarities of sheet music of the late 18th century, the first printing of the "Star-Spangled Banner" (Carr, 1814) and 47 other different editions of the "Star-Spangled Banner," including several rarities.

PEABODY CONSERVATORY LIBRARY, 21 East Mt. Vernon Place, Baltimore, Maryland 21202. The library was founded in 1857, the music library in 1868. Since 1965, **Miss Geraldine Ostrove** has been music librarian. Of the total volumes of 53,480 (January, 1972), there are approximately 9,091 books and 44,389 scores, plus 6,000 disc recordings, 500 tapes, four microfilm reels, and 102 current journal subscriptions. Special collections include clippings and memorabilia, an autograph letter of Ludwig van Beethoven, and the John Charles Thomas collection of music and opera costumes.

MASSACHUSETTS

BOSTON ATHENAEUM, 10½ Beacon Street, Boston, Massachusetts 02108. The library was founded in 1807. There are in the music collection about 1,500 volumes of books, approximately 1,350 volumes of scores, and about 300 volumes of periodicals, in addition to 36 scrapbooks and 12 boxes of sheet music uncatalogued. The entire library contains a total of 453,026 volumes. Special music items include: the only known complete copy of *Primus (Septimus) liber viginti missarum musicalium* (Paris) 1532 by Attaingnant, a sizeable collection of early New England hymn books (pre-1850), a collection of bound volumes of sheet music from before 1850, three boxes of music about Lincoln, six boxes of Civil War music and numerous items printed in the Confederacy, several volumes and boxes of sheet music later than 1850, scrapbooks containing early concert programs of Boston groups, and a nearly complete series of Boston Symphony programs from 1881 to the present. The largest specialized collection is on campanology and includes books, periodicals, manuscripts and ephemera, some of it uncatalogued.

BOSTON PUBLIC LIBRARY, MUSIC DEPARTMENT, Copley Square, Boston, Massachusetts 02117. Library founded: 1854. Music library founded: 1894. Music librarian: **Ruth Bleecker** (1963). Music library includes 80,000 titles (no breakdown provided), 110 periodicals, and some uncatalogued sheet music and programs. There are some incunabula, many manuscripts, early opera scores, Americana, and scrapbooks.

THE BOSTONIAN SOCIETY LIBRARY, 206 Washington Street, Boston, Massachusetts 02109. The library was founded 1882. Music librarian: **Mrs. Ropes Cabot** (1957). The library contains 100 books on music, 400 scores, and 2 recordings. The total library collection is 15,000 volumes. This library is related primarily to Boston history.

BOSTON UNIVERSITY, MUGAR LIBRARY AUDIO DEPARTMENT, 771 Commonwealth Avenue, Boston, Massachusetts 02215. The Audio Department at its present address was founded in 1965. **Miss Elizabeth A. Graves** has been music librarian since 1968. The library has 4,010 books, 6,800 scores, 16,000 recordings, an estimate of 50 titles in all modes of microforms, 41 current titles to periodicals and approximately 2,000 uncatalogued recordings. The complete holdings of Mugar Memorial Library are 600,000 volumes. (All figures are from 1971.) Special collections include 125 tapes of famous artists delivering lectures and interviews, the Albert Spaulding collection of records, tapes, and scores, the Bette Davis collection of tapes and records, a collection of Afro-American tapes. There is a catalogue of holdings of recordings in the medieval and Renaissance period by composer and title.

BOSTON UNIVERSITY SCHOOL OF THEOLOGY LIBRARY, 745 Commonwealth Avenue, Boston, Massachusetts 02215. The library was founded in 1869. There are approximately 4,000 volumes of music books in a library of 105,000 volumes. The collection consists of hymnals published 1700–1900; some are rare.

BRANDEIS UNIVERSITY LIBRARY, CREATIVE ARTS SECTION, 415 South Street, Waltham, Massachusetts 02154. The library was founded in 1948. Creative Arts librarian since 1965 has been **Michael Ochs.** There are, in the music collection, 6,000 book titles including periodicals. There are also 7,000 score titles, 6,500 recordings, 400 microfilm reels and 200 microcards. The University library contains approximately 500,000 volumes.

FORBES LIBRARY, 20 West Street, Northampton, Massachusetts 01060. The library was founded in 1895. **Mrs. Mary C. Lawton** has been music librarian since 1969. There are about 3,400 books, 20,000 scores, and about 3,500 discs in the music library. The library's total number of volumes is 280,940 (as of January, 1970). There are some 18th-century and early 19th-century Northampton imprints as well as a good deal of 19th century music. There are several editions of collected works of composers.

SMITH COLLEGE, WERNER JOSTEN LIBRARY, Center for the Performing Arts, Smith College, Northampton, Massachusetts 01060. College library founded in 1909, the music library in 1924. Music librarian: **Mary M. Ankudowich** (1941). The Josten Library has 41,000 books and scores and 40,000 recordings. The college library has holdings of 800,000 volumes. The music collection is strong in periodicals, definitive editions, and reference works. Unique in the library is a collection of vocal and instrumental music of the 16th and 17th centuries as copied by Alfred Einstein.

MICHIGAN

UNIVERSITY OF MICHIGAN MUSIC LIBRARY, 3239 School of Music, University of Michigan, Ann Arbor, Michigan 48104. Founded in 1941. Music Librarian: **Wallace Bjorke** (1962). The library's holdings are: 19,000 books, 28,661 scores, 13,500 recordings, 40 titles on micro-opaque cards, 1,256 reels of microfilm, 339 periodicals, and approximately 8,500 uncatalogued items. Volumes in the entire university library system: 3,652,521 as of June 30, 1971. The music library's 1,000 rare book items are particularly strong in 18th-century holdings—both books and music. Approximately 7,000 items of 19th- and early 20th-century sheet music of mostly European imprints are housed in the Corning Collection. In general, the Music Library's collection is designed to serve the complete range of academic music studies, from undergraduate through postdoctoral levels.

MINNESOTA

ST. PAUL PUBLIC LIBRARY, 90 West 4th Street, St. Paul, Minnesota 55102. The library was founded in 1882. **Marie D. Peck** is supervisor of Arts and Audio–Visual Services (includes art, films, and music). There are approximately 3,690 volumes of books on music, 8,750 scores, 6,048 recordings, and 10,000 uncatalogued items (mostly popular sheet music to 1950 with index). There are 10 branches of the St. Paul Library in addition to the central library, which contains a total of 366,947 volumes. The branches have comparatively few music books and fewer scores, but each has a record collection. Total volumes with the branches is 698,307.

UNIVERSITY OF MINNESOTA, MUSIC LIBRARY, 103 Walter Library, Minneapolis, Minnesota 55455. The main library was founded in 1851, the music library in 1948. Music librarian: **Katherine Holum** (1950). There are 16,000 music books and 18,000 scores in the library. There are also 11,700 recordings, 460 titles on microfilm reels, 242 titles on microcards, and 345 periodicals. There are 3,000,000 volumes in the general library.

MISSOURI

ST. LOUIS PUBLIC LIBRARY, 1301 Olive Street, St. Louis, Missouri 63103. Library founded: 1865. Music librarian: **Richard Russell** (1969). Of 30,500 volumes of books and scores in the library, approximately 6,500 are books and 24,000 scores. There are approximately 24,000 phonodiscs, 64 titles of periodicals, and approximately 2,000 uncatalogued items. The general library contains a total of 1,427,000 volumes. The music library has a large collection of operas, including phonodiscs and piano–vocal scores. There is a large collection of musicals (piano–vocal scores) plus a sizeable collection of chamber music, including scores and parts.

ST. LOUIS UNIVERSITY, VATICAN FILM LIBRARY, PIUS XII MEMORIAL LIBRARY, St. Louis, Missouri 63103. Founded in 1953. The library's special value lies in its 35,000 manuscript codices on microfilm of the Vatican library. Medieval, Renaissance, and early modern music manuscripts are found throughout the manuscripts of the Vatican library. Special concentrations of music are found in codices *Vaticani latini,* codices *Barberiniani latini,* and the codices of the Chigi Collection. The Film Library also has manuscripts of the Cappella Sistina.

UNIVERSITY OF MISSOURI, ELMER ELLIS LIBRARY, Columbia, Missouri 65201. The library was founded in 1842. The music library was established in 1961–62. Music librarian: **Mrs. Marcia Collins** (1971). It has a collection of about 20,000 volumes (no available detailed breakdown), and 4,094 titles of phonograph recordings. The parent university library has holdings of about 2 million. The microfilm collection of the university library is rated the second largest in the nation among research libraries. It has microfilm copies of nearly every book printed in the United States before 1800 and in England before 1640.

WASHINGTON UNIVERSITY, GAYLORD MUSIC LIBRARY, 6500 Forsyth Avenue, St. Louis, Missouri 63130. Founded in 1947, the library moved into a new building in 1960. Music librarian since 1948: **Mrs. Werner R. Krause.** There are 45,795 volumes (including bound periodicals) and 25,000 pieces of sheet music in the music collection. In addition there are 8,000 pieces of choral music, 10,035 recordings, 145 titles in microfilm reels, and approximately 1,000 volumes of uncatalogued items. Washington University owns the musicological library of Ernst C. Krohn, which is still housed in his home, with the exception of the rare items which are in the Rare Book Department of Olin Library of the university. The 25,000-piece sheet music collection contains about 3,000 items of American publication up to 1875.

NEW HAMPSHIRE

NEW HAMPSHIRE STATE LIBRARY, 20 Park Street, Concord, New Hampshire 03301. The library was founded in 1818. The music division is serviced by the general reference staff. There are 1,900 volumes of books on music, 5,000 titles of scores, 2,279 recording discs, and 10 titles of periodicals. The general library has 584,033 volumes.

NEW JERSEY

NEWARK PUBLIC LIBRARY, 5 Washington Street, Newark, N.J. 07102. The library was founded in 1889 and the music division in 1907. Music librarian: **William J. Dane** (1967). The music collection totals 18,500 including 7,000 music literature titles and 11,500 scores. Also included are 5,100 recordings, 10 titles on microfiche, and 400 bound periodicals with back issues. Uncatalogued items include 14,000 information file clippings plus 2,000 song sheets. The Newark Public Library has holdings totaling 1,075,000. Special items of the music collection include illuminated music manuscripts, 19th-century sheet music covers, John Tasker Howard notes and autographed letters from 20th-century musicians, and about 5,000 items used in the preparation of his books.

PRINCETON THEOLOGICAL SEMINARY, LOUIS F. BENSON COLLECTION OF HYMNOLOGY, SPEER LIBRARY, Princeton, N.J. 08540. The library was founded in 1812. There are 9,905 books of hymnology, both domestic and foreign. The general library contains a total of 305,916 volumes.

PRINCETON UNIVERSITY, MUSIC COLLECTION, FIRESTONE LIBRARY, Princeton, N.J. 08540. Music librarian: **Miss Paula Morgan** (1964). Approximately 12,800 books, 11,100 scores, 1,500 microfilm reels, 100 microcards, and 75 periodicals are in the music library. The general university library contains approximately 3,000,000 volumes. Music and books about music are in Firestone, the main university library building. Records and tapes are in the Woolworth Center for Musical Studies (q.v.). Strong points of the Firestone collection are materials on Bach, Beethoven, and Wagner. The Scheide Photographic Archive of Bach Manuscripts is located with the collection.

PRINCETON UNIVERSITY PHONOGRAPH RECORD LIBRARY, 109 Woolworth Center of Music Studies, Princeton, N.J. 08540. The library was founded ca. 1930. Music librarian: **Miss Ida Rosen** (1965). There are 20,000 recordings in this library.

RUTGERS UNIVERSITY—THE STATE UNIVERSITY OF NEW JERSEY, LIBRARY, New Brunswick, N.J. 08903. The university library was founded in 1766. Music librarian: **Roger M. Jarman** (1966). The central library has a total of 840,889 volumes. The Special Collections Department of the central library contains a large collection of 18th-century editions and manuscripts of works by Handel, 30 of which consist of: 6 editions by John Cluer (1725–1728), 2 editions by John Walsh (1740–1750), and 22 editions printed between 1769 and 1790. In addition, there are 11 18th-century manuscript copies of works by Handel, 9 of which are of anthems. The library has 6,000 recordings.

NEW YORK

BROOKLYN COLLEGE MUSIC LIBRARY, 375 Gershwin Hall, Brooklyn College, Brooklyn, N.Y. 11210. The library was founded in 1930, the music library in 1954. Music librarian: **Raymonde A. Sullivan** (1970). There are 10,000 book titles, 13,000 scores, 7,000 recordings, 400 microfilm reels, 30 microcards, and 200 periodicals in the music library. There are 5,000 uncatalogued items. The general library has 550,000 books (including books on music). Special collections include Americana (many rare hymnals), *Festschriften,* and unpublished translations into English of articles in many languages.

BUFFALO & ERIE COUNTY PUBLIC LIBRARY, Lafayette Square, Buffalo, N.Y. 14203. The Buffalo & Erie County Public Library was a merger, in 1954, of the Buffalo Public Library (founded 1836), the Grosvenor Reference Library (1859), and the Erie County Public Library (1947). Music librarian (acting head): **Norma Jean Lamb** (1971). The library contains approximately 58,000 volumes of books and scores, 71,500 pieces of sheet music, approximately 45,000 recordings, 70 microcards, and 173 periodical titles. The Central Library contains a total of approximately 1,461,000 volumes in a system of more than two and a half million volumes. The library has a special sheet music collection of 19th-century Americana, dating back to the 1820's.

COLUMBIA UNIVERSITY MUSIC LIBRARY, 701 Dodge, Broadway and 116th Street, New York, N.Y. 10027. As part of the music department, the library was begun under Edward MacDowell (1896–1904), Columbia's first music professor, and was augmented by collections of Anton Seidl (1905) and James Pech (1913). In 1934 the library was organized as a division of the university library system. **Thomas T. Watkins** has been music librarian since 1951. There are 18,389 books, 23,617 scores, 15,150 recordings, 796 microfilm reels, 472 microcards, and 3,378 periodicals in the music library. There are approximately 300 volumes of uncatalogued items. Special collections include Béla Bartók's personal studies and transcriptions of southeastern European folk music, and Judah Joffe's collection of recordings showing, in about 3,000 discs and cylinders, the evolution of recording. Unique items include some holographs of MacDowell. There is also a collection of MacDowell first editions and many first and early editions of Beethoven, Haydn, Mozart, and others.

CORNELL UNIVERSITY, MUSIC LIBRARY, Lincoln Hall, Ithaca, N.Y. 14850. The music library was founded about 1935 and incorporated into the university libraries in 1958. The first music librarian was appointed in 1942. **Richard H. Hunter** has been music librarian since 1970. There are 45,830 volumes of books, scores, and periodicals, and 13,780 volumes of recordings. There are also 328 microfilm reels, and 79 microcards. The total of volumes in the university library is 3,779,990. Basically, the music library is a research library with emphases on opera, contemporary music, and 16th-century music. Among uncatalogued items are an extensive sheet music collection and many microfilms.

HISPANIC SOCIETY OF AMERICA LIBRARY, 613 West 155th Street, New York, N.Y. 10032. The Society was founded in 1904. Its building is a combination museum and library. Its approximately 150,000 volumes form an important corpus of material for research on Spanish and Portuguese art, history, and literature. The library's music collection is limited to "some hundreds of volumes" (books, scores, and periodicals) with an emphasis on Spanish and Portugese and some Latin American. It owns a few music titles printed before 1701, as well as the manuscript of Granados's opera "Goyesca." Curator of the library is **Jean R. Longland.**

JULLIARD SCHOOL, LILA ACHESON WALLACE LIBRARY, Lincoln Center Plaza, New York, N.Y. 10023. The Juilliard School library was established in 1906; the Wallace Library is the new library of the school in its Lincoln Center installation. Music librarian: **Bennet Ludden** (1957). The holdings of the library are: 11,800 music books, 26,041 scores, 6,000 recordings, 85 periodicals, and 8,165 uncatalogued items. Special characteristics include the Edwards Collection of minor chamber works of the 19th and 20th centuries; opera piano–vocal scores of the 19th and 20th centuries; 19th-century French opera librettos; the Persinger Collection of violin music; and holograph scores and letters of musicians.

NEW YORK HISTORICAL SOCIETY LIBRARY, 170 Central Park West, New York, N.Y. 10024. The library was founded in 1809. Music is a small part of the general collection, and there is no music librarian. There are a limited number of books on music, a fairly large early American sheet music collection and 200 Edison cylinder recordings. The library contains a total of 500,000 volumes. There are rare items such as pre-1800 sacred music, 18th- and 19-century songsters, music about New York City and State, pictorial covers, New York scenes, campaign sheet music, and music of America's wars.

NEW YORK PRO MUSICA LIBRARY, 300 West End Avenue, New York, N.Y. 10023. Founded in 1954. It is the library of the performing group, New York Pro Musica (see Chamber Groups). The distinction of this library is that it houses one of the largest collections of antique instruments and replicas for performance use. Its over 120 musical instruments include 13 bowed string instruments (viols, vielle, rebec, violin, cittern), 3 organs, 2 harpsichords, 7 brasses (sackbuts, trumpet), 10 flutes and recorders, many reed instruments (krummhorns, rauschpfeifes, kortholts, etc.), handbells, psalteries, bagpipes, etc. Virtually all are in full playing condition. Publications in the library include facsimile editions, microfilms, slides, and books dealing with early performance practices. The library is supported by contributions of friends and benefactors.

NEW YORK PUBLIC LIBRARY MUSIC DIVISION AT LINCOLN CENTER, 111 Amsterdam Avenue, New York, N.Y. 10023. Music Librarian: **Frank C. Campbell** (1959). The main library of the New York Public Library system, Fifth Avenue and 42nd Street, was opened to the public in 1911. Its music holdings at that time came fundamentally from the Astor and Lenox Libraries (founded respectively in 1849 and 1870), the latter containing the Drexel Collection of music books, scores, pamphlets, etc. which formed the musical core of the Lenox Library. The Music Division of the New York Public Library was founded in 1924. It has been part of the Lincoln Center complex since 1963, housed within the Library and Museum of the Performing Arts along with various component libraries: the general library, which is publicly funded and which circulates recordings, scores, books on music, dance, and drama; the research libraries, consisting of the Music Division, the Dance Collection, Theatre Collection, and the Rodgers and Hammerstein Archives of Recorded Sound (q.v. as separate listing)—all privately funded. The following information is confined to the Music Division as a totality (see the separate listing for its constituent Americana Collection). The Music Division's holdings are estimated to be 100,000 books and 145,000 scores (both figures referring to the number of titles); 275,000 uncatalogued recordings; 450 reels of microfilm, 223 micro-opaque cards, 20 microfiche (microform totals refer to cards and reels, not titles); 5,000 periodicals (estimated) with the number of current subscriptions not separately tallied. Uncatalogued items total over five million and include clippings, programs, letters, sheet music, etc. Special collections within the Division include the Drexel Collection of rare books and scores, the Americana Collection (q.v.), Toscanini Memorial Archives of autographs of manuscripts, and original source material gleaned from American and European libraries on microfilm. The Music Division is one of the world's great scholarly collections, the scope of which cannot be delineated in a book of this kind. Its catalog of holdings, as of 1964, has been published by G. K. Hall & Co. of Boston (33 volumes: "Dictionary Catalog of the Music Collection"). Some special features of the library may be mentioned: the libraries of H. F. Albrecht, La Roche, E. F. Rimbault, Julian Edwards, James Huneker, Henry E. Krehbiel, Werner Wolffheim, and the library of the Beethoven Association; extensive folk music representation; opera librettos of the 18th and 19th centuries; historical editions; monuments and collected editions (some in duplicate); incunabula; holograph manuscripts and letters; extensive iconographic holdings; massive clippings and programs files, etc. The Music Division is a vital service institution for the unequaled music publishing, performing, and educational activities of New York City but is often utilized by individuals and organizations from throughout the world who submit requests for information. In 1971, the Research Libraries suffered what seemed to be an irreversible crisis when, for lack of funds, they faced closure to public use. Funds were subsequently raised through benefit performances by leading actors, singers, and musicians and through public and private appeals which satisfied the immediate financial needs of the institution.

NEW YORK PUBLIC LIBRARY MUSIC DIVISION—AMERICANA COLLECTION, Lincoln Center, 111 Amsterdam Avenue, New York, N.Y. 10023. Americana Collection Librarian: **Richard Jackson** (1965). Founded in 1938. The Collection's approximately 12,500 titles consist of 1,400 books and 11,100 scores. There are about 220,000 uncatalogued items including about 2,165 uncatalogued manuscripts. The Collection includes autograph manuscripts of American composers, letters and documents of individuals and organizations in music, a large number of American broadsides (mostly of the 19th century), rare tune books, songsters, and unique sheet music. There are special card indexes including a subject guide to popular songs. Manuscripts include those by Gottschalk, Griffes, George F. Bristow, and large representation of the music of contemporary American composers.

NEW YORK UNIVERSITY MUSIC LIBRARY, Bobst Library, Washington Square, N.Y. 10003.) University library was founded in 1843; the music library in 1945. Music librarian is **Mrs. Ruth B. Hilton** (1968). The music collection consists of approximately 5,200 book titles (totaling some 8,100 volumes) and about 5,488 titles of music scores (totaling some 8,202 volumes). In microforms, the library owns 220 titles on microfilm reels and 35 titles on micro-opaque cards. Periodicals are included in the total count of books; current periodical subscriptions total 130. Uncatalogued are 600 items plus unopened gifts of 3,500 scores and 3,000 books. The main university library has holdings of two million volumes. General characteristics of the music library are those of a library broadly supporting academic undergraduate and graduate music study. Its holdings include some primary sources. Beginning in

1972, it will have some special holdings on the work of Giuseppe Verdi, and in 1973, the music library will cover the curriculum for the school's music education program.

THE PIERPONT MORGAN LIBRARY, 29 East 36th Street, New York, N.Y. 10016. The Morgan Library was opened to the public in 1924. It has no separate music library. The music collection consists mostly of music manuscripts and autograph letters of composers, performers, et al. These are housed as part of the Collection of Autograph Manuscripts, Curator of which is **Herbert Cahoon** (1954). Music holdings are in the following collections: the Mary Flagler Cary Collection (acquired by the library in 1968) of over 3,000 autograph letters; together with the Robert Owen Lehman collection it has some 400 music manuscripts. The Cary Collection, in addition to manuscripts and letters, has printed books, documents, and portraits. The important manuscripts include Brahms's First Symphony, some Chopin mazurkas, Schubert's "Die Winterreise," and "Schwanengesang," as well as the "Death and the Maiden" string quartet, Strauss's "Don Juan," Beethoven's "Ghost Trio," Handel's "Messiah," the Diaghilev manuscript of Stravinsky's "Firebird," etc. Some cataloguing is still being done for both the Lehman and Cary collections. (The latter has been described in a special catalog issued by the library and is available for sale.) Other music items include about a dozen manuscripts from the original Morgan collection, a large collection of Gilbert & Sullivan manuscripts, letters, programs, scores, books, etc.

QUEENS COLLEGE MUSIC LIBRARY, Karol Rathaus Hall, Flushing, N.Y. 11367. The library was founded in 1937, the music library in 1938. **Barbara R. Greener** has been music librarian since 1950. The library has 10,500 volumes of books on music and 18,500 scores in addition to 70,000 choral folios and instrumental parts. There are 12,000 recordings, 960 titles on microfilm reels, 600 microcards, and 1,500 volumes of periodicals. The general college library has a total of 450,000 volumes.

RODGERS AND HAMMERSTEIN ARCHIVES OF RECORDED SOUND, NEW YORK PUBLIC LIBRARY AT LINCOLN CENTER (Research Library of the Performing Arts), 111 Amsterdam Avenue, New York, N.Y. 10023. Established in 1963. Librarian: **David Hall** (1967). This library is a noncirculating library for sound recordings and is apart from the record collection in the circulating division of the Library of the Performing Arts. Its estimated total holdings in discs and tapes is 44,000 plus about 200,000 uncatalogued discs and ephemera. In addition, the Archives has some 3,000 books and record company catalogues, including about 100 periodicals; there are microfilm copies of 10 periodical continuations and record company catalogues. The Archives is the "first major sound archives [in America] open to the general public." The recordings in the collection are extremely diverse, not only in content which includes extensive coverage of classical music, historical performances, jazz and folk music, popular music, Broadway musical plays, film sound tracks, repertory drama companies, music for the dance, as well as languages, sounds of nature, etc., but also in varied forms of original recordings such as LP and 78-rpm discs, piano rolls, cylinders, early Berliner discs, hill and dale recordings, prerecorded tapes, etc. Limited edition and private recordings are also part of the collection. Rare and unique items include the Mapleson cylinders of performances in the Metropolitan Opera House in the years 1901–1903 and the Columbia Grand Opera Records of 1903. All the recordings themselves are inaccessible to listeners. Listening is with headphones in separate booths through a remote control and intercommunication system.

SIBLEY MUSIC LIBRARY, EASTMAN SCHOOL OF MUSIC, 26 Gibbs Street, Rochester, N.Y. 14604. Founded in 1922, the year of the opening of the Eastman School. The origin of the library stems from the collection of Mr. Hiram Sibley, who donated his collection to the University of Rochester in 1904. Music librarian: **Ruth Watanabe.** The total music collection is about 170,000 catalogued volumes and about 25,000 uncatalogued items. Periodical subscriptions are in excess of 200. The Sibley Library is known to be the largest academic music research and reference library in the United States. Manuscript collections include holographs of works by Beethoven, Brahms, Liszt, Mozart, Debussy, Schumann, the American composers **Hanson,** MacDowell, **Harris, Copland,** Chadwick, et al. The library is strong in holdings in early music theory, French opera, contemporary American music, orchestral and chamber music, monuments of music, collected editions of the works of master composers (some in duplicate) and other multivolume music series. It owns a collection of incunabula. Over 400 early music theory and history treatises have been issued by the University of Rochester and the Sibley Library on microcards. In general, the library supports the full range of academic studies and private instruction at the school—from preparatory student and special student to students in doctoral studies and from applied music to music literature and history.

STATE UNIVERSITY OF NEW YORK AT BUFFALO, MUSIC LIBRARY, Baird Hall, Fine Arts Drive, Buffalo, N.Y. 14214. The music library was founded in 1970; the main university library about 1962. Music librarian is **James Coover.** The music collection is comprised of 9,265 books, 20,482 scores, 7,014 recordings, 778 microforms, 4,115 periodicals, and 14,381 uncatalogued items. (Books, scores, records, and periodicals are indicated as volumes.) The library supports the university's broad music needs from popular music cross-disciplinary studies to the doctoral programs in composition, history of music and music education, graduate degree study in performance, music librarianship, etc.

VASSAR COLLEGE, GEORGE SHERMAN DICKINSON MUSIC LIBRARY, Poughkeepsie, N.Y. 12601. The library was founded in 1931. Music librarian: **Frederick Freedman** (1967). There are 16,000 volumes of books, 21,000 volumes of scores, 20,000 discs and tapes, 200 microfilm reels, 200 microcards, and a number of periodicals included in the books total. The college library contains nearly 500,000 volumes in all. The library has especially good reference materials, collected works, and *Denkmäler* ("monuments").

NORTH CAROLINA

THE MORAVIAN MUSIC FOUNDATION, 20 Cascade Avenue, Salem Station, Winston-Salem, North Carolina 27108. (See also under Music Organizations, etc.) The book and manuscript holdings of the Foundation are separately the properties of the Foundation and the properties of the Archives of the Moravian Church but in custody of the Foundation. The Foundation (established in 1956) houses the music books and manuscripts of the latter, the Southern Province of the Church. The archives of the Northern Province are held in the Archives of the Moravian Church, Main and Elizabeth Streets, Bethlehem, Pennsylvania 18018. Further Foundation holdings are in European Moravian Centers, which are the responsibility of the Foundation but are as yet largely unexamined and uncatalogued. The Foundation's direct holdings make up the Peters Memorial Library, which contains modern reference books on music, religion, Moravian Church history, American music, hymnology, and American history, some rare early publications on music and miscellaneous manuscripts. Cataloguing of the collections is incomplete. The Archives of the Church include the Irving Lowens Musical Americana Collection of tune books, hymnals, etc., of which a tentative inventory has been made (the library has since added more Americana on its own initiative including a large uncatalogued collection of popular sheet music from the 19th and early 20th centuries); the Johannes Herbst Collection and the Salem Congregation Collections—both catalogued manuscript collections (the former is fully described in the recent publication, "Catalog of the Johannes Herbst Collection," by **Marilyn Gombosi,** former assistant director of the Foundation and chief of research; published by the University of North Carolina Press, Chapel Hill, 1971). The Herbst and Salem Congregation Collections have anthems for mixed voices and chamber orchestra—altogether about 4,000 to 5,000 items. The Herbst Collection is composed of over 500 manuscripts of approximately 1,000 sacred anthems and arias with instrumental accompaniment compiled and copied out by Herbst (1735–1812). Other Foundation holdings are the Collegium Musicum Collection of manuscripts and early published editions of chamber and orchestral music of the 18th and early 19th centuries, uncatalogued; the Kurth Collection of German-American Music Manuscripts; and uncatalogued collections of 18th century band books, Civil War music, and 100 music copy books containing songs and keyboard music. The emphasis is on the music of the Moravians of the 18th and 19th centuries throughout the Foundation's libraries and the Archives. Librarian–Cataloguer is **Frances Cumnock** (1968).

OHIO

CASE WESTERN UNIVERSITY, MUSIC HOUSE LIBRARY, 11115 Bellflower Road, Cleveland, Ohio 44106. Founded in 1950. The music librarian since 1971 has been **Mrs. Helene Stern.** There are 4,500 music books, 4,000 scores, 5,700 recordings, 200 titles on microfilm reels, 89 titles on microfiche, 66 periodicals (all bound volumes shelved in main library). The Arthur Shepherd Collection consists of manuscripts and scores of his own works as well as letters and other miscellany, all housed in the main campus library (Freiberger Library, Rare Books & Special Collections).

TOLEDO–LUCAS COUNTY PUBLIC LIBRARY, 325 Michigan, Toledo, Ohio 43624. The library was founded in 1838. Since 1961, **Alice Rupp** has been head of art–music–sports division. The music collection has approximately 4,400 titles of music books and 1,600 scores; 2,200 recordings, 24 periodicals; 4,238 uncatalogued pieces of sheet music and 5,464 volumes of choral music. The library contains a total of 1,143,765 volumes.

UNIVERSITY OF CINCINNATI, COLLEGE-CONSERVATORY OF MUSIC, GORNO MEMORIAL MUSIC LIBRARY, 101 Emery Hall, Cincinnati, Ohio 45221. Founded in 1867; since 1968, the music librarian has been **Robert O. Johnson.** There are 10,000 music books, 9,500 scores, 4,800 recordings, and 327 titles on microfilm reels. The general library of the university has 1,156,117 volumes.

OREGON

LIBRARY ASSOCIATION OF PORTLAND, MUSIC DEPARTMENT, 801 S.W. 10th Avenue, Portland, Oregon 97205. The library was founded in 1864, the music library in 1936. Music librarian since 1965 has been **Barbara K. Heiden.** There are 8,850 book titles (includes dance books titles), 17,400 scores (books and scores as of June 30, 1971) and 9,747 volumes of record albums (as of February, 1972). There are also 75 periodical titles. The general library contains 980,679 volumes (June 30, 1971). Special collections include inscribed and autographed photographs of singers, dancers, and instrumentalists who visited and performed in Portland, Oregon during the 1910's and 1920's.

UNIVERSITY OF OREGON LIBRARY, Eugene, Oregon 97403. Library founded: 1881. Music librarian: **Edmund Soule** (1966). There are, in the music collection, 20,500 books, 13,500 scores, 7,400 recordings, 3,300 all types of microforms and 90 periodicals. The general library contains 1,100,000 volumes. Special collections include American sheet music of the 19th and 20th centuries which is organized but not yet indexed. There are about 50,000 items in this collection.

PENNSYLVANIA

FREE LIBRARY OF PHILADELPHIA, MUSIC DEPARTMENT, Logan Square,

Philadelphia, Pennsylvania 19103. The library was founded in 1892, the music department in 1897. Music librarian: **Elizabeth R. Hartman** (1965). It has a total of 62,600 volumes of books and music scores, 39,524 recordings, 10 titles on microfilm reels, 460 periodicals, and 850,000 uncatalogued items. The central library has 800,000 volumes (specified as adult volumes). Features of the music collection are: the Drinker Library of Choral Music, containing 603 titles, chiefly of Bach's works in English translation with multiple copies of the chorus parts and orchestrations for many of the works; American Sheet Music Collection of 150,000 pieces of popular music from the Revolution to the present.

THE LIBRARY COMPANY OF PHILADELPHIA, 1314 Locust Street, Philadelphia, Pennsylvania 19107. Reference Librarion: **Mrs. Lillian Tonkin.** Founded by Benjamin Franklin in 1731, the library is the oldest continuously operating subscription library in the country. The total holdings of the library number somewhere between 250,000 and 260,000 books, of which the music collection is a part. The main collection has superior holdings in Americana with its greatest strength in the period from the Colonial era through the Civil War. The music collection includes items from the Wolfe bibliography of secular music published between 1801 and 1825; songsters; books on music instruction; hymnals; music histories (American and foreign); organ music; opera piano-vocal scores and librettos; a collection from Albert G. Emerick, a Philadelphia musician, consisting of books on music theory, essays, histories, etc., with French imprints. No subject headings in the rare book room catalogue. No appointed music librarian. The library has published "American Song Sheets, slip ballads and Poetical Broadsides, 1850–1870," edited by **Edwin Wolf, II,** Librarian.

UNIVERSITY OF PENNSYLVANIA, THE OTTO E. ALBRECHT MUSIC LIBRARY, Philadelphia, Pennsylvania 19104. The music library was founded in 1953. **Kostas Ostrauskas** has been music librarian since 1958. There are approximately 27,000 volumes of books and music scores. There are also about 20,000 recordings, 160 titles on microfilm reels, 300 microcards, and 115 periodicals.

CARNEGIE LIBRARY OF PITTSBURGH, MUSIC DIVISION, 4400 Forbes Avenue, Pittsburgh, Pennsylvania 15213. Library founded in 1895. Music library established in 1938. Catalogued items total approximately 76,000 bound volumes consisting of 22,730 books and 53,270 scores. Recordings total 12,396 discs. Microfilm reels and microcard holdings are of unknown quantity. Approximate number of periodical titles is 330. Uncatalogued items are about 1,300 titles (popular songs). The Carnegie Library's total volume holdings are 2,266,112, a figure which includes branch libraries, bookmobiles, children's collection—all of which have some music books (figure is for 1971). The Music Division's special characteristics are: Unique items—holographs and manuscripts of works by Andriessen, Cecil Burleigh, Buxtehude (manuscript copy of considerable age), Cadman, Carpenter, Dallapiccola, Ross Lee Finney, Ginastera, Middelschulte, Emil Paur, et al.; letters by W. Damrosch, Victor Herbert, Charles Ives, Saint-Saëns, Varèse, et al.; Karl Merz Musical Library—approximately 1,400 items (Merz, 1836–1890) of 18th- and 19th-century musical literature (Ambros, Burney, Fétis, et al.), and particularly strong in early American music literature. Boyd Memorial Collection: approximately 3,000 volumes of English and foreign language music literature and over 100 scrapbooks of concert programs, clippings, pamphlets, etc. The Collection also includes the personal libraries of other musicians (Zinsmeister, G. Yost, Harvey B. Gaul, H. Ringwalt, Carl Braun, Mrs. Beveridge Webster, et al.). The Division has over 100 pre-1800 publications of histories, treatises, etc. Through the Bald Endowment Fund (over $115,000) the Division has acquired many collected editions, monuments, and musicological series. Of the periodicals held, 78 are of titles beginning publication before 1865.

UNIVERSITY OF PITTSBURGH, THEODORE M. FINNEY MUSIC LIBRARY, Pittsburgh, Pennsylvania 15213. The music library was founded in 1966; **Norris L. Stephens** has been music librarian since that date. There are 8,000 titles of books, 20,000 titles of scores, 3,500 recordings, 2,000 microfilm reels, 250 microcards, 150 titles of periodicals, and 20,000 titles of uncatalogued items. In addition there are another 12,000 titles of literature in the main library. Special collections include the private library of Theodore M. Finney, former chairman of the Music Department. The library has over 1,000 manuscripts of the more than 1,400 works of Fidelis Zitterbart (b. Pittsburgh, Pennsylvania, 1845; d. 1915), the collected works of Adolph Foerster, and manuscripts and early editions of Ethelbert Nevin. Rare items number over 1,000 titles published before 1800, and a manuscript by Joseph Haydn.

TENNESSEE

MEMPHIS PUBLIC LIBRARY AND INFORMATION CENTER, 1850 Peabody Avenue, Memphis, Tennessee 38104. Library founded: 1893. Music library founded: 1955. Music librarian: **Mrs. Jan Karpinski** (1970). The music library contains 5,850 volumes including 3,000 books and 2,850 scores. There are also 5,801 recordings, 38 periodicals, and an unestimated number of uncatalogued items. The general library contains a total of 815,855 volumes. The library is now building a special in-depth collection of books and recordings in the jazz/blues area.

TEXAS

UNIVERSITY OF TEXAS AT AUSTIN, MUSIC LIBRARY, Pierce Hall, 103, Austin, Texas 78712. The library was founded in 1903, the music library in 1941. **Eulan V. Brooks** has been music librarian since 1964. There are 13,000 volumes of books, 16,000 titles of scores, 8,750 volumes of recordings, 900 microfilm reels, 250 microcards, and 2,300 volumes of periodicals. There are also 3,800 uncatalogued items. The general university library contains a total of 2,349,428 volumes.

VIRGINIA

MUSIC LIBRARY OF THE UNIVERSITY OF VIRGINIA, 113 Old Cabell Hall, Charlottesville, Virginia 22903. The library was founded in 1819; the music division in 1940. Music librarian: **Jean M. Bonin** (1971). The music library has 9,000 titles (books and periodicals), 21,000 titles of scores, 4,400 recordings, and 150 titles on microfilm reels. The general library contains 1,256,472 volumes. There is a sizeable amount of rare book material, extensive manuscript collections, principally of traditional music; an extensive collection of miscellaneous imprints of performing editions; a valuable collection of 18th-century imprints including rare tutors, known as the MacKay Smith collection; the Monticello Music Collection; manuscript and typescript, and discs of traditional music; some **Randall Thompson** manuscripts; printed and manuscript collection of the music of John Powell.

VIRGINIA STATE LIBRARY, 11th and Capitol Streets, Richmond, Virginia 23219. The library was founded in 1823. The music collection contains 3,500 volumes of books, 3,500 scores, and about 3,000 pieces of sheet music. There are 100 uncatalogued items. The total number of volumes in the library is 500,000. Most of the sheet music consists of items of Virginia or Southern interest with a large number of Confederate pieces. There are also a number of 19th-century Virginia songsters, hymnals, and other music books.

WASHINGTON

SEATTLE PUBLIC LIBRARY, 4th & Madison, Seattle, Washington 98104. Music librarian: **Mrs. Carolyn Holmquist** (1968). Founded in 1891, the library contains 24,543 music books, 28,157 scores, 13,806 recordings, and 1,552 volumes of periodicals. The total library contains 1,449,870 volumes.

SPOKANE PUBLIC LIBRARY, 906 W. Main Street, Spokane, Washington 99201. Library founded: 1884. **Janet Miller** has been music librarian since 1954. There are 3,550 titles (books and music), 13,167 recordings, and 20 periodicals (plus *Music Index*). Uncatalogued items include some scores and old sheet music. The general library contains a total of 419,405 volumes. The library contains a few 16mm sound/color films and approximately 100 music books in rare book collection.

UNIVERSITY OF WASHINGTON, MUSIC LIBRARY, 113 Music Building, Seattle, Washington 98195. Music librarian: **David A. Wood** (1967). Publications total 37,228 volumes divided as follows: 14,290 books, 21,507 volumes of scores, and 1,431 volumes of periodicals. The library owns 915 microfilm reels and 11 titles on microcards. Features include the Hazel G. Kinscella collection of early American hymnals and tune books; a collection of opera scores, printed and in manuscript, from the late 17th to early 19th centuries; 100 letters to and from Massenet; and 10 letters of Bartók.

WISCONSIN

MILWAUKEE PUBLIC LIBRARY, ART & MUSIC DIVISION, 814 W. Wisconsin, Milwaukee, Wisconsin 53233. Library founded: 1878. Music library founded: 1898. There are approximately 23,500 volumes of music books and the same number of scores in the library. There are also 20,000 titles of recordings. The total number of volumes in the main library is 2,133,215.

Summer Music Camps and Schools

The list of camps that follows emphasizes those offering a variety of music learning opportunities ranging from band, orchestra, choral ensembles, and chamber groups to private instrumental or vocal lessons, instruction in music theory and history, and so forth. Omitted are camps only incidentally concerned with music but which, nevertheless, are often referred to as music camps, particularly in that branch of music education where instructional orientation is derived from the marching band or school athletics band. Thus, not included in the list are summer camps offering primarily, or exclusively, instruction in baton-twirling, cheerleading, drum majoring, etc., of which there are many in the United States.

Also omitted, with some exceptions, are colleges and universities offering the normal semester's music curriculum during the summer term primarily for its own regularly enrolled students. Colleges and universities offering summer music instruction of any kind are to be found in the main listing of schools.

A camp sponsored by or affiliated with a college or university is included here if it provides training to pre-college-age students and if it is otherwise distinguished as something more than a normal credit-bearing summer term.

Certain summer music schools are best known in conjunction with music festivals and are to be found in the festivals section. Special convocations, institutes, or seminars may be mentioned elsewhere in this book (for example, the Congress of Strings, sponsored by the American Federation of Musicians, can be found under Organizations).

Total student attendance at summer music camps in the United States has been surveyed by the American Music Conference: its findings show an annual attendance growth rate of 18 percent. In 1960, there were an estimated 25,000 students attending summer camps of all types; in 1965, 42,500; 1970, 72,000. There has been no corroboration of these figures from any other source.

The listing below is arranged alphabetically by states.

ALASKA

KING'S LAKE FINE ARTS CAMP, P.O. Box 325, Anchorage, Alaska 99501. A camp held in two sessions of two weeks each from mid-June to mid-July. The first session for junior high age, and the second for high school students. Various band and orchestra ensembles plus art and dance are taught.

CALIFORNIA

ARROWBEAR MUSIC CAMP, Winter address: 4220 Heather Road, Long Beach, California 92308. Summer address: Arrowbear Lake, California 92008. A 10-week camp, beginning late June and continuing until late August. For primary school through college age musicians. Instrumental and vocal ensembles are organized. . . . CAZADERO MUSIC CAMP, Winter address: 1835 Allston Way, Berkeley, California 94704. Summer address: 17345 Cazadero Highway, Cazadero, California 95421. Three two-week sessions offered beginning from the end of June through late August; for young musicians from primary through high school age. Instrumental ensembles plus a special flute workshop. . . . IDYLLWILD SCHOOL OF MUSIC AND THE ARTS (ISOMATA) of the University of Southern California (see ISOMATA MUSIC FESTIVAL under Music Festivals, California) . . . (UNIVERSITY OF THE PACIFIC) PACIFIC MUSIC CAMP, Conservatory of Music, Stockton, California 95204. One session (senior camp) of four weeks for students of high school through college age. Instrumental and choral ensembles plus special piano courses are available. Five sessions (junior camps) of one week each offered in special areas of band, choral, or orchestra music, all for secondary school ages. Sessions begin late June through late July; the senior camp coincides with the junior camps.

CONNECTICUT

LAUREL MUSIC CAMP, R.F.D. #2, Winsted, Connecticut 06098 (summer address). R.F.D. #1 Winsted, Connecticut 06098 (winter address). A one-week session from late June through early July for high school and college students. Instrumental and choral ensembles. . . . YALE SUMMER SCHOOL OF MUSIC AND ART. Winter address: c/o Yale School of Music, New Haven, Connecticut 06520. Summer address: Yale Summer School of Music and Art, Norfolk, Connecticut 06058. An eight-week camp from the end of June through late August for graduate students only. Band, orchestra, and chorus ensembles. (See also NORFOLK CONCERTS, under Music Festivals—Connecticut.)

FLORIDA

FLORIDA STATE UNIVERSITY SUMMER MUSIC CAMP, Tallahassee, Florida 32306. A four-week camp from the end of June through late July for young musicians of high school age. Instrumental and vocal ensembles offered; special courses in conducting, improvisation, opera, music appreciation. . . . UNIVERSITY OF MIAMI SUMMER BAND AND ORCHESTRA CAMP, Coral Gables, Florida 33124. A five-week camp from mid-June through mid-July for students of high school age. Band and orchestra ensembles.

IDAHO

RICKS COLLEGE SUMMER ACADEMY OF FINE ARTS, Rexburg, Idaho 83440. A two-week camp from mid- to late June; no age limit. In addition to band and orchestra ensembles, courses in art, ballet, theater, string quartet festival, and organ are held. . . . UNIVERSITY OF IDAHO SUMMER MUSIC CAMP, School of Music, Moscow, Idaho 83843. A two-week camp beginning in mid-June for youth of high school age. Various ensembles plus conducting and composition classes.

ILLINOIS

EASTERN ILLINOIS UNIVERSITY SCHOOL OF MUSIC, Charleston, Illinois 61920. Two sessions from early to late June for high school students, with band, orchestra, stage band, and piano instruction. Two sessions of one-week each and two sessions of two weeks each in specialized courses for directors, teachers, and college students, from early June through early July. . . . EGYPTIAN MUSIC CAMP, DuQuoin State Fairgrounds, DuQuoin, Illinois 62832. A four-week camp from June to July for primary and secondary school ages. Band, chorus, small ensembles, and piano ensembles are offered. . . . ILLINOIS WESLEYAN UNIVERSITY SCHOOL OF MUSIC, Bloomington, Illinois 61701. A one-week band camp for junior high school students, from mid- to late June. A two-week camp for high school students from late June through early July with band, but also offers orchestra, chorus, small ensemble, and stage band. . . . NORTHERN ILLINOIS UNIVERSITY MUSIC FOR YOUTH CAMP, DeKalb, Illinois 60115. A two-week camp beginning mid-July for high school students and older. Instrumental and choral ensembles plus piano. . . . UNIVERSITY OF ILLINOIS—ILLINOIS SUMMER YOUTH MUSIC CAMP, 608 S. Mathews, Urbana, Illinois 61801. Fifteen two-week sessions in specialized areas, beginning mid-June through the end of July. Sessions divided in age groups between junior high and high school students. . . . WESTERN ILLINOIS UNIVERSITY, Summer Music Camp, Macomb, Illinois 61455. A two-week camp from mid-June through early July for secondary school age groups. Instrumental and choral ensembles.

INDIANA

NATIONAL STAGE BAND CAMPS, P.O. Box 221, South Bend, Indiana 46624. Organized in various college campuses throughout the country. No age limits. Provided are stage band ensemble courses in arranging, improvisation, youth music workshop; electronic modulator and synthesizer clinic classes are held. . . . UNIVERSITY OF EVANSVILLE, TRI-STATE MUSIC CAMP, Evansville, Indiana 47701. A one-week camp in late June with instrumental and choral ensembles, plus class piano, history and appreciation of popular music.

IOWA

LUTHER COLLEGE, DORIAN MUSIC CAMP, Decorah, Iowa 52101. Three one-week sessions beginning mid-June: a band camp for junior high school students, a camp offering instrumental ensemble for high school students, and a special guitar workshop the final week. The junior high and high school camps also offer music literature, conducting, and a string seminar. . . . MORNINGSIDE COLLEGE, Sioux City, Iowa 51106. Two one-week summer camps divided into junior and senior high school students. Art is taught in addition to instrumental and vocal ensembles. The camp is held in two sessions, beginning mid-June and ending early July. . . . UNIVERSITY OF IOWA ALL-STATE MUSIC CAMP, Iowa City, Iowa 52240. A two-week camp for youth through high school ages, held from mid-June through early July. In addition to instrumental and choral ensembles, music appreciation, reed-making, composition workshop, and conducting courses are held. . . . UNIVERSITY OF NORTHERN IOWA, TALLCORN BAND CAMP, Cedar Falls, Iowa 50613. A one-week camp held in early August for high school youth.

KENTUCKY

DANIEL BOONE FOREST MUSIC CAMP, Morehead State University, Morehead, Kentucky 40351. Held 12 days in July for youth of pre-high-school age and older. Instruction is in band, smaller instrumental ensembles, some music theory, reed-making, conducting and piano.

LOUISIANA

LOUISIANA TECH SUMMER MUSIC CAMP, Box 5316–Tech Station, Ruston, Louisiana 71270. A two-week camp beginning mid-June for secondary school through college ages, offering instrumental and vocal ensemble training. . . . NORTHEAST LOUISIANA UNIVERSITY SCHOOL OF MUSIC SUMMER MUSIC CAMP, Monroe, Louisiana 71201. A two-week summer camp, offering instrumental and vocal ensembles, beginning mid-July, for youth through high school and junior college age. . . . NORTHWESTERN STATE UNIVERSITY OF LOUISIANA SUMMER MUSIC CAMP, Natchitoches, Louisiana 71457. A two-week camp beginning in early July offering instrumental and vocal ensembles, plus piano and organ instruction. For youth from pre-high school to junior college age.

MAINE

NEW ENGLAND MUSIC CAMP. Summer address: R.F.D. #1, Oakland, Maine 04963. Winter address: Snead Island, Palmetto, Florida 33561. A four- to eight-week camp for youth from primary school age groups through high school, beginning the end of June through late August. If the full eight-week course is taken, lessons in organ, piano, accompanying, and recorder are taught.

MASSACHUSETTS

AMHERST SUMMER MUSIC CENTER. Winter address: 18 Braeburn Road, South Deerfield, Massachusetts 01373. Summer address: Raymond, Maine 04071. A seven-week camp beginning July 1st, for youth through college age. In addition to instrumental and choral ensembles, courses in keyboard, voice, sight-reading, music history, arranging, and composition.

MICHIGAN

BLUE LAKE FINE ARTS CAMP, Twin Lake, Michigan 49457. An eight-week camp which may be attended on a two-week basis. The session runs from the end of June through late August for youth through high school age. In addition to instrumental and vocal ensembles, courses in piano, harp, guitar, music history, ballet, art, and drama are taught. . . . CENTRAL MICHIGAN UNIVERSITY–HIGH SCHOOL MUSIC CAMP, Department of Music, Mt. Pleasant, Michigan 48858. A two-week camp beginning mid-July for high school students. In addition to instrumental and choral ensembles, conducting, music history, music literature, electronic class piano, and electronic synthesizer are taught. . . . NATIONAL MUSIC CAMP, Interlochen, Michigan 49643. Founded in 1928 by Joseph Maddy (1891–1966), it is a music camp of enormous proportion, conceptually and operationally, and is perhaps the most famous institution of its kind in existence. Located on a 1,400-acre campus, it admits some 1,700 students for its 57-day summer season (late June to late August). (In 1972, some 2,300 students of a wide age range, a faculty of 175 and a staff of 625 attended the Camp.) Instrumental and vocal ensemble training is the main emphasis, with public performances culminating the effort. In 1971, in all a total of 325 programs were presented (the number sometimes has been higher), which included student recitals, concerts, preliminary concerto auditions, some faculty recitals, opera performances, etc. Performances take place in a number of locations: Kresge Auditorium, Interlochen Bowl, Jesse V. Stone Auditorium, Grunnow Theater, and the Opera Tent. Certain concerts and recitals are tape-recorded for delay-broadcast over the FM–stereo station, WIAA (88.3 mHz) in Interlochen, and others are broadcast live. WIAA supplies the tapes to member stations of National Public Radio. Other broadcast outlets for the programs are the Voice of America and the National Broadcasting Company's feature called "The Best from Interlochen." Such public exposure to student musical performances suggests the standards applied in the curriculum at Interlochen. Instructional levels include girls' and boys' junior, intermediate, and high school divisions (university level activities also take place) with their respective ensembles: choirs, concert bands, concert orchestras, symphonic bands, symphony orchestras, "World Youth" symphony orchestra, etc. The orchestras are led by music educators as well as guest professional conductors. The faculty is drawn from high schools, colleges, and the professional concert field. Besides ensemble training, there are individual lessons, courses in music theory, history and literature, drama, dance, and some academic subjects. . . . NORTHERN MICHIGAN UNIVERSITY SUMMER MUSIC CAMP, Department of Music, Northern Michigan University, Marquette, Michigan 49855. A one-week camp held in August for late primary grade and high school students. Choral and instrumental ensembles are offered. . . . WAYNE STATE UNIVERSITY SUMMER MUSIC PROGRAM FOR HIGH SCHOOL STUDENTS, 105 Music Building, Detroit, Michigan 48202. A four-week course of instruction held in July and covering training in orchestral, chamber, and choral performance. . . . WESTERN MICHIGAN UNIVERSITY SUMMER MUSIC SEMINARS, Department of Music, Kalamazoo, Michigan 49001. Six simultaneously scheduled seminars lasting for two weeks in July covering respectively chamber music performance training for brass, woodwind, percussion, and string players; choral singing; and piano performance. Music literature is offered throughout.

MINNESOTA

ARROWHEAD MUSIC CAMP. Winter address: 2602 South Rivershore Drive, Moorhead, Minnesota 56560. Summer address: Lake Hanging Horn, Barnum, Minnesota 55707. Four separate sessions for choral, stage band, orchestra (one week each) and band (three weeks), respectively. Age limit is from high school up for the choral camp and junior high through high school for the instrumental camps. Piano and organ lessons may be had at the choral camp and piano at the orchestra and band sessions.

MISSOURI

UNIVERSITY OF MISSOURI ALL-STATE MUSIC CAMP, 140 Fine Arts, University of Missouri, Columbia, Missouri 65201. A two-week camp from mid-June through early July for junior high and high school students. Instrumental and vocal ensembles.

MONTANA

UNIVERSITY OF MONTANA SCHOOL OF FINE ARTS SUMMER MUSIC SCHOOL, Missoula, Montana 59801. A two-week offering, for high school age musicians, of band, chorus, and orchestra training, music literature, art, drama, and dance.

NEVADA

UNIVERSITY OF NEVADA, LAKE TAHOE MUSIC CAMP, Department of Music, Reno, Nevada 89507. A two-week camp beginning early August for grade school students and older. Instrumental and choral ensembles.

NEW HAMPSHIRE

UNIVERSITY OF NEW HAMPSHIRE SUMMER YOUTH MUSIC SCHOOL, c/o Division of Continuing Education, Durham, New Hampshire 03824. A two-week camp from mid- to late August for youth through high school age. Instrumental and vocal ensembles.

NEW JERSEY

GLASSBORO STATE COLLEGE SUMMER MUSIC CAMP, Glassboro, N.J. 08028. A three-week camp in August for high school students. Training is available for band, orchestra, chorus, operetta, and madrigal singing.

NEW MEXICO

EASTERN NEW MEXICO UNIVERSITY SUNSHINE MUSIC CAMP, Portales, New Mexico 88130. A two-week camp beginning early June for high school through college youth. Conducting is offered in addition to all varieties of instrumental and choral ensembles. . . . HIGHLANDS UNIVERSITY, HIGHLANDS MUSIC CAMP, Las Vegas, New Mexico 87701. A one-week camp in early June for students aged 12 and older. Instrumental and choral ensembles.

NEW YORK

CAMP SOLITUDE CHAMBER MUSIC SCHOOL. Lake Placid, N.Y. 12946. A seven-week school beginning late June through mid-August for ages 10 and older. Voice, piano, music history, and composition are taught, in addition to chorus, small ensembles, and music theory. . . . CAMP MINNOWBROOK, c/o 440 West End Avenue, New York, N.Y. 10024 (winter address). Lake Placid, N.Y. 12946 (summer address). An eight-week camp beginning July 1st for students aged 7 to 15. Dance, drama, fine arts, jazz, piano ensembles, photography, and some science courses are offered in addition to various instrumental and choral ensembles. . . . CHAUTAUQUA INSTITUTION, Chautauqua, N.Y. 14722. A seven-week session of significant dimensions from early July through late August. No age limits. Orchestral and choral ensembles plus piano tuning, and choral and opera workshop. (See under Music Festivals.) . . . THE NEW YORK STATE MUSIC CAMP, Hartwick College, Oneonta, N.Y. 13820. A six-week camp from early July through mid-August for primary through high school age youth. Harmony, conducting, and the humanities are taught, in addition to instrumental and choral ensembles.

NORTH CAROLINA

APPALACHIAN STATE UNIVERSITY CANNON MUSIC CAMP, Boone, North Carolina 28607. A four-week camp from mid-July through mid-August for high school students in instrumental and choral ensembles. . . . BREVARD MUSIC CENTER. Winter address: Box 349, Converse Station, Spartanburg, South Carolina 29301. Summer address: P.O. Box 592, Brevard, North Carolina 28712. A six-week camp for ages 12 and older beginning late June. Dance, opera, piano and voice are offered in addition to instrumental and choral ensembles. . . . EAST CAROLINA UNIVERSITY SUMMER MUSIC CAMP, P.O. Box 2517, Greenville, North Carolina 27834. A two-week band and choral workshop for junior high, high school, and junior college students; held in late July. . . . TRANSYLVANIA MUSIC CAMP (see North Carolina, Brevard Music Center above; also, see Music Festivals). . . . EASTERN MUSIC CAMP, 808 N. Elm Street, Greensboro, North Carolina 27401. A six-week workshop held from mid-June to August with conducting, music theory, and piano instruction as well as training in orchestra and small ensembles. For junior high and high school students. (See also Eastern Music Festival under Music Festivals—North Carolina.)

NORTH DAKOTA

INTERNATIONAL MUSIC CAMP. Winter address: Bottineau, North Dakota 58318. Summer address: Dunseith, North Dakota 58329. A seven-week camp beginning mid-June through August 1 for junior high through college students. Art, drama, piano, and dance are offered in addition to instrumental and choral ensembles, music theory, etc.

OHIO

BALDWIN–WALLACE COLLEGE SUMMER MUSIC CLINIC, Berea, Ohio 44017. A two-week session for high school students offering training in instrumental and vocal ensembles, music theory, etc. A piano seminar is also available. . . . OHIO MUSIC CAMP, Box 275, South Bass Island, Ohio 43456. Ten weeks of instruction in special courses, emphasizing string instruments: six-week string master class beginning June 1st; two-week string camp for junior high students; one week each of string teachers, string bass, and recorder school. The string teachers camp is for high school students and teachers, and the string bass and recorder school have no age limit. . . . OHIO UNIVERSITY CHAMBER MUSIC INSTITUTE, School of Music, Athens, Ohio 45701. Offered in the month of July to high school students and in-service teachers. Emphasis is on training in ensemble playing.

PENNSYLVANIA

MANSFIELD STATE COLLEGE SUMMER MUSIC CAMP, Mansfield, Pennsylvania 16933. A six-week camp from late June through early August for high school students. Musical theater is offered as well as instrumental and choral ensembles. . . . WEST CHESTER STATE COLLEGE HIGH SCHOOL MUSIC WORKSHOP, West Chester, Pennsylvania 19380. A four-week workshop in July for students in high school which offers all instrumental and choral ensembles as well as special courses in piano and piano literature, choral literature, and conducting.

SOUTH DAKOTA

BLACK HILLS STATE COLLEGE MUSIC CAMP, Spearfish, South Dakota 57783. One-week camp in late June for high school students. Band, chorus, theory, stage band, group lessons, and music literature are offered.

TENNESSEE

SEWANEE SUMMER MUSIC CENTER, Sewanee, Tennessee 37375. A five-week camp from late June through late July for students aged 12 and older. Orchestra, chamber ensemble, music theory and composition are offered. (See also under Music Festivals.)

TEXAS

LAMAR STATE COLLEGE SUMMER BAND CAMP, Beaumont, Texas 77705. A one-week camp in early July for high school students. . . . SOUTHERN METHODIST UNIVERSITY—MEADOWS SCHOOL OF THE ARTS, Dallas, Texas 75222. Two-week camp (Big D Music Camp) in June for high school students. The University also has five one-week workshops in specialized areas for graduate students and teachers and two two-week camps in specialized areas for educators and graduate students. Sessions run through the end of July.

VERMONT

KINHAVEN MUSIC CAMP, Weston, Vermont 05161. A seven-week camp from late June through mid-August for high school students. Instrumental and choral ensemble training. . . . UNIVERSITY OF VERMONT SUMMER MUSIC SESSION FOR HIGH SCHOOL STUDENTS, Burlington, Vermont 05401. Besides all instrumental and vocal ensembles, there are courses in composition, orchestration and arranging, music literature, and an opera workshop.

VIRGINIA

COLLEGE OF WILLIAM AND MARY SUMMER BAND SCHOOL, Williamsburg,

Virginia 23185. For students in grades 7 through high school. Held from late June to mid-July. . . . NORTHERN VIRGINIA MUSIC CENTER AT RESTON, P.O. Box 307, Reston, Virginia 22070. Over six weeks in duration, the center offers intensive orchestra and chamber ensemble training for students ages 13 to 18. Held from late June to mid-August. . . . SHENANDOAH CONSERVATORY OF MUSIC CAMPS, Winchester, Virginia 22601. Various camp sessions lasting from one to four weeks for training in band and orchestra playing and choral performance. Eligible to enroll are students from grade 7 through high school. . . . VIRGINIA MUSIC CAMP. Winter address: State Department of Education, Richmond, Virginia 23216. Summer address: Massanetta Springs Station, Harrisonburg, Virginia 22801. One-week for junior high and high school students in late June. Music literature, folk dancing, arts and crafts taught in addition to instrumental and choral ensembles.

WASHINGTON

PACIFIC LUTHERAN UNIVERSITY NORTHWEST SUMMER MUSIC CAMP, Tacoma, Washington 98447. One-week camp in late July for junior high and high school students. Courses offered are instrumental and choral ensembles, and beginning guitar. . . . THALIA SUMMER MUSIC CAMP. Winter address: 2626 Eastlake Avenue E., Seattle, Washington 98102. Summer address: Pilgrim Firs, Route 2, Box 530, Port Orchard, Washington 98366. An eleven-day camp in late July for ages 11 to 21. Composition, conducting, orchestra, small ensembles, and music theory are taught.

WEST VIRGINIA

CONCORD COLLEGE SUMMER MUSIC CAMP, Department of Music, Athens, West Virginia 24712. A four-week camp for high school youth from late June to mid-July. Music appreciation and swing choir are taught.

Amateur Music Statistics

For many years the American Music Conference (AMC) has sponsored an annual survey of amateur music making in America. Issued in May, 1972, was the following report, here somewhat abbreviated, based on a survey conducted for AMC by the National Opinion Research Center at the University of Chicago. The statistical base, which provides national projections, is a survey of 1,600 families totaling 5,600 persons.

There are presently 34 million amateur musicians in the United States—3 million more than in 1970. They range in age from 5 to 75. Forty-two percent of all U.S. households have at least one musical amateur, and one amateur in five can play an instrument. Piano, guitar, and organ—in that order of preference—are the favored instruments among amateurs: 15.2 million can play piano (10.9 million play regularly); 7.3 million can play guitar (6.4 million play regularly); 4.2 million can play the organ (4.1 million play regularly). More than 10 million people play two or more musical instruments. Other instruments played by amateur musicians are—in order of preference—clarinet, drums, trumpet, flute, accordion, saxophone, and violin (1.6 million amateurs, including 600,000 who play regularly, are violinists). Fifty-seven percent of all amateurs are women, most of whom play piano, organ, flute, clarinet, and accordion. Instruments played mostly by males are the guitar (66% of amateur guitarists are male), drums, saxophone, and trumpet. One-third of all those surveyed recommended musical instrument playing as an activity for a "child's lifetime enjoyment." As an avocational pursuit, people responding to the AMC survey preferred music to painting 3 to 1, music to crafts 6 to 1, and music to photography 10 to 1.

Part 10 Radio and Television

MUSIC ON AM FM RADIO

The number of nationally heard (network) broadcasts of serious music on commercial AM has dwindled sharply since the relatively abundant days of the 1930's and 1940's. What now remains represents the most meager percentage of total broadcast time. Local network affiliates may, from time to time, present musical events in their areas or find a sponsor willing to support a program of classical music, and, of course, independent stations are free to operate as they please. But the bulk of music heard on AM networks and unaffiliated stations constitutes a mixture of popular and standard music, soul, rhythm and blues, mood music, Broadway musicals, country–western, some genuine folk music, not much jazz, novelty music, and so forth. By far the majority of this is vocal music, which is very nearly always recorded or transcribed. Recorded music is the main source of radio station entertainment, constituting the greatest aid to the radio station revenue. Little live music is presented. The format for a single program is rather similar throughout the nation: two or three hours or more of music entrusted to some local personality, usually a disc-jockey, who announces each selection. There is usually much interspersion of commercial advertising, often between each piece. Local stations, particularly those serving rural areas, are strictly devoted to presenting the music said to be demanded by the average listener in that area. Invariably, this means commercial popular music.

Regularly scheduled broadcasts of serious music on AM include broadcasts that are also available on FM bands. Programs that are made available nationally include the taped broadcasts of live concerts of the Boston Symphony Orchestra, The Boston Pops Orchestra, the Cleveland Orchestra, the Philadelphia Orchestra, the Chicago Symphony, among others. Other orchestras may broadcast locally either throughout their season or for special radio concerts (some examples are cited in the list of symphony orchestras in Part 2). A major live broadcast series features the performances from the stage of the Metropolitan Opera on 20 successive Saturday afternoons beginning in December and running to the end of the season in April. These are carried over a special network of some 218 stations in fifty states: the Texaco Metropolitan Opera Radio Network, created for these broadcasts alone. Sponsorship has been carried by the Texaco Company since 1940, but the broadcasts have been in existence since 1931—one of the longest runs in U.S. radio history. However, the Met broadcasts are not an exclusive AM radio series, since they are also on FM radio in most parts of the country.

There are some 30 commercial full-time classical music FM radio stations currently in the United States: among them are six that broadcast in AM as well. The 30 stations are: New York: WQXR, FM and AM; WNCN. . . . Los Angeles: KFAC, FM and AM. . . . Chicago: WFMT; WEFM; WNIB. Philadelphia: WFLN, AM and FM. . . . Detroit: WQRS. . . . San Francisco: KKHI, FM and AM; KIBE/KDFC. . . . Washington: WGMS, FM and AM. . . . Boston: WCRB: FM and AM. . . . Pittsburgh: WLOA, FM. Baltimore: WBAL, FM. . . . Cleveland: WCLV. . . . Houston: KLEF. . . . Minneapolis: WLOL, FM. . . . Dallas: WRR, FM. . . . Seattle: KING, FM, KXL. . . . Atlanta: WGKA, AM. . . . Milwaukee: WFMR. . . . Miami: WTMI. . . . Kansas City: KXTR. . . . Denver: KVOD. . . . Phoenix: KHEP. . . . San Antonio: KMFM. . . . Louisville: WHAS. . . . Sacramento: KFBK, FM. Syracuse: WONO.

Among the nation's part-time classical music commercial radio stations are: Allentown, Pa.: WFMZ. . . . Baton Rouge, La.: WJBO, FM. . . . Braddock, Pa.: WLOA, FM. . . . Bridgeport, Conn.: WJZZ. . . . Burlington, Vt.: WJOY, FM. Charlotte, N.C.: WYFM. . . . Chattanooga, Tenn.: WLOM. . . . Corpus Christi, Texas: KIOU. . . . Dover, N.J.: WDHA, FM. . . . Fresno, Calif.: KMJ, FM. . . . Greensboro, N.C.: WQMG. . . . Hanover, N.H.: WDCR. . . . Hartford, Conn.: WTIC, FM. . . . Indianapolis, Ind.: WFMS. . . . Lincoln, Neb.: KFMQ. . . . New Haven, Conn.: WYBC. . . . Newport News, Va.: WGH, FM. . . . Poland Spring, Maine:

WMTW. . . . Portland, Maine: WDCS. . . . Reno, Nev.: KNEV. . . . Rochester, N.Y.: WBFB. . . . Wilkes-Barre, Pa.: WYZZ.

The dominant forces in American radio for presenting good music, live, recorded, or transcribed, are the independent FM radio stations located throughout the country. Although only a few FM stations are devoted to the idea of presenting serious music full-time—many FM stations adopt music programming techniques which are identical to those used on AM radio—a sufficient number of FM stations, particularly in large cities or college towns, have maintained high standards consistently enough to influence a general standard.

To the extent that it is possible to exemplify through very limited selection, the following three important full-time classical music commercial radio stations are described in some detail. Two of them broadcast both in FM and AM; the other is exclusively FM. They are located (following the order of time zones, east to west, respectively) in New York, Chicago, and Los Angeles.

WQXR–FM/AM, 229 West 43rd Street, New York, N.Y. 10036. Tel.: (212) 556–1144. Transmits AM on a frequency of 1560 kHz. Transmitter: 50 kW Westinghouse Electric Type 50HG-2; located in Maspeth, Queens County, City of New York. Transmits FM on a frequency of 96.3 mHz, Channel 242. Transmitter is a 10 kW RCA Type BTF-10E Main Transmitter using BTE-10C Exciter and BTS-1A Stereo Subcarrier Generator, located atop the Empire State Building, 5th Avenue and 34th Street in New York City. Effective radiated power: 5.4 kW horizontal polarization (equivalent to 50 kW at 500), plus 3.8 kW vertical polarization. Studio equipment used includes a Dolby B Type processor, Model #320, for all FM broadcasting, Bang and Olufsen SP-12 stereophonic cartridges in Empire Scientific and Rek-o-Kut arms; RCA and Gates 3-speed turntables; Rapid-Q stereo cartridge playback and record machines; Collins and Gates 10-position studio control consoles for monophonic and stereophonic programs; more than 30 microphones of seven different types. The station has its own auditorium–studio with a seating capacity of 189, seven studios, and four control rooms. It maintains recording facilities for making transcriptions (discs), magnetic tapes, and cartridges. There are two timing rooms for prebroadcast testing and timing. The Engineering Department consists of 15 men engaged in the operation and maintenance of the studio and transmitter for both FM and AM broadcasting. The station broadcasts from 6 AM to 12 midnight daily and from 7 AM on Sunday for its AM broadcasting. For FM, it is on the air from 6 AM to 2 AM daily; on Sunday from 7 AM to 2 AM.

The station was founded in 1936, receiving the call letters WQXR at that time; it was developed from a previously assigned station with the call letters W2XR (founded 1934). It was founded by John V. L. Hogan, an electronics engineer, and Elliott M. Sanger, a former advertising executive. The station has been owned and operated by the *New York Times* since 1944. From its inception, the station called itself "the nation's number one fine music station," as it was the first commercial station in America to specialize in broadcasting concert music on a full-time basis. In 1936, it developed its own high-fidelity transmitter; in 1956, it began operating on 50,000 watts, making the station the first to broadcast concert music with the maximum power assignable to U.S. commercial stations. Its FM broadcasting was initiated in November, 1939, the first time in New York City. Also first for New York was the station's transmission of stereo programming (December, 1965), which now accounts for more than 50 percent of its total programming. From 1944 to 1968 the station forbade the use of singing commercials. Its policy currently permits the use of commercials both read and transcribed between music selections; commercials may contain music.

The station has a music library containing some 85,000 recordings, 500 transcriptions, and 2,500 tape reels. Among its collection of recordings are some that are rare (circa 1902) and many 78-rpm discs. In the past, WQXR featured some live-music programming originating from the station; discontinued in 1971 was a remaining vestige of this tradition, the so-called WQXR Young Artist Competition, which featured performances by participants in the station's studios.

Among the station's recorded broadcasts of music are the programs of the Boston Symphony Orchestra, the Philadelphia Orchestra, the Boston Pops, and the Saturday afternoon broadcasts from the stage of the Metropolitan Opera House carried live. The Met series occupies a large block of time on a single day (upwards of three hours). Another large time segment during daylight hours is the "Montage" program running four hours in the afternoon, Monday through Friday. Its content varies but is generally contained within hourly time segments in order to permit the reading of news (on the hour) and commercials. A live talk-show is the two-hour morning program "The Listening Room," with **Robert Sherman,** which presents interviews with famous musicians and recorded and sometimes live performances.

Other station-produced programs (which are sold as well to other FM outlets in the nation) are the weekly "First Hearing," and "The Vocal Scene." "First Hearing" presents a panel of critics, **Martin Bookspan, Irving Kolodin,** and **Edward Downes,** in confrontation with new recordings about which comments are made after first hearing. The moderator is **Lloyd Moss.** Guest panelists, in the absence of one of the regulars, have been **Ned Rorem** and critic **Byron Belt,** among others. "The Vocal Scene" is produced by WQXR's Music Director, **George Jellinek,** who comments on opera, opera singers, opera performance, and other vocal literature while offering recordings, some of which are archival. The balance of WQXR's classical music programming consists of straight recordings formats with such designations as "The Cocktail Hour," "Stereo Concert," "Nightcap," "Symphony Hall," "Steinway Hall" (famous recording artists who use the Steinway piano), etc. Departures from conventional classical music include programs of recorded music of the Broadway theater, folk music, operettas, and others. The station devotes little if any controllable air time to music of the avant garde or experimental music. Some seasonal features include performances of much music by American composers on certain national holidays as commemorative emphasis within one of the programs described above. (Other New York City FM classical music stations have, interestingly enough, a similar tradition.)

In general, the AM broadcasts of WQXR duplicate the overall FM approach to classical music, with perhaps a slighter emphasis on lighter musical fare. This is currently in the process of being altered, due to the granting of a nonduplication waiver by the Federal Communications Commission (June, 1972). Future WQXR classical music programming on AM will therefore be intensified.

WFMT, 500 North Michigan Avenue, Chicago, Illinois 60611. Tel. (312) 644–1900. Founded in 1951 by Bernard Jacobs. The station has no AM facilities. Owned and operated by WFMT, Inc. as an affiliate of Chicago's WTTW, TV Channel 11 (educational television). Its broadcast frequency is 98.7 mHz with an effective radiated power of 15,500 watts. It has stereo transmission. Antenna is atop the John Hancock Building (100 stories) at a height of 1,170 feet. The station broadcasts 24 hours a day (except from 1 to 6 Monday morning).

Facilities at the station include two control rooms with identical consoles, each equipped with two pairs of outputs and four VU meters. There are 12 mixer channels. Reproduction equipment includes two 3M Mincom tape machines with Isoloop head configurations (about 20 percent of the station's programming is through tape). Disc-recording broadcasts utilize two Sony servo-controlled turntables with variable speed control (adapted to use with 78-rpm discs), along with a pitch control strobe device. Tone arms are Audio and Design models equipped with Shure V-15 Type II Supertrack cartridges, elliptical styli for long-play discs. Gram weight at tracking is 1.5. Marantz preamps are used. Other features of the equipment include 12 Neumann and Sony condenser microphones; the monitor system uses AR-3A and Bozak speakers. Some of the control devices have been built by station engineers. The station claims to have been the first to install the Dolby noise reduction system.

WFMT's library consists of more than 50,000 recordings including discs, tapes of foreign-originated programs, and self-produced taped programs. The station staff numbers 21.

The audio standards of the station are rated to be second to none in the nation. Its signal reaches into a six-state, eight-county region north, south, and west of the station (which is close to the city's eastern lakeshore front). This area has the highest density of audience potential in the nation, nearly 85 percent of the homes having FM receivers.

WFMT is often cited as the most successful full-time commercial classical music FM station in the United States, the reference being to its financial stability and growth, audience loyalty, sponsor satisfaction—this despite the station's practicing what is perhaps the most stringent control over commercials in the country—program quality and originality. Billing itself "Chicago's Fine Arts Station," it offers programs of music from commercially available recordings, transcriptions of live concerts by the Boston Symphony, the Boston Pops, the Cleveland Orchestra, the Philadelphia Orchestra, BBC Proms Concerts, Library of Congress Chamber Music Concerts, foreign concerts and festivals of music made available through the Broadcasting Foundation of America (see under Organizations), rare or unusual recordings or transcriptions, full-length opera recordings, and a number of talk shows or combination of music and talk some of which are station-produced.

Among the regularly scheduled music programs are: "The WFMT Morning Program," a daily feature running from 6 AM to 9 AM on weekdays and until 10 AM on weekends; this time slot includes shorter pieces and movements from symphonies, concertos, opera arias, solo pieces for instruments along with weather and time announcements; news comes at 45-minute intervals beginning at 6:15. The tenor of the program—indeed for throughout WFMT's day—is urbane, highly professional, dispassionate, and serene. "Through the Night," is the longest time segment for the Station. Presented six nights a week beginning at midnight during the weekday and continuing until 6 AM, it offers a single host, **James Unrath,** who plays recordings of his selection and sometimes those requested by his listeners. "The First Fifty Years," is a weekly half-hour devoted to vocal recordings from the past. Complete operas are heard every Sunday and Tuesday afternoon. These, plus the nationally available transcribed series of famous orchestras and foreign festivals, etc., are among the programs of music placed in specific time slots. Beyond that, there is music throughout the day and evening scheduled as individual compositions and not framed within any program. These musical selections are of extreme variety. Thus, the bulk of the day and evening offers simple broadcasting of music unobstructed by strict time allotments of hourly segments and without the use of musical themes to herald in a given program—a device commonly used in radio. Apart from the "Morning Program," news is broadcast at noon, 3 PM, (except Sundays and Wednesdays), 6:40 PM, and 10 PM. The newscasts are always read by staff announcers and vary in length according to the amount of relevant news. WFMT never interrupts a work being broadcast. Its commercial policy permits only four minutes of commercial advertising in any given hour; announcements are always read by the announcer—no recorded commercials, jingles, or singing commercials are allowed. These are probably the strictest policies in American commercial broadcasting. Spoken word programs on the air include poetry readings, stories, critical comment on the arts, and various programs made available through the Broadcasting Foundation of America, such as discussions of international events by correspondents of the BBC, recorded drama, etc. Among the station-produced talk-with-music programs are two that are unusual. "Studs Terkel" is a daily program conducted by the well-known author and radio personality, which includes interviews with an enormous variety of people, recordings, documentaries, and sometimes a loose-form session of improvisatory content. This award-winning program, and the Saturday night "The Midnight Special," are two of WFMT's most popular and exportable productions and are the longest continuous running in Chicago radio featuring the same personalities. "The Midnight Special," which is also available for other radio stations, is a three-hour program prepared by **Norman Pellegrini** and **Ray Norstrand.** It is a potpourri of folk music, farce, satire, nonsense, and entertainment music of many kinds presented either pursuant to some random theme of unification or utterly as non sequiturs encapsulated in an attitude perched at a critical point of balance between madness and profundity. There is nothing like it on American radio. For its program listings, WFMT publishes *The Chicago Guide,* which has a total circulation of 80,000 (reputedly the largest city monthly in the nation in terms of subscriptions). A full-fledged magazine, available at 75 cents per copy, it lists all of WFMT's programs in great detail including the record label and serial number of all forecast recorded offerings along with all performers involved in each recording. The balance of the magazine is devoted to the programming of TV Station WTTW, an extensive guide to activities and attractions in Chicago, full-length articles, and graphics, altogether comprising the most ambitious and unusual publication of any radio station in America. President and General Manager of Station WFMT is **Ray Norstrand;** Vice President and Program Director is **Norman Pellegrini.**

KFAC AM/FM, 5773 Wilshire Boulevard, Los Angeles, California 90036. Tel.: (213) 938–0161. Owned by ASI Communications, Inc. Broadcasts AM on a frequency of 1300 kc, 5,000 watts. FM broadcasts transmitted at 92.3 mHz stereo, 59,000 watts ERP. Transmitter is located atop Mt. Wilson at an elevation of 5,700 feet. The station is in operation 24 hours daily. FM penetration is all of Los Angeles County, Orange County, and Ventura County; a substantial coverage of Kern County, San Bernardino County, Riverside County, San Diego County; and partially into Santa Barbara County. Its audience density is one of the highest in the nation. KFAC has called itself "the music station for Los Angeles." It has been broadcasting as a music station since 1931.

Programming for AM and FM on this station is intended to attract two different audiences, both listeners of classical music. In general the AM content is of lighter music, shorter pieces, and mostly from the familiar classical repertory. Audience makeup is of young listeners. The FM programming contains more sophisticated music aimed at an audience that has long listened to the classics.

Among the characteristics of the music programs are one- to three-hour segments of time devoted to whatever the program content may be, on either FM or AM, with a special time slot of six hours beginning at midnight ("Music Out of the Night"). AM continues its programming (all recorded music) with "Breakfast Concert," "Morning Concert," "Luncheon Concert," "Afternoon Concert," etc., into the dinner hour and the evening. Monday through Friday in the late evening there are performances on both AM and FM of live recorded concerts variously of the Boston Symphony Orchestra, the Philadelphia Orchestra, the Boston Pops, the Cleveland Orchestra, and the Los Angeles Philharmonic. On FM, the time segments are more frequently of one-hour duration and are self-explanatory by the program titles: "In a Baroque Mood," "Keyboard Parade," "Concert Stage," "Masters in Miniature," "Luncheon at the Music Center," "World of Opera," "Stereo Omnibus," etc., all of which are presented by regularly assigned announcer hosts. The "Luncheon at the Music Center" is a series of interviews with musicians and other personalities from the the world of art, theater, and films. The opera program is billed as the oldest such program in Southern California. News is presented hourly on the hour. Program Director is **Bernie Allen.**

The foregoing were examples in detail of commercial full-time FM radio broadcasting of classical music and other culturally oriented programs. The following is cited as an example of noncommercial FM radio in the same area of concentration:

MINNESOTA EDUCATION RADIO (MER), 400 Sibley Street, St. Paul, Minnesota 55101. Tel.: (612) 222–5545. This is a "non-profit community corporation organized to provide a public radio service to the people of Minnesota through a network of publicly supported non-commercial radio stations." The MER facilities include two studios and broadcasts from three transmitters. In effect, it is a three-station network. The stations are:

KSJN–FM, 400 Sibley Street, St. Paul, Minnesota (includes the Minneapolis area). Broadcasts on a frequency of 91.1 mHz, with a power of 100,000 watts throughout the Minneapolis–St. Paul area; studios at above address.

KSJR–FM, St. John's University, Collegeville, Minnesota 56321. Tel.: (612) 363–7702. Broadcasts on a frequency of 90.1 mHz, with a power of 150,000 watts from the Weyerhaeuser Studios on the campus of the university.

KCCM–FM, Concordia College, Moorhead, Minnesota 56560. Tel.: (218) 299–3666. Broadcasts on a frequency of 91.1 mHz, with a power of 94,000 watts beamed throughout the Fargo–Moorhead area with auxiliary studios on the campus of Concordia College.

The functions of the three stations are as follows: KSJN is the news unit headquarters and broadcasts programs as scheduled to KSJR and KCCM; it also receives music programming from KSJR for its broadcast area. KSJR is the central source of music programming for KSJN and KCCM. The latter station, KCCM, functions as a transmitting station of broadcasts emanating from the other two stations; these are beamed to the Fargo–Moorhead area.

The combined MER facilities reach an area equal to about 80 percent of the population of Minnesota. Its broadcasts also include stereo and subchannel broadcasts (MER's subchannel is used to broadcast some 17 hours daily of programming for the blind, through the Minnesota State Services for the Blind).

MER is controlled by a Board of Directors which represents education, the arts, and varying sizes of Minnesota communities. It is supported by listener-members (membership entitles listeners to a year's subscription to MER's program guide upon the dues payment of from $12 to $500), funds from the Corporation for Public Broadcasting, foundations, individual grants, and business support for special projects and programs. It also receives some funds from St. John's University and Concordia College.

President of MER is **William H. Kling;** Manager of Stations is **Michael W. Obler;** Chief Announcer and Producer is **Arthur A. Hoehn;** Music Director is **J. Michael Barone.**

The quality of programming, like that of Chicago's WFMT, is of a very high level. The variety of its musical content covers the extreme range from ancient music to the avant garde; its programs of vernacular music are of a cultural orientation. Music is relayed from recordings, transcriptions, and live broadcasts. The transcriptions include the taped programs of live concerts by the Boston Symphony and Boston Pops, the Cleveland Orchestra, the Philadelphia Orchestra, the Chicago Symphony—all weekly presentations. In addition, there are the weekly transcriptions of the "Music from Oberlin" series (Oberlin College), the Library of Congress Chamber Music Concerts, the seasonal broadcasts of the Metropolitan Opera, etc. Among the live broadcasts original with MER are the broadcasts of the Minnesota Orchestra, some seven, taken from the series played by that orchestra in St. Paul; these originate at station KSJN and are relayed to the other MER stations as well as fed to the nine-station Wisconsin FM network and Minnesota stations outside the MER coverage area. The St. Paul Chamber Orchestra, (see Instrumental Ensembles, Part 2) has been presented live in a series of concerts since 1969. Each week throughout the year, MER broadcasts its "Minnesota Recital Series" which features performances by local soloists and musicians and guest artists performing at institutions in the area. Thus, the programs could be recitals of faculty and advanced students in area colleges, chamber ensembles, and well-known national touring artists who play in concerts in the area. Other live broadcasts are those of the St. Paul Opera Company, Minnesota Opera Company, and drama productions of the Guthrie Theatre in Minneapolis.

The MER music programming often features specially created recorded concert series such as the "American Women Composers Series" provided with recordings by the National Federation of Music Clubs with a grant from ASCAP.

The Network's programming begins at 6 AM and signs off at 1 AM. Special time-slots include the 6 to 9 AM "The Prairie Home Companion," with **Garrison Keillor,** a talk program with music; "Midday," with news, consumer and environmental information, public issues, etc.; and "Events, Issues, and Ideas," at the dinner hour. Between these slots are blocks of time devoted to either regularly scheduled programs such as those already described or MER's continuous freely scheduled separate musical works. These and all other programs are published in detail in *Preview,* which is MER's official program guide. Artists, record labels, and serial numbers are indicated.

MUSIC ON TELEVISION

Music on Commercial Television

The first national telecast in the United States of a symphony orchestra occurred on March 21, 1948 when the Columbia Broadcasting System (CBS) presented the Philadelphia Orchestra under Eugene Ormandy. Since that time, America has witnessed little growth on commercial television of regularly scheduled telecasts of full length serious music programs—either concerts or recitals. Most of the good music programs are produced by educational television or local commercial stations. It is not unusual, however, for individual concert artists to make guest appearances on some popular television program produced by the major television networks.

Of the four major American commercial broadcast networks only the National Broadcasting Company [headquarters: RCA Building, 30 Rockefeller Plaza, New York, N.Y. 10020; Tel.: (212) CI 7–8300] and the Columbia Broadcasting System [51 West 52nd Street, New York, N.Y. 10019; Tel.: (212) 765–4321] have, in recent years, managed to schedule national telecasts of music in culturally oriented programs. The concert music commitments of the National Broadcasting Company (NBC) have declined steadily since the days when it sponsored the NBC Symphony; its last regularly scheduled program series were the Bell Telephone Hour and the NBC–TV opera telecasts, both now defunct. Since 1970, only the following "specials" can be cited as network transmissions: A December, 1970 telecast of Beethoven's "Missa Solemnis," from Rome's St. Peter's Basilica (with Pope Paul present). This was a 90-minute program produced in color and televised over Eurovision; the Public Affairs Department of the NBC News presented it for American viewing in association with the National Catholic Office for Radio and Television and it was a production of NBC's Religious Programs Unit, which is to say, it was not conceived as primarily a music program. This program was aired again in 1972. Another program, offered under similar aegis was the 1971 60-minute special, "In Praise," a program of music based on the 150th Psalm and featuring Robert Merrill, David Amram, Eugene Istomin, Seth McCoy, et al. In 1972, an Easter Special, "Music of the Resurrection," taped in the Sistine Chapel with the Chapel Choir, offered a 30-minute program of the music of Palestrina. This was presented by the Public Affairs Department of NBC News, Religious Program Unit, in association with the Division of Film and Broadcasting of the U.S. Catholic Conference. Also in 1972, a two-hour color telecast filmed in Peking and called "The Red Detachment of Women," was shown as a cultural presentation; it featured the Ballet Troupe of Peking. None of these programs were NBC-produced.

The Columbia Broadcasting System (CBS) is far more active in presenting music programs of cultural value. In 1968, it produced two important "specials," the 90-minute "S. Hurok Presents" with Artur Rubinstein, David Oistrakh, and the Bolshoi Ballet; the 60-minute, "Vladimir Horowitz: A Television Concert at Carnegie Hall." The pianist made his television debut with this program, which was taped before a live audience for delayed telecasting. "Beethoven's Birthday: A Celebration in Vienna with Leonard Bernstein," was telecast in December, 1971 and presented the conductor with the Vienna Philharmonic in a taping at the spring Vienna Music Festival of 1971. In terms of logistics, the most impressive television program in years of classical music was the showing on April 30, 1972 of a three and a half hour special called "The Metropolitan Opera Salute to Sir Rudolf Bing." This festive affair involved 43 stars of the Metropolitan, seven conductors, the Met chorus, and its ballet corps. It was taped from a gala evening staged at the Metropolitan Opera House.

A regularly appearing series is that of the New York Philharmonic Young People's Concerts. Over the years these have featured Leonard Bernstein as narrator–conductor–writer in programs of unified content aimed at educating and entertaining. By common consensus, these have been the most successful concerts of their kind for the young in American music not only by virtue of the broad exposure but also in quality. Although Bernstein had been the central figure from the establishment of this series in 1956 until 1972, there have been other guest conductors and narrators. Among them: Dean Dixon, Yehudi Menuhin, and Aaron Copland. Beginning with the 1972–73 season, Michael Tilson Thomas has been the conductor-host. A random selection of titles from the series of the last two years suggests their program content: "Music for the Movies" (music by Aaron Copland), "Anatomy of a Symphony Orchestra," "Thus Spake Richard Strauss," "Concerto for Orchestra" (Bartók's), "Bruckner: the Fourth B?" These programs are generally aired at 4:30 PM in New York City. Three or four are presented in a given calendar year.

A CBS series entitled "Camera Three" has carried a number of programs of music with a cultural orientation. This is a series of half-hour Sunday morning shows. Among the programs from October, 1969, to March, 1972, have been the following: "Alicia de Larrocha Plays 'Iberia'"; "Found: the Lost Schubert" (the so-called Grazer Fantasie as played by Lili Kraus); "The Enigma of Scriabin," with Anton Kuerti, pianist, and Scriabin biographer, Faubion Bowers; "Raga," made in India and narrated by Yehudi Menuhin; "Richard Tucker's 25th Anniversary"; "Portrait of Mischa Dichter"; "Buffy Sainte-Marie: Alternatives," her singing and playing; "Aspects of the Classical Guitar"; "An Elegant Legacy," a program of Irish songs and tales with the Clancy Brothers; "Chamber Music Society of Lincoln Center"; "Knoxville: Summer of 1915" (the Samuel Barber work) sung by Judith Raskin; "The Soul of Verdi," with the CBS Concert Orchestra and Chorus under CBS's Music Director, **Alfredo Antonini** (the only ensemble and conductor attached to any American broadcasting network); "Boulez on Varèse"; "Worship of Music: Dagar Singers of India"; "The Juilliard String Quartet: First Quarter Century"; "John Sebastian: Master of the Harmonica," in performances of the classics; and a program aired on March 5, 1972: "Gisela May Sings Brecht."

Music on Noncommercial Television

The Public Broadcasting Service (PBS) manages the network of noncommercial radio and television. It is funded by the Corporation for Public Broadcasting (CPB) which promotes the financial development of the noncommercial broadcast media. PBS both helps to produce television shows and distributes selected shows which are produced by PBS-affiliated stations throughout the country. One of the important sources of noncommercial television productions is the National Programming Division of New York's WNET/Channel 13, which has assumed some of the responsibilities in this regard once held by the now-dissolved NET (National Educational Television). This summary covers the efforts of both PBS and some of its affiliates in passing, as well as the specific productions in music of WNET/13 that have been distributed nationally by PBS.

WNET/13, Division of the Educational Broadcasting Corporation, 304 West 58th Street, New York, N.Y. 10019; Tel.: (212) 581–6000. President of the Corporation is **John Jay Iselin;** Director of Programming is **Robert Kotlowitz.** The National Programming Division of WNET/13 is located at 10 Columbus Circle, New York, N.Y. 10019; Tel.: (212) 262–4222, 5730.

NET Opera Theatre has produced or has presented in conjunction with foreign TV producers the following operas for the period from December, 1969, to May, 1972 (shown in chronological order): Janáček's "From the House of the Dead," (90 Minutes); Beeson's "My Heart's in the Highlands," (90 minutes); "Peter Grimes," co-produced with the British Broadcasting Corporation (two and a half hours); "Mozart's "Abduction from the Seraglio," (90 minutes); Humperdinck's "Hansel and Gretel" (two hours), a production of NET, BBC, and the Canadian Broadcasting Corporation; "Orpheus Then and Now," which was a presentation of the Orpheus theme as written by Monteverdi and Japanese composer, Akutagawa (90 minutes), produced by RAI, Rome, and NHK, Japan, with NET; Tchaikovsky's "Queen of Spades," (90 minutes); Britten's "Owen Wingrave," (two hours), production by the BBC, members of the European Broadcasting Union, and NET; "Stravinsky Remembered," a presentation of his opera "The Emperor and the Nightingale," (90 minutes); Offenbach's "Tales of Hoffman," (two hours), produced by BBC; Pasatieri's "The Trial of Mary Lincoln," (90 minutes); and Puccini's "La Rondine," (90 minutes). These operas were aired either in their own time-slots or as part of such PBS series as "Fanfare" and "Special of the Week." Music and Artistic Director of the NET Opera Theatre is **Peter Herman Adler.** Singers engaged for the productions that are NET-produced are all from the professional ranks and include many who are very well known.

For the PBS series, "Special of the Week," WNET/13 produced alone or in conjunction with other broadcast organizations the following: "The Black Composer," a 90-minute program presented in June, 1972 which covered the music and work of composers Stephen Chambers, William Grant Still, George Walker, and Ulysses Kay; "Bernstein in London," a program that was taped in London with the visiting Vienna Philharmonic Orchestra under Bernstein. It was a TV-FM simulcast which in New York was aired in cooperation with WQXR; in Washington, D.C., TV Station WETA aired the program through its combined TV and radio FM facilities. Others in the series: "Introducing . . . Roy Buchanan," a 90-minute documentary on the life and music of the rock guitarist and "Jazz à la Montreux," done in cooperation with Swiss Television.

Two series, "NET Festival" and "Fanfare," which no longer exist, ran the following music programs, among others, during the years 1970 and 1971. The programs themselves, although no longer releasable through these series, may remain as individual programs for future use by the PBS system. "Leopold Stokowski," a 60-minute document on the life and work of the conductor; "The Cleveland Orchestra: One Man's Triumph" (about conductor Szell), which was first televised over NBC as part of the Bell Telephone Hour in December, 1966. (Both of these were "NET Festival" programs.) "American Odyssey," a four-part series each lasting an hour; host was Oscar Brand, folklorist; the series documented American heritage through folk music, using four locations to highlight music from this heritage. Concerts were staged by WITF, Hershey, Pennsylvania, at four historic locations: Bar Harbor, Maine; Eckley, Pennsylvania; Cass, West Virginia; Williamsburg, Virginia. These locations were used to recall early American life as it was found respectively in a seaport, coal-mining town, a railroad center, and a colonial community. Performers for "Odyssey" included folk singers Tom Paxton, the Clancy Brothers, Jean Ritchie, Merle Travis, Leon Bibb, Bill Munroe, and others. The four segments were entitled "Off to Sea Again," "Dark as a Dungeon," "The Midnight Special," "Old Colony Days."

Other "Fanfare" programs were: "Georgia Brown Sings Kurt Weill," a 60-minute feature presented through NET as a production of London Weekend Television; "Earl Scruggs: Family and Friends," a 90-minute program with music by Joan Baez, Bob Dylan, et al.; "The Vienna Philharmonic," a 90-minute program on that orchestra, guest conductor Eugene Ormandy, and pianist Rudolf Serkin; this was a production of Austrian Television (music portion) and NET (interview portion); "Jazz at Tanglewood," an hour-long feature with Judy Collins as folksinger–guitarist with the jazz orchestra of Don Ellis, filmed at the Berkshire Music Center in Tanglewood; a production of WGBH, Boston, presented through NET. (Other "Fanfare" productions are described under PBS.)

A new series, "Vibrations," begun in February, 1972, devotes one hour a week to a wide variety of music: jazz, the classics, folk, popular, blues, rock, etc. Its 20 programs thus far produced (with a grant from Standard Oil Company of New Jersey) feature host **Robert Sherman,** who is also program director of New York's FM–AM station WQXR, in conversations with singers, instrumentalists, and others in the performing arts. These talks and interviews are interspersed with performances, films and other illustrative content which outline the present and past activities of the personality, reminiscences, etc. The one-hour programs are usually not devoted to one personality or topic but may cover as many as three or four. Apart from the emphasis on performers, both living and dead, there are programs and segments within them formed around some idea, such as the artist and war, or farce, satire, etc. "Vibrations" is distributed nationally by PBS.

PUBLIC BROADCASTING SERVICE (PBS), 1345 Avenue of the Americas, New York, N.Y. 10019. Tel.: (212) 489–0945/582–2020. Its distributed programs which featured music were (from 1970 to 1972): "Fanfare," a series which ran from October, 1970, to September, 1971; apart from the programs produced for this series by WNET/13 (see above), PBS presented musical performances in such programs as "The Jefferson Airplane Party," with Santana, B. B. King, The Grateful Dead, et al.; recitals by Janet Baker and Dietrich Fischer-Dieskau, and Sviatoslav Richter. Dance programs included the National Ballet of Canada's performance of "Swan Lake," the Royal Ballet of England's performance of "A Midsummer Night's Dream," and a documentary on the training of a dancer by the Kirov Ballet of Leningrad.

NET Opera Theatre (see above under WNET/13).

"Vibrations" (see above under WNET/13).

"Special of the Week" (some of these were produced by WNET/13 including the productions of NET Opera Theatre; see above) included: "UN-Day Concert 1971," presented on October 25, 1971; 90 minutes; featured a work composed by Pablo Casals ("The Hymn") and conducted by the composer–cellist in this premiere which was filmed at the UN; produced for PBS by NET. "Four from Chicago," a production of WTTW in Chicago, offered four classical music performers in the Chicago area in presentation of ballet, opera, and song, and classical guitar music; performers included dancers Christine Du Boulay and Richard Ellis, guitarists Richard Pick and Richard Ferreri, and soprano Carolyn Smith-Reyer. "Boulez—A Portrait in Three Movements"; 90 minutes; color; presented Boulez in performance with the New York Philharmonic, in a session of musical analysis with students of the Juilliard School, and in a discourse about his own musical ideas; produced by NET. "An American Christmas: Words and Music," with Burt Lancaster, actor, as host; one hour; color; besides songs by folk and popular music singers, it presented performances by the Harlem Children's Chorus and the Columbus Boys Choir; produced by NET. These, among others, were part of the series.

"Homewood," a series of 13 one-hour segments which were presented from October to December, 1970 and produced by KCET of Los Angeles; subtitled "An Ongoing Gallery of the Performing Arts," it presented host, **Charles Champlin,** entertainment editor of the *Los Angeles Times,* in conversations and performance sessions with jazz and country musicians, folk singers, classical music performers, et al.; some of the programs, "Jazz in the Round," "Poet Songmakers: The New Breed," "The Romeros," "Profiles in Cool Jazz," etc., indicate some of the content of the series; the programs were known for their sophistication and relaxed attitude.

"Soul," produced originally by New York's Channel 13 (WNET/13), in 1968 for local viewing, has since been distributed nationally by PBS; it is a weekly one-hour series of black entertainment–culture with music, drama, poetry.

"Artists in America"; 11 half-hour programs; presented from July to September, 1971. Each program was produced by a different PBS member station: WETA in Washington, D.C. (on singer Roberta Flack); KPBS, San Diego (on composer Robert Erickson); KUHT in Houston (on blues singer Sam Lightnin' Hopkins), etc.

"Just Jazz," a series of 10 half-hour programs produced by Chicago's WTTW for PBS; presented from May to July, 1971; coproduced by Robert Kaiser and Dan Morgenstern; its format: "outstanding jazz artists in a relaxed and natural environment" with a setting that "simulates a nightclub, including studio audience"; the program had no host or running narration; among the performers, not to mention the sidemen, were Erroll Garner, Dexter Gordon, James Moody, Gene Ammons, Bobby Hackett, Art Hodes, and Don Byas; one program was devoted to the Sounds of Swing, an eight-piece group. The format and content of this series, like so many other folk music, jazz, and pop music programs on noncommercial TV, are not to be found on the commercial channels.

"Doin' It," produced by KCET in Los Angeles; five half-hour programs presented in July and August, 1972; this series "highlights the black experience through drama, dance, music, and poetry"; one program, "Walk on Vinnegar" (Leroy Vinnegar) explored the decline of jazz.

"The Jazz Set," produced for PBS by the State of New Jersey Public Broadcasting Authority; a series of 13 half-hour color telecasts presented in summer, 1972; host was Chris Albertson; the series presented old and new faces in the jazz world; included performances and interviews.

"Guitar, Guitar," produced by KQED in San Francisco; 11 half-hour programs aired between April and June, 1972; featured Laura Weber in a series devoted to the various styles of playing a guitar. Well-known performers joined Miss Weber, who is a teacher of folk guitar, in performances and demonstrations; these included: Jerry Hahn, Christopher Parkening, Elizabeth Cotton, Rey de la Torre, Mark Spoelstra, et al. The range was from jazz, folk, classical, flamenco, rock, to Hawaiian.

"Boboquivari," produced by KCET in Los Angeles; nine half-hour programs (which ran from August to October, 1971) of uninterrupted pop–rock concerts, in color.

"Evening at Pops," produced by WGBH, Boston; 12 one-hour programs (televised between July and September, 1972 but also in previous summers) presents the Boston Pops Orchestra under Arthur Fiedler and a great many soloists, guest performers (nonmusicians including narrators, dancers, et al.), and guest groups; in 1972, the guests included Doc Severinsen, Roberta Flack, Ferrante and Teicher, Chet Atkins, the Boston Ballet, among others. Previous seasons on this series have had William F. Buckley, Jr., political columnist, as narrator; Julia Child, French Chef; José Greco; Max Morath, ragtime pianist; et al. Popular music performances and nonsense sessions are interspersed with performances of orchestral classics.

Miscellaneous individual programs released through the PBS network for 1971 and 1972 were: "Joan Sutherland in Who's Afraid of Opera: The Barber of Seville," a 30-minute program in color, with the London Symphony and a trio of puppets, April, 1972. "A Fresh Breeze Downeast," presenting two of Maine's folk artists, Marshall Dodge and Gordon Bok, produced by the Maine Public Broadcasting Network in association with the Bar Harbor Festival. "Oscar Brand's Easter," produced by WITF in Hershey, Pennsylvania: a 30-minute program devoted to contemporary and traditional songs of Easter. "Easter at Boys Town," produced by KUON

Nebraska and featuring the Boys Town Choir in a program of sacred music. "Philadelphia Folk Festival," produced by WITF in Hershey, Pennsylvania: three one-hour color programs. "The Philadelphia Orchestra," produced by WHYY–TV in Philadelphia. "A Joyful Noise," a one-hour color program produced by WQED in Pittsburgh, featured folk singers Bob and Evelyne Beers in a Christmas program.

Part 11 Music Industries

Record Companies

The listing that follows is primarily of LP disc-producers, including large and small firms as well as a number of obscure ones. Producers of unusual labels, along with firms that are only record distributors, are listed because of the likely educational or archival value of their records.

Merged or acquired companies are listed under the parent firm, but some acquired or merged firms are also given a separate listing if they have had a long-standing separate identity.

Labels shown are those produced or distributed by the company in the main entry. There is usually no identification as to which labels are produced or distributed. In either case, the list of labels for some companies is not exhaustive.

Reference to a firm's ownership of a recording studio is cited only when that fact was specifically provided for this listing.

ABC RECORDS, INC., a subsidiary of the American Broadcasting Corporation, 1330 Avenue of the Americas, New York, N.Y. 10019. Tel.: (212) LT 1–7777. Branch offices: 8255 Beverly Boulevard, Los Angeles, California 90028; 1700 South Michigan Avenue, Chicago, Illinois; 1819 Broadway, Nashville, Tennessee 37203. Divisional firms are: Dunhill Records, Inc., Grand Award Co., Inc., and Westminster Recording Co., Inc. Labels: *ABC, Bluesway, Command, Dunhill/ABC, Grand Award, Impulse, Music Guild, Probe, Westminster, Whitehall.* Labels distributed include: *BBC, Riverside, 20th Century Fox.* Tapes are issued through various licensees.

A & M RECORDS, 1416 N. La Brea Avenue, Los Angeles, California 90028. Tel.: (213) 461-9931. New York: 1855 Broadway. Founded August, 1962. Label: *A & M.* Has its own recording studios. Issues prerecorded tapes.

ACCOMPANIMENTS UNLIMITED, INC., 20259 Mac Avenue, Grosse Pointe, Michigan 48236. Tel: (313) 886–1980. Founded 1964. Distributes some 3,350 tapes of prerecorded piano accompaniment for instrumental and vocal solos. Approximately 150 new tapes released annually. Does not manufacture the tapes but makes selection from tapes submitted to the firm.

ACOUSTO GRAPHIC RECORDS CO., P.O. Box 934, Simpson's Lane, Edgartown, Massachusetts 02539. Tel.: (617) 627–4639. Founded January 1963. Label: *Acoustographic.* A firm specializing in restoring and reissuing antique and historical recordings of the so-called acoustic period (up to 1925). The restoration process is called "acoustoregraphic" by its creator, **Benjamin L. Hall,** who heads the firm. The company distributes its own releases and also offers restoration services to collectors, archives, and other recording firms.

ADVANCE RECORDINGS, 2316 N. Chrysler Drive, Tucson, Arizona 85716. Tel.: 885-0581. Founded in 1962. Label: *Advance*. One series: *FGR*. Established as a nonprofit educational operation to record contemporary music with new, young artists. Releases are all monaural and are sold directly.

AMERICAN MUSIC MAKERS, INC. (formerly World Artists), Suite 310, Carlton House Hotel, Pittsburgh, Pennsylvania 15219. Tel.: (412) 261-4324. Founded 1963. New York City office: 850 7th Avenue (10019). Studios located in Pittsburgh. Labels: *World Artist, Ambassador Artists*.

APON RECORD CO., INC., P.O. Box 131, Grand Central Station, New York, N.Y. 10017. Tel.: (212) 988-0450. Founded 1956. Importers and distributors of the following labels: *Amadeo, Apon, Discapon, Harmonia Mundi, Angelicum, Christophorus, Fidias*. The *Harmonia Mundi* label issues the "Musica Poetica" series (Orff-Schulwerk).

ARHOOLIE RECORDS, INC., P.O. Box 9195, Berkeley, California 94719. Tel.: (415) 841-8624. Founded 1960. Labels: *Arhoolie, Changes*, in six and one series respectively. Also distributes the following labels: *Blues Classic, Old Timey*, and *Raglan*. The repertory of the firm consists largely of field recordings of folk music, blues, hillbilly, etc.

ART RECORDS MANUFACTURING CO., P.O. Box 8935, 251 South West 21st Terrace, Ft. Lauderdale, Florida 33310. Tel.: (305) 584-1904. Founded 1945. Labels: *Art, Citadelle, Souvenir*, and *Unity*. *Art* issued in series 1 to 200; 2000 series consists of Panamanian folk music; *Souvenir* 900 series is of live night club entertainment albums. Tapes are released through Muntz Stereo-Pak, Inc.

ARTIST DIRECT, Blue Mounds, Wisconsin 53517. Tel.: (608) 924-4959. Founded 1955. Label: *Artist Direct*. The entire catalogue on this label consists of the complete keyboard works of Bach, Liszt, and Busoni all played by **Gunnar Johansen** (q.v. under Performers), who has organized the projects. Sales are direct retail.

ATLANTIC RECORDS, 1841 Broadway, New York, N.Y. 10023. Tel.: (212)PL 7-6306. Branch office: 7033 Sunset Boulevard, Hollywood, California. Founded in 1948. Labels: *Atlantic* (main label), *Atco, Bright Star, Dade, Dial, Focus, Instant, Keetch, LeMonde, Lost-Nite, LuPine, Norman, Rosemart, Safice, Shirley, Sound of Soul, Stax*. Prerecorded tapes (reel-to-reel and cartridge) are released through various licensees.

ANGEL RECORDS (see Capitol Records, Inc.). Labels: *Angel, Melodiya/Angel, and Seraphim*.

AUDIO FIDELITY RECORDS, INC., 221 West 57th Street, New York, N.Y. 10019. Tel.: (212) PL 7-7711. Founded (as Audio Fidelity, Inc.) in 1956. Labels: *Audio Fidelity* (in five series), *Mr. G, Karate, Dauntless*. Distributes the *Parallax* label. Tapes are issued through licensees. Produced in 1957 the "stereodisc," introduced by the firm as the "world's first stereophonic high fidelity record."

AUSTIN RECORDS, P.O. Box 9057, Austin, Texas 78756.

AVAKIAN RECORDS, 285 Central Park West, New York, N.Y. 10024. Founded in 1958 to produce a special three long-playing record album of the music of John Cage ("The 25-Year Retrospective Concert") packaged with a 38-page booklet. No other recording issued. Producer is *George Avakian*.

AVANT GARDE RECORDS (and Vanguard Music Corp.), 250 West 57th Street, New York, N.Y. 10019. Tel.: (212) 246-1343/44. Founded 1965. Branch offices are located in Munich and London. Subsidiary firm is Doll Records. Label: *Avant Garde*.

AVOCA RECORD CO., P.O. Box 393, Westbury, N.Y. 11590. Tel.: (516) 433-2910. Founded 1956. Label: *Avoca*.

B & F RECORD CO., INC., 11705 Buckeye Road, Cleveland, Ohio 44120. Tel.: (216) 561-5524. Founded 1954. Label: *B & F* (S and SG series).

BANNER RECORDS, INC., 1290 Avenue of the Americas, Suite 274, New York, N.Y. 10019. Tel.: (212) 265-7760. Label: *Banner* (in one series: 1000). The releases are of Jewish humor and Hebrew liturgical music.

BARCUS–BERRY, INC., 5782 East Second Street, Long Beach, California 90803. Tel.: (213) 439–7785. Founded 1964. Subsidiary: Repeat Records Division. Labels: *Repeat, Conquest.* Maintains own recording studios. Issues tapes in all formats under license agreement through General Recorded Tape, Inc. Barcus–Berry is the originator and developer of the Barcus–Berry Direct Recording Process, which eliminates the use of microphones in the recording process.

BARTÓK RECORDS, 200 West 57th Street, New York, N.Y. 10019. Tel.: (212) 586–2896. Founded 1949. Label: *Bartók.* The music of Bartók dominates the releases on this label.

BIBLE VOICE, INC., P.O. Box 3521, Van Nuys, California 91407. Tel.: (213) 985–5600. Founded 1963. Branch offices in Melbourne and Toronto. Subsidiary: Audio Publishers, Inc. (same address). Has own recording studios. Has released some 84 albums including a recording of a reading of the complete Bible. Label: *Bible Voice.* Tapes also issued.

BIOGRAPH RECORDS, INC., 550 Fifth Avenue, New York, N.Y. 10036. Founded 1968. Label: *Biograph.* Releases consist of field recordings of country music as well as reissues of jazz and blues recordings of historical interest.

BLUE NOTE RECORDS, 1776 Broadway, New York, N.Y. 10019. Tel.: (212) 765–2070. Founded 1939. Division of Liberty Records, Inc., Los Angeles, California. Label: *Blue Note;* recorded in the Liberty studios. Issued in tape cartridges and cassettes.

BOOK–RECORDS ASSOCIATES, 157 West 57th Street, New York, N.Y. 10019. Tel.: (212) CO 5–6585. Founded 1964. Label: *Book–Records.* Distributors of *Evergreen* and *Gp* records. Issues tapes.

BROADWAY MUSIC CORP., 135 West 59th Street, New York, N.Y. 10020. Tel.: (212) CO 5–5767. Founded 1913. Subsidiary of American Metropolitan Enterprises, Ltd., Toronto, Canada. Labels: *Asco, Tap, Harvest.*

BRUNO HI–FI, c/o Musicart International Ltd., P.O. Box 365, Wilton, Connecticut 06897. Tel.: (203) 847–2311. New York Tel.: (212) CY 5–2272. Label: *Bruno.*

BUDGET SOUND, INC., 222 West Orange Grove Avenue, Burbank, California 91502. Tel.: (213) 849–4671. Founded 1963. Labels: *Somerset, Stereo Fidelity, Alshire* (or *Alshire Presents*), *Audio Spectrum, Peter Rabbit* (children's records), *Azteca.* Tapes are issued through Ampex.

CAEDMON RECORDS, INC., 505 8th Avenue, New York, N.Y. 10018. Tel.: (212) 594–3122. Founded in 1952. Labels: *Caedmon, Shakespeare Recording Society, Theatre Recording Society.* Maintains own recording studios. Most of the recordings issued by the firm are spoken word, but some of the recordings have incidental music. Recordings available on tape also.

CAMBRIDGE RECORDS, 473 Washington Street, Wellesley, Massachusetts 02181.

CAMEO PARKWAY RECORDS, INC., 309 South Broad Street, Philadelphia, Pennsylvania 19107. Tel.: (215) KI 5–1140. Branch office: 250 West 57th Street, New York, N.Y. 10019. Founded 1961. Labels: *Cameo, Chariot, Fairmount, Good Time, Little World, Majorette, Parkway,* etc.

CAMPUS FOLKSONG CLUB, 284 Illinois Union, Urbana, Illinois 61801. Labels: *Campus Folksong Club* (CFC 101–301). Three records have been issued under this label containing collections of folk songs of specialized interest.

CANTEMOS RECORDS, P.O. Box 246, Taos, New Mexico 87571. Founded 1964. Records formerly produced by Taos Music Center and Amerecord. Label: *Cantemos.* Distributed by Children's Music Center, 5373 West Pico Blvd., Los Angeles, California 90019. All of the recordings are by one performer, **Jenny Wells Vincent,** who owns and operates Cantemos. Repertory consists of Spanish-language folk songs of the Americas.

CANTOPHONE INSTITUTE, 140 West 55th Street, New York, N.Y. 10019. Tel.: (212)

CI 5–1586. Founded 1957. Label: *Cantophone.* The releases are exclusively of instructional material for singers as taught by four famous singers.

CANYON RECORDS, 834 North 7th Avenue, Phoenix, Arizona 85007. Tel.: 252–1718, 266–4823. Founded 1952. Label: *Canyon.* Utilizes its own recording studio. Exclusively recordings of songs and chants of the American Indian. Some recordings are issued on 78-rpm discs. About 300 titles are in the catalogue.

CAPITOL RECORDS, INC., 1750 North Vine Street, Hollywood, California 90028. Tel.: (213) 462–6252. Founded 1942. Parent firm is Capitol Industries, subsidiary of Electric and Musical Industries Ltd. of Great Britain (EMI). Branch office: 1290 Avenue of the Americas, New York, N.Y. 10019. Tel.: (212) PL 7–7470. Subsidiaries: Capitol Records Distributing Corp., Capitol Records International Corp., Capitol Records (Canada) Ltd., Capitol Record Club, Inc., Toshiba Musical Industries of Tokyo, Beechwood Music Corp., Discos Capitol De Mexico, and Towers Records Corp. The company owns manufacturing and processing plants in Scranton, Pennsylvania, and Jacksonville, Illinois, and records in its own studios. Labels: *Capitol, Angel, Seraphim, Melodiya/Angel* (performers of the Soviet Union), *Tower, Capitol Records International.* Among other achievements within the industry, Capitol Records was the first to record on magnetic tape and the first to release discs on all three playing speeds. Prerecorded tapes are manufactured by Capitol. In addition to producing recordings, Capitol also manufactures phonographs and accessories.

CHESS PRODUCING CORP., 320 East 21st Street, Chicago, Illinois 60616. Tel.: (312) 225–8802. Founded in 1948. Branch offices: c/o Paul Gayten, 1607 El Centro, Los Angeles, California. Divisional firms: Tel Mar Studios, Chess Record Co., Checker Record Co., Cadet Record Co., IIIC Tape Corp. Records from its own studios. Labels: *Chess, Chess Sermons, Checker, Checker Spirituals, Cadet* (formerly *Argo*), *Cadet/Concept, KR.* Tape: 4- and 8-track, cassette, reel-to-reel. No classical issues.

COLGEMS RECORDS, INC., 711 Fifth Avenue, New York, N.Y. Tel.: (212) PL 1–4400. Branch office: 7033 Sunset Boulevard, Hollywood, California. Label: *Colgems* (distributed by RCA Victor).

COLOSSEUM RECORDS INC., P.O. Box 365, Wilton, Connecticut 06897. Tel.: (203) 847–2311.

COLUMBIA RECORDS DIVISION OF COLUMBIA BROADCASTING SYSTEM, INC., 51 West 52nd Street, New York, N.Y. 10019. Tel.: (212) 765–4321. Founded 1889 (Columbia Phonograph Company). A division of CBS (Columbia Broadcasting System) since 1938. Through its CBS International Division it has branch offices throughout the world. The Columbia Records Division has as its labels: *Columbia, CBS, Odyssey, Harmony,* and *Date.* It distributes *Barnaby, Fillmore, Gazette, Kinetic,* and other labels. It utilizes its own recording facilities and manufactures its own prerecorded tapes, cartridges, etc. The firm has branch offices in the U.S. in Hollywood; Skokie, Illinois; Elmhurst, N.Y.; and in Dallas. Columbia first began to record celebrity opera singers in 1903; made its first electric recording in 1925; its development of a workable 33⅓-rpm microgroove recording in 1948 revolutionized modern recording; in 1955 it introduced the marketing innovation, its own mail-order record club which is now the world's largest. Columbia owns large record manufacturing and distribution centers in Indiana, California, and New Jersey.

COMMAND RECORDS (Grand Award Record Co., Inc.), 1330 Avenue of the Americas, New York, N.Y. 10019. Tel.: (212) LT 1–7777. Founded 1954. Wholly owned subsidiary of ABC Records (American Broadcasting Company); has its own recording facilities. Labels: *Command, Command Classics, Grand Award.* Tapes issued through licenses.

COMPOSERS RECORDINGS, INC. (CRI), 170 West 74th Street, New York, N.Y. 10023. Tel.: (212) TR 3–1250. Founded 1956.

Label: *CRI* (*Composer Recordings Inc.*). Has the largest catalogue of recorded American concert music: about 185 long-playing records of over 270 20th-century composers. Most are first and only recorded performances. Recordings are never allowed to go out of print.

CONCERT CLASSICS RECORD CO., 120 Schenck Avenue, Great Neck, N.Y. 11021. Tel.: HU 2–7810. Founded 1960. Label: *Concert Classics.*

CONNOISSEUR SOCIETY, 470 West End Avenue, New York, N.Y. 10024. Tel.: (212) 873–6769. Founded 1961. Label: *Connoisseur Society.* Distributor of *Supraphon* records. The recordings of Connoisseur Society are licensed to Philips Phonographic Industries for production in Northern Europe, the United Kingdom, and Japan.

CONTEMPORARY COMPOSERS GUILD, P.O. Box 1012, Grossmont, California 92030. Tel.: 465–5248. Founded 1962. Label: *CCG* (*Contemporary Composers Guild*).

CONTEMPORARY RECORDS, 8481 Melrose Place, Los Angeles, California 90069. Tel.: (213) OL 3–1560. Labels: *Contemporary, Good Time Jazz, Society for Forgotten Music.*

COOK LABORATORIES, 101 Second Street, Stamford, Connecticut 06905. Tel.: (203) 348–7578. Label: *Cook.*

COUNTY RECORDS, 307 East 37th Street, New York, N.Y. 10016. Tel.: (212) MU 6–2659. Founded 1964. Label: *County* (in two series). Recordings are exclusively of the music of rural America (past and present).

CRITERION RECORDS, 6124 Selma Avenue, Hollywood, California 90028. Tel: (213) HO 9–2296. Branch office: 150 West 55th Street, New York, N.Y. 10019. Labels: *Criterion, Prince, Tiare Tahiti, Reo Tahiti, Palm.*

CRYSTAL RECORD CO., P.O. Box 65661, Los Angeles, California 90065. Tel.: (213) 225–3820. Founded 1966. Label: *Crystal.* Tapes are issued on special order. Specializes in chamber-music recordings with American groups only.

CUCA RECORD CO., 123 Water Street, Sauk City, Wisconsin 53583. Tel.: (608) 643–3304. Founded 1960. Labels: *Sara, Sounds of Wisconsin, Night Owl, Polka Dot, Shamrock, Lucky Leprechaun, Top Gun.* Uses its own recording studios.

DECCA RECORDS, a Division of MCA Inc., 445 Park Avenue, New York, N.Y. 10022. Tel.: (212) 759–7500. Founded August 4, 1934. Has branch offices in major U.S. cities. Labels: *Decca, Coral, Brunswick, Vocalion.* One of the largest record companies in the United States. Each of the labels is issued in many series and in all speeds. Tapes are manufactured for reel-to-reel, cartridges, and cassettes. Decca claims to have issued the first original-cast music, as well as dramatic, album, and the first spoken-word album.

DELMARK RECORDS, 7 West Grand, Chicago, Illinois 60610. Tel.: (312) 222–1467. Founded 1952. Label: *Delmark* (issued in four series monaural and three series stereo). Recordings are traditional and modern jazz, blues and folk music.

DESTO RECORDS, (See Madison Sound Studios, Inc.)

DEUTSCHE GRAMMOPHON GESELLSCHAFT (DGG). (See Polydor, Inc.)

DIAMOND RECORDS, INC., 1650 Broadway, New York, N.Y. 10019. Tel.: (212) 586–3876. Founded 1961. Label: *Diamond.* Tapes issued through RCA Victor.

DORIAN RECORDS, Robert B. Brown Music Co., 1709 North Kenmore Avenue, Hollywood, California 90027. Tel.: 661–4860. Founded 1957. Wholly owned by Robert B. Brown Music Co. Label: *Dorian.*

DOT RECORDS, a division of Paramount Pictures Corp., 1507 North Vine Street, Hollywood, California 90028. Tel.: (213) 462–3141. Founded 1951. Branch offices in New York, Atlanta, New Jersey, Chicago, Miami, San Francisco, Cleveland, Dallas, New Orleans. Labels: *Dot, Acta, Stax, Volts.* U.S. Distributor of *Dynovoice, Viva, Bravo.* Tapes are licensed to Ampex, Muntz, Playtape.

DOVER RECORDS, Dover Publications, Inc., 180 Varick Street, New York, N.Y. 10014. Tel.: (212) 255–3755. Dover Publications founded in 1945. Divisional firm: The Spoken Word, Inc. Labels: *Dover, Hayward, The Spoken Word, Listen & Learn Language Series, Say it Correctly Language Series.*

DROLL YANKEES INC., Box 2447, Providence, Rhode Island 02906. Tel.: (401) 245–8705. Founded 1960. Produces a small number of recordings of natural sounds, bird songs, etc.

DUKE UNIVERSITY PRESS, Box 6697, College Station, Durham, North Carolina 27708. Tel.: (919) 684–2173. The Press was founded in 1921. Has produced one two-record album under the label of *Duke University Press* entitled "The Art Song in America."

DYER-BENNET RECORDS, P.O. Box 235, Woodside, N.Y. 11377. Labels: *Dyer-Bennet Records.* Catalogue contains 14 LP records of the performances of **Richard Dyer-Bennet** and one recording of **Aksel Schiøtz.**

EDUCO, INC., Box 3006, Ventura, California 93003. Tel.: (805) 648–4381. Founded 1953. Label: *Educo.* Maintains its own studios. Recordings are issued in the following series: 3000 (piano solos for teaching use), 4000 (music appreciation), 5000 (master class recordings of instruction and performance of piano music), 6000 (piano accompaniments to art songs).

ELEKTRA CORPORATION, 1855 Broadway, New York, N.Y. 10023. Tel.: (212) 582–7711. Branch office: 6725 Sunset Blvd., Los Angeles, California. Labels: *Bounty, Checkmate, Elektra, Nonesuch.* Tapes (*Elektra* and *Nonesuch*) licensed to Ampex and Muntz. *Elektra's* catalogue consists mainly of popular, folk, and blues singles and albums; *Checkmate* issues are of the staple repertory works recorded in Europe in stereo only and sold at low prices; the *Nonesuch* series, initiated in spring, 1964, was the forerunner of what is now an important aspect of the classical recording field: the so-called budget LP label. The *Nonesuch* catalogue spans the music of all periods including today's avant garde.

E.M.S. RECORDINGS, INC., P.O. Box 86, Becket, Massachusetts 01223. Tel.: (413) 623–8718. Founded 1950. Label: *EMS.* Despite its limited catalogue, EMS has undertaken some notable ventures in the field of recording including the first complete disc devoted to works of Varèse and the first disc side of songs by Griffes.

ESOTERIC INC., 26 Clark Street, East Hartford, Connecticut 06108. Tel.: 289–3491. Label: *Haydn Society.* Esoteric, Inc. is the distributor of *Haydn Society* records.

ESP-DISK', LTD., 156 Fifth Avenue, New York, N.Y. 10010. Tel.: (212) 255–4800. Founded 1965. Branch office: ESP-Disk' (U.K.), Ltd., 102 Southampton Row, London, W.C.1, England. Labels: *ESP-Disk', ORO.* Tapes licensed to General Recorded Tape. Repertory on these labels consist primarily of folk–rock and avant-garde jazz. The company is unusual in that all ESP performers are also author–composers who produce and edit their own releases with financial assistance from ESP, which shares ownership with the artists for each recording.

EUPHONIC SOUND RECORDINGS, c/o Jazz Report Magazine, P.O. Box 476, Ventura, California 93001. Tel.: 649–2437. Founded 1960. Divisional company: Jazz Record Exchange (mail order record sales). Label: *Euphonic.* The releases thus far indicate primary interest in preserving and documenting early American ragtime, jazz, and blues.

EUROTONE INTERNATIONAL, LTD., 130 West 42nd Street, New York, N.Y. 10036. Tel.: (212) 594–9670. Founded 1963. Subsidiary: International Recording Industries, Inc., 135 West 41st Street, New York, N.Y. 10036. Branch office: International Record Industries, Inc., 32 Oxford Street, Lynn, Massachusetts 01901. Label: *Eurotone.*

EVEREST RECORDS, INC., 10920 Wilshire Blvd., Suite 410, Los Angeles, California 90024. Tel.: (213) 272–4391. Founded 1962. Utilizes its own recording studios. Labels: *Archive of Folk Music, Archive of Piano Music, Arvee, Baroque, Cetra Opera Series, Concert Disc, Counterpoint/Esoteric, Everest, HiFi/Life,*

Janus/Pirouette, La Comédie Française, Period, Renaissance, Scala, Stradivari, Tradition. U.S. distributors of *Fonit/Cetra* of Italy (Turin) and *Ricordi* (Milan) labels. Tapes licensed to Ampex, Muntz, General Recorded Tape, and American Tape Duplicators. Everest is the first company to record using 35mm film.

FANTASY RECORDS, 855 Treat Avenue, San Francisco, California 94110. Tel.: (415) MI 8–7750. Labels: *Fantasy, Early Bird, Galaxy, Scorpio.*

FESTIVAL RECORD DISTRIBUTORS, 2769 West Pico Blvd., Los Angeles, California 90006. Tel.: (213) 737–3500. Founded 1949. Branch office: 161 Turk Street, San Francisco, California 94102. Primarily a distributing company of mainly "nationality" records; produces one label: *Fest* (formerly Festival).

FIDELITY SOUND RECORDINGS, 23 Don Court, Redwood City, California 94062. Tel.: (415) 366–3173. Founded 1952. Subsidiary: Salem Record Co., Wellington, New Zealand. Labels: *FSR, Five Star.*

FOLK-LEGACY RECORDS, INC., Sharon Mountain Road, Sharon, Connecticut 06069. Tel.: 364–5661. Founded 1961. Label: *Folk-Legacy.* The catalogue of this firm consists of some 40 albums of field recordings of folk music. The emphasis is on authentic traditional performers of America, England, Eire, Scotland, and Canada.

FOLKWAYS/SCHOLASTIC RECORDS, 50 West 44th Street, New York, N.Y. 10036. Tel.: (212) 867–7700. Founding dates: 1936 (Folkways), 1967 (Scholastic). Labels: *Folkways, Scholastic, Ethnic Folkways Library.* Although the company has an extensive catalogue of folk music of many world regions, there are some unique classical music anthologies, instructional records in music, historical documentaries, religious series, etc.

FRATERNITY RECORDS, Sheraton Gibson Hotel, Cincinnati, Ohio 45202. Tel.: (513) 381–3166. Founded 1954. Label: *Fraternity.*

GNP-CRESCENDO RECORDS, 9165 Sunset Blvd., Los Angeles, California, 90069. (213) 275–1108. Founded 1954. Labels: *GNP-Crescendo, Carole, Dixieland Jubilee.* Tapes licensed to Muntz, General Recorded Tape, RCA, International Tape Cartridge Corp. (ITCC).

GOLDEN CREST RECORDS, 220 Broadway, Huntington Station, Long Island, N.Y. 11746.

GREGORIAN INSTITUTE OF AMERICA, 2115 West 63rd Street, Chicago, Illinois 60628. Tel.: 436–6700. Founded 1945. Labels: *GIA* (*Gregorian Institute*). Record production is a divisional activity of the Institute.

GUILD PUBLICATIONS OF CALIFORNIA, INC., 3929 Fredonia Drive, Hollywood, California 90028. Tel.: (213) 469–3358. Founded 1950. Label: *GP Records.* Has its own recording facilities. Tapes issued on special order. Guild Publications is a publisher of motion picture and television music primarily. Releases are distributed by RCA-Victor, Columbia, MGM, Capitol, and others.

HEIRLOOM RECORDS, Wiscasset, Maine 04578. Tel.: (207) 882–7016. Founded 1959. Labels: *HL* (*Heirloom*), *AHLP, HLED.* HL 503 ("The Civil War"—Its Songs and Ballads) won the Freedoms Foundation Award in 1963.

HICKORY RECORDS, 2510 Franklin Road, Nashville, Tennessee 37204. Tel.: (615) 297–8558. Label: *Hickory.* Tapes leased through M & S, Muntz, Mercury, and General Recorded Tape.

HISTORICAL RECORDS, INC., P.O. Box 4204, Bergen Station, Jersey City, N.J. 07304. Tel.: (201) 252–0252. Founded 1965. Label: *Historical.* The recordings issued by Historical are very rare, old performances of jazz, blues, and country music never before available on long-playing records. Most of the performances date from the 1920's.

IBO RECORDS, INC., 40–08 Hampton Street, Elmhurst, N.Y. 11373. Tel.: (212) 899–5909. Founded: 1965. Label: *IBO.* The releases on this label consist only of the popular dance music of Haiti.

JAMIE/GUYDEN DISTRIBUTING CORP., 919 Broad Street, Philadelphia,

Pennsylvania 19123. Tel.: (215) CE 2–8383. Founded 1959. Has its own recording studios. Labels: *Guyden, Jamie.* Distributors of (in addition to its own labels): *Phil–L.A. of Soul, Arctic, Dionn, First Amendment.* Tapes also released.

JANSCO RECORDS, INC., 5914 N.E. Circle, Chicago, Illinois 60631. Tel.: (312) 772–2259. Founded 1964. Labels: *Jansco* (for Jan Scobey) and *Ragtime.*

JAZZOLOGY RECORDS/GHB RECORDS, P.O. Box 748, Columbia, South Carolina 29202. Tel.: (803) 252–2177 or 256–4548. Founded 1949. Subsidiary firms: GHB Records, Audio Precision Records. Labels: *Jazzology, GHB* (for initials of head of company). Labels are devoted to authentic early jazz.

KAPP RECORDS, INC., 6430 Sunset Boulevard, Hollywood, California 90028. Tel.: (213) 466–5221. Labels: *Kapp, Four Corners, Congress.* Kapp Records is a Division of Universal City Records, Inc. of MCA (Music Corporation of America), Inc.

KAYDAN RECORDS, 12240 Ventura Blvd., Studio City, California 91604. Tel.: (213) PO 2–0966. Founded 1966. Labels: *Kaydan, Travelanguage Series.*

KEY RECORDS, P.O. Box 46128, Cole Station, Los Angeles, California 90046. Tel.: (213) 876–5930. Founded 1954. Maintains separate manufacturing facilities in Calgary, Alberta, Canada. Label: *Key.* Primarily producers of spoken-word records for classroom use, with three records of music including one consisting of the tables of multiplication rhymed and set to music.

KING RECORDS, INC., 1540 Bewster Avenue, Cincinnati, Ohio 45207. Tel.: (513) 761-2211. Founded 1942. Has own recording studio. Labels: *King, Federal, Deluxe, Audio-Lab.*

KISMET RECORD COMPANY, 227 East 14th Street, New York, N.Y. 10003. Tel.: (212) GR 7–2891. Founded 1942. Label: *Kismet.* Producers of Russian popular and folk songs and dance music, international music, square dance recordings.

LA LOUISIANNE RECORDS, 2827 Johnston Street, Lafayette, Louisiana 70501. Tel.: (318) 234–4118. Founded 1957. Labels: *La Louisianne, Tamm, Belle.* Recorded in the company's own studios. Tapes also produced.

LEXINGTON PRODUCTIONS, INC., Pleasantville, N.Y. 10570. Tel.: (914) 769–6332. Founded 1953. Branch office located in London, England. Lexington is a wholly owned subsidiary of Educational Audio Visual, Inc. Labels: *Lexington, EAV.* Tapes issued.

LIBERTY RECORDS, INC., 6920 Sunset Blvd., Los Angeles, California 90028. Tel.: (213) 461–9141. Founded 1957 (?). A division of United Artists Pictures (a subsidiary of Transamerica Corp.; the latter acquired Liberty in March, 1968). Branch offices (distributing companies): 1024 N. Orange Drive, Los Angeles; Charlotte, N.C.; Miami; Atlanta; Chicago; New Orleans; Memphis; St. Louis; Long Island City; Valley View, Ohio; Pennsauken, N.J.; New York. Foreign offices in London and Munich. Maintains its own recording studios. Labels: *Liberty, Imperial, Minit, World Pacific, Pacific Jazz, Sunset, Soul City, Blue Note, Veep, Unart, Solid State, Dolton.* Tapes are issued through Liberty Stereo-Tape and through Musictapes.

LONDON RECORDS, INC., 539 West 25th Street, New York, N.Y. 10001. Tel.: (212) 675–6060. The firm is an American subsidiary, founded 1947, of the parent firm, Decca Record Co., Ltd., London, England (not affiliated with the American Decca firm). Branch offices are in Gardena, California, and Niles, Illinois. Labels: *London* (issued in some 34 extensive series including such special project-series as Wagner's complete "Ring" cycle with 19 LP records, the complete symphonies of Dvořák on 9 records, Winston Churchill's speeches and memoirs on 12 records, etc.), *Coliseum, Deram, Hi, Parrot, Press, London-Stereo Treasury Series,* and *Richmond-Opera Treasury Series* (low-priced reissues). The London catalogue is particularly distinguished for its recordings of complete operas and collections of operatic arias and scenes, and recordings in the so-called international category. Distributors of *Argo, Telefunken,*

L'Oiseau Lyre, and *Société Française du Son* (actually all sold through McGraw-Hill Book Co.). Issues prerecorded tapes, cassettes, etc., licensed through Ampex.

LOUISVILLE ORCHESTRA FIRST EDITION RECORDS, Louisville Philharmonic Society, 211 Brown Bldg., 321 West Broadway, Louisville, Kentucky 40202. Tel.: 587–8681. Label: *Louisville Orchestra First Edition.* The recordings have been issued since 1954. Through 1967 the catalogue contains 82 LP discs of 191 compositions by 137 contemporary composers. Through 1960 all records released are commissioned works. From 1961, the works recorded are first recordings but are not works commissioned by the Louisville Orchestra. All of the works recorded through 1967 were conducted by **Robert Whitney;** from 1968, by **Jorge Mester.** The recording program has operated since 1958 without foundation support and is totally reliant on the income from record sales. (The Louisville Orchestra is a nonprofit organization.)

LYRIC ART RECORDINGS, 425 West 57th Street, New York, N.Y. 10019. Tel.: (212) 581–3047. Founded 1957. Label: *Lyric Art.* Only one unusual recording has been issued under this label: "The Psalms of David" for violin and speech, with a choric ensemble. The violinist, **Ralph Hollander,** is the composer.

LYRICHORD DISCS, INC., 141 Perry Street, New York, N.Y. 10014. Tel.: (212) WA 9–8234. Founded in 1950. Labels: *Lyrichord, Expérience Anonymes, Eterna.*

MGM RECORDS, 1350 Avenue of the Americas, New York, N.Y. 10019. Tel.: (212) 262–3131. Founded 1947. Branch offices: 2053 Venice Boulevard, Los Angeles, California, Tel.: (213) 733–2114; 1112 South Wabash Avenue, Chicago, Illinois, Tel.: (312) 241–0660; 547 West 52nd Street, New York, N.Y., Tel.: (212) CO 5–1872. A division of Metro-Goldwyn-Mayer, Inc. Labels: *MGM, King Leo, Leo the Lion, Verve* (black and blue labels), *VSP, Verve/Forecast, Metro, Vando, Cub, Poppy, Way Out, Spring, Blue Valley.* Distributors of *Lyra, Kama Sutra.* Tapes licensed to Ampex.

MADISON SOUND STUDIOS, INC., 1855 Broadway, New York, N.Y. 10023. Tel.: (212) 582–5560. Founded 1960. National distributor is Lake Record Sales Corp., Loch Road, Franklin, N.J. Tel. (N.J.): (201) 891–1540. Has its own recording studios. Label: *Desto.* Approximately 80 percent of catalogue consists of contemporary American music. Among the notable recordings are the complete piano works of Charles Ives.

MAINSTREAM RECORDS, INC., 1700 Broadway, New York, N.Y. 10019. Tel.: 247–0655. Label: *Mainstream.* Its 5000 series (Contemporary Sound Series), begun in 1960, are albums of music of the avant garde including Americans Feldman, Brown, Cage, et al. These albums now total 16 in number; some are reissues of recordings once released under the now-defunct *Time* label. Tape issues are licensed with Ampex.

MARK EDUCATIONAL RECORDINGS, INC., 4249 Cameron Drive, Buffalo (Williamsville), New York 14221. Tel.: (716) 634–5149; 741–3100. Founded 1967. Branch office: 6010 Goodrich Road, Clarence Center, N.Y. 14032. Subsidiary: Century Records (Custom Recording Service), Buffalo, N.Y. Uses its own recording studio. Label: *Mark Educational Recordings.* Records are issued in the following series: Recital Music Series (MRS), Concert Band Series (MCBS), Ensemble Series (MES), Music of the Greats (MMG); other projected series include a vocal series and a stage band rehearsal technique series. Tapes are available on special order only.

MEDEA RECORDS, c/o Fleetwood Records, 321 Revere Street, Revere, Massachusetts 02151.

MERCURY RECORD PRODUCTIONS, INC., 35 East Wacker Drive, Chicago, Illinois 60601. Tel.: (312) DE 2–5788. Branch offices: 110 West 57th Street, New York, N.Y. 10019, Tel.: (212) 245–7300; 6922 Hollywood Boulevard, Hollywood, California 90028, Tel.: (213) 469–3937; 817–16th Avenue S., Nashville, Tennessee 37202, Tel.: (615) 242–1607. Labels: *Fontana, Limelight, Mercury, Mercury*

Wing, Philips, Smash, Emarcy. Tapes issued through Mercury, Muntz, and Ampex.

METHODIST STUDENT MOVEMENT, P.O. Box 871, Nashville, Tennessee 37202. Not a record-producing organization primarily but has recorded works of three composers (**Alan Stout, Alan Hovhaness,** and **Bernard Rogers**) on two discs. The works were composed for the Eighth Quadrennial Conference of the Methodist Student Movement in 1964. The discs are available from the above address.

MILESTONE RECORDS, INC., 22 West 48th Street, New York, N.Y. 10036. Founded 1966. Label: *Milestone.* Specializes in jazz including reissues of early recordings.

MIRA PRODUCTIONS, INC., 9028 Sunset Boulevard, Los Angeles, California 90069. Tel.: (213) 278–1128. Founded 1965. Branch office in New York City. Labels: *Mira Records* (3 series), *Mirco* (3 series), *Mirwood Records* (2 series), *Surrey.* Tapes issued through Mira and International Tape Cartridge Corp.

MIRROSONIC RECORDS LTD., 502 East 84th Street, New York, N.Y. 10028. Tel.: (212) RE 7–2592. Label: *MirroSonic.*

MONITOR RECORDINGS, INC., 156 Fifth Avenue, New York, N.Y. 10010. Tel.: (212) YU 9–2323. Founded 1956. Divisional firm: Miro Music, Inc. Label: *Monitor;* issued in folk and popular music series ("Music of the World"), language series, and a budget classical series (Monitor Collectors Series—MC). Tapes licensed to Ampex and Muntz.

MONTILLA RECORDS, c/o Spanish World Records, Inc., 151 West 14th Street, New York, N.Y. 10011. Tel.: (212) 989–3177. Label: *Montilla.*

MONUMENT RECORD CORPORATION, 530 West Main Street, Hendersonville, Tennessee 37075. Tel.: (615) 824–6565. Founded 1958. Branch office: 9000 Sunset Boulevard, Hollywood, California 90069. Has various subsidiary companies in the recording field: Fred Foster Studio, Combine Music, etc. Records in its own studios. Labels: *Monument, Sound Stage 7, Rising Sons Records, LTD International.* Tapes issued through Ampex, GRT, and Muntz.

MOTIVATION RECORDS, Division of Argosy Music Corporation, P.O. Box 156, Mamaroneck, N.Y. 10543. Tel.: (914) OW 8–0074. Founded 1947. Label: *Motivation Records.* Producer of "motivational" records for educational use, with music and song as the medium for conveying instruction and knowledge to the young. ("Nature Songs," "Weather Songs," "Energy and Motion Songs," etc.)

MOTOWN RECORDS, INC., 2457 Woodward Avenue, Detroit, Michigan 48201. Tel.: (313) 965–9250. Branch offices: 6290 Sunset Boulevard, Los Angeles, California; 9517 Fieldcrest Court, Dallas, Texas. Labels: *Motown, Gordy, Soul, Tamla, VIP.* Tapes issued through Motown, Ampex, and Playtape.

MUSIC LIBRARY RECORDINGS, Route 1, P.O. Box 545, Lakeport, California 95453. Tel.: (707) 263–6029. Founded circa 1949. Label: *Music Library, Belvedere.* Catalogue consists of significant amount of contemporary music, most of it performed, at the time of recording, by young, new artists.

MUSIC MINUS ONE, 43 West 61st Street, New York, N.Y. 10023. Tel.: (212) CI 5–4861. Founded 1950. Branch office: 121 Kinderkamack Road, Montvale, N.J. Labels: *Music Minus One, Classic Editions, Proscenium Records, Guitar World.* The Music Minus One releases constitute the world's largest catalogue (over 400 discs) of participation recordings designed for a variety of instrumental and vocal performers (jazz, popular, classical) to play or sing along with the recording. Distributed to the music trade by Belwin Mills, music publishers (q.v.).

MUSICAL HERITAGE SOCIETY, INC., 1991 Broadway, New York, N.Y. 10023. Tel.: (212) 873–6130. Founded 1962. Labels: *MHS* (*Musical Heritage Society*), *Orpheus.* Also licensee for *Muza* (*Ars Polona*), *Amadeo, Angelicum, Erato,* and *Arcophon* (foreign labels). Some notable achievements of this company include the first recordings of all the Haydn symphonies and Haydn's complete keyboard music. In general, the Society attempts to record music from all periods, but with an emphasis on the music of the past—particularly works not often heard. The records are available only from the Society and are budget priced.

MUSICOR RECORDS, 240 West 55th Street, New York, N.Y. 10019. Tel.: (212) 581–4680. Founded 1964. A division of Talmadge Productions, Inc. Maintains own recording facilities. Labels: *Musicor, Dynamo.* Distributes the *Downeast* and *Hurricane* labels. Tapes issued through International Tape Cartridge Corp. and General Recorded Tape.

NASHBORO RECORD CO., INC., 1011 Woodland Street, Nashville, Tennessee 37206. Tel.: (615) 227–5081. Founded 1954. Division of Crescent Company. Labels: *Nashboro, Creed, Excello, Abet, Nasco.* Records in its own studios. Tapes issued through General Recorded Tape.

OHB RECORDS CO., P.O. Box 34, Woodmere, Long Island, N.Y. 11598. Tel.: (516) 295–2358. Founded 1960. Label: *OHB.*

OLYMPIA RECORD INDUSTRIES, INC., 239 West 18th Street, New York, N.Y. Tel.: (212) 989–7200. Founded 1954. Subsidiary companies: Arovox Record Corp., Kelit–Aurora Record Corp. Labels: *Galiko, Kelit, Aurora.*

THE ORIGIN JAZZ LIBRARY, P.O. Box 863, Berkeley, California 94701. Founded 1961. Label: *Origin Jazz* (*OJL*). Reissues of vintage country blues and jazz exclusively.

ORPHEUM PRODUCTIONS, 235 West 46th Street, New York, N.Y. 10036. Tel.: (212) 765–1330. Labels: *Riverside* (jazz), *Washington* (classical), *Offbeat, Battle* (gospel), *Jazzland, Popside, Wonderland* (children's records).

OVERTONE RECORDS, 216 Stratford Street, Syracuse, N.Y. 13210. Tel.: 472–5644. Founded 1953. Label: *Overtone Records.* A small catalogue distinguished by some first and presently only available recorded performances of Renaissance and baroque music. The Overtone recording of Scarlatti's St. John Passion won the Grand Prix du Disque for 1958.

OWL RECORDS, 1229 University Avenue, Boulder, Colorado 80302. Tel.: 443–4480. Founded 1963. Subsidiary of Thorne Films, Inc., producer of educational films for classroom use. The firm has its own recording studios. Label: *Owl.* Among the notable issues in *Owl*'s small catalogue are the only recording of Quincy Porter's and **Cecil Effinger's** Seventh and Fifth String Quartets, respectively, and the "organized sound" (electronic music) works of **Tod Dockstader.**

PENN STATE MUSIC SERIES, c/o Pennsylvania State University Press, University Park, Pennsylvania 16802. Tel.: (814) 865–1327. Founded 1956. Label: *PSMS* (*Penn State Music Series*). The Press is a publisher of scholarly books and a limited number of practical editions of musical scores (Renaissance and baroque). The limited number of records now in the catalogue are, in a sense, complementary to the editions.

PETERS INTERNATIONAL, INC., 600 Eighth Avenue, New York, N.Y. 10018. Tel.: (212) LA 4–4020. Founded 1964. Importers and sole U.S. distributors of finished recordings produced by the EMI group companies throughout the world: *Odeon* (England, India, Greece, Denmark, Holland, Sweden, Germany, Italy, France, Spain), *Parlophone* (England, Sweden, Italy), *Regal* (England, Italy, Spain), *Pathé* (Italy, France), etc. Has produced a limited number LP discs. Label: *Peters International* (*PI*).

PFEIFFER COLLEGE, Music Department, Misenheimer, North Carolina 28109. Tel.: 483–3111. Two discs have been issued by the school: *Pfeiffer No. 1* and *No.2* (see composers **Copland** and **Creston.**) Produced and recorded at Pfeiffer College. Disc No. 2 was produced as a fund-raising project for the touring college choir.

PHILLES RECORDS, INC., c/o Phil Spector Productions, 9130 Sunset Boulevard, Los Angeles, California 90069. Tel.: (213) 273–8661. Founded 1961. Branch office: 440 East 62nd Street, New York, N.Y. Subsidiary company: Mother Bertha Music Publishing Co. Label: *Philles.* Tapes issued through Ampex and Muntz.

PICKWICK INTERNATIONAL, INC., 8–16 43rd Avenue, Long Island City, N.Y. 11101. Tel.: (212) EM 1–8811. Founded 1953. Branch offices in Los Angeles and Atlanta. Subsidiary firms are Pickwick Records of Canada, Ltd. and Pickwick International Ltd. (Great Britain). Also owners of Barth–Feinberg, Inc. (purchased from Seeburg Corp. in 1967) and Mourbar Music Publishing Co. Labels: *Pickwick/33, Design, Happy Time, Hilltop, Cricket, Showcase, P.I.P., Instant Learning.* Tapes issued in stereo cartridges. Pickwick International is not a creator of new recordings but rather a merchandiser of commercially successful records produced by other famous firms. The recordings are re-packaged and sold as budget labels.

PINNACLE RECORDINGS, 5358 South Wells Street, Chicago, Illinois 60609. Tel.: (312) WA 4–2974. Founded 1960. Label: *Pinnacle.* Recordings are generally of live performance tapings of Franz Jackson and the Original Jass All-Stars.

PIONEER RECORD SALES, 701 Seventh Avenue, New York, N.Y. 10036. Tel.: (212) 586–7260. Labels: *Asch, Broadside, RBF.*

PLAYETTE CORPORATION, 585 Ninth Avenue, New York, N.Y. 10036. Tel.: (212) BR 9–5379. Founded 1940. Labels: *GMS-Disc.* Also distributes *Deutsche Grammophon, Amado, Festival, Pleiade, Vogue, Lumen, Studio SM, Ades.* The firm specializes in recordings of spoken word in many languages.

PLAYHOUSE RECORDS, P.O. Box 36061, Los Angeles, California 90036. Tel.: (213) 935–4654. Founded 1958. Has its own recording studios. Label: *Playhouse.* Children's records.

POLYDOR INC., 1700 Broadway, New York, N.Y. 10003. Tel.: (212) 245–0600. Branch office is in Los Angeles. labels: *Polydor, Deutsche Grammophon Gesellschaft (DGG), Archive, Heliodor.*

PRESTIGE RECORDS, INC., 203 South Washington Avenue, Bergenfield, N.J. 07652. Tel.: (201) 384–6900. Founded 1949. Labels: *Prestige, Prestige Folklore.*

PROTONE RECORDS & TAPES, 6114 Santa Monica Boulevard, Hollywood, California 90038. Tel.: (213) HO 2–6058. Founded 1956. Branch office: Nashville West Recording Studios, 5505 Melrose Avenue, Hollywood, California 90038. Labels: *Protone, Cornuto, Recotape.* Tapes issued by Protone and M & S.

PUCHITO RECORD MANUFACTURING CO., INC., P.O. Box 445, Hialeah, Florida 33010. Tel.: 887–0831. Founded 1963. Labels: *Puchito, J. & G, Adria, Dardo.*

QUALITON RECORDS, LTD., 39–38 58th Street, Woodside, N.Y. 11377. Tel.: (212) TW 7–1820. Founded 1964. The company is the distributor of *Qualiton* and *Hungarotone* recordings, manufactured in Hungary.

RCA RECORDS, 1133 Avenue of the Americas, New York, N.Y. 10036. Tel.: (212) 586–3000. Founded 1901 as Victor Talking Machine Co.; merged with Radio Corporation of America in 1929. Branch offices are located throughout the world. Parent firm is RCA (Radio Corporation of America), 30 Rockefeller Plaza, New York, N.Y. 10020. Divisional firms; Sunbury/Dunbar Music, Inc., Colgems Records, Calendar Records. Labels: *Victor, Camden, Red Seal, Victrola,* and *Vintage.* Distributes *Colgems* and *Calendar* labels, among others. RCA is one of the world's great recording companies and one of the very limited number of firms in America that dominate the recording field. In 1903, it issued its first Red Seal disc which initiated an era of celebrity recordings (Caruso, et al.); the first "authentic" jazz recording was issued by the company in 1917; in 1925 it made the first electrical recording of symphonic music; in 1931 it demonstrated a 33⅓-rpm recording; it issued the 45-rpm seven-inch disc in 1949. The company uses its own recording facilities and issues its own prerecorded tapes, cartridges, etc.

R.S.V.P. RECORDS, INC., 1650 Broadway, New York, N.Y. 10019. Tel.: (212) 586–6707. Founded 1964. Label: *RSVP.*

RECORDED TREASURES, INC., P.O. Box 1278, North Hollywood, California 91604.

Tel.: (213) 763–3173. Founded 1964. Producers of the series, *The Welte Legacy of Piano Treasures,* which is the label of the firm. In two series, "Premiere" and "Encore," totaling 24 albums, the Piano Treasures are high fidelity recordings of the performances of master pianists of the past (early 1900's) as reproduced on a modern piano by the Edwin Welte sound-transfer invention. The albums are priced at $12.50 each. Tapes issued through Ampex.

REENA RECORD CORP., 570 Seventh Avenue, New York, N.Y. 10018. Tel.: (212) WI 7–7115. Founded 1947. Labels: *Reena, Zimra, Zamir.* Israeli and Jewish liturgical music.

REPRISE RECORDS (See Warner Bros.—Seven Arts) Branch office: 44 East 50th Street, New York, N.Y. Tel.: (212) 832–0600.

REQUEST RECORDS, INC., 66 Mechanic Street, New Rochelle, N.Y. 10801. Tel.: (914) NE 3–6055. Founded 1950. Subsidiaries: Family Records Corp. and various music-publishing firms. Studios are maintained for record editing. Labels: *Request, Family, Library Editions.* The Request releases are recordings in the international (ethnic) idioms, and are distributed solely in the U.S. by RCA Victor. Tapes are licensed to General Recorded Tape.

RHYTHMS PRODUCTIONS RECORDS, Whitney Building, Box 34485, Los Angeles, California 90034. Tel.; (213) 836–4678. Founded 1954. Uses its own recording studios. Labels: *Rhythms Productions, Tom Thumb, Capricorn.* The recordings are mainly for classroom use, encompassing music for dance and rhythm instruction and activity as well as participation musical performances.

RIVERBOAT ENTERPRISES, 141 Columbia Street, Cambridge, Massachusetts, 02139. Tel.: (617) 868–9788. Founded 1962. Label: *Riverboat.* Also distributor for a number of other labels.

ROPER RECORDS, 48–16 43rd Avenue, Long Island City, N.Y. 11104. Tel.: (212) HA 6–1190. Founded 1964. Label: *Roper Records.* Producers of records designed for dancing (popular, ballroom, etc.). Tapes also issued.

ROULETTE RECORDS, INC., 17 West 60th Street, New York, N.Y. 10023. Tel.: (212) PL 7–9880. Founded 1957. Labels: *Roulette, Tico, Alegre, Mardi Gras, Gone, End, Prancer.*

ST. JOSEPH ABBEY, Spencer, Massachusetts 01562. Tel.: 885–3147. First recording made in 1957. The Abbey has made only three LP discs of Gregorian Chant sung by the monks' choir at the Abbey (Trappist). The discs were pressed by RCA Victor and are available commercially from the Abbey.

SAVOY RECORD CO., INC., 56 Ferry Street, Newark, N.J. 07101. Tel.: (201) MA 3–7470. Founded 1939. Uses its own recording studios. Labels: *Savoy, Regent, World-Wide, Gospel, Sharp.* Tapes issued through Livingston Audio Productions.

SCANDINAVIAN MUSIC CO., 2631 Seminary Avenue, Oakland, California 94605. Tel.: (415) 569–6281. Founded 1947. Label: *Harmony Music* (Scandinavian music only).

SCEPTER RECORDS, 254 West 54th Street, New York, N.Y. 10019. Tel.: (212) CI 5–2170. Founded 1959. Branch offices in Los Angeles, Houston, and Chicago. Labels: *Scepter, Wand, Hob,* and *Mace.* Maintains its own recording studios. All labels are of popular music except *Mace,* which is a classical music budget label. Also distributors for the following labels: *Pepper, Toddlin' Town, Cap City,* and *Dewmis.*

SCOPE RECORDS, INC., 170 West 73rd Street, New York, N.Y. 10023. Tel.: (212) 873–5666. Founded: 1963. Label: *Scope.* Three discs thus far issued consisting of the first solo record albums of singers **Ezio Flagello, Jeanette Scovotti,** and **Raymond Buckingham.**

SEATTLE SYMPHONY ORCHESTRA, INC., 627 Fourth & Pike Building, Seattle, Washington 98101. Tel.: MU 2–1675. Label: *Seattle Symphony Recording Society.* Two discs issued of performances of the Orchestra.

SERENUS CORPORATION, 44 East 75th Street, New York, N.Y. 10021. Tel.: (212)

628–4440. Founded in 1964 as the recording affiliate of General Music Publishing Co., Inc. (q.v.) and releases only recordings of works that are published by General. Labels: *Serenus Recorded Editions, Serenus Records.*

SHEFFIELD RECORDS, Box 5332, Santa Barbara, California 93103. Tel.: (805) 969–3731. Founded 1965. Label: *Sheffield.* Some eight discs have been made thus far; includes some first recordings.

SINGCORD CORPORATION, 1415 Lake Drive, S.E., Grand Rapids, Michigan 49506. Tel.: (616) 456–5406. Subsidiary: Zondervan Publishing House. Labels: *Crown V, Zondervan, Singcord.* Gospel music specialists.

SOCIETY FOR THE PRESERVATION OF THE AMERICAN MUSICAL HERITAGE, P.O. Box 4244, Grand Central Station, New York, N.Y. 10017. Founded 1958. Its Archive of Recorded Performances is a continuing project within the framework of this essentially nonprofit organization. The Society adds to its Archive annually. Well over 40 discs have been released. All of the recordings are of worthy unknown or neglected American works dating onwards from the 18th century. Sustaining members of the Society receive all of the recordings produced during the year of their contribution. Nonmembers may purchase single recordings directly from the Society.

SOCIETY OF PARTICIPATING ARTISTS, INC., 404 Broadway, Saratoga Springs, N.Y. 12866. Tel.: (518) 584–2222. Founded 1951. Label: *SPA.*

SOUND BOOK PRESS SOCIETY, INC., 36 Garth Road, Scarsdale, N.Y. 10583. Tel.: (914) SC 5–1571. Founded in 1948. Described as "musical sound books," the recordings issued by this firm are for classroom use and home listening in the following series: "Music to Remember" (69 records), "Music for Young Listeners" (51 records), "Edward MacDowell Piano Music for Young Listeners" (8 records), "Tiny Masterpieces for Very Young Listeners" (20 records—supplementary series has seven additional records), "Fairy Tales," "Modern Children's Books," "Folk Song," "Children's Classics." The music series were edited by the late Lilian Baldwin and can be used in conjunction with her books, published by the Silver Burdett Co.

SOUTH EASTERN RECORDS MFG. CORP., 150 West 29th Street, Hialeah, Florida 33012. Tel.: 888–7411. Founded 1964. Labels: *Kubaney, Kristal, Regio, Alma, Belter, Vergara, Ekipo.*

SPOKEN ARTS, INC., 59 Locust Avenue, New Rochelle, N.Y. 10801. Tel.: (914) NE 6–5482. Founded 1956. Label: *Spoken Arts.* Also distributor of *Bordas* (*Selections Sonores Bordas*) and *LVA* (*La Voix de l'Auteur*). Producers of LP recordings, prerecorded tapes, and sound/filmstrips in the language arts, history, and the humanities including music. All recordings are graded for the appropriate instructional level.

STARDAY RECORDING & PUBLISHING CO., INC., Box 115, Madison, Tennessee. Tel.: (615) 228–2575. Founded 1952. Labels: *Starday, Hollywood, Nashville, Look.* Tapes issued through ITCC, M & S, and through Starday.

STINSON RECORDS, P.O. Box 3415, Granada Hills, California 91344. Tel.: (213) 892–3540. Founded 1941. Label: *Stinson.* Folk music is the mainstay of the Stinson catalogue along with some jazz and ragtime.

STYLE RECORD PRODUCTIONS, 3373 Park Avenue, Memphis, Tennessee 38111. Tel.: (901) 324–6786. Founded 1964. Branch office: 3635 Allandale Road, Memphis, Tennessee 38111. Subsidiary firms: Stylecraft Music Co., Allandale Productions, Inc., Style Wooten Productions. Has its own recording studios. Labels: *Style, Allandale, Styleway, Camaro, Designer, Pretty Girl, Torino.*

SUE RECORDS LTD., 265 West 54th Street, New York, N.Y. 10019. Tel.: (212) 581–9290. Founded 1957. Labels: *Sue, Symbol.*

SUPREME RECORDINGS, INC., P.O. Box 352, Glendale, California 91209. Tel.: (213) 245–3646. Founded 1961. Branch office: Supreme Productions (South East Asia) Limited, 564 Oxford Street, Levin, New Zealand.

Exclusive distributors in the English-speaking world of *Hemmets Harold* (Sweden) records. Labels: *Supreme, Console, Cornerstone.* Recordings are mainly of gospel music.

TAKOMA RECORDS, P.O. Box 3233, Berkeley, California 94711. Tel.: (415) 548–1513. Founded 1963. Label: *Takoma.* Folk music and jazz.

TIKVA RECORDS, 1650 Broadway, New York, N.Y. 10019. Tel.: (212) JU 6–4934. Founded 1948. Subsidiary of San Juan Music Publishing Corp. Labels: *Tikva, Rivoli.* The firm specializes in Jewish–Israeli music.

TIOGA RECORD CO., 6620 Kindred Street, Philadelphia, Pennsylvania 19149. Founded 1964. Branch office is in Atlantic City, N.J. A subsidiary of Herb Ostrow Productions. Labels: *Tioga, Impex, Margate, Oxford, Top-Pop.* Producers of popular music record singles only, including rock, rhythm and blues, and some jazz instrumental records.

THE TOTAL SOUND, INC. (Project 3), 1270 Avenue of the Americas, New York, N.Y. 10020. Tel.: (212) 765–9760. Founded 1966. Labels: *Project 3* (issued in three series), *Sock-O.* Tapes also issued.

TWENTIETH CENTURY FOX RECORDS, 444 West 56th Street, New York, N.Y. 10019. Tel.: (212) 957–5000. Labels: *Movietone, 20th Century Fox* (distributed by ABC—q.v.).

ULTRAPHONE RECORDS, INC., 69 South Moger Avenue, Mount Kisco, N.Y. 10549. Tel.: (914) 666–5287. Founded 1962. Label: *Ultraphone.*

UNITED ARTISTS RECORDS, 729 Seventh Avenue, New York, N.Y. 10019. Tel.: (212) CI 5–6000. A division within Liberty/UA, Inc., a subsidiary of Transamerica Corporation. Liberty/UA has offices at 6920 Sunset Boulevard, Los Angeles, California 90028. Tel.: (213) 461–9141. Other offices are in England, France, and Germany. Labels: *Blue Note, Imperial, Liberty, Soul City, Sunset, Talespinners, United Artists, UA International, UA Latino.*

UNIVERSITY OF MISSOURI PRESS, 103 Swallow Hall, Columbia, Missouri 65201. Tel.: (314) 449–9449. Founded 1958. The University of Missouri Press has had three records produced under its name.

UNIVERSITY OF OKLAHOMA, Educational Materials Service, Extension Division, Norman, Oklahoma 73069. Two discs were produced by the School of Music of the university, containing works by **Harris, Harrison Kerr, Copland, Krenek, Piston,** and **Sessions.** Label: *University Recordings.*

U.S.A. RECORD CO., INC., 3035 West 47th Street, Chicago, Illinois 60632. Tel.: (312) 254–4612. Founded 1958. Subsidiaries: Destination Record Co., MG Production Co. Label: *USA.*

THOMAS J. VALENTINO, INC., 150 West 46th Street, New York, N.Y. 10036. Tel.: (212) CI 6–4675. Founded 1932. Label: *Major.* Producers of background music and sounds for use with movies, TV, radio, live theater, slide shows, etc. Recordings are available as LP discs and tapes. Catalogue consists of some 54 hours of sound (85 discs of music and 12 discs of sound effects).

VANGUARD RECORDING SOCIETY, INC., 71 West 23rd Street, New York, N.Y. 10010. Tel.: (212) AL 5–7732. Founded 1949. Labels: *Vanguard, The Bach Guild, Vanguard Everyman Classics, Cardinal.* Tapes issued through Ampex. The company has an important catalogue of classics and contemporary music, including the works of American composers, European and American ensembles and performers, and folk music.

VARIETY RECORDS, 1971 Venetian Drive, S.W., Atlanta, Georgia 30311. Tel.: (404) 758–8349. Founded 1957. Label: *Variety.* Repertory is popular music.

VAULT RECORD CO., 2525 West Ninth Street, Los Angeles, California 90006. Tel.: (213) 386–1821. Founded 1964. Labels: *Fat Fish, Vault.*

VENUS RECORDING COMPANY OF AMERICA, P.O. Box 1451, Beverly Hills, California 90213. Tel.: (213) 275–6801.

Founded 1959. Label: *Venus.* Has produced a series of discs in the Venus studios of the singing of **Miliza Korjus.**

VOCARIUM RECORDS, 112 Vernon Street, Hartford, Connecticut 06106. Tel.: (203) 249–4984. Founded 1950. Label: *Vocarium.*

VOX PRODUCTIONS, INC., 211 East 43rd Street, New York, N.Y. 10017. Tel.: (212) TN 7–9360. Founded 1947. Labels: *Vox* (in the series Vox Boxes, Vox Twins, Vox Music Masters), *Turnabout* (budget), and *Candide.* An important catalogue of classical releases with a limited number of contemporary composers. The Box and Twins series includes many complete recordings of lengthy works or series of works (e.g., complete piano music of Beethoven, Mendelssohn, etc.).

WARNER BROS.–SEVEN ARTS RECORDS, INC., 4000 Warner Boulevard, Burbank, California 91503. Tel.: (213) 848–6621. Founded 1958. Branch office: 44 East 50th Street, New York, N.Y. A division of Warner Bros.–Seven Arts Pictures, Inc. Labels: *Warner Bros./7 Arts, Reprise, Loma.* Tapes issued through Greentree Electronics, Ampex, Muntz, Playtape, and 3M.

WASHINGTON UNIVERSITY, Department of Music, St. Louis, Missouri 63130. Tel.: VO 3–0100 ext. 4582. Label: *Washington University.* Has produced a limited number of discs of the music of **Pisk, Robert Wykes,** and **Harold Blumenfeld.**

WESTMINSTER RECORDING CO., INC., 1330 Avenue of the Americas, New York, N.Y. 10019. Tel.: (212) LT 1–7777. Founded 1949. A division of ABC (q.v.).

WINDSOR RECORDS COMPANY, INC., 5530 North Rosemead Boulevard, Temple City, California 91780. Tel.: (213) 286–1167. Founded 1950. Label: *Windsor.*

WORD, INC., P.O. Box 1790, Waco, Texas 76703. Tel.: (817) PR 2–8750. Founded 1952. Labels: *Word, Sacred, Canaan, Sword.*

High-fidelity Equipment Manufacturers and Importers

ACOUSTIC RESEARCH, INC., 24 Thorndike Street, Cambridge, Mass. 02141. Tel.: (617) UN 4–7310. Founded 1954. Officers: **A. J. Hoffman,** President; **R. Allison,** Vice-President of Production; **G. Landau,** Vice-President of Marketing. Factory at above address. Manufacturers of *AR* high-fidelity loudspeakers: AR-4X, 2X, 2AX, 3 and 3A, etc.; turntables: AR-Single Speed, 2 Speed, AR-Universal; amplifiers. The firm designed and introduced the first speakers to use acoustic suspension woofers and hemispherical dome tweeters. Sells wholesale only.

ALTEC LANSING, 1515 South Manchester Avenue, Anaheim, California 92803. Tel.: (714) 774–2900. Factory located at same address. A division of LTV Ling Altec, Inc., P.O. Box 30385, Dallas, Texas 75230. Officers: **A. A. Ward,** President; **A. Fiore,** Vice-President for Engineering and Manufacturing; **H. S. Morris,** Vice-President for Marketing. Manufactures portable musical sound systems, microphones, and guitar speakers, all bearing the *Altec* brand name. All products sold through The Ampeg Co., sales representatives.

AUDIO DEVICES, INC., 1370 Avenue of the Americas, New York, N.Y. 10019. Tel.: (212) 757–7470. Cable: TWX 710–581–2895. Factories located in Glenbrook, Connecticut. Tel.: (203) 324–6761. Founded in 1945. President: **W. T. Hack.** The firm is owned by Capitol Industries, Inc. Manufactures magnetic tape: *Audiotape* and *Audiopak.* Sells wholesale only.

AUDIO DYNAMICS CORP., Pickett District Road, New Milford, Connecticut 06776. Tel.: (203) 354–3911. Officers: **P. E. Pritchard,** President; **M. Selkowitz,** Vice-President, Marketing; **J. Menduks,** National Sales Manager. Manufacturers of *ADC* cartridges, loudspeaker systems, FM stereo receivers/amplifiers for consumer use. Sells wholesale only.

BRITISH INDUSTRIES CORPORATION, Westbury, N.Y. 11590. Tel.: 334–7450. Founded in 1937. A division of Avnet, Inc. **Leonard Carduner,** President; **A. M. Gasman,** Vice-President, Promotion; **F. S. Hoffman,** Vice-President, Sales. Imports and distributes *Garrard* automatic turntables, *Wharfedale* speakers and systems, *Ersin* multicore solder. Sold through dealer outlets only.

CONCORD ELECTRONICS CORPORATION, 1935 Armacost Avenue, Los Angeles, California 90025. Tel.: (213) 478–2541. Cable: CONCORLEC. Founded in 1959. Officers: **Howard P. Ladd,** President; **Robert**

Halpern, Vice-President. Divisional firms: Consumer Products Division, Concord Communications System Division, Premium Division. Products are designed and engineered by Concord and manufactured in Japan. Manufacturers of *Concord* audio and video tape recorders. Maintains some 225 service depots in the U.S. Sells wholesale only.

DYNACO, INC., 3060 Jefferson Street, Philadelphia, Pennsylvania 19121. Tel.: (215) 232–8000. Cable: Dynaco Philadelphia. Founded in 1955. President: **David Hafler.** Manufactures *Dynaco* high-fidelity speakers and components (*Dynakit*) and imports *B&O* tape recorders, radios, and microphones. Sells wholesale only.

ELECTRO-VOICE, INC., 619 Cecil Street, Buchanan, Michigan 49107. Tel.: (616) 695–6831. Established in 1927; acquired, in 1967, by Gulton Industries, Metuchen, N.J. Factories are located in Buchanan, Michigan, and Newport and Sevierville, Tennessee. President: **Wayne Beaverson;** Vice-President, Marketing: **Lawrence Lekashman.** Manufacturers of microphones, speakers and speaker systems, tuners, amplifiers, phonograph and recorder accessories, and electronic organs for institutional use. Sales are wholesale only.

ELPA MARKETING INDUSTRIES, INC., Thorens Bldg., Atlantic and Thorens Avenues, New Hyde Park, N.Y. 11040. Tel.: (516) 746–3002. President: **E. L. Childs.** Products are manufactured in England, Germany, Switzerland, and Denmark. Distributors of *Editall* tape-splicing equipment (a domestic product) and importers of *Thorens* turntables and tone arms, *Watts* record-cleaning equipment, *Ortofon* tone arms and cartridges, *Perpetuum Ebner* turntables, and *Beyer* microphones. Wholesale only.

GREG ELECTRONIC CORPORATION, 3650 Dyre Avenue, Bronx, N.Y. 10466. Tel.: (212) 994–7000. Cable: MATTSTU. Manufacturers of *Gregory* and *Bryan* amplifiers. Wholesale only.

HARMON-KARDON,INCORPORATED, 55 Ames Court, Plainview, L.I., N.Y. 11803. Tel.: (516) 681–4000. A subsidiary of Jervis Corporation, the firm manufactures and distributes the *Nocturne* stereo receivers, *Nocturne* stereo compacts, and distributes stereo tape decks. Wholesale distribution only.

HEATH COMPANY, Benton Harbor, Michigan 49022. Tel.: (616) 983–3961. A division of Schlumberger, Ltd., the firm has offices in Toronto; Gloucester, England; and Frankfurt, Germany. Founded in 1947. **D. W. Nurse,** President. Manufactures and distributes some 300 different kits ranging from high-fidelity playback components to electronic organs. Sales are mail order retail direct to consumer.

KENWOOD ELECTRONICS, INC., 72–02 Fifty-First Avenue, Woodside, N.Y. 11377. Tel.: (212) 478–6220. Founded November 14, 1961. Main office: 15777 South Broadway, Gardena, California 90248. Officers: **George Aratani,** President; **Jiro Kasuga,** Vice-President and Chief Engineer. Distributes *Kenwood* products made in Japan; receivers, amplifiers, tuners, test equipment, ham-radio equipment, tape recorders, players, cartridges, and speakers. Wholesale only.

JAMES B. LANSING SOUND, INC., 3249 Casitas Avenue, Los Angeles, California 90039. Tel.: (213) 665–4101. Founded in 1946. President: **William H. Thomas.** The sales and marketing of all *JBL* products is handled by JBL International, a subsidiary, **T. J. Jennings,** President. Manufactures and sells wholesale *JBL* musical instrument loudspeakers.

MCINTOSH LABORATORY, INC., 2 Chambers Street, Binghamton, N.Y. 13905. Tel.: (607) 723–3512. Founded in 1949. President: **F. H. McIntosh.** Manufacturers of *McIntosh* stereo amplifiers, tuners, preamplifiers, and receivers. Sells wholesale only.

NORTH AMERICAN PHILIPS COMPANY, INC., 100 East 42nd Street, New York, N.Y. 10017. Tel.: (212) OX 7–3600. Warehouse and service headquarters are located at 30-10 Review Avenue, Long Island City, N.Y. 11101. President: **Pieter Vink.** Executive Vice-President: **Matthew Doren-**

bosch. Assistant Vice-President and Manager of Norelco High Fidelity Products Department: **Wybo Semmelink.** *Norelco* is the domestic trademark for products imported by North American Philips Co., Inc. The firm distributes *Norelco* cassette and reel-to-reel tape recorders. *Norelco* first introduced the cassette system for tape recorders in 1964. In addition to distributing its products, the company maintains *Norelco* service centers throughout the country.

RHEEM MANUFACTURING COMPANY, 5922 Bowcroft Street, Los Angeles, California 90016. Tel.: (213) 870–9631. Cable: TELEX 6743550. Vice-President and General Manager: **Charles E. Phillips.** Makers of *Rheem Mark VII* Organ, *Kee-Bass,* and microphones. *Roberts* tape recorders stereo components, such as speakers, receivers, compact systems. Wholesale only.

SANSUI ELECTRONIC CORPORATION, 34–43 56th Street, Woodside, N.Y. 11377. Tel.: (212) 446–6300. Cable: SANSUILEC, NY. This firm is the American distributing center for products made by the Sansui Electric Co., Ltd. of Tokyo, Japan. American office established in October of 1966. President: **K. S. Kanai;** Vice-President: **H. Tada.** Imports and distributes wholesale tuner/amplifiers, receivers, amplifiers and speaker systems, and headphones.

H. H. SCOTT, INC., 111 Powder Mill Road, Maynard, Massachusetts 01754. Tel.: (617) 897–8801; 868–7151. Cable: HIFI. Established in 1946 (incorporated in 1947). Officers: **Hermon H. Scott,** President and Treasurer; **Victor H. Pomper,** Vice-President. Manufactures under the brand names of *Scott, H. H. Scott,* and *Stereomaster* high-fidelity stereo components, consoles and compacts, sound and vibration-measuring and analyzing equipment, and electronic instruments. The company is responsible for many "firsts" in the industry. The firm repairs and services its own products, occasionally has published books on high fidelity, and sometimes engages in consulting work. Sells wholesale only.

SHERWOOD ELECTRONIC LABORATORIES INC., 4300 North California Avenue, Chicago, Illinois 60638. Tel.: IR 8–7300. Factory located at same address. Founded in 1955. Makers of high fidelity amplifiers, tuners, receivers, and speakers Sells wholesale only.

SONY CORPORATION OF AMERICA, 47–47 Van Dam Street, Long Island City, N.Y. 11101. Tel.: (212) 361–8600. Cable: SONYCORP. Established in 1960. Officers: **A. Morita,** Chairman of the Board. Has branch offices in El Segundo, California; Rosemont, Illinois; Palo Alto, California; and Vancouver, B.C. Subsidiary firm is Videoflight, Inc. Sony's parent organization is the Sony Corporation, Tokyo, Japan. The American firm imports and distributes *Sony* products which are sold wholesale only.

TANDBERG OF AMERICA, INC., 8 Third Avenue, Pelham, N.Y. 10803. Tel.: (914) PE 8–1275. Cable: REEVESQUIP. Established circa 1958. This firm sells products (tape decks, cassette decks, etc.) made by Tandberg Radiofabrikk A/S, Oslo, Norway. President: **E. Darmstaedter.** Imported products are *Tandberg* tape recorders, *Grampian* microphones, and *Stentofon* intercommunication systems. Maintains facilities for repair of tape recorders. Sells wholesale only.

TELEX COMMUNICATIONS DIVISION, 9600 Aldrich Avenue South, Minneapolis, Minnesota 55420. Tel.: (612) 881–2636. The Communications Division is a division of the Telex Corporation of Tulsa, Oklahoma. Factories are all in Minnesota at Glencoe, Savage, and Blue Earth. **A. Kleinman** is President of the Division. Principal companies of the Communications Division in the field of high fidelity equipment manufacture are the Magnecord (founded in 1946 and acquired by Telex in 1956) and the Viking (acquired in 1966) Companies. The Division manufactures audio equipment and acoustical devices for consumer use as well as broadcasting, industry, education, and aircraft; among them: headphones, headsets, microphones, tape recorders. Wholesale only.

UNITED AUDIO PRODUCTS, 120 South Columbus Avenue, Mt. Vernon, N.Y. 10553. Tel.: (914) 664–6211. Branch office located in

Woodside, Long Island, N.Y. President: **H. Gorski.** The firm imports and distributes (wholesale) *Dual* automatic turntables made in Germany.

UNIVERSITY SOUND, P.O. Box 26105, Oklahoma City, Oklahoma 73126. Tel.: (405) SU 9–1220. Cable: UNIVERLABS, N.Y. Founded in 1935. Officers: **H. A. Blair,** President; **F. D. Johnson,** Executive Vice-President. A subsidiary of LTV Ling Altec, Inc., the firm manufactures a wide range of products with various model names but sold under the brand name of *University Sound:* public address speakers and accessories, high-fidelity systems, microphones, stands, receivers, and amplifiers. Sales are wholesale only.

Music Publishers

Publishing firms listed in this section are, for the most part, restricted to those pertinent to the scope of this book: that is, to those who have published the music of composers listed in the section on composers, who have published music of use to schools, orchestras, bands, instrumental and choral groups, etc., and who have a record of steady growth.

It will be seen that a few firms are included not so much for their importance as publishers, but because they are selling agents for domestic and foreign publications of significance to music making in America, particularly on educational and professional levels.

As selling agents, some firms may have only a partial representation of another publisher's catalogue. Thus, more than one selling agent will be found for that particular publisher.

Founding dates were provided by the publishers themselves. When it was known or suspected that the dates differed from those found in other sources, an attempt at clarification was made directly with the publisher's cooperation. The result should be accurate.

An attempt is made to describe the general nature of each publisher's catalogue in terms clearer than those used by the trade—a tricky task at best and one that is sidestepped altogether in some cases.

A special point should be made of the term, "educational music," since it looms large on the American publishing scene. The term has a varied connotation, depending on the publisher's intent. It can sometimes be understood only when a particular catalogue is studied. All that can be said beforehand is that most publishers listed here imply that "educational music" is neither "art" music nor "popular" entertainment music but that it can be either (or both) only as a by-product of its being primarily functional for the purposes of use in teaching performance. On the other hand, a number of publishers (if not the majority, when one considers the many thousands of publishers in the U.S.) use the term to refer to all music that is not of the "popular standard" category—itself a term of more precise meaning in the music field. This can be ironic when a popular standard is arranged for school band, or chorus, or orchestra, for it is then called "educational."

The reference to the number of titles in print ought, hopefully, to mean titles that are actively stocked and sold and not titles that have been printed over the years and shown as a cumulative figure. There is no guarantee that the request for this precise meaning of "titles in print" was properly interpreted by publishers supplying the information.

By the same token, the number shown of new titles added annually to a given publisher's catalogue excludes reprints of titles which have previously appeared in the catalogue.

In either case, figures are approximate.

When known, performing rights agencies are shown (BMI, ASCAP, SESAC). Where none are indicated, the obvious surmise is that the publisher has no licensing agreement for performing rights, or that he failed to supply the information.

There are some 135 publishers shown below as main entries; the actual number of imprints represented is much larger, since one publisher may also represent several other publishers. In some cases the "owned" catalogues are those of publishers no longer in existence but whose imprint continues, sometimes because of its historical weight or because a tradition refuses to be broken.

The number of publishers who have licensing agreements with ASCAP, BMI, and SESAC, judging from the reports of these performing-rights organizations, totals over 13,000. However, lest it be thought that the publishers listed below are a paltry fraction of the total in existence in America, it should be pointed out that many so-called publishing firms are in reality owners of a single piece of copyrighted published property —usually a popular song in one of the possible extant styles—and exist solely for the full exploitation of such property to whatever extent possible. Often the exploitative potential is quite negligible.

Such firms are not within the scope of this book.

ABINGDON PRESS, Methodist Publishing House, 201 Eighth Avenue South, Nashville, Tennessee 37203. Tel.: (615) 242–1621. Music publishing begun in 1959. President and Publisher: **Lovick Pierce.** Manager, Music Section: **Robert O. Hoffelt.** The Methodist Publishing House has the Abingdon Press as its publishing division; its sales division is Cokesbury, which distributes the Abingdon publications. Publishes music for church use: for organ, chorus, solo voice, etc. Music titles in print: 450; about 40 titles published yearly.

ALFRED MUSIC CO., INC., 75 Channel Drive, Port Washington, N.Y. 11050. Tel.: (516) 883–8860. Founded 1928. Officers: **Morton Manus,** President; **Arnold Rosen,** Vice-President. Subsidiaries: Claire Music Co., Inc., Capri Music Corp., Alfred's Musical Merchandise Corp., Play-A-Long Co. Publishes educational music (guitar, piano, organ, etc.) with some 400 titles in print and approximately 30 titles published annually. Recordings are also produced in conjunction with publications. Licenses to ASCAP and BMI.

AMERICAN COMPOSERS ALLIANCE. (See Composers Facsimile Editions.)

AMERICAN INSTITUTE OF MUSICOLOGY, P.O. Box 30665, Dallas, Texas 75230 (subscription and distribution office). Founded in 1944; the work of the Institute began in 1945. Founder and current director is **Armen Carapetyan.** Since the Institute engages in much research in Europe, various offices have been established temporarily, over the years, in France, Spain, Holland, etc. Current editorial office: C. P. San Silvestro, Rome, Italy. The Institute concentrates its activities on the music of pre-17th-century

Europe. Although more than a publisher, since it encourages and sometimes sponsors scholarly research by both well-established and young music scholars, the Institute's publications are its outward manifestation. Its 105 titles, involving some 220 volumes, are organized under the following categories: Corpus Mensurabilis Musicae, Corpus Scriptorum de Musica, Musicological Studies and Documents, Corpus of Early Keyboard Music, Miscellanea, and *Musica Disciplina* (see Periodicals). The music and treatises cover the medieval, Renaissance, and some of the baroque eras. All are newly edited and printed editions. Ten to twenty new volumes are published annually. All publications are sold directly except to Britain and the Commonwealth nations (Canada excepted).

AMERICAN MUSIC EDITION, 263 East 7th Street, New York, N.Y. 10009. Tel.: (212) 477–0028. Founded in 1951. Proprietor: **Ray Green.** A catalogue estimated to be from 300 to 500 in-print titles comprised mostly of U.S.-born composers (Green, Hanson, Josten, Riegger, Bacon, Bowles, Ruggles, Nordhoff, Van Vactor, et al.). Categories are concert music, band, choral, chamber music, educational, music for orchestra, etc. License is with ASCAP.

AMSCO MUSIC PUBLISHING CO. (See Music Sales Corp.)

APOGEE PRESS, 2145 Central Parkway, Cincinnati, Ohio 45214. Tel.: (513) 421–1090. Founded 1965. A division of World Library Publications, Inc. (q.v.). Publishes avant garde contemporary instrumental and vocal music: 30 titles in print; 30 titles published yearly. Scores are made from the composers' own plate signature. Issued in series, about two a year, with several works to a series. Recordings will eventually be added to the series. Licensed to ASCAP.

ASSOCIATED MUSIC PUBLISHERS, INC., 866 Third Avenue, New York, N.Y. 10022. Tel.: (212) 935–5100. Cable: MUSICPUB NY. Officer: **Benjamin V. Grasso,** General Manager. Subsidiary: Schroeder & Gunther, Inc. (q.v. this section). Associated is itself a subsidiary of G. Schirmer, Inc. (q.v.) and is also an importer of published music. Its own publications include many contemporary works with a large American representation. The company is the American representative for: BMI-Canada, Ltd.; Don Mills, Ontario; Bote & Bock, Berlin; Breitkopf & Härtel, Wiesbaden, and Leipzig; Deutscher Verlag für Musik, Leipzig; Ludwig Doblinger Verlag, Vienna; Enoch & Cie., Paris; Editions Max Eschig, Paris; Friedrich Hofmeister Verlag, Leipzig; F. E. C. Leuckart, Munich; Nagels Verlag, Kassel; Oesterreichischer Bundesverlag, Vienna; Schauer (Simrock), London and Hamburg; Union Musical Española, Madrid. Performing rights license is issued to BMI.

AUGSBURG PUBLISHING HOUSE, 426 South Fifth Street, Minneapolis, Minnesota 55415. Tel.: (612) 332–4561. **Randolph E. Haugan,** General Manager. Branch offices: 2001 Third Avenue, Seattle, Washington 98121; retail store: 57 East Main Street, Columbus, Ohio 43215. The firm is a division of The American Lutheran Church. Publishes sacred choral and organ music as well as instructional textbooks (for choir directors, organists, et al.). Publishes 65 titles annually; 675 titles in print. Performing rights licensed to SESAC.

AULOS MUSIC PUBLISHERS, Box 411, Montgomery, N.Y. 12549. Tel.: (914) 565–5094. Founded 1967. Publications Director: **Howard M. Felsher.** Twelve titles in print of mostly educational music for wind instruments.

M. BARON COMPANY, P.O. Box 149, Oyster Bay, N.Y. 11771. Tel.: (516) WA 2–3377. Founded 1938. Proprietor: **André Baron.** Publishers of instrumental methods and solos, choral and music for solo voice, orchestral scores. Many titles are arrangements of well-known classics for educational use. Catalogue contains many works by Maurice Baron, founder of the firm. About 500 titles in print; 3 to 4 new titles are published yearly. Active as music dealers and importers, the firm is selling agent for the following publishers: Alphonse Leduc & Cie, Paris; Editions du Siècle Musicale Edward Richli, Geneva; Editions Costallat, Paris; Noël-Pitault; Andrieu & Leblanc; J. & W. Chester, London; Editions Gras; Robert Martin, et al. Licensed with ASCAP.

MEL BAY PUBLICATIONS, INC., 107 West Jefferson, Kirkwood, Missouri 63122. Tel.: (314) 965–3818. Founded 1947. President: **Mel Bay.** Publishes primarily music and method books for guitar and other fretted instruments. Seventy-five titles in print.

BELMONT MUSIC PUBLISHERS, P.O. Box 49961, Los Angeles, California 90049. Tel.: (213) 472–2557. Cable: BELMUSIC. Founded 1965. President: **Lawrence Schoenberg.** Publishing emphasis is on the music of Arnold Schoenberg. About 100 titles in print with about 5 titles added annually. The firm is also sole U.S. selling agent of the music of Arnold Schoenberg from the catalogues of Universal Edition, A.G., Vienna; B. Schott's Söhne, Mainz; and Faber Music Ltd., London. Licensing agreements with ASCAP.

BELWIN MILLS PUBLISHING CORPORATION, Melville, N.Y. 11746. Tel.: (516) 293–3400. Cable: BELMIL–Melville–NY. New York City office: 16 West 61st Street, New York 10023, Tel.: (212) 245–1100. International offices are in Canada, England, France, Germany, Brazil, Holland, Spain, Australia, and New Mexico. The firm is a merger of Mills Music, Inc., founded in 1928, and Belwin, Inc., founded in 1918; the merger took place in 1969. Mills was totally owned by Utilities & Industries Management Corp., which now shares with Belwin the ownership of Belwin Mills Corp. All subsidiary catalogues and agencies of both Mills and Belwin were merged. Following the merger, the new corporation, in rapid sequence, acquired the following publishing houses: Franco Colombo (1969); J. Fischer & Bro. of Glen Rock, N.J. (1970); and H. W. Gray (1971). All three (q.v.) are divisions of Belwin Mills. The sole selling agencies acquired during that period were: Schott's Söhne, Mainz, Germany; Schott & Co., Ltd., London (1969); and J. W. Chester, Ltd., London (1970); among others. Other publishers for whom Belwin Mills has selling rights in the United States are: Amphion, S.A.R.L., Paris; Belwin-Mills, Ltd., London; F. Bongiovanni, Bologna; Editions Bornemann, Paris; Moeck Verlag, Celle, Germany; Novello & Co., Ltd., London; Otos, S.A.S., Florence; G. Ricordi & C., Milan and elsewhere; Musikverlage Hans Sikorski, Hamburg; Casa Musicale Sonzogno, Milan; Symphonia Verlag, Basel. Divisional firms of the former Mills Music, Inc. are also part of the Belwin Mills catalogue; they are: American Academy of Music (ASCAP), Ankerford Music Corp. (ASCAP), Multimood (BMI). The original Belwin, Inc. catalogue included the publications of Singspiration, Inc. (Zondervan Publishing House) of Grand Rapids; it also had the selling rights for Mininome Co. (metronomes). Foreign firms for whom Mills Music acted as sole U.S. selling agents include the following (among others which are now part of the merger of the two firms' operations): Associated Board of Royal School of Music, London; Amphion, France; Bessel, France; Israel Composers League Publications, Tel Aviv; etc. Prior to its merger, Mills had about 20,000 titles in print with about 200 new titles published annually. The Belwin catalogue had some 7,000 published titles. The combined catalogues plus all foreign representation cover every possible area of music publishing, making Belwin's list one of the most varied in the United States. President of Belwin Mills is **Martin Winkler.**

THE BIG 3 MUSIC CORPORATION, 1350 Avenue of the Americas, New York, N.Y. 10019. Tel.: (212) 262–3131. Vice-President: **Arnold Maxim.** Subsidiaries: Robbins Music Corporation; Leo Feist, Inc.; Miller Music Corporation. Branch office: 1777 North Vine Street, Hollywood, Cal. 90028. The combined catalogues of The Big 3 Music Corporation cover music in each major category, with a particular emphasis on popular music arranged for band (both school and dance band), combos, chorus, organ, piano solo, etc. The separate catalogues have some distinguishing features: Robbins contains a significant amount of Latin-American dance and vocal music; Feist is noted for its large number of popular standard music; Miller claims to have the world's largest catalogue of Hawaiian popular music. The firms have kept abreast of popular tastes through the years and now carries much rock and roll, folk music, and so on. Foreign representation includes the catalogues of Francis, Day, and Hunter (England), Hans Gerig (Germany), Curci (Italy). Big 3 is licensed with ASCAP.

BOELKE–BOMART, INC., Hillsdale, N.Y. 12529. Tel.: (518) 325–3449. Founded 1948. President: **Walter R. Boelke.** The firm has published mostly modern music under its International Contemporary Series. A smaller listing is its Old Masters Series. The contemporary composers include some of the most distinguished. Thirty titles in print. All titles are sold through Associated Music Publishers (q.v.). Licensed with ASCAP. The company also does music engraving.

BOOSEY AND HAWKES, INC., 30 West 57th Street, New York, N.Y. 10019. Tel.: (212) PL 7–3332. Cable: SONOROUS. Founded in London in 1816; existed for many years as Boosey & Sons; merged with the firm of William Henry Hawkes in 1930; a branch of Boosey & Sons was founded in New York in 1892 but discontinued business between 1900 and 1906. Since the merger, branch offices have been opened in many major cities of the world. The New York office is a subsidiary of Boosey and Hawkes Limited, London, and has a branch office in Oceanside, Long Island, N.Y. 11572. Officers: **W. Stuart Pope,** Managing Director; **John J. White,** Secretary-Treasurer; **Sylvia Goldstein,** Assistant Secretary. The firm's catalogue covers all areas of serious music, with some 35,000 titles in print and an annual issue of about 200 new titles. The firm is the selling agent in the U.S. for: Arrow Press; Artia, Prague; Edwin Ashdown, Ltd., London; Barry & Cia., Buenos Aires; Besson & Co., Ltd., London; Carisch, Milan; Cavendish Music Co. (England); Cos Cob Press; Editions Russes; Enoch & Sons, London; Carl Gehrmans, Stockholm (partial representation); Edition Gutheil; Israel Music Institute, Tel Aviv; Kultura, Budapest; J. Lafleur & Son, England; Norman Richardson Ltd., England; Rudell Carte & Co., England; Winthrop Rogers Edition, London. The musical instruments manufacturing operation of the company, the largest for brass and woodwinds in Europe, is represented in the U.S. by C. Bruno & Son, Inc.

BOSTON MUSIC COMPANY, 116 Boylston Street, Boston, Massachusetts 02116. Tel.: (617) 426–5100. Founded 1885. **John J. Cranley,** President and Treasurer; **Warren W. Norris,** Vice-President and Secretary. Publishers of educational music for keyboard, solo instruments, chorus; church music; instrumental method books; approximately 12,000 titles in print; 125 new titles added yearly. Sole selling agents for Bruce Humphries (textbooks). Music retailing at the above address for records, instruments, etc. Performing rights license to ASCAP. The firm was acquired by Frank Music Corp. (q.v.) in fall, 1968.

BOURNE CO., 136 West 52nd Street, New York, N.Y. 10019. Tel.: (212) CI 7–5500. Officers: **Bonnie Bourne, B. Scherer.** Branch office: 6381 Hollywood Boulevard, Hollywood, California 90028. Affiliates and agents for: ABC Music Co.; Bach Music Co.; Bourne–Filmusic Inc.; Bogat Music; Harborn Music, Inc.; Lady Mac Music; Murbo Publishing, Inc.; Oakland Music Inc.; Schumann Music Co. Publishers of popular and educational music. Licenses with ASCAP and BMI.

BOWDOIN COLLEGE MUSIC PRESS, Gibson Hall, Bowdoin College, Brunswick, Maine 04011. Tel.: (207) 725–8731, ext. 320. Founded 1964. Managed by Profs. **Robert K. Beckwith** and **Elliott Schwartz** of the College Music Department. Publishes exclusively the music commissioned by Bowdoin College for special occasions (the works are also performed at an annual New York recital). Twelve titles currently in print with one or two titles planned for publication yearly. (Some commissioned works have been published by other publishers.) Licensee is ASCAP.

BROADMAN PRESS, 127 Ninth Avenue North, Nashville, Tennessee 37203. Tel.: (615) 254–1631. Founded 1891. **James L. Sullivan,** Executive Secretary-Treasurer. Affiliated with the Sunday School Board of the Southern

Baptist Convention. Has representation in Australia, New Zealand, Nigeria, and Union of South Africa. Publishes church music primarily (choral, organ, piano); produces children's recordings and teaching aids and supplies. About 1,400 titles in print; 120 titles added yearly. License with SESAC.

BRODT MUSIC CO., P.O. Box 1207, Charlotte, North Carolina 28201. Tel.: (704) 332–2177. Retail store: 1409 East Independence Boulevard. Founded 1934. Owner: **Mrs. C. D. Brodt.** The firm has published 300 titles of educational piano, band, and choral music. Sole selling agent for Banks & Son, Ltd. (England) and The Frederick Harris Music Co., Ltd. (Canada). The company also handles the music of a number of foreign firms, mostly English. Performance rights are licensed with ASCAP.

ALEXANDER BROUDE, INC., 1619 Broadway, New York, N.Y. 10019. Tel.: (212) 586–1674. Founded 1955 (music dealership); publishing begun in 1962. Works thus far published are those of contemporary American composers and scholarly editions of older choral music. About 125 titles in print with 45 titles published yearly. The firm is sole selling agent for Tetra Music Corporation and Continuo Music Press, Inc. (both U.S. publishers) and Aldo Bruzzichelli Editions (Italy). The firm is primarily a music dealership. Publication performing rights are licensed to ASCAP and BMI.

BROUDE BROTHERS LIMITED, 56 West 45th Street, New York, N.Y. 10036. Tel.: (212) MU 7–4735. Cable: BROUDEBRD. Founded 1939. Subsidiary: Rongwen Music, Inc. Publishers of scholarly editions of the masters, contemporary music for solo instruments, chamber ensembles, voice, chorus, orchestra, full scores, study scores; some rental items. The firm is active in music reprinting (see Publishers of Music Reprints). About 500 titles in print; 30 to 40 titles published annually. License with ASCAP.

ROBERT B. BROWN MUSIC CO., 1709 North Kenmore, Hollywood, California 90027.

CANYON PRESS, INC., P.O. Box 1235, Cincinnati, Ohio 45201. Tel.: (513) 721–8170. Founded 1950. Director: **Alison Fahrer.** A division of the Baldwin Piano & Organ Co. Publisher of music for band, chorus, and keyboard. About 200 titles in print; 20 titles published yearly. Licensed with ASCAP.

CARLIN MUSIC PUBLISHING CO., Oakhurst, California 93644. Tel.: 683–7613. Owner: **Sidney A. Carlin.** Publishes arrangements for school band and orchestra of the music of the classical repertory. Forty-seven titles in print.

CENTURY MUSIC PUBLISHING CO., INC., 263 Veterans Boulevard, Carlstadt, N.J. 07072. Tel.: (201) 935–1113. Cable: CENTMUS. Founded 1900. President: **Abe Schlager.** Vice-President: **Monroe Gumer.** Subsidiaries: Heritage Music Publishing Co., Inc., J. J. Kammen Music Co. About 4,000 titles in print; 50 to 75 titles published annually. Publications are music editions for educational use. License to SESAC.

CHAPPELL & CO., INC., 609 Fifth Avenue, New York, N.Y. 10017. Tel.: (212) PL 2–4300. Cable: SYMPHONY NEW YORK. Founded 1811 in London. Officers are: **Jacques René Chabrier,** President; **Wallace E. J. Collins,** Vice-President and Secretary; **St. Clair M. Marshall,** Vice-President and Treasurer; **John Cacavas,** Director of Publications. Branch offices are located in Chicago, Los Angeles, and Cincinnati. Divisional firms are: DeSylva, Brown & Henderson, Inc. and Victor Young Publications. Chappell & Co. was acquired by North American Philips Co. in 1968 but sold to Polygram GmbHs in 1972. The firm has some 30,000 titles in print and publishes about 300 titles a year. Publications include songs from musical plays, vocal scores of musical plays, popular songs, music for band and orchestra, sacred and secular choral music, and folios for organ, piano, accordion, etc. Chappell is primarily known for its publications of the music of the Broadway theater and its songs. The firm is selling agent for the following publishers: Williamson Music, Inc. (q.v.); T. B. Harms Co.; DeSylva, Brown & Henderson, Inc.;

Mara-Lane Music Corp.; Mutual Music Society, Inc. and its subsidiaries; Ivy Music Corporation; Victor Young Publications, Inc.; G & C Music Corp.; McHugh & Adamson Music, Inc.; The Players Music Corp.; Dorella Music, Inc.; A–M Music Corp.; Arlou Music, Inc.; A T & Z Music Corp.; Buxton Hill Music Corp.; Chappell–Styne, Inc.; Douglas Music, Inc.; Dubey Karr Corp.; Earleon Music Corp.; Fairway Publishing Corp.; Florence Music Co., Inc.; Sam Goldwyn Music Publishing Corp.; Jubilee Music, Inc.; Lu-Jac Music, Inc.; Midas Music, Inc.; New Dawn Music Corp.; Putnam Music, Inc.; Pamela Music Corp.; Radview Music, Inc.; Remington Music Co., Inc.; Sahara Music, Inc.; Stanfred Music Co., Inc.; and Thomason Music Corp.

CHORAL PRESS, INC. (See Harold Flammer, Inc.)

THE JOHN CHURCH CO. (See Theodore Presser Company.) Founded in 1854; licensed with ASCAP.

CIMINO PUBLICATIONS, INC., 436 Maple Avenue, Westbury, N.Y. 11590. Tel.: (516) 334–3076. Founded 1961. President: **Michael Cimino.** Vice-President: **Peter L. Cimino.** Publishers of popular music arrangements (vocal and instrumental), instrumental method books. Some of the arrangements are for school ensembles. The combined catalogues of the firm represent some 10,000 in-print titles with about 500 new titles released yearly. The company is selling agent for the following publishers: Vogue Music, Inc.; Bibo Music Publishing Co.; Blue Seas Music Corp.; Jac Music Co., Inc.; Baron Music Corp.; April Music Inc.; Blackwood Music Inc.; Sunbury Music Inc.; Dunbar Music Inc.; International Korwin Corp.; Music Music Music, Inc.; E.D.C. Publications, Inc.; Broude Bros. (limited representation); Encino Music; Spanka Music Corp.; Rayven Music Corp.; Tobey Music Corp.; Alpane Music Co.; Leo Talent, Inc.; Song Smiths, Inc.; Bayes Music Corp.; Helios Music Corp.; Sevborg Music Ltd.; Kali Yuga Music Press; Neal Hefti Inc.; Flanka Music Corp.; and others. Cimino Publications, Inc. is licensed with ASCAP.

M. M. COLE PUBLISHING CO., 251 East Grand Avenue, Chicago, Illinois 60611. Tel.: (312) 527–2160. Founded 1910. Director: **Shepard Stern.** Publishers of educational music, particularly method books for solo instruments. Three thousand titles in print; eight titles added annually.

FRANCO COLOMBO PUBLICATIONS, Division of Belwin Mills Publishing Corp., 16 West 61st Street, New York, N.Y. 10023. Tel.: (212) 582–5300. Cable: COLOMUS. Founded 1911 (formerly known as G. Ricordi and Co.; in 1962 was changed to Franco Colombo, Inc.) Acquired by Belwin Mills in 1969 (q.v.). Executive Director: **Donald N. Griffith.** Opera and Symphonic Administrator: **John R. Bogne.** Subsidiaries: Colfranc Music Publishing Co., Inc., and Educational Record Reference Library. The Franco Colombo company publishes varied forms of instrumental music for band, orchestra, mixed ensembles, winds, brass, guitar, etc.; vocal music for solo voice, chorus, opera; educational music. In the Colombo catalog are some 2,600 in-print titles (excluding titles from represented publishers); the firm added about 50 new titles yearly, prior to the Belwin–Mills acquisition. The firm is agent in the U.S. (under Belwin) for the following publishers: G. Ricordi & C., Milan, and all subsidiary and affiliated companies; Musikverlage Hans Sikorski, Hamburg; Editions Musicales Amphion, Paris; A. Forlivesi & C., Florence; F. Bongiovanni, Bologna; Edizioni Musicali OTOS, Florence; Edizioni De Santis, Rome; Casa Musicale Sonzogno, Milan; W. Bessel & Cie., Paris; Gli Amici della Musica da Camera, Rome; Novello & Co., Ltd., London; Forsyth Brothers, Ltd., London; Berben Editore, Modena and Milan, Symphonia Verlag, Basel. Also sole agents for Louisville House Autograph Editions, Louisville, Kentucky. License agreements are with ASCAP (Colombo) and BMI (Colfranc).

COMPOSERS FACSIMILE EDITION, INC., 170 West 74th Street, New York, N.Y. 10023. Tel.: (212) TR 3–1250. Founded 1955.

A subsidiary of American Composers Alliance (see Organizations). Composers Facsimile Edition, or CFE, permits any composer to submit unpublished works in the form of transparent master sheets suitable for ozalid reproduction. The reproductions are made by CFE to order and are sold in bound copies at prices lower than those of the average music publisher. The composer receives a 25 percent royalty from the sale of each reproduction. Composers who are members of the American Composers Alliance (ACA) receive additional benefits resulting from the assignment to ACA of worldwide performing rights which includes mechanicals, broadcast performances, etc. A significant number of ACA-controlled titles are available through CFE.

COMPOSER/PERFORMER EDITION, 330 University Avenue, Davis, California 95616. (See also *Source* Magazine.) Publishers of new music. Over 50 titles in print. Music includes that in printed form as well as works that require use of tape, film, slides, and other materials. Works published are usually those of newer, younger composers.

COMPOSERS PRESS, INC. (See Southern Music Co., San Antonio, Texas.) Founded by **Charles Haubiel** (see Composers) in 1935. Has a catalogue of over 500 titles by 139 American composers. Licensed with ASCAP. From 1941 to 1963, Composers Press sponsored an annual Composers Publication Contest.

CONCORDIA PUBLISHING HOUSE, 3558 South Jefferson Avenue, St. Louis, Missouri 63118. Tel.: (314) MO 4–7000. Founded 1869. President: **A. T. Leimbach.** Vice-President: **Ken R. Hoffman.** Treasurer and General Manager: **O. A. Dorn.** A branch office is maintained in London, England: Concordia Publishing House, Ltd. Catalogue consists of choral, organ, solo vocal, and brass ensemble music and books. Virtually all of the publications are or pertain to sacred music. Titles in print: 1,100; about 50 new titles added yearly. The firm is the sole U.S. selling agent for the "Organum Series" of the German firm of Kistner & Siegel, Cologne. License issued to SESAC.

CONSOLIDATED MUSIC PUBLISHERS, INC. (See Music Sales Corp.)

PIETRO DEIRO MUSIC PUBLICATIONS, 133 Seventh Avenue South, New York, N.Y. 10014. Tel.: (212) 675–5460. Founded 1928. Owner: **Pietro Deiro, Jr.** Affiliated firms are: Santee Music Press, and Momac. The company specializes in music for accordion and has 2,000 titles in print; 50 new titles added yearly. Sole selling agent for McGinnis and Marx, Music Publishers (q.v.) and represents Berben Music Co. of Italy. The Pietro Deiro firm is licensed to SESAC; Santee to ASCAP; Momac to BMI.

OLIVER DITSON CO. (See Theodore Presser Company.) Established in 1857 as a continuation of a business formed in 1783. Licensed with ASCAP.

EASTMAN SCHOOL OF MUSIC PUBLICATIONS. (See Carl Fischer, Inc.)

EDITION MUSICUS, NEW YORK, INC., 333 West 52nd Street, New York, N.Y. 10019. Tel.: (212) PL 7–2742. Founded 1945. President: **Quinto Maganini.** Has in print 750 titles of music for band, chorus, and orchestra. Publishes 10 titles annually. Licensed to ASCAP.

ELKAN–VOGEL CO., INC., Bryn Mawr, Pennsylvania, 19010. Tel.: (215) LA 5–3636. Cable: ELKVOG. Founded 1927. Publishers of instrumental and vocal music in all categories; agents representing these publications are established in London, Paris, and Berlin. Acts as selling agent for the following foreign firms: Durand & Cie., Paris; Jean Jobert, Paris; H. Lemoine & Cie., Paris; Hamelle & Cie., Paris; Editions Musicales de la Schola Cantorum et de la Procure General de Musique, Paris; Ars Nova, The Netherlands; Dolmetsch, England. Licensed with ASCAP. In 1970, the firm merged with Theodore Presser Co. at above address.

HENRI ELKAN MUSIC PUBLISHER, 1316 Walnut Street, Philadelphia, Pennsylvania 19107. Tel.: (215) PE 5–1900. Founded

1956. Owner: **Henri Elkan.** Publishers of educational music, some scholarly editions, and band music with about 250 titles in print and approximately 10 titles issued annually. Main activity of the firm is that of selling agency for various Belgian and Dutch publishers: CeBeDeM, Brussels; Editions Musicales Brogneaux, Brussels; Editions A. Cranz, Brussels; Editions Metropolis, Antwerp; Arthur Meulemans-Fonds, Antwerp; Edition Heuwekemeijer, Amsterdam; Molenaar, Wormerverr; J. A. H. Wagenaar, Utrecht; Edition Eugene Ysaÿe, Brussels. Also represents Concord Music Publishing Inc., New York. Henri Elkan has license agreement with ASCAP.

ENSEMBLE PUBLICATIONS, INC., Box 98, Bidwell Station, Buffalo, N.Y. 14222. Founded 1958. President-Treasurer: **D. Miller.** Publications are mostly music for brass ensembles. About 100 titles in print with about 5 published annually. Music covers the early periods as well as contemporary. Licensed with ASCAP.

EVAN–GEORGEOFF MUSIC PUBLISHING CO. 5003 Ridgebury Boulevard, Cleveland, Ohio 44124. Tel.: (216) 381–8549. Founded 1920. Owner: **Helen E. Kuczmarski.** Editor and Educational Director: **John V. Kuczmarski.** Branch office: 1650 Broadway, New York, N.Y. Subsidiary firms: Concert Music Publishing Co., Northeast Publishing Co. Publishers (under Concert Music) of educational music for band, orchestra, string orchestra, chorus; popular music (under Evan-Georgeoff). Combined titles in print total about 135 with 10 or 12 new titles added annually. License is issued to ASCAP.

FAMOUS MUSIC CORPORATION, 1 Gulf + Western Plaza, New York, N.Y. 10023. Tel.: (212) 333–7000. Branch office: 5451 Marathon Street, Hollywood, California 90038. A subsidiary of Paramount Pictures Corp. (Gulf + Western Industries). Publishers of popular music including songs from film scores. Music is arranged for all categories. Licensed with ASCAP and BMI.

CARL FISCHER, INC., 62 Cooper Square, New York, N.Y. 10003. Tel.: (212) SP 7–0900. Cable: CARFISCHER NY. Founded 1872. Branch offices are located in Boston, Chicago, Dallas, and Los Angeles. The firm has published extensively in all categories of instrumental and vocal music, music for educational use, and musical literature. The combined catalogues of the firm contain a large number of works by American composers. Representatives for the following publishers: A. V. Broadhurst; Appleton Music Publishers, Inc.; Composer's Music Corp.; Cundy–Bettoney Co., Inc.; Eastman School of Music Publications; Ensemble Music Press; Evans Music Co.; Fillmore Music House; Charles Foley, Inc.; Charles W. Homeyer & Co., Inc.; Edgar Newgass Publications; Paterson's Publications, Ltd., London; William A. Pond & Co.; R. D. Row Music Co., Inc.; Signature Music Press (formerly Kickapoo Music Co.); Somerset Music Press, Inc.; and works published by the trustees under the will of Mary Baker Eddy. Carl Fischer publications are licensed for performing rights with ASCAP.

J. FISCHER & BRO., Harristown Road, Glen Rock, N.J. 07452. Tel.: (201) 444–2700. Founded 1864. Publishes music in all categories with a significant number of choral works for the Catholic Church. The firm also engages in retail sales at its location. License is held with ASCAP. In July, 1970 the firm was acquired by Belwin Mills Publishing Corp. (q.v.).

H. T. FITZSIMMONS COMPANY, INC., 615 N. LaSalle Street, Chicago, Illinois 60610. Tel.: (312) WH 4–1841. Cable: FITZCO. Founded 1926. President: **H. T. FitzSimons.** Treasurer: **R. E. FitzSimons.** Secretary: **R. G. FitzSimons.** Publishers of music for church and school use, recreational materials, and textbooks. Distributors of the Melody Way Class Piano Course (Miessner Music Co.). Licensed with SESAC.

HAROLD FLAMMER, INC., Founded 1917. Subsidiaries: Choral Press Inc.; Luckhardt & Belder. Publishes choral, organ, piano, and handbell music. About 2,500 titles in print; 90 to 125 titles added annually. Agents for Faith Press, London. Licenses are with ASCAP and SESAC. Acquired by Shawnee Press, Inc. (q.v.).

CHARLES FOLEY, INC. Founded 1940. Publishers of the music of Rachmaninoff and Fritz Kreisler in both original forms and in arrangements. Large-scale works of Rachmaninoff also included. About 300 to 400 titles in print. Purchased by Carl Fischer, Inc. in 1970 and is now a division of that company. Licensed with ASCAP.

MARK FOSTER MUSIC CO., P.O. Box 783, Marquette, Michigan 49855. Tel.: 226–7310. Founded 1961. Owner and Editor: **James McKelvy.** Affiliated firms: Marko Press and Fostco Music Press. Publishers of choral music with some 60 titles in print; publishes 10 to 15 new titles a year. Sole selling agent for Helios Music Edition. Licenses are with ASCAP and BMI.

SAM FOX PUBLISHING CO., INC., 1540 Broadway, New York, N.Y. 10036. Tel.: (212) 247–3890. Branch office: 1443 Manitou Drive, Bel Air Knolls, Santa Barbara, California 93105. President: **Frederick Fox.** Founded 1906. Publishers of music in most categories including Broadway musicals, methods, solo instrumental, ensemble music for band and orchestra, choral music, textbooks, etc. Agents for Movietone Music Corp. (ASCAP), Reynard Music Corp., MJQ Music Inc. (q.v.), Choral Art Publications, David Gornston, Pace Music Co., Gate Music Co., and others. License is with ASCAP.

FRANK MUSIC CORP., 119 West 57th Street, New York, N.Y. 10019. Tel.: (212) CO 5–3600. Cable: MANAKOORA NEW YORK. Founded 1949. Subsidiary or affiliated firms are: Andrew Music Corp.; Audubon Music, Inc.; Carmichael Music Publications, Inc.; Desilu Music Corp.; Empress Music, Inc.; Saunders Publications, Inc.; The Walter–Sterling Reade Music Corp.; Fideree Music Corp.; Frank Music Corp.; Rinimer Corp.; and Boston Music Corp. (q.v.), with its subsidiary Morris Music Co. of Newark. Publishers of all categories of educational music: for band, orchestra, chorus, piano, etc. The company is particularly known for its musical theater and motion picture scores, popular standards, etc. Approximately 500 titles in print with a yearly output of between 50 to 100 titles. All publications, including those of the affiliated firms, are distributed through the Frank Distributing Corp. located at the same address above. Performing rights license is with ASCAP.

GALAXY MUSIC CORP., 2121 Broadway, New York, N.Y. 10023. Tel.: (212) TR 4–2100. Founded 1932. President: **John M. Kernochan.** Treasurer: **George Thompson.** Subsidiary: Galliard Ltd., London. Publishers of concert music, choral music (both sacred and secular), and serious contemporary music. About 1,500 titles in print; 25 titles published yearly. The firm is sole selling agent for: Highgate Press, New York (q.v.); Galliard, Ltd., London; Stainer & Bell, Ltd., London; Elkin & Co., London; Delrieu & Cie., Nice, France; Les Editions Ouvrières, Paris; American Musicological Society (see Organizations); University of Washington Press. Performing rights license is with ASCAP.

GENERAL MUSIC PUBLISHING, 414 East 75th Street, New York, N.Y. 10021. Tel.: (212) 628–4440. The firm has published many works by contemporary American composers covering a variety of categories. Licensed with ASCAP. (See also Serenus Corporation under Record Companies.)

THE H. W. GRAY COMPANY, INC., 159 East 48th Street, New York, N.Y. 10017. Tel.: (212) PI 5–4323. Cable: NOVGRAY. Founded 1906. Since 1971, the firm has been a division of Belwin Mills Publishing Corp. Publishers of choral music for church and school, organ music, music for solo voice, and musical literature. About 8,000 titles in print with about 100 titles added annually. Agents for: Bornemann Editions, Paris; Plainsong Publications Committee, London. Performing rights license is held with ASCAP.

HANSEN PUBLICATIONS, INC., 1842 West Avenue, Miami Beach, Florida 33139. Tel.: (305) 532–5461. Cable: MIAMUSIC. Branch offices: 1834 Marietta Boulevard,

Atlanta, Georgia; 4555 Kingston Street, Denver, Colorado. Wholly owned subsidiaries: Chas. H. Hansen Music Corp.; Ethel Smith Music Corp.; Music of Today, Inc.; Folk World, Inc.; Sounds of Jazz, Inc.; Silhouette Music, Inc.; Shattinger International; California Music Press. Also operates Hansen Publications/Sheet Music Institute, a sales outlet for a large number of other publishers. Most of the publications of Hansen and affiliates is of popular vocal music. Other categories include educational music, band music, choral music, etc. Over 5,000 titles in sheet music form are in print; 250 new titles annually (sheet music), and about 150 titles in folio form. License agreements are with ASCAP and BMI.

HARGAIL MUSIC INC., 28 West 38th Street, New York, N.Y. 10018. Tel.: (212) 245–7246. Cable: HARGAILMUS. Founded 1941. President is **Harold Newman.** Publishing emphasis is on music for recorder with other publications in the general classification of educational music and some contemporary American music for voice, orchestra, piano, etc. In print publications: 200; annually publishes about 20 titles. An important activity of the firm is the sale of recorders and guitar kits (see Wholesalers, Distributors). Selling agent for: E. J. Arnold & Son, Leeds, England; Zen-on Music, Tokyo (recorder and guitar music); Edition Melodie, Zürich. License is with ASCAP.

HARMS, INC. (See Warner Bros.–Seven Arts Music.)

HIGHGATE PRESS, 2121 Broadway, New York, N.Y. 10023. Tel.: (212) TR 4–2100. Founded 1956. President: **Adelaide Kernochan.** Publishers of all categories of serious music; about 50 titles in print and about 10 titles published each year. License with BMI. Does not sell its publications directly (see Galaxy Music Corp.).

INSTITUTE OF MEDIAEVAL MUSIC, LTD., 1653 West 8th Street, Brooklyn, N.Y. 11223. Publishes scholarly books and editions of music in the following series: Publications of Mediaeval Musical Manuscripts, Musical Theorists in Translation, Collected Works, and Musicological Studies. Some publications are outside the area of medieval music. Over 40 titles in print.

INTERLOCHEN PRESS, National Music Camp, Interlochen, Michigan 49643. Tel.: (616) 276–9221. Founded 1957. **Lyman A. Starr,** Executive Vice-President. About 60 titles in print of music for band, orchestra, chorus, various instrumental ensembles, and solo instruments. Most of the works published are by American composers and arrangers. Publications are distributed by Crescendo Music Sales, Inc., 440 West Barry, Chicago, Illinois 60657. Licensed with ASCAP.

EDWIN F. KALMUS, P.O. Box 1007, Opa-Locka, Florida 33054. Tel.: (305) 681–4683. New York City Office: 154 West 57th Street, New York, N.Y. 10019. Tel.: (212) CI 5–8920. Founded 1927. Catalogue consists of some 5,000 miniature scores, full scores of symphonic music, and Urtext editions. License issued with ASCAP.

KENDOR MUSIC, INC., Delevan, N.Y. 14042. Tel.: (716) 492–1254. Founded 1953. President: **Arthur Dedrick.** Publishes music for educational use with a large number of works for school band. About 1,000 titles in print with about 100 titles published yearly. Selling agent for Almitra Music Co., Inc. (ASCAP) and Dedrick Bros. Music Co. (BMI). Also engages in the production of recordings. Kendor is licensed with SESAC.

KENYON PUBLICATIONS, 17 West 60th Street, Eighth Floor, New York, N.Y. 10023. Tel.: (212) 246–9675. Founded 1961. Publishers of educational music for piano, organ, voice, and chorus; also has published a series of chord books for teaching piano, organ, guitar, etc. Forty titles in print; five added annually. License with ASCAP.

KING MUSIC PUBLISHING CORPORATION,351 West 52nd Street, New York, N.Y. 10019. Tel.: (212) JU 6–4470. Officers: **Walter Kane, Jr., Angel Tomaselli,** and **Irwin Gewirtz.** Subsidiary firms: Clef Music Publishing Corp., Lane Music Publishing Co., McKinley Publishing Co., Cerutti Publishing Co., Central Music Co., Wangir Music Co.

Publishers. The firm and its subsidiaries publish educational and recreational music in adaptations, collections, and arrangements of standard popular and classical pieces for guitar, accordion, electronic organ, autoharp, harmonica, and piano. License is with SESAC and ASCAP.

ROBERT KING MUSIC CO., 7 Canton Street, North Easton, Massachusetts 02356. Founded 1940. Owner: **Robert D. King.** Has published 300 titles of music for brass instruments, which is the exclusive interest of the firm. Approximately 6 titles are added each year. Sole selling agents for W. D. Stuart Music, New York. In addition to publishing, the company engages in music jobbing and retail sales of the brass music of all publishers.

NEIL A. KJOS MUSIC CO., 525 Busse Highway, Park Ridge, Illinois 60068. Tel.: (312) 825–2168. Founded 1936. Publishers mainly of music for educational use for band, chorus, and school orchestra, and sacred choral music. Affiliated firms for which the Kjos company acts as sole selling agent are: J. A. Parks Music Co., Loop Music Publishing Co., General Words and Music Company, and The Pallma Music Company. The Kjos, Parks, and Pallma firms have licenses with SESAC; General Words and Loop with ASCAP.

LAVELL PUBLISHING CO., INC., P.O. Box 717, Omaha, Nebraska 68101. Tel.: (402) 451–2146. Founded 1940. General Manager: **Royce Kent.** Publishers of piano music by contemporary American composers for educational use. About 75 titles in print; 3 titles added annually.

LAWSON-GOULD MUSIC PUBLISHERS, INC., 866 Third Avenue, New York, N.Y. 10022. Tel.: (212) PL 2–3920. Founded 1954. The firm is under the direction of **Walter Gould.** Specializes in the publication of choral music with some 900 titles in print and a publishing schedule of 50 titles a year. Publications are sold only through G. Schirmer, Inc. (q.v.). Licensed with ASCAP.

LEA POCKET SCORES, P.O. Box 138, Audubon Station, New York, N.Y. 10032. Tel.: (212) 866–4026. Founded 1951. Proprietor: **F. Steinhardt.** Exclusively publishers of pocket scores drawn from well-known full-size editions (e.g., Bach–Gesellschaft, Chrysander–Handel, etc.) with most of the scores for solo instruments or chamber groups. Titles in print: 146; published yearly: 10. Sold in the U.S. through Theodore Presser Co. (q.v.).

THE LEBLANC PUBLICATIONS, INC. (LPI), 7019 30th Avenue, Kenosha, Wisconsin 53141. Tel.: (414) 658–1644. Founded 1960. Director of Publications: **Lucien Cailliet.** A division of the Leblanc Corporation, Inc. (see Manufacturers). Publishers of strictly educational music for concert band, symphony orchestra, clarinet choir, woodwind and brass ensembles, pedagogical studies, and method books. In print: 90 titles; 8 to 10 titles published yearly. Licensed with ASCAP.

LEEDS MUSIC CORP. (See MCA Music.)

HAL LEONARD MUSIC, INC., 64 East 2nd Street, Winona, Minnesota 55987. Tel.: (507) 454–2920. Founded 1946. President: **Roger Busdicker.** Branch office: 6223 Selma Avenue, Hollywood, California 90028. Publishes mainly music for school bands, some popular music, and guides and tests for the school band director. About 200 titles are published annually. License is through ASCAP.

LILLENAS PUBLISHING COMPANY, Box 527, Kansas City, Missouri 64141. Tel.: (816) 531–4646. Founded 1924. **R. W. Stringfield** is Manager, Music Department. Music Editor is **Floyd W. Hawkins.** Sales outlets are also located in Pasadena, California, and Toronto, Canada. A division of Nazarene Publishing House. Sacred music publishers. Publications include choral (with collections for children's choir), solo vocal, keyboard, some instrumental music, record-and-songbook albums, director's kits, hymnals, religious dramas and pageants, and some music materials and supplies. In-print publications are as follows: 310 collections, 400 octavos, 60 titles in sheet music form; 40 titles are published yearly. Licensed with SESAC.

LORENZ PUBLISHING CO., 501 East 3rd Street, Dayton, Ohio 45401. Tel.: (513) 228-6118. Founded 1890. Operated by members of the Lorenz family. Founded 1890. Divisional firms are the Sacred Music Press and the Heritage Music Press (founded in 1967). Publishers of music for all Christian faiths (Heritage Press publishes secular music for school use). Over 2,000 titles in print with 120 titles published annually. License is with ASCAP.

LOUISVILLE HOUSE AUTOGRAPH EDITIONS. (See Franco Colombo, Inc.)

LUDWIG MUSIC PUBLISHING CO., 557–67 East 140th Street, Cleveland, Ohio 44110. Tel.: (216) 851–1150. Founded 1921. President: **Carl F. W. Ludwig.** Publishers of music for school band and orchestra and various forms of instrumental and vocal music for educational use. Over 2,000 titles in print and about 20 titles published each year. Licensed with SESAC.

LYRA MUSIC CO., 133 West 69th Street, New York, N.Y. 10023. Tel.: (212) 874–3360. Founded 1960. Owner: **Don Henry.** Affiliated firms are Hendon Importing Co., Inc., and Hendon Music. The firm is a division of International Music Service. Publishers exclusively of music for harp including studies and textbooks. About 125 titles in print; 10 to 15 titles published annually. Lyra has a license agreement with ASCAP; Hendon with BMI.

MCA MUSIC, 445 Park Avenue, New York, N.Y. 10036. Tel.: (212) 759–7500. Cable: MUSICOR. Formerly Leeds Music Corporation. Vice President: **Salvatore T. Chiantia.** Branch offices: Leeds Music (Canada) Ltd., Toronto; Leeds Music Ltd., London. Subsidiary firms: Leeds Music Corporation, Duchess Music Corp., Pickwick Music Corp., Northern Music Corp., Champion Music, Hawaii Music Co. MCA Music is itself a division of MCA, Inc. The combined catalogues of the firm equal some 6,000 titles in print, with about 150 new titles published annually. The catalogues cover a large variety of publications in the popular music and educational music fields, as well as serious classical and contemporary works in most genres. The firm is the U.S. selling agent for these foreign publishers: Edizioni Suvini Zerboni, Milan; Arno Volk/Hans Gerig, Germany; Le Chant du Monde, France; Mezhdunarodnaya Kniga, Moscow; British and Continental Agencies, Ltd., London. MCA Music and its publishing affiliates have licensing agreements for performing rights with ASCAP and BMI.

MCGINNIS & MARX, MUSIC PUBLISHERS, 201 West 86th Street, Apt. 706, New York, N.Y. 10024. Tel.: (212) 799–5214. Founded 1945. Proprietor is **Josef Marx.** Subsidiary is Josef Marx Music Company (ASCAP). Publishers of serious music both old and contemporary. About 120 titles in print; 20 publications issued annually. In addition to printed music, some publications, particularly those of contemporary works, are issued in blueprint or Xerox reproduction and are not offered to the trade. The remaining publications are sold through the firm of Pietro Deiro (q.v. this section). The firm is licensed with BMI.

MCLAUGHLIN & REILLY CO., formerly of Boston. Acquired by Summy–Birchard Company (q.v.). Founded 1909. Publishers of sacred and educational music. About 3,000 titles in print. Licensed with SESAC.

EDWARD B. MARKS MUSIC CORPORATION, 136 West 52nd Street, New York, N.Y. 10019. Tel.: (212) CI 7–7277. Cable: MARKBRO N.Y. Founded 1894. President: **Herbert E. Marks.** Vice-Presidents: **Stephen S. Marks** and **Joseph Auslander.** Branch office: 7235 Hollywood Boulevard, Suite 321, Hollywood, California 90046. Subsidiaries: Piedmont Music Co., Inc.; Alameda Music, Inc.; George M. Cohan Music Publishing Co., Inc. The Edward B. Marks catalogue and that of its affiliates represents music in every style, with a total of over 17,800 titles in print and about 180 new titles published yearly. Originally publishers of popular music including a large number of Latin-American popular songs introduced in the U.S. in the 1930's. Many of these and other American popular songs have long since remained standards in the field of popular music throughout the world. The catalogue now includes educational music and the music of contemporary composers in the categories of symphonic works, operas, chamber music, etc. The publication formats include folios, octavos, rental music, full scores, pocket scores, and books. Selling agent for Ars Polona, Warsaw, and J. & W. Chester, Ltd., London (limited representation). Performance rights licenses are held mainly with BMI and some with ASCAP. (Beginning April 1, 1973, Belwin Mills has handled all shipping, billing, warehousing, selling and promotion of the Marks catalogues.)

MERCURY MUSIC CORPORATION. Affiliated firms are Merrymount Music, Inc. and Beekman Music, Inc. (licensed with BMI and ASCAP, respectively). Since 1959, the Mercury firm has had Theodore Presser Co. (q.v.) as its sole selling agent. Mercury has performing rights license with SESAC.

MERION MUSIC, INC. Established in 1953 (see Theodore Presser Company). Licensed with BMI.

MERRYMOUNT MUSIC, INC. (See Theodore Presser Company and Mercury Music Corp.) Licensed with BMI.

MJQ MUSIC, INC., 200 West 57th Street, New York, N.Y. 10019. Tel.: (212) CI 5–2836. Founded 1958. President: **John Lewis.** Executive Vice-President: **Peter Kameron.** (The initials of the firm are derived from the Modern Jazz Quartet.) Publications in the MJQ catalogue are largely those of the so-called third stream music—or music attempting the fusion of certain tenets of "classical" music (classical in the broadest meaning of the term) and modern jazz. (See also Third Stream Music, Inc.) These works are published by MJQ for concert and educational use. The catalogue includes instrumental music in many categories and some vocal music. Some works are available in composer facsimile editions (ozalid reproductions). Certain titles are available only from Sam Fox Publishing Co. (q.v.). Over 50 titles in print, excluding titles for rental only. Performing license agreement is with BMI.

EDWIN H. MORRIS & COMPANY, INC., 31 West 54th Street, New York, N.Y. 10019. Tel.: (212) 582–5656. Affiliated firms: Arko Music Corp.; Carwin Music, Inc.; Charling Music Corp.; Harwin Music Corp.; Jerryco Music Co.; Mayfair Music Corp.; Melrose Music Corp.; Mesquite Music Corp.; and Morley Music Co., Inc. Publishers of popular music and music for educational use for band, chorus, orchestra, piano solo, and other categories. Licensed with ASCAP.

MUSIC FOR PERCUSSION, INC., 17 West 60th Street, New York, N.Y. 10023. Tel.: (212) 246–9675. Exclusively publishers of music for percussion. Over 110 titles have been issued, grouped as follows: ensemble series, snare series, and a series each for bass drum, mallet instruments, timpani, and a text series. Performing rights license is through BMI.

MUSICORD PUBLICATIONS, INC., 1871 Victory Boulevard, Staten Island, N.Y. 10314. Tel.: (212) 981–8550. Founded 1941. President: **Mrs. David Hirschberg.** Has published over 154 titles of piano music for instructional use; about 3 new publications are released yearly.

MUSIC PUBLISHERS HOLDING CORP. (See Warner Bros.–Seven Arts Music.)

MUSIC SALES CORP., 33 West 60th Street, New York, N.Y. 10023. Tel.: (212) CI 6–0325. President: **Herbert H. Wise.** Vice-President: **Robert Wise.** The firm represents the following publishers: Amsco Music Publishing Co. (SESAC); Consolidated Music Publishers, Inc. (ASCAP); Oak Publications; Yorktown Music Press (ASCAP); Villa-Lobos Music (a special piano series); Embassy Music Corp. (BMI); Weintraub Music Company (ASCAP). Other divisional firms are: Passantino Brands (music writing supplies); Music Sales Book Division (sales of mostly folk-song books and some instructional books for fretted instruments, etc.); Mastertouch Piano Rolls (of Australia). The 10 firms above are all serviced from the central location of Music Sales Corporation. The publishing emphasis of each divisional publisher and the number of titles in print, according to the Music Sales Corp. catalogue, follows. Amsco: 154 titles;

has published the "Everybody's Favorite" series, anthologies of instrumental and vocal pieces for various levels of performance. Each book has a particular emphasis, sells at low cost, and numbers about 192 pages. Consolidated: 172 titles; mainly noted for the "Music for Millions Series," low-cost volumes containing many pieces arranged for piano, organ, wind instruments, etc. Oak Publications: 100 titles; publishers of folk music and "protest" music and instruction manuals for folk instruments. Yorktown: 28 titles; publishers of the so-called Joy series ("Joy of Guitar," "Joy of Bach," "Joy of Jazz," etc.) and early-grade piano recital booklets. Villa-Lobos Piano Music: 21 titles edited by the composer. Weintraub: 114 titles; compositions by contemporary American composers from piano pieces for the young to large-scale symphonic works. Embassy: 19 titles; publishers of "The Whole World Series"; collections of familiar music for piano, violin, voice, etc. Music Sales Corporation operates music retail outlets throughout the United States and also manufactures metronomes.

NEW MUSIC EDITION, founded in 1930 (see Theodore Presser Company). Licensed with BMI and ASCAP.

NEW VALLEY MUSIC PRESS, Sage Hall, Smith College, Northampton, Massachusetts 01060. Tel.: (413) 584–2700, ext. 261. Founded 1942. Publishers of contemporary American music with an emphasis on works of composers who are not published elsewhere. About 65 titles in print; approximately 2 titles issued annually. Most of the catalogue consists of vocal music—solo voice and choral music—and chamber music.

OKRA MUSIC CORPORATION, 177 East 87th Street, New York, N.Y. 10028. Tel.: (212) 879–1960. Founded 1963. President: **Raoul R. Ronson.** Publishes contemporary American serious music, much of it chamber music and popular music. Catalogue of titles issued in combination with Seesaw Music Corporation (q.v. this section). Titles in print: 120; titles published yearly: 20. License with BMI.

OXFORD UNIVERSITY PRESS, 200 Madison Avenue, New York, N.Y. 10016. Tel.: (212) OR 9–7300. Founded in England in 1478; first published music in 1659. The American office is a branch of the English firm and is the sole U.S. selling representative. President: **J. R. B. Brett-Smith.** Manager of Music Dept.: **John Ward.** Not primarily a music publisher, Oxford nevertheless is important to the music field. Its total list of publications, some 25,000 including music, is one of the largest among world publishers. Approximately 4,000 music titles are in print, including 2,000 choral titles. About 250 new titles are published annually. These figures represent the publications emanating both from New York and England. Categories include music for chorus, solo voice, orchestra, band, solo instrumental, instructional books such as the Oxford Piano Course; most categories have works for concert as well as educational use. The Oxford book catalogue has some 275 titles in the field of music. License agreement is with ASCAP.

THE JOSEPH PATELSON MUSIC HOUSE, 160 West 56th Street, New York, N.Y. 10019. Tel.: (212) PL 7–5587. Founded 1920. Headed by **Joseph Patelson** and **Henry Patelson,** the company is primarily a music dealership but has published some classical music reprints and some contemporary works. Titles in print number 80, with about 5 titles published yearly. License is with ASCAP.

O. PAGANI & BRO., INC., 289 Bleecker Street, New York, N.Y. 10014. Tel.: (212) CH 2–6744. Founded 1905. President: **Frank Gaviani.** Secretary: **Theresa Costello.** Titles in print: 3,000; published annually: 50. The firm is known primarily as a publisher of music and method books for the accordion. Other categories include publications for stage bands, brass bands, classical guitar, among others. The firm also sells music merchandise. Publications are licensed with SESAC.

C. F. PETERS CORPORATION, 373 Park Avenue South, New York, N.Y. 10016. Tel.: (212) 686–4147. Founded in 1948. The firm is headed by **Mrs. Walter Hinrichsen,** President, wife of the founder (d. 1969), and although it cooperates with the German firm of Edition Peters (Frankfurt) and Peters Edition, London, it is a separate company. Publications cover a wide range of music: American contemporary, classical, chamber music, pocket scores, Urtext and scholarly editions of the classics, an important music rental catalogue, etc. Represents the following American publications: Alpeg Editions, New York Public Library Music Publications, American Music Award Series of the Sigma Alpha Iota, American Wind Symphony Editions (see American Wind Symphony), and Henmar Press. Foreign publishers for whom C. F. Peters Corporation acts as selling agent in the United States are: Alsbach, Broekmans, Harmonia, Donemus—all in The Netherlands; Goodwin & Tabb, Hinrichsen Edition, and Cell (England); in Germany: Robert Forberg Musikverlag, Bruckner Verlag, Heinrichshofen's Verlag, Kahnt, Robert Lienau, Musikverlag Ries & Erler, Merseburger, Musia, Noetzel, Taunus Verlag, Vieweg Verlag, Hänssler Verlag of Stuttgart, Westend Verlag, and the firm of Wilhelm Zimmerman; Editions Choudens, Paris, France; in Denmark: Dania, Engstrøm & Sødring; Dessain, and Schott Frères—both in Belgium; Eulenburg (pocket scores), Hug & Co., Kneusslin, Reinhardt (Switzerland); Lyche in Norway; Zanibon in Padua, Italy. Recently became sole agent for M. P. Belaieff, Paris, for distribution in the Western Hemisphere, Japan, and the Philippines.

THEODORE PRESSER COMPANY, Presser Place, Bryn Mawr, Pennsylvania 19010. Tel.: (215) LA 5–3636. Cable: RESSERP BRYNMAWRPENN. Founded in 1883. Officers: **Arnold Broido,** President; **Nicholas J. Elsier, Jr.,** Vice-President; **Calvert Bean, Jr.,** Director of Publications. Branch office: 111 West 57th Street, New York, N.Y. 10019 (Tel.: [212] 246–5311). Subsidiary is Elkan–Vogel, Inc. of Philadelphia (q.v.). The combined publications available from the firm cover all areas of music for the school, concert hall, church, and private recreation. Originally founded with the intention of providing music, method books, and textbooks for music teachers, the company retains this emphasis in large measure throughout its catalogues. Music published includes choral and solo vocal music, operas and operettas, music for school bands and orchestras, music for symphony orchestra and other instrumental ensembles, music for solo instruments, collections, musical literature, etc. The rental music catalogue of orchestral and instrumental music includes over 2,500 works. Many contemporary composers including the so-called avant garde are published by the firm. The total number of active publications issued by Presser is about 22,000. About 125 new titles are published annually. The firm represents the following domestic publishers, some of which are owned by Presser: Oliver Ditson Company (acquired in 1931); John Church Company (acquired in 1930); Merion Music, Inc. (acquired in 1953); New Music Edition (acquired in 1959); Liturgical Music Press, Inc.; Mercury Music Corporation; Merrymount Music, Inc.; Weaner–Levant; Society for the Publication of American Music; Music Press; Beekman Music, Inc.; Columbia Music Company; Tritone–Tenuto; Mowbray Music Publishers; Lea Pocket Scores. Foreign publishers represented are: Universal Edition, London, Vienna, and Zürich; Heugel & Cie, Paris; Impero Verlag, Wilhelmshaven, Germany; Editions Musicales Transatlantiques, Paris; Haydn–Mozart Presse, Vienna; Josef Weinberger, London (selected publications only); Philharmonia Pocket Scores, Vienna; Ongaku No Tomo Edition, Tokyo (limited representation); Gerard Billaudot, Paris. The combined domestic publishers represented and owned are licensed for performing rights variously with ASCAP, BMI, and SESAC.

PRO-ART PUBLICATIONS, INC., 469 Union Avenue, Westerly, L.I., N.Y. 11591.

REMICK MUSIC CORP. (See Warner Bros.–Seven Arts Music.)

ROCHESTER MUSIC PUBLISHERS, 358 Aldrich Road, Fairport, N.Y. 14450. Tel.: (716) 377–1503. Incorporated in 1965. **P. L. Toland,** President and Treasurer. About 37 titles in print, most of them the works of American composers; 1 or 2 titles published annually. Licensed with ASCAP.

RONGWEN MUSIC, INC. (See Broude Brothers Limited.) Publishes music of contemporary composers.

RUBANK, INC., 16215 N.W. 15th Avenue, Miami, Florida 33169. Tel.: (305) 625–5323. Publishers of instrumental and ensemble method books and music. Agents for Musica Rara Publications, London, England.

E. C. SCHIRMER MUSIC COMPANY, 600 Washington Street, Boston, Massachusetts 02111. Tel.: (617) 426–3137. Founded 1921. President: **Robert MacWilliams.** Subsidiary: Ione Press, Inc. Has published some orchestral and instrumental music, but the firm is mainly devoted to publishing choral music of a wide variety suitable for church or concert use. Composers represented are not only those of the past, but contemporary Americans and others. Has over 4,000 titles in print and publishes from 40 to 50 titles yearly. The firm acts as selling representatives for Foetisch Frères, S.A. of Lausanne, Switzerland. Licensing agreements are with ASCAP and BMI.

G. SCHIRMER, INC., 866 Third Avenue, New York, N.Y. 10022. Tel.: (212) PL 2–3800. Cable: SCHIRMER NEW YORK. Founded in 1861 as Beer & Schirmer as a continuation of another firm originally established in 1848. (In 1866, the company was renamed G. Schirmer.) Subsidiary company is Associated Music Publishers, acquired in 1964 (q.v. this section). G. Schirmer maintains music retail stores at 4 East 49th Street, New York, N.Y. 10017 and at 3330 Wilshire Boulevard, Los Angeles, California 90005. The firm has its own music printing plant (located at 48–02 48th Avenue, Woodside, Long Island, N.Y.), which is reputedly the world's largest. In 1962 it was reported to print an average of 140 million pages of music yearly; in 1971 an average of about 520 million pages. In September, 1968, preparations were made to sell G. Schirmer, Inc. to Crowell Collier & Macmillan, Inc. The sale was subsequently made with G. Schirmer becoming subsidiary. President of G. Schirmer is **Rudolph Tauhert.** Chairman is **Rudolph Schirmer.** The Schirmer catalogue includes music in all genres and covering nearly all historical eras—with a significant number of contemporary works—for educational and concert use: music for band and orchestra, vocal solo, and choral sacred and secular music, operas and operettas, works for organ, piano, string instruments, and music for elementary instruction. A rental library, musical literature, and textbooks are also published. A series, begun in 1892, called the "Schirmer Library of Musical Classics" (now 1,900 volumes) is particularly well known. G. Schirmer is also publisher of *The Musical Quarterly* (see Periodicals) as well as the standard reference work, "Baker's Biographical Dictionary of Musicians." The exact number of titles in print has not been made known, but it has been estimated to be between 40,000 and 50,000. The company reports that it publishes about 200 titles a year. G. Schirmer, Inc. is the selling agent for the following publishers: W. Hansen, Sweden; J. Curwen & Sons, London; Lee Roberts Music Publishing, Inc. (U.S.); Lawson–Gould Music Publishers, Inc. (U.S.); Faber Music, London; Amberson Enterprises (U.S.); Ascherberg, Hopwood & Crew, Ltd., London. The firm has licensing agreements with ASCAP.

SCHMITT, HALL & MCCREARY COMPANY, 110 North Fifth Street, Minneapolis, Minnesota 55403. Tel.: (612) 336–4367. President: **Robert P. Schmitt.** The firm is a subsidiary of Schmitt Music Center, Inc., also of Minneapolis. Publishers of some 3,000 in-print titles for music for band and sacred and secular choral music. Approximately 65 titles are published annually. The company distributes for Schmitt Music Center and Sacred Design Associates, Inc. The firm is represented in Japan by Nippon Gakki of Tokyo. Licensing is with SESAC; the parent firm is licensed with ASCAP.

ARTHUR P. SCHMIDT CO. (See Summy–Birchard Co.)

SCHROEDER & GUNTHER, INC., 866 Third Avenue, New York, N.Y. 10022. Tel.: (212) 752–3800. Founded in 1879. A division of Associated Music Publishers, Inc. (q.v. this section). The firm specializes in publishing piano-teaching material written by American composers. All sales are through Associated. License is with BMI.

SEESAW MUSIC CORPORATION, 177 East 87th Street, New York, N.Y. 10028. Tel.: (212) 879–1960. Founded 1963. President: **Raoul R. Ronson.** Publishers of contemporary American concert music. Titles in print: 150; published annually: 25. (See also Okra Music Corp., this section.) Licensed with ASCAP.

SHAPIRO, BERNSTEIN & CO., INC., 666 Fifth Avenue, New York, N.Y. 10019. Tel.: (212) 247–3553. Cable: BERNSTEIN. Founded 1898. Board Chairman: **David Schenker.** President: **Richard Voltter.** Branch offices are located in London, England; Nashville, Tennessee; and Los Angeles, California. Divisional firms are: Skidmore Music Co.; Sheffield Music Co.; Shapiro, Bernstein & Co., Ltd. (London); Scarsdale Music Corp.; Painted Desert Music Corp.; Ponderosa Music Co., Inc.; Mood Music Co., Inc. Publishers of popular and standard music primarily. Other categories include band music, sacred and secular choral music, instrumental methods. Titles in print number 10,000 and about 50 titles are published annually. The firm is selling agent for the following publishers: Heugel & Cie., Paris (classical miniature scores only); The Claridge Music Group (which includes Claridge Music, Inc., Cannon Point Music, Inc., Chicory Music, Inc., and Conley Music, Inc.); The Alarm Clock Music Co.; MRC Music, Inc.; Columbia Pictures Music Corp.; Pomona Music Corp.; Seven-Eleven Music Corp.; as well as the divisional firms listed above. The company has license agreements with ASCAP and BMI.

SHAWNEE PRESS, INC., Delaware Water Gap, Pennsylvania 18327. Tel.: (717) 476–0550. President: **Ernest R. Farmer.** Sales Manager: **Robert O. Schell.** Branch offices: 2821 Willowhaven Drive, La Crescenta, California 91214; 434 South Wabash Avenue, Chicago, Illinois 60605. Subsidiary firms for which Shawnee is sole selling agent are: Paull–Pioneer Music Corp.; Maxwell–Wirges Publications; Templeton Publishing Co., Inc. (formerly Alec Templeton, Inc.); Malcolm Music, Ltd.; Axelrod Music Publications; Modern Music Press; Frederick Charles, Inc.; Dartmouth Collegium Musicum Series; Harold Flammer, Inc. Shawnee's combined catalogues include a particular emphasis on educational music for chorus (secular, including popular music, and sacred) and concert band. The Fred Waring Choral Arrangement series is important to the choral catalogue. Also published are a number of works by contemporary composers for orchestra and various instrumental ensembles, including some avant-garde music. Performing rights are licensed with ASCAP—except the Malcolm catalogue, which is with BMI, and Flammer's Choral Press, which is SESAC.

SILVER BURDETT COMPANY, Park Avenue and Columbia Road, Morristown, N.J. 07960. Tel.: (201) 538–0400. Cable: SILDET. Founded 1885. Branch offices: 435 Middlefield Road, Palo Alto, California 94301; 3272 Peachtree Road, N.E., Atlanta, Georgia 30305; 460 South Northwest Highway, Park Ridge, Illinois 60068; 4640 Harry Hines Boulevard, Dallas, Texas 75235. Officers: **John D. Backe,** President; **John H. Williamson,** Executive Vice-President; **Ira Singleton,** Managing Editor. Silver Burdett is a Division of General Learning Corporation and operates as the educational publishing subsidiary of Time, Inc. The firm's music publications include elementary and high school textbooks, instrumental instruction books, and phonograph records. It has produced a teaching and learning series called *Making Music Your Own,* which is a "structured program" covering music instruction for kindergarten to grade 6 and consists of pupil's books, teachers' editions, and recordings and an instrumental music series for beginners called *Play Now.* The music section of the company has published some 82 titles. Publications are licensed with ASCAP. Silver Burdett also distributes the TIME–LIFE library books and the *Story of Great Music,* a mass-market series of recordings covering music stylistically and historically with the aid of printed text and illustrations.

SOCIETY FOR THE PUBLICATION OF AMERICAN MUSIC (see Theodore Presser Company). Licensed with ASCAP. (This society is now dissolved.)

SOLO MUSIC, INC., 4708 Van Noord Avenue, Sherman Oaks, California 91403. Tel.: (213) 762–2219. Founded 1965. President: **Paul Mills.** Has published under 10 titles of mostly popular music; about 2 titles a year are added. Licensed with ASCAP.

SOUTHERN MUSIC CO., 1100 Broadway, Box 329, San Antonio, Texas 78206. Tel.: (512) 226–8167. Founded 1935. Vice-President: **Arthur Gurwitz.** Publishers of music for school band and orchestra, instrumental methods, studies, collections, solo pieces; music for instrumental ensembles such as saxophone quartets, brass groups, clarinet quartets, etc.; choral collections; textbooks; and certain music-teacher supplies and aids. The firm also owns the catalogue of the Composers Press, Inc., which it distributes. Over 1,600 titles in print, with about 50 published annually. The firm is also active as sheet music jobbers and retailers of other publishers' music. License is with ASCAP.

SOUTHERN MUSIC PUBLISHING CO., INC., 1619 Broadway, New York, N.Y. 10019. Tel.: (212) CO 5–3910. Cable: SOUTHMUSIC. President: **Mrs. Monique Peer-Morris.** Branch offices: 6922 Hollywood Boulevard, Los Angeles, California 90028; 2001-A Four Ambassodors Building, Miami, Florida 33131; 1819 Broadway, Nashville, Tennessee 37203. The firm has offices established in major cities throughout the world. Subsidiary and affiliated publishing firms for which Southern is distributor are: Charles K. Harris Music Publishing Co., Inc.; La Salle Music Publishers, Inc.; Melody Lane Publications, Inc.; Panther Music Corp.; Peer International Corp.; Peer-Southern Productions, Inc.; Pera Music Corp.; and R. F. D. Music Publishing Co., Inc. The company is a publisher of music in virtually all categories. It has an important catalogue of serious music by United States and Latin-American composers; a large number of Latin-American popular titles in many arrangements, collections, etc.; a rental catalogue of symphonic music, contemporary popular music, publications for educational use, and so on. Southern (or Peer International) is selling agent for the following: Israeli Music Publications, Ltd. (Tel Aviv) (agents for the Western Hemisphere and Japan); Pan American Union Music Publications, Washington, D.C. (world agent is Peer); Ediciones Mexicanas de Musica, A.C. (Mexico City) (Peer is sole world agent outside Mexico); Editorial Cooperativa Interamericana de Compositores (Montevideo) (Southern is sole world agent); Edition Cranz (Wiesbaden) (study scores); Editorial Argentina de Musica and Editorial Saraceno (both of Buenos Aires) (Southern is sole agent in Western Hemisphere and Japan). Southern's affiliated firms are all licensed with ASCAP except Melody Lane, Peer International, and Pera which are all licensed with BMI.

SUMMY–BIRCHARD COMPANY, 1834 Ridge Avenue, Evanston, Illinois 60204. Tel.: (312) 869–4700. Cable: SUMCO. Founded 1872. President: **David K. Sengstack.** Secretary: **John A. Kelly, Jr.** Formerly the Clayton F. Summy Co., Chicago, and the C. C. Birchard Co., Boston. Other divisions of the firm are: Chart Music Publishing House, Inc.; Arthur P. Schmidt Company; Traficante/Polyphonic Publishing Co.; Creative Music Publishers; Odowan; James Allan Dash/Baltimore Music Co.; Southwestern Music Publishers; McLaughlin & Reilly Co. Titles of all the foregoing firms are sold through Summy–Birchard, which currently publishes only under the Summy–Birchard Company and A. P. Schmidt Co. imprints. Branch offices: 66–33 Myrtle Avenue, Ridgewood, N.J.; 1100 Glendon Avenue, Los Angeles, California 90024. The firm publishes primarily music, method, and textbooks for educational use. The music titles include an extensive series of piano instruction material as well as instrumental solo and ensemble music, band music, and some music for orchestra, choral sheet music and books, and music for solo voice. Also published are "source books" which are books containing miniature reproductions of virtually the entire firm's catalogue (in four categories) in order to facilitate purchasing. About 1,000 titles in print with a schedule of about 20 titles published annually. The firm is distributor in the U.S. for Zen-On Publications of Japan and the violin materials developed by Shinuchi Suzuki. It also produces recordings related to its instructional series and owns Civic Concert Service, a concert booking firm. Performing rights licenses are with SESAC and ASCAP.

TETRA MUSIC CORP. (See Alexander Broude, Inc.)

THIRD STREAM MUSIC, INC., 200 West 57th Street, New York, N.Y. 10019. Tel.: (212) CI 5–2836. Founded 1964. (For officers, see MJQ Music, Inc.) Licensed with ASCAP.

TRANSCONTINENTAL MUSIC PUBLICATIONS, 1674 Broadway, New York, N.Y. 10019. Tel.: (212) CO 5–4973. Founded by Josef Freudenthal (d. 1964). in 1938. Owner: **Mari Freudenthal.** Publishers exclusively of Jewish secular and sacred music and some concert music by Jewish composers. About 800 titles in print with about 45 titles published annually. License agreements are with ASCAP.

VOLKWEIN BROS., INC., 117 Sandusky Street, Pittsburgh, Pennsylvania 15212. Tel.: (412) 322–5100. Founded 1888. President: **Carl R. Volkwein.** Vice-President: **Carl W. Volkwein.** Secretary-Treasurer: **Walter E. Volkwein.** Publishers of music for band, chorus, and instrumental solo music. About 3,000 titles in print; an average of 25 titles published yearly. The firm is also active in the sale of musical merchandise and the music of other publishers. License is with ASCAP.

WALTON MUSIC CORPORATION, 17 West 60th Street, New York, N.Y. 10023. Tel.: (212) 246–9675. Publishes educational music with an emphasis on choral music of past masters and contemporary composers. Particularly prominent are the compositions and arrangements for chorus by **Norman Luboff.** The firm has about 1,000 titles in print with about 40 published each year. Selling agent for Walton is Plymouth Music Co., Inc. of the same address. Licensing agreement is with ASCAP.

WARNER BROS. PUBLICATIONS, INC., 1230 Avenue of the Americas, New York, N.Y. 10020. Tel.: (212) JU 6–0800. Cable: WANG. Founded 1929. The firm is headed by **Victor Blau.** A division of Warner Bros.–Seven Arts, Inc., located at 4000 Warner Boulevard, Burbank, California 91503. A branch office is located at 610 South Broadway, Los Angeles, California 90015. Formerly known as Music Publishers Holding Corp. (M.P.H.), the company consists of the following publishing subsidiaries: Harms, Inc.; M. Witmark & Sons; Remick Music Corp.; Advanced Music Corp.; New World Music Corp.; Pepamar Music Corp.; Weill–Brecht–Harms Co., Inc.; W-7 Music Corp.; and Warner–Sevarts Publ. Corp. Publishes music in all categories including scores and songs from films, Broadway musicals, popular and standard music. Educational music includes piano-teaching material, band and choral music for all school grades, etc. Some 30,000 titles are reportedly in print with about 100 to 150 titles published annually. Licenses for performing rights are with ASCAP and BMI.

WEINTRAUB MUSIC CO., 33 West 60th Street, New York, N.Y. 10023. Tel.: (212) CI 6–0325. Founded 1950. Publications are sold through Music Sales Corp. (q.v. for further details). Publishes about 10 new titles a year.

ROBERT WHITFORD PUBLICATIONS, 8277 N.E. 2nd Avenue, Miami, Florida 33138. Tel.: (305) 757–4961. Founded 1937. **Robert Whitford** is President and owner. Publishers of educational piano music and methods exclusively, all arranged or composed by Mr. Whitford. Some 500 titles in print; about 30 titles published yearly.

WILLIAMSON MUSIC, INC., 609 Fifth Avenue, New York, N.Y. 10017. Tel.: (212) 752–4300. Founded in 1945 by Richard Rodgers and Oscar Hammerstein, 2nd. Publishers of songs, arrangements, and vocal scores of the musical plays of Rodgers and Hammerstein, as well as religious-oriented musical plays and the music of other composers for the Broadway theater. Sole selling agents are Chappell & Co., Inc. (q.v.). License for performance rights is with ASCAP.

THE WILLIS MUSIC COMPANY, 440 Main Street, Cincinnati, Ohio 45201. Tel.: (513) 721–6050. Founded 1899. President: **Edward R. Cranley.** Treasurer: **John J. Cranley.** Branch offices: 43 The Arcade, Cleveland, Ohio 44114; 8 West Pike Street, Covington, Kentucky 41011. Subsidiary is the Clark-Jones Music Company with offices in Knoxville, Oak Ridge, and Nashville, Tennessee. Publishers of piano and other instrumental methods, band music, choral music, children's music books, operettas. Some 9,500 titles in print; about 25 titles issued annually. Represents the following publishers: R. L. Huntzinger, Inc., Ralph Jusko Publications, Delhi Publications. The Willis Company engages in retail sales of music, recordings, musical gifts. Licensed with SESAC.

M. WITMARK & SONS. (See Warner Bros. Publications, Inc.)

WORLD LIBRARY PUBLICATIONS, INC., 2145 Central Parkway, Cincinnati, Ohio 45214. Tel.: (513) 421–1090. Founded 1950. Divisional firms: World Library of Sacred Music, Westwood Press, Apogee Press (q.v.). Publishes music for the Catholic Church, secular and sacred choral music, and music for organ and piano. About 2,000 titles in print; publishes about 200 new titles yearly. Selling agents for the following firms: St. Francis Production, Los Angeles, California; Annie Bank Publications, Amsterdam, Holland; Van Rossum Co., Holland; Zanibon, Padua, Italy; Boileau, Barcelona, Spain. The firm also produces phonograph records. Licenses for performing rights are with BMI, ASCAP, and SESAC.

YBARRA MUSIC, Box 665, Lemon Grove, California 92045. Tel.: (714) 469–6352. Founded 1959. President: **Richard Braun.** Subsidiary company: Harlequin Records. Publishers of chamber music for woodwinds and elementary orchestra music. About 75 titles in print with about 10 to 15 titles published annually. License is with ASCAP.

PUBLISHERS OF MUSIC AND MUSIC LITERATURE REPRINTS

AMS PRESS, INC., 56 East 13th Street, New York, N.Y. 10003. Tel.: (212) 777–4700. Has reprinted musical literature and periodicals, some on microfilm.

BROUDE BROTHERS LIMITED, 56 West 45th Street, New York, N.Y. 10036. Tel.: (212) MU 7–4735. Reprinters of many works of musicological interest including important collections and series. The core of the firm's reprinting activity is its "Monuments of Music and Music Literature in Facsimile" (MMMLF), which consists of three series: music, music literature, and facsimiles. Some of the titles included in the series date from the earliest era of music printing. The entire series consists of over 180 titles either in print or in preparation.

DA CAPO PRESS, 227 West 17th Street, New York, N.Y. 10011. Tel.: (212) 255–0713. A division of the Plenum Publishing Corporation. Music literature reprints and some music including an American music historical series.

DOVER PUBLICATIONS, INC. 180 Varick Street, New York, N.Y. 10014. Tel.: (212) 255–3755. Publishers of low-cost reprints of music books in the following general categories: histories of music, composers and their music, analysis, orchestration, form, instruments, organology, acoustics, sound, aesthetics and philosophy of music, opera guides and librettos, folk music and folklore, self-instruction books, miscellaneous essays, etc. Many are reprints of modern publications. Music reprints have included the Schubert Collected Edition among others. (See also Record Companies.)

JOHNSON REPRINT CORPORATION, 111 Fifth Avenue, New York, N.Y. 10003. Tel.: (212) 677–6713. Branch offices in England, France, Germany, India, Italy, Australia, and Lebanon. Music reprints are a small part of the Johnson reprint catalogue. Music titles are books including series, periodicals, and some music collections. Most titles are of foreign origin.

EDWIN F. KALMUS, P.O. Box 1007, Opa-Locka, Florida 33054. Tel.: (305) 681–4683. Has reprinted practical music editions as well as a number of collected scholarly editions, some in full-size score and others in miniature score sold as sets.

KRAUS REPRINT CORPORATION, 16 East 46th Street, New York, N.Y. 10017. Tel.: (212) MU 7–4808. Reprints, announced and issued, covering the music field are American and foreign periodicals, both continuing and out of print, books, and some music. Music is a minor category in the Kraus catalog.

ANNEMARIE SCHNASE, Reprint Department, 120 Brown Road, P.O. Box 119, Scarsdale, N.Y. 10583. The firm is active as an antiquarian bookseller. Its reprints consist primarily of important French and German music periodicals of the 19th and early 20th centuries.

UNIVERSITY MUSIC EDITIONS, P.O. Box 192, Fort George Station, New York, N.Y. 10040. Tel.: (212) 569–5340. Founded in 1967. A division of High Density Systems, Inc. Publishers in microfiche (4″ × 6″ transparent film cards containing up to 60 pages) of low-cost reprints of large, scholarly, collected editions of the music of great composers and of music literature. It is the world's only exclusive microfiche music publisher and the largest publisher–reprinter of collected editions in any format. The unusual feature of their publications is a booklike binder which contains and organizes the fiche in proper volume sequence by providing pages with pockets—each pocket the equivalent of a normal book volume—and a bound eye-readable index detailing the contents of each volume and each component microfiche.

Music Industries: Instruments and Accessories

Manufacturers, Importers, Exporters, Distributors, and Wholesalers of Musical Instruments and Accessories

The following points should be cited in conjunction with the listing below of companies in the musical instruments and accessories field: (1) Addresses are mailing addresses. Plant locations are mentioned, when known, if they are located elsewhere. (2) Brand names are in italics. Many brand names are identical with the names of the firms. Brand names handled by distributors and importers are generally those reported to be on an exclusive distributor basis (which exclusivity may be mean national, regional, or local in application), but it is understood that other brands not listed may be handled by a given company. (3) No firm engaged in retailing is listed unless it also manufactures and sells directly. Some firms are both wholesalers and retailers. (4) The classification under which some firms are placed is often that best identified with the company. It should be understood, however, that a firm does not always confine itself to that activity; it is not unusual for a musical instrument *manufacturer* to be an *importer* of a totally different kind of musical instrument.

Piano, Organ, and Harpsichord

ABBOTT AND SIEKER, ORGAN-BUILDERS, 2027 Pontius Avenue, Los Angeles, California 90025. Tel.: (213) 473–2058. Founded 1961. Partners: **Richard L. Abbott** and **Uwe Sieker.** Manufacturers of pipe organs with plant at the above address. Also distributors of the pipe organs of the Canadian firm of Casavant Frères, Lte. Sales are retail. Other activities include pipe organ servicing, rebuilding, and repairing. Organs built or rebuilt include 2 to 4 manuals, from 3 to 49 ranks, which, for the most part, have been installed in various locations in Southern California.

AEOLIAN–SKINNER ORGAN CO., 549 E. Fourth Street, Boston, Massachusetts 02127. Tel.: (617) 268–2232. Custom manufacturers of pipe organs.

AEOLIAN CORPORATION, 33 West 57th Street, New York, N.Y. 10019. Tel.: (212) PL 1–0050. Executive offices also in Memphis, Tennessee. Aeolian is the largest firm in the world devoted exclusively to the manufacture of pianos. Its corporate structure and manufacturing facilities are as follows:

Aeolian American Corporation, East Rochester, N.Y. 14445, Tel.: (716) 586–1330, which controls the following subsidiaries: Mason & Hamlin Company, Inc.; Wm. Knabe & Co., Inc.; Chickering & Sons, Inc. (oldest piano firm in America, founded 1823); J. & C. Fischer Company, Inc.; George Steck Company, Inc.; and Weber Co., Inc. Other firms under the parent Aeolian Corporation are: Winter & Co., Inc.; Cable Piano Co.; Ivers & Pond Piano Co.; Mason & Risch, Ltd.; Sterling Action & Key Co.; Aeolian Music Rolls, Inc.; and Hardman, Peck & Co. Manufacturing facilities are located in the Bronx, N.Y.; East Rochester, N.Y.; Memphis, Tennessee; Oregon, Illinois; Toronto, Ontario; Brantford, Ontario; and Woodstock, New Brunswick, Canada. Officers of the Aeolian Corporation are: **W. G. Heller,** Chairman of the Executive Committee; **Henry R. Heller, Jr.,** President; **J. E. Furlong,** Executive Vice-President; **A. W. Linter,** Treasurer. President of Aeolian–American Corporation is **Elmer F. Brook, Jr.** The firm was founded in 1899, the date of founding of Winters & Co., the forerunner of the Aeolian group. The combined manufacturing resources of the firm makes pianos, player pianos, and music rolls. Brand names are: *Mason & Hamlin, Knabe, Chickering, Steck, J. & C. Fischer, Weber, Winter, Hardman, Kranich & Bach, Sterling, Melodigrand, Ivers & Pond, Henry F. Miller, Mason & Risch, Cable, Emerson, Aelian Music Rolls,* and the player pianos *Pianolo, Musette,* and *Duo-Art.* Pianos are made in a wide price, style, and model range (reportedly about 700 different kinds). Sales are primarily wholesale. The firm owns and operates retail stores and showrooms in Brooklyn, N.Y.; Manhasset, Long Island, N.Y.; White Plains, N.Y.; Stamford, Connecticut; and at the corporation address in New York City. There is a general sales office at 2722 Pershing Avenue, Memphis, Tennessee 38112. Tel.: (901) 452–1151.

ALLEN ORGAN COMPANY, Macungie, Pennsylvania 18062. Tel.: (215) 965–9801. Cable: AOCO. Founded 1945. President: **Jerome Markowitz.** Vice Presidents: **Robert Pearce** and **Eugene Moroz.** Subsidiary: Rocky Mount Instruments, Inc., Rocky Mount, North Carolina. Makers of *Allen* electronic organs for home, church, and theater. Sells both retail and wholesale.

ANGELL PIPE ORGANS, INC., 155 Irving Avenue, Port Chester, N.Y. 10573. Tel.: (914) 939–0225. President (and Tonal Director): **Bruce Angell.** Vice President and General Manager: **James Fetherolf.** Maker of *Angell* custom-designed and -built pipe organs. Tunes and maintains instruments of its own manufacture.

AUDION INDUSTRIES INC., 200 Fifth Avenue, New York, N.Y. 10010. Tel.: (212) OR 5–4700. Factory located at 41–06 DeLong Street, Flushing, N.Y. Founded 1960. President: **Herbert Merin.** Makers of *Audion* electronic and electric reed organs; importers of *Kimberly* electric and bass guitars; imports drums, amplifiers, and other musical products. Items priced generally at low cost at retail end. Sells wholesale only.

D. H. BALDWIN COMPANY, 1801 Gilbert Avenue, Cincinnati, Ohio 45202. Tel.: (513) 621–4300. Cable: BALDWINCO. Founded 1862 in Cincinnati, Ohio, by Dwight Hamilton Baldwin; incorporated in Ohio in 1898 as the Baldwin Company, later changing its name to the Baldwin Piano Company. Its present name has been in use since 1963. Chairman: **Lucien Wulsin.** President: **Morley P. Thompson.** Vice-Presidents: **A. J. Schoenberger, John F. Jordan, James M. E. Mixter, Eugene Wulsin.** Secretary: **R. F. Coghill.** Vice-President and Treasurer: **R. S. Harrison.** The D. H. Baldwin complex consists of the following subsidiary firms (with dates of acquisition or formation): Baldwin Piano & Organ Company (1963); The Baldwin Piano Company (Canada) Limited, Toronto (1955); Baldwin Electronics, Inc., Little Rock (1958); Baldwin Export Corp. (1964); C. Bechstein Pianofortefabrik A.G., Germany (1963); Baldwin–Burns, Limited, London (1965); The Baldwin Company; Canyon Press, Inc. (see Music Publishers); The Fred Gretsch Company, Inc. (1967, q.v. Wholesalers, etc.). The company is also affiliated with Siliconix Incorporated of Sunnyvale, California (formed in 1962). The firm owns and operates retail stores in Boston, Cincinnati, Chicago, St. Louis, San Francisco, Los Angeles, Louisville, Atlanta, Denver, New York, and Pittsburgh. Some of these stores have branches in their areas. Over 700 piano and organ dealers in the United States, Canada, and overseas handle Baldwin pianos and organs; the company claims over 900 music dealers handle the other musical products of the Baldwin companies. The combined manufacturing facilities, their location, and the products made are as follows: Cincinnati: general headquarters; Greenwood, Mississippi: piano and organ cases and assembly of vertical and grand pianos; Fayetteville, Arkansas: electronic organs, amplifiers, and assembly of guitars; Conway, Arkansas: vertical and grand piano assembly; Little Rock, Arkansas: electronics and research; DeQueen, Arkansas: guitar amplifiers and small organs; East Camden, Arkansas: rocket motors and fuses; Booneville, Arkansas: organ parts and guitar amplifiers; Boulder, Colorado: banjos (the former Odé Company); Downsview, Ontario, Canada: electronic organs, and guitar amplifiers; Essex and London, England: guitars and amplifiers, organ assembly; West Berlin and Karlsruhe, Germany: manufacture of the Bechstein piano. Although the firm's activity in the electronics field is growing, the manufacture and sale of musical instruments provides the greatest percentage of income for the company, with the *Baldwin* piano reportedly responsible for over half the company's dollar volume. In addition to pianos, organs, guitars, and amplifiers, Baldwin has been active in the manufacture of band instruments since its acquisition of the Gretsch firm and since an agreement made with the E. K. Blessing Co. of Elkhart, Indiana. Band instruments made are cornets, trumpets, trombones, sousaphones, French horns, clarinets, baritones, drums, and others. Baldwin is also sole distributor of *Sho-bud* steel guitars. Most Baldwin musical instruments bear the *Baldwin* brand name. Under the *Baldwin* and *Howard* trademarks 11 basic grand piano models are made; 26 styles of vertical pianos are made under the *Baldwin, Hamilton,* and *Acrosonic* brands. Sales are wholesale and through the company-owned retail outlets.

BANNISTER HARPSICHORDS, Spur Route 518, Hopewell, N.J. 08525. Tel.: (609) 466–1530. Founded 1959. Owner: **Christopher F. Bannister.** Makers of *Bannister* harpsichords and clavichords. Instruments are custom-built and tonally organized in the manner of the 18th-century English harpsichords. Sizes range from spinets to concert doubles. Special types of piano are also custom-made. The company also rebuilds modern grand pianos for private clients and the trade. Sales are direct to customer.

BURTON HARPSICHORD COMPANY, Box 80222, Lincoln, Nebraska 68501. Tel.: (402) 477–1001. Founded 1959. President and owner: **Herbert William Burton.** Factory is located at 917 "O" Street, Lincoln, Nebraska. Makers of one style of harpsichord, the 1648 Ruckers, either assembled or unassembled, and the *Burton Jack.* All instruments are handcrafted; the firm manufactures about 70 instruments yearly. Sells wholesale and retail.

HOBART M. CABLE Co., 7373 North Cicero Avenue, Lincolnwood, Illinois 60646. Tel.: (312) 675–5900. Makers of the *Hobart M. Cable* piano. The instrument is manufactured in Grand Haven, Michigan, with special arrangement of the Story & Clark Co.

CONN ORGAN CORPORATION, 1101 East Beardsley Avenue, Elkhart, Indiana 46514. Tel.: (219) 264–7511. A Division of C. G. Conn, Ltd. (q.v. Brass and Woodwinds). Manufacturers of electronic organs and console and spinet pianos.

DELAWARE ORGAN COMPANY, INC., 252 Fillmore Avenue, Tonawanda, N.Y. 14150. Tel.: (716) 692–7791. Founded 1956. President: **Robert C. Colby.** Makers of custom-built pipe organs designed and built under the *Delaware* name. Installed in churches, schools, and residences. Pipework is imported from Germany (Aug. Laukhuff of Weikersheim/Wttbg.). Keyboards are from Herrburger–Brooks, Ltd. of London, and also from London are many of Delaware's electrical components supplied by Kimber–Allen, Ltd. All sales are direct to customer.

DORIC ORGAN COMPANY, 128 James Street, Morristown, N.J. 07960. Tel.: (201) 539–1040. Founded 1965. Warehouse located in Clifton, N.J. Products are manufactured in Italy and Holland. President: **Alfred Mayer.** Manufacturer of *Doric Light Columns* (colored lights moving to musical sounds) and covers and accessories for the *Doric* organs and amplifiers. Importers of *Doric* transistorized organs and amplifiers; agents for *Eminent* organs. Models are mass-market combo and home types and are generally priced low. The firm also publishes combo organ music folios. Wholesale only.

ESTEY MUSICAL INSTRUMENT CORP., Harmony, Pennsylvania 16037. Tel.: (412) 452–7400. Cable: ESTEY-HARMONY. A division of Miner Industries, Inc. Branch offices located in Lynbrook, N.Y. and Huntington Beach, California. Founded in Brattleboro, Vermont, in 1846. Began making electronic organs in 1950. Current manufacture includes the *Estey* solid-state electronic organs, chord organs, and reed chord organs. Also makers of *Estey* and *Magnatone* amplifiers. Wholesale only.

ESTEY PIANO CORPORATION, 237 North Union Street, Bluffton, Indiana 46714. Tel.: (219) 824–0800. Founded 1869 in New York; located in Bluffton since 1927; known as the Estey Piano Corporation since 1935. The firm is owned by Realty Equities Corporation, 375 Park Avenue, New York, N.Y. 10022. President: **Robert C. Mehlin;** Vice-Presidents: **John K. Geist** and **Roy Trimble.** Manufacturers of pianos bearing the name *Estey* and *Estey–Knight* (the latter is created under a special arrangement with Alfred Knight, Ltd. of London and uses, under an agreement exclusive in the U.S., the *Knight* scale, action, and keys). Some other secondary brand names are also made by Estey. Wholesale sales only.

EVERETT PIANO COMPANY, Indiana Avenue and Elkenburg Street, South Haven, Michigan 49090. Tel.: (616) 637–2194. Founded 1883 in Boston by the music-publishing firm of John J. Church Company, located in South Haven since 1926, when Everett merged with the Cable–Nelson Piano Company. Everett is now a wholly owned subsidiary of United Industrial Syndicate, Inc. President: **Louis C. Amrein.** Treasurer: **George P. Chapman.** Manufacturers of *Everett* (in two lines) and *Cable–Nelson* pianos. Makes only spinets and consoles. Sales are to retail outlets only.

C. B. FISK, INC., Box 28, Gloucester, Massachusetts 01930. Tel.: 283–1909. Factory located at 105 (rear) Maplewood Avenue in Gloucester. Founded 1949; incorporated 1955. President: **Charles B. Fisk.** Makers of custom-designed mechanical action pipe organs. Sales are on a contractual basis only. The company also does organ repairing, tuning, and consulting work.

GRAND PIANO CO., INC., P.O. Box 842, Morganton, North Carolina 28655. Tel.: (704) 437–7135. Factory is located at U.S. Highway 64-70. Founded 1962. President: **Dennis Kincaid.** Manufacturers of spinet and console pianos under the name of *Grand,* all parts of which are American-made. The firm claims to be the first to manufacture a full-sized, complete spinet to sell for about $400.

THE GRATIAN ORGAN BUILDERS, P.O. Box 216, Decatur, Illinois 62525. Tel.: (217) 877–5277. Factory located in Kenney, Illinois. Owner: **Warren B. Gratian.** Makers of pipe organs.

GRESS–MILES ORGAN COMPANY, INC., Washington Road, Princeton, N.J. 08540. Tel.: (609) 799–1421. Founded 1959. President: **Roger H. Miles.** Vice-President: **G. Edgar Gress.** Makers of *Gress–Miles* pipe organs custom-designed and -built for churches and educational institutions. Sales are retail.

GULBRANSEN INDUSTRIES, 8501 West Higgins Road, Chicago, Illinois 60631. Tel.: (312) 693–6262. Founded 1904; was a division of The Seeburg Corp. from 1966 to 1971, when it again reverted to independent ownership. Chairman and Marketing Executive: **Henry E. Carter.** President: **T. A. Delaney.** Manufacturers of *Gulbransen* organs and pianos. Introduced the first marketed transistor electronic organ in 1957 and also the first such instrument with internal *Leslie* speakers. Wholesale sales only.

HAASE PIPE ORGANS, P.O. Box 295, Marengo, Illinois 60152. Tel.: (815) 568–7421. Founded 1931. Owner: **Erich O. Haase.** Makers of custom-built and installed pipe organs. Also services and rebuilds pipe organs. The firm also sells and services pianos. All business is retail.

HAMMOND ORGAN COMPANY, 4200 West Diversey Avenue, Chicago, Illinois 60639. Tel.: (312) 283–2000. Factories located at above address and at 5008 West Bloomingdale in Chicago. President of the Hammond Organ Company is **John A. Volkober.** The firm is owned by the Hammond Corporation, with offices at 100 Wilmot Road, Deerfield, Illinois. Founded in 1929 as the Hammond Clock Co., its name was changed to Hammond Instrument Co. in 1937. It received its present name in 1953. Subsidiaries of the Hammond Corporation include: Gibbs Manufacturing and Research Corporation of Janesville, Wisconsin; Accutronics Division of Geneva, Illinois; Hammond Organ Western Export Corporation (for sales in the Western Hemisphere outside the United States); Wells Lamont Corporation (glove manufacturers). Since 1971 the former International Division has been merged into the Hammond Organ Company, which is now responsible for all world sales. In addition, there is Hammond Organ (U.K.) Ltd. in London, Hammond Organs S.A. (Proprietary) Ltd. in Johannesburg, and Organos Hammond de Mexico in Mexico City. The foreign firms assemble and distribute Hammond organs for sale in their respective regions. Formerly, foreign sales for the Hammond firm consisted of exportation of finished products. (Approximately 10 percent of the firm's business is in the foreign market.) The Hammond Organ Company is a manufacturer of electronic organs bearing the *Hammond* brand name. The firm was the first to produce an electronic organ. Its patent was granted in 1934 with first sales following in 1935. The firm, in effect, created the electronic organ industry. It is one of the world's largest organ manufacturers. Through its subsidiary, the Everett Piano Co., Hammond began making the *Hammond* piano in 1963. These were discontinued when, in 1971, Hammond sold off the Everett subsidiary. Both the organs and pianos are marketed exclusively through franchised dealers.

HOFFMAN PIANO COMPANY, P.O. Box 99, Northvale, N.J. 07647. Tel.: (201) 768–4080. Factory located at Industrial Parkway in Northvale. Founded 1945. Owner: **Wilbur Hoffman.** Makers of *Hoffman* pianos. The firm also rebuilds, refinishes, and repairs pianos for the piano trade. Sales are both wholesale and retail.

HILLGREEN, LANE & CO., P.O. Box 397, Alliance, Ohio 44601. Tel.: (216) 823–7238. Founded 1898. Owner: **R. L. Hillgreen.** Manufacturer of pipe organs; also services and repairs pipe organs. Sells retail.

E. H. HOLLOWAY CORPORATION, P.O. Box 20254, Indianapolis, Indiana 46220. Tel.: (317) 637–2029. Factory located at 2065 Martindale Avenue, Indianapolis, Indiana 46223. Founded 1888 as E. E. Holloway; incorporated in 1953. President: **E. H. Holloway.** Vice-President: **John W. Goulding.** Makers of pipe organs bearing the name of *E. H. Holloway Corp.* Sales are factory-direct through representatives. Area representatives are located in New York, Florida, Chicago, and California. The firm also services all organs.

JANSSEN PIANO, INC. Founded in 1904 and once located in Elkhart, Indiana. The firm was closed down in 1969. It had been a subsidiary of C. G. Conn, Ltd. Certain patents, machinery, and inventory have been subsequently purchased from Conn by Walter Piano Co., 700 W. Beardsley Avenue, Elkhart, Indiana 46514.

KIMBALL PIANO & ORGAN CO., East 15th and Cherry Streets, Jasper, Indiana 47546. Tel.: (312) 482–1600. Factory located in West Baden, Indiana. Founded 1857. Became a division of The Jasper Corporation in 1959. The Jasper Corporation's other divisions include the piano firm of Bösendorfer of Vienna, Austria, and the firm Herrburger–

Brooks of Long Eaton, England. Chairman of the Board (both of the Kimball and Jasper companies): **Arnold H. Habig.** President: **Thomas L. Habig.** Vice-President: **John B. Habig.** Manufacturers of *Kimball* and *Whitney* pianos, and *Kimball* organs (electronic). The pianos are made in spinet, console, grand, and player piano models. The organs are made for both home and institutional use. The firm imports Bösendorfer grand pianos and Herrburger–Brooks keys and action. Sales are retail and wholesale.

KOHLER & CAMPBELL, INC., Granite Falls, North Carolina 28630. Tel.: (704) 396–3376. Cable: KOHBELL. Founded 1896. Chairman of the Board: **Julius A. White.** President: **Charles L. Clayton.** Manufacturers of pianos under the brand name of *Kohler & Campbell.* The firm traces its origins back to the 18th-century American firm, The Astor Piano Company. (Kohler & Campbell acquired the Bacon Piano Company, an outgrowth of the firm of Bacon and Raven which had developed from the Astor company.) Models made are grands, consoles, consolettes, studio, and auto pianos (player pianos). The firm also owns the following trade marks: *Auto Piano, Behning, Behr Bros., Brambach, McPhail, Milton, Francis Bacon, Bjur Bros., Stultz & Bauer, Waldorf, Astor* and others. Wholesale only.

KRAKAUER BROS., 115 East 138th Street, Bronx, N.Y. 10451. Tel.: (212) CY 2–0573. Founded 1869. President: **Robert Krakauer Bretzfelder.** Vice-President: **A. S. Zeisler.** Makers of pianos under the name of *Krakauer.* Pianos are made in upright and console models and a special patented design model which consists of a console piano with certain features of the grand piano. The firm also owns the *Haddorff* piano name. That piano is no longer in production. Sales are both wholesale and retail.

LOWREY ORGAN COMPANY, Division of Chicago Musical Instrument Company (q.v. Wholesalers, etc.). Sales are through the marketing facilities of C.M.I. Organs are electronic and feature innovations that are intended to ease the playing of the amateur.

LOWREY PIANO COMPANY, c/o Asheville Industries, Inc. Black Mountain, North Carolina, A Division of Chicago Musical Instrument Company (q.v.). In 1968, the Lowrey Company moved its piano-making facilities from Grand Rapids, Michigan, to Black Mountain, where, as Asheville Industries, all *Lowrey* pianos are made. Lowrey began making pianos in 1963. The firm makes console, spinet, studio (or school) models. Wholesale.

MAGNUS ORGAN CORPORATION, 1600 West Edgar Road, Linden, N.J. 07036. Tel.: (201) 925–8700. Founded 1957. A subsidiary of Dero Industries, Inc. President: **Roy L. Swanke.** Branch office: 2700 South Garfield Avenue, Commerce, California 90022. Manufacturers of *Magnus* electric organs. Servicing and repair work is offered for its own products by the firm.

MCMANIS ORGAN COMPANY, 1903 North 10th Street, Kansas City, Kansas 66104. Tel.: (913) 321–9696. Founded 1938. Owner: **Charles W. McManis.** Makers, designers, and installers of pipe organs under the name of *McManis Organs.* Sales are retail. The firm does a limited amount of organ maintenance and consulting.

M. P. MÖLLER, INC., Hagerstown, Maryland 21740. Tel.: (301) 733–9000. Founded 1875. President: **W. R. Daniels.** Vice-President Treasurer: **W. F. Slifer.** Pipe organ architects and builders of *Möller* pipe organs. The firm sells directly to the purchaser through some 20 sales representative branch offices located throughout the country.

ROBERT NOEHREN, Organ Builder, 815 Oakdale Road, Ann Arbor, Michigan 48105. Tel.: (313) 662–8620. Established in 1954. **Robert Noehren** (see Organists in instrumentalist performers section), a well-known organist, designs and custom-makes pipe organs under contract to schools and churches. Organs made are usually of large dimension. As an organ builder, he represents himself and has no company as such.

REID ORGAN COMPANY, P.O. Box 363, Santa Clara, California 95052. Tel.: (408)

244–9696. Founded 1944. Owner: **William N. Reid.** Makers of pipe organs. Rebuilding and maintenance service also offered.

RODGERS ORGAN COMPANY, 1300 N.E. 25th Avenue, Hillsboro, Oregon 97123. Tel.: (503) 648–4181. Founded 1958. President: **Laurence A. Morin.** Vice-President: **Frederick B. Tinker.** Manufacturers of *Rodgers* electronic organs in nine standard models and in custom installations. Sales are through franchised dealers. Is exclusive U.S. representative for Fratelli Ruffatti, pipe organ builders of Padua, Italy.

SAVILLE ORGAN CORPORATION, 2901 Shermer Road, Northbrook, Illinois 60062. Tel.: (312) 272–7070. Makers of *Saville* custom-made electronic organs. Sold primarily to churches and schools.

SCHANTZ ORGAN COMPANY, Orrville, Ohio 44667. Tel.: (216) 682–6065. Founded 1873. President: **Paul S. Schantz.** Vice-President: **Bruce V. Schantz.** Makers of custom-built pipe organs. Sales are retail.

SCHLICKER ORGAN CO., INC., 1530 Military Road, Buffalo, N.Y. 14217. Tel.: (716) 874–1818. Founded 1933. President: **Herman L. Schlicker.** Designers and builders of pipe organs with sales direct to customer. The firm also does tuning and maintenance work on pipe organs.

THE SCHOBER ORGAN CORPORATION, 43 West 61st Street, New York, N.Y. 10023. Tel.: (212) JU 6–7552. Cable: SCHOBORGAN. Founded 1954. President: **Richard H. Dorf.** Vice-President: **Alfred M. Rosenberg.** Manufacturers of *Schober* electronic organs sold primarily in kit form. Sales are retail mail order, worldwide. Organs are in four basic models; accessories, such as organ testers, autotuners, reverberation units (registered trade mark: *Reverbatape*), mixer compressors, etc., are also sold. Demonstration records, instruction music books, and other publications are made available by the firm.

FELIX F. SCHOENSTEIN & SONS, 3101 20th Street, San Francisco, California 94110. Tel.: (415) 647–5132. Founded 1877. Officers are **Otto H. Schoenstein** and **Erwin A. Schoenstein.** Makers of pipe organs. The firm also does rebuilding, tuning, and maintenance work on pipe organs. Retail sales.

SOHMER & CO., INC., 31 West 57th Street, New York, N.Y. 10019. Tel.: (212) PL 3–9235. Factory located at 11–01 31st Avenue, Long Island City, N.Y. Founded 1872. President: **Harry J. Sohmer, Jr.** Treasurer: **Robert H. Sohmer.** Makers of the *Sohmer* piano in console, grand, baby grand (a size originated by the firm), and studio upright models. Sales are both wholesale and retail.

P. A. STARCK PIANO COMPANY, 5302 North Milwaukee Avenue, Chicago, Illinois 60630. Factory located at 229 Northfield Road, Northfield, Illinois 60093. Tel.: (312) 577–0777. Founded 1891. President: **Brent Starck.** Makers of *Starck* pianos, a piano-organ combination instrument called the *Combinette* (transistorized), and the *Pianotron,* a portable, electronically amplified piano. Sales are wholesale and retail.

STEINER ORGANS, INC., P.O. Box 895, Louisville, Kentucky 40201. Tel.: (502) 583–5032. Factory located at 1138 Garvin Place, Louisville (40203). Previous to incorporation in 1968, the firm was known simply as Steiner Organs, founded 1958. President: **Phares L. Steiner.** Vice-President: **Gottfried Reck.** Makers of custom-built and installed pipe organs under the *Steiner* name. Sold primarily to churches and music schools; direct sales. Consultant services also offered.

STEINWAY & SONS, Steinway Place, Long Island City, N.Y. 11105. Tel.: (212) RA 1–2600. Cable: STEINWAY, N.Y. Founded 1853. Branch offices: London and Hamburg. Showrooms at 109 West 57th Street, New York, N.Y. 10019. Subsidiary firm: Wilking Music Company, Indianapolis, Indiana. President: **Henry Z. Steinway.** Vice-President and Secretary: **John H. Steinway.** Makers of *Steinway* pianos, grands and uprights. The firm's piano is particularly well known for its use by professional pianists. Sales are retail and wholesale.

STORY & CLARK PIANO COMPANY, 7373 North Cicero Avenue, Lincolnwood, Illinois 60646. Tel.: (312) 675–5900. Factory located at 100 Fulton Street, Grand Haven, Michigan. Founded 1857. President: **Robert P. Bull.** Subsidiary: Hampton Keyboard Company. Story & Clark is a subsidiary of Chicago Musical Instrument Company of the address above in Lincolnwood. Manufacturers of *Story & Clark* pianos and organs, and *Hobart M. Cable* pianos (q.v.). The *Story & Clark* piano is made in console, spinet, and upright models, the latter in specific church and school models. Wholesale only.

TELLERS ORGAN COMPANY, 2419 Holland Street, P.O. Box 1383, Erie, Pennsylvania 16512. Tel.: (814) 456–5306. Founded 1906 by former employees of the A. B. Felgemaker Company (dissolved in 1918). Sole owner: **Herman J. Tellers.** Makers of *Tellers* pipe organs, which are sold through representatives in various parts of the United States. Organs are custom-made, installed, and tested. Sales are on a contractual basis. Churches and institutions of higher learning are the prime customers. The firm does repair and maintenance work as well as rebuilding organs of original good quality.

THOMAS ORGAN COMPANY, 8345 Hayvenhurst Avenue, Sepulveda, California 91343. Tel.: (213) 894–7161. Founded 1956. President: **Robert F. Gunts.** A division of Warwick Electronics, Inc., itself a subsidiary of Whirlpool Corporation. Makers of *Thomas* electronic organs, *Vox* electronic guitars, amplifiers, and sound equipment (made in England); *Vox* musical instruments made specifically (but not exclusively) for direct amplification. The last-named group consists of some 64 instruments of the brass, woodwind, and string families and are sold under the name of *Vox Ampliphonic.* All sales are wholesale.

THE TURNER CORPORATION, P.O. Box 1461, Charlottesville, Virginia 22902. Makers of *Turner* harpsichords. Wholesale.

WESTBROOK PIANO CO., INC., 1 Westbrook Avenue, Marion, North Carolina 28752. Tel.: (704) 695–2332. Founded 1964. President: **Thad M. Poteat.** Financial Vice-President: **J. P. L. Johnston.** Vice-President: **Sam E. Westbrook.** Manufacturers of spinet and console pianos under the brand names of *Westbrook, Coronet,* and *Spinet.* Sales are wholesale only.

WICKS ORGAN COMPANY, Highland, Illinois 62249. Tel.: (618) 654–2191. Founded 1906. President: **Martin M. Wicks.** Manufacturers of *Wicks* custom-made pipe organs. Sales are direct to consumer. The firm also provides pipe organ servicing and organ design and architectural consulting. Among the innovations of the firm is the trademark "Direct Electric Action," which eliminates the use of leather in the organ action.

THE WURLITZER COMPANY, 1700 Pleasant Street, DeKalb, Illinois 60115. Tel.: (815) 756–2771. Founded 1856. Board Chairman: **R. C. Rolfing.** President: **W. N. Herleman.** Senior Vice-President: **W. A. Rolfing.** Plants are located in Dekalb (the largest); North Tonawanda, N.Y.; Corinth, Mississippi; Holly Springs, Mississippi; Logan, Utah; and Hüllhorst, Germany. The company owns retail stores in Boston, Buffalo, Chicago, Cincinnati, Columbus (Ohio), Detroit, Indianapolis, Kansas City, New York, Philadelphia, as well as some 25 smaller branch stores in suburban communities throughout the country. An overseas division, apart from the Hüllhorst plant, is Wurlitzer Overseas, A. G., situated in Zug, Switzerland. That branch is responsible for sales in Europe, North Africa, and other foreign territories. The Wurlitzer Company is a manufacturer of pianos and electronic organs. Pianos are made in the DeKalb plant (which produced its millionth piano in 1968, thus establishing the company as the largest in America making that instrument) in some 50 styles of spinets, consoles, studio pianos, grands, player pianos, and electronic pianos. In 1973, piano making will be phased out of the DeKalb plant and concentrated in Holly Springs and Logan. The *Wurlitzer* organs are made in Corinth, Mississippi; the firm made its first electronic organ in 1947, although it had made pipe organs earlier in the century.

W. ZIMMER & SONS, INC., P.O. Box 11024, Charlotte, North Carolina 28209. Tel.: (704) 525–2748. Factory located at Airport Industrial Center, 4900 Wilmont Road, Charlotte, North Carolina 28208. Founded 1964. The firm is headed by **Wilhelm Zimmer.** Makers of custom-made pipe organs for churches and other institutions and for use in residences; the organs are built with mechanical tracker and electro-pneumatic action. The company provides tuning and maintenance for its own organs. Sales are direct to customer.

ZUCKERMANN HARPSICHORDS, INC., 115 Christopher Street, New York, N.Y. 10014. Tel.: (212) WA 9–1838. Founded 1953. President: **Wallace Zuckermann.** Vice-President: **Michael Zuckermann.** Manufacturers of harpsichord, clavichord, and spinet assembly kits. The *Zuckermann* kits are sold retail primarily as a mail-order business. The firm has discontinued making finished instruments, although it still does harpsichord repair work. The kits provide for a low-cost instrument of basically classical design.

Brass and Woodwind

W. T. ARMSTRONG CO., INC., 200 East Sycamore Street, P.O. Box 963, Elkhart, Indiana 46514. Tel.: (219) 522–5290. Founded 1931. President: **Carl E. Burket.** Manufacturers of flutes and piccolos in various models for school and professional use. Makers of *Heritage* and *Emeritus 21* solid silver flutes and piccolos, in addition to the *Armstrong* brand. Flutes are made in G alto and Eb soprano; the traditional C flute is made with either closed or open key. Products sold wholesale.

ARTLEY, INC., P.O. Box 2280, Nogales, Arizona 85621. Tel.: (312) 325–7080 (Oak Brook Illinois office). Makers of *Artley* piccolos and flutes sold exclusively by C. G. Conn, Ltd. (q.v. this section.)

VINCENT BACH CORP., Box 310, Elkhart, Indiana 46514. Tel.: (219) 264–4141. Plant located at 225 East Jackson Boulevard in Elkhart. Founded in 1918. Since 1961 has been a subsidiary of H. & A. Selmer, Inc. (q.v. this section). Officers of the firm are those of the Selmer corporation. **Vincent Bach** is consultant to Selmer's brass instrument and mouthpiece production. The firm manufactures the *Vincent Bach* trumpets, cornets, fluegelhorns, trombones, and mouthpieces for these instruments in models ranging from those for student use to those for professional performers. Other activities are instrument repair and servicing, consulting, and publishing.

THE BENGE TRUMPET CO., 1122 West Burbank Boulevard, Burbank, California 91502. Tel.: (213) 849–7847. Founded 1934. Owner: **Donald E. Benge.** Makers of *Benge* trumpets and cornets. Instruments are handcrafted; trumpets are made in Bb, C, D and Eb keys. Sells both retail and wholesale.

BUESCHER BAND INSTRUMENTS, Box 310, Elkhart, Indiana 46514. Tel.: (219) 264–4141. Founded in 1888. Acquired by H. & A. Selmer, Inc. (q.v. this section) in 1963 and is operated as a division of that firm. Buescher is a manufacturer of woodwind and brass instruments from piccolos to low brasses. New instruments include plastic alto and bass clarinets and oboes, and a line of electronic winds under the name of *Varitone.*

BUGLECRAFT, INC., 43–01 39th Street, Long Island City, N.Y. 11104. Tel.: (212) 361–3052. President: **Jay M. Berman.** Makers of *Rexcraft* bugles and fifes. Also makes whistles.

C. G. CONN, LTD., 616 Enterprise Drive, Oak Brook, Illinois 60521. Tel.: (312) 325–7080. Founded 1875. Divisional firms: Scherl & Roth, Inc., Cleveland, Ohio, Conn Band Instrument Division, Conn Organ Corporation (q.v.). In 1968, the Conn firm and its divisions were acquired by Crowell Collier & Macmillan of New York. Chief Operating Officer: **T. L. McSwine.** C. G. Conn, Ltd. is the world's largest manufacturer of band instruments, but it also has important manufacturing and sales in the field of organs and pianos. Band instruments made, all with the *Conn* trademark, are: trumpets, cornets, French horns, slide and valve trombones, alto horns, mellophones, baritone horns, euphoniums, tubas, sousaphones (made also in fiberglass), saxophones, piccolos, flutes, oboes, clarinets, bassoons. The Conn Organ Corporation makes both *Conn* electronic organs and pianos. Organs are made in some 11 models for all levels of use. Recently the firm introduced an electronic pipe organ. Conn is also exclusive distributor for *Artley* piccolos and flutes and *Roth* string instruments. The firm publishes educational aids and the quarterly publication, *Connchord,* which is sent out free to a large number of music educators, music dealers, et al. The company maintains a large and important repairing and servicing department and has plants and warehouse facilities in Atlanta, Georgia; Santa Rosa, California; Nogales, Arizona; Abilene, Texas; and Madison, Wisconsin. Sales are wholesale to franchised dealers.

CUSTOM MUSIC COMPANY, 107 Allenhurst Street, Royal Oak, Michigan 48067. Tel.: (313) 546–7502. Founded in 1947 as American Music Instrument Co.; present name in use since 1962. A subsidiary of the American Musical Instrument Co. President: **Fred Marrich.** General Manager: **William Kurth.** Branch office: 3919 Sevilla Street, Tampa, Florida. Manufacturer of *Vue-Strobe* electronic tuner; the firm is mainly engaged in distributing and importing. Exclusive distributor for the following foreign brands: *Cooper–Puchner* bassoons and *Cooper–Kroner* bassoons; *Sanders, Alexander, Mirafone,* and *Kroner* tubas and French horns; *Marzan* tubas; *Lucerne* and *Chauvet* oboes and English horns; *Dolnet* and *Lucerne* woodwinds. The firm also handles instruments and accessories made by other foreign and American firms and has a department devoted to instrument repair and servicing. Wholesale business only.

FOX PRODUCTS CORPORATION, South Whitley, Indiana 46787. Tel.: (219) 723–4888. Founded 1949. President: **Hugo Fox.** Vice-President: **Alan Fox.** Manufacturers of *Fox* bassoons, reeds, and bassoon accessories. Bassoons are made in plastic and wood models. Repairing and servicing is also done by the company. Wholesale only.

K. G. GEMEINHARDT CO., INC., P.O. Box 788, Elkhart, Indiana 46514. Tel.: (219) JA 2–1339. Factory located on Route 19 South in Elkhart. Founded 1948. President and Chairman of the Board: **Daniel J. Henkin.** Honorary Chairman: **Kurt G. Gemeinhardt.** Makers of flutes and piccolos under the *Gemeinhardt* name. Some 26 different models are made including open-hole flutes, Eb soprano and G alto flutes and conical bore piccolos. Instruments are made in nickel, nickel silver and sterling, solid silver, sterling silver, etc. Sold wholesale.

THE GETZEN COMPANY, INC., 211 West Centralia, Elkhorn, Wisconsin 53121. Tel.: (414) 723–4221. Founded 1939. Transferred to current owners in 1960. President: **Harold M. Knowlton.** Vice-President: **Howard Sandberg.** Subsidiary: Meinl–Weston, Division of Getzen Co. Manufacturers, importers and distributors of brass wind instruments: bugles, trumpets, cornets, fluegelhorns, trombones, valve trombones, baritone horns, single French horns, double French horns, sousaphones, tubas; also makers of instrument cases and mouthpieces. These products are made variously under the *Getzen* name and model line such as *Eterna, Capri, "300", Titleist, Deluxe,* and *Elkhorn.* Getzen is the world's leading manufacturer of piston bugles. As an importer, the Getzen firm is the exclusive distributor in North America of *Meinl–Weston* tubas and baritone horns. Sales are wholesale. The firm has a repair department for *Getzen* and *Meinl–Weston* instruments.

WM. S. HAYNES CO., 12 Piedmont Street, Boston, Massachusetts 02116. Tel.: (617) 482–7456. Founded 1888. President: **Janet A. Cox.** Vice-President: **Lewis Deveau.** Treasurer: **Lola A. Haynes.** Branch office: 157 West 57th Street, New York, N.Y. 10019. Makers of solid silver flutes and piccolos bearing the brand name, *Haynes Flute.* Sales are retail. Repair services are offered for Haynes products only.

FRANK HOLTON COMPANY, A Division of G. Leblanc Corporation, 7019 30th Avenue, Kenosha, Wisconsin 53241 (q.v. this section). Founded 1898. A manufacturer of band instruments under the *Holton* name and instrument accessories such as oils, mouthpieces, reeds, etc.

KING MUSICAL INSTRUMENTS, 33999 Curtis Boulevard, Eastlake, Ohio 44094. Tel.: (216) 944–6425. Cable: KING FLAIR. Founded 1893. President: **N. Dolin.** Vice-President: **A. F. Brancae.** The firm is a division of the Seeburg Corporation and was formerly known as The H. N. White Company. Manufacturers of band instruments under the brand names of *King, Cleveland, Tempo, King Marigaux, King Excella,* and *King Lemaire.* Instruments manufactured include piccolos, flutes, clarinets, trumpets, trombones, and baritones. The firm also manufactures its own instrument cases and *Manhasset* music stands. Sells wholesale only.

KOHLERT, INC., 14 Bixley Heath, Lynbrook, N.Y. 11563. Tel.: (516) 599–3003. Division of Wm. R. Gratz Co., Inc. (q.v. Importers, Distributors, etc.). Importers of *Kohlert* woodwind instruments made in Germany. The *Kohlert* line includes flutes, oboes, clarinets, bassoons, saxophones, alto and bass clarinets, and English horns. Wholesale distribution only.

LARILEE WOODWIND COMPANY, 1700 Edwardsburg Road, Elkhart, Indiana 46514. Tel.: (219) 264–3417. Founded 1946. Makers of *Larillee* hand-crafted oboes. Instruments are made in both wood and plastic models and range from those designed for students to those for professional use. Eight models are presently manufactured. Sales are both retail and wholesale. The firm has a repair service for its own oboes.

G. LEBLANC CORPORATION, 7019-30th Avenue, Kenosha, Wisconsin 53141. Tel.: (414) 658–1644. Founded 1946. Manufacturing facilities include plants in Kenosha; Nogales, Arizona; Elkhorn, Wisconsin; a yet-to-be finished plant in Rio Rico, Arizona; and locations in France in Paris, Moulins, Mantes, and La Couture. Subsidiaries and acquired companies are Leblanc Publications, Inc. (see Music Publishers), The Holton Company of Elkhorn, Wisconsin, The Woodwind Company (the last two were acquired in 1964 and 1967, respectively), and Martin Band Instruments, recently of the Wurlitzer Company. President of the Corporation: **Vito Pascucci.** The firm is the U.S. affiliate of G. Leblanc Cie. of France insofar as the importation of the French firm's goods is concerned. The Kenosha corporation, in its total operation, is a manufacturer and importer of musical instruments and accessories and a music publisher; it also offers instrument repair and service. Instruments manufactured are: *Vito* clarinets and saxophones, *Holton* trumpets, cornets, trombones, saxophones, double horns, single horns, baritones, sousaphones, *Martin* brass instruments and saxophones, and other brass instruments. Imported brands are: *Leblanc* (Paris) clarinets (including soprano, alto, bass, and contra), flutes, oboes, saxophones, and other wind instruments; *Noblet* flutes, oboes, clarinets, piccolos, and English horns; *Normandy* clarinets and flutes; *Vandoren* mouthpieces and reeds. Sales are wholesale only.

LESHER WOODWIND CO., INC., Box 310, Elkhart, Indiana 46514. Tel.: (219) 264–4141. Plant located at 1306 West Bristol Street in Elkhart. Since 1967, the firm has been a wholly owned subsidiary of H. & A. Selmer, Inc. (q.v. this section). Manufacturers of *Lesher* oboes and bassoons made respectively in eight and five models each. Sales are only through authorized dealers.

LINTON MANUFACTURING COMPANY, INC., 711 Middleton Run Road, Elkhart, Indiana 46514. Tel.: (219) 293–8578. Founded 1937. Chairman of the Board: **R. Jack Linton.** President: **Jack M. Linton.** Manufacturers of *Linton* woodwinds and woodwind accessories. Instruments made are: soprano oboes; oboes d'amour; alto oboes; baritone oboes; bassoons; contra bassoons; soprano, alto, and bass clarinets; alto, tenor, and baritone saxophones; flutes; piccolos. Reeds and mouthpieces, oils, accessories and tools are also marketed. The instruments are made in several models each and range from student to professional models. Instrument repair service is offered. Wholesale only.

MIRAFONE CORPORATION, 1239 South Olive Street, Los Angeles, California 90015. Tel.: (213) 746–3625. Founded 1898 in Germany. Manufacturers (in Germany), importers, exporters, and wholesale distributors of *Mirafone* brass instruments and double-reed woodwinds. Brass instruments include: tubas, French horns, "Deskant" horns, contralto horns, "Wagnerian tubins," fluegelhorns, baritone horns, alto and bass trumpets, contra bass trombones, and other brass in several models and usually employing rotary valves. The reed instruments made are oboes, English horns, bassoons, and contra bassoons. The instruments range from student quality to those for professionals.

MOENNING MUSIC COMPANY, 9427 Las Tunas Drive, Temple City, California 91780. Tel.: (213) 286–3714. President: **Alicia M. Davis.** Vice-President: **Elise Baxter Moenning.** Importers and distributors of woodwinds made by Gebrüder Moennig in Germany. Instruments include all those of the woodwind family from piccolos to contra bassoons.

F. E. OLDS & SON, INC., 350 S. Raymond Avenue, Fullerton, California 92634. Tel.: (714) 525–0221. Founded 1910. President: **James E. Caldwell.** Vice-President: **R. V. Madden.** Subsidiary of Chicago Musical Instrument Company (q.v. Distributors). Manufacturer of brass and woodwind band instruments under the *Olds* brand. Instruments made are cornets, trumpets, French horns, trombones, baritones, mellophones, tubas, sousaphones (also made in glass fiber), piccolos, flutes, oboes, clarinets, saxophones, bassoons, and others. The firm offers instrument repair and service. Sales are wholesale through L. D. Heater Music Company (q.v.), a Chicago Musical Instrument Company subsidiary.

PENZEL, MUELLER & CO., INC., 36–11 33rd Street, Long Island City, N.Y. 11106. Tel.: (212) BE 3–7940. Cable: BRILLANTE NY. Founded 1901. President: **E. Chiassarini.** Manufacturers and distributors of *Penzel–Mueller* clarinets; *A. Laubin* oboes and English horns (both American-made); *F. Lorée* (Paris) oboes, English horns, oboes d'amour, and bass oboes; *A. Robert* (Paris) clarinets. Also sold are clarinet mouthpieces, caps, ligatures, oboe reeds, and other woodwind accessories. The firm owns the brand names associated with the former firm of George Cloos, Inc., manufacturers of fifes. The company has an instrument repair and service department. Sales are wholesale only.

POLISI BASSOON CORPORATION, 244 West 49th Street, New York, N.Y. 10019. Tel.: (212) 245–5259. Founded 1962. President: **William Polisi.** Manufacturers of *Polisi* bassoons and bassoon bocals. The firm repairs and services bassoons.

VERNE Q. POWELL FLUTES, INC., 295 Huntington Avenue, Boston, Massachusetts 02115. Tel.: (617) 536–5359. Founded 1927. President: **Elmer W. Waterhouse.** Chairman: **Richard W. Jerome.** Manufacturers of flutes and piccolos in gold, silver, and platinum models. Instrument repairing is also offered. Sales are retail only.

G. PRUEFER MFG. CO., INC., 185 Union Avenue, Providence, Rhode Island 02909. Tel.: (401) 942–8150. Founded 1906. President: **Michael A. Scungio.** Vice-President: **Americo L. Scungio.** Manufacturers and importers of woodwinds. Instruments sold include: *Pruefer* clarinets, *Haynes–Schwelm* flutes, oboes, bassoons, and piccolos, and *Festival* recorders. The firm sells woodwind accessories and has a repair service. Sales are wholesale.

F. A. REYNOLDS COMPANY, INC., A Division of Chicago Musical Instrument Company (q.v. Distributors) with plant in Abilene, Texas. Formerly of Cleveland, Ohio, the firm was part of the corporate structure of the former Richards Musical Instruments, Inc. prior to its acquisition by C.M.I. Manufacturers of trumpets, cornets, trombones, French horns, tubas, mellophones, sousaphones, alto horns, and other brass instruments. Sales are through Chicago Musical Instrument Company and its subsidiary, L. D. Heater Music Company (q.v. Distributors).

SCHILKE MUSIC PRODUCTS, INC., 529 South Wabash Avenue, Chicago, Illinois 60605. Tel.: (312) 922–0570. Founded 1958. President: **Renold O. Schilke.** Manufacturers of *Schilke* trumpets, cornets, and mouthpieces for brass instruments. Trumpets are made in the keys of Bb, C, D, Eb, F, Bb piccolo; cornets in Bb. Both instruments are made in a combined total of some 29 models. Mouthpieces are made for trumpets, cornets, alto horns, tenor trombones, baritones, euphoniums, bass trombones, tubas, and sousaphones. Custom-made mouthpieces are also made. Sales are both wholesale and retail.

H. & A. SELMER, INC., mailing address: Box 310, Elkhart, Indiana 46514. A division of the Magnavox Company since 1969. General offices and woodwind plant located at 1119 North Main Street, Elkhart. The firm consists of the following subsidiaries or divisions: Ampeg Company, Vincent Bach Corp., Buescher Band Instruments, Lesher Woodwind Division—H. & A. Selmer, Inc., (see separate listings for these firms), and Vincent Bach International. Plants include the Bach plant (also used for the manufacture of Buescher products), the Lesher plant, a plant for the manufacture of instrument cases located at Elkhart Industrial Park, and the former plant of C. G. Conn Ltd. in Elkhart. President: **Jack F. Feddersen.** Executive Vice-President: **Charles L. Bickel.** The Selmer firm is a manufacturer of the following instruments and accessories: *Vincent Bach* brass instruments and mouthpieces, *Buescher* woodwinds and brass instruments, *Varitone* electronic devices for amplifying wind instrument sound, *Lesher* oboes and bassoons, the Selmer-made *Signet* and *Bundy* lines of band instruments (respectively for advanced and beginner players), *Brilhart* saxophone and clarinet mouthpieces, *Fibercane* reeds, *Selmer* oils, batons, and a number of other accessories. H. & A. Selmer is the sole U.S. representative for *Henri Selmer* (Paris) clarinets, saxophones, trumpets, cornets, and trombones (an arrangement in effect since 1904), and *Besson* low brasses. Selmer provides instrument repair and servicing and publishes a number of educational aids. All Selmer products are sold through some 3,000 authorized dealers. Final sales are primarily to schools on all levels.

JACK SPRATT WOODWIND SHOP, Box 277, 199 Sound Beach Avenue, Old Greenwich, Connecticut 06870. Tel.: (203) 637–3812. Factory and branch office: Jack Spratt Music Publishers, 17 West 60th Street, New York, N.Y. 10023. Founded 1946. The firm is headed by **Edward N. Spratt.** Manufacturers, publishers, importers, and distributors of woodwind-related materials: reeds, swabs, mandrels, etc. Sells *Lamott* instruments and *Prestini* reeds. Woodwind repair work is also offered. Sales are both retail and wholesale.

Fretted Instruments

CODÉ CORPORATION, 8 Hope Street, Jersey City, N.J. 07037. Tel.: (201) 792–1955. Founded 1959. President: **Frank Colonese.** Vice-President: **Leonard De Felippis.** Manufacturers of classic and standard guitars and baritone ukuleles. Wholesale only.

ELECTRO STRING INSTRUMENT CORP., P.O. 1321, Santa Ana, California 92702. Tel.: (714) 545–7255. Factory located at 3117 South Kilson, Santa Ana, California 92707. Founded 1931. President: **F. C. Hall.** A division of Rickenbacker, Inc. (q.v. this section). Manufacturers of *Rickenbacker* and *Electro* guitars and amplifiers. Wholesale sales only.

ELGER COMPANY, Chestnut and Biddle Avenue, Ardmore, Pennsylvania 19003. Tel.: (215) MI 9–1652. Founded 1961. President: **Harry Rosenbloom.** Manufacturers of *Elger Custom* guitars. Also importers of guitars, amplifiers, and guitar accessories. Wholesale only.

NORMAN ENGLISH SALES, INC., 1131 East Michigan Avenue, Lansing, Michigan 48912. Tel.: (517) 484–8368. Founded 1954. President: **Norman English.** Vice-President: **Margaret English.** Makers of *Tonemaster* guitars, amplifiers, and music accessories. These products are distributed wholesale by the firm.

FAVILLA GUITARS, INC., 36-38 Grand Boulevard, Brentwood, N.Y. 11717. Tel.: (516) 273–1011. Founded 1890. President and owner: **Herk Favilla.** Manufacturers of classic, Spanish acoustic steel-string, and 12-string Spanish guitars; also makes ukuleles and baritone ukuleles, strings, and cases. All products carry the *Favilla* brand name. The firm has also published two books on the baritone ukulele and one book of guitar solo music.

FENDER MUSICAL INSTRUMENTS, 1402 East Chestnut, Santa Ana, California 92701. Tel.: (714) 836–5141. Cable: FENDER. Founded in 1947; purchased by Columbia Broadcasting System in 1958 and is a division of CBS Musical Instruments. Factory for Fender products is located in Fullerton, California. Branch office: 912 West Skelly Drive, Tulsa, Oklahoma. Service centers are also located in New York and Nashville. President: **D. D. Randall.** Vice-President: **J. J. Lorenz.** Fender is a manufacturer of *Fender* guitars, microphones, amplifiers, and solid-state electronic organs, *Fender/Rhodes* electric piano (73-key) for classroom piano instruction with teacher console, tape deck, etc. Guitars are acoustic and electric hollow-body models. The firm also makes banjos and string basses and is a wholesale distribution outlet for the following products made by other firms: *Regal* guitars, string basses, amplifiers, and ukuleles; *Tarrega Classic* guitars (made in Sweden); *Starmaster* organs; and *D'Andrea* picks. The firm repairs its own products only. Sales are wholesale.

GIBSON, INC., 225 Parsons Street, Kalamazoo, Michigan. Tel.: (616) 381–7050. Founded 1894. President and General Manager: **Stanley E. Rendell.** The firm is a wholly owned subsidiary of Chicago Musical Instrument Co. (q.v. Distributors) and is a manufacturer of *Gibson* acoustical and electric guitars, banjos, mandolins, amplifiers, and strings. Distributed exclusively by Chicago Musical Instruments and its subsidiaries.

GOYA GUITARS, INC., 1010 West Chestnut, Chanute, Kansas 66720. Founded 1940 as Hershman Musical Instrument Co., Inc.; name changed to Goya Music Corp. in 1966; merged into Avnet, Inc. in 1967; was sold to Kustom Electronics in 1970. The firm is the national distributor of *Goya* guitars. (However, see also Targ & Dinner.) The *Goya* acoustic guitar is made in Sweden; the *Goya* electric is Italian-made. The company is also distributor and importer of *Greco* guitars, which are made in Germany and Japan, and the *Avalon* line of guitars and accessories.

GUILD MUSICAL INSTRUMENTS, 225 West Grand Street, Elizabeth, N.J. 07202 Tel.: (201) 351–3002. Founded 1947. President: **Alfred Dronge.** Vice-President: **Leon Tell.**The firm is a division of Avnet, Inc. Has a manufacturing plant at Westerly, Rhode Island. Manufacturers of *Guild* guitars, amplifiers, organs, public address systems, and guitar strings. Also makers of *Sonola* and *Rivoli* accordions, *Guild* microphones, and various sound reproduction equipment. Sales are wholesale only.

THE HARMONY COMPANY, 4600 South Kolin Avenue, Chicago, Illinois 60632. Tel.: (312) 523–0721. Founded 1892. Vice-President and Sales Manager: **Charles A. Rubovits.** Reputedly, one of the largest manufacturers of fretted instruments in the world; some sources state that an estimated 50 percent of the industry's guitars are made by the company. Instruments made are the acoustic and electric guitar, banjos, mandolins, ukuleles, and guitar amplifiers—all under the *Harmony* brand name. The firm's products are sold to some 25 major wholesale distributors in the U.S. and about six in Canada. Foreign sales are through distributors in several countries.

C. F. MARTIN & CO., INC., P.O. Box 329, Nazareth, Pennsylvania 18064. Tel.: (215) 759–2837. Cable: MARTINCO. Founded 1833. Chairman: **C. F. Martin.** President: **F. H. Martin.** Subsidiaries: C. F. Martin Sales Co.; Vega of Boston, banjo manufacturers; Darco Music Strings, Inc.; Fibes Drum Corporation. Makers of guitars and other fretted instruments, strings and cases, under the *Martin* brand name. Instruments include acoustic, classic, folk, and Spanish guitars totaling some 20 models, tiples, mandolins, and ukuleles. The company repairs its own instruments. Wholesale only.

MERLIN MANUFACTURING CORP., 3545 North Clark Street, Chicago, Illinois 60657. Tel.: (312) 348–2640. Founded 1962. President: **L. McCabe.** Vice-President: **J. Smith.** Divisional firm is Protect-A-Book Division (makes an adjustable bookend device). Manufacturers of *Merlin* aluminum and fiberglass banjos. Sales are wholesale only.

OVATION INSTRUMENTS, New Hartford, Connecticut 06082. Tel.: (203) 379–6083. President: **Richard Della Bernarda.** Branch office: 1680 Argyle Avenue, Hollywood, California 90028. Ovation is a Division of Kaman Corporation, Bloomfield, Connecticut. Manufacturers of *Ovation* guitars (electric, acoustic, and bass in some ten models), instrument amplifiers (34 models), and stage lights. Instruments and amplifiers are designed and sold for the rock-folk music market. Wholesale only. Exports to Canada, Mexico, and Europe.

RICKENBACKER, INC., P.O. Box 2275, Santa Ana, California 92707. Tel.: (714) 545–5574. Factory is located at Electro String Instrument Corp. (q.v. this section), 3117 Kilson, Santa Ana, California 92707. Founded 1931. Officers: **F. C. Hall** and **C. H. Hall.** Divisional firms: Electro I.D.E.A., Electro String Instrument Corp., F. C. Hall & Associates. Manufacturers and distributors (wholesale only) of *Rickenbacker, Electro, Ryder,* and *Astro* electric guitars; *Rickenbacker, Electro,* and *Symfonia Grand* amplifiers; and *Rickenbacker* guitar strings. The firm claims to have patented the first electric guitar (1931) and to have made the first 12-string electric guitar.

SHO-BUD GUITAR COMPANY, INC., 416 Broadway, Nashville, Tennessee 37203. Tel.: (615) 244–4770. Founded 1952. President: **Harold B. Jackson.** Manufacturers of *Sho-Bud* steel guitars. Sells both retail and wholesale. Instrument repair and service offered also.

VEGA INSTRUMENT COMPANY, INC., 155 Reservoir Street, Needham Heights, Massachusetts 02194. Tel.: (617) 449–1150. Founded 1889. Now a subsidiary of C. F. Martin & Co., Inc. Consultant: **William W. Nelson.** General Manager: **Paul L. Badger,** both former officers. Manufacturer, importer, and distributor. Manufacturers of *Vega* guitars, banjos, and *Vega Nu Sound* strings. Selling agents for: *Harmony* and *Supro* guitars (domestic); *Hauser* guitars (made in West Germany); *De Vegas* guitars (Spain); *Ideal* guitars and drums (Japan); *Odell* and *Meyer* band instruments (from Czechoslovakia). Other standard brands handled on a regular jobbing basis are: *Artley* flutes, *Oscar Schmidt* autoharps, *Kohlert* clarinets, *Zildjian* cymbals, etc. Wholesale business only.

Percussion

CAMCO DRUM CO., 9221 South Kilpatrick Avenue, Oaklawn, Illinois 60453. Tel.: (312) 423–2900. Formerly known as Geo. Way Drums, Inc. Founded 1955. President: **John Rochon.** Secretary and Treasurer: **Claire Mayer.** Makers of *Camco* drums and drum accessories: pedals, stands, plastic drum heads, etc. Wholesalers of *Zildjian* and *Krut* cymbals. Sells wholesale. In 1971, this firm was acquired by Kustom Electronics, Inc. and is a division of the latter.

CAPPELLA WOOD ENTERPRISES, INC., Applegarth Road, Hightstown, N.J. 08520. Tel.: (609) 448–1153. Founded in 1963. Manufacturers of drumsticks. Produces 45 models of drumsticks and 18 of beaters. President and owner is **John C. Cappella.**

J. C. DEAGAN, INC., 1770 West Berteau Avenue, Chicago, Illinois 60613. Tel.: (312) 525–4364. Cable: DEAGAN CHICAGO. Founded 1880. A subsidiary of American Gage and Machine Co., Elgin, Illinois. Chairman: **Wallace E. Carroll.** President: **Jack C. Deagan.** Executive Vice-President: **John Martin.** Manufacturers of *Deagan* mallet percussion instruments: vibraharps, marimbas, xylophones, orchestra chimes and bells, bell lyras; also makers of electronic carillons, organ chimes, tuning forks and bars. The vibraharp was developed and introduced by Deagan in 1927. All sales are wholesale only except electronic carillons, which are also sold retail.

DRUM CITY ENTERPRISES, INC., 6226 Santa Monica Boulevard, Hollywood, California 90038. Tel.: (213) HO 7–5002, HO 7–1060. Founded 1947. President: **Roy Harte.** Wholesale and retail distributors of a wide range of brands of percussion instruments and accessories. Repairs and services percussion instruments.

THE G.H.W. CO., 1401 North Nappanee Street, Elkhart, Indiana 46514. Owner: **Mrs. Elsie Way.** Distributors of domestically manufactured percussion instruments and accessories including cymbals, drum heads and covers, and drumsticks. Wholesale only.

G. C. JENKINS COMPANY, 1014 East Olive Street, Decatur, Illinois 62526. Tel.: (217) 423–7777. Founded 1919. President: **James B. Jenkins.** Manufacturers of vibraphones, marimbas, xylophones, tubular chimes, orchestra bells, glockenspiels, celestes, bell lyras, timpani, tuned handbells, and other melodic percussion instruments. All instruments are sold under the brand name of *JeNco.* Sales are wholesale only.

E. W. KENT MANUFACTURING COMPANY, INC., 1189 Military Road, Kenmore Road, N.Y. 14217. Tel.: (716) 873–9650. Founded 1946. President: **Edward W. Kent.** Vice-President: **William J. Kent.** Manufacturers of drums including drum sets for modern popular music, portable drum kits, snare drums, tom-toms, bass drums, parade drums, cymbals, bongo drums, timbales, and drum accessories such as foot pedals, stands, etc. All products carry the brand name of *Kent.* Wholesale only.

LEEDY DRUM COMPANY, 6633 North Milwaukee Avenue, Niles, Illinois. Tel.: (312) 763–3664. Founded 1895. Makers of *Leedy* drums, timpanis, and drum accessories. National sales are handled by the following firms: C. Bruno & Son, Inc., New York and San Antonio; Southland Musical Merchandise Corp., Greensboro, North Carolina; David Wexler & Co., Chicago; J. M. Sahlein Music Co., San Francisco.

LUDWIG INDUSTRIES, 1728 North Damen Avenue, Chicago, Illinois 60647. Tel.: (312) 276–3360. Cable: LUDRUM-Chicago. Founded 1910 as Ludwig & Ludwig, Inc.; merged with C. G. Conn in 1929 and repurchased from Conn in 1955. Ludwig Industries formed in 1968. Chairman: **William F. Ludwig, Sr.** President: **William F. Ludwig, Jr.** Divisional firms: Ludwig Drum Co.; Musser, Inc.; Kitching, Inc.; and Schuessler Case Company (q.v.). Ludwig Industries is an outgrowth of Ludwig Drum Company's exclusive distributorship of the Musser, Kitching, and Schuessler products. *Musser* products include marimbas, vibraphones, xylophones, orchestra bells, chimes, and other mallet percussion. *Kitching* items include scientific tuning devices, band lyras, rhythm bells for educational use, and other similar products. *Ludwig* products include drums, timpani, and drum accessories. The Ludwig company is also exclusive U.S.A. distributor of the Swiss-made *Paiste* cymbals and gongs. Sells to Ludwig dealers only.

PREMIER DRUMS, INC., 825 Lafayette Street, New Orleans, Louisiana 70113. Tel.: (504) 525–4235. Formed in 1963 from a business originally founded in 1947 (Hall Drum Company). Officers are **Warren L. Campo, Jr.** and **Lloyd A. Campo.** Principally importers and distributors of *Premier* percussion instruments and accessories made in London, England. Wholesale distribution.

THE ROGERS DRUM CO., 1000 East 2nd Street, Dayton, Ohio 45402. Tel.: (513) 223–4275. Founded 1849. Acquired in 1966 by CBS Musical Instruments, a division of the Columbia Broadcasting System. Manufacturers and distributors of percussion instruments. Instruments made are: *Dyna-Sonic* snare drums, parade drums, Scotch drums, *Powertone* snare drums; *Swiv-o-matic* percussion-accessories hardware (holders, tilters, etc.); *Rogers* drum sets (models include such designations as *Celebrity, Headliner, Timbale-Twin, Twin-Bass, Citadel, Constellation, Londoner,* etc.); stands, hi-hat cymbals, foot pedals; Sampson drummer thrones; a number of smaller percussion instruments and *Accu-Sonic* timpani are also made. Percussion accessories made include drum covers and cases, drum heads, sticks, brushes, etc. Publishes a series of educational aid sheets called *Percussion Pointers.* Wholesale only.

SISTEK MUSIC CO., 4628 Broadway, Cleveland, Ohio 44127. Tel.: (216) MI 1–0257. Founded 1904. Owner: **James J. Sistek, Jr.** Makers of drums, drum sets, trumpets, and accessories. Brand names: *New Wonder, New Jewel, Allstate, Gem, Spacemaster,* etc. Sales are wholesale and retail.

SLINGERLAND DRUM COMPANY, 6633 Milwaukee Avenue, Niles, Illinois 60648. Tel.: (312) 647–0377. Founded 1916. Subsidiary of Crowell Collier and Macmillan, Inc. President (since 1970, succeeding **H. H. Slingerland, Jr.** who retired after serving as president for 25 years): **Don Osborne.** Manufacturers of drums, drum sets, timpani, mallet percussion instruments, and drum accessories under the *Slingerland* brand name. The firm claims to be the world's largest manufacturer of drums, timpani, and percussion accessories.

AVEDIS ZILDJIAN COMPANY, 39 Fayette Street, North Quincy, Massachusetts 02171. Tel.: (617) 471–2200. Cable: AVEZIL, QUINCY. Founded in Turkey in 1623; American firm founded in 1929. President: **Avedis A. Zildjian.** Secretary: **Armand Zildjian.** Subsidiaries: Azco, Ltd., and A. Zildjian Export Company, Inc. Makers of *Zildjian, Zilco,* and *Azco* cymbals and gongs. Wholesale only.

Accordion

ACCORGAN CORP., 581 Bergen Boulevard, Ridgefield, N.J. 07657. A division of Ferrari Musical Instrument Corp. (q.v. this section). Makers of an instrument—the *Accorgan*—that is basically an accordion containing a transistorized unit which uses the miniaturized organ tone generator, giving off organlike effects when desired.

ATLAS ACCORDIONS, INC., 319 West John Street, Hicksville, N.Y. 11801. Tel.: (516) GE 3–2260. Founding date: "over 40 years ago." President: **J. Terranova.** The *Atlas* accordion is made in the firm's own plant in Italy and distributed in this country through the above address in the *Century, Supreme,* and *Sterling* models. Other instruments bearing the same model names are drums, guitars, and organs—all imported. The firm also imports the *Gregorius* violin, viola, cello, and string bass. All products are sold wholesale.

BELL ACCORDION CORPORATION, 115 East 23rd Street, New York, N.Y. 10010. Tel.: (212) 475–2885. Founded 1948. President: **A. Mencaccini.** Vice-President: **K. Berwin.** Manufacturer and distributor of *Bell, Bellcordion,* and *Milanti* accordions and guitars (all imported) and *Bell* amplifiers (domestically made). Repairing and servicing also offered. Accordions distributed by the Chicago Musical Instrument Co. and its Northwest subsidiary, L. D. Heater Music Co.

BIANCO ACCORDIONS, 7220 S.E. Powell Boulevard, Portland, Oregon 97206. Tel.: (503) 775–8208. Founded 1955. Factory located in Castelfidardo, Italy. Owner: **J. Bianco.** Importers and distributors of *Bianco* accordions and accessories. Sales are wholesale and retail.

CASTIGLIONE ACCORDION AND DISTRIBUTING COMPANY, 12644 East Seven Mile Road, Detroit, Michigan 48205. Tel.: (313) 527–1595. Cable: CACIE. Founded 1920. Headed by **Vincent Castiglione.** Manufacturer, importer, and distributor of drums, guitars, amplifiers, and the *Castiglione* accordion. Wholesale and retail.

EXCELSIOR ACCORDIONS, INC., 333 Avenue of the Americas, New York, N.Y. 10014. Tel.: (212) 929–0171. Founded 1924. President: **Mario Pancotti.** Vice-President: **Edward Pancotti.** Branch office: 37 Leland Avenue, San Francisco, California 94134. Manufacturer and importer of accordions (some models made in New York, others in Italy). Accordion brand names sold by the firm are: *Excelsior, Excelsiola, Accordiana,* and *Savoia.* Also makes *Rotunda* accordion pickups, *Americana* amplifiers, and *Courier* organs. Also offers repairing and servicing. Wholesale only.

FERRARI MUSICAL INSTRUMENT CORP., 581 Bergen Boulevard, Ridgefield,

N.J. 07657. Tel.: (New Jersey) (201) 943–8432; New York City: (212) 244–6676. Factory is the Ferrari Electronics Corp., 422 54th Street, West New York, N.J. President: **Martin P. Kafka.** Subsidiaries are R. Galanti & Bro., Inc.; Beacon Music Co., Inc.; Ferrari Electronics Corp.; and Accorgan Corp. Manufacturers, importers, and distributors of accordions (see R. Galanti this section), guitars, small organs and the "accorgan" (see Accorgan Corp. this section). Acts as selling agent for *Accorgan* and *Galanti.* Wholesale only.

R. GALANTI & BROS., INC., 581 Bergen Boulevard, Ridgefield, N.J. 07657. A division of Ferrari Musical Instrument Corp. Makers of *Galanti* accordions and guitars.

GIULIETTI ACCORDION CORPORATION, 257 Park Avenue South, New York, N.Y. 10010. Tel.: (212) 254–5450. Cable: GIULACCORD. Founded 1914 as L. Giulietti & Co.; present name since 1951. President: **Julio Giulietti.** Subsidiary: Anjay Importers, Inc. at same address as parent firm. The firm is a manufacturer, importer, and distributor of accordions under the brand names of *Giulietti, JG,* and *Bassetti;* also imports and distributes *JG* guitars, amplifiers, and strings. Products are manufactured in Italy. Repairs and services accordions and guitars. Wholesale sales.

IMPERIAL ACCORDION MANUFACTURING COMPANY, 2618 West 59th Street, Chicago, Illinois 60629. Tel.: (312) 476–4702. Founded 1945. Partners: **Carl Gasparetti** and **Merico Malatesta.** Makers of *Imperial* accordions; importers and distributors of *Lindo* accordions, *Cougar* organs, *Tonemaster* guitars; also distributes the domestically made *Magnatone* amplifier. Wholesale only. Does repair and service work.

INTERNATIONAL ACCORDION MANUFACTURING COMPANY, 28504 Riverside Drive, Mt. Clemens, Michigan 48043. Tel.: (313) HO 8–1371. Founded 1932. Plants located in East Detroit and Italy. Owner: **Anonte Bernardi.** Manufacturers and importers of *Super, Golden Chorus* and *Lira* accordions. Sales are both wholesale and retail.

ITALO AMERICAN ACCORDION MANUFACTURING CO., 3137 West 51st Street, Chicago, Illinois 60632. Tel.: (312) 776–2992. Founded 1910. President: **Joseph Romagnoli.** Manufacturers and importers of *Polytone, Concertmaster* and *Polkamaster* accordions. Sells wholesale and retail.

PETOSA ACCORDIONS, 313 N.E. 45th Street, Seattle, Washington 98105. Tel.: (206) ME 2-2700. Founded 1922. Owner: **Joseph G. Petosa.** Manufacturers, importers, and distributors of *Petosa* accordions and amplifiers, and *Gian-Scala* accordions. Repairs and services accordions. Wholesale only.

ROWE ACCORDION DISTRIBUTING COMPANY, 2841 Greenbriar Parkway, S.W., Atlanta, Georgia 30331. Tel.: (404) 344–4023. Founded 1952. President: **B. G. Rowe.** Importers and distributors of *Rowe* accordions, made in Italy, and *Ro-Co* electric and acoustic guitars. Sales are both retail and wholesale.

SANO CORPORATION, 1281 Springfield Avenue, Irvington, N.J. 07111. Tel.: (201) 373–0700. Founded 1952. President: **Joseph Zon-Frilli.** Secretary: **Louis Iorio.** Manufacturers of *Sano* and *Zon-Rio* accordions. Instruments are made with amplifiers and pickups. The firm imports guitars sold under the *Sano* brand name as well as the *Sanovox,* a transistorized accordion with a simulated organ sound. Wholesale only.

SYN-CORDION MUSICAL INSTRUMENT CORPORATION, 32–73 Steinway Street, Astoria, N.Y. 11103. Tel.: (212) 278–7422. The firm represents a merger including Iorio Instrument, Inc. The Iorio firm, a manufacturer of accordions, was founded in 1907. Plant located in Castelfidardo, Ancona, Italy. General Manager: **Amedeo Iorio.** Imports and distributes its foreign-made instruments and accessories. The firm's brands are: *Iorio* and *Candido* accordions, *Iorio Accorgans* (an instrument with a combined organ and accordion sound produced electronically), *Iorio Combo Rhythm Accordion, Iorio Rhythm Amplifiers, Syn-Co* guitar picks and remote sound systems. Instrument and amplifier repairing is also done by the company.

TITANO ACCORDION COMPANY, 230 Herricks Road, Mineola, Long Island, N.Y. 11501. Tel. (516) 746–3100. Founded 1890. Factories are located in Mineola and Italy. The firm is owned by Ernest Deffner Affiliates (New York, N.Y.). Manufacturers of accordions, amplifiers, and accessories under the brand names of *Titano, Titan, Titanorgan.* Wholesale only.

String Instruments

HULL'S SUPPLY HOUSE, Fort Hunter, N.Y. 12069. Tel.: (518) VA 9–4495. Founded 1882. Owner: **John S. Hull.** Importers and jobbers of violins, violas, cellos, string basses, string instrument supplies. String instruments repair is a major aspect of the firm's operations.

INTERNATIONAL VIOLIN COMPANY, 414 East Baltimore Street, Baltimore, Maryland 21202. Tel.: (301) 727–3335. Founded circa 1928. President: **Abraham Quall.** Importers of violins, violas, cellos, and string basses and their accessories; also sells violinmakers materials and tools. Manufacturers of nylon and horsehair bowhair and oil varnish. Wholesale only.

WILLIAM LEWIS AND SON, 7390 North Lincoln Avenue, Lincolnwood, Illinois 60646. Tel.: (312) 677–1800. Founded 1874. President: **H. Benson.** Branch office (salesroom): 30 East Adams Street, Chicago, Illinois 60603. A subsidiary of Chicago Musical Instrument Company (q.v. Distributors). Importers and distributors of string instruments and their accessories; also appraisers, restorers, and repairers of old, rare, and new violins. The firm's repair service is an important aspect of its business (the term "Strad-justed" is used by the company to identify its repair procedure). Some of the brands sold include *Gustav August Ficker* and *Tonklar* violins, violas, cellos; *Kay* cellos; *Laurel* and *Kay* string basses; *William Lewis* violin, viola, cello, and bass bows; *Lifton* instrument cases; *Pieroni, Joachim, Imperial, Rao, Lycon, Dr. Thomastik, Pirastro, Kaplan* strings, *Gibson* guitar strings. The company has published some books and pamphlets on the violin and other string instruments and for a number of years published a regularly appearing periodical, *Violins and Violinists* (discontinued in 1960).

C. MEISEL MUSIC CO., INC., 2332 Morris Avenue, Union, N.J. 07083. Tel.: (201) 688–8500. Founded 1878. President: **Chris Kratt.** Importers and distributors with an emphasis on string instruments and accessories. Brands handled are: *Karl Meisel* violins, violas, cellos, and string basses; *Hausmann,* and *Carlo Micelli* string instruments; *Pohlmann* string basses; *Andrè Piccard* woodwinds; *Gagliano-Hopf* guitars; *Chris-Kratt/A.R. Huettl* band instruments; *Deri* drums; *Meisel* strings; *Werner* bows; *Chris Kratt* mouthpieces; other national standard brands also handled in instruments and accessories.

METROPOLITAN MUSIC COMPANY, 222 Park Avenue South, New York, N.Y. 10003. Tel.: (212) 254–6320. Founded 1925. President: **Robert Juzek.** Manufacturers, importers, and distributors mainly of string instruments and bows. Exclusive distributors of *John Juzek* violins, violas cellos, and string basses, *Dupree* and *Voirin* bows, *Taperfit* tuning pegs. Also imports *Artex* guitars and accessories. Sells wholesale only.

SCHERL AND ROTH, INC., 1729 Superior Avenue, Cleveland, Ohio 44114. Tel.: (216) 861–7640. Founded 1910. President: **J. Frederick Muller.** The firm is a division of C. G. Conn, Ltd. of Elkhart, Indiana (acquired in 1968). Manufacturers of *Roth* violins, violas, cellos, and string basses, and distributors of string instruments accessories (distribution is handled through the Conn firm). Instruments are sold mainly to schools.

A. SCHROETTER CO., 303 Park Avenue South, New York, N.Y. 10010. Tel.: (212) 254–3285. President: **Andrew Schroetter.** Wholesale distributors of string instruments and their accessories. Exclusive distributors of instruments manufactured abroad by the firms of *Roman Teller* and *Wenzl Fuchs.* The firm also handles standard national brands of strings, bows, accessories, etc.

Miscellaneous Manufacturers

AMERICAN HANDLE SALES COMPANY, Unruh and Milnor Streets, Philadelphia, Pennsylvania 19135. Tel.: (215) 332–8000. Founded 1963. Manufactures and distributes handles and handle accessories for portable amplifiers and musical instruments. Sells wholesale only.

AMERICAN PLATING & MANUFACTURING CO., 2241 South Indiana Avenue, Chicago, Illinois 60616. Tel.: (312) 225–4906. Founded 1902. President: **C. T. Urban, Sr.** Manufactures musical instrument accessories: *Stevens* guitar steels and picks, and *Amplate,* which is a single unit folio and lyre for band instruments. The firm also does instrument repair, plating, polishing, etc. Product sales are wholesale only.

THE AMPEG CO., INC., 345 Dalziel Road, Linden, N.J. 07036. Tel.: (201) 925–6700. Founded 1950. Plant is located at 330 Dalziel Road. President: **A. J. Dauray.** Executive Vice President: **R. Mucci.** The firm is owned by the Unimusic Corp. of New York. Makers of *Ampeg* amplifiers, electric string basses and guitars, and accessories to amplifiers and instruments. The firm is exclusive U.S. distributor of Altec Lansing products (see manufacturers of high fidelity equipment). The firm also repairs and services amplifiers and instruments. Sales are through franchised dealers.

AMRAWCO (American Rawhide Manufacturing Co.), 8550 West 43rd Street, Lyons, Illinois 60534. Tel.: (312) 447–3400. Founded 1928. Makers of *Amrawco* calfskin drum and banjo heads, cymbal polish, and percussion accessories; also distributes other brands of the latter. Wholesale sales only.

BERDON, INC., Box 5151 Seattle, Washington. 98107. Tel.: (206) MA 2–3987. Founded 1961. Manufacturers of reeds and reedmaking tools for bassoon, contra bassoon, oboe, and English horn. The firm repairs and services instruments of the double-reed family. Sells retail and wholesale.

DARCO MUSIC STRINGS, INC., 33–35 35th Street, Long Island City, N.Y. 11106. Tel.: (212) 786–3041. Factory is located at same address. Founded in 1962 as a merger of C. D'Addario & Son of Jackson Heights (New York) and Archaic Music String Manufacturing Corp. (Long Island). Now a subsidiary of C. F. Martin and Co., Inc. Manager: **John D'Addario, Sr.** Makers of strings for musical instruments under the following brand names *Darco Black Label, Puccini, Campus, Canora, Serenata, Classic, Gemini, La Rita, New Yorker, Acoustic, Funky.* Wholesale and retail sales.

DELTEX MUSIC CORP., Box 168, Monsey, N.Y. 10952. Tel.: (914) EL 6–2097. Factory located at 14 West Maple Avenue in Monsey. Founded 1930. President: **M. Waldman.** Manufacturers of *Old Kent* rosin and *Glyd-Oil* products for valves, slides, woodwinds, etc. U.S. distributor of *Krut* cymbals (English); also importer of violins, guitar accessories, etc. Wholesale only.

EMENEE INDUSTRIES, INC., 200 Fifth Avenue, New York, N.Y. 10010. Tel.: (212) OR 5–4700. Cable: KWH. Factory located at 41–06 DeLong Street, Flushing, N.Y. Founded 1950. President: **Herbert L. Merin.** Vice-President: **W. J. Kreizel.** Divisional firm is American Audion Corp. (q.v.) Emenee Industries is owned by Emenee Corporation. Manufacturer (presumably the world's largest) of musical toys of all varieties. Also makers of electric chord organs, batons, art and skill games. Sales are wholesale only.

EVANS PRODUCTS, INC., Box 58, Dodge City, Kansas 67801. Tel.: (316) 227–3971. Factory is located at 201 W. Trail Street, Dodge City. President: **Robert C. Beals.** Secretary-Treasurer: **Shirley J. Beals.** Manufacturers of *Evans All Weather* plastic drum heads. Sold wholesale.

GALE PRODUCTS, INC., 4540 Hollywood Boulevard, Los Angeles, California 90027. Tel.: (213) 664–0620. Founded 1950. Owner: **C. A. Tschudin.** Makers of hard rubber woodwind mouthpieces and mouthpiece blanks for clarinets, saxophones, etc. Importers of pads for woodwind instruments. Products sold wholesale only under the *Gale* brand name.

GEIB INCORPORATED, 1751 North Central Park Avenue, Chicago, Illinois 60647. Tel.: (312) 235–1694. Founded 1899. Factory located at 3704 West North Avenue, Chicago, Illinois 60647. President: **N. J. Geib.** Vice-President: **A. C. Geib.** Manufacturers of musical instrument cases under the brand names of *Archcraft, Economo,* and *Vac-A-Bond.* Wholesale only.

GIARDINELLI BAND INSTRUMENT CO., 1725 Broadway, New York, N.Y. 10019. Tel.: (212) 757–0641. Founded 1947. Owner: **Robert Giardinelli.** Manufacturers of screw-rim mouthpieces for brass instruments; custom mouthpieces also made. All sold under *Giardinelli* name. Repair work is an important aspect of the firm's business. Sales are retail and wholesale.

HARMON MUTE COMPANY, 8030 North Ridgeway, Skokie, Illinois 60076. Tel.: (312) 676–0404. President: **Sidney A. Greenspan.** Makers of mutes for brass instruments. Wholesale only.

HERSHMAN MUSICAL INSTRUMENT CO., INC., 43 West 24th Street, New York, N.Y. 10010. Tel. (212) 255–0709. Founded in 1940; in 1966 changed its name to Goya Music Corp., which was sold respectively to Avnet, Inc., then Kustom Electronics (see Goya Guitars); the firm has reverted to its original name. It distributes the *Toyota* line of acoustic and electric guitars and cases, *Bellair* guitar accessories, etc. A subsidiary, Herco Products, makes band instrument mouthpieces, strings, cleaning supplies, musical awards and pins, etc. under the *Herco* name. President and Treasurer: **Jerome Hershman.**

JET-TONE MUSICAL PRODUCTS, INC., 226 Kings Highway, Fairfield, Connecticut 06430. Tel.: (203) 368–0453. Factory located at 1126 Kings Highway in Fairfield. Founded 1964. President: **William Ratzenberger.** Makers of mouthpieces for trumpet, cornet, trombone, and fluegelhorn. All carry the brand name of *Jet-Tone.* Sales are retail and wholesale.

KAPLAN MUSICAL STRING CO., P.O. Box 427, South Norwalk, Connecticut 06856. Tel.: (203) 866–3455. Founded 1907. Factory located at 104 Highland Avenue in South Norwalk. President: **Otto Kaplan.** Manufacturers of strings for musical instruments and bow rosin. Strings are manufactured under the brand names of *Golden Spiral, Tru-Strand, Red-O-Ray, Tonecraft,* and *Maestro;* bow rosin is made under the *Art-Craft* and *Art-Craft Deluxe* brand names. Strings are made for instruments of the violin family, guitars, and harps. Wholesale only.

WM. KRATT CO., 988 Johnson Place, Union, N.J. 07083. Tel.: (201) 688–8600. Business begun in 1920; incorporated in 1947. President: **William Kratt.** Vice-President: **Emily Kratt.** Manufacturers of vocal and instrumental pitch pipes and harmonicas under the *Wm. Kratt* brand name. Reputedly largest manufacturer of brass reed harmonicas in the U.S. Some ten harmonica models are made. Pitch pipes are made for tuning fretted instruments; a chromatic model is made for vocal use. Wholesale only.

KRAUTH & BENNINGHOFEN, INC., 30001 Symmes Road, Hamilton, Ohio 45012. Tel.: (513) 892–7033. Founded 1883. The firm is a subsidiary of Chicago Musical Instrument Company. Manufacturers of music stands under the *Hamilton* brand name and is the oldest music stand manufacturer in America. Sold through wholesale jobbers only.

KUSTOM ELECTRONICS, INC., P.O. Box 669, Chanute, Kansas 66720. Tel.: (316) 431–4380. Factory is located at 1010 West Chestnut in Chanute, Founded 1965. President: **C. A. Ross.** Subsidiaries: Kustom Promotions, Inc.; Kustom Recreational Equipment, Inc.; Goya Guitars; and Camco Drum Co. Manufacturers of amplification systems: guitar amplifiers, bass guitar amplifiers, public address systems; electric guitars, bass guitars, and electronic combo organs—all under the *Kustom* brand name. Service and repair operations are maintained by the firm. Wholesale only.

LYON-HEALY, INC., 243 South Wabash Avenue, Chicago, Illinois 60604. Tel.: (312) 922–7900. Manufacturers of harps bearing the company name. At the above address the firm also operates a retail store, one of the largest in the Midwest.

MAAS-ROWE CARILLONS, 3015 Casitas Avenue, Los Angeles, California 90039. Tel.: (213) 661–1185. Formerly a manufacturer of pipe organs, the firm has been known by its present name since 1954. President: **Paul H. Rowe, Jr.** Makers of organ chimes and carillons. Products sold through dealers.

ROY J. MAIER CORPORATION, 8484 San Fernando Road, Sun Valley, California. Tel.: (213) 875–0767. Makers of woodwind reeds and accessories. Brand names: *La-Voz, Reedgard, Mitchell Lurie, Roy J. Maier Signature.* Sales are wholesale.

MANHASSET MUSIC STANDS (Manhasset Specialty Co., Inc.). This firm, formerly of Yakima, Washington, was acquired by King Musical Instruments (q.v.).

E. & O. MARI, INC., 38–01 23rd Avenue, Long Island City, N.Y. 11105. Tel.: (212) 278–4005. Cable: EOMARI. The company traces its history back to a firm founded in Italy in 1600. President: **Olinto Mari.** Secretary-Treasurer: **Laura Mari.** Manufacturer of strings for instruments of the violin family, fretted instruments including Spanish, electric, and bass guitars, autoharps, and harps. Brand names are: *La Bella, Nu-Tone, La Preferita, Sweetone, Criterion, Regina,* and *Senorita.* Wholesale distribution only.

M. M. MEASON, INC., 162 Halpine Road, Rockville, Maryland 20852 (formerly of Washington, D.C.). Tel.: (301) 427–4447. Founded 1959. President: **William A. Roscoe.** Manufacturers and importers. Makers of *Meason* double reeds for oboes primarily and, beginning recently, also for bassoons and English horns. Reeds are handcrafted, ready-made for student use. Raw materials are imported from France. Wholesale only.

MICRO MUSICAL PRODUCTS CORPORATION, 10 West 19th Street, New York, N.Y. 10011. Tel.: (212) 929–7954. Founded 1923. President: **Dorothy Schwartz.** Secretary: **E. Herrlitz.** Manufacturers of the following musical instrument accessories: *Black Line* clarinet and saxophone reeds; *Classic* and *Duplexo* saxophone straps; *Micro* cleaners and swabs, cork grease, cement, *Micro* clarinet and saxophone pads, oils, polishes, *Grafslide* grease, lip balm; mutes, batons, picks, guitar cords, rosin, and other items for repairing and maintaining musical instruments. Sales are wholesale.

MULTIVOX CORPORATION OF AMERICA, 370 Motor Parkway, Hauppauge, Long Island, N.Y. 11787. Tel.: (516) 231–7700. Cable: LOUISORKIN. Founded 1952. Officers: **Joseph Saltzman, Harold Sorkin, Florence Sorkin.** Manufacturers of *Premier* electric guitars, amplifiers, reverberation units, sound systems, accordion pickups; and *Marvel* amplifiers.

ED MYERS CO., INC., 3022 Pacific Street, Omaha, Nebraska 68105. Tel.: (402) 342–4793. Exact founding date not known; the firm is over thirty years old. President: **Helen Matcha.** Vice-President: **Harold Kappus.** Subsidiary: W. R. Dalbey Co. Manufacturers of *K-C* and *Myers* pads for woodwind instruments, and, through its subsidiary firm, *Dalbey* valve and slide oils. Also sells supplies and tools for band instrument repairing. Sales are wholesale only.

NAREN INDUSTRIES, INC., 1214–22 West Madison Street, Chicago, Illinois 60607. Tel.: (312) 243–1766. Founded 1952. President: **M. J. Reed.** Manufacturers of *Naren* music stands (in five models) and spotlights for photography, commercial display, theater lighting, etc. Sells wholesale only.

NATIONAL MUSICAL STRING CO., 120 Georges Road, New Brunswick, N.J. 08903. Tel.: (201) 545–0038. Founded 1898. Since 1970, a subsidiary of Kaman Corporation. President: **E. Sonfield.** Vice-President: **H. Hagel.** Makers of *Black Diamond* and *Bell Brand* strings for guitars and other instruments. Wholesale only.

NATIONAL RAWHIDE MANUFACTURING CO., 1464 West Webster Avenue, Chicago, Illinois 60614. Tel.: (312) 248–5737. President: **V. J. Surak.** Founded 1954. Makers of calfskin drum heads for snare drums, timpani, tom-toms, bass drums, conga heads, bongo, timbale and tambourine heads, and banjo heads. Brand name is *National.* Also makes platic heads. Wholesale.

THE NORWOOD COMPANY, 8040 North Austin Avenue, Morton Grove, Illinois 60053. President: **Charles A. Geib.** Manufacturers of music and drum stands under the *Norwood* brand.

PERIPOLE, INC., 51–17 Rockaway Beach Boulevard, Far Rockaway, N.Y. 11691. Tel.: (212) 474–2500. Founded 1945. Subsidiaries: Carl Van Roy Company (music publishing) and Periscope, Record Division. Products of both companies are sold exclusively through Peripole, Inc. President: **Mack Perry.** Vice-President: **Sylvia Perry.** Manufacturers of what the company calls "informal" musical instruments for educational use by the young. These products include: *Peripole* rhythm instrument kits, Latin American rhythm instruments, drums, mallet percussion, autoharps and guitaros, simple wind instruments, *Rhythm Zoo* (for mentally retarded children), *Sound Kits* (in plucked, blown, or struck varieties) for self-made sounds, *Musikits* (fretted and string instruments to be assembled), *Sonor-Hohner* percussion (made in Germany) for the Orff Method, and *Stratco* audiovisuals.

B. PORTNOY CLARINET ACCESSORIES, INC., 1715 Circle Drive, Bloomington, Indiana 47401. Tel.: (812) 339–5820. Founded 1962. President: **Bernard Portnoy.** Secretary-Treasurer: **Barbara Portnoy.** Importers and distributors of *Portnoy* clarinet mouthpieces, reeds, and ligatures (all designed by Mr. Portnoy). Sales are both retail and wholesale.

PROLL PRODUCTS COMPANY, 104 Verona Avenue, Newark, N.J. 07104. Tel.: (201) 482–1250. Founded 1945. President: **Gustave Proll.** Manufacturers of musical toys and cello string adjusters. Toys are made under the brand name of *Proll-O-Tone* and are designed after such instruments as trumpets, French horns, saxophones, clarinets, cornets, accordions, harmonicas, flutes, among others. Wholesale only.

REED-O-MATIC, INC., 2700 East Main Street, Columbus, Ohio 43209. Factory is located at A. & Z. Eng. Co., 4th and Court Streets, Covington, Kentucky. Founded 1956. President: **H. L. Fenburr.** Manufacturers of *Reed-O-Matic* reed dispenser (coin-operated) for clarinet and saxophone reeds, plastic reed holders, and guitar wall mounts. Wholesale only.

REMO, INC., 12804 Raymer Street, North Hollywood, California 91605. Tel.: (213) 764–7417. Cable: REMORHEADS. Founded 1957. President: **Remo D. Belli.** Vice-President: **Samuel N. Muchnick.** Manufacturers of plastic drum heads under the brand names of *Weather King, Sound Master,* and *Sparkltone; Remo* tuneable drum practice pads, *Remo* practice drum sets, a tuneable drum called *Roto-Tom,* and *Remo Mano* (hand) drums. The company also offers a drum-head painting service for school or band emblems, etc. The firm is known to be the first to introduce a successful plastic drum head. Sales are wholesale only.

RICO CORPORATION, P.O. Box 5028. Bendix Station, North Hollywood, California 91605. Tel.: (213) 767–7030. Founded 1937. General manager: **Belle Hoffer.** Makers of *Rico* clarinet and saxophone reeds and reed dispensers, and *Gregory* mouthpieces. Wholesale only.

OSCAR SCHMIDT–INTERNATIONAL, INC., Garden State Road, Union, N.J. 07083. Tel.: (201) 964–1074. Founded 1879. President: **Glen R. Peterson.** Treasurer: **Margaret N. Peterson.** Manufacturers known mainly for their *Autoharp* (an instrument generically known by that name, which actually is a registered trademark owned by the company). The firm also makes zithers and *Guitaros.* The *Autoharp* is made in several models. Oscar Schmidt publishes instruction and song books for the *Autoharp.* Repair and service of their instruments is offered by the company. Sales are wholesale.

WM. SCHUESSLER, DIVISION OF LUDWIG INDUSTRIES, 361 West Superior Street, Chicago, Illinois 60610. Tel.: (312) 787–6869. Founded 1903; merged with Ludwig in 1968. Manufacturers of fibre drum cases and timpani trunks; cases also made for marimbas, string basses, chimes, cellos, sousaphones, harps, and other instruments. Wholesale only.

SCHULMERICH CARILLONS, INC., Carillon Hill, Sellersville, Pennsylvania 18960. Tel.: (215) 257–2771. Founded 1930. Chairman of the Board: **George J. Schulmerich.** President: **F. Roy Levy.** Manufacturers of *Schulmerich* carillons, bells, and chimes. Retail sales.

SKLENARIK MUSICAL STRING CO., P.O. Box 90, South Norwalk, Connecticut 06856. Tel.: (203) 866–9476. Factory located at 84 Keeler Avenue in South Norwalk. Founded 1935. Partners: **Mrs. Vlasta S. Erdmann** and **Mrs. Josephine Gedney.** Makers of strings for violin, viola cello, and string bass sold under the brand name of *Artone.* Wholesales directly to music retail stores.

V. C. SQUIER COMPANY, 427 Capital Avenue, S.W., Battle Creek, Michigan 49015. Tel.: (616) 968–8191. Founded 1890. A Division of CBS Musical Instruments, of Columbia Broadcasting System, Inc. General Manager of the Squier firm is **David L. Towns.** Makers of fretted and bowed instrument strings under such brand names as *Esquier, Concert Master,* and others.

THE STANDEL COMPANY, P.O. Box 709, El Monte, California 91734. Tel.: (213) 442–0301. Factory located at 4918 Double Drive in El Monte. President: **R. C. Crooks.** Makers of *Standel* electric guitars and basses and amplifiers. Wholesale only.

UNICORD, INCORPORATED, 75 Frost Street, Westbury, N.Y. 11590. Tel.: (516) 333–9100. Cable: ACCORDIM. Founded 1959. President: **Sidney Hack.** Executive Vice-President: **Ernest J. Briefel.** A subsidiary of Gulf & Western Industries, Inc. Manufacturers of *Univox* amplifiers and public address systems; *Unicord* amplifiers and systems. Importers of a number of musical instruments and accessories brands sold through its subsidiary, Merson Musical Products Corporation (q.v.).

WENGER CORPORATION, 90 Park Drive, Owatonna, Minnesota 55060. Tel.: (507) 451–3010. President: **Harry J. Wenger.** Manufactures movable stages, platforms, seated and standing risers, *Rollaway* acoustical shells, demountable practice rooms (study modules), instrument "chairstands," rolling cabinets for music, *"Mobile Performing Arts Centers"* (consisting of stage, acoustical roof, back and sides—all truck deliverable), and other similar devices for use by school performing groups and professional ensembles. Sales are direct to customer.

WERCO–WHITE EAGLE RAWHIDE MFG. CO., 1652 North Throop Street, Chicago, Illinois 60622. Tel.: (312) 276–0872. Founded 1924. President: **John R. Janac.** Vice-President: **George W. Janac.** Manufacturers, importers, and distributors of musical products and toys. Makers of skin heads for drums, banjos, timpani and other instruments using skin vibrators and resonators. Plastic heads are also handled by the firm. Makers of percussion accessories, tambourines, and rhythm band instruments and accessories. Imports Latin American instruments and fretted instruments. Wholesale only.

Importers, Distributors, Wholesalers, etc.

CHARLES ALDEN MUSIC CO., INC., Southwest Industrial Park, Westwood, Massachusetts 02090. Tel.: (617) 326–6040. Wholesale distributors of music merchandise including *Yamaha* guitars, drums, and band instruments; *Hohner* accordions and harmonicas, among a wide range of standard brands.

ANTIGUA CASA SHERRY–BRENNER, LTD. OF MADRID, 3145 W. 63rd Street, Chicago, Illinois 60629. Tel.: (312) 737–1711. Founded 1939. Head of firm is **James Sherry.** Importers and distributors of classic or flamenco guitars of the following makes: *José Ramirez, Antonio Lorca, Domingo Esteso, Santos Hernandez, Marcelino Barbero, Frederico Garcia, Manolo Rodriquez;* lutes: *Franz Josef Stainer, Karl Werner von Strasbourg.* Also sells stringed instrument accessories and guitar makers' supplies of foreign manufacture. The company publishes *Guitarra Magazine,* which is distributed worldwide.

C. BRUNO & SON, INC., 55 Marcus Drive, Melville, N.Y. 11746. Tel.: (516) 694–9090. A Division of Kaman Corporation since 1971. Founded 1834 and is reputedly the oldest distributor of music merchandise in the United States. President: **Edwin Sonfield.** Branch offices: 3043 East Commerce Street, San Antonio, Texas 78206; 1215 West Walnut Street, Compton, California 90220. The main activity of the company and its branches is wholesale distribution of a variety of musical merchandise. Selling agents for *Bruno* bell lyras and instrument stands; *Harmony, Kay* guitars; *Black Diamond, Gibson, Fender* strings (all domestic products); and the following foreign-made brands: *Boosey & Hawkes* (woodwinds); *Hohner* harmonicas; *Ventura* guitars; *Majestic* drums.

BUEGELEISEN & JACOBSON, INC., 5 Union Square, New York, N.Y. 10003. Tel.: (212) AL 5–6433. Cable: DURRO NEW YORK. Founded 1898. President: **Harry Buegeleisen.** Sales Manager: **Austin Lempit.** Branch offices: 534 Armour Circle, N.E., Atlanta, Georgia 30324; 2350 Charleston Avenue, Mountain View, California 94040; 469 King Street, West, Toronto 2B, Ontario, Canada. Importers and distributors of the following products and brands: *España* guitars and *Val Dez* guitars (made by *España* in Finland), *Kent* guitars (all models), microphones and pickups, *Winston* guitars, *Martin Frères* woodwinds, *Lamont* band instruments, *Stewart* drums, *Marc Laberte* string instruments, *Duro* string instruments and bows, *Serenader* recorders and a number of national standard brands. Wholesale business only.

CARROLL MUSIC INSTRUMENT SERVICE CORP., 351 West 41st Street, New York, N.Y. 10036. Tel.: (212) 868–4120. Founded 1946. Headed by **Carroll C. Bratman.** Importers and distributors of celestas and keyboard glockenspiels (U.S. representatives for the *Mustel* brand made in France) and producers of sound effect devices and equipment and original sound effects for rental to the broadcasting industry, theaters, and concert halls. Retail sales.

CHESBRO MUSIC CO., Box 2009 Idaho Falls, Idaho 83401. Tel.: (208) 522–8691. Founded 1911. President: **Joan Chesbro Briggs.** Distributor, wholesaler and retailer of a variety of musical merchandise. Exclusive distributor of *H & H* strings and *Gold Medal* reeds.

CHICAGO MUSIC SALES CO., 1838 South Halsted Street, Chicago, Illinois 60608. Tel.: (312) 421–2126. Founded 1941. Owner: **Harry Fistell.** Wholesalers and jobbers of musical accessories.

CHICAGO MUSICAL INSTRUMENT COMPANY; Executive offices: 7373 North Cicero Avenue, Lincolnwood, Illinois 60646. Tel.: (312) 463–5616. Cable: CMICO. Founded 1920. Honorary Board Chairman and founder: **M. H. Berlin.** Chairman: **H. Norton Stevens.** President and Chief Executive Officer: **Arnold M. Berlin.** Plants are located at subsidiary companies: Asheville Industries, Inc., Black Mountain, North Carolina; Ciccone Reeds, Inc., Lincolnwood, Illinois; CMI Electronics Co., Lincolnwood, Illinois; Gibson, Inc., Kalamazoo, Michigan; L. D. Heater Music Company, Beaverton, Oregon; Krauth & Benninghofen, Inc., Hamilton, Ohio; William Lewis & Son, Lincolnwood, Illinois; Lowrey Electronics Company, Chicago, Illinois; F. E. Olds & Son, Inc., Fullerton, California; Olds Properties, Inc., Fullerton, California; F. S. Reynolds Co., Inc., Abilene, Texas; Story & Clark Piano Company, Lincolnwood, Illinois; Turner Musical Instruments Limited, Scarborough, Ontario, Canada. (See separate listings for most of these companies.) The products manufactured or marketed by C.M.I. are: *Lowrey* pianos and organs; *Story & Clark* pianos and organs; *Olds* band instruments; *Reynolds* band instruments; *William Lewis* orchestral string instruments; *Gibson, Epiphone,* and *Kalamazoo* guitars and amplifiers; *Maestro* electro-musical products; *Symmetricut* reeds; *Farfisa* spinet and compact organs; *Cordovox* accordions; *Buffet-Crampon* (France) clarinets, including alto and bass clarinets, contra-alto and contra-bass clarinets, basset horns, oboes, English horns, saxophones, piccolos, flutes, trumpets, and cornets; *W. Schreiber & Söhne* (German firm sometimes known as *Wenzell–Schreiber*) bassoons and clarinets. (Both Buffet and Schreiber were acquired through Tolchin Instruments, Inc.) The *Farfisa* products are foreign-made. The company also distributes *Pearl* drums (foreign-made) and some musical products of other domestic manufacturers. Sales are wholesale only.

COAST WHOLESALE MUSIC CO. OF LOS ANGELES, 3701 South Broadway, Los Angeles, California 90007. Tel.: (213) 235–4161. Cable: COSMULA. Founded 1946. Subsidiary of Kaman Corporation, Bloomfield, Connecticut. President: **Eric Emerson.** Vice-President: **Harold Talbot.** Importers and distributors. (See also Coast Wholesale Music Co. of San Francisco.) Exclusive distributors in the Southwest for a number of brands, among them: *Hohner; Ludwig* drums and marimbas; *Astro* band instruments; *Schuster* violas and cellos; and others. Wholesale only.

COAST WHOLESALE MUSIC CO. OF SAN FRANCISCO, 274 Brannan Street, San Francisco, California 94107. Tel.: (415) 781–4840. Cable: MIDI. Founded 1905. President: **W. I. Molis.** Vice-President: **Robert M. Gamble.** A division of Kaman Corporation of Bloomfield, Connecticut. Importers and distributors covering the states in the Northwest, Alaska, and Hawaii. The firm works on a cooperative basis with Coast Wholesale Music of Los Angeles, a separate company (see foregoing). Exclusive Northwest distributor of *Ludwig* drums, *Martin* and *Harmony* guitars, *Currier* pianos, *Hohner* products (accordions, harmonicas, etc.), and *Astro* band instruments; also importers of *Aria* guitars, *Anton Becker* violins and cellos, and *Johann Rauner* string basses. Only wholesale.

R. CRAM & CO., 1595 Broadway, New York, N.Y. 10019. Tel.: (212) CI 6–0678. Cable: CRAMNOS. Founded 1925. **Ralph Cram** heads the firm. Export agents for American-made musical products including instruments and accessories for band and orchestra.

DAVITT & HANSER MUSIC CO., 415 Greenwell Avenue, Cincinnati, Ohio 45238. Tel.: (513) 291–0918. Founded 1924. President: **John Hanser, Sr.** Distributors and wholesalers of instruments and accessories.

DORN & KIRSCHNER BAND INSTRUMENT CO., P.O. Box 705, Newark, N.J. 07101 Tel.: (201) 622–4223. Founded 1926. Plant location is 77 Springfield Avenue, Newark, N.J. 07103 and 26 Washington Street, Morristown, N.J. 07960. President: **Renée Kirschner.** Divisional firm is DeKay Musical Instrument Repair Service. The firm is a wholesale and retail outlet for musical instruments and accessories and music publications.

CARL FISCHER MUSICAL INSTRUMENT CO., formerly of 105 East 16th Street, New York, N.Y.; now a subsidiary of Tolchin Instruments, Inc., Lynbrook, Long Island, N.Y. Founded 1872. President: **Carl Schwartz.** Subsidiary (of Carl Fischer Musical Instrument Co.): York Band Instrument Company, Grand Rapids, Michigan. Wholesalers and distributors of York band instruments; *Evette–Schaefer & Cie.* (France), woodwinds (subsidiary of *Buffet–Crampon,* a firm whose woodwinds were once distributed by Carl Fischer but, since the purchase by Tolchin, have been transferred to Chicago Musical Instrument Co. for distribution); *Robert Malerne* (France) woodwinds; *Rudy Mück* (New York) band instruments; *Hüller* (Germany) French horns, trumpets, and other brass instruments; *Moreschi* (Italy) accordions; *La Marque* (France) clarinets; *M–L* (Mitchell Lurie) mouthpieces.

JOSEF FRIEDMAN MUSICAL SALES, INC., 31 Union Square West, New York, N.Y. 10003. Tel.: (212) 989–3574/5. Cable: MUSIBROKERS. President: **Josef Friedman.** Importers, manufacturers' representatives to the music trade. The firm assists manufacturers in the marketing, sales, and distribution of their products. Among the firms and the products represented are: Ace Musical Strap Co. (fretted and wind instrument straps), Atco Case Co. (cases), Bejod Industries, Inc. (instrument covers and bags), Electro-Mat, Inc. (metronomes), Frey Mfg. Co. (pitch pipes), Herco/Goya (musical accessories), Jet-Tone (mouthpieces), E. W. Kent Mfg. Co. (drums, cymbals, and other percussion), Veri-Sonic Inc. (drumsticks), and other firms and products.

GAR–ZIM MUSICAL INSTRUMENTS CORP., 762 Park Place, Brooklyn N.Y. 11216. Tel.: (212) 756–5450. Cable: NYZIMGAR. President: **Larry Zimmerman.** Manufacturers, importers, and distributors. The firm deals in a wide variety of musical instruments and accessories including string instruments, fretted instruments, percussion, amplifiers, Latin American instruments, rhythm band and school instruments. Products are sold under the names of *Zim-Gar* and *Rhythm-Craft.* Sales are both wholesale and retail.

JACK GOODMAN MUSIC CO., 1011 Chestnut Street, Philadelphia, Pennsylvania 19107. Tel.: (212) WA 5–3585. Owner: **Jack Goodman.** Importers and wholesale distributors of domestic and foreign musical instruments and general music merchandise.

WILLIAM R. GRATZ CO., INC., 14 Bixley Heath, Lynbrook, N.Y. 11563. Tel.: (516) 599–3003. Cable: GRATZ BROOM. Founded 1915. General Manager: **John M. Connolly, Jr.** Subsidiary firm: Kohlert, Inc. (q.v.). Importers of *Hofner* guitars; *Hofner* string instruments; *R. Buchner* string instruments; *Thomastik* strings, tailpieces, and rosin; *Kohlert* woodwinds; *Bohm-Meinl* brass instruments. These instruments and accessories are made in Germany. The firm maintains a repair and service department. Sales are wholesale only.

THE FRED GRETSCH COMPANY, INC., 60 Broadway, Brooklyn, N.Y. 11211. Tel.: (212) 387–5200. Cable: DRUMJOIN. Founded 1883. Midwest wholesale office: 777 N. Larch Street, Elmhurst, Illinois 60126. Manufacturing plant is in Booneville, Arkansas. President: **Fred Gretsch, Jr.** The firm is a wholly owned subsidiary of D. H. Baldwin Co., Cincinnati, Ohio (q.v.). Manufacturers of drums, guitars, and amplifiers under the *Gretsch* brand name; also makers of *Bacon* banjos. Importers and distributors of *Couesnon* woodwind and brass instruments made in France, *I.M. Grassi* flutes and saxophones, *La Tosca* accordions. Also distributes domestic merchandise such as *Harmony* guitars, *Hohner* harmonicas, *Hamilton* stands, etc. In addition, the Gretsch firm distributes the products made by Baldwin's Musical Instrument Division. All sales are wholesale.

GROSSMAN MUSIC CORPORATION, 1278 West 9th Street, Cleveland, Ohio 44113. Tel.: (216) 696–1234. Founded 1922. President: **Henry S. Grossman.** Vice-President: **Leo Handel.** Secretary-Treasurer: **Melvin Euzent.** Divisional firms: Trophy Products Company and Duplex Products—both manufacturing divisions of Grossman Music Corporation. Affiliated company is Grover Musical Products, Inc. All of the foregoing firms are located at the above address and are headed by the same officers. Subsidiary is Harris–Fandel Co. of Needham, Massachusetts. Grossman Music corporation is one of America's largest wholesale distributors of musical instruments, accessories, and music publications. Both domestic and imported merchandise is handled. Brands exclusively distributed are *Hamilton, Champion, Buckingham, Lavelle,* and *Bellmore* band instruments and accessories; *Dumain* woodwinds; *Rondini* and *Masterfonic* accordions; *Pasha* cymbals; *Cambridge* and *Heidelberg* recorders; *Duplex* and *Dixie* drums and accessories; *Kreutzer* violins; among others. In addition, the firm handles a large number of standard brand merchandise. Through its manufacturing subsidiaries, Grossman makes and distributes the *Flutophone,* a plastic flute for educational use, the *Cambridge* recorder, *Duplex* drums and accessories, and *Grover* accessories and instrument parts. The firm also provides its customers with a subscription service catalogue which is up-dated periodically.

L. W. HAGELIN COMPANY, 16 Glenwood Avenue, Minneapolis, Minnesota 55403. Tel.: (612) 338–7037. Founded 1926. President: **L. W. Hagelin.** Vice-President: **R. P. Hagelin.** Importers and wholesale distributors of musical instruments and accessories. Some of the many brands handled (both domestic and foreign) are: *K. Heidel* brass instruments, *Stetson* drums and fretted instruments, *M. Vernier* woodwinds, and *Serena* accordions.

HARGAIL MUSIC INC., 157 West 57th Street, New York, N.Y. 10019. Tel.: (212) 245–7246. Cable: HARGAILMUS. Founded 1941. President: **Harold Newman.** The firm is primarily engaged in the distribution and sale of recorders and music for recorder some of which is published by Hargail (see Music Publishers). Hargail also manufactures the *Harvard* plastic recorder. Its importation activities include being sole U.S. selling agent for the *Küng* (Swiss), *Coolsma* (Dutch), *Purcell* (German), and *Corelli* (German) recorders. It is the Eastern U.S. distributor for the *Rokkomann–Hargail Do-It-Yourself* guitar kit. Sells both wholesale and mail order retail.

THE HARRIS–FANDEL CO., INC., 200 First Avenue, Needham, Massachusetts 02194. Tel.: (617) 444–3910. Founded 1937. A subsidiary of Grossman Music Corporation since 1969. President: **Martin Harris.** Subsidiary: Electric Guitar Cable Co., located at the same address. Importers, wholesale distributors of musical instruments and accessories. Among brand names handled are: *Aria–Diamond, Black Jack, Eko, Fandel* guitars (imported); *Rosita* strings; *Kay* guitars and basses; *Jordan* amplifiers; *Supro* guitars and amplifiers; *Hilgen* amplifiers; *JeNco* mallet percussion; *Premier* drums; *Zildjian* cymbals; *Gregory* amplifiers; *Gretsch* strings and drumsticks; Oscar Schmidt *Autoharps;* and many more standard domestic and foreign brands.

HARRIS–TELLER, INC., 56 West 103rd Street, Chicago, Illinois 60628. Tel.: (312) 785–0700. Founded circa 1938 as Henry Teller & Son; present name and new owners since 1967. President: **Edward Harris.** Secretary: **Michael Harris.** Importers and wholesale distributors of musical instruments and accessories. Among the products handled are: *Beverly* drums and cymbals from England; sitars and tablas from India; *Vivant* drums and amplifiers from Japan; *Noble* accordions from Italy; *Nobility* accordions from Germany.

L. D. HEATER MUSIC COMPANY, 1975 S.E. Allen Avenue, Beaverton, Oregon 97005. Tel.: (503) 646–8121. Cable: LYLECO. Branch office: 306 Second Avenue West, Seattle, Washington 98119. Founded 1917. Since 1966, a division of the Chicago Musical Instrument Company. President: **Lyle D. Heater.** Vice-President: **C. J. Wolf.** A wholly owned subsidiary is The Lyle Corporation. The firm is a wholesale distributor covering 11 Western states and also exports to Pacific countries. Music merchandise sold is that of some 100 manufacturers including the manufacturing subsidiaries of the Chicago Musical Instrument Company.

M. HOHNER, INC., Andrews Road, Hicksville, Long Island, N.Y. 11802. Tel.: (516) WE 5–8500. Cable: HOHNER HICKSVILLE NY. Factory is located in Trossingen, West Germany. Firm founded in Germany in 1857. Branch office: 790 San Antonio Road, Palo Alto, California 94303, and 1742 Armitage Court, Addison, Illinois 60101. President: **Frank Hohner.** National Sales Manager: **Galen E. Stine.** All products are manufactured in Germany. The American company is thus an importer and distributor of *Hohner* instruments. The *Hohner* line includes harmonicas, melodicas (a mouth wind keyboard instrument), accordions, portable electric organs, and other electronic instruments. The firm also distributes *Sonor* drums, *Echolette* portable sound reproduction equipment, *Contessa* guitars, and various educational percussive instruments. The firm is particularly noted for its manufacture of harmonicas, of which it makes some 260 models. Sales are wholesale.

IDEAL INSTRUMENT COMPANY, 889 Broadway, New York, N.Y. 10003. Tel.: (212) GR 7–0130. Cable: IDEALMUSIC. Founded 1952. A division of Ideal Musical Merchandise Company at the same address. President: **Jack Loeb.** Secretary-Treasurer: **Kate Loeb.** Importers of musical instruments and accessories; exclusive importers of products from Czechoslovakia. Items imported are *Artia* instruments and accessories; *Cerveny* and *Lidl* rotary valve instruments; *Tatra* classic guitars; *Meyer* clarinets, oboes, and bassoons;

Riedl bassoons; *Cremona* string instruments; *Lignatone* guitars and mandolins, *Sonorex* accordions and concertinas; *Berg Larsen* reeds; *Ideal* guitars, drums, and accessories; *Porto-Organs; Concord/Benelux* band instruments; *Pfretzschner* string instruments. Wholesale only.

KANSAS MUSIC CO., 228 North Market Street, Wichita, Kansas 67202. Tel.: (316) AM 4–6516. Founded 1925. President: **Henry M. Puls.** Wholesale distributor of musical instruments and accessories. Handles a large number of domestic and foreign brands. Exclusive distributor of *Star* drums, timpani, and banjo heads, *Criterion* instruments and reeds, *Peerless* woodwinds, *Trovatone* fretted instruments and strings, among others.

K & K MUSICAL INSTRUMENT CO., INC., 5 Union Square West, New York, N.Y. 10003. Tel.: (212) AL 5–7285. Founded 1945. President: **Robert Q. Diamond.** Treasurer: **Max Freedman.** Importers and distributors of musical instruments and accessories. Some of the brands handled including those on an exclusive agency basis are: *Victory* brass instruments; *Regent; Cortez* electric and acoustic guitars; *Dynamic* band instruments, guitars, and amplifiers; *Melofonic, Jean Bussion, Kay* guitars and mandolins; and others. Sells wholesale and offers repair services.

LA PLAYA DISTRIBUTING CO., 3725 Woodward Avenue, Detroit, Michigan 48201. Tel.: (313) 831–5440. Cable: LAPLAYA. Importers and distributors. Exclusive distributors of the following brands: *Crestwood* guitars, *Starlight* drums, drum accessories, *La Playa* Latin-American musical instruments, *Belcrest* band instruments. Wholesale only.

LEBAN IMPORTS, INC., 2315 Hollins Street, Baltimore, Maryland 21223. Tel.: (301) 945–0212/6612. Cable: LEBAN-PORTS, BALTIMORE. Founded 1960 (incorporated in 1967). President: **Ralph C. Levy.** Vice-President: **Michael Leban.** Importers and wholesale distributors. The sole importing and distributing agency for *Leban* guitars and accessories, *Leban* drums and accessories and *Club Date* drums. Other brands are handled including *Teisco* microphones, *Straton* trumpets, *Rampone* band instruments, and *Ariana* classic guitars.

LIMMCO, INC., 98 Tec Street, Hicksville, N.Y. 11801. Tel.: (516) 681–0006. Cable: LIMMCO HICKSVILLE NY. Founded 1964. President: **R. Seidman.** Vice-President: **F. Rose.** Manufacturers of *Nomad* and *Kimberly* brand amplifiers. Main activity is the importation of musical instruments from Japan and England particularly drums, guitars, and portable organs. Sales are mail-order wholesale only.

MAURICE LIPSKY MUSIC CO., INC., 30 Irving Place, New York, N.Y. 10003. Tel.: (212) 673–4300. Cable: MISTAMUSIC. Founded 1935. Officers are **Maurice Lipsky** and **Jack Lipsky.** Manufacturers, importers, distributors, and wholesalers of a large number of musical instruments and accessories. Manufacturers of *Plush* musical products; selling agents for *Domino* guitars, *Olivieri* reeds, *Harmony* guitars, banjos, ukuleles, mandolins, *Supro* guitars, *Orpheum* guitars, amplifiers, *Elettra* accordions. Other brands handled are *Louis Schild* string instruments, *Berkley* hand instruments, and *Jewel* drums. Wholesale only.

LO DUCA BROS. MUSICAL INSTRUMENTS, INC., 3034 West Walnut Street, Milwaukee, Wisconsin 53208. Tel.: (414) 344–5410. Cable: ELLEDIA. Founded 1940. President: **Thomas S. Lo Duca.** Vice-President: **Guy Lo Duca.** Subsidiary firm: Eko Sales Division. Manufacturer, importer, and wholesaler. Manufactures *Lo Duca* chord organs and musical instrument cases and amplifiers. Importers and selling agents of *Lo Duca* accordions (designed and assembled in the U.S.; manufactured in Italy), *Eko* guitars (made in Italy), *Duke* drums, *Commander* cases, *Eko/Triumph* amplifiers (made in England), *Eko* strings, *Galli* strings (Italy). Wholesale only.

MAXWELL MEYERS, INC., 830 East Houston Street, San Antonio, Texas 78205. Tel.: (512) CA 7–0211. Since 1965, a division of Targ & Dinner, Inc. (q.v.). The firm handles the combined catalogues of both its own and the parent firm. (For a partial indication of items handled see Targ & Dinner, this section.)

MERSON MUSICAL PRODUCTS CORPORATION, 33 Frost Street, Westbury, N.Y. 11590. Tel.: (516) 333–9100. Cable: ACCORDIM. Founded 1946. President: **Ernest J. Briefel.** Executive Vice-President: **Sidney Hack.** Branch offices: 2182 North Lewis Avenue, Portland, Oregon 97217; 570 West 53 Place, Denver, Colorado 80204; 771 Burlway Road, Burlingame, California 94010; 7800 West Park Drive, Houston, Texas 77001. A division of Unicord, Incorporated (q.v.), a subsidiary of Gulf & Western Industries, Inc. Merson is a distributor of music merchandise including products manufactured by Unicord. Brands and items handled include: *Hagstrom* guitars (electric, bass, classic, etc.); *Giannini* classic and folk guitars; *Univox* electric guitars and amplifiers; *Unicord/Panther* portable organs; *Tempo* guitars, drums; *Marshall* amplifiers; *Univox* amplifiers; *Thibouville Frères* woodwinds; *Warner* brass instruments. Repairing and servicing is offered for the firm's products. Wholesale only.

MUSIC DISTRIBUTORS, INC., 2106 East Independence Boulevard, Charlotte, North Carolina 28205. Tel.: (704) 377–3694. Founded 1964. President: **J. N. Tillman.** Secretary: **Gloria Faye Tillman.** Distributors of musical merchandise, mainly throughout some nine Southern states. Handles national brands. Wholesale only.

NEWARK MUSICAL MERCHANDISE CO., 472 Broad Street, Newark, N.J. 07102. Tel.: (201) 642–3331. Founded 1948. President: **Armond Ciarfella.** Importers and wholesale distributors of general musical merchandise. Exclusive foreign brands include: *Yamaha* guitars, band instruments, and drums; *Suzuki* guitars, *Bernini* accordions; *Schiller, DiLeo, Duray* band instruments; *Drumcraft* drums. Domestic brands include: *American Plating, Carpenter, Harmon, Atlas, Herco, Trophy, Elton, Walberg & Auge, Camco,* and *Micro* accessories; **Oscar Schmidt *Autoharps, Kratt* harmonicas,** *JeNco, Kitching* mallet instruments, among others.

PENNINO MUSIC CO., INC., 1732 West Washington Boulevard, Los Angeles, California 90007. Tel.: (213) RE 5–1621. Founded 1947. President: **Jeannette Banoczi.** Secretary: **Evelyna Boulay.** Wholesale distributors of a large number of foreign and domestic standard brands of musical merchandise. Among the brands handled on an exclusive basis are: *Yamaha* band instruments and drums; *Slingerland* drums; *Deagan* and *Jenkins* (*JeNco*) mallet percussion; *Pierre Mauré* flutes, piccolos, clarinets, and saxophones; *Getzen* brass instruments.

J. M. SAHLEIN MUSIC COMPANY, INC., 1174 Howard Street, San Francisco, California 94103. Tel.: (415) 621–0626. Cable: JULSALEN. Founded 1919. Wholesalers and distributors of general musical merchandise. Western U.S. distributors of the following brands and products: *Premier* drums, *Gregory* amplifiers, *Olivieri* reeds, *Cabart* oboes and flutes; *J. Heinrich Hammig* and *Rudolf Buchner* violins, violas, and cellos; *Hofner,* and *Hausmann* violins, cellos and basses; *Leedy* drums and timpani; *Hohner* harmonicas and accordions, *Merano* accordions, *Chapelain* woodwinds; *Karl Hauser, Supro, Harmony, Kay, Crest,* and *Granada* guitars; *Carlton* brass instruments, *Paesold* bows, *André Revan* saxophones and clarinets.

ST. LOUIS MUSIC SUPPLY CO., 1400 Ferguson Avenue, St. Louis, Missouri 65133. Tel.: (314) 727–4512. Founded 1922. Subsidiary: Musical Products Corporation President: **Bernard Kornblum.** Importers. manufacturers, and distributors of general music merchandise. Brands handled include: *Orsi* band instruments, made in Italy; *Apollo* drums and accessories, guitars, and chord organs; *René Dumont* woodwinds; string instruments made by *Conrad Heberlein* and *Karl Knilling,* both brands made in Germany; *G. Mueller* flutes; *Pioneer* band instruments. The firm also sells rare, old violins. Wholesale sales only.

SCOTT MUSIC SUPPLY, INC., P.O. Box 36, 500 South Grand, Monroe, Louisiana 71201. Tel.: (318) 325–1724. Founded 1965. The firm is headed by the owners, **Jack Dew** and **Joseph Wollam.** Wholesale distributors of musical merchandise. Brands include *Scott* band instruments; *Conn* band instrument accessories; *Holton* accessories; *Yamaha* band instruments, guitars, and drums; *Kapa* guitars, and others.

SORKIN MUSIC COMPANY, INC., 370 Motor Parkway, Hauppauge, Long Island, N.Y. 11787. Tel.: (516) 231–7700. Cable: LOUISORKIN. Founded 1914. President: **Harold Sorkin.** Vice-President: **Joseph Saltzman.** Distributors and importers of musical instruments and accessories. Brands handled include: *Hofner* guitars, *Multivox* electric organs (see Multivox Corporation of America, this section), *Ace Tone* electric portable organs, *Kohlert* woodwinds, *Bohm–Meinl* brass instruments (the foregoing are foreign-made); *Premier* electric guitars and amplifiers, *Marvel* guitars and amplifiers, *Strad-O-Lin* guitars and mandolins, and other products. The firm engages in instrument and accessories repair and service. Wholesale only.

SOUTHLAND MUSICAL MERCHANDISE CORPORATION, P.O. Box 6125, Greensboro, North Carolina 27405. Offices and facilities are located at 826 Winston Street in Greensboro. Tel.: (919) 279–7319. President: **Harry Greenberg.** Executive Vice-President: **Lee Ingber.** Importers, distributors, and wholesalers of musical merchandise. The firm handles many national standard brands; its own lines include: *Marathon* brass instruments, string instruments, drums and accessories, woodwinds, and electric guitars; *Paul Jarman* brass and woodwind instruments; *Remington* brass and woodwinds; *Grenier* woodwinds; *Melodier* brass, string, and woodwind instruments; *Cortley* and *Le Coultré* woodwinds; *Southern* string instruments; *Dixie Leader* string instruments. Other brands are: *Harmony, Kay, Hohner, Gibson, Fender, Leedy, Yamaha, Goya, Sony,* etc. Sales are wholesale only.

STRUM & DRUM, INC., 177 West Hintz Road, Wheeling, Illinois 60090. Tel.: (312) 537–7777. Acquired firm is the former Don Noble and Co., Inc. Importers and wholesale distributors of musical merchanise bearing the brand name of *Norma* and *National.* The lines include electric and acoustic guitars, amplifiers, guitar strings, ukuleles, mandolins, drums, accessories.

FULVIO TALSO INCORPORATED, 381 Park Avenue South, New York, N.Y. 10016. Tel.: (212) 683–2346. Cable: FULVIOTAL. Founded 1939; incorporated 1967. President: **Andrew Pappalardo.** Importers and manufacturers' representative of the following foreign-made products: *Prestini* reeds and pads; *Roma* and *Marinucci* accordions; *Rampone & Cazzani* brass and woodwind instruments; guitars and accessories.

TARG & DINNER, INC., 4100 West 40th Street, Chicago, Illinois 60032. Tel.: (312) 384–6200. Cable: TARDIN. Founded 1920. Since 1971, a division of the Harmony Company. President: **Edward A. Targ.** Executive Vice-President: **Fred Targ.** Secretary: **Solomon Dinner.** Divisional firm: Maxwell Meyers, Inc., 830 East Houston Street, San Antonio, Texas 78205. (Tel.: (512) CA 7–0211.) (q.v.) Additional facilities include a warehouse–shipping plant at 1290 Collier Road, N.W., Atlanta, Georgia 30318. Importers and wholesale distributors of musical merchandise. The company is one of the largest distributors in the music field. The combined lines handled by Targ & Dinner and the Maxwell Myers firms consist of a large number of brands including the following domestic items: *Aztec* music paper, *Billotti Trinome* (metronome), *Blessing* band instruments, *Martineaux* flutes and piccolos, *Don Sellers* record course, *Jensen* recorders (now *Olenick*), *Olympian* mouthpieces, *Burton* harpsichords. Foreign items include: *Martin Busine* brass and woodwind instruments, *Jean Cartier* clarinets and oboes, *Jan Kriml* string instruments, *Dolnet* saxophones and clarinets, *Maynard Ferguson* mouthpieces, *Goya* guitars, *Olympian* band instruments and recorders, *Princetti* accordions. The firm also offers instrument and accessories repairing and servicing. Wholesale only.

TELE-STAR MUSICAL INSTRUMENT CORPORATION, 651 Broadway, New York, N.Y. 10012. Tel.: (212) 674–4900. Cable:

TERSTARTRAD. Founded 1962. President: **Maurice Laboz.** Subsidiary firms: Tele-Star Trading Corp., Music-Craft Electronics. Importers and distributors of musical instruments and accessories. Brands handled are: *Tele-Star* electric portable organs, melodicas (mouth wind keyboard instruments), drums and drum sets, Latin American rhythm instruments, some brass instruments, clarinets, saxophones, recorders, harmonicas, accordions, banjos, mandolins, violins, violas, cellos, and string basses, ukuleles, microphones, guitars, amplifiers; *La Boz* drum sets and practice accessories, classic guitars; some items sold under the name of *Music-Craft.* Wholesale only.

20TH CENTURY MUSIC (formerly Mexican Traders, Inc.), 7510 N. Ashland Avenue, Chicago, Illinois 60626. Tel.: (312) 338–8900. Founded 1954. President: **Gilbert G. Fernandez.** The firm imports musical merchandise which is distributed internationally and acts as Midwest distributor for certain domestic products. Importers of the *Azteca* brand (Mexico) of congas, bongos, claves, castinets, etc. Distributes *Teisco, Kingston,* and *Matador* guitars and drums. Wholesale only.

U.S. MUSICAL MERCHANDISE CORPORATION, 860 Broadway, New York, N.Y. 10003. Tel.: (212) OR 4–3100. Cable: MUSICALUS. Founded 1947. President: **Carl Davidoff.** Vice-President: **Sidney Schneider.** Importers and exclusive distributors of *Sekova* guitars, strings, drum accessories, and other products. National standard brands are also handled by the firm including: *Hohner* harmonicas, *Blessing* band instruments, *Brilhart* mouthpieces and reeds, *Emil Lyon* woodwinds, *Sonata* recorders, and others. Wholesale only.

VOLKWEIN BROS., INC., 117 Sandusky Street, Pittsburgh, Pennsylvania 15212. Tel.: (412) 322–5100. Founded 1888. President: **Carl R. Volkwein.** Distributors of standard brands of musical merchandise (see also Music Publishers). Lines handled include: *Vincent Bach* mouthpieces, *Buffet–Crampon* clarinets, *Ciccone* reeds, *Gibson* strings, *Geib* cases, *Harmony* instruments, *Hohner* instruments, *Kratt* products, *Krut* cymbals, *Micro* products, *Remo* drum heads, *Slingerland* drums, *Yamaha* musical instruments, and many others. Sales are both wholesale and retail.

WESTHEIMER IMPORTING & MFG. COMPANY, INC., 1331 South Michigan Avenue, Chicago Illinois 60605. Tel.: (312) WE 9–0913. Cable: WESURP. Founded 1959. President: **Jack Westheimer.** Vice-President: **Max Wasserman.** Importers of musical merchandise bearing the firm's own brand name: *Kingston.* Products include guitars, drum sets, microphones, and other items made in Japan and elsewhere in the Orient. Distributes to music jobbers.

DAVID WEXLER & CO., 823 South Wabash Avenue, Chicago, Illinois 60605. Tel.: (312) 427–0560. Cable: DAVEWEXCO. Founded 1943. President: **David Wexler.** Executive Vice-President: **Bernard Roy Wexler.** One of the world's largest distributors of musical instruments, accessories, and general music merchandise. A large selection of national brands are handled by the firm, but the following represent brands handled by Wexler on an exclusive basis. Guitars: *Conrad, Wabash, Cordova, Harmony, Kay, Supro, Multikord; Haberline* violins, cellos, and basses; *Cortini* and *Helicon* accordions; *La Paree* wind instruments; various mallet percussion: *Vesta* vibraphones, *Tone Educator* bells, *Swiss Melode* bells, *Prelude* xylophones; *Hofner* and *Buchner* violins; *Whitehall* drums, chord and portable organs, and clarinets; *Leedy* drums; *Kohlert* wind instruments; *Picato, Red Dragon,* and *Mersey Beat* strings; *King David* batons, *Wesner* recorders, and such music-related products as tape recorders, music boxes and novelties, phonographs, piano lamps, metronomes, etc. In total, some 14,000 items are listed as available from the Wexler firm. All sales are wholesale.

WEYMANN COMPANY, 21 South 11th Street, Philadelphia, Pennsylvania 19107. Tel.: (215) MA 7–8191. Founded 1864. President: **Herbert W. Weymann.** Distributors of *Hohner* harmonicas, *Hamilton* music stands, *Black Diamond* and *Gibson* strings, *Seth Thomas* and *Franz* metronomes, *Harmony* fretted instruments, *Rico* and *Symmetricut* reeds, and other products. Sales are retail and wholesale.

WORLDWIDE MUSICAL INSTRUMENT CO., INC., 404 Park Avenue South, New York, N.Y. 10016. Tel.: (212) 679–3110. Cable: WORLDMUSIC. Founded 1944. President: **Morris Levine.** Importers and distributors of *Savarez* nylon guitar strings; *Herwiga, Alexander Heinrich* and *Concerto* recorders; *Lindholm* harpsichords (made in Germany); French horns with the brand names of *E. D. Kruspe, Walter Moennig, Hans Hoyer, Carl Wunderlich, Gebrüder Alexander; Adler–Sonora* and *Hüller* bassoons; *Grünert* cellos and string basses. Sales are wholesale only.

W.M.I. CORPORATION, 1228 Emerson Street, Evanston, Illinois 60201. Tel.: (312) 328–4588. Founded 1963. President: **Sylvain Weindling.** Vice-President: **Barry Hornstein.** Branch office: 2715 South Main Street, Los Angeles, California. Importers and distributors of *Teisco/Del Rey* guitars, *Teisco* combo organs, *Checkmate* organs and amplifiers, *Marlin* guitars, *Del Rey* drums. Wholesale only.

Music Industry Statistics

The following tables of statistics taken from the compilations of the U.S. Bureau of Census for the years 1967 and 1963 (1960, 1965, and 1968 for printed music exports and imports) are the most complete and recent available figures. They were published in 1971 (printed music figures in 1969). The growth of the music industry as a whole in the years since 1967 is a well-established fact, details of which are not yet available from government sources. However, some indication of the extent of music industry growth can be seen by the figures for sales in 1971 and 1970 compiled by the Recording Industry Association of America and the American Music Conference.

The statistics from the Bureau of Census were extracted from the publications cited and are grouped comparatively here for the first time. The grouping of music and music-related industries will make possible easier comparisons with other industry groups in the United States.

Manufacturers' Statistics, Industry Summaries, Music Related Industries, 1967.

		Establishments		All Employees		Production Workers		
Industry	Companies (No.)	Total No.	With 20 or More Employees	Number (in Thousands)	Payroll (in $ Million)	Number (in Thousands)	Man Hours (in Millions)	Wages (in $ Million)
Musical Instruments and Parts	304	343	121	24.9	143.7	20.8	39.9	106.0
Phonograph Records	306	321	73	13.6	766	11.0	22.2	54.0
Radio and TV Recording Equipment	604	661	260	130.2	720.1	107.2	205.6	516.6
Radio and TV Sets	303	341	187	116.7	643.6	96.2	183.4	462.6

Source: U.S. Department of Commerce, Bureau of the Census, *Census of Manufacturers: 1967,* Vol. I, *Summary and Subject Statistics,* 1971.

Music Industry Wholesalers with Payroll, 1967.

	Phonograph Records and Pre-recorded Tapes	Musical Instruments and Sheet Music
Number of Establishments	882	321
Sales (in $ Thousand)	$814,504	$206,276
End-year Inventories (at Cost)	$93,036	$35,938
Percentage of Operational Expenses to Sales	17.1	22.5
Payroll	$71,078	$26,120
Number of Proprietors	338	104

Source: U.S. Bureau of the Census, *Census of Business: 1967,* Vol. III, *Wholesale Trade Subject Reports,* 1971.

Wholesalers exported 1.2 percent of their sales of phonograph records and tapes; 2.9 percent of the sales of musical instrument and sheet music wholesalers were exports.

The largest percentage of sales by both groups of wholesalers were to other wholesalers and retailers. Direct-to-consumer sales were 1 percent for records and tapes and 1.9 percent for musical instruments and sheet music.

Value Added by Mfr. (in $ Million)	Value of Shipment	Capital Expenditures, New: Total (in $ Million)	Capital Expenditures, New: Add. to Plants (in $ Million)	Capital Expenditures, New: Machinery, Equip. (in $ Million)	Inventories, End of: 1967 (in $ Million)	Inventories, End of: 1966 (in $ Million)	Specialization Ratio, %	Coverage Ratio, %
237.8	434.3	10.6	5.4	5.2	123.6	118.6	97	98
182.3	276.4	7.1	1.1	6.0	38.7	38.6	99	96
1586.7	4122.7[1]	93.2	31.9	61.2	764.8	772.1	—	—
1404.5	3846.3	86.1	30.8	55.3	726.0	733.5	94	99

1. The total value of shipments for industry groups includes extensive duplication arising from shipments between establishments in the same industry classification.

Paid Employees and Payroll Entire Year in Retail Establishments by Kind of Business, U.S.A., 1967 and 1963.

	1967	1963	% Change
Radio, Television, and Music Stores*			
Total Paid Employees (Number)	75,088	54,862	36.9
Payroll Entire Year (in $ Thousand)	$366,961	$224,188	63.7
Percentage of Payroll to Sales	13	13.1	

*Categorized as one kind of business.

Source: U.S. Bureau of the Census, *Census of Business: 1967,* Vol. I, *Retail Trade Subject Reports,* 1971.

Sales, All U.S.A., 1967 and 1963.

	1967	1963	% Change
Sales (in $ Thousand)	$3,003,232	$1,712,809	75.3
Percentage of Total U.S. Retail Sales	1.0	0.7	

Source: U.S. Bureau of the Census, *Census of Business: 1967,* Vol. I, *Retail Trade Subject Reports,* 1971.

The 75.3 percent change showed the largest increase in sales over all other kinds of retail businesses; however, its share of the total retail sales (1% and 0.7% for 1967 and 1963) was low. The amount of increase for all U.S. retail sales of 1967 over 1963 was 27 percent.

Distribution of Products within Broad Merchandise Line by Selected Kinds of Business: 1963 and 1967.

Kind of Business (Product Name)	Sales (Number)		
	1963	1967	% Change
Household Appliance Stores:			
Major appliances, radios, TV's, and musical instruments (total)	1,671,378	2,229,418	33.4
New major appliances	1,245,273	1,747,531	40.3
New radios, TV's, etc.	362,049	430,619	18.9
Used major appliances, etc.	53,032	41,022	–22.6
Radio and TV stores:			
Major appliances, radios, etc. (total)	840,960	1,655,298	96.8
New major appliances	120,196	285,545	137.6
New radios, TV's, etc.	662,959	1,301,432	96.3
Used major appliances, radios, TV's	30,529	29,188	–4.4
Records, tapes, musical instruments	27,276	39,133	43.5
Department Stores:			
Major appliances, radios, TV's, and musical instruments (total)	1,521,723	2,625,738	72.6
Major household appliances	933,309	1,493,391	60.0
Radios, TV's, musical instruments	586,414	1,129,347	92.6

Source: U.S. Bureau of the Census, *Census of Business: 1967,* Vol. I, *Retail Trade Subject Reports,* 1971.

The above indicates what portion of the increase in sales of the broad category "major appliances, radios, TV's, musical instruments" is due to increased "major household appliance" sales and what portion is due to increased sales of "radios, TV's, musical instruments" for such retail outlets as "household appliance stores," "radio and TV stores," and "department stores." For example, the 72.6 percent increase in department store sales in these categories is due mainly to the 92.6 percent increase in sales of radios, TV's musical instruments, etc.

American Music Conference (AMC) Statistics: Retail Sales of Musical Instruments, Accessories, Sheet Music, and Self-instruction Aids, 1971, 1970, and 1960. (Includes products produced domestically and imports. Unit and dollar figures are of new instruments sold in the U.S. Exports not included. Dollar figures are estimates.)

	1971		1970		1960	
	Units	Dollars	Units	Dollars	Units	Dollars
Pianos	205,214	$178,741,000	193,814	$164,000,000	197,200	$148,650,000
Organs*	145,000	241,170,000	137,500	215,000,000	106,000	141,400,000
Fretted instruments and amplifiers	2,556,640	200,693,000	2,214,686	159,910,000	420,000	35,000,000
String instruments (e.g., violins, bows, cases)	51,138	12,989,000	75,700	19,720,000	40,600	7,300,000
Band instruments						
Woodwinds	303,000	68,902,000	304,000	66,150,000	241,000	45,300,000
Brass	218,000	51,644,000	225,000	51,000,000	153,000	29,700,000
Accordions, concertinas	21,800	5,100,000	31,800	6,400,000	100,000	18,000,000
Drums	NA	34,880,000	NA	32,000,000	NA	12,000,000
Miscellaneous (e.g., autoharps, chimes, harps, melody percussion)	—	79,304,000	—	78,509,000	—	—
Accessories	—	120,866,000	—	108,400,000	—	—
Sheet music	—	98,820,000	—	91,500,000	—	—
Self-instruction aids	—	13,230,000	—	12,250,000	—	—

*Organ figures for 1971 and 1970 include organs with a retail value of $500 and over.
NA = Not applicable. Blank columns indicate unavailable figures.

Manufacturers' Sales of Phonograph Records and Pre-Recorded Tapes. Recording Industry Association of America, Inc. Report of May, 1972.

	1970	1971
Sales (list price, combined records and tapes)	$1.660 billion	$1.744 billion (5% increase)
Records*	1.182 billion	1.251 billion (5.8% increase)
LP's alone*	1.017 billion	1.086 billion
Pre-recorded tapes	473 million	493 million (3% increase)
8-Track cartridges	378 million	385 million
Cassettes	77 million	96 million
Reel-to-reel tapes	18 million	12 million

*Increase in sales is partly due to the rise in list prices of a number of record companies in 1971.

The RIAA reports that a greater increase in tape sales was stunted by increasing piracy and counterfeiting activities, particularly of 8-track tapes, which cost the legitimate industry about $150 million in annual sales.

MUSIC PUBLISHING: EXPORTS AND IMPORTS

Value of Shipments of U.S. Exports of Printed Music, 1960, 1965, and 1968.

Country or Region of Destination	1968	1965	1960
Grand Total	$1,180,604	$978,850	$570,955
Canada	738,519	650,670	430,508
Latin America	12,846	20,424	3,637
Europe	355,954	—	—
Asia-Australia	58,391	59,936	46,420
Africa	14,894	7,132	505

Source: U.S. Department of Commerce, Business and Service Administration, *Printing and Publishing,* Quarterly Industry Report, July, 1969.

Value of Shipments of U.S. Imports of Printed Music, 1960, 1965, 1968.

Country or Region of Origin	1968	1965	1960
Grand Total	$414,590	$571,082	$266,463
Canada	24,585	8,294	2,058
Latin America	659	1,115	480
Europe	370,713	551,532	263,668
Asia-Australia	15,103	10,141	737
Africa	3,530	—	—

Source: U.S. Department of Commerce, Business and Service Administration, *Printing and Publishing,* Quarterly Industry Report, July, 1969.

Imports for 1966 are not comparable with earlier years because of changes in classifications. Low-valued shipments have been omitted in the above tables.

Canada, the United Kingdom, Australia, New Zealand, and the Republic of South Africa received about 88 percent of all U.S. printed matter exports in 1968. Imported music comes largely from the United Kingdom, West Germany, France, Hungary, Italy, and Japan.

The figures shown in the following table are in the thousands of dollars. Totals include exports from 14 nations: United States, Belgium–Luxembourg, Austria, Canada, Denmark, France, West Germany, Italy, Japan, Netherlands, Norway, Sweden, Switzerland, and the United Kingdom. The source of the statistics is the United Nations Statistical Office.

Export Data of the World's Largest Exporters of Printed Music, 1962–1967.

	Totals	U.S.	W. Germany	U.K.	France	Netherlands	Austria	Denmark	Sweden
1962	$2,193	$ 519	$ 831	$344	$ 85	$160	$ 87	$71	$14
1963	2,296	511	839	367	94	121	92	91	26
1964	2,580	741	915	397	77	104	90	88	15
1965	3,072	979	1,086	392	97	124	117	99	16
1966	3,312	1,033	1,309	352	74	120	135	53	33
1967	3,242	851	1,363	319	148	145	122	57	43

West Germany is the world's largest exporter of printed music; the United States is second largest. The United Kingdom, the United States, and West Germany are among the prime purchasers of each other's music publications.

Part 12 Music Periodicals

It is impossible to discuss music periodicals categorically. Singly they can be erudite, perfunctory, technical, simple, literary, journalistic; they can aim for the mass of amateurs or the corps of professionals, the teacher, the performer, the listener, the composer, the merchant, or the consumer. Some periodicals can be purchased off the magazine stands; others are rarely seen by any except librarians, editors, administrators, and researchers. In short, they reflect most precisely—as no other communications medium can—the multiformity of musical interests and participation in this country. Neither radio, television, phonograph records, nor live concerts can entirely exhibit or cater to these interests and the nuances existing within them.

A large percentage of music publications are organized without profit motivation. Some have become indispensable sources of information and their continued existence is a compliment to the determination and dedication of publishers and editors. Most periodicals with five or more issues a year can survive, albeit precariously in some instances, if their circulation runs from 15,000 to 70,000. This is the broad median range, and it is not occupied by one type of periodical only. Included in this group are: *Music Educators Journal, Diapason, Instrumentalist, Harmonizer, Music Journal, American Record Guide, Billboard,* and *American Music Teacher.*

Periodicals with circulation below 15,000 include many specialized publications with quarterly or annual distribution. Newsletters, bulletins, and other official organs of musical groups fall into this category. Publications distributed to members only have per se limited circulation, as do magazines circulated mainly to institutions such as libraries and schools. Highly specialized magazines such as *Brass and Woodwind Quarterly* and *American Music Teacher* are conceived in and thrive on exclusivism, are tailored within predetermined and nearly fixed budgets and editorial policies, and seemingly do not overextend themselves economically. Many such periodicals have hardy histories and intensely loyal subscribers. None have glamor appeal, but as a unit they are the quintessence of the very notion of American musical diversity. Among them are *Notes* (3,150), *Accordion and Guitar World* (3,500), *American String Teacher* (3,800), *Fretts* (8,200), *Hymn* (2,000), *Jazz Report* (2,500), *Journal of Church Music* (4,218), *Journal of Music Therapy* (1,650), *The Music Trades* (7,200), *Musical Merchandise Review* (11,500), *Musical Quarterly* (5,500), *National Association of Teachers of Singing Bulletin* (3,300), and *Sing Out!* (15,000).

Judging from the circulation figures made available, only seven of the periodicals in the listings rank at the top. (The *Schwann Catalog* has no subscription plan; a widely distributed publication, it nevertheless falls outside the category of circulated magazines under discussion.) Appealing to readers with a broad interest in the arts, *Bravo* magazine, a quarterly, has a distribution of 500,000 concertgoers. Music is stressed in articles and photographs, and famous performers, conductors, and singers are covered in feature stories.

The *Saturday Review,* a magazine which covered politics, social trends, education, literature, and the lively arts, gave a great deal of space to record reviews, special articles in conjunction with new records, and other articles of topical value in the music world. Its high circulation must be considered in the light of its varied contents. What percentage of the circulation was drawn by the magazine's musical content is probably an unknown factor. It can be said, however, that the music section of the *Saturday Review* was of great importance to the magazine in view of its prominence.

The *International Musician* is distributed for 60 cents a year to members in good standing of the American Federation of Musicians. It can therefore claim a paid circulation of 260,000. A combination labor–trade–professional journal, it deals with much information of use to practicing musicians regardless of their specialty. All union business is disseminated through the publication. *Opera News,* with its 85,000 subscribers, is testimony to the steady interest in this branch of music. This Metropolitan Opera Guild publication is a companion, during the season, to the live Saturday afternoon broadcasts of opera performances coming from the stage of the Metropolitan Opera House. It is a standard guide for opera lovers in this country.

Among the most popular music magazines are those primarily devoted to the world of recordings and recording equipment and which additionally offer attractively written articles for the well-cultivated listener, the intelligent neophyte, and sometimes for the professional musician. Since the experience of listening to recorded music can be shared on a mass-scale basis, in the same manner as movies or television, record reviews and the concomitant shoptalk engender wide reader interest. Both *Stereo Review* and *High Fidelity* magazine are eminent examples of popularly directed publications of this kind in America. They claim respectively 300,000 and 252,000 in circulation.

Almost all music magazines now contain record reviews. The reviews found in specialized magazines are usually those most pertinent to the publication. *Harmonizer* (barbershop quartet performances), *Clavier, Opera News, Choral Journal,* and others, all follow this pattern.

Most publications cannot match the utility of periodicals having omnibus contents, that is, reviews of live concerts in metropolitan centers, schools, and festivals in this country and abroad; record, book, and published music reviews and notices; educational news, items on the activities of performers, composers, conductors; editorials, photographs, pedagogical columns, concert management bookings, and feature articles on anything from recollections of prima donnas to the discussion of acoustics.

Musical America, Music Journal, Music & Artists, and *International Musician* all have varied approaches to the omnibus format. *Musical America,* as did the defunct *Musical Courier,* uses a string of correspondents in key cities of the United States and overseas. The work of the correspondents is mainly that of reviewing live concerts. In the *Musical Journal* and the *International Musician* this is not a main feature. *Down Beat* is the jazz counterpart of *Musical America* in the field of magazines with omnibus contents. However, in recent years, almost all general contents magazines have made concessions in both directions: popular music or jazz-oriented publications have included articles on classical music, and periodicals with long histories of serving the classical music field now admit reviews of jazz books, rock books, records, the Broadway theater, and folk music.

With the exception of some newsletters and bulletins, most publications carry paid advertising from the music industries, allied fields, and individuals. The kind of advertising accepted is usually in keeping with the purpose of the magazine. *Musical America,* and a few others, rely a great deal on personal artist-teacher ads, concert management rosters of artists, and school advertisements, with sometimes a back or inside front cover devoted to a piano or organ advertisement. The scholarly *Musical Quarterly* and *Notes* magazine include ads on published music and books and select record releases. *School*

Musician, Music Journal, Instrumentalist, and *International Musician* carry much advertising for band and orchestral instruments and accessory items. *Music Trades* and *Musical Merchandise Review* are almost totally given over to advertising instruments, accessories, and sheet music. Written columns elsewhere in these publications sometimes are virtually other forms of advertising. *Saturday Review's* music advertising ran from records to recorders, but the entire publication was sustained by a variety of clients, as is *Bravo,* which has carried ads for cigarettes and live sea horses.

From the breathless tone and weekly flash of *Variety* to the somnolent and annual *Musica Disciplina,* American music followers have as much reading contrast as is possible to attain in one field. Here one can see the moiling world of music as a speculative ingredient in entertainment commerce, or music as an art-science in the service of a kind of paleontology. Whereas the former publication uses the sometimes cryptic vocabulary of show business, the latter will not hesitate to print entire articles in Latin, Italian, or German. Both, therefore, manage a form of exclusivism.

In between the extremes are the multiple approaches to a field so uniquely open it may be viewed at once as hobby, profession, national resource, or business, serving the home, concert hall, church, or juke box.

The *National Music Council Bulletin, Symphony News* of the American Symphony Orchestra League, *International Musician,* the editorials of *Musical America,* and *Music Journal* and others reach out to feel the pulse of what is ailing or well in American musical life and are quick to suggest treatment when the former condition prevails. The *Musical Quarterly, Perspectives of New Music,* and others try to keep the work and thought of American composers on steady parade before what is felt to be a still unaware public.

The *American Music Teacher, Music Educators Journal, American String Teacher,* the *Instrumentalist, Piano Quarterly,* the *Piano Technicians' Journal,* and others speak directly to select groups on mostly professional questions that cannot be taken up in like manner by other publications. That the substance of music itself—sound—can be viewed from different angles is implied merely by the names of the *Journal of Music Theory, Journal of the Acoustical Society of America,* and the *Journal of Aesthetics and Art Criticism.*

Finer subdivisions and contrasts go on: the *Journal of Ethnomusicology* may not necessarily appeal to the reader of *Sing Out! Fretts* manages to find a different audience from *Guitar Review.* With the impressive array of publications confronting him in America, the critic, musicologist, performer, teacher, and free-lancer is inspired to give literary vent to his interests. Among them: **H. C. Robbins Landon, Paul Henry Lang, Glenn Gould, Gilbert Chase, R. D. Darrell, Robert C. Marsh, Martin Bookspan, Eric Salzman, David Hall, Nat Hentoff, John S. Wilson, Leonard Feather,** to mention a very few, have written for a variety of publications. Established critics sometimes move from their regular base of operation, be it newspaper or magazine, to write reviews or feature articles for another publication. **Alfred Frankenstein, Roger Dettmer, Martin Mayer, Irving Kolodin, Donal Henahan, Michael Steinberg, Paul Hume,** and **Harold C. Schonberg** can be cited in this regard.

Musicologists occasionally find outlets other than those normally suited for their special work. Much of their investigative and analytical writing is found in the *Musical Quarterly, Musica Disciplina, Journal of Music Theory, Journal of the American Musicological*

Society and the *Journal of Ethnomusicology.* However, certain among them are found reviewing books, published scores, or recordings for *High Fidelity, Notes, Musical America,* and other periodicals. **Paul Henry Lang, Karl Geiringer, Bruno Nettl, Robert Stevenson, Gibert Chase, Donald J. Grout, Irving Lowens, Charles Warren Fox,** and **Willi Apel** have been some such writers.

Many magazines give small or no remuneration for submitted articles even in cases where the publication has a definite commercial format attracting advertising revenue. Official organs receive most manuscript contributions from member-subscribers who use the publications as forums for ideas, research papers, and so on, and authors are therefore rewarded in this way. On the other hand, top-circulation magazines will give good to excellent compensation for well-written manuscripts. The more famous the writer, of course, the greater the payment.

Current and future researchers should feel no lack of sources for following and studying America's musical growth in the present era. The periodicals below, and some now extinct, provide ample opportunity for study. To make the task simpler, INFORMATION COORDINATORS, INC., 1435–1437 Randolph Street, Detroit, Michigan 48226, has published since 1949 *The Music Index,* in an *Annual Cumulation* in book form, plus monthly pamphlets. (The cost is $345 for the yearly service.) It lists alphabetically, by author and subject matter, articles from a large number of American and foreign periodicals. The difficulty of preparing the *Index* can be seen by the length of time needed to weed through the current literature. Generally, the annual *Index* is approximately three years behind, and the monthly issues are a year behind.

Other source material publications are *Music Article Guide,* and the *Quarterly Check-List of Musicology, RILM Abstracts,* and, for recordings, *Polart Index to Record Reviews.*

Most of the following periodicals have national circulation. Wherever necessary, the organization responsible for the publication is listed after the name of the periodical. For official organs, bulletins, and newsletters not listed here consult the list of musical organizations. Subscription prices are given in order of domestic (including the U.S. territories) and foreign (F) rates on the basis of annual subscription unless otherwise stated. Subscription prices for Canada (C) sometimes coincide with the domestic rates, at other times with foreign rates. In some cases there are special Canadian rates.

ACCORDION & GUITAR WORLD, 20 Hessian Drive, Ridgefield, Connecticut 06877. Founded in 1936. Published by Gerstner Printers and Publishers. Editor: **John C. Gerstner.** Bi-monthly. Circulation: 3,500. Subscription rates: $3, $3.50 (C), $4 (F).

AFTER DARK, The Magazine of Entertainment, 10 Columbus Circle, New York, N.Y. 10019. Founded in 1960 as *Ballroom Dance Magazine,* expanded into a magazine with broad coverage of the entertainment fields (theater, opera, dance, films, television, popular music, cabarets, etc.) beginning with the May 1968 issue. Publisher: **Jean Gordon;** Editor: **William Como.** Monthly. Circulation: 16,000. Rates: $8 (also C), $10 (F).

AMERICAN CHORAL REVIEW (American Choral Foundation, Inc.), 130 West 56th Street, New York, N.Y. 10019. Founded 1958. Editor: **Alfred Mann.** Quarterly. Circulation:

1,500. Rates: $7.50 (minimum membership dues); single issue: $1.75. Articles, many of scholarly bent, cover points of professional interest to choral conductors. Some issues are in fact monographs: "Choral Performances 1968–1969," "The Choral Music of Beethoven," by Elliot Forbes, "American Panoramas of Twentieth Century Music," by Hans Nathan, "The Anthems of Henry Purcell," by Franklin B. Zimmerman, "The Choral Conductor," by Kurt Thomas (an English language adaptation from the German).

AMERICAN COMPOSERS ALLIANCE BULLETIN (American Composers Alliance), 170 West 74th Street, New York, N.Y. 10023. Founded in 1938. This periodical expired in 1965. Back issues, valuable for information about ACA composers, are still available at 50 cents a copy.

AMERICAN MUSIC TEACHER (Music Teachers National Association), 1831 Carew Tower, Cincinnati, Ohio 45202. Founded May, 1951. Editor: **Homer Ulrich.** Published six times during the academic year. Circulation: 14,786. Rates: $4, $5.50 (F). Single copy: 75 cents. Sent free to members of MTNA.

THE AMERICAN ORGANIST, One Union Square West, New York, N.Y. 10003. Founded January, 1918. Published by Organ Interests, Inc. Editor: **Charles Bradley.** Bimonthly. Circulation: 4,000. Rates: $5 (also C and F).

THE AMERICAN RECORD GUIDE (Incorporating The American Tape Guide), P.O. Box 319, Radio City Station, New York, N.Y. 10019. Founded May, 1935 as *The American Music Lover;* given its present name in 1944. It is the oldest record review periodical in America. Editor and Publisher (since 1957): **James Lyons.** Monthly. Circulation: 44,000. Rates: $6, $6.50 (Pan American Republics), $7 (all other foreign).

AMERICAN STRING TEACHER (American String Teacher Association); Subscription address: **Robert C. Marince,** Lawrence Township Schools, 2596 Princeton Pike, Trenton, N.J. 08638. Editorial and advertising: **Anthony J. Messina,** 1745 Hannington Avenue, Wantagh, N.Y. 11793. Founded in 1950. Four issues a year. Circulation: 3,800. Rates (membership subscription): $6. Single copy: 85 cents.

BEST SONGS, Charlton Building, Derby, Connecticut 06418. Founded in 1955. Published by the Charlton Publishing Corp. Editor: **James Delehant.** Bi-monthly. Circulation: 100,000. Rates: $1.20, $1.50 (C), $1.80 (F). Single copy: 20 cents.

BILLBOARD, 165 West 46th Street, New York, N.Y. 10036. Founded in 1894. Published by Billboard Publications, Inc. of Cincinnati, Ohio, **Hal B. Cook,** New York publisher. Editor: **Lee Zhito;** Music Editor: **Paul Ackerman.** Covers these areas in the music field: marketing of phonograph records, playback equipment, musical instruments, music publications, radio and television, coin music-machine operators and distributors. Weekly. Circulation: 27,755. Publishes special annual buyer's guide. Annual rates: $30 (also C); foreign rates on request. *Annual Buyer's Guide:* $5.

BRASS AND WOODWIND QUARTERLY, Box 111, Durham, New Hampshire 03824. Founded in 1957. Publisher: Appleyard Publications. Editor: **Mary Rasmussen.** Irregularly published. Circulation: 1,000. Rates: $6.50; $2 single copy.

BRAVO, 485 Lexington Avenue, New York, N.Y. 10017. Founded October, 1961. Publisher and Editor: **Kenneth Boyer.** Issued four times a year during the concert season. A magazine of the performing arts, it is used as a concert program in halls throughout the country where there are subscription concerts. (Publication temporarily suspended for the 1972–73 and 1973–74 seasons.)

THE CHAUTAUQUAN, Chautauqua Institution, Chautauqua, N.Y. 14722. Published by the Institution. Two issues in January, three in February, one in March, one in April, two in May, and one in November. Distributed free upon request. Covers activities at the Institute.

THE CHORAL JOURNAL (American Choral Directors Association), P.O. Box 17736, Tampa, Florida 33612. Founded in 1958. Editor: **R. Wayne Hugoboom.** Sent to all members of the ACDA and nonmember subscribers. Covers, in addition to ACDA affairs, music, record, and book reviews pertinent to the choral field. Issued nine times a year, September through May. Circulation: 4,500. Rates: $4 (libraries only), $4.50 (C), $5 (F).

CHORD AND DISCORD (Bruckner Society of America, Inc.). Founded in 1932. Editor: **Charles L. Eble.** Editorial Address: P.O. Box 1171, Iowa City, Iowa 52240. Irregularly issued. Last issuc, as of this writing, was dated 1969. Next issue is proposed for 1973.

THE CHURCH MUSICIAN, 127 Ninth Avenue North, Nashville, Tennessee 37203. Founded in 1950. Published by the Sunday School Board of the Southern Baptist Convention. Editor: **William Reynolds.** Published monthly. Circulation: 30,000. Rates: $5.

CLAVIER, A Magazine for Pianists and Organists, 1418 Lake Street, Evanston, Illinois 60204. Published by the Instrumentalist Co., same address. First issue: March–April 1962. Editor: **Dorothy Packard.** Nine issues annually. Rates: $6; 60 cents additional for foreign and Canadian subscriptions. Circulation: 19,500.

COMPOSIUM, P.O. Box 65661, Los Angeles, California 90065. Published by the Crystal Record Company (same address). President and Editor: **Peter Christ.** First issue: January, 1970. Once a quarterly; suspended as such in 1973, but continues as an annual. Estimated circulation: 8,000. An ". . . index of contemporary [music] compositions," this publication is sent out to music schools and college libraries, conductors of major symphony orchestras, etc. Listings of new music, published and unpublished, are submitted in detail by the composer. Included is information as to where the music can be obtained (the composer himself, the publisher, etc.). An annual *Directory of New Music.* As a related publication, when the quarterlies were issued, it was made of the listings in the quarterly indexes for the year plus composers' biographies and cross-indexes. Price of the Directory: $3.95, soft cover, $5.95, hard cover, plus 35 cents for mailing.

CONSOLAIRE, World Library Publications, Inc., 2145 Central Parkway, Cincinnati, Ohio 45214. Published by the World Library of Sacred Music. First issued January, 1968. Contains organ music (3 stave—with pedal; see also *Manualiere*) intended to be performed with little or no practice by the average organist. Almost none of the music has been published previously. Some music commissioned specifically for the magazine. About eight works in each issue. Bi-monthly. Circulation: 500. Rates: $5, $6 (C). Single issue: $2.

COUNTRY & WESTERN HIT PARADE, Charlton Building, Derby, Connecticut. 06418. Founded 1947. Published by the Charlton Publishing Corp. Editor: **William Anderson.** Bi-monthly. Circulation: 50,000. Rates: $3, $3.75 (C), $4.50 (F). Single issue: 50 cents.

COUNTRY DANCE AND SONG (The Country Dance and Song Society of America), 55 Christopher Street, New York, N.Y. 10014. Editor: **James Morrison.** One issue annually supplemented by three issues of *CDSS News.* Membership subscription.

COUNTRY SONG ROUNDUP, Charlton Building, Derby, Connecticut 06418. Founded in 1947. Published by the Charlton Publishing Corp. Editor: **William T. Anderson.** Monthly. Circulation: 100,000. Rates: $3.50, $4.38 (C), $5.25 (F). Single copy: 35 cents.

CURRENT MUSICOLOGY, Department of Music, Columbia University, New York, N.Y. 10027. Published by the Department of Music of Columbia University and the Trustees of the University with support from the Alice M. Ditson Fund, and the American Musicological Society. Founded in spring, 1965. Editor (1972): **L. Michael Griffel.** Reportedly the only music magazine edited entirely by graduate students who work without remuneration or professional guidance. Graduate students serve as corresponding editors (58 throughout the United States). Some 39 foreign correspondents (including some professionals) also make contributions to the contents. Two issues annually. Circulation: about 1,100. Rates: $5 for individuals; $7 for institutions. Single copies: $3 for individuals; $5 for institutions.

DANCE MAGAZINE, 10 Columbus Circle, New York, N.Y. 10019. Editor: **William Como.** Monthly with a special annual directory, *Dance Magazine Annual.* Rates: $12 (U.S. & C); $14 (F). Annual issue: $5.

DANCE NEWS, 119 West 57th Street, New York, N.Y. 10019. Editor: **Mrs. Helen V. Atlas.** In newspaper format. Published monthly except July and August. $5, $5.50 (F); single copies, 60 cents.

DANCE PERSPECTIVES, 29 East 9th Street, New York, N.Y. 10003. Published by Dance Perspectives Foundation. Founded 1958. Editor: **Selma Jeanne Cohen.** Devoted to critical and historical monographs on the dance. Quarterly. Circulation: 2,000. Rates: $8 (also C), $8.50 (F). Single issue: $2.95.

THE DIAPASON, 434 South Wabash Avenue, Chicago, Illinois 60605. Sponsored by The Royal Canadian College of Organists and Union Nacional de Organistas of Mexico. First issue: December 1909. Editor: **Robert Schuneman.** Monthly. Circulation: over 22,000. Rates: $4 including foreign; single: 40 cents.

DOWNBEAT, 222 West Adams Street, Chicago, Illinois 60606. Published by Maher Publications. Editor: **Dan Morgenstern.** Biweekly. Rates: $7, $1.50 (C and F), $1 (Pan American countries).

ETHNOMUSICOLOGY (Society for Ethnomusicology), Wesleyan University Press, Middletown, Connecticut 06457. Editor: **Norma McLeod.** Three issues annually. Free to members (see Organizations); membership dues: $7.50 (student), $12.50 (individual); $15 (individual or institutional subscription only). Circulation: 1,450.

THE FOLK DANCER, 47–05 5th Street, Long Island City, New York, N.Y. 11101. Published by the Folk Dance House at same address. Editor: **Michael Herman.** Music editor: **Mary Ann Herman.** (The Folk Dance House also publishes an annual syllabus of folk-dance music and directions.) Monthly. Circulation: 4,000. Rates: $5, $6 (C and F).

FRETTS, P.O. Box 928, Santa Ana, California 92701. Founded 1958. Published by the Randall Publishing Co. Editor: **James M. Williams.** Bi-monthly. Circulation (includes all major music stores and individual subscribers): 8,200. Rates: $1.75 (also C); an additional $1 for foreign rates.

GUITAR REVIEW (Society of the Classic Guitar, Inc.), 409 East 50th Street, New York, N.Y. 10022. Founded in 1946. Editor: **Vladimir Bobri.** Issued three times annually. Rates: can be purchased for $8; single issue, $3.

THE HARMONIZER (Society for the Preservation and Encouragement of Barbershop Quartet Singing in America), 6315 Third Avenue, Kenosha, Wisconsin 53141. Editor: **Leo W. Fobart.** Six issues a year (January–February, March–April, etc.). Rates: $2.

THE HARRISON TAPE GUIDE, 143 West 20th Street, New York, N.Y. 10011. Founded November, 1955. Editor and Publisher: **Mrs. Molly Harrison.** Issued every other month. Circulation average: 55,000. Not a periodical but a catalogue in the tradition of several now serving records and tape consumers. Copies are purchasable from tape dealers; single copy subscriptions are handled by the publisher as a special accommodation. Rates: $4.50 and $6 (F). Single copy: $1 everywhere.

HI FI/STEREO REVIEW (see STEREO REVIEW).

HIGH FIDELITY MAGAZINE, Publishing House, Great Barrington, Massachusetts 01230. First issued in spring, 1951. Published by Billboard Publications, Inc., **Warren B. Syer,** Publisher. Editor: **Leonard Marcus.** Content includes record and tape reviews, reports on new high-fidelity equipment, articles on recording or playback technology, composers, musicians, etc. Also issued in combination with *Musical America* (see below). A special *Stereo* annual is also published by the magazine ($1.25). Monthly. Circulation: 252,000 (1972). Rates: 60 cents single issue; $7, $8 (C and F).

HIGH FIDELITY/MUSICAL AMERICA, 165 West 46th Street, New York, N.Y. 10036 (Musical America editorial office). A division of *High Fidelity Magazine* (see above). *Musical America* was first published in 1898. It merged with *High Fidelity* in 1965. Editor: **Shirley Fleming.** Covers reviews of live concerts in the U.S. and abroad and in general is a news magazine of most aspects of the classical music field. Monthly. Circulation: about 25,000 (1967). Rates: $14; elsewhere: $15. Single copy: $1.25. Annual (published in December) *Directory of the Performing Arts:* $6.

HIT PARADER, Division Street, Derby, Connecticut 06418. Founded in 1942. Published by the Charlton Publishing Corp. Editor: **Ian Dove.** Monthly. Circulation (with *Song Hits*): 275,000. Rates: $4.20, $5.25 (C), $6.30 (F). Single issue: 35 cents.

THE HYMN (Hymn Society of America) 475 Riverside Drive, New York, N.Y. 10027. First issued in October, 1949. Editors: **William W. Reid** and **J. Vincent Higginson.** Quarterly (published in January, April, July, and October). Circulation: 2,000. Membership subscription. Rates: $6.50 ($4 for students).

THE INSTRUMENTALIST, 1418 Lake Street, Evanston, Illinois 60204. First issued in September, 1946. Editor: **Kenneth L. Neidig.** Devoted to covering only the instruments of the band and orchestra with main emphasis on those ensembles in public schools and colleges formed within the framework of the general curriculum. Articles are directed to instrumental teachers and directors of school bands and orchestras. Monthly, except July. Circulation: 16,500. Rates: $7; all foreign, an additional 90 cents.

INTER-AMERICAN MUSIC BULLETIN, Music Division, Pan-American Union, Organization of American States, Washington, D.C. 20006. Three issues annually. Free on request.

INTERNATIONAL MUSICIAN (American Federation of Musicians), 220 Mt. Pleasant Avenue, Newark, N.J. 07104. Established in 1900. Editor: **Stanley Ballard.** Published as an offset tabloid. Monthly. Circulation: 260,000. Rates: 60 cents to members of the AFM and $5 to nonmembers.

JAZZ & POP, 1841 Broadway, New York, N.Y. 10023. Published by Jazz Press, Inc. Founded in 1962 as *Jazz.* Present name used since August 1967 issue. Editor: **Patricia Kennely.** Monthly. Circulation: 40,000. Rates: $6 (also C), $6.50 (F), 50 cents single copy.

JAZZ NOTES (Indianapolis Jazz Club), P.O. Box 55, Indianapolis, Indiana 46206. Founded 1957. Co-editors: **Laura Fend** and **William Fend.** A nonprofit publication with no paid advertisements. Four issues a year. Circulation: under 500. Rates: $2.

JAZZ REPORT MAGAZINE, Box 476, or 357 Leighton Drive, Ventura, California 93001. First issue: September 1960. Editor-Publisher: **Paul E. Affeldt.** Incorporates the magazine *Jazz Digest.* Traditional jazz, blues, ragtime and swing is the main emphasis in record and book reviews, feature articles, auction lists, etc. Mimeograph print. Bi-monthly (approximately). Circulation: 2,500. Rates (six issues): $2.50 (also C), $3 (F). Single copy: 50 cents.

JUILLIARD NEWS BULLETIN AND JUILLIARD REVIEW ANNUAL, Juilliard School, Lincoln Center Plaza, New York, N.Y. 10023. Established October, 1962. Published by the Juilliard School. Editor: **A. J. Pischl.** Six times a year; one annual *Review.* Circulation: 5,000. Rates: $2.

JUNIOR KEYNOTES (National Federation of Music Clubs), Suite 1215, 600 South Michigan Avenue, Chicago, Illinois 60605. Editor: **Phyllis Lations Hanson.** Issued four times a year. Circulation: over 7,000. Rates: $1 (also C), $1.25 (F). Single copy: 50 cents.

THE JOURNAL OF THE ACOUSTICAL SOCIETY OF AMERICA (Acoustical Society of America), 335 East 45th Street, New York, N.Y. 10017. Founded 1929. Published by the American Institute of Physics. (The Society's former publication, *Sound,* has been discontinued.) Editor: **R. Bruce Lindsay;** Music Editor: **R. W. Young.** Monthly. Circulation: 7,000. Rates: $22 (also C), $24 (F). Single issue: $3.

THE JOURNAL OF AESTHETICS AND ART CRITICISM (American Society for Aesthetics), Wayne State University, Detroit, Michigan 48202. (Printed at Waverly Press, Mt. Royal and Guilford Avenues, Baltimore, Maryland 21202.) Editor: **Herbert M. Schueller** (Wayne State); Book Review Editor: **Helmut Hungerland.** Summer issue contains a current bibliography of fields covered by the *Journal,* with a section on music and musicology. Quarterly. Circulation: 2,550. Rates: $15 (also C), $16 (F).

JOURNAL OF THE AMERICAN MUSICOLOGICAL SOCIETY (American Musicological Society), c/o Editor, Department of Music, Cornell University, Ithaca, N.Y. 14850. First issue: 1948. Editor: **Don M. Randel.** Issued three times a year. Circulation: over 3,600. Rates: $15 (membership subscription); $15 to institutions and recognized agencies. Student membership subscription: $7.50. Single issues: $3 to members; $2.50 to students; $4.25 to others ordering three or more. An annual *Index* covering the three issues making up the yearly volume is printed in the fall Issue.

JOURNAL OF BAND RESEARCH (American Bandmasters Assn.), University of South Florida, Tampa, Florida 33620. Subscription address: Iowa State University Press, Press Building, Ames, Iowa 50010. First issue: 1964. Editor: **Gale Sperry.** Four categories of material are published in the *Journal:* band music analysis, aesthetics of band music performance, scholarly studies of composers of band music, and reports of events and people in the band field. Two issues annually (autumn and spring). No advertising. Rates: $2.50. Single copy: $1.50.

JOURNAL OF CHURCH MUSIC (Board of Publication, Lutheran Church in America), 2900 Queen Lane, Philadelphia, Pennsylvania 19129. Established January, 1959. Published by the Fortress Press. Monthly except a joint issue for July and August. Editor: **Robert A. Camburn.** In addition to articles of interest to church musicians, there is published music. Circulation: 4,218. Rates: $4.75 (also C); single copies 75 cents.

JOURNAL OF MUSIC THEORY, School of Music, Yale University, New Haven, Connecticut 06520. Published by the Yale Press. Founded in 1957. Editor: **David W. Beach.** Semi-annual. Circulation: 1,200. Rates: $6.

JOURNAL OF MUSIC THERAPY (National Association for Music Therapy, Inc.), P.O. Box 610, Lawrence, Kansas 66044. Published at the Allen Press, Lawrence, Kansas. Founded in 1964 superseding the *Bulletin of the NAMT,* which was published between 1952 and 1963. Editor: **Jo Ann Euper.** Publishes articles on member activities, techniques in music therapy, research, the papers presented at the Association's annual conference and an annual directory of members. Quarterly. Circulation: 1,650. Rates: $5 everywhere. Single issue: $1.50.

LIST-O-TAPES, Trade Service Publications, Inc., 2720 Beverly Boulevard, Los Angeles, California 90057. Founded in June, 1967. Editor: **Ola Corelli.** A loose-leaf publication available on subscription providing a weekly updating of available tape recordings. Circulation: 6,000. Rates: $3 a month; $4 (C).

MANUALIERE, World Library Publications, Inc. 2145 Central Parkway, Cincinnati, Ohio 45214. Published by the World Library of Sacred Music. Contains organ music for manuals only (see *Consolaire,* a companion publication), much of it published for the first time. Bi-monthly. Circulation: 500. Rates: $5, $6 (C). Single issue: $2.

MUSART (National Catholic Music Educators Association, Inc.), 4637 Eastern Avenue, N.E., Washington, D.C. 20018. Established in 1948 (official NCMEA brochure states 1943). Managing Editor: **Michael D.**

Cordovana. Chairman of Editorial Board: **Rt. Rev. Msgr. Sylvester J. Holbel.** A professional magazine covering all areas of activity involving Catholic music teachers in the Catholic school systems. Issued in fall, winter, and spring. Circulation: 5,200. Rates (membership subscription): $8 everywhere. Library subscription: $5. Single issue: $1.

MUSIC/THE A.G.O.–R.C.C.O. MAGAZINE (American Guild of Organists), 54 West 40th Street, New York, N.Y. 10020. First issue: October, 1967. Managing Editor: **Peter J. Basch.** Publishes news, reviews, and articles of interest to organists, choirmasters, and others involved in the field of sacred music. The activities of thc A.G.O. arc covered as well as those of concert organists. Monthly. Circulation: 22,000. Rates: $7.50 (also C); single issue: $1.

MUSIC & ARTISTS, 200 West 57th Street, New York, N.Y. 10019. Published by the *Music Journal.* First issued Feb.–Mar., 1968. Publisher: **Al Vann.** Editor: **Ralph Lewando.** Emphasis is on reviews of live performances throughout the nation, activities of musical artists, organizations, schools, concert managers, composers, etc. Five issues a year: February/March, April/May, June/July, September/October, December/January. *Annual Directory* is published in November. Circulation: 16,000. $7. $8 (C), $8.50 (F). Subscription includes the *Directory* (sold separately for $5).

MUSIC ARTICLE GUIDE, 156 West Chelten Avenue, Room 5, Philadelphia, Pennsylvania 19144. Founded in 1966. Editor and Publisher: **Morris Henken.** "A comprehensive quarterly reference guide to signed feature articles in American music periodicals." (Some 150 periodicals are covered in the indexing.) Published as photo offset of typescript. Quarterly. Rates: $12, $13 (C and F). Single issue: $3.

MUSIC CLUBS MAGAZINE (National Federation of Music Clubs), Suite 1215, 600 South Michigan Avenue, Chicago, Illinois 60605. Founded in 1921. As official organ of the NFMC, the magazine is distributed to the leaders of the 600,000-member organization. Editor: **Mrs. Frank A. Vought.** Five issues a year. Circulation: 6,000. Rates: $2.50 (also C), $3. Single issue: 70 cents.

MUSIC EDUCATORS JOURNAL (Music Educators National Conference), 1201 Sixteenth Street, N.W., Washington, D.C. 20036. First issued in 1914. Editor: **Malcolm E. Bessom.** Monthly during school year (nine issues). Circulation: 70,000. Rates: $4, $6 (also C), $8 (F). Free to members of MENC.

THE MUSIC FORUM, Columbia University Press, 136 South Broadway, Irvington, N.Y. 10533. Established in 1968. Editors: **William J. Mitchell, Felix Salzer.** Scholarly articles discussing various aspects of music from the middle ages to present times. One issue a year. Rates: $8.50 (discount for continuation subscription).

THE MUSIC INDEX, 1435–1437 Randolph Street, Detroit, Michigan 48226. Founded January, 1949. Published by Information Coordinators, Inc. Editors: **Florence Kretzschmar, Betty Stack, Norma B. McDonald.** A subject–author guide to current music periodical literature. Published monthly and cumulated annually clothbound. The *Index* is drawn from over 270 music periodicals from 32 countries. Circulation: over 500. Rates (restricted to annual subscription only): $345 (beginning in 1972). Monthly issues not sold separately, but back issues of annual cumulations are sold at varying prices.

MUSIC JOURNAL, 200 West 57th Street, Suite 1408, New York, N.Y. 10019. Founded in 1943. Publisher: **Al Vann.** Editor: **Robert Cumming.** Ten issues annually. Circulation: 25,000. Rates: $9, $10 (C), $10.50 (F). Single issue: $1.

THE MUSIC TRADES, P.O. Box 432 (80 West Street), Englewood, N.J. 07631. Founded in 1890. Publisher: **George Magliola.** Editor: **John F. Majeski, Jr.** Monthly. Circulation: 7,200. Rates: $4, $5 (C and F). Subscription includes the annual *Purchaser's Guide to the Music Industries,* published continuously since 1897.

MUSICA DISCIPLINA (American Institute of Musicology), P.O. Box 30665, Dallas,

Texas 75230. One issue a year. Editor: **Armen Carapetyan.** Rate: $10.

MUSICAL AMERICA. Not published separately (see HIGH FIDELITY/MUSICAL AMERICA).

MUSICAL MERCHANDISE REVIEW, 437 Madison Avenue, New York, N.Y. 10022. Established in 1879. Published by Select Publications, Inc. Editor: **Hugh Gile Swofford.** Monthly. Circulation: 11,500. Rate: $9.

MUSICAL NEWSLETTER, Box 250, Lenox Hill Station, New York, N.Y. 10021. Published by the Musical Newsletter, Inc. at the same address. First issue: January, 1971 (copyright dated 1970). Editor and Publisher: **Patrick J. Smith.** Published quarterly and sold through subscription only. No advertising or illustrative matter. Directed towards the "interested amateur" insofar as articles are detailed criticisms, reviews, and expositions on music, performances and performers, and areas of musical activity of interest to the serious devotee of music. First issue: 18 pages typeset, offset print. Rates: $10 per year; $18 for two years. Student rate for one year: $5. Single copy: $3.

THE MUSICAL QUARTERLY, 866 Third Avenue, New York, N.Y. 10022. Founded in 1915. Publisher: G. Schirmer, Inc., New York, at the same address. Editor: **Paul Henry Lang.** Quarterly, issued in January, April, July, and October. Circulation (estimated): 5,573. A musicological publication covering a very wide range of subjects treated in depth, some exhaustively. Continuous pagination throughout the volume year. Contains, besides articles, editorial essays or comments, music and book reviews, record reviews, and reviews of recent significant live performances. Annual Index. Rates: $9, $9.75 (F). Single issue: $2.50.

THE NATS BULLETIN (National Association of Teachers of Singing, Inc.), 430 South Michigan Avenue, Chicago, Illinois 60605. Established in 1944. Editor: **Harvey Ringel.** Quarterly. Circulation: 3,300. Rates (membership subscription): $6, $6.50 (C) (and Mexico), $7 (F); single copies: $1.75 each.

NATIONAL MUSIC COUNCIL BULLETIN (National Music Council), 2109 Broadway, Suite 15–79, New York, N.Y. 10023. Editor: **Leslie Rubinstein Kallmann.** Published in fall, winter, and spring. No paid advertising. Covers news of interest to member organizations as well as information of the activities of member groups. From 28 to 36 pages each issue. Circulation: 2,000. Rates: $5. Single copy: $2. Introduced graphic changes and illustrative matter for the first time with the spring, 1973 issue.

THE NEW RECORDS, H. Royer Smith Co., 10th and Walnut Streets, Philadelphia, Pennsylvania 19107. First issue: March, 1933. Editor: **E. Hamilton.** Monthly. Circulation: 10,000. Rates: $1.50, $2 (C and F). Single copy: 15 cents.

NOTES (Music Library Association), c/o Editor, Research Library of the Performing Arts, 111 Amsterdam Avenue, New York, N.Y. 10023. Founded 1934. Editor: **Frank C. Campbell.** Contains articles, detailed book and music reviews, checklists of published books and music, index to record reviews, various annual surveys, lists, and description of publishers' and dealers' catalogues, index to music necrology, etc. Indexed annually. Quarterly. Circulation: 3,150 (net). Rates (membership in MLA): $6.50 (students), $12 (individuals), $15 (institutions). Rates without membership: $10. Single copy. $4.

NUMUS-WEST, P.O. Box 146, Mercer Island, Washington 98040. Published by Numus-West, an organization "devoted to disseminating knowledge of new music through publications, concerts, and lectures." First issue was published in April, 1972 and was distributed free to some 8,000 persons and institutions. As of May, 1972, the plan of publications is two issues annually in November and April in a tabloid newsletter–journal format (first issue, typeset, 32 pages with some commercial advertising). It will contain news reports on new music activity in seven areas of the West Coast from Vancouver, British Columbia to San Diego, California, each area assigned to a professorial composer-correspondent. Reports and articles of a more national and international interest are also to be published. Publisher–Editor: **Louis K. Christensen.** Rates: $2 for North America; $2.30 elsewhere.

THE OPERA JOURNAL (National Opera Association), The University of Mississippi, University, Mississippi 38677. First issue: Volume I, No. 1, winter, 1968. Editor: **Leland S. Fox.** Quarterly. Circulation: 500. Subscription only by membership in the National Opera Association. Membership rates: individuals, $8; organizations, $15; libraries, $5; students, $2.

OPERA NEWS (Metropolitan Opera Guild, Inc.), 1865 Broadway, New York, N.Y. 10023. Founded May, 1936. Editor: **Frank Merkling.** When published weekly (see following), the issues give emphasis to the opera scheduled for matinee performance and national radio broadcast of the Metropolitan Opera for each week during the broadcast season. Otherwise, coverage ranges over the entire field of opera. Published: Sept. 9, 23, Oct. 14, Nov. 4, 25, weekly from Dec. 9 through April 20, May 18, and June 15. Circulation: 85,000. Rates (membership subscription): $15. Single copy: 75 cents.

OVERTONES (National Catholic Music Educators Association, Inc.), 4637 Eastern Avenue, N.E., Washington, D.C. 20018. Founded September, 1965. Editor: **Vincent P. Walter, Jr.** Each issue is devoted to studies within the eight departments of the NCMEA (e.g., elementary music education, secondary, college, instrumental, vocal, etc.) and as such is a "service bulletin" of the Research Division of the NCMEA. Eight issues a year. Issued in a newsletter format. Circulation: 5,200. Rates: included with membership in the NCMEA (see Organizations).

OVERTURE (Local 47, American Federation of Musicians), 817 Vine Street, Los Angeles, California 90038. Editor: **Vince di Bari.** Monthly newspaper. Rates: $2.50.

PERCUSSIONIST (Percussive Arts Society), 130 Carol Drive, Terre Haute, Indiana 47805. First issued in 1963. Editors: **Neal Fluegel** and **James Moore.** Published four times a year, the magazine is now joined with the former *Percussive Notes,* which was also published by the Percussive Arts Society. Circulation: 2,000. Rates (free to members of the Percussive Arts Society): $8 (also C and F); students $5.

PERSPECTIVES OF NEW MUSIC, Box 231, Princeton University Press, Princeton, N.J. 08540. Sponsored by the Fromm Music Foundation (see Organizations) and published by the Princeton University Press. First issued in December, 1962. Editor: **Benjamin Boretz.** Circulation: 2,300. Semiannual. Rates: $6; single issue: $5.

PHONOLOG, Trade Service Publications, Inc., 2720 Beverly Boulevard, Los Angeles, California 90057. Founded June, 1948. Editor: **Ola Corelli.** A publication in loose-leaf format providing a weekly updating service of available recordings. Rates: $11 a month; $12 (C).

THE PIANO QUARTERLY, P.O. Box 707, Melville, N.Y. 11746. Published by Belwin Mills Publishing Corporation. Founded 1952. Publisher: **Martin Winkler.** Editor: **Robert Joseph Silverman.** Reviews books, music, and recordings; contains recommended piano music, etc. Quarterly. Circulation: 3,000. Rates: $6 (also C), $7 (F). Single copy: $1.75.

THE PIANO TECHNICIANS JOURNAL (Piano Technicians Guild, Inc.), Box 1813, Seattle, Washington 98111. First issued January, 1958. Editor: **James H. Burton.** Covers articles and news items on piano technology, piano industry, Guild membership activity. Monthly. Circulation: 2,400. Rates: $15 (also C), $18 (F). Single issue: $1.50.

POLART INDEX TO RECORD REVIEWS (Including Tapes), 20115 Goulburn Avenue, Detroit, Michigan 48205. Founded in 1960. Published by Polart Services at same address. Editor: **Henry J. Polowniak.** The *Index* refers to reviews appearing in some 11 American periodicals, keyed to the identification of the periodical, the exact issue, page, general indication of the length of the review, and whether the review makes a comparison with other recordings. The *Index* appears annually in February and covers reviews appearing in the preceding year; thus the 1968 edition is published in February, 1969. Format is cardboard-bound booklet; offset-printed typescript. Circulation: 1,200. Single annual issue: $2 anywhere, postpaid. All back issues are for sale.

QUARTERLY CHECK-LIST OF MUSICOLOGY, American Bibliographic Service, P.O. Box 1141, Darien, Connecticut 06820. Founded in 1959. Contents covers new and recent nonperiodical publications related to European, American, and Asiatic music history, criticism, analysis, biography, etc. All available bibliographic data is supplied. Annual index. Quarterly. Rates: $5 (same rate for C and F).

RECORD RATING SERVICE, P.O. Box 67, Hudson, New Hampshire 03051. First issued January, 1966. Publisher–Editor: **Michael W. Hutchinson.** Classifies the general quality of approximately 150 recordings of serious music and jazz on disc and tape in each issue. Index and classification of magazine recording reviews is included. Issued quarterly as a bulletin. Rates: $5 everywhere. Single issue: $1.50.

RECORD WORLD, 1700 Broadway, New York, N.Y. 10019. First issued March, 1964. Editor in Chief: **Sidmore Parnes.** Weekly. Circulation: circa 16,000. Rates: $40 (also C), $75 (F). Single copy: $1.25.

RENAISSANCE QUARTERLY (Renaissance Society of America), 1161 Amsterdam Avenue, New York, N.Y. 10027. Founded 1954 (formerly *Renaissance News*). Co-editors: **Elizabeth Story Donno** and **James V. Mirollo.** Not exclusively music, but articles and reviews covering all aspects of Renaissance studies. Quarterly. Circulation: 3,300. Rates (membership): $12.50 (individuals), $16 (institutions).

RILM ABSTRACTS (Répertoire Internationale de la Littérature Musicale–International Repertory of Musical Literature), c/o International RILM Center, City University of New York, 33 West 42nd Street, New York, N.Y. 10036. First issued August, 1967, covering literature from January through April, 1967. A computer-indexed bibliography of literature of music in the form of abstracts. Established in 1966 under the sponsorship of the International Musicological Society, the International Association of Music Libraries, and the American Council of Learned Societies. Deals with current literature: books, articles, dissertations, reviews, etc., appearing after January, 1967. Committees in twenty-three nations assist in gathering material from authors and editors. President, Commission Internationale Mixte and Editor in Chief: **Barry S. Brook.** Editor: **Murray Ralph.** Quarterly. Rates: $36 (library or institution), $12 (individual), beginning August, 1973.

ROCK & SOUL SONGS, Charlton Building, Derby, Connecticut 06418. Founded in 1956. Published by Charlton Publications. Bi-monthly. Circulation: 75,000. Rates: $2.10, $2.63 (C), $3.15 (F). Single issue: 35 cents.

SACRED MUSIC (Church Music Association of America), Publishing office: 584 Lafond Avenue, Saint Paul, Minnesota 55103. Replaces the former *Caecilia* and the *Catholic Choirmaster.* Editor: **Rev. Ralph S. March, S.O. Cist.** Quarterly. Free to members (see Organizations). Rates: $7.50 subscribing member; single issue: $2.

SATURDAY REVIEW, formerly at 380 Madison Avenue, New York, N.Y. 10017; moved to San Francisco after acquisition in 1971 by what was to become Saturday Review Industries (450 Pacific Avenue). Music Editor (Senior Editor): **Irving Kolodin.** Not primarily a music magazine, but contains columns of reviews of music and dance, recordings, etc. The music issue is part of *Saturday Review of the Arts,* issued monthly. Circulation: 550,000. Rates: $12 a year. Single copy: $1. (In April, 1973, the magazine ceased publication pending its merger, later in 1973, with *World* magazine.)

THE SCHOOL MUSICIAN, DIRECTOR AND TEACHER, 4 East Clinton Street,

Joliet, Illinois 60431. Founded October, 1929. Formerly named *The School Musician.* Publisher–Editor: **Forrest L. McAllister.** Used as the official magazine of the American School Band Directors Association and Phi Beta Mu, National Bandmasters Fraternity. Monthly except July and August. Circulation: 15,250. Rates: $5.

SCHWANN RECORD AND TAPE GUIDE, 137 Newbury Street, Boston, Massachusetts 02116. First issued October, 1941. Until February 1971, its name was *Schwann Long Playing Record Catalog.* Published by W. Schwann, Inc. Monthly. Obtainable in record shops and independent record clubs in the United States and some thirty-eight foreign countries. Single copy: 75 cents. In addition to the monthly catalogue, there are the following: *Schwann Supplementary Catalog* (semiannual and covering records not listed in the monthly such as imports, international popular and folk music, monophonic records, domestic popular music more than two years old, etc.); *Schwann Artist Issue* (issued about every three years—last issue in 1970—listing categorically performers and groups from the mainly classical music monthly catalogue); *Schwann Country & Western Tape and Record Catalog; Schwann Children's Records Catalog* (annual); *Basic Record Library* (free for single copy).

SENZA SORDINO, (International Conference of Symphony and Opera Musicians), 4161 Holly Knoll Drive, Los Angeles, California 90027. First issued in 1961. Editor: **Vance Beach.** Deals with information of direct interest to the professional symphony and opera musician such as wages, working conditions, etc. At least four times a year. Published as a four- to six-page newsletter. Circulation: 4,000 (most mailed in bulk to member orchestras for distribution to musicians). Rates: $2 (to members of American Federation of Musicians), $5 (nonmembers).

SING OUT! The Folk Song Magazine, 33 W. 60th Street, New York, N.Y. 10023. First issued in May, 1950. Published by Sing Out, Inc. Editor: **Bob Norman.** In addition to articles, feature columns, etc., there are from 12 to 15 songs printed in each issue. Bi-monthly. Circulation: 15,000. Rates: $6, $6.50 (C and F). Single copy: $1.

SONG HITS, Division Street, Derby, Connecticut 06418. Published by the Charlton Publishing Co. Founded 1942. Editor: **Nadine Drake.** Monthly. Circulation (with *Hit Parader*): 275,000. Rates: $4.20, $5.25 (C), $6.30 (F). Single copy: 35 cents.

SONGWRITER'S REVIEW, 1697 Broadway, New York, N.Y. 10019. First issued in February, 1946. Publisher–Editor: **Sydney Berman.** 11 issues a year. Rates: $3.50, $4 (C and F).

SOURCE, Music of the Avant Garde, 2101 22nd Street, Sacramento, California 95818. Established January, 1967. Published by Composer/Performer Edition. Publishes new works in open score (five in the first issue) along with essays, interviews, reviews, an occasional recording, etc., related to avant-garde music. Twice annually. Issue Number Nine published in 1972. Large format with spiral binding. Circulation: 1,350. Rates: $13 (also C), $15 (F). Single issue: $7.

SOUTHWESTERN MUSICIAN/TEXAS MUSIC EDUCATOR, P.O. Box 9908, Houston, Texas 77015. Sponsored by the Texas Music Educators Association, Inc. First published as a combined magazine in September, 1954. Editor: **Joseph F. Lenzo.** Used as official publication for various Texas music organizations (educators, music schools, bandmasters, orchestra directors, and string teachers). Published ten times a year, August through May. Circulation: about 5,300. Rates: $2.50 (all foreign also except for additional postage). Single copy: 35 cents.

SPECULUM (The Mediaeval Academy of America), 1430 Massachusetts Avenue, Cambridge, Massachusetts 02138. Editor: **Hamilton M. Smyser.** Quarterly. Free to members; otherwise $18. Circulation: 4,400.

STEREO REVIEW, One Park Avenue, New York, N.Y. 10016. Formerly *Hi Fi/Stereo Review.* First issued in February, 1958. Published by Ziff–Davis Publishing Company. Editor: **William E. Anderson.** Approximately 50 percent of the content is devoted to reviews of new recordings. The balance covers high-fidelity equipment and major articles (such as a continuing series on American composers). Monthly. Circulation: 300,000. Rates: $7 (also C), $8 (F). Single issue: 60 cents.

STUDIES IN THE RENAISSANCE (Renaissance Society of America), 1161 Amsterdam Avenue, New York, N.Y. 10027. Established in 1954. Editor: **Richard Harrier.** Annual. Circulation: 3,200. Rates: $8. Single issue: $2.

SYMPHONY NEWS (American Symphony Orchestra League), P.O. Box 66, Vienna, Virginia 22180. Formerly the American Symphony Orchestra League *Newsletter.* Editor: **Benjamin S. Dunham.** Membership subscription (see Organizations). Issued six times a year. Single issues purchasable at 50 cents a copy; 75 cents for double issues.

THE TRACKER (Organ Historical Society), 250 East Market Street, York, Pennsylvania 17404. Editor: **Albert F. Robinson.** Subscription information: **Donald Rockwood,** 50 Rockwood Road, Norfolk, Massachusetts 02056. Quarterly. Circulation: 500. Rates (includes membership in the Society): $5. Single copy: $1.50.

THE TRIANGLE (Mu Phi Epsilon), 1097 Arnatt Way, Campbell, California 95008. National Editor: **Pearl Allison Peterson.** Four issues annually. Rates: $2.

VARIETY, 154 West 46th Street, New York, N.Y. 10036. Founded in 1905. Editor: **Abel Green.** Music Editor: **Herman Schoenfeld.** Weekly. Published in newspaper format. Rates: $20, $22 (all foreign). Single issue: 50 cents.

WASHINGTON INTERNATIONAL ARTS LETTER, 115 5th Street, S.E., Washington, D.C. 20003. Published by Allied Business Consultants, Inc. Founded in 1962. "A letter service and digest concerning 20th century patronage, support programs, and developments." Contents cover arts and government, humanities and education, books and publications. Published ten times a year (omits July and December). Issues are sent first class mail.

THE WHEEL OF DELTA OMICRON (Delta Omicron International Music Fraternity for Women), Curtis Reed Plaza, Menasha, Wisconsin 54952. First issued June, 1915. Published by the George Banta Co., Menasha, Wisconsin. Editor: **Mrs. John Dugan.** Issued four times a year. Circulation: 4,250. Rates: $1.50 everywhere. Single issue: 50 cents.

WOODWIND WORLD, 20 Hessian Drive, Ridgefield, Connecticut 06877. Established in 1959. Editor: **John C. Gerstner.** Issued bimonthly. Rates: $1.50, $1.75 (C and F).

Part 13 Concert Managers

The listings that follow are concert management firms and personal artist representatives in the United States who handle performing artists for the United States. Among them are some who arrange for overseas bookings as well as managers who arrange the American bookings for visiting foreign artists.

An attempt is made in this section to provide a correlation between managements and the performing artists found in Part 5. Concert managements referred to in that section are therefore listed in full here.

A B C, ASSOCIATED BOOKING CORPORATION, 445 Park Avenue, New York, N.Y. 10022. Tel.: (212) 421–5200. Other locations: 9477 Brighton Way, Beverly Hills, California 90211, Tel.: (213) 273–5600; 919 North Michigan Avenue, Suite 2906, Chicago, Illinois 60611, Tel.: (312) 751–2000; 6660 Biscayne Boulevard, Miami, Florida 33138, Tel.: (305) 758–2511; 1100 East Sahara Avenue, Las Vegas, Nevada 89105, Tel.: (702) 734–8155; Lee Park Building, 3511 Hall Street, Dallas, Texas 75219, Tel.: (214) 528–8296. President: **Oscar Cohen.** . . . AGENCY FOR THE PERFORMING ARTS, 120 West 57th Street, New York, N.Y. 10019. Tel.: (212) LT 1–8860. **David C. Baumgarten,** President. . . . ALKAHEST ATTRACTIONS, 1175 Peachtree Street, North East, Atlanta, Georgia 30309. Tel.: (404) 892–1843. President: **Ralph P. Bridges.** . . . RAMON ALSINA, 228 East 80th Street, New York, N.Y. 10021. Tel.: (212) YU 8–2452. . . . AMERICAN PROGRAM BUREAU, 850 Boylston Street, Boston, Massachusetts 02167. Tel.: (617) 731–0500. Cable: LECTURE. President: **Robert P. Walker.** . . . AMERICAN SOCIETY FOR EASTERN ARTS, 405 Sansome Street, San Francisco, California 94111. Tel.: (415) 433–1791. Cable: ASEARTS, Executive Director: **Wallace Thompson.** . . . AMERICAN THEATRE PRODUCTIONS, INC., 1564 Broadway, Suite 902, New York, N.Y. 10036. Tel.: (212) 765–1060. President: **Thomas Mallow.** Vice-President: **Robert T. Gaus.** . . . MARIEDI ANDERS ARTIST MANAGEMENT, 535 El Camino del Mar, San Francisco, California 94121. Tel.: (415) 752–4404. Cable: ALLTRADE. . . . ARN–VACCHINA ASSOCIATES ARTISTS' REPRESENTATIVES, Fontana West, 1050 North Point, San Francisco, California 94109. Tel.: (415) 776–7798. Manager: **Mrs. Irena Arn.** . . . ARTISTS' ALLIANCE CONCERT MANAGEMENT, Box 65833, Los Angeles, California 90065. Tel.: (213) 225–3820, TR 7–0014. Manager: **Peter Christ.** . . . ARTS IMAGE, Box 1041, Newark, N.J. 07101. Tel.: (202) 484–6021. . . . ASEN MANAGEMENT, 111 West 57th Street, New York, N.Y. 10019. Tel.: (212) CI 6–6777. Cable: ASENMUSIC. . . . ASSOCIATED CONCERT ARTISTS, 2109 Broadway, Suite 3-126, New York, N.Y. 10023. Tel.: (212) 787–3300. Co-ordinator: **Miss M. Irgen.** . . . ASSOCIATION OF AMERICAN COLLEGES ARTS PROGRAM, 200 West 57th Street, New York, N.Y. 10019. Tel.: (212) 757–2018. Director: **N. C. Harrison.**

HERBERT BARRETT MANAGEMENT, INC., 1860 Broadway, New York, N.Y. 10023. Tel.: (212) CI 5–3530. Cable: HERBARRETT. President: **Herbert Barrett.** Vice-President: **Joseph A. Lippman.** . . . BERNARD AND RUBIN MANAGEMENT, 255 West End Avenue, New York, N.Y. 10023. Tel.: (212) 877–3735. President: **Cy Rubin.** . . . M. BICHURIN CONCERTS CORPORATION, Carnegie Hall, Suite 609, New York, N.Y. 10019. Tel. (212) JU 6–2349. President: **Mark Bichurin.** . . . JANE BLEYER, 40 Seneca Lane, Pleasantville, N.Y. 10570. Tel.: (914) 769–4162. . . . EASTMAN BOOMER MANAGEMENT, 119

West 57th Street, New York, N.Y. 10019. Tel.: (212) JU 2–9364. . . . FRANCES M. BRACY, Great Northern Shopping Center, 5065 The Mall, North Olmsted, Ohio 44070. Tel.: (216) 777–7170. . . . HERBERT H. BRESLIN, 119 West 57th Street, New York, N.Y. 10019. Tel.: (212) 581–1750.

CELEBRITY STUDIOS, CONCERT DIVISION, 29 West 57th Street, New York, N.Y. 10019. Tel.: (212) PL 3–6356 and 6357. . . . CHIMERA FOUNDATION FOR DANCE, INC., 344 West 36th Street, New York, N.Y. 10018. Tel.: (212) 279–1698 or 1697. Managing Director: **Murray Farr.** . . . BENN CLAY MANAGEMENT, 200 Park Avenue, Suite 303 East, New York, N.Y. 10017. Tel.: (212) 986–2515. . . . CMA (CREATIVE MANAGEMENT ASSOCIATES) DIVISION OF GENERAL ARTIST CORPORATION, 600 Madison Avenue, New York, N.Y. 10022. Tel.: (212) 935–4000. Other offices: 8899 Beverly Boulevard, Los Angeles, California 90048, Tel.: (213) 278–8899; 211 East Chicago Avenue, Chicago, Illinois 60611, Tel.: (312) 943–7100; 2765 South Highland, Las Vegas, Nevada 89102, Tel.: (702) 734–7666. Manager, Concert Division: **Jack Green.** Cable: CREMANASSO. . . . COLBERT ARTISTS MANAGEMENT INC., 111 West 57th Street, New York, N.Y. 10019. Tel.: (212) PL 7–0782. Cable: COLABER. President: **Ann Colbert.** Vice-President: **Agnes Eisenberger.** . . . COLUMBIA ARTISTS FESTIVALS CORPORATION, 165 West 57th Street, New York, N.Y. 10019. Tel.: (212) CI 7–6900. Cable: COLCONCERT. President: **Herbert O. Fox.** . . . COLUMBIA ARTISTS MANAGEMENT INC., 165 West 57th Street, New York, N.Y. 10019. Tel.: (212) CI 7–6900. Cable: COLCONCERT. President: **Kurt Weinhold.** West Coast office: 6464 Sunset Boulevard, Hollywood, California 90028. Tel.: (213) 462–6623 and 461–3401. Divisions: Columbia Artists Festivals Corp., Columbia Artists Theatricals Corp., and Community Concerts, Inc. . . . COMMUNITY CONCERTS, 165 West 57th Street, New York, N.Y. 10019. Tel.: (212) CI 7–6900. Cable: COLCONCERT. President: **George Blake.** . . . THE COMPOSER IN PERFORMANCE INC., Carnegie Hall, Suite 1203, New York, N.Y. 10019. Tel.: (212) 246–4362. Executive Director: **Benjamin Patterson.** . . . CONCERT ASSOCIATES, 68 20th Avenue, San Francisco, California 94121. Tel.: (415) 752–1481. . . . CONTINENTAL AGENCY FOR ARTISTS, 1731 North East 25th Avenue, Portland, Oregon 97212. Tel.: (503) 282–1383. Manager: **John O. Virtanen.** . . . CONTINENTAL CONCERT SERVICE, INC., 119 West 57th Street, New York, N.Y. 10019. Tel.: (212) 757–1035. Board Chairman: **Arthur Judson.** President: **Lois Brannan.** . . . X. COSSÉ MANAGEMENT, 1516 16th Avenue South, Nashville, Tennessee 37212. Tel.: (615) 298–5471. . . . CRITICS CHOICE ARTISTS MANAGEMENT, 1697 Broadway, New York, N.Y. 10019. Tel.: (212) CI 5–9250. President: **Norman J. Seaman.**

JEAN DALRYMPLE MANAGEMENT, 130 West 56th Street, New York, N.Y. 10019. Tel.: (212) JU 6–2828. . . . GIORGIO D'ANDRIA MANAGEMENT, 1005 Carnegie Hall, New York, N.Y. 10019. Tel.: (212) CO 5–3128. Cable: DANDRIART. . . . THEA DISPEKER, ARTISTS' REPRESENTATIVE, 59 East 54th Street, New York, N.Y. 10022. Tel.: (212) 421–7676. Cable: THEADISPEK. . . . DAVID DODDS, 33–05 90th Street, Jackson Heights, New York, N.Y. 11372. Tel.: (212) 639–6718, 564–3250.

ALEXANDRA F. EHRET INC., 4309 Baltimore Avenue, Philadelphia, Pennsylvania 19104. Tel.: (215) 386–6947. Cable: ALEXET. . . . HARRY D. ELLSBERG, 51 Madison Avenue, Room 707, New York, N.Y. 10010. Tel.: (212) 244–1330. . . . ELWOOD EMERICK MANAGEMENT, Wellington Hotel, Seventh Avenue and 55th Street, New York, N.Y. 10019. Tel.: (212) 581–3758.

WILLIAM FELBER AGENCY, 6636 Hollywood Boulevard, Suite 234, Los Angeles, California 90028. Tel.: (213) 466–7629. . . . JOHN B. FISHER MANAGEMENT, 155 West 68th Street, Apartment 801, New York, N.Y. 10023. Tel.: (212) EN 2–4372. . . .

FOLKLORE PRODUCTIONS INC., 176 Federal Street, Boston, Massachusetts 02110. Tel.: (617) HU 2–1827. . . . FROTHINGHAM MANAGEMENT, 156 Cherry Brook Road, Weston Massachusetts 02193. Tel.: (617) 894–7571. Cable: GELFROTH. Chief Officers: **Gelsey T. Frothingham, Margaret L. Luppold.** . . . RICHARD FULTON INC., 200 West 57th Street, New York, N.Y. 10019. Tel.: (212) JU 2–4099. Director: **Richard Fulton.**

ROBERT M. GEWALD MANAGEMENT INC., 2 West 59th Street, Suite 1530, New York, N.Y. 10019. Tel.: (212) PL 3–0450. President: **Robert M. Gewald.** Executive Secretary: **Gertrude Weisbart.** . . . G H V PACKAGES AND PRODUCTIONS INC., 901 Eighth Avenue, Suite 5H, New York, N.Y. 10019. Tel: (212) 581–6838. President: **Vic Vallaro.** Vice-President: **Greg Greene.** . . . SIMONA GLASER, 99–46 64th Avenue, Forest Hills, Long Island, N.Y. 11374. Tel.: (212) 897–6471. . . . LARNEY GOODKIND, 30 East 60th Street, New York, N.Y. 10022. Tel.: (212) EL 5–6560. . . . WALTER GOULD, 609 Fifth Avenue, New York, N.Y. 10017. Tel.: (212) PL 2–3920. . . . GROSSMAN GLOTZER MANAGEMENT, 75 East 55th Street, New York, N.Y. 10022. Tel.: (212) 752–8715. Cable: FOLKTHINK. Representatives: **Albert B. Grossman, Bennett H. Glotzer, Robert J. Schuster.** . . . GUILD OF PERFORMING ARTS, 504 Cedar Avenue, Minneapolis, Minnesota 55404. Tel.: (612) 333–8269. Manager: **Larry Berle.**

ALEXANDER HAAS ARTIST MANAGEMENT, 427 West 5th Street, Los Angeles, California 90013. Tel.: (213) 625–3043. Partners: **Alexander F. Haas, Charlotte D. Haas.** . . . JANET HALL ARTIST BUREAU, 111 West 57th Street, New York, N.Y. 10019. Tel.: (212) 265–1673. . . . JAY K. HOFFMAN PRESENTATIONS, 325 East 57th Street, Suite 1B, New York, N.Y. 10022. Tel.: (212) PL 2–6490. Cable: HOFSCHUCON. . . . BEVERLY HOFFMAN ARTISTS' MANAGEMENT. Milwaukee Office: 3313 North 38th Street, Milwaukee, Wisconsin 53216. Tel.: (414) 445–4458. Los Angeles Office: 805 North Sephora Street, Covina, California 91724. Manager: **Beverly Hoffman.** Associate: **Jan Vroom.** . . . HANS J. HOFMANN, 200 West 58th Street, New York, N.Y. 10019. Tel.: (212) CI 6–1557. Cable: ARTHOFMANN. . . . J. M. HUME ASSOCIATES, 211 Fairlawn Plaza Drive, Topeka, Kansas 66614. Tel.: (913) 272–3948. President: **Joe M. Hume.** . . . HUROK CONCERTS INC., 1370 Avenue of the Americas, New York, N.Y. 10019. Tel.: (212) CI 5–0500. Cable: HURAT. Los Angeles Office: 8255 Sunset Boulevard, Los Angeles, California 90046. Tel.: (213) 656–2363. President: **Sol Hurok.**

IFA (INTERNATIONAL FAMOUS AGENCY INC.), New York Office: 1301 Avenue of the Americas, New York, N.Y. 10019. Tel.: (212) 956–5800. Cable: FAMOUSAGE. Los Angeles office: 9255 Sunset Boulevard, Los Angeles, California 90069. Tel.: (213) CR 3–8811. Chicago office: 166 East Superior, Chicago, Illinois 60611. Tel.: (312) 944–2800. Concert Department Manager: **Ed Rubin.** . . . INTERNATIONAL ARTISTS, 2115 Broadway, Suite 5–41, New York, N.Y. 10023. Tel.: (212) 874–6106. Also: Box 182, Paris, Tennessee 38242. Tel.: (901) 642–2526/0272. . . . INTERNATIONAL ARTISTS AGENCY, 1564 Eighteenth Avenue, San Francisco, California 94122. Tel.: (415) 661–1962. Director: **Pietro Menci.** . . . INTERNATIONAL CONCERTS EXCHANGE FOUNDATION, 9015 Wilshire Boulevard, Beverly Hills, California 90211. Tel.: (213) BR 2–5539. Cable: IPICA. Director: **Irwin Parnes.**

HELEN JENSEN ARTISTS MANAGEMENT, 716 Joseph Vance Building, Third and Union, Seattle, Washington 98101. Tel.: (206) MA 2–7896, 523–0382. . . . LEE JON ASSOCIATES, 18662 Fairfield Avenue, Detroit, Michigan 48221. Tel.: (313) UN 1–6930. . . . JUDD CONCERT ARTIST BUREAU, 127 West 69th Street, New York, N.Y. 10023. Tel.: (212) TR 7–9848. Manager: **William M. Judd.** . . . ARTHUR JUDSON MANAGEMENT INC., 119 West 57th Street, New York, N.Y. 10019. Tel.: (212) JU 6–8135. Cable: NYCJUDSON. Board

Chairman: **Arthur Judson.** President: **Harry S. Beall.** Secretary: **Ruth M. O'Neill.** West Coast representative: P.O. Box 46275, Los Angeles, California 90046. Tel.: (213) 654–0440.

OTTO KAPELL COMPANY, Manorhouse, Paris, Tennessee 38242. Tel.: (901) 642–5852. Booking Director: **Marjorie Jackson.** . . . MELVIN KAPLAN, INC., 85 Riverside Drive, New York, N.Y. 10024. Tel.: (212) TR 7–6310. . . . ALBERT KAY ASSOCIATES INC., 38 West 53rd Street, New York, N.Y. 10019. Tel.: (212) 582–8894 and 765–3195. Cable: ALKAMUSIC. President: **Albert Kay.** Vice President: **Arne Forsberg.** . . . SANDRA KAYE, 20 West 72nd Street, New York, N.Y. 10023. Tel.: (212) TR 7–3800. . . . KENALLEN ENTERPRISES INC., 125 East 63rd Street, New York, N.Y. 10021. Tel.: (212) TE 8–3773. Cable: CHORAGUS. President: **Kenneth Allen.** . . . KOLMAR–LUTH ENTERTAINMENT INC., 1776 Broadway, New York, N.Y. 10019. Tel.: (212) 581–5833. Cable: KOLUTENT. President: **Klaus Kolmar.** Secretary–Treasurer: **Murray Luth.**

DODIE LEFEBRE, 498 West End Avenue, New York, N.Y. 10024. Tel.: (212) 724–8143. . . . LENNY–DEBIN INC., 140 West 58th Street, New York, N.Y. 10019. Tel.: (212) JU 2–0270. Cable: LENNDEB. . . . JACQUES LEISER, 155 West 68th Street, Dorchester Towers, New York, N.Y. 10023. Tel.: (212) 595–6414. Also: 52 rue de Rome, Paris 8, France Tel.: 387–5640. . . . HAROLD LEVENTHAL MANAGEMENT INC., 200 West 57th Street, New York, N.Y. 10019. Tel.: (212) JU 6–6553. Manager: **Irene Bryant.** . . . JUDITH LIEGNER ARTISTS MANAGEMENT, 33 Greenwich Avenue, New York, N.Y. 10014. Tel.: (212) 989–7041. . . . LISARELLI MANAGEMENT, P.O. Box 9061, Berkeley, California 94709. Tel.: (415) 232–8974. . . . MRS. LORNA LA FOND LITOWSKA, 740 Watchung Avenue, Plainfield, N.J. 07060. . . . LUDWIG LUSTIG & FLORIAN, LTD., 111 West 57th Street, New York, N.Y. 10019. Tel.: (212) JU 6–3976. Cable: MUSILUSTIG. President: **Ludwig Lustig.** Secretary: **Louise Florian.**

MARIANNE MARSHALL, P.O Box 3372, Long Beach, California 90803. Tel.: (213) 434–1374. . . . MASTERWORK ARTISTS BUREAU, 300 Mendham Road, Morristown, N.J. 07960. Tel.: (201) 538–1860. Manager: **Mrs. Robert C. May.** . . . JIM MCCLELLAND ASSOCIATES, 2031 Chestnut Street, Philadelphia, Pennsylvania 19103. Tel.: (215) 563–7874/8454. . . . ALBERT MORINI, 119 West 57th Street, New York, N.Y. 10019. Tel.: (212) CI 5–6143. Cable: KONZMORINI.

WILLIAM MORRIS AGENCY INC., New York office: 1350 Avenue of the Americas, New York, N.Y. 10019. Tel.: (212) JU 6–5100. Cable: WILLMORRIS. Other offices: 151 El Camino Drive, Beverly Hills, California 90212, Tel.: (213) 274–7451, 272–4111; 435 North Michigan Avenue, Chicago, Illinois 60611, Tel.: (312) 467–1744. Concert Division Director: **Otto Salomon.** . . . ELEANOR MORRISON MANAGEMENT, 327 Central Park West, New York, N.Y. 10025. Tel.: (212) 865–9420. . . . LILLIAN MURTAGH CONCERT MANAGEMENT, Box 272, Canaan, Connecticut 06018. Tel.: (203) 824–7877. . . . MUSIC UNLIMITED ASSOCIATES, 416 Marlborough Street, Boston, Massachusetts 02115. Tel.: (617) 536–2950. Cable: MUSUN. Artistic Director: **Robert Brink.** . . . MUSICAL ARTISTS INC., 119 West 57th Street, New York, N.Y. 10019. Tel.: (212) JU 6–2747/2759. Cable: MUSARTISTS. Director: **Susan Pimsleur.**

NATIONAL MUSIC LEAGUE INC., 130 West 56th Street, New York, N.Y. 10019. Tel.: (212) CO 5–2472. Cable: NAMULEAGUE. Managing Director: **Ward J. Pinner.** . . . NEW ARTS MANAGEMENT, 33 Wooster Street, New York, N.Y. 10014. Tel.: (212) 691–5434. Director: **Catherine Farinon-Smith.** . . . NEW YORK RECITAL ASSOCIATES, 353 West 57th Street. New York, N.Y. 10019. Tel.: (212) LT 1–1429. President: **Ann J. O'Donnell.**

MICHAEL O'DANIEL—ARTISTS' REPRESENTATIVE (formerly Music and

Drama Associates in New York City), Box 1599, Newark, N.J. 07102. Tel.: (201) 624–1647. . . . ANNE J. O'DONNELL MANAGEMENT, 353 West 57th Street, New York, N.Y. 10019. Tel.: (212) Lt 1–1184. . . . ON STAGE '72–73, 142 West End Avenue, Suite 28U, New York, N.Y. 10023. Tel.: (212) 787–3864. Director: **Robert T. Gaus.** . . . OPERA ARTISTS, 23 Stuyvesant Street, New York, N.Y. 10003. Tel.: (212) GR 7–6212. President: **Richard Flusser.**

P.M.S. CONCERT AGENCY, 3200 37th Avenue, West, Seattle, Washington 98199. Tel.: (206) AT 5–1272. Artists Representative: **Frances George.** . . . PACIFIC WORLD ARTISTS INC., 250 West 57th Street, New York, N.Y. 10019. Tel.: (212) 581–3644. Cable: PACIFICART. Director: **Kazuko Tatsumura Hillyer.** . . . BETTY PARRY MANAGEMENT, 4814 Falstone Avenue, Chevy Chase, Maryland 20015. Tel.: (301) 652–5665. . . . BENJAMIN PATTERSON LIMITED, Carnegie Hall, Suite 1203, New York, N.Y. 10019. Tel.: (212) 246–4362. Cable: BENJPATLIM. . . . PERFORMING ARTS MANAGEMENT INC., 230 Riverside Drive, Apt. 17D, New York, N.Y. 10025. Tel.: (212) 663–8500. Director: **G. Conway Graml.** . . . KAY PERPER MANAGEMENT, 152 West 58th Street, New York, N.Y. 10019. Tel.: (212) 766–2515. Director: **Kay Perper.** . . . PERROTTA MANAGEMENT, 122 East 78th Street, New York, N.Y. 10021. Tel.: (212) 628–6849. Director: **William T. Perrotta.** . . . ANNI PETERS, 303 South Avenue 57, Los Angeles, California 90042. Tel.: (213) 258–1647. SHERMAN PITLUCK INC., 157 West 57th Street, New York, N.Y. 10019. Tel.: (212) 247–0660. Cable: PITARTS. President: **Sherman Pitluck.** . . . MICHAEL PODOLI CONCERT MANAGEMENT, 171 West 71st Street, New York, N.Y. 10023. Tel.: (212) TR 7–1001. . . . BESS PRUITT ASSOCIATES, 819 East 168th Street, Bronx, N.Y. 10459. Tel.: (212) 589–0400. Cable: BEEPEEYEA. Director: **Bessie J. Pruitt.** Associate Director: **Henry J. Pruitt.** . . . PRYOR-MENZ ATTRACTIONS INC., Box 455, 710 Willow Avenue, Council Bluffs, Iowa 51501. Tel.: (712) 328–2361. President: **Clifford W. Menz.** . . . THOMAS PYLE, 711 West End Avenue, New York, N.Y. 10025. Tel.: (212) 663–3087.

RAPSODIA CONCERT MANAGEMENT, P.O. Box 3990, Merchandise Mart, Chicago, Illinois 60654. . . . CHARLES REINHARD MANAGEMENT, 510 Madison Avenue, New York, N.Y. 10022. Tel.: (212) PL 9–8931. . . . JOANNE RILE, ARTISTS' REPRESENTATIVE, 424 West Upsal Street, Philadelphia, Pennsylvania 19119. Tel.: (215) GE 8–0627. . . . HERBERT ROUVAIN, Fountainview Building, 3909 North Murray Avenue, Milwaukee, Wisconsin 53211.

FRANK E. SALOMON, 129 West 56th Street, New York, N.Y. 10019. Tel.: (212) 581–5197. . . . SARDOS ARTIST MANAGEMENT CORPORATION, 180 West End Avenue, New York, N.Y. 10023. Tel.: (212) 874–2559. President: **James Sardos.** . . . DAVID SCHIFFMANN, 60 West 68th Street, Suite 10G, New York, N.Y. 10023. Tel.: (212) 877–8111. Cable: ARTISTSMAN. . . . FRANCES SCHRAM ARTISTS MANAGEMENT, 1860 Broadway, New York, N.Y. 10023. Tel.: (212) 581–9030. . . . ANDREW SCHULHOF MANAGEMENT, 260 West End Avenue, New York, N.Y. 10023. Tel.: (212) TR 4–6697. Cable: CONCERTOUR. Director: **Belle Schulhof.** . . . JIM SCOVOTTI MANAGEMENT, 185 West End Avenue, New York, N.Y. 10023. Tel.: (212) 799–1792. . . . NORMAN J. SEAMAN AND EUGENE L. SEAMAN, 1697 Broadway, Suite 906, New York, N.Y. 10019. Tel.: (212) CI 5–9250. . . . DOLORES SEJDA, 2111 Locust Street, Philadelphia, Pennsylvania 19103. Tel.: (215) LO 8–6765. . . . ERIC SEMON ASSOCIATES INC., 111 West 57th Street, New York, N.Y. 10019. Tel.: (212) 765–1310. Cable: CELLOSEMON. Directors: **Gerard Semon, Marianne Semon.** . . . ARTHUR SHAFMAN INTERNATIONAL LIMITED, 475 Fifth Avenue, New York, N.Y. 10036. Tel.: (212) MU 3–3421. TR 3–1559. President: **Arthur Shafman.** . . . SHAW CONCERTS INC., 233 West 49th Street, Suite 800, New York, N.Y. 10019. Tel.: (212) 581–4654. Cable:

SHAWCONCER. President: **Harold Shaw.** . . . ETHEL D. SIPPERLY, 3312 Perry Avenue, Bronx, N.Y. 10467. Tel.: (212) OL 5–6677. . . . DINA SMITH ASSOCIATES, 72 La Espiral, Orinda, California 94563. Tel.: (415) 254–4929. . . . MARTHA MOORE SMITH ENTERPRISES, 2109 Broadway, Suite 13–102, New York, N.Y. 10023. Tel.: (212) SU 7–3300. . . . SHELDON SOFFER MANAGEMENT, 130 West 56th Street, New York, N.Y. 10019. Tel.: (212) PL 7–8060. Cable: SHELSOFFER. . . . SOUTHWESTERN ARTIST SERVICE, 7612 Bryn Mawr, Dallas, Texas 75225. Tel.: (214) 369–2210. Directors: **Eugene S. Lewis** and **Mildred Sale.** . . . MARY SPECTOR ARTISTS' MANAGEMENT INC., 250 West 57th Street, New York, N.Y. 10019. Tel.: (212) 586–3445. President: **Mary Spector.** Associate Director: **Mary Alan Hoskinson.** . . . WILLIAM L. STEIN INC., 111 West 57th Street, New York, N.Y. 10019. Tel.: (212) CO 5–3715. Cable: STEINWILL. . . . RAY G. STEINER MANAGEMENT, 1300 West Roscoe Street, Chicago, Illinois 60657. Tel.: (312) 248–4849. . . . ANN SUMMERS MANAGEMENT INC., via Mario dei Fiori, 42, Rome, Italy. Tel.: (06) 678–5747. Cable: ANNSUMMERS ROME. . . . SUPER ATTRACTIONS INC., 1015 18th Street, N.W., Washington, D.C. 20036. Tel.: (202) 833–2700. Representative: **Felix W. Salmaggi.** . . . PAUL SZILARD PRODUCTIONS INC., 161 West 73rd Street, New York, N.Y. 10023. Tel.: (212) 799–4756. Cable: PASZILBAL.

SIDNEY TALESNICK ASSOCIATES, 578 East 16th Street, Brooklyn, N.Y. 11226. Tel.: (212) 462–5197. . . . M.N. THOMPSON, 400 East 52nd Street, Apt. 9F, New York, N.Y. 10022. Tel.: (212) PL 3–2492. . . . PHIL TIPPIN, 35–45 79th Street, Jackson Heights, N.Y. 11372. Tel.: (212) HI 6–5595. . . . REGINALD S. TONRY, 4 East 75th Street, New York, N.Y. 10021. Tel.: (212) 249–3500. . . . TORNAY MANAGEMENT, 250 West 57th Street, New York, N.Y. 10019. Tel.: (212) 246–2270. Owner: **Sara Tornay.** . . . RICHARD TORRENCE MANAGEMENT, 394 East Palisade, Englewood, N.J. 07631. Tel.: (201) 569–8616, (212) 927–9700. Cable: ORGANARTS. Booking Director: **Dorothy R. Lake.**

VINCENT ATTRACTIONS INC., 119 West 57th Street, New York, N.Y. 10019. Tel.: (212) 265–4300. Cable: CENTVIN. President: **J. J. Vincent.**

RICHARD WEINER INC., 280 Park Avenue, New York, N.Y. 10017. Tel.: (212) 661–0088. . . . WENDEL ARTISTS' MANAGEMENT, INC., 95 Commercial Street, Plainview, L.I., N.Y. 11803. Tel.: (516) 938–3498. President: **Henry Wendel.** . . . WAYNE WILBUR MANAGEMENT, 1528 South Crescent Avenue, Park Ridge, Illinois 60068. Tel.: (312) TA 3–4952. New York Office: P.O. Box 2862, Grand Central Station, New York, N.Y. 10017. Tel.: (212) LE 5–6024. Cable: WAYWILMAN. . . . LEVERETT WRIGHT CONCERT MANAGEMENT INC., 161 West 57th Street, New York, N.Y. 10019. Tel.: (212) 581–4510. Hartford Office: Bushnell Auditorium, Capitol Avenue, Hartford, Connecticut 06106. Tel.: (203) 525–7455.

YOUNG CONCERT ARTISTS INC., 75 East 55th Street, New York, N.Y. 10022. Tel.: (212) PL 9–2541. Director: **Mrs. Susan Popkin Wadsworth.**

ZAROVICH CONCERT MANAGEMENT INC., 119 West 57th Street, New York, N.Y. 10019. Tel.: (212) 247–5133. Cable: ZARCONCERT. President: **J. H. Zarovich.** . . . ARTHUR D. ZINBERG, 11 East 44th Street, New York, N.Y. 10017. Tel.: (212) YU 6–7077. Cable: ARTZINLAW.

Part 14 Foreign Supplement

Foreign Music Festivals

Australia

ARTS FESTIVAL OF ADELAIDE, Box 1950, GPO Adelaide, South Australia 5001; begun in 1960; Australian orchestras and native and foreign soloists; composers' seminar.

Austria

BREGENZ FESTIVAL, Kornmarkstrasse 7, 6900 Bregenz; founded in 1946; attracts about 80,000 people each year; presents music on the floating stage in Lake Constance (opera, operetta, ballet, concerts); events are also held in the Guild Hall near the lake, the Feldkirch, and the Theater; the regular ensemble is the Vienna Symphony and the Vienna State Opera; about 42 programs are presented.

SALZBURG FESTIVALS, Hofstallgasse 1, 5010 Salzburg; begun in 1920 as an outgrowth of the 19th century Mozart festivals; still retains the music of Mozart as its central idea; festival organizers included Richard Strauss, Max Reinhardt, Bruno Walter, among others; the old Festival House (completed in 1925) is used primarily for performances of Mozart operas; a new $11-million Festival Theater opened in 1960 and is located next to the older house. The new theater is large: 100-foot stage and seats 2,360; in addition to those scheduled for the Festival House, performances are held throughout the city: Landestheater (drama and ballet), Domplatz, Felsenreitschule, the Mozarteum, as well as in churches and the cathedral. Musical fare: operas (about 6), plays, ballets (about 4 performances), orchestral concerts (15 in 1973), chamber concerts, instrumental and vocal recitals, Mozart matinees and serenades (totaling about 18), and sacred music concerts (4). The festival is held in conjunction with a number of other Salzburg events taking place about the same time; among them are the summer courses at the Mozarteum. Usual orchestral ensembles are the Vienna Philharmonic and the Mozarteum Orchestra.

VIENNA FESTIVAL WEEKS (Wiener Festwochen), Rathausstrasse 9, 1010 Vienna 1; founded in 1951; has organized some of its festivals on special themes: choirs (13 choirs from Europe and the United States in 1958), Haydn (1959), centenary of Mahler's birth (1960); as many as nine instrumental ensembles, from chamber groups to symphony orchestras, have appeared at one festival; the orchestras usually include the Vienna Philharmonic and the Vienna Symphony Orchestra plus invited German, Czech, Polish, Russian, and English groups. An imposing list of conductors appear before these groups as well as the two or more productions of the Vienna State Opera; operetta productions form an essential feature of the festival; performances of large choral works abound as do solo recitals. Events take place in front of the Wiener Rathaus (opening ceremony), the Staatsoper, the Burgtheater, Theater an der

Wien, and open air locales. In 1973, the festival was held from mid-May to mid-June.

Bulgaria

INTERNATIONAL MUSICAL FESTIVAL "MARCH MUSICAL DAYS," c/o General Directorate "Bulgarian Music," 56 Alabin Str., Sofia; festival held in Ruse March–April.

INTERNATIONAL MUSICAL FESTIVAL "SOFIA MUSICAL WEEKS," c/o General Directorate "Bulgarian Music," 56, Alabin Str., Sofia; 1972 festival May 24th–June 25th.

INTERNATIONAL MUSICAL FESTIVAL "VARNESKO LYATO," c/o General Directorate "Bulgarian Music," 56, Alabin Str., Sofia; 1972 festival July 1st–20th in Varna.

Canada

BANFF FESTIVAL OF THE ARTS, Banff Centre, Banff, Alberta. A week-long festival begun in 1971. It is held in the Eric Harvie and the Margaret Greenham theaters, on the campus of the Banff Centre School of Fine Arts, respectively seating 1,000 and 250. The 1972 event ran for one week beginning August 13 and included programs and exhibitions of opera, concert music, ballet, film, drama, poetry readings, pottery, weaving, and painting. Workshop-style productions of the performing arts were staged in the afternoon, and the evenings were given over to the major festival performances. One of the objectives of the festival is to display the talents of the students of the Banff Centre along with the work of the faculty. Banff is in the Canadian rockies.

SHAW FESTIVAL, Box 774, Niagara-on-the-Lake, Ontario, Canada. Begun in 1970. The 1972 event was called "Music Today '72" and featured contemporary and traditional music in 10 concerts held in St. Mark's Church in Niagara from August 5 to August 19. The programs consist of music for small ensembles of mixed instrumental and vocal combinations. Ensembles include the Lyric Trio (flute soprano and piano), Orford Quartet, and Nexus (a percussion group of five players). The 1972 series included an all-George Crumb (U.S. composer) concert and an unusual assortment of the music of composers from Czechoslovakia, Taiwan, Japan, Sweden, and Canada, among others.

STRATFORD SHAKESPEAREAN FESTIVAL, 109 Erie Street, Stratford, Ontario; founded in 1952; music festivals began in 1953 and have subsequently increased in scope; fare includes drama, concerts, recitals, and jazz programs in the Festival Theatre, and films in the Avon Theatre; the 1972 festival ran from June 5 to October 21; there are also music master classes.

Colombia

FESTIVAL OF CARTAGENA DE INDIAS, Apartado Aéreo 109, Cartagena; begun in 1945, terminated in 1953, and reorganized in 1959; Musical Director: **Guillermo Espinosa;** concerts, recitals, dance performances, lectures, and exhibitions; held in the Caribbean fortress city of Cartagena during May (10 days); concerts are held in the Teatro Cartagena.

Czechoslovakia

"PRAGUE SPRING" FESTIVAL, c/o Secretary, Prague Spring, International Festival of Music, Dum Umelcu, Alešovo Nábřeži 12, Prague 1; founded in 1946; the festival always begins on May 12th, the date of Smetana's death in 1884, with a performance of Smetana's symphonic cycle, "My Country." Concerts are held throughout the city: the Smetana Hall, Smetana Theater, the National Theater, the House of Artists, the House of the Union of Czech Composers, the gardens of the Wallenstein Palace, Prague Château Court, and other places; exhibitions are held in the National Museum, Villa Mozart, National Gallery, the Smetana and Dvořák Museums. The festival features much Czech music with a lengthy roster of performing ensembles from Czechoslovakia, the countries of East Europe, and other nations; as many as 29 operas are sometimes presented; considered the most lavish music festival in East Europe.

Denmark

AARHUS FESTIVAL WEEK (Aarhus Festuge), Town Hall, 8000 Aarhus C. Performances of drama, opera, ballet, concerts, along with sports, exhibitions, and other activities. Aarhus is on the east coast of the Jutland Peninsula and is the site of a 13th-century cathedral, an opera house built in 1816, an "Old Town" which holds a fair during Festival Week (early September), and an archaeological museum of some fame. Music performances are held in the Jutland Academy of Music, Elsinore Theater, Aarhus Theater, and in the Cathedral. The 1972 Festival included performances by the Royal Danish Ballet, the Aarhus Symphony Orchestra, Mikis Theodorakis and ensemble, the Frankfurt Bach Orchestra, plus open air jazz concerts and concerts of Danish music.

ROYAL DANISH BALLET AND MUSIC FESTIVAL, c/o The Royal Theater, Festival Office, 3 Tordenskjoldsgade DK–1055, Copenhagen K; the festival takes place in Copenhagen, Elsinore, and Odense; a highlight of each festival is the series of performances by the Royal Danish Ballet; events are scheduled for the Tivoli Concert Hall, the Royal Theater (for Ballet and opera), at the State Radio, "Louisiana"—a museum north of Copenhagen, Copenhagen Cathedral, Kronberg Castle, Elsinore, etc.; foreign and Danish artists and ensembles appear.

England

ALDEBURGH FESTIVAL OF MUSIC AND THE ARTS, Aldeburgh, Suffolk; begun in 1948; held for 10 days in June at this seaside resort 99 miles from London; it is now the home of **Benjamin Britten,**the founder and central figure of the festival; there are performances of opera (by the English Opera Group), chamber and solo recitals, lectures, poetry readings, and exhibitions.

BATH FESTIVAL, Festival Society Ltd., Linley House, 1 Pierrepoint Place, Bath BAI, IJY, Somerset; established in 1948; Artistic Director: **Yehudi Menuhin;** in 1973 the festival ran from May 25 to June 3; performances given in the 7th-century Bath Abbey and other halls and churches; concerts are designed around the Bath Festival Chamber Orchestra (led by Menuhin and others); other guest ensembles have included the London Symphony Orchestra, Moscow Chamber Orchestra, etc.; chamber music, drama, ballet, and art exhibitions comprise the remainder of the programs.

CHELTENHAM FESTIVAL OF BRITISH CONTEMPORARY MUSIC, Cheltenham, Gloucestershire (Town Hall); founded in 1945; held for two weeks early in July at the fashionable inland resort 121 miles from London; premiere performances of new works by British composers form the highlight of the festival.

THREE CHOIRS FESTIVAL, c/o Festival Secretary, 3 College Green, Gloucester; held in three towns: Gloucester, Worcester, and Hereford; founded early in the 18th century and features the choirs of the cathedrals of the three towns; takes place one week in September; the towns are from 114 to 150 miles from London; other choirs also perform, and there are orchestral concerts and organ recitals; the 246th gathering of the choirs occurred in 1973; held in association with the Arts Council of Great Britain; in Gloucester performances are held in the Cathedral, St. Mary de Lode Church, and the Technical College.

GLYNDEBOURNE OPERA FESTIVAL, Lewes, Sussex; London Box Office: 23 Baker Street, W.1; founded in 1934; held May to August near the village of Glynde 53 miles from London; founded by John Christie (d. 1962) on the grounds of his 135-acre, 700-year-old ancestral home; the only privately owned opera in England, it is known mainly for its performances of Mozart's operas in a small (800 seats) specially built theater; singers reside at the estate during the festival (rehearsals last about six weeks); the orchestra is usually the Royal Philharmonic.

Finland

FOLK MUSIC FESTIVAL KAUSTINEN, Tourist Office of Central Ostrobothnia, Pitkäsillankatu 22, 67100 Kokkola 10. Founded in 1968. Held for one week in July. Reputedly one of the most popular events of Finland's summer. It offers performances of hundreds of folk players, dancers, and singers with both traditional music and modern adaptations and manifestations of the traditional. Groups from abroad are included in the programs. There are exhibitions of folk instruments and music as well as a folk music camp for youths and an international folk music seminar for teachers.

HELSINKI FESTIVAL, Unioninkatu 28, 00100 Helsinki 10. Founded 1968. The festival is Finland's most prestigious. A two-week affair running from late August to September, it offers concerts of standard classical fare, opera, ballet, theater, film, jazz and pop music, etc. Finland's national music companies and ensembles are featured along with guest performers of world repute. Recent artists have been **Claudio Arrau, Emil Gilels,** and **Martti Talvela;** among the recent invited foreign orchestras has been Japan's NHK Symphony Orchestra under **Hiroyuki Iwaki.** Finlandia House, Helsinki's newest concert hall (opened in 1971), is the location of the regular concerts; other events take place in halls, galleries, churches, parks, and the old fortress of Sveaborg.

JYVÄSKYLÄ ARTS FESTIVAL, Kauppakatu 9 C 36, 40100 Jyväskylä 10. Established in 1955. One of the main features of the annual festival is its series of congresses—lectures, seminars, and discussions on various social, cultural, and ideological problems of international interest. The arts events involve the theme of the congress, which itself lasts about half the duration of the festival in general. The events begin in late June and end after the first week in July. Classical music programs are performed by the local symphony orchestra and chorus in churches and halls and feature soloists, some from the international scene: **Igor Bezrodnyi, Paul Tortelier, Dimitri Bashkirov,** to name some from recent engagements.

KUOPIO DANCE AND MUSIC FESTIVAL, Kuopion Yhteisteatteri, Niiralankatu 2, 70600, Kuopio 60; founded in 1969. This is a festival of music and dance held for about nine days in June. Finnish and international band music is featured with pops concerts, fiddler "jam sessions," and a parade. There are also band competitions for youth and conducting seminars for brass band leaders. The dance part of the festival has presented ballet and folk-dance groups from throughout Europe including such companies as the Estonian Theatre Ballet, the Koco Racin Dance Ensemble from Yugoslavia, the Latvian Daile dance and instrumental ensemble as well as groups from England, Sweden, France, Denmark, the Soviet Union and Rumania. Performances take place in concert halls and theaters with open air performances in the streets and parks.

PORI JAZZ FESTIVAL, Pori Jazz 66 ry, Luvianpuistokatu 2 D, 28100 Pori 10. Founded in 1966. Held for three days in July in various halls and restaurants. The main concert is an open air event located on Kirjurinluoto Island in the middle of town. Late-night jam sessions abound throughout the duration of the festival and there are lectures and seminars for musicians, critics, teachers, and jazz fans, a jazz café, exhibitions, and films. Performers are groups and soloists from the United States and Europe; Finnish groups are represented by some of the big-name bands. Pori is on Finland's West Coast and has population of about 70,000.

SAVONLINNA OPERA FESTIVAL, City Tourist Office, Olavinkatu 35, 57130 Savonlinna 13. Established in 1912. It was interrupted in 1930 and renewed in 1967. Concerts take place in the medieval castle (Olavinlinna Castle built in 1475) which is the town's prime tourist attraction and whose Great Courtyard has an open air stage and seating for 3,000 people. Chamber music concerts, art exhibitions, and theater make up the other programs. The opera festival, which takes place during July (lasting about 10 days), is not the only musical event in the town, since there is a general Savonlinna music festival lasting from June to July as well as a Summer Music Seminar.

TURKU MUSIC FESTIVAL, Sibelius Museum, Piispankatu 17, 20500 Turku 50. Founded in 1959. Festival events are scheduled for a number of locations throughout the city, Finland's oldest and former capital. In churches, museums, manors, in streets and parks, the music concerts and art exhibitions are held for a week in August. Finland's first pop and rock music festival was held in Turku (in 1970) as part of the festival and has since drawn crowds of over 100,000.

France

AIX-EN-PROVENCE FESTIVAL INTERNATIONAL DE MUSIQUE, Casino D'Aix-en-Provence, 13-Aix-en-Provence. Held in July; organized in 1948; offers three or four operas (sometimes six) from the classical repertory in the Théâtre de l'Archevêché; choral concerts take place in the Cathédrale Saint-Sauveur and the Théâtre; concerts and recitals in the Théâtre, Cloître Saint-Louis, and the Hôtel de Maynier d'Oppède; French, German, Dutch, Belgian, Monacan, and Italian ensembles have played there; soloists are of international fame.

FESTIVAL JEAN-SEBASTIAN BACH DE MAZAMET, c/o Mme. Gauthier, 4 av. de la Mairie, Aussillon 81, Mazamet. The 1972 festival of the music of J. S. Bach was held from September 7 to 10 and was the seventh in the series. Performances take place in the town of Mazamet, Gaillac, Castres, and Aussillon in various churches, chapels, etc., such as Abbatiale Saint-Michel de Gaillac, Eglise du Sacré-Coeur d'Aussillon, Grand Temple de Mazamet, etc. The emphasis is on the cantatas of Bach with an evening devoted to chamber music. Performers have included the Gaechinger Kantorei and Bach Collegium Stuttgart under **Helmut Rilling; Pierre Barbizet,** pianist; **Devy Erlih,** violinist. Mazamet is in the province of Tarn, east of Toulouse.

BESANÇON INTERNATIONAL MUSIC FESTIVAL, Parc des Expositions-Planoise, 25 Besançon. Held in conjunction with the International Competition for Young Conductors; founded in 1948; held in September; orchestral events, with chorus or featured soloists, form the heart of the festival; usual orchestras are: Orchestre Philharmonique de l'Office de Radiodiffusion Télévision Française, Orchestre National de l'Office de Radiodiffusion Télévision Française, and the Orchestre de la Société des Concerts du Conservatoire; conductors are world-renowned. Chamber groups, choirs, and ballet troupes also appear. Some concerts are held in the hall of the Parliament of Franche-Comté (18th century); each festival schedules premiere performances. The International Competition for Young Conductors, formed in 1951, is open to young men and women under 30.

BORDEAUX MAY FESTIVAL, c/o Commissariat du Festival, 252 Faubourg Saint-Honoré, 75008 Paris; Bordeaux address: Grand-Théâtre, 33000 Bordeaux; founded in 1950; presents one opera, either a new one or a seldom played one, in two performances in the Grand-Théâtre. Other events take place in the Château de la Brède, Château Mouton-Rothschild, the Cathédrale St. André (and other churches), the Public Gardens, Château d'Youem, and other locations. Orchestras have been the Bordeaux Philharmonic, the Berlin Chamber Orchestra, Munich Pro Art, Philadelphia Orchestra, Madrid National Orchestra, etc. There are chamber recitals, choral events, solo recitals, ballets, drama (by the Théâtre National, among others), and art exhibitions held in the Galerie des Beaux-Arts. World famous performers are always engaged. The festival is under official French patronage.

FESTIVAL INTERNATIONAL DE LA DANSE DE PARIS, Théâtre des Champs-Elysées, 15, avenue Montaigne, Paris 8e. Held in November and presents both modern and classical dance performed by groups from throughout the world.

FESTIVAL DE PRADES (Fidélité à Pau Casals), B.P. No. 2, Mairie de Prades, 66–Prades. Begun in 1951 and for many years under the direction of **Pablo Casals.** Held in July and August, it presents solo recitalists and chamber music groups in a series of consecutive evening concerts (in 1972, from July 25 to August 9). These take place in the churches of Saint-Michel de Cuxa and Saint-Pierre de Prades. Artists from France and other countries are engaged. In 1972 they included **Gaby** and **Robert Casadesus, Alexis Weissenberg, Yehudi Menuhin, Pierre Fournier, Jean-Pierre Rampal, Roger Delmotte,** Mozart Chamber Orchestra of Salzburg, and the Bulgarian Quartet. The repertory played is mostly 18th- and 19th-century. Prades is at the foot of Canigou in the east Pyrenees mountains not far from the sea, in a region of ample tourist facilities.

ROYAN FESTIVAL, Office du Tourisme, Hôtel de Ville, 17 Royan, or: Boîte Postale 517, 17 Royan. Held for seven days in late March. Offers concerts, films, dances and recitals.

SCEAUX FESTIVAL "NUITS DE SCEAUX" (The Nights of Sceaux), 18 bis rue de Penthièvre, Sceaux, Seine; begun in 1947; mainly French music played in the Pavillon de l'Aurore; held in June.

SEMAINES MUSICALES INTERNATIONALES DE PARIS (Paris International Music Weeks), c/o Théâtre de la Musique, 70 rue Réaumur, Paris 3e; begun in 1958; presents about 30 concerts; organized originally by the International Music Council and the Chambre Syndicale des Organisateurs de Concerts de France, but since 1960 has been directed by the French National Committee of the International Music Council; held biennially: 1968, 1970, 1972, etc. in June; devoted mainly to orchestral and chamber music, classical and contemporary; performing ensembles are French, Danish, German, English, Italian, among others.

STRASBOURG INTERNATIONAL MUSIC FESTIVAL, c/o Festival de Strasbourg, 24 rue de la Mésange, F 67081 Strasbourg; founded in 1932 and is considered the oldest of continuing French festivals; held in June; the festival presents a good deal of contemporary music, most of it orchestral and choral, totaling about seven concerts. The resident orchestras are the Orchestre de Radio-Symphonique de Strasbourg and the Orchestre Philharmonique de Strasbourg; guest ensembles have been: the French Broadcasting National Orchestra, Warsaw Philharmonic, Italian Radio Orchestra, Berlin Philharmonic, London Symphony, Stuttgart Chamber Orchestra. Choruses: the Cathedral Choir and the choir of St. Guillaume, both of Strasbourg. Plays are presented by the Théâtre National Populaire; ballet by the Strasbourg Ballet Troupe. Performances take place in the famed Strasbourg Cathedral, the church of St. Guillaume, the Palais des Fêtes, and the courtyard of Château des Rohan; chamber and sacred works of all periods, and chamber and solo recitals are included.

FÊTES MUSICALES EN TOURAINE, Mairie de Tours, 37-Tours (Address is c/o the Mayoralty of Tours.) The festival is a concert series of two consecutive weekends (Friday to Sunday) in late June to early July. They take place in Grange de Meslay northwest of Tours proper, off route R.N. 10. The 1972 event was the ninth annual and featured pianist **Sviatoslav Richter,** the Juilliard String Quartet, Orchestre de Paris with **Georg Solti,** and soprano **Mady Mesplé.** Tickets are available at the box office the day of performance or through advance reservations.

East Germany (German Democratic Republic)

SCHÜTZ FESTIVAL, Dresden; begun in 1955; three days in July; in honor of Heinrich Schütz.

West Germany

ANSBACH BACH FESTIVAL, Städtisches Verkehrsamt, 88 Ansbach; held biennially in July in the medieval town of Ansbach; Bach's secular works are performed in the Baroque Mirror Hall or the Margrave Castle; religious works are performed in the 14th-century Johanniskirche; central musical figure is **Karl Richter,** director, conductor, and performer; the Munich Bach Choir and the Soloists Association of the Ansbach Festival usually perform; well-known soloists appear.

BAYREUTH WAGNER FESTIVAL, Bayreuther Festspiele, Postfach 2320, 858 Bayreuth; founded 1876; held July to August; about 28 performances are presented of Wagner's operas with usually two performances of the entire "Ring" operas; world-famous singers are engaged along with well-known conductors; ensembles are the Festival Orchestra and the Festival Chorus; performances take place in the world-famous Festival Theater.

BERLIN FESTIVAL WEEKS, Berliner Festspiele GmbH, Bundesallee 1–12, 1 Berlin 15; begun in 1951; held September to October; presents as many as nine operas by the German State Opera Company and one staged by a visiting company from another German city; performances now take place in a new opera house built in 1961. Usually included in each festival are two or three premiere opera productions. Two ballet companies perform at each festival, the ballet company of the German Opera, plus a guest group such as the Royal Ballet, London, Ballet de l'Opéra, Paris, an American troupe, etc. Drama is presented by the Berlin State Theater and two to four invited companies: Piraeus Theater, Athens; Frankfurt State Theater; National Theater of Helsinki; and others. Orchestra concerts are presented by two to four orchestras including the Berlin Philharmonic. Guest orchestras have been the Vienna Philharmonic, West German Radio Orchestra, NHK Orchestra of Tokyo, Royal Philharmonic, London; as is the case with the opera program, there is usually a local or world premiere performance of a new orchestral work. The festival also schedules chamber concerts, solo recitals, and exhibitions of works of art.

BONN BEETHOVEN FESTIVAL, c/o Beethovenhalle, Bonn; founded in 1931; usually held in September; organized by the City of Bonn; the new Beethovenhalle was opened in 1959; the music of Beethoven is played by famous ensembles and performers; besides guest orchestras, there is the Bonn Municipal Orchestra.

DARMSTADT FESTIVAL OF CONTEMPORARY MUSIC, Nieder Ramstädterstrasse 190, 61 Darmstadt; held in mid-July, this festival in the front ranks of the avant-grade is organized by the Hessian Radio and the International Summer School on Contemporary Music at Darmstadt; the festival has taken place since 1946; usual fare consists of two orchestral and two chamber concerts, and performances of two operas.

DONAUESCHINGEN FESTIVAL OF CONTEMPORARY MUSIC, Heinrich Strobel, Dir., Städtisches Verkehrsamt, 771 Donaueschingen; organized by the Society of Friends of Music at Donaueschingen as an outgrowth of Duke Max Egon zu Fürstenberg's original events begun in 1921; the first musical event featured music by the then unknown Hindemith, Krenek, and Alban Berg; the festival, which has always lasted two days, was reorganized in 1945 at the Fürstenberg Castle; the orchestra employed is the South-west Radio Orchestra of Baden-Baden; a new Festival Hall was built in 1960; the music is contemporary with a significant amount of electronic or experimental music; usually takes place in October.

HANDEL FESTIVAL, Städtisches Verkehrsamt, 34 Göttingen; held in June and July; the city helped to create a Handel opera revival (1920) and features an opera with each festival; under the auspices of the Göttingen Handel Society; also presents oratorios, chamber works.

KASSEL MUSIC DAYS, c/o Arbeitskreis für Haus und Jugendmusik E.V., Heinrich-Schütz-Allee 35, Kassel-Wilhelmshöhe; held in October; chamber music, choral and orchestral concerts, opera, sacred music, forums, and exhibitions; the City of Kassel and the Arbeitskreis, along with the Amerika-Haus and the Academy of Music, also sponsors (since 1961) a festival week of contemporary chamber music in April.

MUNICH OPERA FESTIVAL, Münchner Opernfestspiele, Brieffach, 8 München 1; founded in 1901; held from July to August; each festival presents operas by Strauss, Mozart, and Wagner, along with other classical and occasionally contemporary composers. The Mozart tradition has remained unbroken since 1903. The festival is especially noted for the theaters which house the productions, among them: the Cuvilliés Theater, which was inaugurated in 1958 as the restored, famous old Residenz Theater, the rococo theater which heard the first performance of Mozart's "Idomeneo." The restoration was necessary as a result of war damage. Other theaters: Prinzregententheater, Herkules-Saal of the Residenz. World famous singers are heard in the operas with the ballet, chorus, and orchestra of the Bavarian State Opera. There are also orchestral concerts and lieder recitals.

NUREMBERG FESTIVALS, a number of musical events held in the city of Nuremberg during the summer months: Serenade Concerts in the Kaiserburg Castle (May to July); Evening Music in the Courtyard of the Holy Ghost Hospital (about 6 concerts from May to September) (both of the preceding are organized by the City of Nuremberg); International Organ Festival, organized by the International Organ Week Society, Nuremberg; the 21st festival was held in 1972; old and new organ works are played by well-known and new performers.

SCHWETZINGEN FESTIVAL, Schwetzingen; May to June; orchestral concerts, opera, recitals—all organized by the town of Schwetzingen and held in the Rococo Theater of the Schwetzingen Castle; dramatic plays are also presented.

WIESBADEN INTERNATIONAL MAY FESTIVAL, c/o Büro der Internationalen Maifestspiele, Staatstheater, Wiesbaden; second oldest German festival (after Bayreuth); a special aspect of the festival since 1950 has been the appearances of foreign opera companies, in two or more productions each, as well as the performances of the resident company, the Hessisches Staatstheater, Wiesbaden. Some of the guest groups: Argentine Chamber Opera, Buenos Aires; Belgrade State Opera; Rome State Opera; Bordeaux Opera; Vienna State Opera; Teatro Massimo di Palermo. Ballet groups have been: American Ballet Theatre, Théâtre Royal de la Monnaie de Bruxelles, Belgrade National Opera Ballet. There are always plays performed by the resident theater or a visiting company.

WÜRZBURG MOZART FESTIVAL, Würzburg; organized by the City of Würzburg; orchestral concerts, choral and chamber music; resident orchestra is the Würzburg Philharmonic.

Greece

ATHENS FESTIVAL, 2, Amerikis St., Athens; begun in 1957; all performances are presented in the ancient open air theater of Herod Atticus at the foot of the Acropolis. Programs include operas performed by the National Opera of Greece; symphony concerts are by Greek and invited orchestras, among them the Berlin Philharmonic, Stuttgart Chamber Orchestra, Orchestre de la Suisse Romande, French Radio Orchestra, Cracow Philharmonic, and others; ballet has been presented by both European and American companies; ancient Greek drama and comedy is performed by the National Theatre of Greece; other European drama groups, such as the Old Vic players, have appeared as guests. July to September.

India

MADRAS MUSIC ACADEMY ANNUAL CONFERENCE AND MUSIC FESTIVAL, c/o 115 E. Mowbsays Road, Madras 14; begun in 1927 and held in December and January; about 50 performances of music and drama from both North and South India; occidental music is also presented.

Ireland

AN FEIS CEOIL (Irish Music Festival), c/o 37 Molesworth Street, Dublin; begun in 1897 and features concerts and competitions of Irish music.

DUBLIN FESTIVAL OF TWENTIETH CENTURY MUSIC, c/o The Music Association of Ireland, Ltd., 11 Suffolk Street, Dublin 2. Founded in 1969, its main purpose is to present a broad representation of solo, chamber, and orchestral music of this century, with special attention given to works by Irish composers. In 1972, the Festival was held June 24–30, in such places as St. Patrick's Cathedral, Trinity College, and St. Francis Xavier Hall. Ensembles included Radio Telefis Eireann Symphony Orchestra, Allegri Quartet, and others. The music was that of a large number of composers: Bartók, Bodley, Boulez, Boydell, Bozza, Debussy, Dutilleux, Joubert, O'Duinn, Potter, Poulenc, Sauguet, et al. There are afternoon and evening events.

Italy

FESTIVAL OF TWO WORLDS, Spoleto; c/o Festival Foundation, Inc., 119 West 57th Street, New York, N.Y. 10019; also: Festival dei due Mondi, Via Marqutta 17, Roma; begun in 1958 and founded by **Gian-Carlo Menotti;**held from June to July; all events are in the Umbrian town of Spoleto (population 12,000) and are staged in two theaters, seating 1,000 and 300 respectively; fare consists of ballet, concerts, drama, art exhibitions, and films; a major goal of the festival is to present a meeting of European and American cultures through music, the dance and drama; many young American performers are engaged.

PERUGIA SAGRA MUSICALE UMBRA (Umbrian Sacred Music Festival of Perugia), Casella Postale No. 341, 06100 Perugia; established in 1946; held in September; located in the country of St. Francis of Assisi, the festivals are mainly dedications of sacred music in a variety of forms: choral works, biblical ballets, operas, and mystery plays. Most of the events take place in Perugia with some in Assisi, Gubbio, Città di Castello, Umbra, etc. There is usually a cycle of Bach cantatas, contemporary works, and a number of large musical forms for chorus and orchestra by Baroque and Classical composers. Important European orchestras and choruses are engaged. Some unusual events have been performances of polyphonic Polish works of the 17th century, Casal's "El Pessebre," the first Italian performance of Handel's "Theodoro" and his Anthems, Schoenberg's "Jacob's Ladder," and the programs dedicated to the 13th century *flagellanti.* Many concerts are held in the Teatro Comunale Morlacchi; others in the Chiesa di Santa-Giuliana, Sala Maggiore della Pinacoteca, Chiesa di S. Agostino, and the Palazzo dei Priori.

VENICE INTERNATIONAL FESTIVAL OF CONTEMPORARY MUSIC (La Biennale di Venezia), c/o Biennale, Ca' Giustinian, Venice; founded in 1930; held in September. Contemporary music, including that by Oriental composers, comprises the main feature of the Biennale. Ensembles have been: Orchestra del Teatro la Fenice, Italian Radio-Television Orchestra, French Radio Orchestra, Cologne Radio Orchestra, Turin Italian Radio Orchestra, the Juilliard String Quartet, and others. There are plays, chamber recitals, and a water festival in San Marco basin. Concerts are heard in the La Fenice Theater, Scuola Grande di San Rocco, and the Cloister of St. Giorgio.

Japan

OSAKA INTERNATIONAL FESTIVAL, New Asahi Bldg., Nakanoshima 2–22, Kitaku, Osaka 530. Begun in 1958; held in April; from its inception, the organizers have invited European and American ensembles and artists to participate with such Japanese groups as the Osaka Philharmonic and the Japan Philharmonic (NHK Symphony); foreign orchestras have been the Leningrad Philharmonic, New York Little Orchestra Society, Pittsburgh Symphony Orchestra, Amsterdam Concertgebouw, Virtuosi di Roma; other guest groups: Amadeus Quartet, New

York City Center Ballet, Salzburg Puppet Theater, Vienna State Opera; there are usually performances of Japanese court music and classical drama, Noh plays, and western drama.

Lebanon

BAALBECK INTERNATIONAL FESTIVAL, Rue Osman Ben Affane, B.P. 4215, Beirut (Beyrouth). Baalbeck is 56 miles northeast of the coastal capital of Beirut and is one of the ancient cities of the world. Its Temples of Jupiter and Bacchus, supposedly the largest and best-preserved remains of Roman architecture left in the world within whose grounds and courtyards the festival is held, have been major tourist attractions for years. The Festival was begun in 1956. It is held in the open air and presents concerts of orchestral music with soloists and conductors from the front ranks of international artists. There are Lebanese ensembles and soloists performing folk music and dancing. Western ballet groups have also been included in virtually every festival of recent years. The 1970 and 1971 events engaged altogether the Stuttgart Chamber Orchestra with Münchinger, the New Philharmonia Orchestra, the Paul Taylor Dance Company, the Amadeus Quartet, Bolshoi Ballet, the Cracow Philharmonic Orchestra and Chorus, the Philippine National Ballet Bayanihan, **John Ogdon,** pianist, **Christian Ferras,** violinist, **Ella Fitzgerald,** "Les Nuits Libanaises Mahrajane," **Oum Koulsoum,** famed Near Eastern singer and others. The Festival is held from July until late August or early September and presents some 12 to 14 evenings of concerts of repeated pairs of programs.

Luxembourg

INTERNATIONAL OPEN AIR FESTIVAL OF MUSIC AND DRAMA, Wiltz, Grand Duchy of Luxembourg. Held from mid-July to mid-August, the festival offers one concert per week, usually on weekends. The programs consist of orchestral concerts, pop concerts, plays, opera, and ballet. Performances take place in the Wiltz castle (seating capacity: 2,100). In 1971, the Chamber Orchestra of Württemberg under **Jorg Faerber,** the pop group, East of Eden, **Grace Bumbry,** the Conservatory of Liège Orchestra under **Jean Jakus,** among others, were the featured presentations.

Monaco

MONTE CARLO FESTIVAL, Concerts du Palais Princier, Service du Tourisme, 2a Blvd. des Moulins, Monte Carlo; July to August; given in the Cour d'Honneur of the palace of the principality, the festival concerts feature the Orchestre National de l'Opéra de Monte Carlo.

Netherlands

GAUDEAMUS INTERNATIONAL WEEK, c/o Stichtung Gaudeamus (Gaudeamus Foundation), Gerard Doulan 21, Bilthoven; first held in 1946; occurs at the end of summer; features new music by young composers of many countries.

HOLLAND FESTIVAL, c/o Bureau du Holland Festival, Honthorststraat 10, Amsterdam; founded in 1948; June to July; held on the same date each summer, the festival is unique in that the events take place in various cities not too far apart: Amsterdam, the Hague, Scheveningen (where most of the events take place), Rotterdam, and Otterloo. The festival is considered Europe's largest. The Festival Foundation receives subsidies from the municipalities involved. All forms of music are performed, and there are many performances of modern works, Dutch and foreign. The list of ensembles—choral, operatic, and symphonic—and soloists who have played during the festival is both extensive and impressive. Over 125 concerts, opera, and dance programs are offered during the four weeks. Dramatic performances, given in the original languages by foreign companies, are included, along with art exhibitions in famous Dutch museums.

New Zealand

AUCKLAND FESTIVAL, c/o P.O. Box 1411, Auckland C.1; may to June; presents concerts by the National Orchestra of the New Zealand Broadcasting Service, the only full-time professional orchestra in New Zealand, founded in 1947; conductor: **John Hopkins;** performances also by the New Zealand Opera Company; imported artists also appear. The festival, begun in 1948, takes place in various locations in Auckland. In addition to music, drama and the visual arts are a part of the annual May event.

CHRISTCHURCH ARTS FESTIVAL, P.O. Box 2600, Christchurch, New Zealand. This festival was begun in 1965, and takes place every 2 or 3 years in March, in various locations in Christchurch. Musical, dramatic, and visual arts are featured.

FESTIVAL OF THE PINES, P.O. Box 354, New Plymouth, New Zealand, Founded in 1958, this annual festival takes place in the Bowl of Brooklands in January–February and offers predominantly light music.

Norway

BERGEN INTERNATIONAL FESTIVAL, c/o Festival Office (Festspillene i Bergen), P.O. Box 183, 5001 Bergen; begun in 1953; May to June; consists of concerts, ballet, drama, recitals, folklore, church concerts, jazz concerts, exhibitions, and a sightseeing tour of Gamle Bergen (Old Bergen). Recitals are played daily in Grieg's home in Troldhaugen, orchestral concerts at the Konsertpaleet, drama in Den Nationale Scene, and the Nationaltheatret, church concerts in the Domkirken, Norwegian folklore outdoors in the Nygårdsparken. Danish and internationally known foreign artists and ensembles perform. The entire festival is a memorial to Grieg.

KONGSBERG INTERNATIONAL JAZZ FESTIVAL, P.O. Box 91, 3601 Kongsberg; Founded in 1965. Kongsberg is a city of 20,000 population 60 miles southwest of Oslo. The festival is a four-day event beginning at the end of June and featuring modern jazz. Performers are Europeans and American jazzmen. There are afternoon and evening concerts.

MOLDE INTERNATIONAL JAZZ FESTIVAL, Postboks 261, 6401 Molde. Concerts, jam sessions, and films. The event has featured American musicians along with those of other countries. In 1972, the festival was held from July 31 to August 5th; Molde is on Norway's west coast on a northwest tangent from Oslo. There is a "jazz camp" for tents which can accommodate about 1,500. The festival is largely youth-oriented.

Poland

"WARSAW AUTUMN" INTERNATIONAL FESTIVAL OF CONTEMPORARY MUSIC, 27 Rynek Sterego Miasta, 00–272 Warszawa; founded in 1957; held in September; composers' music represents a number of European nations as well as the United States. The festival is the only international musical event among the Communist countries to present so much avant-garde music, including electronic music, as part of a series devoted to contemporary music. There are symphonic and choral concerts, chamber recitals, and ballets. Among the ensembles to have performed thus far: the National Philharmonic Choir and Orchestra of Warsaw, Katowice Radio Symphony, Cracow State Philharmonic, Melos Ensemble of London, LaSalle String Quartet of Cincinnati.

Portugal

SINTRA MUSICAL DAYS (JORNADAS MUSICAIS DE SINTRA), c/o Câmara Municipal de Sintra, Sintra; held from August to September, and is considered one of the leading music festivals of Portugal; concerts are organized in various locations in the town.

Republic of South Africa

THE NATIONAL EISTEDDFOD OF SOUTH AFRICA, c/o Witwatersrand Cambrian Society, Secretary, P.O. Box 3552, Johannesburg; founded in 1900; held in April around the Easter season and is presented in the Welsh Eisteddfod tradition; the Cambrian Society is made up of Welshmen mainly; the Eisteddfod is open only to descendants of Europeans, who must be amateurs; music, dancing, speaking, and other activities are judged competitively.

PRAETORIA MUSIC FESTIVAL, 24 Hay Street, Brooklyn, Pretoria; organized by the South African Society of Music Teachers.

Scotland

EDINBURGH INTERNATIONAL FESTIVAL, 21 Market Street, Edinburgh EHI 1BW; the festival is under royal patronage; founded in 1947 with **Rudolf Bing** as the first artistic director; festival lasts from August to September; the festival enjoys substantial attendance; formerly known mainly for its traditional programs of conservative nature, the organizers began in 1961 to present contemporary music. Operas have been staged by the Glyndebourne group, Covent Garden, English Opera Group, and imported organizations such as the Belgrade Opera Company. Four or five operas are usually presented. Orchestras, numbering about five or six for each season, have in the past included the BBC Scottish Orchestra, the Scottish National Orchestra, the Philharmonia Orchestra, the London Symphony, the Berlin Philharmonic, and many others. The Leeds Festival Chorus and the Edinburgh Royal Choral Union have been two of a number of distinguished choral groups. In addition to ballet, solo recitals, and chamber concerts with from four to six guest ensembles, there are master classes, musical theater, drama—with performances by sometimes three different companies, films, etc.

Spain

GRANADA INTERNATIONAL FESTIVAL OF MUSIC AND DANCE, c/o Directión Bellas Artes, Teatro Real, Pl. de Isabel II, s/n Madrid; or the address in Granada: Oficina del Festival, Mesones 1; from June to July; performances take place in the Palace of Charles the V, the Lions Court of the Alhambra, and the Gardens of the Generalife. Each festival has symphonic concerts by the National Orchestra of Spain and sometimes a guest symphonic or chamber group. Leading conductors and soloists appear, the latter usually including **Victoria de los Angeles** and **Andrés Segovia.** I Musici, Saar Chamber Orchestra, Agrupación Nacional de Música de Cámara, have been some of the chamber ensembles to have performed. Ballet performances are always held in the Gardens and have featured such groups as the company of the Paris Opera, the American Ballet Theatre, Antonio's Spanish Ballet, and the Ballet Espagnol.

SANTANDER INTERNATIONAL FESTIVAL, c/o Dirección del Festival, Plaza Velarde, Case postale 258, Santander; founded in 1952; in August; Santander is located on the coast of the Bay of Biscay in Northern Spain, and is famous for its bay and the beaches of Sardinero. Musical substance consists of orchestral concerts, choral concerts, chamber and solo recitals, Spanish ballet and flamenco, opera; drama and fine arts exhibitions are always included. Notable orchestras have been: Madrid National Orchestra, Madrid Chamber Orchestra, and the Orchestra of R.A.I., Turin. Altogether there are about four concerts by the orchestras. The chorus usually featured is the Orfeón Donostiarra of San Sebastian (founded in 1898). Ballet performances, an important aspect of the festival, are produced by such ensembles as Antonio's Spanish Ballet, Mariemma, Coros y Danzas de España, American Ballet Theatre, Paris Opera Ballet, Finnish National Ballet, and others. Performances are held in a square turned into a theater, the Plaza Porticada. The Cathedral is also used. Art exhibitions are shown in the Regina Coeli Monastery, Santillana del Mar.

Switzerland

GSTAAD FESTIVAL, Gstaad; organized in 1958 by **Yehudi Menuhin,** a resident of

Gstaad; performances take place in the 14th century Church of Saanen and often features the Zürich Chamber Orchestra, musicians appearing are chosen by Menuhin.

LAUSANNE INTERNATIONAL FESTIVAL, Lausanne; begun in 1955; some participating groups have been the Belgrade Opera Co., the Budapest Ballet, and the Warsaw Symphony; a full program of operas, concerts, choral performances, and ballet is offered; soloists are world famous.

LUZERN INTERNATIONAL FESTIVAL WEEKS, c/o Internationale Musikfestwochen, Schweizerhofquai 4, 6002 Luzern (Lucerne); begun in 1938 under Toscanini, Nikisch, Ansermet, and others; August to September; a major festival of great symphonic and chamber ensemble performances. The main chamber group is the Festival Strings Lucerne, formed in 1956. Symphonic concerts, including those with soloists and chorus, are held in the Kunsthaus; organ recitals in either the Jesuit Church, or the Hofkirche; other recitals in the Kunsthaus, or the Kursaal; open air serenades at the Lion Monument; and special recitals and master courses at the Conservatory of Music. In addition, there are, sometimes, dramatic performances staged in the Municipal Theater. A special ensemble, the Swiss Festival Orchestra, formed in 1953, was organized for the festival.

"SEPTEMBRE MUSICAL" OF MONTREUX–VEVEY, c/o Secrétariat du Festival, 42 Grand-rue, CH–1820, Montreux; established in 1946 and occurs from August to September or from September to October in the towns of Montreux and Vevey; most of the concerts take place in Montreux's lakeside concert pavillion; outstanding artists abound throughout the programs, and about three orchestras under a revolving roster of eight well-known conductors perform approximately twelve concerts; there are an average of four chamber concerts in each festival.

ZÜRICH INTERNATIONAL JUNE FESTIVAL, c/o Verkehrsdirektion Zürich, P.O.B., 8023 Zürich; along with its regular programming, the festival each year commemorates in particular the music of one country. Resident groups are the Tonhalle Orchestra, the Zürich Opera Company, and Ensemble Schauspielhaus (drama). Some seasons have staged 14 operas, sometimes including a production of a visiting company. The orchestral programs are led by international celebrities. Audiences may hear four languages spoken throughout the festival's entire dramatic programs. Visiting drama companies have included the Oxford Playhouse, Teatro Piccolo of Milan, the National Popular Theatre, Paris, and others. Exhibitions are seen in the Kunsthaus, Zürich Museum, and the Rietberg Museum, the last showing non-European art.

Yugoslavia

DUBROVNIK SUMMER FESTIVAL, c/o Ulica od Sigurate 1, Dubrovnik; founded 1950; held from July to August. The festival has an opening ceremony in front of the Sponza Palace. Performances, due to the mild climate during the festival, take place in the open-air in 20 different locations throughout the city. The festival is Yugoslavia's only cultural event of international consequence. The programs include: orchestral concerts by Yugoslavian ensembles and those from other European nations; recitals and chamber concerts; drama, performed in parks, gardens, and castles which make striking backgrounds for such plays as "Hamlet" and "The Tempest." Every festival schedules performances of Croatian, Serbian, and Macedonian folk songs and dances. Some of the scenic locations are: Fort Revelin, Gradac Park, the Rector's Palace, Držić Square, Fort Lovrjenac, and the Dominican Cloisters. The town, founded in the 7th century, is on the Adriatic coast and is considered one of the best preserved medieval cities in the world.

BIENNIAL INTERNATIONAL FESTIVAL OF CONTEMPORARY MUSIC, Zagreb; begun in 1961; held in May; under the auspices of Radio Zagreb, the Zagreb National Theater, and the Yugoslav Union of Composers; Yugoslav and imported groups perform.

International Competitions and Awards

Arranged in various categories, the following contests are open to Americans and, excepting the Sibelius Prize, are all competitive.

Deadline dates of specific years are given for reference only; the latest application dates and other particulars may be had by communicating directly to the contest authorities. Some past winners are also included. Foreign currency conversions into U.S. dollars are based on exchange rates valid early in 1972.

INSTRUMENTAL CONTESTS

Belgium

QUEEN ELIZABETH OF BELGIUM INTERNATIONAL MUSIC COMPETITION, c/o Secretariat Général du Concours, Musical International Reine Elisabeth de Belgique, Palais des Beaux-Arts, 11 rue Baron Horta, 1000 Brussels; founded in 1951; open to all nationalities and held alternately for pianists, violinists, composers; 1971, for violin; 1972, for piano; 1973 for composers, etc. Performers must be between 17 and 30. The trials take place in Brussels in May. Deadline is January 15 in the year of the contest. Total prizes: 1,045,000 Belgian francs ($20,900); nine prizes are awarded. Those reaching the second-stage elimination contests, but not reaching the finals, receive a small token award. The jury consists of internationally known musicians. The contest is highly regarded.

England

CITY OF LONDON INTERNATIONAL COMPETITION FOR VIOLIN AND VIOLA (Carl Flesch Medal), The Competition Office, Guildhall School of Music and Drama, John Carpenter Street, London, EC4Y OAR, England. Held every two years: 1970, 1972, 1974, etc. Dates for the 1972 contest were May 6 for the deadline of applications and July 9 to 14 for the trials themselves. Violinists and violists of any nationality under the age of 32, as of July 1 of the year of the contest, are eligible. Two elimination stages and a final stage with six candidates selected for the latter make up the trials. All stages are open to the public; the finals take place in London at Guildhall and are accompanied by the B.B.C. Symphony Orchestra. Contestants play from a fixed repertory of pieces which are performed from memory. Any stage may be broadcasted or televised. Prizes are: first prize of £1,000 British and the Carl Flesch Medal; also offered the first place winner are a number of engagements with English and Scottish orchestras (some offered to winning violinists only) including the Birmingham, Bournemouth, Royal Liverpool, the Royal Philharmonic, the Scottish National orchestras, the London Mozart Players, an appearance at the Bath Festival, etc.; these engagements are subject to date and fee negotiation with the winners; second prize is the Corporation of London Prize of £750; third prize is £500; fourth to sixth are respectively £300 to £100. An entrance fee of £10 is required. The competition is under the direction of eminent figures in English musical and cultural life; chairman of the jury is **Yehudi Menuhin.** Winners of the 1970 event were **Stoika Milanova** of Bulgaria (violin) for first place, **Luigi Bianchi** of Italy (viola) for second, and **Caaba Erdelyi** of Hungary (viola) for third place.

Finland

INTERNATIONAL JEAN SIBELIUS VIOLIN COMPETITION, Sibelius Academy, P. Rautatiekatu 9, 00100 Helsinki 10. Held every five years in November and December. The next competition will be held in 1975 and will be the third. Contestants for that contest must have birth dates from 1942 to 1959 exclusive and may be of any nationality. Deadline for entry is usually by August 15, the year of the contest (an entrance fee of $10 was required for the 1970 event, along with various necessary documents attesting birth dates, musical studies, recommendations of references, etc.). Accepted candidates are notified by mid-September. Although the contestant is expected to pay for his transportation to Helsinki, he will be accommodated free of charge with a Helsinki family during the entire period of the competition. The trials are in three stages of elimination involving respectively a solo performance, a performance with piano accompaniment, and finally, with an orchestra. All pieces are played from memory and all stages are open to the public. The repertory is usually fixed and always includes a work by a Finnish composer and, in the final stage, the Sibelius Violin Concerto. A maximum of eight violinists may be chosen for the final examinations. One rehearsal with the orchestra is permitted for this stage. Three Finnish and six international musicians usually make up the jury (among the foreign judges in 1970 were **Gabriel Bouillon, Josef Gingold, Ricardo Odnoposoff,** and **Igor Bezrodnyi.** There are eight prizes, respectively from first to last place, of $3,000, $2,000, $1,000, $700, $400, $300, $200, and $100. An additional prize is available, granted by Finnish Radio, for the best performance of the Sibelius concerto. Various subsequent public performances are arranged for the first three winners. In 1965, the winners were **Oleg Kagan** (USSR), **Joshua Epstein** (Israel), and **Valeri Gradov** (USSR).

France

INTERNATIONAL CONTEST OF FLUTE FOR CONTEMPORARY MUSIC, Royan. Held in conjunction with the International Festival of Contemporary Art. Royan address: P.O. Box 517, 17–Royan; Secretary of the Contest: Festival de Royan, 26 rue Washington, Paris, 8e. In 1972, this was the first event for flute at the Festival. It took place between March 25 and 29; participants could be no older than 33 as of March 25. It was held in the Casino de Royan. The test pieces were all modern music. First prize: 8,000 francs (over $1,600), plus a Paris concert engagement, a performance at the Royan Festival, recording date, and TV appearance. Second prize: 5,000 francs. There are third and fourth prizes plus special prizes.

INTERNATIONAL ORGAN CONTEST "GRAND PRIX DE CHARTRES," Secrétariat du Concours, 75, rue de Grenelle, Paris, 75007. Under the patronage of the President of the Republic. Deadline for the 1973 contest: before July 1, 1973. Competition takes places in Paris for the elimination stages and in Chartres for the finals. In 1973, the event lasted from September 17 to September 30. The finals are public. Age limit: 39. The organ at Chartres is the Grand Organ of Notre Dame. Grand Prize: 10,000 francs, recitals in Chartres Cathedral and in Notre Dame Cathedral in Paris, etc.

MARGUERITE LONG-JACQUES THIBAUD INTERNATIONAL COMPETITION FOR PIANISTS AND VIOLINISTS, c/o Secrétariat Général Concours Long-Thibaud, Immeuble Gaveau 11, ave. Delcassé 75 Paris, 8e. Age limit: 15 to 30; deadline for application: before May 1, 1973; trials for violinists took place in Paris from June 12 to 16, 1973; for pianists: June 18 to 27; first prize for pianists and violinists: 30,000 francs each. Total prizes: 107,500 francs.

Germany

INTERNATIONAL MUSIC COMPETITION (OF THE WEST GERMAN BROADCASTING COMPANIES), c/o Internationaler Musikwettbewerb, 8000 München 2, Rundfunkplatz 1; held in various categories but usually includes singing and piano; other instrumental categories have been viola, violin, oboe, clarinet, and organ; the 1972 contest was open to singers, pianists, violinists, and oboists; singers must be between 20 and 30; instrumentalists between 17 and 30; deadline is July 1st; in 1972 the contests were heard from September 19 to October 6th; first prizes in singing, piano, and violin amount to 6,000 DM with separate prizes awarded to men and women in the singing trials; the prizes in the remaining instrumental groups amount to 4,000 and 2,500 DM each.

KRANICHSTEIN MUSIC PRIZE, c/o Kranichsteiner Musikinstitut, Nieder-Ramstädter Strasse 190, 61 Darmstadt; a series founded in 1952 and sponsored by the International Music Institute for Contemporary Music in Darmstadt; each year the prize applies to different categories (piano, cello, winds, etc.); it is no longer offered in the form of a competition but as an honorary award during the course of attending the Institute; applicants must be between 18 and 30; deadline is about August 1st.

Hungary

INTERNATIONAL LISZT-BARTÓK PIANO COMPETITION, c/o Vörösmarty tér. 1, Box 80, Budapest 5; founded in 1933 (as the Liszt Competition). Age limit: 15 to 32; deadline for application: June 1st (in 1973); the actual competition is held in Budapest in September (1973); prizes range from 40,000 to 10,000 Hungarian forints; contest is held in the Academy of Music.

Israel

INTERNATIONAL HARP CONTEST, P.O. Box 29874, 52, Nachlat Benjamin Street, Tel-Aviv, Israel. First held in 1959. The event takes place every three years. As of this writing, the next contest is scheduled for September, 1973. The deadline for application is usually early in the year of the contest. The contest is held in three stages with each stage having a required repertory in specific published editions. Ten prizes are awarded as follows: first prize, a grand concert harp by Lyon & Healy of Chicago; second, $2,000; third, $1,500; fourth, $1,250; fifth, $750; sixth, $600; seventh, $500; eighth, $400; ninth, $300; tenth, $200. Winners of first and second prize are given subsequent opportunity to perform with orchestras in Europe and the United States. Since the first contest, 110 participants have appeared for the event, the highest number being 34 for the 1965 competition and the lowest being 18 for the 1970 event. Winners of first prize for the contests of 1959, 1962, 1965, and 1970 respectively (an extension of the three-year interval) were **Suzanne Mildonian** of Italy, **Lynne A. Turner** of the United States, **Martine Geliot** of France, and **Chantal Mathieu** of France. Reportedly, the contest has been responsible for the increase in the number of young people undertaking study of the harp and for many new compositions written for the instrument. Generally, judges are selected from the countries sending contestants.

Italy

INTERNATIONAL "F. BUSONI" PIANO COMPETITION, c/o "Claudio Monteverdi" State Conservatory, 39100 Bolzano; contestants must be between 15 and 32; deadline for application is June 30 (in 1972); in 1972, the events were held from August 26 to September 1. The contest consists of an admissions test, elimination tests, and finals. Repertory is predetermined in general categories with some specific required titles. The "Busoni Prize" is 500,000 lire ($800) plus a concert and recitals contract for appearances in Italy. Second Prize is 250,000 lire; the fifth prize is 150,000 lire. The jury is made up of some of the world's greatest pianists and piano teachers. Winners of first prize (not always granted) in recent years: 1961: **Jerome Rose** (U.S.); 1964: **Michael Ponti** (U.S.); 1966: **Garrick Ohlsson** (U.S.); 1968: **Vladimir Selivochin** (U.S.S.R.); 1969: **Ursula Oppens** (U.S.).

INTERNATIONAL COMPETITION "ALFREDO CASELLA" (CONCORSO INTERNAZIONALE "ALFREDO CASELLA"), c/o the Secretary, Accademia Musicale Napoletana, Via S. Pasquale a Chiaia, 62, 80121 Naples. The competition is sponsored by the Ministry of Tourism and Theatre but is administered through the Naples Musical Academy. The 1972 event was respectively the seventh and eleventh competitions for music composition and piano, the two contests being merged to take place in Naples from April 18 to 26. Deadline was March 15 for application and the receipt of the submitted composition. These dates have remained more or less the same through the years. The composition category changes but a chamber work is usually required; the 1972 requirement was for a trio, quartet, or quintet with or without piano. Composers entering the contest may be of any nationality and age. The prize consists of a firm commitment to publication of the winning piece by the music publisher, Casa Editrice Musicale G. Zanibon of Padua, Italy, with the necessary promotional effort for its entry into the music field, etc. Compositions are submitted under a pen name according to fixed rules.

The piano competition is in three elimination stages with the second and third stages open to the public. The finals require the playing of a concerto selected from a list of available choices. Twelve candidates (minimum) are chosen to enter the finals, from whom are chosen eight winners in various prize classifications. First prize is the sum of 600,000 lire (about $970) plus the opportunity to perform publicly with an orchestra and in a series of recitals in Italy and abroad. The second to the sixth prizes range downward from about $485 to $161. The seventh and eighth prizes are merit diplomas. Each monetary prize carries a name in whose honor it is given. An additional prize, the so-called "Clara Haskil" award of $485, is granted to any performer in the second stage who excels in performing a Mozart sonata. Pianists entering may be of any nationality (or stateless) and must be between 18 and 32 within the year of the contest. They may have won only one other first prize in another international contest. An entry fee of 10,000 lire ($16.18) is required for both the piano and the composition candidates.

INTERNATIONAL "NICOLO PAGANINI" VIOLIN COMPETITION, Palazzo Tursi, Via Garibaldi 9, Genoa. Age limit is 35; 1972 deadline was July 15, the contest being held from October 2 to 10; first prize is 3 million lire and second is 1.25 million lire; sixth prize is 200,000 lire (3 million lire = approximately $4,800).

The Netherlands

INTERNATIONAL ORGAN COMPETITION, c/o Stichtung International Orgelconcours, Townhal Haarlem. The event in 1972 ran from July 4 to July 29. This is a combination of concerts and competitive events in organ improvisation based on the old traditions. Events are scheduled for the evenings and are held in St. Bavo's Church in Haarlem and other churches both in Haarlem and in the cities of Alkmaar, Amstelveen, Amsterdam, Beverwuk, and Spaarndam. Concerts include choral performances, chamber recitals, and organ recitals including those by members of the organ competition jury.

Poland

FREDERIC CHOPIN INTERNATIONAL PIANO COMPETITION, c/o Secretariat, Okólnik 1, Warsaw; first established in 1927 and is held every five years or so; the last contest, the eighth, was held in 1970 and was won by **Garrick Ohlsson** (U.S.). First prize is 40,000 zlotys (about $1,700). The eighth contest was held in Warsaw from October 7 to 25, 1970. It involved 122 pianists from 30 countries with 90 proceeding to the actual contest stage.

HENRYK WIENIAWSKI INTERNATIONAL CONTESTS (FOR VIOLIN PERFORMANCE, AND VIOLIN MAKING), Komitet Organizacyjny Miedzynarodowych Konkursow im. Henryka Wieniawskiego, Wodna 27, Poznan. Organized every five years in Poznan; first held in 1935. In 1972 contest was held as follows: violin making: May 4 to 14; violin performance: November 12 to 26. The violin-making event was open to professional makers with the first, second, and third prizes respectively 30,000, 25,000, and 20,000 zlotys. The violin performance competition was restricted to violinists under 30; the prizes (in zlotys) were, for first: 50,000; second: 40,000; third: 30,000; fourth: 25,000; fifth: 20,000; etc.

Portugal

INTERNATIONAL COMPETITION "VIANNA DA MOTTA," Secretaria do Concurso Internacional "Vianna da Motta," Av. Conselheiro Fernando de Sousa, SRF, r/cF, Lisbon. First held in 1957. The 1973 event will be the sixth. It is held every two years and is open to all pianists and violinists, alternately, between 17 and 30 and consists of four stages, two preliminary and two final—all publicly held and taking place in the Hall of the University of Lisbon. Only six candidates can be chosen for the finals; a first prize need not be offered if not warranted in the opinion of the jury. The required pieces by specific composers are selected by the contestant from a list of choices. The final stage requires a performance of a concerto with orchestra (a rehearsal is arranged). First prize (for 1973) is $4,000; second, $3,000; third, $1,500; fourth, $1,000; fifth, $300; and sixth, $200. The jury is always made up of musicians of international repute, e.g., in the 1971 event for pianists were: **Eugene List, Aldo Ciccolini, Fou T'Song, Maria Tipo, Sequeira Costa** (who is Secretary of the Competition), et al. The competition is under the patronage of the President of Portugal and receives the support of prominent individuals and government agencies and organizations. Some past pianist winners include **Naum Chtarkman** (U.S.S.R.), 1957; **Vladimir Krainev** (U.S.S.R.), and **Nelson Freire** (Brazil), both in 1964; **Farhad Badalbeily** and **Victoria Postnikova,** both of the U.S.S.R. (1968). In 1971 no first prize was awarded, but second prize was won by **Roland Keller** of Germany, third prize by **Emanuel Ax** of the United States. Contestants are all granted room and board free of charge. A $20 entrance fee is required of all candidates.

Rumania

GEORGES ENESCU INTERNATIONAL COMPETITION, c/o Concours International "Georges Enescu," 1, Stirbei Voda Street, Bucharest; established in 1958 and held every three years; most recent events were in 1970 and 1973; the contest is open to singers, pianists, and violinists up to age 33 as of the year of the contest; the deadline is in May or June with the actual contest in September; first prize in each category is approximately 30,000 Rumanian lei with six additional cash awards; winners are given the chance to play in several Rumanian cities.

Spain

CONCOURS INTERNATIONAL MARIA CANALS DE BARCELONA, Rambla Cataluña 90, Barcelona 8. Established in 1955. This contest is open to singers, pianists, and flutists of all nations. Age limits for pianists are 15 and 35 as of the first day of January of the contest's current year; for singers and flutists the limits are 18 and 35. The deadline for the 1972 event was February 1, the contest being held in Barcelona from the 17th to the 27th of April. Prizes are for piano: First Prize of 50,000 pesetas; two Second Prizes, respectively for men and women, each of 10,000 pesetas; other prizes consist of medals and honor diplomas. For singing, the First and Second Prizes are respectively 50,000 and 10,000 pesetas, the remainder being medals and honor diplomas. First Prize for flute is 40,000 pesetas; Second Prize is 10,000 pesetas; other awards are medals and honor diplomas. Various additional prizes are available with certain conditions regulating their availability, such as a prize for a resident of Spain who best interprets French music, etc. There are two elimination trials and a final trial which is sometimes broadcasted or televised. Performing repertory is within certain limits, with the maximum time allowed for performances set at between 20 and 35 minutes. An entrance fee of 1,000 pesetas (about $15) is required.

Switzerland

INTERNATIONAL COMPETITION FOR MUSICAL PERFORMANCE (Concours International D'Exécution Musicale), Secrétariat du Concours, Palais Eynard, rue de la Croix-Rouge 4, CH–1204, Geneva. The 1971 competition was the 27th in the series. Two hundred and thirty candidates registered; after preliminary exclusions 157 were admitted to the examinations, from which 49 were selected for the public performances, 15 contestants going to the third stage elimination concert with the Orchestre de la Suisse Romande. The contest is open to any nationality. Each year certain instrumental categories vary, but there is always a category for voice and piano. The other instruments include strings, winds, and percussion, which are changed for each contest (in 1971, these were cello, oboe, and horn; in 1972, they were viola, clarinet, and percussion). Age limits are 15 and 30 for instrumentalists (for wind quintets, the average age of its members may not exceed 35); female singers must be from 20 to 30, and male singers must be from 22 to 32. The age limits apply to birth dates up to October 1st. The deadline for application is usually in July (July 1 in 1972), the trials taking place at the Conservatory of Music in Geneva from mid-September to early October (in 1971: September 18 to October 2). The total amount of prizes offered in 1971 was 64,000 Swiss francs (about $15,250). First prizes for singing (men and women) and piano: 5,000 francs; for instruments: 4,000 to 5,000. Second prizes range from 2,000 francs to 2,500. In addition to the foregoing several special monetary prizes can be won for recognition of one kind or another. Other laurels include the opportunity to perform in orchestral concerts, recital tours (for one of the winners) organized by the Swiss Jeunesses Musicales, etc. The competition consists of three stages: a preliminary audition, a public recital, a public contest with orchestra (the last is preceded by two rehearsals). The jury is made up of well-known foreign and Swiss musicians. The repertory performed is fixed within limits for each stage of the competition and is published in advance. The Geneva Concours is a highly regarded one. Begun in 1939 under the instigation of Henri Gagnebin, the event has attracted a large number of worldwide young artists, many of whom are now in the top level of their profession. Among them: **Georg Solti, Teresa Berganza,** members of the Parrenin Quartet, **Victoria de los Angeles, Wolfgang Sawallisch, Kieth Engen, Arturo Benedetti-Michelangeli, Friedrich Gulda,** to name some. From 1939 to 1970, some 5,947 candidates from 74 countries have entered the contest, winning a total of 419,425 francs exclusive of the special prizes. A registration and an examination fee, both nonrefundable, are required of all contestants.

VOCAL CONTESTS

Bulgaria

INTERNATIONAL COMPETITION FOR YOUNG OPERA SINGERS, c/o Secretariat

18, Stamboliiski Blv., Sofia. The fifth event was scheduled for May 27 to June 18, 1973 in Sofia. First held in 1961; subsequent events took place in 1963, 1967, and 1970. Obligatory repertory includes a song or aria by a Bulgarian composer. Singers cannot be older than 33. The contest is in three stages. There are 17 prizes: 2 first prizes of 3,500 Bulgarian leva, 2 second prizes of 2,500 leva, etc. The Grand Prize is 5,000 leva, a gold ring and medal, and a diploma. Past winners include **Peter Glossop** (England, 1961), **Nancy Tatum** (U.S., 1963), **Joy Davidson** (U.S., 1967), et al.

France

INTERNATIONAL COMPETITION FOR SINGERS, c/o Secrétariat du Concours, Donjon du Capitole, F–31, Toulouse; for singers between the ages of 18 and 34; the deadline for application in 1972 was September 24, the contest being held from October 8 to 14; all events are held in the Théâtre du Capitole; total prizes: 20,000 francs.

INTERNATIONAL SINGING CONTEST OF PARIS, c/o Mme. Jacques Roullet, 14 bis avenue du Président-Wilson, Paris, 16e. Sponsored by the Ministry of Cultural affairs. The fifth event was in 1972, held from May 28 to June 1 in the Salle Gaveau. Age limits: 32 for women; 35 for men. Deadline in 1972: April 30. Works are sung in original languages. Prizes range from 5,000 francs (first prize) to 2,000 francs (third prize); there are also various additional monetary prizes and opportunities.

Germany

See INTERNATIONAL MUSIC COMPETITIONS OF THE WEST GERMAN BROADCASTING COMPANIES (under Instrumental Contests).

Netherlands

INTERNATIONAL SINGING-COMPETITION 's–HERTOGENBOSCH, c/o Secretariat, Stichtung 's–Hertogenbosch Muziekstad. Town Hall, 's–Hertogenbosch. The 19th event was held in 1972 from September 2 to 9 in the Casino-Theatre at 's–Hertogenbosch. The competition is open to singers of all nationalities of a specified age limit (for 1972, those born after December 31, 1938). The categories of repertory include opera, oratorio, and song which are stipulated in the rules as to quantity and style periods. The prizes are: a first prize for each of the basic voice classifications (soprano, mezzo/alto, tenor, bass/baritone) consisting of 2,500 Hfl. (about $700), a medal, a performance with Het Brabants Orkest and a radio performance; second prize for each of the voices consisting of the sum of 1,000 Hfl. (about $280), a medal and a performance with Het Brabants Orkest. Other awards are available for the best interpretation of contemporary Dutch music (1,500 Hfl.), scholarships, 500 Hfl. from the West German government, etc. The contest itself has three stages of elimination with the second and third stages open to the public. Entry deadline in 1972 was July 20. An entry fee of 75 Hfl. ($21) is required.

Rumania

See GEORGES ENESCU INTERNATIONAL COMPETITION (under Instrumental Contests).

Spain

See CONCOURS INTERNATIONAL MARIA CANALS DE BARCELONA (under Instrumental Contests).

Switzerland

See INTERNATIONAL COMPETITION FOR MUSICAL PERFORMERS, GENEVA (under Instrumental Contests).

COMPOSITION CONTESTS

Belgium

See QUEEN ELIZABETH OF BELGIUM INTERNATIONAL MUSIC COMPETITION (under Instrumental Contests).

Finland

SIBELIUS PRIZE (Wihuri–Sibelius Prize), c/o Wihuri's Foundation for International Prizes, Arkadiankatu 21 B25 Helsinki; cannot be applied for but a committee accepts suggested names of likely recipients; grants about $25,000 to internationally famous composers whose work is deemed a benefit to mankind. Founded 1953 by Antti Wihuri. Past recipients: Paul Hindemith (1955); Dimitri Shostakovitch (1958); Igor Stravinsky (1963); Benjamin Britten (1965); Olivier Messiaen (1971).

Germany

INTERNATIONAL COMPETITION FOR WOMEN COMPOSERS, c/o Gedok Studio, Liebfrauenstrasse 19, Mannheim–Feudenheim; categories include a symphonic work, chamber work, and a vocal work; the prizes are 2,000 DM for the symphonic piece and 1,000 DM for each of the other categories; contests were held in 1950, 1956, 1961, 1963, and 1967.

Italy

See INTERNATIONAL COMPETITION "ALFREDO CASELLA" (Concorso Internazionale "Alfredo Casella") for composition contest (under Instrumental Contests).

Monaco

PRINCE PIERRE DE MONACO INTERNATIONAL COMPOSITION COMPETITION, c/o Secrétaire Général du Concours de Composition Musicale "Prince Rainier III de Monaco," Secrétariat Général, Palais de Monaco; founded in 1960; deadline for 1972 was April 1st; prizes are 20,000 French francs for an orchestral work; in 1973 compositions will be for the theater (opera or ballet); in 1974, of chamber music; in 1975 works of sacred music.

Netherlands

INTERNATIONAL GAUDEAMUS COMPOSERS' COMPETITION, Gaudeamus Foundation, P.O. Box 30, Bilthoven, Netherlands. Under the auspices of the Gaudeamus Foundation, an organization devoted to contemporary music which also sponsors the International Gaudeamus Music Week (the 1972 event, held in September, was the 24th in the annual series), of which this competition is an important part. Eligible for the 1972 contest are composers of any nationality who were born after January 1, 1936 (the birth date varies with each year's competition). The composition for 1972 had to be for choir, chamber ensemble, orchestra, chamber orchestra, or electronic music. Deadline for 1972 was January 31. Prizes (first, second, and third): 4,000, 2,000, and 1,000 Dutch guilders, respectively.

Spain

OSCAR ESPLA PRIZE, c/o Secretaria del Ayuntamiento, Town Hall, Alicante; begun in 1960; open to composers of any age and nationality; work must be in symphonic form (suite, concerto, chorus–orchestra, etc.), original, and unpublished; in addition to the 250,000 pesetas first prize, the winning work receives performances throughout Spain. If no single work receives the winning prize, the jury may award a second and third prize of 150,000 and 100,000 pesetas, respectively (100,000 pesetas = approximately $1,400). Detailed regulations govern the submission of scores. Deadline for 1972 contest: March 15.

Switzerland

INTERNATIONAL COMPOSITION COMPETITION FOR BALLET AND OPERA, c/o Radio Geneva, 66 Boulevard Carl-Vogt, CH 12118, Geneva; organized by the City of Geneva and Radio Suisse Romande. The sixth event was in 1973. Held every two years alternately for opera and ballet. In 1973: ballet; 1975: opera. Deadline for 1973 application: September 1. First prize (1973): 10,000 Swiss francs (about $2,600) and the possibility of staging the winning work in Geneva. Open to all composers without age limit. Specific regulations govern libretto and duration, piano–vocal score, instrumentation, etc. The jury is composed of noted composers, stage directors, et al; in 1971 (opera contest), 46 scores from 17 different countries were submitted. First prize was withheld; second and third were awarded.

CONDUCTING CONTESTS

Denmark

THE NICOLAI MALKO INTERNATIONAL COMPETITION FOR YOUNG CONDUCTORS, The Malko Secretariat, Radio Denmark, Radiohuset, DK 1999, Copenhagen V, Denmark. The contest is organized by Radio Denmark, the Danish Academies of Music, and the Danish Symphony Orchestra and is under the patronage of King Frederik IX of Denmark. The contest is held every third year (1971, 1974, etc.) and is open to all nationalities of conductors of specific age limits; the 1971 contest stipulated a birth date for all contestants between May 15, 1940 and May 8, 1951. Deadline for that event was February 1 and the actual trials took place in Radio House in Copenhagen during the period May 9 to 14. The competition is held in four divisions with specified works as the trial compositions. Part of the auditions are made public and are sometimes televised or broadcast by Radio Denmark. Prizes are: a first prize of $1,000; second prize of 5,000 Danish kroner (about $670); third prize of 3,500 kroner; and a fourth prize of 1,000 kroner. Each of the prizes emanates from a different donor. For United States candidates there is a special travel grant of $500 donated by **Mr. and Mrs. Charles W. Lubin,** since applicants must pay for their trip to Denmark (although the Secretariat assists the contestants in certain practical ways once they arrive there). An application fee of 50 kroner (about $7) is needed. The various committees supervising the event, as well as the juries, are composed of many leaders in the field of music. The jury in 1971 contained conductors **Kiril Kondrashin** (U.S.S.R.), **Igor Markevitch** (Monaco), **Mogens Wöldike** (Denmark), to name some. The competition is named in honor of the late Nicolai Malko, the Russian-born conductor who conducted many seasons in Denmark and who led orchestras throughout the world including, for several years, the orchestra of Chicago's Grant Park Concerts.

France

BESANÇON INTERNATIONAL COMPETITION FOR YOUNG CONDUCTORS, c/o International de Jeunes Chefs d'Orchestre, Parc des Expositions, Planoise 25, Besançon. The 1972 event was the 22nd in the series. Held during the Besançon International Festival of Music. Dates in 1972 were from September 17 to 20. Three elimination stages, each permitting professional and nonprofessional contestant category. Repertory is announced in advance. No monetary awards. Open to young conductors under 30.

Italy

INTERNATIONAL COMPETITION FOR CONDUCTORS OF SYMPHONIC MUSIC, c/o Secretariat, Accademia Nazionale di Santa Cecilia, Via Vittoria 6, 1–00187, Rome. The 1974 contest will take place in May; age limit: under 35; first prize includes 2 million lire and an invitation to conduct one of the subscription concerts of the Academy during the following season; second prize is 1 million lire.

MISCELLANEOUS CONTESTS

Bulgaria

INTERNATIONAL BALLET COMPETITION, The Directorate of Bulgarian Music,

Secretariat of the International Ballet Competition, 56, Alabin Street, Sofia. First competition was held in 1964; it was the first international ballet contest ever held. It takes place in the town of Varna, on the coast of the Black Sea, in an open air theater. It is open to all nationalities. The 1972 event took place from July 8 to 25; there are two sections of competition: junior and senior; the latter refers to dancers born after January 1, 1944. Competitors may perform as soloists or duos. Classical and modern dance is included in the trials. Competitors may bring their tapes and disc recordings or avail themselves of a local piano accompanist. Prizes range downward from 3,000 Bulgarian leva. Deadline for 1972: April 15.

Poland

See HENRYK WIENIAWSKI COMPETITION (Violin-making contest under Instrumental Contests).

Music Publishers

Argentina

A.Y.C.A. (Autores y Compositores Asociados Ayca Ediciones Musicales), Av. Olivera 929, Buenos Aires. . . . BARRY Y COMPAÑIA, Montevideo 264, Buenos Aires. . . . CADEM (Corporación Argentina de Ediciones Musicales), Thames 2449, Buenos Aires. . . . EDITORIAL ARGENTINA, Libertad 374, Buenos Aires. . . . EDITORIAL ARGENTINA DE MÚSICA, Bartolomé Mitre 1568, Buenos Aires. . . . EDITORIAL ARGENTINA DE MÚSICA INTERNACIONAL, Lavalle 1494, Buenos Aires. . . . RICORDI AMERICANA, Sociedad Anónima Editorial y Comercial, Cangallo 1570, Buenos Aires.

Australia

J. ALBERT AND SONS, LTD., 137–9 King Street, Sydney, New South Wales. . . . ALLAN AND CO., 276 Collins Street, Melbourne. . . . BOOSEY AND HAWKES, LTD., 250 Pitt Street, Sydney. . . . NICHOLSON'S PTY., LTD., 416 George, Sydney. . . . W. H. PALING AND CO., LTD., 338 George Street, Sydney. . . . G. RICORDI AND CO., LTD., 164 Pitt Street, Sydney.

Austria

AKADEMISCHE DRUCK—u. VERLAGS-ANSTALT, P.O. Box 598, A–8011, Graz. . . . HERMANN BOHLAUS NACHF. GES. M.B.H., den Frankgasse 4. Wien IX/72, . . . L. DOBLINGER, Dorotheergasse 10, Vienna 1. . . . JOSEF DOERR MUSIKVERLAG, Wiedner-Haupstrasse 152, 1050 Vienna. . . . EBERLE-VERLAG, Seilergasse 12, 1015 Vienna. . . . GLOCKEN-VERLAG, Theobaldgasse 16, Vienna 6. . . . FRIEDRICH HAWLIK, Neubagasse 7, Vienna 7. . . . JOHANN KLIMENT, Kolingasse 15, 1090 Vienna. . . . EMIL W. MAASS-MUSIKVERLAG, Grosse Schiffgasse la, Vienna 2. . . . OESTERREICHISCHER BUNDESVERLAG FÜR UNTERRICHT, WISSENSCHAFT, UND KUNST, Schwarzenbergstrasse 5, Vienna 1. . . . PHOEBUS MUSIKVERLAG, Mollardgasse 17, Vienna 6. . . . ADOLF ROBITSCHEK, Graben 14, A–1011 Vienna. . . . RUBATO MUSIK VERLAG, Hollandstrasse 18, 1020 Vienna. . . . SOLISTEN VERLAG, Alser Strasse 43, 1080 Vienna. . . . THALIA, MUSIK, UND THEATERVERLAG, Schoenbrunnerstrasse 48, Vienna 5. . . . UNIVERSAL EDITION, Aktiengesellschaft, Musikverlag und Bühnenvertrieb, Karlsplatz 6, Vienna 1. . . . VAMOE-MUSIKVERLAG, Fischerstiege 4, Vienna 1. . . . JOSEF WEINBERGER, Mahlerstrasse 2, Vienna 1. . . . WELTMUSIK, EDITION INTERNATIONAL, Seilergasse 12, 1015 Vienna. . . . WIENER DREIKLANGVERLAG, Pfeilgasse 35, Vienna 8. . . . WIENER VERLAGSANSTALT, Johannesgasse 12, Vienna 1. . . . JOSEF WORALL, Mariahilfer Strasse 45, Vienna 6.

Belgium

ARCADE, 299, Avenue van Volxem, Brussels 19. . . . CENTRE BELGE DE DOCUMENTATION MUSICALE (CEBEDEM), rue de la Régence 8, Brussels.

Brazil

CASA CARLOS WEHRS, Rua da Carioca 47, Rio de Janeiro GB. . . . EDICOES EUTERPE LTDA., Av. Rio Branco 108, Rio de Janeiro. . . . EDITORA MANIONE S.A., Av. 13 de Maio 13–19, Rio de Janeiro. . . . EDITORA MUSICAL BRASILEIRA, Rua Santa Luzia 799, Rio de Janeiro. . . . EDITORA ARTUR NAPOLEAO, Av. Rio Branco 37, Rio de Janeiro. . . . IRMAOS VITALE S.A., INDUSTRIA & COMERCIO, Av. Almirante Barroso 2, Rio de Janeiro.

Bulgaria

PUBLISHING HOUSE "SCIENCE AND ART," 6, Rouski Str., Sofia.

Canada

ALGORD MUSIC LIMITED, 372a Yonge St., 2nd Floor, Toronto 200, Ontario. . . . ANGLO CANADIAN MUSIC CO., 1261 Bay Street, Toronto, Ontario. . . . ED. ARCHAMBAULT, INC., 500, est rue Ste.-Catherine, Montréal 132, Quebec. . . . BERANDOL MUSIC LIMITED, 651 Progress Ave., Scarborough 707, Ontario. . . . LA BONNE CHANSON, St. Hyacinthe, Quebec. . . . BOOSEY AND HAWKES (Canada) LTD, 279 Yorkland Blvd., Willowdale 425, Ontario. . . . A. J. BOUCHER, 1769 Amherst Street, Montreal, Quebec. . . . CANADIAN MUSIC SALES CORPORATION LIMITED, 58 Advance Road, Toronto 570, Ontario. . . . CAVEAT MUSIC PUBLISHERS LTD., 198 Davenport Road, Toronto 5, Ontario. . . . CHANTECLAIR MUSIC, 29 Birch Avenue, Toronto 190, Ontario. . . . CHAPPELL & CO., LTD., 14 Birch Avenue, Toronto 190, Ontario. . . . A. FASSIO PUBLICATIONS, Lachute, Quebec. . . . HARMUSE PUBLICATIONS, P.O. Box 670, Oakville, Ontario (a Division of Frederick Harris Music Co., Ltd.) . . . FREDERICK HARRIS MUSIC CO., LTD., P.O. Box 670 Oakville, Ontario. . . . HURON PRESS, P.O. Box 3083, London 12, Ontario (a division of Jaymar Music Limited). . . . IROQUOIS PRESS, P.O. Box 3083, London 12, Ontario (a division of Jaymar Music Limited). . . . JARMAN PUBLICATIONS LIMITED, 3–4 Building "A," 435 Midwest Rd., Scarborough, Ontario. . . . E. C. KERBY LTD., 198 Davenport Rd., Toronto 5, Ontario. . . . LEEDS MUSIC, MCA Building, 2450 Victoria Park Ave., Willowdale 425, Ontario (a division of MCA Canada Limited). . . . LESLIE MUSIC SUPPLY, P.O. Box 471, Oakville, Ontario. . . . MANITOU MUSIC, MCA Building, 2450 Victoria Park Ave., Ontario (a division of MCA Canada Limited). . . . MELLO–MUSIC PUBLISHING CO., 507–314 Broadway Avenue, Winnipeg, Manitoba. . . . MUSIQUE CANADIENNE, 4519 Berri, Montreal, Quebec. . . . OXFORD UNIVERSITY PRESS, 70 Wynford Dr., Don Mills 403, Toronto. . . . PASSE-TEMPS, INC. (LES EDITIONS DU), 218 Notre Dame Street West, Montreal, Quebec. . . . PEER INTERNATIONAL (CANADA) LTD., 1405 Bishop St., Montreal 25, Quebec. . . . PETER MCKEE MUSIC COMPANY, LTD., 3 Regina St., North, Waterloo, Ontario. . . . PROCURE GENERALE DE MUSIQUE, ENR., 9 rue d'Aiguillon, Quebec. . . . QUEST MUSIC ASSOCIATES, LTD., 310 Lake Shore Road, Etobicoke, Ontario. . . . G. RICORDI & CO., CANADA, LTD., 1000 Yonge St., Toronto 289, Ontario. . . . SOUTHERN MUSIC PUBLISHING CO., LTD., 1405 Bishop St., Montreal 25, Quebec. . . . SUMMIT MUSIC LTD., 1000 Yonge St., Toronto 289, Ontario. . . . TAYLOR MUSIC CORP., LTD., 311 Lake Shore Road, Etobicoke, Ontario. . . . GORDON V. THOMPSON, LTD., 29 Birch Ave., Toronto 190, Ontario. . . . WATERLOO MUSIC CO., 3 Regina St., North, Waterloo, Ontario. . . . WESTERN MUSIC CO., 570 Seymour Street, Vancouver, D.C., or 229 Yonge Street, Toronto, Ontario. . . .

WHALEY ROYCE & CO., 310 Yonge Street, Toronto, Ontario.

Chile

DEPT. TECNICO DEL CONSERVATORIO NACIONAL DE MÚSICA (Technical Department of the National Conservatory of Music), Calle Agustinas 620, altos, Santiago; reproduces the music of Chilean composers used in the Conservatory. . . . EDITORIAL "CANTICUM," Calle Lira 150, Santiago; choral music publishers. . . . EDITORIAL "CASA AMARILLA," Calle San Diego 128, Santiago; textbooks and music. . . . EDITORIAL "EDUCACIÓN MUSICAL," Calle Agustinas 620, Santiago; educational music. . . . EDITORIAL SOCHIACO, Calle Carmen 82, Santiago; popular music publishers.

Costa Rica

IMPRENTA ATENEA, San José. . . . IMPRENTA NACIONAL, San José. . . . IMPRENTA UNIVERSAL, San José. . . . TALLERES GRÁFICOS LA TRIBUNA, San José.

Czechoslovakia

ARTIA, Ve Smeckach 30, Prague 1 (export agency for cultural publications, etc.) . . . CESKY HUDEBNÍ FOND, ÚSTŘĚDNÍ ARCHIV (Central Archives of the Czech Music Foundation), Staré město, Pařízská 13, Prague 1. . . . ORBIS, Stalinova 46, Prague. . . . S.N.K.L.H.U. (STÁTNÍ NAKLADA-TELSTVÍ KRÁSNÉ LITERATURY, HUDBY A UMĚNÍ), State Publishers for Literature, Music, and Art, Prague.

Denmark

EDITION DANIA-KNUD LARSEN MUSIKFORLAG, Graabrødretorv 7, Copenhagen. . . . DAN FOG (Music Publisher and Antiquarian), 7 Graabrødretorv, Copenhagen K. . . . ENGSTRØM & SØDRING, Musikforlag, Palacgade 6, Copenhagen. . . . WILHELM HANSEN, Musikforlag, Gothersgade 9–11 DK 1123, Copenhagen K. . . . EJNAR MUNKSGAARD LTD., 6, Noerrengade, Copenhagen K. . . . MUSIKHOEJSKOLENS FORLAG, 6040 Egtved. . . . SAMFUNDET TIL UDGIVELSE AF DANSK MUSIK (The Society for Publishing Danish Music), sole selling agents: Dan Fog, Musikforlag, Graabrødretorv 7, 1154 Copenhagen; established in 1871, the Society is a nonprofit organization interested in disseminating the published music of Danish composers. . . . SKANDINAVISK MUSIKFORLAG, Borgergade, Copenhagen.

Irish Free State (Eire)

FOILLSEACHÁIN F.Á.C., 14 Parnell Square, Dublin. . . . GOVERNMENT PUBLICATIONS (AN GÚM), 3–4 College Street, Dublin; publishes native Irish music. . . . PIGOTT & CO., LTD., 112 Grafton Street, Dublin. . . . WALTON & CO., LTD., 2–5 North Frederick Street, Dublin.

England

ALLIANCE MUSIC PUBLICATIONS, 7 Watergate Road, Portsmouth. . . . ANGLO–SOVIET MUSIC PRESS LTD., 295 Regent Street, London. . . . ARCADIA MUSIC PUBLISHING CO., LTD., 18 Great Marlborough Street, London W.1. . . . ASCHERBERG, HOPEWOOD & CREW, LTD., 16 Mortimer Street, London W.1. . . . EDWIN ASHDOWN, LTD., 19 Hanover Square, London W.1. . . . AUGENER'S EDITION (of Augener Ltd.), 18 Great Marlborough Street, London W.1. . . . BANKS & SON, LTD., Stonegate, York. . . . BAYLEY & FERGUSON, LTD., 2 Great Marlborough Street, London W.1. . . . BOSWORTH & CO., LTD., 14–18 Heddon St., London W.1. . . . A. V. BROADHURST, 95a St. George's Road, Brighton. . . . J. & W. CHESTER, LTD., 11 Great Marlborough St., London W.1. . . . CAMPBELL, CONNELLY & CO., LTD., 10 Denmark Street, London W.C.2. . . . L. J. CARY & CO., LTD., 16 Mortimer St., London W.1. . . . CAVENDISH MUSIC CO., LTD., 295 Regent Street, London W.1. . . . J. B. CRAMER & CO., LTD., 139 New Bond Street, London W.1. . . . J. CURWEN & SONS, LTD., 24 Berners St., London W.1. . . . DASH MUSIC CO., LTD., 10 Denmark St., London W.C.2. . . . DE WOLFE, 80–82 Wardour St., London W.1. . . . ELKIN & CO., LTD., 160 Wardour St., London W.1. . . . ENOCH & SONS, 19 Hanover Square, London W.1. . . . FAITH PRESS, LTD., 7 Tufton St., Westminster, London S.W.1. . . . B. FELDMAN & CO., LTD., 64 Dean Street, London W.1. . . . FORSYTH BROS., LTD., 13 Mortimer Street, London. . . . FRANCIS, DAY & HUNTER, LTD., 138–140 Charing Cross Road, London, W.C.2H. . . . H. FREEMAN & CO., 95a St. George's Road, Brighton. . . . GOODWIN & TABB, LTD., 36–38 Dean St., London W.1. . . . GREGG INTERNATIONAL PUBLISHERS LTD., 1 Westmead, Farnborough, Hants. . . . JULIUS HAINAUER LTD., 29 Cranbourne Gardens, London N.W. 11. . . . A. HAMMOND & CO., 11 Lancashire Court, New Bond Street, London W.1. . . . HINRICHSEN EDITION, LTD., 10–12 Baches Street, London, N.1. . . . JAMESONS LTD., 95a St. George's Road, Brighton. . . . ALFRED A. KALMUS, 2–3 Fareham St., London W.1. . . . J. R. LAFLEUR & SON, LTD., 295 Regent St., London W.1. . . . ALFRED LENGNICK & CO., 14 Berners St., London W.1. . . . LEONARD GOULD & BOLTER, 139 New Bond St., London W.1. . . . PETER MAURICE MUSIC CO., LTD., 21 Denmark St., London W.C.2. . . . NOVELLO & CO., LTD., 160 Wardour St., London W.1. . . . OCTAVA MUSIC CO., LTD., 33 Crawford St., London W.1. . . . PATTERSON'S PUBLICATIONS, LTD., 36 Wigmore St., London W.1. . . . W. PAXTON & CO., LTD., 36–38 Dean St., London W.1. . . . PICKWICK MUSIC, LTD., 25 Denmark St., London W.C.2. . . . KEITH PROWSE MUSIC PUBLISHING CO., LTD., 30 New Bond Street, London W.1. . . . MICHAEL REINE MUSIC CO., LTD., 22 Denmark St., London W.C.2. . . . REYNOLDS & CO., LTD., 19 Nassau St., London W.1. . . . WINTHROP ROGERS, LTD., 295 Regent St., London W.1. . . . J. SAVILLE & CO., LTD., Audley House, No. Audley St., London W.1. . . . SCHOTT & CO., LTD., 48 Great Marlborough St., London W.1. . . . R. SMITH & CO., LTD., 210 Strand, London W.C.2. . . . STAINER & BELL, LTD., Lesbourne Road, Reigate, Surrey. . . . SPHEARE PUBLICATIONS, 13 Villiers Ave., Newton Abbot, S. Devon. . . . SUN MUSIC PUBLISHING CO., LTD., 138 Charing Cross Road, London W.C.2. . . . SWAN & CO., LTD., 18 Great Marlborough St., London W.1. . . . SYLVESTER MUSIC CO., LTD., 80–82 Wardour St., London W.1. . . . UNITED MUSIC PUBLISHERS, LTD., 1 Montague St., London W.C.1. . . . UNIVERSAL EDITION, LTD. (London Office), 2–3 Fareham St., London W.1. . . . VICTORIA MUSIC PUBLISHING CO., LTD., 52 Maddox St., London W.1. . . . WARREN & PHILLIPS, LTD., 49 Riding House St., London W.1. . . . A. WEEKES & CO., LTD., 14 Hanover St., London W.1. . . . JOSEF WEINBERGER, LTD., 33 Crawford St., London W.1. . . . JOSEPH WILLIAMS, LTD., 29 Enford St., Marylebone, London W.1. . . . WORKERS' MUSIC ASSOCIATION, LTD., 136A Westbourne Terrace, London W.2. . . . LAWRENCE WRIGHT MUSIC CO., LTD., 19 Denmark St., London W.C.2.

Finland

OY MUSIIKKI FAZER, Aleksanterinkatu 11, 00100 Helsinki 10. . . . OY R. E. WESTERLUND AB, Helsinki.

France

LEON AGEL, 96 rue René-Boulange, Paris 10e. . . . ALLELUIA, Gérard Meys (Productions) 10 rue St. Florentin, Paris ler. . . . ALPHA, 54 rue d'Hauteville, Paris 10e. . . . A.M.I., 67 rue de Provence, Paris 9e. . . . L'AMICALE COMPTOIR DES ARTICLES DE FETE, 32 rue des Vignoles, Paris 20e. . . . AMOUR, 30 rue Pierre-Semard, Paris 9e. . . . AMPHION, 26–28 rue de la Pépinière, Paris 8e. . . . ANDRIEU, FRERES, 17 rue Rodier, Paris 9e. . . . APRIL MUSIC, 3 rue Freycinet, Paris

16e. . . . ARLEQUIN, 6 rue François-Moushon, Paris 15e. . . . ARMAGNAC–MUSIC, 12 blvd. Poissonnière, Paris 9e. . . . ATLANTIC, 60 blvd. de Clichy, Paris 9e. AZNAVOUR (Editions Musicales Charles), 124 rue La Boétie, Paris 8e. . . . BAETZ P. & CIE, 52 rue du Faubourg-Saint-Martin, Paris 10e. . . . BAGATELLE, 10 rue Washington, Paris 8e. . . . BALS DE FRANCE, 82 Faubourg St. Martin, Paris 10e. . . . EDDIE BARCLAY, 44 rue de Miromesnil, Paris 8e. . . . LE BARON, 48 ave. Maurice-Utrillo, 95-Montmagny. . . . BELIER, S.A., 252 Faubourg Saint-Honoré, Paris 8. . . . BERNET–MUSIC, 44 rue de Miromesnil, Paris 8e. . . . BESSEL & CIE, 78 rue de Monceau, Paris 8e. . . . PAUL BEUSCHER, 27 blvd. Beaumarchais, Paris 4e. . . . BILLAUDOT, 14 rue de l'Echiquier, Paris 10e. . . . BONITA, 252 Faubourg St. Honoré, Paris 8e. . . . BOOSEY & HAWKES, 4 rue Drouot, Paris 9e. . . . S. BORNEMANN, 15 rue de Tournon, Paris 6e. . . . BOURNE FRANCE, 10 rue Washington, Paris 8e. . . . H. BOURTAYRE, 56 rue Bassano, Paris 8e. . . . BRETAGNE, 43 rue Fessart, Boulogne 92. . . . RAOUL BRETON, 3 rue Rossini, Paris 9e. . . . MAURICE BRUN, 41 bis rue Vandrezanne, Paris 13e. . . . BYG MUSIC, 29 ave. de Friedland, Paris 8e. . . . CALVI (Editions Gérard) 54 rue d'Hauteville, Paris 10e. . . . CAMIA, 80 rue René-Boulanger, Paris 10e. . . . CARAVELLE, 35 blvd. Malesherbes, Paris 8e. . . . EMILE CARRARA (Productions du Club) 86 Faubourg-St.-Martin, Paris 10e. . . . CARROUSEL, 20 bis. rue Louis-Phillippe à Neuilly 92, France. . . . CLAUDE CARRERE, 89 rue La Boétie, Paris 8e. . . . MARTIN CAYLA, 33 Faubourg-St.-Martin, Paris 10e. . . . CENTRE D'ART NATIONAL FRANÇAIS, 61 ave. de l'Urss, correspondance: B.P. 98 RP, 31 Toulouse. . . . CENTRE NATIONAL DE LA RECHERCHE SCIENTIFIQUE, SERVICE DES PUBLICATIONS, 15, quai Anatole, Paris 7e. . . . J. M. CHAMPEL (Edit.) B.P. ne 2 à Neuville-sur-Ain. . . . CHAMPS-ELYSEES, 5 avenue de l'Opéra, Paris ler. . . . LE CHANT DU MONDE, 32 rue Beaujon, Paris 8e. . . . S. A. CHAPPELL, 4 rue d'Argenson, Paris 8e. . . . CHOUDENS, 38 rue Jean-Mermoz, Paris 8e. . . . C.I.P.E.M., 60 blvd. de Clichy, Paris 18e. . . . LA COMETE, 80 rue René-Boulanger, Paris 10e. . . . LA COMPAGNE, 11 rue de Magdebourg, Paris 16e. . . . COMPTOIR MUSICAL, GALLET-BERGER, 6 rue Vivienne, Paris 2. . . . COMTESSE, 44 rue de Miromesnil, Paris 8e. . . . CONSORTIUM MUSICAL PHILIPPO, 24 blvd. Poissonnière, Paris 9e. . . . CONTINENTAL, 15 rue Saussier-Leroy, Paris 17. . . . COQUELICOT (Editions du), 6 rue Francoeur, Paris 18e. . . . COSTALLAT, 60 Chaussée d'Antin, Paris 9e. . . . COURCELLES, 49 ave. Montaigne, Paris 8e. . . . M. D'ANELLA, 118 rue Legendre, Paris 17e. . . . DANYMUSIC, 134 blvd. Haussmann, Paris 8e. . . . DAUPHINE, 44 rue de Miromesnil, Paris 8e. . . . DE CLERCQ, 44 rue du Colisée, Paris 8e. . . . DEGRUCK, 61 ave. Ray.-Poincaré, Paris 16e. . . . DELRIEU, 45 avenue de Jean-Madecin, 06/Nice. . . . JEAN DREJAC, 60 rue François-ler, Paris 8e. . . . DURAND & CIE, 4 place de la Madeleine, Paris 8e. . . . EDISONOR, 14 rue des Messageries, Paris 10e. . . . EDITIONS ASSOCIEES, 7 rue de la Pépinière, Paris 8e. . . . EDITIONS MUSICALES GRAS, 36 rue Pape-Carpentier, La Fleches (Sarthe). . . . EDITIONS 57, 15 rue Saussier-Leroy, Paris 17e. . . . EDITIONS FRANÇAISES DE MUSIQUE, 26 rue Beaujon, Paris 8e. . . . EDITIONS UNIVERSELLES, 52 rue du Faubourg-St.-Martin, Paris 10e. . . . EMILHENCO MUSIC COMPANY, 88 rue du Faubourg-St.-Martin, Paris 10e. . . . ENOCH & CIE, 27 blvd. des Italiens, Paris 2e. . . . LES EPIS, 14 boulevard des Filles-du-Calvaire, Paris lle. . . . E.P.O.C., 71 rue de Provence, Paris 9e. . . . MAISON ESCHIG, 48 rue de Rome, Paris 8e. . . . ESSEX, 34 Champs-Elysées, Paris 8e. . . . EURO-FRANCE, 18 rue de Provence, Paris 9e. . . . FANTASIA, 3 rue de Gramont, Paris 2e. . . . FLEURUS, 31 rue de Fleurus à Paris 6e. . . . MICHEL FORTIN, 4 Cité Chaptal, Paris 9e. . . . FRANCE CONTINENTALE, 80 rue René-Boulanger, Paris 10e. . . . FRANCE MELODIE, 5 avenue de l'Opéra, Paris le. . . . FRANCE VEDETTES, 44 rue du Colisée, Paris 8e. . . . FRANCIS DAY, Publications, 5 avenue de l'Opéra, Paris le. . . . FRENCH MUSIC, 124 rue La Boétie, Paris 8e. . . . GRAS FRERES, 4 rue de la Rochefoucauld, Paris 9e. . . . JULIO GARZON, 13 rue de l'Echiquier, Paris 10e. . . . LOUIS GASTE (Editions), 5 rue du Bois-de-Boulogne, Paris 16e. . . . GEDALGE (Lib. Music), 75 rue des Saints-Pères, Paris 6e. . . . GRANDE AVENUE, 49 avenue Hoche, Paris 8e. . . . GRANDES EDITIONS MUSICALES (Soc.), 4 rue Drouot, Paris 9e. . . . J. HAMELLE, 22 blvd. Malesherbes, Paris 8e. . . . MICHEL HAVANAIR, 7 rue de Trêtaigne, Paris 18e. . . . HEUGEL & CIE, 2 bis rue Vivienne, Paris 2e. . . . HOMERE (Eds. Musicales & Disques), 3 Cité Magenta, Paris 10. . . . HORTENSIA, Editions Musicales, 46 rue de Douai, Paris 9e. . . . IMPACT, 3 rue de Gramont, Paris 2e. . . . IMPERIA EDITIONS MUSICALES, 14 avenue Hoche, Paris 8e. . . . IRVING BERLIN (Editions) 4 rue d'Argenson, Paris 8e. . . . JACQUET & CIE., 8 blvd. Magenta, Paris 8e. . . . JEAN JOBERT, 44 rue du Colisée, Paris 8e. . . . JOUBERT, 25 rue d'Hauteville, Paris 10e. . . . LABAT, 3 et 5 rue Labat, Paris 18e. . . . LABRADOR, 9, square Moncey, Paris 9e. . . . ALBERT LASRY, 62 blvd. de Clichy, Paris 18e. . . . G. LEBLANC, 70 rue des Rigoles, Paris 20e. . . . B. P. LEBRIOT, no. 7 à Formerie 60. . . . ALPHONSE LEDUC, 175 rue St. Honoré, Paris. . . . GUSTAVE LEGOUIX, 4 rue Chauveau-Lagarde, Paris 8e. . . . LEGRAND (Productions Michel Legrand), 252 Faubourg-St. Honoré, Paris 8e. . . . LEMARQUE (Les Prod. Francis Lemarque), 121 Blvd de la Marne, La Varenne-St.-Maur 94. . . . HENRY LEMOINE, 17 rue Pigalle, Paris 9e. . . . LIMOUSINE EDITION (Segurel) Chaumeil. . . . PÉPÉ LUIZ, 14 rue Chaptal, Paris 9e. . . . MAGALI, 33 rue de La Rochefoucauld, Paris 9e. . . . MAJESTIC LUCIENNE CANETTI, 252 Faubourg St.-Honoré, Paris 8e. . . . MANDY MUSIC, 95 rue Championnet, Paris 18e. . . . MARGUERITAT SCHOENAERS, Millereau, Reunis, 24 rue René-Boulanger, Paris 10e. . . . MARINE, 44 rue de Miromesnil, Paris 8e. . . . B. MARQUE, 109 rue Lecourbe, Paris 15e. . . . MARTIN, 106 La Coupée à Charnay-lès-Mâcon. . . . MASSPACHER, 39 passage du Grand-Cerf, Paris 2e. . . . DE MAURIZI (Tzigania), 8 rue Etienne-Jodelle, Paris 18e. . . . ROBERT MELLIN & CIE., 74 blvd. de la Gare, Paris 13e. . . . MELLOTTEE (Litt. Music), 48 rue Monsieur-le-Prince, Paris 6e. . . . MERIDIAN (Les Nouvelles Editions), 5 rue Lincoln, Paris 8e. . . . METROPOLITAINES, 3 rue Rossini, Paris 9e. . . . MONDE-MELODY, 6 rue Vivienne, Paris 2e. . . . MONEDIERES, à Chaumeil 19. . . . EDWIN H. MORRIS, 4 rue d'Argenson, Paris 8e. . . . MUSICA FILMS, 14 rue Montjuzet, Clermont-Ferrand. . . . MUSIC 18, 10 rue Washington, Paris 8e. . . . MUSIQUE SACREE, 269 rue Saint-Jacques, Paris 5e. . . . NUMERO 7, 15 rue Saussier-Leroy, Paris 17e. . . . OURS (MLLE. JACQUE CARNET, comp.), 56 rue de l'Université, Paris 7e. . . . OUVRIERES, 12 avenue Soeur-Rosalie, Paris 13e . . . PALACE, 8 rue Saint-Marc, Paris 2e. . . . H. PANELLA, 1 bis, rue Bieue, Paris 9e. . . . PARIS-CENTRE ACCORDEON, à Masseret. . . . PARIS TREE MUSIC, 15 rue Saussier-Leroy, Paris 17e. . . . PATHE-MARCONI, 19 rue Lord-Byron, Paris 8e. . . . MAURICE PETER, 15 rue Saussier-Leroy, Paris 17e. . . . PHILIPPE PARES EDITIONS, 15 rue Saussier-Leroy, Paris 17e. . . . PHILIPPO, 24 boulevard Poissonnière, Paris 9e. . . . PICOT (Recueils comiques), 50 blvd. de Strasbourg, Paris 10e. . . . PIGALLE, 89 rue La Boétie, Paris 8e. . . . JACQUES PLANTE, 35 boulevard Malesherbes, Paris 8e. . . . PLEINS FEUX (Georges Bérard) 12 boulevard Poissonnière, Paris 9e. . . . PLOIX-MUSIQUE, 48 rue Saint-Placide, Paris 6e. . . . PRESENCE, 33 Faubourg St. Martin, Paris 10e. . . . PRISMA MUSIC, 40 rue du Faubourg-Poissonnière, Paris 10e. . . . PROSADIS, 14 avenue Hoche, Paris 8e. . . . RADIO MUSIC FRANCE, 15 rue Saussier-Leroy, Paris 17e. . . . RICORDI, 3 rue Roquepine, Paris 8e. . . . RIDEAU ROUGE, 24 rue de Longchamp, Paris 16e. . . . R.M.C. 16 boulevard Princesse-Charlotte à Monte-Carlo et 37 ave. George-V. . . . ROYALTY (Editions Musicales), 25 rue d'Hauteville, Paris 10e. . . . LES RYTHMES NOUVEAUX, 3 rue

Gustave-Goublier, Paris 10e. . . . EDITIONS SALABERT, 22 rue Chauchat, Paris 9e. . . . HENRI SALVADOR, 6 place Vendôme, Paris 1e. . . . ROBERT SALVET EDITIONS, 89 rue La Boétie, Paris 8e. . . . SANDRA MUSIC, 17 rue Monsigny, Paris 2e. . . . SCHMOLL, 15 rue Saussier-Leroy, Paris 17e. . . . SCHOLA CANTORUM ET DE LA PROCURE GENERALE DE MUSIQUE, 76 bis, rue des Sts-Pères, Paris 7e. . . . S.E.M.I., 5 rue Lincoln, Paris 8e. . . . SEPTENTRION (Pierre Celie), 3 rue de Grammont, Paris 2e. . . . SOCIETE ANONYME D'EDITION, 7 rue Gambetta, Nancy. . . . SOCIETE DISTRIBUTIONS MUSICALES, 20 rue de Croissant, Paris 2e. . . . SPANKAFRANCE, 44 rue de Miromesnil, Paris 8e. . . . F. SUDRE, 17 avenue Trudaine, Paris 9e. . . . SUGARMUSIC, 90 avenue des Champs-Elysées, Paris 8e. . . . SYLVIA, 4 rue d'Argenson, Paris 8e. . . . SYRINX, 40 cours Albert ler, Paris 8e. . . . THEVEN, 34 rue Pigalle, Paris 9e. . . . TOP 2000, 12 rue Magellan, Paris 8e. . . . TOURNESOL, 68 et 70 rue Lhomond, Paris 5e. . . . GERARD TOURNIER, 67 rue de Provence, Paris 9e. . . . TRAIN BLEU, 12 rue de Magellan, Paris 8e. . . . TRANSATLANTIQUES, 14 avenue Hoche, Paris 8e. . . . TRO EDITIONS (J. Poisson) 34 Champs-Elysées, Paris 8e. . . . TULSA, 15 rue Saussier-Leroy, Paris 17e. . . . TUTTI, 15 rue Saussier-Leroy, Paris 17e. . . . VENDOME, 5 rue Lincoln, Paris 8e. . . . RAY VENTURA, 14 avenue Hoche, Paris 8e. . . . VIANELLY EDITIONS, 3 rue Rossini, Paris 9e. . . . VOGUE INTERNATIONAL, 20bis, rue Louis-Philippe à Neuilly, 93. . . . WILLIAMS, 62 rue d'Orsel, Paris, 18e. . . . AUGUSTE ZURFLUH, 75 blvd. Raspail, Paris 6e.

Germany (East)

VEB BREITKOPF & HÄRTEL, Musikverlag, Leipzig; publishes musicological literature, orchestral and chamber music, choral music, opera, and ballet. . . . VEB EDITION LEIPZIG, Karlstrasse 20, Leipzig C 1. . . . DEUTSCHER VERLAG FÜR MUSIK, Karlstrasse 10, Leipzig; collections, musicological literature. . . . DEUTSCHER BUCH-EXPORT u. IMPORT, P.O. Box 276, Leninstrasse 16, Leipzig C 1. . . . HARTH-MUSIK-VERLAG, P.O. Box 467 Karl-Liebknechtstrasse, 12, Leipzig; popular music. . . . VEB FRIEDRICH HOFMEISTER, MUSIKVERLAG, P.O. Box 147, Karlstrasse 10, 701 Leipzig; educational instrumental music, miniature scores, folk music, vocal music. . . . VEB LIED DER ZEIT MUSIKVERLAG, Rosa-Luxembourgstrasse 41, Berlin 102; dance and entertainment music, operettas, popular music. . . . COLLECTION LITOLFF, Leipzig; chamber and vocal music. . . . VERLAG NEUE MUSIK, Leipziger Strasse 26, Berlin W 8; musicological publications and scores for contemporary works of the Association of German Composers. . . . EDITION PETERS, Talstrasse 10, Leipzig C 1; chamber, choral, and orchestral music. . . . EDITION PRO MUSICA, Leipzig; teaching materials and music. . . . VOLK UND WISSEN VERLAG, Berlin E.; school music and music for the young.

Germany (West)

BÄRENREITER-VERLAG, Heinrich-Schütz Allee 29–37, 3500 Kassel-Wilhelmshöhe. . . . VERLAG DES BEETHOVEN-HAUS, Bonn. . . . EDMUND BIELER VERLAG, Zulpicker Strasse 85, Cologne. . . . BOTE UND BOCK, Hardenbergstrasse 9A, Berlin-Charlottenburg 2. . . . BRAUN PERETTI, Hähnchen-Passage, Bonn. . . . BREITKOPF UND HÄRTEL, P.O. Box 74, Wiesbaden. . . . F. A. BROCKHAUS, Leberberg 25, P.O. Box 261, 62 Wiesbaden. . . . COLLOQUIUM-VERLAG, Berlin. . . . ALFRED COPPENRATH, Neuottinger Strasse 32, 8262 Altötting/Bayern. . . . RUD. ERDMANN, P.O. Box 471, Wiesbaden. . . . B. FILSER VERLAG, Augsburg. . . . FURCHE VERLAG, Blumenstrasse 57, 2 Hamburg 39. . . . G. HENLE VERLAG, Schongauer Strasse 24, 8 München 55. . . . FRIEDRICH HOFMEISTER VERLAG, Ubierstrasse 20, 6238 Hofheim/Taunus. . . . HIERSEMANN VERLAG, Stuttgart. . . . MATTH. HOHNER A. G., Trossingen. . . . KISTNER UND

SIEGEL MUSIKVERLAG, P.O. Box 101, Gereonshof 38, 5 Köln 7. . . . ERNST KLETT VERLAG, Rotebuhlstrasse 77, 7 Stuttgart. . . . ALFRED KROENER VERLAG, Reuchlinstrasse 4B, 7 Stuttgart W. . . . ROBERT LIENAU VORMALS SCHLESINGER, Lankwitzer Str. 9, 1 Berlin 45. . . . CARL MERSEBURGER, Hindenburgstrasse 42, Darmstadt. . . . VERLAG MERSEBURGER BERLIN, Alemannerstrasse 20, Postfach 130, D-100 W. Berlin. . . . HERMANN MOECK VERLAG, Hannoversche Strasse 43a, 10a Celle. . . . VERLAGSHAUS G. MOHN, Gutersloh. . . . KARL HEINRICH MÖSELER, Hoffman-von-Fallersleben-Strasse 8, 3340 Wolfenbüttel. . . . WILLY MUELLER, Suddeutscher Musikverlag, Heidelberg. . . . VERLAG DAS MUSIKINSTRUMENT, E. Bochinsky, Klüberstrasse 9, Frankfurt. . . . GEORG OLMS VERLAG, Am Dammtor, Hildesheim; primarily music book reprints. . . . C. F. PETERS, Kennedyallee 101, Frankfurt-am-Main. . . . R. PIPER & CO. VERLAG, Georgenstrasse 4, 8 München 13. . . . PUSTET VERLAG, Gutenbergerstrasse 8, 84 Regensburg. . . . PHILLIPP RECLAM VERLAG, Stuttgart. . . . M. SANDIG, Wiesbaden. . . . HANS SCHNEIDER, Mozartweg, Tutzing Obb. . . . C. L. SCHULTHEISS, Denzenbergstrasse 35, 74 Tübingen. . . . SCHULER VERLAGSGESELLSCHAFT, Lenzhalde 28, 7 Stuttgart, N.W. . . . SCHOTT'S SÖHNE, Weihergarten 65, Mainz. . . . L. SCHWANN VERLAG, Charlottenstrasse 80/86, Düsseldorf. . . . STAUDA VERLAG, Kassel/Wilhelmshöhe (c/o Bärenreiter). . . . SUDDEUTSCHEN MUSIKVERLAGES, Willy Müller, Heidelberg. . . . W. SULZBACH, Ringstrasse 47a, Berlin-Lichterfelde. . . . P. J. TONGER-MUSIKVERLAG, Bergstrasse 10, 5038 Rodenkirchen/Rhein. . . . UGRINO VERLAG, Elbchaussee 499a, Hamburg/Blankenese.

Greece

AIKAROS CO., 4 Stoa Diou St., Athens. . . . NICHOLAOS ANDRAEDIS, 2 Pheidiou St., Athens. . . . M. CONSTANTINIDIS, 6 Stoa Arsakeiou, Athens. . . . DEMETRIOS GAITANOS, 25 Zoodochou Pigis St., Athens. . . . STEPHANOS GAITANOS, 10 Stoa Arsakeiou, Athens. . . . PHILLIPPOS NAKAS, 2 Charilaou Trikoupi St., Athens.

Hungary

CORVINA VERLAG, Budapest.

India

LAKSHYA SANGEET KARYALAYA, Hill View, Raghaoji Road, Bombay 26. . . . MUSIC ACADEMY, 115-E. Mowbsays Road, Madras 14. . . . SANGEET AND MUSICAL MIRROR, Sangeet Karyalaya, Hathras (U.P.).

Israel

BENNO BALAN, Zion Square, Jerusalem. . . . HAMERKAZ LETARBUT, Beit Va'ad Hapoal, Arlosoroff St., Tel-Aviv; publishers for the Cultural Department of the Labor Federation. . . . ILLAN MELODY PRESS, 105 Ben Yehuda St., Tel-Aviv; popular music. . . . ISRAEL EDITION, 112 Yehuda Halevy Road, Tel-Aviv. . . . ISRAEL MUSIC PUBLICATIONS LIMITED, 105 Ben Yehuda Street, Tel-Aviv. . . . NEGEN EDITION, 59 Allenby Road, Tel-Aviv. . . . RENEN EDITION, Ramat Gan, Salk Street, Tel-Aviv.

Italy

ALL'INSEGNA DEI BRANDE, Corso Palermo 11, Torino. . . . AUGUSTA, Via Po 3, Torino. . . . FRANCESCO BONGIOVANNI EDITORE DI MUSICA, Via Rizzoli 28 E, Bologna. . . . CARISCH, Via Generale Fara 39, 20124 Milano. . . . CASA EDITRICE, LORENZO DEL TURCO, Via Della Croce 81, Rome. . . . CASA EDITRICE, Leo S. Olschki S.P.A., Casella Postale 295, Florence. . . . CASA MUSICALE GIULIANA, Via F. Venezian 24, Trieste. . . . CASA MUSICALE SONZOGNO, Via Bigli 11, Milano. . . . DESCLEE & CI. (Editori Pontifici e Tipografi della S. Congregazione dei Riti), Piazza Grazioli 4, Rome; known for publications of Gregorian Chant. . . . EDIZIONI CURCI, Galleria del Corso 4, Milano. . . . EDIZIONI DRAGO, Via Roma 6, Magento (Milano). . . . EDIZIONI SUVINI ZERBONI, Galleria del Corso 4, Milano. . . . FRATELLI PALOMBI, Via dei Gracchi, 185, Roma. . . . INSTITUTO ITALIANO DE STORIA DELLA MUSICA, c/o Accademia di S. Cecilia, Via Vittoria #6, Roma. . . . G. RICORDI & CO., Via Berchet 2, Milano. . . . ZANIBON EDITION CO., Padua.

Lebanon

VOIX DE L'ORIENT, A CHAHINE & FILS, Rue Monot, Im. Ingea. . . . VOIX DE L'ORIENT, A. CHAHINE & FILS, Fue G. Picot, Im. Ingea.

Mexico

CASA ALEMANA DE MÚSICA, México D.F. . . . DE LA PEÑA, GIL HERMANOS, México D.F. . . . EDICIONES MEXICANES DE MÚSICA, A.C., Avenida Juárez 18, México D.F. . . . EDITORIAL MEXICANA DE MÚSICA INTERNACIONAL, S.A., Revillagigedo 106, México D.F. . . . HERMANOS MARGUEZ, S. DE R.L., Avenida Chapultepec 43, México D.F. . . . MENZEL, Palma Norte 413 A, México D.F. . . . ENRIQUE MUNGIÁ, México D.F. . . . OTTO Y ARZOZ, México D.F. . . . PROMOTORA HISPANOAMERICANA DE MÚSICA, S.A., Revillagigedo 108, México D.F. . . . WAGNER Y LEVIEN, México D.F.

Monaco

LES EDITIONS DE L'OISEAU-LYRE, Les Remparts, Monaco.

The Netherlands

ACCORDA MUSICA (G. E. den Boer), Weissenbruchstraat 43 Acc., Amsterdam. . . . ACCORDEA, UITGEVERIJ, Besterdstraat 19, Tilburg. . . . ALBERSON EN CO., Groot Hertoginnelaan 182, s'-Gravenhage. . . . W. ALPHENAAR, Kruisweg 49, Haarlem. . . . G. ALSBACH & CO., Leidsegracht 11, Amsterdam. . . . ALTONA JORGENSEN, Leidsestraat 19, Amsterdam. . . . ANTIQUA, Staalstraat 7, Amsterdam. . . . ARSIS (Ward Instituut), Swalmerstraat, Roermond. . . . ANNIE BANK, Anna Vondelstraat 13, Amsterdam. . . . CHR. BOND HARMONIE-EN FANFAREKORPSEN IN DE PROV. GRONINGEN (D. Siccama), Hoogkerk. . . . CREYGHTON MUSICOLOGY-MUSICA ANTIQUA, 45 Lassuslaan/ Bilthoven. . . . LES EDITIONS INTERNATIONALES BASART N.V., Leidsegracht 11, Amsterdam. . . . W. BERGMANS BOEK-HANDEL, Markt 35, Tilburg. . . . E. J. BRILL PUBLISHERS, Leiden. . . . BROEKMANS & V. POPPEL, V. Baerlestraat 92, Amsterdam. . . . J. R. BUSCHMANN, Lange Jansstraat 13, Utrecht. . . . DEKELING & SWART, Leidsegracht 11, Amsterdam. . . . UITGEVERIJ VAN DOMBURG, 2e Const. Huygensstraat 83, Amsterdam. . . . DONEMUS (DOCUMENTATIE IN NEDERLAND VOOR MUZIEK—Documentations in the Netherlands for Music), Jacob Obrechtstraat 51, Amsterdam-Z; a referral agency of the music of Dutch composers; unpublished scores in miniature form (reproduced from manuscript) are in its library and on loan. . . . A. DREISSEN, Leidsegracht 11, Amsterdam. . . . FA. V. DRIESTEN, Schermlaan 47, Rotterdam. . . . DE EERSTE MUZIEK-CENTRALE, Raamgracht 10, Amsterdam-C. . . . GEMENGDKOORUITGAVE, Nieuwe Ebbingestraat 161a, Groningen. . . . N.V. GRAFISCHE INDUSTRIE AFD. DE TOORTS, Nijverheidsweg 1, Haarlem. . . . HARMONIA UITGAVE, Roeltjesweg 23, Hilversum. . . . HANDELMIJ. JOH. DE HEER EN ZN. N.V., Jensiusstraat 54, Rotterdam. . . . N.V. HEES & CO., Choorstraat 1–3, Delft. . . . A. J. HEUWEKEMEYER, Bredeweg 1, Amsterdam. . . . J. HOES, Nieuwstraat 17, Weert. . . . J. HOFMAN, Tuinbouwstraat 59, Groningen. . . . HYMNOPHON (R. R. GANZEVOORT), Damstraat 1, Amsterdam 1. . . . M. ISLER, Rijnstraat 9, Amsterdam. . . . P. J. W.

JONGENEEL, Markt 41, Gouda. . . . KLAVARSKRIBO, Ringdijk, Slikkerveer; publishes music in a novel notational system called "Klaverskribo." . . . FRITS A.M. KNUF, Jan Luykenstraat 52, Amsterdam Z 1. . . . KON. BOND V. CHR. ZANG & ORATORIUM VER., De Perponcherstraat 104, Den Haag (The Hague). . . . KONEFA MUZIEKUITGAVEN N.V., Jensiusstraat 54, Rotterdam. . . . W. F. KOOLS, Waldeck Pyrmontkade 29, The Hague. . . . KOORFONDS MUZIKALE BLADEN (R. R. Ganzevoort), Damstraat 1, Amsterdam. . . . KRIPS–MUSIC, Thorbeckelaan 71, The Hague. . . . J. W. DE KRUYFF, Terborgseweg 8, Doetinchem. . . . ANT. M. VAN LEEST, Hermanus Boexstraat 12–14, Eindhoven. . . . W. FLICHTENAUER, Kruisplein 44, Rotterdam. . . . J. J. LISPET, P.C. Chrysantenstraat 57, Hilversum. . . . MELODIA (C. Smit Jr.), Amstel 52, Amsterdam. . . . ALG. MUZIEKHANDEL EN UITGEVERSMIJ. V. ESSO EN CO. N.V., Leidsegracht 11, Amsterdam. . . . CENTRALE MUZIEKHANDEL, H.N. v.d. GLAS, Albert Cuypstraat 23, Amersfoort. . . . METRO MUZIEK, Bern. Zweerskade 18, Amsterdam. . . . MOLENAAR MUZIEKCENTRALE, Zuideinde 18, Wormerveer. . . . HENRI MOSMANS, Kerkstraat 53, 's-Hertogenbosch. . . . MUZIEKARCHIEF "IN DE BLOCKFLUYT," Oude Gracht 305, Utrecht. . . . MUZIEKGRAVURE "DILIGENTA" (P.J. Wiest), Stationsstraat, Maasland. . . . MUZIEK SMITH, Leidsegracht 11,Amsterdam. . . .MUZIEKUITGEVERIJ ARS NOVA, Oostsingel 92, Goes. . . . MUZIEK UITG. SUPERTUNE, Leidsegracht 11, Amsterdam. . . . J. NAGEL, Singel 160–162, Amsterdam. . . . J. NAUTA (Frisia Cantat), Looxmagracht 18, Sneek. . . . BUR. V. UITGAVE "NED ORGELMUZIEK," Boslaan 18, Bussum. . . . MARTINUS NIJHOFF, UITGEVERS, The Hague. . . . VAN 't HOEN'S PERIODIEKE PERS, 's-Gravendijkwal 165b, Rotterdam. . . . W. PIJLMAN, le Helmersstraat 94, Amsterdam. . . . J. POELTUYN, Deurloostraat 18, Amsterdam. . . . H. A. POORT'S MUZIEKHANDEL POLYPHONIA, Voorstreek 6, Leeuwarden. . . . VAN ROSMALEN & ZN., Roosendaalselaan 18, Velp (G.). . . . FA. WED. J. R. VAN ROSSUM, Achterhet Stadhuis, Utrecht. . . . FIRMA A.V.D. SCHAAF, Parkweg 125, Enschede. . . . SERVAAS MUZIEKHANDEL, Schoolstraat 26, s'-Gravenhage. . . . LEO SMEETS, Roelofsstraat 116, The Hague. . . . C. B. SMIT, Amstel 52, Amsterdam. . . . J. H. SMIT, Singel 115, Amsterdam. . . . C. W. H. SNOEK, Hoogstraat 156, Rotterdam. . . . SPECIAAL REPROGRAFISCHE ONDERN. S.R.O. v.h. MUSICO M.P.S., Nieuwe Molstraat 12, The Hague. . . . STUDIO V.D. RHEE, Hugo Molenaarstraat 16b, Rotterdam. . . . ANT. TIERLOFF, MUZIEKCENTRALE, Markt 92, Roosedaal. . . . N.V. Q.J. v. TRIGT, Albertus Perkstraat 16, Hilversum. . . . OTTO DE VAAL, Oudedijk 90, Rotterdam. . . . J. A. H. WAGENAAR, Oude Gracht 107–109, Utrecht. . . . J. C. WILLEMSEN, Langestraat 72, Amersfoort. . . . WOLTER HATTINK & CREYGHTON, Noord Houdringelaan 20, Bilthoven. . . . N. V. VANWOUW, Molenpad 15–17, Amsterdam.

New Zealand

CHARLES BEGG AND CO., P.O. Box 889, 19–21 Manners Street, Wellington. . . . CHAPPELL & COMPANY (NZ) LTD., Nimmo's Buildings, Bond and Farish Streets, Wellington. . . . E.M.I. MUSIC (Division of H.M.V.) 162–172 Wakefield Street, Wellington. . . . OTAGO UNIVERSITY PRESS, John McIndoe, P.O. Box 56, Dunedin. . . . SEVEN SEAS/SANDY MUSIC, P.O. Box 1431, Wellington. . . . WAI-TE-ATA PRESS, Victoria University, P.O. Box 196, Wellington.

Norway

HARALD LYCHE & CO., Kongensgate 2, Oslo; also located in Drammen. . . . MUSIKKHUSET A/S, Karl Johansgate 45, Oslo 1. . . . NORSK MUSIKKFORLAG A/S, Karl Johansgate 39, Oslo.

Republic of Panama

JORGE LUIS MACKAY, CO., Avenida Central 10, Panama City.

Poland

POLSKIE WYDAWNICTWO, Muzyczne, Krakau, Poland.

Portugal

VALENTIM DE CARVALHO, CASA DE MUSICAS, Rua Nova do Almada 95–99, Lisbon. . . . CUSTODIO CARDOSO PEREIRA & CA., Rua do Carmo 11, Lisbon 2. . . . SASSETTI & CA., 20 B, Ave. Visconde Valmor, Lisbon.

Republic of South Africa

ATHENA PUBLISHERS PTY., LTD., Barclay's Bank Building, 52 Long Street, Cape Town (for Oxford University). . . . BOOSEY & HAWKES, PTY., LTD., Cor. Longmarket & Parliament Streets, P.O. Box 1851, Cape Town. . . . BOOSEY AND HAWKES (South Africa PTY. Ltd.) P.O. Box 3966, Johannesburg. . . . DEPARTMENT OF MUSIC, South Africa Broadcasting Corp., P.O. Box 8606, Johannesburg. . . . STUDIO HOLLAND, Music Printers and Publicity Advisers, Rodene Bldg., 16 Bloem St., Cape Town.

Rumania

UNION OF RUMANIAN COMPOSERS (Uniunea Compozitorilor din R.P.R.), 141 Calea Victoriei, Bucharest.

Spain

BOILEAU BERNASCONI, Alessio, Barcelona. . . . CASA ERVITI, San Sebastian. . . . CONSEJO SUPERIOR DE INVESTIGACIONES CIENTIFICAS, Instituto Español de Musicologia, Epigciacas 15, Barcelona 1. . . . EDITORIAL SERAFICA, Madrid. . . . HARMONIA, Madrid. . . . IBERIA MUSICAL, Barcelona. . . . MUSICAL EMPORIUM, Rambla Canaletas 129, Barcelona 2. . . . UNION MUSICAL ESPAÑOLA (Antigua Casa Dotesio), S.A. Carrera de San Jeronimo 26, Madrid 14.

Sweden

AIR MUSIC SCANDINAVIA AB, Oxenstiernsgatan 27, 115 27, Stockholm. . . . ANDERSSONS MUSIK 1 MALMÖ AB, Box 17018, 200 10 Malmö 17. . . . BARDINGS MUSIKFÖRLAG, Drottninggatan 81A, 111 60 Stockholm. . . . THORE EHRLING MUSIK AB, Box 5268, 102 45 Stockholm 5. . . . EHRLING & LÖFVENHOLM AB, Box 745, 101 20 Stockholm 1. . . . ELKAN & SCHILDKNECHT, EMIL CARELIUS, Sveavägen 45, 111 34 Stockholm. . . . ERIKS MUSIKHANDEL & FÖRLAG AB, Karlavägen 40, 114 49, Stockholm. . . . CARL GEHRMANS MUSIKFÖRLAG, Box 505, 10126 Stockholm; largest publisher of purely Swedish music. . . . KARL GRÖNSTEDT MUSIKFÖRLAG, Borgargatan 4, 117 34 Stockholm. . . . AB ABR. HIRSCHS FÖRLAG, Box 505, 101 26 Stockholm 1. . . . IMUDICO AB, Box 27053, 102 51, Stockholm 27. . . . INTERSONGFÖRLAGEN AB, Box 5222, 102 45 Stockholm 5. . . . KEJVING MUSIK AB, Bastugatan 45, 117 25 Stockholm. . . . KÖRLINGS FÖRLAG AB, Radagatan 34, 123 51 Farsta. . . . EDITION LIBERTY AB, Box 1178, 171 23 Solna 1. . . . ABRAHAM LUNDQUIST MUSIKFÖRLAG, Katarina Bangata 17, S-116 25 Stockholm. . . . NILS-GEORGS MUSIKFÖRLAGS AB, Box 5268, 102 45 Stockholm 1. . . . NORDISKA MUSIKFÖRLAGET, Box 745, 101 20 Stockholm; a subsidiary of Wilhelm Hansen, Copenhagen; annually publishes the serious works of Swedish composers. . . . AB NORDISK FOLKMUSIK, Box 2008, 403 11 Göteborg 2. . . . OKTAV MUSIKFÖRLAG, Box 6038, 200 11 Malmö 6. . . . REUTER & REUTER FÖRLAGS, Brahegatan 20, 114 37 Stockholm. . . . SONET MUSIC AB, Torsvikssvängen 7, 181 05 Lidingö, Sweden. . . . SOUTHERN MUSIC AB, Grev Turegatan 38, 114 38 Stockholm. . . . SKAP (Svenska Kompositörer av Populärmusik), Tegnérlunden 3, Stockholm; unpublished works by Swedish popular music composers in photostatic prints. . . . EDITION SUECIA, Tegnérlunden 3, Stockholm; managed by the Association of Swedish Composers and publishes only Swedish music. . . . SWEDEN MUSIC AB, Box 5265, 102 45 Stockholm 5. . . . EDITION SYLVAIN AB, Box 5268, 102 45 Stockholm 5. . . . WESTLINGS MUSIKFÖRLAG, Box 9039, 102 71 Stockholm 9.

Switzerland

APOLLO-VERLAG (Alb. Kunzelmann), Stockerstrasse 37, Zürich. . . . DIE ARCHE, Rosenbuhlstrasse 37, Zürlich 7/44. . . . ATLANTIS VERLAG, Zeltweg 16, Zürich. . . . BAUMANN-DRUCK, Verlag, Schöftland. . . . R. BOGGIO, Musikverlag, Bätterkinden. . . . H. BONNE, Kreuzlingen. . . . BRONSTEIN, P. MME, Place Madeleine 13, Genève. . . . J. CAVALLI, Grand Chêne, Lausanne. . . . A. G. CLAUDE, Züricherstrasse 10, St. Gallen. . . . EDIFO S.A., Bandenstrasse 332, 8040 Zürich. . . . EDITION "CHANTE-JURA" (H. Devain), La Ferrière. . . . EDITION EULENBURG, Grütstrasse 28, Adliswil. . . . EDITIONS SIDEM, S.A. (E. Liechti), rue de Hesse 8, Genève. . . . EDITION TURICAPHON, S.A., c/o Aberbach, Brunnenstrasse 9, Zürich. . . . EDITIONS DU SIÈCLE MUSICAL, S.A. (E. Richli), Blvd. Helvétique 16, Genève. . . . ELWE-VERLAG (E. Lüthold & Co.), Flössergasse 8, Zürich. . . . FRERES FOETISCH, S.A., Caroline 5, Lausanne. . . . MAURICE & PIERRE FOETISCH, rue de Bourg 6, Lausanne. . . . FRANCKE VERLAG, Hochfeldstrasse 113, Bern. . . . GROLIMUND FRAU, EMIL, Clendy derrière, Yverdon. . . . HELBLING & CO., Pfaffikerstrasse, 8604 Volketswill. . . . HUG & CO., Limmatquai 26/28, Zürich. . . . CH. HUGUENIN, Daniel-Jeanrichard 14, Le Locle. . . . A.G. HÜNI, Fraumünsterstrasse 21, Zürich. . . . F. X. JANS, (Kirchenmusikverlag), Altdorf; church music. . . . JECKLIN SÖHNE, zum Pfauen, Heimplatz, Zürich. . . . KROMPHOLZ & CO., Spitalgasse 28, Bern. . . . ALBERT LÜTHOLD, Oberdorfstrasse 28, Zürich. . . . G. B. MANTEGAZZI, Tessiner-Musikverlag, Engimattstrasse 25, Zürich. . . . L. MARGOT, Pré-du-Marché 37, Lausanne. . . . H. MOSER, Gunten. . . . ERNST R. MÜLLER, NOTENDRUCKEREI UND VERLAG, Tösstalstrasse 45, Winterthur. . . . HANS MÜLLER-LIENHARD "MILGRA-EDITION," Wädenswill. . . . MÜLLER & SCHADE, A.G., Theaterplatz 6, Bern. . . . MUSIKVERLAG ZUM PELIKAN (Dr. A. Brandenberger), Bellerivestrasse 22, Zürich. . . . WERNER NEUKOMM, BLASMUSIK-VERLAG, Wettingen; publishes music for winds. . . . ARTHUR NEY, Villars /Ollon. . . . M. OCHSNER & CO., Einsiedeln. . . . L. G. PANTILLON, rue Numa Droz 29, Le Chaux-de-Fonds. . . . PAULUS VERLAG, Moosmattstrasse 4, Luzern. . . . RAUBER FRERES S.A., Ave. Benj. Constant 2, Lausanne. . . . MAX REINER & SÖHNE, Marktgasse, Thun. . . . ERNST A. G. REINHARDT, Sommergasse 46, Basel. . . . O. RICHARD, Schönenwerd. . . . HANS ROSCHI, Lenzburg. . . . RUH EMIL ERBEN, Adliswil/Zürich. . . . SANER MUSIKVERLAG, Dornach/Sol. . . . F. SCHNEEBERGER, Lerberstrasse 7, Bern. . . . PAUL SCHNEEBERGER, Kanalgasse 13, Biel. . . . F. SCHORI, Zentralstrasse 56, Biel. . . . A. SMETAK, Nelkanstrasse 26, Zürich. . . . SOLOTHURNER MUSIKVERLAG, HANS LEICHT, Zeughausgasse 11, Solothurn. . . . FR. STOCKER, Kanalgasse 13, Biel. . . . GOTTFRIED STUCKI, MUSIKVERLAG, Münsingen. . . . OTTO STUDER, Riedweg 37, Zürich-Höngg. . . . SYMPHONIA-VERLAG, A.G., Angensteinerstrasse 15, Basel. . . . ALESSANDRO TRAVERSI, Bellinzona. . . . TURICAPHON, A.G., Riedikon/Uster. . . . R. WAGNER, ANTRO-MUSIKVERLAG, Schönenbuchstrasse 8, Basel. . . . H. WIDMER, MUSIC-BÜHNENVERLAG, Schürbungert 47, Zürich; publishes music and stage works. . . . WALTER WILD, Aehrenweg 11, 8050 Zürich. . . . WILLI MUSIKVERLAG, Cham. . . . ZÜRCHER LIEDER-BUCH-ANSTALT, Beckenhofstrasse 31, Zürich.

U.S.S.R.

STATE MUSIC PUBLISHING HOUSE (MUZGIZ), Moscow. Through Mezhdunarodnaja Kniga, Moscow 121200; founded 1923.

Uruguay

CASA PRAOS, S.A., Av. 18 de Julio, No. 1080, Montevideo. . . . PALACIO DE LA MUSICA, Av. 18 de Julio esquina Paraguay, Montevideo.

Wales

JACK EDWARDS, Great Darkgate Street, Aberystwyth. . . . GWYNN PUBLISHING CO., Llangollen. . . . HUGHES & SON (including the Educational Publishing Co.), 16 Westgate Street, Cardiff. . . . STANLEY JONES, 6–7 New Arcade, Newport. . . . ROWLAND'S MUSIC STORES, Castle Arcade, Queen Street, Cardiff. . . . D. J. SNELL, High Street Arcade, Swansea. . . . UNIVERSITY OF WALES COUNCIL OF MUSIC, University Registry, Cathays Park, Cardiff. . . . GRIFF C. WILLIAMS, Music Publishers, Llanwrtyd.

Addenda

AMERICAN ACADEMY OF ARTS: New President is **Aaron Copland.**

AMERICAN COMPOSERS ALLIANCE (ACA): Has established a management service for promoting personal appearances of its members as lecturers or performers or both in educational institutions. All fees go to the composers. As of July 1, 1972, all active ACA members could join Broadcast Music, Inc. (BMI) as "composer affiliates," and BMI will now handle all performance rights of all ACA composers. Thus, ACA is now a BMI "publisher-affiliate" as well as a service organization. CFE is a non-royalty-paying printing and storing service for composers who are not members of ACA.

AMERICAN MUSIC CENTER also shares its offices with the American Society of University Composers.

AMERICAN SOCIETY OF COMPOSERS, AUTHORS, AND PUBLISHERS (ASCAP): As of May, 1972: the organization claimed 5,037 music publishers and 14,829 composers and lyricists as members. As of August 30, 1972, the total ASCAP membership reached 20,343.

AMERICAN SYMPHONY ORCHESTRA cancelled its 1972–73 season following the resignation of **Leopold Stokowski,** who now lives in England. The orchestra reorganized for the 1973–74 season as a self-governing orchestra. Music Director and Conductor is **Kazuyoshi Akiyama.** The new season has a schedule of five concerts at Carnegie Hall.

ASSOCIATION OF COLLEGE AND UNIVERSITY CONCERT MANAGERS: **Fanny Taylor** is on leave of absence as Educational Director of ACUCM. She is with the National Endowment for the Arts. Acting Executive Director of ACUCM is **William M. Dawson.**

ASSOCIATED COUNCILS OF THE ARTS and the Partnership for the Arts merged their organizations in November, 1972. The head of the latter organization will become a member of the Board of the merged unit.

BUEGELEISEN & JACOBSEN: new address for the firm since September, 1973: 5 Canal Road, Pelham Manor, New York, N.Y. 10803. Tel.: (914) 738-2252.

EVERETT PIANO COMPANY was purchased by Yamaha International Corp. of Buena Park, California from United Industrial Syndicate on September 27, 1973.

Jacob Druckman, composer, is now Director of the Electronic Music Studio at Brooklyn College and has an exclusive contract with the publishing firm of Boosey & Hawkes.

FESTIVAL OF TWO WORLDS at Spoleto, Italy: Artistic Director is **Romolo Valli;** President is **Gian-Carlo Menotti.**

Irwin Hoffman is also permanent conductor of the Belgian Radio and Television Symphony Orchestra. He is Principal Conductor of Chicago's Grant Park Orchestra.

JACOB'S PILLOW DANCE FESTIVAL: **Walter Terry,** noted dance critic, after having served first as Acting Director and then as Permanent Director of the festival, beginning in January, 1973, resigned the post in September, 1973. **Tom Kerrigan,** serving as General Manager at the time, also resigned.

LENOX STRING QUARTET: **Paul Hersh,** pianist and violist with the group, left the quartet to serve on the faculty of San Francisco Conservatory.

LIMMCO: new address is 211 Park Avenue, Hicksville, New York 11802. Telephone number is unchanged.

Otto Luening has retired from the faculty of Columbia University Music Department.

Gustav Meier has succeeded José Iturbi as conductor of the Greater Bridgeport (Conn.) Symphony.

Musical America's New York City address is now: 1 Astor Plaza, New York, N.Y. 10036. Tel.: (212) 764-7458.

NATIONAL ASSOCIATION OF MUSIC MERCHANTS (NAMM) has a new address since September 10, 1973: Suite 3320, 25 East Wacker Drive, Chicago, Illinois 60601. Tel.: (312) 263-0261.

NEWPORT JAZZ FESTIVAL: For its second season in New York City, the festival ran for ten days from June 29 to July 8, 1973. Total paid admission was about 133,000. Some 56 musical events involving 1,000 musicians were scheduled throughout the city and environs at 13 sites, including Shea Stadium, Carnegie Hall, Avery Fisher Hall (formerly Philharmonic Hall), Radio City Music Hall, Nassau Coliseum, Central Park, and Alice Tully Hall.

NORFOLK (Va.) SYMPHONY's new hall is Chrysler Hall.

PASADENA SYMPHONY ORCHESTRA: New Conductor is **Daniel Lewis.**

New York City's Philharmonic Hall was renamed Avery Fisher Hall September 20, 1973, following a gift of several million dollars to the Hall by **Avery Robert Fisher,** high-fidelity equipment manufacturer.

EDITIONS SALABERT, once available through the firm of Franco Colombo (Belwin Mills), now has its own New York City office.

SEATTLE SYMPHONY: In April, 1972, the orchestra performed some 36 concerts in Alaska. It was the first tour of that state by a major symphony orchestra. The orchestra's new address is: 305 Harrison Street, Seattle, Washington 98109.

SOUTH BEND SYMPHONY: **Edwin Hames** retired as conductor after 40 years with the orchestra on October 22, 1972.

UNIVERSITY OF WASHINGTON SCHOOL OF MUSIC Director is now **John T. Moore.**

NECROLOGY

Victor Babin, pianist and Director of the Cleveland Institute of Music; d. March 1, 1972.

Esther Williamson Ballou, composer; d. March, 1973.

Seth Bingham, composer and organist; d. June 21, 1972.

Jean Casadesus; d. January 20, 1972.

Robert Casadesus; d. September 19, 1972.

Pablo Casals; d. October 22, 1973.

John Cranko, of the Stuttgart Ballet; d. June, 1973.

Giorgio D'Andrea, artists' representative; d. July 5, 1972.

Arturo di Filippi, founder-director of the Greater Miami Opera Guild; d. June 28, 1972.

José Echaniz, pianist; former Artistic Director of the Lake Placid Music Festival and faculty member of the Eastman School; d. 1969.

Richard Ellsasser, organist; d. 1972.

Alvin D. Etler, composer; d. June 14, 1973.

Aurelio Fabiani, founder and General Manager of the Philadelphia Lyric Opera; d. April 26, 1973.

Rudolf Friml; d. November 12, 1972.

Rudolph Ganz, composer; pianist; President-Emeritus of the Chicago Musical College; d. August 2, 1972.

Goeran Gentele; d. July 18, 1973.

Herbert Graf, opera director; d. 1973.

Paul Heinecke, of SESAC, Inc.; d. December 23, 1972.

Bernard Isaacson, Editor of *Musical Merchandise Review;* d. July 17, 1972.

Istvan Kertesz, conductor; d. April 17, 1973.

Paul Kletzki, conductor; d. March 6, 1973.

Emily Kratt of Wm. Kratt Co.; d. September 5, 1973.

Wm. F. Ludwig, Sr., drum manufacturer; d. July 8, 1973.

Jean Madeira, contralto; d. July 10, 1972.

Fritz Mahler, conductor; d. June 18, 1973.

Lauritz Melchior; d. March 18, 1973.

Elemer Nagy, Co-director of the Hartt Opera Theater; d. July 30, 1971.

Carl M. Neumeyer, Director of the Illinois Wesleyan University School of Music; d. December 7, 1972.

Hall Overton, composer; d. November 24, 1972.

Rose Palmai-Tenser, founder of the Mobile Opera Guild; d. August 1, 1971.

Hans Schmidt-Isserstedt, conductor; d. May 28, 1973.

Elaine Shaffer, flutist; d. February 19, 1973.

Alexander Smallens, conductor; d. November 24, 1972.

Joseph Szigeti; d. February 19, 1973.

Al Vann, publisher of *Music Journal* and *Music & Artists;* d. June 17, 1973. His wife, **Dorothy Schwartz Vann** succeeds him as publisher.

Index

Index

This index contains the names of all living persons cited anywhere in the *Handbook*, a number of deceased persons—or musical institutions or legacies in their names, all organizations, and all music industry firms and their products by brand name or label.

Italics are used for periodicals, journals, newsletters, and the like, for record labels, and for the brand names of musical merchandise.

A record label or brand name identical to the name of the producing or distributing company has its citation either as a label or a company name. If the producing company's name differs in any way from that of its product, there is an additional index citation for the company name.

In general, the index citations for record labels, music publishers, and the brand names of manufactured goods refer to their entries in Part 11 (Music Industries). In the case of foreign music publishers, references are to Part 14 and, possibly, Part 11 if the foreign publishers are cited as having American selling agencies. Apart from other information, these references show the relationship between the products and the producing or distributing firms. If an American publisher's or record company's name and address are not included anywhere in Part 11—either directly or through association with another firm—a citation appears for the page on which such information is included.

Through the use of this index it is therefore possible for the reader who may know only a brand name, a record label, a publishing imprint, or the name of an organizational publication to locate the name and address (along with other information) of the producing firm or distributor or of the sponsoring organization, even when such names are not themselves main entries.

The way in which entire sections of the *Handbook* are organized results in the need for certain frequent common references—some numbering in the hundreds. The index necessarily omits these references. For example, the reader seeking information about a particular concert manager will find him in the alphabetical listing in Part 13 (Concert Managers). But in order to find out which performers he represents, the reader must refer to the individual performers' alphabetical listings in Part 5 (Performers). Readers should note other such situations: for who has performed with which major orchestras or opera companies or at which festivals, check Part 5; record labels are listed under the appropriate entries in Part 5 and Part 6 (Composers); music publishers appear in Part 6. Also not to be found as separate index listings are the many references to both the National Endowment for the Arts and the Ford Foundation in the sections on symphony orchestras (in Part 2) and opera companies (in Part 4).

DISCARD